THE STEWART TRILOGY

Book One
LORDS OF MISRULE

In 14th century Scotland, the ruling House of Stewart was a house divided, beset by hatred and jealousy. Descendants of the Bruce's daughter, they kept the throne only by an extraordinary genius for survival – or, as many said, the luck of the Devil.

Their rivals were the Douglases; and when the second Earl was slain in battle, the Stewarts were suspected of foul play.

Young Jamie Douglas, bastard son of the powerful Lord of Dalkeith and esquire to the dead Earl, vowed to avenge his master. But he had only his wits, courage and integrity with which to challenge the most eminent and unscrupulous men in the kingdom, among them Robert Stewart, Earl of Fife and Menteith (later Duke of Albany) and Alexander Stewart, Earl of Buchan, the notorious Wolf of Badenoch.

But while vengeance burned in Jamie's heart, he could not prevent his fatal attraction for the beautiful and spirited Stewart women – and one in particular.

THE STEWART TRILOGY

Book Two
A FOLLY OF PRINCES

Scotland at the dawn of the 15th century was in a
wretched state. While the feeble Robert III still clung to
the throne, his kingdom rang with the sound of conflict
as his son and brother grappled for power.

Sir James Douglas of Aberdour, married as he was to
the King's illegitimate sister, had to tread a hazardous
path through the warring factions. But having a
conscience made life harder still. For in those days – and
in that company of men – a conscience could cost a man
dear.

THE STEWART TRILOGY

Book Three
THE CAPTIVE CROWN

Three generations on from the great Bruce, with the heir to the throne murdered, King Robert III a sick weakling, and his remaining son still a child, Scotland was in a bad way. The destiny of the royal House of Stewart was to depend on two outstanding young men: Alex Stewart, bastard son of the notorious Wolf of Badenoch, and his cousin, Brave John of Coull, a son of the hated Regent.

The Stewart Trilogy

LORDS OF MISRULE

A FOLLY OF PRINCES

THE CAPTIVE CROWN

Nigel Tranter

CORONET BOOKS
Hodder and Stoughton

First published as three separate volumes

Lords of Misrule © 1976 by Nigel Tranter
First published in Great Britain in 1976 by Hodder and Stoughton
First published as a Coronet paperback in 1978

A Folly of Princes © 1977 by Nigel Tranter
First published in Great Britain in 1977 by Hodder and Stoughton
First published as a Coronet paperback in 1979

The Captive Crown © 1977 by Nigel Tranter
First published in Great Britain in 1977 by Hodder and Stoughton
First published as a Coronet paperback in 1980

This edition 1998
A Coronet paperback

The right of Nigel Tranter to be identified as the Author of the
Work has been asserted by him in accordance with the Copyright,
Designs and Patents Act 1988.

10 9 8 7 6 5 4 3 2 1

ISBN 0 340 39115 4

Printed and bound in Great Britain by
Mackays of Chatham PLC, Chatham, Kent

Hodder and Stoughton
A division of Hodder Headline PLC
338 Euston Road
London NW1 3BH

Lords of Misrule

PRINCIPAL CHARACTERS

In Order of Appearance

LADY EGIDIA STEWART, LADY DALKEITH: Sister of the King; wife of the Lord of Dalkeith.

JAMIE DOUGLAS: Illegitimate eldest son of Sir James, Lord of Dalkeith. Esquire to the 2nd Earl of Douglas.

SIR JAMES DOUGLAS, LORD OF DALKEITH: Statesman and wealthiest noble of the kingdom. Chief of the second line of Douglas.

SIR JAMES LINDSAY, LORD OF CRAWFORD AND LUFFNESS: Lord High Justiciar, chief of the name of Lindsay, and son of Lady Dalkeith by an earlier marriage.

JAMES, 2ND EARL OF DOUGLAS: Most powerful noble in Scotland, Chief Warden of the Marches and Justiciar of the South-West.

ROBERT II, KING OF SCOTS: Grandson of the hero-king, Robert Bruce.

JOHN STEWART, EARL OF CARRICK, HIGH STEWARD OF SCOTLAND: Eldest surviving son of the King and heir to the throne — later Robert III.

ROBERT STEWART, EARL OF FIFE AND MENTEITH: Second surviving son of the King; later Governor of the realm and Duke of Albany.

DAVID STEWART, EARL OF STRATHEARN: Fourth surviving son of the King.

WALTER STEWART, LORD OF BRECHIN: Youngest legitimate son of the King.

GEORGE COSPATRICK, EARL OF DUNBAR AND MARCH: Great noble. Justiciar of Lothian.

LADY GELIS STEWART: Youngest of the King's legitimate daughters.

MARY STEWART: One of the King's illegitimate daughters. Maid-in-Waiting to the Lady Gelis.

SIR ARCHIBALD DOUGLAS (The Grim), LORD OF GALLOWAY: Great noble; later 3rd Earl of Douglas.

JOHN DUNBAR, EARL OF MORAY: Great noble. Wed to another daughter of the King. Brother of Earl of Dunbar and March.

MASTER JOHN PEEBLES, BISHOP OF DUNKELD: Chancellor of the realm.

SIR WILLIAM DOUGLAS OF NITHSDALE: Illegitimate son of the Lord of Galloway. Warrior and hero.

SIR HARRY PERCY (HOTSPUR): Great English noble and champion. Heir to the Earl of Northumberland.

JOHN BICKERTON: Son of Keeper of Luffness Castle. Armour-bearer to the Earl of Douglas.

GEORGE DOUGLAS, EARL OF ANGUS: Young noble. Founder of the Red Douglas line.

LADY MARGARET STEWART, COUNTESS OF ANGUS: Widow of late Earl of Mar; Countess of Angus in her own right. Mother of the boy Earl of Angus.

LADY ISABEL STEWART, COUNTESS OF DOUGLAS: Daughter of the King. Wife of 2nd Earl of Douglas.

LORD DAVID STEWART: Eldest son of the Earl of Carrick; later himself Earl of Carrick and Duke of Rothesay.

LADY ANNABELLA DRUMMOND, COUNTESS OF CARRICK: Wife of King's eldest surviving son. Later Queen.

ALEXANDER STEWART, EARL OF BUCHAN: Known as the Wolf of Badenoch. Third surviving son of the King. Lieutenant and Justiciar of the North.

DONALD, LORD OF THE ISLES: Great Highland potentate. Son of eldest of the King's daughters.

MASTER THOMAS STEWART, ARCHDEACON OF ST. ANDREWS: Illegitimate son of the King.

LORD MURDOCH STEWART: Eldest son of the Earl of Fife.

SIR ANDREW STEWART: One of the five foremost illegitimate sons of the Earl of Buchan, Wolf of Badenoch.

SIR ALEXANDER STEWART: Eldest of above. Later Earl of Mar and victor of Harlaw.

SIR WALTER STEWART: Still another of above.

MARIOTA DE ATHYN (or MACKAY): Mother of above, mistress of Buchan.

LACHLAN MACKINTOSH, 9TH CHIEF: *Mac an Toishich*, Captain of Clan Chattan.

FARQUHAR MACGILLIVRAY: *Mhic Gillebrath Mor*, 5th Chief.

MASTER WILLIAM TRAIL, BISHOP OF ST. ANDREWS: Primate.

DOUGLAS GENEALOGY

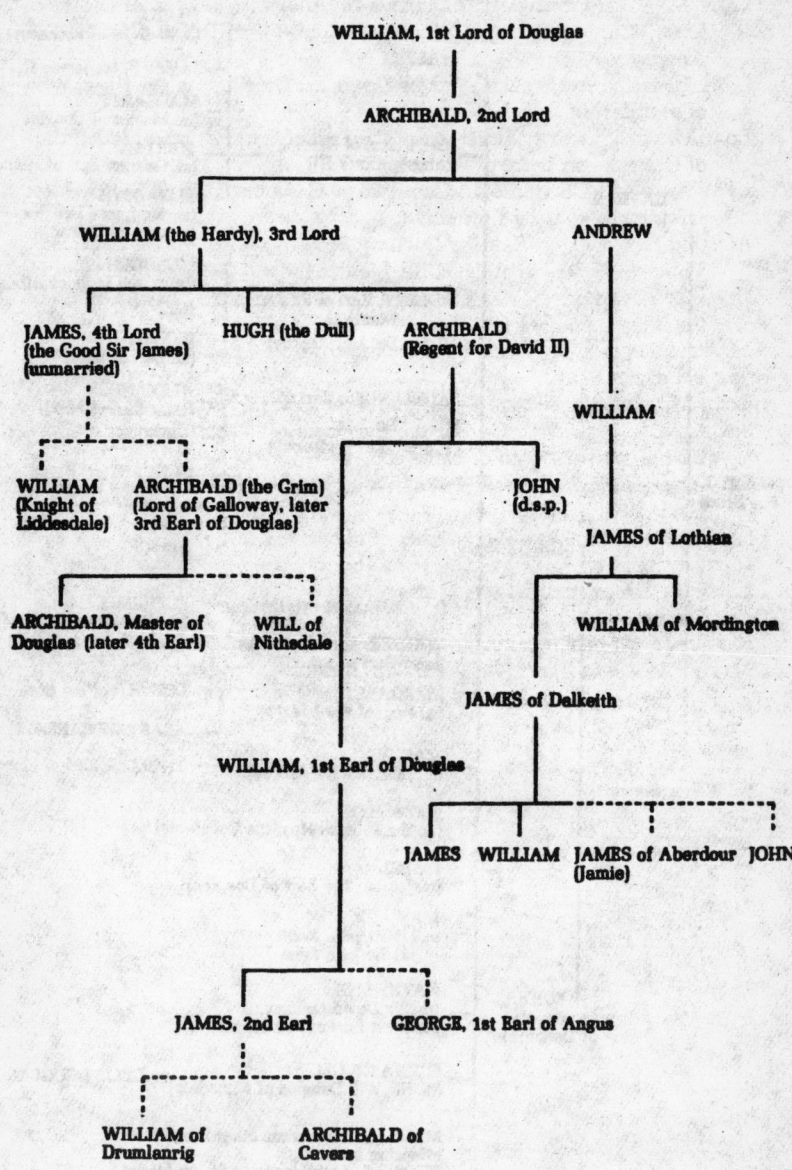

STEWART GENEALOGY

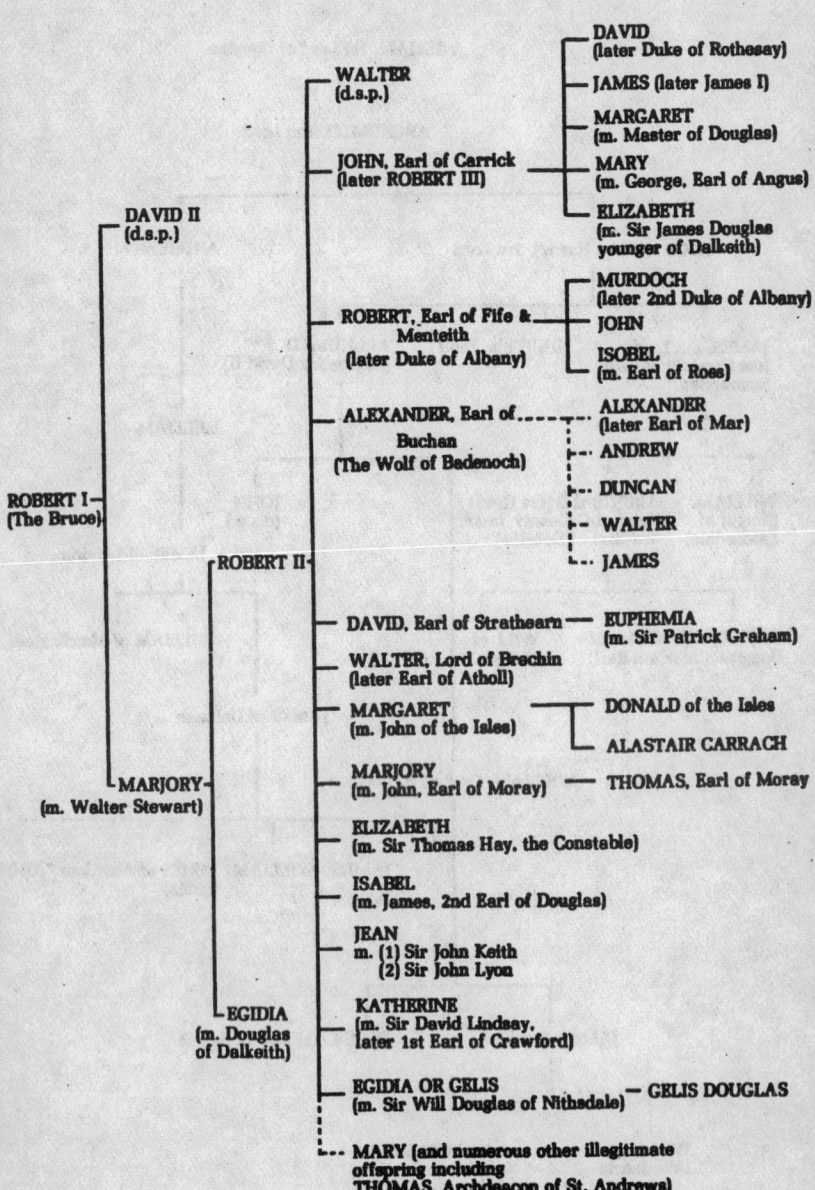

ROBERT I (The Bruce)

DAVID II (d.s.p.)

MARJORY (m. Walter Stewart)

ROBERT II

WALTER (d.s.p.)

JOHN, Earl of Carrick (later ROBERT III)

- **DAVID** (later Duke of Rothesay)
- **JAMES** (later James I)
- **MARGARET** (m. Master of Douglas)
- **MARY** (m. George, Earl of Angus)
- **ELIZABETH** (m. Sir James Douglas younger of Dalkeith)

ROBERT, Earl of Fife & Menteith (later Duke of Albany)

- **MURDOCH** (later 2nd Duke of Albany)
- **JOHN**
- **ISOBEL** (m. Earl of Ross)

ALEXANDER, Earl of Buchan (The Wolf of Badenoch)

- **ALEXANDER** (later Earl of Mar)
- **ANDREW**
- **DUNCAN**
- **WALTER**
- **JAMES**

DAVID, Earl of Strathearn — **EUPHEMIA** (m. Sir Patrick Graham)

WALTER, Lord of Brechin (later Earl of Atholl)

MARGARET (m. John of the Isles)
- **DONALD of the Isles**
- **ALASTAIR CARRACH**

MARJORY (m. John, Earl of Moray) — **THOMAS, Earl of Moray**

ELIZABETH (m. Sir Thomas Hay, the Constable)

ISABEL (m. James, 2nd Earl of Douglas)

JEAN m. (1) Sir John Keith (2) Sir John Lyon

KATHERINE (m. Sir David Lindsay, later 1st Earl of Crawford)

EGIDIA OR GELIS (m. Sir Will Douglas of Nithsdale) — **GELIS DOUGLAS**

MARY (and numerous other illegitimate offspring including THOMAS, Archdeacon of St. Andrews)

EGIDIA (m. Douglas of Dalkeith)

I

I

THE GREAT HALL of Stirling Castle made a fair representation of Bedlam, and had done for some time. It was fuller than usual, of course, with so much of the country's nobility assembled; and the meal and entertainments, hastily arranged but on a lavish scale, had gone on longer than usual also. The more fastidiously-minded of the women had retired discreetly considerably earlier, and that included three of the King's daughters and the Countess of Carrick, wife to the heir of the throne. Those who chose to remain tended to have anything but a restraining influence, their skirls and screams contributing to the general uproar in significant degree, with effect on wine-taken men. And such as had disarranged clothing were by no means all serving-wenches, entertainers and the like; some, in young Jamie Douglas's opinion at least, were certainly old enough and distinguished enough to know better. His own step-mother, for instance — if that was the right description for his father's second wife, when even the first was not Jamie's mother — the Lady Egidia Stewart, was behaving unsuitably, and with the French ambassador, her gown torn open almost to the navel. Her husband, the Lord of Dalkeith, like her brother the King, was asleep, head fallen forward on bent arms amidst a pool of wine at the Douglas end of the dais-table; but her sons by two of her previous marriages were present and very much awake; and Jamie considered that they must find the spectacle embarrassing — although the eldest of them, Sir James Lindsay 12th Lord of Crawford and Luffness, Lord High Justiciar of Scotland, admittedly did not demonstrate anything of the sort, as he knelt on one of the tables further down the hall, amongst toppled flagons and empty platters, boxing with a brown Muscovy bear of the dancing variety, its keeper weeping and declaring that there would be injury done, while most of the wolfhounds in the room bayed and slavered their excitement. Jamie Douglas was no prig, and appreciated his fun as much as most young men; but he felt that the present occasion and company was not the most suitable for it, that things were getting out of hand, and the important business of the evening was still to be concluded.

He himself was heedfully sober. He was rather inclined that way, anyhow, but had been specifically warned by his master, the Earl of Douglas, to hold himself prepared to act scribe, if necessary, in case none of the trustworthy churchmen were in a state to wield a quill. He was sitting near the head of the esquires' and pages' table, at one side of the great smoke-filled apartment, where he was really quite close to his lord at the left of the dais-table — the King's left, that is, the male Stewarts being all on the right, naturally. Normally the table-plan was T-shaped, the dais-table on its slightly-raised platform crosswise at the head of the hall, the main board stretching down the room slightly to one side, leaving ample space for the servitors, the entertainers and spectacles, with the esquires down the far wall. Tonight, on account of the large numbers present, an extra lengthwise board had been inserted, parallel; so there were in fact three tables reaching down the room, complicating precedency arrangements, cramping the service and the entertainment and adding to the present uproar.

Jamie dutifully kept his eye on the Earl of Douglas. He had been only six months promoted esquire to his hero and chief, after serving for four years as page; and he recognised well the great honour the Earl had done him — and perhaps to some extent, his father — in making the appointment. For many young lords in their own right would have been glad to be principal esquire to the puissant head of the most powerful house in Scotland; and for an illegitimate son, even of the wealthy Lord of Dalkeith, aged only eighteen, to be selected, had been unexpected and the cause of some heartburning. Although Jamie would not have admitted as much, he rather suspected that the Countess Isabel of Douglas had had something to do with it. The beautiful daughter of the King, she had always shown him especial kindness, as a page, and had on occasion called him handsome. He did not know whether his typically dark, almost swarthy and somewhat sombre Douglas features were handsome or not, nor greatly cared; but he was glad that he was well-built, tall and wide-shouldered, since so much in life depended on that. He was taller than the Earl, indeed.

James, 2nd Earl of Douglas, clearly was sober also tonight; and likewise and evidently less than approving of the way the evening was shaping. A dark, stocky, thick-set man in his early thirties, with strangely still though rugged features, he sat glowering, shoulders hunched, staring distastefully down on the pandemonium of the hall. But every now and again, he would glance along the dais-table itself, to his right, past sundry notables and his snoring monarch, to where John, Earl of Carrick sat immediately on the King's right, quietly reading in a curling parchment, amidst all the hubbub, an odd sight; and beyond him to the next seat where his brother, Robert, Earl of Fife and Menteith sat back, stiff face raised towards the smoke-dim hammer-beam ceiling, eyes closed — although no one would ever suggest that that man would be asleep. Two more of the King's sons, David, Earl of Strathearn and Walter, Lord of Brechin, the youngest, sat still further along, the first staring moodily, the second sprawling hopelessly drunk; but neither of these concerned the Douglas. It was their elder brothers, John of Carrick, heir to the throne, and Robert of Fife, the real power behind that throne, who were the objects of his assessment and speculation, of his less than patient waiting. And it was not often that the chief of the Douglases had to exercise patience in public.

The two princes, on whom the entire success or otherwise of the evening hinged, could not have been less alike, in appearance as in character, although sons of the same mother — which was by no means always the way with the royal offspring — and only some two years apart in age. John, although but fifty-one years, looked an old man already, gentle, sad and studious in aspect, delicately featured with great expressive eyes, hair and beard already grey, diffident and awkward of manner. He was the second son of Robert the Second, the first of the Stewart kings — the eldest, Walter, had died young — and although he had qualities of intellect and great compassion, these were scarcely those most demanded for the next King of Scots; and it would be safe to say that he represented the major disappointment of the kingdom, to himself most of all. Some of the poor folk loved him after a fashion, for he was kindly towards them, when princes were expected to be otherwise, humble-minded, generous. He had been kicked in the knee by a horse, long ago — it had to be a Douglas horse that did it — and the bone had set badly, so that John Stewart limped through life thereafter, where the Scots expected their leaders to stride manfully.

Robert Stewart, as it happened, was scarcely popular either; nor did he stride with much élan, to be sure. He was not pitied — he was feared. A tall, slender, stern-faced man, good-looking in a spare, long-featured way, he had a tight mouth, watchful almost colourless eyes and a severe manner — an unlikely Stewart in fact. Always well if soberly dressed, where his brother John was untidy and careless to a degree in his clothing, he had for years now taken more and more of the rule of the kingdom into his own long-fingered hands, as the aged, half-blind and failing father Robert the Bruce's grandson, sank towards senility. Although that certainly did not mean that Scotland was well or adequately governed, in the year 1388, nor had been for a decade. If men did not love Robert of Fife, they tended to feel that putting up with him was probably the lesser of evils — they had little choice, anyway — for the next brother was Alexander, Earl of Buchan no less, the terrible and notorious Wolf of Badenoch so-called, not present this night for, praise God, he was apt to confine his outrageous activities to the northern half of the kingdom, where he reigned as Justiciar and Lieutenant of the North; the thought of *him* governing the realm was enough to come between a man and his sleep. And the other two surviving princes, David and the second Walter, were by way of being nonentities.

So the Earl of Douglas watched and waited, with smouldering impatience. That his glance seldom lingered on the slumped and open-mouthed person of King Bleary himself, held its own significance.

Jamie felt for his beloved and admired master, who was patently bored to an extremity. The Countess Isabel, his wife, had left the hall an hour since. The Papal Legate, who sat on his right, spoke Italian, Latin, French and Spanish, but neither Scots nor English; and the Earl of Douglas's scholarship in such matters had been neglected. On his left he had long exhausted the conversational resources of George, Earl of Dunbar and March, a somewhat morose man although a good enough soldier. The entertainment itself was fair enough of its kind, a gipsy troupe now dancing with wild abandon to screaming fiddles, the women half-naked and becoming more so; but there was a time and place for all things, and it had been a long and active day, of tournament and pageantry and chivalric sports, in all of which the Earl had taken his major part, indeed largely organised by himself as an excuse to gather together this large assembly of great and lesser nobles and chieftains without the monarch or his heir suspecting what was afoot. But there was important work to be done this night yet, and the hour was already late. Worse, too many of the lords and knights on whom so much depended, were already either drunk or so drink-taken that they would be increasingly difficult to handle and bring to a state of usefulness. The thing was nearing the impossible.

It was all, as so often, John of Carrick's fault. The man had a genius for upsetting things and people — all with the best will in the world, which made it the more irritating. Tonight he was a danger to the plans of better men — or at least more active and venturesome men. Every endeavour had been made to contrive his absence from the table, but he had confounded all by turning up, late, to sit beside his father, a right which scarcely could be denied to the heir to the throne. Since his arrival, the project had been either to get him to leave early, through offence, disgust or boredom; or else to make him sufficiently inebriated for his presence not to matter. It had not worked. John could drink deeply too, on occasion, like all the Stewarts — but not tonight. And although clearly he was not enjoying the proceedings, he stayed on in his seat, having brought in his wretched parchment with him, the study of which seemed to console him. As far as Douglas could see, it was poetry or something such. Yet the business of the evening could not be proceeded with whilst Carrick was present, or conscious, for fear of his interference, his disapproval, his influence on the King. It was galling in the extreme. Young Jamie recognised all this, since he was in some measure involved himself — but he could not help being a little sorry for the unfortunate prince nevertheless.

At length, the Earl of Douglas could stand it no longer. Pushing his wine-goblet away, he raised his head, caught Jamie's eye and

15

beckoned. The young man rose, and made his way round behind the dais-table to his master's side, stooping between him and Dunbar. The Earl gestured him round to the other side, where the Papal Legate's ignorance of the language would afford better privacy.

"This is damnable, beyond all," he jerked, low-voiced. "We must get him out, somehow, or nothing will be done this night. I swear Robert could have got him away, if he would — but Robert is none so keen on this project himself, a plague on him! I can think of one thing only, Jamie — the Lady Gelis. We must use her."

The esquire's swarthy features flushed. Like many of the younger men there, he was helplessly, hopelessly in love with Egidia Stewart, youngest legitimate daughter of the King, usually called Gelis to distinguish her from her aunt, the Lady Dalkeith. Almost all the Stewart women were handsome but Gelis was a raving beauty, a darkly lively, sparkling creature of just twenty years, all gaiety, verve and challenge, in person as in personality. She now sat at the far right end of the dais-table with the usual bevy of lordlings around her, two of Jamie's legitimate brothers amongst them, a noisy colourful group. Jamie had, in fact, been disappointed in her that she had not long since left the hall with her elder sisters and other discreet ladies — for in his mature opinion that room was now no place for fair and virtuous young women. But, of course, it had been *her* day. As the only unmarried princess, she had been Queen of the Tourney. She was clearly loth to end the day's excitements.

"Get her out of here," the Earl James went on. "You are friendly with her, I hear. She should have been gone long since. Then have her send for the Earl of Carrick, her brother. He dotes on her, all know. Some upset, outside. A tulzie — some young fools. She is troubled — sends for her brother to escort her to her chamber. He would not come back, I think."

The younger man all but wailed. He would gladly have laid down his life for Scotland's greatest soldier and chief of the name of Douglas, his master. But this command was beyond him. "My lord — how can I?" he protested. "She will not leave because *I* ask her to. She smiles on me, on occasion — but that is all. I have no power with her. All these around her are more important than I am. How shall they take it if I come urging the princess to leave them . . .?"

"Damnation — then get your precious brothers to take her out, boy."

"Why should she go? But if *you* asked her? Or better, my lord — if you asked my lord of Carrick to take her, himself. Say that the company grows unruly, too ill-mannered, that she would be better away. He would take it from you . . ."

Douglas frowned. "There would have to be more noise, horse-play, around her before I could do that. But — you go, Jamie, and stir up some buffoonery. Seem the worse for wine, if you like. Raise a turmoil. Then I can approach Carrick. Off with you."

Unhappily Jamie Douglas did as he was commanded. It was appallingly unfair. The very last thing he wanted was to raise an uproar, make an object of himself in the eyes of Gelis Stewart. Damn the Earl of Carrick!

At the end of the table it was as though a separate little party was in progress, heedless of what prevailed in the rest of the great apartment. Seven or eight young men, sons of the highest in the land, eddied around the princess, sitting on her bench, on the table-top itself, even on the floor at her feet, laughing, chattering. One, the Master of Dunbar, heir of the Earl thereof, was singing a madrigal to her, plucking soulfully at the strings of a lute as accompaniment.

Perplexed, Jamie eyed them all. He insinuated himself to the side of his half-brother and namesake, James Douglas Younger of Dalkeith, nearly two years his junior but born in wedlock and so heir to their father. They were good enough friends. The Dalkeith family, like most other noble houses there represented, made little difference between the legitimate and illegitimate, save in the all-important matters of heritable property and titles.

"James," he muttered in the other's ear. "You are to make a to-do. A noise, something of a riot. Fight. It is the Earl's orders. No — hear me. He wants the Lady Gelis to be in the midst of a turmoil. So that my lord of Carrick can take her out. No questions, of a mercy! Do something. Pick a quarrel with Willie — as though you were drunk. Go on."

His brother peered at him. "Are *you* drunk, Jamie? Taken leave of your wits?"

"No. It is the Earl James's orders, I tell you." He grabbed his other brother, William, a year younger still. "Willie — come, pick

17

a fight with James," he urged, in a sort of commanding whisper. "Or with me. All of us. We have to make a noise . . ."

His normally far-from equable and pacific kin gaped at him and at each other. Some of the other lordlings were following their gaze, likewise. All knew Jamie as the mighty Earl of Douglas's principal esquire, and so with his own importance. But they would take ill out of any interference with their evening's pleasure.

"What is it, Jamie?" That was Gelis Stewart herself, kindly enough. "Your brows are even blacker than usual — which is a wonder! Is anything wrong?"

He cleared his throat. "No. That is — no. It is these, my brothers. They, they should be gone. The hour is late. Willie is but fifteen." He reached out to grasp the youngster's shoulder — and whether out of brotherly regard for the command to seem to quarrel, or from a more natural resentment at this high-handed intrusion, the youth twisted violently away. Jamie, however, hung on, and the other brother took the opportunity to join in, an arm round Jamie's shoulder, in turn. The trio, lurching together in a reeling huddle, cannoned against the table — and Jamie judiciously swiped a wine-flagon and a goblet with his free arm, so that both crashed to the floor, spilling blood-red contents. Angrily now, some of the lordlings sprang up, and George Dunbar ceased his serenading.

Turmoil, of a sort, was achieved.

Normally, to be sure, such goings-on in the presence of the monarch would not have been permitted for a moment, and royal servitors would have hurried forward to hustle the offenders out. But this was not a normal occasion, the monarch was fast asleep and had been for an hour at least, as had many another, and the rest of the hall resounded to such noise and uproarious mirth that what went on up here was scarcely noticeable. But it was sufficiently noticeable for the Earl of Douglas, who rose and went to tap the heir to the throne and High Steward of Scotland on his hunched shoulder, to speak and point.

Catching sight of this out of the corner of his eye, Jamie heaved a sigh of relief, and almost relaxed his pushing and pulling at his youngest brother. But the turmoil must not stop too soon, of course, so he continued with some token struggling. Alexander Lindsay, son of Sir David of Glenesk and another princess, the Lady Katherine Stewart, came to separate them, in laughing remonstrance — and was turned upon for his pains. As one or two others came to Lindsay's aid, the scuffle took on a new dimension. Gelis Stewart was scolding them all, only half in laughter.

Jamie had a momentary glimpse of the cold eye of Robert, Earl of Fife and Menteith, considering them remotely from up the table. Then, thankfully, he realised that the Earls of Douglas and Carrick were beside the princess, stooping to speak with her.

Disentangling himself from the other young men took a little while, none sure what it was all about but now roused and the wine in them making its presence felt. Then Jamie, receiving a buffet on the head from his master of all people, staggered aside, to glower distinctly querulously at the entire scene. He saw his brothers scowling at him similarly, the Earl of Douglas stalking back to his seat, and the Earl of Carrick limpingly escorting the Lady Gelis from the hall — although she looked back in some bewilderment as she went.

He found another young woman looking speculatively at him, likewise, and from much closer at hand.

"That was a strange business, Jamie Douglas — and not like you," she said. "What does it mean, I wonder?"

He frowned at her; Mary Stewart, half-sister and lady-in-waiting to the princess, a comely, cheerful and friendly creature, popular with all and particularly well-endowed as to figure, one of the many royal bastards about the Court. Jamie and she, as a rule, got on very well together. "It means that this hall is no place for princesses—or for other decent young women!" he jerked. "Ought you not to be following your mistress?"

"I see," she said, slowly. "I see something — but not all. I shall enquire more, hereafter. Your doublet is torn. If you bring it to me in the morning, I might stitch it for you — and learn the rest, perhaps? A good night, Jamie." And dipping a less than respectful curtsey, she turned and hurried after the prince and princess.

Some little time and explanation was required to achieve detachment from his brothers and the other sprigs of nobility. By the time this was accomplished, his lord was beckoning to him again.

"You did well, Jamie," the Earl said briefly, as though it was all normal duties for an esquire. "Now to serious business." He looked along the table. "His Grace seems sufficiently asleep still. We can make a move. You have the list of the men we want, lad? Have them to come to the Chapel-Royal. Not all at once — one at a time. Such as are not too drunk. But no others, mind. And tell Lyon to bring on his more women dancers — the gipsies. They will keep the rest ogling, for they are to throw off most of their clothing! You have it all?"

"Yes, my lord. Shall I inform the Earl Robert of Fife?"

"No. He would not take that kindly, I think! I will do it. Off with you, now, Jamie."

The Earl of Douglas rose again, and moved along to the Earl of Fife's position, to stoop and say a word or two. That self-contained individual altered neither attitude nor expression, but he did incline his stiff head somewhat. Douglas moved further, to David, Earl of Strathearn, and again spoke quietly. That handsome but rather weak-featured prince looked a deal more interested and would have started up, but the other pressed down on his shoulder and indicated to wait for the elder brother, Fife, to make a move. He glanced at the sprawling Walter Stewart of Brechin, snoring drunk, and shrugging, went back to where the Lord of Dalkeith, second man of the Douglas clan, slept head on arms, and shook him into wakefulness.

"James — waken, man," he urged. "Have you your wits? Aye, well — at last we can move. Not you, not you. The King sleeps on. You and my lord Bishop here, the Chancellor, to stay and see that all is in order here. If any could call this uproar order! The drinking and entertainment are to continue. See that we are not disturbed, in the chapel — that is important. If His Grace wakens, assure him that all is well and we will be back. Not to leave the hall. With wine he will fall asleep again — he always does. You have it?"

Yawning, his older kinsman managed both to nod and shake his head at the same time. "Aye — but I do not know that I like this, James," he said. "It smells of deception, of trickery, bad faith towards His Grace. Our oaths as Privy Councillors . . ."

"Like it or no, it is the only way, man. You know that. God knows I would prefer to have it otherwise — but it is this, or nothing. And I have worked sufficiently hard to bring it thus far. Are we to be tied for ever by a degrading, weakly-signed truce and an old done man's palsy? Ha — there Robert rises now. He has been hard enough to move, I tell you — no warrior that! I will after him. See you to matters here. We will be back anon. Where is Archie of Galloway? Ah, here he comes . . ."

In company with the tall stooping eagle of a man who was Sir Archibald Douglas, Lord of Galloway, third in the Douglas hierarchy, by-named The Grim, the Earl of Douglas slipped out of the hall by the dais entrance, in the wake of the Stewart princes.

*   *   *

In the Chapel-Royal of Stirling Castle, distinctly chilly in bare stone, the illustrious company gathered. Carefully selected, these were the most powerful nobles and most puissant and experienced warriors on the land — with two or three militant churchmen amongst them including the mitred Abbots of Melrose and Dryburgh. Jamie Douglas had found only two or three too far gone in drink to be able to attend, although some were scarcely at their brightest owing to the long wait. Significantly the French ambassador was present, the only non-Scot. The Earl Robert of Fife sat in the chapel's throne, as of right, and looked down on them all coldly, with a sort of steely patience. He did not suffer fools gladly, however high-born.

"Your attention, my lords," he said at length, the very slight impediment emphasising the clipped manner of speech rather than the reverse. "You have been brought here, I hope, to good purpose. A considerable endeavour is intended. On the realm's business. As commander of His Grace's forces, I am concerned. The Earl of Douglas will explain. Proceed, my lord." The Earl Robert was no great talker.

The Douglas was not either, really — although he had his own forceful eloquence on occasion, and a sort of dogged sincerity which could be very effective. "My lords," he said, "and Monsieur le Comte. As you well know, this realm is still smarting from the invasion of King Richard of England of three years back, when he burned much of our land, the abbeys of our good friends here, Melrose and Dryburgh, also the towns of Berwick, Coldstream, Roxburgh, Haddington and part of Edinburgh. And my lord of Dunbar and March's castles of Dunbar and Ercildoune — and attempted mine of Tantallon." A brief hint of a smile flickered on his dark, strong features.

A rumble of agreement, almost a snarl, rose from the company.

"There are stirrings again, over the English March. It could be that Richard Plantagenet, to draw attention from his misrule, thinks to do what his thrice-damned forebear Edward sought to do, and could not — to make Scotland but an English province. The great Bruce and our forefathers stopped that. We may have a similar task. It may not be so, but it behoves us to recognise the danger." He held up his hand. "Wait. We did not strike back at Richard three years ago, as we should have done, and as our French allies desired. For we were weak, lacked armies and armour. His Grace was occupied with other matters, and re-signed a truce, a truce the English had just broken . . ."

"His Grace was feart!" Archie the Grim barked, an outspoken man. "His Grace turns the other cheek. We all know that — and pay the price. Get on with it, James — to the meat of it. Enough of old history!" As Warden of the West March of the Border, the Lord of Galloway was much affected by the constant English threat and the inefficacy of the one-sided truce.

"Quiet, Archie," his chief said, but conversationally. "We never doubted that King Richard must be taught his lesson, my friends — but there has been lack of opportunity. With King Robert otherwise minded." He glanced over at the King's sons briefly, but neither made any comment. "Until now. We have tidings which favour us at last. Richard is beset with troubles. Many of his lords have risen against him, led by his own uncle, Gloucester and nephew Bolingbroke — Warwick, Arundel and the rest. The Lords Appellant, as they are called. They say that John of Gaunt, Richard's other uncle, of Lancaster, is also behind them. You all know of this. They have seized London. This, in the South. Now, in the North too, is trouble. I have sure word that open feud has broken out between the Percy and the Neville. It has been simmering from long, cousins as they are — and now they take opposite sides in this matter. You know what that means — the two greatest houses in the English North at war with each other. Wardens of their East and Middle Marches. The West March will be drawn in — nothing surer. The Border lies open to us, my lords, if we but force it."

There was a stir of excitement now. The Earl of Douglas was Chief Warden of the Marches, on the Scottish side, as well as head of the most powerful Border clan. If he believed that the English Borderline was open to them, none would doubt it.

"What is proposed, my friends, is that we muster a large force. Swiftly and secretly. And strike into England whilst they are thus at odds with each other. As we should have done long since."

Men eyed each other with varied expressions — although undoubtedly the majority feeling was gleefully favourable.

"And the truce, my lords?" the Abbot of Melrose asked. "The signed truce with England."

"To lowest hell with the truce!" somebody cried, and many there shouted agreement.

"No doubt, sirs. But the King's royal signature is upon it," the prelate insisted. "And the Great Seal of this realm. Moreover, the original truce is endorsed and sealed by His Most Christian Majesty of France. Such great raid as is suggested would break it. Break the King's royal word. Can any here think to do that?"

All eyes turned on Robert, Earl of Fife. That careful man examined his finger-nails and made no comment.

The Douglas cleared his throat. "The full truce expired in the spring of this year," he reminded. "Since when, as you may know, there has been renewal only by letter. Not by any meeting or full treaty. The Great Seal not appended. His Grace's signature to the letter, yes. But ... what His Grace has signed, His Grace can unsign!"

There were many exclamations at that, both appreciative and questioning. The other abbot, of Dryburgh, spoke up. "His Grace is a man of peace, my lord. Hating war. He will not revoke that letter, I think."

Douglas looked at the Earl Robert — but still got no help from that quarter. David of Strathearn spoke up, however. "My father will sign," he asserted. "Sign *something*, Master Clerk, never fear!"

Douglas, frowning, spoke quickly. "Here is why we have to go about this matter with some care. Why the tourney was held today, to bring you together. Why it required to be done thus. Why you are all here, in the King's castle and presence. Yet His Grace not to know the reason. Nor my lord of Carrick. If the Earl John was to hear of this, he would inform his father — nothing surer. Since he is of a like mind. We, who are differently minded, must needs use this device — distasteful as it may be. If we are

23

agreed, my lords, the Earl Robert here will present a paper here-after to his royal sire, for signature. He, h'm, assures that it will be signed. For His Grace ever signs what the Earl Robert puts before him. The writing will be small and difficult. His Grace's eyesight is not good. What is needed must be done. For this realm's weal and safety. A copy will be given to the envoy of His Majesty of France, to send to Paris." He looked over at the French ambassador. "You understand, Monsieur?"

The Frenchman nodded. "*Parfaitment, mon ami.* It is well thought of; My royal master, I swear, will be well content. He no more loves Richard Plantagenet than do you!"

Douglas sought not to let his relief show. Much depended on the French envoy. "Good, Monsieur le Comte. And . . . the arms and armour?"

"*Certainement.* The arms and armour you must use, yes. Would that I might come with you, my friends, to use it. At last. *Mais non* — that would be indiscreet, I fear."

Not only the Douglas sighed thankfully. All around major satisfaction was expressed. Three years earlier, the King of France had sent to Scotland the magnificent gift of 1,400 complete sets of the finest armour, with arms to match, along with 40,000 gold livres in money — partly to keep the Scots in alliance but more to be used as a threat against the English, to help ensure that King Richard kept the tripartite truce by not invading France. But though the gold was distributed — Douglas himself had got 7,500 livres, as Warden of the Marches — the arms had remained unused. For King Charles VI had prudently sent the precious goods in the strict care and control of a strong party of French knights, ostensibly to instruct in their usage, but in fact to ensure that they were used only for purposes directly favourable to himself. The projected invasion had never taken place, and the arms went unused and undistributed — although much coveted throughout Scotland. Their French guardians had been constantly and carefully renewed, and so far no appeals had been sufficient to weaken their grip. The getting of these armaments into good Scots hands without offending the King of France and endangering the Auld Alliance, had been a major preoccupation for these three years.

"The plan is this," Douglas went on. "Some of us have discussed it, at Aberdeen, a week past. And put it to my lord of Fife, who I rejoice to say is in agreement — for I need not say that

24

it could not be attempted lacking that agreement. We will cross the Border, as soon as may be possible, in two arrays, one on the Middle March, one on the West. To further divide the English strength and confuse them as to which is the main assault. We shall require powerful forces, for this is no mere raiding, but war. Many men — knights, mounted men-at-arms, foot. You, my lords, have the men. We judge that 50,000 would be an apt number. And they must be mustered swiftly and secretly — secret from Stirling as well as from Newcastle and Carlisle! That will be difficult — but it is necessary. Royal orders to halt, to disperse, would be . . . embarrassing!"

Men considered the implications of that, thoughtfully — although some snorted their contempt for any such orders from any source. Coldly the Earl Robert intervened.

"We must not receive such orders. Or I, as commander of the forces of the Crown, cannot proceed. Mind it."

"Secrecy and haste, then, are vital, my friends. We will muster where we may be well hidden. On the southern skirts of my Forest of Ettrick — where none but shepherds and herdsmen will see, and these my people. Muster at Jedworth. The forces will thereafter divide, one to go south directly, by Tynedale. That will be the lesser force. The other will ride down Liddesdale and Eskdale, to the Sark and Carlisle."

"Who leads?" That was Sir James Lindsay, the Justiciar, the same who had been table-fighting with the bear. Men held their breaths for the answer.

"My lord Earl of Fife and Menteith is commander over all. Under him, my Lord of Galloway leads the West array. I lead the East, with my lord Earl of Dunbar and March deputy."

There was fairly obvious relief at this announcement, although the Earl David of Strathearn stirred restlessly.

"Now as to men." Douglas stared round him at them all, at his most bull-like. "Numbers, my friends. Start with you, Lindsay. How many? Within the week?"

"A thousand," that cheerful young man said promptly.

"Not sufficient. From your lordships of Crawford, Luffness, Byres and Barnwell. Double it, man!"

"It is the time, James. Only a week! But . . . very well. I will try for two thousand."

"Good. Archie?"

"As many. Give me two more days, James and I will make it *three* thousand. From Galloway."

"The extra two thousand must follow. I know that you have many men away in Ireland with your son Will. But we cannot wait. Every day increases the risk of discovery. Dunbar, how many?"

"I will not be beat by Archie Douglas! Four thousand from my two earldoms. But only for the East array. I will not have them under any other command." And he glared at Robert Stewart.

"Let Douglas watch out, then!" David of Strathearn gave back. "He is welcome to you, and them. I would not risk such cattle — or you, Dunbar — in any command of mine! Lest you desert to the English. As is your family's habit!"

There was uproar in the Chapel-Royal.

Between them, Douglas and Fife in time gained approximate quiet.

"Of a mercy, restrain yourselves," the former requested. "Or we are lost before we start. Jamie — are you noting these numbers? On your paper? Moray — you?"

"My lands are all in the North, James. I could not get men down in time. But from my small Merse baronies I can find you a hundred or two. Say four hundred at most. All horsed." The Earl of Moray was Dunbar's younger brother and married to another of the princesses, Marjorie.

"Your Merse mosstroopers are worth three spearmen and more. Now — my lord of Dalkeith knows of this ploy, and promises one thousand. Myself, I will bring six thousand. And I will vouch for another thousand from my young kinsman of Angus. How many is that, Jamie?"

"Ten thousand Douglases, my lord. And, wait — six thousand and four hundred others."

"A start. Hay — my lord Constable? What of you . . .?"

"How many Stewarts?" the Earl of Dunbar demanded, interrupting, and staring at Strathearn and Fife.

There was a murmur of support from not a few present. The Stewarts in fact, fairly new come to a position of major power through the Bruce connection, were much less rich in manpower than many of the other great nobles. And the one who could have raised most, holding their only inherited earldom — as distinct from their earldoms gained by judicious marriage — was John of

26

Carrick, Lord High Steward, not present. He, and the Wolf of Badenoch, in the far North.

"I will bring fifteen hundred," David of Strathearn said, scowling. Most men doubted if in fact he could raise half that.

"And I five hundred." That was Sir John Stewart, Sheriff of Bute, a bastard of the King and a stout fighter.

"Enough!" The Earl Robert raised a hand. "The Stewarts will be sufficiently represented. Leave it so. Douglas — proceed."

And so the count went on, the great magnates now gleefully vying with each other to embarrass the unpopular Stewarts by the numbers of men promised. Eventually Jamie could excitedly announce a total of 45,000.

A day was fixed for the muster, at Jedburgh, eight days hence.

The Earl Robert rose from the throne, to indicate that the meeting was over. He led the way back across the courtyard to the Great Hall.

All appeared to be as it had been there, save perhaps that there was even more noise and cantrips. King Robert still slept soundly — he had a great capacity for sleep — and his youngest son Walter was now on the floor. The Lord of Dalkeith was only just awake, blinking owlishly; and Bishop Peebles of Dunkeld, Chancellor of the realm, was playing cards at the dais-table with his chaplain. Somebody had up-ended two tables, trestles, at the foot of the hall, and using these as barricades, battle was being done by a number of the young nobles, including Jamie's brothers, with tankards, platters, belts, even ladies' shoes, as weapons. The Lord Lyon, as official master-of-ceremonies, had given up all attempt to control the situation, and had retired, with his heralds, to a corner of the room where they played dice, unable to leave until the monarch chose to make his departure.

Distastefully eyeing the scene, the Earl of Fife drew a paper from his doublet, and turning to look for Jamie Douglas, pointed peremptorily at the inkhorn and quill which hung from the esquire's belt. Given these, the Earl moved to his sleeping father's side, and unceremoniously shook the royal shoulder.

The King of Scots came approximately awake, blinking rheumy, red-veined eyes, the reason for his by-name of King Bleary. He had once had quite noble features. "What ... what's to do? What's to do, eh? It's you, Robbie? Och, I must have dozed over. Aye, dozed. Robbie — I'm needing my bed . . ."

"To be sure, Sire. I will have you escorted to your chamber forthwith. But first, here is a paper to be signed. A small matter to do with the Marches, for James Douglas. A crossing of the Border, which requires your royal signature, he says."

"Och, it's gey late for papers, Robbie. The morn will do fine, will it not? Forby, the Douglas seldom begs *my* leave to cross yon Border! He's aye at it. He's Warden, is he not?" The voice was quavering, thick.

"No doubt, Sire. But Percy and Neville are on the rampage and better that Douglas has your authority to deal with them. I might even have to assist him myself. To, h'm, keep the peace. His Grace of England, I fear, cannot keep his lords in order."

"Percy and Neville? Och, the ill limmers. Trouble-makers . . ."

"Exactly, Sire. Sign you here, then, and it's done with."

Mumbling, the old man took the quill in a shaking hand and made some sort of crooked signature where directed.

The Earl Robert straightened up, with the paper. "Very good, Your Grace. And now, to bed." He looked around. "Lyon—His Grace retires."

Thankfully the chief herald signed to his trumpeters, and thereafter a loud if distinctly ragged fanfare blared out. All in the hall capable of doing so stopped whatever they were doing, and stood, if only approximately, whilst the King of Scots, on the Earl Robert's arm, hobbled from the chamber.

The Lord of Dalkeith stretched and yawned. "Thank God that is over," he said. "Did it go as you wished, James?"

"As well as could be expected, yes. We shall require more men yet — but I will find them, never fear." The Earl of Douglas shrugged. "It has been a tiring evening."

"I wonder that you ever got Robert Stewart to play this game of yours, James. It is not like him. That man is no adventurer! You will be advised to watch him well. He may be your good-brother, but I know him better than you do. Ah, well — I'm for my bed. If I can find that wife of mine. Jamie — go seek the Lady Egidia. Or . . . no, perhaps better not, better not . . ."

28

II

THE GREEN HOLLOW of the haugh of the upper Jed Water, at the Kirkton of Southdean, was a stirring sight in the August evening; indeed it stirred like the inside of some vast anthill. Hidden amongst the foothills under the great Cheviot ridge of Carter Fell, it lay some ten miles south of Jedburgh and within four miles of the actual Borderline at the pass of Carter Bar. The Scots leaders had chosen it as the mustering-place, in preference to Jedburgh itself, for secrecy's sake. Jedburgh was on the main Middle March road south, into Redesdale in Northumberland, and there was considerable coming and going along the road when there was no state of war between the two countries. Travellers, packmen, wandering friars and the like would not fail quickly to carry word southwards of any large concentration of armed men at Jedburgh, the nearest Scots town to the Border in this Middle March; and the English would be warned. Southdean, however, was off the main Carter Bar route, where the Jed Water made a major bend westwards amongst the jumble of green braes and hollows, and could be approached inconspicuously from more than one direction. It had the further advantage of offering a hidden west-by-south route, for the division of the army which was going to invade England via Liddesdale, Sark and Carlisle.

Army was indeed a true description of the concourse assembled in the skirts of Cheviot that August evening. Here was no raiding band or skirmishing force, but a vast concentration of well-armed and equipped manpower, and of suitably varied categories. There were widely differing estimates as to numbers; but the total was almost certainly nearer to fifty than forty thousand, and still growing. There were probably forty thousand foot alone, spearmen, halberdiers and the like. Of lords' mounted men-at-arms, or lances as they were usually termed, there were five or six thousand; and as well as these, a couple of thousand Border mosstroopers, also mounted — indeed who could never be parted from their horses,

29

so that it was said, their wives and womenfolk came very much second in importance. There were also some five hundred archers, an arm in which Scotland was always weak, and so representing a major achievement, many of them supplied by Holy Church, and most of these mounted. And, of course, there was the chivalric and knightly host itself, the lords and nobles, the lairds and gentry, with their esquires, standard- and armour-bearers, pages, chaplains and bodyguards, adding up to another five hundred at least. For a private, volunteer and notably unofficial venture, Lowland Scotland had done the Douglas proud — for it was that Earl's idea, of course, from the start.

Jamie Douglas at least swelled with pride at the sight of it all. As chief esquire to the great Earl himself, he was very much concerned, naturally; and moreover he had a personal stake in the business now, for in token of affection and esteem, and especially to mark the occasion, his father had made over to him, illegitimate though he was, the small estate of Aberdour in Fife. He had not yet actually got a charter of the lands, admittedly, only the Lord of Dalkeith's verbal declaration; but that was enough, for his father was a man of his word. And on the strength of it, he had hired three horsed men of his own for this venture. He was a laird now, even if only in a small way, with a 'fighting tail', and a stake in this gallant affair.

Not that Jamie had much time for prideful musings. His master kept him more than busy, and there was a constant stream of tasks to be done — for though in theory Robert, Earl of Fife and Menteith, was commander-in-chief, all the organising fell to the Douglas. Most there accepted this as right and proper anyway, for he was well and away the foremost warrior of Scotland as well as its most powerful subject — and of course chief Warden of the Marches into the bargain. At a lift of the Douglas's finger, more than half of that host would have made a right-about-turn, marched to attack Berwick-on-Tweed, turned for home — or on the Stewarts, to rend them. All knew it, including the Stewarts.

Jamie had come out of the parish kirk of Southdean, or Sooden as the Border folk call it, where a more or less continuous council-of-war had been in progress for the last two hours. The Earl of Douglas wanted Pate Home of Hutton for advice on a scouting party for upper Redesdale. Pate was a freebooter and horse-thief of considerable notoriety, and had appeared before the Wardens on many a charge; but none knew the wild empty hills flanking Rede and Coquet and Aln, over the English March, as did he. He would be found in the Earl of Dunbar and March's assembly, presumably . . .

The lively scene of the huge armed camp spread over the grassy braes and hollows, all colour and movement, was exhilarating for a young man. His attention, however, became concentrated on a particular corner of the whole, near the riverside, where there seemed to be some especial commotion, shouting, quarrelling. It was in the sector occupied by the Mersemen, the East March Borderers, always a contentious lot and followers — if that was the word — in the main of Dunbar and March. It was where Pate Home was to be looked for, anyway, so Jamie Douglas made his way thither.

As might well have been anticipated, the trouble proved to be about a horse, these being Borderers. And no ordinary horse. A magnificent black Barbary stallion, with one white fetlock, was the centre of controversy, amidst a throng of vociferous competitors, with three individuals all apparently claiming if not actual possession, at least some hold on the animal — and to emphasise their claim each gripping some part of its harness. Will's Wat of Foulsyke asserted that he had seen it first, and therefore he had prior claim. Dand Elliot in the Haremyres held that he had reached the brute first. And Mark Turnbull of Ruletownhead, the only one of lairdly status, declared that he it was who had given authority to bring the animal back into camp; therefore its disposal was also a matter for him. The crowd took voluble sides.

Jamie was certainly not anxious to get mixed up in a Marchmen's dispute about horseflesh, being a reasonably prudent young man; but he was intrigued, and much admired the stallion. Innocently he asked to whom it belonged, thus saddled and bridled.

He was all but submerged in a flood of scorn and invective, and was but little the wiser as a result, save for the realisation that there seemed to be an underlying assumption that it was an *English* horse, and therefore fair game. Pricking up his ears, he approached the burly Mark Turnbull, tugging his elbow.

"I am my lord Earl of Douglas's esquire, sir. Where came that horse, friend?" he enquired, civilly.

The other, who undoubtedly otherwise would have shaken him

off, possibly with a blow, paused at the Douglas name. "Ha, cockerel — what's that to you? Or to Douglas?" he demanded. "Will the Douglas buy him off me?"

"That remains to be seen. I but asked where it came from?"

"Och — from a bit den, off the waterside, a half-mile up." Ruletownhead pointed southwards. "Back some ways. Hidden in a clump o' saughs."

"*I* found it," Will's Wat insisted. "It's mine, by God!"

"I set hands on it first. That's Border law . . ."

"Why should it be any of yours?" Jamie enquired. "A fine beast, saddled and bridled, and hitched in bushes. *Somebody* owns it . . ."

All stared at him, pityingly.

"That's an *Englishman's* horse, bairn!" Turnbull explained, with what might pass for patience. "Any Englishman's beast is forfeit, this side o' the March."

"But — how do you know it belongs to an Englishman?"

"Do you reckon we wouldna ken a kenspeckle brute the likes o' this? If it belonged *this* side o' the March, man?"

"But there are thousands of horses in this valley, now, from all over Scotland. Horses you do not know."

"Sakes, boy — how long since you left your mother's breast? This stallion has been ridden long and fast, *today*. Hidden the south side o' this camp. Look at its houghs and hooves. Yellow clay. There's no yellow clay within a score o' miles, this side o' the March. But there is in Redesdale, no more'n eight mile south. In England. Rochester, Otterburn, Elsdon. And why hide the crittur there, if it was a Scots horse? It was hidden — nothing surer."

"Then . . . this is serious! Important. It is not just the prize of a good horse. But what it was doing there. And where is its master . . .?"

"How can we tell that, laddie? There are thousands o' men here. Strangers. He could be any o' them . . ."

"I'm thinking I might know that beast," a new voice spoke up, from the rear. "I'll wager I've seen it running with the mares in Twizel's parks. It's a beast I'd no' be like to forget. Will Clavering of Twizel's stallion."

"Twizel! Clavering!" Jamie turned to the speaker, a thin, hatchet-faced man of early middle years, sardonic as to feature. It was Patrick Home of Hutton himself. "Ha — it's you, Hutton.

Are you sure? The Claverings are well-connected, are they not? Powerful folk? This could mean much. Danger."

"Powerful?" Home shrugged. "I'd no' so name them! But Will o' Twizel is kin to Clavering o' Tillmouth, chief o' the name. Likewise Shellacres and Grindon."

"In other words, an important Northumbrian squire. Here amongst us. And we about to invade Northumberland! A spy. What else? We must take him. Quickly. Hutton—you would know him? By sight?"

"Guidsakes, lad — what's one damned Englishman amongst 50,000 of us?" the Turnbull scoffed. "We've got his horse—which is what matters!"

"Hutton — could you find this man? Clavering?"

"In this concourse? Amongst thousands! I have seen him but twice, close, man . . ."

"Then we must do it differently. Take his horse back to where you found it, Ruletownhead. And then set men, hidden, to watch it. The owner will go back for it, presently . . ."

There was immediate protest. They could watch the den without the horse, to be sure.

"No! If he hid the brute thus warily, he will make wary return. He might well perceive it gone. Take fright. Make his escape. Never fear — you shall have the horse. But get the Englishman first." Young James drew himself up, and raised a hand high. He was not a Douglas for nothing. "I speak in the name of the Douglas. Will you have me go bring my lord Earl to you? And your own Lord of Dunbar? Aye — then see to it, and swiftly, my friends. And you, Hutton—my lord seeks word with you, forthwith. In the Kirk. Come, now . . ."

The little church was packed to overflowing, and with the cream of Scotland's nobility — yet the smell, of a warm summer evening, was as of lesser men, of sweat and leather and horse and unwashed humanity. Men in chain-mail, half-armour and protective clothing tended to smell. The Earl Robert sat in the parish priest's stall, and all others had to dispose themselves as best they could. The Lord Maxwell, Deputy Warden of the West March, was holding forth on the division of forces and objectives, when Jamie brought Pate Home to Earl Douglas's side.

"My lord," he whispered, "here is Hutton. But there is something more. Something amiss. I fear there is a spy in the camp."

The Earl, seated uncomfortably on a saddle on the earthen floor, sat up. "Eh?" A spy? What mean you . . . ?"

Hastily Jamie muttered the essence of the matter, while the Lord Maxwell scowled in his direction.

"Clavering of Twizel, eh? I have heard of him. You sure of this, Pate?" Douglas made no attempt to lower his voice.

"I canna be sure, my lord. But it is a notable stallion, with the one white fetlock. I ken no other like it. And it comes from the English side, I'd swear."

"Aye. Then this must be seen to. Jamie — I need you here, by me, for the writing." The Earl turned to scan the serried ranks of Douglas lords and lairds behind him — and that church might almost have been a Douglas court. "Will — see you to this. Jamie will tell you. And swiftly. Then come you back, Jamie." He faced the front again. "A matter of some urgency, my lord Robert," he mentioned. "Proceed, Maxwell."

Jamie took Sir William Douglas, Lord of Mordington, outside, and informed him of the situation. He was his own uncle, younger brother of the Lord of Dalkeith, a cheerful extrovert. He would cope adequately.

Back in the church, the vital discussion on the division of forces, and who was to go with whom, continued. It had been agreed that the main thrust would be made in the west, for both the Percys' and the Nevilles' home areas were in the east, in Northumberland and Durham, and an invasion on the west side of the Pennines would probably gain greater impetus and get further. The Eastern assault would be more in the nature of a diversion, a distraction to draw off the opposition, hard-hitting and fast-moving but with limited objectives. The question hinged on personnel and personalities.

Archie the Grim, of Galloway, a veteran fighter, was to command the west force, under the Earl Robert his friend, who was no warrior; but a preponderance of the lords wished to accompany the Earl of Douglas, whose dashing reputation as a soldier promised the greater honour, chivalric credit and general excitement. It was this vexed issue which was holding up the planning — to the Earl Robert's distinct offence. The popularity of Douglas as against Stewart, was all too obvious.

As it happened, soon after Jamie's return, there was a diversion which to some extent redressed the balance. A commotion at the church-door heralded the appearance of a small group of new-comers, mud-spattered, travel-stained, clad for war, and led by a slender, long-featured rapier of a man, only in his twenties but with a careless air of leadership. Sufficiently swarthy to be recognised as a Douglas, he was of the sort to grip and hold the attention.

There was a major stir at this development, even the Earl of Douglas rising to greet the newcomer; and the grizzled Archibald of Galloway pushing forward, to grip the young leader by both shoulders. He was indeed Archie the Grim's son, though not his heir, illegitimate but the light of his sire's fierce eye nevertheless — Sir William Douglas of Nithsdale, the most gallant blade in the land, and next to his chief probably the most successful soldier into the bargain, young as he was, and already in line for the title of the Flower of Chivalry. Moreover, it was whispered, he might well be the light in another eye also — the Lady Gelis Stewart's.

"So you are back, lad!" his father cried. "Well come — and in time for a new and fair venture. How did it go, Will?"

"Well, my lord — passing well." For such a long dark face, the young man had a most winsome smile. "We landed at Cairnryan yesterday, rode to Threave — and spurred on here hotfoot when we heard of this venture." He bowed to the Earl of Douglas. "Yours to command, my lord."

"Aye, Will. I rejoice to see you. Safe. And Ireland? Did you prosper?"

"To be sure. We made our mark. Those treacherous kerns will not forget Douglas for a while. Nor will their English masters. We fought two battles, slew their leaders, burned their pirates'-nest of Carlingford, and sank the English fleet based there. And coming back, by Man, we taught that isle that the Scots were its true masters, not the English. There will be no more pirates preying on our Galloway coasts for long, I swear!"

"Good! Good, I say, Will — bless you! The Irish needed that lesson. Man likewise. Here is an excellent token and portent for our present attempt. Not only Galloway and Douglas, but all Scotland is in your debt..."

The Earl was interrupted by a hammering noise from the chancel of the church. The Lord Robert Stewart was banging his dirk hilt on the arm of the priest's stall.

"My lords," he said thinly, tonelessly, into the hush he achieved. "May I remind you that this is a council, and under my authority, as Great Chamberlain of Scotland. Not some Douglas tryst and caleerie. We will proceed with the business. You were saying, my lord of Crawford . . .?"

"Earl of Fife," the Douglas declared, level-voiced but tellingly. "On Douglas territory and in *my* presence, Douglas business is all men's business! Perhaps in the territories of one or other of your ladies, in Menteith or in Fife, it might be different! But not here."

There was a quivering silence at this blunt reminder of basic realities. More than half the men in that building were either named Douglas or linked with Douglas in marriage, interest or vassalage.

The Lord Walter Stewart of Brechin, youngest of the King's legitimate sons, burst out with hot words. But his brother, the Earl David of Strathearn, gripped his arm.

"*I* welcome Sir William of Nithsdale, and rejoice at his success," he said clearly. "His Grace, our royal father, will be grateful, I have no doubt."

Archie the Grim was not usually renowed as a peacemaker, but he essayed the role now, in his strange friendship with the Earl Robert. "I crave the forbearance of all," he exclaimed, his harsh voice creaking in unaccustomed placation. "My son's arrival, and his good tidings, much bemused me. My lord of Crawford — proceed."

Young Lindsay of Crawford, whose mother was a Stewart but now wed to a Douglas, coughed and looked at the Earl Robert — who stared directly ahead of him, expressionless, utterly self-contained, but none doubting his wrath. "Very well," he said, doubtfully. "But, to be sure, here is a new situation, is it not? A new force landed in Galloway, from Ireland. In the west. Will my lord of Nithsdale fight with the west array? Or the east?"

"My son, I think, will ride with his father," Sir Archie said.

"To be sure, my lords — that I will."

There was a new stir in the kirk. If the dashing young Will of Nithsdale with his victorious force, was going to be on the west front, then some of the sprigs of nobility present were prepared to reconsider. Some shifting of positions became evident. Jamie Douglas knew a pang of something like resentment, in that his romantic distant kinsman should seem to be able to steal some of the popularity of the Earl James, his chief. And there was the matter of the Lady Gelis's rumoured favours . . .

At anyrate, the problem of the division of the forces seemed to have become much eased and the council-of-war was able to proceed to tactics. David of Strathearn was advocating a by-passing of Carlisle and a drive down on Lancaster, when there was another interruption. Douglas of Mordington came back with a prisoner.

The stocky, red-faced, youngish man, looking distinctly apprehensive, was indeed Clavering of Twizel. They had caught him returning in round-about fashion for his horse. Mordington presented him urgently before his chief, ignoring the Earl Robert.

"I am Douglas," that man informed the captive grimly. "Chief Warden of the Marches. I require to know your business in this camp on my territories, Englishman?"

"I . . . I had reason to travel to Jedworth, my lord," the other declared, glance darting around the hostile faces. "I saw . . . many men. I came to discover what it might be. So, so great a gathering."

"Why were you riding four miles off the Jedworth road, sir?"

"I thought to ride by, by Fulton, my lord. I could win to Fulton this way . . ."

"Why Fulton?"

"I might buy cattle there. As at Jedworth. On occasion I deal in cattle, my lord Earl."

"You were looking for cattle? Scots cattle? To buy?"

"Yes, lord. To buy."

"Search him, Will. Discover how much siller he has on him."

A rough search of Clavering's person produced only three nobles, a half-noble and some groats.

"You were buying no cattle this journey, sirrah," the Earl declared. "You lie."

"No, lord — no! I was but spying out the prospects. For buying. If the prospects were good, I would come again. With the money. With drovers . . ."

"Aye — spying out the prospects! *That* I will believe, Englishman! But not for buying. For stealing! You ride alone. Secretly.

37

You hide your horse in a brake. Come spying through this camp . . ."

"No, my lord — no! On my soul I swear it! I am an honest man I have broad acres. No need to steal cattle . . ."

"How many Borderers have? Yet cattle-stealing is as life to them. As Warden, I am left in no doubts as to that! On both sides of the March. I say that you were spying the prospects for a raid. Choosing a route, a secret route. To drive back beasts stolen from Fulton and other lands, through these quiet hills and into Redesdale. You planned a prey . . ."

"In the name of the Blessed Mary and all saints — no! I am no reiver . . ."

"Fulton is a vassal of mine, my lord James," Kerr of Altonburn put in. "He is in the camp. Have him in, and see if he knows this man."

"I do not *know* him," Clavering asserted hurriedly. "I was told that he bred good cattle."

"Aye — so you went to spy them out. By back ways. Instead of riding honestly up to his door, from Jedworth. I say you are a liar, and a poor one, Twizel! Enough of this. You were intent on stealing Scots cattle. And you know the penalty for cattle-reiving, in my warden's court. Hanging, sir! You will hang."

With a wail, Clavering sank down on his knees. "My lord Earl — mercy, I pray you! Mercy! Of your lordship's clemency. I did not come to steal. On my immortal soul, I swear it! Hear me. That is not why I am here. I can explain . . ."

"It was not cattle, then? You lied in this also?"

"No, lord — not cattle. I came . . . I came . . . otherwise. To discover what was to do. So many men a-move on the Border. My lord Harry Percy sent me. He was concerned — all were. At Berwick. He feared a raid, a great raid."

"Ha! Here is a horse of a different colour! But equally lies, I'll be bound!"

"Truth, lord — truth. The Percy had had word. In Berwick. He is Governor of Berwick. Word of mustering men. He sent me to discover the truth. Others also. I followed a company of men, riding down Teviotdale. To here. At a distance . . ."

"So! You were spying, indeed? You confess it. Not for cattle, but for men! On Scots soil. Spying on me, Douglas! And you think to escape hanging by confessing it?"

"It . . . it is warfare, lord. Not reiving. I am captured, yes. A prisoner. You cannot hang a prisoner-of-war. A ransom. My kin will pay a ransom."

"Tush! Think you Douglas is interested in ransoming such as you? You are a spy, sir — no prisoner in fair fight. And should hang. Unless . . .?"

"Unless, lord?" The other in his eagerness grabbed the Earl's arm.

Distastefully he was shaken off. "Unless you can offer us some information that is of value to us. Information that is sufficiently valuable to exchange for your valuable life, Twizel! How think you?"

The other bit his lip unhappily.

"Yes or no, man?"

"I know little, sir . . ."

"You come from Berwick. Twizel is near to Berwick. If Hotspur Percy is concerned, does he muster men?"

"Yes, lord. At Berwick. And at Alnwick."

"How many?"

"Not many. As yet. He does not know your numbers. Or . . . or intent. There is the truce . . ."

"You claim a truce? And yet would be treated as a prisoner-of-war! You must make up your mind, Clavering."

"Yes, lord. No, lord. I . . ." Helplessly the man shook his head.

"Percy musters in Berwick and Alnwick? But not in great numbers as yet. What else? What of Neville?"

"There is trouble with the Lord Neville of Raby, sir. Percy and he are at odds, although cousins. There is word of Neville raiding in the south. But I know not . . ."

"Where in the south?"

"They say in Weardale and Allendale and Stanhope. But I have no sure word. The dale country . . ."

"And Clifford? And the Bishop of Durham? On whose sides are these?"

"Both support Hotspur. The Prince Bishop is already in arms on the Percy's behalf. In those south dales. And my lord of Clifford making thither from Cumberland."

"Then why does Hotspur sit in Berwick town, his southlands raided, and leave Neville to be repelled by his friends? It sounds not like Hotspur!"

"King Richard's orders, my lord. The Percy is Governor of Berwick and Warden of the East March. And there have been whispers of trouble in Scotland. His brother, Sir Ralph Percy leads in the south. For the old Lord of Northumberland . . ."

"I say that is not like Harry Hotspur! There is more to it than any King's order, I swear, to keep him. Tell me, sirrah — if you value your neck."

Clavering swallowed. "I think . . . I do not know, lord — but I think that the Lord Harry intends to make a sally into Scotland. From Berwick. Should a raid develop into England. To, to draw the Scots back. I do not *know*, you understand, my lord. I but heard that it was so . . ."

"That sounds more like the Percy! So — we have it, now? You have, I think, earned your neck, Englishman — from us. But earned a hanging, I'd say, from Hotspur! Take him away. But hold him secure. He may aid us further, yet."

The unhappy informant was escorted out.

"What now, then, James?" the Earl David asked. "Do we change plans?"

"Not on the west, I think. Here in the east, we must consider anew."

The Earl Robert made one of his few interventions. Although little of a warrior, he was shrewd of mind. "If Clifford leads a Cumberland array to aid Ralph Percy in the south-east, he will cross by the Irthing, by Gilsland and Haltwhistle and the South Tyne. The hills between grow ever higher and wider to the south. Cumberland, Westmorland, Furness and Lancaster should lie unprotected. Our main thrust should go far and fast. But there is danger. Ralph Percy, Clifford and the Bishop, when they gain word of our Scots thrust, could make their peace with Neville, and march westwards through the hills of Teesdale and Lunedale, across the spine of England, to cut us off. From Scotland. If Neville joined forces with them, we could be caught."

"My own thinking, entirely," Douglas nodded. "They must be diverted, therefore. Into believing the main thrust to be in the east. That will be my task. A swift-moving mounted force, stopping for nothing, until it menaces Ralph Percy's flank in the southern dale country. Then burning and harrying, and a slow retiral. Drawing them after us. Leaving them with little time to spare for you, in the west. *You* to strike fear deep into England."

"It will serve . . ."

"And what of our Scots East March?" Archibald of Galloway demanded. "If Hotspur invades from Berwick, meantime?"

"We must allow for that, yes. Detach a force to hold him. Will Douglas — Mordington is on his way. In the Merse. Take you, say, two thousand or so of Mersemen. They will know and defend their own country best. Keep the English back from the Merse and Lothian. They will not be in large force."

"Not to come with you, my lord? Into England? On this venture . . . !" That was almost agonised.

"Someone must defend the Merse, Will. Your lands are there. You know it all. But, see you — it may not be for long. You may be able to join us. For when Hotspur hears that it is *Douglas* wasting his homelands of Keeldar, Coquet, Alnwick and the rest, threatening his town of Newcastle — as hear he will, I shall make sure — I wager he will ride south in haste, King Richard's orders or none. And either forget the venture into Scotland, or else send but a token force under some lesser man. *I* would, in his boots."

None there found fault with that reasoning.

So it was agreed. The Douglas, with fastest movement requisite, did not want to be encumbered with foot, or large numbers. His force would consist of lords and knights and esquires, with their men-at-arms, plus a contingent of Border mosstroopers and a share of the mounted archers, 3,000 would serve. Another 2,000, a mixed force, would follow along behind him, more slowly, to consolidate, protect his rear, burn and harry, and help confuse Hotspur. Mordington would take his 2,000 and head north-eastwards however reluctantly. And the main body, over 40,000 still, would march south-westwards, over the Note o' the Gate pass into Liddesdale and so down to Esk, to cross into England east of Carlisle, and thereafter southwards for Lancaster.

III

JAMIE DOUGLAS RODE cheerfully down Redesdale, a little
uncomfortable in his new shirt of French chain-mail, but
heart singing within him. Without actually thinking the
matter through, it seemed to him that this was what he had been
born to do, that all his life hitherto had been just a preparation,
leading up to this fine sunny morning's adventure. He, James
Douglas of Aberdour, was off to war, well-mounted, armed,
equipped and 'tailed'; indeed he was now riding on the soil of the
Auld Enemy, and in the most gallant of company. The green
Cheviots rose steeply on either hand, the sparkling Rede sang and
chuckled on their right, the larks shouted their praise above them,
and they clattered down the winding, twisting drove-road, part of
it of Roman construction, they said, at a fast trot, 3,000 strong and
under the proud banner of Douglas. For a young man, it was the
best of worlds.

There were many other banners flying this morning, and no
lack of Douglas colours amongst them; but the main great
undifferenced standard of the house today was not borne by
Jamie, nor yet by Bickerton the armour-bearer, but by the Earl's
fourteen-year-old illegitimate son, Archibald Douglas of Cavers.
The other members of the Earl's personal retinue were present
also—John Bickerton, son of the Keeper of Luffness Castle for Sir
James Lindsay, but still Douglas's armour-bearer; Master Richard
Lundie, chaplain; and Simon Glendinning and Robert Hart,
junior esquires or senior pages. To them, riding immediately
behind the Earl and his supporting lords, were attached a group of
Douglas lordlings — James and William, Jamie's legitimate
brothers, and Johnnie, otherwise; William of Drumlanrig, only
thirteen, the Earl's other illegitimate son — unfortunately he had
no lawful offspring as yet; young Douglas of Mains; Douglas of
Bonjedward and others. There was some regret that the hero, Sir
William of Nithsdale, had gone with the west force — but not on
Jamie's part, who had room in his heart for but one hero at a time.

They made a stirring, lively company in their youthful high spirits, brave armour — most of it worn in earnest for the first time — and colourful heraldic surcoats worn over the steel. Behind them the winding column stretched far out of sight, for even 3,000 horsemen on a narrow road, three-abreast and in close file, will cover well over two miles; and there were the sumpter horses behind that.

The first sizeable English village, Otterburn, fifteen miles from the Borderline at Carter Bar, came in sight of the head of the column, under the grassy braes and outcrops of Fawdon Hill, a cluster of grey, low-browed and reed-thatched cottages, with a sturdy peel-tower on a mound behind. There were some quite fair cattle and sheep grazing on the slopes around, and some useful horseflesh in the in-fields. But though these aroused a succession of acquisitive growls, especially from the mosstroopers, the Douglas had given sternest orders that there was to be no harrying and reiving at this stage, however tempting, indeed no pausing at all. They would have their sport later, he promised.

But Douglas himself was interested in the Otterburn area, as they rode by — as he was in every strategic site. He pointed out to his companions, the Earls of Dunbar and Moray, the Lord of Crawford, Sir William Keith, the Marischal and others, how the place was made for defence, the flooded low ground of the Rede meadows proof against cavalry attack, the river itself unfordable here, the slopes behind steep, with scrub woodland for cover, and retreat-lines into the hills. The Earl was an experienced campaigner, but he also had a natural-born eye for tactical country.

After Otterburn, the valley of the Rede much opened out to high, rolling moorland and wide vistas, with the Cheviots drawing back, the river itself swinging away southwards to join the Tyne at Bellingham. Pate Home of Hutton, in charge of the forward scouting party, was waiting for them at the Elsdon Burn. He reported that the country lay unroused, apparently unsuspecting, the folk at their harvesting. Whatever rumours Hotspur had heard at Berwick, he did not seem to have sent warning south.

All that day the Scots rode southwards, unopposed — and for once not leaving a blazing desolation behind them. By Rothley and the Scots Gap they came to the great Hadrian's Wall of the Romans, and crossing Tyne by a quiet secondary ford near Wylam, were able to camp sufficiently secretly in the extensive

Chopwell Woods, just over the County Palatine border, Durham city itself only some fifteen miles to the south-east, a lively demonstration of the Douglas capacity for swift and prolonged advance.

But the two days that followed were a disappointment, at least to Jamie Douglas and many another non-veteran campaigner. Nothing would shake the esquire's pride and faith in the Earl of Douglas; but it seemed to him that his hero was on this occasion scarcely living up to his reputation. For nothing very gallant or exciting transpired. Scouting parties were sent out into the dale country ahead and towards Durham itself, and these in due course sent back information that Sir Ralph Percy, Hotspur's brother, was in intermittent action against Neville's forces in the Blanchland area of the Derwent valley, aided by the Prince-Bishop of Durham and a considerable contingent. This meant that Durham city would be largely unmanned. The Douglas was not intent on any confrontation — the English forces combined seemed to add up to almost 10,000 against his 3,000. His objective was to distract, divide further if possible and draw the enemy eastwards away from any possible crossing of the Pennines into Westmorland and Lancashire where they might menace the main Scottish thrust. This sort of programme offered little of glory and chivalric élan, such as Jamie and other untried warriors had looked for in the great adventure. It did not seem like the famous Earl of Douglas, somehow, to allow himself to be used merely as a species of decoy, he with the greatest military reputation in Scotland, whilst the western army achieved all the action. After all, it had all been Douglas's idea, in the first place.

What did transpire was less than dramatic. The Scots force was split. The Earls of Dunbar and Moray, with about 1,000 men, went to harry the flanks of Percy's force, up Derwent — not to risk any battle but to worry and mystify the English, and thereafter to retire north-eastwards burning the land as they went. Douglas himself, with the bulk of his force, made a hasty descent, by night, on Durham city, to threaten it — they could not expect to capture it even if they had wanted to, secure behind its strong walls. It was hoped that this would sufficiently alarm the warlike Bishop to bring him back in haste to the rescue, and so not only weaken Sir Ralph Percy but have the effect of bringing Hotspur himself hurrying south to protect Newcastle and the populous coastal plain.

Jamie found the night dash to Durham exhilarating enough. But once there, circling round and round the silent walled city yelling threats, soon palled, with nothing more effective possible lacking siege machinery. Just before dawn they drew away northwards again, the Earl apparently satisfied, but now grimly giving the order to burn, burn.

The setting alight to the surrounding countryside thereafter, with villages, mills, farms and cot-houses going up in flames, over a wide swathe of North Durham, might be strategically sound and even in keeping with the accepted standards of Border warfare; but it seemed scarcely in the chivalric tradition and unsuitable work for a knightly host. Jamie, and others who felt like him, could hardly put this point of view directly to the Earl; but something of disappointment and reaction did become evident in that savage, smoke-filled early morning. Jamie was in fact seeking to comfort his young and vomiting brother, amongst screaming horses and bellowing cattle, weeping women and cursing men, priests and friars on their knees praying, all in the ruddy glare of burning Finchale Priory monastic buildings — not the church thereof, for all churches were being spared, by order — when the Earl James rode by, armour gleaming red.

Reining up, he looked down on them. "You mislike it?" he asked them, harshly. "Your tender stomachs turned, eh? Then remember this night laddies. And remember that we are but babes at it, compared with the Plantagenet — all the Plantagenets. Seek that it will not happen in Scotland again, as it has done times without number — why we are here. Remember Kelso, Roxburgh, Haddington, Teviotdale, Tweeddale, Melrose. Now — have done with your puking and play the man. Remember your name — Douglas! Jamie — come with me."

At last the Scots began to gather again, company by company, on the high heath of Chester Moor seven miles north of Durham. Although the new day was bright ahead of them, behind was almost as dark as night still, under the pall of smoke lit by a red and evil flickering. Few were depressed, unhappy, sickened, it seemed — indeed excitement and elation ran high, destruction clearly engendering its own fierce exultation.

They rode back to Chopwell Woods. The other party was late in arriving; but Dunbar and Moray were also well content with their night's work. Percy had been lured out, and was warily probing behind them, but only slowly, not risking any major confrontation before he could discover the Scots' full numbers and intentions. They had carried out token burnings over a fairly extensive area around Slayley, Dipton and Hedley.

Weary as they all were, Douglas was not prepared to allow them rest. He was anxious to have the Tyne between them and Ralph Percy before they halted — for to be caught on the wrong side of that major river, by a superior force, could be fatal. They headed north, as they had come.

Just before noon they rested at last, in the Horsley Woods, only nine miles up-river from Newcastle. And there, stiff and jaded, as the invaders snatched what rest they could, the news was brought that Harry Percy himself had arrived at Newcastle, having evidently ridden through the night. He appeared to have brought no large force with him.

At this word of Hotspur's near presence, a noticeable change came over the Earl James. He was as a man re-invigorated, personally challenged. For long there had been especial antagonism between the great houses of Douglas and Percy, that of rivalry rather than feud. Their interests tended to clash at points innumerable, their positions almost complementary, the two most powerful families of the Border area. Douglas was Chief Warden on the Scots side, and it was probably the similar appointment of Harry Percy, in place of Neville, on the English side, which had sparked off the present fighting. As well as this, there was the more personal aspect. Hotspur, as his nickname implied, was renowned far and wide as a high-spirited, potent and gallant figure of that age of chivalry, probably the most famous champion in England, headstrong, arrogant, courageous and a law unto himself. Douglas, Scotland's most famed warrior, was born to cross swords with him. Undoubtedly, with Hotspur's arrival on the scene, a new dimension developed. Jamie was not alone in suspecting that this situation lay largely behind the entire present Douglas involvement.

Nothing would do but that the Scots must ride for Newcastle at once. Hotspur must be challenged — and before his brother came up with reinforcements. There would not be any large garrison in the town — Ralph Percy would have taken all he could. If Harry Percy had ridden south, fast, with only a comparatively small company, it could represent a notable opportunity. Newcastle's town walls were not nearly so strong as Durham's, despite the more powerful castle. They might be able to lower the Percy's pride somewhat — and not before time.

Infected by their leader's enthusiasm, they rode out of Horsley Wood, by Houghton to the Roman Wall, and along it eastwards by Heddon, Throckley and Walbottle, until from the Nuns Moor Newcastle came in sight. On a ridge of the rolling common of the Town Moor, hidden by thorn scrub, broom and whins, they halted, to gaze down.

Newcastle, although sunk in the valley of the Tyne, at the first point inland from the estuary at which it might be bridged, was not nearly so tightly enclosed by banks and braes as was Durham. In consequence, the town had spread itself more widely over the valley-floor, sprawled indeed, to the detriment of its defensive capabilities. Protected on the south by the river, its walls tended to ramble and be extended in the other directions, the newer extensions less high and thick than the old, with obvious weak spots. The main gate, leading to the bridge and dominated by the tall castle, looked potent enough, however.

From their viewpoint the newcomers could see two gates, and both were open — as might be expected, in early afternoon. But undoubtedly they could be closed before any rush of Scots could reach them, however swift. There was a wide fosse before the walls themselves, moreover, which would narrow any attack to the recognised crossing-places. No surprise headlong assault was going to get them into the town.

But Douglas had a notion. He had been to Newcastle many times and knew the lay-out of the town. Since these two northern gates were open, it was likely that others were also. It ought to be possible to make their way down fairly close to one of the lesser western ports unobserved, via a wooded ravine of a sizeable burn they had crossed, which dropped from the common land of The Leazes, an extension of the Town Moor south-westwards, near enough perhaps to rush the West Gate before it could be closed. No large numbers would be required, or suitable, for this. It might not prove possible, but would be worth the attempt.

The Earl himself would lead this sally. He selected 300 men only. The rest would remain in their present position until the gate-rushing attempt was launched; then they would show themselves, and ride straight down upon the main northern gate, to cause maximum alarm and distract attention from the western assault, hopefully preventing aid being sent there.

Jamie went with his master, better pleased with this sort of warfare. The 300 rode back on their tracks, into the main open forested lands between Arthur's Hill and Scotswood, until they picked up the Lort Burn they had noted. They were surprised to see no herders or cattle on the Town Moor and The Leazes; no doubt the night's burnings had alarmed the owners and all had been withdrawn to safer grazing. The dean or ravine of the burn wound and twisted, making awkward going, with the men having to dismount and lead their horses; but inevitably it led approximately in the right direction, towards Tyne.

When they reached the level ground and their cover began to thin out, Douglas himself, with Sir James Lindsay, Jamie close behind, crept forward and up a low bank, to reconnoitre. They found that they were on the edge of open waste haughland, which gave the impression of being flooded in winter, with the town walls rising no more than a quarter-mile away. Unfortunately there was no gate opposite. The only one visible on this side, presumably the West Gate, was some distance further to the south-west.

The Earl cursed. "Too far," he jerked. "Near half-a-mile. Unless they were asleep, they could have the gates closed before we could reach them. Even at the gallop."

"We could win further along this burnside, without being seen," Lindsay pointed out. "The bank will give us cover some way yet, so long as we are not mounted. We would get that much nearer yon gate."

"Not near enough." Douglas pointed. "You can see how far we could go, unobserved. It would still leave 600 yards of open ground to cover. And there is the fosse to cross. It will not serve."

"My lord," Jamie put in, diffidently eager. "They would not close the heavy gates, surely, for three or four men, seeming to be unarmed travellers. If these could ride openly, then seek to stop the gates being closed. It might give time for the rest to win across."

"Dangerous work for the three or four, laddie! They could be overwhelmed and cut down. And keeping the gates open might not be easy."

48

"They would have surprise to aid them. And the gates could be blocked in some fashion. *I* would go."

"How would you block the gates?" Lindsay demanded. "You cannot carry anything sufficiently heavy . . ."

It was the Earl who answered him. "Those beasts!" he exclaimed, pointing. There was quite a number of cattle grazing in the haughland, no doubt brought down from the Town Moor and commons for safety. "Use them. Drive a dozen before you. Then hamstring them, in the gate-mouth. They will not easily move hamstrung cattle in a short time. And the brutes will give you some cover, forby. That is it, Jamie — you have it! They will not be able to close the gates till the beasts are dragged clear. And we will ride the moment we see you within the gates. But . . . it may cost you dear, boy. You will not be able to wear armour."

"When they see you all coming at the gallop, my lord, they will not concern themselves with such as us."

So it was decided. Jamie, his half-brother William and two mosstroopers used to handling cattle doffed all armour, shirts-of-mail and helmets, and with only their dirks at their sides, mounted and rode openly out from their cover towards the grazing cattle, while the rest of the party continued on down the burnside, behind the lessening bank, leading their horses.

Jamie and his companions felt exceedingly naked as they trotted unhurriedly towards the gate, slantwise across the haughs. They had no difficulty rounding up sufficient cattle-beasts; indeed they picked up almost too many of the animals which, looking askance at the horses, moved off in front of them fully a score strong. There was a great temptation to rush it, now, to cover the ground as quickly as possible before those gates were closed in their faces and the arrows started to fly. But Jamie resisted the urge, and held back his colleagues. Haste would only arouse suspicions.

A new problem began to materialise, which successfully distracted their minds from their personal fears. This was the tendency of the cattle to run on too far and too fast, ahead, and so enter the gateway before they could be stopped. Fortunately the fosse came to the rescue, the deep and wide ditch dug well out from the wall-foot. It was fairly dry at this season, but much rubbish from the town had been cast into it, making the bottom all but impassable, and the trotting cattle, clearly not liking the look

49

of it, turned at right angles along the lip. The horsemen, cutting across, were able to catch up without hastening unduly.

Before the West Gate, of course, the fosse was bridged by a road. They reached this still with no challenge from whoever kept the gate. Three men were seen to be standing in the entry watching them, but displaying no signs of alarm. The cattle were still in front, and need not appear to be being driven deliberately. With a flash of inspiration, Jamie raised his hand in part salute, and then pointed at the beasts, and shouted,

"Stupid brutes! A plague on them! Turn them back, see you — turn them." He hoped that his voice would not reveal him as a Scot. The Northumbrian tongue was not so dissimilar.

Possibly the three men would have sought to turn back the cattle anyway, since they presumably would not be welcome in the streets. Anyhow, they answered the appeal, waving their arms, shouting, and trying to prevent the beasts' entry. The creatures, confused, had horses behind them however, and pressed on through the gatehouse pend. Chaos ensued.

It could hardly have worked out better for Jamie's purpose, a score of hulking beasts jammed in the entrance pend, men disputing their passage, yelling horsemen behind. Reaching for their dirks, the Scots leapt down.

What followed was not for delicate stomachs. Stooping, four of them slashed with their knives at the great tendons at the back of the hocks of the cattle-beasts' hind-legs, to hamstring them and bring them down, the mosstroopers at least expert at the grim task. Bellowing with pain and fright the wounded animals collapsed by the rear, unable to move. In only a few moments that gateway was a heaving, roaring mass of disabled livestock such as would take much time and labour to clear — and the town-gates, could not be shut until it was.

There was, indeed, no attempt to shut them. Bent low, and busy amidst the distracted animals, the four Scots did not hear or see the eruption of their fellow-countrymen, from the cover of the burnside 6oo yards away, until they were in full charge, well out into the haugh. But the three at the inner end of the gateway did, since they were facing that way — and a terrifying sight it must have been. They turned and bolted; and their flight was joined by two more from the gatehouse above, racing away up a narrow street of thatched houses. The West Gate was left in the charge of the four Scots and the frantic cattle-beasts — such as could still move going pounding after them into the town.

The Earl's contingent came thundering up in great style — and found nothing more dramatic to do meantime than to put out of their misery and clear away about a dozen suffering bullocks. A cheaper entry into a walled city would have been hard to imagine. Congratulations were showered on Jamie and his companions.

The Douglas wasted no time on such inessentials. With Lindsay, Bickerton and others he drove his horse somehow over the struggling mass of bullocks and pressed on beyond the gateway. They found that they were still not within the city itself, but in a sort of adjunct to it, and enclave, with a number of houses, hutments, byres, stables and what looked like a tannery and brewery. Beyond this area rose another and higher wall, with a second and stronger gatehouse.

Pulling up, the Earl frowned. It was clear that this was the original city wall and West Gate, and that, with the place growing, new wall had been added, in this section, further out. Edward I had first walled-in Newcastle almost a century before, and his grandson Edward III had extended it in places. This was one of the extensions.

There was obvious alarm, panic indeed, ahead, with folk streaming from houses and buildings and hurrying off up the central street. The Scots leaders spurred forward. If they could reach the second gate while it was still open to admit these people, they could perhaps hold it open. Douglas yelled for men to follow him.

Jamie left off putting cattle out of their misery, gladly, mounted and rode on. He could hear distant shouting, cheering and clash from northwards. Evidently the main body had moved down upon the northern or New Gate, as arranged.

He came up with the Earl to find him taking cover behind the gable of a house which jutted into the access street, which was the principal road out, to Carlisle.

"Archers!" he was warned, briefly.

Peering round, he saw an open space, used as a bleaching green apparently, with behind it the tall double towers of a gatehouse in the high walling. In the open, two horses lay transfixed with arrows, Lindsay's and Bickerton's, the second the unfortunate

51

armour-bearer had lost thus — although the armoured men themselves were safe. Bowmen could be seen standing between the
crenellations of the tower-tops. The last of the townsfolk were
pushing in through a small postern door at the side of the great
gateway between the towers. This wider entry was not closed by
the usual massive gates, but by a piled-up barricade composed of
carts, ploughs, barrels, joists, furnishings and the like — and was
being added to feverishly as they watched. Presumably the gates
themselves could no longer shut — or they might have been detached and used for the new gateway.

The Earl was swiftly weighing up the tactical situation. "All to
dismount," he told Jamie. "Bowmen forward. The best armoured
to me."

It took some time to organise the attempt, the few archers they
had brought along to seek to keep down the heads of the enemy
bowmen on the towers, those Scots who had protective coats-of-
mail, mainly gentry these, to form up under Douglas himself, to
rush the barrier on foot.

That sally was not a success. For one thing, men weighted down
with steel, whether plate- or chain-mail, or both, were inevitably
slow-moving and anything but agile. Instead of being able to rush
the barricade they only blundered towards it. They might be fairly
proof against arrows, but not against the thrusts of long pikes
which, though they did not pierce the armour, could knock the
men down. And clambering on and over upturned carts, ploughs
and barrels was far from ideal footwork for such burdened men,
used to fighting on horseback. They could not bring their swords
to bear, and the few lances they had brought were no match for
the twelve-feet-long pikes. The defenders had almost every advantage. With townsfolk throwing missiles of all sorts, and more pikes
being rushed up, Douglas regretfully ordered a retiral. The forty
or so who had made the attempt had to support or drag back with
them fully a quarter of their number, mainly with damaged limbs
caused by falling or being knocked over on the unstable barricade.
Jamie aided his half-brother Will, groaning with pain; and young
Archie Douglas of Cavers, standard-bearer, was also amongst the
casualties. This was no more knightly combat than was ham-
stringing cattle-beasts.

The Earl now was in a quandary. If they had had the armoured
war-horses and destriers which were the normal mounts for chiv-

alry, it would have been comparatively easy; but on such slow and heavy creatures they would never have been able to reach here in the first place, covering scores of miles a day. Their light mounts were unprotected against archery. The English were always strong in bowmen, with their long yew-bows and cloth-yard shafts which Scotland could not match. Any attempt to rush this barricade clearly would have to be done by *unarmoured* foot, protected by some sort of portable shield or covering — like the sows for sheltering teams working a battering-ram, in siege-machinery. But that would take time to make. Bringing in large numbers of men from the main body would solve nothing here, for the entrance gateway between those drum-towers was narrow, and only a limited number of attackers could fight therein, at a time. Not having come prepared for siege warfare, they were held meantime.

On the other hand, they had gained a useful salient into the city, here, with houses and buildings for cover, and a safe approach to the outer walls at least. They would endeavour to hold on to this enclave. It was the best place that they were likely to obtain from which to threaten the town. Douglas ordered his men to convert the houses and buildings into strong-points, and the archers to prepare many fire-arrows for an attack on the thatched roofs beyond the inner walls. He also sent for the two Earls and other leaders to come round from the demonstration before the main northern or New Gate, for a conference. And he sent out many more small groups to scout around in all directions but especially south-westwards. They must on no account be caught in the rear by *Ralph* Percy.

What would Hotspur do now, they all wondered? He was certainly not the man to lie low meekly and do nothing.

IV

WHETHER OR NOT Sir Harry Percy was weary, and resting after his hurried dash southwards of sixty miles from Berwick, he gave remarkably little sign of his presence in Newcastle that day — so that, indeed, the Scots began to wonder whether their scouts had been misinformed and he was not there at all. His reputation was such that it was expected that he would react vigorously and at once to their attacks; but nothing of the sort developed that afternoon or evening. There were no counter-demonstrations, no counter-attacks, no intimations that any other than the normal garrison and Town Guard were in control of the city. A stout defence was mounted, admitted — but that would have been looked for, anyway.

The Earl of Douglas was in two minds as to what to do. He was, after all, in a highly dangerous situation, deep in enemy country which he himself had aroused to fury, with a comparatively small force of 3,000 and at least four English hosts in the vicinity—Ralph Percy's, the Bishop of Durham's, Hotspur's own northern column based on the Northumberland's seat at Alnwick, and the Neville's. Not counting what numbers faced them here in Newcastle itself. Prudence suggested that he should withdraw to a secure defensive position somewhere to the north, with good lines of retreat; but of course, it was not prudence which had brought the Scots here in the first place. On the other hand, they had no siege engines or equipment, and therefore little hope now of entering a walled and defended city. It had been Douglas's hope that pride, vainglory and chivalric *élan* would have been strong enough to force Hotspur into some sort of retaliation and challenge, especially against a Douglas presence. None materialised.

It was decided that they should wait until the next day — but ready for immediate retiral, with one-third of their numbers keeping open an escape-route northwards. Meantime they would fortify their enclave within the walls, keep up intermittent demonstrations, sallies and aggressive gestures all around the perimeter, and seek to construct a timber-and-hide shield for an assault on the barriers, with long poles for pushing obstructions out of the way, and scaling-ladders of some kind.

As evening wore on, news from the scouts was that Ralph Percy, with some 4,000 men, largely foot, was now directly south of Newcastle in the Washington vicinity, examining that devastated area but still heading northwards heedfully, possibly awaiting instructions from his elder brother. The Bishop was hastening back to Durham. There were also messengers from Gordon and the Scots rearguard division, announcing that they were now in the Rothbury district and in skirmishing contact with a Percy force of some 2,000 based on Alnwick. Considerably relieved that no immediate threat appeared to be posed by these various enemy units, Douglas set his sentries, and settled to a much-needed night's rest.

Daylight revealed no change in the situation. But over the breakfast fires braising good English beef, a middle-aged knight, fully armoured but without helmet, rode out from the postern at the West Gate, under a white flag, proclaiming himself to the sentries to be none less than Sir Matthew Redman, Captain of the Castle of Berwick, and requesting to be conducted to the Earl of Douglas.

The Earl, sitting in the morning sunlight in the brewery yard, savoury chop in hand, rose courteously to greet his visitor. He suggested that the Englishman dismounted and took breakfast with them.

"I cannot greatly recommend the ale, Sir Matthew — but the beef would be excellent, if only it had had a little longer to hang."

"I thank you, my lord Earl — but I have already eaten," Redman said, remaining in his saddle. "I regret that our English beer is not to your taste. But no doubt we will be able to offer you better hospitality later, when you are the guest of the Lord Harry Percy. He sends me to you to give you welcome to his father's Northumbrian domains. He wishes with all his heart that he had had longer notice of your coming, so that Percy might have greeted Douglas more fittingly."

"That is kind, sir. But perhaps it is not too late for such personal greetings? Assuming that Hotspur is sound in wind and limb? I have feared for his good health since yesterday, when on arrival we saw naught of him!"

"Sir Harry was at his meal when you arrived, my lord — and does not like to be disturbed. Thereafter he slept a little, having been in the saddle the previous night. He trusts you will forgive him?"

"Gladly. I but anticipate our meeting the more. When am I to have the honour, sir? Assuming that Sir Harry is sufficiently rested and able?"

"Any time you choose, my lord. He will be waiting at this West Gate, to receive you, in person. There is some small blockage, impedimenta, chattels lying there, which the townsfolk have left — you know what these burghers are — but that will not stop you? Or if you would prefer to go to the New Gate, to the north, he will meet you there, with pleasure. Unfortunately that gate has jammed shut. The timbers swollen, perhaps. But it may be that if you were to push, whilst we pulled, Sir Harry thinks a meeting might be effected. Or anywhere else you care to choose, my lord, around the walls?"

"I see. Hotspur is not so hot, this fine August morning, that he would venture *outside* his walls to meet me, in more knightly style than in dragging rubbish and pushing ill-made gates, Sir Matthew?"

"Alas, the Percy is desolated. But he must needs remain on hand within, to greet another visitor, his father-in-God the Prince-Bishop of Durham, who is also expected at any moment. Less distinguished than the Earl of Douglas, of course, but a man of venerable years. Also, his own brother Sir Ralph Percy is coming. Obligations, you will understand."

"I understand you, yes. But you can inform Sir Harry that the Bishop has changed his mind, and found pressing business in Durham. And Sir Ralph is making but slow progress northwards, having difficulty with heath-fires and the like. This warm weather. You would observe the smokes? So Sir Harry would have time enough, I think."

For the first time, the other looked a little put out. "You . . . you may have been misinformed, my lord," he said. "But I will tell the Percy what you say."

"Do that, Sir Matthew. But I would not have him to disturb his arrangements one whit. For a man so clearly set in his ways, feeling his years perhaps, that would be troublesome. Tell Hotspur — if I may still name him that? Tell him that I will meet him at this West

Gate just as soon as I have comfortably finished my breakfasting. And gladly. Perhaps we may be able to clear away your ... impedimenta. I give you good morning, sir."

Jamie Douglas had had much ado to restrain his mirth during this exchange. It shed a new light on his beloved but normally rather dour and unforthcoming hero. He had never before heard him speaking like this, so much master in an affray of words, as distinct from deeds. The Englishman went off less pridefully than he had come.

The Earl was less dilatory than he had sounded, when Redman was gone. Tossing aside his meat, he quickly gave his orders, all indecision gone.

The renewed assault on the West Gate was launched within an hour of Hotspur's challenge, although the shields and sows were scarcely complete. There were two of these, each about twenty feet long, of a size to negotiate the entrance gateway. Consisting of planking torn from buildings and coated with raw hides from the slain cattle, to help baffle arrows, they were really no more than simple, angled shelters with slits left at eye-level, and cross-bars for holding up and carrying, behind and beneath which men could advance in comparative safety upon the barriers. Once the obstructions were reached these could be canted upwards somewhat, while some of the men inside worked, still under cover, to clear the obstacles away, reinforced by others bearing long poles and beams, with which to push. Behind would creep the main assault.

Since there could be no secrecy about this attempt, the Earl made the most of it, with trumpets blowing and hundreds of throats shouting the continuous chant of "A Douglas! A Douglas!" Bowmen were stationed at strategic points, to shoot blazing arrows over the walls, in the hope of setting fire to thatch within; and the main mass of the Scots, who could not be employed on this restricted front, were set to galloping to and fro around the perimeter walling, yelling challenge and threat, as at Durham, to alarm and preoccupy the citizenry.

Douglas and his officers did not demean themselves by creeping under the mobile canopies, but stood in a knot under his great banner just out of bowshot, watching, ready to move in whenever opportunity offered. To Jamie, in his shirt-of-mail again, it was frustrating just to stand by idly, whilst others adventured all; but with such limited space as the gateway provided, there was little else that they could do.

The canopies proved very effective, and though arrows stuck quivering in the planking and stones and spears and other missiles were showered down on them from the wall-walk and gatehouse parapets, they continued to move inexorably onward, one behind the other, the bearers secure beneath. Perceiving the uselessness of assailing these, quite quickly the English diverted their assault on to the crouching ranks which followed after. More or less unprotected, these suffered heavily. It was as well that it was only from above that they were vulnerable, the canopies in front also protecting them from low-level attack, or the attempt would have proved costly indeed.

The first canopy reached the start of the barrier, amidst screams and yells and trumpetings, with smoke beginning to billow up from within. Here it moved slightly at an angle to one side, to allow the other to come up alongside so that they formed a sort of wide spearhead. The front curtains were tipped up somewhat now, necessarily because of the obstructions — which themselves, however, tended to form a protection against arrows. Leaving only a third of their number inside to support the things, the others stooped to tug and pull and heave at the miscellaneous obstacles. The polemen, sometimes three to a beam, moved forward to push the more massive objects.

Unfortunately the besieged, in the interim, had greatly added to the pile of impedimenta — were still adding to it. Indeed, faster than the awkwardly-stooping attackers could clear the barrier at one side, it was enlarged at the other. The following men were unable to help or make any real impact on the situation, for so soon as they appeared from behind the canopies, or mounted the barricade, they were the targets for accurate and close-range archery. The armoured knights again pressed ponderously forward, but once more they were halted by their sheer inability to climb effectively over upturned carts, wheels, ladders, barrels and the like, sheathed in heavy and hampering steel. Arrows did them little harm, but the occasional shaft found its mark in crevice, joint or visor. The long pikes, however, were still a menace, and thrown spears and stones helped to topple unsteady armoured feet.

After a grim half-hour of this, with only the fire-arrows appearing to have been very effective, the Earl himself shaken from sundry falls, he recognised that nothing was to be gained as against quite considerable losses, and reluctantly gave the order to retire. To the jeers and cat-calls of the defenders, the Scots began the awkward and dangerous process of disengagement. It was simpler to advance behind those canopies than to retreat, especially with casualties to drag back.

It was Hotspur's turn, now. New trumpets rang out from within the walls and, against a pall of dirty black-brown smoke, a magnificently armoured figure in black plate mail, gold inlaid, over chain, and a great helm plumed with the blue and gold Percy colours, appeared on the gatehouse parapet, flanked by a scintillating group of knights. They all looked a deal more fresh and polished, less travel-worn and smoke-blackened, than their Scots counterparts.

"I am Percy," a strong voice called, casually authoritative though with a distinct burr, as his trumpeter left off. "I regret that Douglas has been unable to join me for the hospitality I promised. Some lack of endeavour, is it not? We must try harder, I say. Strive more manfully to overcome all obstacles! Do you not agree, my lord?"

Douglas drew a deep breath. "I had never thought to see Harry Percy, once named Hotspur, hiding behind old carts and ale-casks!" he gave back. "If these are your favoured defences, sir, my folk will make a song about them, I swear! A song which will resound for generations to come. Can you not hear it? 'Harry Hotspur and the Farmyard Midden!' Or perhaps 'The Percy at the Garbage Gate!' A ballade — a notable ballade!"

"The singing will be otherwise, I think. Scarcely by the Scots! And speaking of such things, is not the Douglas motto *Jamais Arriere*? Never Behind? Yet I vow I saw you, my lord, creeping far behind your front men in their pigeon-cotes or coney-hutches! We must seek a new motto for Douglas. *Toujours Arriere*, perhaps? Always Behind? That would serve. Or, say . . ."

He broke off as an arrow clanged against his breastplate, setting him staggering back a pace, though quickly he recovered his stance, unharmed.

"No!" Douglas cried hotly, to his archers. "Not the Percy. He is mine! The others if you wish. Not the Percy."

Taking him at his word, the Scots archers, furious at the Percy mockery, let fly their shafts at the knightly throng on the parapet-walk. Promptly English arrows came winging back, and the exchange of civilities broke up in a hurry in mutual disagreement.

Douglas did not allow the previous set-back to discourage him. If the barricade was impossible for them, and the shut gates likewise, without siege engines, only the walls themselves were left. He had ordered the manufacture of some sort of scaling ladders. Since normal, lengthy step-ladders with wooden rungs could not be fabricated in haste they had to make do with rope-ladders. These were contrived out of twisted straw and bracken, with wooden cross-pieces inserted at convenient intervals — awkward admittedly but just possible for the task. Great numbers were required, each about twenty-five feet long and with a crosswise pole of about six feet at the top end, which could be thrown up over the wall-head, with the intention of catching in the crenellations, and holding. It would not be easy to make them so catch, and the defenders could of course cast them down or chop the ropes through. So large numbers were needed; and the men manning the walls would have to be kept busy and distracted, on a wide front. To assist in this, orders were given to collect large quantities of straw, hay, dead bracken, whins and anything else burnable, from the surrounding haughs, commons and woodlands, this material to be piled up in heaps to the south and west, from which direction the wind blew, to provide a comprehensive blanket of smoke, under the cover of which the attempt could be made.

While this was being organised, a scout came to report that Sir Ralph Percy had arrived just south of the city. And even as Douglas considered this news, another messenger from Pate Home appeared, to announce that the Percy and his force were in fact crossing the bridge over Tyne into Newcastle itself, making no move to ride round and attack the Scots from the rear, as might have been feared. Presumably he was still uncertain as to their numbers; or he may have been merely obeying his elder brother's orders. This, at least, was a major relief. Ralph Percy would not greatly add to their problems by merely reinforcing Hotspur inside the walls. Still, it would be wise to commence the wall assault before the newcomers had time to be deployed.

So the fires were lit, and the billowing clouds of smoke rolled over on the breeze to envelop all the western and northern portions of the town in their choking pall, to add to that of the burning thatches within. Under the cover, the ladder-throwers advanced against a very considerable stretch of the walling, coughing and spluttering, eyes streaming.

It was difficult and frustrating work. The walls averaged about twenty feet in height, and throwing the ropes up and over in itself was an awkward procedure, with all the protruding rungs and poles. Most casts fell back, and of those which went over, nine out of ten did not catch in the crenellations, and they too slithered back whenever pressure was put on them. Where they did take hold, there was usually a defender nearby to hurl them back, or chop through the ropes. The smoke helped — but it also hampered the attackers. They were unable to call the attention of many of their fellows to a ladder which was holding. Some Scots clambered up on to the wall-head, only to find themselves alone and unsupported.

Jamie Douglas, running up and down the perimeter and weeping copiously, with the task of keeping his master informed of progress, was not long in coming to the conclusion that this assault, too, was going to fail. Even those ladders which had gained a lodgement did not remain long in position, with teams of Englishmen running, crouching, along the parapet-walk, to clear them, with any Scots who had climbed them. The Scots archers did manage to pick off a number of these — but the smoke hindered them equally with the enemy, and some of their own fellow-countrymen fell to their arrows in the murky confusion. And when Ralph Percy's additional manpower began to stream up to reinforce the walls, the balance became quickly less favourable. The fuel situation, too, began to deteriorate, with the stocks of smoke-making material running out, and the sinking fires ever tending to produce more heat than smoke — on an August noontide which had become sufficiently hot anyway. The perspiring, sore-eyed, coughing attackers flagged, visibly.

Once again, the Earl of Douglas had to admit defeat, and call off the attempt.

The Scots morale was not helped when, as they were drawing off, the Percy himself, now accompanied by his brother, appeared once more above the West Gate, this time under a white flag.

"Warm work on a hot day, my friends," he called. "Clearly you are wearied. Sir Matthew tells me, Douglas, that you do not enjoy our simple English beer? So here is a pipe of prime Burgundy wine to cool your gullets. With Percy's much sympathy!"

Down from the parapet was lowered on a rope a huge ninety-two gallon wine cask, infinitely carefully, inch by inch, amidst much English cheering.

Douglas, ignoring the growling of his own people, with a great effort wiped the black frown from his features. He bowed, and as a further gesture removed his plumed helmet and handed it to Bickerton.

"I thank you," he shouted back. "I shall be glad to taste of your so famed hospitality. Which we have hitherto found hard to come at!" He paused. "But see you, Percy, we have, I swear, both had sufficient of this jousting at a distance, which appears to be deciding us nothing. Let us come to a decent decision, as between Douglas and Percy, I say. I have burned your lands — as you have burned mine, in the past. Let us settle this issue between us and our houses as honest knights should. Let us cross lances, you and I, in single combat, here before all. A joust, sir. You are namely at the business, I am told. Show us *how* namely, I pray!"

There was an obvious stir, up there on the gatehouse parapet. And not only there. All around him, Douglas's lieutenants and supporters looked astonished, doubtful or openly hostile to the notion. Most began to declare it foolish at the best, dangerous anyway, possibly disastrous. But the Earl shook his head. They had sustained four rebuffs, he pointed out. He had the spirits of his men to consider — of vital importance, deep in enemy territory. The men were no longer at their best. It was clear to all that they were not going to win into this city, by force nor yet by guile. But just to steal away, in defeat, must wound their spirits further, as indeed their fair name. This way, a retiral could be effected decently. If he won, they could go proudly. If he lost, it would be in fair fight and before the greatest champion in England — no reflection on the Scots.

The Percy seemingly was having a like difficulty in deciding the pros and cons of this unexpected proposition. Before it might be rejected, Douglas sought to clinch the matter by changing it from proposal to dare. He had a trumpet-blast blown.

"I, James Douglas, do hereby challenge Henry Percy in single combat!" he cried. "Mounted or afoot. With lance, sword, battle-axe or mace — the choice Percy's. To be fought until one or other yields or is carried off the field."

There was only a brief pause before Hotspur shouted back. "I accept. So be it. Let it be lance *and* sword. Mounted, to be sure. Prepare to fall, Douglas!"

"It is a match. There is space here, before the gate. I will meet you here, so soon as you are prepared. With no carts or casks to protect you, Percy!"

The total change which came over the entire scene and situation was almost laughable. From an atmosphere of war, anger and bloodshed, suddenly it tended almost to holiday, sportive excitement. With no longer the dread of vicious arrows picking them off, the Scots set about clearing a wide space before the old West Gate, laughing, even shouting wagers to Englishmen who began to work to clear a passage through the barricade. Equally cheerful sounds came from within. The fear of possible sudden death and terrible hurt, abruptly lifted, can produce almost hectic reaction.

Jamie Douglas did not know whether to rejoice or otherwise. He had faith in the ability and expertise of his renowned lord; but Hotspur's martial and chivalric fame was as notable — and he was bound to be fresher as well as being somewhat younger. Possibly better mounted too, for though the Earl had a superb Arab stallion, the sort of animal which was ideal for long and fast cross-country riding, it was on the light side for the tiltyard. Percy probably would not have a destrier available at Newcastle, admittedly; but he would certainly have a choice of heavier beasts. He had chosen the mounted duel, and no doubt knew what he was about. If the Douglas was to fail, and before all . . .

The contest was bound to differ from the normal tournament standard in more respects than the horses involved. The Earl was armoured mainly in chain-mail, with only cuirass of plate back and front, gauntlets and knee-pieces of steel, and no massive jousting helm — and it was likely that Percy would be in the same black plate armour he had been wearing. There might be jousting armour kept in the castle here, but it would be surprising if it fitted Hotspur, who was over six feet tall. Likewise, Douglas had no blunt jousting lance; and it seemed unlikely that, for pride's sake, Percy would insist on them using such, as against the sharp and shorter war lances. In other words, this was going to be a much more dangerous affair than in a normal tourney — just as so much more hung on the result.

The Earl was ready first — indeed little preparation was necessary, although John Bickerton fussed about tightening buckles and straps holding the cuirass-guards in place and testing every item of the stallion's trappings and harness, his lord pooh-poohing impatiently. Jamie attached a long Douglas pennon to the Earl's lance, aided his hero to mount and then handed him up his comparatively small shield, blue and white, with the Douglas heart.

To a lively fanfare, Sir Harry Percy rode out through the gap in the barrier, followed by a throng of knights and esquires, a gallant figure on a splendid bay and leading a matching beast. He did wear the same rich armour as before, with considerably more plate than the Douglas, and being taller anyway, made the more imposing figure. Visor up, he raised a gauntleted hand.

"Ha, Douglas!" he called. "I have brought you a better nag than your grey. It will be weary, perhaps. I would not have you further disadvantaged than you are already!"

"I thank you — but I am well content, sir," the other retorted. "Give your second horse to your brother, Sir Ralph. Then, when I have unseated you, he can seek to redeem the honour of your house!"

Percy laughed aloud. "Crow while you may, Scot! Your time is short." And he reined round, to ride off to the south end of the open space — so that Douglas, not he, would have the sun in his eyes.

"My lord — you should have drawn lots for that position!" Jamie protested. "He has taken the advantage, as of right."

"Let him be, lad — perchance he will need it! Give me my lance . . ."

"See you, Lord James," Bickerton put in, at the other side, low-voiced. "Take you this small mace. It could be useful. Should lance and sword fail."

"No, no. Lance and sword Percy said—so let it be. I need no mace."

"But, sir — he has already taken an advantage. This of the sun," the armour-bearer pressed. "Who knows what other trick he may spring? He has the fresher horse and the longer reach. And more plate-armour. Take the mace — if only as precaution." And he held up a short-handled, heavy spiked club, designed for piercing even steel plate.

"No, I said. Fool — put it away! Would you have all see it? See

64

Douglas doubting the outcome? Taking a weapon disallowed?" And with a back-handed swipe of his steel gauntlet, the Earl swept the proffered mace aside. Unfortunately it struck Bickerton slightly on brow and cheek, one of its spikes drawing blood. Douglas trotted off to the opposite, northern, corner from Percy, Jamie running after, whilst the armour-bearer flung up hand to head, and cursed savagely.

The two principals sat their mounts some 200 yards apart, the furthest the open space would allow. The Earl of Dunbar and March and Sir Ralph Percy paced out into the centre, bowed stiffly to each other, agreed on a signal, decided that second lances would be available should one snap, and that either side had the right to carry off their champion unopposed should he fall. Then, back at his own party, Sir Ralph gave the sign, and a long high blast on a horn proclaimed that the fight was on.

Nothing loth, the protagonists shut down their visors, couched their lances and dug in their spurs, driving their spirited mounts forward, all dash and colour. A hundred yards was not a very adequate distance in which to attain maximum speed, but these were swift riding horses, not heavy destriers, and both were in fact into the full gallop before they met. The sun was strong in Douglas's eyes, it being early afternoon, and he was only too well aware of the handicap. But by keeping his glance lowered and peering through his thick, dark eyebrows, he to some extent countered the effect. He was counting almost every hoof-beat of his stallion — and at the same time warning himself not to underestimate his opponent.

Only a few yards apart, the Earl savagely jerked his horse's head to the right. At that speed, the animal all but fell over its own fore-feet, its rider keeping his saddle only by a remarkable mixture of balance and agility. For moments the grey was directly across the front of the bay, with Douglas's lance rendered useless. If the Percy had been prepared for that extraordinary manoeuvre, the other would have been at his mercy in those brief instants. But they were both right-handed men, with their lances couched each at that side, so it went without saying that they should ride to clash at the same side. Percy did make a wild thrust, but it was uncoordinated and askew. Douglas took the lance-tip on his shield, off which it slid harmlessly. But he himself could make no effective riposte. He plunged on, past.

But already he was urgently, violently, reining back and round, his beast's forelegs now pawing the air. In only a few yards he had managed to turn completely, on the creature's hind-legs, mainly, and thereafter was spurring back whence he had just come, behind the Percy.

That man, possibly because of the restricting effect of his helmet, both as to vision and hearing — and also because the normal procedure after such an inconclusive pass would be for each to ride most of the way back to the perimeter positions before wheeling for another charge — was a little while in realising that his opponent was in fact hard at his heels. But when it did dawn on him, he reacted in no uncertain fashion — for it must look very much as though he was running away, with his rival chasing him, an intolerable situation for England's champion. Indeed, many onlookers, the Scots at least, had begun to howl with mirth. So Hotspur sought to rein round, almost as abruptly as his foe had done half-a-minute before. He achieved the difficult feat almost as effectively as Douglas had done — for both were superb horsemen, necessarily — and so again faced his enemy. But now their respect-ive positions were vastly different. Percy, suddenly, had the sun in his eyes, and moreover was all but at a standstill; whereas Douglas was in full charge. Not only that, the Scot was prepared for the situation, had visualised and contrived it, and the Percy was not. Barely a dozen yards apart, it was too late for the Englishman either to take adequate avoiding action or to gather any speed. He aimed his lance at the other's breast and furiously hacked at his bay's sides with his sharp spurs.

But there could be no comparison between the impact of a lance with a full gallop behind it, and one with little more than trotting speed. The two protagonists met with a resounding crash, and both took the opposing lance-points on their shields. Percy's set back the Douglas in his saddle quite noticeably — more from his own momentum than anything else; but the Scot's weapon smashed Hotspur and his shield clean off his bay's back. The man fell backwards with a mighty clatter, his lance flying wide — and fell, not on peat-dust or soft turf, but on cobblestones, inside a great weight of steel plating. Sparks actually flew up at the impact. Sir Harry Percy lay still, in gleaming, colourful ruin.

The Earl, recovering his seat, glanced round, perceived the

situation, and rode on to his own corner, amidst the wild cheering of the Scots.

Jamie Douglas, all but beside himself with excitement, almost worship, was bubbling breathless enconiums as his lord trotted up. But, turning his mount again, the older man raised his visor and sat still.

"Wait you," he panted. "He may rise. It may not be finished."

But the Percy lay motionless — and clearly his supporters considered that enough was enough for, superintended by Sir Ralph, a large number of the English ran out from their side into the central space, to pick up and half-carry, half-drag the presumably stunned Hotspur back to the entrance gateway. The yells of the watching Scots became fiercer, more jubilant.

Douglas, narrow-eyed, moistened his lips. "It will serve, I think. Scarce my finest hour — but it will serve for our present needs." He raised a mail-clad arm to point. "See, Jamie—they have overlooked something, in their haste. Come with me."

Lance raised high now, its Douglas pennon fluttering, he trotted out again into the middle, Jamie running, all but skipping, behind. The English, with their inert burden, looked at them askance, but the Earl waved them on, genially.

"I pray that Sir Harry be not sore hurt," he called. "Air, and a mouthful of that excellent Burgundy, will revive him, I vow!" Pulling round somewhat, he leant over, to murmur to Jamie. "Hotspur's lance and guidon lad. Lying there still. Get it. Bring it to me. Quickly, before they perceive it."

The young man ran for the forgotten lance. The English began replacing the gateway barrier, presumably fearing a rush at it.

So, carrying both flagged spears, the Earl of Douglas rode back to his own people, barely five minutes after leaving them, to hilarious enthusiasm. He waved down all the plaudits, however.

"That was not a knightly victory," he declared. "That was but a strategem, an artifice of sorts. But necessary, since it was needful that I won. Presently, we can retire with honour, I think. Meantime, a beaker of that Burgundy, in sweet Mary's name!"

"There is a messenger here, James, from Home," the Earl of Moray said. "The Bishop of Durham is on the move again. Northwards."

"Ah! How far? And in what strength?"

"He left Durham an hour before noon, my lord. With a strong force. Horsed, in advance, perhaps 1,400 with 5,000 foot behind," the scout informed. "When last seen, the horse was at Rainton. They will have moved many miles further north, by this."

"Aye." Douglas dismounted. "This means that we must ride the sooner. But . . . decently." He turned to Dunbar and Moray. "My friends — have all our force assemble in groups and troops outside the walls. Save those who are here, within this part. These to show naught of readiness to move, meantime. You have it? Not to *look* as though we prepare to retire until I have spoken with the Percy again. We have a little time yet, I think."

After a due interval, the Earl had his trumpeter sound a summons, and then paced forward on foot, nearer to the West Gate again, Jamie at his side. He raised his hand.

"Englishmen," he called, "I seek word of the Percy. He suffered a misfortune. Too early an end to our joust. How fares he? Is he recovered? No serious hurt?"

After a few moments of silence, Sir Ralph answered, from a window of the gatehouse. "He is well enough, Douglas — after that scurvy trick! Stunned by his fall, that is all. It was no honest fight."

"It was a poor bout, yes. Too swift an end. But honest enough. I fear that the sun got in your brother's eyes. But if you are not satisfied, sir, perhaps you would care to come run a course with me, yourself? To retrieve this!" And in his other hand he held up, and let unroll, the long fish-tailed pennon with the Percy arms. "How say you?" And he flapped the thing casually.

There was a pause at the other side. Then another voice spoke up, not quite so strong and arrogant as before, but clearly Hotspur's.

"I will fight you again, Douglas — anywhere, at any time. Never fear. These fools dragged me off the field. We could have finished the bout."

"Ha, Sir Harry — I rejoice to hear you sound so well recovered. What happened to you was but a mischance, yes. I, too, am ready to meet you at any time. When, I hope, you will give me better sport!"

"Damn you, Douglas . . . !"

"Any time," the Earl repeated, holding up the pennon again.

"But . . . not today, I think? I would not have you riding another course, when shaken from your fall. It would be but a dull contest. Next time, we must not disappoint. Meantime, no doubt you will come for this guidon of yours? I am called back to Scotland, unfortunately. I cannot wait here while you recover your strength. But I will go but slowly. Wait for you between here and the Border. Till after tomorrow's night. Thereafter I shall carry your guidon to Scotland and plant it upon my castle's wall. Where you may come for it, if you care!"

"That you shall never do!" came back hotly, from the gate-house. "This I swear!"

"Very well, Percy — as you will. The remedy is in your own hands. Come take your guidon before I leave Northumberland. You will find it before my tent. I will wait for you until two nights from now — no more. Perhaps we shall see some sport, yet." And flicking the pennon mockingly, Douglas turned and strolled back to his own party. "Prepare to move," he called, but unhurriedly and quite openly.

"Do we give up, my lord — *now*?" Jamie asked, unhappily. "Flee, because of this Bishop's coming?"

"Can you count, boy? *I* count over 10,000 against us, when the Bishop comes up — perhaps more, since we know not how many Harry Percy has in this city. And Neville may be moving against us. We have heard no word of Neville. We flee, then — as far as the Town Moor, yonder!"

"The Town Moor . . .?"

"Aye. There is room there, for action. I will not be trapped down here, pressed against these city walls. When you go to war, lad, learn to use your head! It will help keep it on your shoulders! See, now — take this Percy guidon, and guard it well. Where is Bickerton? To rid me of this cuirass . . ."

"I will aid you, my lord," young Archie of Cavers volunteered. "John Bickerton has gone."

"Gone? How, gone? Gone where?"

"He mounted horse and rode away. Sore angered that you had struck him, my lord," Richard Lundie, the chaplain, explained.

"The fool! I did not strike him. Not of a purpose. I but thrust away that mace. What was he at, giving me the mace before all? The English must have seen it. Giving the Douglas a mace, when Percy had declared for only lance and sword, putting my honour at risk! The man has lost his wits. And now he betakes himself off? Lindsay — what's amiss with the fellow? He is your man. I made him my armour-bearer on your commendation."

"I know not, my lord. He is a good fighter, and namely with horse, hawk and hound. His father keeps my castle of Luffness in Lothian, and sought my good offices with you. I am sorry that he has behaved so. If I had known of this temper . . ."

"Think no more of it, Sir James. I also am sorry — that the mace struck him. I shall tell him so, anon. When he has recovered from his spleen."

"The *Douglas* will never make apology to that, that underling!" Jamie protested. "He is a surly oaf. I have never liked him."

"If Douglas has behaved ill, he will make apology to any soever!" the Earl reproved. "It is the knightly code — and do not forget it. Any of you."

"Only a Douglas should be armour-bearer to Douglas," Will Douglas of Drumlanrig, the Earl's elder illegitimate son put in — who had coveted that position for himself, although only fifteen.

"Bairns — enough!" the Earl cried. "We have more important business than to haver here, about thin-skinned youths! When you find Bickerton, send him to me. Now — prepare to retire. In good order. Up to the Town Moor . . ."

So, in orderly fashion, with a fair amount of trumpet-blowing and marshalling, the Scots turned their backs on Newcastle town and marched up the quite steep braes and banks to the north-wards, to the high common lands. Here, where they could not be approached unawares, there was room for manoeuvre and a choice of retreat routes, Douglas pitched camp. He had cooking-fires lit all along the lip above the city, so that there could be no doubts about their presence there; and before his own tent he set up Hotspur's lance with the Percy pennon. Sentries were posted all around, and scouting parties were out in force.

Just after sunset a messenger arrived from Pate Home to say that the Bishop of Durham had halted for the night at Birtley, just over 4 miles south of Newcastle. A close watch was being maintained on him.

John Bickerton was still not to be found, amongst the leadership, when the camp settled for the night.

V

PONTELAND LAY AT a crossing of the Pont River eight miles north-west of Newcastle, a bridge-hamlet with a small castle, really only a peel-tower, in a good position to levy tolls on the bridge-users. The Scots came to it in mid-forenoon and in no hurry. Douglas, in fact, was disappointed. Hotspur had not ventured out to seek retrieve his guidon, although the Scots had waited as long as they dared, with the Bishop reported on the move again and probing west-about — and moreover, word at last of Sir Ralph Neville with a large force heading north-eastwards from Derwentside. The object of the Scots exercise had been fully accomplished, therefore, and the main thrust, in Cumberland and Lancaster under the Earl of Fife and Archibald the Grim, was safe from any cross-country assault, to cut it off from Scotland. But the Earl of Douglas had hoped for better results in his personal exchange with Harry Percy. So he was dragging his feet somewhat, on his way home.

It was, of course, a risky game to play, for if the Percys joined up with the Bishop they would form an army many times the size of his own, and in their own country. But he based his calculations and hopes on Hotspur's famous pride and arrogance. The man must be smarting indeed, and was known to resent his Prince-Bishop's territorial pretensions anyway. Believing himself to have been bested by something of a trick, in single combat, he should be eager to prove that he was the better man in the field, especially in his own Northumberland territory amongst his father's vassals — without calling upon any churchman to aid him. Douglas would have wagered on him following them up, without waiting for the Bishop. His people most certainly would be keeping him well informed as to the Scots' progress and numbers. Yet rearward scouts reported no move out of Newcastle.

Ponteland was an excuse to delay for a little, at least. The owner of the little castle had the unlikely name, for a Northumbrian, of Sir Aymer d'Atholl. He was not exactly a renegade Scot, since he had been born here and never lived in Scotland; but he was descended from the ancient Celtic Earls of Atholl, and his grandfather had taken the English side in the Wars of Independence, and in consequence had lost all his Scottish lands, and settled here. The Scots had not forgotten them, however, especially as the d'Atholls were not backward in the Border reiving activities.

So a halt was made, to assault and take Ponteland Tower.

John Bickerton had quietly taken his place in the Earl of Douglas's entourage that morning as they assembled to leave the Town Moor of Newcastle. He made no comment on his absence, nor indeed on the previous day's incident, curtly dismissing his colleagues' remarks and queries. The Earl had taken him aside, however, before they moved off, and had spoken with him for a minute or two — none knew to what effect. Now, Douglas sought him out, appointing him to go forward and demand the yielding of this castle. He went, stiff, expressionless.

So far as delay was concerned, Ponteland did not provide much excuse. Quite quickly Bickerton brought back Sir Aymer d'Atholl himself, a middle-aged, heavily-built, anxious man, with a cast in one eye, who had taken one look at the force arrayed against him and recognised the wisdom of a prompt surrender. The Earl made a gift of his person to Bickerton, to take back to Scotland for purposes of ransom — a gesture which drew not a little comment, some of it resentful. It even set Jamie wondering why his master must be so generous and forgiving. The general opinion was that there was more to this than met the eye.

Leaving Ponteland Tower's stables and subsidiary buildings alight, as a beacon for Percy — since the stone tower itself would not burn — they moved on north-westwards.

Two days earlier Douglas had sent couriers to halt their slower-moving rearward force, under Gordon of Huntly and Scott-of Buccleuch, in the Wansbeck valley west of Morpeth. They would be more use there, keeping the Percys' Alnwick and Berwick groupings occupied and in check, and maintaining an open line of retreat for the main body, than they would have been had they come on to Newcastle. An extra 2,000 men, mainly foot, could not have opened that citadel; and they would have been only a hindrance to any swift withdrawal. Now they would join up.

They reached the Wansbeck in the Wallington area in the early afternoon—and had no difficulty in finding the second Scots force. Indeed it could be heard, if not seen, from miles off, with the continuous lowing and complaining of vast numbers of cattle. Gordon and Scott, if somewhat reproachful at the undramatic and pedestrian role allotted to them, had evidently decided to make the best of their opportunities otherwise, and had apparently collected the products of half the farms of Northumberland, such as would travel on the hoof, to compensate for lack of more martial excitements. And, it seemed, this huge concourse by the Wansbeck was not all; two other great herds had already been despatched northwards, under adequate guard.

Douglas found no fault with this. But he refused to halt for the night at this great camp, nevertheless. It was in no very good defensive position, for the Wansbeck was a comparatively shallow stream and could be forded easily at many points. This was no place to await the possible onset of Harry Hotspur. The Percy might come with many times their own numbers—and encumbered with all their booty, his new foot reinforcements would be of little service against a cavalry host. He must secure a very strong position, and adequate escape routes at his back. Otterburn, in the mouth of Redesdale, which they had noted on their way south that first morning, provided more or less what he required. It was another fourteen miles.

The Earl ordered the march to continue, and Gordon and Scott to bring on their people and the cattle at their best speed — but to be ready to disperse should the Percys' array overtake them. Pate Home and his rear scouts would give them warning.

It was dusk before the main force reached the long green Cheviot ridges, all pools of shadow, where the Rede issued from the narrows of its upland valley at Otterburn. But Douglas would allow no respite nor settling-in until he had made his defensive dispositions, pressing on a little way beyond the village. The river, and the wide low haughlands flanking it, wet and swampy, would protect his right; the steeps and escarpments of Fawdon and Greenchesters Hills would cover his left, provided they could deny the enemy the area in between the two heights, where the Otter burn itself came down from the north to join Rede. Admittedly the burn had carved for itself a fairly deep dean, or ravine, and this would make a useful frontal barrier. But there was a wide gap between the two hills to the north, and this would be the weakness of the position, and would have to be thoroughly plugged against

73

any outflanking move. Apart from this, the position was an excellent one, only marred by the fact that in the centre of it all on a steep knoll where a smaller burn joined the Otter, above the deep dean, rose the Tower of Otterburn. And unlike Ponteland, its owner did not acquiesce to the Scots demand for instant surrender. It was a much stronger place, to be sure, although no larger, a tall square parapeted tower of stone, with tiny windows and a door reachable only by a removable timber stair, at first floor level, all within a small, irregular, high-walled courtyard. Taking it would be no easy matter, without siege engines.

Satisfied that he had surveyed the terrain as well as was possible in the fading light, and recognised its advantages and its dangers, and aware that the tower could do him no harm, at least, the Earl allowed his host to make camp, partly on one side of the dean, partly on the other. He made use of the earthworks of an ancient fortified camp, on the higher ground west of the burn, as main base — evidently their Pictish ancestors, who had extended their sway further south than this, had also recognised the strategic usefulness of Otterburn.

During that moonlit night, although there was no word of the Percys, the continuous arrival of contingents of the vast cattle-herd, amidst much bellowing and stir, ensured that few of the Scots leaders, at least, achieved undisturbed sleep. The new arrivals and their noisy and complaining charges, were confined to the low haughland area flanking Rede.

In the morning Douglas held a council-of-war, for there was considerable difference of opinion manifesting itself amongst his principal colleagues and lieutenants. One school of thought, put forward by the Earl of Moray and the Lord Maxwell, mature and responsible men, considered that they had done sufficiently well in this expedition, and should return now safely to Scotland without further adventure or possible risk, their objectives accomplished. This waiting for Percy was perilous as well as unprofitable. Another proposal, put forward by some of the younger lords, was that they should now cross over to the west of the country, by the Tyne, Haltwhistle and the Gilsland Gap into Cumberland, to join up with the larger Scots army. This was supported by Sir James Lindsay of Crawford, Sir John Montgomerie of Eaglesham, Sir John St. Clair of Roslin and others. These, too, were doubtful of the business of waiting for Hotspur.

The Borderers, on the other hand, the Scotts, Homes, Kerrs, Gordons, Johnstones and the like, were in their element here, with the March not far at their backs, and most of Northumberland wide open to their depredations, were quite content for Douglas to wait, so long as they might make Otterburn their base and fan out left, right and centre but especially down into the richer coastal plain around Warkworth, Alnwick and Craster, in a glorious despoiling campaign such as generations of their mosstrooping forebears had dreamed of.

The Douglas heard them all out patiently. Jamie, in attendance, thought that perhaps he was even encouraging the discussion and prolonging the debate in the interests of his own preoccupation with Harry Hotspur, giving that hero more time to come up. As commander, the Earl had of course to balance the pros and cons of over-all strategy; but he also had to take into account the desires of the various component parts of his force. For this was no sort of disciplined military unit, save in that it voluntarily accepted himself as leader. Every man in it was in the fighting tail of some lord or laird, none belonging to any central authority. And none were being paid for attendance, save out of the pockets of the same lords and lairds. There was no such thing as a national army. Therefore a commander had to carry his supporting leaders with him at every step — or they could just depart and either return home or go campaigning on their own; often they did just that.

The Earl of Douglas therefore could not *command* all to his will, even though a fair proportion of those present were in fact Douglases. He had to gain his ends by more subtle means, if at all. He did so now by playing one view against another; and, being a man of action himself and recognising that words were less effective than deeds as a distraction, proposed that they meantime assailed Otterburn Tower, which was impudently holding out against them. None objected to this, at least — and delay was achieved.

The assault was not, and could not be, a very effective exercise. Large manpower was of no advantage. The position of the keep, surmounting a mound of solid rock, meant that there could be no mining or undercutting. The courtyard and outbuildings were fairly quickly taken and destroyed; but thereafter there was a stalemate. A battering-ram, contrived out of a tree-trunk, beat

75

down the basement door and its iron yett; but this merely gave access to the vaulted ground-floor chamber, which had no communication with the upper parts of the building — and unlike a timber floor, the stone vaulting was quite fire-resistant and immensely thick. The only other door was at first-floor level, its removable timber staircase drawn up. The battering-ram could not get at this, even though attempts were made to erect a platform from which to assail it, while the arrows and missiles of the defenders on the parapet-walk high above made the attempt costly. The windows were all so high and tiny, that ordinary arrows could not find a mark, and fire-arrows were useless against a wholly stone building. Picking away at the lower courses of masonry, under cover of mobile shelters, was put in hand; but with walls eight feet in thickness, with iron-hard mortar, this was a slow process indeed. In fact, the little castle could only be starved out, through lack of water and food; but this might take days.

Nevertheless, as far as the Douglas was concerned, the attempt served its purpose. It used up time, constituted a challenge to hot-blooded men, and stilled demands for departure meantime. And it did not prevent quite a large proportion of the Border contingent from pursuing their favourite role of cattle-stealing, ranging near and far for beasts discreetly hidden away in remote valleys, deans and 'beef-tubs'.

In mid-afternoon Pate Home sent the anticipated news at last. The Percys were on their way, having left Newcastle during the forenoon, a host of perhaps 8,000. They had not so far linked up with the Bishop of Durham, who was advancing slowly northwards well to the west — seemingly keeping a wary episcopal eye on Sir Ralph Neville, who was also advancing on a more or less parallel line still further to the west. These two forces were still some thirty miles off; but the Percys only twenty or so when the message was despatched.

Now there was no talk of retiral or heading westwards. All was preparation. Messengers went out in all directions to warn the raiding bands. Douglas was content. He should have his confrontation.

Nevertheless, by dusk, the Percy had still not put in an appearance, and scouts reported him still five miles away on Ottercops Moor, although his forward pickets were probing much nearer. An hour later, Home himself rode into the Otterburn camp to announce that the enemy had in fact settled in camp below Hunterless Hill, at the west end of that moor.

Tomorrow, then, would see Douglas and Percy at grips, at last.

The Earl and his lieutenants made a final circuit and inspection of the position before turning in. He was still a little concerned about a flanking attack from the higher ground to the north. It was the one weakness of the site. He ordered a strong party under Scott of Buccleuch to occupy these heights on either side of the burn. And on the low ground north of the Rede itself he had all the cattle which had not yet been despatched northwards spread in a great belt half-a-mile wide, some thousands of beasts. Any surprise frontal attack would have to negotiate this living barrier. It seemed unlikely that Hotspur would make a night assault; but if he did, they ought to receive ample warning.

Reasonably satisfied, Douglas retired to his tent, as a pale half-moon rose over the ridges eastwards.

*　　*　　*

Jamie, in the esquires' tent behind his master's, was awakened by the horn-blowing from the low ground, an urgent ululant wailing. Only three or four seconds later the Earl's voice was shouting for his aides and leaders. Stumbling heavy-eyed out into the now quite bright moonlight, the young man found Douglas already standing before his tent. There was a confusion of noise from the riverside area now, the clash of steel, shouting and a great lowing of cattle.

"Dunbar, Moray, Lindsay, Maxwell to me — quickly, Jamie!" he jerked. "Archie—get Montgomerie, Gordon, Keith. Will— down to the haugh. Discover for me the position. Synton commands there—Scott of Synton. Richard—up to Buccleuch on the left. Discover if he finds any move there. Ha—Pate! Lacking your own presence this once, your scouts have slept, I think! Get forward and find me what's to do. Rob Hart—the horses. Simon — stay by me. Bickerton — my armour . . ."

Most of the leaders came hurrying, without being summoned. While Bickerton eased the Earl into his chain-mail shirt and buckled on the cuirass back and front, and other armour-bearers did the like for their own masters, Douglas rapped out his orders.

"You know your positions, my lords. All was arranged. From

the noise, Percy has elected to strike by the riverside — the marsh-land — first, hoping to turn our flank. That means he is on foot. Horses would be bogged down, there. No doubt he will try the left flank also. Maxwell — be ready to go to Scott's aid. You are on my left. Afoot, on those braes. Indeed, on this ground, most fighting will be on foot. You have the right, Dunbar. I move to the edge of this dean, meantime, to await information. I will seek to advance in the centre, if I may, towards the village. Is that clear?"

Not all of the awkward business of fitting on and buckling the armour was finished by any means, when Douglas pressed on to the lip of the ravine, where a better prospect of the area to the east was to be had. He was still helmetless, as were some others. Everywhere behind him men were assembling in their troops and companies.

Jamie found the waiting, the staring across the dark wooded trough of the dean, galling, nerve-racking, with the babel of sounds coming from a considerable distance ahead and to the right. Nothing was to be seen of any conflict, however bright the moonlight. But the Earl, fitting on his plumed helmet now, was not going to move further until he knew more, however eager his supporters. If Hotspur had chosen to attack under cover of dark-ness, unexpected for that man, then he was going to use that darkness and consequent confusion for his purposes. With a force apparently some three times as large as the Scots, he could be allowed no other advantages.

At last Will of Drumlanrig came running up from the low ground, all but speechless, partly with excitement. "Cattle . . . Englishmen . . . fighting . . ." he panted. "In the bog. In the river. Everywhere. Beasts crazed. Charging all ways. Blood . . . !"

"Quiet, boy!" his father snapped. "Take your time. Keep your wits. Speak plainly — or not at all."

'Y-yes, my lord. Yes," the fifteen-year-old said, swallowing.

"Answer my questions then, Will. Did you speak with any in command, down there?"

"Aye. With Scott of Synton and the Laird of Swinton. They said . . ."

"Wait. Are these alone? Do they have many men still down there with them?"

"Some, lord. I could not see many. The cattle . . ."

"But they have a front? *This* side of the cattle?"

"Yes."

"The English? *They* are amongst the cattle?"

"Aye — hundreds of them . . ."

"Tcha, boy — we are not concerned with hundreds but *thousands*! Now — what did Synton and Swinton say? Think, Will — did they say aught of the English strength?"

The boy chewed his lip. "Aye, sir. They said . . . Synton said that some were across the river. Mounted. He said to tell you that he believed . . . believed that they could hold them. Those in the haugh. With some more men. He wants more men . . ."

"Now we learn. He believes *he* can hold them, down there — with more men. Then, he cannot think that to be the main force. Of thousands. He could not hope to hold thousands. And the horse across Rede — a diversion, a flanking force, to ford higher and come down behind us. But we know there is no ford till Shittleheugh, three miles up. They cannot ride fast in this light in rough country. We have an hour before these can reach our backs. Did he say aught else, Will? Think."

"The cattle, yes. Swinton said that they had driven many of the beasts uphill. And were seeking to drive more. Up to the village, he said. To block Percy in the streets . . ."

"God's sake, boy — why could you not say that, at the first!" the Earl exclaimed. But he patted his son's heaving shoulders, nevertheless. "They believe Hotspur's main thrust is in the centre, through the village where lies the road. For his horse, to be sure. So Swinton would pack the street with cattle. It makes good sense, for Percy. This I would have done my own self, with another flanking force to the high ground northwards. Now we may hazard a move. My lords — you hear? I conceive Hotspur to advance on four fronts. One in the level haughs. One horsed across Rede, to scare us. One probably on high ground, to our left. And in the centre, moves his main force along the road, through the village where his horse may pass on good ground, thereafter to spread out like a doo's tail, to advance, mounted in the main, on this burn and dean. You have it?"

Cries of agreement supported his assessment.

"We can wait here for him, my lords. He must dismount to cross the dean. But that would give his flanking thrusts time. Time to work around us. Instead, we can go meet him. Seek to engage him before he can form a front in the fields and rigs this side of the village. If the cattle and the Mersemen have managed to hold him

79

up in the streets, his confusion could be our opportunity. If we are too late, we would retire promptly to his dean. How say you?"

There was a great shout for an advance.

"So be it," the Earl said grimly. "We give battle. But against three times our number. Do not forget it, because of this moonlight. If I fall, my lord of Moray commands in the centre, until my lord of Dunbar takes fullest command. If Moray falls, Lindsay of Crawford commands. Then Maxwell. Now — Gordon, take you another two hundred. Down to the haughs to aid Dunbar and Synton. Keith — mount you, and take one hundred horse westwards, to halt this English cavalry which will seek to ford Rede at Shittleheugh. But be prepared to ride to our aid if we need it. Maxwell, on the left, be prepared to turn northwards, swing round without breaking the line, if Buccleuch requires aid. For the rest, leave all horses here. Get your people across this dean. Assemble them in a long front at the other side. No further advance until I order it. There will be no trumpeting before battle is joined. We hope for surprise. Off, now — and quickly . . ."

Assembling all on the eastern lip of the dean took longer than impatient tempers approved, in the darkness of the steep, tree-filled ravine; but at last all was approximately in order. The Scots centre consisted of about 1,600 dismounted men, armed with lances, swords, maces and bows, in four main companies — Maxwell on the left; Douglas himself, with Moray next; Lindsay and the Sinclair brothers on their right; and Montgomerie and Gordon still further to the right, to try keep touch with the Earl of Dunbar down on the low ground. The noise of battle ahead and to the right was still very confused; but clearly the cattlemen and their charges were holding up the enemy advance notably well — although this could not last for long.

Douglas raised the heavy iron mace he carried, high above his head — it would be of more use than a sword in what was to come, he declared — and amidst a low, muttering growl, infinitely menacing, the long line began to move eastwards across the slantwise pasture-land, pacing steadily, unhurriedly.

It was Jamie Douglas's first real battle — as that of many another there. And far from what he, and others no doubt, had anticipated — on foot, in half-darkness, against an unseen enemy, with no brave cheering and slogan shouting, the business sounding more like the approach to a cattle-fair. Banners there were in plenty, but the colours were muted in the greenish moonlight. He carried a sword over his shoulder, the long two-handed war brand — he doubted if his wrists were up to wielding a mace effectively — and had a dirk at his side. He paced directly behind his lord, with Bickerton on his right and young Archie carrying the chiefly, undifferenced standard of Douglas on his left. Rob Hart strode beyond Archie, and Simon Glendinning beyond Bickerton, these last three's ages not adding up to more than forty-four between them. Richard Lundie the chaplain was not yet back from his errand to Scott of Buccleuch on the high ground. This at least was as visualised — the Earl's personal entourage in its due position. To the right of them Moray's gentlemen marched likewise. Behind, the men in their hundreds came on, clanking, rank upon rank. Jamie knew a distinct and awkward admixture of emotions — wild elation and sheer bowel-loosening fear struggling within him.

They seemed to go pacing across that hillside for a long time, opening ranks to pass clumps of whin-bushes or outcropping rocks, and closing again. It all felt highly unreal, somehow. They were nearing the village, but could distinguish nothing of what went on there, save for the noise. The light of the half-moon was peculiarly unsatisfactory in that it seemed to alter the relative sizes and shape of things, near and far, giving the impression of quite distinct prospects but obscuring detail and proportions. However, it would work that way for both sides. Quite a number of cattle-beasts were milling around before them, having escaped presumably from the constrictions of the village. From any way off it was hard to tell whether these were animals or groups of men.

A clash and shouting on their right, at no great distance, brought the line to a halt. Montgomerie's and Gordon's company had apparently come up with the enemy. The noise maintained and grew. Douglas waited, sending word up to Maxwell to pause likewise. They must learn what this signified. Hotspur might be seeking to avoid the village area by making a diversion closer to the river, with his main force. Or it might be no more than some extension or movement of the haughland fighting. The Earl sent runners to discover.

They came back sooner than might have been anticipated,

having met messengers from Sir John Montgomerie. He asked for immediate reinforcement. He believed that he was in fact facing the main strength of the English, who appeared to have left their horses behind also, and were advancing just above the edge of the haughs and water-meadows. Numbers he could only guess at, but it was a major thrust. He was forming a sort of schiltrom or defensive square, lances projecting like a hedgehog's spines — for they were clearly much outnumbered.

The Douglas was still hearing this report when Master Lundie came riding fast from the north, to announce that Buccleuch was under attack from a force which had come round the back of Fawdon Hill, seemingly in fairly large numbers, again afoot. Buccleuch was holding them meantime in the throat of the little pass of the Otter burn; but he required more men if he was to prevent them rounding his position by taking to the hillsides.

The Earl made up his mind with typical swiftness. He sent an order to Maxwell, on their left, to divide his force of some four hundred. To send half up to Buccleuch's aid; and to follow him, Douglas, with the other half. Then he commanded his own array to wheel round, almost at right-angles and right-handed. In line abreast again, but facing southwards now, towards the river, not eastwards to the village, the centre resumed its deliberate advance. Battle sounded straight ahead.

Their approach to the flank of the English host was aided by the presence of a scatter of thorn-trees and a larger than usual bank of whins, at an uneven stretch of the common land. In daylight this would have been of little service; but under the moon its shadows were as deep as though it had been quite a major wood. In consequence, the Scots perceived the line of their foes, indistinct but indubitable, considerably before they themselves were observed — the more so in that they were looking for the enemy in this position and the English were not. First with the bushes and thorns themselves as cover, and then with their dark shadow as backcloth, they were within two hundred yards of the Percy's flanks before the warning was given.

The Earl was ready, therefore, if his opponents were less so. "A Douglas! A Douglas!" the Scots cried, as they charged down the slight slope under a dozen banners.

Obviously there was a great mass of the enemy before them, parts of it engaged in an assault on Montgomerie's and Gordon's schiltrom but the major portion just marching westwards. Turning these two sections into a unified L-shaped front, to face the schiltrom and the north, was not the work of a moment, however alert and expert the leadership. The Scots were in amongst them before it could be achieved.

Jamie, running yelling behind his lord, forgot about fears and unease of stomach. The Earl went in, smiting hugely with his mace, and his esquire followed close. He tried to wield his great sword effectively, but found it awkward. It was altogether too long for such close work, too heavy for easy wielding. The Earl's shorter-handled mace was obviously infinitely more practical. After making two or three ineffective jabs at figures suddenly thrust up against him in the mêlée, and only avoiding an unexpected dirk-thrust by an inch or so, he recognised that practicalities were more important than sentiment and chivalric notions, and tossed his fine sword from him, a gift from his father on his eighteenth birthday. Instead, he snatched out his dirk, and felt the better man therefor.

Others were doing likewise around him. Lances and bows, as well as swords were being discarded as useless meantime. The dagger, the battle-axe, the club and the mace were the weapons for this in-fighting, on foot. The Scots perceived this rather more quickly than did their foes, undoubtedly. And they were aided by the element of surprise. Led by the Douglas and the other lords, Moray still helmetless, they drove on mightily, sending the front ranks of the English reeling back. Men went down before them in swathes, and soon the attackers were stumbling and tripping over the fallen bodies of their victims, their momentum slowing.

Jamie's duty, as esquire, was principally to protect his master in rear and flank. But that did not prevent him from some aggressive initiative of his own. A big round-faced fellow with a wide-open mouth and gapped teeth, presumably yelling, loomed up at his left, and stabbed viciously with a shortened sword, held part-way down the broad blade. Dodging aside, Jamie nevertheless felt the blow glance off his chain-mailed shoulder, leaving it numb, and knocking him back. But somebody close behind butted into him, cannoning him forward against the Englishman, not yet fully recovered from his swipe. Fending himself off with one hand, despite weakness of shoulder, Jamie drove down his dirk with the other, at the thick column of throat. The man went down in spouting blood. Pressure from behind toppled him full length over the fallen Northumbrian — thereby saving him from another English sword-thrust. Thereafter, prostrate, feet kicked, stamped on and tripped over him in all directions, a more horrible experience than any he had yet encountered. He felt little pain, but knew a great indignation, affront. It was some time before he could get to his feet, unsteadily, bruised and breathless, spitting grass from his mouth. His victim lay twitching beside him, but otherwise still. Stepping over the body, dirk held the more firmly, he pressed on, in suddenly trembling excitement, offence forgotten. He had slain his first foe. He was a full man now.

Detached from his group, Jamie recognised that his duty was to get back to his lord's side as quickly as he could. In the press, confusion and half-light he had some difficulty in discovering the Earl's whereabouts; but amongst the banners ahead, reeling and swaying and dipping crazily, he discerned one larger than the others, and thrust his way towards it. For safety's sake he chanted "A Douglas! A Douglas!" as he went, despite lack of breath. In the mêlée he could be attacked by friend almost as easily as by foe.

The Scots were doing less well now, however. The English had rallied, and some of their leaders fought their way back from the front assaulting the schiltrom to take command. Jamie realised, indeed, that the Douglas banner, along with others, was being forced back towards him. He found himself amongst a group of men momentarily at a loss, apparently detached, like himself, from their comrades and leaders, some wounded. He raised his voice urgently.

"I am a Douglas!" he shouted, waving an arm at them, with the dirk. "Come! Shout, all of you. Your loudest. Shout 'A Douglas!' Come on — to the Earl's banner. All shouting!"

There was probably no more than twenty of them all told. But tight-knit and yelling vehemently in unison, they no doubt sounded like reinforcements of many times that number. Especially as other Scots took up the cry in a renewal of vigour and enthusiasm. For a few minutes the tide of battle turned again.

The Earl of Douglas was swift to renew the slackened initiative. Uplifting his great voice, he bellowed "Percy! Percy! Hotspur! Here is Douglas! Percy — to me — and die!"

How far his challenge would reach in that uproar there was no knowing, powerful as were his lungs. But indubitably it had an effect on the ordinary English soldiery in the Earl's immediate vicinity, causing them to hesitate, glance around, even draw back a little, in the recognition that here was no business of theirs, a contest between the giants, a lordly feud not for wise but lesser men to interfere in. If it did not produce Sir Harry Percy, wherever he was, or his brother, at least it allowed Douglas to head a distinct forward movement again, his mace swinging and beating tirelessly.

The Lord Maxwell and his half-company came running from the north, to join the fray, shouting a new slogan, but welcome.

When Jamie at length won back to his due position, it was to find that his place immediately behind the Earl had been filled by John Bickerton. The others, Archie Douglas, Hart, Glendinning and Lundie were all still there, although Glendinning appeared to be wounded and Archie was drooping, tripping and stumbling, to the dire danger of the standard — no doubt its weight was beginning to tell on his fourteen-year-old wrists. Jamie, in fact, grabbed its pole as one more trip over a body all but brought it down.

"Take it, Jamie — take it!" the boy gasped. "I canna . . . hold it up. I'm no' . . . right." Vomit was in fact spilled all down the lad's front. Close range killing is not good for the stomachs of sensitive teenage boys.

So Jamie Douglas found himself acting standard-bearer, and requiring both hands to hold aloft the tall staff and banner. Which meant that there was no more dirking for him, meantime. Young Archie clung close to his side, panting, his own dirk drawn now, in white-knuckled fist.

Douglas, Moray and Lindsay had now swung round somewhat right-handed, seeking to cut their way through in the direction of Montgomerie's schiltrom — where, it was to be assumed, Hotspur himself would be fighting. Certainly several banners could be seen to be upraised thereabouts, although devices were impossible to distinguish in the poor light. As the leading Scots neared these, so the fighting grew ever tougher, with more and more armoured knights mixed amongst the ordinary men-at-arms and spearmen. Moreover, even the Douglas's arm was beginning to flag somewhat, with the weight of that deadly flailing mace. More than once the Earl staggered back from some blow he had failed to avoid, through growing weariness even though his mail protected him from actual wounding. Each time Bickerton, directly behind, caught him and held him up.

It was when a particularly heavy stroke from a knight with another mace sent the Earl reeling back, that it happened. Bickerton caught his master, as before — but this time his right hand rose high and fell again, in a swift gesture which had nothing to do with support for a tottering man. And Jamie had glimpsed the gleam of steel in the moonlight, in that right hand. The Earl's mail-clad body convulsed to a violent spasm, and uttering a loud groan, the bloody mace at last fell from suddenly nerveless fingers. Bickerton now had to hold up his collapsing lord bodily.

Jamie Douglas gazed, appalled.

With an enormous and evident effort, the Earl gained some sort of control of his buckling legs, and managed to stand approximately upright, swaying, mumbling. Bickerton let go of him, and he began to lurch sideways. Throwing the standard at Archie again, Jamie leapt to catch and seek to hold up the weighty person of his hero, babbling incoherencies. The others, Lundie, Hart, Glendinning, perceiving that the Douglas was sore hurt, gathered round him, while Moray, Lindsay and Maxwell moved forward, smiting, to form a protective front.

"My lord! My lord!" Jamie cried desperately. "The dastard! Oh, the foul dastard! My good lord . . ."

"My back!" the Earl muttered. "In . . . my back!"

Horrified, the young men crowded round their lord, young Archie dropping the standard altogether in his distress for his father. They gabbled their questions, and fears.

"Hold me . . . hold me up," Douglas got out, thickly. "Hold. Lead me . . . forward."

"My lord — no! My good lord," Jamie wailed. "Do not so. Rest, you . . ."

"No!" That was vehement, determined, however weak the voice. "I am . . . Douglas! A, a . . . dead man! But . . . old prophecy. In our line. A dead man . . . shall gain . . . a field!"

They were all supporting him now, but even so the Earl's knees gave way. Sagging forward, he was held. Head sinking, he saw his standard lying there before him.

Sir James Lindsay came, panting. "How fare you, Douglas?" he demanded.

"But ... poorly," the Earl gasped. "I die. But ... I die ... like my forefathers ... praise God! On the field ... not in ... my bed!"

"No, no. Not that. We shall save you yet, friend," Lindsay cried. And to the esquires. "Fools! Lay him down. Staunch his wound. Here is folly ..."

"No!" Douglas was still master. "I say ... no! Raise me up. Aye ... and raise my banner ... lying there. No foe ... nor friend ... to see ... what case you see me in. Lest ... lest ..." His voice faded.

The Earl of Moray was there now, questioning.

"Raise me, I say." Almost miraculously there was an accession of strength in the quavering voice. "On, with me. My ... command. I am Douglas. Shout it — my slogan! Conceal ... my death. Forward me ... and my banner. Douglas ... shall win the day ... yet! My last command ... to you all. Shout, I say ..."

They shouted, then, in broken sobbing tones which, however, strengthened as they continued. "Douglas! A Douglas!" On and on they went, three young men staggering, panting, shouting, dragging the now inert figure of their master. And all around them, from other throats, the cry arose once more, "A Douglas! A Douglas!" with renewed vigour. But the Douglas himself spoke no more.

* * *

Although it seemed a long way that they carried their weighty burden over the uneven, corpse-littered ground, banner waving above them, it was of course not far before the esquires were up with the battling front line of the Scots fighters again. Here they must halt. Nor, in the nature of things, and in sheer self-preservation, could they continue to hold up the dead Earl, however loyal to his last command. The Douglas had said that dead he would yet win the battle; to this end they must *fight*, not just stand. So they lowered the mail-clad body to the ground. In doing so, Jamie discovered that the Earl's mace was still attached to his gauntleted wrist with its leather thong. Stooping, he detached it. This would be his, from now on — until he might use it to fullest effect, on John Bickerton, God willing!

If they could no longer bear up the Douglas's person, they could still shout his slogan, as commanded, whilst breath was in them. This they did, standing over the corpse, while above them Archie kept the great standard upright. The sight and sound of them seemed to put new heart into the entire Scots front. But it was no longer a forward-moving front, nevertheless. The fact was that they were now only some two hundred yards from Montgomerie's schiltrom, and in between was wedged the most knightly leadership of the English array, fighting on two fronts and standing fast, out of necessity. It was a matter of sheer ding-dong slogging, until one side or the other gave in.

At least, in these circumstances, it was not a chaotic mêlée and press of bodies, as before. There was room to wield a sword — or a mace. Jamie did so in a strange state of mixed pain, sorrow and utter determination, uncaring for any danger to himself, standing over the body of the man he had most loved and admired, stricken down by blackest treachery. As tirelessly as its fallen owner, he now swung the Douglas mace in that hacking, immobile battle, all but an automaton in his steely inward rage and outward calm. At his left Simon Glendinning had picked up a discarded English sword, and used it with dogged, dour ferocity, hurt already as he was. Rob Hart at the other side had never abandoned his, and made deadly play with it in persistent figure-of-eight pattern. Close at their backs, Chaplain Richard and young Archie of Cavers kept the standard aloft between them, each with a dirk in hand to protect the others' flanks and rear. They had now been joined by the Earl's other son, Will of Drumlanrig, with a battle-axe which he certainly had not had before. They made a tight, tense and dedicated group above their dead lord — and only Richard Lundie out of his teens.

Only esquires as they might be, they were dealing now with the cream of the North of England chivalry, dismounted admittedly but experienced as they were proud.

Rob Hart was the first to fall, struck down by a glancing battle-axe blow to the side of his helmet. Jamie felled the wielder immediately thereafter with his mace, but Rob lay still, over the Earl's legs. Will Douglas of Drumlanrig stepped into his place, straddling both, without pause. They still gasped "A Douglas! A Douglas!" breathlessly, sometimes only mouthing the words, Archie and the chaplain doing rather better at their backs.

88

Some timeless, incalculable time later, Jamie realised that Glendinning, on his left, was on his knees, swaying, sword still at last. Lundie, leaving the standard to the boy again, picked up that sword and took the other's stance at Jamie's side.

The greenish moon shone coldly down on Otterburn, and endless carnage. Will Douglas fell next, pitching against Jamie from a sideways blow. Now there was only the two of them, with Archie behind. It could not go on for much longer.

It did not. Jamie was dazedly, almost blindly, involuntarily swinging his mace at one more armoured figure in plumed helmet who loomed up before him when some corner of his consciousness perceived a difference. This man was waving a steel-gauntleted hand, not thrusting a sword or axe. Then he recognised the coat-armour of Montgomerie of Eaglesham, the three gold fleurs-de-lis on blue. Reeling drunkenly now, he stayed his blow.

"Hold!" Montgomerie was shouting hollowly. "Hold, you!" He raised his visor and spoke more plainly. "Hotspur has yielded! To me. Sir Ralph is down, wounded. Where is the Douglas? The day is ours. Ours, I say! Where is Douglas?"

Lindsay came lurching from the left, as Jamie shook his head wordlessly.

"There is Douglas — dead!" the Lord of Crawford panted. "So we win? Win the day — too late! It is as he said. A dead man shall win it!"

"Dear God — Douglas?"

All around them now the battle was disintegrating, slackening, as the word was shouted, screamed, laughed. Men were throwing down their arms, fleeing or yielding, as the news that Hotspur had surrendered swept the field. Cheers rose above the shrieks and groans of the dying and wounded.

Moray came up, bleeding from a cut brow, fair hair caked with blood. He was leading Sir John Lilburn, his last opponent, as prisoner. Everywhere the Scots were grasping at weary bewildered English knights as captives, the richer-clad the better, meet for ransom, even fighting each other for prize specimens. In only minutes that dreadful scene was changed from one of desperate battle and bravery to one of bickering, huckstering, riot and shameful greed, like some evil fair.

But not around the fallen Douglas, where the young esquires had piled up a quite distinct semi-circular barrier of enemy slain in their protective efforts. Scarcely knowing what he did, Jamie Douglas sank to his knees scrabbling to open his master's visor, sobbing openly now. The dead eyes, open still, gleamed palely in the moonlight.

Lindsay shook his head. "Here is the sorriest victory we shall ever see!" he exclaimed. "The noblest of our race the price of it."

"*Your* price, my lord—yours!" Jamie burst out, voice breaking. "Slain by your man. The dastard Bickerton! Keeper of your castle . . ."

"What? What are you saying? Are you mad, sirrah? Your wits unhinged . . .?"

"I saw him, I tell you. Saw him stab my lord. In the back. Saw the dirk. Oh, my lord, my dear lord!"

"How can this be? His mail . . .?"

"Bickerton? Where is he?"

"I'll not believe it. Here's folly . . ."

"Turn him over," Moray commanded. "Let us see his back."

They rolled the Earl's corpse over — and in doing so had to move Rob Hart's body. He groaned — so he was not dead, at least. But none had eyes for him at that moment. All stared at the Douglas's armour, at the back.

Jamie pointed, jabbing with his bloodstained finger. "See — unbuckled! There — and there! The shirt-of-mail open. Undone. Of a purpose. By Saint Bride — he left him undone! That he might do . . . this!"

There seemed little doubt that this was so. The chain-mail shirt opened down the back, and here was only fastened at the neck by one toggle, instead of all the way down. And the steel back-plate of the cuirass which covered it was loose at the left side, its leather straps unbuckled. It was the armour-bearer's task to fasten both, as he dressed his lord. And only the armour-bearer could have known that neither *was* fastened, and that a dirk, driven in and down sidelong, would meet no resistance from plate- or chain-mail. The thing was clear to all. The Earl of Douglas had not fallen in fair fight, but had been murdered. And by his own trusted servant.

Moray straightened up, set-featured. "Take him to his tent," he ordered. "Find the man Bickerton. We will deal with this anon." Until his elder brother, Dunbar and March, appeared on the scene, Moray was senior commander. "Now — there is much to do. Get the men to order. Marshal the prisoners. Succour the wounded. Discover how it goes with my brother. And with Buccleuch. And Keith the Marischal. My lords — to your tasks. St. Clair — see you to the prisoners. Hepburn — rally our men into their companies. Ramsay — down to the haughs, to my lord of Dunbar . . ."

Keith the Marischal rode up. "Where is my lord of Douglas?" he demanded. "The English horse are in our camp. Ravaging it. They were more than double our strength. We tried to hold them, but could not. They drove us back, right from the ford. Under Matthew Redman. Now they rob our camp . . ."

"So long as that is *all* they do!" Moray panted. "They do not follow you, to attack us here?"

"I think not. They seek booty . . . But — where is Douglas?"

"Douglas is dead. Slain. I command meantime. My lord of Crawford. Take sufficient men, and go attend to this Redman . . ."

Jamie Douglas paid no attention to all this. He was now bending over his fallen friends, removing helmets, loosening armour, Lundie aiding him. Will Douglas was already sitting up, head in hands, rocking back and forth. Simon Glendinning was alive, breathing stertorously. Robert Hart's eyes were open, but wandering, blood dribbling from open mouth. At least none were dead — yet.

A runner came from the Redeside meadows to say that all fighting had virtually ceased there, with the Scots pursuing the fleeing foe. Elsewhere there appeared to be pockets of resistance, but only that. There was still no word from the high ground.

With the aftermath of the battle beginning to be brought into some sort of order and discipline — although a fairly large proportion of the victors appeared to be out-of-touch and chasing Englishmen eastwards — Jamie and the chaplain supervised the careful transportation, by prisoners, of their three friends back to the ravaged camp across the dean. There they found no sign of Redman's cavalry, nor of Lindsay's, though the place was in a sorry state, tents down, gear strewn everywhere, horses running around loose. In one of the re-erected tents they laid the wounded esquires. Lundie, like most clerics, was trained in caring for the sick. He thought that Glendinning would survive. Will Douglas had been little more than stunned. But Hart was grievously hurt and had lost much blood. He doubted whether he would survive till morning.

That young man did, in fact, die without regaining consciousness, just as dawn began to break. Only then did Jamie Douglas allow weariness to overcome his sorrow and anger, and he slept, still in his blood-spattered shirt-of-mail from France.

The sun rose on a scene and situation full of contradictions, of desolation, ruin, the groans of wounded and the smell of blood. The Scots had won a major victory — but there was little of elation in their camp. The death of the country's greatest soldier and most respected leader overshadowed all, even the humbler men-at-arms and mosstroopers recognising that something more than just a great noble had been removed. Those who knew most of the national and political situation in Scotland were the most concerned. And a great many had loved and admired the Douglas as a man, despite his rather stolid and unforthcoming manner, and mourned him truly. There were others to mourn, too — although in fact the Scots losses were extraordinarily light, all things considered — little more than one hundred dead, though four times that number wounded, most not seriously; whereas 1,800 English dead were counted on the various battle-grounds, and the wounded and prisoners amounted between them to another thousand. They had made a clean sweep, almost, of the English leadership, with not only Hotspur and his brother captured but the Seneschal of York, Sir Ralph Langley, Sir Robert Ogle, Sir Thomas Walsingham, Sir John Lilburn, Sir Thomas Abingdon, Sir John Felton, Sir John Copland and many another distinguished knight. As against this, few prominent Scots were lost, though many were injured or somewhat battered. But, strangely, Sir James Lindsay of Crawford was a casualty, at the last. One of his men, who had ridden back into camp soon after daylight, told the extraordinary story. Lindsay and his company had managed to clear the Scots camp of the plundering cavalry under Redman, Captain of Berwick, and had thereafter chased them, and, burdened as they were with the Scots spoils, had caught up with them in the Kirkwhelpington vicinity about eight miles to the south-east, with Redman no doubt heading for Newcastle. There had been another fierce, if lesser battle, which the Scots had eventually won, Lindsay himself defeating and dis-

arming Sir Mathew Redman. He was heading back to Otterburn
with his prisoners and recaptured booty, when in the dawn light
had seen a host moving southwards towards them across Kirkwhelpington Common, which they took to be the main Scots
force — but which in fact proved to be the Bishop of Durham's
fresh army of some 10,000. Lindsay and his party had been captured, in turn, and Redman released — and so far as he knew, this
survivor alone had escaped to tell the tale.

This news, of course, upset the Scots leadership in more than
distress at the loss of the Lord of Crawford, important as he was. If
the Bishop's large force had been only eight miles or so away at
dawn, he could be a deal nearer now. And though he would be
aware of Hotspur's defeat, and presumably the warier, the Scots
were in no state to engage in a new battle with a fresh army of
10,000. Especially as Neville's force might well also now be near at
hand. The Earl of Dunbar and March, now in command, sent off
Pate Home and his scouts with urgent instructions, and ordered
an immediate preparation to march. They were, after all, only
some fifteen miles from the Scots border at Carter Bar.

In all this stir, Jamie Douglas was not concerned. Only little
rested, he was busy on his own, searching the camp and questioning. John Bickerton was nowhere to be found; none had seen him
since the early stages of the battle.

Jamie was summoned from his fruitless quest by Dunbar himself, almost ready to move off but delayed by the difficulties of
coping with so many wounded, the construction of horse-litters
proceeding apace. Batches of prisoners, wounded and cattle—
which no Borderer would consider leaving behind—were being
despatched westwards up Redesdale all the time, in long convoys,
the severely injured in improvised litters or hammocks slung
between two horses.

Jamie found the Scots leadership assembling in an open space.
The Earl of Douglas's body was there in the midst, wrapped in his
own standard now, and standing beside it his two sons, Will of
Drumlanrig, looking very wan, and Archie of Cavers, between
tears and a silly grin, clutching the Percy pennon instead of his
sire's banner. The corpse of Rob Hart lay beside that of his lord.
Simon Glendinning stood shakily at the other side, supported by
Richard Lundie. Jamie was directed to stand beside them. Sir
Harry Percy, and sundry other English notables not seriously

wounded, stood behind, just a little apart from the ranks of the Scots lords and knights.

Dunbar, flanked by his brother Moray and the Lord Maxwell, stepped forward, clearing his throat. "My lords, friends and esteemed foes," he began, a little uncertainly. "We are here to do honour. First, to James Douglas, who lies here. A noble man. A stout friend. A puissant and worthy foe. In him, Scotland has lost much, its greatest fighter and most able councillor. We proclaim that loss. Scotland will mourn him long."

There was a prolonged murmur, part growl. Dunbar was no orator, with a thin and reedy voice unsuited for outdoor heroics; but what he had said so abruptly touched all.

Into the murmur another voice spoke, a voice much more assured, yet with that incipient hesitation of delivery and pronounced burr. "I, Harry Percy, would crave your permission, my lord, to add my word of praise, of honour. The Douglas was the fairest flower of your fair land. I, and all my people, mourn him little less than do you. But he died, as he lived, in honour. On an honourable field. May I do as well!"

If some breaths were caught at that, most were not, and there was a swell of approval. The Scots leaders had decided that nothing was to be gained by announcing to all and sundry that the Douglas had been murdered. It would serve his name and memory nothing. It would not be forgotten by those who knew; but some things were better handled discreetly, it was felt.

"I thank you, my lord Percy," Dunbar acknowledged. "I would expect no other word from one of your renown. It was a well-fought fight, and none who took part will forget it. Or its cost. For many died, beside the Douglas. We honour them all, Scots and English both."

Again the tight-lipped murmur.

"Aye." Dunbar coughed. "And now we have an especial token to pay, in honour. Last night, certain young men played a noble part much in advance of their years. They supported the Douglas — that was their duty. But they did it passing well. And when he fell, they carried him forward as he had commanded, dying and dead, to the forefront of the battle, where he would ever be. They held him up, and his standard above him, and cried his slogan as encouragement and example to all. And when, hard-pressed, they must lay him down, they guarded his body to the last, fighting above it like . . . like ancient heroes!" Even the Earl's reedy voice was vibrant. "One lies dead, here, before us, with his lord. One is wounded, all are hurt."

There were cheers now, unrestrained.

Dunbar held up his hand. "Hear me. Of these young men, one is in holy orders, Richard Lundie from North Berwick, chaplain. Him we must leave Holy Church to honour. Of the others, three are Douglases — William of Drumlanrig, Archibald of Cavers and James of Aberdour. The last is Simon Glendinning, son to Glendinning of that Ilk here present. He who died is Robert Hart, from Douglasdale. I say to the four who may, step forward to the side of him who may not!"

Eyeing each other doubtfully, the four paced, shuffled or limped out to stand directly beside the corpses, Lundie with them, aiding Glendinning. "Kneel," the Earl commanded, drawing his sword. He stalked over to them. "I do hereby welcome these four into the most honourable, worthy, valiant and lofty estate of knighthood," he announced, his voice squeaking a little, with emotion. "Well and truly earned on that field where the honour is doubled — the field of battle. William Douglas, I dub thee knight, young as you are." And he brought down the great blade on the lad's shoulder. "Be thou good and true knight unto thy life's end. Arise, Sir William. And you, Archibald, younger still, who bore your standard to victory, with your sire dead at your feet—arise, Sir Archibald, and be thou good and true knight unto thy life's end."

The boy's gulping sobbing sniff was heard by all; and evoked no single grin nor remark.

"And you, James Douglas of Aberdour, namesake and chief esquire to your puissant lord — the most valiant of all, I am assured. Be thou good and true knight until you rejoin the Douglas! Arise, Sir James."

"Amen!" Jamie muttered — the only one who remembered the due form of what was, in fact, a religious ceremony.

"And Simon Glendinning, who fought on wounded — be thou good and true knight until thy life's end also. Arise, Sir Simon."

Richard Lundie said the Amen for his swaying, dizzy charge, raising him to his unsteady feet again.

95

"And you, Sir Priest, I cannot knight. But I would shake you by the hand!" Dunbar added, reaching out. Then he turned to the body lying beside that of the Earl. "Robert Hart," he jerked, swallowing. "You were one of this knightly band. I would not now hold you apart. You cannot kneel nor rise — but I can still dub you knight. Rest in peace, Sir Robert Hart, and serve your master still, if you may."

A sigh arose, like the breakers on a long shore.

"This I have done," Dunbar ended, "because I believe that James, Earl of Douglas would have had it so." He raised sword on high. "Now, my friends — enough! We march for Scotland, without more ado. My lords — to your places, in column. Sir Harry Percy and his captor, Sir John Montgomerie, will ride with me. Trumpeter — sound the March . . ."

*   *   *

The Prince-Bishop may have been only a few miles away, with his large force; but he evidently preferred to keep that distance from the retiring Scots. No doubt refugees from Otterburn reaching him did not understate the numbers and capacities of the victors. At any rate, the invaders were not attacked on their fifteen-mile march to Carter Bar, although a discreet distance behind the Bishop's people were reported as keeping pace, as it were, seeing them off. By mid-afternoon the Scots had crossed the March and were back in their former camp at Southdean, unmolested. Pate Home sent word that the Bishop had halted his main array at Ramshope four miles from the Borderline, sending forward only a token force to the lofty pass-like junction of the two kingdoms above Catcleuch. Clearly there was to be no attempt at rescue of the Percys and other notables, humiliating as this must be for Hotspur.

The Scots leaders had hoped that there might be couriers from the Earl Robert of Fife and the western invaders, indicating progress or intentions; but none such appeared, although first Douglas and then Dunbar had sent messengers across country to keep the main army informed. There was only minor debate now as to whether any move should be made to join the other force. At this stage, with the Douglas dead, so many wounded and prisoners to see to, not to mention thousands of cattle to be suitably disposed of, there was no enthusiasm for prolonging the expedition. Not only the Mersemen, mosstroopers and other Borderers found home beckoning. The break up of the eastern force commenced.

Jamie Douglas was nothing loth. He had had sufficient of war and invasion, hero as he now found himself to be considered. Normally he would have been highly excited, elated, at his almost unbelievable elevation to the rank of knighthood, something he could scarcely take in, as yet. But any such exultation was at present effectively damped down by his sorrow over his hero's death, and his seething anger at the murderer. He desired no further distracting adventures, meantime; he had but one ambition — to avenge his late master.

The next day, then, only the rump of the host rode northwards, although with most of the leadership still intact. They went by Jedburgh, Ancrum and over Lilliard's Edge to Tweeddale where, at Melrose Abbey, under the three isolated peaks of the Eildons, the Trimontium of the Romans, they laid to rest the body of James, Earl of Douglas — Moray, his brother-in-law asserting that he had once expressed the wish to be buried there, where the great Bruce's heart, which he bore represented on his shield, was also interred. Sir Robert Hart they also buried, beside his lord, in a ceremony which brought tears rolling down many a rough and unshaven cheek. They passed the night at Melrose, the monks giving skilful attention to the wounded. And next morning, as they were about to resume their northwards march, couriers at last arrived from the Lord Robert's force. They declared that this also was on its way home, the messengers having left it at Carlisle. They had had a successful expedition likewise, it seemed — although they had not got so far south as Lancaster. But all to the north of that they had harried and laid waste in traditional style. They had had a brush with the Lord Clifford, to his disadvantage — Sir William Douglas of Nithsdale, Archibald the Grim's gallant son, having apparently challenged the Englishman to single combat, in true chivalric fashion, and been curtly rebuffed. With huge booty they were now crossing back into Scotland unpursued, in high satisfaction — although, of course, mourning the death of the Earl of Douglas. Robert of Fife ordered that the late Douglas's force await his arrival, wherever it might be. No reasons for this were given.

The Earl of Dunbar and March, who hated all Stewarts on principle — and was moreover on his own territory here — was not prepared to comply. He declared that all who wished to take their departure might do so, and rode off himself to his own castle of Ercildoune in Lauderdale, with a selection of prisoners for ransom. But he left his brother Moray with what remained of the force, to await the others.

Jamie seized the opportunity to take his leave. With a group of young Douglases, including Sir Will of Drumlanrig, he set off up Lauderdale also, on business bent. He had ridden southwards a youth; he rode northwards very much a man.

VI

WITH SOUTRA MOOR behind them, and the head of Lauderdale, the travel-stained and battle-scarred group of young men gazed down over the lovely spread of East Lothian, all green pastures barred by the golden rigs of harvest, dotted with demesnes and manors and castles, their villages and hall-touns, to the far blue haze that was the smoke of the fires of Haddington, its capital. Out of it all rose the isolated and abrupt humps of the Garmyleton Hills, Traprain and North Berwick Laws and the soaring Bass, like leviathans from a verdant sea, whilst beyond stretched all the silver-and-blue mirror of the isle-strewn Forth, to the distant cliffs and strands of Fife — surely one of the most fair and fertile prospects in all Southern Scotland, from these Lammermuir heights.

But the horsemen were not concerned with prospects, save as they related to a certain locality.

"You cannot see it from here," young Patrick Ramsay of Waughton declared. "It lies just behind West Garmyleton Hill, yonder, on the edge of Aberlady Bay. You can see part of the wide bay — but not Luffness. Twelve miles? Thirteen? There, east of

Garmyleton, is my father's house of Waughton, also vassal to Lindsay. Five miles east from Luffness." Ramsay, about Jamie's own age, was an extra esquire of Sir James Lindsay's, at a loose end now with his lord captured.

"He may not have returned to his home." The new Sir Will voiced, not for the first time, the doubt that beset them. "Would any of *you* do so? With every man's hand against you? He may have fled deep into England."

"Every man's hand may not be against him. In Scotland," Jamie said levelly. "He may come home to acclaim and reward, the Judas!"

"No! Never that! You are saying . . .?"

"I am saying, Will, that it may not have been merely spite, ill-will, which turned Bickerton assassin. Would a blow from a mace, by chance, serve for that? As all declare? I say that he may have planned his treachery long before. But waited his opportunity. When it might pass undiscerned. If I had not seen that dirk . . .!"

"But why, Jamie—*why*?"

"There are those who do not love Douglas, in Scotland. Who fear Douglas power. Who would bring that power down. Are there not? Some who might welcome this vile deed. Who might possibly have devised it. Some not so far from the Throne!"

"God! You mean . . . the Wolf?"

"The Wolf, perhaps. It could be his style. Or the Lord Robert himself. I trust him little more than his brother. I swear neither will shed a tear for their good-brother, our dear lord!"

Silent now, the young men rode down from Soutra Hill into the green plain of Lothian.

They went by Hundebie amongst the foothills, past Keith the Marischal's castle and through the great Wood of Saltoun to the Tyne, which they forded at the village of Samuelston. Then, keeping well to the west of Haddington, they began to climb over the skirts of the Gled's Muir and up the gentle green slopes of Bangly Hill beyond, till they stood on the summit of the West Garmyleton ridge and could look down directly over the coastal levels around the great V-shaped bay of Aberlady and the woodlands of Luffness at its apex, a bare three miles now. It was late afternoon and the scene was peaceful and very fair.

The Lindsay castle of Byres they passed, like that of Garmyleton to the east — for all this land was Lindsay territory — but they did not halt. At the church and hospice of St. Cuthbert at Ballencrieff, however, they did pause to enquire whether any of their comrades from the English expedition had returned — for churchmen tended to know all that went on in their area, and these were no doubt in fairly close touch with the Carmelite monastery at Luffness little more than a mile away. But the friars here knew nothing of any recent travellers of significance; indeed asked young Ramsay, with whom they were acquainted, for any news of John Bickerton, whose father they seemed to respect. Keeping their own counsel, the party rode on.

Circling the undrained marshlands of Luffness Muir, where cattle grazed knee-deep in the part-flooded meadows of the Peffer Water which flowed into the bay nearby, they came at last to the major Lindsay stronghold of Luffness Castle, rising islanded in a strong position on a sort of tongue of firm land between the Peffer, the bay and the marshes. Here towered a great and massive redstone keep of five storeys, topped by a parapet and wall-walk with bartisans and machicolations, within a large curtain-walled enclosure with circular flanking-towers at each corner and a gate-house to the east. The monastery lay a quarter-mile to the south-west, on the same tongue of firm land. To the north the sea glittered, with the tide almost full over the shallows of the bay.

Now that they were here there was some debate as to procedure. The newcomers could not hope to rush this great castle. If Bickerton had indeed returned, he would presumably hold it against all Douglas visitors, he was its keeper, after all. Guile, on the other hand, was unlikely to gain them entry. It was decided that they should remain hidden in the trees at a short distance, and only Ramsay ride forward alone, to enquire. He was known here, and no Douglas; and one young man would not seem to constitute any great threat.

However, he came back in only moments, to say that the castle stood open, the drawbridge down, the portcullis up, the gates wide, no sign of special caution or alarm. It looked as though Bickerton had not come home.

Considerably deflated, the party rode over the drawbridge timbers, through the pend and into the wide courtyard enclosure, amongst clucking poultry. Servants wheeling dung from the stables gazed at them interestedly — but only that. A wench with a pail, dimpled, giggled and lingered.

At something of a loss, the vengeance-seekers reined up and dismounted. A thick-set, stooping elderly man appeared at the arched doorway of the keep. He eyed them doubtfully, but civilly enough.

"A good e'en to you, my young friends," he greeted. "How can I serve you, at Luffness? I'd say that you have ridden far. And show signs of war." Will of Drumlanrig was not the only one who still wore bandaging. "My son? Do not . . . do not tell me that you have come . . . to give me ill tidings? Of my son . . .?"

Jamie frowned. "I am Douglas of Aberdour," he jerked. "I . . . we come from England, yes. From Redesdale. Your son is John Bickerton, sir?"

"Aye. I am John de Bickerton, tenant of these lands. My son, who keeps this castle in my stead for my lord of Crawford, is not with you? He is not . . . dead, young sir?"

"No. No — would that he . . ." Jamie restrained himself. "Sir — we had looked to find your son here. He, he left the field. Before us. Before all. At Otterburn, in Redesdale. Four nights past. He has not come home?"

"Why should he, friend?" The older man looked from one to the other, warily now. "What is this, of leaving the field? What field? He was with the Earl of Douglas. Armour-bearer. Was there a battle? If the Earl fell, why should John come home betimes?"

"Because he slew him, sir! Stabbed him in the back! That is why," Drumlanrig burst out. "John Bickerton slew my father."

"Slew . . .?" The old man stared. "What folly is this? Are you out of your wits, boy?"

"No! The folly is otherwhere, sir. I am Will Douglas of Drumlanrig — *Sir* William! And your son killed my father, the Earl. Miscreant . . .!"

Others of the Douglases joined in then, in a chorus of accusation and fury. It caused the older man to step back into his doorway in concern, and his servants to move closer, wondering. But it also had the effect of calming Jamie Douglas, oddly enough. He held up his hand.

"Quiet! Quiet, you!" he exclaimed. "This will advance us

nothing." He turned on Bickerton. "You, sir — how did you know that the Earl of Douglas had fallen?"

"Eh? Did I say so? I but said *if* the Earl had fallen. No more. Else his armour-bearer would not leave his side, surely? I meant no more than that."

"Yet it was strangely said. As though you . . . knew!"

"No, no. I swear it. Here is all some sorry mistake. My son would never do what you say. You err, young sirs. You have been misled . . ."

"I saw it, with my own eyes. Saw your son's hand strike, dirk held. At the height of the battle. Armour and shirt-of-mail unfastened. At the back. I was his chief esquire. At your son's side. No mistake, sir. Save that I *saw* — who should not!"

"I'll not believe it," the old man said. "Not John. Not my son."

"Your son, yes. So we think to find him here, in this castle."

"You will not find him here, I tell you. Come search, if you will. There is none here but my wife and daughter."

"We will, yes, to be sure. For found he must be."

All were for pushing into the keep, but Jamie ordered some to remain outside, to search the stables, byres and outbuildings. His knighthood, and the experiences of the last days, had given him an authority unknown previously.

They went over the castle, from lowest pit and vaulted basement to topmost tower and caphouse, and found nothing. Some unhappy and bewildered women watched them, wringing hands and protesting; but there were few men about the place, Lindsay having taken almost all away with him on the expedition.

Jamie had to admit defeat. He made some sort of apology to Bickerton's wife, but in stilted fashion, before they mounted and rode away.

They had barely crossed the drawbridge before the great gates clashed shut behind them, and they heard the rumble of drawn bars. Then the portcullis clanked down into place. Bickerton senior evidently intended to suffer no more intrusions. Even as they gazed back, Ramsay spoke up.

"What kind of horse did Bickerton ride?" he asked.

"Lastly, a tall grey, with dark dappling on legs," Jamie answered. "A good animal. Why?"

"No matter."

"Then why ask, man?"

"I but found a beast strangely stalled. When you were searching the keep. Behind the yard. In the base of one of the angle-towers. A mare stalled. Not in the main stables — apart. No stall at all, indeed — an icehouse for keeping fish and meat, I'd say, with a doocot above. It was a blue roan, with a white left knee. I had a notion that I had seen the beast before, somewhere."

Jamie drew a quick and audible breath. "A blue roan with a white knee? Left knee — and mare! My lord had such as his third horse. A gift from the Lady Isabel. It was with us, at Otterburn!"

They stared at each other, silent now — until they all began to speak at once.

Out of much angry debate and clamour, they came to a decision. Clearly they would not be let back into Luffness Castle—nor could they force their way in to such a strong place. But, if they kept a discreet watch on its gates, day and night, they might either gain entry, or grab John Bickerton if he ventured out. He could not remain shut up somewhere indefinitely. But they would require many more men for such a round-the-clock watch. Ramsay could bring some from Waughton, fairly quickly. But not sufficient. Jamie declared that he would get Douglases from Tantallon. It was only some eight miles away, and he had to go there anyway. The Countess Isabel had gone there when her lord set off for the expedition — it was her favourite seat, by summer seas. He would have to go break to her the news of her husband's death — to his sorrow. Meantime, the rest of the party must stay here on watch, well hidden. Ramsay could also fetch food and drink from Waughton.

Jamie rode away eastwards, along the shallow Vale of Peffer, Will of Drumlanrig at his side. That youth was still not fully recovered of his hurt, and his stepmother's house at Tantallon was as near to a home as he knew.

*   *   *

It was near to dusk when they came to the mighty castle of Tantallon, the impregnable Douglas fortress on the cliffs east of North Berwick, compared to which even Luffness seemed modest. There was no other castle in the land quite like it in design. It consisted, in effect, of merely a simple and long hugely high wall, like part of a city's ramparts, crowned by the usual parapet and wall-walk, which cut off a thrusting small peninsula of the cliffs. Three tall towers rose therefrom, one at each end and one in the centre, the latter a gatehouse-tower very large and strong, almost a keep. No fewer than three deep and wide ditches and their associated banks protected this long frontage landwards, in addition to the steep and narrower moat, water-filled, which lay immediately below the walls, from neck to neck of the peninsula. And seawards the cliffs dropped sheer in dizzy precipices to the restless waves. Offshore a mile-and-a-half the stupendous rock of The Bass soared abruptly from the tide, stark and awesome, the cloud of screaming seabirds a perpetual halo round its lofty head.

The drawbridge under the great central tower was raised for the night when the two young visitors arrived; but the guards had been watching their approach and the bridge was lowered for them promptly enough on the shouting of their identity — both well-known here, of course.

Once through the long dark cobbled pend below the gatehouse-tower, it was as though they had entered a different world. Here was nothing of fortification, grim strength or beetling threat. Suddenly all was light and delight, peaceable domesticity, colour and space — indeed, spaciousness was the dominant impression, with the sky the most evident feature. For although there were minor and subsidiary buildings within the vast curtain wall, these were of no great height and extent and at the sides only, stables, kitchens, storerooms, a chapel. But all the wide centre of that cliff-plateau was vacant, right to the precipice-edge, save for grassy lawns, flower-beds, rose-bushes, winding paths, arbours, a well. So lofty were the cliffs that from here the sea was only visible at a major distance and it was the sky and the wheeling birds which took the eye until the very lip was reached. Then, suddenly, the endless hush and sigh of the creaming waves on the reefs and skerries far below added a new dimension.

Two ladies strolled in that fair green pleasance in the cool of the August evening, and a boy with them. At sight of the dismounting newcomers, the lad came running.

"Jamie! Will!" he cried. "You have come back. How did you fare? Did it go well? I wish I could have gone. My lord would not take me. Though he took Archie, who is not much older than I am. Where is he — my lord?"

Will began to speak, but Jamie gripped his arm tightly.

"He is not here, my lord," he said carefully. "We have come alone. The expedition had . . . its successes. We won a battle. But . . . we must pay our duties to the Countess. And to your lady-mother . . ."

"A battle? You fought a battle? Against the English? And *I* was not there! Tell me, Jamie. You, Will . . .?"

"My lord Earl — the Countess first. Both Countesses. You would not have us fail in our respect?"

"Oh, if you must!" The fair-haired, delicate-featured twelve-year-old shrugged. He was George Douglas, Earl of Angus.

They moved over to the ladies, Jamie's feet reluctant indeed. They bowed.

"Will! And Jamie!" Countess Isabel welcomed them warmly. "I joy to see you back. Safe. But, Will — are you hurt? Not sorely, I hope? You have not brought my lord with you? Shame on you both!"

"No, lady," Jamie said, and swallowed. "I am sorry."

The other woman laughed. "Do not look so concerned, boy!" she said. "I do not doubt that the Lord James did not seek your agreement!" She was a somewhat older woman, but still handsome, bold-eyed, lively, a foil for the more gentle Stewart princess.

Jamie drew a deep breath, his eyes on the Countess of Douglas. "Madam," he began. "My lady — I come bearing ill news. To my sorrow. My lord, my good lord . . ." He stopped, unable to go on.

"Jamie!" The Lady Isabel took a step forward. "Do not say . . .! Oh, God — do not say it! Are you telling me . . . telling me that my lord . . . that my lord is . . .?"

He nodded, dumbly — although he had rehearsed what he should say to her times without number these last days.

"A-a-ah!" A long, shuddering sigh broke from her trembling lips. And turning abruptly, she hurried away from them towards the sea side of the garden.

Will began to blurt out the dire story to the Countess Margaret. But Jamie went slowly after his mistress. He did not go right up to her, where she stood, shoulders heaving, at the cliff-edge and staring out to sea, but waited perhaps a dozen yards back, silent, desolate.

At last she turned and came back to him, drying tears with her long flaxen hair, seeking to control her lovely features.

"Tell me, Jamie," she commanded. "I am myself again. I can bear the worst, now. How . . . how did it befall?"

"The worst is very ill, my lady. It makes sore telling. My lord was slain in a battle. A great battle which he won. In Redesdale in Northumberland. Against the Percy. But . . . he was not slain in fair fight. He was murdered. Stabbed in the back. By his own armour-bearer, John Bickerton. Murdered by that *dastard*!"

Horrified, speechless, she gazed at him.

"He had left his armour undone. And so could dirk him. From behind. I saw him — saw the dirk. So evil a thing . . . !"

"But why, *why*?" That was a wail.

"None know, lady. He . . . Bickerton, thought himself affronted — but I believe it more than that. None would slay his own lord for the like."

Again the Countess turned away, and once more Jamie Douglas waited silent. At length, when she did not speak, he began to talk quietly to her back, telling her all, the entire extraordinary story of treachery, hate and heroism, and of battle won by a dead man — although he did not emphasise the part he himself had played.

In time, tight-lipped but in command of herself, the Countess Isabel allowed him to lead her indoors, to her own boudoir in the castle — and even thanked him for his care and thought for her.

Later, as they ate, with the Lady Isabel sending a message that she had retired for the night, Jamie sought the other Countess's permission to send men to Luffness to aid in the apprehension of Bickerton — and found her co-operative. She was a very different creature from Isabel Stewart, spirited, almost fiery, outspoken, heedless of convention. She had lived here for long, by courtesy of the Earl James, for she had been his father's mistress, although she had lands of her own in Angus. The two Countesses were good friends, however peculiar their relationship.

So a group of Douglas men-at-arms and servants were sent riding through the night to Luffness, with explicit instructions. Only then did Jamie follow Will to bed.

In the morning he was wakened by the Countess Isabel herself coming to his chamber in the east tower — to his minor embarrassment. She was heavy-eyed and pale — but, he thought, the more beautiful for it. He had always admired her greatly, with something almost like awe, not only as his master's wife and the

King's daughter, but for a calmly serene quality and unfailing kindness — not least towards himself, whom she had always befriended, unaccountably to his own mind. If tenser than he had ever known, she was now self-possessed again, and lucid. She came to kiss his brow, before sitting on the end of his bed.

"Jamie — or Sir James, as I hear you are now to be styled — I am come to thank you," she said, with a quiet control which was palpable. "For all your goodness and duty towards my lord and myself. Your kind thought. Your last service to him. Your coming here. I am much in your debt — and would be more so."

"I am yours to command, my lady. Always."

"Scarcely that, Jamie. You are now a knight — and something of a hero I hear. A laird likewise, with your own lands of Aberdour. You are no longer my lord's esquire — nor any lord's esquire. But a man of some substance. Your own man — although but eighteen years. What do you purpose, Sir James?"

"My lady!" he cried. "Do not speak so. I am not other than I was. I am James Douglas, who was my lord's leal servant. Now I am yours, so long as you need me."

"Not servant, Jamie — but friend. And I need you. Yes, need a friend, I think. A stout and leal friend. As I have never needed one before. Will you be my good knight and support, Jamie Douglas?"

"To be sure I will!" he exclaimed, sitting up in bed, forgetting his nakedness. "And gladly, joyfully. But, my lady — why speak so? Of need? You, Countess of Douglas, and the King's daughter, can have the pick of Scotland's lords and knights for your support. What need have you of such as myself?"

"You think so, Jamie? Think again, then. Have you thought at all, my dear? I am the King's daughter — one of many. But . . . have you thought of the King's *sons*? My brothers, God help me! Think you they will cherish the widow of Douglas, sister or none? And my father is but a shadow, a helpless old man, half-blind, and scant protection for me or for any."

The young man swallowed. "He is still King of Scots."

"So they tell me!" She shrugged. "So much for the King's daughter! And what of the Countess of Douglas? Who will be *Earl* of Douglas now, Jamie? Have you thought of that, also?"

He frowned, biting his lip. "I . . . I do not know. I had not thought, no. To me, there was but *one* Earl of Douglas . . ."

"Aye, lad — to me also. But it behoves us now to think differently. Had I had a son to James, or even a daughter, all would have been otherwise. But our child died, as you know — and I have borne no more. Not through lack of will. So there is no heir to all the Douglas power, their lands and wealth. James had no brothers. No clear heir — but there will be hands outstretched to grasp and grab, of that you may be sure. And I in the midst, a weak woman! Now do you see why I need a leal and honest knight in my support, Jamie? Even at eighteen years!"

Appalled, he gazed at her. "I had not thought ..." he muttered.

"I *have*," she said calmly. "I have spent the night thinking. Do you see that as strange? The sorrowing widow? Should I not have been mourning my dear lord? Not thinking thus. But I shall have years to mourn him, Mary pity me! I must needs think *now*. Plan. Enquire. Discover. And I need help."

"My help is yours, lady. Now and always."

"Dear Jamie! But — what did you intend? What think to do? Now, that you are your own man. You must have had some notions?"

"None, no — beyond serving you. All these past years I have been servant to my lord as page and then esquire. Since I was eleven years and I left my father's house for yours. I have no other thought, save to avenge my lord's murder, on that assassin Bickerton. This I have sworn." He stirred restlessly under what blankets still covered the lower part of him. "I should be on my way now, my lady. Back to Luffness. We have trapped him, I believe. And must needs spring the trap. Ramsay and the others await me. I must go ..."

"Bickerton, that foul wretch, can wait, Jamie. Meantime. Let the others deal with him," she said. "They are sufficient, surely at Luffness? I need you. Forthwith. If Bickerton is penned in Luffness castle, he will not escape."

He looked doubtful. "And I must ride to Dalkeith Castle. To see my father. He will look for me ..."

"It is thither I would have you take me, Jamie. For Sir James — save us, you are *both* Sir James now! A confusion. Sir James of Dalkeith, your father, is one of the wisest men in this realm, forby a Douglas. And trustworthy. He will advise me. A member of the Council, he will know what to do. What is best. Today, Jamie — for the tidings of my lord's death will cover the land swiftly. Douglas's death will set the tongues wagging and the agile wits leaping. Grasping hands will move fast, I prophesy! I must move fast also, if I would save what I can."

"As you will, my lady. Allow me to rise, dress and eat, and I shall escort you to Dalkeith."

"I thank you. But — can we not have done now with this of my lady? You are a knight, now — and my friend."

"And you a princess, madam."

"As to that, it signifies little. In especial, now! When we are alone, at the least, Jamie, call me by my name. Isabel. In token of true friendship. I want a true knight to my support, not a servant. Can you bring yourself to do that, Sir James Douglas?"

He nodded wordlessly.

They rode for Dalkeith, leaving Will with the Countess Margaret and the Earl George. It was nearly a score of miles to the west, near Edinburgh, in the Esk valley. They had to pass the vicinity of Luffness on the way, and Jamie took the opportunity to visit his little beleaguering force, now almost thirty strong and with Ramsay very much in command. It was difficult, he said, to keep them all out-of-sight of the castle all the time, and maintain constant observation. The main gate remained shut and the drawbridge up; but a postern-gate to the west was opened now and again momentarily, and servants used this to come and go, especially down to the little haven and boat-strand on the bay shore, where there were fishing-boats. Ramsay's men were watching this like hawks, naturally, lest Bickerton should seek to escape by sea. The castle's occupants were acting very warily—so almost certainly they realised that they were being held under scrutiny. Fortunately the Carmelite monks of the monastery were being helpful. Richard Lundie had had an interview with the Prior before proceeding home to North Berwick, and had been assured of cooperation in the apprehension of Bickerton. For the monastery was a Lindsay foundation, and with their lord a prisoner in England, the monks were anxious that his interests should not be prejudiced. On Jamie's suggestion, the Countess called on the Prior in person, to inform him that she would do all in her power to obtain Sir James Lindsay's release from the Bishop of Durham, possibly in exchange for one or more of the Douglases' own distinguished captives — after all, Lindsay was son to the Lady Egidia of Dalkeith. In return, all Lindsay vassals and supporters must give every assistance in bringing the Earl of Douglas's murderer to justice.

They rode on westwards through the Garden of Scotland, as some named Lothian, from Seton onward becoming almost wholly Douglas lands.

Dalkeith Castle was not a mighty fortress like Tantallon, nor yet a major stronghold like Luffness; but rather a kind of palace, although in a strong defensive position, as befitted the seat of the wealthiest of all the Douglases. Large and with extensive ramifications, it stood in wide parkland on the peninsula where the North and South Esks joined, its town lying a little way upstream, no mere castleton this, but a burgh of barony to rival many a county capital.

The new arrivals found the place in something of a stir, with its lord preparing to ride forth — and the Lady Egidia with him, for she, the King's sister, was not the sort to be left at home in domesticity when anything was toward, and especially now when her captive son was to be rescued, by one means or other. Clearly something *was* toward today, with an air of excitement evident everywhere. Of course the Earl of Douglas's death was now known on all hands; and it was recognised that there would inevitably be changes in the land. And with Lady Egidia concerned for her son, everyone else had to be concerned also.

Sir James of Dalkeith welcomed the Lady Isabel with warmth and sympathy, and his son with real pride and affection. But there was no denying that he was an anxious man — and not too greatly in connection with James Lindsay. He expressed his sorrow, shock and horror at the Earl's murder, and his deep concern for and loyalty to the widow. But that his concern went further and deeper than that he did not seek to hide. While expressing due satisfaction at the victory of Otterburn and the successful outcome of the entire English expedition, he who was statesman rather than soldier, had other preoccupations. If his favourite though illegitimate son's heroics and knighthood did not gain quite as full acclaim as they might have done in other circumstances, Jamie had no complaints to make. At least his younger and legitimate brothers, like Johnnie, were duly impressed.

The Lady Egidia seemed much more indignant that her son had allowed himself to be captured than worried about his state.

It seemed that even before he got back from his raiding, the Earl of Fife and Menteith had called a meeting of the Privy Council for next day, 18th August, at Linlithgow — the Earl Robert, not his father the King, and at Linlithgow not Stirling. This haste was alarming to the Lord of Dalkeith. In theory, of course, it could be said to be a result of the success of, and necessary adjustments occasioned by, the English expedition; but there was no such great hurry for that. Equally, in theory, the Earl Robert had no authority to call any such Council; he did so in the monarch's name — but clearly had not consulted his father in so doing from Carlisle. Almost certainly there was other reason for the meeting — and it would be strange if it was not connected with the death of the Earl of Douglas.

Sir James, senior, suggested that the Lady Isabel and Jamie ride with him and his wife to Linlithgow, another score of miles to the west.

They rode in style, suitable for the richest man in the kingdom, with a large retinue of knights, vassals and men-at-arms — rather more, Jamie felt, than were necessary for mere attendance at a Council meeting. But he did not question his father's motives. Despite the style, the ladies chose to ride saddle-horses like the rest — Stewart princesses tending to be of the kind to eschew horse-litters and other femininities. As they went, the older man amplified some of his disquiets.

"Isabel, my dear — have you considered fully what changes this sorry death may bring to your circumstances?" he asked, gravely if kindly.

"I have, yes. Though how fully, I cannot say. That is why I have come seeking *your* advice, my lord."

"Aye. And you will require advice, I fear. The most powerful earldom in Scotland is fallen vacant, with no sure heir — and there will be many seeking to improve on the situation. You, as Countess, may well be either a target to aim at or a hindrance to be brushed aside."

"That I realise. I have said as much to Jamie here."

"Whoever is Earl of Douglas can control great manpower, see

you. Greater than any other soever in the realm. Who *needs* great manpower, in especial, think you?"

"My royal father needs it — but is not like to want or use it! His sons my brothers, are . . . otherwise!"

"So think I. But they cannot be Earl of Douglas, any of them. And, praise God, you are their *sister* — and even his present Holiness at Avignon cannot grant dispensation for brother to marry sister! So they, at least, must plan otherwise."

The Lady Egidia hooted. "God — I would not put even that past my nephew Alex!"

The Lady Isabel bit her lip. "I think, my lord, we must discern one from another," she said, a little breathlessly. "John needs men, and strength, yes — but he would not stoop to gain it by ill means. That I am sure. David is not concerned greatly with power and riches. Walter is—but he is young and foolish, a babe compared with the others. So we are left with Robert and Alexander."

"Aye — and a sufficiency, these two, by the saints! They have always looked on Douglas with envy."

"Yes. Think you one or other arranged the murder of my husband?"

There was a shocked pause. Even the Lady Egidia, woman of the world as she was, stared at this blunt and terrible suggestion from her pale but lovely niece.

Dalkeith cleared his throat. "My dear — I think that you should put such thoughts from you. They are . . . dangerous."

"No doubt. But I shall find out. Jamie here as good as hinted at it. Others may think similarly. He considers that some small slight, as between lord and armour-bearer, was scarcely sufficient cause for planned murder. Bickerton left my lord's armour part unfastened — and only he knew it. To repay a hot word and a chance scratch from a mace? I think not."

The older man shook his head. "It is passing strange, yes. But the other . . . is scarcely believable. One thing is certain—if it was so, we shall never learn the truth. That I'll swear!"

"Perhaps we shall, my lord," Jamie put in. "I believe Bickerton is hiding in Luffness Castle, despite his father's denial. We have the castle surrounded, watched. When we have the wretch, we will make him talk — that *I* swear!"

His father eyed him sidelong. "You might be safer lacking his information, lad. Folk who will slay once, will slay again!"

"You would have me to fail in avenging my lord's murder?"

"The Earl of Douglas, God rest his soul, would not have you to follow him to the grave, I think! As you might, thus."

They rode in silence, for a while.

"You clearly believe that this shameful deed was more than just a young man's resentment, my lord," the Lady Isabel said, at length. "We have thought of two who might have conceived it. Of these, I would say that my brother Robert would be the one, rather than Alex. He is the plotter, the colder villain. Alex would slay, yes — but would likelier do it with his own hand! He is a rogue—but the more honest rogue, I think! He would strike down whoever got in his way — but with his sword, where Robert might use poison!"

None commented on this elaboration on her assessment of her princely brothers.

"But — there could be others, could there not? Who might have subborned Bickerton? Who could seek to gain by James's death. Who, think you, will win the earldom?"

"I cannot believe that any who could possibly become Earl of Douglas could do such a thing. For they would have to be themselves Douglases — and it is inconceivable that any such would plan the death of their chief. But I agree that others could seek to use a new Earl of Douglas for their own ends, his power and influence. And so might possibly have done this. But again — who is placed so to use him? Or gain by the using? Other than one of the royal house?"

"It would have to be a very great noble," Jamie put in.

"Aye. But which? There are not many of sufficient power and stature to be able to play in such a game, to profit by it. Who are not Douglases or Stewarts. Dunbar? Moray? Or, or . . ."

"Say it," his wife snapped. "Or Lindsay! There are no others of sufficient stature. With Mar and Angus in women's hands. And Fife, Menteith, Carrick, Buchan and Atholl held by Stewart. Sutherland, Caithness, Ross and the Isles take no heed for our Lowland concerns. Which leaves Lindsay! He was there. And it was my son's vassal who did the deed. But I swear that James had no part in this! He is no saint — but this is not his style. And he admired Douglas."

"I, too, would swear that Sir James Lindsay knew naught of this," Jamie declared. "As also my lords of Dunbar and Moray. These all were friends."

"I agree," the Countess said. "We need consider none of them. But there is one, perhaps, whom you have overlooked. Not of quite the same stature, no — not an earl or a great lord. But an ambitious man of an ambitious house. No friend of my family — but linked to the Crown nevertheless. Sir Malcolm Drummond of Cargill. Whose aunt was second queen to King David, and his sister Annabella wife to my brother John. He is married to my dear lord's only sister, the Countess of Mar. He has not claimed the title of Earl of Mar—but he is acquisitive, and might be waiting to do so. If he was to claim also the earldom of Douglas, in his wife's name, he could become the most powerful man in this kingdom!"

"Whe-e-ew!" Dalkeith whistled, turning in his saddle to look long at the princess. "Malcolm Drummond! *That* I never thought on. But it is true. The Countess Isobel of Mar, whatever else, will inherit much by her brother's death. Not the earldom, I think — but wide lands. The unentailed lands of Douglas. Or most of them. Drummond I have never liked — though that may be but prejudice. You have sharp wits in that bonnie head, my dear! Drummond was not in this late expedition?"

"No," Jamie said. "After winning his tourney at Stirling, he went back to Kildrummy, they said. His wife's castle in Mar."

"And Bickerton? He was not at Stirling, I seem to remember. *You* acted armour-bearer to Earl James, there?"

"Yes. Bickerton was not at Stirling."

"So it seems the less likely that Drummond should be concerned."

The Lady Egidia took up the inquisition. "You said, James, that Isobel of Mar will inherit most of the *unentailed* lands of Douglas. But what of the entailed lands? Who gains them?"

"Whoever becomes Earl gets Douglasdale. And part of Ettrick Forest, I believe. But the major part of the landed heritage goes to Archie. Archibald of Galloway. The lands were entailed on him back in '42, by the Earl William, Earl James's father, a cousin, although illegitimate. After James himself, and his heirs. That entail, so far as I know, has never been altered. James leaving no direct heir-male, it will stand, I think."

"Archie the Grim! And will he become Earl of Douglas also?"

"Not necessarily. Others might have as good a claim. And be legitimate! Archie was only a natural son of the Good Sir James, Bruce's friend."

"So! Here we have another possible assassin — Archie the Grim!"

"Never! Archie is leal of the leal, I'd stake my life on that! Leal to Douglas."

"But a friend of Robert Stewart. And that nephew of mine has few friends. Lord — what a tangle!" The Lady Egidia leaned forward to look past her husband at the Countess. "My dear, in all this sorry roll of suspects, do not let it escape your notice that there is another who could have a claim to the earldom of Douglas. And so could become even richer and powerfuller than he is now — James Douglas, Lord of Dalkeith! Do not forget *him*!"

"Egidia, my heart — I find your humour too *Stewart* for my taste!" her lord said coldly. "I pray you, curb it. For Isabel's sake, if not mine."

They rode on in silence, with more than enough to think about.

VII

THE LITTLE GREY town of Linlithgow beside its loch, a few miles inland from the narrow Forth, midway to Stirling, seethed like an anthill disturbed, that evening, with much of the Scots western army encamped around it, the handsome brown-stone Palace on the ridge above the loch occupied by the princes and lords; and most of the houses of the burgh itself taken over temporarily by clerics and lesser nobility and gentry. Newcomers were arriving all the time; indeed Dalkeith's party finished the journey in company with the entourages of the Abbots of Melrose and Kelso and of the Lord of Borthwick. Jamie and his father were immediately struck by the fact that the army was here, and had not been disbanded like the eastern force. Moreover, that large numbers of lesser lords and lairds, Stewarts in especial, who had no connection with the Privy Council and had not been with the English expedition, were coming in also.

"I do not like this," Dalkeith said. "What are all these for? They can only be here because they have been summoned. And since the Earl Robert of Fife is in command, *he* must have summoned them. And that man never does anything without good reason. Or, leastways, without *definite* reason!"

"The Lord Archie of Galloway will, no doubt, tell us what's to do," Jamie suggested.

But it transpired that the Lord of Galloway was not in fact present. He had left the army after it recrossed the Border northwards, with his son Sir William, for his own castle of Threave, near Kirkcudbright. He was expected for the Council, nevertheless.

Bonfires were being lit on all the gentle hill-tops around Linlithgow as they rode up the quite steep causeway, past St. Michael's Kirk, to the Palace. It appeared that tonight was to be an occasion for celebration, festivities, gaiety — little as the Earl of Fife was apt to be associated with such manifestations normally. Presumably it was to celebrate the successful outcome of the English expedition — although the Douglases at least found it scarcely suitable or tactful, with mourning for the kingdom's greatest soldier more fitting. So far as Jamie could ascertain, the western thrust had produced no great achievements anyway; a few skirmishes, a number of not-very-important prisoners and hostages, and some thousands of head of English cattle, were hardly sufficient to account for such large-scale rejoicings. All the dramatics had, in fact, been with the eastern force.

The Dalkeith party's reception at the Palace was not enthusiastic; but then the Earl Robert had never been an enthusiast. He expressed formal condolences with his sister on the sad death of her husband; but that was all. He was more forthcoming towards Dalkeith himself, briefly almost affable indeed — although he eyed his aunt with distaste. Unlike some of his brothers, he was not a lover of women, not even much of a liker. Jamie, needless to say, he ignored. The Earl David of Strathearn was much more friendly and sympathetic towards his sister — but appeared to be as little informed about the reasons for the Council-meeting, and the allied rejoicings, as were the newcomers. Robert told him nothing, he complained. As for the Lord Walter of Brechin, he was drunk as usual, with his whores, and in no state to inform, sympathise or even recognise anyone.

The Palace, though large, was crowded already. Small and inadequate accommodation was found for the Lady Isabel, and better for Dalkeith and his wife; but Jamie had to find quarters where he could in the town, eventually teaming up with some Nithsdale Douglases in the stables of a hostelry. His new knightly status cut little ice in Linlithgow, it seemed.

He did gain some information from his new companions however. According to them, the victory fires and festivities were not only to celebrate the Northumbrian and Cumbrian invasions, but their own earlier victory in Ireland under Sir William of Nithsdale, at Carlingford, their destruction of the English fleet and their taking of the Isle of Man on the way home. These, taken in conjunction with the western thrust almost to Lancaster, were considered to be much more strategically and politically important than the fight at Otterburn — which was, after all, little more than a personal feud and bicker between Douglas and Percy. In token of this, when Sir William, the Flower of Chivalry, arrived with his father, on the morrow, there was to be a great merrymaking, and the announcement of the King's bestowal of the hand of his youngest daughter, the Lady Gelis, on Sir William, in royal approbation. Archie, Lord of Galloway, was also to be honoured in some fashion, it was thought.

Jamie Douglas, lying on straw in that inn's stable, knew a smouldering resentment on behalf of his dead lord, and against the gallant William of Nithsdale and his father. But though he was suspicious enough to perceive a Stewart wedge being driven shrewdly between the main stems of Douglas, he did not recognise that the iron point of that wedge had already penetrated his own mind.

All the following morning and forenoon new arrivals poured into Linlithgow. Sir John Montgomerie of Eaglesham escorted his illustrious captive, Hotspur, treated by all with great respect. The Earls of Dunbar and Moray came, grumbling, but brought with them other important prisoners, by request — although Sir Ralph

Percy was too sorely wounded to travel further. The Lady Gelis appeared, gay and colourful, with a bevy of her ladies, from Dundonald in Ayrshire, where her royal sire had retired. Archie the Grim, his legitimate son Sir Archibald, Master of Galloway, and the illegitimate but renowned Sir William, rode in in fine style, with a large following, with the chief of the Johnstones and the Lord Maxwell with them. These at least paid immediate respects to the bereaved Countess. Sir Malcolm Drummond came from Tayside, and a host of Stewarts from Bute, Renfrewshire, the Lennox, Menteith, Fife and Berwickshire. Two notable absentees however were Earl John of Carrick and Earl Alexander the Wolf. Presumably these had ignored their brother's summons.

The Council was held at noon on the 18th of August, in the lesser banqueting hall of the Palace. Despite the huge concourse assembled at Linlithgow, only a very few were Privy Councillors, of course, so that not more than a score could attend the meeting. The remainder and the women could only wait on events.

Jamie, attending on the Lady Isabel, went with her to call on the Lady Gelis — who had been allotted much superior quarters than those of her elder sister. The young man was less than happy at the prospect. For although he still was hopelessly under the spell of the younger woman and longed to be in her company, the thought of her forthcoming union with William of Nithsdale was like a knife in his breast, he told himself; and close contact with her now would only turn that knife in the wound. Moreover, he felt that this public betrothal was somehow all part of a deep plan to denigrate the memory of his late master and to split the house of Douglas — and, knowingly or not, Gelis Stewart was lending herself to it. He admitted, however, that he might be a little prejudiced.

The two sisters met in a little rush of affection. For although one was an elder daughter of the King and the other the youngest, with fourteen years difference of age, they had always been good friends.

"My dear, my dear!" Gelis cried, and impulsively threw her arms round Isabel. "My heart bleeds for you! My very dear — how cruel, how cruel! I am desolate for you. In your great loss. What am I to say? James — so grievous a blow, so noble a lord!"

"Say . . . say nothing, Gelis sweet," her sister got out. "What is there to say?"

"Isabel, my heart, my brave one . . . !"

They wept on each other's shoulders.

Highly embarrassed, Jamie looked away, looked at the other young woman in the upper tower chamber, Mary Stewart, one of the King's bastard daughters and principal of Gelis's pretty throng. She looked as though she too was going to burst into tears. Clearing his throat, he strode over to the window to stare out at the loch. He should never have allowed himself to be brought here.

Presently out of much sniffing and swallowing and broken words, he heard the Countess congratulating her sister on her forthcoming marriage, saying, in a rush, what a splendid and gallant bridegroom she would have, and how she always had known that her heart was set in that airt. It was not every princess who was permitted to wed the man of her choice. And so on.

Mary Stewart came over to stand beside the young man, tears apparently quickly swallowed, a dimpling, warm-eyed, lively piece, not so beautiful as Gelis but markedly good-looking for all that, in person as in feature. But then, the Stewart women were nearly always good-looking. This one had a very notable bosom, which rose and fell close enough at Jamie's side, and under his regard, to be distinctly affecting.

"So much sorrow and joy in one small chamber!" she murmured. "Stewarts and Douglases! Think you women should so seek marriage? Might they not do a deal better lacking it?"

Startled, he raised his eyes from breasts to face. "I . . . I do not know, Mistress Mary. Have not thought greatly. As to marriage. For women."

"I dare say not. Men seldom do, I think. And yet — you were born out-of-wedlock, were you not? As was I !"

He cleared his throat. "Aye. So you are not a princess, Mistress — and I shall never be Lord of Dalkeith!"

"True. But we may live the happier — who knows? And bastardy does not seem to have done you much other dis-service, Sir Knight!"

"I, ah, did naught to deserve knighthood," he assured. "I but did my plain duty."

"That was not the tale as I heard it, Sir James! But have it as you will. Men have been knighted for less than doing their duty."

"Jamie Douglas!" That was Gelis calling now. "Come — allow that I mark your advancement to new estate, in fitting fashion." And as he approached, and bowed, she reached up, took his cheeks between both hands, and kissed him full on the lips. "There, Sir Knight — another accolade! As well deserved, it may be! Heigho — I have always wanted to do that — to one of the best-looking young men in my father's realm!"

"My, my lady. I ... I ..." Jamie was stammering, flushing hotly, when his lips were closed by another smacking kiss, this time from the girl Mary, a hearty salute the impact of which was by no means lessened by the strong and well-defined pressure of two prominent breasts against his chest.

"I did not dare before, but now I may!" that young woman declared, laughing breathlessly. "For is not every true knight vowed and bound to cherish and serve all ladies in their need?"

"The price you pay, Jamie! For feminine admiration," the Lady Isabel said, smiling away her tears. "As well that you are *my* assured knight, is it not?"

"Tell us," her sister commanded. "Tell us how you did it, Jamie. How you did aid the Douglas to win his last battle. How you bore him forward. Isabel, my heart, will be but proud to hear it again, I vow!"

"I have not truly heard it once, yet! Only the bare facts."

"There is naught to tell," he protested. "After, after my lord was stabbed by, by ... after he was stabbed, he *ordered* that we do it. *He* was the hero, not us. Ordered us to carry him on, dying or dead. To hold him up, to shout his slogan, to keep his banner above him. That none might know him fallen, friend and foe alike. And when we might no longer bear him onward for the English swords and axes and spears, we laid him down and fought above him. We could do no other. Here was no deed worthy of knighthood ..."

"Yet three of the six fell, did they not? On top of the Douglas? And Rob Hart died?"

"So not only did a dead man win a battle, but a man was knighted, dead?" Mary said.

"Oh, I wish that I could have seen that sight!" the Lady Gelis cried.

A choked-off sob from Isabel turned them all — and Jamie chewed his lip as the others went to seek comfort their sister, proclaiming their thoughtlessness.

He made an effort, and changed the subject. "You, Lady Gelis, should seek your tales of heroes not from me but from your Sir William," he said. "All declare *him* to be the true hero. That his battles were those that mattered. That our sallies against the Percy were but by-play!"

If there was a slightly sour note behind that, Gelis did not seem to detect it. "Oh, I will have it all out of him, yes. I long to hear it. But I have scarce seen him. Robert and the others have been so busy making much of him. And now they have him into this Council. A great honour for so young a man, I have no doubt. Ah, well — my time will come. I have waited thus long — I can wait a little longer."

"And what of the King of France, lady?" Jamie surprised even himself by bringing that out. "He waits also, does he not?"

"Why, let him wait, Jamie! I never wanted him. He is fat, they say — and slobbers! Lacks something in wits, I have heard. He has my picture — let him bed with that, if he likes it so well! I would not exchange Will Douglas for any king or emperor! Indeed, there are other Douglases I'd sooner wed than any monarch, if the truth were known!" And she dipped a mocking curtsy.

Confounded, he blinked and flushed again, wordless.

Mary Stewart, laughing, took his arm. "She but would make sure of *some* Douglas or other, lest Sir William be now grown too great to look at her! But come, Sir Jamie — I warrant these two have matters to discuss between them fit only for princesses' ears! Let us bastards go walk a little by the loch and feed bread to the waterfowl. And you can tell me how you broke into Newcastle town behind a herd of stolen cattle!"

"You know of that . . .?" he wondered.

"Ah, we know of many things, sirrah — more than you think. Who knows, I might even tell *you* some!"

"Come back shortly, Jamie," the Countess told him.

Uncomfortable, in that the young woman did not release his arm, even when going down the winding turnpike stair — which occasioned not a little bumping together and close contact in the process — and on amidst the idling, strolling, laughing throng in the great quadrangle and out in the terraced pleasance beyond,

Jamie was not very forthcoming at first; but his companion chattered away inconsequentially for both of them. It was not until they were down skirting the reedy fringe of the loch, where the coots scuttered and the mallard launched out in quacking protest, that she changed her tone and tune.

"Tell me," she said, "do you know much of Sir William of Nithsdale? How he lives? What are his ... ways? As a man — not a hero? Or a lover, perhaps! You are kin to him, in some degree, are you not?"

He looked at her, warily. "So distantly as not to signify. But I *know* him a little, yes. Less well than does the Lady Gelis, I'd think!"

"Perhaps. She knows one side of the man, yes. But there are other sides which a woman may not discover easily *before* marriage! Something of a drawback!"

"No doubt. But it is late in the day, is it not, to think of that?"

"It is not new thought of. But there is a matter the Lady Gelis would know more of. And on which Sir William has not spoken. One appropriate that you and I should consider, bastards both! We have heard that Sir William has already a bastard son. Where, and by whom, we have not yet learned. Have you heard of this?"

"No. But it is not so strange, surely? Many men have, by his years. And he is a natural son, himself."

"Oh, to be sure. Men are ever very generous with their seed, we women have discovered! Perhaps you, likewise? But this matter is more delicate than some. For, from what we have heard tell, Sir William is sufficiently concerned for this child to settle property upon him. So it seems that it is not just some milkmaid's get, to be made into a forester or a falconer. Yet he has not declared it to his bride-to-be. You will perceive the problem, Jamie? The mother! The Lady Gelis is not seeking to lay blame — she could scarce do so, coming from *our* family! She would happily accept such a child, see to its rearing perhaps. But the mother is a different matter."

"I see that, yes. But I know nothing of this. Have not heard of child or mother. Your informant, who knows so much — surely he could tell you more?"

"That is the rub. For the tale came to us less than directly. By second mouth, or third. At Court, you know how it is. We do not even know if it is true. Save that it sounds too particular to be wholly contrived. The Lady Gelis would wish to know the truth. And hopes that you might learn it for her."

"So! I am to play spy on my kinsman?"

"Scarce that. Just to discover, if you may, whether the tale is true or false. She is entitled to know that, is she not?"

"She could ask Sir William."

"Not the easiest question on this happy occasion! All the realm will be lauding Sir William of Nithsdale and his royal bride. And he has not told her of this. If it is untrue . . .! Delicate, as I say. You agree? And Gelis conceives you her friend."

"Aye," he said, heavily.

"You do understand, Jamie? This must be secret. There are none so many we can trust. If there *is* a woman whom Sir William cherishes sufficiently to settle lands on her child, she must be of at least lairdly rank. Yet he professes faithful and undying love for the princess! To start married life with such a hidden mistress could be . . . trying!"

"Very well. I will see what I may discover."

"Do, Jamie. We shall all be grateful. For I, too, am devoted to my sister's interests." She squeezed his arm. "The Lady Gelis's quarters will be open to Sir Jamie Douglas at any and all times!"

He cleared his throat as comment to that.

"Now, alas — we may be required by our betters . . ."

The Council-meeting ended sooner than might have been expected for so evidently important an occasion, and the members came out looking distinctly bemused, where they were not scowling — save for some few, who seemed gleeful. Dalkeith, Dunbar, Moray and indeed David of Strathearn, were amongst the blackest-browed. Archibald the Grim, for once, managed to look uneasy and undecided, his son William equally doubtful.

The Lady Isabel was not long in repairing to the Dalkeith's chamber, Jamie with her. They found his father stamping the floor and haranguing the Lady Egidia — which was not like that equable and moderate individual. He promptly turned on the newcomers.

"It is not to be borne!" he declared. "The man is insufferable! It was no Council but a . . . a presumption, an effrontery! He treated us all like bairns before a tutor. Hectored us, would hear no contrary view. All was decided, arranged — we were there but to be *told*! The King's Privy Council!"

"And you bore it like sheep?" his wife asked.

"We did not. But your precious nephew allowed no vote, overrode all. In his cold, sour fashion. He is to be master in Scotland."

"He has been the power behind my father for long, now," the Countess pointed out.

"Aye. But now it is much more than that. He is to be Governor of the Realm. That is to be his style. As good as Regent. To take over all the functions of government, on your royal father's behalf."

"But . . . can he do that? Is it possible?"

"He says that it is with the King's consent. It will require the confirmation of a parliament. But that is to be called shortly."

"And will he gain that confirmation?" the Lady Egidia wondered. "Robert is not loved in the land. And does not Douglas sway sufficient votes in any parliament to check him?"

"Douglas! Well may you ask! The man is a devil. Cunning. He has waited until now to bring this forward. Planned all. It is all clear now. Why he agreed to the English invasion — which surprised me, I will admit. Why he went with it, unlike himself as this was. He comes home a victor — although *he* gained no victory! Advances Will of Nithsdale as the realm's hero, and gives him his sister to wed, amidst public rejoicings. And splits Douglas in twain! That is Robert Stewart!"

"If Douglas is so weak as to allow Robert to split it!"

"That is the devil of it! Whether or no *he* caused the Earl's death, it plays into his hands. Removes the undoubted leader and chief. He could never have done this with the Earl James living. But now he as good as confers the earldom on his friend Archie of Galloway."

"But even he cannot do that, can he?" the Lady Isabel cried. "Even in his father's name?"

"No — God be thanked! It requires a due process, of law. And earldoms fall to be confirmed by the King in *parliament*. But Archie has the entailed lands — he had the papers there, on the table, to prove it, the Earl William's testament. That is why he went to Threave, from Carlisle; to fetch them. And he is in the running for the earldom itself. I did what I could. I protested. I put in claims for the earldom — to ensure that it was not settled out-of-hand. For myself. And for young Angus, who is a half-brother, though illegitimate. But Archie himself was illegitimate. Drummond put in a claim on behalf of his wife, as we guessed he would. Myself, I do not desire to be earl. But the claim had to be laid. So Douglas is indeed split — which is what Fife desired and planned."

"I esteemed Archie a true man, and no fool," his wife said. "He will not wish this to damage the Douglas power. For though he is friend to Robert, he does not love us Stewarts — makes no secret of that. He might well be the best Earl of Douglas, forby!"

"Agreed. I do not contest that. But not if he is in Fife's pocket."

"Robert is a plotter, yes. A shrewd and hard man. But he is not a man of action, James. No warrior . . ."

"That is why he needs Archie and young William of Nithsdale. They are."

"If he *needs* them, then the power remains. With Douglas."

"He has begun to whittle it away already — and Archie did not seek to stop him. Fife has himself assumed the position of Chief Warden of the Marches, in Earl James's room, a position that has been Douglas's for generations. It gives him additional great power, in the Borders in dealing with the English. It is damnable!"

"Robert had all his plans laid, then," the Countess said levelly. "This was not all contrived in a day or two. And none, or little, was possible while my lord lived! I think that we need look no further for his murderer."

They eyed her with varying expressions, silent.

A knock at the door heralded a servant to announce the Lord of Galloway and Sir William Douglas of Nithsdale to see the Lord of Dalkeith. Archibald the Grim strode in, followed by his son. "James—it is necessary that we speak . . ." he began, in his harsh, strong voice; and then noticed the Countess, and paused, to bow jerkily. "My lady Isabel! My dear lady — I am sorry. Desolated for you. A tragedy. I deeply feel for you."

"I too, lady," Sir William added, bowing more deeply. He had a musical voice, in contrast to his father's. "That your loss is the realm's loss can be scant comfort to you now. All true men grieve with you."

"All *true* men, no doubt, my lords!" That was very cool.

Askance, they eyed her, and transferred their bows to the Lady Egidia.

"We were speaking of you, Archie," Dalkeith said, less than cordially. "And that travesty of a Council."

"Yes. To be sure. I reckoned that you might. That is why I am here."

"Sent by my lord of Fife?"

"Curse you, James — no man sends Archie Douglas! Stewart or other! Now or ever! Mind it, will you?" He paused, and nodded briefly to each of the ladies. "Your pardon. But Sir James should know me better. We have been acquainted, friends, for sufficiently long."

"That is what I thought, Archie. Until today!"

"Why should I change, man? Today? Because of the earldom, think you? For myself, I care nothing to be Earl of Douglas. Lord of Galloway is sufficient for me. And now I have the entailed lands. Enough. And am an old man, getting . . ."

"Yet you let your friend Fife claim the earldom for you."

"Aye. Since I could not stop him. Nor could I say that I would refuse it man. I have as good a right as any. But, see you, James — this is no matter for bickering over, you and me. Or any. You could have a claim, yes. Young Angus, yes. Others perhaps. But are claimants' rights all that is concerned? I think not. That is why I have come to you." The great stooping eagle of a man strode about the room. "What is the Earl of Douglas? What different from other earls and lords? Power, I say. Douglas power. Man-power. Not wealth — you have the most of that. Not lands or name — save insofar as these command men. It is being able to put a dozen of a thousand men in the field, horsed and armed, that makes the Earl of Douglas different from others. Can you deny it?"

Dalkeith shook his head.

"What then? This power. The Earl must be able to *use* these men if he is to be a power in the land. Able and ready. That means he must be a soldier, a fighting-man. I say that is the heart of it. Are you that, James? Could you command ten thousand men in the field? Could the boy Angus? Could the Lady Isobel of Mar, or her Drummond husband? Or any other who could make a claim? *I* can. And my sons after me. That is why I let the Earl

Robert make that claim for me. I, and no other, can hold the Douglas power together today. And so held it must be, for the weal of this realm."

Into the pause, his son spoke. "I believe that my lord is right. Our Douglas power is great — but it could vanish like snow off a dyke, lacking a fighting leader. You must see it, sir? You are greatly respected, trusted. But would armed men flock to your banner? And if they would not, where is the vaunted power of Douglas?"

Dalkeith cleared his throat. "I, or other, as Earl, could call on my leal supporter and friend the Lord of Galloway to lead my host in the field!"

"Aye, but it is not the same thing, my lord . . ."

"I would do it," Sir Will's father said, "but as Archibald of Galloway would all of Douglas rally to me? Galloway and the south-west, yes. Douglasdale possibly. But what of Ettrick and Teviotdale? What of Lothian and Clydesdale? Of Kilpatrick and Lochleven? Of Abercorn? And all the rest? Would these all gladly follow a Gallowayman who was not Earl?"

"Archie is right, James," his wife said, quietly. "If you would retain the real power of your house, Archie had best be Earl of Douglas. And if Robert is to be contained, that Douglas power will be needed!"

"But Archie is supporting him! Douglas power will be used to *aid* Stewart, not contain him!"

"Not so, James," Galloway denied. "I think none so ill of Robert Stewart, unlike so many! But my support for him is not final, unchangeable. Still less so if I was Earl. I support him now because I see him as strong, and would see him stronger. For the realm's sake. This kingdom must have a ruler, James, a governor. You have said so yourself. It has not had that, in truth, for long. My regrets towards your ladyships, but the King has not ruled the land for years. And when a king does not rule, others must, or there is confusion, anarchy. Scotland needs a Governor, and a strong one."

"Perhaps. But . . ."

Sir William spoke up again. "Have you considered the other choice, my lord? If the Earl Robert does not take the rule? Someone must, and will! And who is next in line — since it is sure that the Earl of Carrick will not — the Earl Alexander. Again, with these princesses' forbearance, since I speak of their brother and nephew — would you have the Earl of Buchan ruling Scotland?"

"God forbid! But the Earl John of Carrick *is* the heir to the throne. And a man of sensibility and judgment. Not strong, perhaps — but with the support of the Earls Robert and David — to which he is entitled, but has never had — he could rule well, honestly, whilst his father lives. In preparation for when His Grace dies."

"No avail, James," Galloway said. "You know, as do we all, that Carrick has not the stomach for it. As in the earldom of Douglas, the Kingdom of Scotland requires a strong hand, not a hesitant one. Ever has done. Carrick would not serve, and could not. Alex the Wolf *would*, and might — to our cost! I say we must support the Earl Robert in this pass."

"Even though he may have contrived the murder of my husband to gain it?" That stark question dropped into the heated discussion like a douche of icy water.

"Robert? Murder . . .?" Galloway got out, staring. "What is this? What are you saying?"

"I say that though my lord was slain by the hand of this wretch Bickerton, his was not the *mind* behind it. Would some small slight suffered days previously provoke such cold-blooded assassination? Robert has planned this present entire assumption of power and government? He could not have done it with James alive. Therefore he assumed James dead! I believe he subborned Bickerton to do it."

"Christ God! No — I cannot believe that."

"Who, then?"

"I do not know. But — not Robert. He would not stoop to murder. Of his good-brother. His own sister's husband!"

"Has he ever shown me any love? Affection? Shown any his love and affection! His wife? His son Murdoch? Save perhaps to yourself, my lord! You are his friend. But even with you, I think, Robert will drive a hard bargain. His support for you will not be without price, I swear! You will find that out, one day."

Sir William's quick indraw of breath was obvious to all.

The Countess looked at him. "Something occurs to you, sir? Part of the price? Since you are to become another good-brother of Robert's, you would be well advised to walk warily!"

"It is not that, Lady Isabel," the younger man said. "I had just remembered . . . Tantallon!"

"Sakes, yes — that I also had forgotten! In all the rest." Dalkeith exclaimed.

"What of Tantallon, my lord?"

Dalkeith and Galloway exchanged glances, almost guilty glances. "It is part of Robert's price, I suppose. For supporting Archie's claim — although he gains on every hand, anyway. He is requiring Tantallon Castle to be handed over to himself, he told the Council. For his own use, Isabel. To be *his* property."

"But he cannot do that!" Most of them had probably forgotten the presence of the youngest member of the party, who had sat silent, watchful throughout, not raising his voice in the company of his elders and betters. Now protest burst from Jamie. "Tantallon is my lady's home — which she and my lord loved best!"

Tantallon was in an especial position. The barony of North Berwick belonged of old to the Celtic Earls of Fife. It was the southern end of their ferry across Forth to Fife — as Earlsferry was the northern. The first small castle of Tantallon was theirs, built to protect the ferry-passage. When the Earl William's father desired to build a large castle there, for some reason he did not buy the entire barony, but only leased the old ruinous tower and its ground — why, was not known. Perhaps the then Earl of Fife would not sell. So Fife still owned the ground and superiority—and when the Earl Robert gained the Fife earldom in gift, he must have learned this. And now he sought to resume possession. It was, after all, one of the fairest houses in the Kingdom — and the strongest!

"That is unworthy — even of Robert!" the Lady Egidia declared.

"Yes. But . . . lawful!"

The Lady Isabel drew a long quivering breath. "So! I am to be homeless as well as husbandless! And friendless likewise, it would seem! Am I to have nothing, my lords — nothing? The earldom given to whoever can serve Robert best. The entailed lands to Galloway. The unentailed lands to Isobel of Mar and whoever else may claim them. And now Tantallon, my home. What of the Countess of Douglas, my lords? What is left for this wretched woman, chief princess of Scotland?"

Unhappily the men gazed at her tense loveliness.

"No doubt provision, due provision, will be made," Sir William said.

"Something will be done, my dear," Sir James assured.

"To be sure," Sir Archibald agreed, heavily.

"Ah, I thank you! So kind! And think you that you can affect Robert? My lords, you are but babes to my brother!" the Countess rose. "Jamie — escort me hence, I pray you. I require better counsel than I shall gain here, I think." Proudly she swept towards the door — which Jamie leapt to open for her. But before she passed through, she turned and spoke in a rather different tone. "My friends — consider well. If this is how Robert commences his reign as Governor — beware! *I* am paying, first — but you all will pay before the end! I say — God preserve our land, from Robert Stewart!"

Outside, she took the young man's arm. "Jamie — go find my brother David, and bring him to my chamber. He will like none of this, I swear!"

"Yes. To be sure. But . . . the Earl of Strathearn is scarcely a strong man for you to lean upon. I cannot think that he will avail greatly in this pass . . ."

"Then I must be strong enough for both of us — with your support, Jamie. He is still the King's son, as much as Robert is. And tomorrow we ride to see the King! My father is still King of Scots, however feeble. His royal signature and seal is law. We ride for Ayrshire, Dundonald. And I would have David to ride with us."

"Ayrshire? But . . . I must go to Luffness, Lady Isabel. To see to Bickerton . . ."

"Bickerton can wait. He will not escape. Besides, others can attend to him. I need you, Jamie. I need *somebody* I can trust, close by me."

"Very well. But will you not see the Lord Robert himself, before you go? He may prove less harsh . . ."

"Never! I shall never seek anything from that man, save vengeance! For I am a Stewart too, I'd remind you! Go, now . . ."

Earl David of Strathearn proved sympathetic, indignant at his brother and some comfort to his sister in that he offered her a home at his own castle of Auchterarder, would later find a house for her on his broad Perthshire lands somewhere. But he would not come with her to Dundonald — not meantime. He had to return to Strathearn forthwith. His wife was poorly—and of course he had not seen her since he left for the English expedition. Why did Isabel not come with him, to Auchterarder? She would gain little or nothing from the old man at Dundonald anyway, he said. She thanked him but insisted that she must see her father. Perhaps later she would come to Strathearn. Clearly David was not going to oppose his brother actively.

That night in his stableyard accommodation in the town, Jamie Douglas, by discreet questioning of his Nithsdale companions, learned the gist of the story of Sir William's bastard son — and it seemed to be no secret, in fact. The mother had been the pretty daughter of a small Kirkpatrick laird near Closeburn in Dumfriesshire, who about five years before had died giving birth to the child. The young father had been sorely distressed, and had insisted on taking full responsibility for the boy, as a sort of penance, giving him his own name of William Douglas. No doubt all this would be explained to the princess in due course.

Before they set out next morning on their sixty-mile ride to Ayrshire, Jamie sought out Mary Stewart in Gelis's quarters of the Palace, and retailed this information. It was well received, since it put a much kinder light on the bridegroom-to-be, indeed a somewhat romantic one, which did his renown but little harm. Jamie was uncertain whether to be glad or sorry. Mary's reaction towards himself, like that of her mistress, was positive however, and indeed almost heady for a young man.

In something of an emotional turmoil they left Linlithgow for the west, the Countess, Jamie and his tail of three.

VIII

BY THE HIGH moorlands of the Upper Ward of Lanarkshire, upper Clydesdale and Strathaven, they came to the long valley of the River Irvine at Loudoun Hill, where Bruce and Wallace had both won victories not so long before, and eventually, in the eye of the sinking sun to Kilmarnock, where the hills sank to the coastal plain and the western sea spread golden before them in gleaming molten glory. Four miles nearer the sea, the castle of Dundonald soared out of the green levels on its rocky hillock, a massive thick-walled hold, far from palatial, smaller than Dalkeith and not so strong as Tantallon or even Luffness, but the King's favourite home, where the best years of his life had been spent before the problems of being first High Steward and then monarch descended upon a simple, friendly, unambitious man really unsuited to be either.

The King maintained little or nothing of a Court here, no style nor circumstance, well content to be little more than the Laird of Dundonald —although inevitably there was a chamberlain, chaplain, secretaries and a fairly large guard. Even his illegitimate sons all lived in finer style than this.

The old man was unaffectedly glad to see his eldest daughter, even though he was preparing to retire for the night when they arrived with the dusk. He had always been fond of his bed, and nowadays spent an increasing proportion of his time therein, with a notable capacity for sleep. But whenever Isabel began to mention the reasons for her visit, he waggled a hand in the air.

"Not just now, lassie — not just now!" he quavered, all but pleaded. "I knew you would be wanting something, to have come all this way. But I'm right tired, Isa. The morn — we'll see about it the morn. I am for my bed. I'm an auld man, mind . . ."

His daughter sighed. "Yes, Sire — as you will. But you are still King of Scots, and my father. And it is family matters that bring me here. Tomorrow, I must have the attention I am entitled to, as your daughter."

"Aye — the morn, Isa. I'm right vexed for you, mind, losing your man, lassie. An ill business. Aye, right vexed." He leaned forward, peering from those bloodshot eyes at Jamie. "And who's this laddie you've got? Do I know him?"

"This is Jamie Douglas — now Sir James. Natural son to Dalkeith. Knighted by my lord of Dunbar after ... after that terrible battle. He was esquire to my husband. Now is my true knight."

"Ooh, aye. Douglas, you say? There's a wheen Douglases. Over many, maybe. Over many Douglases and over few Stewarts for the Crown's weal! Forby, mind, I've made as many Stewarts as I could, in my day!" That came out in a little spurt of spirit. "Aye, well — I'm away to my bed. I'll see you the morn, Isa."

"Yes, Father. Sleep well."

"A good night, Your Grace."

But in the morning there was no sign of the monarch, nor any summons to his presence. Fretting, the Lady Isabel waited until nearly noon; and when still her father did not put in an appearance, she told Jamie to come with her. She was going to beard the old and weary Lion of Scotland in its den.

"Not me, Isabel!" he protested. "Not into the King's bedchamber. I cannot go there. Forby, this is no matter for me, between you and His Grace."

"No — I want you with me, Jamie. I have my reasons. Your presence will help me. Come."

They made their way up to the monarch's rooms on the second floor of the keep. Two guards stood at the ante-chamber door, but the princess swept past them without a glance. Within, a secretary sat at a table with sundry papers, quill and ink-horn, and another guard stood at an inner door.

"Countess," the secretary said, rising and bowing "His Grace is not to be disturbed."

"Perhaps not by you, sir. But *I* shall see him."

"But ... no, my lady! His Grace is ... occupied. His royal command ..."

"His command to you — not to his daughter. I shall see my father. Stand aside, sirrah!" This to the guard, peremptorily. "Come, Jamie."

A blast of hot air met them as they passed through the inner doorway, for although it was a muggy August day a large fire of logs blazed in the wide arched fireplace. The King was sitting up in a huge fourposter bed, with a stained and threadbare cloak around him and a woollen nightcap on his white head. Nearby, an elderly monk sat and read aloud in Latin from a large illustrated volume.

"Och, Isa! Isa!" the monarch wailed. "You shouldna . . . you shouldna . . ."

"Sire — I did not ride across the breadth of Scotland to kick my heels in your waiting-chamber! I have important matters to deal with, and will not be put off further."

"Aye — but I'm busy the now, Isa. Hearing Holy Writ, no less!"

"Holy Writ has kept these thirteen hundred years, Father. It will keep an hour longer! Moreover, if I recollect aright, it declares somewhere a father's duty to his children! Sir Priest — leave us."

The chaplain hesitated, recognised realities, and bowed himself out.

"Och, lassie — and you were aye the gentle one! Biddable . . ."

"I am no longer your gentle, meek daughter, Father. I am a woman hardened, Countess of Douglas and first princess of this realm. And I needs must fight for my rights — since it seems none other will do so for me, save Sir James, here."

"Robert will see to it, Isa. Ask Robert. He's the one for seeing to things. He's to be the Guardian or Regent or some such. He'll see to all "

"Robert is the last one to go to, Sire — since it is Robert who assails me. Why, oh why, did you give him this power? Delivering your realm into his evil hands!"

"Hech, hech, lassie — say not so! You must not speak so ill of your brother, I say. It's not right. Robert has wits . . ."

"Wits, yes — of a sort. Wits to look after Robert Stewart and care not who else suffers. I believe he it was who had James murdered. So that he could be quit of the Douglas power — or some of it. Which might curb his own. He offers the earldom to Archibald of Galloway, to gain his support. He will break up all Douglas lands, allotting them to whom he will. Save to me, Countess of Douglas! He takes the office of Chief Warden of the Marches, for himself. It has always been a Douglas office. And he takes from me even Tantallon, my house, for his own. All this within days of James's death."

The King's mouth had fallen open at this recital. He shook his old head helplessly. "No, no, Isa — you have it wrong, I swear. Robert wouldna do the like of that."

"He has done it — and in *your* name, Sire! All is now done in your name, by Robert. As though you were dead, and John likewise. So I have come to you, the King. You are that still. And he can do little or nothing *against* your expressed will and royal command. You must assert your kingship — or not only I but all Scotland go down in ruin."

"But, lassie — that is *why* I let Robert take the rule. I'm auld and done — and I canna see right. I canna read papers and the like. Forby, my belly pains me. Who else can I turn to, girl? Johnnie will take no hand in things. Och, he can read the papers fine — but that's all he'll do. You know Johnnie. He should have been a monk! And Alex! Alex I can do nothing with — nor ever could. There's a devil in Alex, I reckon. Davie's well enough — but he lacks all purpose, the lad. Like Johnnie. He's aye wheenging about this or that, but he never *does* much. And young Wattie! He's but a headstrong laddie, aye drinking over much. When he's older, maybe, he'll serve. But no' now. And I canna set John of Bute, above his lawful brothers — though he's got a good head to him. Others likewise . . ."

"If you will not rule yourself, Father, you could appoint a *Council* of Regency. Jamie's father, Dalkeith, suggested it. Like the Joint Guardians who followed Wallace — the Bruce, Comyn and Bishop Lamberton. Three. Two others to keep Robert in check. Perhaps Traill, Bishop of St. Andrews, my lord of Dunbar, or Dalkeith himself . . ."

"Robert would not have it, Isa. He would not."

"If you commanded it, signed and sealed it, he would *have* to."

"He would not. He'd make me unsign it, lassie. Robert's right masterful." The old voice quavered away.

Helplessly she looked at him. "Oh, Father! Will you do *nothing*! You, crowned and anointed lord of this realm!"

"I canna, Isa. I'm . . . I'm not myself. I'm sick and tired and needing my sleep. You should not come troubling me."

She took a long breath, and spoke in a different voice, almost sternly. "Well, Sire — if you will do nothing for the realm God gave you, I must see that you do something for *me*, your daughter. I must be provided for. I must have my share of the Douglas lands. I demand my jointure annuity be paid to me — three hundred merks each year from the Customs of Haddington. Also the barony of Ednam, at Kelso, settled on James and myself on our marriage — if James could retake it from the English! Which he did. These at least I must have."

"Ooh, aye, lassie — if these are yours, you shall have them. Robert will not keep them from you . . ."

"He must not be allowed to! You have a secretary in the next chamber, Father. He shall make a writing of it. Jamie — fetch him. With paper and ink."

"But, Isa — there's no need . . ."

"Go, Jamie. And bring the priest too, as witness."

So the clerk and monk were brought in; and the Countess Isabel, in firm clear tones, dictated something like a charter to the effect that the King's Grace hereby confirmed to his beloved daughter Isabel Countess of Douglas the annuity granted to her and her late spouse of three hundred merks or £200 Scots paid from the customs of the burgh and port of Haddington; plus fullest possession and all rights in the barony, manor, mill and multures of Ednam in the shire of Roxburgh. And that thereafter the said Countess Isabel's due share or terce in the unentailed lands of the earldom of Douglas were to be allotted to her freely, all sheriffs of counties wherein lay the said lands to make disposition thereof on pain of royal displeasure.

The spluttering quill laboriously set all this down in good Latin, Isabel took it and the paper and put them on the bed before her father.

"Sign," she said, and as he held back, she took his trembling, mottled old hand and guided it into some sort of signature.

"Robert'll not like this," the grandson of Robert Bruce, the hero king, complained. "He said *he* was to do all the signing now."

"He is not Governor of Scotland yet! Not until your parliament confirms it, Sire. Sir Monk — pray witness His Grace's signature here. And you, Jamie, below. Sand it, Master Secretary . . ."

The King crouched further down in the great bed, turning his face away from them all. "Leave me, now. I'm tired," he said thickly. "You're not like my Isa, any more. I . . . I wish I was dead, just!"

For moments she gazed down at the wreck of a man and a monarch, and her eyes filled with tears. She was, in fact, still the gentle, biddable Isabel Stewart, and every word spoken and move made that noontide had been screwed out of her with the most painful resolve and distress. When her father still did not raise his bleary glance to her, abruptly she turned and almost ran from the overheated bedroom, clutching her paper. Bowing unhappily towards the bed, Jamie sighed, and followed.

Going down the twisting turnpike stair within the thickness of the walling, he caught up with her, and perceiving her bent and shaking shoulders he took her arm.

"Do not grieve so, Isabel," he faltered. "He is not himself, as he said. He forgets — and will forget. He will not hold it against you. And it had to be done."

She twisted round, sobbing, and buried her face against his chest, gripping him tightly. "Oh, Jamie, Jamie — what am I to do?" she mumbled. "All, my whole life, is fallen in ruin about me. I have nothing left, nothing! Not just lands or castles but, but . . . I am alone, now. I had so much, so much. With James. And now — nothing. Not even a father, or brothers. All gone. And I must needs harry that old broken man — for this! A wretched paper scratched by a clerk!"

He held her, while the paroxysm of grief and shame ebbed, and gradually she quietened. He even stroked her fine golden head. At last she straightened up, blinking away her tears. "Dear Jamie — you are good, kind. How would I do without you? Forgive me, a weak, silly woman. I promise that I shall not weep on you again! See, take this paper and keep it safe for me — a paper I hate myself for, God knows!"

"Will it serve?" he asked. "Can it gain you what it says? If the Earl Robert wills otherwise?"

"We must make it serve. Robert is not yet Governor in *law*. And the King's signature *is* law. We must work fast to gain what it says. Before the parliament. A parliament requires forty days to call. We have that time, only."

"The parliament will do as the Earl Robert says?"

"I fear so. Almost certainly. Since it is the King's appointment. And he will not change it — you can see that. With no Earl of

Douglas to rally those against. And Archie of Galloway supporting. I fear there is no hope. In forty days Robert will be master of Scotland, in law as in fact."

"So what do we do? Now?"

"We go see the Prince and High Steward of Scotland! John, Earl of Carrick and heir to the throne, no less!" She grimaced. "He is little stronger than his father, an old man before his time. But at least he will not hide in his bed, I hope! And he has power — if he will use it. Robert will not want the heir to the throne publicly against him. We go to Turnberry."

"Do not look for too much," the young man said.

* * *

Turnberry, chief seat of the Earldom of Carrick, and the Bruce's birthplace — his mother had been the Celtic Countess of Carrick in her own right — stood on the coast some ten miles south-west of Ayr. Skirting that town and the smaller burgh of Maybole, capital of Carrick, the little cavalcade was trotting south-westwards through the low green hills and whin-clad braes near to the Abbey of Crossraguel, when a peremptory trumpet-blast turned them all in their saddles. A colourful and glittering body of horsemen had crested a long grassy ridge behind them, presumably come from Maybole. Shouts followed, most obviously directed at themselves.

"Unmannerly ruffians!" the Princess said. "Ride on."

The thunder of hooves behind them, and more trumpeting, made Jamie uneasy. "Perhaps we should wait?" he suggested. "They are many more than we."

"No! In Scotland, the King of Scots' daughter does not wait for anyone. Especially in Carrick! Draw your sword, Jamie."

"Is that wise, my lady? Four against forty?"

"Not to *fight* them. To show that we will not brook brigandage against honest travellers on the King's roads."

Reluctantly Jamie and his trio unsheathed their weapons.

The sight drew a prolonged yell from their pursuers. Coming on at the gallop, they were not far behind now.

"Dod — fetch them to me!" High and vital above the rest, an authoritative voice prevailed, bell-like, assured, its sharp clarity like a woman's. "Bring them here."

A big hulking man, roughly dressed but superbly mounted, detached himself, with seven or eight others, from the main party which had drawn up about seventy yards back, and spurred forwards.

"Steel, heh?" this individual bellowed. "You seek a bout, cocksparrow?" And he whipped out his own blade in a lightning flourish. "Jump, laddie — jump!" he hooted laughter as Jamie jerked back in his saddle to avoid the flickering point an inch from his nose. "Mistress — hide your pretty boy in your arms, lest I collop and skewer him for my supper! And these cattle with him."

"How dare you, sirrah . . . !"

The large man, contemptuously ignoring Jamie now, swung on Lady Isabel and grabbed her bridle. "I dare mair'n that, my bonnie birdie!" he cried, and leaning over, threw a great arm around the Countess and lifted her right out of her saddle to set her before his own. He started to slobber kisses on her shrinking, jerking person.

Jamie slashed sideways with his sword at one of the others who had grasped his own bridle, and the arm went limp as the fellow yelled. In the self-same movement the weapon lunged directly at the back of the man. Dod's thick, red neck. Somehow he prevented the point from actually driving in deep, so that it only nicked a scarlet cut in the bristly roll of flesh, partly aided by the man's turn of head at his colleague's shout. Blood flowed, but only slightly, staunched as yet by steel itself.

"Unhand the Countess, animal!" Jamie cried. "Or this point drives home! And you others — one move, and you will need to bury this oaf!"

Whether it was the blood, the commanding tone so unexpected, the mention of the word Countess or the self-evident fact that they had an expert swordsman to deal with here, there was an immediate and flattering reaction on the part of the attackers, a sort of momentary freezing of motion and sound over the entire scene. Jamie raised his glance — although his sword-tip remained steady, indenting the fleshy back-neck.

"Does he die?" he called towards the group waiting at a distance. "Or do you, whoever you may be, come make amends to the Lady Isabel?"

139

There was a distinct pause, in strange contrast to all the previous vehemence and activity. Then a single rider trotted on from the colourful throng.

At first they thought that it was indeed a woman, despite the clothing, so light a figure bestrode the magnificent black. But then they perceived that this was a boy, not even a youth, slender, straight, assured, sitting the huge horse as though born to it and dressed richly in the height of fashion. To call this child — for he could not have been more than eleven or twelve years — good-looking was an understatement; he was, in fact, beautiful, of feature as of person, with great lustrous eyes, heavily-lashed, long fair hair wavy to his shoulders, with a slender gold band holding it in place around a brow that would one day be noble. A sword hung at his side and a dirk at his hip — but neither were drawn. Instead he carried in his hand a quite substantial riding-whip of stock and thong.

"You are bold, Sir Swordsman!" this apparition called, in that high and flutelike voice as he approached. "I like bold men — so long as they are not *too* bold for their own good! Did you say *Lady* Isabel, sir . . .?"

"He did, nephew!" the Countess declared, pushing back the silken scarf which she wore over her head when riding and which, though somewhat disarranged by the man Dod's attentions, still had partly obscured her features.

"Christ God — Aunt Isabel!" the boy exclaimed. "By the Mass — here's a turn! And a joy, to be sure — aye, a joy indeed! My dear Aunt!" And his trill of melodious laughter rose sufficiently joyous for any.

"Joy, child! Do you call being assaulted and mauled by this . . . this brute-beast of yours a joy? Or being chased like gipsies by your unruly horde!" She wrenched herself out of the big man's now lax grasp as she spoke, and slid to the ground, flushed, angry — her proud beauty remarkably like that of the boy.

She was, as it were, just in time. With a hissing crack the whiplash streaked out to fall right across the face of the unfortunate Dod in abrupt savage punishment. Snaking back, it slashed again and again and again, on face, head, shoulders, wrists.

"Hog! Stirk! Fool! Fool, I say!" the beautiful boy spat out, as he belaboured his servitor in a quite extraordinary exhibition of vicious and sustained vehemence, improbable even in a grown man. "Cur! Creature! How dare you ... so treat ... a Stewart!" he snarled.

The hulking giant sat crouching but still under the rain of blows, not even raising an arm to protect his face — although his horse reared and sidled.

"Enough, David — enough!" the Countess cried, quite quickly. "Have done boy — of a mercy! This is too much. Unsuitable. Especially when *you* so ordered it!"

"Ah — you think so, my dear Aunt? Very well — if you say so." Following up a final slash with an elaborate bow from the saddle, the lad beamed an angelic smile on her. "So, my lady Countess — I hope that I see you well? Despite my lord's sad death. All grieve for you, I am sure." He was panting only a little from his punitive exertions.

"Thank you," she answered, very coolly. "Jamie — this is the Lord David, son and heir to my brother the Earl of Carrick. David — Sir James Douglas of Aberdour. To whom you owe most profound apology."

"Sir — I grovel at your feet!" the lad cried, with the sweetest smile imaginable, and something of a flourish. "If my oafs offended you they shall pay for it, believe me! I know not where Aberdour is, but welcome you to Carrick. We Stewarts must ever make Douglases welcome, must we not?"

Distinctly warily, Jamie eyed this remarkable and precocious sprig of the royal tree — who presumably one day would be his monarch, a notion apt to give pause. "I thank you, my lord," he said carefully. "I trust that I have not damaged your servant. But Douglas tends to look after its own! Even in Ayrshire!"

"To be sure." The youngster laughed happily. "Care nothing. Dod will mend his ways — and watch heedfully for Douglases in the future, I swear! As do I. But ... there are many bands of rogues roaming the land, see you, robbing, burning, slaying. Irish scum in the main, broken men from the Irish wars — but insufficiently broken yet, by God's eyes!"

"And did *we* look like broken Irish scum, David?" the Lady Isabel demanded. "Even at a distance?"

Laughter tinkled. "Save us, Aunt — but you might have been! They steal good horseflesh. They much trouble the good folk of Maybole. I have three here that I am going to hang." And he turned and pointed back to the main mass of his band, where certain bound and battered individuals sat slumped in the midst.

"Hang . . .?" the Countess echoed.

"Why, yes. I could have done it at Maybole, but conceive that they will hang more prettily at Turnberry! I like to keep our gallows-tree there well stocked, you see! It serves a useful purpose."

"Indeed! And your father . . .?"

"Oh, Father concerns himself otherwise. He studies chronicles and verse and the like. Myself, I write some poetry, mind — but I seek not to neglect my other duties!" Again the joyous laughter. "But come, Aunt — and Sir James. It *was* James? I will escort you to my father and mother. They will be much pleasured to see you. As am I. We can hang these creatures afterwards . . ."

Isabel and Jamie exchanged glances, as he assisted her back into her own saddle.

They came in resounding style to Turnberry, therefore, on its green terraces above the bay-scalloped shore. It was a great sprawling establishment, more of a fortified township than a castle, a community of miscellaneous buildings within a lofty and extensive perimeter wall, in the old Celtic patriarchal mode rather than any Norman-type feudal fortress, although there were sundry later castellated works, towers and barracks, erected by the English invaders during the Wars of Independence. The place now had an afternoon rural quiet about it, as of a village dozing in the early autumn sun, with leisurely harvesting going on in the surrounding rigs and fields. But the young Lord David soon changed all that. Obviously he was very much the master here, sending everybody about their business in no uncertain fashion. He brought the visitors to the long central hall-house with its attached chapel, which formed the centre-piece of the entire establishment; but could find neither parent here, even in the chapel where apparently his father spent much of his time. Racing off, in a sudden reversion to more typical boyish energetics, he presently hallooed them to follow him into a most pleasant orchard and rose-garden, contrived within the walling, where the ground fell in gentler shelves towards the beach in a south-facing enclave. Here, in an arbour facing out over the blue plain of the sea, he brought them to Annabella Drummond, Countess of Carrick, sitting at her needlework.

"Mama, Mama — see whom I have found for your delight!" this surprising juvenile called. "Aunt Isabel of Douglas, no less. Come all the way from Lothian. And Sir James Douglas of Aber-somewhere. Is this not a joy?"

The tall, calmly Junoesque woman, of a serene and quiet loveliness, rose to greet them, clearly pregnant, the future Queen of Scotland. She smiled slowly but warmly, and came forward with a sort of gentle deliberation — which was indeed how she did all things.

"My very dear Isabel," she murmured. "The dearer for your great loss. My heart aches for you." She opened her arms wide for her sister-in-law.

Watching them embrace, interestedly, the Lord David turned to Jamie. "Are women to be envied or pitied, think you, Sir James?" he asked speculatively.

"Eh . . .? Sakes — I do not know! That is scarce something for *us* to decide."

"You think not? I would not wish to be a woman, of course. But there are some things they do better than we do. How old are you, sir?"

"I shall be nineteen at Yule, my lord."

"Not very old," the young-old prince remarked. "I thought not." There might have been a certain criticism implicit in that. But the issue was not pursued, for the Countess Annabella spoke over Isabel's shoulder.

"Sir James — forgive us. I bid you welcome to Turnberry. We shall talk later. Davie — look to Sir James's comfort and refreshment."

"Yes, Mama. Where is Father?"

"With Abbot Colin, I should think. At Crossraguel. When you have attended to Sir James, have my lord informed, Davie."

"Yes. Come," the boy said. But as they were passing out of the orchard he addressed Jamie confidentially. "Are you much in need of rest and refreshment, Sir James? Or would a tankard of ale or wine serve you meantime? You see, I think that I will hang those three Irish *before* I go get my father. You will wish to watch the sport, no doubt?"

Jamie swallowed. "Thank you — no! But . . . *can* you do this? Yourself? You — hang men! Without trial . . .?"

"To be sure. No need for any trial. They were caught in the act,

143

inflagrante delicto indeed! Rape and robbery. At Myremill. They hang. And better before my father comes. Kinder. He has over-soft a heart — and would suffer as much as they, I swear! I seldom tell him of such matters. Do not say that *you* are of a like kidney? And you a swordsman, clearly? Unlike Douglas, I think!"

"I prefer my sport ... otherwise! And despite what you say, I would counsel you to refer the issue to the Earl of Carrick before you do anything more, my lord."

"Nonsense!" The youngster laughed. "We do not trouble father with the likes of this. But, come — you shall have your refreshment, Sir James. Each to his taste!"

Later, drinking wine and munching bannocks alone in the vast cavern of the great hall under the smoky hammer-beam rafters and thatch, Jamie listened to prolonged cheering from somewhere not far off. He did not doubt but that it signified the successful exercise of justice on the part of the second heir to the throne.

When Limping John of Carrick eventually arrived from nearby Crossraguel Abbey, that he was pleased to see his sister was not in doubt. But his gladness was nevertheless overlaid, clouded, by the sort of wariness and mild alarm, mixed with apology, which had become the man's general reaction to life, as though he knew well, from sad experience, that even the simplest and most modest of pleasures fell to be paid for by demands which were either painful, distasteful or quite beyond him. It was, admittedly, easier when his beloved wife was present — for then he could push all on to her calm and capable shoulders. And the lad Davie undoubtedly saved him from much troublesome decision.

No specific discussion of the Lady Isabel's problems took place until after the evening meal in the hall, with sixty or seventy present, and Jamie sitting at the end of the dais-table with the Lord David and the three Carrick daughters, Margaret, Mary and Elizabeth, aged ten, nine and seven respectively. Thereafter, with the children dispersed again, and the Earl John muttering about time to be going to the chapel for prayers, the Lady Annabella steered the adults firmly into her own small music-room which opened on to the orchard, and where they could watch the sun sinking over the jagged mountains of Arran to the north-west. Jamie would have excused himself, but Isabel held him close, clearly desiring such small support as his presence might offer.

Once started, she poured out her troubles in a flood. Her brother listened with sympathy but still more manifest and growing discomfort, sighing a lot, shaking his head, and fidgeting. His wife was less demonstrative, quietly intent; but at the end, when she had given her lord ample opportunity to groan, spread his hands helplessly and bite his finger-nails, the Countess Annabella it was who expressed a practical reaction.

"It is clear then, John, that your brother Robert must be countered in some measure, for Isabel's sake, but also for the realm's likewise. Robert is an able man, but he need not be permitted to rule all at his own devices. We must contrive otherwise."

"Counter Robert!" her husband exclaimed. "How can we, Anna — how can we? I canna do anything with Robert — nor ever could. You know that. He never heeds me, goes his ain gait."

"Yes, my dear. But there are ways in which he can be curbed. Until he be Governor."

"Not by me."

"By the King, your royal father's writ, John. If I understand it aright, and from what Isabel says, until the Governorship is confirmed by parliament, it is not valid in law. And the King can order undone anything done in the interim. Is that not so?"

"Aye, but . . ."

"Moreover, only the King or his Governor can summon a parliament. Robert cannot yet do this, without your father's signature. Such signature then, my heart, is *your* strength and weapon. On Isabel's and the realm's behalf. We know that your father is as wax in Robert's hands. But you must keep him from signing the necessary summons for a parliament. Prevent it until your sister's affairs are decently settled."

"How can I do that, Anna? Even if he heeded me in the matter, the moment Robert came stamping down to Dundonald with his papers, my father would sign. You know he would."

"In Dundonald he might, yes. In Turnberry, he might heed his eldest son the more."

"Eh? Turnberry? You mean . . .?"

"Bring him here, John. He is a sick old man, and not like to live long, I think. You are his eldest son. Bring him into your house, whether he would come or not. We shall look after him. I shall nurse him well. And guard him from Robert's servants, as all others. Robert will come in person, in time, yes — but we can keep him from seeing his father alone. It will all delay the day. A parliament requires forty days calling, does it not? Six weeks. If we can delay even one month, in the summons, it will put it off until mid-November. A little longer and we shall be into Yule — no time for a parliament. Mid-winter, with the fords and passes closed and the roads impassable, will not serve, since but few could travel the country to attend. Parliaments are never held in mid-winter. So it would be spring . . ."

"Annabella! How clever you are!" Isabel cried. "I swear I had not thought of that! The longer we can delay, the better. Meanwhile Jamie's father Dalkeith, with Bishop Trail, Dunbar, Moray and the rest, can seek rally the forces of good, of moderation."

"My brother Malcolm would help."

Her sister-in-law blinked, and found no comment. After all, Sir Malcolm Drummond was one of the possible suspects in the murder of the Earl James. This could hardly be hinted at here.

The Earl John provided a suitable if involuntary distraction by getting up and limping about the little room, dragging that right leg — the leg which indeed might be held as partly responsible for much of Scotland's present woes. For until the age of eighteen, John Stewart had been a stalwart enough young man, not exactly excelling at tournaments and field sports, but a fair enough performer. He had even led one or two minor military expeditions with some success. Then, at a hunt, a Douglas horse — and Jamie's own uncle's horse — had lashed out a hoof and shattered the youth's knee-cap, turning the High Steward's heir at one blow into a cripple for life. And worse than the physical was the mental effect. Suddenly John Stewart became inadequate, and grew ever more so. For a leading Scots noble, especially an eventual heir to the throne, to be incapacitated from sitting a horse properly and all that that implied, from sword-fighting, hunting, archery, and manly sports, as well as from going to war — especially with the brothers this one had — was utter invalidation. Only a man of the strongest character and will-power could have overcome such handicap.

"You make it sound simple, Anna," he objected now. "But my father will not *want* to come here. And if come he does, we canna keep Robert from seeing him. Robert is masterful. He will order all from the chamber, see you . . ."

"Robert cannot order you, the High Steward of Scotland, to do anything, John. Especially in your own house. You must stand up to him, in this — to your *younger* brother. Isabel will stay with us here. And she, I doubt not, will not bow to Robert's commands! She will support you . . ."

"To be sure I will. We could have Gelis here also. Until she marries. She little loves Robert. Even brother David might come. Never fear, John — you will not be left to outface Robert alone. And meantime, with your support, I shall take all lawful steps to save what I can of the Douglas heritage. With the King's signed paper I have, and the High Steward's backing, surely even Robert will be able to do little — until he is confirmed Governor."

"You are over-sanguine, lassies, over-sanguine . . ."

So it was decided, however doubtful and unhappy the Earl John. Isabel would spend the winter months at Turnberry — she was as well there as anywhere, in the circumstances; and this area was really home to her, for she had been brought up mainly at Dundonald. Moreover, Gelis would be summoned home to her father's side also; and since Nithsdale was just over in the next county of Dumfries-shire, she should find no fault with that. With Tantallon having to be vacated, the Countess Margaret of Angus and her son would have to move out, and should be invited to come to Turnberry also. The Angus Stewarts were only distantly connected with the royal house; but she was a strong-minded woman and would make a stout ally against Robert. With the King clearly weakening, and at seventy-three not likely to live long, the heir to the throne must inevitably become the focus of much manoeuvring and positioning — however little he liked the prospect. The Stewart women would, as it were, hold these two feeble but essential cards in their slender hands, hold them close. Robert of Fife and Menteith was not master yet.

Jamie Douglas would go east again, shortly, with a varied mission — but mainly to bring back the Lady Gelis Stewart to her father's side. He was distinctly uncertain as to his feelings in this matter; not that that would be allowed to weigh in any balance soever.

IX

WITH THE LEAVES already beginning to curl, crinkle and mottle with autumn — here, with the salt winds off the North Sea, they did not achieve quite the brilliant scarlets and gold of the inland trees — Luffness Castle glowed a mellow rose-red in the declining September sun, so very different a pile at the edge of so different a bay. Jamie was surprised and concerned to find no guard keeping watch on it, no sign of Richard Lundie or young Ramsay, nor even the Tantallon Douglases. The place looked quietly normal, with the harvest being led in from its fields to the adjoining farmery buildings and stackyards. Reluctant to present himself at the door again to face old Bickerton, he rode round to the Carmelite Priory in the demesne, established by the Crusading Sir David Lindsay, one-time Regent of Scotland a century earlier who, dying of a fever on his way to the Holy Land, had arranged for his body to be brought back home by dispossessed monks from the monastery on Mount Carmel, these being given land at Luffness to set up a new establishment.

He found the brown-and-white habited brothers at vespers in their chapel above the long snaking quarry which ran down to the shore, and from which the stone for castle and priory had been hewn, a pleasant quiet place now under tall old trees, with a yew-enclosed little graveyard adjoining and fish-ponds nearby. Here Jamie waited patiently, listening to the sweet singing coming from within the chapel. He wondered, amongst other things, how the lord of this fine barony was faring as a captive in England — whether perhaps he had already been ransomed. It would undoubtedly be best for the entire Bickerton business to be cleared up before he returned.

The singing ended. When the monks came out, he approached Prior Anselm, an elderly, gentle man, bastard uncle of Sir James Lindsay himself. To him he put his questions.

The old man eyed him sombrely. "So you do not know, young man?" he commented, shaking his grey head. "There has been shame committed here, at Luffness. Murder. Four days ago. My lord of Crawford would be sore affronted. Young John Bickerton may have done ill, in England — I know not. But he should not have been murdered."

"Murdered! Bickerton? What do you mean?"

"I mean, sir, that that unfortunate young man lies there." He pointed to a spot just outside the square of dark yew trees which marked the graveyard, where six feet of newly-turned earth scored the green sward. "He was hiding in the castle, as you know. Four days back he ventured out, rashly — by the postern to the boat-haven. He was seized by your waiting men. And then that young man Ramsay, from Waughton, came up and dirked him, there before them all. A most vile slaying — a man held and defenceless. Without opportunity for confession or absolution. Whatever his fault, this was shame and evil, against the laws of God and man. We buried him there, outwith our holy acre, his old father sorrowing. We dared not place him in consecrated ground . . ."

"Ramsay did that? Why? Why?"

"I know not. Vengeance. Misplaced vengeance . . ."

"But it was not for Ramsay to take vengeance. He was not one of the Earl of Douglas's men. He is a follower of Lindsay's. Bickerton was to be taken, and questioned as to why he slew the Earl. I must see Ramsay forthwith."

"I fear that you will not, Sir James. He is gone from Waughton, none knows where the very next day, in guilt, no doubt. An evil business, my son . . ."

Jamie went and looked down at the grave of John Bickerton, tight-featured, before he rode on from Luffness.

At Tantallon he found the Earl Robert's men already taking possession, the Countess Margaret in a white-faced fury, with what amounted almost to a state of war existing between the Fife men and the Douglas retainers. The Countess, of course, had no legal right to remain there; but it had been her home for long. Earl James's father, Earl William, had installed her there as his mistress — although she owned large lands elsewhere as Countess of Angus in her own right and widow of the Earl of Mar. Earl William's lawful wife, James's mother, had queened it at Douglas, Drumlanrig, Cavers, Liddesdale, Ettrick, Abercorn and the other Douglas castles, but left Tantallon to her rival — although, indeed, that was no correct description of their relationship, for they remained good enough friends, being in fact sisters-in-law, the Countess of Douglas being the sister of the deceased Earl of Mar and bringing that earldom to her husband the Earl William when her brother died. It was a peculiar and involved situation, but the arrangement seemed to suit all parties. When his father died, Earl James allowed the Countess Margaret to stay on at Tantallon with her child, his half-brother; but he often stayed there himself also, with Isabel, who loved the place. There had been room enough for all, anyway, and the two Countesses got on very well. Now, all was to be changed.

Jamie had no difficulty in persuading the Lady Margaret and her son to go to Turnberry, especially as part of a scheme to counter the machinations of Robert Stewart. A fiery creature when roused, she would have travelled to the ends of the earth to do just that, she declared. She had been refusing to budge, for the Fife men; but clearly that could not go on indefinitely. She had many Angus houses she could have retired to; but Turnberry represented positive action. She gave orders for immediate packing.

Jamie questioned the Douglas men-at-arms who had been at Luffness, and who had returned here when their vigil there had so abruptly ended. But he learned no more than Prior Anselm had told him. Two of them had been at the postern when Bickerton had been apprehended, presumably on his way to escape by boat from the little haven. They had taken him in triumph to where the rest of the party were gathered — and there and then, without warning or consulting other, Ramsay had snatched out his dirk and knifed the man they held. Afterwards he had cried vengeance and declared that this was a murderer's due deserts. Master Richard Lundie had been there, and was much upset. He had had them take the body to the Priory. Then they had all dispersed, Ramsay the first to go.

The next day, while the Countess was still packing up her goods and chattels, Jamie rode into North Berwick to see Lundie. He found the young chaplain, son of a small laird on the outskirts of the town, still much distressed at having been the witness of a cold-blooded slaying, so very different from blood-letting in the heat of battle — indeed inclined to blame himself for not having been able to prevent the attack. But it had been so swift, so totally unexpected, all over in a moment.

"There was no provocation then? No words passing between them? To account for Ramsay drawing on Bickerton?"

"None. The others had just brought Bickerton up, ungently but no more. I was asking them how and where they had taken him, when Ramsay pushed me aside, no word spoken. I only saw that he had a dirk in his hand when it flashed down on Bickerton's unprotected breast. He . . . he went on dirking him, Jamie, till we dragged him off. But by that time Bickerton was as good as dead. His . . . his throat cut. Blood . . ."

"He cut his throat?"

"Yes. After he was down. After many stabs. Neither had spoken a word. Afterwards he said it was just punishment. It was a terrible scene, Jamie. A taste of hell, no less!"

"Aye. But — you said something there, Richard. That neither spoke a word. Could that be what was behind it all? That nothing *should* be said! That Ramsay, for his own reasons, wanted Bickerton's tongue silenced at all cost? That he had intended all along to silence him thus?"

"But why? Ramsay surely had nothing to do with Earl James's death. He fought bravely enough at Otterburn. In *Lindsay's* array."

"I believe that somebody paid Bickerton to slay our master. Might not the same pay Ramsay afterwards to ensure that Bickerton revealed nothing? No names. And now Ramsay has gone none knows where!"

"The blessed saints! Who? Who, Jamie?"

"That I mean to discover, if I may — God helping me! It must be one who will much profit by the Earl's death. Someone very powerful."

"Or someone who hated him."

"Perhaps. But — think you not that all this has the marks of cunning and greed and calculation, rather than hatred and anger? I think of three. First, the Earl Robert Stewart, who I conceive to be capable of any infamy. Secondly, Sir Malcolm Drummond, married to our lord's sister and only near lawful kin. And thirdly, Sir Archie the Grim himself — who is like to be third Earl of Douglas."

"Oh, no! Not he — not a Douglas!"

"I hope not. But he had more to gain than any other — save the Earl Robert. And he is the Earl Robert's friend."

"That I cannot believe, Jamie. He is a hard man, but noble enough. A great warrior, not a back-hand killer. A true Douglas. Might it not be, rather, the Lord Alexander — the Wolf? He is an evil man — and often quarrelled with our Lord James."

"He has been in the north all this time. He could scarce have arranged it all. Especially this last. Besides, this I think has little of that man about it. He would slay and murder and cheat, yes — but he would do it *himself*, not use others at long range. No — I think his brother Robert is the more like. If we could but trace a link between him and Ramsay . . ."

Next day, Jamie, now with all the Tantallon Douglas men-at-arms as tail, escorted the Countess of Angus and the young Earl George to Dalkeith, on their way to Turnberry. There were some forty of these stalwarts, well armed and mounted, and in default of other master they were glad enough to attach themselves to the young knight who had been their lord's chief esquire. Presumably they were really the Lady Isabel's men now — if she had the wherewithal to pay them. But meantime Jamie was well content to use them in her name — and found his status the more greatly enhanced.

At Dalkeith, he explained to his father the situation at Turnberry and the opposition developing against the Earl Robert's designs. Also, of course, the death of Bickerton, which might or might not be related. Dalkeith was interested, but doubtful. He did not see any coalition of women, however spirited, defeating Robert Stewart; and the King's and Carrick's contributions he dismissed as valueless, save insofar as the royal authority could be utilised. On the subject of Bickerton, he agreed that it had almost certainly been a silencing killing — but drew the self-evident lesson that any further enquiry would therefore be highly dangerous and best left alone.

His son kept his own counsel.

That evening, he and his father and brothers with Uncle Will of Mordington, discussed the national situation long and earnestly. The older man saw matters from a slightly different angle, more concerned with the maintenance of the power of the house of Douglas than with the mere policy of countering the Earl Robert. After much thought, he told them, he had come to the conclusion that Archie the Grim was the key to the entire situation. He was satisfied that he was honest, strong and able, if irascible, and the best man to be Earl of Douglas. Moreover, he could have more effect on Robert Stewart than could anyone else. The country had to be governed, and with a strong hand, not allowed to drift as it had been doing for too long. Robert Stewart could undoubtedly provide that strong hand, for he also was an able man, if less than honest. If he could be steered, influenced, pushed towards the good, his evil tendencies restrained, the realm might well do none so badly under his Governorship. After all, but for the accident of primogeniture, *he* might well have been the heir to the throne instead of John. He might have made a passable King. Archie of Galloway was a possible bridle to curb and guide the Earl Robert, in the realm's interests as well as those of Douglas. Therefore he, Dalkeith, was prepared to offer Archie his support, and try to sway other Douglases to do the same. And in return he would seek Archie's aid and cooperation in a policy of containing Robert Stewart. This by no means need run contrary to the Turnberry developments. Indeed, if they had Archie's cooperation, anything done there would be much more likely to be effective.

It was Jamie's turn to be doubtful. But he was so very new to politics and statecraft, so recent a recruit to the ranks of knighthood, and so comparatively humble a member of this family, that he must needs defer. His father, however, sufficiently accepted the validity of his doubts and questions to suggest that he should accompany him on a visit he had planned to pay to Threave Castle in Galloway, to see Archie. They would go the very next day, and would travel so far on the way with the Countess Margaret, then leave her in the Cumnock area, to continue on to Turnberry, whilst they turned southwards for Galloway. Jamie could return to Turnberry and the Countess Isabel's service thereafter.

This was accepted as a sound programme, the urgency doubted by none. It appeared that the Earl Robert was intending to have a parliament at Edinburgh in the first week of November, and planning, as a popular spectacle to enhance the start of his regime, to have the marriage of his sister Gelis and Sir William of Nithsdale at the same time. Any contrary moves would have to be made quickly.

It was a major cavalcade that left Dalkeith next morning, for its lord usually travelled in style as a matter of policy. With the Tantallon Douglases they made a company of over two hundred.

Even such as the young Lord David of Carrick would think twice about assailing these travellers. They rode in cheerful, colourful fashion, with even mounted musicians to while away the tedium of travel, Douglas of Dalkeith being one of the very few Scots lords rich enough or sufficiently old-fashioned to indulge in such conceits — although he did it to maintain the prestige and image of the house of Douglas as much as anything else. The Lady Egidia came along too, determined to be involved in whatever went on, and with perhaps some part to play at Turnberry as the King's sister; and she and the Countess Margaret made a lively chattering pair. Also, Sir Will of Mordington was a hearty extrovert, of very different character to his brother. Jamie indeed felt the almost holiday atmosphere to be unsuitable. But perhaps all his recent responsibilities and commitments were making him too sober-minded, old before his time — for he was basically a high-spirited young man.

He rode with his three brothers, all younger than himself, the legitimate James and Will and the bastard Johnnie — and though he would hardly have admitted it, even to himself, he was not a little pleased to note the new respect all three accorded him. Even though he had been the eldest — and their father never made any real distinction between those born in wedlock or out of it — he had always been very much aware of his bastardy. But now he was promoted, the only knight amongst them, something of a hero, and deeply involved in current affairs. Moreover, he had a tail of over forty men-at-arms who trotted behind *him*, not part of their father's following, most respect-inspiring. So, even though Jamie felt that music and laughter were somewhat inappropriate in the present state of affairs, with his master so recently murdered, the realm in crisis, not to mention the implications of the Bickerton business, he was not altogether displeased to be riding so gallantly through the golden autumn forenoon.

They followed the south-eastern slopes of the green Pentland Hills, crossed into the Upper Ward of Lanarkshire at Dolphinton and traversed the high moorlands beyond, ever with the lofty isolated cone of Tinto beckoning them on. From there onwards they were in Douglasdale, which was accepted as running from Tinto Tap to Cairntable, tall summits fifteen miles apart, with the Douglas Water threading the low ground, the fair and fertile land from which they all took their name. Fifty miles from Dalkeith they halted for the night at Douglas Castle itself. The great fortress — another which had been partly razed and then rebuilt and enlarged by the English occupiers in the bad years at the beginning of the century — was held at present only by its keeper and a small garrison; but these hastened to welcome and provide for such distinguished Douglas travellers — and Jamie that night occupied his own old room in the south tower, which had been allotted to him when he was the Earl's page and then squire. The earldom possessed a score and more of castles; but though Tantallon had been the Earl James's favourite house, this was the seat and centre of all. Just who owned it now was still to be decided.

The following morning they rode on out of Douglasdale and over the shoulder of Cairntable, by Muirkirk and more heathery watershed, to Cumnock, with the Ayrshire plain beginning to spread wide before them. Here they left the two ladies and the young Earl of Angus, with half Jamie's tail as escort, to proceed on westwards another twenty-five miles to Turnberry, while the main party swung southwards through the hills to Dalmellington and the Doon valley, which they followed up to Loch Doon, scene of some of the Bruce's early adventures, and so over another watershed to the south-flowing Ken and into Galloway. Riding hard now, with music and singing a thing of the past, they reached the river Dee by dusk, and Threave Castle amongst its marshes as night fell, weary but satisfied. The Douglases could still cover eighty miles in a day when so they chose.

The Lord of Galloway was not at home, but was expected back the next day from a justice-ayres visitation, with his son and heir Archibald, in Wigtonshire. Meanwhile the visitors were entertained by Joanna, Lady Galloway, now an elderly handsome dame inclining towards stoutness but once a noted beauty, heiress of the rich and powerful Morays of Bothwell, whose hand Archie, in his young and dashing days, had fought five knights for in succession, in single combat. She had brought him the great lands and castle of Bothwell and also the hereditary office of Pantler, or Butler, to the King; and this Threave Castle had been largely built from her money. It was an unusual fortalice, rising from a sort of island in a widening of the Dee where the river spread almost into a loch, amidst marshlands, a safe and mighty place, approachable only by water — with a zigzag under-water stone causeway for knowledgeable horsemen, an exceedingly tall and massive square keep within a walled and towered enclosure built to the exact shape of the island. All its stables, farmery, mill, brewery and castleton necessarily were some little way off, on the 'mainland', which had its inconveniences; but for security it was all but impregnable, not quite so strong as Tantallon but nearly so.

When its lord returned next day, he welcomed his guests in his gruff, jerky way, warmly enough, but bluntly wanted to know why they had come. His old friend Dalkeith did not make a habit of visiting him, nor indeed stirring far from his own domains — especially not, as it were, in force like this. Had he come to challenge him for the earldom?

It was not until considerably later, in the privacy of his personal chamber at the top of the keep, that he got his full answer. With his son Archibald — Sir William was still sweethearting in the Stirling area with the Lady Gelis — he was closeted with Dalkeith and Mordington and Jamie, stalking long-legged about the floor like a restless crane, frowning and puffing, whilst his friend and distant kinsman held forth. Archibald, Master of Galloway, listened very differently, a quiet, thoughtful, unsmiling man in his mid-thirties, well aware that though his heir he was not his father's favourite son.

"So Robert Stewart must be held," Dalkeith wound up. "He has his virtues, no doubt, and is capable of rule in this land — if kept within bounds and not allowed his head. But he is untrustworthy, unscrupulous and secret, and could serve both the realm and Douglas mighty ill if let and allowed. Already has done, it may be. You are closer to him than most — for he has few friends, as you well know, Archie. With your help, I believe, he can be held and guided aright."

The other snorted. "Guided where, man? I do not know that I could guide Robert Stewart anywhere. But if I could — where? Who chooses the direction? Not I, 'fore God!"

"There are many who would aid you in that, Archie. Many of them Douglases!"

"Oh, aye — we could look after our ain! But think you Robert Stewart would accept that? Douglas control?"

"It would not be done so bluntly. The Privy Council is there to advise the ruler — if the ruler will heed its advice. As has not been done for long. Douglas, I think, can still sway a majority of the

Council. So it can be the Council's guidance you press on the Governor. He will not always heed you. But it could make the difference between tyranny and honest government."

"You are naming Stewart tyrant before he has so much as taken office, James! I say that you misjudge him. I think not so ill of the man as you and many do. What makes you so sure that he will act the tyrant?"

"What he has already done. Since Earl James's death. Whether or no he had anything to do with that slaying. He immediately assumes the rule. Takes to himself the Douglas office of Chief Warden of the Marches and Justicier of the South. Seeks to divide up the Douglas patrimony. Grasps Tantallon for himself and excludes the Countess Isabel from her rights. All before he is even confirmed in office . . ."

"All this seems more hurt to his sister Isabel than to the realm at large. Or even to Douglas."

"And you would allow him to mistreat the Countess of Douglas, your chief's widow?"

"Not so. But I would not turn the realm upside-down over a Stewart family quarrel."

"You would not turn that quarrel amongst Stewarts to Douglas advantage, Archie?" That was Sir William of Mordington.

"Ha! And there we have the meat of it! You want me to weaken Stewart that Douglas may gain? The old ploy!"

Dalkeith frowned at his brother. "That is not my intention — although Douglas can be, *must* be, a useful halt on Stewart power. Else we are all like to suffer. I fear that we shall have great power abused — what we have seen already but a warning. Nor are the fears only mine. The Stewarts themselves dread the future — and are taking steps to counter it. Jamie — tell my lord."

The young man cleared his throat. "At Turnberry, my lord, the Countess Isabel, the Countess Annabella of Carrick, the Countess Margaret of Angus and the Lady Egidia, are all of one mind. They will do what they can to delay the Earl Robert's rise to supreme power . . ."

"A confederation of women! What can *they* do, boy?"

"I believe, my lord, more than you might think. The future queen, two princesses and the Lady Angus, have much influence. And they hold the King."

"Eh? The King? What is this?"

"The Earl John by now should have His Grace at Turnberry. They will cherish him there. Others may join them — the Earl of Strathearn, the Countess Marjorie of Moray, the Lady Gelis it may be. Surrounded by these, the King will be the less likely to sign what the Earl Robert puts before him. The summons for a parliament, and the like."

"I see. Yes, I see. But Robert will not be long in putting that bees' byke to rights! They will not keep him from his father."

"No. But they can keep him from being alone with His Grace, they declare. Which may serve."

The older man stared at him, from under shaggy, beetling brows.

"You see it, Archie?" Dalkeith said. "My *wife* does, I assure you! And she lacks not shrewdness. She was not to be left out of it. Robert Stewart needs his father's signature to gain supreme power, in calling the first parliament. The old man is weak, yes. But with these close around him . . ."

"And what do you want of me?"

"That you will aid us — and them. Urge moderation on your friend. Help delay the parliament. To give time for moderate men to rally, for moves to be made to secure our positions."

"And why should he heed me?"

"Because he *needs* you, Archie. He has few friends, as I have said. And the support of the Earl of Douglas could be important indeed."

"But I am not the Earl of Douglas."

"Not yet. But you could be. I could hope, *will* be."

"Ah! So that is the way of it?"

"Yes, my friend. With *my* support, and that of other Douglases I can sway, Earl Robert can have you appointed to the earldom — as is his desire. The Lady Annabella, I swear, could persuade her brother, Malcolm Drummond, not to make any claim on his wife's behalf. And Margaret of Angus make no claim for her son."

"And the price I pay for all this?"

"No more than you might choose to pay anyway, Archie. No more indeed than your simple duty, I think. To take the lead and uphold the name and power of Douglas. And, where necessary for the weal of the realm, to help restrain Robert Stewart. As his friend, this would be in his own best interests, to be sure."

"You make it sound mighty simple, James. And this was what you came to Threave to put to me?"

"It was. And I charge you, Archie — do not dismiss it lightly."

There was silence in that upper chamber for a little. It was Jamie who, greatly daring, broke it.

"My lord of Galloway may be loth to become Earl of Douglas and then to run counter to the Earl Robert," he suggested.

They all eyed him doubtfully now.

He did not realise that he was frowning almost as blackly as Archie the Grim. "If the Earl Robert can perhaps have one Earl of Douglas slain, who was in his way, might not he do likewise with another?"

"Curse you, boy!" That came out in a great explosion from their host. "Mind what you say in your betters' presence. Jumped-up puppy! How dare you!"

Jamie sat his bench tensely. "I meant no offence, my lord. I but would point out the danger . . ."

"Danger! To *me*. It would take more than Robert Stewart to endanger Archibald of Galloway! God's wounds — who do you think I am! I was leading armies when Stewart was a babe at breast — and a sickly one!"

"Forgive me, my lord. I . . . misjudged."

"Aye, you did! Watch your callant tongue, in future. Forby, there is no reason to believe that he had aught to do with the Earl James's death. *That* is dangerous talk, see you! I'd counsel you to watch your tongue there also, boy. Or you might find it shortened!"

"Yes, sir. Like, like John Bickerton's has been shortened!"

"Bickerton? Is he taken, then?"

"He is dead, my lord. Stabbed to death before he could utter a word from that tongue! By Ramsay of Waughton — who is now none knows where. Silenced, sir."

The breath came from Archie the Grim in no explosion this time, but in a long exhalation. "Is that so?" he said slowly. He started to pace the floor again.

"It obliges one to think, Archie," Dalkeith put in quietly.

"Think, aye. But who did this thing? Not Robert Stewart, I'd swear!"

"Who else fell to gain greatly by the Earl James's death?"

"*You*, sir!" That was the Master of Galloway's first contribution to the conversation, as he looked at his father.

That man's bark was eloquent as it was wordless.

"We can think of only Malcolm Drummond, other than the Earl Robert, who would so gain. And yourself, Archie, as Archibald here points out," Dalkeith added. "And Drummond has been all the time in Perthshire. There could be something in what Jamie says. As to risk, danger . . ."

"Bah! Danger! Are you all out of your wits? Do you think fear of a dirk would prevent me from becoming Earl of Douglas?"

Archibald Douglas looked at Jamie, and smiled thinly. "*I* think there are wits here sufficiently sharp!" he murmured. "But I conceive this, this compact a good one, sir. I would say agree to it."

"When I require your counsel I'll ask for it, sirrah!" his father jerked. He jabbed a finger at Dalkeith. "If I accept this thing, James, I shall be no slave to your Council. Or to any soever. I shall use my own judgment."

"I should expect no other."

So, without any further actual undertaking, the matter was agreed, and what could be a decisive step taken in Scotland's journey.

A hawking was planned for the morrow, in the great Dee marshes; and a hunt for the day following — whereafter the Dalkeith party would return whence it had come.

X

DESPITE HIS AWARENESS of the situation and its implications, Jamie was unprepared for the state of affairs prevailing at Turnberry. It had become a household of women, and masterful women with strong personalities, each used to having her own way and controlling large establishments. Although they were united in the policy which brought them there, in other respects they were less so, and harmony was scarcely automatic. Moreover, the Lady Annabella was the only one who was not a Stewart, but was mistress of this castle and would one day be Queen; yet was accepted as distinctly inferior by those who were born royal — which now included the Lady Elizabeth, fourth daughter of the King and wife of Sir Thomas Hay of Erroll, the High Constable. Fortunately Annabella Drummond was a woman of quiet dignity and serenity and though as strong-minded as any, did not display it habitually. She indeed was the peace-keeper and catalyst. Her lord kept himself out of sight as far as possible, spending most of his time at Crossraguel Abbey — and very little with his father, immured at the top of a tower and approachable only via a single, narrow turnpike-stair. For all the impact *he* made on the establishment, King Robert might hardly have been present, well content to stay in his bed, with his confessor and clerk to minister to him when he was not pleasantly dozing, no trouble to anyone and glad when his daughters and sister found it unnecessary to attend upon him. Young Lord David, unfeignedly pleased to see Jamie returned, confided that he would positively welcome the appearance of his Uncle Robert, or his Uncle Alex, or anyone else who would deliver him out of the hands of all these women, male and female.

Inevitably Jamie was much in the boy's company, for there was little for him to do in the Lady Isabel's service, in these circumstances, and escape from the castle precincts became something of a daily preoccupation. Unfortunately, he found that he was expected to act as something of a controlling influence on this precocious child, at least by his mother — for the Earl John appeared to have given up all attempts at restraint, if he had ever made any. Needless to say, David Stewart's main reaction to Jamie Douglas's representations and chidings was amusement and enhanced extravagances. He did not so much resent the young man's tentative strictures as invite them, challenge them, enjoy them. Indeed, he seemed to both admire and pity his companion, adjudging him painfully out-of-touch with the realities of life, and taking upon himself the onus of widening that experience. In this quest, Jamie was led hurtling about the countryside, usually at the head of a large cut-throat band, looking for trouble in whatever shape it might offer itself, allegedly seeking out law-breakers, disturbers of the King's peace, petty oppressors, remiss payers of feudal dues and the like, but in fact stirring up the desired disharmony and turmoil for the satisfaction of putting all drastically to rights. Nothing pleased David Stewart more than a hanging, a beating, a ducking and the general chastising of wrong-doers, multiple if possible; or a burning or demolishing of offenders' premises. All in the name of justice, feudal or royal, of course — his father's name. He was on the young side for personal rape, but was always interested in seeing women's reaction to stress and punishment, especially if deprived of their clothing. His men were allowed a long rein — but were notably careful to keep an eye on their young lord throughout all activities, alert for any sudden change of mood or withdrawal of approval; for he could be as devastating towards his own minions as towards their victims. Jamie by no means enjoyed these expeditions, and did all he could to tone them down. He sought, wherever possible, to divert his young host's energies towards the hunting field, fowling, exploratory voyages by galley to Arran and the Stewart island of Bute, archery and athletic contests, horse-racing and the like. The boy had never had anyone with whom he could compete and identify on, as it were, equal terms, with only sisters, and no friends of his own age and status. Now he had an associate, a companion who, although not of his own rank, was of the superior status of knight and who had actually proved himself on the battlefield, and as such was worthy of youthful approval. Gradually Jamie's influence began to tell.

But before all this developed, that other and anticipated development on the national scene began to evolve. Two days after Jamie's arrival from Threave, a messenger from the Earl Robert came riding to Turnberry, via Dundonald. In fact, it was Sir John Stewart of Bute, bastard brother of the princesses, probably the King's favourite child and most popular member of the family generally, a genial, darkly handsome and capable man. He brought a paper for the royal signature — the summons for a parliament to be held at Edinburgh on 4th November. Surprised not to find the monarch at Dundonald, he had come on in haste — since there was some urgency.

Sir John was not long in being apprised of the situation — and found himself escorted upstairs to see his father by the entire regiment of ladies, who then remained in the bedchamber throughout the interview. After initial surprise and mild protest, when the King waved away the paper and refused to sign, rheumy old eyes darting from one daughter to another, John Stewart took it all in good part; but he emphasised that his half-brother of Fife would certainly take a very different attitude. He was only a courier, a messenger, with no responsibility beyond the carrying of the summons. He would have to send word back to Robert at Doune Castle, whom he feared would be very angry. After all, the King had *agreed* that Robert should be Governor, and this parliament only necessary to confirm it, a mere legal formality. He imagined that Robert would come in person, and swiftly.

At his aunt's and sisters' urgent request, he agreed to delay sending his own report to the Earl Robert for two or three days more — since every day counted. It was now turned mid-September, and by another week it would be too late to give the necessary forty days' notice for a parliament by 4th November. Postponement would therefore become inevitable. For his own skin's sake, Sir John told them ruefully, he would betake himself on to Rothesay, the main Stewart castle on Bute, of which he was hereditary keeper, and stay there meantime, leaving some unfortunate servant to be the bearer of the tidings to Doune. But he wondered whether the ladies knew just what they were doing?

Ten days passed after the departure of Sir John, ten distinctly anxious days at Turnberry — although the anxiety by no means transmitted itself to the Lord David, who was in the highest of spirits and kept Jamie fully occupied on a variety of ploys. On the ninth day there was an excitement. When out on a sea-fishing competition — one of Jamie's suggestions — in Maidenhead Bay, the boy was aroused by the sight of a column of smoke rising from a hilltop inland; and nothing would do but that they all must pack up this stupid fishing at once and return to the castle for horses and men. Shouting orders to this effect to the other boats involved, David revealed that he had, of his own authority, arranged for beacons to be prepared on prominent view-points, to be lit as warning of the approach of the Earl Robert's party, from the east. It would not do if the Earl of Fife was not properly met and escorted to his brother's house.

Jamie's doubts over-ruled, they hastened up from the boat-harbour to the stables, calling for men, mounted and were off north-eastwards, a smaller company than was the boy's usual, about a score strong. Some four miles on, under Mochrum Hill where the beacon was now but a smouldering heap, they were able to see a cavalcade approaching.

"A Stewart banner," the boy pointed out, presently. "Blue and gold. At least he does not ride under the Lion Rampant — yet!"

"True. But see you the other flying beside it?" Jamie asked. "Blue and white, with gules for difference. That is the Red Heart of Douglas, for a wager."

"Your friend Sir Archie of Galloway with him?"

"I would think not . . ."

As they neared, it became evident that there were women in the oncoming company, quite a number of women. And the Earl Robert was no lover of the opposite sex and unlikely to travel so encumbered. David groaned.

"More of them!" he said.

But Jamie's heart thumped. That tinkling laughter sounding across the hillside turf he would know anywhere — Gelis Stewart. And . . . others. "Your Aunt Gelis, my lord," he exclaimed. "And Sir William Douglas of Nithsdale. Not the Earl Robert, at all."

"Jamie! Jamie Douglas!" a cry rang out. "Here's joy! Ha — Jamie!"

The Lord David glanced at his companion sidelong. "My Aunt Gelis seems more concerned for Jamie Douglas than for her nephew!" he said. "And I see you flushing, do I not? Here's joy, indeed!" And his own laughter was as musical as the young woman's.

Belatedly the rest came. "And young Davie! Grown almost into a man! I scarce knew you, Davie."

"We cannot all be Douglases!" the boy returned. "Welcome to

Carrick, Aunt Gelis. At least, you are the prettiest of them! Is she not, Sir James?"

Fortunately any reply to this was unnecessary in the general greetings as they came together.

Gelis leaned over in her saddle to kiss her nephew — and then leaned further to grip Jamie's arm impulsively. "How kind to come to meet us!" she said. "How did you know that we were coming?"

David laughed again. "Ask Sir James, Aunt," he advised.

Jamie cleared his throat. "We did not *know*, Lady Gelis. For sure. But my lord's beacon, the smoke yonder, made it ... a possibility. A signal. The Lord David was on the watch ..."

"How clever! I thank you both. Will — this is my nephew, the Lord David of Carrick. Who will one day be liege-lord for us all, God willing. Sir William of Nithsdale, my betrothed ..."

"Another Douglas hero! I' faith — where would we be without them? How fortunate you are, Aunt Gelis — two of them!"

Sir William considered the boy warily. "*I* am the fortunate one, my lord," he corrected. "And the more so if I win your regard. As Sir James seems to have done."

"Sir Jamie wins wherever he turns, I swear! Ask Aunt Isabel!"

Jamie, frowning a little, sought to cut this short. "The Countess Isabel will be happy to see you, Lady Gelis. As will the Countess of Carrick and the other ladies. You have come ... to aid them?"

"I do not see my coming aiding any, Jamie. But Isabel besought me. And, and ..."

"My father added his persuasion," Nithsdale added, significantly.

So this was the first-fruits of Archie the Grim's compact — a hopeful sign. "All aid will be required, I think," he said gravely.

He was assessing the value of Sir William's presence — who was, after all, something of a protègè of the Earl Robert's, and partly beholden to him for Gelis's hand — and turning his mount's head westwards again, when his thigh was jostled a little by another, as a horse sidled close, and a voice spoke quietly.

"So very sober, Jamie! Such weight on these young shoulders! Where is the smiling lad who was esquire to Douglas?"

He turned to find Mary Stewart's comely features near, and none the less attractive for being flushed with riding into the autumnal wind. Despite her concerned tone of voice, her eyes were dancing.

"I am sorry," he said. "Sorry if I seem heavy, dull. I have matters on my mind, yes. Problems . . ."

"To be sure. But she is betrothed to Sir Will, and there's naught to do about it! You must needs content yourself with lesser game, Sir Knight."

He darted an alarmed glance around lest any other should have heard. "No!" he jerked. "You mistake. It is . . . quite otherwise. Nothing of that sort. Problems laid on me. The Countess Isabel. That of the Earl Robert. And now this Lord David. His mother seeks my aid in curbing him. It is difficult . . ."

"He seems a knowing child!"

"Too knowing! He is a devil! But likeable also, in some fashion. He greatly lacks his father's hand."

"So Jamie Douglas must act father, in place of the heir to the throne? Father to a devil — though not yet himself, himself . . .!" She let that go. "I can think of a better part for you to play, at your age, Jamie."

"And you so old and wise, yourself, Mistress Mary!"

"I am older than you by a full six months! Yes, I asked your brother Johnnie. Besides, women are always older than men at our age."

"You tell me so? You scarce look it, I vow! All lightsome fairness and winsomeness." His glance was drawn down inevitably towards her prominent bosom, by no means negatived under her riding-habit. "And, and grace of form."

"Ha — that is better!" she approved, reaching out to pat his arm. "No problems with Mary Stewart, at least! Remember that, Jamie, will you?" He looked at her thoughtfully for a long moment, and then nodded, with a sort of decision, but unspeaking.

The Lady Gelis looked back over her shoulder. "Mary — what are you muttering to Jamie? Watch her, Jamie — for she is a scheming minx! You would be safer riding by *my* side, I vow!"

"Would I, Princess? I do not think that I am safe with any of you! Unlike Sir William, perhaps."

"Stewart women are no man's safety," Nithsdale gave back. "But we Douglases never learn, do we? We are but moths to their flame."

"Nor do the Stewart men ever learn.it, I swear!" David put in. "My Uncle Robert, now — think you *he* will learn?"

That silenced them—for the Earl of Fife was no character to joke about, at any level.

As they rode on, Mary spoke again, low-voiced. "All is well now, between these two, Jamie. Over the child. Gelis told him that she knew of it — saying nothing of you. And he explained all. He was relieved to, I think. They will care for the boy, both of them. Instead of being a stone for stumbling, it may become a blessing."

"I am glad."

She considered him. "I believe that you are. How strange a man is James Douglas!"

So they returned to Turnberry more companionably than might have been anticipated. There the coming of the new arrivals cheered all at the castle greatly — save perhaps its lord, who saw every addition to his household as only portending further trouble. Gelis's presence was important for their project — but Will Douglas's could be more so, in the circumstances. And Gelis's young ladies were a colourful and cheerful boon to any company — even though with one accord they all spoiled young David Stewart deplorably.

Jamie Douglas found himself in a highly unsettled state.

It was the following noontide that the smoke-signal rose again from Mochrum Hill, and archery, with the young women competing, was abruptly dropped forthwith, at the Lord David's command, he insisting that Jamie should come with him. William Douglas preferred to stay where he was, sensibly, and this would have suited the younger man better. But the boy was as imperious as he was impetuous. The Earl Robert must be met and welcomed. They left the castle behind them in a state of excitement — with the young Earl George of Angus, a quiet, retiring lad, despatched to Crossraguel to fetch back the Earl John.

The welcoming party discerned the newcomers in much the same area as they had met the Lady Gelis's party the day before — and again the Stewart colours waved at its head, although on a much larger banner and unsupported by other. Young David grinned cheerfully.

"Look not so glum, Sir Jamie!" he cried. "My Uncle Robert

will not eat you! Nor me, either. Come!" And he spurred onward, into a gallop.

The company they approached in such headlong fashion was a large one, with fully a score of gentlemen besides five times that number of men-at-arms. It drew up, nevertheless, in an approximately defensive posture as the Turnberry party of about forty came pounding on. Though Jamie would have reined back considerably, he was unable to do so without being over-run by their tail, which was being waved and hallooed on by the Lord David, as though at a stag-hunt. Arrows pointed at them from the drawn bows of mounted archers following their line of approach, they thundered up, and in a wide circle rode right round the stationary cavalcade, the men yelling "A Stewart! A Stewart!" The complete circuit made, the boy pulled up his black rearing on its hind legs right in front of the tight group of staring gentry, and doffing his velvet bonnet with a flourish, bowed extravagantly from the saddle.

"Who are you who come to Carrick in force and unannounced?" he cried. "Even under the Stewart colours? Welcome if you are friends. Beware, if not!"

As the astonished and indignant notables spluttered, the thin and so slightly impedimented voice of Robert Stewart was raised. "Insolent!" he said. "I am the Earl of Fife and Menteith. What is the meaning of this, this outrage?"

"Ah — Uncle Robert, is it? I am David of Carrick, your nephew. You should have warned us of your coming, should you not?"

"I do not require to warn any of my coming, boy. I am the Great Chamberlain of Scotland and Governor of the realm."

"You say so, my lord?" Another laughing bow. "Then I welcome, in my father's name, my lord Chamberlain, who has strayed from his chambers to Carrick! But scarcely as Governor — since there is none such, I understand, until parliament in its wisdom so agrees. Am I right, Uncle?"

The Earl Robert was neither eloquent nor glib-tongued, unlike his nephew, however agile his wits. He stared in cold disapproval now. "Insolent!" he said again. "Remove your rabble, boy — I would proceed. On the King's business."

"Ha — the King's business, is it? That is different, Uncle," the boy allowed, smiling dazzlingly. "Come — I will conduct you to

His Grace's presence. If he will see you. For he is sickly, these days. Taken to his bed. But if His Grace cannot see you, my father will serve, no doubt. To conduct the King's business."

His uncle sought for words. "Boy!" he got out. "Are you so great a fool as you sound? This is intolerable! I need none to bring me to my father's presence. In especial, such as you! I speak with the King's voice — and do not forget it. As for your father . . ."

"My father will be King before long, my lord. And I heir to his throne. I would remind all here, likewise, not to forget it!"

There was an appalled silence as men eyed each other and looked from still-faced ice-cool uncle to brilliant beautiful nephew. Undoubtedly the thought that shared alarm in most minds was that here was a very different son from father, a difference which Scotland would have to reckon with.

The Earl summoned his dignity. He shrugged, spoke a word to his closest companions — who barked appropriate laughter — and then urged on his horse.

The Lord David caracoled his mount around, and reined over to his uncle's side. "Back!" he said briefly, with an authoritative flick of his slender hand to those who flanked the Earl. And, after a momentary hesitation, these did pull back — for he was, after all, the King's senior grandson and third in precedence in the kingdom, outranking anyone present. As he drew alongside, he waved over to Jamie to take the place of the dismissed riders at the other side of the Earl. "This is Sir James Douglas of Aberdour," he informed.

His uncle did not so much as turn his head. "I am acquainted with the young man," he said shortly. "And I do not seek his escort — nor yours!"

"Ah, but it is our pleasure. Is it not, Sir James?"

Highly uncomfortable, Jamie mumbled something incoherent.

"You do not often honour us with your presence, Uncle," the boy went on. "Indeed, I cannot recollect you being at Turnberry before."

He got only a grunt in response; but continued to make ostensibly polite but essentially barbed conversation all the way back to the castle, betraying no least awareness of the hostility he had so successfully generated. Jamie marvelled at the sheer ability of the lad, quite apart from his brazen effrontery.

But at Turnberry Castle, of course, the situation changed dramatically. The Earl Robert could ignore young David with his father, mother and aunts present — and these were less expert and successful in dealing with him. From the moment of arrival, he adopted an air of complete mastery and command, the chill assumption that all would fall out as he intended. He was curt with his brother, still more so with his sister-in-law, looked disapprovingly at his three sisters, but strangely enough paid a certain wary heed to his Aunt Egidia and the Countess of Angus, older women both, and formidable. Will Douglas he was formally cool towards, clearly indicating that he found his presence there unfortunate. After the initial greetings, and some brief introductions of his gentlemen, he crisply announced that he was going to see his father, and at once. He intended to return to Dundonald that evening.

Everybody looked at the Earl of Carrick.

That reluctant protagonist evidenced more than his usual unhappiness. "Maybe you'd better not, Robert," he said. "He's, he's not well, mind. Sleeping. Not himself. We had to bring him here . . . for his health."

"Nonsense, man. Where is he?"

"Och, Robert — he's not just fit to see folk. He's up in his room . . ."

"God's eyes, man — I have come all this way to see my father on business of state! The realm's affairs must go on — or have you forgot? We cannot all hide ourselves away, reading poetry and mumbling prayers! Take me to my father, John — and then I will relieve you of my presence. Which I find is scarce welcome here!"

Helplessly the Earl John looked at the others, and moved slowly towards the door.

His brother, following, waved to certain of his gentlemen to accompany him.

Immediately the ladies moved into action. In a rustling phalanx they hurried after the two princes, all six of them — and inevitably, the non-royal visitors had to hold back to allow these precedence. As the Countess of Angus, last of them, passed through the hall doorway, young David took swift charge. He held up his hand against the group of his uncle's attendants.

"You will wait here, my lords and gentles," he ordered. "We

cannot have His Grace's chamber of sickness throng with folk. A family audience only." There were protests, pointing out that the Earl Robert had commanded them to follow him; but he was peremptory. "In this house, sirs, my royal father or myself give the commands. Sir James — come with me. Sir William — entertain these gentlemen *here*." And grasping Jamie's arm, he drew him out and slammed the door behind them.

"My lord — not me!" Jamie protested. "I have no place in this."

"Aunt Isabel said to bring you," the boy assured, gurgling appreciative laughter. "Did you see their faces? Is this not a notable ploy? As good as a play-acting."

"I fear it will be no play-acting. The Earl Robert is not to be played with, see you. Others have discovered that. I urge that you walk more warily, my lord — even you!"

But the boy was already racing up the twisting turnpike stairway, hooting his scorn.

They caught up with the panting women near the topmost landing, and pressed on into the King's bedchamber behind the Lady Angus as the chaplain and clerk were expelled. Jamie squeezed himself into an inconspicuous corner of the overcrowded and over-heated room, but David pushed forward to the bedside.

The monarch was already in a state of alarm and distress, a protective arm across his brow as though to ward off a blow. He was mumbling a general protest — and none there paying the least attention.

"I will not have this, John!" the Earl Robert was saying sternly. "I insist on seeing my father. Alone. Have this, this crowd removed from the room. Forthwith. It is unseemly. Disgraceful."

"I canna do that, Robert," his brother said. "They're his bairns, the same as we are. And his sister. Besides — they'll not go!"

"They will go," the other declared grimly. He turned. "All of you — leave this chamber. At once. I would speak with my father alone. On the realm's business."

Nobody moved.

"Fools!" he jerked. "Bairns and women! Out, I say — and quickly."

"Robert — you will speak to *me*, at least, more respectfully!" the

Lady Egidia declared. "You will not order me out of my brother's presence."

"Nor me! Nor me!" That was a chorus.

Belatedly the Earl turned to his father. "Sire — command this, this rabble to leave your presence. A royal command."

"Och, Robbie — I canna do that," the King moaned. "They're my bairns — and not doing any harm. But . . . but I'd fain see you *all* gone. I would so!"

"I have come a hundred miles to see you, Sire. On important business."

"Aye, well. Another time, Robbie. Not the now. Later, see you. I'm not well . . ."

The Earl Robert's lips tightened to a thin band. "Very well, Sire — if that is your royal will." He drew out a folded paper from his doublet. "Just sign this document, and I will be gone. And the others with me, I think!" He looked round. "Have the clerk in, with his ink-horn."

The monarch wagged his white head, and would not touch the proffered paper, eyes darting from one to the other of his visitors. "I'm no' for signing papers the day, Robbie. I'll no' can hold the quill."

"I will guide your hand, Sire."

"No, no — I tell you, not today."

"Sire, the business of your realm must go on, whether you are well or ill. You are King of Scots, do I have to remind you? *I* do your work for you, not these idlers! And have done, for long. I cannot do it without your royal signature. The seal I can have affixed. But this signature I require. If the realm's business is to continue to be transacted. It will take you but two moments." He looked round. "Where is that clerk?"

"He's gone, Uncle Robert," the Lord David informed him. "Down the stairs."

"Then go fetch him back, boy. With his quill and ink-horn. Quickly."

"Shall I, Father? Mother?"

As John Stewart bit his lip, his wife answered for him. "His Grace says that he does not wish to sign anything, Davie. Not today. So there is no need to fetch pen and ink. Is there, my lord Robert?"

"*I* say, fetch it!" the other snapped.

172

Again none moved, save for the King who sank lower in his bed and sought to cover his red eyes.

"Blood of Christ God!" the Earl cried, driven into unwonted vehement wrath. "Have you all lost what little wits God gave you? This paper is to call a parliament of the realm. I have already sent it to be signed, as is my right — and have had it returned to me unsigned. How dare you! How dare any of you hold up the calling of a parliament? Part of the kingdom's right and duty. This could be named treason!"

"Can the King commit treason, Robert? And his heir? Or his heir's heir?" That was the Lady Isabel, her voice quivering, but strong enough. "Our royal father does not consider that a parliament is necessary at this time. Nor do many who advise him. Your paper will not be signed."

The murmur of agreement from all around left her brother in no doubt but that this was the case. He drew a long breath.

"Very well," he said. "If this is your bairns' plot. Think you it will serve you aught? I have another paper, at Doune. Duly signed by the King. Appointing me Governor of this realm. I shall not fail to govern the realm, I assure you. With or without parliament called. Until parliament meets. I am master of this land — and you will all discover it! When parliament does meet it will confirm my appointment — only that. And I am Governor whether parliament confirms or no."

"But is that not unlawful, Uncle Robert?" the boy asked interestedly.

The other ignored him. "I warn you all — you are playing with fire. When your foolish fingers are burned, do not come greeting to me!" Folding up the paper, he put it back in his doublet. "Sire — I do not congratulate you on your present advisers. I'd counsel you — change them! You would be better back at Dundonald, likewise. Where I am going now." And nodding curtly to his father, he turned, and pushed his way through the press of them to the door, and out.

There was a throbbing silence when he had gone, until the Lord David's gleeful crowing.

"A victory!" he cried. "A notable victory. He has not got his signature that he came for, and cannot have his parliament. We have him beat!"

None of the others were quite so sanguine.

A sort of sob from the bed drew all eyes, and brought Gelis impulsively to grasp her father's hand. But he withdrew it fretfully and burrowed lower in the bedclothes.

"Go away!" the King mumbled. "Go away — all of you. Let me alone, will you. I wish, I wish I wasna here." And he sought to draw the covers over his head.

After a moment or two, with one accord they all moved to the door — some even remembering to turn and bow as they went out.

XI

THE CONCENTRATION OF accomplices could not remain at Turnberry indefinitely, especially once the Earl Robert had returned to the east and the immediate tension was relaxed, although even David Stewart was not so optimistic as to believe that they had heard the last of the matter. But there would be no parliament in November. Sir William Douglas was the first to go — although only over into Dumfries-shire, to his house of Gilmour in Nithsdale from whence he could visit Gelis in half-a-day's riding. The Ladies Egidia and Marjorie had to return to their respective husbands and households. The Countess of Angus and her son stayed on for the time being, but she said that she must proceed to Angus to collect rents and deal with affairs before the winter set in.

Lady Isabel herself decided that she must make a few visits to specific places and persons in order to seek salvage what she could of her inheritance and rights while still she might — this being, after all, one of the reasons behind the plan to delay the parliament and Robert's assumption of complete power. The Lord of Dalkeith had said that he would act for her, do what he could; but that was scarcely sufficient. And it would be wise to go sooner rather than later, not only on account of the weather for travelling but in that Robert would surely be unlikely to stage another descent upon Turnberry immediately. She would go almost at once, then, in the first days of October, and seek to be back within the month. Gelis was well enough content to stay and help Annabella sustain and strengthen the Earl John's feeble will-power meantime; Turnberry was much the nearest royal house to her betrothed's home.

The Lord David, restless and chafing at being left alone with the women — for of course Jamie Douglas was to escort his mistress on her journey — pleaded vehemently to be allowed to accompany them; and it was a marked change for that autocratic juvenile to be pleading instead of commanding. But he obtained no encouragement and was told that his place most certainly was to remain at Turnberry supporting his mother and acting for his father where possible. Jamie added his own recommendation — namely that the boy should be available to act escort for his Aunt Gelis when she rode abroad; since, as he would be the first to admit, escorts for ladies were entirely necessary in Carrick.

"Ha — that from the practised knight-errant and escorter of ladies, Sir Jamie Douglas!" the other exclaimed. "Shall we change places, then? You stay here and squire my Aunt Gelis, while I escort my Aunt Isabel on her travels? I think you would prefer that? But would your kinsman, Sir William?"

They were walking together along the shore-line where the castle gardens came down to the sea, a favourite promenade of an evening. These two were much in each other's company, the boy clearly finding Jamie more to his taste than any other in the castle; the young and gentle Earl of Angus, who was his own age, he despised utterly. It would not be accurate to say that they had become friends; there were too many differences of outlook and background, as well as of years, for that. But they had developed an understanding and companionship, and possibly a sort of respect — however wary on Jamie's part. He eyed the other sufficiently warily now.

"I am the Lady Isabel's servant," he said stiffly. "As I was her husband's. I go where she goes."

"How splendid for Aunt Isabel! She finds that to her taste, I vow! But do *you*?"

He frowned. "To be sure I do. The Lady Isabel is kind and true as she is fair. And she needs aid. She has been sorely misused. Such service as I can render her, I do so gladly."

"No doubt. And she will find your service welcome — since you are a good-looking fellow, are you not? Well set-up and dark enough for any woman. Women like dark and personable men, I am told! One of the best-advised young men about the Court, one lady named you!"

"My lord — I would be grateful if you would not speak in these terms. Of the Lady Isabel and myself. It is unsuitable. We are princess and servant . . ."

"Yet the princess approves Jamie Douglas's various parts, as escort, I swear! I have watched her. And noted that she *disapproves* of my Aunt Gelis's approval of the same parts!"

Jamie halted. "Lord David — I must ask you not to speak so. Or I must leave you. You are wholly in error, talk of matters you know nothing of. The Lady Gelis is kind towards me only as she is towards all."

"I would not judge you a fool, Sir James! Nor yet blind. But . . . nor am I! My aunts find Jamie Douglas agreeable to their tastes — or some of them do, for I have over-many aunts! And that does not exclude my bastard aunt, Mary! Who, I think, would fight either of the others for you, if need be! Tell me — is it pleasing to you to be so approved by women? Or a weariness? Myself, I find it trying, at times."

Jamie swallowed and shook his head helplessly at this impossible but all too percipient stripling. "I do not know of what you speak, my lord," he said shortly. "Nor wish to know. If we are to walk further together then I request that we speak of other things."

"Heigho — do I touch you so shrewdly? Very well, Sir Knight — as you will." The boy pointed. "That ninny, there — playing with my sisters like any bairn. Why is he not to be Earl of Douglas instead of your Archie the Grim? Who is himself a bastard. This of bastardy — what means it? In such matters?"

The young Earl George of Angus had come into view amongst the tidal rocks, with the three young Carrick girls, evidently collecting little crabs and starfish in the pools.

"I cannot tell you for sure," Jamie admitted. "In law, a bastard does not inherit title or lands. He can win them, but not inherit them. But if there is no lawful heir, it can be arranged. By special destination I think is the way they say it."

"George Angus is a bastard. Son of the Countess of Angus in her own right. But also of the Earl William of Douglas. If he can be Earl of Angus, why should he not be Earl of Douglas also, now that his half-brother Earl James is dead? None are so close as he."

"I do not rightly know. He *could* be, I think. And one day might wish to be. But there are two reasons that come to me. The first, that to be chief of Douglas is an especial position—as all know. It is not the oldest or most senior, but it is the most powerful earldom in the land. Since the Comyns were put down by the Bruce. It fields ten thousand men. *That* is the reason. It is meet, and necessary, that Douglas should have an earl who is strong, a warrior, a grown man of proven ability. No child. Second, the realm, the Council, parliament, your uncles, would not wish Douglas any *stronger*, I think! Angus is a great earldom too, though it lacks the Douglas manpower. But it is rich and controls wide lands. Add Angus to Douglas and many would consider it too much for one man. Especially Stewarts! So Earl George is not considered. Perhaps wisely."

"Wisely! If I was my Uncle Robert I would take and cherish this . . . this bairn! Make him Earl of Douglas and Angus both. Then hold him fast. Make him my servant, to use as I would. And so have the power of Douglas and Angus and Stewart combined. I think my terrible uncle, whom all so fear, is something of a fool! Do you not agree, Sir Jamie?"

The other stared at this great-great-grandson of the Bruce, and wondered anew what sort of monarch Scotland was going to have in a few years' time. The era of weak kings appeared to be moving towards its end. Rounding another little headland of the shore-line, they perceived three women strolling back towards them on the green machair just above the beach—the Ladies Isabel and Gelis and their half-sister Mary. They themselves were walking on the sand and shingle of the strand itself, and Jamie would have continued to do so, even edged a little seawards perhaps and raised a hand to salute from a distance. Not so David Stewart. He headed straight for the ladies, determinedly.

"My dear Aunts!" he cried. "Well met. I have been offering to change places with Sir Jamie here. To act escort for you, Aunt

Isabel, on your travels, while he squires Aunt Gelis. But he pretends to have none of it! Is not this a pity?"

Jamie looked black as any Douglas, and the women exchanged glances.

"It seems to me an excellent exchange," the boy went on. "I am penned here at Turnberry all my days, like a stalled ox. Or, not an ox, perhaps — but stalled, at least!" He laughed, and winked. "I never get opportunity to see the country — which one day I am to rule, after all. My father takes me nowhere — would go nowhere himself if he might. Whereas Sir James is for ever riding abroad. Moreover, he would, I swear, better entertain Aunt Gelis in the absence of her betrothed, than would I! And Mistress Mary also, of course! Do you not all agree?"

"Not so, Davie," the Countess told him. "We have spoken of this already and decided otherwise. You would make a very good guard against thieves and robbers, I have no doubt. But I require Sir James for other services than that."

Her nephew grinned wickedly. "Aye — I feared as much! Indeed, I said so to Jamie, did I not? And I *am* on the young side for such services — and moreover, your brother's son! Ah, me! But we could both come, could we not? When my presence was uncalled for, I could successfully absent myself."

"Davie — I do not think that I like your tone of voice. You, you lack respect for your elders."

"Ah, my aged Aunt! I would not name you elderly — yet. Three times *my* age, yes — but barely twice Sir Jamie's! And what, after all, are years? My father, and his royal sire, are both babes compared with myself! Even this Douglas here, I sometimes think, has the simplicity of a bairn! Especially where women are concerned. And I swear you all trade on it!"

"Davie — enough! We will have no more of this," the Lady Isabel exclaimed. "You will keep your flyting tongue better curbed when speaking to me."

"And to me," Gelis agreed. "And when speaking of Sir Jamie, too."

"Ha — yes! Sir Jamie. You hear that, my friend? How they support you, seemingly, these princesses. At the expense of one who will one day be your liege lord—and theirs! Be warned, my simple friend. They will make you pay their price . . ."

"Nephew!" Stepping forward, the Countess grasped the boy's

arm, quite sharply, and tugged him round. "Come with me. We shall have a word together you and I! Gelis—I think that you should come also."

"It is high time," her sister asserted, nodding, and took the other arm. Over his shoulder, the irrepressible Lord David glanced back. "At least we leave you with the best endowed, Jamie — to my mind. You will thank me yet!"

Jamie, holding back with Mary, watched the trio walking over the sandy greensward of the machair towards the castle. "That boy is a handful, i' faith!" he got out. "I never knew the like. He has a tongue like a whiplash — and a mind as quick!"

"I have not failed to notice it," the other admitted.

"Where he gets it, God knows! With his quietly strong lady-mother and his humble saint of a father . . ."

"Perhaps that is it, Jamie. His father may be a humble saint, but he is little of a man. David has had to act the man, for his quiet mother. And not all the Stewarts are spiritless! Alexander was something of this sort, when young, perhaps — though lacking such wits. And the Drummonds lack not for fire — as Queen Margaret Logie taught all!"

He shrugged. "Who knows? But I find David hard to bear with. There is no handling him. And yet, not always. At times, he can be a very good companion. And in a fight, I'd sooner have that boy at my back than many men I know."

"Still fathering him, Jamie!" She paused, and laid a hand on his arm. "See you — he talks much nonsense, and hurtful non-sense. But he is sharp, and there is some truth behind his fleering words. I think that you might be well advised to heed it, Jamie."

"Which of his follies and insults should I heed?"

"What he hints about my royal sisters. This is difficult to say, for I love them both dearly. But . . . they would both use you, Jamie, I think. Not only as a loyal and trusty servant, but as, as a man! A personable and even desirable young man." She stopped, swal-lowing, as though she perhaps had said too much.

He frowned. "The Lady Isabel is my mistress. I am her knight. Of course she will use me — as is *my* desire. As for the Lady Gelis, she is kind — that is all. *She* has never used me — even though I would serve her gladly!"

Mary shook her fair head at him. "Jamie — is that boy right, then? *Are* you a simple bairn, in some things? Do you not know when you are being used? By women!"

He smiled. "I would have thought that it would scarce pass my notice! You now, Mistress Mary — I would not fail to notice if *you* were using me kindly! Or otherwise."

"I wonder! One day, perhaps, we shall see! But . . . do you not see what I mean? What that insolent nephew of mine was meaning also? Isabel needs a friend and helper, yes. A man she may rely on. But she finds you more than that, I warrant. Tell me that she has never put herself into your strong arms? Or perhaps wept on your broad shoulder?"

He coughed. "I have sought to comfort her, to be sure. When she was sore troubled. Over my lord's death. It is my simple duty. She was always kind to me — before my lord was slain. I believe that it was through her good offices that he chose me as his principal esquire . . ."

"Exactly!"

"What mean you by that? She stood friend to me. Should I not stand friend to her, now that she needs me?"

Mary Stewart drew a long breath. "Jamie — believe me, I would not turn you against my sister even if I could. And she *does* need you. But in the ways of women, I think you are little more than the babe Davie said. You are not yet twenty. Isabel is thirty-five. Almost old enough to be your mother. For you to be accepted by all as too close to her could be no good thing for you. But that is what folk will say. She is an attractive woman still — and attracted by you, clearly. And a widow. With strong passions, however seemingly gentle. We Stewart women were always like that. I think, perhaps, you might yet be wise to take young Davie with you on your travels, as he suggests!"

"No! This is a great foolishness. You misjudge the Lady Isabel, Mary. Shamefully. She is good and kind and has been much ill-used. I am her knight, and shall remain so — so long as she will have me."

"As you will. Perhaps once away from Gelis she may be less . . . heedful!"

"Gelis? Dear God — what is this you are at now? What has the Lady Gelis to do with it?"

"That you need ask such question proves you an innocent,

Jamie! For long you have made sheep's eyes at Gelis, we all know. You are scarce clever at hiding it! Not only you, I agree — most of the men at Court are like to do the same. But you, you have a *longing* in your eyes, at times. And Gelis, being Gelis, and a Stewart, plays on it. For she is fond of you also—oh yes, no question of that. If Sir Will had not come along first, older, a great hero, knighted and with an inheritance ...! But we Stewarts can be generous with our affections! Look around you! So to some extent Gelis encourages you — which is less than kind, perhaps. And Isabel sees it all too clearly. And, and resents it. And so acts accordingly."

Bewildered he huffed and puffed. "But this is crazy-mad! Women's tattle grown monstrous! It is not true. None of it. Like some play-acting, making much out of nothing. I swear, you it is Mary who plays the bairn now. You must be simple indeed, to believe all this!"

"You think so, sir? Simple, lacking in wits to have *told* you, perhaps! Doing my poor self no good in your knightly eyes! But — at least you have been warned. Whether it will preserve you remains to be seen."

They had come to the castle gatehouse. Briefly she laid her hand on his arm again. "Forgive me, Jamie, if I have hurt you in this. I, I meant well."

Stiffly he bowed to her and hurried away to his own quarters.

*　　*　　*

They left next day, without David Stewart but with a jingling escort of Tantallon Douglases, heading east by south. They were making for Ednam, across on the other side of Scotland, on the edge of the Merse near where Teviot joined Tweed north of Kelso the barony, English-held at that time, granted by King Robert to Earl James as dowry for his daughter Isabel, on their wedding — if the Douglas could capture and hold it. A somewhat doubtful dowry, as the bridegroom had observed at the time — caring not, since he was five times as wealthy as the Crown anyway. But he had made a point of taking and holding Ednam, or more properly Edenham, nevertheless — and surely no property in Douglas possession was more properly the Countess Isabel's now. Gelis accompanied them as far as Castle Gilmour in Nithsdale, any excuse to see Sir William a good one. With Mary present too, for that first day, Jamie was distinctly distant and aloof towards all three ladies, stiffer than he knew — and the kinder they seemed the stiffer he grew. Mary at least had no cause to grumble.

The Countess's party did not linger at Castle Gilmour but left quite early next day, due east now. Jamie, without actually forcing the pace, pressed ahead smartly, glad to stretch himself after the constrictions of Turnberry — and Isabel seemed by no means averse. She was a good horsewoman and physically fit. They rode up the fast-flowing Mennock Water, through the high, steep Lowther Hills, with only sounds of baaing sheep and yittering curlews to compete with the hollow drumming of their horses' hooves. Through the green jaws of the Mennock Pass they trotted, after a long climb, to Wanlockhead, and then down the east-flowing Elvan Water beyond, to Elvanfoot — no country for lingering in, anyway, empty, inhospitable. Now they were in the upper Clyde valley, still deep in the shouldering hills, Lindsay of Crawford country, only a few miles south of Tower Lindsay. It occurred to Jamie that Ramsay of Waughton, son of a Lindsay vassal, might just possibly have come here to escape the consequences of his crime; but the Lady Isabel was not in favour of going to see, declaring that there was nothing that they could do about it if he was there. She was, oddly enough, much less concerned over the murder of Bickerton than was Jamie, averring that the wretch had merely got his deserts.

After resting their horses in a meadow of the Clyde, fifteen difficult miles behind them, they started another long climb over the high watershed of southern Scotland, where the west-flowing Clyde, the south-flowing Annan and the east-flowing Tweed all rose from a single mountainside, using the old Roman road to take them across the lofty bleak moors to near the head of Tweed, eight more peat-pocked, broken miles. In late afternoon, mud-spattered, weary but thankful to have the worst over, they turned down that stripling river, their way more or less uncomplicated and straight-forward from now on. Another eight miles and they halted at lonely Oliver Castle for the night, to a kindly welcome. Oliver of that Ilk was a vassal of Douglas, and two of his sons had been at Otterburn.

Isabel had stood the gruelling test and pace well, and Jamie found himself to be proud of her, his stiffness of manner replaced by mere stiffness of joints. The emotional strains of recent days faded into tired good companionship.

Next day's riding was comparatively easy, drove-roads following Tweed all the way, north and then east, by Drumelzier, Lyne, Peebles and the northern edge of the Ettrick forest, Traquair, Elibank and Yair, to the confluence of Ettrick and the greater river, all in Douglas country now, forty miles. Another five and they came to fair Melrose, where emotion of a different sort took over. Here, of course, the Earl James was buried, and his widow — and to some extent Jamie also — was preoccupied with grief and memories. Abbot Bernard, their host, was kind, thoughtful, refraining from discussing the matter of the handsome tomb the Countess had ordered to be erected until she raised the subject herself. Arrangements were thereafter made for a chaplain's fee to be paid for all time coming in order that perpetual prayers and masses should be offered for the soul of Earl James Douglas. This had all been proposed and outlined previously; now it was finalised — in the hope that the Countess's revenues would in fact be such as to stand the cost, which included the eventual building of a new side-chapel.

They spent all the next day, Sunday, at the lovely red-stone abbey under the green Eildon Hills, a bitter-sweet interlude in which the monastic peace and quiet regimen, the chanting of the monks and the mellow tolling of bells, was mixed with sad memories, hurt and resentment at what lay behind it all. True peace of spirit was more than even Melrose could offer them.

But mourning, of the passive devotional sort, was not really in the Stewart nature — for which Jamie was thankful — and on the Monday morning they rode on, in a drizzle of rain now, by Leaderfoot and Smailholm to the Eden Water at Nenthorn, and so to Ednam, where the gentle green hills finally died away and the great fertile plain of the Merse spread towards the distant sea — which seemed indeed none so distant that noon-tide, with cold rain driving in from the east and a grey curtain over all. They were only four miles from the Borderline at Carham.

The small stone tower of Ednam, within its courtyard, had been burned so frequently by the English that it had finally been left abandoned. But the thatched steward's house nearby, surrounded by the barony's hamlet of cottages, was reasonably roomy and probably more comfortable than would have been the tower. Dod

Ormiston the steward, a big, burly, red-faced Merseman was much put about by the unprecedented necessity to entertain the Countess of Douglas in his house, but rallied nobly and, aided by his sonsy wife, provided excellently well. Jamie was a little ashamed to find himself relieved that their quarters here permitted little of privacy. Despite himself, Mary Stewart's absurd warnings were having their effect, and he was on his guard against any unsuitable intimacies.

They had three days of typical east coast chilly thin rain, which hampered their survey of the barony inevitably. It was a bigger property than either of them had realised, comprising a rough triangle with two-mile sides, and a three-mile base where the Eden Water flowed into Tweed, almost touching the abbey-burgh of Kelso on the south and reaching within a mile of Birgham village on the east. Within this area were many farmsteads, two corn-mills a lint-mill, a tannery, a brewery and much pasture heavily grazed by good cattle. The rents, multures and vassalage from all this should amount to a goodly sum, and Ormiston confirmed the fact. He also informed that he conveyed the whole, in cash and kind, quarterly to the Abbot of Melrose — an item Abbot Bernard had omitted to mention during their conversations. It seemed that the Earl James had granted the whole revenues of this barony to the abbey as a token of piety — along with how many another, who could tell? It was a side of his character and behaviour unknown to wife or esquire.

Much exercised by this revelation, the visitors left the steward in no doubt as to procedure in future. Expensive if creditably secret piety might be all very well for the rich and powerful Earl of Douglas, to ensure his warrior's soul's entry into eventual bliss; but his deprived widow would have to rely on a more humdrum behavioural virtue, and Holy Church must get along without her jointure-house and barony's revenues. Jamie had some unkind epithets for the so kindly Abbot of Melrose, with whom they had so recently been discussing the financing of side-chapel, tomb and chaplaincy.

From Ednam they rode a short day's journey northwards across a corner of the Merse, by Eccles, Fogo and Duns, to Evelaw Tower high in the southern skirts of the Lammermuir Hills, another small Douglas lairdship which had been alienated, for debt, to the Abbey of Dryburgh, but which the Earl James had repurchased a few years previously — and which therefore could by no means be considered as part of the entailed lands of the earldom. Here they found the indebted vassal, John Douglas, an elderly soured man, still in control as tenant. He was in turn instructed where to send his rents and dues in future. Compared with Ednam, Evelaw was a poor place; but it had 10,000 acres of high hill pasture, and the wool of its sheep-flocks, exported from Berwick-on-Tweed to the Low Countries, produced sizeable revenues annually. The bare and draughty little tower was a comfortless shelter, and the Lady Isabel slept that night in a chilly garret which no princess certainly had ever previously occupied, while Jamie had to make do with a blanket on the hall table.

Their next call was a deal more civilised, no less than the royal burgh and sheriffdom of Haddington, some twenty miles across the grassy heathery Lammermuirs northwards and down to the plain of Forth, where their business was with the Abbess Margaret, who oddly enough farmed the royal burgh's customs, and those of its port of Aberlady. In the Cistercian nunnery a mile east of the town she was shown the Countess's letter with the King's signature confirming his daughter in the customs and revenues. Unenthusiastically, the distinctly masterful Mother Superior agreed that it seemed she must pay the Lady Isabel the dues in future — less of course her fair percentage for collection thereof, which naturally fell to be greatly increased from what it had been owing to the general difficulties and uncertainties of the times. The Countess was quickly out-manoeuvred by an obvious expert, and though Jamie sought to haggle he was not long in admitting a measure of defeat. Lady Isabel would be fortunate to net even half of the customs duties, he reckoned, royal edict or none.

Nevertheless, he considered that their tour of inspection had been well worth-while, an estimated average of £600 Scots per annum being more or less assured — no princely income for a princess admittedly, but a deal better than had seemed likely a few months before. Harboured carefully — if he could persuade any Stewart so to behave — it ought to serve to keep his mistress in modest comfort. But not to pay for extravagances such as a tail of Douglas men-at-arms, to be sure. That was a different problem. However, there were still one or two other sources of possible revenue to be investigated in due course.

Leaving Isabel at the nunnery next day, low with her feminine monthly troubles, Jamie took the opportunity to ride the five or six miles northwards across the Garmyleton Hill to Luffness and Waughton, to see if there was any news to be gleaned as to the whereabouts of young Ramsay. In this quest he drew a total blank; but was interested to discover that Sir James Lindsay himself was back home at Luffness Castle, having been not so much ransomed as exchanged for the wounded Sir Ralph Percy. He was somewhat on the defensive over the behaviour of his two vassals, Bickerton and Ramsay, though of course deploring their deeds. He could add nothing by way of explanation or exoneration. But he was clearly shocked at the entire situation, sympathetic towards the Countess Isabel and prepared to see the Earl Robert as principal villain of the piece. In any eventual power-struggle he almost certainly could be looked upon as an ally of Douglas. He assured Jamie that if he could discover Ramsay's whereabouts, he would — and would take steps to get the truth out of him. He also congratulated Jamie on his knighthood, declaring it to be well-earned — and indeed treated the younger man with the respect due to an equal, not a little flattering in the circumstances — not that the Lord of Crawford and Luffness was yet thirty, himself.

The day following the travellers proceeded from Haddington the fifteen miles to Dalkeith, to report to Jamie's father and to seek his advice as to further moves on the Lady Isabel's behalf. They were warmly enough welcomed, and approval was expressed over what they had achieved; but there was something, just something that was not quite right; and Dalkeith was a little restrained about what should be done next. On the wider front, he informed them that the Earl Robert was proceeding steadily, but meantime fairly discreetly, to gather all power in the kingdom into his own two hands, preparatory to parliamentary confirmation. Archie the Grim was seeking to exert a restraining influence, as agreed; but the man's progress was inexorable notwithstanding. Robert Stewart was going to rule Scotland—nothing was surer. Perhaps he would do it better than they feared—since someone must. It behoved all who could, therefore, to look out for their own interests.

And those of such as could not do so themselves, his idealistic son added — to his sire's non-committal grunt.

That evening the Lord of Dalkeith summoned Jamie, alone, to his private sanctum in the west tower of the castle, a circular room lined with books and parchments and charters and genealogies, indicative of Dalkeith's wide range of interests. Many an hour the boy had spent in this chamber, unlike any of his brothers, who had shunned it — although it had been the romances in the main, which surprisingly were to be found there, well-thumbed — rather than the more serious works, which had been apt to attract him; his father, who clearly had catholic tastes in reading, only mildly censorious. Tonight he seemed a little preoccupied to say the least, less at ease than was his usual with his favourite bastard.

"Jamie," he jerked, rather abruptly, after some markedly casual remarks far from typical of the man. "I want a word with you, lad. A . . . a word for your own good. Sit you — sit down, a God's name!"

Warily son eyed father. "Yes, my lord."

"Tcha, boy — do not my lord me! This is a serious matter, see you. You will pay me due heed."

"Do not I always, Father?"

"Aye. Well. This is it, then. For your own good, lad, as I said." He coughed. "There is talk, see you. Ill talk. Who set it about, I know not. But I hear tell of it from more airts than one. Of you and the Lady Isabel. It must stop, boy. It is folly, I know — damnable folly. But . . . it will not do."

Jamie felt himself flushing hotly. "What must stop, sir?" he asked, demanded.

"Do not speak so to me, sirrah! Remember your place, boy. I, ah, I mean that this ill talk must be stopped. And quickly. Once and for all."

"There is no truth in it."

His father peered at him from under down-drawn brows. "No? You deny it — yet I have not said what the talk is! You have known of it, then?"

"You said it was . . . of the Lady Isabel and myself, sir. Ill talk. There is nothing that is wrong between us. I am the Lady Isabel's servant, as I was her lord's. I am her knight, her protector. It is a knight's duty to protect helpless ladies, is it not? I seek to aid her in her affairs. That is all."

"Aye. Worthy, very worthy. But she is an attractive woman — and you are a man now, Jamie. I was wed two years before I was your age. Folk *will* talk."

187

"Some folk! Must we needs heed them? The Lady Isabel is kind, good, fair — but she is old enough to be my mother, almost."

"I am relieved that you recognise it, lad. But such talk, in Court circles, could do you harm — do her harm also. For she is a princess, remember, and one in a difficult position. Precarious — aye, precarious is the word. No ordinary woman. And one the Earl Robert has discovered cause to consider his enemy, sister as she is. Archie says that he blames all the trouble with the King on her — and on you! Scarce an enviable position for a young man of barely nineteen years."

"So we know now whence the talk stems!"

"Perhaps. But the talk must be stopped, for all that. It is entirely necessary for my name, and the name of Douglas."

"Sir Archie has not forgiven me for what I said at Threave, I think. That if he became Earl of Douglas he might have cause to fear the Earl James's fate."

"Tcha! Archie has more to consider than your laddie's haverings! He wishes you no harm — indeed only good. Hence these steps we must take. For your good and hers, Jamie."

"Steps . . .?"

"Aye. We have decided on it. The Lady Isabel must marry again. And quickly."

"But . . . but . . . dear God — how can this be? You cannot mean it? Truly? Marry . . .!"

"It is the only way, boy. She needs a protector, yes — and not a mere youth, but a man of substance to provide the King's daughter with what she requires. A man in whose name and state she will be secure again."

"And where will she find this paladin, sir? And, and at short notice?"

"We already have him. I have sent for him to come see her. Tomorrow. Edmonstone. Sir John Edmonstone of that Ilk."

"Edmonstone! That, that lumpish Lothian lairdie! Johnnie Edmonstone, who hunts and drinks and sleeps and does naught else! To wed the Countess of Douglas!"

"Watch your tongue, boy! How you speak of your elders and betters. Sir John is a sound man, honest, and of good ancient lineage. Ninth of his line. Moreover, he is a vassal of my own.

Under my superiority he holds large lands. And his mother was a Douglas. He has been widowed these five years. He will serve very well."

"But . . . she can scarcely know the man!"

"That is small matter, in a marriage of this sort. We have chosen carefully, never fear. He is rich enough to provide for her every need, of respected name and standing to be her second husband — but of rank sufficiently below her own to leave her, the King's daughter, free to live her own life as she wishes. And it will keep her within the Douglas camp, so that our own protection can be called upon, if required."

"She will never wed Edmonstone — Isabel Stewart!"

"I say she will. And gladly. It answers most of her difficulties, can you not see? She can make of the marriage what she will, much or little. Edmonstone is a good-humoured man and scarce lusty. He will not trouble her if she does not wish it. Besides, she requires Douglas support. Without our backing the Earl Robert would quickly bring her down — as she knows full well. She will do what we say."

"I wish you well in the telling her, my lord! She is a Stewart, remember!"

"Ah — that will come better from her aunt! My wife, another Stewart, should be telling her even now! And making the position clear, I hope."

For a little there was silence. "What does Edmonstone get out of this?" Jamie asked, at last, dull voiced.

"Why, some enhancement of standing, wed to the King's daughter. Certain further lands from myself, to aid him in his extra expense. And the castle and barony of Tulliallan, in Perthshire, from Archie. Though this is partly to have his support in his claim to the earldom of Douglas."

"I see. All is thought of. Save for the Lady Isabel's desires! And myself, to be sure. What of me, sir, in all this?"

"You, lad, will be much advantaged. Once she is wed, the talk will cease. You will see. And the Earl Robert will have less cause to judge you as in his road. Which is important, Jamie — whatever *you* think. You are too young to be making an enemy of the most powerful man in the land."

"I was not too young to fight my good Lord James's enemies, by

189

his side. At Otterburn. I shall not cease to fight them because he was murdered."

"Vengeance, lad—there speaks the voice of vengeance. Too expensive and too dangerous a voice for an eighteen-year-old in this Scotland! Forget the past and Earl James Douglas, my boy — and think of the future of Sir James Douglas of Aberdour! That is a father's counsel — and command!"

"Yes, sir." Jamie rose. "Have I your lordship's permission to retire?"

"Aye." His father sighed. "Go, then. But ... God give you a head as well as a heart, lad. Go use it, of a mercy!"

Jamie went straight to his own bedchamber. He had no wish to have to speak with Isabel Stewart, or anyone else, that night. His mind in a turmoil of conflicting emotions, he lay on his bed and stared up at the four-poster's canopy for hours before he slept.

* * *

In the morning, when the Lady Isabel came down to break her fast, he found that he just dared not meet her eyes. And yet she seemed almost as though nothing had happened, a little thoughtful perhaps but cheerful enough and still apparently on good terms with her host and hostess. It was as though nothing important had been decided and she, at least, had not had anything like a disturbed night.

Jamie did not see her alone until nearly noon, when the chill November rain ceased and they might walk down to the Eskside in the watery sunlight. He blurted it out as soon as they were out of hearing of the others.

"This, this of marriage, Isabel! This folly, this impertinence! What is to be done? And John Edmonstone — that clod! What is to be done?"

"Why, marry the man, Jamie! What else?" she replied, shrugging. "I have little choice in the matter, it seems."

"But ... but ..." He stared at her. "You would *do* it? Wed Edmonstone?"

"Why, yes — if I needs must. There are many men I'd sooner *not* marry than Sir John, if marriage it is to be. And it seems to be necessary. I have feared this must come, for some time. Princesses must have husbands, they tell me — and husbands who are not over-ambitious for power and who will not embarrass the Crown. Sir John Edmonstone fulfils these requirements. And he is a civil enough man, genial, kindly they say, well thought of . . ."

"But he is a drunken boor. Lives only for his hounds and his hawks and his flagons!"

"So much the better for me! I have learned that the best virtues in a husband are such as bespeak the least trouble for the wife! I do not seek, and shall not find, another Lord James. You, dear Jamie, had you been but ten years older . . .!" She took his arm and squeezed it. "But, alas—ifs and buts will serve me nothing. I must have a husband of name, lands and substance, to protect my *own* name and substance. If I can gain such a one who will not trouble me unduly, then I am fortunate. Or so I am assured!"

Jamie bit his lip. She kept her hand on his arm.

"I understand that Edmonstone Castle is not strong but comfortable — and in need of a woman's hand. A bare three miles from here, so we shall be close neighbours. And Douglas will continue to support my cause."

He could not bring himself to look at her, despite the pressure on his arm, for disappointment in her. Somehow she seemed to have failed him, become less than herself, less than the mistress he had delighted to serve, the Princess-Countess. Johnnie Edmonstone . . . !

"And myself?" he got out, looking away across the river. "What becomes of me? You will need *me* no more, I think. And James Douglas will never serve John Edmonstone!"

"Jamie, my dear!" she cried, turning to throw her arms around him. "I will ever need you. You are my valiant knight — and must always remain so. If you will. Of course Sir James Douglas will never serve Sir John Edmonstone — you, knighted on the field as hero! Sir John will be but a husband, a *second* husband — you remain my true knight and friend, Jamie. I would not wed him were it to be otherwise — that I swear."

Glancing hastily around him to see that they were not observed, he managed to disentangle himself. "John Edmonstone may see it differently."

"John Edmonstone will heed my wishes — or do without Isabel Stewart as wife!"

"My father, likewise, may have other notions . . ."

He got no further regarding his sire's probable doubts, the drumming of hooves, many hooves, on the castle approach drowning his words. A hard-riding party of about fifty were beating across the parkland, to thunder over the drawbridge — a bridge Jamie had scarcely ever seen raised. A large Douglas banner, differenced with the white lion of Galloway, fluttered at their head.

"Archie the Grim!" he exclaimed. "The other marriage-maker! And in haste it would seem. Why, I wonder? Not wedding-bells, I warrant, to bring *that* one hot-foot, to Dalkeith."

By mutual consent they turned back to the castle postern.

It was not, indeed, any thought of weddings or reputations which had fetched the warrior Lord of Galloway from Linlithgow that day, but much more serious matters. He came to inform his friend and colleague Dalkeith that Alexander Stewart, Earl of Buchan and Lord of Badenoch, had at last elected to issue out of his Highland fastnesses, where he acted Justiciar and Lieutenant of the North, to take a hand in affairs of the South — and a high hand at that. They had all begun to forget Alexander the Wolf, something Scotland could never afford to do for long.

XII

THE FIRST THEY knew of the trouble, at Turnberry, was the actual clamour at the castle-gatehouse just at daybreak of a dull November morning. The Earl of Carrick was still at his devotions, with his wife and children, in the castle chapel when Pate Boyd, the steward, came urgently. It was perhaps significant that it was not to the Earl his master that Boyd tiptoed but to young David Stewart, kneeling at the end of the line before the candle-lit altar.

"My lord," he whispered hoarsely. "Visitors. Fell strange visitors. Seeking entry."

"Visitors? At this hour?" David did not trouble to lower his musical voice, despite the priest's intonations. "What insolence is this? Who comes to the High Steward's door before sunrise? Tell them to be off, before they are taught better manners."

"I canna do that, lord — I canna. It is my lord Earl o' Buchan, he says. Your lordship's ain uncle." Boyd looked over towards the Earl John, who, head bent, was either too deep in his devotions to hear or preferred not to do so.

"Buchan! My Uncle Alex? The Wolf!" The boy stared. "God be good — what brings *him* here? From his Hielands. You are sure, man? It is not some impostor . . .?"

"He shouted it loud enough, my lord — right lordly and strang. And a wild pack wi' him, Hielantmen a', by the looks o' them. He'd have me to lower the drawbridge there and then, and no' keep him waiting. But I didna. I said I maun needs ask . . ."

The youngster rose from his faldstool, and caught his mother's eye on him. He smiled to her, with a small wave of his hand, reassuring, assured, strangely so to come from one so youthful. He turned and went out with the steward, while the priest's voice droned on uninterrupted.

"Why, in God's name were we not informed, man?" David demanded, once clear of the chapel. "None should be able to approach Turnberry unannounced. Even my uncles. They must have been seen coming here. Someone will suffer for this!"

"Aye, my lord — but it's my notion that they have come frae the beach. Come by sea. There isna a horse amongst them."

"Sakes — the sea! Uncle Alex! Well, now. And with a pack of Hielandmen, you say? This is . . . peculiar." David paused. "Pate — send a man up to the topmost tower. All the shore can be seen from there. See if there are boats, ships — galleys perhaps. It will be well to know."

"Yes, lord. But — what can it mean?"

"We shall see. But, if Uncle Alex comes visiting, he might well choose to come by sea. From his Lochaber, down through the Isles. And none would know. Which might be his desire . . ."

They came to the gate-house and David Stewart slowed his pace to stroll out unhurriedly on to the parapet wall-walk. Before him, across the water-filled moat, in the thin drizzle of chill rain off the Firth of Clyde, a crowd of men stood waiting, huddled in wet plaids and cloaks, a strangely silent, watching, menacing throng, strange in their ragged tartan clothing, their curious wary tense-seeming stance, their absolute quiet, and the fact that two splendid banners flapped above them damply in the blustery westerly breeze, both gold and blue, one showing the fesse checky of Stewart, the other the yellow sheaves on azure of the earldom of Buchan.

The boy had hardly shown himself, with Boyd, before a tall figure stepped out from the crowd, wrapped in a plaid like the rest but different from all others in the long, silver-gilt shoulder-length hair of his bare head, as in his commanding presence, a spectacularly handsome, splendidly-made man in his early forties. He raised his powerful voice.

"Where is the Earl of Carrick?" he demanded. "My brother. I sent for him. Lower this drawbridge. I have stood waiting here over-long already. Down with it, I say. I am Buchan."

"Ha, Uncle — and I am David Stewart, your nephew. My father, the High Steward, is at his devotions. As is suitable at this hour. No doubt he will welcome you anon. Meantime it falls to me to do so, all unworthily. Thus early in the day!"

"Then let us in, boy. Get the bridge down. I am not used to standing at doors."

"To be sure. It will take only a little time . . . when I have given the order."

"Saints of mercy — then give it, sirrah!"

"Oh indeed yes, my lord of Buchan. If you *are* my lord of Buchan! We have not met, have we? You are ever in your far Highlands, I have heard tell. You must agree, sir, that I have to be sure that it is my father's brother who comes chapping unannounced at our door before sun-up of a winter's morning. Before I open up. The merest precaution — like the swords I perceive beneath your company's cloaks. How do I know that you are the Earl of Buchan, sir? It is an odd hour for visiting, is it not?"

"God's blood, boy — have you taken leave of your wits? Or have you none? Would any man in my father's realm *say* that he was Buchan if he was not?"

"As to that, sir, I know not. Men have strange ambitions. But no doubt you can think of some means to identify yourself, to my satisfaction?"

"*Your* satisfaction!" Suddenly and surprisingly the big man down there burst into loud laughter, slapping his thigh — and in so doing revealing that he was clad in chain-mail under the enveloping plaid. "Lord save us — your satisfaction!" he shouted. "Boy, I like you — on my soul I do! But this of identity — you scarce sound like your father's son. My brother Hirpling Johnnie Stewart's brat!"

Boyd at David's shoulder, was speaking now, low-voiced. "Six Hielant galleys beached on the boat-strand, my lord. Big boats," he reported. "More men, forby. Hundreds. Hech, hech — had we no' better lower the brig? You canna keep yon one out . . ."

"Not him, perhaps, but *them*!" The boy clenched his slender fists, but the features he turned back towards the visitors were as sunny as ever. "I rejoice that I find favour in your eyes, sir," he called. "But I shall still require my father's permission before I may lower the drawbridge. Far be it from me, however, to keep my uncle standing in the rain — if such you are. Will you come round to a small postern we have in the wall, where but one at a time may enter? The Sea Gate we call it. Just yourself my lord. And I can take you to my father."

"The Fiend take you—no, I will not! Alexander Stewart does not go creeping to back doors like some whipped cur! Damnation, boy — I was *born* in this house. Enough of this, I say. I have come to see my royal father, the King's Grace, who I hear is held here. Would you, or any, dare stand between me and the King, you insolent cockerel?"

"There are orders for the protection of His Grace's person, sir. You would not have it otherwise, I swear? I will go . . ." David Stewart paused as a shuffling step sounded at his back, and turned to find his father peering anxiously past him down the bridge-end.

"Och, Alex — it's yourself," the High Steward of Scotland said. "Man, man — it's you? Here's a surprise — a right surprise. Alexander, by all that's wonderful . . ."

"Alexander perished with the cold and needing his breakfast, Johnnie," the other gave back. "That brat of yours will not have me inside. Does not know his own uncle when he sees him. Have down this bridge and let me in, a God's name! I've come to see you. And my father."

"Yes, yes, Alex — to be sure. Boyd, man — have the bridge down and the portcullis up. We must not keep my lord of Buchan waiting."

"Father," David said urgently, beneath his breath. "Have a

195

care. He has a large force of Highlandmen with him, come secretly by sea. We do not want all that rabble of savages in here."

"Nonsense, Davie — we cannot keep my brother out. We cannot keep him from seeing the King."

"Bring him in at the Sea Gate, then. Alone . . ."

"No, no. Not my own brother, Davie. That would not do. Alex is none so ill as he's named. Boyd—let down the bridge, I say."

And so the Wolf of Badenoch strode into Turnberry Castle, a vigorous, commanding figure, all large laughter and bonhomie now, although his fine but curiously colourless grey eyes glittered with other than benign good-nature. And in behind him flooded his Highlanders, silent, wary and armed to the teeth.

Slapping John of Carrick on the back to the extent almost of knocking him over, his brother was loud in greeting. When he turned to his nephew he appeared to have forgotten all offence and patted the fair head, not altogether unlike his own, with avuncular approval, declaring that here was a fine spirited gallant who would one day, God willing, make a fine spirited king. And when, presently, he came into the presence of the Countess Annabella he was polished gallantry itself, bowing, kissing her on both cheeks, admiring with frankly masculine appreciation whilst retaining her hand in his own. As for the Lady Gelis, just down from her bedchamber, he took her in his arms and kissed her comprehensively lingering on her lips in no mere brotherly salute and then letting a knowledgeable hand stray over her bosom speculatively. Alexander Stewart it seemed, loved them all and bore no grudges.

He shared breakfast with them, in a small chamber off the hall, while his multitudinous followers were being fed in the main apartment — and being eyed askance by the castle retainers. Since the former spoke only the Gaelic, there was no communication between the brothers' entourages; indeed most obvious mutual suspicion. But Alexander made up for any stiff uneasiness, even if John did not, being excellent company, affable and amusing.

"Now to our respected but burdensome parent, Johnnie," he announced, when he rose from the table.

"Eh? Och, Alex, he'll scarce be awakened yet. It's early enough for an old, sick man . . ."

"Tush — he has nothing to do but lie in his bed all day, has he, man? Unlike myself. And you, to be sure. As well now as later. I am in something of haste to be on my way, see you. Much as I would wish to linger in such peerless company."

"You . . . you are not biding then, Alex? You are for off again . . .?" His brother quite failed to disguise the relief in his voice.

"I fear so. This is but a call in passing, as it were. I am apt to have much to see to when I venture out of my northern fastnesses, Johnnie. I cannot let my business wait overlong on an old bed-ridden man's sleep."

"He is your monarch, as he is mine!" the elder brother reproved, although less than decisively.

"So he is, on my soul — so he is! So I'll up and pay my best respects, without further delay. Lead the way, nephew."

"You do not wish to trouble him with, with papers and the like?" Carrick put to him unhappily, eyeing his womenfolk.

"Papers? God — no! I leave papers and the like to Robert." Alexander hooted a laugh. "I heard how you had cheated Robert of his precious paper about the parliament. A notable ploy — excellent. Now — I'll see my father." That was crisp.

The other shrugged. "Davie . . ."

They climbed the winding turnpike stair in file, with young David well ahead, his uncle close behind and then a lengthy gap before the slower limping and panting heir to the throne, followed by his wife and sister. At the King's lofty quarters, the Earl of Buchan entered the ante-room, swept aside the protesting friar and clerk and marched straight into the royal bedchamber without so much as a knock, like a gust of sea breeze.

"Ha, Sire! Father — here is your prodigal!" he called out loudly. "Awake, awake — here's no occasion for sleeping. It is not every day that you see your son Alex, Your Grace of Scotland!"

"Eh? Eh?" The monarch peered up from the bed in alarm. "Guidsakes, guidsakes . . . is it . . . is it yourself, Alex? It's Alex, is it? I canna, I canna see right . . ."

"To be sure it's Alex. Your favourite son, is it not? Come all the way from Badenoch to see you. God — it's hot in here."

"Alex — aye, it's yourself. I can hear it's you." The old man reached out a trembling hand — and touched a cold chain-mail sleeve. "Och, guidsakes — what's this? What's this, Alex? Mail, aye link-mail. You're, you're clad for war, Alex! What's this, eh?"

"I came by sea, Sire. From far Lochaber. And when a man sails your western seas, by the powers, he does well to wear mail, with your grandson Donald of the Isles around! You should keep him in better order, I say. Or let me do so!"

"Och, Alex — he's headstrong. Like yourself, mind — aye, like yourself. And I canna do all I'd like. I'm no' well, lad — no well . . ."

"We'll get you better, never fear. That is why I am here."

"Eh? Na, na, lad — there's no betterment for me, I fear. It's ower late for that, Alex. My days are numbered. Numbered, aye . . ."

"All our days are numbered, Father — even mine. But you'll have many yet, I wager. I'll see to it. I've come to take you in hand. Over-much lying abed and sleeping. We will have you on your feet again — the King of Scots! Never fear, Sire."

Something like a sob came from the bed.

A quiet voice spoke from behind. "What mean you, my lord? When you say that you have come to take His Grace in hand?" That was the Countess Annabella, who with the others now stood near the foot of the bed.

"Just what I say, my dear good-sister. My father needs a change. Of air and of company. He has had too much of women's cosseting, too much of being treated as though he was a-dying! You mean him well — but he is being coddled into his grave! I have come to take him into my care, for a while. And he will do the better, I swear."

"No! You cannot do that. It is out of the question."

"Alex — you'll not mean it? You jest, cozzen us . . .?" his brother gasped.

The other ignored them. "Sire — come with me to Rothesay. To your own house there. You ever liked the place. Away from women's pampering for a space — lest they smother you in their too-kind thralldom. You are the King — a man! With a realm to rule. We'll make a man of you again. At Rothesay."

The monarch had crept further, deeper, into the bed-clothes. He was staring up in horror, shaking his white head wordlessly.

"Alex — do not be a fool!" the Lady Gelis exclaimed. "Are you mad? Father is sick. And of great age . . ."

198

"Are you coming, Sire? With Alex. A change from Johnnie."

"No-o-o!" That was a wail, quavering, agonised.

"I say that you are!" His son bent swiftly to grasp the old man, bed-linen and all, and snatch him up in strong arms. King Robert had been a large man himself, and was still no light-weight; but Alexander Stewart was strong, six feet three inches in height and powerfully built. Bundling his parent in the blanketing, he swung around. "Out of my way!" he cried, and marched for the door.

Although Carrick held out imploring hands to stop him and the two women stood in his way, Buchan pushed past them all unheeding. Only young David Stewart actually sought physically to halt him, hurling himself bodily at his striding, burdened uncle, to try to bring him down by grasping him about the legs. The other raised knee and foot and lashed out, kicking the boy violently across the floor to crash against the arras-hung stone walling, heavily. Reaching the door to the ante-room, he again raised foot to smash it open with his booted heel and so stamped through, past the gaping, hand-wringing clerk and friar.

"Open that door, fools!" he cried, and so authoritatively that the clerk hurried to do so even as he gabbled pleas and incoherencies.

Down the winding corkscrew stairway son and father descended, at anything but a careful pace.

The Ladies Annabella and Gelis were now at Alexander's heels, trying to halt him still. But there was little that they could do, in the circumstances, since they could not win past to get in front, and he ignored entirely their ineffective efforts at obstruction. Shaken and dizzy from his head's contact with the bedchamber wall, David only made up on them as his uncle reached the hall doorway — and the hall of course was full of the Highlanders, who came to crowd round their striding master at once, precluding any rescue attempt.

Not yielding up his precious burden to any, Alexander Stewart pushed on, within his circle of now grinning clansmen, across the hall and out into the courtyard, making for the gatehouse-pend; and though many of Carrick's servitors and retainers stared in amazement, none was so bold as to seek to interfere — even when young David's voice rang out in urgent command. The Highlanders now produced naked dirks from under their plaiding.

Out they swept, unimpeded, through the gatehouse-passage, over the echoing drawbridge timbers and off down the wet slippery track to the beach and the waiting galleys. If the King of Scots protested, it was from under smothering blankets.

The Wolf of Badenoch seldom left his upland fastnesses for purely social occasions.

II

XIII

THE GREAT ABBEY-CHURCH of Holyrood was packed to the doors, and the noise emanating therefrom could be heard even at the foot of Edinburgh's Canongate and no little way up the steep green slopes of Arthur's Seat to the south — which would scarcely please the mitred Abbot. It was an odd situation, really, for more than the Abbot and his monks; for parliaments in Scotland were not usually attended by hundreds; indeed seventy or eighty was normally considered a good turn-out. But here was a rather special parliament, this April noontide of 1389. It was the first for many a long day, and called in highly significant, not to say irregular, and dramatic circumstances; it was only very doubt-fully constitutional, since it did not, in the end, have the King's written authority as summons; and it was being held, unusually, here in Lothian, for the very good reason that the Earl Robert did not dare hold it anywhere further north or west — for here, where Douglas influence was paramount, he could rely on sufficient se-curity, a highly important matter, with his brother Alexander south of the Highland Line. Edinburgh town was as full of Douglas minions and supporters this day as was the Abbey itself of their betters. Archie the Grim had seen to that. Moreover, the occasion was abnormal, and the church packed, because for the same security reasons, not only the parliament's members were present but hundreds of spectators also, something new in pro-cedure. If a high proportion of these onlookers were named Douglas, that was only to be expected in Lothian — and of course they had no voice nor say in the debates or votes, however much noise they made at this preliminary stage. But at least they ensured that few others would interrupt and perhaps seek to dominate the proceedings. It had been a bitter decision for the Earl of Fife to take; but confronted with the situation engineered by the Earl Alexander of Buchan, he had little choice.

Jamie Douglas had an excellent position and viewpoint, sitting beside the Lady Isabel Edmonstone — although she never called herself that — and her husband, in the high clerestory gallery on the south side, where the April sunlight shone in warmly from above the crags of Arthur's Seat in dancing mote-clouds. The smell of humanity was very strong. Annabella Countess of Carrick, now recovered from an unfortunate miscarriage, and her son the Lord David Stewart, sat nearby; also the Lady Gelis, the Lady Marjorie of Moray, the Countess of Mar, the Countess of Angus and the young Earl George, and other notables linked with the royal house. Below, in the chancel, the members of the parliament itself sat or stood — for there were insufficient stalls for all — and there sundry familiar figures could be picked out, such as Jamie's father, Sir James Lindsay of Crawford, Sir John Montgomerie of Eaglesham, Sir Will Douglas of Nithsdale and many another Douglas, Sir Malcolm Drummon of Stobhall, Sir Walter Scott of Buccleuch and so on, amongst all the bishops, mitred abbots, lords of parliament, sheriffs and representatives of royal burghs. The nave of the church was full of the less privileged onlookers, standing close as herrings packed in a barrel.

Sir John Edmonstone, not a commissioner of parliament, a big, burly red-faced man whose bullish manner was redeemed by a simple almost childlike smile — though this could deteriorate into a braying laugh — was trying to identify all the commissioners below and decide who were in the Earl Robert's pocket, who in Archie Douglas's and who might vote against both. He was not very good at it, lacking insight and judgment. Often he irritated Jamie — and no doubt his new wife more so — but basically they all got on a lot better than the younger man had anticipated. He had misjudged the man, indeed, for he was in truth honest, good-hearted, even-tempered and undemanding. Also predictable, which can be a help. He now declared loudly that the churchmen were the doubtful entity — one could never be sure of clerks, slippery as eels. Save that few of *them* would be apt to be in the Wolf's camp, at least . . .

A trumpet-flourish quelled these assessments, like the noise generally, and the earls of Scotland filed into the chancel to take up their positions in the choir stalls. There were only five of them present, for there were gaps in the august total of fifteen meantime. Countesses in their own right, such as Mar, Athol and Lennox were represented by their nominees; minors such as Angus and Sutherland could not sit; and the royal brothers now accounted for five, Carrick, Fife and Menteith, Buchan and Strathearn — and David of Strathearn had died suddenly, in allegedly mysterious circumstances, only two months before, leaving a daughter of ten years. So, since Alexander of Buchan was not honouring this assembly with his presence, and Henry of Caithness—who was also Earl of Orkney and considered himself a Norseman — did not deign to attend, there were represented only Dunbar and March, his brother Moray, Ross — who was the Earl Robert's son-in-law, and Carrick. This last's role as heir to the throne being unprovided for in parliament, he sat merely as senior earl — but his modest, limping entry was quite overshadowed by the simultaneous arrival of a resplendent figure in full Highland panoply, who drew all eyes and considerable exclamation, Donald, Lord of the Isles, son of the King's eldest daughter Margaret. The Earl Robert's success in coaxing this almost legendary potentate to his parliament preoccupied all present, and most were still talking about it when another trumpet-blast heralded the appearance of Master John Peebles, Bishop of Dunkeld, Chancellor of the realm, in richest episcopal canonicals, with behind him the sober spare figure of Robert, Earl of Fife and Menteith. At the same time, by a side-door, Archie of Galloway slipped into his place as a lord of parliament, lower in the chancel.

The Chancellor, bowing to all, took his seat in the throne-like chair behind the table set before the high altar, Earl Robert positioning himself on a bench a little way aside, but facing the assembly. It was the Scots usage for the monarch to preside in person over his parliaments, taking a full part in the debates, the King in Parliament being no idle formula. When he was not present, the Chancellor was in procedural charge; otherwise he acted as something between secretary and working chairman. Peebles was a big, old stooping man, thin-bearded, with an unctuous voice but shrewd little eyes. He now raised all to their feet, opened with a brief Latin prayer, waved all to their seats again but remained standing himself, and went on, almost without pause and in the same sing-song voice, to announce that by God's will and the King's royal authority, this ninth parliament of the reign, duly called and constituted, was hereby in session.

A voice from the back of the nave interrupted him to declare that it was not duly called but most unduly, and indeed was no true parliament.

Amidst the general stir and exclamation, the Bishop went on unmoved, as though he had not heard, not so much as raising his eyes from his papers on the table. He read out that their business, of grave import for the realm, had been much delayed by ill-disposed persons interfering in the due processes of summons, and in especial seeking to influence and counter His Grace the King's royal will in the matter. It would be most necessary for parliament to take the necessary steps to ensure that such infamous, indeed treasonable, activities were nullified, brought to an end and their perpetrators duly punished.

Dead silence greeted this announcement. Some eyes were raised towards the royal ladies in the clerestory gallery, nobody looked at the Earl of Carrick, and most present were carefully non-committal. The Wolf of Badenoch might not be present, but he cast a long shadow, and none knew for sure who might be in his pay and service.

The Bishop went on. "My lords and commissioners — before proceeding to the general business of this parliament, it is entirely necessary that His Grace's expressed will relating to the rule and governance of his realm be made effective, belated as this must be. The King's Grace has nominated and appointed to be Governor of the Realm, in his royal name, with all and full powers and authority so to rule, the Lord Robert Stewart, Earl of Fife and Menteith, Great Chamberlain of the kingdom and Chief Warden of the Marches. It falls to this parliament, the first assembled since the King's pronouncement — which I here hold in my hand, duly signed and dated the 8th day of September last — to confirm and homologate that royal will. Does any present so move?"

"I, Archibald of Galloway, so do." That was brief, but swift and clear from mid-chancel.

"And I, James of Dalkeith, second," Jamie's father added quietly.

A tremor of excitement ran through the great church, as everywhere men exchanged glances, smiled, grimaced or otherwise recognised realities as distinct from sentiments and prejudices. If the whole power of Douglas was being placed behind the Earl Robert, then parliament, like most of the rest of the realm, would not say otherwise — meantime. Up on the clerestory, however, a high and musical laugh rang out, mirthful, unconstrained but somehow shocking in those circumstances, drawing every gaze. The young Lord David Stewart of Carrick smiled down beatifically on all, and then glanced along the gallery to his left.

"You hear, Sir Jamie?" he called, clearly. "You hear?"

At the gasps from all, Bishop Peebles banged his gavel on the table. He opened his mouth, then shut it again almost with a click. Even the Chancellor could hardly shout 'silence' at the second heir to the throne, especially when his father sat there, head bent, unmoving. Instead, he cleared his throat and said hurriedly,

"The motion is moved and seconded. Is there any contrary motion?"

In the hush that followed, with many breaths held, Jamie stirred uncomfortably. "That was ill done," he muttered, to the Lady Isabel. "He is Satan itself, that boy! But then, it is *all* ill done, I say!" And he gestured down to the chancel below.

She shook her head. "I know not. We can but trust your father and Sir Archie. We must."

"You do that," her husband agreed.

Another voice was speaking down there, a voice which made all the others sound slightly harsh and jerky, speaking in the softly sibilant lilt of the West Highlands. "I, Donald, do not offer any contrary motion, my lord Bishop," the Lord of the Isles observed mildly. "I but make support of my grandsire's expressed will — so long as it is exercised for the weal and benefit of the realm in *all* its parts and peoples. Which exercise it will be my concern and duty to see carried out hereafter, whatever — as the good God is my witness!"

That also set tongues wagging and heads nodding. If Donald of the Isles, almost an independent prince who practically controlled the entire West Highland seaboard and the Hebrides, like Douglas, supported the Earl Robert, then any opposition was going to be cramped and limited indeed. It escaped the recognition of few that all the Wolf's great territories of Lochaber, Badenoch and Highland Moray were flanked by those controlled by Donald of the Isles. Yet the soft-spoken Highlander, who so seldom interested himself or intervened in Lowland affairs, was giving plainest notice that his support was conditional on his own interests being served, and that he could and would withdraw it at will.

The Chancellor coughed. "I, ah, thank you, my lord," he said, a little doubtfully. He glanced sidelong, quickly, at the Earl Robert, as though for a cue. Receiving none from that stern-faced, ice-cold individual, he drew a hand over his mouth, and added, "I say again — is there any contrary motion to that proposed and seconded?"

If any had come prepared so to move, they could scarcely fail to recognise the inutility of anything such now. Any small and feeble vote would be worse than none at all. There was a heavy silence.

"Very well," the Bishop said, obviously relieved. "I declare that this parliament confirms the expressed will and command of the Lord King Robert in appointing the Earl Robert of Fife and Menteith as Lord Governor and Guardian of this realm of Scotland, during the King his pleasure. Let all men, high and low, heed, accept and note well, else at their peril." He turned, and bowed low to the Earl Robert, vacating his chair.

The other rose, nodded and stalked forward, to seat himself without hint of ceremony in the Bishop's place, pushing aside the papers on the table — the Chancellor hastily gathering these up and standing aside. There was no cheering, no demonstration of any sort, any more than on Fife's part. Undoubtedly few there felt what was done was any occasion for celebration.

Robert Stewart stared levelly out over the assembly for long moments. Then he jerked his head at the Chancellor. "Continue," he said, shortly, his first word spoken so far.

Peebles coughed again. "Yes, my lord Governor." One of his papers fluttered down at the far end of the table. He seemed less assured than heretofore. "Ah . . . the next business. Aye, the next business is that of the French treaty. His Grace of Scotland's compact with His Grace of France expired before Yule last. It should have been renewed, but required parliament's confirmation, likewise. Our King's letter might have served, but such was not sent — for reasons known to all. My lord Governor sent his own letter of intent. It is now required that this parliament should confirm full renewal of the treaty. It is suggested, for a period of three years. On the same terms. Such accord being necessary in order to ensure the mutual defence of both realms against the aggressive designs of the King of England. Is it agreed?"

"I so move," Walter Trail, Bishop of St. Andrews, the Primate, called.

"And I second," Sir James Lindsay added. "I have been lately tasting of English hospitality, and can confirm the need for education in that nation!"

There was a cheer for that, on all sides — the first sign of enthusiasm in the gathering.

The Chancellor took this as implying no contrary motion, and went on, "Further to this, His Grace of France has, in his good pleasure, newly concluded a truce with King Richard of England, in the hope that this will further limit the Plantagenet's war-like designs. None set great store by this, but King Charles did seek to have this realm of Scotland included in the truce, as good ally should. But King Richard would have none of it, and we are excluded. Wherefore my Lord Governor is minded to apply some persuasion." He looked up from his papers. "My lord of Galloway will speak to this."

Sir Archie rose. He was not much more of an orator than was the Earl Robert — and scowled the more blackly in consequence. "I have little to say," he jerked, resentfully. "Richard Plantagenet needs a lesson. Added to that we gave him at Lancaster and Otterburn. To bring him to sign a truce with us. He has newly appointed the Earl Marshal of England to be Chief Warden of the Marches. In place of Hotspur — who is still aiding Montgomerie build his new Polnoon Castle."

This drew a general laugh. It was an open secret that Sir Harry Percy's ransom money was being used to erect a handsome new fortalice at Eaglesham for his captor, Sir John Montgomerie; and that Hotspur was not to be released until the work was more or less complete.

"Richard has ordered his Earl Marshal to prosecute offensive warfare and rapine against our Borders with all vigour," Sir Archie went on, warming a little to his task. "Therefore, I say — and the Earl Robert says — let us strike first. This Marshal has taunted that he would meet us on any fair field, were our numbers twice his own. Let us show the Englishman, and his liege lord, that the Scots are better neighbours when seated at a treaty-table than when threatened with rapine and war! How say you?"

There was, of course, a great and continuing shout of acclaim. That sort of talk, however far short of eloquently delivered, could always be relied upon to arouse a Scots audience. But there was a questioner, nevertheless — the said Sir John Montgomerie, Lord of Eaglesham, when he could make himself heard,

"That would make better sense, Archie, if it was not broadcast to all the world in advance, here in this church," he observed conversationally. "Last time, we kept it secret, and took them by surprise. Now, I warrant their Earl Marshal will know of this in two days' time. And take steps."

There was some murmuring of agreement from the older com-paigners.

"Let him," Galloway declared. "That will serve us well enough, Johnnie. So we considered. We have heard that he plans an attack on Annandale. This news will perhaps make him less eager to attack meantime. To look to his defences, rather. He cannot know when we will come, nor where. Let him sweat over it, I say!"

That was accepted. No vote was required to confirm this strat-egy.

"My lord Governor," Chancellor Peebles resumed, "further to this matter, if it is necessary to assemble large numbers of men-in-arms, then certain steps will require to be taken to aid in it. As all will recognise. Foremost, there is the matter of the earldom of Douglas. That earldom can, and should, field a greater number of men than any other. But at present owing to the lamented death of the late and noble Earl James, it stands in disarray. It is, more-over, right and proper for the weal of the realm, that this issue of the earldom be resolved. It is a matter for this high court of par-liament. The Earl James of Douglas left no direct heir. It falls for a new earl to be appointed with His Grace's royal consent — as exercised by the Lord Governor — and with the agreement of this parliament. And, to be sure, that of the House of Douglas itself. Who will speak to this matter?"

"I will." Sir James of Dalkeith rose. "And I speak, not only for myself but for all of the name of Douglas. We declare, represent and advise that Sir Archibald Douglas, Lord of Galloway, heir of entail of the earldom lands, should forthwith be appointed, accepted and confirmed as 3rd Earl of Douglas, in the room of the late Earl James, of noble memory."

"This I support . . ." Sir William of Mordington, as nominee in the parliament for the young Earl of Angus, jumped up to second; but his voice was drowned in the great shout of agreement from the ranks of Douglas present, both members of the parliament and spectators. The applause went on for some time, the Chancellor making no attempt to halt it. Earl Robert sat inscrutable.

When it could do so and be heard, a single voice was upraised. "I demur, my lords," Sir Malcolm Drummond of Stobhall cried. "I do demur. My lord Chancellor, you erred when you said that the Earl James left no direct heir. No direct male heir, perhaps. But he left a lawful sister, the Countess of Mar, who is my wife. In her name I demur. She is the rightful Countess of Douglas. When the Earl William, of Douglas and Mar, died, she heired his earldom of Mar. Now that her brother the Earl of Douglas has died, leaving no lawful child, she heirs this earldom also. So I claim, my lord Chancellor."

"H'mm." Peebles cast a quick glance at the Earl Robert. "Does, does any support that claim?"

"I protest!" Sir Archibald of Galloway exclaimed, rising. "No woman shall lead Douglas! This is understood. It has all been considered. God's eyes — will your wife take ten thousand Douglas lances into battle, man?"

"The Countess can appoint her captain to do that, my lord."

"*You*, Drummond? You?" That was a snort. "Think you one single Douglas blade would follow you to war!"

"Damn you, Douglas . . ."

"My lords, my lords!" the Chancellor quavered. "Of a mercy — address the Throne, the Lord Governor, I'd mind you. I bid you to curb your tongues."

Dalkeith rose, pressing Sir Archie down to his seat, probably the only man in the realm who might do so. "My lord Governor — permit me to intervene," he said, quietly, soothingly. "There are, I submit, two points relevant to Sir Malcom Drummond's claim. One is that while an only female child may be accepted as heiress to an earldom — as is not infrequently the case — a *sister* is in a different case. There is no such ruling. It *could* be so, lacking a better claim. But in this instance there *is* a better claim. As has been said, the earldom of Douglas fields the largest fighting force of any in this land, and it is only suitable that a man, and a soldier, should control it. Such was foreseen by the Earl William himself, the Earl James's father, who forty years ago entailed the earldom lands on Sir Archibald as next heir to Earl James and any lawful son of his. This, to ensure proper and strong rule of the earldom. I myself, my lords, who might have claimed the earldom, I accept that decision of the Earl William, and withdraw any claim, in favour of the Lord of Galloway."

Loud and prolonged Douglas applause, and angry gestures towards Drummond, left that man in no doubt as to how any vote would go. He must have known all along, of course; and therefore was only making this demand as a formality, or for other advantage or bargaining power.

"My claim, on behalf of my wife, stands," he said, with some dignity, and sat down.

"Do you wish it put to the vote, my lord?"

"Since that would be without effect — no."

"Very well. I declare that this parliament accepts and confirms Sir Archibald, Lord of Galloway, in the earldom of Douglas — which lord now to step forward before all."

Sir Archie, puffing and snorting in his own sort of embarrassment, rose and came stamping up the steps to the table before the altar, amidst loud plaudits. He could be seen to be carrying in one hand a clearly heavy weight that gleamed brightly golden. Coming to the side of the table he halted, and bobbed his grizzled head — he was never much of a man for bowing. Then he held out his golden burden to the Earl Robert, who rising, took it — and required both hands to hold it. Even then it part-fell to the table with the weight, unrolling, and proved to be a magnificently-wrought massive shoulder-belt of close-linked golden chain. This, after a little awkward fumbling, the Governor managed to put over his friend's head and one shoulder, where it hung down on the left side, the recipient half-crouching his great height to facilitate the business. He had never looked grimmer.

"In the name of the King's Grace, I belt you earl," Fife said levelly, thinly. "Stand, Archibald, Earl of Douglas."

Straightening up, the other nodded again, looking as though he might speak, changed his mind, and turning, stamped down the steps again — although this time he made for the earls' stalls not to his own former seat. Less ceremony and display could scarcely have been shown by either principal. Yet nothing more significant had taken place in Scotland for long.

But if Archie the Grim was no play-actor he quickly demonstrated that he was far from averse to action of a more practical nature. No sooner had he sat down, next to the Earl of Moray, than he was on his feet again, whipping off the golden earl's belt and tossing it aside.

"My lord Governor," he grated, "I, Archibald, Earl of Douglas, do declare and inform that Sir Malcolm Drummond of Stobhall, in the name of his wife, Isobel, Countess of Mar, has wrongfully and unlawfully taken possession of certain lands belonging to my earldom — to wit, the northern parts of the Forest of Ettrick — these three months past, and moreover takes and holds the revenues and rents thereof, contrary to all right and custom. These lands have long been part of the entailed property of the earldom of Douglas. I demand his, and her, immediate ejection therefrom, compensation and restoration of revenues to be made. Moreover censure to be passed on the said Malcolm by this parliament." He sat down, amidst uproar.

What the Chancellor could not thereafter achieve in the way of order and silence, young David Stewart, up in the gallery, did without apparent effort. His silvery laughter, high enough to be heard above all, rang out again, with its own dramatic effect.

"My poor Uncle Malcolm!" the boy cried, in mock sympathy. "Fallen amongst thieves, Border thieves! Seek you a Samaritan speedily, Uncle! I suggest my other uncle, Alexander of Buchan!"

Appalled, alarmed, outraged or merely intrigued, the company stared — all save the Earls of Carrick and Fife. In the ensuing hush, the latter tapped the table with one knuckle, a small sound but somehow more pregnant with meaning than the Chancellor's gavel; and the former sank his greying head between his hands, shoulders hunched.

Drummond, biting his lip, rose. "My lord Chancellor," he said, "my wife took possession of those lands in token. Token of her claim to the earldom — which I have here put forward. As was surely just. No single oxgate of land has been given or offered to her out of the vast lands of Douglas. She, the only lawful close kin to the late Earl. His bastards have received the great properties of

Drumlanrig and Cavers. It is inconceivable that his sister and true heiress should receive nothing. So this land at Ettrick was taken in token. Will you censure her for that?"

Peebles coughed. "In that these lands are entailed in the earl-dom, yes," he answered. "This was meet and proper for censure. Some, some other lands might have been chosen."

Dalkeith stood, and quickly, ever the smoother of the way. "My lords — the Chancellor is right. Some other lands *should* have been chosen. For this token. It is true, as Sir Malcolm declares, that the Countess of Mar should not be denied some due portion of her brother's lands and wealth. But there are other lands, more personally held. I say that some such may be decided upon, for transfer to the Countess — some suitable lands. I offer my word upon it. And, I make sure, the new and noble Earl of Douglas will concede likewise." He looked hard at Archie. "That this issue may be equitably resolved."

Drummond and the new Earl glared at each other. Then the former inclined his head. "I accept my lord of Dalkeith's under-taking. In the name of my wife," he said. Undoubtedly this was what his hopeless claim to the earldom had been made for.

Earl Archibald frowned, but shrugged. "So be it — so long as censure is passed on this ill deed." As an afterthought, he added, "That the King's law be upheld."

Relievedly the Chancellor nodded vigorously. "The law, yes. The law. In that this was contrary to law, it is most meet for censure. This parliament must indeed pass censure. I so declare. No need for further debate. May we proceed to the next business, my lord Governor?"

A curt nod from the throne.

"Yes, then." The Bishop made great play with his papers. "We now come to a more grave and lamentable matter, my lords. As must be known to you all, a notable and heinous wrong has been perpetrated in the realm, in that our liege lord King Robert's royal presence has been rudely invaded and his sacred person seized upon and apprehended. By . . . by persons of note. Who, I say, ought to know better, my lords. His Grace even now is in a state little short of captivity, to the shame of this his kingdom, par-liament and people. It is entirely necessary that due steps be taken to right this great wrong, relieve our liege's unhappy situation, and, deal with the offenders." That came out in something of a spate. The Bishop, in an unenviable situation himself, looked up. "The Lord Walter of Brechin to speak to this."

The stir aroused by this ominous challenge was enhanced as everywhere men peered about them looking for the King's youngest son, whose presence in the church was not obvious. No sign of any response to the summons to speak was forthcoming.

Boyish laughter from the gallery *was* forthcoming however, once more. "Seek the nearest whorehouse!" the Lord David advised blithely.

Unhappily the Chancellor looked at the Earl Robert.

That man smoothed a hand over tight mouth. "Call on the Earl of Carrick," he said.

"Ah, yes. My lord Earl of Carrick — will you speak to this matter of the seizure and holding of your royal father, the King's Grace?"

The Earl John raised a protesting, trembling hand. "No! No, I will not!" he got out. "I cannot. Not me. I . . . I cannot condemn in others . . . what I myself have done. God pity me — I cannot!" And jumping up from his stall, he turned and stumbled over to the vestry door, and out.

Up in the gallery the Countess Annabella rose quietly and made for the nearest stairway, while her son raised his all too clear voice helpfully.

"Uncle Robert — you must needs do your own dirk-work your own self, for once."

There were moments of tense silence. The Lord David had, as was quite usual, exactly the rights of it, of course. In any move to condemn and take parliamentary action against one of the King's sons, none who was not himself a prince of the blood could dare take the initiative. Alexander the Wolf still held the King bedbound prisoner in Rothesay Castle, issuing threats and defying his brother Robert and all who might support him. He was demanding, in his father's name, all sorts of appointments, privileges and powers. The Lord Walter, lined up for the task, had failed to appear. The Lord John had refused and was gone. The Lord David of Strathearn was dead. Which left only the Lord Robert himself, able to speak. That prince's reluctance to do so was self-evident. Robert Stewart always used others as mouthpiece and sword-hand both. Although every motion hitherto considered had been at his instigation and devising, all knew, he had not had to enunciate or speak to any. Now he found himself in a corner, and his distaste was daunting to witness. Looking at none but considering his own fingertips, he spoke.

"A kingdom may lack a king, but must still be governed. His Grace my royal father is sick, old — but still, under God, our sovereign lord. He has appointed me to govern, in his name. In despite of this, Alexander, Earl of Buchan has elected unlawfully to abduct and constrain His Grace, holding him fast and preventing him from signing papers, issuing writs and doing other needfuls for the governance of the realm. Such is treason." He paused, letting that dread word make its own impact. "Treason. And the penalty for treason, by whomsoever, is death."

There was a still longer and shocked pause, made nonetheless tense for the even, unemotional tone in which that had been enunciated. Not for long, not since the Baliol aftermath of the Ward of Independence, had anyone suffered death for treason in Scotland.

Robert Stewart leaned back in his chair, eyes upturned now to the stone-groined roof. "I am now Governor, appointed and confirmed, and require no longer His Grace's signature for any action of rule I may take. Let all note well. But I am a merciful man. And sensible that my brother's folly is more to blame than is his sin, for he was ever headstrong. Therefore, whilst I condemn his action as treason, I do not seek his death. This time." Another lengthy pause. "But penalty there must be. Sanctioned by this parliament. I declare that Alexander Earl of Buchan is no longer a fit person to be Lieutenant of the North and Justiciar North of Forth. I therefore pronounce his removal from these high offices under the Crown, and from all revenues and emoluments therefrom. And I nominate in his place the Lord Murdoch Stewart of Menteith, as one who may be trusted to sustain faithfully the duties and responsibilities of these offices. The Earl of Buchan to be seized and apprehended so soon as may be. And the King's Grace to be enlarged forthwith to the freedom of his own house of Dundonald, or wherever else he may elect." That was as lengthy a speech as anyone could recollect that man making.

The clipped cold voice was, as it were, bitten off sharply, and the speaker closed his eyes. Apart from chuckles from the gallery, none thought fit to comment.

"Thus ... and thus!" David Stewart observed. Clearly he now

216

considered himself to be the voice of the silent majority, a voice that none would find easy to silence. "This to be the way of things! And Cousin Murdoch is a ninny! Uncle Alex will eat him! Unless yonder Heilantman takes a hand? Eh, Cousin Donald?"

Despite themselves, everyone present had to admit the uncanny shrewdness of this precocious juvenile who one day should be their King David III. Mere spectator and with no right to raise his voice, he was yet holding a sort of balance in this charade of a parliament — and the only one who was. All eyes turned more or less involuntarily towards the large and colourful figure of Donald of the Isles — who smiled gently but held his peace meantime. All eyes save the Governor's that is, which remained closed.

When the lack of comment or reaction began to become embarrassing, the Chancellor recognised that his was the responsibility again. "My lords — we have heard the Lord Governor's decision and, h'm, merciful pronouncement, on this matter. Does any wish to speak to it?"

"Move acceptance," the Earl of Douglas jerked, shortly.

That should have been all there was to be said, in the circumstances, with Douglas and Stewart lined up together. But as young David had reminded them, there was a third and very relevant force to be considered here. It was all very well to talk of depriving the Wolf of Badenoch of his offices of Lieutenant and Justiciar of the North, virtual ruler of the entire North-East of Scotland; but quite impracticable to remove his power as such, whoever bore the titles, unless with the full and active cooperation of the man who ruled the North-*West* — Donald, Lord of the Isles, whose territories marched with the Wolf's for hundreds of wild and mountainous miles. That potent individual now rose to his impressive height.

"I do agree, my good lords, that my uncle the Earl of Buchan is sorely at fault in laying violent hands on my grandsire the King," he said, sighing sorrowfully and shaking a noble head — the jaw-line strength of which much belied the mild and gentle manner. "May I not suffer for so admitting? *Auribus teneo lupum!* But then, if you consider it, my friends — *homo homini lupus!*" he added, for further confusion. For this was no untutored if picturesque barbarian, as the Lowlanders were apt to name all Highlanders, but possibly the most highly-educated man in that assembly, the churchmen included, a graduate of the University of Cambridge, a poet of some renown, a historian, and with it all one of the greatest warriors in the land and certainly the most feared captain of galleys on the Western and Irish Seas — some would say pirate. "I would but remark that it is less difficult to condemn the Earl Alexander's activities than to enforce his better .behaviour, see you. More than motions of parliament are necessary, whatever. Even when seconded by the most puissant Earl of Douglas."

The new earl scowled, but warily.

"The Lord Alexander, my uncle, hearing your lordships' strictures and threats in Rothesay Castle, has only to take one of the many galleys always moored at that quay, place His Grace of Scotland therein, and sail for one hour, to Cowal or two hours to Kintyre, from that Isle of Bute, and he is quite beyond your reach. Not beyond *my* reach, my lords — for these are in my domains. But beyond yours. Do you not agree? Thereafter he may travel by land, or in his galley if so he wills, up through the Suderies and Lorn to Loch Linnhe and his own lands of Lochaber and the North — where not only you, but I myself, may not touch him at all. You will take my point?"

None, not even the least knowledgeable in geography, failed to do so.

"So, my lord, you require Donald's aid in this matter. No? But to help you effectively, Donald also is requiring *your* aid, in some measure. North of Lochaber and the Great Glen is the large earldom of Ross, whose present lord, my cousin's husband, sits here. This earldom marches, all to north and west, with the Lord Alexander's northern territories. But . . . can it be used against him? My lord of Ross will forgive me if I say that he is scarce a soldier! Moreover, he is not even a Gael, a Highlander, being of the Lowland house of Leslie, whose father but *married* the Lady Euphemia, daughter of the last true Earl . . ."

Alexander Leslie, Earl of Ross, jumped to his feet. He was a mild young man, and no warrior indeed, but he could scarcely sit still under this attack, however genially framed.

"My lord Robert," he exclaimed, to his father-in-law, "I protest! The Lord of the Isles has no call to abuse me. I have done him no hurt . . ."

The Earl Robert pursed his thin lips, but said nothing.

"My good cousin — I do not abuse you," Donald assured,

almost kindly. "I but remind this parliament that to prosecute action, successful action, against your uncle, and mine, all powers in the North must be wielded, and wielded strongly. You, Cousin, are scarcely a wielder of the sword, and your earldom of Ross, which could be a bulwark against Badenoch and Lochaber and Braemoray, is not. I say that, meantime, it should be in more swordly hands — or part of it. For the realm's weal."

There was considerable indrawing of breaths.

Donald addressed himself to the chair again. "My Lord Robert, as you and all know, the late King David, for his own purposes, forfeited my kinsman, the last true Mac-an-t'Sagairt Earl of Ross, William, and bestowed the earldom on his *second* daughter, Euphemia, married to Leslie, ignoring the elder daughter, my wife Margaret. Which Countess Euphemia, her first husband dead, is now the wife of the same Earl Alexander of Buchan, although deserted by him. Her son, Alexander Leslie, my lords, sits here as Earl of Ross. I know naught to his disfavour — save that he lifts no hand against the Earl of Buchan. I, who I say *should* be acting Earl of Ross in the name of my wife, the elder sister, would do so, and could, since my lordship of the Isles makes one with much of the Ross territories. In especial Skye, which island was unjustly taken from my father and given to Ross and which the Countess Euphemia took as her portion on her second marriage, and is now ruled by Alexander of Buchan. The Isle of Skye is mine of right, my lords. I say now, give Donald back the Isle of Skye, and in his wife's right, control of the western territories of Ross, meantime — and you need fear no more from Alexander of Buchan. If not . . . *incidis in Scyllam cupiens vitare Charybdim!*" Bowing, he sat down.

The young Earl of Ross half-rose to his feet, chewed at his lip and sat down again, silent. This was beyond him, he recognised. Only the Earl Robert, his father-in-law, might deal with the mighty Lord of the Isles — and the Earl Robert it was who had invited the man here, no doubt knowing the consequences.

Men eyed each other. This then was the price of the Islesman's unaccustomed journey south and his further co-operation, the Isle of Skye and control of much of Ross. The Governor must have offered him inducement to come — therefore this might well be Robert Stewart's own policy against the Wolf. In which case, it would stand, nothing surer. The boy David had already spelled it out, had he not? No contrary or protesting voice was raised, then, in all the Abbey-church.

The Chancellor looked uncertain, but got no help from the Governor. "How say we to my Lord Donald of the Isles?" he asked.

When still Robert Stewart did not speak, Dalkeith rose. "I move that the Lord Donald be granted the Isle of Skye and control of the western lands of the earldom of Ross, meantime, during the pleasure of parliament and the assent of the King's Grace, through his Governor," he said. "The Earl of Ross's interests to be sustained, and compensation granted."

Fife's nod was almost imperceptible — but the Chancellor perceived it.

"Very well. If none controvert it, that is agreed. The Lord Donald's requests granted meantime, the Earl of Ross's interests to be upheld and maintained by parliament."

The Wolf of Badenoch was a useful scarecrow, if nothing else.

Seeing the Governor yawn, the Bishop spoke briskly, relievedly. "This session must draw to a close. Tomorrow at noon another session will deal with matters of sheriffdoms, allocation of customs-duties, royal burghs, wapinschaws and the like. However, there is one other item which would seem to be best considered today — since it refers to another earldom, that of Strathearn. Unless, my lord Governor, you would prefer it to be held over. Until the Lord Walter of Brechin might be here to speak to it?"

"No." Robert Stewart presumably having abandoned all reliance on his youngest brother, and committed himself to advocacy once, if need be could do so again. "I will speak," he said, if acidly. He raised a minatory finger. "My brother, whom God rest, David, Earl of Strathearn, died two months past. He left but one child, a daughter of ten years, the Lady Euphemia Stewart. The earldoms are the prime support of the Crown. It is not meet that they should remain in the hands of females of tender age, who can nowise render the Crown due aid. Since this is a royal earldom, I advise that the said Euphemia of Strathearn should wed, and forthwith. I advise that Sir Patrick Graham, brother to Sir David Graham of Montrose here present, a knight of proven worth, be selected. He can be relied upon to uphold and manage the earldom for the benefit of my piece and for the good weal of the realm. I *inform* parliament. But this being a royal fief, I do not require its confirmation by any." Without altering his level and factual tone, and making no pause, he went on. "My lord Chancellor, you may prorogue this session." He rose, and without a backward glance, stalked from the chancel.

Into the surge of excited clamour that arose on every hand, Jamie Douglas added his contribution. "Saints of God — did you hear that!" he exclaimed. "The man is beyond all! I say we have raised a monster to rule over us — and will tell my father so."

"Hush, Jamie," the Lady Isabel warned. "If it is so, you must watch your words the more."

"I care not. All, all was a mockery, I say! Even that last. If Strathearn is a royal earldom, it should have gone to one of his father's other sons. The Lord Walter had first claim. But he does not trust Walter of Brechin to do as he tells him — so he weds this wretched child to one of his own vassals of Menteith, Graham, who *will* do as he is told. So Strathearn becomes another earldom to add to Fife and Menteith. Which will be the next . . .?"

"Ha, Sir Jamie — so now we see what a parliament means!" the Lord David interrupted, pushing forward — and certainly not lowering that resounding voice. "Was it not an enlightenment? The true voice of the King's subjects assembled — as issuing from the lips of my Uncle Robert. Every voice that spoke was his — save perhaps Cousin Donald's. Your own father's, no less. And your Sir Archie's. Where stands Douglas now, heh?"

Jamie swallowed his own seething doubts, necessarily. "Sir Archie is now Earl of Douglas. And as such, he will speak otherwise than in a parliament, to be sure. You will see . . ."

"When I hear him speak otherwise than with my uncle's words, I will believe you!" The boy stared round at them all, as they waited to descend the narrow turnpike stair from the clerestory. "That, then, was a parliament, my friends! God's blood — it will be different when I am King — that I promise you!" And he thrust his way through the press to the stairway.

XIV

THE SCOTS WERE riding southwards again through the rolling English countryside, armed for war and in superficially gallant style — yet all so differently from that last and truly gallant occasion, at least so far as Jamie Douglas was concerned. Perhaps he was prejudiced, comparing the leadership but poorly with that of the other. He was loyal enough to the new Earl of Douglas, of course — although, to his mind, Archie the Grim was but a poor successor to the Earl James. But that hard-bitten character was not in fact in charge today, the Governor himself being in command, despite the fact that over half the 12,000 horsemen involved in this adventure were Douglases or their vassals. It was the first major display of Douglas strength under the new regime, and all wrong that the overall commander should have been Robert Stewart.

Jamie himself was relegated to a very minor and inconspicuous position. Not only was he not up in front in the personal train of any of the leaders; he was not even in the hundred-strong Dalkeith contingent, the command of which had been given to his legitimate brother James, specially knighted for the occasion by the Governor — part of the price for the Lord of Dalkeith's support at that parliament. Jamie got on very well with his half-brothers; but James was a year and more younger than himself, something of a scatterbrain so far and totally inexperienced in war and military matters. The next legitimate brother, William, was his second-in-command, although no knight and barely seventeen. Jamie had preferred to attach himself and his own small 'tail' to the joint company of his former colleagues-in-arms, Sir William Douglas of Drumlanrig and Sir Archibald Douglas of Cavers, the bastard son of the Earl James. These three young Otterburn knights, still with an aura of the heroic about them, however little regarded by the present leadership in Scotland, rode together well down the long column, at the head of some three hundred men-at-arms, Jamie's contribution being ten of his own, ten of the Lady Isabel's former Tantallon men, all she could afford, and a score of her husband's retainers, Sir John Edmonstone himself not being of a warlike disposition.

This expedition was unlike the Otterburn one, in other ways. It was differently routed, adopting an invasion course midway along the Borderline but trending ever towards the west. This was because the English Earl Marshal, the Earl of Nottingham, acting Chief Warden, whose challenge the Scots were hereby accepting, was not on good terms with the Earl of Northumberland and the Percys, who considered the Wardenship to be hereditary in their house and Harry Hotspur's present unfortunate absence in Scotland no reason for installing strangers. In consequence Nottingham found it politic to make his base at Carlisle in the west, avoiding the Newcastle-Alnwick Percy country. The Scots were not exactly heading for Carlisle, it being no part of their policy to assail fortress cities. The strategy was to strike down the centre of the country and then cut diagonally across, behind and below Carlisle, making for the Gilsland Gap, in the Haltwhistle Fells, and so into the Upper South Tyne valley, constituting a dire threat to sundry unprotected areas and thus, hopefully, drawing the Earl Marshal out of his Carlisle Castle, to meet them in the open field. At Lanercost they would be within seven miles of the vital Gilsland Gap — which surely Nothingham would never allow them to take and exploit.

Jamie's part of the Scots host heard little of tactics or policy. But they trusted the Earl Archie to keep the Governor right on strategy, for he at least was a seasoned campaigner. They would have been happier however, had his son Sir Will of Nithsdale been present; for his father, at sixty-four, might be less vigorous and adventurous than once he had been, and the expedition was already somewhat depressed by rumours that the whole enterprise was really only something of a gesture, no serious fighting being envisaged, the object being to bring pressure to bear on King Richard Plantagenet to include Scotland in his peace-treaty with France. Unfortunately Will of Nithsdale was not with them, he having departed immediately after the parliament on a semi-diplomatic, semi-chivalrous mission to the Prince of Danzig who was organising a Crusade against the Saracens, and at the same time seeking to re-negotiate the harbour-dues of the great port in favour of the Teutonic Knights—which could gravely affect the trade of the many Scots merchants exporting to Poland. Sir Will was said to have left the Lady Gelis six months' pregnant. Jamie and his friends were not alone in thinking that a warrior of

Nithsdale's renown might have been better employed on this expedition than in traipsing off to Danzig.

They were beginning the gradual descent into the broad Vale of Irthing, south of Bewcastle, when scouts sent back word that they were in touch with light enemy forces just north of the great Roman Wall. This was presently amplified with news that there were further forces at and behind the Wall itself, larger than seemed likely for mere patrols out from Carlisle. The Scots array halted. It could mean that the Earl Marshal had already moved out to oppose them, better informed than they had given him credit for. Caution, it seemed, was advisable.

They moved forward again, more slowly. But with Lanercost Priory coming into sight from the last modest heights before the Wall and the Irthing, they were halted again. They could see for themselves, without scouts' reports, a large body of men drawn up under flags and banners on a hilltop site to their half-left, less than a mile away.

The mighty Hadrian's or Picts' Wall, stretching from coast to coast, here followed the Irthing, on the higher ground of its north side. Although superficially broken down and breached, it still constituted a prominent and formidable barrier, reinforced at fairly regular intervals by mile-castles and turrets, minor forts of considerable strength. These tended to be set on heights, and the highest in this area, where the ground rose fairly abruptly to a sizeable hill, had been chosen as stance for this large waiting force, or for the centre and hub of it, for the Wall and flanking fortlets were obviously manned also.

It represented a poser for the Scots leadership, which had not for a moment anticipated that the old Roman defensive system would be used in modern times. They had not expected the enemy to thus stand prepared for them, and in a purely defensive posture, as seemed to be so. A score of miles within England, the English Earl Marshal, who had been challenging the Scots for weeks, might have been expected to be rather more assertive. To attack this fortified hill, and the massive Wall itself, would be almost as costly a business as besieging the walled city of Carlisle. None doubted that here was Nottingham himself, for the Leopards of Plantagenet were blazoned on a great banner.

There was much debate as to what should be done. The hotter, younger spirits urged an immediate and direct assault, first on the flanks, then from behind where the ascent was less steep. The Earl Archibald advised that they seem to ignore the entrenched enemy, swing off before them eastwards for the Gilsland Gap, as originally intended, leaving the English high and dry on their hill or forcing them to come down and follow, when they could be attacked on lower ground. But the Earl Robert would have none of either proposition. The one was much too dangerous and liable to defeat; the other ran the risk of them being cut off from Scotland. Who knew what the Marshal might have arranged? Let them all remember that they were here to make a demonstration, not to court defeat and disaster.

The Scots army seethed with frustration. This was not the way the Douglases, at least, went to war. But the Governor was coldly adamant. And so long as their new Earl deferred to him, they could do nothing. Camp was set up on the hillside opposite and in full view of the enemy. Trumpets challenged them from the Roman heights.

Presently, although the Earl Robert would indulge in no undignified shouting-match, the Earl of Douglas, under only his own Crowned Heart banner, rode forward with a large group of his supporters, Jamie included, to as near the Wall and hill as they dared, to remain outwith arrow-shot — for nothing was more certain that those ramparts would be lined thickly with English bowmen. Here, below the central fort, they blew trumpets in return, and eventually a party of notables came a little way down the slope towards them. Since these brought a Leopard flag, presumably they included the Earl of Nottingham, Earl Marshal of England.

The Earl Archibald, who did not enjoy shouting any more than did his friend, had brought a herald to do it for him.

"In the name of the high and mighty prince, Earl Robert of Scotland, Governor of the realm; and of the noble and mighty Earl Archibald of Douglas, Lord of Galloway, we ask if we have the honour to address the excellent and renowned Earl Marshal of England, acting Chief Warden in room of Sir Harry Percy presently prisoner in Scotland?" this functionary called.

After a moment or two the reply came, sufficiently clear. "I am John of Nottingham, Earl Marshal, yes. And I am Chief Warden of these Marches — but not in the room of any, especially not of the captive Henry Percy. I demand to know what does the

Lord Robert Stewart and the Earl of Douglas, with an armed host, on English soil?"

Archie muttered to the herald, who shouted again. "They are here at your lordship's invitation. You besought them to come and cross a lance with you and yours, saying that wherever you found any Scots you would give them battle, and more potently than did the Percy at Otterburn."

The response was immediate. "I am rejoiced, sir, that these Scots are come to show their mettle. As distinct from raiding farms, burning churches and raping women, as is their usual. By all means let them now prove their worth and ability in war. We are most ready. Make your onset my Scots friends. We await you."

Amidst an outburst of disbelief and abuse the Scots eyed each other. The man was inviting them to assail a strongly fortified position behind which he and his force sheltered. It was inconceivable. Was this English chivalry?

The herald began to interpret this righteous indignation, when the Earl Archibald pushed him roughly aside.

"My lord!" he cried — and he had quite as loud a voice in fact as had the herald, with noticeably more rasping harshness. "You cannot truly mean what you say? Surely between knights of name and renown, a fair fight is the only way to resolve differences? Yet you enclose yourself in a fort and ask us to assail it with lances and swords! Or did I, Douglas, mishear you?"

"Ha — is that the new-made Earl Archibald?" Nottingham had a fine carrying voice, though slightly and proudly nasal. "I greet you well. But if you have failed to come provided with due and proper weapons, am I to blame? When visiting England you should come better prepared, sir."

"Damn you — we came prepared to meet knights and men of honour, in answer to challenge. Not hill-top forts and skulking defenders!"

"You invade our kingdom and yet would pick your own battle-ground, my lord? Surely not. Come up here, sirrah, and see how we skulk."

Cursing, the Douglas sought to change his tone. "My lord — you cannot mean that you are content to sit behind those ramparts and do naught?" he demanded. "No true knight could hold up his head after such cravenry. In especial the Earl Marshal of England. Come down, sir, with many or with few and let us settle our scores in fair fight, as honest men should."

When he was vouchsafed no reply at all, swearing, he tried again. "See you — we Scots are 12,000. I know not how many are you. But bring down 5,000 and we will field 4,000. Or bring 500 and we will field 400. Any five against four. Can I say fairer?"

Silence from above.

One last throw. "Englishman," Archie shouted, "if you be indeed knight, or man at all, I, Archibald Douglas challenge you to single combat. I conceive you to be a deal the younger. Choose you the weapons. Let it be an honest trial of strength."

"Not so, old man!" came back the haughty rejection. "I, of the blood of kings, do not cross swords with Border cattle-thieves."

Archie gulped, swallowed, but still found voice. "Because you know better Englishman! But you will not then refuse to fight the Governor himself? The Earl Robert Stewart, the King's son — you of the blood of kings."

The listening Scots drew quick breaths. This was tempting Providence with a vengeance — for nothing was more sure than that the Earl Robert would not indulge in any single combat. But they need not have been anxious.

"No, sir," came the reply. "I represent here His Grace of England, King Richard. In his name I fight no such childish contests. If you think to defeat us, try you! If not, then I command that you leave His Grace's territories forthwith, without further hurt or harassment to this land. I have no more to say to you." And turning about, he led his party back up the hill.

The Scots burst into wrath and scornful denunciation; but that was all that they could do.

Later, however, the argument waxed hot and furious. Those for direct assault on the line of forts had gained many more adherents. Douglas himself still advocated an outflanking move towards the Gilsland Gap. Others suggested a surprise dash on Carlisle itself, now presumably left only partly defended. But the Governor would have none of it. Surprisingly he was not displeased with the outcome here. According to him it was a moral victory, an English defeat on their own soil — and without a life lost for the Scots. They had demonstrated that they could march into England without let or hindrance, and put the Earl Marshal's forces on the defensive, helpless. This would not be long in reaching King Richard's ears — and he would read the due lesson. Possibly they had achieved all they set out to do.

Extraordinary as this attitude appeared to his fellow-countrymen, Robert Stewart held to it — and in this new dispensation his word stood as law.

In mid-afternoon, then, despite resentment almost amounting to revolt, the camp was struck and the Scots turned to face north again. But before they could move off, the Earl Archie insisted on riding back to where he had hailed the English previously. This time nobody came down to speak with him although an arrow or two winged over, to fall well short. He was accordingly forced to bellow the louder.

"Englishman — you named Douglas cattle-thief, and the Scots ravagers and burners. I promise that you will regret those words! I will make them true, see you. All the way back to Scotland. Your folk here will curse your name, Nottingham — curse you. I swear it!" He reined around, shaking his fist.

It is to be feared that the Earl of Douglas redeemed his promise, that July day and the next — for the Scots did not return as they had come, the direct way, but headed north by east over the fells to the North Tyne valley, where there were much richer pickings in the Barrasford, Wark and Bellingham areas, cattle-country which they despoiled with a ruthless thoroughness, burning, looting and ravishing at leisure, knowing well that there was unlikely to be any danger at their heels. The sky darkened with the well-known smoke-clouds, the cattle-herds grew and grew, their dust and lowing protest seeming to fill the Middle March. The Governor did nothing to stop it — probably recognised that he could not do so, with 12,000 angry and all but mutinous troops under commanders almost as disappointed and thwarted as their men.

Jamie Douglas rode homeward as discontented as the rest, but with the added depression engendered by what might have been, the recognition that this was all a grievous downfall, a degeneracy and blot on Scotland's escutcheon. Also the recognition that Archie the Grim would never be another Earl James, and that the high zenith of Douglas pride, power and prestige was past. He feared greatly for Scotland hereafter under this new and ignoble regime. As for the cattle-reiving, he was not against it on prin-

228

ciple — of Border stock he could hardly be that. But he deplored
the violence and savagery which now went with it, and which
should not have been sanctioned by the nobles. He allowed none
of the men under his control to take part in excesses — but that
was a mere drop in a loch.

It was not that he was wholly committed to the chivalric code,
now declining throughout Christendom. He recognised its follies
and contradictions, its outdated arrogances and preoccupation
with personal fighting valour as against the well-being of the majority. But he greatly endorsed the noble ideals of knighthood, and
the disciplines these imposed — and was young enough to try to
apply them wholeheartedly. And what he had seen around him on
this expedition, on both sides, he felt to be the negation of knighthood.

Another part of Jamie's trouble was that, for the first time in his
life he was at odds with his father. He believed that Dalkeith had
made a grave mistake in coming to terms with and then actually
supporting the Earl Robert, letting down the Lady Isabel in the
process. Always he had greatly respected his father, believing in
his judgment, wisdom, integrity. Now he was less sure of all three.
Perhaps the preference shown to his legitimate brothers in this
unfortunate raid rankled more than it should.

At any rate, back in Scotland unpursued, Jamie did not return
to Dalkeith but went straight to Edmonstone, a significant gesture. There dire news awaited him. The Lady Isabel had gone to
Dunfermline to be with her sister Gelis. Sir Will of Nithsdale was
dead, slain at Danzig, vilely.

Within the hour Jamie was on his way to Fife.

XV

THE PALACE OF Dunfermline stood back a few miles, on the
rising ground, of the north shore of Forth, in Fothrif, the
western division of Fife, beside the large and wealthy abbey

where the Bruce and his queen were buried. It was an ancient place and had been one of the favourite seats of the old Celtic kings, Malcolm Canmore's in especial. Here the present monarch had been brought on his release from the Wolf's clutches at Rothesay. Donald of the Isles had surrounded the Isle of Bute with his entire fleet of hundreds of galleys, as only he could do, and the Wolf had quickly understood the realities of the case and slipped away in a small boat, by night, for the far north, leaving his royal father to be collected by the Islesman. The Earl Robert had had him brought to Dunfermline, as being conveniently near to his own Fife castle of Falkland, where he could keep a close eye on him in future, lest anyone else sought this short-cut to power in the land.

Jamie and his twenty men crossed the Forth at Queen Margaret's Ferry, and reached the grey town of Dunfermline, crowding around the twin eminences of palace and abbey, as the sun was sinking behind the Ochils to the north-west, on the first evening of August. To his surprise he was welcomed by the jangling cacophony of the bells of the abbey and of the other churches and chapels. He was more surprised still when, on enquiry, he elicited the information that the Governor himself had arrived earlier that afternoon, from the South, and this joyous pealing was to signalise his great victory over the Earl Marshal of England, near Carlisle.

At the old rambling palace, part of it half-ruinous, Jamie, avoiding the finer quarters where the Earl of Fife might be looked for, found his way to the princesses' chambers in the ancient east wing. Here he discovered Mary Stewart in sole charge, who greeted him with a hug and a warm kiss.

"Jamie himself—back from the wars!" she exclaimed, with undisguised pleasure. "Safe and unhurt, too, God be thanked! Here's joy, Jamie — and we could be doing with some, I swear, here at Dunfermline."

He snorted, with scant appreciation of her fine welcome. "Unhurt! Would God some of us *had* been hurt! Then we might at least have been able to hold up our heads, like men. Not hang them, like cheats and cozeners!"

"Sir Jamie Douglas hanging his head in shame? I'll not believe it!" she cried. "Besides, you won another victory, did you not? Hear those clanging bells — which I would to God would stop . . .!"

"Those bells are as great a fraud as the rest," he told her. "There was no victory. Not even a battle or a skirmish. Nothing. Not a sword was drawn or a lance couched, save against the English countryfolk on the way home. It was all a folly, from start to end. The English would not fight, and sat in their forts behind stone walls — and the Earl Robert was scarce keener. So he turned back without a blow struck. He never intended that there should be any true fighting. A demonstration, he named it. He would allow no move further into England — and our new Douglas earl yielded to him. We turned tail, unblooded, and came home — assailing only farms and villages and reiving cattle. And for that, your precious half-brother rings Dunfermline's bells."

She stepped forward to put a finger against his lips. "Hush, Jamie — in this house speak not so. I love Robert little better than do you — but I do not shout it aloud in his own palace! That one has ears and eyes everywhere — spies. And he mislikes you sufficiently already."

"I care not . . ." he began. But his voice faltered and faded. She had come very close to him, to touch his lips, and the sheer power of her vivid femininity literally took his breath away. Mary was not really beautiful, like her half-sisters Gelis and Isabel, but she was lovely, warm and so much woman that a man was roused, challenged and yet to some extent disarmed, inevitably. Or Jamie Douglas was, at least.

He drew back, in sheer self-defence, changing his tone when he could. "But . . . but I did not come here to talk of the Governor and his ill ways," he said. "I had tidings at Edmonstone, and so came . . ."

"Aye, came in haste seeking your two princesses!" She finished for him. "Ever their fond knight! And my warnings unheeded! Well, Sir Knight, they are both presently dining with the said and unbeloved Robert. He summoned them to his table — a modest banquet to celebrate his victory, see you. So you must needs put up with me meantime, my friend and fellow-bastard!"

"Not so," he objected. "Or . . . I mean . . . No. You mistake me. I came to find out, to discover. What ill befell Sir Will of Nithsdale. I heard only that he was slain. And how it is with the Lady Gelis . . .?"

"To be sure. I have a shrewish tongue, Jamie. It is a bad

business. We got the word the very day you rode South. Sir Will was basely slain. At Danzig. Set upon by bullies, in the street, and stabbed to death. It is said hired by the Lord Clifford. Though . . ."

"Clifford? You mean the English lord from Carlisle?"

"The same. He was in Danzig also for this Crusade folly. It seems that in the previous raid on England, when you were at Otterburn, in the West array Sir Will came up against Clifford somehow, who miscalled him pirate and assassin. Over the Isle of Man campaign. Clifford had certain interests in Man. Sir Will challenged him there and then to prove his words in fair fight or single combat, or to retract them. But Clifford refused. So they met again in Danzig, and Will repeated his challenge before all. And again Clifford would not. But that night, hired bullies waylaid Will in a dark lane and did him to death — presumably that there be no more uncomfortable challenges. So Gelis, ten months wed, is a widow—and expecting a bairn in eight weeks' time."

"Dear God — how dastardly a deed! Clifford! I will not forget that name!"

"If Clifford it was. I suppose that Sir Will might have had . . . other ill-wishers."

He brushed that aside. "What sorrow for the Lady Gelis, what pain and hurt. Hurt for Scotland also, for he was a notable soldier. We have not many of his like."

"And yet, you did not greatly love him, I think, Jamie?"

"I admired him, esteemed him. Was it necessary that I should also love him?" That was a little stiff.

"Perhaps not." She smiled.

"How is Gelis? How does she bear this great blow?"

"Well. Bravely. But, she is a Stewart — and she is angry too."

"Aye. And with cause. Like her sister. Both widowed, and by assassination. An evil fate indeed."

"That thought has not escaped them both. As you will discover."

"Both husbands Douglases. And two of the realm's finest leaders, fighters. Is there a curse on Douglas? Or is it on Stewart?"

"I think not. I do not believe in curses. Save human ones, such as my brothers Robert and Alex! And perhaps young David? Although he may grow out of his accursedness — who knows?"

232

"You make the Stewarts sound sufficiently accursed!"

"Not the women, I hope?"

"No," he agreed. "Not the women. But — now *you* it is who talk dangerously. No?"

"No doubt. Let us go walk in the orchard then, Jamie — where none shall overhear our . . . indiscretions!"

Warily he eyed her. But he felt that he could scarcely refuse—nor particularly wanted to.

So they went strolling along the avenues of fruit-trees which sloped down into the glen of Pittencrieff below Malcolm's Tower, in the cool of the August evening, she with her rounded bare arm tucked in his, he very much aware of the pressure and motion of a shapely breast against his side. They made a handsome pair, for other strollers of the Court — but sought private ways in the interests of security. Mary did most of the talking, but despite her warnings about precautions and the like, they spoke little that was particularly significant or controversial. Indeed much of the time they did not speak at all, and this was undeniably pleasant — for the man, at least. He recognised that he was by no means at his best in making conversation with young women. Yet he liked their company, some more than others. After he had left such, he could always think of a hundred witty and devastating things he could have said, but had not.

Although they did not speak incessantly, perhaps Mary Stewart learned more than she wanted to know about Jamie Douglas than in other more talkative sessions.

They visited Queen Margaret's Cave, but unfortunately it was already occupied. Whereafter they sat decently in a rose-arbour, slightly cramped as to space but uncomplaining — until the midges drove even the stalwart Mary into retreat, she being scarcely clad for midge-resistance. Jamie was suitably concerned and helpful about brushing the creatures off.

Soon after their return to cover, the two princesses came back from the banquet, early, and there was quite an emotional scene as they welcomed their knight-errant with more embraces and kisses — and Jamie, ill at ease, wishing that Mary had not been standing there in the background smiling gently. That they were both glad to see him, despite a certain preoccupation, was obvious; and though Isabel naturally was the more demonstrative, Gelis was far from backward, with unshed tears in her violet eyes as she greeted him. Oddly enough, although he instantly blamed himself fiercely for it, his fine sympathy for her was distinctly eroded by a sort of offence at her so evident state of pregnancy. Unfair and ridiculous as this was, it was somehow basic, elementary — and he was still only nineteen, after all. The feeling of her great belly pressed against him as she threw her arms around him undoubtedly displeased. He sought to keep his eyes studiously on her face thereafter — not with entire success.

The subject of Sir Will's death, although in all their minds, was not mentioned at first, as though deliberately. Instead they spoke of the fraudulent victory at Lanercost, the humiliations of the Douglases, the declining health of the King, and the Lord Robert's probable intentions in the immediate future. Jamie in fact wondered at the Governor inviting these two so uncooperative sisters to his table here, and the sisters, exchanging glances, agreed hurriedly that this certainly represented very much a change in tactics. Perhaps he felt the need of some superficial royal family support, now that David of Strathearn was dead, he had for the moment alienated the Lord Walter, the Earl Alexander was in open revolt, and the Earl John eyed him ever the more askance. The Stewarts at present could scarcely be called a united family; but it was probably necessary for Robert to try to preserve an illusion of concord as far as possible. Isabel, biting her lip, said that she hated her brother more than ever, but that Gelis and she could not wholly abjure and renounce his company meantime, unfortunately. The King was undoubtedly sinking fast, and in duty bound, as well as in their own interests, they could not abandon him wholly to Robert's sour ministrations and manipulations.

Jamie accepted that, of course. When, after a curiously uncomfortable interval of silence, he felt bound to raise the subject of the assassination in Danzig, stiltedly expressing sympathy and revulsion, he was unprepared for the reaction. It was as though a dam had been breached. Both princesses burst out in exclamation of pent-up feelings. In a babble of incoherent and jumbled assertions, they vied with each other in completely confusing as well as embarrassing their hearer — who was unable to get the gist of their hot accusations, save that once again their brother Robert was the target. Clearly they had been bottling this up all along.

But quite quickly they recollected their dignity, and Isabel, presumably recognising her sister's priority in this, fell silent, while Gelis spoke, more quietly but still tensely.

"I should have known, have guessed," she said. "I blame myself. He has been ill disposed towards Will, ever since Turnberry, when we came between him and our father. Will had but little to do with it, but *I* had, and Robert has not forgiven me. He never forgets—and he is a man who will strike a woman through her husband. Moreover, Will had opposed him in more than one matter, since. I should have guessed, when *he* was chosen to go on this mission to Danzig, that he might never come back."

Jamie stared. "But . . . but . . ." he floundered. "What are you saying. What is this . . .?"

Isabel took up the charge. "Who sent Sir William to Danzig? Robert — he only. His father, Sir Archie, did not want him to go. He would have had him with him on this planned raid on England. Robert sent him, for his own purposes."

"But Mary said that it was the Lord Clifford who slew him. Or planned it."

"Clifford takes the blame, yes. No doubt Clifford hired those evil bravoes," Gelis said. "But who was behind Clifford?"

"The man Bickerton slew James," her sister added. "But we believe that Robert it was who caused Bickerton do it. He could as readily have arranged it with Clifford. Robert never soils his own hands."

James shook his head. "Clifford is a powerful English noble. He would scarce act assassin for the Earl Robert. Go all the way to Danzig . . ."

"He could have been bound for Danzig and this great Crusading gathering anyway. Robert is ever well-informed. If he learned of it, what more simple than to send a secret courier to Carlisle and suggest this? After all, Robert was with the western array when Sir Will and Clifford exchanged words. He knew Clifford would bear resentment — and was a craven into the bargain. The man he needed."

It was all possible, certainly — but somehow even Jamie, loathing Robert Stewart as he did, could not quite bring himself to believe it.

"You have not taxed him with it? The Governor?" he asked.

"What use in that? He would deny it, and we could prove

235

nothing. And then he would be the more on guard against us, menacing us the more."

"On his guard . . .?"

"You do not think that we shall not seek our vengeance? And rely on *your* help to gain it, Jamie!"

He shook his head. "Do we not need proof before we seek vengeance? You say yourself that you could prove nothing. And your brother is not the man to leave proofs lying for folk to find. Since Otterburn I have managed to learn nothing, of either Bickerton or Ramsay. No single word. My lord Governor is a clever man, and if he is also what we fear he will not easily be discovered. Not that I can credit this of Clifford and Sir Will . . ."

"Why do you say that?" Gelis demanded. "You believe that he planned the Earl James's death. If he can murder one good-brother, he can murder two. Three, indeed, perhaps . . ."

"Three?"

"It could be. Not good-brother, but brother itself. He could have slain David. David of Strathearn."

"Oh, no . . .!"

"Why not? None knows of what David died. He ailed and died suddenly, without warning. His wife believes that it was poison. Who should poison David of Strathearn? He was a gentle man, without enemies. Who, then, gained from his death? Only Robert. He immediately took the child Euphemia into his own guardianship, and has now married her, bairn as she is, to his own vassal Patrick Graham. So he has the great earldom of Strathearn firmly in his hands — to add to the others. I say that we are dealing with Satan Incarnate!"

Jamie looked from one to the other of the women. This seemed to him to be a sort of hysteria — no doubt caused by Gelis's pregnant state, allied to shock over her husband's death. But Isabel nodded grimly. Mary shook her head, and half-shrugged. He sighed.

"I do not know. We cannot tell. We would be wise, I think, not to seek to go too far, or too fast, in this. All is but supposition, see you. We should hold to our course meantime, I say. Bide our time. Make no rash moves, to give him cause to suspect us . . ."

"What do you conceive us to be doing, Jamie?" Isabel was almost sharp with him. "Why are we living under this roof? Why did we sit at his table, eating his meat which all but choked us? Is that rash, unwise? Think you we need telling that we deal with a viper?"

"Forgive me. I spoke unthinkingly, Princess." Abruptly he sought to change the subject. "Lady Gelis — how shall you do now?" he asked. "Where live? How contrive your affairs? If there is aught that I can do to aid you . . .?"

"I may need call on you yet, Jamie. Meantime, I shall contrive by learning from Isabel. Who has trod this road before me! At least I will have this child." She patted her stomach. "Will's child. In this, to be sure, I am blest. I have the young William, also. For though he is bastard, he is Will's son likewise, and a proper child. I shall continue to rear him, as Will would have wished. And one day, perhaps, one or both will avenge their father!"

Jamie had nothing to say to that.

*　　*　　*

Jamie Douglas would have preferred not to remain at Dunfermline Palace for long. The atmosphere he found little to his taste. It was impossible to avoid the Earl Robert's presence entirely, and that self-contained individual, although he did not actually order the young man to leave, left him in no doubt that his company was not welcome. The quite large entourage which attached itself to the Governor — it could hardly be called a Court, since he seemed to exist quite independently of it, indeed ignored it most of the time — took its cue from him nevertheless, and in the main treated Jamie as a sort of leper. Only in the princesses' quarters was he welcome — but these were so poor and restricted that he found lodging, amongst the men-at-arms, in the little town. Moreover, the King was very ill, and this produced its own sombre but tense reaction — for all recognised that the end could not be very far off, and that there were bound to be great and fundamental, not to say alarming, changes in the state of affairs in Scotland thereafter. What would happen in the new reign was anybody's guess — but Lady Gelis at least was convinced that Robert Stewart would seek the death of the Earl John and so gain the Crown for himself. Indeed so sure was she of this that she sent off one of the Tantallon men as messenger to Turnberry, to warn her eldest brother of his danger.

Had it not been that the princesses urged him to stay, Jamie would have been off in a day or two, about business of his own.

But to get away from the palace and its hostile aura for a little, he decided to pay a visit to the barony and lairdship his father had so generously settled on him — Aberdour. He had been there only once before, content to enjoy its modest revenues from afar. But this seemed a suitable opportunity to inspect it, especially as there was an old-standing dispute anent certain revenues connected with it and the Abbot of Inchcolm, which would be better cleared up if he could discover the facts. Since Aberdour lay only some seven miles to the east, along the Fife coast, he suggested that it would make a pleasant excursion on a warm August day for the Stewart ladies, a break from the palace and its strains. But Gelis decided that in her condition she could not risk horse-riding; and Isabel, after agreeing to go, the previous night, announced that her royal father's state of health that morning was such that she ought not to leave his side. Mary, however, appeared to have no such scruples, and said that she at least would keep Jamie company. He, as usual, was uncertain if this was altogether wise; but he could hardly refuse her, especially as Gelis decided that her half-sister and companion deserved an outing and that it would do her good.

So, seeing no need for an escort in the circumstances, they left Jamie's own tail of ten behind, to trot off companionably through the pleasing and fertile Fothrif countryside, well-tended church-lands in the main, by Pitreavie and Letham to the sea at Doni-bristle, and so along the scalloped shoreline of reefs and skerries and headlands, linked by sandy small bays. It was a day of heat-haze and little colour, with the Forth's islands seeming to float in flattened outline above the surface of the gently-lapping sea. Jamie pointed out Inchcolm, the closest inshore of these islands, on this north side, as the site of the abbey whose abbot was in some way involved in the controversy over revenues — though he was unsure of the details. Mary declared that she had met the Abbot of Inchcolm, and liked him little — he lived most of the time, it seemed, not at his island monastery, but in some style, with his crony the mitred Abbot of Dunfermline, two princes of Holy Church. They could see the square tower of the abbey, for the island was only a mile off shore from Braefoot Point of Dalgety Bay.

Mary Stewart appeared encouragingly concerned about his revenues from the Aberdour barony, asking sundry businesslike not to say searching questions such as he had scarcely expected from a young woman, especially one of the King's bastards.

They came, just before noon, round a long and broken headland of skerries and low crags, to a wider and more open bay than that of Dalgety, or rather to twin bays separated by a grassy tongue — though not quite twins either since, oddly enough, that to the west had a golden strand and that to the east a silver. White sands are highly unusual on the east coast of Scotland, however common on the west, and this of Aberdour was renowned, Mary duly admiring it. Behind the strands, on the higher ground but under the green Cullalo Hills, towered the quite massive square keep of a medium-sized castle, with nearby on one side a circular stone doocot and on the other the gables and traceried windows of a fair-sized chapel.

"So that is your inheritance, my lord of Aberdour!" the girl said.

"A small barony, much neglected," he admitted. "But . . . it might be restored and improved."

"What I was thinking my own self," she agreed.

Aberdour Castle, on closer approach, proved to be a tall and fairly rude oblong tower of four storeys and a garret, its thick walls surmounted by a parapet and wall-walk, rising to the east of a courtyard with subsidiary lean-to buildings, all on an eminence above the Dour Burn — and in a poorer state of repair than had appeared from a distance. The steward, whom they found ensconced in what had been the priest's house of the chapel of St. Fillan, was apologetic. The place was not in good order, no — but his instructions from my lord of Dalkeith had been to spend as little upon it as might be and send all possible monies accruing to Dalkeith for the young master's benefit. The young master conceded, rather shamefacedly, that he had indeed been glad to accept all revenues thus produced, without any great enquiry as to how obtained. The responsibility undoubtedly was his. He asked what, in fact, these revenues of his comprised?

The steward, who seemed an honest if somewhat garrulous individual, revealed that the rents of the farmeries and holdings, plus the multures of two mills and the salmon fisheries and harbour dues — all received in kind, of course, but sold for the best prices obtainable at Dunfermline market — constituted the main revenues. But the oyster-fishing in Whitesands Bay was becoming increasingly valuable, and accounted for the slow but steady rise of the late years. If only half of it all was not having to be handed over to the Abbot of Inchcolm each quarter, the barony's affairs could be said to be in a reasonably healthy state. But Holy Church was hard, hard, to the last groat, ever at him . . .

It was Mary who interrupted him. "I have met the Abbot of Inchcolm, and like him but little," she said. "What is this matter in dispute?"

Like a flood released the complaint poured out. "It is a right iniquity, lady," the steward said earnestly. "An auld story, but nane the less ill, for a' that. It was forty years back, when my grandsire was steward here. This barony then was the Mortimers'. You'll mind, sir, this was before your faither's faither bought it. The Lord Alan de Mortimer was the last o' his line. His son died before him, leaving but a lassie. Years before he died, with the son still living, he gave a bit charter to the Abbot o' Inchcolm yonder, leaving him a moiety o' the revenues o' the parish o' Dalgety — o' which this barony is the main portion — on condition that he and his heirs and successors should be given place o' burial before the high altar o' the abbey church o' Saint Colm yonder . . ."

"And were they?"

"They were not, lady. The son was killed in foreign wars, his corss God kens where. And when the Lord Alan died, in 1350 it was, and his corss in its coffin o' lead was being ferried oot yonder to the island, some o' thae ill-disposed and black-hearted monks tipped it oot, over the side, to sink in the sea." The steward's stubby finger pointed south-westwards across the bay. "See you yon bit, between Braefit Point and the island? Yon's still ca'd Mortimer's Deep, and nae fishermen will net there, by God!"

"But why, man? Why throw the body out?" Jamie demanded.

"Why? For that they wanted the jewels and gold to be buried wi' the corss. A gold belt he wore, they said. And his lady's jewelled crucifix. None kenned then — but one o' the oarers told o' it a year after. He was one o' thae serving brothers, and was put out o' the abbey for some trouble wi' the abbot. He told the Lord Alan's daughter, and she found another oarer to vouch for it. But the Abbot denied it, would hae nane o' it. On oath . . ."

"So you are saying that the conditions of the charter are unfulfilled and therefore void?" Mary took him up eagerly.

"Neither this Alan nor his heir were buried in the church, and there were no other Mortimers? So the grant of this — what did you name it? Moiety, yes. This moiety should not have to be paid?"

"Aye, lady — you have it. And a moiety is a full half, mind! The Lady Jean Mortimer said then, and we have aye said since, that nae moiety is due, and the charter forfeit."

"The monks must do more than just deny it, surely?" Jamie said. "If the body is not in the sea, where is it?"

"Och, they say it's in its place, right enough. In its bit coffin in the kirk. Under yon muckle slab. They've aye said that . . ."

"You mean buried?"

"No' just buried, no. There's a bit arch in the wa', up in the choir. To the side o' the altar. A stone coffin, just, wi' this muckle slab o' stone carved like a knight lying on top. The Lord Alan had it carved for himsel'. They say that the corss is in there—as it should be. I say it's no'. Nor the gold or the geegaws."

"Then here's a simple matter," Mary declared, laughing. "Let us go and see. Out to the island. Look under this slab, this stone effigy. If the bones are there, and the jewellery, we are satisfied, and you continue to pay your moiety, Sir James. If not, then you know where you stand."

"Och, they'd no' let you, lady—they would not. No' in the kirk . . ."

"Why not? Sir James, here, is the lord of this barony of Aberdour. That barony has long been paying large dues for right of sepulture in the abbey church. The barony has surely the right to inspect its leasehold! He could be concerned for his own future burial! What say you, Jamie?"

He grinned. "It seems an excellent ploy to me. And perchance profitable I confess, I'd not have thought of it. But since *you* have . . ." He turned to the steward. "Can you find us a boat to take us out to the island?"

"I can that, sir. My ain bit boat's doon at the haven. It's a fine flat sea. I'll oar you oot mysel', wi' my son. Aye, wi' pleasure, sir. God kens, I'm sweer to see under yon slab!"

So, leaving the horses, they strolled down to the little harbour, the steward's husky son, Tom Durie, about Jamie's age, less tall but more heavily built, hurrying after. Mary was in great spirits and holiday mood, finding it all a pleasing adventure. Steward

Durie and his son were clearly much more impressed by her than by their new-found laird.

The row out in the small boat was enjoyable — although undoubtedly it could be much otherwise in different conditions, Inchcolm often being stormbound it seemed. The two Fifers pulled strongly, scattering the rafts of crooning eiders and sending sooty scoters scuttering off right and left, patterning the glassy surface with their busy feet. Further out, gannets from the Bass Rock were diving hugely for fish, dropping from great heights with uncanny accuracy, masters of air and water both.

As they neared it, Inchcolm proved to be a fairly rocky island about half-a-mile in length, cliff-bound to the east, green to the west, kidney-shaped, the two halves all but separated by a low isthmus — over which, the steward said, the winter seas often surged, making it two islands indeed. The abbey, with its church, monastic buildings, chapterhouse, outhouses, farmery and gardens and even small patchwork fields, was on the western and lower half.

There was a jetty at the isthmus, where they landed, watched idly by two serving-brothers in their black Augustinian robes as they fished from nearby rocks. Mary skipped ashore gleefully, with skirts kilted up.

"They will not put me off, a woman, from this so holy island, will they?" she wondered. "They will have to carry me, screaming, if they do."

"I think it will not come to that," Jamie told her. "I would have my knightly and baronial say, first!"

Even mock-anxiety was unnecessary, however; for having climbed the track from pier to abbey gatehouse, and passed the untended porter's lodge, all seeming to sleep in the warmth of the August mid-day, the first person they saw was a woman, who answered their continued knocking at a door — and a cheerful, plump and bold-eyed woman at that, far from over-dressed above the waist and as approximately monastic-seeming as was Mary Stewart.

"We seek the Abbot of this place, mistress," Jamie said. "I am Sir James Douglas of Aberdour and this is my steward."

"Hech, hech — the laird, is it?" she exclaimed, with a whinnying laugh and a sketched curtsey. "Braw, young sir, braw! As the lady'll no' contest, I jalouse!" Another laugh. "Auld Durie I

242

ken — aye, and young Durie something better! Eh, lad?" That was added with a chuckle that sounded significant, and set the young man flushing. "But you'll no' find the Lord Abbot here, young sir — Durie could ha' tell't you that. It's Dunfermline toun for the likes o' him. But I could bring you to Master Ramsay, the Prior, if that will serve your Honour?"

"*Ramsay*, you say?" He paused. "Yes, mistress — the Prior will do very well. I thank you."

She led them through a succession of rooms and along corridors, rich with smells of cooking, stacked with victuals, stores, wines and the like. In the large refectory, set for a meal, two elderly monks dozed. In the inner courtyard, surrounded by the arcaded cloister-walk, with a fountain playing in the midst, a portly man sat in a chair beside it, open-mouthed and fast asleep.

"Father Prior!" the woman declared, gesturing. She strode forward, to shake the sleeper vigorously. "Wake up, wake up!" she cried, with scant deference. "Here's no way to greet the quality, I declare. The young laird o' Aberdour, nae less. And a bonny leddy, forby. Aye, and auld Durie, the big stot . . .!"

"Eh? Eh?" The stout cleric started up in alarm. "A mercy . . .!"

"Do not fret yourself, Master Prior," Jamie soothed. "It is a hot day, and we intrude. I am James Douglas, seeking your aid. But hurry there is none."

"Ah. Yes. To be sure, Sir James. It is . . . we are honoured. In this poor house. If you had sent me word . . ."

"No need for that. Since I seek only a very small service. I wish to see my barony's burial-place in your church. That is all."

"Oh!" Prior Ramsay had a face rather like a seal; and now the round eyes popped even more prominently. "Burial-place . . .?" he faltered.

"Yes. Burial, interment, sepulture — name it what you will. In the choir of the abbey-church here. We would inspect it."

"But . . . sir, my lord — that is *Mortimer's* tomb. Sir Alan de Mortimer. Scarce yours . . ."

"It was paid for, and still is being paid for, out of the revenues of my barony of Aberdour, Master Prior. It was Mortimer's once — but it is Douglas's now. Or would you have me to withdraw my revenues?"

"Ah no, sir — no! Not that. Not to be thought of. But — this is a matter for the Lord Abbot, not for me. I have no authority . . ."

"Then I shall speak with your Abbot — later. But now we are here, we will see the tomb."

"Not now, Sir James — not now. See the Lord Abbot, first. At Dunfermline . . ."

"I shall do no such thing. We have come out to this island, and we shall see what I have been paying for. A moiety of my barony revenues, no less. You say that you have no authority to discuss the issue — therefore you have no authority to prevent me from seeing it, either. Do you take us there, Master Prior—or do we go look for ourselves?"

Muttering, the stout man girdled his robe about him and led the way across the courtyard to the north side, where rose the church, with its tall square battlemented tower. Church and monastery had been founded by Alexander I in 1123, when he had been driven ashore here in a storm whilst crossing Queen Margaret's Ferry, and had been forced to shelter for three days and nights, until the gale abated, in the cell of a hermit, living on shellfish and the milk of the Columban anchorite's cow. The King's fright, on this occasion, resulted in this oddly-sited abbey of the Augustinian canons.

Opening the door into the church nave, cool and lofty in pillared stone, Prior Ramsay crossed himself elaborately and spoke in exaggeratedly hushed voice.

"Your lady, Sir James, must abide here, by the door."

Jamie shook his head and refused to whisper. "No, Master Prior — she will remain with us."

"But . . . but it is forbidden, sir. In our Order . . ."

"The woman who led us in would be forbidden to your house by your Order, likewise, I think? Moreover, this lady is the King's own daughter, the Lady Mary Stewart, and she bides at no door in her father's realm!" He promoted her to the title of lady, as though she had been legitimate — and she squeezed his arm.

The cleric's eyes popped again, and he made awkward obeisance. He hurried forward into the church without more ado. The Duries, father and son, looked further impressed.

The chancel or choir, at the east end of the long building, was directly under the tower, up three steps. Here, the feature that they sought was readily apparent. To the left of the altar, inset in the walling, was a wide arched niche or alcove, with the recumbent effigy of a knight in full armour, life-size, shield on breast and sword at side, feet crossed at the ankles to indicate that he had been on Crusade. There was another niche and effigy on the opposite side, likewise, but this was carved in clerical robes with a crozier—an abbot. The Prior, genuflecting towards the altar, pointed.

"The Mortimer tomb, Sir James. And Princess."

"The *Aberdour* tomb," Jamie corrected, stepping forward for closer inspection. "Handsome. But then, it should be, for £150 Scots each year, should it not?"

Their guide murmured something indeterminate.

Jamie stooped to peer at, and then to try to lift the massive sculptured lid — whereat the Prior cried out in agitation, and indeed grabbed the younger man's arm.

"No, no, sir! I pray you — do not touch it."

"Why not? I desire to look inside. I pay for a sepulture, not just an effigy, Sir Prior. I must see its state. Stand back."

"No, Sir James — no! This is sacrilege! The property of Holy Church. You may not touch it. Without, without my Lord Abbot's permission. None may."

"Has he ordered so, Master Prior? The Abbot?"

"Yes. Yes, indeed."

"Why should he do that, tell me? Did he guess that someone would come looking? Or is he afraid of what maybe found therein?"

"No, no, sir. But all within the choir is holy, sacrosanct. Not to be touched by unconsecrated hands . . ."

"*You* will help me lift this stone cover then, Prior. Moreover, my hands are consecrated after a fashion, for I have taken knightly vows. You will not deny the validity of the knightly order?"

"No. But . . . I cannot, I cannot, sir. Cannot permit this." The cleric turned away, however, to go kneel before the altar, wringing his plump hands.

Jamie, ignoring him, jerked his head at the Duries, and nothing loth, they also stooped to help him lift the massive lid. But though it moved slightly, their fingers could gain insufficient purchase. Only a narrow crack appeared beneath, and closed again as their pressure relaxed.

"We need bars. Of iron. It would snap my dirk-blade . . ."

"Spades," young Durie suggested. "They hae a graveyard here. They'll hae spades."

"Go find some, then."

"No-o-o!" That came in a groan from the altar, as the Duries hurried out.

"Do not distress yourself, Sir Prior," Mary said, soothingly. "We will do no hurt to anything. Merely raise this slab and look inside. See the state of the, the remains. See what space remains. We shall replace all as it was."

The other burst into gabbled Latinities.

The Duries came back with two spades. Also two serving-brothers, whom they had evidently recruited, and who gaped at all, and crossed themselves for safety's sake.

"Ah — helpers," Jamie greeted them. "Come, friends — aid us with this lid."

"You will not! I forbid it!" Prior Ramsay exclaimed, turning his head though still on his knees. "I . . . I . . ." He seemed as though he might be considering more drastic commands, but thought better of it, and returned to the comforts of Latin.

"You lift, all," Mary said, taking one of the spades. "I will put the blades in."

The three men stooped to their task, and into the opening crack between lid and coffin the young woman deftly slipped the spades. Then, with the leverage, it was a simple matter to raise the effigy-carved cover. Save for some scuttling spiders, the space beneath was entirely empty.

"What did I say!" old Durie exclaimed. "Nae corss. Nae gold nor jewels either. Nor ever has been. Devil-damned monks!"

"Sir Prior — come you here and see this emptiness. You others likewise — as witnesses!" Jamie invited. "Neither Sir Alan de Mortimer nor his gold is here. As we feared."

Ramsay held back. "It . . . it is long," he quavered. "Many years. Half a century. All has decayed away. Dust, no more. Dust and ashes. *Requiescat in pace*."

"There is not even dust here, man. And bones do not decay away, in a dry place, in fifty years or a hundred. Nor do gold and jewels! Mortimer is not here, nor ever was, I vow. Tipped into the sea, in Mortimer's Deep, and his golden belt and crucifix stolen. Douglas has been paying for a fraud for thirty years!"

The cleric was up and plucking at his lower lip now. "I know

246

nothing of this," he protested. "I have been here but eight years. My Lord Abbot but a dozen. There has been some mischance . . ."

"Mischance, yes. One does not cozen Douglas, with impunity! Even Holy Church! This mischance will fall to be righted."

"Thirty times £150 is a notable mischance!" Mary observed, judicially. "I make it £4,500 — although, it may be my summing is wrong? And the Lady Mortimer's heirs, before that, may be interested!"

The Prior let out a strangled wail. "Saint Colm and Saint Bridget — save us! Saint Augustine, our founder, protect us, come to our aid! Mary Mother of God, hear us — for we are a poor and humble house, lacking in the world's gear . . . !"

"You say so, sir? I have seen no sign of it," Jamie told him. "I think you prosper most genially, on this isle. And will scarce notice the loss of my £150 each year."

"Ah, no, sir. You have not seen. Broke buildings. The wreckage of storms. Timbers wormed. Dykes fallen. Salt winds killing the apples . . ."

"Then if you are so poor, where do all the revenues go? Mine, with the rest? Perhaps your Abbot, in his fine town-house in Dunfermline, could tell us? And will! Now, we shall leave you, Master Prior, and return to that good town." Jamie paused. "But before we go, I have a small matter to ask of you . . ."

"Anything, sir — anything!" the other said earnestly. "Our poor house is at your service. And the Princess's. If you will tell my Lord Abbot that I, that I . . ."

"Sought to prevent us from looking into yonder tomb, sir? Surely, I shall tell him so, never fear. But my question is this. I think that I heard that your name is Ramsay?"

"Indeed yes, sir. Joseph Ramsay."

"I am interested in the name of Ramsay, Prior Joseph. And it is no common one in these parts. The Ramsays of Dalwolsey are renowned. In Lothian, not far from my father's house. But few others, I think, save at Waughton near to Haddington, vassals of Lindsay . . ."

"Waughton is the line I come of, Sir James. An old house, somewhat decayed, but honourable. Ramsay of Waughton is my cousin-german."

"Ah — he is? Then, Master Ramsay, perhaps you can give me tidings of his son Patrick, my one-time companion-in-arms?

We fought side-by-side at Otterburn. I have been seeking him . . ."

"Pate? You know young Pate, Sir James? A good lad, a fine lad — if headstrong a little, perhaps. But no ill to him. And like to do great things. He was here, to be sure, not long since . . ."

"Here? Pate Ramsay — on Inchcolm? Do not tell me that he was thinking to turn monk — that one!"

"No, no — the saints forbid! He was but biding here a while, with me his father's cousin. Lying quiet, I would suspect, after some youthful escapade! He did not confide in me—but he is a spirited lad. As you will know."

"Spirited, yes. That is true. So he was here? Small wonder I could not find him! And now — he is gone again?"

"Yes. Near a month now."

"But not home. There was no word of him at Waughton."

"No. I think that he headed into the north. The Highlands. On great affairs." That last was said with a sort of knowing pride.

"Great affairs? Patrick Ramsay?"

"To be sure. We Ramsays are well thought of, see you." The cleric nodded portentously. "Twice whilst he was here, on the island, he went to Falkland. Twice. Aye, and once to St. Andrews . . ."

"To Falkland! Why? Did he say why?"

"Falkland is my brother Robert's house," Mary mentioned. "But — a town, besides."

"Yes, Princess—the Governor's castle. What he did there, he did not say. Some privy matter." The Prior sighed, clearly regretful. "But he was concerned in some ploy, I swear. For he had money to spend — as I have never known him to have. And a fine horse he came back with. He stabled it with this Durie." The steward nodded confirmation. "Good new clothes, besides . . ."

"I see. So whatever he did at Falkland, whoever he saw, it was profitable."

"Profitable and important, yes. And at St. Andrews, he went to the castle, I do know — the Bishop's castle."

"M'mmm. You think, on the same ploy?"

"Belike. He went to St. Andrews between the two visits to Falkland."

"But it was not to Falkland nor St. Andrews that he went,

248

finally? You said that he headed northwards. Into the Highlands."

"North, yes. He told me that he was travelling on a long journey. That he required good horseflesh. Much siller. And a sharp dirk — for he was going amongst Hielant savages."

"He had ever a sharp dirk! But ... amongst Highlandmen? For why?"

"He would not say, Sir James. Save that he would do well out of it. For he conceived the Bishop more generous than the Earl Robert! That is all he said."

"He said that? Generous. The Bishop? And he *named* the Earl Robert, in this? The Bishop of St. Andrews, he meant?"

"I cannot tell what he meant, sir. Or which bishop. He would tell me no more."

Jamie and Mary exchanged glances, hers distinctly mystified.

Try as he would, the young man could get no more out of the Prior. Ramsay was, in fact, a simple man, not notably intelligent; and almost certainly all that he knew had been wormed out of him.

They left the abbey, then, amidst pleas to be merciful, generous, understanding, to be good and faithful members of Holy Church, and to think well of the future of their immortal souls.

They went back down to the jetty. But there, as the Duries were preparing to aid them into their boat, Mary demurred.

"The day is young yet," she pointed out. "Whilst we are here, I would wish to see the rest of the island. Who knows, I may never be here again. Our friends can wait. Fish, or sleep, or row back to Aberdour, and then return for us. No? And we shall make a round of this rock in the silver sea, and discover its secrets. I have ever had a notion for islands."

Jamie found nothing really wrong with this suggestion; and old Durie said that he and his son would go back to the mainland and return in two or three hours with a flagon of wine, some cold fowl and bannocks with honey. The two monkish fishermen were still where they had left them.

As they strolled off southwards to climb the quite steep ascent to the modest clifftops, the girl took Jamie's arm.

"It has been an interesting day, has it not?" she said. "Is it always thus when Jamie Douglas takes the air?"

"I would say that *you* it is who gave the day its spice," he told her. "I would not have thought of coming out to this island to see that tomb."

"No. You do not care greatly for such things, do you, Jamie — moneys, revenues? For gear and goods. But they are important, also. We Stewarts are perhaps over-well aware of that! But if you will not look to your own interests, someone else must! We have made a start today. You must keep it up, see you."

"You mean in refusing to pay this wretched Abbot of Inchcolm his £150 each year? I shall certainly pay no more of that. So that I shall be that much the richer. For which I have to thank only you . . ."

"I mean far more than that, Jamie Douglas. That is a mere nothing, as I see it — although it may double your yearly revenue. I was not wholly playing the foolish woman with that fat Prior when I spoke of thirty years of wrongful payments. I say that you must claim back from the Church your due moneys. Scarce the total, of course — I cannot conceive of you winning £4,500 from the coffers of Holy Church. But a large sum should be demanded, nevertheless. For false assessment. In amends and repayment. We will have Sir Jamie Douglas a rich man, yet! Although I suppose that your father might claim some of it?"

"Lord — this is folly, Mary!" he protested. "You dream! £4,500 is a fortune . . ."

"Yes. Are you not fortunate, then? But I must warn you, Sir Knight — you will become the target for scheming women! With all that in your coffers, they will be after you, like wasps round ripe fruit! Even, perhaps, king's daughters!"

"Oh!" he said, looking at her sidelong. "I . . . ah . . . umm."

"Yes. So you are warned, my friend. Once more! Keep all such at arm's length — and keep your siller to yourself!"

He conjured up a laugh. "The warning I note. But the need I doubt. For this I swear — I will get no penny of your £4,500 out of Holy Church. None can hold on to their siller better than the churchmen. This Abbot will scorn me. I can hold back the £150 each year — although they will try to gain that, too. But to get money *from* them — never! You do not know churchmen, I think!"

"Which is where you are much wrong, Jamie. I do. Notably

one. *I* think that you have not considered this as closely as I have done, in my so feeble woman's head! Inchcolm Abbey has its Abbot, yes. Who is no doubt all that we say. But he is not supreme. Inchcolm, and Dunfermline Abbey likewise, come under the supreme authority of the metropolitan diocese of St. Andrews, the greatest and wealthiest see in the land. And who is in charge of the revenues and moneys of that diocese? The Archdeacon. And who is Archdeacon of St. Andrews, and right-hand of the Primate-Bishop? Who but my own favourite brother, *full* brother, son of both my mother and my father, Thomas Stewart! You have it now?"

He whistled soundlessly.

"So very soon we shall go and see Master Thomas. I would have wished to go, anyhow. He will not come to Dunfermline, I think, for he does not love Robert and keeps his distance."

"But ... but ... even so, Mary, the Church will not pay out large moneys. However much your brother may regard you. Bishop Trail, the Primate, will have other notions."

"Perhaps. But even Bishop Trail will not wish to offend too greatly the Lord of Dalkeith's son. Nor his Archdeacon, the King's bastard. He will, I think, wish to seem at least fair. Moreover, we have a strong card to play. In that gold belt and crucifix amissing. Theft by fraud Holy Church may belittle — when done by itself. Theft by secret stealing is another matter. They will wish this kept quiet, I swear — and must needs pay for it!"

He gazed at her, astonished, part-admiring, part-askance.

"So, you see — those riches may be within your grasp, Laird of Aberdour."

"I do not know what to say," he got out. "To you. Who have contrived all this. Whether to thank you, or, or ..." He swallowed. "None other that I know could have done it, that is certain sure."

"There you are wrong, Jamie. Many others could — made otherwise than yourself! However, let us agree that neither of my sisters Isabel nor Gelis could. For this is not princess's work — despite the title which you gave me to yonder Prior! Mind it. And do not thank me until you hear that siller jingling in your pouch." She pointed, with her free hand. "Now, since climbing cliffs and teaching high-minded knights their business is tiring work, I suggest that we go sit on yon grassy shelf for a space.

251

Watch the gannets dive. We have earned a rest, have we not?"

He could not deny that. Just below the cliff-edge there was a ledge above the sheer drop to the waves, and here, between sea and sky, they sat themselves down. The ledge was deep enough for safety, but sufficiently constricted by ribs of rock that they must sit close together. It was very warm, such breeze as there was, from the west, not penetrating here where they faced east, down Forth. Mary threw off her riding-doublet, and after a little, the man did likewise.

"This of St. Andrews," he said. "Why did Patrick Ramsay go to St. Andrews?"

"Do not ask me," she told him. "I did not understand all of that. What you were at, seeking out. This Ramsay was the man who stabbed Bickerton, was it not?"

"Yes. He came here to hide, it seems — and an excellent place. But from here he made these visits to Falkland and St. Andrews. Falkland I can understand — since I conceive him to be in the pay of the Governor. But St. Andrews . . .?"

"Perhaps Thomas may be able to tell us. Save that, if this Ramsay was on Robert's business, Thomas would be unlikely to be concerned."

"It is all most strange. This of going on a long journey, into the Highlands. Why? And talk of a bishop. The Bishop, he conceived, might be more generous than the Earl Robert, he said. Is this Bishop Trail, the Primate? Although, as the Prior said it, I thought it more as though the bishop he referred to was in the Highlands. Where he was going. Did not you?"

She shrugged. "I do not know. See you that gannet? The splash it made. They are very large birds . . ."

"Yes, yes. But this bishop. It is important, Mary. You must see it . . ."

"Perhaps, Jamie. But . . . none of it was very clear to me. Did you reckon that it meant so much?"

"Would that I knew what it meant! For I would seek out that Ramsay to the uttermost end of Scotland! Is he indeed in the Earl Robert's service? If so, why send him into the Highlands? Since it seems that somebody did — with money, new clothes and a fine horse. And a bishop at the end of it, perhaps? There are none so many bishops north of the Highland Line. Moray, Ross, Argyll and the Isles. These three, since Caithness and Orkney are scarce Highland. Argyll is west, not north. So we have Moray and Ross. Ross is far away. Moray, then? What might the Governor want of the Bishop of Moray that he must needs send such as Pate Ramsay as messenger?"

"Who knows? Such a great edifice to build out of so little, Jamie." Mary did not sound very interested. "How do the gannets dive on moving fish? From so great a height? Surely the fish will have swum on . . .?"

"I know not. It is a wonder. But — this of Ramsay. The secret, I think, must lie at St. Andrews. We shall learn nothing at Falkland or Dunfermline, I swear. But at St. Andrews . . ."

"Very well. We shall go to St. Andrews, and soon. As I said. But, now . . ." She yawned prettily, and leaning back, closed her eyes.

At least he had the sense not to go on. He watched the gannets, and gradually the frown of concentration eased from his dark brow. A vessel under full sail was tacking up-Firth between Inchcolm and Inchkeith.

Presently, with no further remark from Mary, he turned to look at her. She lay back, one firmly-rounded arm outflung towards him, fingers loosely curled, eyes closed, lips slightly parted. She breathed softly, regularly, flushed with the sun, tiny beads of perspiration on brow and upper lip. And as he had been all but overwhelmed, the first evening at Dunfermline, by her vital femininity, now, in a rush he was again by her naturalness, her frank unconcern, her seeming trusting helplessness there at his side. She appeared to have dropped straight off to sleep, uncaring for his presence. The linen bodice she wore under her doublet was part open, and anyway did little to hide the full shapeliness of her person.

Leaning on one elbow, he considered her, rather ashamedly at first, as though somehow he stole what he should not. But most clearly she had cared little in this respect, or she would not have lain back thus. So perhaps he was entitled to his gazing. Whether he was or not, he gazed his fill, something he had never done nor had had opportunity to do before with any woman, watching the gentle movement of her breathing, the rhythmic rise and fall of the rounded bosom, the faint pulse beating in the hollow of her throat, the sweep of eyelashes on cheek, the tiny occasional twitchings at the tip of her nose. He was strangely moved, as well as physically stirred.

Indeed, he was more moved and stirred than he realised. For without actually being aware of it, he had moved ever closer to her, identifying with the warm vitality of her, until his face was close enough to the girl's to feel the regular little puffs of her breath against his skin — and found it a delight.

Then, suddenly, her eyes were open and she was gazing into his own, long, steadily, untroubled, until most naturally her hand came up and gently pressed down the back of his head so that his mouth bore down on her own. Their lips met and gradually stirred, then became eager, questing.

"Jamie! Jamie!" she murmured into his mouth. "It has taken you long, long!"

He did not now waste time nor breath nor tongue in answering her, not in words, at least. His hands found employment to match his lips and he all but sobbed at the rich feel of firm breasts and the thrust of hard nipples. Her arms were round him now and holding him fast — and despite his ever-present doubts, it was all the most natural development in the world.

It continued that way, and the August afternoon stood still for them.

When at length they reluctantly moved on from that ledge on Inchcolm's cliff, it was hand-in-hand, slowly, in a companionable silence. Now and again they smiled to each other, that was all.

The Duries had to wait longer than they expected for their passengers.

XVI

JAMIE HAD HIS interview with the Abbot of Inchcolm Master John Dersy, two days later, in much finer quarters than the princesses occupied, in a wing of Dunfermline Abbey, to which the Abbot had just returned, hawk on wrist — and as the younger man had anticipated, got little or nowhere with the smoothly arrogant prelate. He admitted nothing, conceded no whit, deplored Sir James's sacrilegious descent upon his abbey without his permission, declared the revenues of Holy Church inviolate and scoffed at any suggestion of compensation. Jamie kept his temper, stated his case clearly, made no threats. He did declare, however, that the Aberdour-Dalgety moiety would no longer be paid. The Abbot pronounced this to be unthinkable, impossible, and murmured about higher authority and the dire penalties which the Church could impose against its intractable sons. On that note the interview ended.

A few days thereafter they rode to St. Andrews, quite a major journey of nearly forty miles, across Fife from south-west to north-east. The old King had rallied again somewhat meantime, and the Lady Isabel decided that on this occasion she might accompany Jamie — and indicated that, in the circumstances, there was really no need for Mary to go, since she could equally well make all necessary representations to the Archdeacon Thomas, her brother also. But Mary was determined, and since she was Gelis's lady-in-waiting, not Isabel's, she found no call to accede — especially as Gelis encouraged her, for some reason. Jamie was uncertain whether to be disappointed or relieved — anyway, he had no least say in the matter.

The weather was less kind to them, being dull and grey; but it did not rain and they made good time riding across hilly Fothrif and the fertile Howe of Fife, this time with an escort befitting a princess. Once they were started, the two half-sisters were good enough friends, and Jamie rode between them without the feared discomfort and with only occasional pangs of disloyalty when he found himself riding sufficiently close to rub knees with Mary rather than with his mistress the Countess-Dowager. Moreover she was, he reminded himself, the wife of Sir John Edmonstone, after all.

The journey took them most of the day, and an early evening sun came out at their backs to light up the spires and towers and pinnacles of the ecclesiastical city on the edge of the restless sea, the wide ocean here and no longer the Firth of Forth. It seemed a fair place as they gazed down from the heights of Magus Muir, with a host of proud and prominent buildings, the great cathedral and Bishop's castle dominating all. There were literally scores of religious edifices in this the ecclesiastical metropolis of Scotland, churches, chapels, priories, monasteries, nunneries, seminaries, hospices, colleges and shrines, with a large population to staff and support them. Here the Primate, Bishop Walter Trail, held sway, every second man in the street was monk or priest, and the sound of chiming bells was seldom absent.

It was a walled town, and the travellers hastened to win through the gates before they might close at sunset. Within, the main streets were broader than in most cities — although there were narrow wynds and lanes between — and the buildings of consistently superior architecture. This was a community where wealth was not in short supply.

The castle stood above the shore on a small cliff, many-towered in warm red sandstone. They had some difficulty in getting past the porter's lodge and gatehouse, for Bishop Trail was from home and the Archdeacon was, it seemed, out hunting still on Tent's Muir. However, identities were established and they were allowed inside; and soon afterwards Master Thomas Stewart and a cheerful, notably unclerical-seeming company arrived, all hooded hawks and slavering, tired hounds, loud in praise of an excellent day's sport.

Jamie was surprised to find Thomas Stewart a young man, only a few years older than himself. He had assumed that to be an archdeacon would require more mature years, forgetting that this was Mary's full brother and therefore likely to be not so very different in age. He was good-looking, stylish, with no hint of the ecclesiastic about him, in dress or manner. He welcomed his sisters warmly and Jamie genially.

A deal better fed than they would have been at Dunfermline, at length they found themselves alone with their host in the east tower of the castle. Mary wasted no time in introducing the subject of the Inchcolm tomb and payments. Any notion that the Archdeacon Thomas might prove unsympathetic, difficult or even particularly cautious, was quickly dispersed. In fact he shouted with laughter, slapped his knee and appeared to find the entire story much to his taste. He was not, evidently, in the least shocked at the monastic theft, fraud and treatment of the departed, nor was he surprised nor put out by Mary's claim on Jamie's behalf, for compensation for years of moneys paid out under false pretences. Without hesitation he agreed to see what he could do to ease matters along.

Jamie, at least, felt that this was all too easy, too casual altogether, and in consequence little likely to come of it.

"Can this Abbot be made to pay?" he asked. "Unless he can be forced, he certainly will not. He made that very clear to me, even talking of penalties of the Church against me should I persist."

"Ah, I doubt if *you* could make John Dersy pay a groat," the other laughed. "But we here can squeeze him somewhat, in various ways. He is an unpleasant knave and I rejoice at opportunity to bring him down a notch or two. Leave John Dersy to me."

"How much will you get out of him, Thomas? For Jamie?" Mary demanded. "I say it should be a great sum, many hundreds of pounds, thousands indeed. That Abbey has been defrauding the Mortimers and the Douglases for thirty-five years. That is £4,500 mis-spent."

"Sakes — so much! But you were ever greedy, my dear Mary!" her brother accused. "A glutton for what you wanted! I fear that we cannot reach for such great treasure as that. But some solatium we should achieve for you."

"How much?" she insisted. "Do not cozen us, Thomas. How much, think you?"

"A plague, vixen — how may I tell? As yet . . ."

"Sir James should accept no less than £2,000!" Mary asserted crisply.

"Mary . . . !" Isabel exclaimed. "Have you taken leave of your wits?"

Jamie swallowed. No such figure had been mooted. He would never have suggested any such vast sum, and well pleased with a fifth of it. He stirred uncomfortably.

"Heigho — ever the same Mary Stewàrt!" the Archdeacon chuckled. "That would be a mountain of siller, girl! I fear even *our* treasury would look askance at that. What will Sir James do if it is not forthcoming?" That was interested, easily conversational.

"Why, at the next Privy Council, or parliament, one of the Douglas lords, Sir Jamie's father perhaps, could announce the secret theft of gold belt and jewelled crucifix by the canons of Inchcolm and require their restoration, with due penalty and penance by the said abbey. And, to be sure, due solatium, as you call it. Our brother Robert will be anxious to retain the goodwill of Douglas, I think — since he needs it. I say that it would be less expensive for Holy Church to pay now!"

Her sister at least looked shocked. "You cannot threaten and assail Holy Church so, Mary! Like — like some common merchant!"

"I can, and will. Or Sir Jamie can. Why not? The Church is not above the law. And even the Church's law says Thou shalt not steal!"

Her brother shook a rueful head. "You should have been the man, and Archdeacon of St. Andrews, sister!" he said. "I vow you would have set all by the ears! But you, Sir James — I fear for you! With this one at your heels. She requires a strong hand. Are you so equipped? I, for one, never could master her. Who are these great moneys for? You — or Mary? If you let her get a grip on them . . . !"

"Pay no heed to him, Jamie. A brother's blethers. But at least he clearly believes that there will *be* great moneys to be gripped! We will hold him to it. Perhaps you should offer him some small . . . encouragement?"

"Mary — enough!" Isabel commanded. "You have a wicked tongue. Enough of this. I say we should pass to the other matter . . ."

"So long as Thomas remembers to do his utmost — if he would save his Church trouble!" the irrepressible younger woman put in.

"Other matter?" Thomas Stewart groaned elaborately. "Do not tell me that there is more? A further claim on the long-suffering Body of Christ?"

"No. Nothing of that sort," Isabel said. "A more important matter. Which in some measure concerns me also. Concerned with the death of my husband. Jamie will tell you."

"We seek to learn, sir, what one Patrick Ramsay was doing at St. Andrews a month past, or six weeks? When he came here on some . . . ploy."

"Patrick Ramsay, you say? Ramsay? Should I know? Who is he? This is a large town, Sir James, with many folk, much coming and going. Should I have knowledge of this Ramsay?"

"I had hoped that you might, Sir Archdeacon. Or at least

recollect the name. For he came *here*, we are told. To this Bishop's castle. On some seemingly secret mission."

"A month ago? I know no Ramsays, save Neis Ramsay of Banff in Angus. But he has not been here ..."

"A young man, sir. Younger son to Ramsay of Waughton, in Lothian. Biding for a time on St. Colm's Inch. Come here to see the Bishop, we believe ..."

"Ha! St. Colm's Inch, again! I reckon I have you now, yes. A young man came here, some weeks past, from Inchcolm Abbey. Though not from Abbot Dersy, I think. To see Bishop Trail. I had naught to do with it, nor him. Did not know his name. This was your Ramsay?"

"Yes. Do you know, sir, what was his business with the Bishop?"

"M'mm. I do, yes. But that business was, shall we say, privy."

"You cannot tell us? Even some small word of it? It is ... important."

"Important, yes. That is why I am reluctant to speak of it. Save to, to ..." He looked at his sisters.

"Can you speak of it to *us*, Thomas?" Isabel asked. "For if you can, there is naught, I swear, that we would not wish Jamie to hear. He is my very good friend and leal knight. As he was my husband's ..."

"I know how Sir James won his knighthood," her brother nodded. "But — this matter has naught to do with the death of the Earl of Douglas, Isabel."

"Are you sure?" Jamie said. "I think that there may be some link in that ill chain."

Thomas Stewart stared closely at him. "How much do you know, Sir James?" he demanded.

"I saw Bickerton of Luffness, the Earl's armour-bearer, stab my lord in the back at Otterburn — and believe that he was set to do it by someone much more important. We sought to take Bickerton, at Luffness, to make him tell all. But this Ramsay reached him first and slew him before he could talk. Most certainly to close his lips for ever. Murder, of a set purpose. I have been seeking him since, to learn who paid him to do it!"

"We believe that it was our brother Robert," Isabel added factually.

259

The Archdeacon's handsome and mobile features had turned very still, set.

"On Inchcolm we learned that this Ramsay had been hiding there, on the island. After the murder. The Prior is his father's cousin." Jamie went on. "Whilst there he twice visited Falkland — this before the Earl Robert's recent expedition into England. He gained at Falkland money, a good horse, new clothing. And came here to St. Andrews Castle. And then left, to travel North, in the Highlands. Telling his cousin that he believed that the Bishop would be more generous than the Earl Robert!" He paused. "There seems to be proof, therefore, of a link between the Governor and Ramsay. But . . . we need more than that."

Stewart drew a long breath. "What makes you believe that Robert was behind the Earl James Douglas's murder?" he asked. "Even for Robert, it seems a, a long step!"

Isabel answered him. "He misliked James. He had most to gain by his death. Within days he was grasping at James's properties and offices. And he got the power of Douglas into the hands of his friend, Archie of Galloway. Moreover, who else could have done it? Only one or two could, or would. And such we think to have ruled out."

"So-o-o! Robert is a hard and harsh man. But . . ."

"Gelis believes that he also is behind the slaying of *her* husband. In Danzig . . ."

"God's eyes! This is too much . . .!"

"Yes, too much," Mary agreed. "I think that folly. The delusions of a woman stricken and pregnant. Poor Gelis, she has siezed on this. But I say it serves our present quest nothing."

"Aye so would say I. But what *is* your present quest?" her brother asked. "For I cannot see any link between the murder of Earl James and this mission of the man Ramsay to Moray."

"Ha — to Moray!" That was almost a chorus from his three hearers.

Jamie answered him. "We do not seek a link, necessarily. What I seek is Patrick Ramsay. I must see him. Get the truth from him. I have taken a vow on it. Wherever he has gone, I will follow him — to Moray, or further. He closed Bickerton's lips; I will open his!"

"To prove Robert guilty? Suppose you do so, man? What then? What can you do, any of you, against Robert? He rules this land now, all-powerful. He can bend all to his will. What will it serve to prove that he did this deed? You cannot bring him to trial. No court in the land could try the Governor, no tribunal heed you. And he will deny all. You but beat your fists against a wall."

"Somehow, sometime, we will find a way of being avenged," Isabel said levelly. "Tell us, Thomas — was this mission of Ramsay's on Robert's concerns?"

He nodded.

"I was sure of it!" Jamie exclaimed. "Ramsay *is* in the Governor's pay, then. Even though his present employ is naught to do with the Earl James's death. Or other concern of ours."

"I shall believe that when I hear what it is, Thomas," Isabel said.

Her brother shrugged. "You are determined," he sighed. "But it is in truth a *family* matter. Of the Stewarts. If you care not that Sir James hears it, and promise secrecy, I suppose that I may tell you, since you are sisters of both concerned." He paused. "Robert is in fact, seeking to force our brother Alexander of Buchan's hand. He has a subtle mind, has Robert, and he has conceived a scheme whereby he may perhaps win advantage on two scores. It is to do with Alex's wife — whom he has not lived with scarce since he married her seven years ago. He wed Euphemia only for her great lands and titles, for she was Countess of both Ross and Buchan, Lady of Skye, Badenoch and Lochaber. Alex got the earldom of Buchan, and Badenoch and Lochaber, with her — but not Ross, which went to her first husband's son, Alexander Leslie, the present Earl and Robert's good-son. Since when Alex has deserted his wife, to live mainly with this Mariota de Athyn."

"Euphemia is well quit of him, I say!" Mary observed.

"No doubt. But that is scarce the point. What signifies is that Euphemia could be said to be denied of her conjugal rights. Robert has seen an opportunity here. If the marriage could be said never to have been consummated — and there are no children of it — then, with Euphemia's agreement, the Church could proclaim it null and void, however Alex objected. In which case his earldom of Buchan, and other lands he gained, could be taken from him, his power utterly ruined. All came to him through Euphemia—Skye, Lochaber and the rest."

"Ha — Donald of the Isles!" Jamie exclaimed.

"Exactly. Our nephew Donald could find his position much affected, if these great lands all reverted to Euphemia."

"But is this not folly?" Mary broke in. "We all know Alex. At first hint of this, he would go straight to the Countess Euphemia, take her and consummate their marriage there and then, for all to see, whether she would or no! Then there could be no decree of nullity."

"To be sure," Thomas nodded. "Hence present secrecy. Alex must not learn what is afoot until the trap is set. If you could think of this, Mary, so could Robert! And has done, to some effect. He has sought an order of Holy Church from the Diocesan — that is the Bishop of Moray, Alexander Barr — and backed by the whole power of the College of Bishops as represented by the Primate here, commanding Alex to take up co-habitation with his lawful wife, deserting the other, under penalty. This is why your man Ramsay is acting secret messenger, why he came here with Robert's text, to gain Walter Trail's agreement, and now is in Moray, conveying it secretly to Bishop Barr for ratification. And to gain Euphemia's signature, at Forres."

"But ... but ... what will that serve?" Jamie cried. "The Wolf — the Earl of Buchan, will no more obey such bishops' order than he will give up the earldom and lands. He will pay no heed, and cannot be turned out by force, in those fastnesses."

"Save perhaps by Donald! But that is true, Sir James. Save that, I think, you have not duly noted that phrase I used. Under penalty. That penalty is not fully stated in the first order — lest Alex perceives his danger. All that will be declared is under penalty of £200 payment. But the true penalty is, in fact, excommunication for disobeying the command of Holy Church. Excommunication, swift and final. And being ratified by the Primate, the Pope will confirm it without doubt."

"Will excommunication greatly trouble the Lord Alex? He is scarcely a religious man!"

"God's death, it ought to! Religious or not. For an excommunicate forfeits all rights in law, in state as well as Church. He becomes as good as dead before the law. So Alex would be unable to contest forfeiture of his earldom and lands, unable to claim any rights soever, his hands tied. Not his sword-hand, perhaps — but if he reverts to the sword he becomes a mere outlaw and brigand, with all who value their immortal souls ranged against him. Including, of course, Donald. So says Holy Church."

They stared at him.

"Robert has planned all this? Against his own brother!" Isabel said.

"He has. Alex has defied him, and is too powerful. He is the only man who might challenge Robert's rule, the next prince in succession—since John will challenge nothing. That Alex could never do, as excommunicate."

"It is clever," Mary conceded. "For Alex will scorn and ignore the order — before he knows of the excommunication. And then, no matter if he does go back to his wife and consummates the marriage, it will be too late. For he will have no rights in this, either."

"Precisely. The Church will not accept an excommunicate's cohabitation as valid, or any woman bound thereby. Such would become a rape!"

"Almost I am sorry for Alex," Mary said. "Although I never thought I would say so."

"Be sorry for us all," her sister amended. "For all Scotland is now ruled by this — this devil."

"The more reason to heed my warning," her brother pointed out. "Do not seek conclusions with Robert — any of you."

Jamie shook his head stubbornly. "Nevertheless, we cannot lie down under evil," he said. "You, sir, a churchman, will not deny that? I shall still go after Patrick Ramsay, to Moray. Find him, and wring the truth out of him. About Bickerton and Earl James's murder. I can do no less, now I know where he is gone."

"No, Jamie!" Mary exclaimed. "Do not do it. What value or virtue in it?"

"Neither virtue nor point," Thomas declared. "Since such knowledge can do you no good. Besides, why go to Moray now? Ramsay will have been gone five or six weeks belike. Difficult as travel is in the Highlands, it should not have taken him all such time to reach Bishop Barr at Elgin. He is but a messenger, and the business should not occupy him overlong. The Countess Euphemia lives at Forres — which is not far from Elgin. Ramsay may well already be on his way back. He will, no doubt, return to report to Robert. If see the fellow you must, then await his return."

"That makes sense, Jamie," Isabel agreed. "No need to go travelling the barbarous Highlands. You might well miss him, indeed. We can wait."

"They are right," Mary added earnestly. "It is here, in the South, that all will be decided, not in the North. Bide here with us, Jamie."

He could be an obstinate young man, and he did not commit himself.

Although there appeared to be nothing more to be learned or gained from the Archdeacon Thomas, they stayed for a few days at St. Andrews, where the atmosphere was considerably more cheerful than at Dunfermline. But Isabel was still anxious about her father's health, and Jamie that Ramsay might come back early and he miss him. After an active interlude of hunting, hawking, feasting, music and even play-acting — which gave the young man, at least, an altogether new impression of high ecclesiastical living — they made their return journey westwards, with promises from Thomas Stewart that he would do what he could about the Inchcolm business, and that if any vital word of Ramsay or his mission came to St. Andrews, as distinct from Dunfermline, he would let them know.

With that they had to be content.

XVII

THE AUTUMN AND winter of 1389 was an unsatisfactory period for Jamie Douglas — as well as for sundry others. Having allowed himself to be persuaded not to set off northwards through the Highlands looking for Ramsay, he found himself forced to hang about the vicinity of the Governor's Court, at Dunfermline and elsewhere, indefinitely, to be sure of seeing that elusive young man when he eventually put in an appearance — which in fact he did not do. For an active and not particularly patient character, this endless and more or less idle waiting was a misery — the more so as, the King's health slightly improved, the Lady Gelis removed herself to Dumfries-shire to have her childbirth at Nithsdale, and took Mary with her. Actually the Earl Robert himself did not remain for very long at a time in one place, moving around to Falkland, to Doune, to Stirling and Linlithgow and Edinburgh, although leaving his ailing parent, under heavy guard, at Dunfermline. Since Isabel felt it to be her duty, as well as in her own interest, to remain with the King, with no others of his daughters near, Jamie would have been hard put to it to find excuse to travel round with, or near, the Governor — who so clearly disliked him — had it not been that the new Earl of Douglas came up from his Border fastnesses to be with and support his friend, and Jamie could attach himself not so much to the Earl's company as to his heir's, the Master of Douglas. Archie the Grim was hard hit by the death of his favourite son, Sir Will, and grimmer than ever. He did not particularly love his eldest and legitimate son, but insisted that the Master danced attendance. The latter had his own little coterie of gentlemen and knights, as befitted the heir of Douglas, and in this group Jamie found himself welcome. Drumlanrig, Cavers and other young sprigs of the house of Douglas, were loosely of its number, and gradually more joined it, including Jamie's own brothers Sir James, William and young Johnnie. The Master was a rather gloomy and reserved young man of twenty-seven, but honest enough. He tended to be more preoccupied than usual in that his marriage was imminent and he a less than enthusiastic bridegroom. It was a union planned by his father and the Governor for political and prestige purposes, the bride being the Lady Margaret Stewart, fifteen-year-old eldest daughter of the Earl of Carrick, the Lord David's sister. The marriage would serve to tie the next generation of Douglas to the Stewart cause and at the same time act as a possibly useful lever on the Carrick family. If the Master of Douglas had had other plans, he was not permitted to air them.

Jamie, with the others, was in the little town of Doune, in Menteith, which served the Earl Robert's great main castle — and where the hunting at least was excellent — when the news came that the Lady Gelis had given birth to a daughter, to be called

Egidia. Earl Archie, the grandfather, snorted his disgust and became worse-tempered than ever. Jamie would have sought to go visit mother and child — and Mary — had he not been tied, waiting for Patrick Ramsay to appear.

In late autumn, the fruits of the expedition into England, of the early summer, where displayed, however futile and abortive it all had seemed to most of the participants, in the arrival of a joint embassage of French and English envoys. A decision had been reached at Boulogne, at last, by these two realms, to include Scotland in their mutual treaty of non-aggression; and the ambassadors brought with them a document signed by Kings Richard and Charles agreeing to a three year truce between all concerned, with the recommendation of renewal thereafter if all went well. This was the first major success of Earl Robert's rule, and seemed to justify his peculiar behaviour at Lanercost and the Roman Wall — although few Douglases at least saw it that way. The envoys came to Dunfermline, where the king was still bed-ridden, so that the Governor's Court had to go back there temporarily to greet them. It is to be feared that the Englishmen got but a cool reception, despite their errand, for Robert Stewart was never effusive, and the Douglas faction, being no weathercocks, remained hostile. Archie the Grim went so far as to send the envoys back with a demand to the King of England for the extradition of his subject the Lord Clifford to stand trial in Scotland for the murder of Sir Will Douglas of Nithsdale. The French had a rather kinder welcome and the truce was signed.

As early winter rains and snows and frosts developed, Jamie began to give up hope of Ramsay's return. Travel anywhere in deep winter was difficult enough, with roads turned to quagmires, low ground flooded, rivers too deep to ford and food for man and beast hard to come by; but in the Highlands it was all but impossible, with the passes blocked and the glens closed. If Ramsay had not got through by this time, then he was unlikely to appear before late spring. The same, of course, applied to any idea of Jamie's going looking for him. All development in his quest seemed to be at a standstill meantime.

All was not gloom with Jamie Douglas, of course, as his twentieth birthday approached — not an age for unrelieved depression. For one thing, in early December a preaching friar brought him a letter from the Archdeacon of St. Andrews. In it he announced that, on his instructions, the diocesan chancellor would pay to Sir James Douglas of Aberdour, on return of the enclosed document duly signed and witnessed, the sum of £100 Scots yearly for ten years, in full adjustment and quittance of his claim against the Abbot and Chapter of St. Colm's Inch. A postscript to this added that there was word from Moray that Bishop Barr had issued the desired command to cohabit and sent it to the Earl of Buchan, presently apparently residing in some outlandish mountain hold called Lochindorb Castle in Braemoray, with no reported results to date. Three months were being given to obey. There had been no sign nor word of the man Ramsay, at St. Andrews.

If, in fact, Jamie was more exercised by the postscript than by what went before, this is not to say that he was not grateful and gratified over this financial windfall — although perhaps his first reaction, that Mary would be pleased, was significant. £100 for ten years, £1,000 in all, was far more than he had ever really anticipated, whatever Mary's extravagances, and, added to his own doubled Aberdour revenues, gave him an income of £400 a year, a sum that many a lordling might envy. He had managed well enough on £150; this would be nothing less than riches.

He would have gone, thereafter, to Nithsdale, to pay his respects to mother and child and to convey the news. But with the Douglas-Carrick wedding to be a Yuletide one at Dunfermline Abbey — so that the King's near presence at least would give it added significance — most of the royal family would be assembling, Gelis allegedly intending to make the winter journey in a horse-litter.

He would wait.

It was to be an especial Yule all round, apart from the wedding. It was the first of the new regime; the first of truce with England. The Governor was not the man to court popularity, nor yet to enjoy festivities; but he could recognise the value of public favour for any government, especially that of the lesser nobility and the Church. So this Christmastide he was prepared to spend money fairly lavishly. It would not be his own money, after all.

Isabel disapproved strongly. Her father believed that he was dying and only wanted to be taken home to Dundonald in Ayrshire, to pass away in peace. It was not much to ask, for the King of Scots. This was no time for his family to be celebrating and capering in his house.

Nevertheless, most of the Stewarts came, from one side of Scotland or the other, despite bad weather for travelling — none from the Highlands of course; but then there was only the Wolf and his illegitimate crew, and his sister and nephew of the Isles, who dwelt in those heathenish parts; for Alexander Leslie, Earl of Ross, and his wife, preferred to live in the Lowlands, being no true Highlanders. The Earl John, of course was there, however reluctantly, with the Lady Annabella and their family, the Lord David to be groomsman. The Lord Walter of Brechin came, with his inevitable entourage of giggling young women. The Lady Egidia of Dalkeith brought such of that family as were not already present. The Lady Elizabeth, married to Sir John Hay of Erroll, the High Constable, came with the Lady Jean, widow of the former Great Chamberlain, Sir John Lyon of Glamis, slain in a brawl with the Lady Egidia's son, Sir James Lindsay. The Lady Marjorie attended on this occasion, with her husband the Earl of Moray, however much the latter disapproved of the Governor. And the Lord Murdoch Stewart, Robert's heir, was there, despite his presence underlining the fact that he was not up where he should have been, as new Justiciar of the North, all knowing that he was in fact frightened to venture into his jurisdiction for fear of the uncle whom he was supplanting. Most of the illegitimate offspring were present also, including the Archdeacon Thomas for once, judiciously keeping his distance from the Governor.

The Douglases, naturally, were there in force, to see their young chief wed. Dunfermline had seldom been so full.

Gelis's litter cavalcade, slow-moving necessarily, was one of the last to reach Dunfermline, and after days of hard frost, Jamie, along with most of the other younger folk, was away curling and skating on frozen Loch Leven eight miles to the north, when it did arrive. Indeed, he was back, starting to eat his evening meal in his very humble quarters in the lower part of the town when, of all people to act messenger, the Lord David Stewart burst into the room.

"Your particular friends have come, Jamie," he announced. They were on familiar terms now, the youth seeming to find Jamie's company more to his taste than that of others; indeed they had been skating together most of the day.

"You mean . . .?"

"I mean my beautiful and well-endowed aunts, on whom Jamie Douglas delights to dance attendance! And does not know which he loves best. They came this noontide, it seems, having taken ten days to travel from Nithsdale — God knows how. Although, of course, they have this puling babe with them. And an insolent lad, whom I have already had occasion to put in his place, the late Sir Will's bastard. But . . . man, finish your eating, of a mercy. They will not run away."

But Jamie was on his feet and hastily tidying himself. Nothing would do but that they must hurry off up to the palace, through the nightbound, slippery streets. With the overcrowded state of Dunfermline, there were lights everywhere however, bonfires on eminences, drink flowing and drunken men-at-arms brawling in the wynds, women skirling and coaxing, packmen selling their wares even at this hour, fisherfolk with braziers vending boiled cockles and mussels and oysters for instant eating, preaching and begging friars going about their business, dogs barking, pigs grunting in the gutters and poultry pecking, a lively and inspiriting scene despite the cold.

The palace and abbey were just as full of folk and movement and noise, with even the illustrious of the land having to bed down in ante-rooms, mural-chambers and corridors. Gelis and her party had no option but to share Isabel's apartment in the old wing, and here David brought Jamie. Throwing open the door, he announced him with an elaborate flourish.

"Sir James Douglas of Aberdour, Knight — a man of wealth and substance and the scourge of Holy Church! To pay his too humble duties to beauty, high-born and base-born — having foolishly left his own meal uneaten to do so!"

Frowning blackly, Jamie stood in the doorway. His eyes lighted at once upon Gelis — and remained there. Always she had been lovely. Now she had somehow added an almost ethereal beauty, a fining-down and spiritualising of her features as of her expression, perhaps as the result of childbearing, motherhood and sorrow, which elevated, exalted, her looks to the exquisite, the utterly heart-catching. Certainly they caught at Jamie Douglas's heart. Gone in a moment his former discomfort and slight offence at her pregnant state, his feeling of alienation on account of her so obvious worship of the memory of Will of Nithsdale. He could not take his eyes off her at first, though there were four others in the room.

"Jamie!" she cried. "How good. How kind. We were but talking of you." She rose, near the fireside — although this time she did not hurry to him but waited for him, arms out.

He did the hurrying — although actually he was almost afraid to embrace her, so fine-wrought and fragile-seeming she had become. Not that her person felt fragile in his arms; it was more an aura of delicacy, rarity, which she appeared to have developed. Her kiss, on his lips, was warm but calm, lingering rather than impulsive. Gelis Stewart was a girl no longer, but a full woman.

"Dear leal Jamie," she murmured, stepping back a little to look at him, but still holding his hand. "Darker than ever, I do declare." A brief touch to the hair at his temple. "But, come. Come and see my poppet. She sleeps, after her long journey . . ."

Only then, as he turned, had he eyes for Mary, sitting back with tambour-frame in a corner of the arras-hung room. She was watching him, smiling just slightly, and looking bonny, bonny — but, of course nothing like so beautiful as her half-sister. He raised his free hand to her, wordlessly, as Gelis led him over to the crib.

The baby was pink and plump and fair, with eyes closed, lips slightly open and tiny fists clenched. Jamie, with no great experience of the like, thought it lacking in interest — but did not say so.

"Very good," he pronounced. And, as an afterthought, "And fat."

"Fat! She is not fat. Do you not think that she is beautiful?"

He was not a good liar. "Not, not as beautiful as her mother!" he got out. He pointed to the rolls of fat at the little wrists. "When she has some hair, perhaps . . ."

"All babies are so . . ."

A tinkle of laughter from across the room. "You have much to teach him, Gelis," Mary said. "But . . . he learns quickly!"

"I dispute that last!" David declared.

From the other side of the fireplace, Isabel spoke. "Perhaps he would prefer your other . . . acquisition, Gelis?" she suggested. "More recognisably Douglas."

Where she pointed, a boy stood, quiet, alert, watchful, and slender, dark, almost swarthy. Douglas he was indeed, every inch, and the young image of the late Sir Will. Small wonder that Gelis cherished him.

"Young Will," she announced. "Young Will of Nithsdale. Who grows apace. And will one day grow sufficiently to avenge his father." That was said quietly, without emphasis, as though common-place — and all the more telling for that. The boy did not so much as blink his bright eyes or alter expression — although David made a face.

Jamie stirred uncomfortably. There were too many currents and cross-currents in this room — not all for the best, he felt. Although on vengeance bent himself, he conceived this last to be unhealthy. He went over to the boy and shook his hand. In their lean darkness they displayed a marked similarity.

"Your father was a fine man, young Will," he jerked. "Grow like him if you would please him best. That is enough."

"As one hero of another," David mocked.

"My lord — I am no hero," Jamie said stiffly. "But this lad's father was. If the house of Stewart could produce stock of this sort, but one or two, it would require to fear the future less."

"Bravo! Bravo! Up, the Douglas!" the youth cried, grinning cheerfully. "I love you when you are embattled thus. Eh, Aunts? Are not we Stewarts a poor crew? Not a hero amongst us. So we needs must marry Douglases — and hope."

Into the uncomfortable silence, Isabel spoke. "We none of us heed Davie," she mentioned, in a general way. "Jamie — I have been telling them of your great good fortune, which Thomas has gained for you. We rejoice . . ."

"Though it is but half of what I asked," Mary put in. "Even so, it is excellent, Jamie."

"It is *you* I have to thank," he said. "As I do, Mary. I am truly grateful. £100 a year is a notable sum. Added to the moiety, it is riches. The Archdeacon has been good, kind. He is here for the wedding — I have thanked him . . ."

"Had my esteemed but unfortunate father known of your so great wealth, Jamie, he could have come to you for siller, instead of having to sell his eldest daughter." David observed.

"Sell . . . ?"

They all gazed at him.

"Why, yes. Did you not know? My revered and saintly sire is a babe in many things, I fear. Like some others I know. Siller is one

271

of them. Rents, dues, revenues — he lets his tenants and vassals off with them, on any sorrowful tale. In consequence is ever indebted to others, less kind. Certain matters have grown pressing — so my Lord High Steward of Scotland must needs find some hundreds of siller swiftly. His kind brother the Governor found it for him — on condition that he wed his daughter to the heir of Douglas. So, no doubt, the Earl Archie paid for it. Heigho — my valuable sister, at fifteen!"

Struck silent, they digested this.

"I had no notion of such a thing," Isabel said, at length. "It is shameful. So, so lacking in dignity. She will be the first princess of Scotland . . ."

"If her father ever reaches the throne!" Mary put in.

"You think . . . he might not?"

"I think it possible."

"You think father might go the way of Uncle David of Strathearn, Aunt?" young David asked, interestedly.

"I did not say that, Davie. Only that it is possible that he might not reach the throne. Other, other hindrances might come between."

"As such?"

"Your father might be persuaded. To renounce the crown. Or to abdicate when the King dies . . ."

"In favour of Uncle Robert? Then it would be necessary to get rid of *me*, would it not? For I am the next heir, not my uncle. And I would not renounce nor abdicate, I assure you. So I am equally at risk, with my father. Do not think that I have not conceived of it. I keep my eyes and ears wide, whatever my father does."

Jamie looked at the youth, wondering, as so often before. It crossed his mind that here undoubtedly was someone the Earl Robert would have to dispose of eventually if he wanted unchallenged control of Scotland.

It was as though David Stewart read his mind. "So you see, I am in my uncle's road even more than is my father. He considers me child, as yet. But that will change. In another year or two . . ." The boy laughed and shrugged. "In another year or two, my father will either be King, or dead, or else I King. In any case, better able to look after my Uncle Robert! What one Stewart can do, so can another. Let Robert Stewart watch for himself!"

If Jamie, or the Stewart women, had any notion of dismissing

272

that as adolescent bravado or posturing, they had but to remember the rows of dangling bodies at Turnberry Castle, hanged on this boy's orders; or indeed the manner of their initial introduction to him there. David Stewart did not go in for idle posturing.

Smiling at their alarmed expressions, he went on. "As token that two can play this game, I too can take Douglas to be my shield and support. God save Douglas, I say! So I offer myself as groomsman for this wedding. Persuade my lady-mother that Archibald, Master of Douglas is the finest goodson she could find for her firstborn, a true, honest and kindly husband, if something sober. That my uncle would seem to think the same in this, is no matter. Archibald Douglas will be *my* friend, not his. I might even wed a Douglas myself, before too long — the grim and ancient Earl Archie has a belated daughter Marjorie, has he not? I already have made many Douglas friends, and shall make more. Have I not, Jamie? So now you see why I so cherish Sir James Douglas of Aberdour as my dear and close companion. He is as a key to the door of this Douglas strength — as well as being a likeable carl, to be sure." And the insufferable youth patted Jamie's shoulder.

Even as that young man jerked away, however, he knew doubts, misgivings. How much of all this was folly, how much stark truth? This boy could well be King of Scots in a few years' time — if he lived. All that he said, however fleeringly spoken and outrageous, in fact made sound sense. Even the last mocking reference to himself. Put a crown on this beautiful head, and the words became not vapourings but pregnant with meaning, fateful, perhaps prophetic. And that crown was in a highly unstable state, none would deny.

Gelis it was who changed the subject, or at least brought it back to where it had been, young Will Douglas.

"Do not heed Nephew Davie too closely, Will," she advised. "He talks much nonsense. Wiser to heed Sir Jamie, who uses words more carefully! He acts, as one day you must act. Learn from him."

Embarrassed, Jamie looked around him. "I, I fear that I cannot act in anything on an empty stomach!" he said. "I but came to greet you. With your ladyships' permission I go back and finish my meal. Tomorrow there is to be another great bonspiel, skating, curling, jousting on sleds, races, feasting on the ice, at Loch Leven. If I may act escort for any or all . . ."

"It will be *all*, I assure you!" David prophesied. "You will see. Now, I shall come with you, back to your lodging. Perhaps I may win a few more Douglases as friends. Unlike you, I never hazard myself alone with these aunts. I bid you all a good night . . ."

*   *   *

Loch Leven, wide and level under the thrusting Benarty and Lomond Hills, presented a gay and extraordinary scene, basically white with ice and hoar-frost but splashed and dotted with colour as hundreds disported themselves on the ice. Lists, enclosures and even pavilions of a sort had been erected, the servitors and men-at-arms dragged sleds of food and drink and fuel out to the islands, where bonfires blazed and groaning trestles were set. Half-a-dozen curling-matches were in progress, players sweeping busily with birch-brooms to ensure maximum runs for their stones; skating and sledge races were taking place; tumblers, acrobats, wrestlers and even dancers entertained, and groups of instrumentalists dispensed music throughout. There was ample room for all, for the heart-shaped loch was in fact almost four miles long by two wide, with seven islets, two quite large, and the little towns of Kinross and Milnathort huddling on its northern, marshy shore. All save St. Serf's Priory Island belonged, as it happened, to Jamie's father, like so much else in Lowland Scotland, and he it was who was paying for all the festivities, here and elsewhere, as contribution to the Douglas side of the wedding.

Jamie's party did indeed include all the group of the previous evening — save for the baby, left with a nurse; but others also had attached themselves, more to the princesses and the Lord David than to Jamie, Gelis being as a magnet for a large proportion of the well-born males on the loch. The fact that the bride of two days hence was also with them made a deal less stir. She was a quiet modest girl, with the warm beginnings of Stewart good looks — and her brother was unexpectedly kind to her. The bridegroom was nowhere to be seen.

Jamie had bought, begged or borrowed as many sets of bone-made skates as he could find in the little towns, and they all were displaying their differing stages of expertise, those who had been reared on the east side of the country being notably better at it than those from the west, where intense frosts were rare. The Stewarts were mainly from the south-west, and Jamie suitably had elected to teach Gelis the art. Not that he would have had the least chance with her, in view of the many eager and more highborn instructors, had she not made it clear that he was her own choice. The business, of course, involved much clinging and clutching and holding up, which neither appeared to find distasteful. Nevertheless, Gelis did not shout and laugh and skirl as so many young women were doing in like circumstances, but maintained the air of calm dignity that went with her new sort of beauty — however little dignity and learning to skate might seem to match. She was looking utterly lovely in that bright, cold air, cheeks flushed, great eyes glowing, heavy coiled hair golden against the black-and-white hood of her fur cloak. Jamie suffered little of his normal slight impatience.

"You must think me very awkward, clumsy, Jamie?" she panted, not for the first time. "I vow my little Egidia might perform as well at this as do I! Perhaps I am too old to learn this skating?"

"Too old? You are twenty-one years four months. Is that old?"

"So — you know, to the month. Am I to be flattered, or otherwise?"

"I have no concern with flattery," he told her, holding her straight on course. "But I have long grieved that you were sixteen months older than am I. It seemed a sad gap, once."

"But not so sad now, I think?"

"No," he admitted. "Not now."

"I feel a deal older."

"I do, also. But you — you have suffered much. Yet look . . . the fairer."

"Suffered much, yes. And learned much, I hope . . ." She collapsed into his arms again. "Save in this nonsense! How strong you are, Jamie. How secure I feel, in your strong arms."

"They are yours to command, Gelis. Always."

"I wonder!"

"Why say that? What mean you? It is truth."

"Yes, Jamie. Truth in one fashion. I know that you are the lealest of the leal. But . . ."

"But what?"

"These strong arms have held others, have they not? Even more closely perhaps?"

He caught his breath and could not answer her, cursed by his inability to lie convincingly. Was it possible, conceivable, that Mary could have told her?

She searched his face, so near her own. "It is true, then. You see, Jamie? True, the other — only after a fashion." She pushed away. "Now — let me try this again . . ."

"But . . . but . . ." He shook his head, and concentrated on supporting her delectable person. Many watching undoubtedly marvelled that any man, in the circumstances, could manage to look so frowningly displeased — although indeed his dark brows had much to do with it.

Isabel glided close. After years of marriage in the east, she was a good skater. "Spare poor Gelis, Jamie," she called. "She has suffered enough, surely! Come — escort me over to the isle where they are roasting beef. I vow I can smell it, from here. I am hungry." That was slightly imperious.

"Yes," he nodded. "Very well. Perhaps the Lady Gelis is hungry also? Will you come . . .?"

"Not now, no, I thank you. It may be that I can find some other strong arms, meantime. Later, perhaps . . ."

His frown unabated, he skated off with Isabel.

"Gelis wearies easily," her sister mentioned. "In her present condition. I scarce think it wise for her to try to skate, meantime."

"She seems well enough. And nothing loth."

"She is not eight weeks from childbirth. Not truly herself. Do not encourage her towards foolishness, Jamie."

"Yes, Princess."

She looked at him sharply, as they sped together over the ice. "I mean it kindly, Jamie. For you both. Gelis is too recent a widow, and mother, for, for cantrips! And folk will talk."

He seemed to have heard that before, somewhere. He forbore to enlarge on it, however.

They came to the islet, not far from that of the castle, where the food was being dispensed. A dozen fires blazed here, whole sides of oxen roasting on two of them, on spits, wildfowl, capons, venison on others, with boiled lobsters, crabs and shellfish on braziers.

There were wines and spirits and ale, hot if desired. A gipsy with a fiddle and a dancing-bear entertained here.

The Lord Murdoch Stewart sat on a sled, watching the bear with lack-lustre eyes, and toying morosely with a whole roasted mallard. His young gentlemen had drawn some distance back, so that it seemed that he was in one of his moods. He was a strange and difficult man — perhaps not to be wondered at, with the father he had — tall, well-made with reddish hair, and good-looking in a heavy way that could frequently turn to sullenness. In his late twenties and still unmarried, he had been kept too closely under his father's thumb, and while resenting it, lacked the strength to break free.

"I hear that you almost won the sled race, Nephew," Isabel greeted him civilly.

"Almost — but did not!" he returned shortly. "How should I, when others have better horses?"

"You showed the greater skill, then."

He shrugged.

"Cousin Murdoch will remedy his lack of good horseflesh soon enough now," a musical voice declared behind them. "When he can take the best from all the North. A poor Justiciar and Lieutenant who could not!" The Lord David, who must have skated after them, had come up quietly.

Murdoch eyed his young kinsman without delight, and made no comment.

"To be sure, it will be necessary to take over from Uncle Alex first," David went on judiciously. "He, now, will have a fine stable, I warrant. Perhaps he will leave it for you, Cousin. When do you go?"

"When I am ready."

"Ah, yes. Good. Readiness is vital, in dealing with our good uncle. And discretion likewise. But I have little doubt but that you are most suitably discreet, Cousin Murdoch."

Hastily Isabel intervened. "I would think that Murdoch is waiting for tidings from the North. To determine when he should go."

Her older nephew nodded. "That is so."

"And it is scarce the time for journeying, my lord," Jamie put in. "For couriers or for Justiciars." He had no urge to rescue the Governor's sullen son from his gadfly relative, but he hoped that this conversation might be steered to the subject of Ramsay — of which, of course, David knew nothing.

Murdoch nodded again.

"What tidings do you await?" David asked interestedly. "That Uncle Alex has died a death? Or perhaps so dreads your coming that he sends abject terms. For the surrender of his powers and offices?"

Stung, the other raised his head. "The Earl Alexander will have good reason to be abject!" He jerked. "You speak truer than you think, boy."

"Ha — you say so? That will be a new role for the Wolf of Badenoch!"

"A new role, yes. He has never yet been, been . . ." Murdoch swallowed the dread word just in time. He coughed. "Been faced with the full rigours of Church and state," he substituted.

"*Church* and state?" the quick-witted David asked.

"And you await a courier bringing tidings of this?" Isabel inserted.

"We do. He is delayed. Or I could well have been in Elgin by now."

"Delayed? Or lacking the desired tidings?" his cousin wondered, sceptically.

"Delayed. He left Elgin in mid-October. A friar of Bishop Barr's brought the word to the Abbot of Dunfermline. But the Highland passes were closed early, with snow, floods . . ."

"But insufficiently to halt the friar, it seems!"

"He came came round the coasts."

"So you still await this courier and his message before you venture North?" Isabel asked.

"I mislike your word venture, Aunt." That was heavily said.

"Travel, if you will. Journey. And if he comes not?"

"We have sent another. To ascertain conditions."

"Such caution, Cousin, will serve you but oddly in dealing with Uncle Alex, I think!" the youngster observed, pulling a face. "Come, Aunt, Jamie—let us see if the beef here is as tender as is Murdoch Stewart." And he strolled off.

After a moment or two, Jamie followed him, leaving Isabel apologising to one nephew, who scowled, for the behaviour of another who smiled.

"Ox-roasting is but poor sport!" David commented, as the other came up with him. "How think you, Jamie?"

"I think you make enemies needlessly, my lord."

"You do? That one is my enemy whether I make him so or not. His kind, one might bait into indiscretion, I say." He paused. "What is this of the rigours of *Church* and state?"

Jamie shrugged, and moved faster, ahead.

At the true ox-roasting they found Mary and her niece, the bride, nibbling daintily but effectively at steaming ribs of beef, and joined them gladly. But when, presently, the Countess Anabella of Carrick came and carried off her two children to present them to the Primate, Bishop Trail, who would conduct the wedding service two days hence, Jamie was less at ease. He had not been alone with Mary since her arrival from Nithsdale, hardly indeed since the day on Inchcolm, and he was uncomfortably aware that the young woman might well have remarks to make. He chewed the more attentively at his rib.

"I saw you talking with that odious Murdoch," she said, after a space. "You would get little out of that one, I think?"

Much relieved, he answered her, his mouth full of meat. "More than I thought to. We learned that Ramsay left Elgin in October. They still look for him to come. So they wait as impatiently as do I. They have sent another messenger to the Bishop of Moray meantime."

"To learn how Alexander has received the cohabitation command?"

"Yes. That, and to discover if may be what reception would greet the Lord Murdoch should he venture into his new jurisdiction. He mislikes the word venture, which Lady Isabel used — but it is clear that he is afraid to go North until he learns that his uncle is sufficiently cowed. But if what the Archdeacon Thomas said is so, then the Earl Alexander could not yet be cowed. If ever. For he was given three months to comply with the command. Under threat only of fining. The excommunication, which they think alone could cow him, not to be mentioned. Three months are not yet gone."

"So-o-o . . .?"

"I think that the Earl Robert may not have told his son all. That Murdoch believes the excommunication threat to have been made, and does not know of the deceit, the trap."

279

"It could well be so. Robert would deceive his own self, if he might. Does, perhaps." She paused. "It may be that we all do."

"In what fashion?"

"Why, in our everyday hopes and fears and wishes. *I*, see you, had believed that you had been weaned from your doting on Gelis. But I find that it is not so. You are more besotted than ever, I think! I it is who deceive myself."

He drew a sharp breath. "You have no right to say that," he protested.

"No? Even after, after ..." She shook her head. "No *right*, Jamie, perhaps. But must a woman have a right before she may speak her mind? To one who, who has been close to her?"

It was that word close which sparked off the little blaze — that and his own too lively conscience. Gelis had used the same word, or closely. These arms, she said, had held others even more closely.

"So you must needs tell Gelis of this closeness!" he jerked. "Was that why you did it? There on Inchcolm? To unbesot me of your sister!"

She drew back from him as though struck. "Jamie — how unkind. How cruel!"

'Belike, for the same reason, you gained me those moneys from the Church," he blurted on, his long-repressed doubts and emotional tearings bubbling up unchecked at last. "I did not desire those moneys. I was well enough, lacking them. *You* shall have them — for they are yours. You plotted for them and won them, not I. Take them, then. I will make a charter of gift ..."

"Stop!" she commanded. "Before you say the unforgivable! Before you call me whore, harlot! And keep your moneys. For you will need it all, and more, if Sir James Douglas seeks to wed himself to a princess. Not that Gelis will ever wed *you*, or any. She will use you, yes. Hold you to her side. But not wed. She is wed to the memory of Will of Nithsdale, only. And the person of his son. She will wed no other. I ... I ..." she turned and ran from him then, voice choked in her throat.

Almost he went after her, but did not and stood biting his lip, hating himself.

Isabel found him, presently, staring at his rib of beef unseeing. She linked her arm in his. "Come — take me to see this castle on the other island," she said. "My brother Alex was imprisoned there by Queen Margaret of Logie, when a young man, twenty years ago. Did you know . . . ?"

He went with her, wordless.

*   *   *

Two days later, the wedding itself was something of an anti-climax. It was, indeed, a strange admixture of extravagance and parsimony, of splendour and apathy, of the formal and the make-shift. The fact was that, when it came to the bit, neither Earl Robert nor Earl Archibald had been prepared to dip their hands too deeply into their pockets for the business, and the Earl John could not afford to. As a result much was skimped. Where the Lord of Dalkeith had had a hand, and sundry other Douglases, there was amplitude, colour, richness — but this was only on the perimeter, as it were, the inessentials, where they were spending to enhance the credit of their house. The churchmen were, as always, magnificent to look at; and Dunfermline Abbey a brilliant setting. Most of the guests were at their finest. But that said, the proceedings were all but humdrum, the ceremonial cut to a minimum. The Master of Douglas looked well enough and suitably clad, but scarcely interested — indeed much outshone by his lively and youthfully beautiful groomsman in royal cloth-of-gold and scarlet, who for that matter, equally outshone his light and shrinking sisters, all three of them, the bride included. The wedding-feast after the ceremony was lavish enough but lacked sparkle—the Governor's presence something of an inhibiting factor perhaps, and neither the Earl Archie nor his son at their best in such social occasions; while the bride's father contributed nothing to gaiety. Indeed, the Lady Egidia of Dalkeith was heard to exclaim loudly that they required her nephew Alex to liven matters up suitably, by God!

Jamie himself added little enough to the jollity. He stood through the ceremony and sat through the banquet, in lowly position and dark reserve, at odds with himself and all else. He could have placed himself near Mary, but she would have nothing to do with him — and of course in such formalised proceedings the princesses were far out of his reach. Not that Gelis was being very gracious to him either, and he was finding Isabel trying. He cursed himself for what he had said to Mary — but that would not unsay it. Yet, in a way, she had deserved it, undoubtedly; he was tired of

281

being warned and reproved and tugged this way and that. He had never felt less of a knight or hero, less chivalric, less sure of his direction. He was, in fact, not good at waiting, at inactivity and looking on.

After the wedding there were the usual Yuletide festivities. But somehow conditions were not favourable, despite official encouragement, Holy Church's cooperation and the unusual peace with England. For one thing, the weather broke down to continuous rain, chill and windy, and with outdoor occasions excluded, all indoors became so overcrowded as to lose appeal. But there was more to it than that. There was a kind of undefined and unexpressed fear hanging over the land, a fear for the future. The old man slowly dying up in his tower-room scarcely helped.

Folk began to leave for home early. Jamie's twentieth birthday passed almost unobserved.

It was, in fact, the King who achieved for Jamie his immediate desire — to get away from Dunfermline quickly; or, at least, Isabel it was who persuaded her brother to allow her father to go home to Dundonald, his childhood home, as he wished. The monarch was scarcely rational now and seldom spoke lucidly. But when he did it was of his longing for Dundonald, to die there. The Governor at last agreed. He was himself a restless man. He decided to wind up affairs at Dunfermline and take the King home himself, with a large guard, of course. Isabel was not to be parted from her father — and Jamie, as ever, provided her escort.

The parting from Gelis and Mary was a strained and straining business, with the boy Will watching, level-eyed, silent. Neither of the young women had ever looked more fair. Stilted farewells expressed nothing of what might have been said, should have been said. Gelis kissed him goodbye, with a sudden little rush. Mary did not. But as he moved to the door, it was Mary who had the last word.

"Take heed, Jamie, how you go. Always," she said. "Be not . . . so great fool as . . . as sometimes!"

After a moment he nodded his head at that, and left them.

III

XVIII

USED AS HE WAS, by this time, to the rugged and spectacular, in scenery, Jamie Douglas involuntarily reined in his garron as they topped the rise, to stare at what opened before them, beyond the birches. Two massive, hulking mountains reared themselves threateningly a few miles ahead, steep-sided from this angle, harsh, sombre even, with the forenoon April sunlight gleaming on their still snow-clad flanks — where the flanks were not so abrupt or riven by corries and ravines that the snow could not lie. In that vast welter of hills in which they rode, and had ridden for days, these two stood out dramatically, menacingly; and between their mighty buttresses a great abyss yawned, dark, daunting. There appeared to be no other break in the solid phalanx of mountain and ridge in front.

Nodding towards it all, he turned in his saddle to the young Highlander, Gregor MacAlpin, whom he had hired on the advice of the Bishop of Dunkeld, when they entered Atholl, as necessary guide and interpreter.

"Those mountains? That gulf? What are they?" he demanded.

"*An Muc Ath-Fodla* and *An Torc Baidheanach. Druimochdair* between," the other said, in his pleasing, lilting voice. "The Sow of Atholl and the Boar of Badenoch. Also the Pass of Drumochter."

"Badenoch . . . !" Jamie, despite himself, repeated that ominous name with a hint of dread.

"Badenoch, yes. Och, Atholl ends at the Sow — with the Boar

seeming like to be mounting her!" Gregor smiled briefly at the significance of his little joke. "But it is through this Badenoch that you are after coming to travel, is it not, lord?"

He part-nodded, part-shrugged. "Yes. To be sure. And that pass — must we go through that?"

"There is no other way, at all."

He signed to the other three to ride on.

They were five days north of Dunkeld — and in this land one counted distances by days rather than miles — eleven since they crossed the Highland Line at Aberfoyle in Menteith. It seemed scarcely credible for Border horsemen, but they were averaging no more than a dozen miles in the day. They had left their good horses at Dunkeld, of course, and now rode the stocky, short-legged, broad-hooved Highland garrons, which nothing would make speedy but which were sure-footed and tough enough to cover country which would have foundered any ordinary mount. Jamie had heard plenty about the difficulties and dangers of Highland travel; but he had not fully realised the scale and scope of the problem until he actually experienced it — made worse, to be sure, by his own impatience in starting out too soon, before the worst of the spring snow-melt and flooding was past. With every burn a hazard, every river a rushing torrent, every loch swollen, every glen-floor a bog, every drove-track — for there were no true roads — a succession of peat-broth quagmires, progress was as slow as it was uncomfortable and dangerous. And devious — for circumnavigation was the constant procedure; often half-a-day was spent reaching a spot tantalisingly in view only a mile ahead. The fact that beauty and grandeur were everywhere around quickly lost appeal, in the circumstances — although every now and again sheer and dramatic scenic loveliness did halt the Lowland travellers in their tracks.

Progress had proved to be expensive as well as slow, and Jamie had reason to be glad of his new-found wealth whatever he had said to Mary Stewart. Not that food and forage cost the wayfarer more than in the Lowlands; considerably less in fact, although the choice was severely limited, for human consumption, to oat products, beef, venison, salmon and scraggy poultry, with milk and cheese. The expense arose from a sort of passage-toll. Every area of the long route, however vacant-seeming, was in fact the territory of some clan, or part of a clan, under its chief, chieftain or tacksman; and each of these exacted payment for way-leave or so-called safe-conduct across their domain, however small, barren or empty. They might pay as much as three such tolls in a single day, with fierce-looking if superficially polite clansmen assessing them shrewdly at each stop, deciding on how much to make the charge, on the basis of how much the victim could probably afford to pay — and it was by no means always the greater territories and more powerful chiefs who charged the most. Jamie at least had had the sense to take good advice on this matter before setting out, and had decided to limit his escort to a mere three – for the larger the party the larger the toll, it seemed. It was of little avail to use a numerous and heavily-armed retinue, evidently — short of a small army — for food and forage was just not provided for such, and the Highlanders had innumerable ways of blocking the already difficult passage of those whom they did not like, without actually resorting to arms; although this they could do also, for these chiefs could call up surprising numbers of savage swordsmen from the apparently empty mountains and glens, who were far more at home fighting in bogs and on steep hills than could be the travellers. Three, therefore, was probably sufficient for immediate personal protection from small robbers and the like, whilst being no provocation to the more powerful. That last thought had been very much in Jamie's mind, also, for the final stages of his journey and quest, where any seeming provocation towards a much more dire authority fell to be avoided at all costs.

There was one advantage, however, about this expensive toll-paying process, other than the fact that it was usually linked with providing hospitality — if that was the word — in the form of elementary food and shelter; and that was, since it was compulsory on all travellers, it provided a fairly reliable means of checking who and what had come this way recently. So Jamie, through Gregor MacAlpin the interpreter, could question each wild toll-gatherer anent Patrick Ramsay. There were, in fact, very few Lowland travellers in the Highlands, save for the ubiquitous churchmen, wandering and mendicant friars who moved continually between monasteries, abbeys and dioceses wheresoever situated, and tended to act as couriers, messengers, even packmen for other than religious institutions. Church advice at Cambuskenneth, Dunblane and Dunkeld had been unanimous that this, by mid-Atholl and Drumochter, was the route almost certain to have been taken by Ramsay or any other wayfarer to and from Elgin. The alternative, by Ericht and the passes of Glen Shee and the Mounth, was longer and higher with many more hazards — whilst the route round the east coast would take a half-month longer. Despite all his questioning, however, Jamie could glean no hint nor trace of anyone approximately resembling Patrick Ramsay. Young, red-haired, broad-built and hot-eyed, he was the sort of Lowlander the clansmen would note and remember. Some indeed said that they could recollect one such travelling northwards in the autumn, alone. It seemed that Ramsay was still in the North.

Now, as they approached the beetling Pass of Drumochter, under the rearing Sow of Atholl, they were as usual accosted by typical tartan-and-calfskin-clad brigands, with ingratiating smiles and bows but armed to the teeth, requesting *màl*, or mail, as they called it, in the name of the mighty and potent chieftain MacConachie of Dalnamine, own cousin to *Donnachaidh Mor* himself, lord of all Atholl. They had to pay not a few contributions to this resounding potentate already, but this was the costliest of all, as final quittance, as it were, for after this they would be into the lands of the barbarous Macphersons, Cattanachs, Shaws and other members of the unspeakable Clan Chattan — where the good God preserve them! Jamie, who had anticipated any threat to come from the Wolf of Badenoch and his minions, was concerned to hear of these new terrors. But MacAlpin indicated that this was likely to be no more than exaggerated clan rivalry and animosity, or else a desire to detain the travellers here for prolonged 'hospitality' — which assessment seemed to be substantiated when the MacConachies switched their pressure to the dangers and appalling horrors of the Pass of Drumochter just ahead, than which there was apparently, nothing to compare and which demanded days of preparatory feeding and toughening for man and beast, here in the clan township of Doire Dhonaich, as well as no doubt expensive escort through eventually. Warnings were also given as to the extortionate habits and sheer wickedness of the thieving monks in front — from which it transpired that the Church, in its charity, has established a hospice of sorts for wayfarers in the very mouth of the Pass, which the MacConachies clearly resented. Pressing on to this, despite almost tearful dissuasion, in a mile or two, at Dalnaspidal, they found a small and modest establishment, not to say primitive, although no doubt a very grateful haven for many a stormbound or weary traveller. It was kept by three Cistercian friars and half-a-dozen very tough lay-brothers. These likewise did their utmost to prevail on Jamie to linger, harping on the dramatic severities of the Pass rather than on the Clan Chattan bandits — though, the visitors suspected, really only desiring more prolonged converse and gossip with folk who spoke other than the local Erse. However, it being no more than noonday, Jamie was determined to press on. When they took their leave, the friars reluctantly admitted that there was, in fact, another similar hospice at the other end of the Pass which they ought to be able to reach before nightfall, if God and the Virgin were kind.

Drumochter, which now engulfed them, was certainly a daunting place, as befitted the main and major access from the Southern Highlands into the wilder upland fastnesses of Badenoch and Braemoray, one of the greatest such gateways in all Scotland. One thousand five hundred feet above the level of the sea, it was a six-miles-long deep defile between close-shouldering high and barren mountains, so steep that for much of the year the sun never reached its rocky and narrow floor. Cataracts poured whitely down its harsh flanks, so that the noise of falling water prevailed, punctuated by the frequent scream of eagle and buzzard circling above, all against a strange rumbling sound like distant thunder, which MacAlpin said was actually the noise of wind amongst the high tops — although there was little wind here in the gut of the Pass. Apparently these mountains, outliers of the mighty Monadh Ruadh to the north, made their own weather, and storms of great fury could rage up there about the peaks and corries, in a totally different climate unsuspected below. Many a hillman, herdsman or hunter had perished for failing to remember that. Sometimes that weather descended into the Pass itself — and then let travellers beware.

As well as these hazards, Drumochter was declared to be the haunt of wolves, wild boars and other terrors; but Jamie, considering its bare and stony sides argued that any such creatures would be highly unlikely to seek out these singularly barren and unproductive hunting-grounds if they had a grain of natural sense.

In fact, although the traversing of that great defile took them the remainder of the day, it was water, bog and fallen rocks which delayed them rather than animate creatures or climatic conditions. Apart from the eagles, buzzards and ravens, and a few deer and white hares, they did not set eyes on anything that moved throughout — save for the everlasting cascading white water which scored the hillsides and made a prolonged marsh of the boulder-strewn floor, eventually to turn into the north-flowing River Truim.

Weary, soaked and splattered with peat-mud to the eyes, they came to Dalwhinnie, where this river, running fast now, began to drop somewhat to a wider though still high and enclosed upland valley. Here was the second hospice, with a scattering of turf cabins and more mail to pay, this time to Macphersons whose patronymic, the Sons of the Parson, possibly only enhanced their cupidity. Fortunately, by Lowland standards, the scale of these tolls was small, a single silver piece obviously representing great wealth to a people whose normal medium of exchange was in kind not coin. The Macphersons proved to be no worse than the MacConachies however, in other respects.

They spent the night at this hospice, and Jamie found great difficulty in keeping awake during the prolonged session of questions, discourse and report which followed the meal and went on by the hour, with Friar John, from Stirling, avid to gain and dispense news and views with one of his own race. But out of all the talk, the travellers did learn something of value other than that no one answering the description of Patrick Ramsay had passed this way. They gained a new insight into the ways and regime of Alexander Stewart, Earl of Buchan, still Justiciar and Lieutenant of the North so far as the local inhabitants were concerned.

Clearly there was a sort of love-hate relationship between the Wolf and the people here. He was a hard, cruel man, yes — but he kept the warring, plundering clans in order. He took his own heavy taxes and dues from all, but let them off others' claims, including the King's. He allowed no robbers, thieves and sorners to operate in all Badenoch, Braemoray and Lochaber — other than his own sons and minions. Above all, he made constant war and frequent descents upon the fat lowlands of the Laigh of Moray and the like, which all Highlanders were prone to do, and did not prevent others from doing likewise. It ill became a churchman to defend such raidings, Friar John admitted, especially as the Prior of Pluscarden and the Bishop of Moray were his superiors in God; but the fact was that all these low-countrymen were rich, and arrogant in their riches, referring to all Highlandmen as caterans and Erse savages and treating them accordingly whenever they might. Clearly the good friar had become somewhat contaminated through his long stay in the mountains.

Jamie was too sleepy to pursue the matter at length, rarified mountain air and Highland travel tending to have that effect; but he did gather that the Wolf had three main strongholds, strategically sited where they could best control his vast domains, or at least the accesses and drove-roads and passes through them — Lochindorb, on the high moors of Braemoray, above the Moray plain, to the north, which was his favourite seat and home; Loch-an-Eilean, a smaller fortress, also on an island in a loch, amidst the great pine-forests of Rothiemurchus, in the centre and heart of the territory; and Ruthven, not so very far from Dalwhinnie, guarding both this route to the south and that which probed right across the Highlands to Lochaber and the West, as well as all the great upper Spey valley. He had lesser holds too, of course, but these three represented the government of one-fifth of Scotland, as far as acreage went. Their captains were all sons of the Wolf, young men as hard and tough as their sire, illegitimate to be sure but none the less authoritative for that. There were five of them, all by Mariota de Athyn, a noted concubine; and though he had innumerable other brats by other women scattered over the face of the land, these were very much the ruling family, with more power, according to the friar, than any prince or earl in the South.

The Wolf, it seemed, was a king in all but name — and a far more potent one than ever his father had been.

Jamie sought his couch heavy-eyed, that night — but with a correspondingly heavy feeling that he ought to be exceedingly thoughtful.

Next morning, as they rode on down Glen Truim, his mind was indeed very busy. It seemed clear that with the Wolf's grip so strong and all-embracing, nothing was likely to be achieved in these territories lacking his permission, since it seemed that he was not to be avoided as Jamie had hoped. On the other hand, if anyone was apt to know the whereabouts of Patrick Ramsay, the Wolf was, undoubtedly. So instead of avoiding him, if possible, as intended, might it not be more profitable actually to seek his presence? He had no reason to think well of the Earl Alexander, but nor had he reason to loathe him as he did his brother. And since the Wolf also loathed his brother, might he not in fact be sympathetic towards this quest? Moreover, he had the where-withal to bargain, had he not? The knowledge of this excommuni-cation trap. For that knowledge the Earl should be prepared to pay. And if it was to help convict his brother Robert of the murder of the Earl of Douglas . . . ?

Would such approach and revelation be in some way wrong, a tale-bearing, a breach of faith even? But against whom? Isabel? She did not love Alex — but again she did not hate him as she did Robert. She could not particularly desire his excommunication, her own brother, just to further an evil plot in Robert's game of power? The Archdeacon Thomas, then, who had revealed it? The same applied to him; and though it was partly a churchmen's plot, he had had no hand in concocting it. None would suffer, then, from its revelation save the instigator, Robert Stewart. Which was as it should be. Well, then!

He had got so far in his debate with himself when, as on the previous day, he suddenly drew up his garron, to stare. Not, this time, at ominous, threatening grandeur but at sheer heart-break-ing loveliness. Rounding a corner of the steepening glen of the now rushing, foaming Truim, there far-flung before them opened a tremendous prospect of dizzy immensity, a vast low-lying am-phitheatre, all colour and light, rimmed by range after range of mountains slashed with snow and shadow, purple and mauve and every shade of blue. All the foreground was the rich dark-green-and-copper of Caledonian pine-forest, stippled with the verdant emerald of young birch-buds and just bursting out. It took a moment or two to realise that half the colour of the middle-ground was in fact water faithfully reflecting hills and woods and sky. After the constriction of the Pass and close-shouldering mountain-sides, the vista was breath-taking.

"Badenoch," MacAlpin nodded. "The Drowned Land."

"Drowned . . . ? It is beautiful. I had no notion . . ."

"Drowned, yes. That is the great valley of Spey, twenty miles long and a mile broad, lord. In this season of melting snows, the Spey cannot contain it all, and is after spreading over all the valley. Each year it does so, for it carries the waters of all the land.

That is no mighty loch, but flooded meadows. *Bàth-eanach*, the Drowned Land."

"It is beautiful, nevertheless."

It was amazing how abrupt was the transition from bare, bleak and stony heights to green and heavily-forested uplands, grassy slopes and wide vistas. A populous land, too, such as they had not seen since South Atholl, for though villages as such were not in evidence, cabins and little townships were everywhere and blue smoke-columns rose out of all the woodlands, the sweet scent of burning birch-logs on the air.

Jamie now saw that any idea he might have had to avoid the Wolf's whereabouts, at this Ruthven Castle or elsewhere, would have been in vain, without actually taking to the mountain-sides like goats — where they quickly would have been spied anyway. The configuration of the land, the hills, the rivers and the flooding, all conspired to channel the travellers into a very limited choice of route. And where spurs of low hill jutting from either side narrowed the strath to a waterlogged half-mile or so, in the centre, like an island in the floods, rose a steep-sided, flat-topped mound crowned by the towers of a castle. The Wolf certainly knew where to site his strongholds. Nothing could move up or down this upper Strathspey without being observed from this hold.

Seeing it from some miles distance, to the south, Jamie was congratulating himself on having decided to visit it anyway, when his thoughts were rudely interrupted. Out from the cover of pines and junipers flanking the track, near the junction of Truim with Spey, without warning, leaped a rough and ragged crew of Highlanders brandishing swords and dirks, shouting and gesticulating threateningly. Less alarmed than they would have been six days earlier — for this was not an entirely unusual approach for the toll-collectors — the travellers reined in, and sighing, Jamie prepared to dip once again into his pouch. But fairly quickly he recognised that this hold-up differed from the normal pattern. There were considerably more of the clansmen than usual. There were no smiles; indeed they all looked distinctly hostile and prepared to use their weapons.

Jamie raised a hand above his head, and turning, nodded to MacAlpin. That man made his accustomed speech, in Gaelic, explaining that this was Sir James Douglas of Aberdour, a peaceful traveller, and pointing out that they had paid mail back at Dalwhinnie, but if further payment was customary, then let their leading man speak and it would be considered.

There was a pause at this, and many dark eyes turned towards the woodland from which the caterans had emerged. Looking, Jamie perceived a youth sitting a garron there, under an ancient, gnarled pine. He was the youngest of the band undoubtedly, but the only one mounted, though bareback, and clearly the leader.

"I am not a mail-collector!" this youth called, in English, though with a Highland accent — and managed to make it sound as though he had been insulted. He rode forward. "Who are you? Where are you going? And what does any of the name of Douglas do in Badenoch?" That was peremptory. "I considered you all Border thieves?"

Jamie eyed him assessingly. Although dressed in stained and ragged tartans, short kilt and plaid, with the usual calfskin sleeveless jerkin, this one had an air about him. He seemed to be about sixteen years old, with quite good features — had they been recently washed — and a mass of tawny hair to his shoulders, badly in need of a combing. Youthful and ragged as he was, he bore the unmistakable stamp of authority. Also there was something slightly familiar about those features — a Stewart, at a guess.

Jamie took a chance. "I am Sir James Douglas, as you have heard. And we Border thieves at least do not demand payment from lawful travellers crossing our lands! I come to Badenoch seeking my lord Earl of Buchan. With information for his private ear. I request, sir, that you aid me on my way to his house."

The youngster rode close, beardless chin high. "You are bold with your request, Douglas!" he said. "I advise a more respectful tone!"

"Respect from a Douglas requires to be earned. Civility I offer to all." That was evenly said. "I have not won my way here through all your Highlands by bowing in respect before all who challenge me. On the other hand, I have offended none, paid all asked of me . . ."

Quick as a snake might strike, the youth leant over from his garron's broad back and slapped Jamie sharply across the face, first one side then the other, with fierce efficiency. Clearly he had done this many times before.

"*Learn* respect, fellow!" he snapped. "I am Sir Andrew Stewart." Jamie had drawn back in his saddle, cheeks flaming from more than the blows, eyes flashing. His hand fell to the hilt of his sword — but immediately gleaming steel tips of broadswords and dirks thrust forward within inches of him by dismounted caterans on all sides.

"Curse you — you will pay for that!" he panted. "Pay, Stewart! Pay for those felon's strokes. *You* will learn that no man strikes Douglas and does not suffer. Call off your, your animals, boy!"

The other looked as though he was about to repeat the blow, but thought better of it. "We will teach you how to be respectful, in Badenoch!" he said briefly, and rapped out some Gaelic commands to the clansmen.

Swiftly these leapt upon the five horsemen and dragged them down to the ground. There was no point in fighting or struggling. Expertly if ungently their wrists were pinioned behind their backs. Then, surprisingly, they were ordered to mount again, their horses' reins held by caterans. Stewart turned his beast round, and without another word kicked it into a smart trot. Promptly the entire company set off after him at a loping run, the lead horses in the midst.

So they went northwards, at an astonishingly fast pace, through the woodlands of birch and pine and juniper. Jamie had heard of the running gillies of Highland chiefs. Now he knew the reality.

In about three miles they came to the floodlands of the main Spey valley, the great river presumably flowing somewhere through the midst. Keeping up their spanking pace they skirted the eastern edge of the water, scattering large herds of grazing cattle from the open woodland slopes. Another two or three miles of this and ahead, islanded amongst the floods, rose the lofty walls of Ruthven Castle on its mound, a strong and extensive place. Could this arrogant youth be its captain? It seemed scarcely credible. Yet Stewart he seemed to be — although the *Sir* Andrew part Jamie very much doubted.

Almost opposite the castle their leader rode straight into the water, without hesitation or casting about, although at a somewhat odd angle. Splashing out on this course, he abruptly changed direction after about a score of yards, through almost a right-angle, but without pause, the gillies running after heedless of the water up to their bare thighs. Another change of course halfway out made it clear that they were in fact on a zigzag underwater stone causeway.

Still without moderating their speed, the caterans wet and breathing deeply but far from gasping, they breasted the steep slope by a spiral track which wound round the mound, all of it entirely vulnerable to defensive assault from the sheer walls above. The mound itself, which Jamie had taken to be a natural outcrop or moraine, now, from its regular outline and smooth stoneless sides, appeared to be artificial, a work of men's hands. But not the motte-hill of a typical motte-and-bailey castle; by its great size, prehistoric rather, a monument to silent, giant races long gone. A couple of standing-stones on the summit, near the entrance-gateway, further testified to this.

Through that gateway they ran, into a wide courtyard surrounded by low, thatch-roofed lean-to buildings within the high walled perimeter, more like a village than a castle — and a slovenly village at that, with a high central midden of dung in the midst, poultry clucking around, deer- and calf-skins stretched to dry, peat-stacks in corners and half-naked children at play. Here young Stewart barked a few cryptic orders, leapt down from his garron and strode off into the main tower or keep without a backward glance. The prisoners were pulled down from their saddles and hustled away to the keep basement, where MacAlpin and the three Tantallon Douglases were flung into one small vaulted cell and Jamie alone into another, the door slammed on him and the key turned.

He had reached the Wolf of Badenoch's domains, with a vengeance.

*　　　*　　　*

Jamie spent two days and nights in that vaulted basement. The fact that he was held alone in it appeared to be his only privilege, for otherwise conditions could scarcely have been less privileged. A heap of old and distinctly smelly skins in a corner of the stone floor for bed, a wooden bucket and the tiny grilled window represented the sole amenities. He could not complain about the food, for it was no worse and no better than they had been able to purchase all the way up through the Highlands, plain but adequate as to quantity, though thrust wordlessly into the cell twice a day by a grinning gillie who knew no English. This was his sole contact with his fellows, his shoutings and door-bangings going quite unanswered. There were no facilities for washing or shaving, only the sanitary bucket — which was soon far from sanitary.

In those two days and nights, Jamie had opportunity for serious thought. He could not see where he had gone wrong. They could not have avoided this encounter. Their approach had obviously been reported to this Ruthven Castle and they had been deliberately ambushed. He could not admit that he should have reacted differently to that slap on the face, nor said other than he had anent respect. He had told this young insolent the truth. A man, and a Douglas, had to keep his *self*-respect. He had also informed him that he was seeking the presence of the Earl Alexander — presumably his father — with tidings for his private ear. Surely the youth could not ignore that completely, however arrogant? Detaining him like this might please his vanity — but it was inconceivable that he would not send to the Wolf to inform him. In which case it was to be assumed that the Wolf would wish to hear the alleged private information. Even he would not dismiss as of no interest a Douglas come all this way north on a special mission? In which case he could look for developments before very long. The Wolf would either send for him, or send an intermediary to question him, someone less high-handedly autocratic than this deplorable Andrew. And he could then refuse to speak until he saw the Earl himself.

With this line of reasoning Jamie consoled himself during his lonely incarceration.

When, on the forenoon of the third day however, the cell door opened to admit three men, none of them ordinary gillies, it was not quite as he had anticipated. Indeed to call them men was scarcely accurate, for all were younger than himself. There was the insufferable Andrew, a slightly older, taller youth dressed in somewhat tarnished finery of Lowland style, and a heavier, more stolid individual, seemingly older again, in kilt and shirt, though this last was of tattered silk not the usual coarse linen, but none the cleaner for that. It was the middle one who drew the eye. He might have been the Lord David, save that he was fairer, older, taller, a brilliantly handsome, slender and debonair character, all smiles and self-confidence, with long and lustrous well-combed hair, a tiny silky beard and scimitar of moustache. The finery which he wore with such élan did not quite fit him, having clearly been made for a somewhat heavier-built man — the Wolf himself probably by its richness. This character bowed with a flourish to Jamie. The others did not.

"Sir James Douglas, I am told. Of Aberfoyle, is it? I greet you kindly. I hope you find your quarters, er, secure? And have had a sufficiency to eat?" Even the voice was like David's, musical and light, but with the typical Highland lilt and sibilance — and the mockery not amissing either.

"Aberdour, not Aberfoyle. Son to Douglas of Dalkeith — of whom even you may have heard!" Jamie gave back stiffly. "And not used to such accommodation or such treatment, sir."

"To be sure. Sir Andrew, my brother, is plaguey short on accommodation here, unfortunately. And other things, perhaps." That came out with a cheerful laugh. "But sound at heart, see you. I am Alexander Stewart, at your service, Sir James. And this is another of the family our half-brother Rob, of Glentromie. A stalwart — although lacking the accolade as yet."

The third individual glowered like a Highland bull, and said nothing.

"I am relieved to hear that you, at least, are at my service, sir! And appear to have better manners than this brother of yours. I am rejoiced that *I* do not have to claim him brother!" Jamie said. "Perhaps you will bring me out of this stinking hole and convey me to the Earl of Buchan, to whose house I was bound when this savage waylaid, struck and imprisoned me here. I demand release, escort and redress."

"God damn your soul, Douglas . . .!" his captor began, when his brother Alexander gripped his arm. Seemingly the one had some authority over the other, for Andrew stopped speaking, though obviously with a major effort.

"All shall be attended to, I assure you," the other said soothingly. "But I would prefer if you would speak of Sir Andrew more courteously, sir. We do not like the term savage, on Lowland lips!"

"Then, Stewart, school your brother not to act like one! He struck me twice, unprovoked. And one does not strike Douglas without paying for it."

"In your Borderland perhaps not, Sir James. But in Badenoch, Douglas may cut less wide a swathe. Still, if Sir Andrew struck you without due cause, I am sure that he will give you due satisfaction — as one knight to another. And in this regard, Sir James, it would pleasure me if you addressed me as *Sir* Alexander, rather than just Stewart. Since we have been knighted just as truly as yourself—although admittedly not on the field of battle. But at least by a royal prince, not a Border earl! And we are all bastards together, are we not?" That was said with a winning smile.

Jamie considered, and decided that perhaps it was time for some civility, at least towards this less barbarous individual — who presumably was in fact King Robert's grandson. They all were, to be sure. Evidently the Wolf knighted certain of his offspring, but not others — as, of course, he was entitled to do, and they were as true knights as he was.

"You know much of my circumstances, sir," he said, less stiffly. "I am surprised at that, up here . . ."

"We are not wholly ignorant, my friend. Even in Badenoch! Especially where deeds of valour are concerned. But we hear of other matters also. Such as the fact that you, sir, enjoy the intimate favours of more than one of our aunts, our father's royal sisters. A matter we, in our ignorant northern fashion, found strange to account for — and you younger than seemed likely! I . . ."

"How dare you! How dare you speak so!" Jamie burst out. "Of these ladies. The princesses. Your own kin. It is false — false, I say! They are noble and virtuous ladies . . .'

"My, oh my! Such heat, such fervour! Have we been misinformed? It is not like our royal sire to have his notions wrong. Especially of his own sisters . . ."

"Nor has he, I swear!" Sir Andrew declared. "This, this insolent Border adventurer would deceive in this, as in all else."

"Hush, Andrew! We must respect Sir James's knightly word! In especial where ladies are concerned." The sarcasm was only slightly veiled. "Moreover, it may be that it is the same royal ladies who have sent him on this journey to our father? It would ill become us to seem to doubt their goodwill! As their virtue. Or indeed, their messenger's. Not so, Sir James?"

Jamie began to speak, and then perceived the possibility of

benefit in this. "The Ladies Isabel and Gelis *are* concerned in the matter," he agreed. "I am but their servant and courier. I left them at Dunfermline, to journey north."

"And our aunts' message, sir?"

"That is for my lord Earl's ears alone, Sir Alexander."

The brothers exchanged glances.

"*We* shall decide on that," Sir Andrew said. "We have the means to open close lips, believe me! Our father does not suffer impostors and interlopers gladly. You will do better to tell us first."

"No!" the prisoner said baldly.

"I think, Andy, that we should take him to Lochindorb," his brother said. "This is your territory — but in a matter between our sire and his sisters it might be wise. If it is indeed so. The hazard is Sir James's!" He turned to Jamie. "You understand, my friend, that if our potent father deems you a liar, or in deceit, you will be happy indeed, in due course, to hang! I swear that you might be safer, more comfortable, to let us be judge, first!"

Despite himself, Jamie swallowed — for he had no reason to believe that this young man exaggerated or misrepresented. But he shook his head nevertheless. What he wanted, had come all this way for, he would not gain here, he was sure.

"Very well, Sir James — to Lochindorb you shall go. I shall take you there myself — with Sir Andrew's permission. For he is captain of this castle and territory. And I wish you pleasure of the exercise!"

"I thank you. I would wash, cleanse myself. My men the same, no doubt . . ."

* * *

They rode away from Ruthven Castle within the hour, Sir Alexander Stewart, with the silent Rob of Glentromie and a troop of mounted caterans. Now Jamie and his men rode unbound, even with their swords and dirks restored to their sides, their new escort adopting a totally different line from that of his brother, and chatting pleasantly as they trotted through the bright noontide. For all that, they were none the less prisoners, and all knew it. They could no more have escaped than taken to the air.

Their route, north by east, took them through a wonderland of scenic beauty and attractiveness. The vista seen from afar was not belied by closer acquaintance. On every hand was colour and light and fairness of form and outline. The hills near at hand were gentle, green, wooded, those behind sculptured in granite, blue shadow and white snow-cornices. The woodland glades on every hand were mainly of graceful silver birch, purple branches and twigs bearing their lightsome pale tracery. The Caledonian pines, growing often out of heather, were ancient giants spaced well apart, massive rounded trees quite unlike the pines of the South, combining strength with grace. In every glade the juniper bushes not only glowed rust-red amongst their rich green but were festooned with myriads of glistening spiders'-webs which the night's heavy dew had decked with tiny diamonds. There was water everywhere, not only the flooded meadows and tributary burns but still, dark pools in hollows and shaws of the wood where water-lilies floated. Through it all the roe-deer flitted like silent, brown shadows, the occasional woodland stag stood at gaze, the caper-cailzie and blackcock swooped and blundered and all the lesser birds of the forest twittered and sang.

After a few miles, Jamie remarked on it all. "You live in a land of surpassing beauty," he said. "How many perceive it, I wonder?"

"Ha — a lover of more beauty than women's, Sir James! But — do I detect blame here? Accusation? That we barbarians cannot perceive such delight? Pursue only our own un-couthnesses?"

"I meant nothing such. Only that when seen every day, even such beauty might pall. I think you wear thin skins in Badenoch, Sir Alexander."

The other paused, and then laughed. "You are right there, no doubt," he agreed. "Or some of us. The result of being . . . who we are, perhaps, Lords of all here — but despised and hated whenever we set foot out of our own glens and forests."

"Feared, also."

"Feared also, yes — for that is necessary. The Douglases — are they not feared in the South, on the Border? Is not fear necessary? For respect. Even in the so courtly Lowlands? I understand that men respect our Uncle Robert. But do not respect our Uncle John — since none fear him. Although he heirs the throne."

Jamie could not deny it. "If that is so, it is a sorry judgment on us all!"

"True. But . . . we have strayed far from beauty, have we not, Sir James? Myself, I much rejoice in the fairness of this land. On all we see around us. But it is a matter of taste. I doubt if Rob, here, sees it all so lovely?"

That stolid individual, thus brought into the conversation, shrugged. "I see this as difficult and dangerous land. When we most need the meadow pastures, for the beasts after winter, they are flooded. These forests harbour wolves, wild-boar — and worse, broken men. Those mountains breed storms, and little else. We cannot eat beauty, nor yet keep our enemies from hiding in it."

"And there you hear the voice of most sensible men, my friend! We stand rebuked, do we not?"

"No," Jamie said shortly.

Alexander Stewart laughed aloud. "On my soul, I like the rocky style of you, James Douglas!" he exclaimed. "A man who knows his own mind, and speaks it. Let us hope that our lordly father finds a similar liking — for I would not wish to hear that sturdy voice choke on the end of a rope!"

On that ominous note they rode on through beauty.

They presently skirted round the eastern shore of what was more than just flood-water, a large loch, although still only a widening of Spey, Insh by name. This lay at the mouth of the major glen of Feshie, opening from truly mighty mountains, still wholly snow-covered, the Monadh Ruadh, highest range in all Scotland. Here they had to ford the magnificently rushing River Feshie, a hazardous business even for sure-footed garrons, with the tremendous weight of white water to be negotiated in channels cut in solid rock. Thereafter, however, the floodlands ended, the valley sides drew closer, and the track lifted high above the Spey.

It was here that they began to smell burning, not the sweet scent of birch-logs in domestic fires but a more acrid smell, heavy, persistent. The breeze was from the east.

Rob Stewart quested the air. "Inchriach?" he jerked. "Tullochgrue?"

"Further than that," his brother judged. "Thin on the wind.

And nothing to be seen. No smoke-clouds. No blue haze. More like Glen More. Beyond Rothiemurchus. Aye, Glen More."

"Then a big fire. If we smell it here."

"Yes." Both brothers had involuntarily urged their mounts to a faster trot.

"Who? Seath Mor Shaw? The Cattanachs? MacGillivray? Or just a chance fire?"

"Too early in the year for a chance fire. Undergrowth is still damp. Who knows who it is? But discover we shall."

Soon they left the main north-going track to turn away from the river, due eastwards, climbing quickly to a tiny pass between two rounded birch-clad hills of no great height. At the summit of the coll, though none paused in their hurried progress, Jamie at least drew a quick breath.

They were on the lip of a huge basin, many miles across, wholly covered by dark pine forest save for a loch just below them, tree-grown to the very edge, and just the glimpse of another far beyond to the east. All around this wooded depression high hills stood guardian, wholly isolating it from the main Spey valley and all else. On an islet in the middle of the first loch below, a castle rose, much smaller than that at Ruthven, consisting only of two square towers of no great height, linked by curtain-walling, but taking up every inch and angle of the islet nevertheless so that the grey walls seemed to rise straight from the still waters. It was a fair place, as castles went, a jewel in a sylvan setting.

But Jamie's companions were not looking at castle or loch, but beyond, towards the far north-eastern side of the great basin. There great clouds of brown smoke were billowing high, tinged with a murky orange and every few moments slashed with bright red bursts of flame as whole pine-trees went up like torches. It was indeed a big fire, possibly half-a-mile wide and approaching twice that in depth, a terrifying sight even at this distance.

"The Luineag! Geadas!" Rob Stewart exclaimed. "That is not Seath Mor and the Shaws. So near their own places. Damnation — if it is those Cattanachs again . . .!"

Sir Alexander was pointing, stabbing with urgent finger. "See that! And that! The line of that fire. Where it has been lit. How it burns. Whoever raised that blaze knew what he was at! It is controlled. Look — the ravine of the Luineag that side. The line of

Geadas Burn at the other. The flames will not pass these. They are eating back into the east wind. Those two sides narrow in, run almost together at length, to Loch Morlich. Yonder." He stabbed again. "Do you not see? As good as an eel-trap! An ever-narrowing funnel of fire."

Jamie could not tell what he meant, but his half-brother appeared to understand. "Then . . . what? Who?"

"Not the Cattanachs, for sure. How could that serve them? I know but one man who would think of that device! Come, you." Alexander pushed on, at speed.

They pounded down to the loch, and along its shore, threading the trees, until opposite the castle-island. There Sir Alexander drew rein.

"Sir James," he said, "I regret that I must leave you here. Rob also. To discover this of the fire. Here is the castle of Loch-an-Eilean, formerly mine, Rob now its captain. In this Rothiemurchus. You will be comfortably enough bestowed here, for this night. Lochindorb is too far to reach in a day. Some of these gillies will see to you. A boat will come for you . . ."

"Do not be fool enough to attempt an escape!" the brother put in, roughly. "You would not get far — and could have your throats cut before nightfall!"

"Truly if crudely put," Alexander nodded, smiling. "But Sir James is no fool."

"If you doubt my safety, allow that I ride with you," Jamie suggested. "I have languished behind stone walls sufficiently these last days. I would rather ride — and learn how you deal with your forest afire."

The two Stewarts exchanged glances.

"You may learn more than you reckon on!" Alexander said grimly. "But, as you will. No harm in it."

The entire party beat on round the west side of Loch-an-Eilean.

Thereafter, round the loch-foot, they turned to ride east by north through the vast forest, all pine this, with the great trees well scattered and growing out of heather and juniper-clumps, the surface hillfoot country with the high Monadh Ruadh rising steeply, close on the right. Vistas were intermittent and seldom lengthy, save up towards the tall summit ridges. But ever the dark smoke-clouds thickened ahead, and the smell of burning became harder on the nostrils and throat. There were many cabins in the forest, single and in groups, some quite large communities, for foresters, wood-workers, charcoal-burners, herdsmen — for shaggy and semi-wild herds of cattle roamed amongst the glades — and hunters to protect these from wolves and the like. This Rothiemurchus seemed to be something of a world unto itself, with quite a large population living under the canopy of the great pines. Pine-needle-carpeted tracks criss-crossed the vast area everywhere. Clearly it would be an easy place to get lost in.

It was difficult to judge distances in the forest, with its twisting tracks and lack of lengthy prospects; but they seemed to go for some three or four miles before the noise of the fire before them, the crackling roar, became evident above the hollow drumming of their garrons' hooves on the pine-needles, a grim and frightening sound. Presently they could feel the heat of it, on the easterly breeze. They came to a sizeable stream, the Geadas, and moved along its north bank. Ahead now all was darkened by the pall of smoke.

At last they emerged from the trees into the area of devastation, a blackened, smoking desolation stretching widely across their front, patterned still with flame and glowing red, out of which thrust innumerable great skeleton trees not yet wholly consumed and blazing like torches. It made a hellish scene. As Sir Alexander Stewart had predicted, it was half-a-mile wide, and more; also, as suggested, its flanks were controlled, limited, on this south side by the stream they had been following — or by its course, at least, no ravine but a broad belt of bleached stones and pebbles ten times as wide as the Geadas itself, witness to the fury of the floods which could sweep down from the high hills behind laying down this wrack of stones two hundred yards across; the other, northern side apparently would be similarly confined by the still larger River Luineag's course.

Many men, clad in short kilts, some entirely naked, blackened with soot and streaming with sweat, laboured all along this base-line of the fire, wielding besoms of birch-twigs to beat at the creeping flames to prevent them from spreading further westwards. The head of the conflagration was far to the east now, almost a mile probably, although it was hard to judge in the smoke and heat-quivering air. Alexander Stewart shouted brief words, in Gaelic, to the first of the men they came to, who grimaced, shrugged, and pointed away north-eastwards.

They rode on northwards, along the base of the fire-area, without pause, panting and choking with the heat, the garrons rearing and nervous. Small wonder that the beaters looked exhausted. Presently they reached the south bank of the Luineag, a wider stream and, oddly enough, flowing in the other direction, westwards not east. This had no margin of stones, for it flowed out of Loch Morlich ahead, not into it as did the Geadas; but it ran in a wide grassy course nevertheless quite sufficient to prevent the flames from leaping across to the trees on the other side. Along this grassy corridor, coughing and spluttering, they turned eastwards again.

In just under a mile they were gulping deeply, their mounts all but unmanageable, for now they were level with the actual fire-front, an appalling inferno showering out sparks and blazing fragments, exploding in constant bursts and reports, the flames fifty feet high and more, the heat blistering, intolerable even here a hundred and fifty yards from the edge. But it was less dark now, the smoke itself largely left behind, what there was lit up by the red glare. Ahead could be sensed rather than seen, light and space.

At last, streaming-eyed, they were ahead of the fire — and suddenly all was clear, open, bright, the sinking sun gleaming on the wide levels of Loch Morlich, backed by all the soaring magnificence of the Monadh Ruadh mountains and the Glen More hills. But it was not so much that abrupt widening of the background which held the riders' painful and bleary gaze, but the men in the foreground. For, a few hundred yards in front, where the Luineag River emerged from the loch, at the sandy shore itself, many men and horses stood waiting behind a screen of junipers. Two or three boats also lay just a little offshore south of the river-mouth, oars at the ready. Nobody here was sweating, active or seeking to deal with the fire, most obviously. Just waiting.

But even as the riders pounded up, there was a flurry of activity. Out from the small unburned area of forest still left between the fire and the loch-shore, burst two animals, strangely matched, racing most differently, one long-legged the other short, one a great-antlered woodland stag the other a massive-shouldered and tusked wild-boar. Bounding gracefully, head up, and rushing purposefully, head down, these made straight for the sandy shore, the stag quickly gaining on the other. Then the shouts arose, as men out there in the boats yelled, waved arms and plaids and splashed oars. In fresh alarm the stag swerved and turned left, to race instead for the mouth of the Luineag; and after a moment or two the boar did likewise. And hidden behind the barrier of uprooted bushes, the main group of watchers waited, arrows strung, spears at the ready.

There was only a fairly narrow corridor between the row of junipers and the shore, for the fleeting animals to pass before the river-mouth. Arrows sped, and the stag's graceful bounding suddenly changed to a desperate shambling scrabble, before it pitched forward and lay still.

An authoritative shout then rang out above the roar of the flames, and right over the barrier of bushes a single figure vaulted, tall, lithe, in Lowland clothing, spear in hand. Out to meet the rushing boar this individual ran, on a collision course. Only a pace or two from the charging animal he somehow achieved a leap to one side, an approximate halt and a rising on his toes. Down drove the spear into the massive bristling flank, just a hand's breadth behind the heavy shoulder, as the crazed brute went hurtling past with a bare inch or so to spare. Spear standing out from its side the creature careered on almost to the river's edge, dead on its feet, before the heart gave out and it fell, tusks goring the sand. Its slayer turned to face them all, laughing, handsome head thrown back.

"My father loses little of his art with the years — in this as in other matters!" Alexander Stewart the Younger observed. "You are spared the ride to Lochindorb. Though — I shall not announce you yet, Sir James. My lord's sport must not be spoiled. you understand? Achieved at such . . . pains!"

Jamie nodded, silent.

XIX

THE EARL OF BUCHAN and his companions paid no least attention to the newcomers, being much too busy. Clearly these had arrived just in time for the climax of this extraordinary proceeding, with the fire reaching this apex of the long triangle between the rivers, and all trapped within now penned in this diminishing corner — or else burned to death. Creatures had been seeking to escape for some time previously for the ground between Luineag, loch and fire, the killing-ground, was already littered with carcases. Now, the Earl Alexander, leaving his boar, had barely got back to his cover before three grey-brown shadows slipped out from the woodland and ran swiftly, belly-down, directly for the river. These were lean and fast, and one was badly burned as to coat and tail, limping on one foreleg — wolves, yellow eyes glaring, red tongues hanging from parched mouths. Arrows sped at them, and two fell, twitching; but the limping one ran on, although transfixed by a crossbow shaft. A couple of wolf-hounds leapt out from the junipers after it, and managed to pull it down in snarling fury just as it reached the water.

There were already further creatures bolting from the shrinking cover — a mixed bag now, two dainty roebuck leaping high, a stag and three hinds in great-eyed terror, and a female boar. The deer all fell under the hail of arrows. But a young man emulated the Earl — he looked like another Stewart — racing forward with spear to meet the boar. He was less expert at the business than the other however, drove in a slant-wise blow which failed to penetrate the tough hide and glanced off, the spear jerked out of his grip. Whether it was the hooted scorn from behind or on his own initiative, the youth thereupon hurled himself bodily after the animal as it rushed past, falling upon it, arms encircling its hind-quarters. Down they both crashed.

"God-sakes — Walter was ever a headstrong fool!" Sir Alexander exclaimed. "As well it is only a sow, or he would have himself killed!"

But in fact this new brother of his was fortunate, however foolhardy — and determined. For though a female wild-boar could be almost as dangerous as a male, this one was terrified by the noise and the fire, rather than angry, and already scorched by blazing embers. This new attack probably seemed to it just a continuation of the horror in the wood, and instead of rounding on its assailant it merely struggled to regain its feet and continue its flight, squealing loudly the while. The youth hanging on grimly, was dragged along the ground — to the shouted laughter from behind the junipers. Walter Stewart was actually clutching the sow's little tail now, to the further delight of the watchers. But he was by no means put off in his determination by this ridicule. Bumping over stones, roots and pebbles, whilst clinging to the tail with one hand he was reaching with the other for his belt, where hung his dirk. Somehow he managed to unsheath it.

But to use the weapon effectively on the sow, in his present position was well nigh impossible. Desperately he sought to get to his feet. The brute was running too fast, and had enormous strength in those massive forequarters. Young Stewart managed to get approximately to his knees, still being pulled along, and from this most awkward and unsteady of stances began aiming a series of wild stabs at the only part of the creature's anatomy he could reach, its hindquarters and rear orifice — with delighted and distinctly rude advice yelled by the bystanders.

Right to the river the animal ran, the King's grandson still attached and smiting. In the water, however, all was changed, for the pig family are not the best of swimmers and Walter Stewart was. The pressure went off him, likewise the friction on his legs. Now he could use his dirk to better effect and at a better target-area. It was still a messy, protracted, splashing and bloody affair, but the end was no longer in doubt. Presently the poor brute was in its death-throes and being towed back to the bank.

"I warrant you have never seen boar hunted so!" Alexander cried. "But then — nor have I! My brother Walter goes his own way."

The exodus from the burning forest had by no means stopped for this interlude, and most of the hunters were too busy to watch the end of it. Creatures of all kinds were emerging now, mainly deer, but more wolves, singly and in groups, foxes always alone, bewildered-seeming badgers, even a great wild-cat in spitting, tail-lashing fury — which the Earl shouted was his, and slew with a crossbow-bolt, laughingly shouting death to Clan Cattanach. There were hordes of lesser animals also, of course — red squirrels, mountain hares still half-white, stoats, weasels, marten, the ground a moving carpet of voles, mice, shrews and the like. Most of the birds had already flown but some there were still low-fliers like capercailzie, woodcock, blackcock and owls.

Then suddenly Jamie gasped, and pointed. "Look!" he cried. "A man! Dear God — a man! There, behind those alders. Save us — another! Men — in that inferno! Why? Why do they linger? In there. Are they mad? With safety here."

Alexander Stewart did not answer. The figures in the trees disappeared.

"Are they *your* men? Your father's?" Jamie demanded. "What do they there?"

"Wait, you," Rob Stewart advised shortly.

"More! Saints alive — there are more! See yonder. Beyond the fallen tree. The upturned roots. Two more — no, three."

The others were not looking where Jamie Douglas pointed. For, a little further forward, a single man had run out to the very edge of the trees, staring towards them, clad only in a philabeg or short kilt, body blackened and gleaming with sweat. He paused, pant-ing. And even as he did so, an arrow zipped out from the juniper barrier and took him full in the throat. With a bubbling scream, hands up trying to tear the thing out, he fell, spewing blood.

"God in Heaven!" Jamie whispered.

Almost immediately thereafter two more men burst out at the front of the woodland, with a red deer hind alongside, and ran straight to the loch-shore. One was in ragged tartans, the other completely naked, with all hair burned off. They got almost to the water's edge before marksmen in the boats dropped them both. The deer sped on, unchallenged now.

A cheer rang out from the junipers.

Jamie turned to stare at the Stewart brothers. "Murder!" he choked. "Cruel, bloody murder! The most heartless kill-ing . . .!"

"Killing, I agree," Sir Alexander nodded, although with less calm confidence than his usual. "But not murder, no. Justice, shall we say? Execution. These are Cattanachs, a broken clan. Rejected by the chiefs of Clan Chattan. They live by robbery, rapine, slaying. As fierce as yon wild-cat — which is their emblem . . ."

As he spoke another blood-curdling scream rang out, and a fourth racing refugee dropped, to thrash about in agony.

"Murder, I said!" Jamie repeated, hoarsely. "Savage, merciless murder. Hunted down like brute-beasts . . . !"

"Justice, fool!" Rob Stewart grated, gripping his arm hard. "Watch your tongue, Douglas! I warn you! Our father is Justiciar of the North. These are felons, outlaws. The scourge of the forests. They can be taken no other way . . ."

"Burned out! Hunted as though for sport! All the fire was for this? Not the wolves and boars and deer? *This!* For *men*! The rest but by-play waiting? This is your father's justice? Small wonder that he is named the Wolf of Badenoch!"

"I advise that you hold your tongue, Douglas!" Sir Alexander said gratingly. "For your own sake. Since *you* are now within that jurisdiction!"

Small point in reminding that any such jurisdiction was now withdrawn by Crown edict. These Stewarts would make their own edicts and laws. Jamie, belatedly sensible, kept his lips tight closed.

There were fourteen of the so-called Cattanach slain, the last two with hair and beards aflame, before the fire reached this last corner of the trap and the sport was over. Gillies gathered up the game and began to gralloch the deer. But there was no attempt to collect the human victims, who were left to lie where they had fallen — on the principle apparently that they were not fit for Christian burial and that their own kind would no doubt deal with them in due course.

Jamie found himself curiously dealt with. He was not brought and presented to the Earl, but indeed kept carefully out of that man's way, by the young Alexander. He could not believe that the Wolf had not noticed his presence, even recognised him — for he had seen him often enough in the past in the Earl of Douglas's company; but no move nor sign was made towards him. Alexander went and spoke with his father, alone, leaving Rob to guard the prisoner. When he came back, it was to order a turn-around and the ride back to Loch-an-Eilean.

It was some little time before Jamie realised that the Wolf's party was not following them. He mentioned the fact.

"My father has set up a hunting-camp for this night in Glen More," Alexander told him. "There is no accommodation for you there. Moreover it is best, I think, that you do not see my lord in your present state of mind, Sir James. I have no cause to love you, but I conceive you to be honest after your own fashion. I would not wish to see you sealing your own fate by hot words to our sire — who suffers such less than kindly! Some breathing-space is advisable, I say — during which it is my hope that you will learn to mind your words, and take that black Douglas scowl off your face! Tomorrow we shall ride for Lochindorb."

"You are very . . . careful, sir!"

"Perhaps I am the careful one of a scarcely careful family. Though not all would call me that, I think! Eh, Rob?"

That youth smiled, for the first time in Jamie's experience.

*   *   *

It seemed that this Lochindorb Castle lay something under a score of miles to the north, well beyond the Spey valley and amongst the high moorlands of Braemoray. Why it should be necessary for Jamie to be taken there for his interview with the Earl was not fully explained; but leaving the churlish Rob behind at Loch-an-Eilean, Alexander took him off next morning, wrapped in plaids against the chill rain-storms. They went through the dripping woodlands, by Inverdruie and Loch Pityoulish, through a small pass close above the Spey and so into another vast forest area, that of Abernethy, separated from Rothiemurchus by outliers of the Glen More hills.

There was no fording Spey, so wide and deep a river; but there was a ferry at a township called Boat of Garten, where quite a fleet of large flat-bottomed scows were maintained by brawny Highlandmen, seemingly in the Stewart pay. Clearly no one would cross Spey from north or south unless with the Wolf's permission. The cattle-droves of the North on their way to the southern markets had to come here — and pay the required mail.

In the distance, eastwards, down the great valley, they could glimpse from sundry eminences another smallish stronghold; Castle Roy, Alexander explained, of which the boar-slaying Sir Walter Stewart, his younger brother, was captain. It seemed that the Earl had knighted all his five sons by the Lady Mariota de

Athyn, to distinguish and raise them above his other innumerable bastards, as the ruling family of Badenoch.

They forded another quite major river, the Dulnain, and soon thereafter began to climb out of the woodlands, and the wide Spey valley itself. Gradually open heather succeeded the pine trees, bare rolling moorlands the glades and glens. In intermittent rain-showers, the change was not for the better.

Nevertheless, Alexander Stewart was friendlier again today, good company indeed. Perhaps it was because he had none of his brothers with him, as witnesses. No direct references were made to the fire or the slaying of the Cattanachs, indeed little to his father at all. But of his mother he spoke warmly, of his brothers amusingly, and of their life here in the North spiritedly. In return he asked a great many, and pointed, shrewd and intelligent questions about conditions and personalities in the South and at Court. Clearly this Wolf's whelp hankered after a wider and fuller life than Badenoch offered him.

As well that their converse was interesting, for the journey was not. Jamie had not realised that there were such endless barren moors in the land, treeless, almost featureless, seemingly extending almost to infinity. In the Douglasdale country of Lanarkshire there were long, dreich moorlands; but nothing to compare with these. It was a high plateau, really, and they often were riding through the skirts of chill clouds, far from flat, dotted with legions of small dark lochans and peat-pools. But the unending brown desolation of the heather, pitted with black and ominous peat-hags, was what predominated. When that heather was in bloom it would be a scarcely believable sea of purple; but meantime it was a lost and dreary wilderness. Great herds of deer were there, as brown as the heather; but apart from these, the whirring grouse and the circling buzzards and eagles, the entire land appeared to be empty.

It was mid-afternoon, and the weather improving, before there was any major change. Summits and ridges with some definition had gradually been taking the place of the everlasting heather billows and troughs. Ahead these now steepened and grew into true hills, not so very high above the surrounding plateau but no doubt of quite substantial height above sea-level. Ascending the long southern flank of one of these, they topped a shoulder and there opened before them, with no prior indication, a wide amphitheatre, an oval green hollow amongst all the surrounding and prevailing brownness, perhaps three miles long by half that in width, not actually forested but dotted with trees, pine and birch, the first seen for hours. In the centre the hollow cradled a loch of the same general shape, of approximately half its dimensions; and in the loch was an island from which rose a many towered castle. A more unlikely place in which to find a fortress would be hard to imagine.

"Lochindorb?" Jamie exclaimed. "That? There?"

"None other. You are surprised?"

"This your *home*? The Earl your father's seat? Lost in this wilderness?"

"Scarcely lost. But well hidden, is it not? Secure. There is no more secure hold in all Scotland than that, I swear!"

"Secure, perhaps, yes. But to what purpose? Out here? Well hidden from what? Eagles? Deer? Your Cattanachs? Security must serve a purpose, surely? What, here?"

"An excellent purpose, my friend," Stewart asserted. "From that secure hold most of the North is governed. In the wilderness, yes — but none so remote. From Loch-an-Eilean and upper Spey, perhaps. But from what is important here, not so. See those stout towers. Why think you Edward Plantagenet built them here? For the King of England it was who turned this from a mere eagles' nest of the Comyns into a strong fortress, near a century ago. One of the greatest soldiers of Christendom, however much he hated Scotland. Not for any whim or fancy. From this hold two or three hours' riding will put you astride every route into the North, or out of it — by Findhorn and the Streens, the Slochd and Strath Dearn, Strath Nairn and Drommossie, Strath Errick and the Great Glen, Latterach, Glen Lossie and Lower Spey. The Laigh of Moray lies open to the east, Cawdor and Inverness to the north, with the Ness crossings, and all the Mondath Liath passes to the west. He who holds Lochindorb not only sleeps secure in his bed but has all the North by the throat! English Edward knew it, if *you* did not!"

Suitably abashed, Jamie rode on down towards the loch.

Halfway down the slope the horns were ululating from the castle.

"That is to inform all hill-top guards and outposts that it is a

314

friendly party which approaches, that boats will put out from the island — for none are permitted to linger at the shore — and that no aid or reinforcement is required," Alexander explained, with a hint of pride. "We keep but fifty of a garrison — but a thousand can be here within the hour. Your wilderness is less empty than you think perhaps, Sir James!"

"They cannot tell *who* we are, at this range, surely?"

"They have known who we were and where we were since we left Dulnain ford," the other asserted cryptically.

As they drew near, Jamie could see that any superficial resemblance to Loch-an-Eilean was confined to both castles being built on islands. This was a major strength by any standards, five times as large as the other perhaps, a great oblong of high curtain-walls with round towers rising at every angle. There were outer defensive walls to form a bailey or basse-cour, all strengthened by earth-works, ditches and portcullis gateways and draw-bridge — although any attack, necessarily by boat or raft, would have to be on a vast scale and long maintained ever to win a toehold on the island, which had been artificially extended and steepened by timber and masonry to provide only one possible landing-place. The castleton for men-at-arms, stables, byres and farmery were all on the mainland.

Used as he was to powerful castles, Jamie was impressed.

Boats were waiting for them, and Jamie and his four attendants were ferried out to the island. A large cheerful woman and a good-looking girl of about fourteen awaited them at the landing-stage. Alexander embraced them both warmly.

"Here is Sir James Douglas of Aberdour come seeking my lord, Mother," he announced. "Come the long road from Fife, on some especial mission. He looks stern, but is less stiff than he seems!" He laughed. "Sir James — the Lady Mariota de Athyn. And our sister Margaret."

The lady beaming on them, Jamie bowed warily. He was after all a prisoner, and this was the most notorious concubine in the land, in a situation with its own delicacy.

The woman at least appeared to feel no need for wariness nor yet delicacy — which indeed was a word scarcely appropriate to her. In her forties, she was generously made, tall, still handsome with much red hair, open, comely features, a wide mouth, a ready smile and great vitality. She was, in fact, of chiefly Celtic blood, being a daughter of Mackay of Strathnaver, in Sutherland, chief of the name, descendant of the noted MacEth line from which also sprang the Earls of Ross. So she was oddly enough distantly connected with the Wolf's true wife Euphemia, Countess of Ross. Her brother Farquhar Mackay of Strathnaver was physician to King Robert. The Celtic MacEth, meaning the Son of Hugh, had like so many another, been 'Normanised' to De Athyn.

"Welcome to my house, Sir James," she said genially, as though this was the most ordinary domestic establishment. "I have heard of the brave Sir James, and Otterburn fight. I rejoice to meet such a hero! In especial one who looks the part!" And she half-curt-seyed to him smiling, like any girl a third of her age. "We live very quiet here, at Lochindorb — I fear you will find us exceeding dull. We cannot offer you the excitements of the Court." She chuckled. "Not that I have ever experienced them! But my house is yours. Use it as your own." She had a deep, throaty voice, highly attractive.

Astonished at such a reception to the Wolf of Badenoch's lair, Jamie swallowed and muttered disconnected inanities — the more so as, turning towards the great portcullis-hung gateway, they were confronted by a long beam, on the left, projecting from the southern corner parapet of the outer bailey walling, a beam from which dangled six men, in varying stages of decomposition.

Alexander noted the visitor's expression, if his mother did not. "Prime malefactors those, Sir James," he sang out. "We have to keep the King's peace, here. Fortunately the wind is very seldom from the south."

The girl Margaret trilled a laugh. "I think Sir James is shocked!" she said.

"We certainly must have them taken down soon," the Lady Mariota nodded.

Within the curtain-walled enclosure, the castle was not unlike Ruthven, save that it was larger and cleaner, a small walled town in miniature. There was almost a street down the centre, with single-storey subsidiary buildings on either side, all of stone here, with no dangerous thatching to burn, and including a quite hand-some chapel, kitchens, brewhouse, laundry and the like, also an armoury. At the upper end of the street were the great and lesser halls and a two-storeyed range of domestic quarters, where Jamie was conducted, his men being bestowed near the kitchens.

There was no sign of the master of the house.

A peculiar interlude followed, almost unreal to Jamie's mind. For two days he was the honoured guest in a hospitable, comfortable and well-found house, treated with courtesy and respect. There was no least hint that he was, in fact, a captive, that his very life might be in danger, that any sort of threat hung over this establishment. Only those dangling bodies in their creaking chains in the outer bailey spoke of any sort of abnormality. He was free to go where he would to see what he would — and if he did not say all he would, that was of his own choice. Of course, he was unable to leave the island without requesting the services of boatmen; and once over there, it had been made entirely obvious that he would be under observation all the time and could go no further in any direction than his hosts desired. He went hunting and hawking with Alexander and the girl Margaret, although it was now May, and the breeding-season limited sport. He fished in the loch and chased mountain-hares with greyhounds. He attended chapel — for there was a resident chaplain. He talked much with the Lady Mariota — and came to the opinion that in many ways she was a woman to be admired. More than once he was on the point of touching on the subject that had brought him here, and the matter of the Bishop of Moray's injunction. But each time he drew back, in embarrassment, believing that it might be the end of the good companionship—moreover, for best effect, it would be put directly to the Earl, when he elected to return.

That happened on the evening of the third day. Just as dusk was falling, there was a blowing of horns from hilltop outposts, answered loudly from the fortress, and presently a large cavalcade of horsemen, laden pack-horses and running gillies appeared over the skyline to the south. An air of anticipation came over the castle, Jamie's contribution less than joyous.

He kept discreetly out of the way while the Earl was being welcomed home with three of his sons, Duncan, Walter and James. When, later, Jamie was summoned to the lesser hall for the evening meal, the Wolf greeted him with superficial civility, although with the arched eyebrow and fleering smile which was more or less habitual.

"Ha—the Douglas knight-errant!" he exclaimed. "One of the paladins of Otterburn come to my poor table in the wilderness. I regret that I was not here in person to receive you, Sir James. But

317

my lady and young Alexander would serve you well enough? Perhaps better than might I!"

Uncertain what that last might mean, the other bowed. "I have been most kindly used, my lord — since I reached Lochindorb," he said, with emphasis on that last word. Two could barb their remarks at the end.

"Say you so? Journeying in these parts can have its hazards, young man. We all suffer them on occasion. Even I, the Justiciar! However, you have reached my house safely — for which you may think to thank your Saint Bride. Your Douglas saint, yes? Was she not burned to death, poor woman? Or do I mistake?"

Jamie moistened his lips, recognising the warning. He inclined his head.

"My lord — how gloomy an invitation to your table! You will quite put our gallant guest off his meat," the Lady Mariota said cheerfully. "You will all be hungry, I swear. Sir James — sit you beside me, and tell me more of Sir Will of Nithsdale's son and the Lady Gelis. I have not understood this . . ."

That meal was a very different one from the others Jamie had had at Lochindorb. There was a tension in the air, a lack of ease — although to be sure, neither the Earl nor his lady appeared to be aware of it. Alexander and his sister certainly were restrained, almost anxious — whatever the attitude of their brothers. Jamie came to the conclusion that this aura of wariness, discretion, was endemic when the Wolf was present, an inevitable reaction to his dominant, predatory and unpredictable character. If he did not frighten Mariota de Athyn, she was alone in that. The three sons who had arrived with him, aged about fifteen, fourteen and twelve, Sir Walter, the middle one, a twin brother of Margaret's, had the air of savage cubs ready to snarl and bite — but not in their father's presence. Alexander appeared to be the only one with a mannerly veneer. Jamie's efforts to respond frankly and cordially to the Lady Mariota's amiable conversation were less than successful.

His relief when the Earl abruptly rose from the table was shortlived. For when the older man strode off, it was to pause at the door.

"Young man," he called back. "If, as you say, you have a privy message for me, I will hear it now. Come."

"Allow that he finishes his meat, Alex," the lady protested — but Jamie got to his feet, bowed, and followed the Wolf out. This thing had been put off for sufficiently long.

In a small first-floor chamber of the domestic range, the Earl shut the door on them and turned on his visitor.

"Well?" he demanded — and there was no attempt now to disguise hostility and impatience, as they stood facing each other. "Who sent you? And why?"

Jamie endeavoured — more successfully than he knew — not to show his trepidation. "My mission in the North, my lord, is two-fold," he said. "Firstly to find a man whom I believe may give *me* information as to the murder of my lord the Earl of Douglas. Secondly to bring to *you* information which you may find to your advantage. I come from Dunfermline and your royal sisters, the Ladies Isabel and Gelis."

"My sisters never sought to advantage me ere this, Douglas!" the other barked. "Why should they do so now? Why should they think that they *could*? And send such a stripling as yourself. To me!"

"As to that, my lord, I cannot answer you. But I was coming anyway. On my own quest. To try find this man I spoke of . . ."

"Well, well — out with it, boy! What is this information to advantage me?"

"It concerns the matter, the delicate matter, of, of your mar-riage, my lord. And the Bishop of Moray's injunction . . ."

"Christ God! You, *you* dare come here to talk of that! You, sprig of Douglas, to me — Buchan!"

"Only as a messenger, sir. If the message I bring is to your advantage, does my lowly estate concern you?"

"Boy — do not use that tone of voice with me! 'Fore God — I have hanged better men than you for a deal less than that!"

"No doubt, my lord. But you will not hang me, I think, until you have heard my message! When you may have cause to thank me, instead."

"That we shall see. But I warn you — speak with care. For I am not gentle with those who offend — and I like not your tone of voice."

"I little require your warning, my lord. Since I have seen your way with those who you esteem offensive — in Rothiemurchus fire! So I speak with due care. If I may?"

"Speak, then."

"The injunction I spoke of. From the Bishop of Moray. That you should forthwith forsake the Lady Mariota to cohabit with your true wife, the Countess of Ross, under penalty of £200 . . ."

"Damnation — how know *you* this?"

"You think that it comes from Bishop Barr, my lord. But in fact it is your own brother, the Governor's doing. In conjunction with the Primate, Bishop of St. Andrews. And it was your *half-brother*, the Archdeacon Thomas, who learned of it at St. Andrews and informed your sisters. I was there."

"Go on."

"You have not obeyed the injunction, my lord — as they conceived that you would not. It is a trap. For though they declare the penalty to be but £200 payment if you do not, the truth is far otherwise. You were given three months to comply — which is now overpast. Then the true penalty is excommunication — the greater, not the lesser. Excommunication by Holy Church!"

If Jamie had hoped for astonishment, dismay, even fury, he was disappointed. The other merely nodded, hot eyes narrowed.

"And they think that clerks' rigmarole and ranting will terrify me, Alexander of Buchan! My brother Robert at least should know me better."

It was Jamie who was astonished. "You, you knew?" he said.

"Aye, I knew. I am none so ill-informed, in my wilderness. Your precious information is a mite stale, boy!"

"But, but . . ."

The Wolf snapped his fingers. "That for your excommunication!" he added.

Floundering, the younger man sought to recover his lost confidence. "My lord — have you considered well? What excommunication can mean? Not just prelates' pronouncements and anathemas. But the loss of all rights, in law. The excommunicate becomes as dead before the law. They will declare your earldom, titles and lands forfeit. All rights and privileges as the King's son likewise. All offices taken from you. And you unable to contest it, in law . . ."

"*I* make the laws in Badenoch, boy!"

"Perhaps, my lord. But in the realm at large? In the South? There the Governor controls all. It would serve you ill to become an outlaw there, with no rights . . ."

"When I go south, my young friend, I will take my rights with me, never fear! A thousand broadswords will speak louder than any bishops' anathemas!"

"Yet your brother, the Earl Robert, does not think so. Or he would not be going to this trouble. And he is not a man to misjudge in such things."

"Then I must teach brother Robert that he can misjudge indeed! Teach him, and his bishops, a lesson they will not forget. I will teach him who rules in the North — and what will be the fate of his wretched son Murdoch should he show nose north of Atholl! I have already made plans to do the like. It may be that, if I do not hang you first, you may have the pleasure of witnessing that showing and teaching, Douglas!"

"Why should you hang me, sir?" Despite himself, Jamie's voice quivered a little. "I have done you no hurt. I came to *serve* you, with this information — not knowing that you already had it. Wherein do I offend?"

"You came from my brother's Court — and I trust none who do so. I mislike the liberties you take with my sisters, Douglas — even though they may encourage you. And you called my son Andrew savage, did you not?"

Jamie cleared his throat. "He struck me. Twice. Imprisoned me without cause. You knighted your sons, my lord. You know that one knight does not strike another. As to your royal sisters, I have taken no single liberty. They have been kind to me — but only as to a servant they favour. And I am not of the Governor's Court, misliking it — as it mislikes me!"

The Wolf was eyeing him assessingly. "You talk overmuch for a stripling," he said softly. "Even for a Douglas! I may have to still that tongue, I think. As I stilled the other from the same airt."

"I, I cannot stop you, my lord — since I am in your power. But ... I am your guest, am I not?"

"Not mine, boy — not mine! *I* did not bring you here. You are my captive — which is something different."

"But why should you conceive me your enemy? When I came to serve you. And when our true enemy is the same, my lord. The Governor. He it is who seeks to trap you and bring you down. And he it is who, I believe, caused the murder of the Earl James of

Douglas, at Otterburn. Why I came seeking Patrick Ramsay, his minion . . ."

"Patrick Ramsay, you say? You came seeking Ramsay?"

"Yes. He is the man who can tell me whether the Governor paid Bickerton to slay the Earl James . . ."

The Wolf hooted a laugh. "Ramsay will tell you nothing! Come, boy — over here." He strode to the window, and threw open the lower timber-shutter. "See you, yonder. The second from this end. Or it may be the third — I mind not. There is your Patrick Ramsay." He was pointing at the row of hanging corpses.

Jamie stared. "You mean . . .? Ramsay — he is dead? You hanged him? Hanged Ramsay."

"To be sure. Few more deserved it. I hanged him in November. Or it may have been earlier."

Jamie let out his breath in a long sigh. Here, then, was the end of his quest — and nothing decided. Ramsay silenced, like Bickerton, for ever. This hazardous journey into the North for nothing. All but wasted time and effort. He would never now uncover Robert Stewart's guilt.

"Why did you hang him?" he asked, flatly.

"For the best of reasons. He it was who carried the insolent Bishop's letter to me. As to this of my wife. I made him talk. We have means here to open the tightest lips! From him I learned of this excommunication. Before he died."

"Need you have killed him?"

"Why not? He was a rogue, employed by rogues. Working against me. All such that I lay hands on die. I warn you! Besides, it was necessary, having spoken, that his lips be closed."

"He said nothing of the Earl James? Of his murder? Of Bickerton?"

"I did not ask him, boy. I know naught of that. Nor greatly care."

"Yet could you prove that the Governor had my master slain, my lord, you would have forged a strong weapon against him. The Douglas power. Even the new Earl Archibald could not save him from the Douglas wrath!"

The other stared at him for long moments. "And this was what you sought?" he demanded. "To prove this — to seek to bring down my brother?"

322

"Yes."

"And my sisters? They are in this with you?"

"Yes."

"I see. Aye — well, then, I may come to think a little less ill of you, Douglas! Who knows? Though do not rely on it, my friend! I will think on what you have said. Have you more to tell me?"

Jamie shook his head. "Nothing that I would think would interest you. But . . . may I go now, my lord? Leave your house? Return to the South? For what I came to do is done. Or no longer able to be done. My purpose here . . ."

"That you will not, sirrah. You will bide here, during my pleasure. Go when I say you may go, not before — *if* I say it!"

"Then I am your prisoner still? Why?"

"Was it not guest you said, earlier? Guest will sound better meantime. My lady's guest — not mine!" The Earl laughed, and waved towards the door.

More depressed than he had been for long, even in the Ruthven vault, Jamie followed him out.

XX

IT WAS NEARLY a month later, strange and difficult weeks, before there was any major development, any sign of the reason for Jamie's detention at Lochindorb. During that period he was well-treated by the Lady Mariota, her daughter and Alexander, ignored or mocked by Duncan and Walter, and tolerated by the youngest son, James. Fortunately or otherwise, the Wolf himself, with one or more of his sons, was from home for most of the time, on and off; when present at the castle he varied his reactions towards the reluctant visitor through careless bonhomie and utter disregard, to scornful railing and sheer abuse. In the period Jamie saw three men hanged, others lashed with whips, and one old woman, allegedly a witch, thrown into the loch to drown. All in the name of the King's justice. Otherwise he hunted, hawked, coursed, fished, fed well, listened to Alexander on the lute or singing — and he was a notable performer — and talked much with the lady of the house.

Then, one evening in early June the Earl, who had been away overnight, this time with all his sons, came riding back in especially boisterous state, seeming to be in a strange combination of satisfaction and frustration. All who had been with him were noisier than usual, save Alexander, who was indeed more silent, preoccupied. Clearly something significant had happened, but what was not vouchsafed to the captive; and when a few leading questions elicited no explanations, his pride forbade him pressing the matter. Alexander was undoubtedly unhappy, however, his brothers distinctly elevated, and their father varying between extreme irritability and loud cheer. The Lady Mariota remained her friendly, genial self, but there was no question that she was concerned about something and that there was tension in the air.

It was a few nights afterwards that Alexander came to the prisoner's little chamber, with the rest of the house retired to bed. "Your waiting is over, Sir James," he announced, though somewhat grimly. "We ride tomorrow — and you with us. You have been chafing, I know, in this idleness. Well, at least there will be an end to that."

At the distinctly ominous tone of voice, Jamie reserved expressions of rapture. "You ride where? To do what? And in what way am I concerned? I gather that it is not that I am to be released?"

"Scarcely that. Since you have been kept here for a purpose. No — my father has been waiting. Waiting for too long for his patience — or yours, perhaps. Now there is to be an end to waiting. But whether you will enjoy the doing, instead of the waiting, remains to be seen."

"I have been waiting for my release, Sir Alexander, for some reason for my confinement here. Any reason may be easier to accept than none. But . . . what have *you*, and your father, been waiting for?"

"In the main, for the old King, my grandfather, to die. He is gone now, at last. We had word from the South some days ago. Now it is confirmed. So there is no longer need to wait."

"The King dead? Poor old man — but he is better away. He had no pleasure in his life, for long."

"As to that I know not. I never saw him. But he has died at Dundonald, his own house. At a great age, seventy-four years, no less."

"God rest his soul," Jamie said. "The Lady Isabel will mourn him, at least. It, it will mean great changes."

"Changes, yes. And so we act quickly, here in the North."

"Act quickly?"

The other nodded, but did not amplify.

"What does the Governor now? Do you know?"

"He continues to govern. But not us! As my father will demonstrate."

"But the Crown? What of the Crown? The Earl John is heir. But . . .?"

"The Earl John is now King. By the Grace of God and his brother Robert! Though not King John. John is considered an unlucky name for a king — too many Johns have come to grief. So he is to be crowned King Robert the Third. An apt enough style, since the true Robert Stewart will rule him and through him!"

"So! I, many, feared that the Earl Robert might seize the Crown for himself."

"As did we all. That is why my father waited. Much depended on it. But he, Uncle Robert, has chosen to remain Governor . . ."

"Governor, *still*? But—will his brother the new King, permit that? An old bed-ridden man might appoint a Governor; but the Earl John is none so old."

"Nevertheless, the word is that he has reappointed his brother as Governor to rule in his stead — or Robert has appointed himself and the King has acceded. He is weak, gentle, as we all know. He will be just as wax in Robert's hands, even more so than the old man, who had some strength once. In this way Robert will have all the power — but when aught goes wrong, the King it is who will bear the blame!"

"Yes, I see it. Though, John is weak and gentle, yes — but he has a son who is neither. And the Lord David, your cousin, is now heir to the throne. Young as he is, I swear there will be trouble."

"The more trouble for Robert Stewart the better! *We* plan to make some, forthwith!"

325

"What trouble will you make which can hurt the Governor, far in the South?"

"That is for my father to show you, not me. We have already made a start — but only a start." He shrugged and sighed in one, but left it at that. When Jamie pressed for details, the other shook his head and made for the door. "I came but to prepare you, Sir James," he said. "To be ready to ride tomorrow. For the rest — you will find out. A good night."

Next day, then, a major cavalcade rode out northwards from the castleton of Lochindorb. Always the Earl went heavily escorted and well armed; but on this occasion the company not only bristled with arms but went dressed in their finest, a colourful admixture of Highland and Lowland, tartans, Celtic jewellery, velvet doublets, chain-mail shirts, calf-skins and breast-plates, the Wolf himself splendid in gold-inlaid half-armour. Sir Andrew from Ruthven and Rob Stewart from Loch-an-Eilean arrived to join them, with another half-brother named Thomas, captain of some castle called Drumin. All five of the Lady Mariota's sons were present, however many other of her lord's bastards were included in the noisy, laughing retinue — and certainly there were not a few who might have claimed Stewart features. They rode, or ran, under many banners and pennons, a gallant-seeming concourse.

Parties began to join them almost at once, from every valley and township — and there were more of these latter than was apparent. The Dorback Burn, quite a major stream, flowed out of the north end of the loch, and down this they proceeded in the brilliant early summer sunshine. Soon, on the slightly lower levels of the vast Moor of Dava they had collected contingents large and small, doubling their strength to fully five hundred, all wild-looking, bare-shanked Highlandmen under their chieftains and tacksmen. Only a small proportion were mounted, the rest no less mobile for being afoot. They went at a tireless lope which easily matched the garrons' trot.

Presently they left the Dorback and the well-trodden droveroad to turn away eastwards and climb up and up over the shoulder of a long low double-summit hill and across a bleak upland watershed of mosses, peat-hags, pools and tall old heather, with the prominent landmark of the pointed Knock of Braemoray rising blue out of the prevailing browness some miles to the north-west. It was the sort of terrain no Lowland force would dream of traversing; but these Highland caterans took it literally in their stride, caring nothing for the quaking bogs and the splattering peat-broth, leaping the tussocks, skirting the emerald-green treacheries, splashing through the burns and shallows, and making rather better time indeed than did the garrons.

Jamie rode between Alexander and the boy James, a little way behind the Wolf and his chieftains. He had been so far vouchsafed no hint as to their mission and objective, his enquiries eliciting only that they were making for Dallas, on the River Lossie, only some half-dozen miles from the sea at Findhorn Bay.

Dallas, when reached in its own hidden valley amongst the lower cattle-dotted foothills, proved to be a quite large community, and now something in the nature of an armed camp. The Wolf had already proved Alexander's assertion that he could summon up a thousand men within an hour or two; now fully another thousand was awaiting him here. It was a notably secure place, at a joining of waters amongst low green hills, for a secret mustering of an army. But why should the King's Lieutenant and Justiciar of the North require such secret army?

It was mid-afternoon when they arrived at Dallas, having covered fifteen difficult miles. They appeared to be halting here for some time, with fires lit by the riverside, cattle being roasted whole, liquor available in abundance and a general air of good cheer. The Wolf seemed to be in the best of spirits now — but evidently was not in the least interested in his prisoner, who was left to languish alone, although strictly guarded. More clansmen kept coming in as the day wore on.

Jamie was dozing, sitting with his back against a tree, seemingly the only non-cheerful individual of that great company, when Alexander brought him a smoking rib of beef, for his evening meal, with a beaker of ale, and sat to partake with him.

"What does your father want with me?" he demanded, sourly. "Has he any reason? Any reason, at all? For bringing me today? Or for holding me captive these months? I do not believe that he has — only that I am in his power and he enjoys showing that power. A despot. He oppresses for the sake of oppression . . ."

"Have a care of your words, Sir James!"

"Care? I am past caring. I can see nothing in which I may be of use to him. Is there to be no end to this . . .?"

"You have a use, yes. My father does nothing without due purpose." The other spoke thoughtfully. "I am not sure, but I believe that it is partly because of your friendship — if that is the word — with his sisters, my aunts. The princesses. He conceives you to have a possible value there. In his continuing battle with his brother Robert, he might well find his sisters' support useful. He believes you to be very close to aunts Isabel and Gelis, and thinks that they might be prepared to do much to gain your release. I heard him say as much to my mother."

"But surely he cannot keep me endlessly a captive in case such opportunity arises?"

"Not endlessly, no. Matters come to a head, now. It is a trial of strength, between these two brothers of the King. And you are caught up in it. We all are. But *you*, to be sure, entangled yourself! You came here, to Badenoch, for that purpose."

"I cannot see that it is necessary to hold me prisoner . . ."

"Do not think that I have not sought to convince him of that. But you have given him much offence, with your too outspoken tongue. I have warned you, many times. He has told me that you are fortunate — and that is true, I assure you. He could as easily have killed you, for crossing him, struck you down with his sword, or had you hanged. As he has done so many. That he has not done so is because he thinks to find you useful. As a witness. And possibly out of some respect for your courage — for he much admires courage. But he has no patience with foolhardiness."

Jamie shook his head. "This possible usefulness I cannot see. Even if he does believe that my safety may carry some weight with the princesses, why bring me on this expedition? What is the object? You said something of witness? Of what am I to be a witness?"

"Let us say of what can happen to those who oppose the Earl of Buchan and Lieutenant of the North. For he still is that, whatever the Earl Robert may say."

"And what parliament may say?"

"Parliament, indeed! What power has your parliament here? My father rules the North, and will continue to rule it. If he must needs take stern measures in that rule, he is not the first to do so. This land needs a strong hand. No dispensing of edicts and decrees will rule the North — only the clenched fist. And not only the North, in the end, but the entire kingdom. The Governor recognises that, and uses deceit, plot, murder, to enforce his clenched fist. That is not my father's way. He is a more honest man, whatever else. He uses his power openly, before all men. He stabs in the front, not the back!"

"And for whom am I to witness his stabbings?"

Alexander drew a quick breath, but controlled his voice. "For Robert himself, I would think. And your Douglas earl. The King also, it may be. Certainly the princesses. All those who have influence in the South. A Douglas witness will be believed. See you — my father does not confide in me, in any of us. But I would say that he reasons thus. The new King is an even weaker monarch than his father. He will not *rule*, only reign. So others must rule for him. He, my father, hates and despises his brother Robert, and would displace him, as Governor of the whole realm, if he could. There is only a year or two between them in age, both strong men. You do not love the Earl Robert. Which would you prefer as Governor?"

"God save me — I do not know!"

"Aye. So there you have it. Even the man of convictions, Sir James Douglas, does not know! My father, then, will seek displace Robert. But if he cannot, he will at least seek to maintain his rule of the North. He will not be turned aside by excommunications and threats. Hence his present harsh measures. Edward of England burned Berwick-on-Tweed and slew 17,000. As warning, to save him burning all Scotland . . ."

"Harsh measure? What mean you by that? Is that what we are at, here? Imposing harsh measures?"

The other shrugged and rose to his feet. "We shall see. As I say, I am not in my father's full confidence." He was moving away when he paused. "I would sleep now, if you can. I understand that we ride three hours before sunrise."

"Three hours before sunrise? Why that, in God's name?"

He was not vouchsafed an answer.

Sunrise was in fact timed for five thirty a.m., and in the small hours of the morning the Wolf's augmented force, now perhaps 3,000 strong, left the Dallas area to proceed down the valley of the Lossie, a lengthy column. Scouts rode ahead and to the flank, along the wooded slope of the Hill of the Wangie.

Through the sleeping and quite heavily wooded foothill country they rode and marched, by the side of a now quite large river, by Kellas and Buinach to where the Latterach joined Lossie, and on by Manbeen, with the land ever sinking before them and the hills lessening and drawing back. It was not so dark, of a northern Scotland June, that much of the landscape was not fairly evident, and it was clear that they were coming down into more settled lowland country — although of course Jamie Douglas had scant idea as to where they were. They halted for a while, after perhaps ten miles, at a ford and milling community called Pittendreich, apparently waiting for a flanking company to arrive, which had for some reason been sent round by an alternative and more northerly route.

"Where are we?" Jamie demanded of Alexander, who alone of the leadership ever troubled to come to his side. "We near the coastal plain, that is clear."

"We are at the mouth of the Vale of St. Andrew. Wherein lies Pluscarden, up yonder. It is a populous vale, and a small force has been sent round that way, to ensure that all is well, there."

"All well! For whom — at this hour of the morning?" Jamie frowned. "Pluscarden, you say? There is a famous monastery there, is there not?"

"There *was*. A great Priory. But it underwent a ... chastening!" On that cryptic remark, Alexander moved off.

When the newcomers arrived, and the Wolf seemed to be satisfied that his rear was secure, they proceeded for another mile or so, and it was noticeable how a quiet had descended upon the entire force now, a sort of furtiveness. When, presently, they emerged from woodland, on a well-defined drove-road, to the Lossie again, which it seemed they must now ford, it lacked less than an hour to sunrise. And Jamie was surprised to see before them, in the strengthening light to the east, the towers and pinnacles of a town black against the yellow. Soon he recognised that it was more than a town; the soaring spires and steeples of a mighty cathedral dominated a host of lesser columns and turrets. That could only be the celebrated Lantern of the North, Elgin Cathedral, seat of the Bishopric of Moray and capital city of the greatest province north of Tay.

Here, having crossed the river, the force divided, swiftly, silently now, into four sections, the Earl retaining perhaps one-third of the whole with himself, the other three being placed each under a son — but not Alexander, who was ordered to stay near his father, and Jamie kept with him. The others had apparently received their orders already, and melted away with their ragged but well-armed companies, in various directions.

The Wolf's thousand proceeded south-about around the city's perimeter at a distance of about a mile, by Hardhillock and Dunkinty. Although the sun had still not actually risen, it was now possible to see most of the city in outline, a dark shadow on its gentle ridge, the towering cathedral at its far, east, end. There was a castle at Elgin too, and a royal one, to the west — actually official seat and court-house of the Lieutenant and Justiciar, Alexander pointed out; but compared with the famous Lantern of the North it was but a poor place, crowning the low Lady Hill — and clearing the Justicar was not making for it now. There were many other steeples and spires, including the tall square tower of a large church midway between castle and cathedral, indicating numerous fine buildings, rather after the style of St. Andrews it seemed to Jamie.

The eastern approaches to the city were through a succession of low sandy banks grown with birch scrub, providing good cover, if that was required, for even a large body of men. Amongst the last of these the Wolf drew up his contingent, facing west now, whilst he and his lieutenants moved quietly forward to an isolated mound beside a deep, glooming pool in a hollow, unusual in being some little way from the river and apparently unconnected therewith. This pool was evidently well known to all, an adjunct of judiciary known as the Ordeal Pot, for the drowning of witches. On the knoll, where a few trees hid them, they waited, Jamie now brought up with the leaders. The air of hushed secrecy and damped-down elation and anticipation was very evident.

Low-voiced, Alexander described at least the physical situation to the prisoner — who certainly did not pretend lack of interest. Just ahead, they could see the quite large buildings, *outside* the walls of the city, of what he identified as the Lazarite leper hospital. This was one of the largest such places in Scotland, and the brothers of the knightly Order of St. Lazarus of Jerusalem who manned it, were noted for their dedication. Just beyond this, in the high perimeter walling, was the gate known as Pann's Port, where the lepers each morning got their daily bread — hence the name — issued to them from the Bishop's bakery within the city; the lepers were not allowed, of course, to enter this, or any other town, as unclean. At sunrise this charitable distribution was made.

It was at this stage that Jamie realised that he was not the only unwilling spectator of this curious enterprise. A tall white-robed friar was now also included in the leadership group, although manifestly holding back from the others. A powerfully-built man of notably proud carriage for a monk, he had been brought to the Pittendreich rendezvous by the company which had there joined them from the Vale of St. Andrew, and so was presumably one of the clerics of the Priory of Pluscarden which Alexander had described as having undergone a chastening. Although there was no communication between the prisoners, it seemed as though he was being held as some sort of hostage.

Alexander was further quietly describing the scene, as they waited. The walls in which this Pann's Port opened were actually those of the cathedral precinct, or chanonry; for the great church had its own walled city-within-a-city, wherein rose innumerable religious edifices and establishments, monasteries, nunneries, friaries, hospices, chapels, shrines and the manses of the cathedral clergy. The secular city had its own walls and gates, of course; but at this eastern section of the perimeter the chanonry wall was the outer one, and this Pann's Port opened directly into the cathedral-yard.

Jamie began to understand, and stared from speaker to leper-hospital to walled gateway, with dawning apprehension, almost horror.

Alexander's voice tailed away as his father came strolling up to them, at length apparently prepared to recognise the existence of his captives.

"So, Douglas," he said genially, holding out a leathern bottle. "A mouthful of wine, for your sustenance, as we await our churchly friends. Come, drink with me — to your further education!"

Jamie bowed stiffly from the saddle of his garron, warily—but did not refuse the proffered refreshment, whatever was meant by this of education.

"Alex has looked after you well enough, I hope?" The Earl seemed to be in expansive mood. "Perhaps you have found it all dull, lacking incident? But we will put that right, never fear. Show you incident in plenty. For you to relate hereafter to your so notable friends in the South. In but a short while now, to be sure. That is, if our churchmen are not over-lazy — like so many of their kind. Eh, Master Sub-Prior?"

The tall Valliscaulian Order friar inclined his tonsured proud head briefly, silently.

"The Church, *Holy* Church, has its uses for once, this day," the Wolf went on. "Prior Moray will no doubt guide us in the matter, where necessary. Keep us right. As is suitable. After all, he has learned our methods. And if he is sufficiently helpful — who knows? He may greatly benefit, rise much higher on the road to Heaven than mere Sub-Prior of Pluscarden — especially as Pluscarden no longer needs a sub-prior, or a prior either! With the good offices of the Lieutenant and Justiciar of the North, he might even aspire to a bishop's mitre! And, by God, the See of Moray is going to require a new Bishop after this day!" And he barked a laugh.

Neither captive said a word.

"So, Sir James," the Earl went on, conversationally, "we have both spiritual and military advice here, eh? You are a soldier of a sort, are you not? Experienced in war and siegery? Although I do not think that you won into any of the cities you assailed, yon time in England! But perhaps you know the business, in theory? How would you advise that we gain entry to this walled city of Elgin, wherein lies my castle and courthouse — aye, and my lady-wife, mark you, my *wife*! Yet whose gates remain ever shut against me, the King's Lieutenant, on the orders of Bishop Barr, the Excommunicator! Your good counsel, sir — since it lacks yet a few minutes to sun-up."

Jamie moistened his lips. "Do I understand, my lord, that you mean to *attack* this city?"

"Attack? I mean to *enter* it, sir, one way or another. And thereafter remonstrate with Master Barr. He claims that it is *his* city, the Bishop's city. I say, as in duty bound, that it is the King's city. We must come to a conclusion on this matter, if there is to be any rule in the North."

"And you require 3,000 men, my lord, to speak with the Bishop?"

"Why, we must needs find a way in, somehow. Many gates to ask at. By stealth — or as we did at Pluscarden last month. Eh, Master Moray? So, Sir James — what is your advice?"

"I scarce think you need any from me, my lord. Clearly you plan a surprise assault at sunrise. On an unsuspecting city, on citizens of your own brother the King. My fellow-subjects, and yours. Who have done no hurt to any." Jamie drew a deep breath. "I would counsel restraint, since you ask me."

"A-a-ah!" That was very quiet. "So you offer me advice on policy. Not tactics, boy? Ah, well, I must be grateful! Meantime, we shall just have to use our own poor wits, lacking your experienced military guidance. This city is guarded. But at sunrise its night guards may be weary and heedless, their duty over. And the day guards may still be part-asleep. There are six gates in all, four in the town-wall, two into this precinct. We seek admittance at them all! But here at Pann's Port, Douglas, we shall seek with especial humility. The lepers from yonder Lazar-house each morning come out to get their bread — provided by Master Barr's bakers. They are not permitted to enter this godly city — but the Pann's Port is opened to let them draw their loaves. So, this fine morning, we shall join the unclean — and in our modesty win more than bread! Will it serve, think you?"

The younger man swallowed. "Only you, my lord, would have thought of that. To use the Bishop's charity to destroy him . . . !"

Jamie Douglas got no further. A mighty backhanded swipe struck him full on the throat, snapping back his head and toppling him from his saddle. He crashed to the ground, and lay still.

* * *

When he came to himself again, he was sitting up, against Alexander Stewart's knee, held by the other's arm. His head throbbed, his vision swam and his throat ached so that it was an agony even to swallow. The friar, Moray, stood nearby, watching. The Earl had gone back to his chiefs. He must have been unconscious, but only for a very short while, presumably.

"You are a fool!" Alexander said, when he saw that the other was conscious again. "Will you never learn, Douglas?" He bit his lip. "I am sorry — but the blame was your own. My father will not be spoken to so. You should know it."

Jamie sought to speak, found it too much of an effort, and forbore.

"Are you hurt, man? Sorely?"

334

"I think not. My throat . . ."

"Why cannot you hold your tongue? As must others. He might have taken his sword to you, instead of his fist. Why?"

There was no answer to that.

The first dazzling golden level rays of the sun were just surmounting the dark band at the seaward horizon as Jamie struggled to his feet, dizzily. With the sudden increase of brightness the scale and detail of the city ahead became more evident, a riot of towers and gables, spires and turrets, domes and battlements. Something of the power and wealth of the Bishop of Moray — and of the reasons for the Wolf's envy and malice — became apparent. But it was the cathedral itself which inevitably drew the eye, quite the most splendid Jamie had ever seen, more noble than St. Andrews or Durham, its two great square towers to the west balanced by a lofty turreted gable to the east, and in the centre another and still mightier tower with soaring spire, the whole edifice three-hundred feet in length, its buttresses, clerestoreys, blindstoreys, arches and triple-tiered windows a challenging symphony in golden-brown stone. The Lantern of the North was well-named.

As the golden dazzle from the east lit up the magnificent building, a deep, sonorous but tuneful, joyful pealing of bells rang out from the cathedral towers to meet the new day, a rich and commanding paean of praise and thankfulness which throbbed and swelled and maintained — and which, even when joined and supported by what seemed to be scores of lesser bells from the other religious houses of Elgin, still clearly sounded through, behind and above all, so that the rest appeared to be no more than a background harmony to a major theme.

Soon after the bells began to ring people started to emerge from the leper hospital, people who limped and scurried and hobbled and crawled, a few at first, then a stream, a crowd, and all making for the Pann's Port gate.

Rob Stewart was already hurrying back to the main body of the Wolf's thousand behind.

Quickly thereafter, in ones and twos, Highlandmen came unobtrusively from this side and that to mingle with the waiting throng before the gate, seeking to appear not too strong and lusty for the pathetic company they kept, wrapped in their plaids, stooping, stumbling. Then the gates were unbarred and opened, from

335

within, and the crowd surged forward. Trestles laden with steaming loaves were pushed and carried through the gateway by black-robed Lazarite brothers, some actually set up within the entrance itself.

The Earl of Buchan hooted. "They could scarce be kinder!" he declared. "No need for our would-be lepers. They could not close those gates in time, now. Come, friends — to our sport! Master Prior — come break your fast!"

The leadership, mounted and otherwise, trotted down to the Pann's Port unhurrying. In through the pitiful crowd of lepers they rode and pushed, knocking the unfortunates over like nine-pins, the white-robed friar striding amidst all in frowning stern-ness. Leaning from his saddle, the Wolf snatched up a warm loaf of bread from a trestle-table and tossed it to him, and another for Jamie.

"Of Bishop Barr's bounty!" he called, grabbing a third for himself. "He bakes good bread," he added, as he bit into it appreciatively. "I might put him into my kitchen at Lochindorb instead of hanging him!"

The Sub-Prior stared ahead of him, expressionless.

Everywhere now the caterans were snatching up the lepers' bread, knocking over the tables — and any of the black-robed, green-crossed brothers who got in their way or made protest.

The Earl rode on into the cathedral precincts, his fierce horse-men behind. It was as simple as that. They were in Elgin, and had not even had to draw a sword, as yet.

Before the great fluted and shafted western door of the cath-edral, twenty-four feet high, the Wolf reined up, just as the bell-ringing died away. "You all know your tasks," he said to his lieutenants. "*I* will attend to Barr and to his property! They will be singing the Angelus in yonder, now. But not the Bishop, I warrant! He will still be in his bed, with a whore on either side, like as not. Wattie — have your men guard all these cathedral doors. Do not enter yet — but none to leave. They will have heard nothing, because of the bells' din. Alex — bring Douglas and the Prior with me. Mackintosh — the Dean's manse is yonder, behind that wall. See to it. Next is the Chanter's, I think, MacPher-son." He pointed again. "That one is the Chancellor's, Mac-Gillivray. Aye, and the Sub-Dean's. God in Heaven — they serve themselves well! Off with you. And remember — tinder and fuel

336

to be sent back. Thatch, straw, plenishings, timbering. Plenty of citizenry to carry it! Aye, and find that Archdeacon Spynie for me — he who brought the Lady Euphemia here from his Forres. I want him, alive — and my wife!" He rode on.

Jamie looked at Alexander Stewart. "This is beyond belief!" he said. The other did not answer but gestured him onwards.

A short distance west of the cathedral rose a tall, slender building, in dressed stone, of three storeys and an attic, within its own little courtyard and walled garden, the Bishop's town-lodging. It was more of a little castle than the senior clergy manses round about, defensible — but within the walled precinct and city its defences were left latent, its courtyard gate wide, its door shut but not locked and barred. This last the Wolf discovered when he rode up. It was a massive door and he made no attempt to kick it open but ordered a gillie to try it. When it opened, he laughed, and shouted, "Barr! Barr, I say! Knave! Clerk! Rouse yourself, ex-communicator! Come down and break your fast with me. I have some bread here — lepers' bread. Come share it with Alexander Stewart!"

There was silence in the house.

"Come, man! Slug-abed! Come and tell me whether I should hang you or drown you or burn you! Your St. Lawrence toasted on a grid-iron, did he not? Will you follow the good Lawrence? Or prefer that I slit your throat for the rogue you are? Come — aye, and bring my wife with you!"

When still there was no least response, he hurled his loaf at the statue of a saint in a niche of the vaulted vestibule, sending it crashing to the floor and shattering. "Ho — servants! Scullions! Rascals! To me — to me, I say!"

A scared face peered round from the turnpike stairfoot. "Lord — he is not here! From home," the apparition wailed. "My Lord Bishop is not here."

"God's Death! Where is he?"

"He is gone to Spynie, sir. He is at Spynie."

"God damn and shrivel his soul! The foul fiend roast him! He came back from Spynie three days agone. I had sure word."

"Yes, sir — yes. But he left again. Yesterday's noon. He entertains company at Spynie . . ."

"Christ in Heaven!" The Wolf's fury all but choked him. He made an awesome sight, purple in the face, gasping for breath like a landed fish, his clenched fists raised above his head. Spynie Castle, the Bishop of Moray's episcopal palace, lay some three miles to the north, a powerful stronghold set most securely in the saltmarsh of the Lossie estuary.

Storming out, the Earl spurred back to the cathedral, speaking to none. At the great western entrance, where the boy Sir Walter stood on guard with a score or so of caterans, he pushed past all, gesturing peremptorily for the door to be opened, and rode inside. Behind him surged his party — but none of these had quite sufficient of their lord's spirit to ride horses into God's house.

Within, the scene and aura, the tenor and tempo, was so utterly different as to be scarcely believable, acceptable. The building itself was so vast and lofty and glorious as to completely dwarf all men, even mounted men, and their puny doings, the orderly forest of tall pillars, the multi-storeyed arches criss-crossing, the soaring vaulting and groined ribbing so high above as to be but dimly seen in the mellow light of the rank upon rank of stained-glass windows and the blue haze of generations of incense. The prolonged narrowing vista of aisles and transepts, side-chapels and galleries, was all but overpowering — and uniquely so, for this was the only cathedral north of France to boast double aisles in the nave. The wall-paintings and hangings and memorials were so rich and varied and colourful as to take away the breath at first glance, the gold-coated screens of the choir a glowing joy. In all this sublime splendour the presence of men was scarcely to be noticed; but their music and praise was. Far ahead, up in the choir, sweet chanting rose high and clear, the pure notes of boys' treble voices lifting through the undertones of tenor and bass, as those cathedral bells had risen through the cacophony of the rest. There was no congregation; only the lesser cathedral clergy and choristers at early morning worship, up there below the high altar.

The Earl of Buchan was not impressed; or if he was he betrayed no sign of it. Without pause he drove his garron up the great central aisle. Presently the hollow clatter of its hooves penetrated to the singers' ears, and gradually the chanting died away as men and boys turned to stare appalled. Behind the Wolf, but at some distance, came his distinctly doubtful and overawed minions.

Past the golden screens and up the steps into the choir or chancel he went. Opposite the stalls where the gaping, white-surpliced choristers waited, he reined over to where a massive multi-armed candlestick stood, and, lashing out with his foot, kicked it over, to crash on the tiled flooring, as introduction. He jabbed a finger towards the officiating priest and his assistants up before a secondary altar.

"Begone!" He barked the single word, and gestured away.

Terrified, the clergy hurried off, only one remembering to bow briefly towards the Presence-light above the high altar. The choristers were commencing to depart likewise when the Wolf turned in his saddle to his followers.

"These," he said pointing at the singers, men and boys. "Use them. All woodwork to be stripped. All timbering. All vestments and hangings. All that will burn. In heaps. Where it will best serve. In especial at the stair-foots, in the galleries, under the roof-trusses. Find where the lamp-oil is stored. And candles. More fuel will be coming from the town — thatch, straw, wood — much more. See to it. And quickly. Andrew, Wattie — all vessels of gold and silver, crosses, gewgaws and the like, to be collected."

Thus commanded, like a horde of destructive ants, the caterans swarmed off over the magnificent edifice, smashing, breaking, wrecking, dragging and heaping. Instead of sweet music and chanting was shouting, laughter, cursing, banging, splitting and clanging. The Earl sat his horse in the midst throughout, stationary but overseeing all.

"May we go outside?" Jamie said, voice cracking. "If we . . . stay here, I swear . . . I will assail him! With my bare hands . . . !"

"If you will." Alexander sounded little loth.

In silence they hurried out, through the spoliation. The smell of burning met them before ever they emerged through the western portal, carried on the westerly breeze. Outside, great gouts and billows of smoke and flame were already surging up from various parts of the town, with near at hand the clergy manses beginning to blaze.

"They should not have excommunicated him!" Alexander Stewart said heavily.

"Can you do nothing? *Nothing?*"

"What can I do? What can anyone do? You have seen him. He is not as other men. You know that. He is a law unto himself. He *is* the law, in all the North!"

Jamie shook his head, beyond words.

Presently the first of the columns of fuel-bearers began to arrive at the cathedral, frightened citizens, men, women and children, driven by dirk-brandishing caterans, burdened with their own or their neighbours' furnishings and roofing. They made a sorry sight.

To burn a lofty, stone-built cathedral was, of course, a very difficult and major task. The Earl had anticipated this, and went about the business with a carefully thought-out and grim efficiency which gave the lie to any suggestion of mere savage wrath. He permitted no firing until a vast quantity of tinder was accumulated, and disposed at heedfully selected points where it would achieve most damage. With much of the city alight, a terrifying sight, the cathedral itself was darkened, all but hidden, huge as it was, in the roaring, swelling smoke-clouds pouring down on the wind, creating their own hot wind. Before all was ready for the torches, conditions within were menacing enough. The final touch was somehow the more odious, the wholesale smashing of the richly lovely stained-glass windows the better to create ample through-draughts to fan the flames. Only then were the fires lit.

Even so, it took a while for the blaze to get a grip. But when it did, the effect was tremendous. The many narrow turnpike stairs which led up to the clerestory galleries in especial acted like great chimneys, with the flames roaring up in daunting fashion. The galleries and the nave roofing took fire first, therefore, with added frightening effect for those still working dragging fuel below, showers of sparks and flaming fragments raining down. With the choking smoke, conditions inside became quite horrifying. But still the Earl remained there, dismounted now since he could no longer control his maddened horse, directing, superintending.

The tall person of the Sub-Prior of Pluscarden materialised out of the smoke before Alexander Stewart and Jamie, just outside the western doorway, his eyes running, as were all others.

"Where is he? Where is the Earl?" he demanded. "In the name of God, tell me! This is ... beyond all. Even Pluscarden and Forres..."

"My father is within, Sir Prior," Alexander said, shaking his head. "But it will serve you nothing to see him, speak with him."

"It must. It *shall*. God in Heaven above — the mighty Trinity to which this church is dedicated — should strike him down! The King's brother . . . !"

An explosion of flame and smoke above them burst out a window too high for the wreckers to have reached, showering all below in broken and molten glass. Starting back, seeking to protect themselves, they scattered.

"Perhaps God will!" Jamie panted, to the cleric. "Since the Earl is still in there."

Without a word the other pushed past the cowering guards and plunged within.

"The fool!" Alexander jerked, when he realised what had happened. "He can do nothing. None can do anything now. Even my father himself." He shook his fair head. "This is madness. He should be out — my father. He could die. This smoke could overcome him . . ."

"And just retribution! I pray that he does die."

The other only frowned. "He is my father. And my brothers are in there still, also . . ."

"Only because their own savage lust for destruction keeps them there."

"I am going in. I must! Wait you here . . ." Alexander Stewart, in turn, hurried back into that inferno.

Jamie waited, a prey to conflicting emotions. Should he also go in? What good could he do? Alexander was the only one he would lift a finger to aid. And the Prior, of course. On the other hand, for the first time in long weeks he was in a position to try to escape. None stood close guard on him. If he could make a dash through the smoke and into the city? Better still, out through Pann's Port and into the open country. Lie low somewhere, then make his way south. He had no arms, no money, only the clothes he stood up in. But he could steal a garron . . .

He gnawed his lip. Alexander Stewart would suffer for it, if he did. Could he help that? He had given no sort of parole. He had been maltreated, threatened, wrongly imprisoned. He owed nothing to any of this wretched family. He peered around him in the lurid flame-fingered gloom. Caterans were milling about everywhere — but most might not know who he was. Or conceive him any responsibility of theirs. The smoke could be his opportunity.

He edged a little way further out from the doorway, peering.

Then, just as he was preparing to stroll away, a hand fell on his shoulder and jerked him round. Two Highlandmen stood just behind, dirks held at the ready, threatening. They said nothing, but there was no mistaking their warning. He had been in error in thinking that he was no longer closely guarded.

Shrugging, he moved back to his former position.

In a short while the Sub-Prior Moray came stumbling out of the cathedral, coughing, clutching a burned hand, his white robe blackened by embers. Gulping the slightly better air, he stood beside Jamie.

"The man is Satan incarnate!" he panted. "Filled with the spirit of hell. Sheerest hatred. Possessed. Nothing avails with him."

"Nothing. Save a sword keener and stronger than his own!"

"Who is there to raise that sword? You are also held captive? I saw you struck down. You at least are no friend of his."

"No friend," Jamie agreed. "I am James Douglas of Aberdour. His prisoner."

"Douglas? You are far from your own country, sir."

"Aye — too far. Would God I were home again. Out of this devil's clutch."

"He is a destroyer. And must himself be destroyed. If we would save Holy Church in the North."

"Less easily done than said."

"I will do what I can, God willing. A month past he burned down my priory of Pluscarden. After burning the whole town of Forres . . ."

"Forres? He burned Forres? And Pluscarden. That is what he was doing! They did not tell me. But why? Why Forres?"

"Because his true wife dwelt there. The Countess Euphemia, whom he has long deserted. Over whom he was excommunicated." The Prior was having to shout, above the roar of the flames and the cries of men. "Holy Church cared for her. Archdeacon William de Spynie, in particular. He is Rector of Forres as well as Archdeacon of Moray. He escaped this evil prince, and brought the Countess to Pluscarden. Then on here to Elgin, to the Bishop. So now he comes destroying here. Beelzebub, the prince of devils. Flinging down God's houses. Defiling His altars. Abusing His servants. Stealing His treasure. I shall make him pay, by all the saints of glory! I shall go South forthwith. To the Primate. To the Governor. To the King himself."

"What can they do. Even the King?"

"They can, and must, do something. I have powerful friends, kin. I am of the great house of de Moravia. If it is the last thing I do, I shall see that he suffers for this. I will go to the Vatican, even!"

"The Vatican can do no more than your Bishop of Moray, I fear — excommunicate. That is the direst sanction — and he scorns it. But, sir — if you do win to the South, will you inform the Lady Isabel Stewart, who was Countess of Douglas, of my state? Or the Lady Gelis . . ."

"But these are princesses. Sisters of this royal monster!"

"I rejoice to call them friends, nevertheless. I am the Lady Isabel's knight and servant. If you cannot win to them, see Mistress Mary Stewart, their half-sister. Tell her. Indeed, best tell her first. Say that I am the Wolf's prisoner. But will return as soon as I may, God willing. And tell her . . ." He paused, and shook his sore head. "Aye — tell her that, sir."

"I will do so. If I can. If either of us escape with our lives from this monster, this fiend in human form."

"You are not a prisoner as I am, are you? Brought here but for this day? You they will not hold, I think. Why not try to slip away now, sir? I tried — but me they know for long, and restrained me. You, a churchman, might move around. Slip away in the smoke, if you may. You can serve no good purpose here."

Looking around him in the thick gloom, Sub-Prior Moray nodded. "I can attempt it. God keep and preserve you then, my son," he murmured. And head down, clutching his burned hand, he paced slowly off and was quickly lost to sight. None appeared to see it as their duty to follow him.

Presently Alexander emerged again, with his father and brothers, all staggering, blinded with tears, lungs bursting, faces red. Sack-loads of valuables were dragged out after them, some of the bags on fire. The Earl coughing terribly, hair and beard singed gasped in debate whether to ride on the three miles north to Spynie and launch immediate assault on the Bishop's palace, whilst his sons pointed out that Barr would have had ample warning. Moreover his hold, protected by the saltmarsh, was impregnable, save by surprise.

The Earl allowed himself to be convinced. In fact, he was exhausted with the heat, the smoke and lack of any sleep the night before, a man in his fifties, for all his physical strength and energy.

Gazing blearily, for once like his late father, on all blazing Elgin, he nodded. He handed his horn to someone with more available wind than he had left, to blow the Retiral.

Only a small number heard that summons, of course. Leaving most of his force, now largely dispersed, drunken and ungovernable, to wreak their wills on what was left of the capital of Moray, the Wolf trotted off south-westwards, with his long train of booty.

At the crest of the ridge of Hardhillock he looked back. Out of the holocaust of the city the cathedral now towered like a mighty furnace, spouting flame.

"We have lit the Lantern of the North!" he exclaimed huskily. "Douglas — you perceive? You have seen how Alexander Stewart deals with those who misuse him. Remember it. Remember all of it. So that, one day, you can tell those who ought to know. For their own good. If God and I spare you!" Without waiting for answer, he rode on.

XXI

DESPITE THE WOLF'S repeated mentions of his role as witness, he seemed to be in no hurry to despatch Jamie upon this duty. He was taken back to Lochindorb from Elgin — which at least was better than Loch-an-Eilean or Ruthven — and thereafter the Earl more or less ignored him. He could scarcely be said to forget him, for the reluctant visitor was permitted to revert to the status of restricted house guest, and therefore could not be entirely overlooked by the master of the house. Fortunately or otherwise, the Wolf was much away from home in the weeks that followed, apparently holding justiciary courts here and there, at Inverness, Nairn, Rothes and as far away as Lochaber — of which he was also lord — however extraordinary a proceeding this might seem for the man who had just deliberately burned two towns, a cathedral and a monastery. What sort of justice he meted out must be debatable — although Alexander defensively declared that his father made an excellent, shrewd and fair judge. He took different sons with him on these journeys, so that Jamie suffered a variety of jailers, not all so accommodating as Sir Alexander. However, the Lady Mariota was consistently kind and indeed seemed to enjoy the captive's company; as, to a lesser extent did the girl Margaret.

Jamie was intrigued by Mariota de Athyn. A woman of character, intelligence and considerable charm, and gently bred, she nevertheless appeared to be quite content with her life and situation. Stranger still, she clearly was very fond of her savage paramour. To be sure he was apt to behave comparatively well when in her company, so that she undoubtedly saw the best of him. But how she could condone his behaviour elsewhere was beyond Jamie Douglas's understanding. Despite his own evident attraction for the other sex, he still had a lot to learn about women. They never actually discussed the Earl's outrages together, of course; although they came near to it time and again, the woman always skilfully turned the conversation. But they discussed much else, and Jamie had constantly to remind himself that he was talking with a notorious courtesan and not a perfectly normal and admirable wife and mother.

Had it not been for the sense of freedom restricted, plus the uncertainly as to the future, Lochindorb Castle would have been none too bad a place in which to pass a Highland summer. The immediate surroundings were scenically attractive, activities for an energetic young man numerous and unfailing — although he was never permitted to indulge in them unescorted — and the provender excellent. When Alexander was at home, he had no complaints as to the company. But with anyone as unpredictable and unrestrained as the Wolf as arbiter of his fortunes, none of all this permitted easement of mind.

As to repercussions from Elgin and Forres burnings, strangely enough, they heard nothing at all. No word came from the outside world, and the matter was seldom referred to at Lochindorb — although Jamie did gather that, as well as what he had seen to be burned at Elgin, the Maison Dieu Hospice, the Greyfriars and Blackfriars monasteries the main parish or Muckle Kirk and no fewer than eighteen clergy manses had been destroyed. But as far as reactions and retributions were concerned, it might all never have been.

The captive, of course, made constant demands to be allowed to leave for the South. But none could give him that permission, save the Wolf; and he would not until he was ready, he said. And Jamie was past the stage of protesting more than automatically, formally. Having learned all too clearly of what the man was capable, in one of his rages, and perceiving at long last that argument, like protest, was profitless in the circumstances, he held his peace.

In a period of some seven weeks, one quite welcome and enlightening interlude did occur. For reasons undisclosed but probably because he desired to have Alexander with him and none of the other sons happened to be at Lochindorb that week, the Earl elected to take Jamie with him also on one of his judicial excursions. This trip, far up the valley of the Findhorn, according to Alexander, was in a somewhat different category from the usual, where courts were held in towns and castles and populous areas. This one involved the settlement of a dispute between two Clan Chattan chiefs, the Mackintosh himself, Captain of Clan Chattan, and MacGillivray. Apparently it was the sort of problem which would formerly have been decided by simple recourse to armed conflict — in which case the Mackintosh would presumably have won, for he was much the more powerful, and as head of the Chattan confederation could have called on other members for support. But, surprisingly enough, under the Wolf's regime as Justiciar, such age-old customs were frowned upon and the matter fell to be settled by due process of law — the King's Justiciar's law. Hence this journey.

A party of about two-score, they rode off northwards across the bleak Braemoray moors in the last week of July, in no hurry, enjoying a fine summer's day in what were presently pleasing surroundings when they came down into the fairly narrow and picturesque Findhorn valley at Ardclach. Jamie was surprised indeed at the general holiday atmosphere, something he had by no means associated with the Earl. In fact it was almost like a royal progress, on a small scale, with Buchan greeted at every small community with smiles, respect, acclaim even, himself genial, friendly and consistently good company. Gone was the savage tyrant; instead a father-figure, authoritative but benevolent and accessible, prepared to talk and listen to the humblest of the cateran families and clansmen, the herders, peat-cutters, woodmen and the like. That they responded, indeed came to welcome him, showed that this was no unusual manifestation, no mere demonstration for the occasion. It occurred to Jamie, belatedly, that these Highlanders must in fact approve of their fierce overlord or they would scarcely turn out at such short notice and in such large numbers to fight for him.

They crossed the lofty area known as The Streens, wild and supporting no townships or settlements but at this season pastured by great herds of cattle, up from the lower lands for the summer grazings. Parties of young people tended the herds in some fashion, living an idyllic and carefree existence up there on the roof of the land, untrammelled by their elders' presence, domestic drudgery or indeed much in the way of moral codes. The life of the shielings, as it was called, given passable weather, was obviously a pleasant one, a kind of prolonged annual holiday. Yet, according to Alexander, it was about just such shieling controversy that the present errand was concerned.

The Streens crossed, they came down into the wider strath of Moy, The Mackintosh country, wooded and more like Strathspey, and here they found the Captain of Clan Chattan himself waiting, with a large company of his clansmen, Lachlan, 9th chief and Baron of Moy, an elderly but still powerful man of huge stooping frame, hooded eyes and beaked nose. But he greeted the Earl warmly and they seemed to be on excellent terms.

The augmented company, now with pipers to cheer them on their way, proceeded on up the Findhorn, whose valley now assumed the character of a normal Highland glen, the hills rising ever higher as they pushed deeper into what were now the mountain masses of the Monadh Liath. This Strathdearn as it was called was a fairly populous valley, with strips of oats on every level haugh and terrace, cot-houses dotted the length, even a little church at Dalarossie, low-browed and thatch-roofed like the cabins. Everywhere the Earl and Mackintosh were hailed and welcomed, clearly popular, in a way no great lord would be greeted by common folk in the South.

Where the side-glen of Kyllachy came in from the north-west, another company awaited them, Farquhar MacGillivray, 5th of the name, with a selection of his chieftains and tacksmen, from

Strathnairn to the north. He was a youngish man, thick, stocky, rather like a bull, with a sort of brooding stillness to him which might well explode into sudden and drastic action. He was stiff with The Mackintosh but gruffly amiable towards the Earl, who handled him jovially. The two sets of clansmen eyed each other like wary dogs.

A mile or two further up the main valley another glen came in, Mazeron by name. This was their destination. For the tacksman of Glen Mazeron, one Conal Dubh MacGillivray, was the transgressor and cause of the present trouble. He was accused of stealing cattle up on the shieling pastures between this Strathdearn and Strathnairn, one of the most heinous crimes in the Highland calendar, which struck at the very roots of a pastoral way of life based on common grazings. It appeared that he had been caught actually with the stolen beasts, red-handed, so that there was no doubt as to guilt. What was being contested, and what had brought the King's Justiciar all this way, was who should try him and what the sentence should be. The MacGillivray chief, *Mhic Gillebráth Mor*, claimed that as the offender was a tacksman of his, the duty and privilege fell to him; whereas the Mackintosh held that, since the beasts had been stolen from the Kyllachy shielings, Mackintosh land, the jurisdiction was his. The aggrieved owners certainly could not rely on adequate penalty being meted out by any MacGillivray trial, or even be sure of getting their cattle back. So the chiefs brought in the Justiciar. It was interesting that the Wolf agreed to come.

It was early evening before they reached Glen Mazeron, over thirty miles, and much too late, all agreed, for any serious debate or trial. Strangely enough the atmosphere at the township was anything but gloomy and foreboding, almost the same holiday spirit prevailing as elsewhere, even the offender himself playing host with a fair degree of aplomb. He was a swarthy eager little man of early middle years, voluble, lively and far from crushed by the enormity of his sin. He was not locked up. There was no place here to incarcerate him and nowhere to which he could effectively flee anyway. In the Highland polity a man stayed within his own clan, right or wrong. But he was the tacksman here, superior tenant, and recognised his duties towards the distinguished visitors.

The two chiefs had come well provided, and the encampment

348

suffered no lack of cold meats — more beef carried, undoubtedly, than could have been produced from the stolen cattle which brought them here — venison, oatcakes and *uisage-beatha*, the fiery spirit of the North. A lively evening developed, with singing, tale-telling, piping and dancing. Even the cattle-stealer contributed notably on his fiddle, for he was a renowned performer, and was roundly applauded. The Wolf himself was not above singing powerfully, dancing, and finally impersonating a pompous cleric at his devotions — which went down well. He insisted that Jamie, after Alexander had borrowed the tacksman's fiddle and played with expertise and feeling, should render an offering, so he sang a haunting Border ballad of lost love and hopeless sacrifice — which, of course, being in English, was understood by few, but with most of his hearers three-parts drunk anyway, this mattered little.

Presently all who were sober enough to do so wrapped themselves in their plaids and slept under the stars, around the aromatic birch-log fires.

In the morning a brisk purpose prevailed, although many of the company seemed to breakfast on whisky. They all moved to a nearby knoll, whereon the Earl and the two chiefs seated themselves. The clansfolk, reinforced now by what must have been a large proportion of the local population, gathered round in a wide circle, in the best of spirits. When Conal Dubh MacGillivray was escorted to the judgment seat he had to pass through the crowd, to cheerful raillery. It was noted that he brought his fiddle.

The proceedings were, of course, conducted wholly in the native Gaelic, and had to be translated for Jamie by Alexander Stewart. After a brief introductory speech by the Earl, here known as *Alastair Mor Mac-an-Righ*, Big Alexander Son of the King, genial, even humorous, the MacGillivray chief launched into a prolonged and vehement declaration that it was elementary and age-old custom that a *ceann cinnidh* or clan chief was responsible for the administration of justice within his own clan and its territories, save insofar as this did not conflict with the jurisdiction of the *Ard Righ*, the High King. If a chief was held responsible for the actions of his clansmen by the Crown, it followed that he must be able to discipline, try and punish offenders. Conal Dubh was undoubtedly his clansman, tacksman of this clan territory of Glen Mazeron. There was no possible cause for dispute. He, *Mhic Gil-*

lebráth Mor, had in fact sat in judgment, and adjudged Conal Dubh as guilty of the crime of cattle-stealing from open shieling grazings, and passed sentence. This sentence was that the said Conal should have his right hand struck off from his right arm; that he should thereafter be banished from the clan and its territories for five years and five days; and that restitution should be made from his goods to the owners of the said cattle. Confident of the correctness and fairness of this judgment, he, *Mhic Gillebráth Mor*, submitted the case to the superior jurisdiction of the High King's Justiciar.

Nodding, the Wolf turned to The Mackintosh.

That fierce old man, who introduced himself as *Mac an Toishich Mor*, Captain of Clan Chattan, Senseschal of Badenoch and Baron of Moy, poured scorn upon MacGillivray's pronouncements, on various counts. While there was no question that the wretched and infamous Conal Dubh was a clansman of MacGillivray, yet *Mhic Gillebráth Mor* was himself a clansman of *himself, Mac an Toishich Mor*, since MacGillivray was only a sub-clan of the great and mighty Clan Chattan federation of which he, *Mac an Toishich Mor* was Captain and chief. The greater included the lesser before the law. Secondly, the cattle had been stolen from Glen Kyllachy shielings, which were and always had been Mackintosh territory, the aggrieved owners Mackintosh clansmen, entitled to look to their chief for justice on his and their territory. Thirdly, he was Baron of Moy, which rank and status conferred upon him a superior jurisdiction to that of *Mhic Gillebráth Mor*, including the right of pit and gallows over the entire barony lands of Strathdearn, to which Glen Mazeron indubitably belonged. *Mhic Gillebráth Mor* held no such baronial status. And, since this was undoubtedly a hanging matter, the power of pit and gallows was involved. He therefore claimed the right to try and sentence the said Conal, as inadequately tried and sentenced by *Mhic Gillebráth Mor*.

The Earl, who of course knew all this anyway, thanked both contestants for their clear and concise statements of the position. He pretended to ponder for a little, and then put forward his own observations, in entirely moderate fashion. Both sides appeared to have much to be said for them, he held. Much seemed to depend on the definition of the terms sub-clan and federation. It seemed to him that a clan was a clan, or else it was not. A federation was an association or alliance, in which the members, in this case the constituent clans, were partners. This, to his mind, did not lessen the status of the members, which remained clans, with all their privileges and responsibilities. There might be greater and lesser clans within the federation, but they were all *clans*. A captain was necessary in such a confederation, but for leadership in war rather than before the law. MacGillivray was undoubtedly a clan, and had been one from early times. Therefore, it seemed that *Mhic Gillebráth Mor* had uncontestable right to try and sentence his clansmen.

While The Mackintosh frowned darkly, MacGillivray's bull-like features broke into a grin.

Nevertheless, the Earl went on, judicially, there was much in what *Mac an Toishich* had put forward, not so much as Captain of Clan Chattan as Baron of Moy. The barony *was* a superior jurisdiction, just as the Crown was superior to both. In this regard, the right of pit and gallows was important. Had *Mhic Gillebráth Mor* sentenced the offender, Conal, to death, there might have been no dispute — save perhaps that the Crown might possibly have contested the sentence as infringing on its prerogative. But he had not done so, imposing a lesser penalty. So the Baron of Moy might well claim that the sentence was inadequate, as he did, and since he held the right of pit and gallows, it might be that there should be a re-trial with a view to revising the sentence. Was not cattle-stealing normally considered to be a hanging matter, on open grazings?

The Mackintosh forcefully declared that of course it was so. All knew that. It was merely that this Conal Dubh was a tacksman, not just an ordinary clansman, and a distant cousin of *Mhic Gillebráth Mor* — who was therefore shielding his kinsman. Mac-Gillivray hotly asserted the contrary saying that it was within his right to impose what sentence he thought fit. But that if hanging it was to be, then *he* would impose that sentence and do the hanging, not Mackintosh.

The two chiefs were now glaring at each other angrily, and clansmen on either side beginning to growl ominously and finger their dirks.

Smiling benevolently, easily, the Earl raised his hand. It would be a pity he asserted, if his good and true friends were to come to blows over such a small matter as who should conduct a hanging!

If they were both now agreed that hanging was the most suitable penalty, he would be glad to resolve the difficulty for them by himself, as Justiciar, carrying out the sentence. Would this be agreeable? As between friends? He could insist, of course, since they had both appealed to him for a final decision.

Both protagonists, after a doubtful moment or too, looked relieved, and nodded their agreement.

The Wolf beamed on all. A most happy outcome, he declared. All should be satisfied, and the Clan Chattan federation preserved from schism. There was only the one point remaining outstanding. Had the guilty party Conal Dubh MacGillivray any relevant observations to make? And he turned to the offender.

That man, who had listened to the debate with the greatest of interest now bobbed his head eagerly and launched into a monologue which Jamie would have assumed to be a plea for mercy but which did not seem to be in the right tone for that. Alexander explained that the little man was in fact expressing his favour for the amended sentence. He had never relished the notion of his right hand being cut off — for it would mean that he could never play his fiddle again; which was his greatest joy. He would far rather be comfortably dead, especially if he was to be banished from Strathdearn which had been his home always, the valley he loved and about which he had composed more than one fiddle tune. There was only the one thing that he would ask, of the lord's mercy and goodness. Might he be disposed of some other way than by hanging? He had always disliked the idea of hanging on a rope, an awkward, uncertain and undignified end for any man — he had seen a few hangings.

The Earl nodded kindly. He would prefer not to die by hanging, himself, he admitted. Cold steel was much to be preferred. Might he make a suggestion? As a younger man he had been rather good at beheading people with a sword. On a chivalric expedition to France he had had the privilege of winning a tourney where the prize was the opportunity to execute six malefactors. He had whipped off the heads of four of them with single strokes. Only with his arm flagging a little had he required two strokes each for the final pair. Would Conal Dubh like to essay that?

Conal Dubh would be delighted, it seemed. He was at his lordship's disposal, there and then. There was only one small matter first. He would very much like to play them all a piece on his fiddle before he went. If he might, he would give them his own favourite composition, *In Praise of Strathdearn*. It was not very long and would not delay their lordships unduly.

This request was graciously granted, to general applause. The little tacksman took up his instrument, briefly tuned the strings, and plunged into a lively, spirited and tuneful air, linked by a simple but effective refrain, which soon had all feet tapping while the Wolf beat time with his dirk. Imperceptibly, however, the lilt changed to a sweet and lingering melody, wistful, poignant. He ended on a high note, pure, quivering, which brought lumps to many a throat.

Beaming round, Conal Dubh bowed to the Earl and the chiefs. Holding up his fiddle, he said something which Alexander failed to finish translating. He was asking the Wolf if he might present the instrument to one whose fiddling he had admired the previous evening? In the fiddle he was leaving behind the best of him, he said, and wished the creature to be in good hands. He would break it over his knee if he was not permitted to present it . . .

Alexander Stewart's interpretation faded away as the little man turned to him and held out the instrument. With the Earl nodding agreement, the young man stepped forward to accept the gift, his face a study. Haltingly he promised to look after the fiddle well and truly.

The Wolf sent a gillie for his great two-handed sword, and came down from the mound. The tacksman turned to face him and spread his hands eloquently, ready.

"He says that, since there is no priest present, he trusts the good God to receive a sinner's soul unshriven," Alexander reported unsteadily.

"Must this be . . .?"

"I fear so. Cattle-stealing is a more grievous crime here than is murder."

The sword handed over to the Earl, he tried a few swishes with it, in the air to flex his muscles, the condemned man watching, critically concerned. Then the latter asked whether he should kneel down on the grass, thrust his head forward or how otherwise dispose himself? He was told that the other usually did his decapitating standing up, and that since he was only a small man there should be no difficulty.

Conal Dubh bowed again, half-smiling — and on impulse the Wolf outthrust his hand to shake that of his victim. Then, stepping back, with great swiftness and a remarkable explosion of strength, he swung the five-feet-long blade up, back and forward again without pause, his eyes and those of the tacksman remaining locked until the very moment of impact.

With a notably final snapping sound, the grinning dark head flew right off, to land on the grass feet away and roll over and over, still smiling. The headless trunk, however, spouting blood like a fountain, stood its ground for a few timeless moments before taking three or four uncoordinated steps, sideways and backwards oddly enough, then, as the knees gave way, pitching forward.

A great sigh arose from the company. A woman began to wail, some way off, presumably the wife.

The Justiciar of the North, *de facto* if not *de jure*, had dispensed justice, maintained the royal authority, prevented a clan squabble from escalating into wholesale bloodshed, and kept the favour and support of two useful lieutenants.

The air of holiday had reasserted itself well before the Earl's party left Glen Mazeron to ride down Findhorn again, with Jamie Douglas meditating on Badenoch and the Wolf. He was beginning to suspect that judgment, like justice, was less straightforward north of the Highland Line than he had supposed.

XXII

THE WOLF AND his household knew of the impending visitation, of course, an hour and more before it arrived, knew even that a woman was involved. But identities they could not know, for this company was large enough to escape the escorting attentions of Sir Andrew Stewart of Ruthven, unlike lesser predators. When, eventually, in the late afternoon of the last day of July, the cavalcade did appear in sight of Lochindorb

Castle, over the final shoulder of Carn nan Clach Garbha, it was to reveal something that the busy scouts had omitted to mention — that it now rode under two banners, one that of Stewart, the other no less than the Lion Rampant standard of Scotland.

That set tongues urgently to wag in the island stronghold.

The Earl, presently, sent his son Alexander in a small boat to meet the newcomers at the opposite shore, to enquire their business and to question the presence of some fifty armed men in his territories, uninvited and unheralded, Stewart banner or none.

Sir Alexander was rowed back notably quickly, alone and in some agitation. He had just a little difficulty in enunciating his message to his father. "It is the new High Steward," he declared. "David, Earl of Carrick and Prince of Scotland. He, he requires your presence before him. He said . . . forthwith!"

"God's eyes—*requires!*" The Earl all but choked. "Requires, he says? Me! That insolent brat, my nephew Davie!"

"He says that he comes directly from the King, his father, my lord. And sounds . . . confident."

"Let him, the pup! Now — what has he come here for, young David Stewart? This is passing strange. And the woman? The woman — what of her? Who is she?"

"He did not say, my lord. She did not speak. Save that she is mighty good to look at, I learned naught of her. He was short in speech. Most masterful."

"So-o-o! We will change that! But . . . good-looking, eh? He is on the young side to be trailing a doxie around with him — although perhaps I did at his age! She would not be one of the princesses, my sisters?"

"I know not, sir. I have never seen them."

"They have come a long way. Why? Why, I wonder?" The Wolf turned to look speculatively at Jamie, when there sounded a loud and continuous blowing of horns, peremptory, imperious, from the shore. "Curse the malapert!" he barked. "This one needs a lesson — and will get it."

"Perhaps you should go, Alex," the Lady Mariota suggested mildly. She did not often do the like. "This is the heir to the throne. It will serve you nothing to give unnecessary offence. Your brother is not young, nor strong. This David could be king sooner than you think. Better not to have him as enemy."

355

"Let him learn discretion, if he is to be king! Aye, and manners too. In the North, *I* rule. He will discover it — as others have done!" He swung round. "How say you, Douglas? You have learned who is master here. You will know this stripling, I swear?"

"I know him, yes, my lord. And would counsel you — beware!"

"Save us — you would? Then you are a bigger fool than I thought you! When Alexander Stewart begins to heed striplings and shavelings, it will be time to bury him!"

"This stripling, sir, is ... unusual! And does not resemble his royal father."

The Wolf began to speak, then stopped, staring. There was some commotion over there, which resolved itself into men-at-arms, dismounted, pulling heather-thatch off the roofs of two or three of the castleton cot-houses. Even as they watched, the heaped roofing began to smoke, burst into flames.

"As I said, the Lord David is an unusual youth ..." Jamie commented — but the Earl was already striding down to the island landing-stage. When Alexander hurried after his father, Jamie went also.

The Wolf did not speak once during the row over to the mainland, and no others sought to intrude on his thoughts. Anyway, by halfway across Jamie's interest was elsewhere. Against the background of blazing thatch and smoke columns, a small group of riders still sat their horses, apart from the busy men-at-arms a little, waiting. The slender figure of the Lord David, now Earl of Carrick, was easily picked out. And beside him sat a rather less slender but still trim figure, even better-known to Jamie Douglas — unmistakably Mary Stewart, and the only woman there. His heart gave sufficient leap within him almost to make him splutter a sort of cough.

After that recognition, for a little while, he was less than sure of the exact sequence of events, his mind and emotions in a whirl. He was vaguely aware of the boat grounding, of leaping out after the others, of David's ringing call — which should of course have been directed towards his uncle but was in fact addressed to him — of shouts and hot words and tension. What he was entirely aware of was Mary's lovely face, flushed, eyes sparkling, lips parted, gazing at him — and him only. That made up for a lot of captivity.

He pulled himself together. The Wolf and his nephew were confronting each other, a sufficiently dramatic situation in all conscience. The barely fourteen-year-old High Steward, with the musical, high-pitched and mocking voice, had assumed the initiative.

". . . and having come so far, looked for a kinder welcome than this, my lord," he was saying. "To be kept waiting, like packmen at a gate. After insolent attentions by sundry creatures of yours since we entered this Badenoch."

"How dare you! How dare you fire those my cot-houses!" the Wolf thundered.

"I dare more than that, in this kingdom," the boy answered easily. "A deal more, Uncle, as you shall discover. I am here representing its liege lord, by his express command. Let none forget it."

"Damn you, boy — keep that sort of talk for those it may impress! Here *I* command — in the King's name. And by my own right hand!"

"Then command to better effect, sir. To receive me, and your sister here, better than this."

"How am I to know who may come chapping at my door, unannounced . . .?"

"You did not know that we came, then?" That was quick. "Your bastard at, at — I misremember the barbarous name — declared that none approached your robber's hold unknown and unannounced. An idle boast, it seems?"

The Wolf, frowning, drew a great breath. And Mary Stewart took the opportunity to put in a word.

"My lord Alexander," she said. "Greetings. It is no little time since we saw each other. But you may recollect my identity, nevertheless! I hope that I see you well?"

Her half-brother ignored that, entirely. "You will discover no idle boasting at Lochindorb, Nephew, I promise you," he said. "Indeed you will discover much that you ought to have been taught before this! Including regret for allowing your ruffians to damage my property." And he gestured to the burning thatch.

"Ha!" The boy tinkled a laugh. "I thought that such would commend itself to you, Uncle. Are you not an expert with torch

357

and tinder? We hear of whole towns and even cathedrals set alight. Is it only *Alexander* Stewart who may burn houses? Besides, was it not effective? To bring you, belatedly, to your duty."

It appeared that the youth had actually achieved the well-nigh impossible. The Earl of Buchan was rendered speechless.

Pressing his advantage, David spoke more formally — yet the subtle mockery was unmistakable still. "That duty, my lord, is to hear and receive the King's command. I am sent to summon you, as His Grace's brother and an earl of this realm, to attend the royal coronation at Scone on the 14th day of August next. God save the King's Grace!"

The Wolf moistened his lips. "What folly is this?" he demanded.

"Folly? You name the King's coronation folly, my lord? Before witnesses? The crowning of the Lord's Anointed! Is that not as good as high treason?"

"The folly is in sending such as you all this way to tell me. As good as a play-acting. Why?"

"You are entitled to be summoned, my lord. Would a lesser messenger have better pleased you? Or should it have been a greater? Is the heir to the throne insufficient to invite the Earl of Buchan? Must the King himself come to Badenoch and humbly seek your lordship's attendance?"

"Think you I care who acts messenger? I would no more attend this coronation flummery than seek to fly in the air!"

"So — that is the answer I am to take back to my father? In response to his royal command."

"Take what answer you like, boy. I care not. But not to Johnnie, or whatever he now styles himself. He is but a puppet. Take it to him who sent you, to my brother Robert, the Governor."

"The Earl Robert did not send me. Indeed he knew naught of my coming. We are scarce the best of friends. I came from the King alone."

"Think you that should comfort me? If I appeared at Scone, it would be to deliver myself into Robert's hands. He would have me taken and bound within the hour."

"So that is it, Uncle? You are afraid! The Earl of Buchan and Wolf of Badenoch is afraid to venture out of his lair! For fear his sins may catch him up? I will tell my father that."

"Fool! If it is fear to beware of treachery, then I am afraid, yes. I know my brothers. Even if the King were honest in this, he could not save me from Robert. So — would you have me take an army down to Scone? Perhaps I should!"

"Take whom you will, my lord. I but bring the royal summons. But I have another royal command, see you. You are holding here, without right or cause, a leal subject of the King, who has served him well. Sir James Douglas, a friend of the princesses. And of my own. It is my father's express command that he be released forthwith. To return with us."

The Wolf turned, to stare at Jamie with that blank yet calculating look of his, which could be frightening. "The wind blows that way, does it?" he said. "Now, how did that tale arise? So far away?"

"We had it on excellent authority," David said briefly. "I rejoice to see him here, and in seeming good health. Despite ... blows!"

"And why not? He has been my guest, my welcome guest, these two months and more. Although he came unbidden. He has fared well, dining at my table. My son here, Alexander, has looked after him like any brother. Is it not so, Douglas?"

Jamie hesitated. "I have no complaints as to Sir Alexander's treatment of me," he said.

"I think not!" That was grim, warning. "Held without right or cause, heh? So much for your excellent authority."

"Then, my lord, he *can* come back with us, without hindrance?" Mary put in.

"To be sure. If he so wishes." Narrow-eyed now, the Earl looked at his captive.

"I do so wish, my lord," Jamie contented himself with saying. He was only too well aware that this was a very much more delicate game than probably either of his friends realised. He knew a great deal better than they did of what the Wolf was capable, and how utterly devastating one of his rages could be. The fact that David had fifty men-at-arms immediately available might look decisive, for the moment; but that was not likely to affect his uncle's reactions in any major way. Nor was the nephew's now lofty status. Alexander was looking exceedingly anxious, on edge — and Jamie had found that was the best guide to watch.

The older man suddenly seemed to have had sufficient of this verbal exchange. "Enough!" he jerked, in a different voice. "Come, you. Over to the castle. We have stood here over-long. Nephew, and you Mary, come in this small boat. Leave your men and horses. I will send over a barge for such as you would have with you there."

"No, Uncle."

"Eh? What mean you — no?"

"I mean that we bide here. With my men. Who knows, if we went out to your island yonder, some h'm, some storm might blow up! And we could not win back. We will bide here, very well. Send us victual . . ."

"But — God's eyes! You cannot roost out here. All night. Lacking all comfort."

"We have journeyed over two hundred miles of mountains, Uncle, lacking better comfort. And will do so again. We return to the South tomorrow. In the morning."

"Tomorrow? What nonsense is this? Not yet dismounted and talking of riding again. Come — over to the castle and rest you."

"I say no. Here we stay."

"Mary — you at least will have a grown woman's wits. Come."

"I have, my lord — and elect to stay likewise."

"Save us all! The bairns' folly of it. What of your two hundred miles of mountains, to journey back? Unrested."

"The reason for our swift return, Uncle," David said. "We have little time. The coronation is in but fourteen days. And it seems that it is necessary that I be present! Whether you are or not. We must start back in the morning."

Tight-lipped, the Wolf considered them. Then he shrugged. "As you will. I shall send over some meats. Alex — come. And you, Douglas."

"Sir James stays here, with us," David said, "since he rides with us, in the morning."

"Curse you — he is my, my . . ."

"Your captive, Uncle? Hostage?"

The Wolf glared around him, at the watchful ring of men-at-arms. Many of his own people stood behind them, the occupants of the castleton; but mostly they were women and children.

Almost all the men were away at the bog-hay harvest in the floors of the side-glens, so vital for winter forage. A supreme realist, he recognised realities now. Without another word he swung about and strode back to his boat.

Alexander waited a little, then shook his head unhappily at Jamie, and hurried after his father.

The boat was barely launched on its return journey before Mary had slipped from her saddle and run to fling herself impulsively into the young man's arms.

"Oh, Jamie, Jamie, Jamie!" she cried. "I feared ... that I would never ... see you again! Jamie, my dear — my very dear!"

He could not answer anything, just then. Not that he tried so very hard. Her lips were very close to his own, lips he had thought of, dreamed of, at some length in recent weeks. He conceived of better use for them than chatter. There had been a sufficiency of talk, anyway. He closed them with his own, onlookers or none.

David Stewart, however effective and mature-seeming, did lack certain of the attributes of the grown man, prominent amongst them an inability to take this sort of situation seriously. He did not give them long, therefore, before dismounting, to come and clap Jamie on the shoulder in cheerful reproof.

"Come, Sir Jamie man — have you no better greeting for your future king than slobbering over his auntie!" he exclaimed. "Here's gratitude, by the Mass! And me coming all this road just to rescue you! Shame on you!"

"Aye, my lord — to be sure." Jamie released Mary — who still kept hold of his hand, however. "I am sorry. I crave pardon. Forget myself. In my, my ..."

"Yes, yes — we all know your weaknesses, friend! It is our royal pleasure to forgive you, this once. At least, it seems that you are little the worse for all your troubles."

"I am entirely well, yes. Is it true, what you said? That you came all this way for *my* sake?"

"Of course we did," Mary assured. "This of the coronation was but an excuse. To gain the King's permission. And this escort. We never believed that my curious brother would come to Scone ..."

"She would have come for you if she had had to walk all the way!" David interrupted. "As, perhaps, might I! But this way we

361

journeyed secure, in a troop of the royal guard. At the Treasurer's cost!" He chuckled. "Which guard I had better see to . . ."

While the boy and an officer ordered the men-at-arms to prepare camp, Mary sought reassurances that Jamie was as well as he looked, had not suffered hurt at the Wolf's hands. "That friar, Alexander Moray, told us that he had seen you knocked off your horse. By that brutish brother of mine. When you tried to stop him burning the cathedral. We have been direly anxious, Jamie."

"No need," he told her. "He is a hard and savage man, and I have seen some ill things. But he has his own honesties — if that is the word. Once he decided not to hang me, he has treated me fairly, by his lights, preserving me as some kind of witness. Little as any witness would seem to his credit! I was to testify to his power and ruthlessness, as warning to others. In the South. That none would dare oppose him. He has held me prisoner but has done me no hurt."

"Thank the good God for that. When we heard of the burnings and slayings . . ."

"And yet, you, a woman, came all this way! Into like peril. I can scarce credit it, Mary — even yet. Through all these wild and dangerous Highlands. You, a king's daughter . . ."

"I am no shrinking flower, Jamie. Nor have I to play at being a princess! Neither Isabel nor Gelis could come. It would scarce have been suitable. But Isabel is in Galloway and Gelis has the child to see to. So I went to David. Now that his father is King, and he the High Steward, he can do much. Too much, perhaps, for one so young. Though Robert hates him, and seeks to clip his wings. He leapt at this venture. For he admires you greatly . . ."

The young prince came back. "Will that uncle of mine truly send us food and drink, Jamie?" he asked. "If not, we must see what these caterans' cabins can provide."

"He will, I think — if only to save *them*. He looks after his people well — and will guess that you would do that. But do not think, my lord, that he will forgive you for this. Or allow you to outwit him. He is a dangerous man to cross. And no fool."

"So we understood — and so we planned it. We were not going to be lured out to his island, and held. We were not to be parted from our men. We were not going to stay sufficiently long for him to be able to gather together a force to overwhelm us. If he had not

362

brought you across with him, it would have been more difficult. We would have had to bargain for you."

"With what?"

"With another dear cousin of my own!" He grinned. "A surly oaf, calling himself Sir Duncan Stewart, who thought to interfere with our free passage, some leagues back. We taught him otherwise and took him into our custody to teach him manners, bringing him with us in case of use! He is in a herd's cabin in a valley a mile or so back under guard. If his sire had refused to yield you up, I would have offered this oaf in exchange — if you will forgive the insult, my friend? Hanged him, if need be. Now it may not be necessary."

Jamie swallowed. "Praise be you did not do that!" he said. "For assuredly I would have hanged likewise, and promptly. And you never won South again. You do not know the man, I tell you. Even now, I fear that he will seek to counter you. He will not like being outreached. And by one so young, and on his own doorstep. He will do *something* to stop you."

"What can he do? He can have no force, large enough to stop us, on that island, to bring over against us. If he sends out messengers, we shall see them and stop them. I have men on watch. Any boat leaving the castle will be seen . . ."

"Under cover of darkness?"

"It is never so very dark of a night, we have discovered. But such darkness as there is will serve us as well as Uncle Wolf! We shall not wait until morning, but slip away during the night. We have all we came for — you! We shall be many miles away from this Lochindorb by daylight."

"He would follow."

"Let him. I still have his bastard as hostage."

Jamie was doubtful still. Presently his doubts were justified. A barge was rowed across from the castle, laden with cold meats, oatmeal, ale and whisky in generous measure. With it came Alexander, again with the invitation for the visitors to come over to the island, to meet its chatelaine at least, whose provender was thus provided. When this was politely refused, Alexander sent back the unloaded barge but remained behind himself, with half-a-dozen tough and well-armed Highlanders as a sort of bodyguard, explaining that in this case his father had told him to stay and offer such aid as he might to their comfort, all night if he must.

This of course, upset the plans for stealing away unobserved. Jamie, who had scarcely believed that the project could be successful anyway and was likely to have unpleasant consequences, was almost relieved; especially as Alexander was his usual civil self again and seemingly in excellent spirits. His doubts gathered again however when, almost casually, the other announced that he had decided to come with them, to the South. It was a notable opportunity. Always he had wanted to visit the Lowlands, to attend the King's Court, to see the life led there. He loved this mountain land — but a man should know more than that, especially a Stewart. So he intended to travel with them, if they would take him. He would represent his father at the coronation — for nothing was more sure than that the Earl would not go.

Jamie stared. "But . . . but . . . do you realise what you say?" he demanded. "If you come south with us, alone, without your father, for how long do you think you will remain a free man? The Earl Robert would sieze you, almost certainly."

"If I was in this young prince's protection? He is High Steward and heir to the throne. Surely his name and state would protect me?"

"You do not know the Governor. He is as hard a man as your father, however cold. I say that you dare not risk it, man."

"And you would care, so much? You so long *our* prisoner!"

"*You* have always treated me well. And your lady-mother." That was gruff. "What does your father say?"

"He calls me a fool," the other admitted. "But will not gainsay me if I am resolved. As I am. He too says I will be taken and held — for he despises your young Earl David, as I do not. But he declares that *he* would get me out of such imprisonment quickly enough! He will have his own methods, see you. Moreover, I think he sees some advantages in having me in the South for a space, speaking directly with the King, my uncle, and with others. It would also ensure that he was not accused of deliberately disobeying the royal command to attend the coronation — which might be used against him. If he sends me as deputy. The fact that he has not forbidden me to go means something of the sort, I am sure."

The news of this change of stance on the part of the Wolf put the visitors in something of a quandary — as was no doubt anticipated. David suspected a trap, and said so; but Alexander assured that it was not so. That young man was so obviously pleased with the prospect that it seemed highly unlikely that his part was not genuine. As to his father's, they reserved judgment. It would, of course, enable the party to take their leave of Badenoch without further difficulty.

Although still wary, the sudden improvement in the situation brought about a general relaxation. The food and drink was distributed and appreciated. Mary was found quarters, of a sort, in one of the cot-houses; but the rest of the company remained encamped in a fairly tight group. There was now no point in planning to leave before sun-up, but an early start would still be advisable, for time was indeed short.

When he decently could, Jamie steered Mary off a little way along the lochside — although there might in fact be some small doubt as to who actually initiated the move. Alexander and David were discussing routes for the southward journey. In the gloaming light, the young woman may have found a variety of obstacles, roots and the like to trip over, and took Jamie's arm. They went unspeaking for a while.

He made three false starts, and then in sheer disgust with himself burst out, "A mercy, Mary — here have I been thinking of you, dreaming of you, longing to talk with you, all these weary months, and now, now I cannot think what to say or how to say it! I am the greatest fool . . . !"

"You are doing fairly well, I think, so far," she said.

"No. How can I say what I want to say? To thank you . . ."

"If that is what is troubling you, Jamie, say no more. Am I to be thanked for doing what I wished and sought and planned to do?"

"You are, yes — if that is so. For wishing it. To come all this way. Yourself. Not just to send another. For me. Endangering yourself."

"I could not allow David to come alone. He is able, yes, and keen. But young, headstrong. And I it was who sought *his* aid. I could not leave you in the Wolf's hands. Has he really treated you none so ill?"

"Yes and no. He has held me captive, threatened me with hanging — as he hanged Ramsay of Waughton, the man I came seeking — mocked and made fool of me. Yet, save when he felled me at Elgin, he has not mistreated me. For much, I have to thank his son, this Alexander, much the best of his brood. And his — I was going to say his wife, for wife is what she is to him in all but marriage — his concubine, the Lady Mariota. She is kind, warm-hearted, keeps a good house. She has treated me as guest . . ."

"Then I need scarce have come?"

"No, no — save us, no! I have been waiting, hoping. Not knowing when he would let me go — if ever he would. I hoped and prayed that Prior Moray would not forget, would deliver my message. I told him that *you* would be best. To tell. But never intended that you should come, in person . . ."

"Did you hope for Gelis?"

"No. I never thought of any woman coming."

"At least you conceived me to be the one to send to. I must console myself with that!"

"I believed you to have the soundest wits of, of my friends."

"I thank you, kind sir! Further consolation. Although I much mislike clever women! It was not as such that I hoped to commend myself!"

"I am sorry. I was never very good at saying the right word. I . . . I did not dream of you as a clever woman, Mary."

"No? This is better." She pointed to a bleached tree-trunk cast up on the shore by a flood. "Come, let us sit on this and you can tell me how you dreamed of Mary Stewart."

"That I would not dare!" he asserted, as he sat down.

"So bad as that, was it?" She smiled. "You but make me the more eager to hear. Was it worse than on Saint Colm's Inch?"

He swallowed. "To be honest — yes!" he said.

The young woman laughed aloud. "My dear honest Jamie! I love you for your honesty — as perhaps you love me for what you call my wits! So I am a fallen woman, am I — or as good as one? Does not Holy Writ declare that for a man even to desire a woman in his heart is as good — or as bad — as to have bedded her? Alas for my poor virtue!"

He shook his head. "Mary — I wish that you would not mock at me so. Laugh at my, my feelings for you . . ."

Sensing actual distress, she quickly changed, "I am sorry, Jamie — we Stewarts have the tongues of scorpions. Our men flay with their swords; we women do it with our lips! Forgive me. But . . . these feelings for me, that I laugh at? What are they? Will you not tell me?"

Thus abruptly brought to direct decision, as it were, he drew a long breath and stared straight ahead, across the darkling waters, to the Wolf's castle.

"I think I need you," he said. Which was not really what he intended to say, out of his sudden acceptance of commitment.

She waited for more; but when it did not seem to be forthcoming, she spoke. "Need? What does that mean? There are many needs."

He nodded. "Many. I need you in many ways. I have had long to think on this. As a prisoner, in cells, on journeyings, in the heather. I need your *wits*, yes — but also your courage, your steadfastness, your resolve, your swift strength. Aye, and your disregard for all obstacles . . ."

"You have me sounding like a good mare for breeding, with your catalogue!" she observed. This time there was no laughter in her voice.

But he was not to be put off his recital, now he had screwed himself up to it. "No. But I lack much that you have, could give me. I am dull, slow-spoken, stiff of manner. Lacking your laughter, even . . ."

"Certainly you might laugh more," she agreed.

He had not finished yet. "These things you have. As well, you are very lovely. Of face as of person. These I need too, I have found. Your . . . your body."

"Ah! So we do come to that!"

"Yes, I fear so. These months I have learned about myself. Found myself longing for you, Mary, these qualities, yes — but also your person. All of you, lass. I have near cried out for you . . . !"

"Me? Not Gelis? Or just a woman, perhaps? A ready woman?"

"You. You only. I know now. Gelis was . . . otherwise. I did not know myself, then. My need is for you . . ."

"*Need*, again!" she interrupted him. "What is this, Jamie? A declaration of dire need, necessity? A proposal to cohabit? Or could it even be marriage, as last resort!"

"Of course it is marriage, Mary. Think you I am like the Wolf, a lecher . . . ?"

"Both our fathers were lechers, were they not — since we are bastards," she exclaimed. "It would be none so strange. But . . .

367

dear God — here is Jamie Douglas proposing matrimony to Mary Stewart at last, at very long last! And she talks of parents and bastardy! And he of qualities and excellences and bodies — but never a word of love nor yet fond affection!"

"But — but Mary! Of course I love you. Love you most dearly. With all my heart. You must *know* that. It is to be understood. I would not be talking this way otherwise . . ."

"Then *say* so, of a mercy! Do something. Why sit we here, debating . . .?"

They stared at each other, then, on their tree-trunk. And simultaneously both burst into laughter, a strange, rueful, frustrated but releasing laughter, which had tears somewhere behind it on the girl's part and helpless apology on the man's, yet was basically joyful, joyful.

Leaning over, he fondled her in his arms, still laughing. Kissing and being kissed, he declared incoherently, most interruptedly and with monotonous repetition — although entirely convincingly — that he loved her, loved her more than anything else in this world or the next, loved her wholly, entirely, exclusively, and would she be his wife? Would she? Would she? Her answer was implicit rather than explicit, but entirely positive, not in any doubt — even though they both appeared to require repetition, even continuous confirmation of the entire situation, however gasping and breathless a process, Mary's splendid bosom partly responsible for this last, being considerably compressed on the one hand and obtrusively impact-making on the other.

They were still in this state when David and Alexander Stewart came up to interrupt. The latter would have held back, considerately; but there was nothing like that about the High Steward.

"Come, come, you two!" the former reproved. "You have been at this sufficiently long, surely? Besides, it is no way to behave, in decent company! In fullest view of the camp! We have been observing you this considerable while, and wagering on how long you could maintain it . . .!"

"Not so," Alexander asserted hurriedly. "My lord jests."

Jamie glared at them both, with comprehensive hostility.

"For the aunt of the heir to the throne, it will not do," the boy went on. "Even the illegitimate aunt! The royal house must ever present an example. And in front of this son of the Earl of

Buchan! What if his sire was to perceive you from yonder castle? Corrupting all . . . !"

"I'll thank you to speak more respectfully of the lady who is to be my wife," Jamie began stiffly — but was interrupted by Mary's peal of laughter, in which the Earl David promptly joined. When Alexander commenced to chuckle also, Jamie had no option but to relax to a somewhat shamefaced grin. He rose to his feet — and was surprised to find the High Steward throwing his arms around him in an impulsive embrace.

"Bless you, Jamie! God be praised!" he cried. "So you have come to it, at last. I will be groomsman at your wedding! Here is the best news we have heard for long. Mind — what sort of a wife she will make I know not. But she is the right shape for child-bearing and like frolics . . ."

"Nephew — hold your tongue!" Mary commanded. "And wait until you are asked to attend the wedding before you offer your services . . ."

David stopped more of that by going to kiss his aunt heartily, while Alexander came to grip Jamie's hand with obvious pleasure.

After that they had to drink more of the ale and whisky the Wolf had sent over than was really good for them, in celebration. Even the men-at-arms got extra, until all was finished.

When at length, the night well advanced and all sleepy with the drink and the camp-fire heat and smoke on top of a long day, the trio escorted Mary to her cot-house quarters, it was David who completed an elaborate goodnight slapping Jamie on the shoulder and pushing him towards the cabin door also.

"With your troth pledged before all, you will be thinking to share this night's accommodation, I swear!" he asserted.

Jamie looked at the young woman — who paused but did not speak. He sighed a great sigh. "No," he said. "Not so. We will do this thing decently, properly. Mary . . . Mary deserves no less."

She turned to consider that, and him, for a long moment, then nodded. "No doubt I will thank you, Jamie — one day," she said. "Good night." And she hurried within.

"M'mmm," her nephew said. "And you may make a kirk or a mill out of that, Jamie Douglas!"

"A kirk, surely!" Alexander adjudged, but soberly.

Together they went back to the camp-fire.

In the morning, and earlier than might have been expected, the Earl came over, with the Lady Mariota and their daughter, to suggest again that the visitors delayed their departure; also to urge Alexander to change his mind about this journey to the South. But since it was altogether out-of-character for the Wolf to urge and suggest anything, rather than to command and since Mariota had brought a bundle of Alexander's best clothing and gear for her son to take with him, it looked as though they were reconciled to his going — which was as good as saying that his father wished him to go.

All was now approximate amity, with good wishes for the travellers, and even congratulations forthcoming to Jamie on his betrothal. Also regrets, from the ladies at least, that they were going to lose their visitor. That young man was perhaps suspicious of mind, but he remained cautious, feeling that there was probably something more behind all this than met the eye or ear.

As they were preparing to move off, and Alexander had embraced his mother and sister warmly, the Wolf raised his voice to rather more like his normal tone and manner.

"Nephew — and you, Douglas," he said, "remember that I am placing my son in your care. He is going with you, amongst men of ill will, against my advice. I have told him that if he does this, if he makes his own bed, he must needs lie in it! Nevertheless, I shall expect you both to ensure his good treatment. As part price of my releasing you, thus. Mind it."

David shrugged. "We shall try, to be sure," he said. "But as you well know, Uncle, none can ensure anything in this realm as it is governed today. Sir James discovered that, when he came here to your Badenoch, did he not? Sir Alexander may be more fortunate, but we cannot swear to it."

"No? The King's only son cannot warrant protection for one in his care? I think you can. I shall require it of you, have no doubts. Unless Alex prefers to think again? More wisely?"

"No, my lord," his son said firmly. "I wish to go. Moreover, I think that I perhaps can look after myself."

"We shall see. Although, to be sure, I think even Robert Stewart, or any other, will consider twice before interfering with a son of mine! For I promise you, if I hear aught of hurt to Alex, I will not sit idly in Badenoch wringing my hands! Let all know that." The Wolf stared round at them all. Then he jabbed a finger at Jamie. "Douglas—you will not fail to remember what you have learned here. What you have been shown." That was no question, but a statement. "You will tell those who ought to know. You have seen what sort of hand rules the North. Let none mistake or forget it. I let you go, now — and might not have done. See that you are duly . . . grateful!"

Jamie inclined his head, wordless. He moved forward to salute the Lady Mariota and her daughter, more hurriedly than he would have intended. Then he leapt on to his garron's broad back.

The Wolf had the last word, hand and voice raised. "Make no mistake, all of you," he called. "It might have been otherwise, here — much otherwise. The decision was mine. Go in peace."

*   *   *

The journey south was a deal less trying and prolonged, for Jamie at least, than it had been northwards. A good summer had dried up the land, and the innumerable rivers and lochs and the unending marshes and peat-bogs were less of a barrier. Also, of course, having *Alastair Mor Mac-an-Righ*'s eldest son with them, as well as the force of men-at-arms, greatly facilitated progress, the endless haggling about mail and passage miraculously evaporating, smiles and bows ushering them from one clan territory to another, food and forage provided at much more modest rates throughout; so that frequently Jamie and his three Tantallon Douglases, with MacAlpin the interpreter — all of whom the Wolf had returned to him the morning they left Lochindorb — exchanged rueful glances. For all that, he would have been well content had their progress been less expeditious, since it developed into something of an idyll for him, traversing a most lovely country day after day with Mary ever at his side. Even though they could seldom be completely alone for any length of time, they did manage to lag behind quite frequently, wander apart of an evening, make small unaccompanied ventures. On occasions when there was no separate sleeping accommodation for the young woman, Jamie had the joy of lying side by side with her, on sweet-smelling bog-hay or straw. It was all one of the happiest episodes of his life, young and cheerful company, long carefree days in the saddle, learning sides of Mary's character which he had not known — and rejoicing in all he learned.

This carefree aspect of the journey was something new for

Jamie Douglas. Since Otterburn he had never been carefree. He had been plunged from youth into manhood too swiftly, had saddled himself with responsibilities in the Lady Isabel's service, taken his knightly status perhaps too seriously; above all been oppressed by the horror of the Earl of Douglas's murder and his own vow of vengeance. Now, the failure of his quest here in the North, far from depressing him actually lightened his mind. The deaths of both Ramsay and Bickerton somehow seemed to clear the account. And it was evident now that if the Earl Robert was indeed guilty, it would never be confirmed, much less established before all men. Jamie had, at last, come to accept that he, a very minor figure on the realm's stage, could never hope to bring the Governor to book — and that acceptance was like a weight off his shoulders. Admittedly this journey was only a sort of timeless interlude, a very temporary hiatus; but he knew an abiding sense of relief, of freedom from onus and obligation, nevertheless. For that, of course, Mary Stewart was to be thanked in large measure.

Only one incident marred the pleasant tenor of their progress, and that at the very beginning. When they released young Sir Duncan Stewart from his incarceration, under guard, in a rude shieling cabin in Glen Tarrock, a bare hour after leaving Lochindorb, he had not taken the situation well, being surly and resentful to a degree, despite his brother Alex's soothings and explanations. He had ridden off eastwards, not to Lochindorb, without farewell. But later in the day, in the Forest of Abernethy, they saw him again, with the other brother Andrew and a small group of mounted caterans. They sat their garrons high on a hillock above the track, to watch the south-bound party go by. They did not come down or seek to waylay them. But as the travellers passed below, the two brothers raised clenched fists high, shook them, and cursed with a ferocious violence and intensity. Even David was taken aback, and Alexander remained silent for a long time thereafter. But there was no pursuit nor further demonstration.

They won out of the true Highlands at Dunkeld, collected Jamie's Lowland horses and said goodbye to Gregor MacAlpin. Then on to Stirling, where the King was said to be in residence prior to moving to Scone in a few days' time. They saw many fine and colourful cavalcades already on their way to the coronation. The heir to the throne was just in time.

XXIII

THE CORONATION OF Robert the Third was a strange affair from the start. The new King himself would probably have been glad enough to dispense with the entire occasion; certainly to have had it on a very abbreviated and modest scale, a mere gesture. But this did not suit his brother the Governor. Just why the Earl Robert was so determined that it all should be a great and memorable proceeding was not entirely clear, for he was not a man who cared much for display and was no waster of money. Yet that August of 1390 nothing was spared, all was conducted with much formality and dignity, and everyone who mattered in Scotland was expected to be present. It might indeed have been the Earl's own crowning. Perhaps he felt that it established his own position as king-maker more clearly. Perhaps it served his purpose to summon all the realm together under his eye — for although a summons to parliament might be ignored or rejected, to refuse to attend a coronation could be construed as treasonable. Possibly he felt that the Stewart hold on the throne was still too new and less than secure — this was only the second of the line, after all — to risk dispensing with any of the traditional formalities. Whatever his reasons, the Governor arranged all, decided all.

The Abbey of Scone, considering its importance as the principal shrine of Scotland, was surprisingly modest compared with such as Dunfermline, Melrose, Cambuskenneth and the like. It had belonged, of course, to the ancient Celtic Church polity, ever much less spectacular in its display than the Romish; and Scone had been the capital of Pictavia, the Pictish kingdom, retained as such by Kenneth MacAlpin when he united Picts and Scots. Here was installed the semi-legendary talisman of the Scots monarchy, the Stone of Destiny; and here all Kings of Scots had been crowned from time immemorial. But its modest size meant that there was but little accommodation for such great state occasions, and with the King's and the Governor's personal households occupying the abbot's and monastic quarters, there was no room for others. Large numbers of the commonality, servitors, scullions and the like were installed in tents and pavilions in the haughland of the Tay nearby; but for the quality this would not do. Fortunately Saint John's town of Perth was only three miles to the south, and there the great majority of the nobility, gentry and dignified clergy found lodging, riding to and fro each day, the burghers of Perth charging exorbitant sums for the use of very inferior houses for the few days of the event.

Although the Lady Gelis had not yet arrived from Nithsdale, so that Mary had to wait for her, Jamie found his father installed in a wing of the large Blackfriars monastery of the Dominicans, on the north side of Perth, with the Lady Isabel and her husband, Sir John Edmonstone, allotted a room therein. His father greeted him rather after the style of the returned prodigal — for Jamie's journey into the North had been taken contrary to Dalkeith's advice — rejoicing at his safe return. He had been uncertain as to how his sire would react to the news of his betrothal, for he was not yet of full age by a few months, and fathers could be awkward about such matters. Mary, a more or less penniless bastard, was not provided with the tocher or dowry normally so important. But the old lord took it very well, making no objection and declaring that although Jamie was young he had shown himself to have a mind of his own; and having gone his own way for these past two years, he was entitled to choose his own bride — especially one who had shown her acumen by improving his financial position notably, as she had done over the Inchcolm affair. That would serve in lieu of dowry. And the link with the royal family was in the Douglas tradition and might well prove useful. Moreover, it was probably time that Jamie married, if he intended to remain in the Lady Isabel's service; it would look better thus. That was as far as the careful Lord of Dalkeith committed himself, in words, on what he fairly evidently considered was his son's unsuitable entanglement with the former Countess of Douglas. Clearly this betrothal was something of a relief.

This first duty over, Jamie went in search of the said Lady Isabel, and in some little trepidation.

He found her, with the Lady Egidia, strolling in the orchard of the monastery, which lay just within the city wall, overlooking the open parkland of the town common called the North Inch — and did not know whether to be glad or sorry that she was not alone. At sight of him she came quickly over to embrace him, with undisguised delight — to his rather more than usual embarrassment.

"Jamie, my dear! My very dear!" she exclaimed. "How good, how good! Praise God that you are safely back. Oh, Jamie — I have been so worried. In those terrible Highlands. And in that ogre's hands! How you must have suffered . . ."

"I did not suffer at all," he jerked. "I . . . I am very well."

From the background her aunt hooted. "He does not look to me like a great sufferer! Never seen him look better — if you would stand back somewhat, girl, so that I *may* see him!"

Isabel ignored that, still clutching him. "We heard grievous tidings of you. At the sack of Elgin. Made prisoner. Struck down by that monster. You should never have gone, Jamie — I told you it was too dangerous."

He shook his head. "Not so. But it is all past. I suffered no hurt. Learned much. And now — now I am betrothed to be wed." That came out in a rush.

She drew back now indeed, staring at him. She parted her lips but did not speak.

"Ha!" the Lady Egidia said. "Are you now? To that minx Mary, for a wager!"

"Mary, yes." It was at Isabel that he looked, half-defiantly, half-pleadingly.

"You will *wed*?" she said, almost in a whisper. "Wed . . . Mary?"

"Yes. I love her. She is . . . good."

"High time, too," his father's wife put in briskly. "Time you were wed, young man. You are too fond of women — without being able to take care of yourself! And women too fond of you! That Mary has a good head on her shoulders. She will keep you right. This is best. Is it not, Isabel?" That was almost a command.

The younger woman touched her hair, her cheek. "No doubt," she murmured.

"She came. To gain my release. A long way. With much courage. She loves me well, she says. And, and she is a bastard, as am I!"

375

"So! My own leal knight no longer!"

"But yes. To be sure, I am. Why not? I made my knightly vow to serve you. I will not cease to do so because I am wed. I am ever yours to command."

"Unless your Mary says otherwise!"

He shook his head. "Why should she do that? She is your sister. She loves you also. She has always known me to be in your service."

"Yes. No doubt. Yes — forgive me, Jamie. If it is your wish, if you are happy . . ."

"Then I may continue to serve you?"

"If you so will."

"I will, yes." He paused. "But — I fear that I achieved little in that service, in the North. I failed. Failed to find what I sought. The Wolf, the Earl of Buchan, had hanged Patrick Ramsay. As bearer of the excommunication letter. So I learned nothing. Nothing which would establish the Lord Robert's guilt. With Ramsay dead, I fear we shall never establish it."

"For which you should praise God, I say!" Egidia Stewart asserted. "A less profitable employ I never heard tell of! I swear your life is the safer lacking that information, Jamie. Yours also, it may be, Niece. Dangerous knowledge."

Isabel spoke levelly. "I will discover that knowledge if it is in my power to do so, nevertheless. And charge Robert with it, before all. If it is my last act!"

"Then do not also sign this lad's death-warrant in doing it, girl! Enough is enough. Three young men have died. Is that not sufficient, Isabel?"

When the other did not answer, Jamie spoke. "I do not think that it will be possible to learn more now. None can keep a closer mouth than the Governor. If he ordered Bickerton to do the deed, he will never tell. Bickerton will not tell! And Ramsay, who could have told who paid him to silence Bickerton, will not tell either. Who else would know? None, I doubt. So I fear our quest is ended, Lady Isabel."

She turned and hurried away from them, back into the monastery buildings, without word or backward glance.

"Let her be, boy," Lady Egidia told him, as he made to follow her. "She will be herself again presently. You dealt her two strokes there. Give her time."

The Lady Gelis arrived that night, in the Earl of Douglas's train, from the South-West. Since the death of Sir Will of Nithsdale, Archie the Grim had taken more interest in his royal daughter-in-law than when her husband had lived — although it was probably more on account of the boy Will, in whom he seemed to find something like a reincarnation of his favourite son. The lad was with the party also, and dressed like a prince by his grandsire.

After his interview with Isabel, Jamie was a little anxious as to how Gelis would react to his news. He need not have worried. Once again he did not see her alone, for she had the boy Will with her — indeed she seemed to keep him at her side always. She was looking as beautiful as ever, almost more so, with her features more chiselled, her eyes seeming larger. But there was something strange about those eyes, a fey look which he had not seen before, a sort of preoccupation as though she was concerned with something which she alone could see — and which was certainly not himself. She greeted him warmly enough, but fairly quickly seemed to grow almost abstracted. The impression grew on him that it was not lack of affection but rather lack of interest which was the trouble. Her mind was not on what he had to say. It turned out that she knew of his betrothal, for she had already seen Mary; but it did not appear to make much impact upon her. She made conventional remarks of congratulation and goodwill, but there was little conviction therein. As assuredly, however, she was not in any way resentful or hurt. On the subject of Patrick Ramsay she listened attentively enough, but made little or no comment, expressing no emotion either way. He noticed that, all the time he was talking to her, her eyes kept turning back to the boy Will, as though that was where her true concern lay. As for himself, Jamie discovered no regrets, no hankering for what might have been, no trace of what he now could look upon as a former infatuation with the princess. If she had changed, so presumably had he. He still could admire her, have an affection for her; but the ache and the desire had gone — to be replaced, indeed, by a disquiet for her, an anxiety. There was something far from right about her. If it was still preoccupation with her murdered husband and vengeance therefore, it had taken an even more unhealthy turn than had her sister's. There seemed to be a strange balance in the Stewart nature, which if upset could grievously swing to direst

377

extremes. Mary, thank God, appeared to have escaped this flaw—unless an occasionally flying tongue might be an aspect of it!

The following two days were busy ones, with preparations for the coronation interrupted, strangely enough, by a state funeral. This was the Governor's idea, and many were the questions and discussions as to why he ordained it, the significance of the thing — for Robert Stewart seldom did anything without due calculation. It was the old King's burial. Robert the Second had died on May 13th; but his body, embalmed, had been kept unburied until now. He was to be interred at Scone Abbey on August 12th, and the new monarch crowned there the next day. The Governor said this was to emphasise the continuity of the royal line and kingship, that Robert II was theoretically king until he was interred; and Robert III was not really king until he was crowned the next day. But most men saw it as one more device for ensuring Robert's own supreme power in the new reign. He was still constitutionally Robert II's Governor and Regent, so long as his father remained unburied. There was to be no possibly dangerous hiatus between that event and the next day's when the new monarch would confirm him in the rule.

The funeral, in the end, was in fact a somewhat hurried and makeshift affair, grief and regard for the old man having tended to cool, and the morrow's more dramatic and vital celebrations overweighing all — indeed the elaborate decoration and festooning of the Abbey and its surroundings was more apt for a wedding than a funeral. Isabel Stewart was possibly the only one to shed tears.

That evening, however, tongues were more busy than ever in speculation and debate, with even more significant tidings. All in Perth and Scone were agog with two further items of news. One, that the Queen's personal coronation was to be postponed until the day after her husband's; and two, that the Governor himself intended to place the crown on his brother's head. The King had apparently agreed to both these departures.

After the evening meal, the group at the Lord of Dalkeith's lodging were discussing the implications, with a variety of reactions. The general opinion was that both were deliberately insulting to the monarch — and the first, of course, still more so to his wife; but that the second might be the more significant.

The women were indignant about the slight to Queen Annabella, whom they had all come to admire, and some to love, during the Turnberry affair. Even Egidia forgot to be cynical and voiced her disgust at her brothers, both brothers, one for being so hard and the other so weak. Isabel declared that it was Robert's bitter way of paying back Annabella for his rebuff at Turnberry, and that they all ought to unite again to demand a reversal. Gelis said nothing, but Mary pointed out that they had not much time to do anything such. Robert had heedfully delayed the announcement until the last moment no doubt for that very reason. The ceremony would be beginning in not much more than fifteen hours.

"Too short a time to achieve anything to any purpose," Dalkeith agreed, shaking his grey head. "It is a sorry business — but not really important. The Queen remains the Queen whether her coronation is one day or the next. Nothing alters that. As an example of Robert's spleen it is vexatious, but only that. What is more important is this of the actual placing of the crown on his brother's brow. This, I fear, is symbolic of much greater danger."

"Why?" his wife demanded.

"Do you not see? He, Robert, is demonstrating to all that he, and he alone, is making his brother the King. The Crown is *his* gift. Not only does it make his position as Governor more secure, but it could be used to imply that what he could do he could also undo! The king-maker might unmake. Or, even put him in a position hereafter to refuse to crown the boy David. He must have good reason for this move — he always has. I do not like it."

"He is Earl of Fife," Sir John Edmonstone pointed out.

"Only by a trick, a device. The right to place the Crown on the King's head is hereditary in the MacDuff family — not necessarily in the earldom of Fife. Up till this, the head of the MacDuff line has been Earl of Fife — but today is not. When old Earl Duncan died, eleventh of his line, he left only a daughter, Isabella, to succeed to his earldom. She wed, as her second husband, the Lord Walter, the King's eldest son. They had no bairns — she was forty-six years old when they married, to be sure — no more than a ploy to get the premier earldom in the land for the Stewarts. When Walter died young, and the Countess wed yet again, an Englishman, by an intrigue she and he were prevailed upon to settle the earldom on Walter Stewart's brother, Robert, in exchange for lands elsewhere. The true heir of the MacDuffs was otherwise. The senior of them, the Lord of Abernethy, by tradition should have the privilege of crowning the monarch at his coronation — not the holder of the Fife earldom."

"Are no MacDuffs here to uphold their claim?" Jamie asked. "This Lord of Abernethy — where is he? I know nothing of him."

"He is a quiet man, retiring, older than am I. He will never oppose the Earl Robert, I fear."

"Can we do nothing, then?" Isabel demanded.

"What is possible? At this stage. He lives far away in the sheriffdom of Banff. If he has not come South . . ."

It was at this juncture that there was an interruption. An esquire came hastening from Scone, from the Earl David, seeking Jamie Douglas, to announce that the Governor's men had arrested Sir Alexander Stewart. Sir James was to come, at once.

"You heard?" Jamie cried, to his father. "He has taken Alexander! Despite all. Despite the Earl David's protection. Despite the King's own kindness towards him. We believed that he was safe, since he had fair audience of the King. The Earl Robert has held his hand these three days. Now . . . ! What can we do?"

Dalkeith eyed him unhappily. "I do not know," he admitted. "He *is* the Governor. Where the affairs of the realm are concerned only the King can gainsay him. And if the King will not . . ."

"He relied on us to preserve him. His father put him in our care . . ."

"His precious father is scarce in a position to demand care from *you*, boy — or any other who has suffered his attentions! I wonder greatly why he allowed this young man to come. He needed not to be a seer to foretell this . . ."

But Jamie had gone, with the esquire, to ride hard for Scone.

He found David Stewart in the Abbot's quarters of the monastic wing, displaying rather more agitation than he had ever seen in that self-possessed youth — but it was the agitation of anger rather than dread or uncertainty.

"You have heard?" the prince exclaimed. "The insult of it! He has taken him in despite of me. And of my father. Fall foul him — he scorns us both! This is not to be borne, I say!"

It occurred to Jamie that David was more concerned for his

own pride than for Alexander's safety. "What has he done with him? Alexander? Where is he, my lord? Is he in any danger of hurt?"

"God knows! He was here, talking with one of my sisters, when my uncle's creatures came for him. This afternoon. I was in Perth, so knew naught of it till I returned. They rode off with him — that is all I am told."

"And your father? What does the King say?"

"My royal sire wrings his hands and moans! Prays, belike! But will *do* nothing. He says he will talk with Robert anon — but, God be good, that signifies nothing! Oh, to have a *man* for a father!"

Jamie sighed. "What can we do, then? If the King will do nothing. When a guest, his own nephew, is taken from his own house . . ."

"Do! We will go speak with my accursed uncle here and now! I but waited for you. He is here in the monastery, with that oaf Murdoch. And your precious Earl Archie . . ."

"Me? *I* cannot go denounce the Governor to his face! A mercy — not me, my lord. I am only a small man, a mere knight . . ."

"You are the Wolf of Badenoch's witness, you told me? You can tell Robert Stewart matters no one else can. Come, you."

"But . . . this is folly . . ."

"Do you not desire to aid your friend? Never fear, I will say most of what has to be said. You will know when to support me." Without further instructions, David hurried off.

Across a pleasant courtyard and into the cloisters the young prince strode, with a very reluctant Jamie behind. Guards stood at the door of the refectory — but none dared to halt the heir to the throne. Pushing through the crowded eating-hall, full of the Governor's minions who eyed the pair askance but did not seek to question them — some even bowing uncertainly — David made for a far door protected by two more guards. When one of these began to interpose himself and ask, respectfully enough, his lordship's business with the Governor, he was actually dug in the stomach by a sharp elbow.

"Out of my way, fool!" the boy snapped. "Do you dare oppose *me*, Carrick?"

Hastily the other guard opened the door, and they marched in. David slammed it shut behind them.

Four men lolled at ease behind a table, with wine-flagons and platters — at least, three lolled, for Robert Stewart never did such a thing but sat stiffly upright. The others were the Earl of Douglas, the Lord Murdoch Stewart and Bishop Peebles of Dunkeld, the Chancellor. The last got heavily to his feet, while the rest stared.

"What is this, this intrusion . . .?" the Governor was saying, frowning, when he was interrupted, and vehemently, as his nephew shot out an accusing hand and pointing finger.

"My lord of Douglas — do you not stand when the High Steward of Scotland enters the chamber?" he demanded. "On your feet, sir. As for you, Cousin Murdoch, I swear you have not the breeding to know how to behave. Learn, then!"

Astounded, that awkward young man rose, looking alarmedly at his father, whilst the Earl Archie, muttering, raised posterior a few inches from his bench before sinking back again, craggy brows down-drawn.

"Nephew — how dare you burst into my chamber, with your infantile arrogance!" the Governor jerked, remaining seated. "I will have a word with your father on this, believe me!"

"I dare a deal more than that, sir," the boy gave back, strongly. "And refer to me more respectfully in the presence of these . . . persons! I am here because a friend and kinsman has been shamefully, unlawfully and indeed treasonably taken out of my father's house by your ruffians, whilst under the King's and my own protection. I require Sir Alexander Stewart returned to that house forthwith, sir, and due apology made to him, and to me!"

His uncle considered him expressionlessly. "Have you overlooked the fact, boy, that *I* rule this kingdom, as its lawful Governor? And do not require to answer to you, or any, for my actions."

"You were Governor for my late grandsire, now buried, sir. My father, after tomorrow's coronation, *might* continue you in office, in some fashion — or might not. *I* certainly would not. But meantime you only *act* Governor. Whereas I am High Steward and Prince of Scotland, next in rank to the King. Do not forget it." He turned. "Chancellor Bishop — you are aware of the truth of this, if my uncle has forgotten. Am I right?"

The heavy old cleric cleared his throat unhappily. "I . . . ah . . . my good young lord. That is so, in a manner of speaking. But . . ."

"Manner of speaking, sirrah? Is it true or is it false?"

"Er, true, my lord. But . . ."

"But nothing! Uncle — you will return Sir Alexander Stewart to my father's lodging here, immediately."

"I shall do no such thing, boy."

"Not if the King commands it?"

"Has the King commanded it?"

"*I* command it. And His Grace will, if I ask him, confirm. He is much disturbed by your action."

"I shall see His Grace then, in due course, and inform him of the matter. And of your insolence. Now leave us, Nephew — we have important matters in hand."

"You have important matters to *explain*, sir! And I will have that explanation, now! Where is my cousin Alexander? Where, and why, have you taken him?"

"I need not answer your ill-mannered questions, Nephew — even as *acting* Governor! But for your information, your Uncle Alexander's bastard is by now halfway to my house of Falkland, in Fife. For his own security. His father is an outlaw and excommunicate, and has grievously injured many. Not only in Elgin and Forres. His son could be endangered. I will see that he is preserved, secure."

"Do you expect any to believe that? Only you would dare assail him, when in the King's care and protection. I say that you have taken him for your own ill purposes. Out of hatred for his father. And, no doubt, because you think to use him to force his father to your will. In which case, I say, you have made your greatest mistake, Uncle. And are like to pay dearly for it. Indeed, I believe that you may have fallen into a cunning trap."

The Governor looked coldly unimpressed. But the Earl Archie spoke.

"Trap, my lord? What mean you — a cunning trap?"

"I mean that my Uncle Alex is fully as clever as is my Uncle Robert, my lord! He as good as *sent* Sir Alexander south with us. He would never have permitted him to come had he not wished it. And he warned his son, before all, that you might act to his hurt. Demanded *my* protection for him. Why send him then, think you? The Wolf knows well what he is at. I say that he *wanted* you to move against his son. So that he might have excuse to move against you! And now you have given him it, my lord acting Governor."

Robert Stewart moistened thin lips. "My shameless brother can do nothing against me, from his barbarous mountains. He may burn and slay in the North — and we shall halt that in due course. But he is powerless here in the South."

"You believe so?" The boy smiled. "*He* does not believe so — and Uncle Alex is a man of action, remember. Unlike some others! He has, h'm, designs on this southern part of my father's realm, I am told." He turned. "Has he not, Sir James? You were held by him for months, in his house of Lochindorb. To be his witness — chosen to give his warnings. Were you not?"

Jamie drew a deep breath. "Yes, my lords. He told me so. Said that I should make it known to you all, to all who have the rule in the South."

The Governor sniffed, not even looking at the speaker. He sipped from his wine goblet.

The Earl Archie sat forward, however. "What did he say, Jamie?"

"He said that he would come South, one day. And when he did he would claim his rights. Rights the excommunication had sought to take from him. He, he knew of the excommunication device, my lords, and what was behind it, before ever I reached Badenoch."

"Ha! He did? And you say he spoke of coming South?"

"Yes. He promised to do so. And said that he would bring his rights with him. That was the way he said it. And that a thousand broadswords would speak louder than any bishops' anathemas."

"Wind!" the Governor said. "Bluster. Vain pretence — such as is Alex's custom."

"Sir James has it otherwise," David put in. "Was Elgin, Forres, Pluscarden wind and bluster?"

"Aye, my lord — these things were done by way of warning and example," Jamie went on, looking from one to the other. "I was taken to see, as witness. And told to tell you. How, he, my lord of Buchan, acts. And will act. To other than Elgin and Forres. If he has to come South. He meant it — that I swear. And it was ... terrible."

For a moment or two there was silence in that chamber.

"You see?" the prince resumed. "The Wolf is sufficiently wolfish! He refused to come to my father's coronation — but he sent his son. Why? Now you have taken his son. May not this be the excuse he looked for? Now he can come, to rescue his son. You said a thousand broadswords, Jamie? But he has more than that, I think?"

"He had over 3,000 at Elgin, my lord. Sir Alexander told me he could raise 10,000 and more in a week."

"Wild savages — Highlandmen!" the Earl Robert snapped, scornfully. "Mere threats, bairn's boastings. What could such do against our knightly array and armoured chivalry? Burning cathedrals and defenceless towns is one thing, assailing a steel-clad host another. Alex is not fool enough to risk that. You will not frighten grown men with such tales, boy."

"Then you refuse to heed? You, in whose hands the safety of my father's realm is supposed to lie?"

"I refuse to heed the tales and threats of fools and bairns. Now — leave us, if you please, to our important business. Tomorrow's observances occupy my time sufficiently."

David Stewart moved forward, to lean over the table towards his uncle. "There are more sorts of fools than bairnly ones!" he said. "I declare that my father is ill-served — and shall not cease to tell him so. And when *my* time comes, my lord of Fife and Menteith — watch you, I say! Watch you!" He swung about and strode for the door, Jamie hastily following. But before opening it he paused. "You may resume your seats, my lord Bishop and Cousin Murdoch," he said, and so left them.

It was a fair exit — but they had failed in their task and no flourish would disguise it. The boy mouthed blasphemies all the way back to his room.

Coronation day, August 14th, dawned bright if breezy — and with much of the ceremonial taking place outdoors, the weather was important. The exodus from Perth started early, and even by sun-up the roads were packed with folk making for Scone, from all over the Lowlands, in holiday mood and in their best clothing. Even the mounted nobility and gentry, ploughing their impatient way through the unending crush, could not spoil the popular good humour.

Isabel not requiring his services today, and Mary in attendance on Gelis, Jamie attached himself to his father's party — otherwise, undoubtedly he would not have gained admission to the Abbey-church, which was not nearly large enough to contain all who wished and considered themselves entitled to occupy it. Even so, although his father had a prominent place amongst the lords of parliament, he and his brothers were installed in only a fairly lowly position at the back of the south aisle, where sundry pillars tended to interfere with the view. But it had its advantages for young people who might seek to lark about somewhat during the long period of waiting, and moreover provided a visual alleyway to the seats reserved for the princesses and their ladies at the front of the opposite aisle. Jamie at least could see and make signs to Mary.

The Scottish coronation was a mixture of religious service and secular ceremonial, its procedures laid down and ordered over the centuries, with little scope for innovation. Only in minor details could there be variations — as, for instance, in this of the Queen's share in the programme being put off till the next day. Annabella walked to the church from the Abbot's house, in a small procession of her own, to take her seat in a chair-of-state in front of the princesses. Her eventual arrival signalled the start of the ceremony proper.

Sweet chanting introduced a choir of singing boys, and, flanked by acolytes swinging censers, the Lord Abbot of Scone led in the prelates, the bishops and mitred abbots and priors, in their gorgeous copes, dalmatics and canonicals. These paced up to the chancel, which was hung for the occasion with magnificent tapestries, and seated themselves in the stalls on either side. Then, to the sound of fifes and tap of drums came the lords of parliament, in their robes, two by two, Dalkeith among them with half-a-dozen other Douglases, Lindsay of Crawford, Montgomerie of Eaglesham, Maxwell, Seton and others to the number of some two score. These did not sit but went to stand just above the chancel steps facing the altar but leaving a passage in their midst.

Clash of cymbals heralded the earls, led by Dunbar, and all present save only Buchan, resplendent in scarlet and gold — Carrick and Fife having different roles to play. The earls went to sit on chairs in front of the prelates on the north side of the chancel.

There followed a flourish of trumpets, high and clear, to announce the royal approach. Lyon King of Arms brought in the great officers of state, the High Steward, a slight but brilliant figure in cloth-of-gold, the Chancellor, Chamberlain, Treasurer, Standard-Bearer and Keepers of the Great and Privy Seals, who brought the symbols of their offices to lay on a green-velvet-covered table before the altar. As these took up position in front of the prelates on the south side, the Primate, Bishop Trail of St. Andrews, led in the limping monarch, flanked on one side by the Constable, Sir Thomas Hay, bearing aloft the sword-of-state, on the other by the Marischal, Sir William Keith, bearing the sceptre. Behind, looking inscrutable, walked the Earl of Fife and Menteith, bearing the Crown of Scotland on a crimson cushion, his son Murdoch at his heels.

The King, of sadly noble appearance, wore the white velvet of purity and truth under a prince's robe of crimson, his hair and beard already almost as white as his doublet — scarcely credible as brother to the Wolf. A throne without canopy was set on a small dais behind the green-covered table; but the monarch was led by the Bishop to a lesser chair at the side. The sword, the sceptre and the crown were placed on the table. All was ready.

The Abbot of Scone, a dignified and venerable figure, moved up to the high altar, with his assistants, and commenced the coronation mass. This said, the celebrant and monarch alone partook of the elements. The Abbot then turned to bow to the Primate, who moved over to the royal chair and raised the King to his feet. Standing thus together, he administered the Oath, in which the monarch swore in a husky voice to be a father to his people, to keep the peace in his realm so far as God allowed, to forbid and put down all evil, crime and felony in all degrees, and to show mercy and righteousness in all judgments — in the name of God Almighty, merciful and compassionate. By the time he came to an end, the royal voice was the merest whisper.

The Bishop was then given a vial of consecrated oil from off the high altar, by the Abbot, and with this he anointed the King's head and brow in the name of the Father, the Son and the Holy Ghost.

A great shout arose within the crowded church; and led by the choristers, the company burst into the singing of the Twenty-third Psalm. But when the fourth verse was reached, all fell silent

for a high, clear solo voice which sang heart-breakingly the
significant lines:

Yea, though I walk through the valley of the shadow of death,
  I will fear no evil;
For Thou art with me; Thy rod and Thy staff they comfort me.
Thou preparest a table before me in the presence of mine
  enemies;
Thou anointest my head with oil; my cup runneth over.

When there was silence again, Bishop Trail led the monarch
down from the dais, which he negotiated only with difficulty, and
a little way towards the ranked lords and people.

"I present to you the Lord's Anointed, your liege-lord and
undoubted King!" he intoned impressively.

The building all but shook to the eruption of bellowed chanting. "God save the King! God save the King!" The monarch
blinked, shaking his head.

Now the Lord Chamberlain came forward to divest the King of
his prince's crimson and put on him instead the robe of royal
purple. He was led to the throne, not to his former chair, and
seated. The Constable came over with the sword-of-state, the
monarch rising to have it girded on by a shoulder-belt — for it was
five feet tall and two-handed. Sitting again and finding the sword
awkward to dispose at his side, he was brought the sceptre by the
Marischal, easier to hold, in the left hand.

Another flourish of trumpets, loud in the enclosed space of the
church, heralded the actual crowning. The Earl Robert came up
with the crown on its cushion, still with Murdoch behind. Many
present beside the Douglases undoubtedly resented the Governor's
appropriation to himself of this especial honour. The emphasis
was obvious. He handed the cushion to his son, took the handsome, indeed magnificent crown from it, lavishly made by Robert
the Bruce out of the spoils of Bannockburn, and placed it on his
brother's brow with the minimum of ceremony. Stepping back, he
inclined his head slightly, rather than bowed.

The trumpets sounded a prolonged fanfare.

The crowned and anointed King sat, one hand high on the hilt
of the great sword, the rod of the psalm, the other holding the
sceptre, or staff, while the coronation anthem surged out from

hundreds of throats. Although some of the throats were a trifle choked for singing, just then, some from emotion at the age-old and significant thing that was done, representing their pride of nationhood; some at the essential mockery of all so solemnly represented; some at the personal tragedy of the gentle, kindly, ineffectual man whose twisted fate it was to sit there.

Just before the singing ended, there was an unrehearsed incident. Out from the line of officers of state the dazzling, slender figure of the High Steward stepped, to sink before the throne on one knee, head bowed to his father, hands out. Relinquishing his awkward grip of the sword-hilt, the King extended his own hand, trembling, towards his son, who reaching up, took it between his palms, in the traditional gesture of fealty. Kneeling there, he repeated the fealty oath, his young voice firm, unhurried, whilst the Earl Robert frowned blackly but could not interfere, and from the nave a great sob came from Queen Annabella, hastily suppressed.

Rising to his feet, relinquishing the royal hand, David Stewart bowed low to his father, turned to stare blankly at his uncle, and then returned easily to his place. Jamie Douglas, for one, could scarce forbear to cheer. The great sigh that went up from the congregation was eloquent.

But now it was the Governor's turn. Striding forward, he raised his brother from the throne in brusque fashion, and with two flicks of his forefinger summoned the Constable and Marischal to come and take the sword and the sceptre. A further beckon brought Sir Alexander Scrymgeour, Constable of Dundee and Standard-Bearer of Scotland, to lift the Lion Rampant standard from off the table and hold it aloft above the royal brothers. Then, without further ado, and gripping the King's arm, he set off at a pace on the fast side for a man with a limp. He led the monarch, who still wore the crown, down through the ranks of the bowing lords, out of the chancel and into the nave, making for the great west doorway. He did not pause or even glance at the Queen as he passed her chair, although his brother attempted a shambling bow.

Out of the church they passed, and hurriedly the officers of state, the earls and prelates and lords, sought to form up in their due order and follow on, the Constable and Marischal to get into their flanking positions and the Standard-Bearer to come close behind with the banner.

The church stood on a kind of terrace above the level haughlands of the Tay, with the monastic buildings to east and west. But to the north, a little way back, was a slightly higher ridge, grassgrown, and all about this a vast crowd was congregated. In their thousands the people of Scotland waited to hail their newcrowned sovereign on the famed Moot-hill of Scone. Unfortunately, the renowned Stone of Destiny, on which the new King should have seated himself, was not available. When Edward of England had come storming for it in 1296, it had been hidden away, and the invader palmed off with a lump of Scone sandstone roughly quarried, instead of the ornate and highly carved talisman long known as the Marble Chair. The true Stone had been produced for Bruce's hurried coronation; but on the hero-king's death-bed, he had entrusted it to his loyal supporter, Angus Og, Lord of the Isles, well knowing the dangers to it implicit in his infant son David's succession and the unending English threats. Angus Og had taken it to the Hebrides, and there it still was, succeeding Lords of the Isles refusing to yield it up until their claims to the earldom of Ross, and otherwise, were met — the present Donald being no exception. So there was no Stone today. But the Moot-hill presentation could still be made, the motions gone through.

As the now distinctly straggling procession began to climb the hill, another royal brother arrived from Perth. Walter, Lord of Brechin, had somehow managed to miss the church ceremony but was in good time for the feasting. His two elder brothers ignored him entirely.

To the ringing cheers of the populace the principals reached the top of the Moot-hill, the King distinctly breathless. There, turning to face the crowd, the Earl stooped to pick up a fistful of the sacred earth, already loosened for the purpose, and thrust it into his brother's hand.

"I, Robert of Fife and Menteith, give you the land of Scotland!" he said, level-voiced. "I will aid you to hold it secure." And his hand clenched over the other's. With the other hand he gestured towards the assembly, and raised his voice — a thing he seldom permitted himself. "On this Moot-hill of

Scone," he called, "I, Robert, give you your crowned King."

The cheers rang out, unperceptive of the double meaning, and continued. The monarch inclined his head; but it was more an act of infinite regret, almost of apology, rather than a bow of acknowledgment. His son came and stood beside him, at the other side from his uncle.

Presently the Lyon King had his trumpeter blow a flourish for silence, and, as successor to the ancient Celtic sennachies, commenced to intone from a lengthy parchment roll.

"Hear me, all men high and low — behold the High King of Scots, *Ard Righ Albannach*, Robert, son of Robert, son of Marjorie, daughter of Robert, son of Robert, son of Robert ..." On and on he went, tracing the royal descent back through the Bruce generations to David, Earl of Huntingdon, brother of William the Lion and Malcolm the Fourth and so by Malcolm Canmore through seven more generations to Kenneth MacAlpine who united Picts and Scots, and on through the misty Celtic names to Fergus MacErc of the semi-sacral Fir-Bolg who followed the missionaries from Ireland, but who claimed descent from the pagan Eochaid, the Horseman of the Heavens, god-spirit of the early Celts. It took a considerable time to rehearse, but the huge crowd listened intently throughout. The Scots had ever been a race of genealogists.

Now servitors came carrying the throne from the church, on which the King seated himself thankfully. He was barely thereon when his brother Walter, the second Walter of the family, came to drop unsteadily on one knee and take his hands between his own in token of fealty, muttering something approximating to the oath — for he was three parts drunk as usual — seeking the prominence of being first to do so. Thereafter, in more dignified fashion and due order of precedence, starting with the earls, all the great ones of the land — save the ecclesiastics — formed up to do likewise, a lengthy process; and not only the great ones, for every holder of a barony was expected to make fealty, although not all on coronation-day, and even Jamie in due course came forward to swear loyalty for the barony of Aberdour. He was moved with real compassion as he took those soft hands within his own, wishing that he could say something of what was in his heart instead of the oft-repeated and all but meaningless formula. And he was much aware of the stern features of the Earl Robert regarding him unfavourably from behind the throne on one side, and those of David Stewart half-smiling at the other.

At last it was all over, and Lyon could announce that the King graciously invited all and sundry, high and low, to come feast with him in the Abbey-park below, to celebrate together this great day. Long live the King's Grace!

Later, Jamie sat with Mary, and other dependants of the lofty, at a modest but well-placed trestle-table not far from the royal and Douglas ones. Well-fed, they discussed the day's events. All around them was repletion, satiety, even excess, gluttony and drunkenness, folk great and small, young and old, gorged with meats and wine and ale and now being entertained by a variety of musicians, jugglers, tumblers, bear-dancers and the like. Only at the royal table itself was there little aspect of ease, relaxation and content. The King sat exhausted but still tense, only toying with his food, the Queen on his right seeking to sustain, encourage and comfort him, David on his left making no major attempt to disguise his boredom but amusing himself by intermittently baiting his cousin Murdoch who sat next to him. The Governor was on the Queen's right, but sat at a distinct remove, expressionless, staring straight ahead of him, Isabel on his right finding no more to say to him than to her other brother Walter who sprawled asleep over the board. Gelis and the other princesses present sat at the far side of Murdoch. However good-looking, none would have called the royal family a happy or congenial company.

"By all the saints, when may we slip away?" Jamie murmured, not for the first time. "Must we sit here all day? I planned to take you to Shortwood Shaw and Kinclaven, where Wallace fought the English — fair woodland and river. It is but eight miles . . ."

"I cannot leave until Gelis does — as you know well. And she may not until the King does, as you also know. What has happened to my staunch and patient Jamie?"

"You have! I am weary of being patient, of putting up with other folk, of *sharing* you! I want you to myself, Mary — do you not understand? We are never alone . . ."

"I understand only too well, foolish one," she said. "Since my need is as great as is yours — immodest as it may be to admit it! Perhaps you should not have chosen a princess's maid-in-waiting for your betrothed? But — wait you lad. Rein in! I shall make it up to you, I promise!" And she gripped him beneath the table.

"That makes it but the worse, woman! If I could catch young David's eye. He looks sufficiently wearied of it all, himself. He might induce his father to make a move . . ."

"His unhappy Grace, my brother, would welcome a move, I swear. But until his master, there, gives the word . . . !"

"How can a man be so, so helpless? So lacking in all spirit? *He* is the master now, King of Scots. He can command, and none gainsay him. Why submit to the Governor so?"

"Well may you ask. John was born tired, I think. And being the weary one of a forceful family must have been a sore business, wearing him down. Alex and Robert ever dominated him harshly. Being lamed was the final blow. The habit of deferring to others will not change now, at his age, I think. Being king will mean nothing to him, save irksome duty and more pain. All he seeks is peace, quiet and his books."

"Yet he could make a good king. He is kind, honest, just . . ."

"No, Jamie — these are not the qualities demanded of a king, today. Or ever, I believe. If the king has them, so much the better. But what he *requires* is rather strength, vigour, ruthlessness, an ability to be harsh and to frighten men. Some might love John, but none could ever fear him. And the ruler needs to be feared." She pointed at the Earl Robert. "Yonder is the man who *should* have been king. And does he not know it! He has all those qualities I named, and none love him. But all fear him. I mislike the man with all my heart — but my head tells me that he might have made a good king for Scotland. As even might Alex. Both have been denied what could so easily have been their birthright. And have fought against that denial differently. But they are strong, determined men, and could have given this land the strong rule it has lacked since the Bruce died. Robert may do so still, as Governor. John never would, or could."

"You talk like my father."

"I am glad if I do — a mere woman! For your father has one of the wisest heads in Scotland, Jamie. If you were to choose to follow *him*, instead of dancing attendance on Isabel, you could rise high in this realm, Sir James Douglas!"

He looked at her thoughtfully. "Do you want me to rise high, Mary?"

393

"No-o-o. I think not. But I am a Stewart also, see you, and the lust for power is in us. So beware! I would sooner have you always the true and modest Jamie I know and find to my taste! But you may have little choice, lad. Do you not see it?" She pointed again, on either side of the King, to Robert and David Stewart. "Those two will, and must, come to blows, one day. Over the rule of this kingdom. The Governor and the heir to the throne. Nothing could be surer. In not many years from now, I vow, there will not be room for both of them in Scotland. For Davie has the qualities a king needs also. And Robert, I swear, will never yield the power to him, gracefully. Many will have to choose whom they will support. And Davie calls *you* his friend. He will demand not a little of his friends, that one. I think that you will need all your father's wisdom one day, Jamie."

"I would not wish to be caught up in any struggle for power."

"Perhaps not. But you have to choose sides. And if you choose for the boy you have come to like, as against the man you have come to hate, you will not keep out of it."

"You are warning me? *Against* David and *for* the Governor?"

"Lord, no! Since I mislike Robert as much as you do, even though he is my own kin. I but remind you that it may not be so easy to remain aloof when battle is joined. For Jamie Douglas in especial."

They sat in silence for a space, watching yet scarcely watching a juggler.

"What will he do now? With Alexander?" Jamie demanded. "Your precious Governor!"

"Who knows? But he will not heed *us*, in the matter, that is certain. There is nothing you can do, Jamie."

"I have tried the Earl Archibald. He is the only man the Governor heeds. But he will not act. He says it is for the best. That the Wolf and all his brats deserve nothing better, but worse indeed. My father besought him also, but could do no better. My hope is that David may later prevail on the King to assert his authority and order a release. He says that the Queen will keep reminding his father on this. Will you speak with her also?"

"To be sure. But, I grieve for Annabella. Her lot is the sorriest of all. For John can blame none but himself; or, at least, his nature. But the Queen, although quiet, calm, is a woman of spirit. It must greatly try her to see her husband so used. And herself slighted."

"Tomorrow she will do better. At her own coronation."

"We must seek to see that she does. For that is not Robert's intention, I swear. The service here is to be direly short, and held early in the day. Moreover, Gelis says that he is contriving a great tourney, race-meeting and wapinschaw, on the Inch at Perth, for all day long. As a celebration, he says — but it will mean that a great many will not come to Scone. He will ensure, I vow, that few indeed do come . . ."

"This is shame! A sorry, contemptible stroke. Does David know of it?"

"I do not know. We must ensure that *many* learn of it."

"And yet you say that Earl Robert might have made a good king!"

"If his ambition and yearning for the crown had not been soured and twisted thus, I think he might have been, yes. For he is able, competent, shrewd, forceful. He is a man thwarted, seeing others doing ill what he could do well. He has become a man eaten up with resentment."

"And all Scotland must pay . . .!"

XXIV

JAMIE DOUGLAS, MAKING plans now, with Mary, for their wedding in October, spent the next few weeks on the move between the houses of Edmonstone, Dalkeith and Aberdour — where they were going to set up home and where much refurbishing was necessary after years of neglect, before any self-respecting man could bring a bride to it. Mary's position, in this interim period, was difficult. Gelis had retired again to Nithsdale in Dumfries-shire, with her step-son, the remote situation of which seemed to suit her present withdrawn mood — but was highly inconvenient for Mary. Besides which, the coronation over, she seemed neither to require nor desire her half-sister's attendance. So Mary, who would have relinquished her position as maid-in-waiting anyway, on marriage, did so in advance. But being illegitimate and having no property of her own, this left her more or less homeless. And though, as a royal bastard she could have always found some sort of lodging and employment about the Court, this did not suit her independent frame of mind, especially as the Court was now really the Governor's, the King himself retiring to the seclusion of Turnberry on every possible occasion. The young Earl David had been allotted a suite of rooms for himself in Stirling Castle, in recognition of his advancement as heir to the throne and High Steward, although he used them but seldom. The boy was glad to bestow one of these chambers on his favourite aunt, so that she might have somewhere that she might call her own meantime, and keep her belongings; but that great hilltop fortress was hardly a suitable residence for a single young woman, when the Court was not present, and she was no more often there than was David. Moreover, she felt slightly less then welcome at Edmonstone, for though the Lady Isabel had fully recovered her equanimity and treated Jamie almost as before, there was still a reserve between the half-sisters, and Mary's aforementioned independence of spirit made her avoid Isabel's house. Happily she was always welcome at Dalkeith, where the old lord, and Lady Egidia also, had come to approve of her. Since it would not do that she should openly cohabit with Jamie before the marriage ceremony, when he went to Aberdour she found quarters with her half-brother the Archdeacon Thomas — or at least provided by him, at a nunnery at Dysart, reasonably convenient. It was all in rather irritating contrast, nevertheless, to their fine free ride south from Badenoch; but they put up with it in moderate patience since it would soon be over — and, to be sure, they contrived to be alone together with fair frequency.

They were, in fact, busily planning and arranging their house at Aberdour one day in late September when a messenger from Dalkeith summoned Jamie urgently to his father's bedside. The old lord was ill and desired to assemble his family around him. Much concerned, for neither his sire nor the Lady Egidia were of the alarmist type, Jamie, and Mary with him, set off for Queen Margaret's Ferry without delay.

They reached Dalkeith Castle to find a large family concourse, in considerable gloom, for the lord thereof was well loved. He had suffered some sort of heart attack four days before, and though he had shown some small improvement since, he seemed to be convinced that he would not recover. Presently Jamie was summoned to the bed-chamber, alone.

His father did not look so very different from when last seen, hale and well, but his eyes somehow appeared to have grown larger. His voice also was less strong, and breathless.

"Jamie, lad," he said, mustering a faint smile. "You gladden my old eyes. You are the eldest of my brood. And though born out-of-wedlock, you have ever been close to my heart. For I loved your mother dearly. She was not such as I might wed — a small farmer's daughter. But we were close, close." His voice sank to a whisper. "Closer than ever were my two wives!"

Embarrassed, Jamie gripped the older man's arm. "God rest her soul," he said. "I never knew her."

"To your loss, boy — to your loss. The plague took her, young." He sighed. "If only I might have wed Meg ..." A pause. "But *you* are more fortunate, Jamie. You can wed the lass of your own choice, as not all can. Your Mary — she will serve you very well. A young woman with a head on her — as well as the parts young men show more interest in! You have chosen well, in the end."

"I thank you, sir. But ... you must not tire yourself. The Lady Egidia said I was not to stay long, to tire you ..."

"Heed her not, lad — heed *me*! I have two matters to speak of. And I may not be spared for another chance. I have made up my will and settlement of my affairs. I have left you certain tokens. When I pass on. The lands of Stoneypath and Baldwinsgill, in Lammermuir, with the castle of Stoneypath. And Roberton, in Teviotdale. The tower there is long broken by English raiding. But the barony itself is well enough. These are larger, richer lands than your Aberdour ..."

"But, my lord — there is no need! I thank you — but I have sufficient. I do not seek wide lands ..."

"Wheesht, lad. You will have bairns soon enough, you and yon lassie. They will need to be provided for. Forby, Jamie, I leave you to look to and provide for young Johnnie. Your brother, your *full*

397

brother. He has not your wits nor steadfastness. Belike he will grow in sense. But I durst not leave him lands yet. He would but squander them. So see you to him, out of yours. For the rest . . ." He paused, panting. "For the rest, I would have you to have my second gold girdle — you'll mind it. And my suit of tilting-armour. It will fit you well enough. Inlaid with gold. And two silver plates, with my arms. To remember me by . . ."

"My lord, my lord — do not speak so! Do not talk as though you were, were dying. You are not, I swear. And I do not require such tokens to remember you by. You have always been a true and kind father to me, a bastard though I am . . ."

"I have tried to be, lad. I . . . I . . ." A fit of breathlessness shook him. Jamie straightened up.

"I will go now, sir. You have spoken more than enough."

"No, no. Bide you, boy — a little longer. I told you. I had two matters to speak of. Hear me. You know that the lassie Borthwick died a while back? Her your brother James was betrothed to. Janet, Sir William's daughter. Aye, poor lass. But I have arranged another match for James. With the new King's second daughter, the Lady Elizabeth. Aye, a more suitable match. For my heir."

"But . . . but, sir, she is but fourteen. A child, yet . . ."

"Old enough to be wed. Her sister wed but a year older. To Archie's son."

"And James? What says he to this?"

"It is not what James says, boy — it is what *I* say. Forby, James knows his part and place. He is heir to Dalkeith and Morton. Unlike you, he may not wed just whom he fancies. James will be the second man of the Douglas power. One of the richest lords in the land. So he weds the King's daughter, a princess — where you wed a King's bastard! There is the difference. Aye, the difference."

Jamie said nothing.

"They are to wed on St. Martin's Mass. Here in my church of St. Nicholas, Dalkeith. My wish . . . that you are wed together, you and James. A double wedding, Jamie . . ."

"But we are to wed the month before. In October, not November."

"A month's wait will not hurt you, boy. And it will serve you well. A great occasion. Although I will not be there to see it, I think. The King, the Governor, Archie, all the highest in the land. To see you wed."

"I care naught for that. Nor does Mary, I swear. We would be wed quietly . . ."

"No doubt, my son — no doubt. But I choose to make the decision mine, not yours. You are not yet of full age. The cost of all will be mine. You are a Douglas, and will accept the responsibility of that." His father's eyes glowed almost eerily, even though his voice was little more than a dry whisper. "It will be a great day for Douglas, for Dalkeith. I am near my end, but this I can do. The Stewarts, and therefore the Crown, will be bound closer than ever to Douglas. Do you not see it, lad?" In his eagerness, the old lord half-raised himself from the pillow, but fell back, unable to sustain the effort. His gasping, rustling voice however, went on. "My wife, the Lady Egidia, the King's aunt. James's bride, the King's daughter. Your bride, the King's half-sister. All wed to Douglas. Archie's son wed to the King's eldest daughter — just as his bastard Will wed Gelis, the King's sister. His second son is to wed the Governor's second daughter. Young George of Angus is to wed the Lady Mary, the King's youngest. You see? The Douglas design!"

Jamie swallowed. "I see . . . something. Something I had no thought to have part in! Mary and I are not for this design, my lord. Marrying for design, for power. And I would scarce have thought that Douglas was so admiring of the Stewarts to wish to be allied only to them! I have heard you name them upstarts, sir, have I not? Compared with our own more ancient power."

"Fool! Do you not see?" The mottled hand, surprisingly strong, gripped his own. "The Stewarts themselves are naught to care for. It is the Crown! The day will come when most Stewart lines end in a Douglas! And there are none so many lawfully-born males in line for the throne. Young David. The Governor. The Governor's two sons. Walter of Brechin. That is all. And none save the Governor married. Bastards innumerable, but these cannot succeed. You see? Douglas meantime will surround and support the throne. One day, Douglas may mount it!"

The younger man shook his head. "So this is what the Earl Archibald and you plan. With other's lives! I . . . I mislike it, my lord. And cannot see why Mary and I, illegitimates both, have to contribute to it. Why involve us?"

"You add weight, boy. To this wedding ceremony. A double wedding is the more notable. And you are something of a hero, Jamie. Since Otterburn. And now your Badenoch venture. Aye, and your Mary riding North to rescue you. She is bonny, well liked. Folk speak of you both. You will add weight."

"I mislike it . . ."

His father spoke sharply, seeming to forget, for the moment, that he was reputedly on his death-bed. "It is my will. You will obey. Remember it." Then he sighed, and wearily waved a hand. "Pleasure an old done man, Jamie. It is not much to ask. Go now, lad. I will see Mary later. Not now — for I am tired . . ."

Distinctly upset, Jamie went to tell the young woman. Surprisingly, Mary was less perturbed than was he. If it would please his father, she said, it would not greatly hurt them. They would survive the added three weeks. This design for linking Douglas and Stewart so closely was scarcely new, after all. And anyway, no concern of theirs. She could see nothing sinister about it, as Jamie seemed to do. Nor, clearly, could the King and the Governor think so, since they must agree to all these marriages. Indeed, she would not be at all surprised if it was not so much a Douglas design as a Stewart one. For the Earl Robert was ten times more of a plotter and planner that ever could be the Earl Archibald and the Lord of Dalkeith; and if he allowed these marriages, then he had his reasons. Let their wedding be held at St. Martin's Mass, and before all the Court — it would but serve to demonstrate how well and truly wed they were. And Isabel and Gelis would have to be present to acclaim them! She laughed cheerfully. Besides, these great new lands willed to Jamie, in Lammermuir and the Borderland, were well worth three weeks of waiting.

Jamie Douglas, it is to be feared, was due to learn what it meant to have a wife with a clear and practical head on her bonny shoulders.

The next day, delayed by events, the Earl of Douglas arrived, in his usual striding stir scarcely suitable for invalid visiting. Indeed, when Jamie escorted him upstairs to his father's bedchamber, he was in grave doubts as to the wisdom of admitting him — not of course that he could have kept Archie the Grim out had he decided that was best. Stamping in, panting from the climb, the Earl wasted no breath on sick-bed sympathies.

"Sakes, man James — you lying there yet!" he cried. "Here's a

400

poor state of affairs! This winna do, James. With a wedding, two weddings, to get by with. Aye, and worse than weddings, a sight worse!"

"Archie ...!" the sufferer faltered. "I'm sick, direly sick. I doubt I am not long for this life. Aye — maybe the next will be better, kinder ..."

"Faugh, man — the next life'll need to look to itself! This one needs looking to with a deal more haste and swink. Precious soul of God — I'm like to be needing five hundred men from you any day now, weddings or none!"

"Eh? Eh?" Dalkeith stared. "Men ...? What's this? What's this, of a mercy?"

"Trouble, James — trouble. Alex Stewart — a curse on him! He's on the move — or his heathenish bastard sons are! They've come spreenging out of their Hielant hills, with thousands of their bare-shanked caterans. Over the Mounth passes into the lowlands of Angus, Strathmore and Gowrie. Fire and sword and dirk ..."

"God a mercy!"

"The Wolf has struck, my lord?" Jamie demanded, at his back, forgetful of his place. "In force? Invaded the South?"

"Struck, yes — a plague on him! No warning or declaration. He's loosed his barbarian horde on to honest men's lands, slaying, burning, ravaging. It is no cattle-reiving, this, but bloody war."

"Not war, Archie — never war!" Dalkeith quavered. "They'll be making a bit stramash, a gesture, just ...?"

"If this is a gesture, man, it's a sore one. They've already defeated the force sent against them — God knows how! At a bit called Briarachan or something such — Glen Briarachan, north of Glasclune on the edge of Strathmore. We'll need to do something about it, James. I doubt I'll have to muster Douglas."

"But ... but ..." The invalid spread his hands, helplessly.

"This is the Wolf's answer," Jamie said. "To his son's arrest and imprisonment. I ... I ..." He could hardly say I told you so to the Earl of Douglas. "I feared something of the sort. He warned me. Who commands this Highland host, my lord?"

"Some brigand sons called Duncan and Andrew Stewart, they say. A pair of savages, by God! But they must be stark fighters — for they've routed the Sheriff of Angus, slain him indeed — Sir Walter Ogilvy of Auchterhouse, a fair enough soldier. And Lindsay of Glenesk and a wheen more. A bad business."

"There has been a battle?"

"You could name it that. When the word of this inroad came in, I wasna there. I was in the Borders and knew naught of it. Robert, the Governor, sent his good-brother, Sir David Lindsay of Glenesk to deal with it, with the Sheriff — since it was his own country. They mustered a force from the knights and lairds of Angus and Strathmore, a fair force by all accounts — but these caterans defeated them. A slaughter, no less. Hundreds slain, including the Sheriff and his brother, Guthrie of that Ilk, the Lairds of Ochterlony, Cairncross — och, many more. David Lindsay himself sore wounded, like Sir Patrick Gray and other knights . . ."

"Armoured chivalry defeated by the scum of Hieland bogs!" Dalkeith exclaimed, in agitation.

"It seems so. They should never have fought them in these upland glens — damned folly! But, even so . . ." Douglas shrugged. "When Robert heard of it, he sent for me. All Angus and Gowrie and the Stormonth, even Fife itself and Strathern, lies open to these barbarians. He'd have me raise the power of Douglas. But that will take time. God knows what they may be at before I could hold them."

"There's others besides Douglas, Archie," the sick man protested. "Nearer to the bit. Mar, Crawford, Drummond, Hay, Lyon . . ."

"Aye — no doubt. And they'll no' be standing idle. But none can field an *army* as can we, James." That was said not in any pride and eagerness but almost wearily. Archie the Grim had reached sixty-six years.

Jamie spoke, greatly daring. "You do not *wish* to raise Douglas, my lord? To engage in war. For an ill cause, if ever there was one — the, the Governor's folly!"

"Of course I do not, boy — do you take me for a sword-brandishing fool! Fighting the English is one thing; fighting our own countrymen, even these bare-shanked Hielantmen, and on our own land, another. But we canna let them over-run and destroy the realm."

"I do not think that they will aim to. They will not keep up any sustained campaign, I reckon. How would that serve the Wolf?"

"The foul fiend knows! What does he want? Is he coming South to try to release that precious son of his?"

"More than that, I think." Jamie frowned in concentration. "I

402

believe that he expected this. Sent Sir Alexander with us knowing that his brother might well lay hands on him. And so give him good and extra cause to make this invasion. I believe he would have invaded anyway — but that shameful arrest, when under the King's and prince's protection, aided him. I know what he wants — he made it very clear. He wants to ensure the continuation of his rule in the North, as Lieutenant and Justiciar. And he wants the excommunication lifted. To this end, and for vengeance on Bishop Barr, he burned Elgin and the rest. As example. For the same reason he sent this host South—and can send many more ..."

"Well, man — well? What of it? How will this save us from outright war? And me from raising Douglas?"

"It may not be too late to save both, my lord. And to spare much bloodshed. The Governor's policy towards his brother has failed. The excommunication plot, his substitution of his son Murdoch as Lieutenant, and how this of Sir Alexander. He has *provoked* this invasion. But surely it is not too late to change his policy, perceiving his mistake?"

"Robert Stewart does not easily change his mind. And he is a proud man. Besides, it is too late by the Mass!"

"Perhaps not. If the Wolf gets what he really wants? And to give him it will cost the Governor little, save in his pride. If he released Sir Alexander, said he would press the Primate to withdraw the excommunication, and offered to restore the Justiciarship, in return for his brother calling back his forces to Badenoch?"

"He would never do that. Give way on all these — to a lawless brigand and his unholy tribe!"

"Why not, sir? What would it cost him, in truth — compared with civil war? Alexander held in a Falkland cell serves him nothing. The excommunication would be lifted by the *Church*, not seemingly by the Governor. And the Wolf *is* still Justiciar, and accepted as such by all in the North — the Lord Murdoch's appointment never taken up. He would rejoice to be relieved of it, I vow! Three scrapes of the Earl Robert's pen, and the danger would be lifted."

The Earl Archie tugged his beard. "Would it be sufficient? And would Buchan credit it? Believe it would all be done? He trusts none, that one."

"I think he trusts *me* — however humble an instrument! Else why make me his witness? Why release me to come South again? If I sent him a message, assuring him that Alexander was released, and would not be taken again — on *your* surety, my lord! — I think that he would agree."

"Robert would never lout so low to his younger brother, boy. He could not do it. To restore the Justiciarship would be as good as eating dust before all the kingdom. And parliament, mind, confirmed that dismissal . . ."

The invalid took a hand. Dalkeith was sitting up now, indeed, and looking a deal less near death's door than when his friend had entered, despite the alarming news. "It might be done judiciously, discreetly, Archie," he declared. "Made to sound better — so that Robert Stewart might swallow it. A contrivance. He need not actually restore his brother — since it was only in name that he was ousted. If Robert was to announce that his son Murdoch wished to resign his appointment — which all know he has never desired — this would serve. No other being appointed. Would it not?"

"That is right," Jamie agreed eagerly, "no need for more."

"And this of the excommunication," his father went on, life in his voice again. "Since the lifting of it would in fact be Holy Church's doing, not Robert's — if Alex could be persuaded to express some form of regret for what he has done. Not so much in the matter of his wife perhaps but in this burning of the cathedral and towns. Then the Governor's name need scarce come into it."

"Express regret — Alex!" the Earl exclaimed. "As well expect the Devil to! Or Robert!"

"A form of words could be devised — only words, man. To cover the matter. I could contrive such, I believe. Something Alex Stewart could say, or sign, which would save the faces of the churchmen. Make some small payment, perhaps. A token, just . . ."

It was Jamie's turn to look doubtful, even though he rejoiced at his father involving himself, rousing from his despond, displaying the shrewd and experienced statecraft again for which he was renowned. "It would be difficult," he said. "With the Wolf holding all the cards. He is not a man to be cozened by skilful words. Any more than he is to express regrets . . ."

"But neither is he a fool, Jamie. He must know that Holy Church would have to have *something* before the Primate could lift the anathema. To preserve the bishops' credit. He cannot expect to be freed of excommunication without at least a gesture that they could call repentance. Even Alex Stewart! I say that he will recognise that."

"This *I* say, my lord — that he will never apologise to any bishop, to his brother. The Governor, that is. To the King himself it might be different. That might serve. But to none other, I'd swear."

"Aye — that might be contrived, likewise. John — King Robert — will do anything to save his realm from war, I think. How say you, Archie? Could you convince Robert? He needs must listen to you, after all — for he requires you. And he must see that only something such as this can save him, in this pass."

"I can try," the Earl agreed. "Aye, devil burn all stiff-necked Stewarts — I can try! James — can you write a letter? For Robert to send to Alex. You are good at words. And I will tell him to sign it — or whistle for Douglas support! And you, boy — write one to Buchan himself, as you said. To go with it. And by the fastest courier we can send to Badenoch."

"And Sir Alexander? You will get him out of Falkland Castle, my lord?"

"To be sure, to be sure. God help me, I'll get him moved out of there and back to the King's keeping — damn him for a plaguey pest! Aye, and meantime I'll have to set up some sort of a defence to keep his ruffianly brothers from splurging further South into decent country. While we treat with their father. A curse on them all, I say . . .!"

"Better that than flinging all Douglas into war, Archie — all the realm. Jamie — fetch me paper, quill and ink, lad . . ."

XXV

THE ATMOSPHERE IN the church of the Dominican or Blackfriars monastery at Perth was tense. It was already well past noon, and the small but illustrious company waited uneasy, on edge, offended in some cases. It was unthinkable that the King himself should be seen to wait for anybody, even his own brother, and he remained hidden in the chapter-house, young David shuttling to and fro cheerfully enough, probably the only non-tense member of the congregation. Bishop Trail of St. Andrews, the Primate, and Bishop Peebles of Dunkeld, Chancellor, looked distinctly nervous in their stalls up near the altar, Archdeacon Thomas Stewart demonstrating greater ease by strolling constantly from one to the other with a sort of alert reassurance. The Earl of Douglas, representing the Governor, also paced about, huffing and snorting. The Ladies Isabel, Elizabeth and Jean Stewart sat silent, no longer even whispering, with Mary in attendance behind — the other royal sisters unable to be present for one reason or another, Marjory because her husband, the Earl of Moray, had just died as a result of a tournament wound in England, Katherine being at the bedside of her wounded spouse, Sir David Lindsay of Glenesk, Gelis preoccupied in Nithsdale, and Margaret, as ever, lost in Donald's barbarous Isles. Walter of Brechin should have been there, but was not. The remainder of the congregation, apart from the prior of the monastery and one or two priests and monks, consisted of Jamie and Sir Alexander Stewart, released for the occasion, standing beside Mary and behind the princesses.

Jamie himself was agitated, undeniably. Although both Mary and Alexander kept reassuring him that no real responsibility rested with him, he could not but feel that it must, to some extent. The details and timing of this encounter had been no concern of his, admittedly, but the general situation was — or at least he had been the vital link and largely the instigator. People kept looking at him. Alexander revealed little concern, but there was a stillness about him unusual in that lively character. He looked pale from his confinement.

David came back, a gay figure in peacock clothing. "Look not so fearful," he called out, grinning, to Jamie but loud enough for all in the church to hear. "We are entirely comfortable here, are we not? And Holy Writ enjoins us to pray as well as watch, I seem to recollect. I perceive little praying in progress — but perhaps my lords Bishop are doing so silently, for us all!" He laughed, uninhibitedly. "My royal father, at least, is an example to all. He is lost, through there, in a dusty manuscript, sacred I have no doubt. And Her Grace contemplates, as is her wont — eternity perhaps."

Archie the Grim emitted a choking sound. Otherwise the heir to the throne's observations were received in silence.

Jamie whispered to Alexander. "We should have posted a lookout, up on the monastery bell-tower. To tell us if he approaches. From the north. We still could do so."

"What benefit in that? If he comes, he comes. If not, no watchman will bring him. He may already be in the city. But never fear, my friend — if he said that he would come, come he will. Sooner or later."

"Thank God that it is the King, in there, not the Governor! He would have been long gone ere this, and all lost."

"Perhaps. But my father knows his brothers."

The Lady Isabel turned in her seat. "Jamie — you are sure it was noon?" she murmured. "Not mid-day — which might mean a less certain hour. Or noon*tide*, perhaps?"

"I did not make the arrangement, Princess," he said. "The Governor planned it all. Used his own messengers . . ."

"My esteemed Uncle Robert said *noon*," David declared. "And we all know what weight he puts on truth and accuracy. In small matters!"

More than one throat gulped at that.

The Archdeacon Thomas, after conferring with the bishops, came down to the lower chancel area to speak with his royal relatives.

A noise, a disturbance, from outside, galvanised the company — clattering hooves, shouting and the clank of mail. And since the church opened off the cloisters, deep within the monastery complex, this was unlooked for, to say the least.

Jamie had a vivid mental vision of the Wolf riding his horse right into the cathedral of Elgin, and something quailed within him.

Then the west door of the nave was flung open in unceremonious style, and a knight in full armour, helmeted, came clanking in bearing aloft a large banner displaying the arms of Buchan, three golden sheaves on blue. Behind him paced a gaudily-tabarded herald in the Stewart colours, and thereafter two trumpeters. These blew a resounding fanfare which set the hammer-beam roofing ringing. The herald then raised his powerful voice.

"The mighty prince Alexander, Earl of Buchan, Lord of Badenoch, Lochaber and Kinneddar, Lieutenant and Justiciar of the North, *Alastair Mor Mac-an-Righ*!" he announced.

Shaken, all stared.

There was a distinct pause before the Wolf walked in. He had elected to dress simply, if rather oddly for the occasion, wholly in gleaming chain-mail, girded with a golden earl's belt. A great two-handed sword hung from a shoulder-belt, also of gold, and over the other shoulder was draped a voluminous tartan plaid. His head was bare, his shoulder-length silver-gold mane gleaming to match the chain-mail. He was chatting easily with his two sons, Sir Duncan and Sir Andrew, leaders of the current invasion, these dressed as though straight from the field of battle. Behind came a colourful throng of Highland chieftains in an eye-catching display of varied tartans, eagles' feathers and Celtic jewellery, all armed to the teeth. The excommunicate of Holy Church had arrived to offer penance, oblation and satisfaction.

Brushing past his banner-bearer, herald and trumpeters, the Wolf walked up the nave some way, and paused to stare round the church. His eye lighted on his son. "Ha, Alex!" he called, but did not move forward or discontinue his survey. He greeted none other. "Where is my brother the King?" he rapped out. "Douglas — where is he?" It was not at the Earl thereof that he looked, but at Jamie.

David Stewart stepped out. "Greetings, Uncle," he called pleasantly. "What delayed you?"

He was ignored. "Sir James Douglas — I said, where is the King? Whom you engaged would meet with me here."

"My lord, he is here, I assure you . . ."

"Earl of Buchan, His Grace is occupied, in the chapter-house," the nephew announced, now fully as stiffly as his uncle. "I shall enquire whether he is ready to receive you!"

The Wolf started forward angrily, but restrained himself with an effort. He did not know this church and where might be the chapter-house. Undoubtedly it would look highly undignified to go trying at various doors. He stood still, frowning. The boy by no means hurried off.

Archdeacon Thomas cleared his throat, in the hush. "My lord — the Primate and my lord Bishop of Dunkeld have been awaiting you . . ."

His half-brother eyed him remotely, up and down, and then looked away, unspeaking.

The Earl of Douglas hurrumphed strongly. "We have been here a long while waiting, Buchan," he jerked. "I have more to do with my time."

"Then go do it, man. Your presence is not required."

Hotly the Douglas snarled something incoherent; but he had no answer to that.

No one else ventured a remark.

Presently, preceded by his son, the King came limping through a sidedoor near the chancel-steps, Queen Annabella on his arm — or more accurately, he on Annabella's arm, since she it was who did the supporting. He looked around him, moistening his lips, a stooping, nervous figure, as all rose and bowed, managed both to shake and nod his head at the same time in acknowledgment, and without further ceremony hobbled over to the high-chair provided, and sank down, opposite the bishops. The Queen remained standing at his back, to one side, the young prince at the other. An entrance more different from his brother's would be hard to conceive.

He cleared his throat. "Aye, Alex," he said thickly. "You've come, then."

"We have both come," the Wolf returned shortly. "I hope to some purpose."

"Oh aye, to be sure — to be sure. But . . . this is all none of my doing, Alex. Much here."

"Meaning, Sire?"

"I mean that it is Robert's contrive. All of it. I would not have had yon excommunication . . . if I had been asked. Nor this end to

409

it. It was ill done. But, Alex—you shouldna have burned Elgin. You should not. The cathedral. Yon was a sin, a great sin. I wouldna like to have that on my conscience, Alex. No, no . . ." The hesitant voice trailed away. Only one or two there knew how much resolution it had taken to enunciate those words.

The Wolf knew, and his pale eyes narrowed. "There are sins and sins, Brother," he said, levelly for him. "You at least will never have *that* sort on your conscience! And Robert's conscience died at birth!" He took a deep breath. "Shall we say, Sir, that, like yon fire, I, I got something out-of-hand! To my. . . regret." That last was like a trap shutting. Undoubtedly it represented fully as great an effort as had the King's statement.

There was silence then, as people eyed each other, wondering. When it was clear that the supreme sacrifice had been made and that they would not get more, the monarch cleared his throat again. "Aye, well," he said. "So be it. God forgive us our sins—and *I* have ower many! But see you, Alex—the Bishop here, my lord of St. Andrews, has this matter in hand. This of excommunication — the lifting. There is some form of words for it. My lord Bishop . . .?" Thankfully the King pushed, almost physically, all over to the Primate.

"My lord of Buchan," Trail began, in sepulchral tones, rising to his feet, "where grievous sin has been committed, in especial sin against the Holy Ghost, Christ's Holy Church has power to pronounce solemn excommunication, the supreme anathema, banishment of the creature from before the face of the Creator."

"Who said so, man? Christ?" the Wolf interrupted.

The Primate coughed. "Holy Church says so, my lord. The successors of Saint Peter . . ."

"Not even Saint Peter himself? Only his successors! But which one, Clerk? He in this Avignon? Or he in Rome? There is a difference, is there not?"

"My lord — this is a solemn matter . . ."

"God's truth, man — do I not know it! My eternal soul, no less — as you would have me to believe! Have done with your preachings, Sir Priest — if you would have me to bide in this kirk much longer!"

The Primate twisted his hands together and looked unhappily from the King to his fellow-bishop. "I protest!" he exclaimed. "I do most solemnly protest!"

410

"So do I, sirrah — so do I! So there are two of us! Now — get on with it a God's name! Or I leave, you hear — leave!"

"Alex," the King quavered, "the Bishop is your friend. Here to do you a good service . . ."

"Then let him perform it, and be done. I did not come here to be preached at."

Drawing a quivering breath, Trail tried again. "My lord of Buchan — before excommunication may be lifted, repentance is necessary. Repentance in sackcloth and ashes . . ."

The guffaw which interrupted that was sufficiently eloquent.

"Do, do you so repent, my lord?"

"How think you, Clerk?"

The Bishop drew a hand over his lips. "You have *come* here. Presumably for that purpose. You have said that you, h'm, you regret . . ."

"So I seem to recollect."

"M'mm. God's judgment against impenitent sinners is terrible, my lord. I, ah . . . the regret you speak of, to my mind referred to the wicked burning of Elgin Cathedral. But . . . but that is not what the excommunication was pronounced for. Indeed it pre-dated it. The excommunication was on account of the failure of your marriage to your lawful wife, the Countess Euphemia, and, and . . ."

"And that, Christ God, I *do* regret!" the other shouted. "More than anything else on this earth — a curse on it!"

"Ah. I . . . m'mmm . . ."

The Bishop of Dunkeld plucked at the enriched loose sleeve of the Primate's magnificent cope, and muttered a few words.

"I, ah, can take it then, that your lordship repents sufficiently on both scores," he said. "Which is . . . satisfactory." He coughed. "There is but the matter of the robe, now. This of sackcloth and ashes." Hurriedly he stooped, to pick up a coarse grey gown which lay on the floor beside his stall. "To, to ease and expedite the matter, my lord, we have here a garment, a vestment. Made of sackcloth. It, it is already sprinkled with ash. If you would . . . if your lordship might . . . the required formality . . ."

The Wolf barked a great laugh, and slapped his mailed thigh. "Mary Mother of God!" he cried. "Here's the best jest I've heard these long years! Holy Church comes prepared for all! Sackcloth — with the ash provided. And no doubt dust, likewise? Lord,

411

I make profound reverence!" And he bowed low, with a flourish. "It would take a clerk to think of that." He turned. "Duncan, lad — go fetch me this notable provision, without which naught can be done. I would inspect this wonder, this miraculous mummock! Fetch it."

The youth left his side to stride forward, up to the chancel where, smirking and without ceremony he grabbed the grey robe and returned with it to his father. The Earl held it up, to examine it with assumed interest, this way and that, and turned to display it to the chiefs behind him, laughing. Mystified, not understanding anything that had been said, they laughed dutifully, in turn. Draping the thing casually over his right arm, amongst the folds of his plaid, he looked at the Bishop again.

"I swear you could have done better than this!" he commented. "More ash. But proceed, Sir Priest. What now? What further mummery have you in store?"

The Primate began to speak, thought better of it, and stooped for a hurried word with Bishop Peebles. Shrugging as he straightened up, he adjusted his cope. "It is intended that the garment should be *worn*," he muttered. "But perhaps this will serve, so." He shook his head, sighing, and moving over to before the high altar, turned to face them all, raising a beringed hand.

"Dearly beloved in the Lord," he announced, in a sort of weary monotone. "With God's mighty assistance I do hereby ordain and declare, before all here present as witness, that the awful and condign sentence of excommunication, duly pronounced upon our erring brother in Christ, Alexander, in person before us, be lifted, removed, effaced and nullified; the said Alexander by God's grace, being duly penitent and seeking the forgiveness of the Lord Jesus Christ and of His Holy Church. In the name of the Father, the Son and the Holy Ghost. Amen." He paused. "I also . . ."

"I agree," the Wolf announced loudly, briskly. "That's over, then. And not before time!"

The Primate blinked, mouth open to continue. Clearly he had by no means finished his rite. "But . . . there is more, my lord," he said.

"More? What need we with more? You have said the word. Before witnesses. The thing is done. Why waste more time on more words? *You* may, if so you wish. For myself, I am off. This has taken overlong, as it is. And my good caterans up in Strathmore may be growing restless. Heigho — I'll have them turned and marching back to Badenoch by nightfall — for I have matters to attend to with all the rule and governance of the North on my unworthy shoulders — not so?" He chuckled. "See you, my lord Bishop— I will keep this notable garment of yours, as memento! I will put it on the man Barr when next I see him. With some additional ash of my own! Alex — come you home with us, lad."

"My lord, my lord — there is more yet, I say . . ."

"I told you — enough is sufficient. Sire — I bid you a good day. All of you."

The Primate hurried down to the royal chair and spoke urgently to the monarch, the Bishop of Dunkeld also coming over, anxiously.

"Alex," the King called, as his brother turned away. "There's the matter of the compensation, mind. Restitution. For the damage. Making good, man. Was that not agreed? Their lordships are exercised on that score, see you."

"Indeed? Filthy lucre! Sordid gain, to be chaffered over in this house of prayer — making it but a den of thieves! My lords, my lords — here's a fall from all the sanctity! But, as you will. Two thousand merks."

There was a tingling silence, with even the bishops exchanging astonished glances. Undoubtedly not only had they expected to have to fight for their money, but this was far in excess of what they might have hoped for.

When no verbal response was forthcoming, the Earl swung on one of his lieutenants, who bore a satchel in place of a claymore. From this he took two leather bags, obviously very heavy. The Wolf tossed these in the direction of the chancel, scornfully, where they fell to the floor with a clinking sound.

"Gold!" he jerked. "Two thousand — with thirty pieces of siller, in addition. As seems suitable for the occasion, my friends! Will that serve you?"

The Primate seemed to have difficulty in swallowing. "My lord," he got out, "this is, this is . . . munificent! A, a signal contribution. It will not pay, of course, for all the damage done to the Cathedral of Elgin. The Bishop of Moray will require a deal more. But . . ."

"A pox — it has naught to do with Elgin!" the other snapped. "And not one plack will I give to the man Barr. That gold you may use as you wish — save that none goes to Barr. Perhaps you will purchase a better sackcloth gown, in the place of this! Aye — and let it buy for me and mine some place of sepulture before an altar. A fair place of sanctity, for when I am gone. As befits so repentant a prodigal! You will see to this, my lords spiritual?"

"In, in Elgin Cathedral . . .?"

"Not so. Never in Barr's rickle o' stanes! Besides, yon will not be rebuilt in a lifetime! No—in some other kirk as yet unburned!" He grinned. "It might keep such a one safe, to be sure!"

Bishop Peebles spoke up. "My lord of Buchan — you may have sepulture under the shadow of my altar at Dunkeld. If so you desire."

"Ha — that you may win a moiety of the gold, Sir Chancellor! So be it — as you will. I will hold you to that. Dunkeld, eh? It will serve as well as any other." He shrugged, and looked round. "Alex—I said, come you."

Sir Alexander pressed Jamie's arm. "Another day, friend," he murmured. "We shall celebrate this! And—my thanks, my true thanks." With a bow towards the King and a smile at Mary, he went to his father.

As the young man moved across the flagged aisle, Mary gripped Jamie's arm. Turning to her, he discovered, alarmed, that she was repressing laughter only with a major effort, her eyes dancing, her features working.

"He is going!" she whispered. "Jamie — he is going *now*, I do believe! No more — that is it all. Saints of mercy — it is beyond belief! If only Robert could have been here, to see and hear!"

"Hush! He is here," he told her, frowning. "David has just told me. Watching unseen through yon lepers' squint."

"Lord — you say so?" She all but choked. "That makes it perfect. I shall never forget this day, so long as I live!"

"It is all mockery, Mary, almost a blasphemy. From start to finish. On both sides. The bishops merely out-mocked . . ."

"Sssh!"

"Brother—God save you," the Wolf was now calling, his hand on Alexander's shoulder. "God save the King — especially from Robert Stewart!" He bowed elaborately, and turned. "Nephew — I wish you well, but tremble for you! Sisters — my

414

salutations." He looked at the Earl of Douglas slightingly, but said nothing to him. To Jamie he nodded. "Watch you the company you keep, young man. You might do better in Badenoch!" He signed to his trumpeters, and to their somewhat ragged flourish, without even a glance towards the clerics, he laughed and swinging around, pushed his way through his colourful entourage, marching out, the penitent at large.

"Aye, well," the King said, and with a sigh heaved himself to his feet. "That was Alex, aye." And on the Queen's arm, he limped slowly whence he had come.

David, joy writ large on his beautiful face, skipped gleefully down towards his friends.

The clergy clustered together for a few urgent moments, seeking to school their features, and then paced out with great dignity. From the small congregation the buzz of talk and exclamation arose and maintained.

Scotland, it seemed, could breathe again. The terrible Earl of Buchan had been brought to heel, had confessed, repented and made restitution, and in the infinite mercy of Holy Church, was restored to the communion of saints. The Governor of the realm was the Governor still, and had disposed of armed invasion and the threat of disaster to his rule. Even John, the King, had been forced for once to play monarch, in some degree, and to demonstrate that he could do what his Governor could not.

Jamie Douglas drew a long quivering breath, and turned to his bride-to-be. "That is it, then," he said. "What now?"

"Now—*us*!" she declared strongly. "For in three days' time we shall be man and wife. I charge you, sir — forget all else . . .!"

A Folly of Princes

PRINCIPAL CHARACTERS

In Order of Appearance

SIR JAMES DOUGLAS OF ABERDOUR (JAMIE): Illegitimate eldest son of the Lord of Dalkeith. Knighted at Otterburn.

DAVID STEWART, EARL OF CARRICK: Youthful High Steward of Scotland and heir to the throne. Later Duke of Rothesay.

SIR DAVID LINDSAY OF GLENESK: Brother-in-law of the King. Later 1st Earl of Crawford and Lord High Justiciar.

SIR ALEXANDER STEWART OF BADENOCH: Eldest and illegitimate son and heir of the notorious Earl of Buchan, Wolf of Badenoch.

LADY ISABEL STEWART: Sister of the King. Former Countess of Douglas, now married to Sir John Edmonstone of that Ilk.

LADY ISOBEL DOUGLAS, COUNTESS OF MAR: Countess in her own right. Sister of the late 2nd Earl of Douglas and wife of Sir Malcolm Drummond.

MARY STEWART, LADY DOUGLAS OF ABERDOUR: One of the King's illegitimate sisters. Married to Jamie.

ROBERT III, KING OF SCOTS: Great-grandson of the Bruce.

QUEEN ANNABELLA DRUMMOND: Wife of the King. Sister of Sir Malcolm Drummond.

THOMAS DUNBAR, EARL OF MORAY: Son of one of the King's sisters.

ROBERT STEWART, EARL OF FIFE AND MENTEITH: Next brother of the King, Governor of the Realm. Later Duke of Albany.

HAL GOW, called OF THE WYND: Perth blacksmith and sword-maker.

GEORGE COSPATRICK, 10TH EARL OF DUNBAR AND MARCH: Great noble.

GEORGE DOUGLAS, EARL OF ANGUS: Young noble. Founder of Red Douglas line. Half-brother of late Earl of Douglas.

LADY MARGARET STEWART, COUNTESS OF ANGUS: Mother of above. Countess in her own right.

SIR HENRY PERCY (HOTSPUR): Great English noble and champion. Heir to the Earl of Northumberland. Warden of the Marches.

ARCHIBALD (The Grim), 3RD EARL OF DOUGLAS: The most powerful noble in Scotland. Also Lord of Galloway.

JAMES DOUGLAS, LORD OF DALKEITH: Statesman and wealthy noble. Father of Jamie.

JOHN PLANTAGENET, DUKE OF LANCASTER (JOHN OF GAUNT): A son of Edward III. Uncle of Richard II of England.

MARIOTA DE ATHYN (or MACKAY): Mother of Sir Alexander Stewart of Badenoch. Late mistress of the Earl of Buchan.

LORD JAMES STEWART: Younger son of the King. Later James I.

BISHOP GILBERT GREENLAW OF ABERDEEN: Chancellor of the Realm.

SIR MALCOLM DRUMMOND OF CARGILL AND STOBHALL: The Queen's brother. Husband of the Countess of Mar.

BISHOP WALTER TRAIL OF ST. ANDREWS: Primate.

SIR WILLIAM LINDSAY OF ROSSIE: Fife laird. Kinsman to Lindsay of Glenesk.

SIR JOHN DE RAMORGNIE: Fife laird. Prolocutor-General.

ARCHIBALD, MASTER OF DOUGLAS: Eldest son of Archie the Grim, 3rd Earl.

SIR WILLIAM DOUGLAS OF DRUMLANRIG: Illegitimate son of James, 2nd Earl.

SIR ARCHIBALD DOUGLAS OF CAVERS: Illegitimate son of James, 2nd Earl.

KING RICHARD II: Deposed by Bolingbroke, Henry IV. Possibly an impostor.

DONALD, LORD OF THE ISLES: Great Highland potentate. Son of eldest of King's sisters.

SIR JAMES DOUGLAS, YOUNGER OF DALKEITH: Half-brother of Jamie. Husband of the Princess Elizabeth.

THOMAS STEWART, ARCHDEACON OF ST. ANDREWS: Illegitimate son of Robert II. Brother of Mary.

HENRY IV: Usurping King of England.

MURDOCH STEWART, EARL OF FIFE: Eldest son of Albany.

JOHNNIE DOUGLAS: Illegitimate full brother of Jamie.

DOUGLAS GENEALOGY

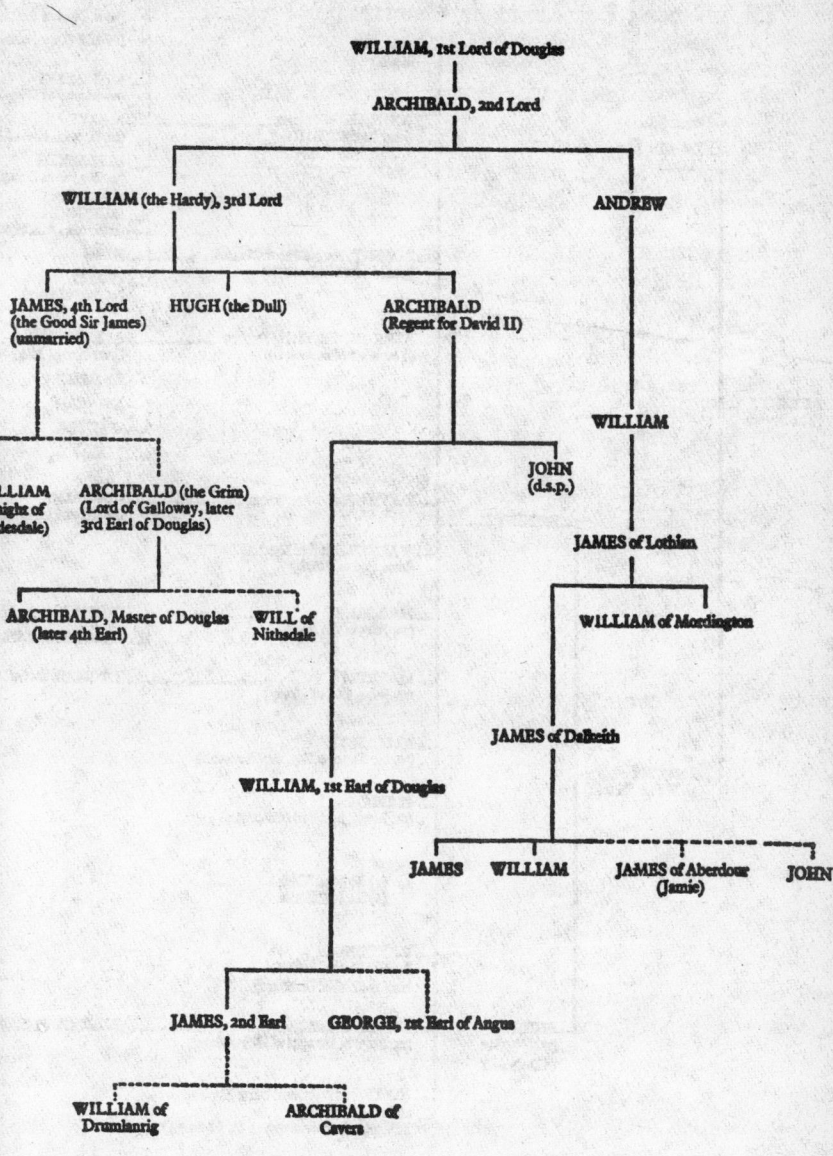

WILLIAM, 1st Lord of Douglas

ARCHIBALD, 2nd Lord

WILLIAM (the Hardy), 3rd Lord

ANDREW

JAMES, 4th Lord (the Good Sir James) (unmarried)

HUGH (the Dull)

ARCHIBALD (Regent for David II)

WILLIAM

JOHN (d.s.p.)

WILLIAM knight of Liddesdale

ARCHIBALD (the Grim) (Lord of Galloway, later 3rd Earl of Douglas)

JAMES of Lothian

ARCHIBALD, Master of Douglas (later 4th Earl)

WILL of Nithsdale

WILLIAM of Mordington

JAMES of Dalkeith

WILLIAM, 1st Earl of Douglas

JAMES   WILLIAM   JAMES of Aberdour (Jamie)   JOHN

JAMES, 2nd Earl   GEORGE, 1st Earl of Angus

WILLIAM of Drumlanrig   ARCHIBALD of Cavers

STEWART GENEALOGY

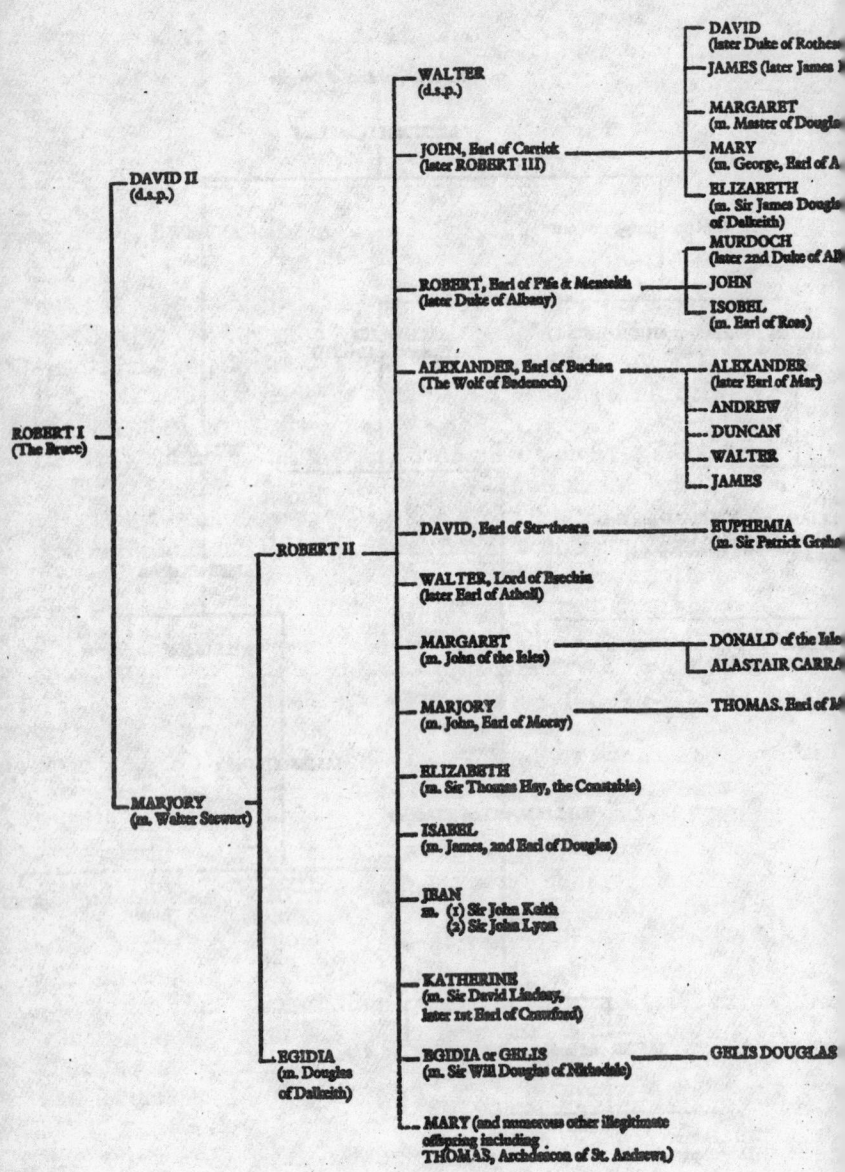

I

SAINT JOHNSTOUN OF Perth seethed. Being the nearest town
to the Abbey of Scone, where the coronations of the Kings
of Scots took place, it was quite accustomed to being overcrowded on occasion. But today's thronging went beyond all
experience and report. Not only the walled city itself, on the
bank of Tay, but all its environs and surroundings, was so
crowded with folk that it seemed that scarcely another could be
crammed in; yet still more arrived by every road — and Perth
was a great hub of roads and routes from all directions, the first
point at which the long estuary of Tay grew sufficiently narrow
to be bridged, the gateway to Scotland's North and East. It was
claimed that 20,000 people converged on the town that October
day of 1396. It was as likely an under- as an over-estimate. No
King's coronation had ever drawn such a concourse.

Poor old King Robert was there, to be sure, third of his name
— although his true name was John and he had only been
crowned as Robert to capitalise on the fame of his mighty great-
grandfather, Robert the Bruce, John being considered an unlucky
name for kings; which fame and capital he direly needed. He
was installed in the Dominican or Blackfriars monastery, on the
northern edge of the walled city, overlooking the wide, green
levels of the North Inch, a favourite haunt of the gentle monarch, who himself was something of a monk by inclination. His
Court filled the other religious establishments and best houses
of the town — these too in much larger numbers than normally
troubled to grace the presence of the self-effacing and studious
monarch. His brother's, the Governor's Court, of course, was
larger, but he had taken over Scone Abbey, three miles to the
north, for the occasion, preferring always to keep his stiff
distance from the King.

9

Sir James Douglas of Aberdour pushed and struggled his way through the crush of people in the narrow streets, seeking to preserve his patience and a modicum of good humour. Good humour was indeed all around him, the folk in holiday mood — galling for a young man on urgent business. He had left his horses and small escort behind at the Red Bridge Port, being there assured by the porters that he would by no means get them all through the press short of using the flats of their swords to beat a path — which would be likely to provoke a riot in present circumstances. He was not of an overbearing character but he *was* in a hurry.

Once out of Shoegate and High Street, into Meal Vennel, the going was easier, the crowds less dense; and by the time he was into Blackfriars Wynd there were few people to hamper him. At the north end of the wynd royal guards stood watch at the monastery gates; but Sir James was well known to all such and he was let through without question.

The Blackfriars monastery was a haven of peace compared with the packed city so close by. It was indeed an unlikely place to find within the perimeter of a walled town, open, spacious, with large gardens and orchards all around the conventual buildings, very rural-seeming for its situation, with pleasant paths and arbours, cow-sheds and dairies, stables, beehives let into the walling to supply wax for the chandlery, doocots with their strutting cooing pigeons everywhere. There were people here too, of course, strolling amongst the fruit-trees and rose-bushes, but these were courtiers and their ladies, in couples and small groups, not packed together in noisy, smelly propinquity like the commonality without. Not a few of the ladies especially smiled or raised eyebrows towards the hurrying young man, for he was attractive to the other sex, good-looking in a dark almost sombre way, tall and well-built, with an air of preoccupation that was alleged to intrigue womenfolk. He acknowledged their salutations civilly, with nod or brief word, without pausing in his stride. Only once did he smile, and that to his young sister-in-law, the Lady Elizabeth Stewart, second daughter of the King and wife to his own namesake and half-brother, Sir James Douglas, Younger of Dalkeith — and when twenty-six-year-old Jamie Douglas smiled, his sober, almost stern features were transformed and lightened remarkably. Getting a smile out of this young man was something of a ploy, indeed, at the Scots Court.

Making for the monastery guest-house, which the King had taken over for his own use meantime, the newcomer asked where was the Earl David, and was informed that the prince had gone over to the Gilten Arbour, to ensure that all was in readiness for the comfort of his father. This did not sound like the nineteen-year-old David Stewart, for whom comfort, the King's or any other's, did not normally mean much; but he hurried in the indicated direction nevertheless.

The Gilten Arbour was a summer-house, at the extreme northern edge of the monastery gardens, a rather special summer-house; more of a pavilion perhaps in that it was two storeys high, circular and with a wide balcony above a pillared portico all round, the whole decorated with gold paint, classical figures and signs of the zodiac, the fancy of some former Prior — a sports-lover presumably, for the upper storey was so contrived that it looked over the high town-wall here into the North Inch directly beyond, the hundred-acre riverside parkland which constituted the best disporting-ground and tourney-court in Scotland.

At the arbour door a single large and tough individual stood. He raised a cynical eyebrow at the visitor.

"He is . . . occupied!" he said. "Wearied of waiting. Do not go up, Sir James."

"I must see him. And at once."

"I tell you, he is not to be disturbed. Bide you for a whilie . . ."

"No. Stand aside, Pate. You have done your duty. Let me do mine. This is urgent. I come from the Clan Chattan camp. I am going up. Or would you, or he, prefer that I went to the Governor instead?"

"I warn you, he is drink-taken . . ."

"I never yet knew drink to blunt his wits. And I will risk his temper." The Douglas brushed past the other, and ran up the wooden stairs.

On the balcony, a woman's shoe and a silken bodice, none too clean, was preparation for what was to come. Feminine skirling choked off to breathless laughter, from near at hand, offered further guidance. There were two apartments on this upper floor. At the second, James Douglas rapped sharply on the door, took a deep breath, and stepped inside.

"Fiends of hell! How dare you! How dare you, I say — curse and burn you! God's eyes — get out!" Very strangely, despite the abrupt ferocity of that, the voice that spoke managed to sound almost musical, mellifluous, without thereby lessening the anger.

"I dare for good reason," the other asserted, his own voice more raspingly gravelly than he knew. "And would dare still more, my Lord David, in your service and your royal father's, if need be!"

"Damn you, Jamie . . .!"

The room, simply furnished with a rustic table and benches, row upon row of stored apples on shelving around the walls, was a shambles. Clothing lay scattered, male and female; an upset wine-flagon spilled its contents, like blood, over the wooden floor; a bench was upturned, with a gleaming golden earl's belt flung across it; apples had rolled everywhere. In one far corner, on a spread cloak, a young man was half-rising, bare from the middle downwards, and under him sprawled a wholly naked young woman, notably well-endowed, all pink-and-white lush invitation and challenge, seeking to hold him down.

The two men stared at each other, the younger glaring hotly, the other frowning with a sort of determined concern.

"If the Lady Congalton will excuse me for a few moments," Douglas said stiffly, "I have matters for your privy ear, my lord, which will not wait."

David, Earl of Carrick, High Steward of Scotland and heir to the throne, rose to his feet, took a pace forward and then halted, his face flushed with wrath, wine and his immediate exertions. It was a remarkable face, beautiful rather than handsome, winsome with a delicacy and regularity of feature that any woman might envy, yet somehow redeemed from any suggestion of weakness by the firm mouth and chin, the keen sparkling eyes and the autocratic carriage of the head. There was nothing of femininity there — nor indeed was the lower part of him, so very patently on display at the moment, lacking in any degree in masculinity; much the reverse, in fact, being at least complementary to the lady's plenitude. At nineteen years, David Stewart's manhood was not in doubt.

"Jamie Douglas!" The apparition raised a hand to point an accusing finger at the intruder — and suddenly, surprisingly, burst into a cascade of melodious laughter. "Jamie Douglas — only you, in all this realm, I swear, would so behave! Aye, and from only you, by God, would I bear with it! Well — what is it, man? Out with it?"

"My lord . . ." Jamie glanced from the other's nether parts

12

to the still recumbent woman — who had now elected to place one small hand over the joining of her legs and the other amidst the opulence of her swelling breasts — neither of which achieved more than an emphasis on what was there.

"Never heed Kirsty," the Earl advised, apparently untroubled by his own state of undress. "She'll bide. Speak up — and stop nodding your head at yonder door. I am not going outside. I am not finished here, as even you can see!"

The intruder shrugged. "As you will. I come from Luncarty, six miles north. The Clan Chattan company is halted there. About thirty-five strong. They will come no further. They have been shadowed for some time, they say, by the Governor's men. They captured one and put him to the question. He revealed that the Governor was waiting, at Scone, requiring word of their progress. At Scone, between them and Perth, here. Sir Alexander Stewart is with them, and fears a trap. He has reason, after all! I tried to persuade him to come on, but he would not . . ."

"A plague on it! He has the King's safe-conduct."

"He requires more than that, my lord. He asks that you yourself come. With the royal guard for escort. Only so will he trust the Governor not to attack them."

"But . . . saints above! My wretched uncle will not assail them. He is a devil, yes, and hates us all. But he would not dare to interfere in this. It is *my* affair, mine and Moray's. With my father's agreement and blessing."

"This I told Sir Alexander. But he is not convinced. The Earl Robert imprisoned him once before, contrary to your word, and mine. He asks why the Governor should lie at Scone when all others are at Perth. If he smells knavery, can you blame him?"

"Curse them all . . . ?"

"To be sure. But curses will not bring Clan Chattan to the North Inch this day! It lacks but a bare two hours until the contest is due to start — so it will be late anyway. Sir Alexander says that he will wait at Luncarty until the hour set for the affrayment. If you, and the escort have not come by then, they turn back for their own Highland fastnesses."

"But, save us — what is Alexander Stewart that Clan Chattan comes and goes at his word? My bastard cousin — what has he to do with it?"

"They appear to trust him. Look on him as guide and protector. Against Southron treachery. In place of his dead

13

father. The Wolf was long their overlord, however savage his rule. These Mackintoshes, Shaws, Macphersons, MacGillivrays and the rest of the Clan Chattan federation, they have taken his eldest son in his place."

"Are other of his oaflike brothers with them?"

"No. Only Sir Alexander. With one Shaw Beg MacFarquhar, who seems to be their champion, and he they call *Mhic Gillebrath Mor*. Not the Mackintosh himself, Captain of Clan Chattan."

"Well, Jamie — we must pleasure them, I suppose. Since my own credit depends on it. If this contest does not take place, now, my name and repute suffers. And my intolerable uncle smiles — if smile he can! Which is no doubt his object in this business — to frighten off these Highlanders and so bring the entire project to naught. To my hurt."

"That same thought came to me, my lord. So — you will come?"

"I will not! I have more to do meantime — as you can see! — than to run to and fro at the beck of the unlamented Wolf of Badenoch's bastard! But I shall send him the royal bodyguard, to comfort his faint heart! You will take it, Jamie — and bring those clansmen to the North Inch, within the hour."

Douglas shook his head. "It will not serve, my lord. I myself suggested as much — but Alexander said no, that the Governor could countermand such escort, dismiss it. You, the heir to the throne, he could not countermand — you in person. So it has to be yourself . . ."

"I tell you it has not, man! Are you deaf? See you — take Moray. He is my cousin, the King's nephew. He will serve. Cousin to your Alexander too. If he will not have *you*."

Again the stern shake of the dark head. "The Earl of Moray has always been against Clan Chattan, in this feuding. He champions the Comyns, who are his own vassals. They would never accept their enemies' protector as escort."

"Damnation — who are they, this Hielant rabble, to refuse this earl and accept that? I'm minded to let my Uncle Robert at them! Teach them a lesson . . ."

"And lose your great contest? And bring your Lieutenancy of the North to an ill start indeed."

"God's sake, Jamie Douglas — you must ever have the rights of it! Ever the last word. Does that bonny aunt of mine, tied to you in wedlock, not find you beyond all bearing?"

A brief glimmer of his famous smile flickered across the other's sombre features. "She says so, yes — frequently."

"Aye — and much good it will do her!" The Earl David chuckled, himself again. "See, then — take Lindsay. My Uncle David, of Glenesk. He is here, at this Blackfriars — I saw him but an hour back. My father's good-brother. He will do as well as Moray. Better, for he is older, a seasoned warrior. And he does not love the Governor. Aye, Lindsay will do. Now, of a mercy, man — be off! This lady has been patient — you will agree? If she catches her death of chill, *your* blood her husband will be after! Myself, I was contriving to keep her warm! Eh, Kirsty?"

Douglas bowed stiffly. "I will do what I can, my Lord . . ."

"Do that, Jamie. And haste you. Hasten, both of us. You a-horse and me astride, eh?" As the other left the room to that silvery laughter, he heard the High Steward of Scotland add, "Now, lassie — let us see if we can raise this issue to its former heights, blackest Douglas or none . . .!"

* * *

The hard-riding company pounded northwards, parallel with Tay again, five-score strong, under no less than three proud banners, the royal Lion Rampant of Scotland, the red chevron on white of the earldom of Carrick, and the blue-and-white fess chequey on red of Lindsay — signs and symbols enough, surely to prevent anyone seeking to interfere with their passage, even in this ungoverned and ill-used kingdom. Jamie Douglas, leading the way, was now flanked by two somewhat older men, both dressed a deal more splendidly than he — Sir David Lindsay, Lord of Glenesk and Sheriff of Angus on his right, and John Stewart of Dundonald, Captain of the King's Body-guard, on his left. Both, oddly enough, were brothers-in-law, of a sort, of himself and of each other, for Lindsay was married to the King's lawful sister Katherine, John the Red was that sister's illegitimate brother by the former monarch, and Jamie's wife was the King's illegitimate sister Mary. King Robert the Second, the Bruce's grandson, had made up for his lack of prowess on the field or in the council-chamber by his prowess in the bed-chamber or anywhere else convenient, with fourteen legitimate children and innumerable otherwise. His grandson David but followed in the family tradition — although he had wits far in advance of his grandsire's.

Sir David Lindsay was none too pleased at being dragged away on this unsuitable and unnecessary errand at his nephew's second-hand command. He was a vigorous, stocky and powerful man in his early forties, the most renowned tourneyer in two kingdoms, lord of two-thirds of the county of Angus, as well as Strathnairn in the North, a proud man in his own right and considering himself of better blood than any Stewart, cousin and heir to the chief of his name, Sir James Lindsay of Crawford and Luffness, Lord High Justiciar. Adding injury to insult, he had been grievously wounded six years before, at the deplorable Battle of Glasclune, by one of the disreputable brothers of the man he was being sent to escort, all bastards of his late brother-in-law the Earl of Buchan and Wolf of Badenoch, to the praise of God now safely deceased. He rode tight-lipped.

John the Red of Dundonald was a very different and less reputable character, huge, with a fiery head and beard, loud, boisterous, cheerful, an unlikely Stewart and taking after his Kennedy mother. He made a curious captain for the guard of his mild and inoffensive half-brother. He laughed and shouted now, at Jamie's other side — who preferred the Lindsay silence.

They had less than six miles to go, fortunately. Half-way there, they came in sight of Scone Abbey across the Tay. They all eyed it, but only John Stewart commented.

"Robert will see us fine, from yonder," he cried. "And I'll wager he mislikes what he sees!"

Three times thereafter, Jamie's keen eyes picked out silent groups of motionless horsemen, sitting their mounts beneath the cover of trees back from the roadside, wearing the Stewart colours and the Governor's badge of the earldom of Fife. None moved or made any sign as the company cantered by.

At a bend of the great river, presently, was Boat of Luncarty, a ferry and milling hamlet, with a little parish church crowning a mound on the higher ground behind. Here, on the level haughland where the progenitor of the Hays had helped Kenneth the Third to defeat the Danes four centuries before, with the outliers of the blue Highland hills not so far distant, the Highland party they sought had halted, where they could still retire into the security of their mountains if need be.

As the newcomers clattered up, bulls' horns were blown in warning and many fierce hands dropped to sword-hilts, dirks and the shafts of Lochaber axes, amongst the colourful tartan-clad warriors. These numbered about thirty, plus sentries placed on points of vantage, and all in their best array, armed to the teeth. They stared at the royal guard, tense, suspicious, ready.

It was a peculiar situation, from any standpoint — for these were amongst the best fighting-men in Christendom, and courageous to the point of folly, the pick of a mighty clan. Moreover they were here on an entirely lawful occasion, on the heir to the throne's personal invitation and under royal safe-conduct. It was unlike such to display fright, trepidation, in any circumstances; yet their alarm and tight wariness was very apparent here. It was all eloquent testimony to the state of chaos and insecurity in Scotland in the last decade of the fourteenth century, and to the reputation of the Earl Robert of Fife and Menteith, Governor of the realm for his elder brother the King.

From amongst the crowd a young man stepped forward, the only man there not wearing tartans, but dressed in approximately Lowland fashion, without armour. He was fine-featured, slenderly built, handsome in a fair way, and with a marked resemblance to the Earl David of Carrick although older by about five years, Sir Alexander Stewart, eldest of the late Wolf of Badenoch's bastard brood and, since that prince left no legitimate offspring, Lord of Badenoch in fact if not in name and character. He looked from one to the other of the leaders of the newcomers.

"No Earl of Carrick, Sir James?" he said formally — but his voice had a pleasing Highland lilt and softness. "What of our compact?"

"My lord was engaged, Sir Alexander," Jamie told him carefully. "He could by no means leave Perth. But he sent his fair salutations and asked my lord of Glenesk, here, to act his deputy. With John Stewart of Dundonald, His Grace's captain of guard. Both kin of your own, and his."

"I see. It is my pleasure to meet Sir David. I am aware of his fame and prowess, to be sure. John Stewart I know, of course — and greet kindly. But my requirement was the High Steward himself, the only man under the King who ranks higher than the Governor. And on whose invitation, I, and these, are here."

"Boy!" Glenesk barked, "who think you that you are? That you can summon the heir to the throne! And turn up your nose at Lindsay! You, Buchan's bastard!"

"Who I am, my lord, matters nothing in this issue. What matters is that the Clan Chattan accept me as my father's heir.

17

And that we have come South to Perth on the King's safe-conduct. Although such should scarcely be necessary for the King's lawful subjects in his own realm! Yet we are threatened by the Governor . . ."

"He has not assailed you? Nor even sought to halt you?"

"His men have dogged us since Dunkeld. Now they line the road ahead, our scouts say. The Earl Robert does not wish us to come to Perth . . ."

"But the Earl David does, by God — and we will see that you get there!" John the Red cried. "He, Robert, but thinks to scare you off, man."

"I have tasted of his scaring off methods, sir! And wish to taste no more. *Why* should he seek to do so?"

Lindsay shrugged. "He disapproves of the Earl David his nephew's appointment to be Lieutenant of the North, and Justiciar. He appointed his own son, the Lord Murdoch Stewart, to that position six years back. Murdoch durst never take it up, whilst your father lived. So the Governor has never been able to extend his rule to the northern half of the kingdom. He still would have his son Lieutenant and Justiciar. He says that the Earl David is too young, lacks experience. He would discredit his appointment. This contest David has conceived as a means of settling the feud which has been tearing apart much of the North. If it is successful, then David's reputation is much enhanced — a good start to taking up office. If it fails, or never takes place, after half Scotland has come to watch, then . . .!" He left the rest unsaid.

Jamie intervened urgently. "That is all true. But there is need for haste. Already there must be delay. The King waits. The folk will grow impatient. Let us be on our way."

Sir Alexander turned to consult with the leaders of the watching, listening Highlanders, fierce-looking men with the softest voices in the land.

"Tell them who and what I am, young man," Lindsay said loudly, as though to penetrate their Gaelic-speaking ignorance by sheer volume of sound. "Tell them that they need have no fear — the Governor will not seek to interfere with *me*."

"I have done so, my lord. And they agree. We will come . . ."

So, mounted on their stocky, sturdy Highland garrons, the Badenoch party took the road again, flanked by the superbly horsed royal guard, heading southwards at a brisk trot under the streaming banners.

Not a single man-at-arms wearing the Governor's colours did they observe *en route*. Evidently there was nothing wrong with the Earl Robert's eyesight, nor with his recognition of realities, when it came to the bit.

When they reached the North Inch of Perth it was to find that great park already crowded with people. A central area of about six acres had been fenced off, and at the south end of this the Clan Comyn, or Cumming, contingent was already in place, waiting, a piper strutting up and down before them. Elsewhere the spectators thronged the approximately one hundred acres of common land, riverside meadows from which the cattle had been driven for the occasion — save for the clear space left immediately in front of the Blackfriars monastery wall. The folk were entertaining themselves meantime, in good spirits, with games, dancing, fiddling and horseplay — although one or two minor fights had inevitably broken out amongst rival lords' retinues. Pedlars, hucksters, tumblers, gypsies, fortune-tellers and the like were doing a roaring trade. It all resembled a gigantic fair, in the crisp October noontide.

Leaving the Clan Chattan party, with John Stewart and part of the guard, at the north end of the railed-off enclosure, the object of much interest, staring and pointing on the part of the crowd thereabouts, Jamie Douglas, with Sir Alexander and Glenesk, rode on into the town. The streets were much less thronged now, with most of the people already assembled in the Inch. At the monastery, Jamie was in doubt as to whether to seek the High Steward in the Gilten Arbour again or in the more conventional royal quarters in the guest-house; but the sight of his henchman, Pate Boyd, talking with a group of others at the guest-house door, and a jerk of that man's head upwards, seemed to indicate that the prince's recreational activities were for the moment over. The Douglas, dismounting, led Sir Alexander upstairs two steps at a time, the Lindsay following the young men more sedately.

In a large upper room, from which emanated much chatter and laughter, they found the Earl David in the midst of a gay and richly-dressed company of both sexes, beakers and flagons of wine being much in evidence. He had his arm around the shoulders of a handsome and statuesque woman almost old enough to be his mother, his hand inside the low-necked bodice of her gown, whilst he talked animatedly with sundry others. He seemed to be in excellent spirits, certainly without any aspect of anxious waiting. The Lady Congalton was reunited with her husband, over near one of the windows.

"Come, Alex," Jamie said, as the young man from the North held back a little in the doorway. "That is he, in the scarlet-and-gold. With the Countess of Mar."

"I see him, recognise him. As he has seen and recognised me — although he gives no sign. He seems . . . fully occupied!"

"Tush — never heed that, man. It is his way with women. Even his real aunts must needs put up with it — although some appear to like it. Come!"

"I am not clad for this peacock throng . . ."

"Sakes, Alex — do not be a fool! You are worth any score of these put together — and *he* knows it! What do clothes matter? See, we shall . . ."

"Ha, Jamie my dear — I have been looking for you." A good-looking woman in her late thirties came up to them, fair, almost beautiful, though with her fine-chiselled features just slightly lined with care. "Where have you been? And who is this? Kin of my own, in some sort, I swear! But then, we Stewarts have almost a surfeit of kin, have we not?"

"Ah, to be sure — you have not met. This is Sir Alexander Stewart of Badenoch, whom I aspire to call my friend, my lady. And this is the Lady Isabel, His Grace's sister, former Countess of Douglas and now wed to Sir John Edmonstone of that Ilk."

"I might have known it. Another of my multitude of nephews — Alec's son. And the best of that brood, from all accounts. Certainly the best-looking, I'd vow! Welcome to Court, Sir Alexander — if this Court is any place to welcome one to!"

The young man bowed courteously. "My father spoke much of you, Princess. As has Sir James, here. And always much in your favour. I perceive why, to be sure."

"Gallant, Nephew! Who would have looked for the like from your wild mountains?"

"There are worse places to be reared than our Highland mountains, Lady Isabel — some nearer here, I think!"

"So-o-o! We have claws as well as smiles, Sir Alexander!"

"My lady — your pardon," Jamie intervened, with a trace of impatience. "We must speak with the Earl David. Forthwith. We have been hastening, to come to him . . ."

"Yes. It is ever the Earl David nowadays, Jamie. David this, David that! I must not delay you, and him, no!"

20

The Douglas bit his lip. His position at Court had grown difficult of late. He was, in fact, the Lady Isabel's man, her knight and man-of-affairs, her late husband the Earl of Douglas's former chief esquire who had remained loyal servant and friend to his widow although she had in time been forced to remarry. But ever more noticeably, in the last year or so he had tended to gravitate into the orbit of the young and masterful heir to the throne — who indeed most evidently liked and trusted him as he did few others. Whomsoever the Prince David wanted to serve him, served him — it was as simple as that. Just as he would have none near him who did not please him. Wilful in all things, spoiled in one way from earliest years, he had nevertheless come to approve of Jamie — admire would be too strong a word — ever since they had first clashed and then worked together in some measure at Turnberry seven years before, at the task of circumventing his Uncle Robert of Fife and Menteith. They were still at it, united in this at least, that the Governor had to be countered. David had plenty of aides and servants more in keeping with his own style and temperament; but he had recognised something in Jamie Douglas lacking elsewhere, and more or less purloined him from his aunt's service when he had come to set up his own establishment at Court. The Douglas was not altogether happy with this position — although serving the Lady Isabel had its own difficulties and embarrassments, especially for a happily-married man. The Stewarts were an autocratic lot; and since aunt and nephew were by no means always on the best of terms, the situation could have its problems.

Shaking his dark head unhappily, Jamie took the young Stewart's arm and led him over to the prince's group. He did not hesitate to interrupt what he conceived to be the inanities there being discussed.

"My lord — Sir Alexander Stewart of Badenoch, representing the Clan Chattan party," he said briefly.

"Ah, yes. Welcome, Cousin — I thought it must be you. Though what you may have to do with the Clan Chattan I am eager to learn! It is long since we forgathered." With no undue haste he withdrew his hand from the Countess of Mar's fine bosom, stroking her neck and dark hair as he did so.

"I greet you, my lord Earl. After six years. Clearly I find you in excellent shape and spirits! As to the Clan Chattan, they do me the honour to make me their spokesman and, to some extent,

21

guide — since they are unaccustomed to your Southron ways and tongue."

"Indeed. How fortunate they are! And where are your picturesque barbarians now? We have been awaiting them overlong, it seems."

The other young man, so strangely like the prince, drew a deep breath — and Jamie Douglas plunged in, to avert the clash.

"They are in their place at the north side of the lists, my lord. The Comyns face them. All is now in train. No need for further delay . . ."

"Our Jamie is a notable foe of delay and dalliance," the Earl mentioned conversationally. "Highly admirable, I am sure. Myself, I fear that I am less concerned over who is kept waiting — so long as it is not Davie Stewart! How is it with you, Aunt? Are you of the impatient sort?"

"For some things, yes, I think I am."

Something in the Countess's husky voice made the prince look at her quickly. But she was looking only at Alexander, with an assessing, almost lustful expression in her dark eyes. She was a strong-featured, handsome woman, well-made, with a high complexion and a smouldering aspect to her — a fairly typical Douglas. She was, in fact, sister to the murdered 2nd Earl of Douglas, only daughter of the 1st Earl of Douglas and Mar, and had inherited the Mar earldom in her own right. She was married to Sir Malcolm Drummond of Stobhall, chief of the name and brother of Queen Annabella, David's mother.

"To be sure. That I can well believe," the quick-witted prince acceded. "You hear that, Cousin? Beware — as I do! Now — we must not keep Jamie waiting — or even Clans Chattan and Comyn. Still less, my royal sire — although I cannot conceive of him being eager for the fray! Where is Lindsay? Ah, there. Uncle David — you and Moray will take charge in the lists, you with Clan Chattan, Moray with his Comyns. Lyon and his heralds and trumpeters to the Gilten Arbour. Indeed, all of you to the Arbour, to await His Grace's coming. Wines and refreshments are already there, never fear . . ."

Sir Alexander bowed briefly. "I shall return to my, h'm, barbarians and friends, my lord!"

"And I with you," Jamie said.

"You shall not," the prince declared. "I require you by my side, Jamie. Take my aunts over to the Arbour meantime."

So a move was made across the gardens, amidst much donning of cloaks and plaids against the October air. Jamie, collecting the Lady Isabel, her sisters Marjorie, widowed Countess of Moray, and Jean, widow of Sir John Lyon, now wife to Sir James Sandilands of Calder, looked around him for a fourth to escort. He found her having a brief word with Sir Alexander at the door before he hurried back to his Highlanders — Jamie's own wife Mary Stewart, illegitimate daughter of the late monarch, Robert the Second, a dancing-eyed, high-spirited creature, comely, highly attractive and of strikingly excellent figure, whom six years of marriage to the seriously-minded Douglas and two young children had totally failed to repress. She now pressed her equally illegitimate nephew's arm and came across to her husband and half-sisters cheerfully.

"Alex grows more to my taste than ever!" she announced. "Is he not good-looking? Jamie will have to keep his eyes open, I swear! He says that the Clan Chattan are sure to win, that he knows the Comyns — or should it be Cummings? — and they are not truly Highlandmen. They will break first."

"I say that the entire contest is shameful," the Lady Isabel declared. "Davie is not to be congratulated. In this, as in much else. Nor your Thomas, Marjorie — who put him up to it."

"I agree," the Lady Marjorie of Moray said. "It is to treat men like dumb animals. Like a bear-baiting or a dog-fight. I shall not watch for long, I promise you!"

"No need to come watch at all then, Marjorie," the Lady Jean pointed out.

"It will not be a pretty spectacle," Jamie admitted, "I sought to convince the Lord David against it, to be sure. But good could come of it, to be sure. Much good, for the North. An end to this terrible feuding and bloodshed."

Over at the Gilten Arbour, the high-born throng squabbled for the best seats and view-points; also started at once on the victuals. The view over the North Inch was tribute to the monkish builder of the summer-house; and of course the railed-off enclosure for the lists had been chosen to be immediately below and in front of the royal vantage point. A great stir and swell of noise arose from the crowded park, punctuated by the high and distinctly discordant strains of the bagpipes, for the Clan Chattan party had produced one of their own pipers to pace and blow before them — which caused the opposition to field two further instrumentalists to outplay their rivals. At some two hundred yards apart, the resultant din was notable, and even the royal band of fiddles, flutes and cymbals which the Earl David had thoughtfully provided failed to drown the competition.

Presently, however, a brassy fanfare of trumpets rang out, and under its imperious blare even the pipes wailed and sobbed into silence. Flanked by gorgeously tabarded heralds, the Carrick and Strathearn Pursuivants, the venerable Lyon King of Arms came pacing along the Arbour balcony, clearing a passage. When the trumpets died away, Lyon raised hand and voice.

"Silence and due obeisance from all!" he called into the hush. "Bow low before His Grace the Lord Robert, by God's will and anointing High King of Scots, our most noble and puissant prince."

Unfortunately there was something of a hiatus after this resounding introduction. The stairway up to the balcony was steep, and King Robert was lame, having been kicked on the knee by a Douglas horse when a young man, with disastrous effects on more than his walking. Bowing low, even more or less metaphorically, was not something which might be maintained indefinitely.

At last, leaning on the arm of his Queen, with his son David on the other side, the monarch appeared at the head of the stairs. Although in fact only fifty-eight he looked at least fifteen years older, a frail, stooping figure, white-haired and white-bearded, with a finely sensitive face and lofty brow but the lines of weariness and weakness etched deep. He was wrapped in a voluminous furred cloak, for he felt the cold. Limping heavily, he kept his eyes downcast, a man miscast for his role if ever there was one. At his side Annabella Drummond looked every inch a queen, tall, serene, quietly assured without any trace of prideful haughtiness. She was not beautiful like her son, but of pleasing looks and a kindly expression. She aided and supported her husband solicitously. The prince did not actually hold his father's other arm but strolled close by, smiling and nodding to all.

The King and Queen took their seats at the centre of the gallery, to the prolonged cheering of the populace in the Inch — for strangely enough Robert was popular, in a quiet way, more perhaps out of comparison with his brothers than for more positive reasons, although he had a reputation for generosity, patience, kindness, the Good King Robert who would not hurt

24

a fly. The Queen too was gracious and accessible, much more so than was normal. And the beautiful High Steward was the people's darling, despite the nature of many of his activities. David did not sit but remained behind his father's chair, beckoning Jamie Douglas to his side.

"No sign of my Uncle Robert?" he murmured. "He can scarce expect us to wait for him!"

"As Governor of the realm he may feel so entitled, my lord."

"Then he must learn otherwise." The prince raised his voice. "Lyon, proceed, if you please."

After another long flourish of trumpets, the principal herald bowed to the King and spoke again. "By His Grace's royal command," he cried, "I declare that a judicial trial of strength and armed contest shall now take place before His Grace and all men. Between the House of Comyn, or Clan Cumming in the Erse, and Clan Chattan. This as final decision and judgement between these two tribes and contestants in the dispute which has long maintained between them, on the matter of the lands and castle of Rait and the barony of Geddes, in Strathnairn, in the province of Moray in the northern parts of this realm; whereby there has been much scaith and hurt to the lieges of His Grace in those parts, to the King's sore sorrow."

The elderly Lyon King of Arms paused for breath, and the buzz of anticipation grew, far and near.

"This contest," he went on, "will be decided by thirty champions of these tribes or clans, duly selected. They will fight here, before His Grace, as is their custom, with sword, dirk, axe and arrow, but without armour or shield other than the small leathern targe. The fight will be to the death or until one side concedes complete victory to the other, and therewith the undisputed possession of the said lands of Rait and Geddes, which Mackintosh of Clan Chattan claims the Clan Cumming have unlawfully taken from him and his. Moreover it is to be accepted by both sides that the losers will hereafter abide by this decision and disturb the King's peace no more, by placing themselves under the dominion and authority of the winners. Assurance of their full acceptance of these terms to be made here before the King's Grace by right and proper sureties — namely the noble Lord Thomas, Earl of Moray for the Comyns, of whose earldom they are vassals; and the potent Sir David Lindsay, Lord of Glenesk and Strathnairn, who has consented to act surety for the Clan Chattan of Badenoch in the absence of a reigning Lord of Badenoch. My lords — in the King's name do you accept the terms aforesaid?"

The young, red-faced Moray and the older Lindsay paced out from their respective sides, bowed to the royal gallery and indicated that they did.

"So be it." Lyon turned to face the Earl David. "And do you, my lord of Carrick, High Steward and Prince of Scotland, appointed to be Justiciary and Lieutenant of the North, accede that such decision by trial of arms shall be binding and final in the jurisdiction of your northern territories hereafter?"

"I do."

"Then, my lords, it is His Grace's royal pleasure that you return to your clans and prepare them to commence the contest. You will signal when ready."

Throughout Lyon's long announcement the King had sat, head bent, eyes on his clasped hands. He did not raise either now. A less convincing picture of royal pleasure would have been hard to conceive.

Jamie touched the Earl David's arm, and pointed. Above the mass of the crowd, away to the north, could be seen waving banners and the glint and gleam of sun on steel armour.

The prince nodded. "He comes, then. Damn him — just in time!" Frowning, he jerked. "Jamie — haste you and get these Hielantmen started. Before he comes up. Quickly!"

Even as the Douglas hurried through a postern gate in the town wall, he heard the Earl of Moray shouting that the Comyns were ready. But when he reached the Clan Chattan party it was to discover consternation. One of their number was missing. They had all been present only a short time before. They had only twenty-nine men to face the Comyns' thirty. It was a catastrophe.

"Is it so bad?" Jamie demanded, of Alexander Stewart. "One man in thirty? A loss, yes — but not too great a challenge for stout fighters . . ."

"*Dia*, James — do you not see?" the other exclaimed. "It is not that. Clan Chattan would fight five short, ten short, and win! It is the disgrace. One turned craven and fled. Or been suborned."

"Suborned? You do not mean that?"

"Why not? We know the Governor would wish this contest to be stopped."

"He is coming. That is why I am here. The Lord David

26

wants a start made without delay. I think that he fears the Lord Robert might prevail on his father to stop the contest, even yet."

"No doubt. But we cannot start with a man short. It is not that we are weakened but that the terms of the engagement are broken. The compact was for thirty on each side, no armour, no spears or lances, no surrender, no truce or interval. If any of these terms should be broken, the trial is over and the victory adjudged to the other side. Now do you see?"

Just then, only now visible from this lower position, the Earl of Fife's column of about two hundred armed horsemen forced its way past, some way to the east, along the line of the road which threaded the North Inch, swords out to beat a way through the crowds with the flats of the blades. In the midst, surrounded by his gentlemen, the stiffly erect figure of the Governor looked neither left nor right. Curses followed him, but low-voiced, and fists were shaken, but not where they might be seen by the horsemen.

"What will you do, then?" Jamie demanded.

"We have men out, searching for the man in the crush. If they cannot find him, we must seek to enroll another. If we can."

"That will take time. The Earl David wants a start made. At once. Before the Governor . . ."

"*Could* he stop all? If the prince and the King say otherwise?"

"He is strong, harsh — and the King fears him. Moreover the King himself does not like this contest. He might well be persuaded. But, once started, it could scarce be stopped."

"Give us but a little longer." Stewart spoke briefly in Gaelic with the enormous man near him, Shaw Beg MacFarquhar, leader of the Clan Chattan group, a magnificent figure of a proud young Highlander, nearer seven than six feet tall. He turned back. "We shall seek a substitute. At once. But he must be of Clan Chattan, or linked with it. While still we search for this wretch . . ."

"Perhaps none would perceive it? Twenty-nine will look much like thirty, in a fight."

"The Cummings would see it, never fear. Every man will count, before the end. No — go back to my Cousin David, Jamie. Tell him that one man has fallen out — sick, say. We shall find another. A few minutes only . . ."

Lindsay had come up, with Sir Thomas Hay, Lord High Constable, who had an overall responsibility for supervision of

27

trials of strength, referee. The Lord of Glenesk was frowning blackly.

"This is shameful!" he declared. "Would God I had never allowed myself to be talked into this folly. Moray will never cease to point his insolent finger at me . . .!"

"Grieve not too soon, my lord," Alexander advised. "We shall fight, and win. Even if I myself have to take part . . ."

"That would not serve, man. You are a Stewart, though base-born. All know it. No member of Clan Chattan. Such it must be, the Constable says."

"The piper . . .?" Jamie suggested.

"He is no sworder. Besides, they will need his piping to spur them on. But off with you, Jamie. We will find a man. Gain us but a few minutes . . ."

When the Douglas won back through the throng to the Gilten Arbour balcony, it was to find the Earl Robert Stewart, Governor of Scotland, standing before the King, in no very respectful attitude, and speaking coldly. He was a tall, slender man, good-looking in a stern-faced way, thin-lipped, long-featured, pale-eyed, with a watchful and severe manner. Although he had a faint impediment in his speech, his clipped voice lacked nothing in chill authority.

". . . as wrongful and ill-conceived as it is barbarous!" he was saying. "Folly and worse. I say that it must be stopped. Forthwith. You, Sire, must command a halt."

"*Must*, Uncle . . .?" That was the Earl David, interestedly. "I am the Governor of this realm. The rule is mine . . ."

"Governor for His Grace, is it not? When the King is present in person, his word is supreme, I think? Tell me, Uncle, do you conceive the Governor superior to the King of Scots?"

The other kept his steely gaze on the unhappy monarch not on the insouciantly smiling heir. "Not superior — effectual," he said briefly, without change of tone. "The King has ordained me Governor, to rule — confirmed by parliament. Therefore *I* rule — not the King, who reigns. There is a difference, Nephew."

"To be sure. But whom the King has ordained, the King can unordain. And the Governor cannot *over*-rule the King's expressed wishes, at any time. Is that not so?"

His uncle spoke directly to the monarch. "Sire — *is* it your expressed wish that this great slaughter of your subjects should proceed?"

His brother gnawed his lip. "Not, not slaughter, Robert —

28

no, no. A fair fight, just — no more. To save many lives. Davie says it is the best way. To end this strife in the North . . ." The only certainty about the royal voice was its pleading note.

"Davie is young and rash, Sire. Well-meaning no doubt, but lacking in experience and judgement. You must heed sound, proven advice, not the wild notions of a lad not yet of full age."

"*Must* again, my lord! I think that you forget to whom you speak!" The prince turned. "Sire — the word is given to commence this combat. The Governor has come late. I urge you to request him to be seated and let all proceed."

"Aye, Robert — that would be best . . ."

Jamie Douglas, at the Earl David's back, touched his elbow. "Sir Alexander seeks time," he whispered, "a little time. One man of Clan Chattan gone. Bolted, they fear . . ."

"God's damnation!" the other swore, but beneath his breath, and somehow managing to retain a smiling face. "This could ruin all."

"Yes. But he says they *will* fight. Find someone. Give him time . . ."

The Governor was now appealing to Queen Annabella, as a woman, to make her husband stop the contest, adding that, moreover, the King was in duty bound to heed the advice of his appointed Governor above that of any other, even the heir to the throne, where the public weal was concerned. The Queen, who was in fact much against the entire project but desired to support her husband and son, looked less serene than usual. The prince interrupted, strongly.

"Your Grace — I am appointed Justiciar of the North. Thomas Dunbar is Earl of Moray and the Clan Cumming are his undoubted vassals. The Clan Chattan are vassals of the lordship of Badenoch, represented by Sir Alexander Stewart. All three agree on this contest. Does the Governor claim that his authority can over-rule the juridical and feudal rights of all? If he so claims, I suggest that we call for a ruling from the Lord High Justiciar of the realm, Sir James Lindsay, Lord of Crawford. Where is the Lord of Crawford?"

Although the Governor asserted that he was not interested in the opinion of Crawford or anybody else, the cry went up for the Lord High Justiciar — who was Sir David Lindsay's cousin. He was not in the best of health, and it could be anticipated that he would take some time to find.

The Earl of Fife and Menteith seldom permitted himself the luxury of anger, but he showed it now, striding up and down in front of the nervous monarch, declaring that all was folly, insolence, a deliberate affront and attack on himself. Heads would fall for this . . .

Vigorous argument and the taking of sides resulted amongst the Governor's gentlemen and the courtiers of the King — or, more truly, of the Earl David, since it was around him that all revolved. Time was well and truly wasted.

In the midst of it all, with the Lord of Crawford still not found, his cousin Glenesk appeared below the gallery, with the High Constable, to announce that all was now ready, Clan Chattan having found a replacement for one of their number who had fallen sick. A certain Perth blacksmith and armourer of Mackintosh blood, commonly called Hal Gow of the Wynd, had volunteered to aid his fellow-clansmen, a doughty swordsman as well as a sword-maker, it seemed. The Constable had approved this replacement . . .

Cheers greeted this intimation. The Earl David quickly signed to Lindsay to get on with it.

So, while argument and protest still continued, the bagpipes struck up anew and a great shout arose from the ranks of Clan Chattan, to be taken up immediately by the Clan Cumming. Not to be outdone, Lyon's trumpeters blew a high blast or two. All talk died away and all eyes lifted to the tourney-ground. Even the Earl of Fife turned to watch, frowning. Jamie Douglas heaved a sigh of relief — even though he was none too happy, himself, about the entire contest.

Hay, the Constable, flanked now by Moray and Lindsay, moved over to a platform erected in a commanding position against the town-wall and below the royal gallery, where they could oversee all. He bowed towards the King then to each of his colleagues, and raised his hand. Only the strains of the bagpipes sounded.

As his hand dropped, the two groups of contestants moved forward, at the walk, pipers pacing behind. Most of the Clan Chattan were bare to the waist, having discarded all clothing save for the philabeg or short kilt — all save one who was seen to be a short, stocky man in ordinary artisan's attire of hodden grey breeches, grey shirt and blue bonnet — the volunteer blacksmith Hal Gow, somewhat bandy-legged but immensely broad across the shoulders. Like the rest he carried on his left

30

arm a round leather-covered targe, as shield, and a crossbow of hunter's type in the right hand. The long two-handed sword, sheathed at his back, which looked comparatively modest on Shaw Beg's tall frame, seemed huge indeed behind the smith. A cheer went up, especially for the bow-legged auxiliary champion, from the vast crowd of Lowlanders. The Cummings, being less truly Highland, retained more of their clothing, but were similarly armed and looked a fine stalwart crew, under the leadership of one Gilchrist mac Ian, or Christie Johnson.

Marching warily forward, the two leaders were watching each other like hawks as they drew closer. They had started about two hundred yards apart, which was overlong range for maximum effect for these hunters' crossbows, however short for the typical English longbows of war. Mac Ian was fractionally the first to act. When each side was some forty yards from its base, slightly in front of his extended line, he dropped on one bare knee and whipped out one of three arrows from his belt. Immediately all his men followed suit.

Shaw Beg adopted a different tactic, and swiftly. His men, who had been bunched much closer together, at his shout leapt and bounded closer still, to hurl themselves into a tight group, in approximately three layers, the lowest crouching down, the middle stooping forward, the rear standing upright. All thrust their targes out, the lowest held fairly close, the second rank out a little to protect the heads of those beneath, the standing men fully extended over the men in front. This manoeuvre, although undoubtedly often practised, took precious seconds to perform; and before the last targes were in position the first arrows were on their way. Screams rang out as three men fell transfixed, one in the rear rank through an eye, two in the middle rank through throat and breast. Their comrades closed still tighter, their targes forming a fairly continuous shield now — although, being circular, they inevitably left gaps.

Each man was provided with three arrows only. The Cummings now shot off their remaining shafts; but the toughened leather of the targes was impenetrable and they almost all fell harmlessly; but three more of the sixty found marks, one man pitching forward in the bottom rank, one hit through a gap in the middle to yell in agony, the third arrow piercing the left forearm of Shaw Beg himself, who being the tallest man there was the least well protected. He remained standing, with the shaft protruding back and front.

Five Clan Chattan fallen and their leader wounded in the first few moments.

Now the scene changed dramatically. It was the Badenoch men's turn. They had five, possibly six, fewer marksmen but their opponents were now disadvantaged in that they were not huddled together but extended in a long line, each man's targe only partially able to cover him. Gilchrist mac Ian yelled at them to close on him, and this they raced to do — but not before the Clan Chattan shafts were flying. Four men fell, in that unprotected race, two more before they could form up their targes as a consolidated shield, two more still from the final flight of arrows which found gaps and niches.

Eight Cummings down as against five — for Shaw Beg had demonstrated that he was by no means out of the fight, using his crossbow with the best of them. Now, tossing the bow away, he twisted his arm around, grasped the barbed end of the shaft, and with a vicious jerk which must have caused excruciating pain, snapped the wooden shank in two. Drawing out the remaining feathered end, he threw it from him; and almost in the same motion reached back for his great two-handed claymore. All his men had likewise thrown away their bows, and drawn swords. Yelling their slogan of *"Loch Moigh! Loch Moigh!"* they went forward at the run, in an ever-extending line, to give room for effective swordplay, the Perth blacksmith well to the fore, bow-legs or none. They left the five bodies behind, lying still or writhing in torment.

The clash, as the two sides met headlong, was shocking, to watch and hear as well as to experience, twenty-five against twenty-two. The clang and shriek of steel, the yells and screams of men, the shouts and howls of the crowd and the high discordant strains of the pipers who continued to play as they strode up and down behind their respective sides, and only some fifty yards apart now, made a frightening accompaniment to a scene of fury and heroism, savagery and anguish, bloodshed and death.

There could be no description of this extraordinary struggle, since it was really a score of different struggles, all to the death, all competing for description. In swordsmanship and axemanship and dirksmanship the two sides were fairly evenly matched; and in courage and determination there was nothing to choose from. Wounded terribly, men fought on, even when stricken to their knees. Swords and Lochaber axes falling from one nerve-

32

less hand were grabbed and wielded by the other — and when neither had the strength left to brandish such weighty weapons, dirks were snatched out to thrust and stab. Flesh and blood wilted and spouted and failed, but the spirit maintained, triumphed whilst breath and consciousness remained — worthy of a better cause.

Up on the Arbour balcony, as no doubt elsewhere around that arena, Jamie Douglas was not alone in feeling that it was shameful, almost obscene, to sit and watch this desperate encounter. He had fought long and hard on the bloody field of Otterburn, and had suffered hurt in sundry tournaments; but being an idle spectator of men in extremity and dying horribly, was not for him. Many, especially amongst the women, found the spectacle more than they could stomach, and there were hasty retirals, vomitings, even swoonings. But by no means all, or even a majority, felt this, as was proved by the shouting, egging-on, wagering, the cursing and cheering which prevailed. The King, however, crouched low, hand over his eyes, his Queen stroking the bowed head. His brother the Governor watched expressionless.

Of all the individual combats, two were apt to rivet the attention — those between Shaw Beg and Gilchrist mac Ian, and between the smith Hal Gow and a variety of opponents. The two leaders singled each other out, from the start, and went at it with tremendous vigour, despite the Shaw's wounded arm. As swordsmen there was little between them — although fighting with the five-foot-long two-handed claymores demanded sinew and endurance more than finesse; nevertheless skill of a sort was important, especially in the recovery from missed strokes. Basically a figure-of-eight motion was more effective than any indiscriminate jabbing and poking and slashing, since it enabled the wielder to remain in control of his weapon; but it had the disadvantage of predictability. Sundry variations on the theme were possible however, switchings of figure, direction, extent and level; at these Shaw Beg probably had the greater expertise as well as the longer reach — which helped to counter-act the obvious pain and increasing stiffness of his left arm. But it seemed apparent that he was going to tire soonest, if he could not finish off the combat with a vital stroke.

Hal of the Wynd, as the Perth folk called the volunteer, was in a different case. He quickly demonstrated that he was no mere rash townsman taking on his betters in weaponry, but a man who knew all there was to know about swords and swordsmanship. His first opponent he disposed of in a couple of minutes. His second took longer, having a more extended reach and notably quick footwork; but a dextrous backhanded reverse stroke eventually laid him low — and everywhere men began to wager on the blacksmith personally.

Elsewhere honours appeared to be fairly equal — although Clan Chattan's extra three men did make a difference. It was an unwritten law that, although it was a battle between sides, within that context combats were single — so that two men did not assail one, and when a man felled his opponent, he waited until one from the other side was free to engage him — and usually much needed the momentary respite to regain breath.

Although there was no official interval in that dreadful battle, there came a time when, in mutual if temporary exhaustion both groups, or more accurately all sets of combatants still on their feet, gradually came to a halt. Indeed, at one stage, only the two leaders were still circling and slashing at each other. When Mac Ian tripped and fell over one of many bodies which littered the field, Shaw refrained from striking down at him but instead stepped unsteadily back a little, staggering, to lean heavily on his tall sword, panting grievously. The other rose, and he too backed away. Everywhere, men who could do so leaned on swords and axes, swaying, clutching at wounds, some doubled up in pain. Few were not covered in blood, their own or others'. The trampled grass around them was more red than green.

In this grim hiatus the pipers came strutting to the front again, to march up and down before their respective sides, blowing and playing at their strongest, passing and repassing within only a few feet of each other, weaving in and out amongst the fallen, the jangled strains of their rival instruments helping to drown other demoralising sounds — for even the most determined and stoical sufferers could not entirely still their groans and cries, and somewhere a man was screaming thinly in mortal agony. Some wounded were dragging themselves about, even in circles.

Not all the spectators were appreciative of this interval, some even claiming that they were being cheated, that this was no fight to a finish. Others, of the wagering sort, were busy assessing and seeking to count and allot the slain and survivors to their two sides; since most combatants stood, panting, approximately where they had paused and there was no clear front, this was not entirely clear. But there was no doubt that there were still thirty-three men on their feet; and of the twenty-seven fallen over half appeared to be dead. The general consensus was that there were eighteen to fifteen, in favour of Clan Chattan, still in the fight.

After only two or three minutes, the pipers' revitalising efforts seemed to be sufficiently effective for a restart to be made. By unspoken consent the two leaders moved off laterally, in the direction of the riverside, a little distance, this to make use of a clean stretch of greensward; for the blood everywhere made footwork hazardous, and the litter of bodies was a major impediment for the remaining fighters. The others were not slow at following, even though the majority now reeled, limped or hobbled.

The fight recommenced, with three Clan Chattan men waiting, disengaged.

At first, the clash seemed to be only fractionally less vigorous and furious than heretofore. But in fact, after a few minutes, it was evident that the pace had slowed. The urgency and resolve was still there, but thews and sinews and breath just could not maintain the fullest expression. Strokes were less accurate, reaction slower, footwork heavier, swords being increasingly discarded for dirks. Nevertheless, men fell faster and blood flowed still more copiously — for weary men were tardier in avoiding blows, in ducking and dodging. In the next quarter-hour sixteen men fell, ten of them Cummings. Of these, Hal the Smith slew two, though twice wounded himself now, with a gashed brow and a slit forearm. Only five Cummings remained capable of fighting, to face twelve opponents. But the terms declared that there was to be no yielding, and none there questioned it. Only up on the Gilten Arbour balcony was there some talk of calling an end to the slaughter, and that only by a minority, mainly women. The King had not once raised his head to look during the second stage.

The end came quite suddenly. The leaders were fighting only with dirks now, and therefore at closest quarters. In making an arm's length stab, Gilchrist mac Ian Cumming lost his balance and stumbled forward, actually cannoning, bent, into his foe. And this time the Shaw did not step back but drove down with his dirk between the other's bare and unprotected shoulder-blades. Pierced to the heart, the Cumming fell.

35

Although it is to be accepted that the others still fighting were much too busy to have eyes for anything but their opponents, somehow the fact of the fall of their leader communicated itself to the remaining four Cummings. This affected men differently. One red-bearded individual, although already bleeding from multiple wounds, it maddened to a final desperate outburst of furious energy wherein he hurled himself bodily upon his foe, ignoring the dirk-slash which laid his cheek open from ear to chin, and stabbed the other to death in a wild flurry of vicious blows — indeed went on stabbing crazily even with his man inert on the grass. But the other three reacted otherwise, recognising that fate was against them, accepting it at last, and quite literally yielding up the ghost. In a bare minute after mac Ian's fall, these three also lay twitching on the ground.

The fight was over. Eleven men of Clan Chattan's thirty, including the blacksmith, remained on their feet, although all were more or less seriously hurt; the one red-head of Clan Cumming, gibbering inanities. The pipers did not stop their playing but, unasked, changed their tunes from fierce arousal to merge their offerings to a slow and dignified coronach for the dead, no longer in competition but united in the same lament.

The High Constable, with the lords of Moray and Glenesk, turned about, bowed to the royal balcony, then stepped down from their platform and came almost hurrying to the scene of conflict.

The entire North Inch of Perth seemed to erupt in cheering. "God's eyes!" the young Earl David cried, "that was a fight! The greatest, I say! And I am three hundred merks the richer! That blacksmith shall have it all, I swear. Come, Jamie." And forgetting all about the dignity expected of the heir to the throne, the High Steward of Scotland or the Justiciar of the North, he swung himself over the balcony-rail, hung by his hands from its flooring, dropped to the ground, landed on all fours and ran for the postern-gate.

Sir James Douglas, with a wife present, was less precipitate, bowing towards the King and more vaguely towards the princesses, before pushing his way to the stairway and down.

The monarch arose, and without a word to any, limped away. Any acknowledgement towards the bowing courtiers, the Queen made. The Earl of Fife briefly ordered a return to Scone.

Jamie caught up with the prince, who was having to fight his way through the surging, excited throng to the battle-ground. Owing to the fact that the combat had moved riverwards, they had to cross ground which had been fought over; and the Douglas, for one, all but spewed when he realised that what he, and others, had kicked and tripped over was a hacked-off arm. Despite his battle experience, he had not realised that human blood smelled so sickeningly strongly.

They reached the ultimate arena to find arguments and confusion, the triumph confined to the spectators, the victors suffering from reaction, pain, loss of blood and weariness. Monks from the Blackfriars and other monasteries were already there seeking to comfort the hurt, to staunch and bind up wounds; and a priest, kneeling in congealing blood, was administering extreme unction to the dying. The one Clan Cumming survivor was still shouting Gaelic incoherencies, to the embarrassment of all, while his wounds were being dressed. The pipers continued with their sobbing coronach; but the young Earl of Moray was involved in an argument with the Constable over what he claimed, at second-hand, was the unfair introduction into the conflict of another and especial kind of music, from a mysterious chanter, the flute-like portion of the bagpipes on which the finger-work was played. This, he asserted, according to his Cumming supporters, had been enchanted or incanted over by witchcraft or other such devilry before-hand, and played during the combat by persons unknown, enabling the Clan Chattan contestants to fight on with supernatural vigour long after their wounds should have laid them low. In token of which he held up a slender black pipe perforated with holes, which someone had picked up from the field. Lindsay was treating this extraordinary objection with hooted scorn, while the Constable looked highly sceptical; and Sir Alexander Stewart was declaring that not only had he not heard this alleged unworldly music but had never seen the chanter before, and that the Clan Chattan did not require witchcraft to win their battles for them.

On this confused scene, the prince's arrival had some calming effect. He commended the Constable's handling of the contest, congratulated Shaw Beg, through Alexander Stewart, on his well-deserved victory, dismissed the black chanter complication as nonsense — he did not like his cousin, Thomas Dunbar, Earl of Moray — and made much of the smith, Hal Gow of the

37

Wynd, declaring that he should have the full three hundred merks, £200, which he had won on his wagering. It seemed that the smith had agreed to act volunteer for a mere half-merk of silver, plus the assurance that if he survived the fight he would receive suitable compensation — a sporting arrangement. This royal windfall, a huge sum for any working craftsman, relieved the Clan Chattan representatives of any financial responsibility — although Sir Alexander told the tough little man that if he elected to come back to the North with or after them, to the land of his fathers, he would give him a good croft in Badenoch to be held by him and his heirs in all time coming, an offer accepted on the spot.

There was some discussion as to the circumstances which had led up to the smith's enrolment. It was now established that the Clan Chattan defaulter had been seen to hurry off eastwards, run down to the riverside and thereafter swim away across Tay; yet the man was known as a considerable swordsman, with some pretensions to gentility and certainly not lacking in courage. The assumption that he had been bought off by someone who wished to stop the contest was reinforced and logical. And the Governor seemed to be the likeliest buyer.

"It was my noble uncle, I swear!" the Earl David declared. "It has the smell of him about it! Not that we will ever prove it against him — he will, as ever, see to that. But when the reckoning comes, I shall not forget it."

"Such reckoning could cost you dear, my lord," his Uncle Lindsay warned. "I would advise that you forget it, lad."

"Not so," his nephew contended. "I have an excellent memory. And the score lengthens. One day, see you, I shall be king in this realm."

"God willing!" his uncle said.

The prince stared at him for a long moment. Then he turned to Alexander Stewart. "Come, Cousin — we shall dine together. Celebrate your victory, and mine. I swear that we have much to talk over. I am going to require a deputy in my justiciarship — for I promise you I am not going to bury myself up there in your wilderness, however magnificent!"

"I thank you, my lord — but no. We head back over the Highland line, forthwith."

"With all these dead and wounded?"

"Even so. The wounded will do better in their own country. We shall bear them in horse-litters. The good brothers at

Dunkeld will attend to them, tonight. They would have it so, I assure you. The dead we will carry with us, for burial in their own glens."

"But why the haste, man? Wait until the morrow, at least."

"Tomorrow might be too late, my lord."

"Too late? For what?"

"For our safety."

"Safety from whom, of a mercy?"

"From the same man as heretofore — the Governor of this realm. Think you that he will love us any the more for this day's outcome?"

"God's eyes, man — you are under *my* protection, now! The Governor will not touch you, I tell you."

"You tell me, yes, my lord — and I thank you. But is our Uncle Robert aware of it? Or heeding? You are heir to the throne, and with much influence. But he it is who still governs this kingdom and wields *power*. Men must obey his word — unless you or His Grace are there to controvert it. So, being in even less good state to withstand him than we were on our way south, we retire behind our Highland hills forthwith. Where even he dare not follow us, I think. So I promised *Mac an Toiseach Mor*, Captain of Clan Chattan."

The prince seldom displayed his anger — although Jamie Douglas at least could recognise the signs, the lifted left eyebrow, the slight flaring of fine nostrils, the increased brilliance of the smile. Now he positively beamed.

"I could almost conceive you to insult me, Cousin," he murmured. "But have it as you will, since you judge me unable to protect you and your hillmen. Perhaps one day you will learn who rules this Scotland. Jamie — have Red John Stewart and his guard escort our doubting friend back to the skirts of his precious mountains. My lords, if you are finished here . . . ?"

Jamie Douglas lingered for a few moments with Alexander Stewart. "That was . . . a pity," he said.

"Perhaps. But as well to know always where we stand."

"The Earl David could be as valuable a friend as a dangerous enemy, Alex."

"No doubt. I have no wish to have him enemy, God knows. Uncle Robert is enemy enough! But first dangers first! I gave my word to the Mackintosh — as *you* once gave your word to my father, in like case. As did David also."

39

"I have not forgotten. So be it. But . . . you heard what he said anent a deputy in the North justiciary? Play your hand aright, Alex, and you might ride high on that tide."

"But — is it a tide I wish to rise on, Jamie . . . ?" the Wolf of Badenoch's son wondered.

II

FIVE-YEAR-OLD David Douglas frowned darkly at his father, his mother, his three-year-old sister Alison and his nurse Janet Durie, in turn; but it was at the last that he pointed his small imperious finger.

"She is bad!" he asserted. "Janet is bad. An ill woman. I will *not* go to bed with Alie. She is younger than I am and goes to bed first. Everybody knows that."

"But you are late already, Davie," his mother pointed out, reasonably. "Both of you. Janet is quite right . . ."

"She is not. I will not go." Straddling his stocky little legs widely, the heir to Aberdour, Roberton, Stoneypath and Baldwinsgill stood, rock-firm, and summoned up his blackest scowl — which could be black indeed, like the rest of him.

"On my soul, he grows more like his father every day!" Mary Stewart declared. "A true Douglas — black in manners, habits and conduct as in appearance! And so overweening as is beyond belief!"

"To be sure," Jamie agreed. "I fear it is the bad Stewart blood in him. He minds me more of his uncle the late Wolf than of any Douglas I know. And as for overweening, he is after all the grandson of one king and like to be the godson and namesake of another."

It was the little girl's turn to assert herself. "I gave Davie an apple with a worm in it," she announced informatively. "A white, curly one. He ate it in half." Her expression angelic, she sighed, with all the sympathy in the world. "Poor curly worm."

"And there, further, speaks the voice of Stewart womanhood!" her father exclaimed. "Seldom have I heard it more eloquently expressed!" Certainly the child had all the renowned

41

good looks of the female Stewarts, of exquisite features, flaxen fairness, purple-blue eyes and a grace of manner to charm the sourest.

But not, in this instance, the ill-used Davie Douglas. "I hate her," he announced simply. "And I hate Janet too."

"Sirrah!" his father declared, "for that unknightly word, *you* shall go to bed first. And if the other half of the curly worm remains uneaten, Alison shall have it!" Sternly he strode over to the children, picked one up under each arm and marched off with them up the winding turnpike stair of Aberdour Castle keep, right to the little garret bedroom within the parapet-walk, the giggling young nurse following.

When he returned to the modest first-floor hall, it was to be chided by his lively and lovely wife.

"I vow those poor bairns never know whether their father is carping at them or cozening them. Sometimes I do not know myself. I never met a man who could proclaim his mirth under so sombre a visage!"

"Would you have me smirking and leering all the while, like some of those half-men at Court, woman?" he demanded.

"I would but have you to smile, say twice a day, my love — thrice on saints' days! And fill my cup of happiness. Once at the bairns' bed-times, once at your own. The warm results might surprise you, sir!"

He achieved a grin at that, at least. "Sakes, girl — if the results were warmer than your usual at such times, I doubt if I could stand up to it!"

"Craven! Poltroon! We shall put you to the test this very night!"

"Lord — as well that I am off the morn for a spell of only hard *horse*-riding! You Stewarts are devils between the blankets, male and female!"

"At least I may send you off on your travels in suitable state to be a leal husband, until we forgather again! How many days, Jamie? And nights?"

"Nine. Ten at the most. All must be at Cortachy by Saint Gregory's Eve, 11th of March, at latest. And I with them. And you must be there by then likewise, with the Lady Isabel — since you prefer to escort her, rather than that I should! It is fell important that she should come, David says. He cannot be sure that the Lady Katherine will come, Lindsay's wife — and he would wish *some* royal support."

female side from the English royal house also. Beside him, the Stewarts, Douglases, Lindsays, even the Bruces, seemed comparative newcomers on the Scottish scene, gaining their high positions by the sword, intrigue or judicious marriages with Celtic-line heiresses. George Cospatrick Dunbar let none forget it.

After being handed a sealed letter from the Earl David, Dunbar left Jamie to eat a solitary meal, in the company only of a bevy of shaggy deer-hounds, in a corner of the vast shadowy great hall lit by smoky pitch-pine torches. The Earl was a widower, his sons from home, his only daughter not on view, and the huge rambling stronghold, loud with the sound of waves, was a chilly, echoing, gloomy place where draughts constantly stirred the arras hanging against the stone walls. Dunbar owned a score of castles in a dozen counties of Scotland, the entire Isle of Man also; and it was strange that he should choose to make this one his principal domicile, dramatic history notwithstanding.

Fed and refreshed, Jamie was led by a servitor through a succession of winding vaulted corridors, their walls running with damp, which were, he could sense, bridges over the swirling tide, to a small private chamber in a detached tower, hung with tapestries and lined with books and parchments, where the Earl George stood in front of a well-doing log fire, the warm comfort contrasting notably with the spray which every few moments splattered against the shuttered windows.

"Draw in to this fire, Sir James," his host said civilly. "It is chilly again, after the softer weather we have been having. Ill conditions for riding the country."

"None so bad, my lord. I have ridden abroad in much worse. As well, since this gathering I come to tell of has been planned for the earliest date possible when the lower Mounth passes should be clear of snow. Hard weather now could ruin all."

"Aye, no doubt. Angus in fact came of age in January, did he not?" The Earl waved the opened letter in his hand. "You know what is written in this?"

"Only in general, my lord. The Earl David honours me with his confidence in sundry matters."

"You will know, then, that he seeks my aid in a league against his uncle, the Governor — whom God rot! This aid he seeks — what is it for? What does he plan?"

"That, my lord, I cannot tell. I do not know. This is what

the gathering at Cortachy is to debate — under the cover of the Earl of Angus's coming-of-age celebrations. A secret gathering . . ."

"Yes, man, yes — I understand that. But before I go traipsing off to Angus on this young man's caper, to my much discomfort, I must know at least in some measure what he proposes. There could be danger in this . . ."

"There is ever danger. my lord, where the Earl Robert is concerned. This is to seek to lessen it."

"A plague on it, man — that goes without saying. Do you have no notion as to what young Carrick plans? What action he envisages? He must have something in mind."

"No doubt, sir. But he has not confided it to me. I am but his messenger, in this. He does not wish it talked about at large, bruited abroad, lest it come to the Earl Robert's sharp ears. The Governor has his creatures everywhere . . ."

"Of that I am well aware also. But not in Dunbar Castle, I think!" He waved the letter. "David Stewart must require my help badly, I swear — since to obtain it he offers to marry my daughter! Did you know of that, Sir James?"

The younger man blinked. "No, my lord — no. I . . . ah . . . this is a surprise to me."

The other smiled faintly. "And to me. My daughter is but fourteen years. Young for her age. I had not considered her marriage, as yet, seriously. Certainly not that she might be the future Queen. Yet this letter offers just that. Why? What does he want of me, at that price? He knows that I have no love for Robert Stewart, anyway. Any move against him would have my sympathy. So what is this for?"

Jamie was nonplussed. On the face of it, this suggestion of marriage to Dunbar's daughter was an unlikely one. The girl was little more than a plain-faced, gawky child as yet, scarcely an attraction in herself as bride for the dashing heir to the throne. As an alliance of houses it did not seem to reveal obvious advantages. Admittedly, Dunbar was very rich, owning vast lands apart from much of this Lothian, and Man, in the Merse, Lauderdale, Annandale, Nithsdale, Clydesdale, Galloway and Ayrshire, capable of producing great numbers of men as well as riches. But these territories had never been integrated into any strategic man-raising block, united by name and clanship, as were those of Douglas for instance. Nor was George Dunbar a particularly notable warrior; indeed his record of treasonable activities was worse than that of any other noble in Scotland — although undoubtedly he would not call it that, since he considered himself a free agent, a semi-royal and all but independent princeling, who contrived alliances as he would. He had gone over actively to the English side in disputes twice already — as indeed had his forefathers — once in 1385 and again in 1393, when he considered his interests thus best served. In every way, he seemed an unlikely choice as prospective father-in-law for the future monarch. Yet David Stewart, however impulsive, seldom made major moves without good reason. It might even be that it was Dunbar's English links which interested the prince, at this juncture — and the fact that Dunbar controlled the vital East March of the border. The Governor, whatever else he was, was consistently anti-English. Who could tell — David might even be prepared to play with such dangerous fire . . .

"I know not, my lord — save that an alliance with your great and illustrious house could advantage any . . ."

"Pshaw, man — spare me that! The Stewarts have always hated and feared my house. I think it may well be merely that, with Douglas firm on the Governor's side, the Earl Archibald and to a lesser extent your own father, he thinks to use me as a counter-weight. Well, we shall discover — if I come to Cortachy."

"I pray that you do so, sir — for the realm's sake. If it comes to a struggle between the Earl David and the Governor, every man's support is like to be vital. And you are one of the greatest in the kingdom . . ."

"I do not require you, young man, to tell me of my duty towards the realm!" the other snapped. "But we shall see . . ."

Next day Jamie proceeded due southwards through the Lammermuir Hills, by the pass of Monynut, to the Whitadder Water and so to Duns and the Merse. A long day's stiff riding brought him to Roxburgh, where Tweed and Teviot joined, forty miles without making any calls — for this was all still within the earldom of Dunbar and March, and its lords and lairds would do as the Earl said. Fourteen further miles up Teviotdale, deep in the Borderland now, and wearily, with the dusk, the traveller came to Cavers, in a hanging valley amongst green whin-clad knolls high above the river and under the thrusting conical hill of Ruberslaw. Here was the massive peel-tower of a friend and distant kinsman of his own, Sir Archibald

Douglas, illegitimate son of the previous Earl of Douglas, knighted like himself on the field of Otterburn where his father had fallen. Now aged twenty-four, he was a stocky, dark young man, like his sire, of a cheerful, outgoing and uncomplicated nature. Jamie had no difficulty in convincing him to come to Cortachy. Nor did he require persuading to take the risk of offending his present chief, Archibald, Earl of Douglas, his father's successor. None of the murdered Earl James's kin and close followers were greatly enamoured of Archie the Grim, who had disappointed the entire clan by his support of the Governor. Many indeed claimed that he should never have been appointed Earl of Douglas, and that the earldom should have gone to another, notably to this Sir Archibald of Cavers' elder brother, Sir William of Drumlanrig. Admittedly Sir William was illegitimate — for the Earl James had had no lawful offspring — but then, so was Archie the Grim himself, Lord of Galloway and natural son of the great Bruce's heroic friend, the Good Sir James Douglas, greatest of the race. Jamie was not desirous of promoting any sort of revolt against his chief, nor against his own father who supported the Earl Archie and therefore the Governor; but, along with many another Douglas, he-felt that their great and powerful house was not playing the part it should, and could, in faction-torn Scotland.

Sir William of Drumlanrig, whose tower rose right in the midst of the little town of Hawick, only three miles from Cavers, was presently from home, tending his lands in Dumfries-shire; but his brother assured that he would send for him and have him at Cortachy likewise, within the week. Satisfied — for these two between them largely controlled much of the Middle March, and could muster almost a thousand tough and mounted Border mosstroopers — Jamie headed on westwards the following morning, over the lofty watershed of Southern Scotland, for Moffat, Upper Nithsdale, Carrick, Kyle and Cunninghame, where he had many more calls to make. It was indeed going to take him all his time to reach Angus, nearly two hundred miles to the north-east, by the due date.

* * *

Cortachy was not a castle in the accepted sense, but rather a fortified private township, in the old Celtic tradition, a seat of the former Celtic Mormaors and Earls of Angus and now the temporary domicile of their successor the young George

Douglas, dispossessed of Tantallon in Lothian by the Governor. It was a sprawling, untidy establishment which had outgrown its containing stone walls and earthen embankments and ditches, set pleasingly in the green haughs where the South Esk and Prosen Water joined at the mouth of the great Glen of Clova, under all the snow-capped Highland mountains. It guarded the southern exit from the White Mounth pass from Upper Deeside, part-Highland, part-Lowland. It was crowded this St. Gregory's Eve, in mid-March 1397, but few there were Highlanders.

George Douglas was an unlikely figure to be the focus of so much stir and excitement, a pale and frail young man, almost fragile-seeming, with large anxious eyes and a diffident air — although there was more to him than might appear at first glance. His mother was the power here, Margaret Stewart, Countess of Angus, a lusty, hearty woman still, with an unusual and complicated history, countess in her own right, widow of the last Earl of Mar and mistress of the 1st Earl of Douglas. This young man was the illegitimate son of the said William of Douglas, to whom she had conveyed the earldom of Angus. He had been accepted by all to be a Douglas, not a Stewart. Undoubtedly he found his lively mother and stirring ancestry hard to live up to.

On this occasion, although friendly to all, he made little attempt to act the host. That duty was taken over with entire authority by David, Earl of Carrick — in between flirting outrageously with his hostess, who was almost old enough to be his grandmother. The Stewarts were apt to be like that. The heir to the throne was at his brilliant best, gay, witty, winning, approachable, putting all at ease — save for the women, none of whom seemed to remain unaffected by his rampant sensuality. He should have been drunk throughout, from the amount of liquor he consumed — and possibly was, although he gave little sign of it.

It was a great gathering, in those rather odd surroundings, skilfully selected and assembled, with half the nobility of Scotland represented, as well as certain members of the royal house. Not a great deal was attempted to emphasise the theme of Angus's coming-of-age; that was merely the excuse for the bringing together of so great and diverse a company so that suspicion would not be aroused in the Governor's circle. It was as well that the Earl David was so able a host, for many of the guests were antipathetic if not downright enemies, their only common ground a hatred of the Governor and all his works.

Jamie was delighted to reunite with his Mary — who actually had reached Cortachy before him, in the company of· two of her half-sister princesses, the Lady Jean Stewart, formerly married to Sir John Lyon the Chamberlain and now to Sir John Sandilands, Lord of Calder; and the Lady Isabel, wife of Sir John Edmonstone. The latter's husband was not present, for he was a vassal and supporter of the Lord of Dalkeith, Jamie's father, and therefore in the opposite camp; but his wife, widow of the murdered Earl of Douglas, hated her brother the Governor sufficiently to‿insist on attending in person.

The banquet held in the great hall of the place, a long detached building of its own in the midst of the township, had to be a carefully managed occasion. Food and drink were available in rich profusion, and all must be satisfied; yet it was important that drunkenness on a major scale should not overtake any large percentage of the guests before decisions were reached, a difficult matter to ensure. Deliberately therefore the wines and spirits were held back in some measure, and elaborate entertainment provided throughout the meal, so that the deprivation might be the less noticeable; singers, jugglers, dancers, acrobats and the like performed without pause in the cleared space to one side of the long tables, amongst the hurrying servitors and the roaming, stealing and squabbling deer- and wolf-hounds — a lively scene under the smoky, flickering blaze of the torches. Even so, not a few of the company managed to get distinctly noisy and elevated on the light ale — or perhaps they had been indulging beforehand — to the extent of joining in with the entertainers, one pair of young lords capering up and down the table-tops themselves, weaving in and out amongst the viands and flagons, whilst Jamie's own half-sister, wife of Philip Arbuthnott of that Ilk and a bold piece, left the board to dance a wild jig with a handsome gypsy, pushing aside his partner to do so.

The Earl David, up at the transverse dais-table and flanked by young Angus and his mother, watched all heedfully whilst apparently by no means stinting himself of food and wine and jollity. Deciding that the moment had come, he rose to his feet, a resplendent, glittering figure. At a sign from him a servitor rang a bell, and gradually quiet was established. The enter-

50

tainers were hustled out, the capering lordlings coaxed down from the table and the panting and dishevelled Lady Arbuthnott restored to her place on the bench between her equally disapproving husband and half-brother Jamie. Amidst sundry hushings, the High Steward and Prince of Scotland spoke, pleasantly, conversationally.

"My lords and ladies and friends all," he said, "we are here gathered for the most happy and felicitous of employment, the celebration of the coming to full years of our good friend and host, George Douglas, Earl of Angus and Lord of Abernethy. His reaching of this great age, something I myself cannot aspire to for two years yet, mark you, should be a source of joy and satisfaction to us all, and indeed to this ancient realm, in the councils of which he will now be able to play his full and important part. In urging you all to rise and drink to the health, well-being and success of George Douglas, I say that we should couple with it that of his lady-mother, whose beauty, talents and attractions grow but the more dazzling with each year that passes. I tell you . . ."

The rest was drowned in shouted acclaim, as all who were able to do so lifted to their feet to pledge the Earl and Countess in vociferous if less than decorous fashion. It was perhaps noticeable that many more eyes lingered on the mother than the son.

After a little, Angus rose from his chair, said simply, "I thank you all," and sat down again. The Countess Margaret threw kisses at large and then pulled down the Earl David at her side to salute him full and protractedly on the lips, to the cheers of the company.

Murmuring something in the lady's ear, David Stewart straightened up. "I thank the good God that this is not *my* mother!" he observed, with a joyful laugh and significant pause, and received a slap on the wrist for his pains. "However," he went on, when he could make himself heard, "something of the sort is proposed. My esteemed royal father, to express his pleasure in the occasion and his favour towards George of Angus, has graciously consented to bestow the hand of his second daughter, my sister Mary, on the said George, in betrothal. Which will make him and myself brothers, and therefore his mother perilously near to being mine!"

As the din occasioned by this pronouncement continued, Jamie looked at his wife. He had had no inkling of this. Clearly it represented a major departure in policy, David's policy, since it was unlikely that the King had done more than merely accede. It was one thing to use Angus's majority as an excuse to assemble supporters from far and near in this remote hold, altogether another to ally him intimately to the royal house in marriage. To what advantage? George Douglas was an inoffensive young man and no warrior. Nor was he particularly rich or strong in manpower. Personally therefore he was of no great value to the prince's cause. Yet this especial mark of favour must have some good reason — for the King had only three daughters and the eldest already married to the Master of Douglas, the Earl Archie's heir; and the third to Jamie's own half-brother, heir to the Lord of Dalkeith. It could only be the vital Douglas connection, then, Jamie concluded, the determination to support the Crown with Douglases, in the next generation. No doubt also as warning to Earl Archie and his son that their hold on the Douglas earldom might not be all that secure. After all, this George Douglas was a son of the first Earl, and half-brother of the second, much closer to the main stem than was Archie the Grim. Wed to a princess, he might be used conveniently to supplant the Galloway line should cause and opportunity arise. That would be it . . .

"The Earl Archie is not going to like this!" Mary whispered in his ear, indicating that she had reached the same conclusion. "Nor is Robert. But many Douglases will."

He nodded. "He is making a bid, I think, to separate Douglas from the Governor. Possibly even to challenge the leadership."

The prince was continuing. "Whilst we are on matters matrimonial, it is my further great satisfaction to declare that His Grace is likewise pleased to accede to my own betrothal to the Lady Elizabeth Dunbar, with my lord Earl of Dunbar and March's kind agreement, a match and alliance which, I am sure, will give all cause for much rejoicing." He turned towards where that Earl sat at the dais-table between the Princesses Isabel and Jean, and raised his wine-cup. "My lord, I drink to our mutual felicity."

This time there was no riotous din as reaction but something of a hush as men and women groped in their minds for the reason for this utterly unexpected and unlikely intimation. So much was involved in this. Dunbar was unpopular with most of the nobility, resented by many and distrusted by almost all. His wealth and power were not belittled; but his suitability as father-in-law of the future monarch, his unknown daughter as the next Queen, were highly questionable.

Dunbar rose, bowed gravely to the prince, sipped his wine, and sat down unspeaking.

Recognising, as no doubt he had planned, that the time had come to dispense with pleasantries and side-issues, the Earl David changed his tone and manner to a suitable seriousness.

"My friends," he went on, "these matters of kindly goodwill and celebration are to our comfort and satisfaction. But we announce them in ill times, our ancient realm in sorrowful state. My royal father's kingdom is divided, misgoverned, endangered. There is chaos and faction and discord within, and threat from without, our friends at enmity, our enemies like to seize their opportunity against us. I have secret but sure word that the English plan to beset us, taking advantage of our divided state, although there is truce, but recently renewed, between the realms."

The growl from his listeners proclaimed their predictable rising to that age-old but unfailing bait.

"At home here, as we all know, the King's law is disregarded on all hands. Men are permitted to do as they will, he who has power taking what he covets, the weak and the helpless crushed."

The prince paused at that, looking around him slowly, significantly. There were not a few of the powerful present, used to doing just as he said. Many pairs of eyes concentrated on their plates and wine-goblets. No comment was forthcoming.

"The Treasury, moreover, is empty, the King's taxes, revenues and customs uncollected or handed over as pensions and bribes and fees of support. Due and proper charges are not paid, the trade of the merchants and craftsmen is stolen, the King's roads, bridges, fords and ferries are not maintained, the ports and harbours are choked, sea-walls broken, flood-banks breached, town-walls crumbling. Even my royal mother's yearly portion, established by parliament, has been withheld these three years by the Chamberlain's deputies."

Again he paused. All knew who was now Great Chamberlain of Scotland. The growl which had remained muted over the depredations of the powerful barons rumbled satisfactorily again.

"Who is responsible for this evil state of the realm?" the speaker demanded. "My royal sire, the King, reigns, yes. So he cannot avoid some blame. He sorrows for it. But owing to age, ill-health and infirmity, His Grace is unable to *rule* his

53

kingdom as he would, and should. So he appointed a Governor to rule it in his name. That Governor and Great Chamberlain, his brother the Earl of Fife and Menteith, has ruled the land these eight years. In these years, evil has multiplied and triumphed and good has been put down, justice set at naught, the revenues squandered, place-seekers and lickspittles are raised up and honest men slighted. I say that it is enough, that it is time for change!"

A great shout greeted that declaration, and continued. Flagons, beakers and fists beat on table-tops. There was no doubt as to the support for that sentiment amongst those present, divided as they might be otherwise. But doubts were implicit.

"How?" Lindsay of Glenesk barked, when he could make himself heard. "Change, yes — but how is it to be effected? When the Governor controls all?"

Many voices echoed that vital question.

"Bear with me, Uncle and my lords, for a moment," the prince said. "There must be change. And change, to be effective, means that the Governorship must be changed. Although the Earl Robert of Fife is my own near kin, I say it. Fife must go. And although, as you, my lord, say, he presently controls all, I believe he can be *made* to go. And must . . ."

"How? How?" The demands came on every hand now.

"I have thought long on this, my friends," David assured. "I am young, yes — but I have consulted with wise heads, my royal mother in especial, who grieves sorely for the realm. I have come to the conclusion that there are four means by which we may unseat my uncle. It will take time, for we must by no means risk war, civil war amongst our people. But the four together, I am convinced, will do it. And, I say, within a year or eighteen months."

He had the keen attention of all, even the drink-taken leaning forward, ears cupped.

"Here is the gist of it. Four heads, but all linked. To be spoken to more fully hereafter. First, the English threat — for nothing will more swiftly unite our folk. The English threat — with the Governor shown to care nothing, taking no steps to counter it. Second, money, siller, the empty Treasury — and the Governor giving bribes to his friends and shown to be but lining his own pockets. Third, a parliament to deal with this, a parliament called to *our* tune, not his. Lastly, and necessarily, to detach Douglas from his support."

54

Into the buzz of excited comment and exclamation, Mary spoke to her husband. "I did not know that he had it in him. This, this state-craft. He is more able than I knew."

"Aye — but can he carry it further? Can he convince that all this is possible? He has made a good start, yes. But he must convince. And there are hard heads here . . ."

It was as though the prince had heard them. But then, many, no doubt, were saying or thinking the same. "My friends — you may consider that I but beat the air. Hear me, then. Take the last first — Douglas. The Earl Archibald is close to the Governor, unhappily. But he could be detached, I swear — at least in large enough measure for our purposes. His son and heir, the Master, my own good-brother, married to my eldest sister, loves Fife a deal less. He is unhappy at the role of Douglas today — as are many here. The Douglases are fighters ever, and even Archie the Grim must gravely doubt the policy of appeasing the English. Especially as much of his great lands lie along the Border, and suffer. My Uncle Robert made one great mistake. On the death of Earl James Douglas he snatched the Chief Wardenship of the Marches for himself, because of its revenues, when it should have gone with the Douglas earldom. Always the Chief Warden was Douglas. Now, with the English threat, the Border Marches come to the fore. And they are not being protected. We have, in this room, the Hereditary Sheriff of Teviotdale, Sir William Douglas of Drumlanrig, who with his brother of Cavers, all but controls the Middle March. Also here is the Earl of Dunbar and March, who controls the East March. The West March is the Earl Archibald's, deputed to his son the Master. Where, I ask you, does that leave the Chief Warden, the Governor? I say all but powerless in a most vital area. But *responsible!* If we cannot use that situation to prise the Earl Archie and the rest of Douglas further from Robert Stewart, then we are poor creatures indeed. Moreover, we now have another Douglas earl, of full age, and to be allied to the royal house, with a more ancient earldom than that of Douglas. How say you, my friends?"

There was no question about the reaction. Even the most sceptical were impressed. The Douglases were the most powerful house in the land, and essentially a Border clan. Use the Borderland and English threats thereto as lever, in skilful hands, and almost anything could be done with them. Most there indubitably had forgotten that amongst the innumerable offices and positions the Earl Robert had appropriated to his own uses was that of Chief Warden of the Marches. The Douglas brothers of Drumlanrig and Cavers were loudest in their acclaim. Dunbar looked thoughtful and young Angus uncomfortable.

"This English threat?" Lindsay demanded. "I have heard naught of any such. What substance is there to it? Other than casual raiding, which is always with us."

"I come to that, Uncle. There is substance indeed. It is like a pitch-fork, double-pronged. Carefully planned. Donald of the Isles, my esteemed cousin, has entered treasonably into what he terms a treaty with Richard of England whereby he will make an attack by sea in the West, at the same time as Richard sends a force into the East and Middle Marches. Donald, injured over Skye and the earldom of Ross which he claims as his and which the Governor conveys to his daughter's husband, will descend with his galley-fleet on the Galloway, Carrick, Kyle and Cunninghame coasts."

"When, by God?" Sir John Montgomerie of Eaglesham cried, whose lands lay in Kyle and the Ayrshire coast.

"Before summer, I am told. When the season is apt for coastal landings and campaigning . . ."

"Save us — and we do nothing!"

"I, Carrick, intend to do something, my lord of Eaglesham! As you will hear. It is the Governor who does nothing."

"Curse him . . .!"

There was uproar in the hall now, for there were many present from Galloway and Ayrshire, the fruit of Jamie's patient calls.

"Wait you, my friends — cry out not too soon," the prince advised. "My father's lands of Dundonald and Bute, and my own of Carrick and Turnberry, are thereabouts. So I am as much concerned as any here. But I believe that we can turn this to our great advantage, well before Donald is ready to strike." He paused. "We are fortunate, I think, in that Richard of Bordeaux, King of England, is a fool! Rash and arrogant, setting his own nobility, even his own kin, against him. He has had his uncle, Gloucester, arrested and slain, likewise Arundel. Which much offends his other uncle, John of Gaunt, Duke of Lancaster. Now, to distract his people's attention from his follies at home, Richard will adventure into Scotland, as he has done before. For this he requires commanders and men, for he is no warrior himself. So he must needs turn again to the stalwart Lancaster, his best soldier still. And for men, in the North, he needs the Earl of Northumberland — or Hotspur, his son. These are to invade the East and Middle Marches when Donald descends on the West. If we do not halt them first."

"Halt them with what? John of Gaunt will not halt lightly!" Lindsay asserted.

"It is my hope to halt him with words rather than men," he was told. "See you, my lord of Dunbar has the advantage over the lave of us, in that he has good friends and even kin south of the Border." The prince said that straight-faced, although most would not have done so. "John of Gaunt is one of them, Hotspur likewise. I say that we could turn this to good effect. Hotspur, the Percy, is Warden of the English East March as is my lord on our side. The Wardens meet, ever and anon, to settle Border differences. I say, with my lord's good offices, we will call a greater meeting, letting the English know that we are aware of their projected invasion, prepared for it, and requesting John of Gaunt to be present, as well as Hotspur. We could claim this meeting under the terms of the truce. On our side, as well as my lord of Dunbar and myself, we would ask Earl Archie of Douglas but also Earl George of Angus, here. Others likewise, including our friends of Drumlanrig and Cavers. This well before Donald can move. I believe we could force Lancaster to come, and thereafter prevent the venture. The Earl of Dunbar is Lord of Man. If a host was to be mustered on that isle, directly opposite John of Gaunt's Lancaster coast, with many boats assembled for transport, I think the Duke would think twice of obeying his arrogant nephew Richard. And all done with the Governor not having stirred a hand!"

There was a pause whilst men took all that in. Gradually heads began to nod in appreciation. No objections were put forward, although not a few glances were cast doubtfully at Dunbar. The prince's gesture towards him in the matter of the betrothal was now better understood, tying him to the Scots side; but not all were disposed to trust him, even so. He sat, toying with his wine-cup, a half-smile on his tough features.

"So much for Douglas and the English threat," the Earl David resumed cheerfully. "Now, as to the revenues, siller. Next to English invasion, naught effects men more than the belief that moneys are being stolen from them! The misappropriation of the King's funds is a large subject and not easily brought home to ordinary folk, I agree. But actual sums, figures, charged against a single man can be understood, and telling." He

57

reached into a doublet pocket and brought out a paper. "Here are some, for you to remember and speak of, my lords and ladies. All relating to the Earl of Fife and Menteith, his private purse. As Governor, £1,000, or 12,000 ounces of silver yearly. As Chamberlain £200, although he is demanding £900 more for sundry expenses. As Keeper of Stirling Castle, £200. As protector of the Abthania of Dull, of the old Celtic Church, £200. From the royal customs of Cupar, £200. The same from Linlithgow. All the wool and hides from his two earldoms permitted to be exported free of the customs charged on others. There are more, many more than these. But these will serve. Remember some of them. We can use this to bring him down."

There were due cries of outrage; but likewise queries as to how this shameful catalogue could be used to effect their purpose. As Lindsay did not fail to point out, the Governor would care nothing for their mere condemnation.

"This is where my fourth charge to you arises," David Stewart told them. "The parliament. A parliament called, and these facts presented before it. An indictment of the Governor. The facts would tell, then. It could not be a true parliament, to be sure, since in effect now the Governor must call that, in the King's name — or the Chancellor calls it on the Governor's instructions — and Chancellor Peebles is in my uncle's pocket. But the Privy Council can call a Convention or General Council of the realm — also in the King's name — and I swear that I can muster sufficient votes thereon to carry the day, to outvote my uncle if he objects. There are seven members of the Privy Council here present. This will be the last of our steps against the Governor, and we must all ensure its success. Persuade all our friends and kin. Convince the people that we can, and must, unseat him. Especially the churchmen. The Church votes in the Estates are vital. We shall not put down Robert Stewart without them. He has much offended many of the clerics. Peebles the Chancellor, Bishop of Dunblane, is his man; but Bishop Trail of St. Andrews, the Primate, does not love him, and is close to my mother the Queen. Glendinning of Glasgow, and other bishops, are likewise against him. We must all work hard on this. By then I believe the English business will be settled, and my uncle discountenanced therein. The Douglases, also, should be deserting him, if I judge aright. We can do it, I say. A year, eighteen months . . ."

The gathering was getting noisy now, with enthusiasm mounting. But there were still some hard heads.

"An indictment of the Earl of Fife on this of moneys might be passed by such Convention, my lord — yet not achieve our aim." A new voice spoke, that of Sir James Sandilands, Lord of Calder, fairly recently become the husband of the widowed Lady Jean Stewart, and so one more uncle of the prince, a solid and influential man of middle years. "He might well bow to it, but no more. Not stand down. And we should be little the better."

"True. But after such vote, we can further force him, I believe. It will require a device, but will serve almost certainly. The Council must first declare misgovernment of the realm. This against my royal father — who already admits as much, to his sorrow. He will then acknowledge it to the Council, but declare that his officers have failed him, in especial the Governor, and charge the parliament or Convention, to judge the matter and put it right. This a royal command. The Convention would then *have* to arraign my uncle. And since the King had thus expressed no confidence in him beforehand, the vote could scarcely be other than against him — after this of the moneys."

That produced the loudest cheering of all. Lindsay had difficulty in making his strong voice heard.

"When you have unseated the Governor, Nephew, who will then govern in his place?" he demanded.

Smiling genially, the younger man spoke briefly, simply. "*I* will."

As all digested that, some with glee, some with sober approval, some with doubts, the prince turned to look along the dais-table to where his aunts sat on either side of Dunbar. He caught the Lady Isabel's eye and raised his brows.

That princess, now in her early forties, her lovely face showing the lines of strain and sorrow, nodded and moistened her lips. With some reluctance she spoke.

"My lords. My lords, I say . . ."

Her comparatively soft tones quite failed to penetrate the clamour of talk until the Earl of Dunbar banged his flagon on the table for quiet. She went on.

"Hear me, my lords. I speak as one close to His Grace the King, and much concerned for the welfare of this his realm. Hear a woman's voice, if you will. I say that what we have heard tonight should rejoice us all. I say indeed, thank God for my nephew the Earl of Carrick and High Steward. That he is such as he is. Thank God that the heir to the throne is grown to man's stature in fashion as he has, strong, able, vigorous. For too long this kingdom has been weakly governed, and all have suffered for it. I say it, who have reason to know — although it has been my own royal father and brother from whom that weakness has stemmed. Kindly and gentle, they have not been of the stuff of kings. But at last we have one who is. My other brother, the Governor, has brought the realm to its knees. If it is to be saved, it must be saved soon, swiftly. I have come far to say this, and at some cost to myself. I urge that you support the Earl of Carrick with all your strength and will. The Earl of Fife can be put down from the high place he has held for too long — and must be. He has done . . . enough harm." Her voice choked a little at that, and for a moment it seemed that she would not go on. Then she rallied. "Unseat him, my lords, for the realm's sake and your own sake — and mine! And raise up in his place him who will one day be your rightful king."

There was a sympathetic murmur as she ended, into which the Lady Jean, her sister, exclaimed, "I say the same."

Mary whispered to her husband. "She did it well, in the end. I know how she dreaded it. To speak thus. And she has ever had her doubts about David. But she did well."

He nodded. "Yes. Her hatred of the one much outdoes her doubts of the other. I feared that she might fail him. But, no . . ."

The prince, assessing the approval which greeted his aunts' support, as indication that the royal family was largely behind him, judged the moment apt to bring the talking to a close. "I thank you both," he said. "Indeed I thank all here for heeding me so patiently, for showing that you are with me." He raised his wine-cup. "Drink with me," he urged. "Drink to His Grace, to the downfall of Robert Stewart and the reform of the realm's government."

All, enthusiastic, more soberly in general favour, or positively doubtful, must needs drink to that cunningly worded toast — since to fail to honour the King's Grace was as good as high treason. So all present were, in a measure, committed.

Summoning back the entertainers, and further supplies of wine, the Prince of Scotland sat down, prepared to enjoy the rest of the evening.

III

THE BORDERLAND WAS a joy to behold, with the spring green stippling the trees, the golden gorse ablaze on every knowe, the corn-spears beginning to thrust up, the lambs and calves frisking on the hillsides, the cuckoos calling in the valleys and all the Cheviots, snow-free to the summits at last, looming a purple-blue barrier to the south. Few failed to respond, in some measure, however subconsciously.

Jamie Douglas whistled tunelessly as he rode, with moderate content and no immediate responsibilities. He had done all that he could, and success or failure lay on more important shoulders than his own. He was not a wagering man, and would not have liked to stake a lot on the outcome of this day, one way or the other. But at least it was action of a sort, a start in putting to the test David Stewart's theories and plans, after much labour, persuasion, bargaining and drumming up of support. By this night, they should know if it had been worth while or mere wasted — and dangerous — effort; whether Scotland was likely to take the first faltering steps on a new course, or not.

The Earl David, at least, could not complain of lack of interest in his project — too much interest, rather. His own retinue was a distinguished one, for as well as the Earl of Angus, and the lords of Errol the Constable, Keith the Marischal, Eaglesham, Calder and Glenesk — although Sir David should now more properly be called of Crawford, since his cousin Sir James thereof had died of his sickness leaving no nearer heir and he had become chief of all the name of Lindsay — it included Bishop Walter Trail of St. Andrews, the Primate, Bishop Matthew Glendinning of Glasgow, the Archdeacon Thomas Stewart of St. Andrews, and the Abbot of Melrose, all

61

entitled to sit on the Privy Council. Not far behind, but keeping a careful distance, was the Earl of Douglas's cavalcade, also illustrious, with the Master, the Lord of Dalkeith, Jamie's father, the lords of Mordington, Strabrock and other Douglas barons plus the Bishop of Galloway and the Abbots of Dundrennan and Newabbey.

This was fair enough, indication that Archibald the Grim took the business sufficiently seriously to come in some strength. But what was less encouraging was the fact that, not far behind the Douglases, rode still another glittering contingent — and this, like David Stewart's, under the royal banner of the Lion Rampant of Scotland. The Governor himself, Earl Robert Stewart of Fife and Menteith, had elected to come, uninvited, to this meeting at Haddonstank. As nominal Chief Warden of the Marches, of course, none could question his right to attend, furiously angry as he was known to be over this arrangement entered into with the English outwith his authority.

The meeting, whatever it effected, could hardly fail to be lively.

Haddonstank, on the Redden Burn, four miles east of Kelso but on the south side of Tweed, was the recognised meeting-place for the East March Wardens. Situated on steadily but gently rising ground, where the Borderline swung away southwards from the great river, it was just a few hundred yards inside Scotland. Because of the welter of Cheviot foothills behind, it seemed to turn its back on England and the South, to look out northwards over the farflung, extensive and undulating plain of the Scots Merse, a rich and fertile land of corn and pasture in marked contrast to the high heathy moors of North Northumberland, to make Englishmen's mouths water in contemplation — the goodly heritage of George Dunbar.

Today the broad shelf of grassland, normally cattle-strewn, was as busy and as colourful as any fair — as indeed to some extent it was, for these periodical Days of Truce were accepted as something of a holiday by the Border folk on both sides, and people who had no connection with Wardens' meetings and cases to be tried, flocked from far and near to attend, to meet friends, to make bargains, do business and possibly witness a hanging or a scourging. Packmen, pedlars, dealers, begging friars and the like seized the opportunity to ply their trades, and vendors of ale, wine of a sort and even hot cakes and shellfish did a good traffic. Always tents and pavilions and shelters were erected for the Wardens and their followers; but on this occasion the number of these was vastly increased, and to add to the colour, vivid and variegated heraldic banners flapped in the breeze above many, as above the men-at-arms' camps and horse-lines.

When the Earl of Carrick's company arrived half-an-hour before noon, George of Dunbar and March was already there, he being responsible for arranging the meeting. His opposite number, Sir Henry Percy, the famous Hotspur, English East March Warden and heir of the old Earl of Northumberland, was also present; and the two, who were old friends, indeed kin, had all ready and were drinking wine together. Hotspur, a gallant figure now in his late thirties, was well known to most of the Scots notables, for he had been taken prisoner after Otterburn in 1388 and had thereafter spent over a year in Scotland whilst the new castle of Polnoon was being built for his captor, Sir John Montgomerie of Eaglesham, its cost being the price of his release. He was a cheerful character, however arrogant, and good company when he considered that company up to his exacting standards — for to be sure he was one of the foremost champions of England, indeed Christendom, in the lists if not necessarily on the battlefield. He now greeted David Stewart with an easy, half-mocking deference, and Montgomerie his former captor with real warmth. He had a distinct burr, almost stammer in his speech — but none would dare call it a hesitancy or impediment.

These greetings were still in progress when the Earl of Douglas arrived, and he and his entourage were included in the welcome. Archie the Grim, although still a formidable, not to say daunting, character, at seventy-three had mellowed somewhat. Tall though bent, like a great stooping eagle, beak-nosed, iron-grey, harsh-voiced, irascible, he nevertheless was less feared than formerly, although few could ever be close to him — including his silent, watchful, scarcely likeable son, the Master of Douglas. The Earl's hot temper was proverbial, but he was reckoned an honest man, insofar as his position as head of the most powerful house in Scotland permitted, his long-term support and even friendship for the Governor wondered at but accepted as an idiosyncrasy — and possibly, conceivably, implying some virtue in Robert Stewart not generally discoverable. He greeted the heir to the throne warily, was barely civil to Hotspur, looked pityingly at Angus, ignored Dunbar entirely, and clanked and

63

stamped about in half-armour and great spurs, hawking and spitting, glaring at all and sundry but not actually attacking anyone. More diplomatic Douglas relations were left to James, Lord of Dalkeith and Morton, a grave, courteous man in his mid-sixties, statesman rather than warrior, comfortably built, reputed to be the wealthiest noble in the kingdom. Jamie was, as almost always, quietly proud of his sire, who tended to show up well in most company, although he had chosen to adhere to the opposite side in the Scottish dichotomy from his illegitimate son. That Dalkeith supported the Earl Robert, as at least capable of holding a strong hand on the chronically unstable helm of Scotland, instead of the King's nerveless grasp, was apt to be a source of unease, not only to Jamie but to others who liked and admired him, not least the Lady Isabel Stewart, to whom he had acted protector on her husband's murder. He was, moreover, known to think but poorly of the Earl of Carrick.

The Governor's arrival could have provided a dramatic moment — save that there was little of the overtly dramatic about Robert Stewart, however much so his actions might be, on occasion. Cold, reserved, disapproving, he gave no impression of being emotionally involved in any way as he rode up to the meeting-place, save in a general distaste for all he saw. Soberly but richly clad, spare of figure, upright of carriage, he remained in his saddle, waiting until others came forward to receive him suitably.

David did that, cheerfully unabashed. "So, Uncle — you honour us with your presence!" he called, but without haste or coming close. "Excellent. I am glad that you have come to recognise the importance of what we seek to do."

"I recognise folly, insolence and youthful rashness, Nephew," the other answered thinly. "As I have had occasion to do ere this! And so am come, to seek undo such ill as folly may breed, in affairs best left to men of full age and experience."

"Ah — that is kind! To come aid us, in our immaturity. All here will be grateful, Uncle, I have no doubt — including the Earl of Douglas, whose immaturity and inexperience I had scarce recognised! Sir Harry Percy, here, you will remember ...?"

"Where is Lancaster? John of Gaunt?"

"He is not yet here. But he is not far off, I am told. Come — a cup of wine while we wait ..."

The Earl Robert ignored that, and urged his horse aside,

64

over to where the undifferenced banner of Douglas waved above a pavilion — the only one, presumably, in which he was prepared to bestow his person.

"It looks ill," Angus said unhappily. "He is set against us. He will ruin all."

"Never think it," the prince assured. "He can do little here against us, without offending his friend Douglas — I shall see to that! Jamie — you are able to enter the Douglas tent unannounced, to speak with your father, if naught else. Go you, and try to hear what goes on between them. I need to know how the Earl Archie will behave, if I can. How he is disposed towards the Governor's strictures. John of Gaunt is an old friend of Douglas's, I am told, but mislikes my Uncle Robert. Watch and listen, for so long as you may . . ."

Jamie Douglas had indeed no difficulty in slipping into the Earl of Douglas's large pavilion, for the Master was standing in the doorway, with his overweight brother known as Sir James the Gross, and with them he was on good enough terms. Within, it was uncomfortably crowded, many of the Governor's supporters having followed their master in. Jamie's presence went scarcely noticed. The Lord of Dalkeith was talking with the two earls, and his son moved as close as he might, waiting ostensibly for speech with his father. It was not easy to hear all that was being said, however, for the noise of the general chatter.

It was sufficiently clear that the Earl Robert's displeasure was not being confined to his nephew, and the Douglas was finding it necessary to defend his own presence there in no uncertain fashion, Dalkeith as ever seeking to pour oil on troubled waters. Archie the Grim was barking out that he must needs protect his own interests, not only as West March Warden but because lands of his own were being preyed upon by English raiding parties, and especially by the impudent English garrison of Roxburgh Castle. The captain there was indeed demanding no less than £2,000 of compensation from him for his son James's breaking down of Roxburgh bridge — and this five miles within Scotland! Moreover, the Percy was claiming actual rights of use and want within Ettrick Forest, *his* Forest, seeking damages from him, Douglas, for having fired his camp there. To such a state had matters come in this Borderland . . .

Testily the Governor replied than none knew better than he that the English were insolent ever. But far more was at stake

65

this day than any mere Border bickering. The due and proper rule of the realm was being challenged.

With the Douglas earl spluttering that the continued occupation of Scots' castles by Englishmen, and demands for thousands of pounds compensation, was scarcely mere bickering, Dalkeith soothingly suggested that it was all a question of which to deal with first, the cause or the effect. If they could strike at the roots of the English trouble, rather than the branches, they would achieve the more.

This seemed to mollify both men somewhat, since each evidently considered it to substantiate his own contention. The Governor's further assertion that his nephew's head was swelled altogether too large for a youth not yet of full age, and required to be reduced not a little, was accepted. But when he added that the young man was a fool and a dangerous fool, Dalkeith demurred, declaring that he believed him far from a fool; and that the danger could well lie in treating him as such. Rash and impetuous, yes — but these were common failings in young men of spirit. Safer to deal with him in such fashion, than to deem him fool and so underestimate him. Was that not why they were here? This point of view seemed to irritate the Earl Robert, who snapped that he required no advice as to how to deal with his brother's son, and was not going to have an arrogant stripling summoning English leaders to meet him, without the authority of the kingdom's Governor. He alone was competent to deal with Lancaster — as he would demonstrate. Why the proud Plantagenet had consented to come in the first place, he did not know. But if come he did, it was not for young Carrick to deal with him.

Archie the Grim was declaring that he did not care who dealt with his old gossip John of Gaunt so long as he obtained his rights, when a cry from outside intimated that the Duke of Lancaster approached. As they all trooped out to watch, Dalkeith perceived his son's presence.

"Ha, Jamie — I heard that you were here. You would be, to be sure. You have a habit of being where trouble is, these days — if not stirring it up! What are you at, here? What does the prince think he can achieve?"

"Much, my lord. For the good of the realm. Much that the Governor has not done, and appears to care naught for."

"Concerned with Lancaster?"

"Yes. In part." Jamie was wary. For though he loved and

admired his father they were seemingly on opposite sides in this, as in much. "But since you support the Governor, sir, we shall not agree on it."

"I do not support him blindly, lad," the older man said, low-voiced. "Nor wholly. Where what he does seems to be in the realm's interest, I support him, yes, in the cause of good government, of *any* firm government. He *is* the Governor, and until another is appointed it is all true men's duty to support him insofar as their consciences allow."

"How can you say that, in honesty, sir? When so much that he does is evil, oppressive, dishonest, contrary to all good conscience. You, a man of religious faith . . ."

"Perhaps, Jamie, I see things less clearly-cut, at sixty-seven years, than you do at twenty-seven! Kings and rulers cannot be judged by the same standards as ordinary men, they frequently must do deeds, in the interests of government, which would be wrongful in lesser men. You will learn as much, if so be you grow in wisdom with the years! All is not conveniently black and white, lad. I love not Robert Stewart — but the nation had *no* government until he took it in hand. Remember that. He has many faults — but so have I, to be sure. Even you may have one or two! We must make do with what we have, in matters of state."

"Thank God, then, that we have a prince and heir to the throne who is otherwise. Who will rule honestly, fairly."

"You think so? How good to have your young certainty. Does David seek the rule, then? Think to replace his uncle?"

Jamie bit his lip. "In due course," he said, more carefully. "His time will come."

"No doubt. But he would hasten it a little, perhaps? And hopes this meeting with Lancaster might aid in that?"

Unwilling to be questioned further, the young man made for the tent-door. "As to that, I cannot say, my lord. Ask him yourself. I must go to him, now . . ."

"Hear this, son," his father said, at his back. "I am not so thirled to Robert Stewart that I would seek spoil young David's chances, this day or other, should they seem to me to be for the realm's good. And you can say the same for Archie Douglas. We are no creatures of the Governor's. I made a compact with Archie, you will recollect, lang syne, to support him so long as he sought to counter his friend Fife's excesses. That stands — but our interest is the realm's, and Douglas's, weal, not Stewart's. Mind it."

Jamie turned to look at his sire for a moment, searchingly; then nodding, moved outside the pavilion.

A splendid cavalcade, ablaze with heraldry and banners, under the great standards of the Plantagenet leopards and of Lancaster, was quite close at hand, perhaps two hundred strong, approaching from the south-west, from the woodlands of Haddonrig, emitting the music of instrumentalists as it came. Sir Henry Percy and the Earl of Dunbar were already moving out to meet it.

Jamie hurried through the crowd to where the Earl David waited, some way apart from the Governor and Douglas.

"See there," the prince said. "We have achieved our first aim. We have brought John of Gaunt to parley with us. He would not have come, I vow, had he not been prepared to treat. Now I needs must play my fish to best advantage. But the invasion will not take place, I think, and Donald of the Isles be disappointed. Islanded, indeed!" He turned. "Well, Jamie—did you discover aught?"

"Only that the Governor deems himself alone able to deal with the Duke of Lancaster. Intends to do so. But that the Earl of Douglas and my father are by no means wholly thirled to him. They will choose their own course, as they see best. Best for the kingdom. And for Douglas."

"Ah! Then we must see that my uncle learns a lesson — and that Douglas is well served. Eh, Jamie Douglas?"

The leaders of the newly-arrived English party had dismounted, their musicians still playing a rousing air, and were now approaching on foot, with the Wardens Percy and Dunbar. These two had their instructions to bring the visitors directly to the Earl David; but, from his flanking position, the Earl Robert stepped forward to intercept.

"My lord Duke — welcome to Scottish soil," he called, having to raise his voice — something that man very seldom permitted himself — although his words remained clipped, flat as ever.

John of Gaunt paused, half-turned and inclined his head. He was a heavily-built, florid man in his late fifties, with prominent features which might have been graven in stone, and an imperious mien and bearing. Splendidly dressed and bejewelled, with gold-braided tunic and fur-lined travelling cloak, he was the fourth son of Edward the Third, born in Ghent, and had for a time assumed the crown of Castile, in right of his wife, moreover succeeding his brother, the Black Prince, as Duke of Aquitaine.

"My lord," he acknowledged, briefly.

"It is our pleasure to see you once more — and in more comfortable state," the Governor went on, with rather obvious lack of warmth. The last time that Lancaster had been in Scotland he had been taking judicious refuge after the revolt of the peasants led by Wat Tyler, in 1381, in which he was suspected of having a hand — although a few months later he had led an armed host over the Border on a limited raid which almost got to Edinburgh.

Lindsay of Crawford gripped the Earl David's arm. "He is seeking to oust you, here," he declared. "To take command of the meeting."

"Let him be," the prince said. "He will find that difficult. He has little that Lancaster wants — whereas I think that I *have*."

"Greetings, my lord Duke!" the Earl Archie cried — who had been both host and opposing commander to the Plantagenet on various occasions.

The other inclined his head but did not answer. He looked towards the Earl of Carrick. That young man took a couple of steps forward, as acknowledgement and encouragement; and gravely Lancaster resumed his onward pacing, a man of inbuilt dignity and formal behaviour. David of Carrick, although less powerful than the Governor, nevertheless held precedence there, as heir to the throne, High Steward and second man in the kingdom. Only to him could the Duke speak, in the first instance.

"Cousin — well met!" the younger man said genially. They were not any sort of cousins, in no kinship at all; but the term emphasised their special status, both sons of kings. Fife could have said the same, but had not. "You have ridden far today? You are not wearied, I hope? Your presence here gives pleasure and satisfaction to us all. Your fame precedes you."

John of Gaunt eyed the speaker keenly and took his time to answer. "I thank you," he said. "I am not wearied. Your letters I read — and understood. I deemed it best to talk with you." Clearly the Duke was a man of few words.

"Best, yes. We have much to discuss. First, however, wine to refresh you. My tent is yonder. But — here is my lord Bishop of St. Andrews. And my lord Bishop of Glasgow. Likewise, my lord of Crawford. Of Erroll, the Constable. Of Calder. Of Eaglesham . . ."

After the introductions, as Lancaster was led into the prince's pavilion, the Earl of Douglas stamped over to join them, muttering into his beard. The Earl of Fife however, did not. Expressionless he watched, and then turned and pushed past the Lord of Dalkeith, back into the Douglas tent, alone.

* * *

It suited both parties that the proceedings should seem to take the form of an ordinary Wardens' meeting, within a recognised framework. Face had to be preserved, dignity maintained intact, if anything real was to be achieved. This way was best, enabling the true principals to seem merely to sit in on the transactions, making their interpolations as and when it suited them, masking the significance of their contributions under the guise of advice and guidance. Moreover, for David Stewart, it had the very important advantage that it forestalled any move by the Governor to chair or manage the meeting. The two Wardens were automatically in charge, and since it was being held on Scottish soil, the Earl of Dunbar and March opened the proceedings.

George Dunbar was no more a wordy man than was Lancaster. The proceedings were held, as usual, in the open air, so that as many as possible might see and hear justice being done according to the special Border law. He commenced by declaring that this was a duly constituted court of justice for the East March of the Border, binding on both sides thereof, called as was their right and duty by himself and Sir Henry Percy of Northumberland. They were privileged to have with them on this occasion the lord Duke of Lancaster, uncle to King Richard, on the English side; and David, Earl of Carrick, High Steward and Prince of Scotland on the Scots side. Also the Governor, the Earl of Fife and Menteith, honoured their deliberations with his presence. Let the first issue be raised.

A typical Borderline case was put before them, in which one Wattie Home, in Thortersyke in the parish of Birgham, in the Scots Merse, claimed that Samuel Payne, known as Fenwick's Sam, in Chatton-on-Till, had crossed the March on the night of November 15th last, St. Margaret's Eve, and driven off from his outfield five of his best kye, two in calf. Because his, Home's, wife was labouring with their first child at the time, he was unable to follow up the raiders until the child was born, which was a day and a night later. When he rode over the March into the Vale of Till with his friends, to regain his beasts, as was his right, they were assailed by Fenwick's Sam and his neighbours, to the effusion of blood, and were driven off and sorely pursued back to Scotland, contrary to all the law of the Marches. He now claimed the return of his beasts, with the two calves, plus due compensation.

Sir Henry Percy then called Samuel Payne, in Powsall Rig, Chatton-on-Till, who admitted that he was known as Fenwick's Sam and that he had, on the night stated, taken the said kye from Thortersyke over in the Scots Merse, this because of injury done to him by the said Walter Home, at Bellingham Fair three months earlier, over the sale of a broken-winded nag. He asserted that the said Wattie Home was no better than a Scots rogue and thief and well-known as such. Moreover he could not claim hot-trod rights to recover the kye, since as all knew it was necessary for the trod to be hot that it should be ridden within twenty-four hours of the alleged offence. This had not been done; indeed it was nearer forty-eight hours than twenty-four before the Homes crossed the March. Therefore their lordships should dismiss the claim as incompetent.

All this in the broadest of Border accents, unintelligible to certain of the illustrious hearers, who indeed looked thoroughly bewildered.

The two Wardens eyed each other, Hotspur raised one shoulder fractionally. Dunbar nodded, and demanded whether Fenwick's Sam had never heard of the *cold*-trod, whereby action could be taken for recovery within six days?

The Northumbrian was vehement that there was no such thing.

A debate developed over the legal effectiveness of the so-called cold-trod, Borderers on both sides joining in loudly, until Hotspur held up his hand.

"Enough!" he cried, in his slightly stammering though commanding voice, "or we shall be here all day, on this one issue. My decision is this. The cold-trod, right or wrong, can be debated on another occasion. In this case I say that the man Home was entitled to remain with his wife over the birth of their firstborn, and in a difficult labour. He should not be penalised thereby. He followed the trod as quickly as he was able, and should not have been assailed. But Sam Payne was not necessarily to know this. Therefore my judgement is that the kye be returned, lacking the two calves, which Payne has

71

nurtured since November. And no compensation to be paid."
He raised eyebrows at Dunbar.

That man nodded. "Accepted," he said. "But since Home is
tenant of a vassal of my own, I shall pay him compensation for
the calves. This for judgement. Next?"

There was no argument by the litigants, nor delay in bringing
forward the next case. It was fairly straightforward. Returning
from the last Day of Truce six months earlier, when the Wardens
had met at Cornhill-on-Tweed, one Pate Swinton, dealer in
Kelso, had in the ale-house of Mother Shipley at Learmouth,
struck the complainer John Robson also a dealer, of Branxton,
known as Robbie Doddie, whereby he was unable to ride
abroad on his lawful occasions for the space of many months —
indeed could not be present today on account of the said injury,
wherefore his claim was being presented by his brother. The
man Swinton had ridden fast over the March, after the offence,
and no punishment nor recompense had been obtained. Such
was demanded now, the offence being committed on an
undoubted Day of Truce.

Pate Swinton, who admitted the assault, pointed out that he
had been grievously insulted by the said Robbie Doddie, himself
a notour horse-coper; moreover, he had been drink-taken at
the time.

Dunbar imposed a fine of one silver merk to the Warden's
Fund and two silver merks compensation to the injured man,
Hotspur agreeing.

It was during the succeeding hearing concerning a trespass
committed on ground which was debatable, that is, where the
Borderline was less than distinctly defined on a hillside on Steer
Rig near Old Halterburnhead, that signs of restiveness amongst
the more important onlookers became too apparent to ignore.
The Earl David nudged Dunbar's elbow, and that man, catching
Hotspur Percy's eye, intervened to declare that he would
appoint two commissioners to proceed to the spot in question,
there to decide whether the offence was in fact committed on
Scots or English ground, and whether the offenders paid fealty
to Scots or English feudal barons, or both, as some were con-
tending. He hoped that Sir Henry Percy would do likewise. If
agreeable, case continued until commissioners reported.

Hotspur acceding, looked round. "My brother, Sir Ralph
Percy, to speak. In another matter," he announced, almost
without pause.

The quality, if not the local Border folk present, drew deep breaths. Now they would get down to matters of some moment.

Sir Ralph Percy was a very different man from his gallant and extrovert brother, quiet, thoughtful, restrained. He had been badly wounded at Otterburn nine years previously and still walked with a pronounced limp.

"I speak to this, my lords," he began, almost apologetically, "since my brother is Warden here and so may feel prevented from speaking to it with freedom. But the matter concerns his interests, and those of our father, the Earl of Northumberland. I hereby make complaint against Archibald Earl of Douglas, his son Sir James, called the Gross, and others, servants of theirs, that they did violently attack and burn the camp of my brother, Sir Henry Percy, within the Forest of Jedburgh, on the 20th day of October last, to the death of four of King Richard's lieges, the destruction of much valuable property and the theft of nine good horses. For which shameful and warlike act, due reparation is demanded, punishment required upon the offenders, however illustrious, and assurances given that such assault will not be repeated."

There was silence round that great circle as men considered the significance of that statement.

The harsh, gravelly voice of Archie the Grim broke the hush, and strongly. "It will not have escaped the notice of you all, my lords, that the alleged offence was committed in the Forest of Jedburgh, in Scotland, and against Englishmen. Moreover, on *my* property! On whose authority were Sir Henry Percy's men in Jedburgh Forest, far beyond their own borders. And what doing?"

Sir Ralph looked at his brother, who nodded and took over. "Easily answered, my lord," Hotspur said. "They were hunting buck in that part of the Forest near to Roxburgh Castle, known as Sunlawshill. As was their right. As all know the Forest extends far beyond Jedburgh, and the offence was committed in that part which comes within the demesne of Roxburgh Castle. Which castle is held by Sir Philip Stanley, under my overall authority, for the King of England . . ."

"God damn you, Percy!" the Earl Archie snarled. "Roxburgh is in Scotland."

"But held by King Richard, as is Berwick Castle, and so agreed and accepted under the terms of the current truce, renewed three years ago, my lord."

"No. No, I say! No truce gives Englishmen the right to ride abroad at will in Scotland, and on *Douglas* property. To hunt *my* deer. To fray with my servants."

The Percy shrugged. "Are Douglas deer excepted from the truce? That truce, my lord, confirmed the *status quo* at date of renewal. Roxburgh and Berwick Castles, with their demesnes, were and are occupied by English garrisons, and as such are covered by the terms of truce." He turned to look directly at the Earl of Fife. "You, my lord Governor, signed that renewal, in the name of your royal father. Can you deny that this is so?"

Robert Stewart moistened thin lips. "I signed, yes," he said coldly. "The truce confirmed the *status quo*. But it gives no especial rights or privileges to Englishmen in Scotland."

"Is it an especial privilege not to be attacked by Douglas bravoes when on peaceable and lawful employ?"

"Mind you words, sirrah!" Archie the Grim exclaimed.

The Governor stared blankly but said nothing more.

"If my words offend, Douglas, show me how they err," Hotspur went on. "You cannot deny the attack and damage. You cannot deny that the east portion of Jedburgh Forest has long been the demesne of Roxburgh Castle. You cannot deny that the English occupation of that castle is confirmed by the truce which your Governor signed. If you have any quarrel, it appears that it should be with him, not with us!"

"Insolent!" Douglas swung on Lancaster. "Do you permit your spokesman so to insult us, on Scots soil?" And when John of Gaunt made no answer, he turned to Robert Stewart. "You, my lord Governor — teach this arrogant Percy to curb his ill tongue. And not again to challenge Douglas on Douglas territory — or suffer another Otterburn, by God!"

"I did not call this meeting," Fife said. "I did not invite Sir Henry Percy on to Scots soil. Address your complaints, my lord, to him who did!"

Every eye turned to the Earl David. That young man smiled pleasantly. "Let us discuss this matter reasonably, my good lords," he suggested. "It seems to me that the Earl of Douglas has much right on his side. He is undoubtedly feudal superior of the Forest of Jedburgh, and the deer in that forest his. If the Percys were indeed hunting buck therein, then he or his had the right to interfere. If that was, in fact, the true reason for the English presence there? After all, I would have thought that

Sir Harry had a sufficiency of deer to hunt in his own wide territories?"

There was silence at that, from Hotspur as from all others.

"I put it to you, Sir Harry," the prince went on, conversationally, "that when the Douglases came upon your men, they were not indeed hunting but clad and equipped for war. Wearing steel jacks and helms, not hunting green, bearing lances and swords, not greenwood bows."

Hotspur shrugged. "In the lawless and ungoverned state of Scotland, all who venture abroad are well advised to go so provided!" he gave back. "Whether so be they hunt, journey or attend Wardens' meetings!"

"Ha! So you claim that Scotland is misgoverned? Or was it ungoverned?"

"Why, I do, my lord — since that is my experience. And that of others."

All glances swivelled back to the Governor, as breaths were held. That self-contained individual did not rant or bluster. He merely turned to where John of Gaunt sat stroking his jowelled chin.

"My lord of Lancaster — restrain this man," he snapped.

The Duke gave a single shake of his grizzled head. "Sir Harry Percy is Warden of this March, and may speak his mind here," he said heavily.

"I insist, sir," the Governor declared, steely-voiced.

"No-one insists to *me*, my lord."

"In Lancaster perhaps not, sir. In England, even. But you are here on Scottish soil. And I govern in Scotland. I insist that you restrain your Englishry. I will not be insulted by any soever, on my own territory."

"Any more than will I!" Archibald Douglas cried.

Lancaster rose from his wooden bench. "Then I shall leave your territory, and gladly, my lord," he said evenly. "But . . . I do not promise that I will not be back! In different garb!"

David Stewart spoke up. "My lords, my lords — here is no cause for offence, I swear. Probably the fault is mine. I may have seemed to accuse Sir Harry of sending his men into Scotland on warlike intent. Spying out the land, or something such. That was not my mind. Merely that they seemed not to be hunting, from what I have heard. But with all this talk of English invasion imminent, we Scots are perhaps over delicate."

Men eyed each other wonderingly. To most present indubitably this was the first they had heard of any projected invasion. Lancaster, who had been turning to move away, paused. Moments passed, without a word spoken.

With an easy laugh the young prince waved his hand. "Forgive us then, Sir Harry. And do not accuse my good uncle of misgovernment! And you, my lord Duke, be pleased to sit again, I pray. For we have much to discuss yet, have we not? Of more profit."

Most of the English who had seats had risen automatically when their leader did. Now they sat down, one after another, and the Duke, dignity suddenly at stake, appeared to decide that it was probably less feeble to sit again than to remain standing uncertainly, alone.

"This of profit, then," he jerked, resuming his seat. "Let us have it."

"To be sure. If the Lords Warden will permit? And leave Sir Harry's claim meantime, for another. This concerns a claim also against the Earl of Douglas and his son, this time made by Sir Philip Stanley, English captain in Roxburgh Castle, for £2,000 compensation for the destruction of Roxburgh bridge. My lord Governor, do you wish you speak to this?"

His uncle stared out of these colourless eyes, mouth like a trap. But as all watched, he had to speak. "I know nothing of any such," he said flatly. "Nor can conceive it possible."

"Ah. Yet the claim is made, Uncle, and falls to be considered." David did not add that the claim had been made only two days earlier, direct to the Scots Warden, and Dunbar had been instructed to keep quiet about it.

Percy spoke. "Sir Philip Stanley cannot be present but has given me the terms of his claim. The moneys are for the cost of rebuilding the bridge, and for inconvenience and delay caused by lack of the bridge."

"Insufferable!" the Governor said.

"My son destroyed that bridge, as he did others, for good and sufficient reason," Douglas asserted. "For the better security of this realm. It is a Scots bridge, built by Scots hands, within Scotland and on my land. How can any Englishman claim anything concerning it."

"The bridge served Roxburgh Castle across Teviot, my lord. All who travel to Roxburgh, from the South, from Berwick, even from Kelso, must use it."

"Precisely. That is why it was destroyed."

"And why we who hold **Roxburgh** and **Berwick**, by treaty, demand compensation."

"You do not hold these Scots castles by treaty, but by armed invasion and conquest."

"The signed truce is a treaty, as is its renewal. Confirming, whilst it lasts, the *status quo*."

"Damn the truce and the *status quo*!"

"You damn the man who signed it, Douglas!"

David appeared to come to the rescue of his uncle again. "We must not wholly blame what seems to be an ill-made treaty or truce on he who signed it," he objected, moderately. "The greater good of the whole realm, of the two realms, was no doubt paramount over Douglas and Border interests. Was it not, my lord Governor?"

Only the quiver of Robert Stewart's slender nostrils betrayed his fury. "Enough of this folly," he jerked. "No such claim is to be considered."

"The claim is against Douglas," Percy insisted. "On behalf of King Richard, not myself. I but speak for his captain of Roxburgh." And he looked at Lancaster for support.

"The claim is fair," that man nodded.

It was Robert Stewart's turn to rise to his feet. "This is not to be borne," he said. "Such English arrogance is beyond belief."

"Are you speaking to me, sir?" Lancaster demanded. "Watch your words. I would have you know that . . ."

"Dunbar," the Governor ordered, breaking in. "Close this travesty of a meeting. I will have no more."

"How dare you interrupt my speaking, sir!" John of Gaunt exclaimed. "No man in Christendom may do that. I am not finished . . ."

"But I am! And this is Scotland, where *I* rule. The meeting is closed — as it should never have been opened."

"And I say no!" Lancaster thundered. "I have not come so far to be spurned aside thus."

"Will you outface me, sir? Me, the Governor?"

"Aye, will I! Governor of what? A sub-kingdom of which my nephew is Lord Paramount. As was my father. And his. Mind it. And mind who I am, man. I am Duke of Lancaster, Duke of Aquitaine, former King of Castile and Leon, nearest heir to the throne of England. You will give me the respect that is my due."

"I will give you nothing, sir — save permission to leave my borders, and forthwith!"

David Stewart stepped in once more. "My lord — *I* asked the Duke to come to this meeting. So that, in some measure, he is my guest, under my safe-conduct. In due course I shall escort him honourably over the March. When we have finished our deliberations."

"Then do so speedily."

"In my lord Duke's good time, Uncle. After all, he outranks us both in dignity, does he not? Not, I say, in this fable of English paramountcy, but as duke — where we, to be sure, are but earls!" The prince's smile indicated what he thought of such titular niceties.

"Young man," John of Gaunt said ponderously. "Hitherto I have discovered nothing to have made my journey from Lancaster worth the making. I have been miscalled, and I find all profitless. It is not my custom to suffer such treatment. I warn you all, I have the means to demonstrate my displeasure."

"No doubt, my lord Duke. You have already intimated as much, I think. Did you not say that you did not promise not to return, and in different garb? I took that to mean, at the head of an army? As you have done ere this."

Plain speaking at last, however pleasantly enunciated.

"You may take it as you will, sir."

"A threat, a palpable threat!" the Earl of Douglas asserted, grinning fiercely. "Will you cross swords with me again, my friend? In your other garb?"

"Hear who speaks of threats!" Hotspur cried. "Was it not Douglas who threatened another Otterburn, a little back? Invasion of England. War, in fact."

"To be sure. Two can play that game, Percy. You think to march into Scotland at will. What of your truce, now? What of this *status quo*?"

"You dream, Douglas — dream! You are getting old — an old man's delusion . . ."

"Old enough to recognise an insolent pup in need of schooling!" The Douglas–Percy feud seemed in no danger of dying. "Why think you my son broke down Roxburgh bridge? And others along Teviot and Tweed, Jed, Rule and Slitrig Waters? To hold up and hamper projected invasion, that is why! Invasion planned by you and Lancaster, to link with Donald of the Isles' descent upon my lordship of Galloway, in the west. That is why. We know it all."

In the succeeding hush the wheepling of curlew on the moorland rising behind was the only sound. It was out, now — the reason behind this entire assembly. And the Earl Archibald had been forced into the making of the disclosure, not David Stewart. Jamie Douglas looked at the prince with enhanced respect. It had all been masterfully done, the others, however illustrious, little more than puppets to dance to his skilful manipulation.

The Earl David's gaze was directed, not at Douglas, Percy or Lancaster, but at his Uncle Robert — on whose account everything had been plotted and guided, of course. As far as was possible with that sternly disciplined and unbending character, the Governor was looking almost bewildered, at a loss. Clearly no hint of the English invasion threat had reached him, despite his multitude of spies — as had been David's major preoccupation. That the Douglas had kept it to himself, as requested, was in fact the most hopeful indication of all, proof that Archie the Grim could be detached from the Governor's party, that he resented still the Chief Wardenship having been filched from him and then left contemptuously neglected; proof that he recognised misgovernment, especially in the policy towards England and in the terms of the truce which had been used to hurt him so. He might only be teaching his former ally a lesson, of course. But it all represented a notable advance for the Earl David's cause.

That young man saw the moment as ripe for the further and final pressure. "My lord Duke has come here to speak to this matter of invasion talk, I think," he observed. "No doubt he will dispel all such fears as groundless?"

Lancaster took his time to answer that. "If we are threatened, we protect ourselves," he said, at length, carefully.

"To be sure. So must all. But Scotland poses no threat to England, at this time. Has not my uncle here signed this notable truce? It may not comfort Douglas and the Borders, but at least it must comfort England!"

"What but a threat to England, my lord of Carrick, are the many Scots troops massed on the Isle of Man, opposite my Lancaster shores? Troops and ships."

"Ah, that. You have had your answer from the Earl of Douglas. My seditious cousin, Donald of the Isles, in what he deplorably calls treaty with King Richard, assembles galleys and birlinns for a descent on Galloway and the West March. The word is that King Richard will despatch forces to join him, over our Marches. But on this we are confident that you can reassure us. So my lord of Dunbar, who is also Lord of Man, takes due precautions. Against the Islesmen. For Man is but twenty miles from Galloway. In sight, indeed. No threat need be looked for, towards *Lancaster*. Which is somewhat further off, is it not? Thirty miles?"

They eyed each other levelly for a few moments. This was what John of Gaunt had come for, this and nothing else. All the rest was, in a sense, unimportant, but play-acting, setting the scene.

"I am well pleased to hear it, sir," Lancaster said, at length — although he scarcely sounded it. "No such venture was envisaged. No such invasion. Whatever your barbarian Donald might devise."

"I was sure of it, my lord Duke. We may take it, then, that the only threat to our peace comes from the Islesmen? No English will support them?"

"Have I not said so, sir?"

David laughed, in friendliest fashion. "We are great sticklers for words, in Scotland. One of our many weaknesses. There is a word for it, which escapes me! You said, my lord, that no such invasion was *envisaged*. Not that no invasion would take place! A mere equivocation, admittedly. As though, when I said that no threat need be *looked* for from the Scots forces on Man, I meant that there still might be *un*looked-for developments! It would be a pity to misunderstand, or suffer ambiguity — eh, my lord Duke?"

The other frowned. "There need be no misunderstanding. I am a man of plain words. And not used to having my word doubted, sir."

"Of course not. And I the last to doubt it. Then, all is as it should be. We have the word of John of Gaunt, Duke of Lancaster, that there will be no English invasion over the Scots March; and you have mine that the Scots forces on Man will move only against Donald's Islesmen. What more might any desire? Your journey has not been wasted — nor that of any here. Eh, Uncle?"

The Governor, who had listened to this exchange in tight-lipped hostility towards all concerned, inclined his head slightly but did not commit himself to speech.

"The claims against Douglas?" Hotspur put in. "King Richard's and my own?"

"I suggest that you reconsider them, sir," David answered,

with just a touch of asperity. "Sir Philip Stanley likewise."

"Saints of God, yes!" the Earl Archibald agreed.

"*I* might reduce my claim somewhat," the Percy admitted judicially. "But I cannot commit my liege lord Richard to do so."

"No? I swear King Richard knows naught of this. But, since the claim is only made in his name, no doubt the Duke here, his uncle, can modify it. Especially as the bridge was broken in error, as it were. To counter this supposed invasion. After all, my lord of Douglas will have to build it up again!"

John of Gaunt shrugged. "We shall not bicker over a bridge," he said. "Forget the matter."

"Well spoken, sir. That, then, can conclude our business, my lords . . ."

"Save for *my* claim against Douglas," the persistent Hotspur reminded. "In this pass, I will accept £1,000 for damage to my camp, horseflesh and men, in Jedburgh Forest . . ."

"By God you will not!" That came out like an explosion from the hitherto genial, patient and smiling prince. In the twinkling of an eye, he was transformed to the personification of blazing royal rage and startling authority, quite frightening to see. "Jedburgh Forest may be Douglas's, but in the final instance it is the territory of *his* liege lord, my father, the King of Scots. Not one merk of £1,000 will I allow that Douglas or any other pay to any Englishman for rights claimed therein. Is it understood, sirrah?"

Surprise, shock even, registered on every face, shading to consternation and alarm where English, to delight, glee, where Scots. The Percy, dumbfounded at last, found not a word.

"My lord of Dunbar," the prince went on, crisply. "Close this meeting, if you please. I thank all who have attended. My lord Duke, I shall now escort you over the March — and consider it an honour." Most evidently in complete control of the situation, the Prince of Scotland called for horses.

After briefest leave-taking, variously stiff, and with the Earl David riding off with Lancaster in a southerly direction whilst Percy headed eastwards without delay and the Governor north-westwards still more expeditiously, Jamie Douglas found his father at his side.

"Well, son," the Lord of Dalkeith said, "that was a remark-able accomplishment. I have seldom seen the like, in a long life. Your prince has more to him than I had reckoned."

"*Your* prince also, sir."

"To be sure. We seem like to have a new kind of King in Scotland! It was masterly, from start to finish — especially the finish! As good as a play-acting."

"It was no playing," Jamie assured. "That was a bid for the governance of this realm. Before ever he ascends his father's throne."

"No doubt. And Robert Stewart perceived it as such. He will not take that kindly, mark you."

"No. But David, having planned thus far, will not be out-smarted easily."

"I hope not . . ."

"*You* hope not, Father — you who have supported the Governor hitherto? Do you change sides, then?"

"I told you before, lad, it is no question of taking sides. I seek first the weal of the realm, then the weal of Douglas. After this day, few will doubt where both lie! As, to be sure, was the prince's whole purpose."

"Will the Earl Archie then think as you do?"

"Need you ask? You heard him. His interests are made to seem to suffer most from the Governor's actions, or lack of action. The mockery of this truce. The danger to the Borders and Galloway — all now lifted by the heir to the throne! Who himself still accuses none of anything. What sort of a son has our sorry monarch produced?"

"One who intends to see justice and good government in the land."

"I hope so — I hope so, indeed. I hope that he is not . . . *too* clever, for his own and the kingdom's good."

"Why should he be?"

"He moved men around like pawns on a chess-board this day, Jamie. And few men, proud men, like that. The Governor he made look a fool and less than competent — and he is no fool. Lancaster he manipulated into committing himself not to invade. Hotspur he led on to his own destruction. Dunbar he used. All before other men. Today David Stewart demonstrated his ability, yes — but he made enemies in doing so, powerful enemies. He is going to need friends, lad, *friends* — not enemies."

"He made friends of Douglas, at least . . ."

IV

THEY DREW REIN on the long, rounded hill-crest and gazed down thankfully, all but wonderingly, on the vast green amphitheatre with the wide loch at its centre, so little to be anticipated in that seemingly illimitable wilderness of rock and peat and heather. Farflung, the bare hills reared on every hand, with here and there to be glimpsed the misty blue outlines of higher, farther mountains. To come across an enclave of greenness in the barren midst, not the emerald warning of bog and moss but the kindly green of hayfields and pasture, of water-meadows and even strips of tilth, of spreading birch-woods and the darker richness of Caledonian pines, was a joy and relief to the eyes of weary travellers. The entire Highland scene was beautiful, of course, although somewhat inimical to Lowland eyes; but the lofty moorlands of Braemoray, north of Strathspey, were particularly daunting, extensive, unrelenting, and all that August day Jamie Douglas's party had been traversing their heather wastes without sign of settlement, or even a house or the works of men — although not without sign of man himself, for well behind them, not always visible but ever present, the shadowy figures of men, many men, dogged them, dismounted wild Highlandmen, but apparently well able to keep up with the mounted Lowlanders on this rough terrain, even though the travellers had wisely exchanged their fine horses for shaggy, sturdy sure-footed garrons, six days ago back at Dunkeld in Atholl, on entering the true Highlands. Jamie at least knew who those shadows would be, and what they portended — for he had been here before.

"What place for a castle, by the Powers!" Pate Boyd exclaimed, pointing. "Whoever built yon hold must have misliked his fellow-men! Forby, it is a large place. What good can it serve, hidden away here?"

"More than you might think," Jamie told the prince's tough henchman. "This Lochindorb may seem lost, far from all. But, in fact, just to the north, beyond that ridge and col, is a notable hub of routes, coming out of sundry glens and passes, from the Laigh of Moray, from lower Strathspey, from Strathdearn and Strathnairn and Inverness and the Great Glen, as well as this we are on from upper Badenoch and the South. Whosoever holds Lochindorb Castle can control most of the North-East. That is why Edward of England, the first of the name, curse him, built it! The place was a small Comyn hold before that, a mere hunting-house. But Edward was a notable soldier and campaigner, whatever else, and saw its value. Like the late Wolf, who perceived that he might rule the North from here. And did."

In the midst of the roughly circular loch which lay in the centre of the great green hollow of the hills, a small island projected, wholly occupied by the towers and walls and battlements of a sizeable courtyard-type castle, with gatehouse-keep, flanking towers, curtains and outer and inner baileys. A flag flew from the gatehouse parapet, blue-and-gold, for Stewart. They rode down towards the loch, thirty well-armed horsemen of the royal guard, under Douglas and Boyd. It represented long journey's end.

"They will have been warned of our coming — unless Sir Alexander differs greatly from his late father," Jamie informed. "They maintain look-outs on every hill-top. And no doubt these behind us have sent a messenger hastening ahead."

That this was an accurate forecast was soon proved by the fact that boats were to be seen, presently, pulling out from the castle-island, a large flat ferry scow for horses and a smaller craft. These, and only these, were waiting for them at the jetty beside the scattering of rude cot-houses and cabins which comprised the castleton, at the mainland shore opposite the island; clearly no access to the castle was possible unless boats were despatched therefrom.

The young man who awaited them, with a group of gillies, at the jetty, was clad in simple short kilt, shirt and calfskin sleeveless jerkin, like the rest, but by his bearing and features was obviously of a different background — Sir James Stewart, youngest brother of Sir Alexander, now in his twentieth year, and good-looking in a raffish way. The late and alarming Earl of Buchan, the King's brother and so-called Wolf of Badenoch, who had for so long ruled these parts as Lieutenant and Justiciar of the North, had produced no legitimate offspring, for sufficient reasons though a surplus otherwise; but this family at Lochindorb, five sons, the children of the Lady Mariota de Athyn, his concubine, he had singled out from all the rest by knighting them all at an early age, in a gesture part-defiant, part-mocking, part-significant, so that they had constituted a kind of ruling family of the North. This one, probably the most presentable, next to his eldest brother Alexander, of a wild bunch, had become comparatively friendly with Jamie Douglas when he had been a hostage, if not prisoner, here seven years before.

"Jamie Douglas — it is yourself!" he cried, in a sibilant Highland lilt. "And nothing changed, by God — save that you are better escorted than once you were! We wondered who came, so well provided with steel, whatever."

"To be sure, friend — one learns caution if not wisdom, with the years. And you — you are a man now, and a brave one, I swear. Around the age I was then. When last I was here. I trust I find you all well at Lochindorb? It is three years now since your father died. But I saw Alexander near a year back, at the North Inch fight at Perth."

"Aye, that was a notable ploy — would I had been there. But someone must needs keep this place, when Alex is from home. As he is now . . ."

"He is not here? A plague — we have travelled a long way to see him. He is not far off . . . ?"

"Far enough. He is in Lochaber, with Andrew and Duncan. With swords unsheathed! Would God I was with them, instead of biding here looking after my mother and sister . . ."

"Lochaber! Dear God — so far! Is it this of Alastair Carrach MacDonald?"

"The same — the murdering brigand! He lays Lochaber waste."

"It is partly on his account that we are come. This is ill news. We shall have to follow him — Alexander. Follow your brothers . . ."

"Not this night, whatever," the young Stewart declared. "Come you over to the castle. My mother will joy to see you. She ever thinks well of you, often speaks of you. As does Margaret . . ."

So Jamie and Boyd were rowed over to the island, leaving their troop of thirty men-at-arms at the castleton.

The Lady Mariota de Athyn welcomed Jamie most warmly, almost embarrassingly so. Now in her late forties, she was a large, generous, cheerful and handsome Highland woman of character, one of the chiefly Mackays of Strathnaver, improbable to a degree as a notorious courtesan who had set the tongues of Scotland wagging. The fact was that she had been a good wife to the Earl of Buchan, although he could not marry her, having been wed to the heiress Countess Euphemia of Ross and Buchan at an early age, although he had never lived with her. The Lady Mariota had loved that extraordinary man, accepted all the difficulties and contumely that went with concubinage, made an excellent mother to his children, maintained this remote northern home of his, and exercised a beneficial influence upon one of the wildest characters ever Scotland had produced. She and Jamie had got on well, from the first. He had always treated her with respect, as wife and chatelaine.

Now she embraced him affectionately, comprehensively, and not really in motherly fashion, kissing him, holding him at arm's length for inspection and then pressing him back to her ample bosom for further kisses. He did not exactly struggle to be free — but would have preferred that the cynic Boyd should not have been an interested witness. Moreover, she was a strong woman.

When they could exchange more than breathless incoherencies, and he had muttered conventional sympathies over the death of the Earl — since when he had not seen her — he launched into an explanation of his presence there, and with an escort of the royal guard. He came on behalf of the Earl David — of whom the Lady Mariota in general approved — on an important, composite and quite difficult mission. The prince was seeking to unseat his uncle, the Governor, in a lengthy and elaborate campaign carefully thought out. In this cause it was necessary that the heir to the throne's own credit should be maintained and enhanced. One of the weaknesses of his position was that he had made scarcely an adequate Lieutenant and Justiciar of the North, indeed had not as yet so much as shown his face in these parts — this because of his great and many commitments in the South and the demands of this campaign. Jamie did not emphasise the large demands on the prince's time of whoring, drinking and general merrymaking, although no doubt the lady, who was not unfamiliar with the Stewart character, could assess that for herself. The Earl David had had to leave all in the North to deputies, up till now, notably Sir Alexander, her son. But it was important that, at a parliament or general council of the realm to be held in a few months' time, no stones should be hurled at him on account of any seeming neglect of his duties as representative of the Crown up here. So he planned a major visit or progress through the Lieutenancy before the winter set in; and he, Jamie Douglas, was here in the nature of a forerunner and smoother of the paths.

The Lady Mariota expressed herself as delighted at the prospect of seeing the prince again, and hoped that she would have the pleasure of entertaining him at Lochindorb.

Jamie's acknowledgement of that was somewhat preoccupied. The difficulty was, he pointed out, that there must be no *trouble* during the Earl David's tour. The situation demanded that it should be more in the nature of a triumphal progress, the holding of a few selected justice ayres, the appointment of sheriffs and officers, and so on. But no fighting or disputes. As for this wretched Alastair Carrach, Donald of the Isles' brother, his raiding and ravaging from the West, this must be stopped at all costs. Undoubtedly it was being done as a form of reprisal for Donald's intended descent on Galloway, and linking with the English, being countered by David.

Their hostess pointed out that this was what Alex and her other sons were now doing down in Lochaber, seeking to deal with Alastair Carrach. He had attacked and captured the royal castle of Urquhart, near Inverness, and left Maclaine of Lochbuy installed as keeper. Then he had retired again down the Great Glen, and was now dispossessing the Camerons and running riot around Arkaig and Lochy. Her boys were doing all they could, and manfully.

Jamie shifted his stance uncomfortably. "I am sure of it," he agreed. "And their prowess is not in doubt. But it is a matter of time, see you. The prince must make his progress here in the North before the onset of winter when the passes are closed and the rivers in spate. Not later than October. Less than two months now. And there must be no warfare, or the echoes of warfare, to mar it. His enemies would seize on that. So there is no time for any campaign against this Alastair. We must gain our ends . . . otherwise."

"Otherwise?" the lady repeated. "How think you to do that, Jamie my friend?"

He looked away. "Terms," he said. "We must come to terms, I fear."

"Terms! With Alastair! Save us — you do not know what you say! This is not like you, Jamie."

"No," he agreed unhappily. "But these are the prince's commands. I am sent to treat with the man and get him out of Scotland and back to his isles. At almost any price. And swiftly."

"Here is foolishness. Alastair will not be bought off cheaply, if at all. And no trust be put in any treating with him. He is a hard man. My lord knew how to deal with him. He would never have dared this raiding whilst the Earl lived. Cold steel he understands, only that. If not that what have you to offer him?"

"Sufficient, perhaps. This is no ordinary raiding, see you. It is not, in truth, Alastair whom we have to buy off, but his brother Donald. The Lord of the Isles is angry that his plan against Galloway and Man was brought to naught. We know now, what we had not understood earlier, that he intended to seize Man. And to keep it, to incorporate it in his island kingdom. And to use his alliance with King Richard to win complete independence from the Scottish Crown. So now he sends his brother raiding, not so much for gain, or in Highland feuding, but against the Crown. Why think you Alastair assailed and took a *royal* castle — Urquhart? That is not raiding, but a gesture. If Donald is making gestures, it is for a purpose — for he is no fool. So perhaps he will talk, bargain."

Doubtfully the woman shook her head. "And *you* think to bargain, to outwit Donald of the Isles, Jamie?" Undoubtedly that was not meant to be insulting, but there was no mistaking the implication.

He shrugged, and sought to change the subject.

Next morning early they left Lochindorb, returning as they had come, over the empty heather hills to mid-Strathspey, at Duthil on the Dulnain, young James Stewart glad to escort and guide them to his brothers, as excuse to get away from Lochindorb. Nothing was said about the shadowing hillmen who had dogged their heels the day before, minions undoubtedly of one of the Stewart half-brothers — for the Wolf had left a varied and sufficient progeny to ensure a kind of dynastic leadership

88

over all these vast territories. These men had followed them from the vicinity of Ruthven Castle, near to Kingussie, another of the Wolf's strongholds, and thus far the party reached that evening, with Stewart insisting that they spend the night there. It was a grimly amusing situation for Jamie, not only in that these same shadowers, who had found them too strong a company to interfere with on the way north, now must needs act hosts, after a fashion; the fact was that last time Jamie Douglas had been within these walls, it was as an ill-used prisoner in a cell. The Sir Andrew Stewart who then captained this fortress was now away in Lochaber with Sir Alexander, and only a surly half-brother by some undistinguished paramour, Rob Stewart, was in charge. Although considerably older than Sir James, and clearly disliking having to offer hospitality, however elementary, to the Lowlanders, he did not argue — an interesting commentary on the power and supremacy of the Lady Mariota's offspring over the rest of the Wolf's numerous brood. Considering this oafish Rob, it did not fail to cross Jamie's mind that he also was, nevertheless, a grandson of King Robert the Second and no more illegitimate than were Sir Alexander and his brothers.

Ruthven was a very different place from Lochindorb, set on a lofty mound amidst the flooded water-meadows of Spey, strong and quite large, but internally more like an encampment of gypsies, a sordid caravanserai, than a powerful baron's castle. No chatelaine kept this hold, however many slatternly women roosted therein. The visitors were glad to escape, with the sunrise.

They rode south by west through a lovely land, one of the fairest, so far as scenery went, in all Scotland, following the waterlogged meadows of Spey by Nuide and Ralia, through hanging woodlands of birch and forests of ancient and gnarled Caledonian pine, fording foaming, sparkling rivers, and with the great mountains ever shouldering close, a place of deer and wolf and wildfowl, of eagle and buzzard and blundering capercailzie. Where Glen Truim came in from the south, down from the lofty bare pass of Drumochter, the Spey took a pronounced bend almost due westwards into what seemed almost a new valley. This they followed, through Cattanach and Macpherson country. All the way they would have been challenged, obviously enough, for it was a fairly populous land, with cattle in all the open woodlands and the cabins of the clansfolk sending up their columns of blue woodsmoke into the August air; but young Sir James bore aloft his father's dread banner of Buchan and Stewart colours, which clearly still represented authority hereabouts. Following a well-defined drove-road, one of the main Highland routes into the West, they made fair progress, and camped for the second night a few miles beyond the foot of long Loch Laggan, Spey far behind now. They were here on the watershed of Highland Scotland, on the edge of the great lordship of Lochaber.

By noon of next day they were beginning to see traces of Alastair Carrach MacDonald's work, in the Braes of Lochaber, burned homesteads and cabins, slaughtered cattle, here and there the unburied bodies of men, women and children, not a few hanging from roadside trees. The local folk now remained in hiding, but the condition of the corpses indicated that the killing had been done possibly a week previously. Eventually they came across a couple of cowherds, Camerons, who either recognised the Stewart banner or else were of bolder stuff than their fellows, who told the travellers that the word was that the accursed Islesmen were now ravaging and butchering in the Arkaig and Glen Loy areas, to the west, and that *Alastair mac Alastair Mor* — the Gaelic name for Sir Alexander Stewart — had followed them this way five days earlier.

They pressed on with enhanced urgency, their way fairly consistently downhill now through long Glen Spean, with the tang of the western ocean not infrequently in their nostrils, on the breeze, to add its piquancy to the prevailing scents of heather, pine, bog-myrtle — and burning.

By evening, they came down the frothing, spouting, cataract-strewn Spean to the more open levels of the lower end of Glen More, the Great Glen of Scotland, between Loch Lochy and Loch Linnhe, the latter but an arm of the Firth of Lorne and the Sea of the Hebrides. Emerging from Glen Spean, now indeed they were challenged, and fiercely — but by Badenoch men, Macphersons attached to Alexander's force. On ascertaining young Stewart's identity, although they eyed the Lowlanders with undisguised suspicion, they provided an escort to convoy them the few miles further to the main Badenoch camp. There had been no major clash with the Islesmen as yet, they reported.

The travellers came up with Alexander Stewart, at length, at Gairlochy where Spean joined Lochy under the abruptly-rising hills of Locheil and Wester Lochaber, here forming the west wall of the Great Glen. This was the traditional gathering-place of the Clan Cameron. Alexander and his brothers were waiting here for the fullest assembly of the Cameron manpower, for they were under no illusions as to the size of the task ahead in seeking a confrontation with the Islesmen. They had brought about eight hundred men from Badenoch, mainly Mackintoshes, MacGillivrays and Macphersons, of the Clan Chattan federation; but it had become very evident as they progressed that Alastair Carrach had far larger numbers with him than had been reported previously, possibly as many as 3,000 — and none underestimated the fighting qualities of the Clan Donald Islesmen, sea-rovers of the toughest breed. So every Cameron that Lochaber could produce was going to be required. Some nine hundred of them were already assembled, under the chieftains of two of the three branches, the MacGillonie of Strone and the MacMartin of Letter Finlay. But more, many more, were needed; the question was whether Alastair Carrach would give them time to muster. He was up the long side-glen of Arkaig, to the west, but known to be retracing his steps.

Alexander was as delighted as he was surprised to see the Douglas again — even though his brothers Andrew and Duncan were less so. He eyed the royal escort thoughtfully however.

Jamie was interested to see how very much in command the other was, without in any way making a display of it. Slighter, finer-made and superficially at least, gentler than any of his brothers, he nevertheless exercised his authority seemingly effortlessly — over the wild-looking Cameron chieftains also. His father, to be sure, had been Lord of Lochaber as well as Badenoch, through his lawful wife, who had inherited ancient Comyn lordships; and now Alexander was accepted as lord in his place, here in the North at any rate, whatever the Governor and parliament might say. Being a deputy of the Justiciar, too, enhanced his authority, giving him legal power; but it was the power of personality, of blood and birth, and of the sword, which really counted. However, his quiet air of mastery and leadership was obviously innate, a personal attribute rather than stemming from his position. Jamie had never had occasion to see him as a commander, hitherto, and was impressed.

But it was not long before they came to disagreement, nevertheless. When Alexander heard about the proposed coming to terms with the island invaders, he was as critical as his mother had been, declaring the whole notion as impossible as it was

91

unprofitable. Alastair would never treat, especially when he was in a position of strength, as now; besides, he required to be taught a lesson, not encouraged in aggression. His own cousin he might be, in blood, but he would hang him for a pirate and murderer, if he could lay hands on him.

"That would not please the prince, Alex — whose cousin he is also," Jamie pointed out, as they paced back and forth along Lochyside in the August gloaming light. "And you are here as the prince's deputy, in part. Alastair may deserve hanging — and David used to be a great one for hanging folk in the name of the realm's weal, in his father's Carrick! But, for policy's sake Alastair, and through him his brother Donald, must be kept quiet meantime, until David gains the governorship. Then it may be different."

"And what, my friend, will keep Alastair Carrach quiet, whatever, in this situation? He lives by the sword, the dirk and rapine, a captain of pirate galleys and gallowglasses; cold steel and the torch's flame the language he talks and understands. He may be a king's grandson — as are some of the rest of us! — but his standards are those of a jackal. You saw what he has done in Glen Spean and Glen Roy?"

Jamie nodded. It was on the tip of his tongue to say that his friend *ought* to know how to deal with such, since his own father had been the prince of jackals of all the land, a greater pirate and blood-letter than ever Alastair MacDonald could hope to be; but that would be to defeat his own case, for the Wolf at least had known how to keep the Islesmen in their place, and would have hooted at the Earl David's project in derision.

"See you, we — or at least the prince — has something to offer," he explained. "It is a most privy matter, but I can tell *you*, so long as no others learn of it. The offer, though made to Alastair, is for Donald's consideration. It is the earldom of Ross, no less. Donald has ever claimed it, in his wife's right. The Governor saw that her sister gained it, and through her, her weak son, the present Earl, who is wed to the Governor's daughter. Murky work. Once the Governor is unseated, David is prepared to support Donald's claim, and to move the King to support it. All the earldom save Easter Ross and the lordship of Ardmeanach and Cromartie, which the present Earl should be left. So Donald would get all Skye and Wester Ross. Is that not sufficient price for Alastair's return to his islands? That is what I am empowered to offer."

The other stared at the speaker for a long moment before commenting. "Changed days for Jamie Douglas!" he said, at length. "Is your Earl David corrupting you? You named it murky work, what Robert Stewart did with the Ross earldom. Is this less murky?"

"It is . . . statecraft."

"Perhaps. But less than honest, I think."

"Why should it be? If David is to oust his Uncle Robert from power, and keep him so, he is going to require friends, many and powerful friends. Or allies. If he could make his peace with Donald, he could be a most powerful friend. They are full cousins, after all . . ."

"The prince has over many full cousins! And Donald the least likely as friend. And the most dangerous. Better to have him as declared enemy, I say. See you, Donald is different from all others in this realm, Jamie — he considers himself *outside* it. He seeks independence from Scotland. Once, his forebears were Kings of the Isles — he seeks return to that state. And to advance his territories, to recover all that once was the great Somerled's — the earldom of Ross, yes, and much more. This Lochaber. Much of Argyll. Indeed, most of the North-West. And if he does gain all that, as price for his support of David, think you he will be content? Donald is clever, and of boundless ambition. I do not think you know what you attempt, you and your prince."

"*Your* prince likewise, Alex! And Donald's. One day to be King — and before long, perhaps, for King Robert is in poor health. And David is clever too. He has outwitted Donald once, at Haddonstank. He can do so again . . ."

"And does he intend to, in this of the earldom? Is it only a cheat?"

Jamie frowned. "No. Or not that I know of. He offers to bargain . . ."

"At *my* cost!"

"Yours? Why that?"

"I should have thought that easy to understand, friend. Lochaber was my father's, and is now mine, by right. Donald makes no secret of claiming it — why Alastair is here now. Not only that. The earldom of Ross flanks all the lordship of Badenoch to north and west. Alexander Leslie, the present Earl, is a quiet man, little menace. But let Donald of the Isles establish himself here on the mainland, and it will be constant war. As

Earl of Ross little of Badenoch will be secure from his ambitions. War not only with me and mine, but with the mainland clans — Clan Chattan, these Camerons, the Mackenzies, the Grants, the new Frasers, the MacMaths. Can you not see it? This may look like statecraft from Stirling or Perth. But from here it is the promise of war and bloodshed."

The Douglas looked at his friend concernedly, perplexedly. "Surely you mistake?" he objected. "Fear unnecessarily?" But he said it without conviction, for he did not underestimate Alexander's wits nor shrewdness.

The other shook his almost delicately handsome head. "No. Here we have cause to know Donald MacDonald better than you in the South do. And it is we who will suffer, in the first instance. I warn you, Jamie — say nothing of this your mission to my brothers here, as *I* will not. Or I fear not only for the mission but for your safety!"

"They would threaten the heir to the throne's envoy?"

"They are my father's sons — and see your Lowland affairs as little concern of theirs. Whereas Donald and Alastair are! And these Cameron chiefs I scarce think have ever heard of the Earl of Carrick!"

"Must I hide, then, within my escort of the royal guard? In *your* camp, Alex?"

"Not so. But — keep your lips closed on what you have told me."

"But I must get to Alastair. For that I have come all this long road."

"How do you propose to do that, my friend?"

"Go seek him out — what else? Up this Arkaig, where you say he is."

"He may welcome you less warmly than you think."

"Never fear — *he* has heard of the Earl of Carrick, if the Camerons have not! And I have my guard."

"Thirty against 3,000! Do not rely on Alastair's courtesy. He is a man who strikes first and talks afterwards! I fear for your mission as much as I fear its consequences." He looked away, at the now darkling hills, and slowly he spoke. "I do not know that I can allow it, Jamie."

From anyone else that would have brought forth a fairly harsh and unequivocal response. But these two knew and respected each other. Nevertheless, Jamie frowned blacker than he knew. "You would not seek to *halt* me!"

Alexander Stewart sighed and changed his tune a little. "See here — I think you still do not understand the position, Jamie. This is war we are at, here in Lochaber. Alastair has laid waste much of our land, and must be stopped, punished. He knows that we are here, waiting for him, and marches back down Arkaig — though he takes his time, sure of himself. He is much stronger in men than am I. We await reinforcement, more Camerons and the like. He will know that also. Think you he will delay and parley whilst we grow stronger? Accept your word and withdraw, whilst we sit here? His galley-fleet awaits him in Loch Linnhe; he must pass us here to reach it. Will he be prepared to believe that you can hold back us, and the Camerons, after what he has done to their glens? Not fall on him as he emerges from the *Mile Dorchaidh*, the Dark Mile, at the mouth of Arkaig? *I* would not so believe."

"You are set on fighting, then?"

The Stewart inclined his head. "I fear so. That is why we are here. You cannot assemble hundreds, thousands of Highland fighting-men who have seen their glens smoking, and then turn and say that talking will serve, that they should go home peaceably. Could you do that with Douglas mosstroopers? I do not know. But clansmen — no. You know the Cameron motto? *Chlanna nan con thigibh a so's gheibh sibh feoil*. Sons of the hounds, come here and get flesh!" He paused. "Jamie — give me two days. Till tomorrow night, at least. I shall then know better Alastair's position, his strength and my own. If I can check him, even in a limited fashion, he will be the more ready to talk, perhaps. That I *must* attempt — or my name and repute as Lord of Badenoch and Lochaber is discredited. Give me until tomorrow's night."

Douglas shrugged. "It seems that I have little option, does it not? Very well. Till tomorrow night . . ."

*   *   *

Jamie did not have to wait so long. By mid-forenoon next day reports were coming in of Alastair Carrach moving down Loch Arkaig-side with all speed now — and significantly, on both sides of the loch. Latest word put his forward parties at near Ardachvie on the north side and at the River Mallie crossing on the south — but three miles from the foot of the loch. Not only that, he had scouts out ahead in both the entrances to the glen, which could only indicate a tactical move. He was looking for a fight.

Arkaig was one of the many long valleys which branched westwards from the Great Glen, probing for nearly a score of miles into the mountains towards the western sea, but coming to something of a dead end well before reaching salt-water. It was a reasonably fertile and populous glen by West Highland standards, the main holding of the MacGillonie Camerons. But it differed from most similar east–west valleys in that it was something of a hanging valley, averaging some 150 feet above the Great Glen level, and all but blocked at its entrance by a great intrusive wedge of hill called *Torr a Mhuilt*, a glacial deposit. Two narrow exits skirted this land-mass to north and south, the former the main entrance to Arkaig through the constricted mile-long ravine known as the Dark Mile, a rocky and gloomy trough, wood-hung, threaded by the twisting, awkward drove-road. The southern pass was much more open, and through it the River Arkaig itself found its way, but the road did not follow it nevertheless, because that river, in its mile-long descent presented a mixture of cataracts and flooded flats, still more difficult to negotiate than the Dark Mile's constrictions. Both represented awkward exits militarily, and it looked as though Alastair was going to use them both. Alexander meantime, of course, had pickets lightly holding both.

He summoned his leaders, Jamie attending — but it was clear that this was not to be any council-of-war; only the details of his tactics remained to be worked out. He spoke to them in the musical sibilant Gaelic, so Jamie understood none of it, though gaining just a hint here and there from the finger pointing to various features of the landscape as he went on. He was interrupted frequently, especially by his brother Sir Andrew, with evident doubts, questions and suggestions; but clearly he held firmly to his own theme and decisions. These seemed to be accepted in the end, and presently his bearers hurried off, shouting for their own lieutenants.

Alexander turned to Jamie. "We must do the best we can," he explained. "Alastair divides his force — which might aid us. Or again might not. We do not know which route his main body will take — by the Dark Mile or the river. I think the river. We do not even know his full strength. I am sending companies to seek block both passes. But he will expect this — it is what any man would do. So there can be little surprise. All I may do is not to commit *my* main strength at first. Only comparatively weak parties into the passes, under my brothers. To delay

Alastair, and at the same time perhaps make him over-confident. He is a confident man, and has had these weeks all his own way. Pray that he remains that way, today!"

"And where *will* you place your main strength?"

He pointed. "Hidden, up there on the ridge of yonder hill, *Torr a Mhuilt.* In the birch-scrub and hollows. From up there I will be able to see down into both passes, in some measure. Can send my strength where most needed. Alastair will not know my numbers, either. It will provide little enough of surprise, but it may just serve."

"You are still determined to fight? Why not let me talk, instead?"

"No, Jamie. You may talk if we are defeated! I have drawn the sword, and must use it — or cease to lead Highlandmen."

The other shrugged. "As you will. What would you have me do then?"

Alexander eyed his friend keenly. "I would have you aid me this day, Jamie. In some small degree. Will you?" That was a question and no plea; but the Douglas could not fail to sense something of appeal.

"How aid you?" he asked, warily. "*I* am not here to fight."

"No. I do not ask you to fight. Only to, to make a gesture. See you, oddly, *you* in fact represent the only true surprise with which I can confront Alastair Carrach — cavalry. The Islesmen do not fight horsed — Highlanders seldom do. They cannot carry horses in their galleys. He may have captured a few garrons, for use as pack-animals for booty — that is all. His is a foot host — as is mine. But you have come with thirty horsed men-at-arms, of the royal guard. Armoured, and with banners and pennons . . ."

"Thirty only! A mere escort, not a fighting force . . ."

"True. But in this camp there are over a score of garrons — my own and my brothers' and some of the chieftains' riding-horses. Around here I could raise more, many more. There are plenty of garrons — only they are not used for fighting. We could mount men on them, contrive what would look like lances and banners, at a distance. Add these to your thirty. Then you could take up your stance on the high ground, where you would seem to threaten Alastair's flank. Let yourself be seen, a quite large cavalry force, ready to ride down upon the Islesmen. I believe that would cause him some alarm, give him pause."

97

Jamie stared. "You mean that I should just stand? On a hill? Do nothing? Play-acting . . . ?"

"To be sure, my friend. That is all I ask."

"But . . . I should feel the greatest fool."

"The hero of Otterburn, eh? But if the Douglas is prepared to come all this way to talk with Alastair, surely he is prepared to show himself? As being at least fit for more than talking."

The other chewed his lip. "Is there such a place? Where such stand could be made? Where cavalry could hope to operate?"

"There is, yes. Part way up the River Arkaig, on the south, the Achnacarry side. At the widest part of the pass, high above, is a lesser ridge, a half-mile back from the river. If you lined the crest of that. See you, I believe Alastair will come that way, with his main force, not through the Dark Mile. At this season the flooded meadows will be dry, passable. He will be laden with booty, his people sure of their strength. The Dark Mile is difficult and narrow. They would be much more strung out and apt for ambush. I will seek to trap him, nevertheless, by the riverside. And if cavalry, which he cannot have looked for, hold the high ground, he will be much distracted. Will you do it, Jamie?"

The Douglas spread his hands. He could not say no.

"My thanks. It may mean much. And Jamie — do not show yourselves until the enemy is well forward, so that he cannot change his advance. Now, sufficient of talk. Let us be doing . . ."

*　　　*　　　*

On the high bare heather slopes of the *Meall an t-Seamraig* ridge, with much of Lochaber spread below and the lochs of Lochy, Linnhe, Eil and the farther Firth of Lorn shining in the afternoon sun, Jamie Douglas looked back at his motley following, which straggled over a large area of the hill. From thus close-at-hand it certainly did not look like any sort of cavalry force — a gypsy encampment on the move, rather. The thirty troopers looked the more formidable and effective in contrast; but for the rest, it was an almost laughable sight. Alexander had scraped together almost a hundred beasts, of a kind, shaggy garrons and work-horses for carrying peats in panniers, in the main, some rather better riding animals, many mere ponies whose low-slung bellies brushed the high heather and whose riders' feet were apt to all but trail the ground. The said riders were as heterogeneous as their mounts, largely old men and boys unfit for the Cameron fighting strength, rounded up at short notice from herding, peat-cutting, from the cowshed and the cabin door, armed with every variety of weapon, however rusty and antique. They seemed cheerful enough, most appearing to look on it all as in the nature of a holiday — although none could speak other than the native Gaelic and so were unable to communicate with the Lowlanders. Not that there was any fraternising between the two parties anyway; the royal guard men-at-arms, in their gleaming breastplates and helmets, could scarcely have shown their scorn and disapproval more eloquently even if they had spoken the Gaelic.

Pate Boyd, riding beside Jamie, gestured. "This rabble wouldna frighten a coven of auld wives!" he asserted, not for the first time. "Guidsakes — we'll never hear the end o' this when we get back hame!"

"From a sufficient distance they may look better, Pate. But as well that we are only to stand and watch! That low ridge ahead — this guide keeps pointing to it. I take it that is where Sir Alexander would have us stand."

From up here, facing north, they could not see down into the short, deep valley of the Arkaig River, the swelling of hill ahead, a mere long fold in the heather rather than any ridge, preventing. There was a distinct dip, wet with black peat-hags, before it; and here Jamie ordered his curious company to wait, whilst he rode on with Boyd and the Cameron guide. Nearing the crest, if so it could be called, they dismounted and went carefully forward on foot.

They were unprepared for what they saw. Although it was comparatively level up here, really only a sort of heathery plateau, the terrain changed entirely before them, the ground falling away in a long and continuous grassy slope, quite steep, scored by small watercourses and dotted with carpets of bracken. At the foot, possibly six hundred feet below, there was a belt of green levels, no doubt flooded in winter but now meadowland of a sort, then the river, quite wide, and the opposite hillside rising much more abruptly, clothed with hanging woods of oak and birch. But it was not the sudden prospect of the Arkaig valley which surprised them so much as what went on within it, the violent activity of men. The valley-floor was full of men. Battle was already joined.

"Dear God — it is started! We are too late. Or Alastair early. Look — they are fording the river. There — and there.

These must be the Islesmen. Alexander was to be up the hill there, opposite, he said." Jamie shook his dark head as though to clear it of indecision. "Pate — back with you. Bring up our people. Mounted. On to the crest. Quickly. Spread them out in line abreast. Mix our men-at-arms amongst them. A long line, so that they seem more than they are. Haste you . . ."

While he waited impatiently for his horsemen to come up, Jamie sought to comprehend the most evidently confused situation below, half-a-mile away. There appeared to be roads, or tracks, on both sides of the river, and both were crowded with men over a long stretch. At first he assumed that these represented the two embattled forces, Alexander on the north side, the Islesmen on the south. But many were to be seen splashing across the shallows from south to north, and not being opposed; so clearly Alastair's men must be on both sides, having advanced along each bank. It was not easy to see just what was happening on the north side, for the woodlands came down almost to the river there; but it seemed that fighting was proceeding on the lower slopes, amongst the trees. Continual splashes in the river — and they must be large splashes to be visible at this distance — puzzled him at first. Then he realised that these were being caused by rocks, and possibly logs, being rolled down upon the Islesmen by Alexander's men on the higher ground.

Evidently then his friend was using the hill opposite, this *Torr a Mhuilt*, as a sort of fortress, and had coaxed Alastair Carrach into the costly task of assailing its steep side. Sound tactics for the weaker side, forcing the other into the difficult role almost of a besieger against a strongly-entrenched garrison. But though this might inflict heavy losses on the enemy, it could hardly result in Alexander's victory — for if the cost proved too great, the Islesmen could always withdraw their attack and, with their greater numbers, merely sit around the foot of the hill waiting, like any other besieger. Eventually Alexander would either have to come down and fight it out on the less advantageous low ground, or else try to steal away quietly, by night. Both of which would mean defeat. It was, in fact, a defensive strategy.

Jamie had reached this conclusion when his horsemen came pounding up around him, scarcely in the long and careful line abreast formation he had commanded. His men-at-arms sought to carry out the order, in some fashion, but the Gaelic-speaking contingent had either not understood or were otherwise minded. These came in bunches and groups, to yell and point at the scene below and brandish weapons and shake fists, a sufficiently aggressive demonstration but lacking any appearance of a disciplined cavalry force. Some indeed promptly urged their beasts, and their friends, on down the hill towards the battle.

Jamie shouted and gesticulated for these to come back and for all to line up as arranged — but he might as well have saved his breath. He called for his single trumpeter to sound a summoning blast or two — and though this, echoing and re-echoing amongst the hills, did have the effect of turning most heads in his direction, it produced no other positive result save to increase if possible the warlike ardour of his ragbag throng, who presumably took it as some kind of challenge or encouragement. It occurred to him indeed that the fighters down in the valley-floor might consider it in the same light, since undoubtedly they would hear it also.

"We will never hold the critturs!" Boyd asserted, coming up with Jamie's own horse. "They will be off, down there, like a pack o' gangrel curs."

The Douglas mounted, fists clenched, staring downhill. Clearly Boyd was right. Everywhere the Cameron riders were edging forward raggedly, in ones and twos and little parties; only the royal guard sat their mounts on the ridge, as ordered.

"It will be a massacre!" he exclaimed. "These fools, with their hatchets and dirks — the Islesmen will cut them to pieces!"

"Nae mair'n they deserve, the witless, godless heathens!"

"No! They are fighting for their homes, their folk. Look up there, at Arkaig-side burning . . ."

But Boyd did not glance up the long smoking glen to the west. "There they go!" he shouted. "They're off, the crazy-mad spawn of . . ." The rest was lost in the fierce and prolonged yelling of the rest of the Highland horsemen as with one accord now they surged forward, after the group of about a score who had started the downward rush.

"God Almighty!" Jamie cried. "We cannot sit here and watch. Watch our friends fight and die, and do nothing. Damnation — I am going down! Trumpeter — sound the Advance." He drew his sword and raised it high. "Forward!" he shouted.

Pate Boyd cursed obscenities behind him but did not hold back. And whatever their feelings in the matter, the outstretched line of the thirty royal guardsmen dug in their spurs, lances brought forward to the ready.

This was the craziest cavalry charge since Bruce's camp-followers made their wild rush at Bannockburn. In no sort of order, scattered over a wide front and brandishing their diverse weaponry, they thundered downhill bellowing their wrathful challenge. The Lowland men-at-arms fairly quickly managed to coalesce into something of a recognisable formation, but this was well towards the rear. Jamie discovered himself to be shouting "A Douglas! A Douglas!" in true Border style, and though it was not taken up by his following, he kept it up.

It was as well that the Highland garrons were sure-footed creatures and used to coping with treacherous conditions. There were a few spills amongst the unaccustomed horsemen but somehow the vast majority reached the bottom of the hill and plunged on across the soft level meadowland, a disorderly, yelling rabble.

At least their spectacular eruption on the scene had had a major effect on the enemy. The tide of men splashing across the river's shallows had all but died away, as all were called on to turn and face the new threat. And if the charge was a wild and headlong one, the defence was as little co-ordinated, likewise strung out along the riverside over a considerable distance in no formation or commandable state. The Islesmen were in greatly larger numbers than the horsemen, but they were at some disadvantage through being stationary in the face of violent impetus, lacking any strategy for dealing with such unprecedented attack, and being insufficiently concentrated to take concerted action.

The clash, inevitably, was less impressive than the approach, the impact individual rather than general. Momentum carried the shouting horsemen through, in the main; but once that momentum was spent, at the river's edge, the attackers tended to be at a loss. Many, indeed, flung themselves down from their mounts, unused to fighting on horseback, and hurled themselves into battle on foot.

Confusion reigned.

On a scene of utter chaos, Jamie Douglas suddenly perceived that he and his men momentarily could represent the only ordered and disciplined entity present, and as such might exercise a major influence on events. He could see a point in the long enemy line, a knot as it were, where it was thickest, densest, and where there seemed to be less disorder — the leadership almost certainly, possibly Alastair Carrach himself with his chiefs. With instant decision he turned in his saddle, reining up a little, to wave up the cohort of the royal guard behind, using the clenched-fist close up signal, swinging his arm up and down on either side.

"Back me! Back me!" he cried. "Tight. Arrow-formation — arrow, I say!"

Probably few if any heard him; but these were trained cavalrymen and knew very well what was intended. Swiftly they closed in behind into a solid phalanx, with little lessening of speed, and Pate Boyd and the under-officer spurred up alongside Jamie. He brought down his sword in a slashing gesture forward, pointing towards that knot of the enemy leadership some three hundred yards away, half-left a little further up the valley, kicking his beast into a full gallop.

The Islesmen were no cravens and amongst the fiercest fighters in the land. But they were wholly unused to the terrifying task of standing up to a charge of semi-armoured cavalry and had no tactics to deal with it. There might have been two hundred or so men clustered round what were now clearly the chieftains of the invading host, and only thirty men bore down upon them. But those thirty were on pounding, turf-scattering, snorting horses, long lances levelled now, and wearing steel breastplates and helmets. The waiting half-naked men wilted and broke before ever impact could be made.

Jamie, keeping his eye firmly on the chiefly figures, evident from their arms and attire and barbaric jewellery, drove unswervingly at these. They did not linger for him much longer than the rest, but scattered likewise. His beating, seeking sword never so much as made contact with any as they darted away in all directions, desperate to get from under lashing, flailing hooves. In a matter of only moments the leadership group of the invaders was no more, dispersed.

As the river-bank loomed up, Jamie sought to pull up and rein round, urgently, in danger of being ridden down by his own followers; but training told, and the men-at-arms managed to swing away right and left, and wheel about, retaining something of formation.

"After the leaders!" the Douglas yelled. "Hunt them down. Only them. The leaders . . ."

Now indeed all *was* confusion on that south side of the

Arkaig, as the Lowlanders rode off after the individual fleeing chiefs and all semblance of a front on either side was broken. Jamie was gambling on preventing any overall enemy command from being able to operate and control the situation; but he recognised the risks and dangers inherent. He and his were still vastly outnumbered, this side of the river; and though the Islesmen had been scattered, few casualties had actually been inflicted. Moreover, he himself had now little in the way of control over his people — although the trumpeter still clung close and his blared summons could fairly quickly recall the men-at-arms to his side. Their surprise had been highly effective, but if the enemy rallied now all could be as swiftly lost.

It was at this critical stage that, of all things, music took a hand in the struggle. Suddenly, above the shouting and clash, the sound of bagpipes came sobbing and shrilling up the valley, turning Jamie's head as it turned many another. There, down-river but on this south side, a host was coming into view, marching westwards, led by half-a-dozen pipers. Banners of a sort waved above this also, and steel gleamed in the sunlight. From the direction, it could only be Alexander's men, more Camerons presumably.

The effect on the Islesmen was dramatic. Any possible rally was halted there and then. Reinforcement for their foes was just too much, at that moment. Men began to disengage, to turn and flee, in ones and twos and small groups, some westwards towards Loch Arkaig again, some across the meadowland to the hills from which the horsemen had descended.

Promptly the noise of battle began to increase on the north side, amongst the woodlands, as the attack there was stepped up, to coincide. The trickle of flight became a flood. Soon all the invaders who could move were streaming away from that highly unconventional battlefield, casting weapons from them, abandoning booty, every man for himself. Moreover, the panic quickly spread across the river. There, too, flight became general.

It was not Alexander himself but young Sir James Stewart who came hastening up behind the pipers — and his company proved to be only superficially like a fighting-force, in fact a similar collection of old men and boys to Jamie's own, another example of Alexander's talent for improvisation.

The elder brother was not long in coming leaping down through the birch-woods of *Torr a Mhuilt* to splash across the

104

Arkaig shallows to them. He ran up, to grasp Jamie by both arms.

"My friend, my good friend!" he cried. "A joy, a very triumph! I thank you, I thank you with all my heart! A victory, a notable victory — and all yours, Jamie. You took Alastair wholly by surprise — aye, and myself also! Your charge of cavalry won the day. How can I sufficiently thank you, friend?"

Embarrassed, Jamie shook his head. "It was no charge. Only the merest chance," he asserted. "We could do nothing else. They plunged on, out of hand. I could not control them . . ."

"You controlled them sufficiently to make Alastair Carrach turn and run, man! I asked you only to stand and show yourselves — and instead you charged, and won the battle for me! The Islesmen will not rally now, this side of the Hebridean Sea — I shall see to that. Thanks to Sir James Douglas . . .!"

Protest as he would, that was the way of it. Jamie was a hero again, and nothing that he could say would alter it. Even the other Stewart brothers relaxed much of their hostility.

Alexander was right, at least, about Alastair Carrach being unable to rally his forces. No doubt he tried to, but, harried by Alexander's men, now being continuously reinforced by new Cameron contingents coming from all over Lochaber, he was unable to make a stand. Moreover, his galley-fleet lying there in Loch Linnhe, beckoned men enticingly. Within forty-eight hours he was sailing back to his isles, a discredited man.

Jamie, of course, had no opportunity to deliver his message from the Earl David — nor indeed did it seem any longer necessary. Circumstances had changed radically — and he had had his part in changing them. What the prince would say to it all was debatable — but the sooner he was informed the better.

The Lowland party rode with the returning Badenoch contingent as far as the northern mouth of the beetling Pass of Drumochter, and left them there to head southwards, with the plaudits and thanks of Alexander Stewart loud in their ears. However much of a hypocrite Jamie felt, he was glad of that young man's esteem nevertheless. He recognised him as a figure it would be unwise to underestimate on the Scottish scene. Unfortunately the chances that he and his cousin David might come to a clash was distinctly possible — two Stewarts of similar spirit if very dissimilar natures. Though if he, Jamie Douglas, could do anything to prevent it, he vowed to himself that he would do so.

V

IT WAS STRANGE to be back amongst the Highland hills again, and in Alexander Stewart's company likewise, so soon, however different the circumstances. Strange too how different the land itself looked, after a bare two months interval, if possible even more colourful, more beautiful. Already the mountain tops wore caps of snow, their lower slopes with the heather turning from purple to a rich sepia, and further down still the tracery of the birches changed from delicate green to pale gold. The October air was like wine. It was good to be off, footloose as it were, on this special mission for the prince, instead of proceeding on to Elgin and Inverness with the large, slow-moving and far from harmonious official cavalcade.

Jamie Douglas had been thankful when, at Lochindorb, the Earl David, concerned with the continuing delays in their progress through his Northern lieutenancy, had decided that the itinerary must be curtailed drastically. The Governor himself, no less, with a large entourage, had insisted on accompanying his nephew on this Highland tour, and could nowise be dissuaded or prevented. With as result an inevitable sourness and ill-feeling throughout, as well as a general slowing up. Just what the Earl Robert's purpose had been in coming on this prolonged and uncomfortable peregrination was not entirely clear; presumably he suspected David of designs which could damage his own interests—and with reason, of course; possibly he felt that he could act as a brake and counter-influence on the young man's all-too-evident ambitions. But the effect had been depressing, and restricting in results as in pace. And to none more galling than to Jamie Douglas, towards whom Robert Stewart never attempted to conceal his chill hostility.

A large part of David's design in making this progress was, of course, to try to ensure the support of the northern magnates in the forthcoming struggle for power. Naturally it much hampered him to have his rival with him, and in consequence, many of the intended interviews with the lords and chiefs had either to be abandoned or conducted at second-hand, by envoys sent out on detachment as it were. Jamie had been so used on not a few occasions, primed with appeals, promises and disguised threats. It was not work greatly to his taste, although he proved fairly successful at it. The word of his dramatic intervention into the battle on the Arkaig had spread far and wide throughout the Highlands, exaggerated out of all recognition, and he now found himself accepted as something of a major military leader, a reputation which no denials from him could eradicate, and which the Earl David found a distinct asset. He had been as delighted as he was amused at the result of Jamie's August excursion in the North, which had enabled him to preserve intact the bargaining powers of the earldom of Ross and at the same time bring pressure to bear on Donald of the Isles — who indeed had further drawn in his horns and agreed to the gesture of theoretically punishing his brother for unauthorised raiding on the mainland by allegedly committing Alastair Carrach to token imprisonment on the isle of Islay for a year. Also the royal castle of Urquhart had been yielded up again to the King's officer — in this case Sir Alexander Stewart.

The slow progress of this less-than-happy joint Lieutenant's and Governor's tour had meant that, if indeed the travellers were to get back safely to the South before the snows came down from the mountain-tops to choke the passes, a large part of the programme would have to be abandoned. It had been intended to return from the Inverness area by the vast and populous territories to the east, by the sheriffdoms of Banff and Aberdeen and the great earldom of Mar. That was now ruled out, and Jamie in consequence sent on this independent journey, to the Countess of Mar and her husband Sir Malcolm Drummond, at Kildrummy in Strathdon, thereafter to find his way home on his own. He had been glad to go — and Alexander, as Deputy Lieutenant, glad to accompany and escort him through the seventy-odd miles of wilderness — for he, of course, was even less popular with the Governor than was the Douglas.

So the two friends, this time with a bodyguard of a score of running gillies, Clan Chattan men, trotted south-eastwards through the glowing October uplands with a great relief from cramping restrictions and strained relations, and a consequent almost carefree cheer. Affairs of state and the power struggle could be forgotten for the moment, and the natural friendship and mutual esteem of spirited young men allowed its head.

They had crossed Spey and threaded the Abernethy Forest to climb the eastern skirts of the great Monadh Ruadh range beyond, up and up on to even higher lands than Lochindorb. Spending the first night in the narrow gut of steep Glen Braan, they had crossed over the desolate heights to the south, the very roof of Scotland, by Tomintoul and the Lecht passes through the Mounth, by a route which would be impassable in little more than a week or two. By testing even their sturdy garrons, not to mention the tireless gillies, they reached the lower lands around Corgarff at the head of Strathdon for the second night. And now they were riding down that lovely strath, eastwards still, amongst the gentler hills of the wary Forbes clansmen, immediate destination not far ahead.

Kildrummy Castle, principal seat of the mighty earldom of Mar, was strategically sited to dominate more than one route through the Mounth passes from the lowlands of Aberdeenshire, Angus and the Mearns. Strongly sited on the hillside above the Don, and protected on all sides save the approach by steep ravines, it was a great and powerful hold, larger than Lochindorb or any other further north, from which its owners ruled a territory large as many a Continental princedom — all the Mars, Braemar, Cromar, Midmar, Formartine and the Garioch, with much of the Firmounth and parts of Strathbogie besides. Although theoretically under the authority of the Lieutenant, because oft he mighty masses of the Monadh Ruadh mountains which soared between, the earldom of Mar was in practice almost independent. Hence this visit.

The travellers came to Kildrummy in mid-afternoon, and were received in very cautious fashion by the steward, being scrutinised and interrogated at some length from the gatehouse drum-towers before being admitted. Clearly Highland caterans were less than welcome here.

It seemed that the Countess of Mar was out hunting stags, and Sir Malcolm her husband had left to visit his Strathearn domains far to the south-west.

The young men were disappointed, for Malcolm Drummond,

Queen Annabella's brother, was an important man to win to the support of the prince in the forthcoming struggle. It might seem strange that he should require to be coaxed to his nephew's side, but there was sufficient reason. First of all, he did not love any of the Stewarts — had been brought up so. His aunt, Margaret Drummond of Logie, had been Queen and second wife to David the Second. Although admittedly a lady of doubtful virtue, the King had known that when he married her — she had, after all, been his chief mistress for years before his first wife died. But when King David himself died, his nephew and successor, Robert Stewart, treated her and her family vilely; and the Drummonds did not forget. Moreover Sir Malcolm hated the Douglases — or at least the present Earl Archie, considering that he had wrongfully supplanted his wife in titles and estates. He had married Isobel Douglas, sister of the late Earl James, and Countess of Mar in her mother's right; but she had been excluded as heiress of Douglas in favour of Archie, Lord of Galloway. So, a man with a grievance, he found little on the Scots governmental scene to attract him, and seldom appeared at Court or council. Nevertheless he was powerful, when he wanted to be, not only because of his wife's great earldom of Mar but on account of his own large Drummond lands in Perthshire. He was a strangely proud man, yet had never sought to be created Earl of Mar, in his wife's right, as was his entitlement.

However, when that lady returned from her hunting, she at least greeted the visitors warmly — and Alexander notably more warmly than Jamie. They had met before briefly, of course, prior to the North Inch contest at Perth, when the Earl David had been fondling her, in his usual fashion with attractive women whatever their age. She was a handsome creature, now in her thirty-ninth year, dark and tall, of statuesque build, big-bosomed and with a hot eye. The so-pronounced swarthy Douglas colouring gave her almost a Latin look, and she was as forthright in manner as most of the clan.

"So, my young friends," she declared, when she came down to join them for the evening meal. "You bring me Stewart requests, do you? Seeking favours? Brave knights!" She had changed from her hunting attire into something more suitable for evening wear — or at least for some sort of evening, though whether it was apt for this occasion was a matter of taste, for the rich gown was so low-cut and off-the-shoulder as to provide a challenge to masculine susceptibilities and the laws of gravity both. How it kept approximately up was a mystery which continued to preoccupy the two guests. Momentarily they expected to see one or both of the great white breasts burst out of the purely token grip of the bodice whenever the Countess drew deep breath or laughed, both of which she did frequently and heartily. Now and again she hitched the material up somewhat, but with a casual lack of concern. She ate and drank heartily too, and gave the impression that the evening might not be altogether uneventful.

Jamie allowed Alexander to answer this first verbal challenge. His position *vis-à-vis* his friend was a little uncertain here. He was the prince's man and direct envoy; but he was only an unimportant knight and small Douglas laird in fact, the lady's brother's former esquire. Whereas Sir Alexander, although a bastard also, was son of a royal earl, grandson and nephew of kings, Lord of Badenoch and moreover acting Deputy Justiciar of the North.

The other demonstrated a sort of wary courtesy and charm. "We did not fear too greatly, Countess, since we have heard only good of your ladyship, to rival your beauty. Moreover, does not the Earl David look on you as his friend?"

"Does he? You tell me, sir."

"Er . . . that is my understanding. He spoke most kindly of you, Lady Isobel."

"My husband's nephew will speak most kindly of any who can serve him — *while* they can serve him! Being a Stewart — like yourself, Sir Alexander." She chuckled throatily. She had a deeply husky voice.

Dragging his eyes from the endangered bosom, the other glanced at Jamie.

"Yes," the lady went on. "Let us hear a Douglas on this."

Jamie coughed, applying his gaze to his rib of cold venison. "The prince ever speaks well of you, madam," he said, with as much certitude as he could summon up.

"That comforts my heart, Sir James. Yet he sends you two to ensure my support? He conceives it necessary — but does not come himself."

Neither guest was in haste to answer that. Jamie spoke, at length. "His lordship conceives you his sure friend, Countess. It is more to your husband, I believe, that he sends us. It is unfortunate that Sir Malcolm is not here."

"Ah. So he is sure of me, but not sure of his Uncle Drummond — is that the way of it? He knows my husband's opinion of the Stewarts, so keeps his distance and sends you?"

Her guests applied themselves to their viands, aware that they were not doing very well, and that this woman was shrewd as well as bold, formidable in fact.

"Come," she went on cheerfully. "No need to look so glum. It is always as well to know just where one stands, is it not — where the Stewarts are concerned, in especial! Have you come seeking anything of *me*, a mere woman? Or is it Malcolm only your prince needs?"

"No, Countess — by no means," Alexander assured in his softly pleasing Highland voice. "It is you who are Mar, not Sir Malcolm. You who control this great earldom and all its powers and men and resources. Sir Malcolm and the house of Drummond are important also, and the prince seeks their aid. But Mar is of much larger influence, and could mean much to his cause."

"David Stewart wants those powers and men and resources for his own purposes? Why should I lend him them — even though it does suit him to call himself my friend?"

"It is not the men and resources he wants, lady, but your support. The votes of your vassals at a parliament. In the spring, in April most like, he intends to challenge his uncle the Earl Robert for the power and governorship of his realm. He is going to need every vote that he can raise, and all possible support in the land likewise. Mar comprises many lordships, not a few votes. And a large number of knights' fees . . ."

"I see. So that is it. David Stewart would displace Robert Stewart, the young lion for the old fox — and his love for me comes down to votes in a parliament!" She actually snorted. "Is there any reason why I should so aid him?"

"The young lion will be your king one day, lady."

"Perhaps, perhaps not. Only if he wins his fight. If Robert wins, then *he* will no doubt be king one day, instead. What of those who supported David, then? Safer to support neither, is it not? I fear that you have shown me no reason why I should risk all for David Stewart."

Alexander looked towards Jamie.

That young man frowned. "Lady Isobel," he said, almost challenged, in his jerky forthright way. "You have no cause to love the Earl Robert, I think?"

111

"That is true, at least," she agreed.

"He it was who made sure that you did not get the Douglas earldom, at your brother's death. He it was who, I believe, had your brother, my master, foully slain at Otterburn."

"I have heard that tale, yes. But there is no certainty, no proof."

"No proof — but he gained most from the Earl James's murder. And the murderer was slain in turn, secretly, before he could talk. And the slayer was in the Earl Robert's pay. Your brother's widow, the Governor's own sister, believes that he did it. Is your ladyship less . . . concerned?"

She eyed him levelly. "You speak very directly, sirrah. But the Douglases are apt to, are we not?"

"I judge that you would wish me to do so, Countess."

"Perhaps. Then tell me, as directly, what I gain by supporting David Stewart, Sir James."

"Vengeance on the Earl Robert. And a better, more honest, rule in this kingdom."

"What makes you believe that exchanging David for this uncle will better the rule? I conceive the one no more honest than the other."

"I believe it — although I cannot prove it, any more than I can prove that the Governor slew Earl James. But I have known the prince since he was but a boy. He has his failings, but I believe him honest in his wish to govern well the realm which will one day be his own."

She looked at him for long moments, silent. Then she laughed, and bit into her venison with strong teeth. "We shall see," she said, mouth full.

Alexander felt the need to change the subject. "It much interests me to be in this house, Countess," he said. "For another reason, as well as the delight of your company. It was here that a forebear of mine suffered grievous betrayal. My great-grandmother, Marjory Bruce, with her stepmother the Queen Elizabeth de Burgh, and her uncle, Nigel Bruce, were betrayed here to the English invaders, Nigel to his execution, only a few months after the good King Robert's coronation. It was an evil chance."

"No chance, my friend. The smith here, one Osborne, bore a grudge against his master, Gartnait of Mar, for some slight. This was his revenge. Although Gartnait himself escaped. That slight cost the King his favourite brother, his wife and daughter

112

eight years in English prisons — aye, and his sister Christian, Gartnait's wife also."

"A dastardly deed. I hope the smith suffered for it, in due course?"

"Oh, he did. And quickly. Oddly, at the hands of the English themselves — who seem to have misliked traitors also. Osborne had covenanted with them for a large sum in gold, for the deed. They paid him by melting the gold and pouring it molten down his throat." She laughed. "No doubt they slit him open after, and retrieved their outlay!"

"Lord . . .!" Jamie muttered.

Later, they sat before the great log fire and listened to a silver-voiced singer render the haunting ballads of the North-East, accompanying himself on a harp. The Countess sat on a deerskin-piled settle between the two young men, wine goblet in one hand but the other free to touch and stroke and caress Alexander on her left. Jamie, at the other side, was sufficiently aware of this, but managed not to feel deprived or resentful that he was not equally favoured. If Alexander found the process distasteful, in a woman old enough to be his mother, he did not show it. But when the minstrel exchanged his harp for a fiddle and the Lady Isobel, evidently still more affected by that sobbing, romantic music, leant still further over to her left so that one magnificent breast at last escaped from its tenuous confinement to rest heavily white on the Stewart shoulder, Jamie felt that in merest friendship he ought to seek the other's rescue. When the musician paused, he cleared his throat and announced that Alexander himself was a notable performer on the fiddle, and singer likewise, and should demonstrate his skill.

Their hostess took this, as it were, in her stride however. Expressing unqualified delight, she imperiously summoned the minstrel over to the settle, to give his fiddle to their visitor, who would play it there at her side, without disturbing himself or her. This Alexander proceeded to do, however cramped the accommodation and possibly distracting the attentions on his right, and demonstrably to the satisfaction of their chatelaine, seemingly unperturbed.

After some time of this, and finding his role unrewarding, and moreover tending to nod off, what with the heat of the fire, the large meal and a long day in the saddle, at the end of a Gaelic love-song of infinite yearning, Jamie got to his feet and sought the Countess's permission to retire. This she graciously granted

113

— whilst keeping her strong hand pressing Alexander firmly down in his seat.

Jamie had one more try. "We shall be riding early on the morrow, Lady Isobel," he informed. "For I have other calls to make and little time to make them. I hope that I may give the prince a favourable answer as to the valuable support of the earldom of Mar?"

"A mercy — what an hour to consider such matters, man! The Douglas single-mindedness carried almost too far, I vow! A weak woman, I have not yet reached a conclusion on this important issue. But . . . seek you your couch, Sir James. Sir Alexander will sing me another lay or two, and then we shall have some small exchange and see if we cannot come to agree on the matter. I am hopeful of a mutual accommodation — eh, Alex? So, off with you, and a good night to you."

Jamie looked down at his friend, who smiled up at him guilelessly but made no suggestion of a move.

Thoughtfully he left the private hall and found a sleepy servitor to light him to his tower chamber. Here, then, was a side of Alexander Stewart new to him. Hitherto he had no knowledge and insight on his friend in relation to women, other than unfailing courtesy towards his mother and sister. It seemed that he was either susceptible or opportunist — or both. He could well understand that the other's almost delicate good looks and engaging manner could have great attraction for the opposite sex, especially for older women; even the hint of steely and wholly masculine determination beneath the mild and slightly diffident exterior could probably have its fascination. But on this evening's showing, the inclination was two-sided. He was a Stewart, of course. Did such seemingly mutual partiality add up to weakness or strength? It might be important to know.

Jamie was pondering thus as he undressed for bed when there was a knock at his door. Assuming that he was perhaps misjudging his friend after all, he went to draw the door-bar — a precaution he had early learned not to neglect in an imperfect world. But he found not Alexander Stewart but a smiling young maid-servant there waiting on the draughty stair-landing. She slipped inside and bobbed a sort of curtsy — in the process the voluminous plaid in which she was wrapped opening to reveal that she was wholly naked beneath, a rounded, buxom creature of very definite femininity, strongly but comfortably made.

"Her ladyship sent me to warm your bed for you, sir," she

explained cheerfully. "She wouldna have any guest o' hers deprived!"

"Indeed. That was kind in her — and in yourself, lass. And I am grateful," he declared. "But when weary, as I am this night, I sleep better alone, see you. My good wife assures me that, after a long day ahorse, I twitch grievously — to my bedfellow's discomfort!" Turning the young woman around, he guided her back to the door — although for both their sakes he did not fail to run his hands appreciatively over her generous curves and undulations, and patted her substantial bottom as he propelled her out. "I thank you. Both. An undisturbed good night to you!"

The Countess of Mar, then, had not been quite so lost in lust for Alexander as she had seemed — or at least did not forget her chatelainely duties towards her other guest.

In the morning, despite what might have been anticipated, both Alexander and the Lady Isobel were early on the scene — earlier than Jamie indeed. More hunting, it seemed, was on the programme, this being the best time of the year for upland stags, just before the rutting season started. Fond as he was of the chase, Jamie had more to do than hunt deer this October; but it transpired that Alexander was otherwise minded — at least the Countess evidently assumed that he was accompanying her on the day's expedition.

When the Douglas could get his friend alone, it was to learn that this was indeed the parting of the ways. Alexander felt that, here on the verge of the Lowlands, his presence was no longer necessary, or in fact advantageous, for Jamie's further calls, in Angus and the Mearns. He had played his part for his Cousin David, would stay a little longer at Kildrummy and then return over the mountains to his duties in Badenoch.

The other eyed him with his direct Douglas gaze. "You find it to your liking here?" he asked — and sought with only partial success not to make it sound like an accusation.

"Why, yes," Alexander acceded, with no hint of embarrassment. "The Lady Isobel is good company, and kind, when you come to know her. I find her something of a challenge."

"Is that what she is? I would have called her a masterful woman — of the sort I would admire from a distance!"

"Masterful, yes. And all woman. As I said, a challenge."

"Almost as old as the Lady Mariota, your mother, I swear."

"Four years younger. She told me she is thirty-nine. And so

115

has almost twenty-five years of experience of being an attractive woman! Is there not something in that, some dare, some gauntlet to be picked up? Much more so than with some milk-and-water wench or untried virgin. No?"

Jamie shrugged. "A matter of taste, let us say. I prefer something ten years and more younger."

"You prefer Mary Stewart! But I have not that good fortune and felicity. Every man to his inclination. But, you should be grateful, Jamie, for mine — for your prince's sake. I think that I convinced the Countess last night to throw the whole weight of Mar behind David. And to urge her husband thereto, likewise. Whilst you but slept!"

"M'mm. Aye, well . . ."

Presently Jamie Douglas rode away alone southwards for the Dee and the Cairn o' Mount pass to the Howe of the Mearns and the land of the Lindsays and the Ogilvys, leaving his mild-mannered and delicate-seeming friend and his forceful, mettle-some hostess to their sport. Not for the first time, he wondered about Alexander Stewart — almost as much as he wondered about David Stewart.

VI

"THIS ACCURSED WEATHER!" David Stewart exclaimed, beating fist on the window-ledge of an upper room of the Blackfriars monastery at Perth. "Snow — in April! It is damnable. This could ruin all — all we have worked so hard to achieve. Infernal, devil-damned snow!"

"I think not, my lord," his cousin Alexander said soothingly. "It commenced only at noon yesterday. Insufficient time to harm us greatly."

"But it is heavy, man — heavy. Look at the size of those flakes, of a mercy! If it has blocked the passes again, or some of them, we are lost. It could have been a close enough thing as it was. This could hold up and delay many. Even turn some back. Defeat us."

"Will it not be apt to hold up the Governor's supporters equally as much as your own, my lord?" Jamie Douglas asked.

"Not so. My uncle, having held the rule all this time, has his support all around him, near at hand. Those who love him least have stayed at a distance, furthest away; those who fear him most — for who could love the man? — remain close. Moreover his earldoms of Fife and Menteith, with Strathearn also, which he dominates, are nearby. Snow will not keep these away. Whereas *my* friends, from the North, from Galloway, from the far ends of the realm . . .!"

"I say that you fear unnecessarily, Cousin," Sir Alexander contended. "I know the snow, and the Highland and Mounth passes, better than you do, since I live amongst them. There is no wind today, and it is the wind which blocks the passes — drifting snow. Days and nights of wind. This snow will not last nor lie long — not in April, almost May. Prolonged rain would have been worse, for that could flood the glens and make the rivers impassable. I say that few, if any, from the North will be turned back. Delayed a little only . . ."

"Few is all that is required to defeat us," the Earl David asserted. "Delay also."

"Could it not be postponed?" Jamie asked. "Even a day or two might serve."

"A parliament, duly called under the Great Seal with the required forty days of notice, cannot be postponed. Not when all the principals are already assembled. It would require the King in special Council — and Robert still dominates the Council."

The three young men stared out at what they could see of the white expanse of the North Inch of Perth. It was exactly thirty months since the extraordinary clan battle had been fought there; and on the morrow, 28th April 1399, the town was the chosen venue for another sort of battle, less bloody perhaps but of much greater significance for the entire kingdom. It was not like David Stewart to be gloomy or depressed, but so much was at stake, the culmination of months, years of work and planning.

The prince shrugged and mustered a rueful smile. "Well, what will be, will. And meantime, I keep a lady waiting — and an impatient lady at that! Eupham Lindsay is a hot piece in more ways than one. As well, perhaps, since it may well be chilly in yonder Gilten Arbour!"

The other two exchanged glances. Jamie coughed. "My lord — the Earl of Dunbar and March is arrived. Here, in this very building. Is it wise . . .?"

"George Dunbar, I think, will scarce be haunting the Gilten Arbour summer-house in a snowstorm!" He paused. "Besides, he may be the less concerned, presently! And he is a dull fish. So — I leave you, my friends. Pray you to your various saints that the snow stops. And at tonight's banquet keep sober, since I may need you . . ."

The prince gone, Alexander looked thoughtful. "What think you he meant when he said that Dunbar might be the less concerned presently? I thought I heard a strange note there?"

"I do not know." Jamie frowned. "But I mislike this of Mistress Eupham Lindsay. At this moment. She is, after all, niece to Sir David Lindsay of Crawford and Glenesk, the King's good-brother. And the Lindsays are proud. To be playing with her now, betrothed as he is to the Earl of Dunbar's daughter.

Dunbar may be dull, but he is prouder even than the Lindsays — and more powerful. This could be folly, I say."

"He plays with many women, Jamie."

"Aye. But he might choose them with more care . . .!"

Even although many parliamentary attenders had not yet arrived, the refectory of the Blackfriars monastery, the largest apartment in Perth, was thronged for the King's banquet that night, so that it was difficult to see where the others would have been fitted in had they been in time. But more than mere numbers are requisite for a successful evening's entertainment, and this occasion was ill-starred from the start.

Although Lyon King of Arms, as master of ceremonies, had been carefully busy, at Earl David's instigation, in seeking to seat judiciously the membership of the two great factions, as far as these were known, there were other sub-factions, private feuds and various divisive causes, in an appallingly discordant realm. Due consideration for precedence and complicated pride of birth and rank had to be balanced likewise, and there were inevitable complaints, resentments and clashes amongst the guests long before the people at the dais-table came in to take their places. Although this had been foreseen, and music and entertainers brought on from the very start, to help damp down and disguise hostilities, the atmosphere nevertheless was more reminiscent of two armed camps than of a celebratory feast. Although none knew exactly what was likely to transpire, there was little doubt that goodwill and harmony would require much cherishing.

Jamie Douglas and Mary Stewart sat well down the third of the three lengthwise tables — for however close to the prince, the young man held no official position and was, of course, not a commissioner to the parliament; indeed he could not have found any justification for being present had not his wife been an illegitimate sister of the King. Sir Alexander Stewart chose to sit between them — although he indeed could have occupied a somewhat higher place as *de facto* though not *de jure* Lord of Badenoch and acting Deputy Lieutenant of the North.

Jamie was anything but at ease as they waited, much aware of the brittle atmosphere, concerned that there might be serious trouble; but his companions appeared to be happily carefree. Mary was of a cheerful and non-worrying disposition; and Alex, despite his sensitive appearance, seemed to be able to shrug off apprehension, secure in some inner confidence.

119

"There are a deal too many of David's unfriends here," Jamie declared, not for the first time. "Or, leastways, too few of his friends come. There is Sir John Stewart of Darnley, now, with Sir David Dennistoun. Sir John Ramorgnie, too . . ."

"Is Ramorgnie not friendly with David? I have seen them together."

"Aye — but I do not trust him. He is a deal too clever, that one. And his lands are in Fife. Like yonder Sir Walter Bickerton of Kincraig. I trust none of the name of Bickerton."

"Jamie is scarcely the most trusting of mortals," his wife confided. "Sometimes I wonder if he wholly trusts *me*! Even with quite elderly admirers! As well that he considers you harmless, Alex! Perhaps it is a Douglas failing?"

But Jamie was in no mood for banter. "There are too many *Douglases* here for my comfort!" he added. "At least, those following Earl Archie."

"But the Earl Archibald is less firm in his support of the Governor, is he not?" Alexander said. "Since that business on the Border and the trouble with Percy and Lancaster."

"Yes. But when it comes to the vote tomorrow, I fear that he will side with the Earl Robert. Out of old custom and friendship. So my father believes. And his son, the Master of Douglas, has taken a mislike to David, more's the pity, although he is his good-brother. Over some slight . . ."

"Ha — here is Eupham Lindsay, looking sleek as a cat at the cream!" Mary observed. "The whisper is that David is so besotted with her that she is growing ambitious."

"Ambitious? You mean . . . ?"

"Marriage," his wife nodded. "*I* do not think so, knowing my nephew. But that is the talk. Elizabeth Dunbar is a dull child and will never satisfy David. But Eupham Lindsay is scarce of the rank to threaten her."

"He'd never marry her. His wife will one day be Queen. But he could offend the whole Lindsay clan with this folly . . ." Jamie paused. "The saints be praised — here's two Douglases we can rely on, come in time. Will of Drumlanrig and his brother Archie of Cavers. They are sure, at least . . ."

The dais-table occupants began to file in, from the Prior's door at the back of the refectory. Jamie's own half-brother, suddenly greatly enhanced in status, came first, with his wife, the Lady Elizabeth, second of the King's daughters. Then the Master of Douglas, with the elder sister, the Lady Margaret;

and George, Earl of Angus with the Lady Mary, the youngest. There followed three of the princesses of the previous generation, two with their husbands, Sir David Lindsay and Hay of Erroll, the Constable, although the Lady Isabel, former Countess of Douglas, was alone. Then, after a pause, came the Earls of Moray, Ross, Dunbar and Douglas, with the senior Bishops of St. Andrews, Glasgow, Aberdeen and Dunkeld.

Jamie, counting pros and cons, glowered blackly. His calculations were scarcely encouraging.

Finally the awaited fanfare of trumpets heralded the monarch, the music and entertainment ceased, and all rose. The King of Arms led in five persons, the Earls of Carrick and Fife, nephew brilliant in white satin and gold, uncle soberly fine in black and silver; then King Robert, noble in appearance but undistinguished and untidy as to dress, leaning heavily on his Queen's arm, Annabella on the other hand leading a small, wide-eyed boy in scarlet velvet, the Prince James, born unexpectedly five years before and now the monarch's joy and consolation — although joy is too happy and positive a word ever to use with reference to King Robert the Third.

"Why have they brought the child?" Mary whispered to her husband. "Late as this. Is he not a poppet!"

"There will be a reason, you may be sure."

The King, bowing but eyeing the throng nervously, seated himself in the high chair at the centre of the dais-table, with David on his right and the Queen on his left, then the little prince between her and the Earl Robert — who sat as far away from the child as he might without having to be too close to the Primate, Bishop Trail, of whom he much disapproved. This last raised a beringed hand and declared a Latin grace-before-meat, before all resumed their seats.

"David looks in good spirits," Alexander commented. "A deal more cheerful than the Governor."

"He is ever that. And the more spirited the less the cause!"

"Jamie is ever a fount of cheer, himself!" his wife confided.

The banquet thereafter proceeded normally and without incident, other than the odd squabble between antipathetic neighbours which the music and singing was sufficient to cover up. As course succeeded course however — although April was a difficult month for game and fish — and the wine began to flow ever more freely, disagreements became more vehement and black looks were more common than amiable converse, even up on the dais. Presently Jamie found the Earl David's eye upon him, with the summons of an almost imperceptible jerk of the head.

He made his way unobtrusively round the side of the refectory, amongst the busy servitors, to the back of the dais where he could approach the prince from behind, to bend discreetly.

"Get Dennistoun out of here, Jamie," David murmured. "He is drunk and ripe for mischief. He is picking on Montgomerie of Eaglesham — who is sufficiently hot-tempered as it is. Anything of trouble could spark off a blaze here now. Get him out."

"But . . . how can I, my lord?" the other demanded in an anxious whisper. "He is much senior to myself. Chief of his name. And of the Earl Robert's party."

"Tell him . . . see you, tell Montgomerie also. Tell him I command it. Both to leave, in the King's name, to settle their differences outside. The guard then to take Dennistoun in charge. Montgomerie can come back. Speak with Montgomerie first. Quickly now, man."

Doubtfully Jamie moved down to midway along the second table, where he whispered to the angry Sir John Montgomerie, Lord of Eaglesham, whom he knew well since Otterburn days. That man seemed disposed to question the command, but a glance at the dais-table, and the prince's nod, convinced him. He rose — and at his rising, Dennistoun, across the table, also got to his feet, presumably taking it as challenge. Jamie indeed had to do little persuading with the younger man, for with Montgomerie gesturing far from kindly towards the nearest door, he was nothing loth. Fists clenched threateningly, he turned to stumble in that direction, pushing servitors aside roughly.

Jamie pressed back into his seat Sir Thomas de Eglinton, who would have gone with his friend Montgomerie, and then hurried to the door himself, to alert the guard there, and his colleagues outside. In the end, the entire contrivance went naturally enough, for Dennistoun had barely got through the doorway before he began to lay violent hands on Montgomerie, so that the guards' duty to prevent fighting in the monarch's vicinity was plain and straightforward, scarcely requiring Jamie's relayed instructions from the prince to take Sir David Dennistoun of that Ilk into custody meantime for his own good. There was something of a scuffle before the protesting laird was led away. Jamie advised Montgomerie to wait a little while before returning to the banquet, for appearance's sake.

When he himself re-entered the chamber, it was to find the music and singing stopped and the King of Arms on his feet and declaring,

". . . all love and royal goodwill and for the better repute and report of this his realm. His Grace therefore decrees and ordains that the style, title and degree of duke in this kingdom of Scotland be herewith established, to rank above that of earl, as in other kingdoms of Christendom, that henceforth none such Englishman as the Duke of Lancaster or other shall seek to claim superiority or precedence over princes of this our more ancient realm, to their just offence. In pursuance of which royal ordinance, His Grace the King hereby is pleased to nominate his entirely well-beloved son and heir, David, Earl of Carrick and High Steward of Scotland, to be known and styled hereafter as Duke of Rothesay, with all such honours, privileges and dues as may be deemed suitable to support that rank . . ."

Lyon's fruity intonations were lost in the surge of comment and speculation, as the company demanded of each other the meaning of this wholly unexpected and unprecedented development, and what advantage there was in it for the prince.

"Further . . . further, I say," Lyon went on loudly, "His Grace appoints and ordains his well-beloved elder surviving brother, Robert, Earl of Fife and Menteith, likewise to be a duke of Scotland, with the style and title of Duke of Albany . . ."

Again the swell of remark and exclamation, louder now.

"Silence, I say — silence in the King's royal presence! In consequence of these elevations, the King's Highness is graciously pleased to appoint his second and entirely well-beloved son, the Prince James here present, to be Earl of Carrick and Lord of Renfrew, in the room of his brother, with all due appurtenances. And likewise the Lord Murdoch Stewart, His Grace's nephew, absent through indisposition, son of the said Duke of Albany, to be Earl of Fife — although not of Menteith. All as from this day henceforth, by royal command."

David Stewart rose to his feet, smiling, and bowed low to his father, then to his mother, and waved an all-embracing genial hand to the company — which mustered a somewhat ragged and less than enthusiastic cheer. It was then seen that the little boy, James, was also standing and bobbing his head. Their Uncle

123

Robert evidently felt himself compelled to do likewise, although he dispensed with the smiling.

"Now, what is the meaning of this?" Mary demanded of her husband new back at her side. "Did you know of it, Jamie?"

"No. Nothing. It is a strange device. But since I swear the King did not think of it himself, it must have been David's, or Robert's doing. Yet David is not one for styles and titles. He must have seen this as a means to sweeten his uncle, to cozen him perhaps? For even if it was the Governor's notion, it could not have been contrived without David's agreement. Robert *was* angry, at Haddonstank, when Lancaster sought to take precedence of him, as duke. But . . ."

Lyon was not finished yet. "These appointments, the first dukedoms in this realm of Scotland, will be confirmed and celebrated, as is fitting, before God's altar in the abbey-church of St. Michael at Scone tomorrow, at noon. Which means that the parliament to be held thereafter will be of necessity postponed until the hour of three in the afternoon . . ."

"Ha! There is David's hand, at least! Delay for four hours," Jamie muttered.

"Moreover, His Highness, in his gracious favour and love, desire to honour two of his most important and puissant subjects, to make acknowledgement of their long and excellent services to his realm and person. Therefore he calls Archibald, Earl of Douglas, father of his daughter Margaret's husband, likewise to the rank and style of duke of Scotland. And Sir David Lindsay, Lord of Crawford and High Justiciar of this realm, to be belted Earl of Crawford."

This new announcement achieved a deal more interest and excitement than had the previous ones — especially the last. For although dukedoms as such meant little or nothing to the Scots, being a wholly alien conception, earldoms were very much otherwise, being part of the nation's very fabric and polity, positions of vast hereditary power and influence. The earls of Scotland, fourteen in number hitherto, were a tight and exclusive group of the supreme nobility, based on the ancient Celtic mormaorships, and semi-royal in a way that their English counterparts were not. They were, in fact *Righ* in the Gaelic, sub-kings, giving point and meaning to the monarch's proud title of *Ard Righ*, or High King of Scots, king of these kings. No new earldoms had been created since that of Douglas in

1357, and that had been a special case and had aroused a furore as an unsuitable precedent, not one of the antique Celtic patrimonies. Now Crawford was being elevated to this jealous estate, the Lindsays raised to dizzy heights.

Sir David Lindsay rose and bowed, clearly surprised, bewildered, indeed.

"Nephew Davie again?" Mary wondered. "Buying Lindsay to his side?"

Jamie was fingering his chin thoughtfully. "I would scarce have thought it necessary. Lindsay is on his side, anyway. He hates the Governor. Look at him now — the Governor. His face . . .!"

Certainly the new Duke of Albany was showing grievous displeasure frozen on his handsome features.

"I wonder if it is not Douglas's elevation, rather than Lindsay's, which hurts him most?" Alexander suggested. "A dukedom, level with his own. Moreover, must it not mean that the King, and therefore David, is seeking to bind Douglas to his side, thus? Our David has not been idle!"

"Is the Earl Archie drunk, think you?" Mary asked. "He has not risen. See, he sits there grinning and shaking his head."

Others too were noting the Douglas's behaviour, notably Lyon, who was looking significantly at the Earl.

"My lord of Douglas," he called. "You heard the King's most gracious appointment? Do you make due acknowledgement?"

Into the sudden hush, Archie the Grim hooted a harsh laugh. "I heard!" he cried. "But . . . na, na! I'm beholden to His Grace. Och, aye — beholden. But by his royal leave, I'll just bide the way I am, man!"

Lyon gasped — and not only Lyon. "But, sir — a duke! A duke, do you hear?"

"Sir Duke! Sir Duke!" the Earl quacked. "Why no' Sir Drake, Sir Drake?" His hoarse laughter, on top of his efforts to sound like a duck all but choked him — and laughter in turn swept the assembly. In braid Scots the word duck is pronounced juke.

Lyon, looking appalled, banged his baton of office on the table. "My lord," he exclaimed, "do I understand that you *reject* His Grace's honour?"

The other leaned forward, smile gone. Indeed he had seldom looked more grim. "Not reject, sirrah — but decline. Aye, humbly decline. With my thanks. For if I became this new-fashioned duke, who then would be Earl of Douglas? Tell me that!"

There was silence then, as his fellow-guests stared, at each other, at the King and his son, at the Governor and back to the old Earl, weighing the implications, the significance and the consequences of this unprecedented disclaimer. Even Jamie, although he sensed the danger, knew a surge of sheer elation. Never, surely had the power and pride of the house of Douglas been more vividly if crudely demonstrated, the Stewarts more clearly put in their place.

"Oh, dear," Mary murmured. "Now what will happen?" But her eyes danced.

David Stewart required none to point out the danger — nor how to deal with it. He slapped down his open hand on the table-top, to make the goblets and flagons jump, and throwing back his beautiful head, laughed silvery mirth.

"God save us — and bless the Douglas!" he cried. "Juke! Juke! Here's a joy! My potent goodsire-to-be, in no doubts as to who is to be Earl of Douglas! Not the Master yet awhile — no, no, not the Master yet!"

"Clever!" Alexander commented, beneath his breath. All knew that the Earl did not get on well with his son and heir, the moody Master of Douglas — who, as the two Stewart dukedoms foreshowed, as heir would become Earl if his father was Duke.

But Mary, brows raised, was following a different line. "Goodsire-to-be?" she repeated. "You heard what he said? What does that mean?"

"A slip of the tongue? The Earl is his *sister's* goodsire."

"David does not make slips of the tongue," Jamie jerked, tensely.

The prince proceeded to prove him right — and effectively to banish from men's minds the possible injury to the royal authority and patronage implied in that rejection of the dukedom. Still standing, he went on.

"This, my lords, ladies and friends, would seem a suitable moment to acquaint you with my, h'm, felicity. As all know, I had the honour to be betrothed to the Lady Elizabeth Dunbar, daughter of my good friend the Earl of Dunbar and March. This, because of purely personal reasons, and owing to delay because of youth, has been broken off, with no least reflection on the young lady concerned. And it is now my pleasure to

126

inform you that I am to be wed, and shortly, to the Earl Archibald's daughter, the Lady Mary Douglas. You will rejoice with me, I am sure!"

The breathless pause which greeted this announcement was rudely broken by the noise of a chair being forcefully pushed back, as George, Earl of Dunbar and March, rose abruptly to his feet, white-faced. He stared around him, threw a curt nod in the direction of the monarch, and stamped out of the apartment without a word to any. The Earl of Douglas grinned.

In the clamour of talk which followed, Jamie looked at his wife, sombre features working. He could find no words.

"Our Davie outdevils the Devil!" she said. "But he will overstep himself one day, I fear."

"If he has not already done so," Alexander added. "Dunbar is too powerful a man to offend so. Tomorrow, how will he vote, he and his?"

"David assesses Douglas as a deal more powerful — tomorrow and every day. And would bind him close," the young woman said. "But . . . it is not well done."

"It is damnable!" Jamie declared. "I it was who took his offer of betrothal to Dunbar. This is beyond all. And to say nothing of it . . ."

Mary touched his arm and nodded. Near the foot of the first table there was a commotion. Sir William Lindsay of Rossie, illegitimate half-brother to the new Earl of Crawford, and his daughter Eupham, were also in process of leaving the room, and angrily. It was forbidden, of course, to leave any function at which the King was present without specific royal permission; but the calls of nature had to be met, especially with so much wine being consumed, and it was usually politely assumed that such departures were thus motivated and only temporary.

"So — the whisper was true!" she said. "The Lindsays *were* ambitious. And now see their hopes dashed. But to prevent more lapsed votes, their chief is made earl!"

"Even David would not be so cynical as that!" Alexander protested. "Although it is no doubt no accident that the earldom was announced tonight, before the parliament . . ."

Their exchange was halted as the new Duke of Albany got to his feet to speak. He seldom so indulged, being no orator and preferring to wield power from the background.

"Your Grace," he said, although he did not look along at his brother, and spoke without the least hint of warmth,

127

"believing this advancement in style and rank to be advisable and to the advantage of the realm in its rule and governance — which rule and governance are my responsibility — I accept it with due approval. I say, however, that my friend the Earl of Douglas was right and wise in declining such elevation. I advise that the dignity of duke should be restricted wholly and only to members of the royal house, lest unnatural envies and intrigues as to station be aroused. I am rejoiced also that my lord of Douglas's daughter is to wed my nephew, and so in God's providence may one day be Queen-Consort — which day, it is to be hoped, will however be long delayed. The lady is well known to me, and I am satisfied that she will be an excellent and steadying influence on the prince, of whose youthful spirits we are all aware . . ."

"To be sure, Uncle Albany — to be sure!" David called out cheerfully. "But you need not make the Lady Mary sound quite so . . . venerable! She is but six years older than myself, I believe!"

If there was considerable amusement at this significant sally, the Governor demonstrated none — nor did the Earl Archibald. "Such steadying being also in the realm's interests," Albany went on levelly. He paused. "But these matters, although of some import, are minor compared with the business of the morrow. I have agreed to the calling of this parliament because there is a dangerous spirit of lawlessness, and denial of due authority, in the land, fostered I fear by persons who should know better and who manifestly therefore lack due responsibility of judgement. This parliament must take fullest steps to crush such hurtful spirit and dangerment to the good government of the kingdom. To which end I will address myself tomorrow — and expect all others to do likewise, and enact accordingly. On pain of my direst displeasure, as Governor of this realm." He stared round the suddenly sobered gathering with a kind of chilly menace which left no doubts in the minds of practical men that stern reality as distinct from clever manipulation had belatedly come to this banquet. "Mind it tomorrow, I say, lest much that you all deem secure held in your hands is wrested out of them, to your sorrow." Again the telling pause. "That is all I have to say — save that the hour grows late and tomorrow will demand clear heads and firm wills. Roystering can await another occasion. With Your Grace's permission I will now retire — and advise those who have any part to play in the parliament to do likewise."

As the Governor turned to move from the table, King Robert raised his gentler voice, for the first time that evening. "Aye, Robbie," he said. "I'm for my bed, my own self — and you will be pleased to await my departure, see you." And as the company all but gasped audibly at this extraordinary assertion of the royal identity, the monarch added, "I agree that the morn's parliament is important, fell important — otherwise I'd not have called it. But I'd remind you, remind all, that dire displeasure is *mine* to display, on this realm's behalf. Not yours, Robbie, nor yet Davie's, here, but mine — so long as I wear the Crown. Your advice I shall ay cherish, and whiles act on. But the Lord's anointing is on my head, God help me, and mine only. Mind *that* tomorrow. I bid you all a good night."

As the King heaved himself up, with his wife's aid, and Lyon gestured urgently for the trumpeters to sound, Robert, Duke of Albany stood stiff, silent, expressionless, whilst everybody else rose hurriedly. Men, it might have been noted, bowed lower than they had done for many a day as their sovereign lord limped off, even David, Duke of Rothesay.

"Who won this night's jousting, then?" Mary Stewart wondered — and received no answer from either of her escorts.

*   *   *

The service of installation of the new dukes, conducted by Bishop Trail the Primate and the Abbot of Scone, was solemn and impressive, but there was an unreality about it, a sense of play-acting whilst more major matters loomed large. Few conceived these titles and dignities as of any vital importance, whereas the clash which must follow between the two beneficiaries could shake the kingdom. No great numbers attended.

Jamie Douglas reined over to the prince's side as the company formed up outside the abbey for the ride back to Perth. "Pate Boyd has just brought word, my lord, that the Countess of Mar and Sir Malcolm Drummond have arrived at St. Johnstoun, with their train. Also the Bishops of Aberdeen and Moray, and the Lords of Arbuthnott and Philorth and the Thane of Cawdor."

"Praise God for that — for some of them, at least! They are all going to be needed. You heard of George Dunbar, damn him?"

"That he has ridden off for his Borders, aye. With his lairds. And so you lose his votes. That . . . could have been avoided, my lord," Jamie declared with dour emphasis.

The Duke smiled. "Perhaps. But I think I made a fair exchange — in the parliament and Council, as well as in my purse, if not in my bed! As to that last, we shall have to see, Jamie. You Douglases are dark ones, in more than your faces! Ah — there goes my puissant sire. Heaven grant that he did not use up all his hard-won resolution last night! Keep me informed, Jamie, as to all arrivals, right up till the end, the vote. I will give orders that you may come and go, by the Prior's door." And he spurred off.

The parliament was held in the same Blackfriars refectory as the previous night's banquet, and for the same reason. There was little room for spectators here, but David had arranged for space to be reserved, and seats, for certain special onlookers, notably such royal ladies as wished to attend, and countesses in their own right who would have been entitled to be present as commissioners had they not been women. Despite the weather— although the snow had now disappeared — there was a fair attendance, seventy-odd votes being represented.

The King presided in person, as was the correct if not invariable procedure; but the Chancellor acted as chairman, a sort of programme-director. Old Bishop Peebles of Dunkeld had died, and the Governor had swiftly ensured that another nominee of his own, Bishop Gilbert Greenlaw of Aberdeen, succeeded him in this post of chief minister, an able and ambitious cleric who could be relied upon to be on the winning side. The line-up of forces appeared to be very evenly divided, although there were a number fairly doubtful of allegiance and the prince's faction still hoped for sundry belated arrivals.

After prayers for God's guidance on their deliberations, and loyal expressions towards the monarch, the Chancellor outlined the agenda. Because of the unavoidable delay in starting, the proceedings would have to be extended over two days, with His Grace's permission. The detailed business of sheriffships, revenues, customs and taxes, trade, foreign envoys and the like would be held over till the morrow, and this day's consideration devoted entirely to high policy in the rule and governance of the realm.

No comment, indeed profound silence, greeted this pro-

130

nouncement; and the Bishop, coughing slightly, went on after a pause, with more than a hint of nervousness evident in even his assured and sonorous tones.

"Your Grace," he said, "there has been much talk, some of it malicious and ill-informed, of misgovernment, misfeasance and impolicy, in the realm. To put an end to such talk and accusation, my lord Duke, Your Grace's Governor, agreed to this parliament making specific enquiry into the matter that the truth of the situation may be established beyond a peradventure. He who has ruled the land these ten years has nothing to hide nor any regrets to make. Contrariwise he is entirely confident of his rectitude and the fairness and honesty of his rule. Although, to his grief, he has certain charges to make against, against persons here present."

"My lord King," the Lord of Eaglesham, bold man, called, "is this clerk from Aberdeen making a homily on behalf of the Governor? Or conducting the business of this parliament?"

The groundswell of both agreement and dissent rose, making ominously evident the deep divisions and passions represented in that room. Jamie Douglas, standing near the door behind the dais, silently cursed Montgomerie's impatience. This was no time for hot words and losing tempers, with so much so delicately balanced.

The monarch raised a hand in an uncertain gesture, but made no comment.

"Sire — my lords — bear with me," the Chancellor pleaded. "All must be done in due and decent order. It is proper that, since the rule is being challenged, he who has borne the rule must make his attitude and position clear. My lord Duke, whilst permitting this discussion and voicing of opinions, in no fashion accepts that he is open to censure or obliged to heed it. As duly appointed Governor, his is the rule, his the authority, and decision therefore his alone."

"His alone, then, the blame!" That was Sir Malcolm Drummond of Stobhall — and Jamie gave thanks at least that he was thus early coming out on the right side, and strongly, hopeful for the Countess of Mar's attitude.

"Perhaps, my lord. If blame there be. But who can apportion blame, save he who knows all the facts behind the decisions? And only the Governor is in that position."

The groan that went up at that was promptly drowned in cheers from the opposition. The two dukes sat silent throughout, watchful, waiting. It was some time before it was perceived that the monarch's hand was raised again.

Silence gained, King Robert spoke, in his mild and slightly hesitant voice. "My lord Chancellor — there is truth in what you say. But you mistake, mind, when you say that the Governor permits this discussion. He can neither permit nor refuse, see you. The King in parliament is sovereign. The *King* therefore permits this discussion. Aye, and there's another bit. You said that the decision in rule is the Governor's alone. That isna so. The rule and governance of this realm is vested in the Crown. The Crown may decide to rule by the hands of others. But the decision is the Crown's — aye, and the responsibility likewise."

Of all there, probably only his wife and son had ever heard John Stewart speak thus firmly, and with authority undeniable however unhappy the voice.

Glancing across to his Queen, amongst the watching ladies, the King drew a long, tremulous breath. "See you, my lords of parliament," he went on. "If my brother Robert, now of Albany, has no regrets to voice, *I* have. If this realm has been misgoverned — and I accept that it has — then I must bear the responsibility since I am its ruler, not Robert. He has but governed in my name. If there has been ill done, then this parliament must say so and condemn it. That is your duty, aye your duty. You must censure such failure in the rule. And censure who is responsible — myself."

There was confusion, almost consternation, amidst cries of No! No! But Jamie noted that David Stewart was smiling quietly. This, then, was no surprise to him at least.

There was a pause. The monarch seemed to have completed his extraordinary intervention. Nobody appeared to know just what to do now, least of all the Chancellor, who kept looking towards the Governor for guidance — and receiving none.

Jamie saw David turn and sign towards his other uncle, by marriage, the new Earl of Crawford. Somewhat doubtfully the Lindsay stood up.

"Sire," he said, "this taking on your own royal shoulders of the blame for the misgovernment, and what is amiss in the land, is noble, most noble. Though few would say the fault was Your Grace's. Yet it is true that if there is misrule in a kingdom, the King must, in the first instance, bear the responsibility. If matters are to be righted, then the righting must start at the head. This parliament is called so to do, that your realm may regain its health, and the rule of law, justice and peace be restored. Therefore parliament's blame must be declared and recorded, and censure passed on . . . on the guilty. Before there can be betterment, reform."

From his throne the monarch held out empty hands. "So I recognise, my lord. So indeed I do command. Censure there must be, unmistakable. And it is necessary that the censure of parliament must be passed upon myself, as head of the realm's government at fault. For all to perceive. I, I command that you proceed to do this, my lord of Crawford." If those strange words were sufficiently strong, certain, the voice enunciating them was not.

"Yes, Sire. H'mm." The Lindsay looked around him. "I move, then, that this parliament of our Scottish realm here assembled declares solemnly that there has been grievous misrule and wrongous handling of the nation's affairs these sundry years past. And hereby makes due censure of the King's Grace, and his government, as responsible therefor." And he sat down abruptly.

"And that motion I second," Sir Malcolm Drummond called strongly.

"As do I," Montgomerie added.

The stir and excitement was intense. Never before, so far as anyone there had heard tell of, had the King of Scots been publicly and formally censured in his own presence. Even though it was by royal command, and presumably within the power of parliament, it seemed little short of high treason, almost of sacrilege.

The Chancellor-Bishop, chairing his first parliament, looked about him in unhappy agitation. "Is there any contrary motion?" he quavered. "Is any otherwise minded?"

As men shuffled and eyed their neighbours, suddenly aware of the danger, that any denial of this censure itself would in fact be a disobedience of the King's expressed command, and therefore likewise to be rated as treasonable, a dry cough from the Duke of Albany drew all eyes. That self-contained man did not rise, but spoke flatly.

"Before any such motion can be accepted or rejected, it is necessary to establish that there has indeed been the misgovernment alleged. Unless this is proven, there can be no cause for censure." He made that sound like a douche of cold

133

water, so that the heady temperature in the refectory dropped immediately by degrees.

Thankfully the Chancellor seized on this lifeline. "True, my lord Duke, assuredly. Before my lord of Crawford's motion be put, if its relevance is contested, such must be spoken to. My lord Earl, do you so speak?"

Crawford snorted. "What need of that, man? Everyone knows the realm has been mismanaged for years. Lawlessness is on every hand. The Treasury is empty. The sentences of sheriffs and justice-ayres are not carried out — I, as High Justiciar can vouch for that! Men mete out their own justice. Lands are raided. What more establishing do you need?"

"My lord Chancellor, these are general assertions," Albany observed. "Not specific charges. Not evidence, as the Justiciar knows well — or should. Indeed, even as such, they would seem rather to indict the High Justiciar himself, for failing to enforce due justice in the land."

"How can I, Stewart, when the very Governor himself flouts all law and justice!" Crawford cried hotly. "The power and force of the realm is in *your* hands, not mine."

"Specific charges — and named witnesses to speak thereto, my lord Chancellor," the Duke went on frigidly. "We have heard sufficient of wild accusation. Else I leave this travesty of a parliament for more profitable activity. And not only I!"

In the ominous growling from both sides which greeted that threat, David, Duke of Rothesay rose from his seat, smiling as ever.

"Your Grace, my lord Chancellor, my lords all," he said easily, "I agree entirely with the Duke of Albany. Enough of generalities. Likewise of hot words. This is the King in parliament assembled, the weal of the realm our only concern. But our solemn duty also. None of us enjoy the laying of blame and the passing of censures — in especial upon our own close kin and friends, to say nothing of our liege lord. It is distasteful to all men of goodwill. Let us, then, dispense with blame and accusation, and confine ourselves to a calm and reasoned consideration of facts and problems, that we may ensure due amendment, if this is necessary, in all amity."

Warily men weighed that, his own supporters equally with Albany's and the uncommitted, doubtful of such sudden sweet reasonableness.

"Let us be done with this issue as swiftly as possible," he

went on. "And I crave your sympathy in having thus to make dispraise and denunciation of my own royal father's government. To prove its failure, as at present administered, it is only necessary to present to you certain proven cases of ill-management to the realm's hurt. Not by any means all. As herewith. The Treasury is empty and owing moneys to many. In especial the sum of 10,000 merks, being four years payment due to Her Grace the Queen, secured nevertheless on the customs of certain ports and burghs, including those of this same St. Johnstoun of Perth, of Dysart, Montrose and Aberdeen. Yet these customs have been uplifted each year and duly paid to the Lord High Chamberlain of the realm. This in time of peace when no major charges have been required of the Treasury. Many other such defaults I could list — but one is sufficient for our purposes. My lord Chamberlain may, to be sure, assure us that such customs, dues and taxes have not reached his coffers. But if so, since they have been uplifted from the shippers and traders, who hold papers to prove it, then failure in government is evident."

There was silence in the chamber. Silence likewise from the Chamberlain — who, of course, was none other than the Governor himself and who certainly did not fail to perceive the trap set for him. If he denied that he had received the moneys, then his system of tax-collecting was grievously at fault; if he had received them, but had not paid them out in accordance with parliament's express provision for the Queen's expenses, then he was still more at fault. And where were the moneys gone, with the Treasury empty?

When none other spoke for him, Albany shrugged. "There are many calls on the Treasury," he said, without rising. "Were my nephew more conversant with the difficulties of government, he would know of these. Such as the payment of life pensions, heritable pensions and pensions of retinue — these last to ensure supplies of armed men for the defence of the kingdom in case of need — payments made to many of those lords here assembled! There are payments of clerks, officers of state, keepers of castles, notaries and the like. There is the upkeep of embassages and the sending of envoys to other Courts. The repairs of fortresses, ports, bridges. Many more. I do not come to parliament armed with clerks' books and papers; but such can be seen hereafter by those so minded."

"To be sure, my lord — to be sure. None would expect the King's Chamberlain to act as clerk. And with so great and many moneys amissing, it would be beyond all reason to bring to mind even a few of these piddling matters. But, as it happens, I am in a position to aid you in this, in some small way, to recollect some of these grievous items at the realm's charges. Such as 12,000 ounces of silver paid yearly, for the Governor's support; £200 yearly for the Chamberlain's support — with £900 more required as sundry expenses; £200 yearly from the royal customs of Linlithgow, for the Governor's support; £200 from the customs of Cupar, likewise for the Governor's support; £200 yearly for the support of the Keeper of Stirling Castle, my lord Duke of Albany; £200 yearly to the Lord Protector of the Abthania of Dull — which some here may never have heard tell of, but which is an office connected with the ancient Celtic Church of this realm which has been non-existent now for two centuries. That former Church is fortunate in having as the Protector of its Abthania none other than my lord of Albany — than whom none could be more sure a shield, you will agree! I could considerably further aid the Governor's memory — but here is sufficient, I think?"

As the catalogue was spelled out, faces had grown grimmer, and a muttering noise, almost a snarl, accompanied the final stages of the recital, all but drowning the prince's mellifluent tones. Some of it undoubtedly emanated from the Governor's own supporters, resenting this damning attack. But the shock sustained by many of the uncommitted was probably the more telling, whilst David's own adherents sought to cover their glee by cries of shame and the like.

But glee was suddenly quenched, on the prince's side at least, as the door opened to admit a new group of commissioners to the parliament, still travel-stained from long and muddy riding — the Bishops of Moray and Ross and the Abbots of Deer, Kinloss and Fearn. The churchmen's votes could be vital to the outcome today, and all these five could be guaranteed to support the Governor. Jamie all but groaned.

The interlude, with the newcomers from the North bowing to the King and then taking their seats, gave Albany opportunity to collect his thoughts, if that was necessary; and when he spoke he did so carefully, precisely.

"Again the Duke of Rothesay fails to recognise the realities of government, Sire," he said. "These sums accrue to me, or more properly to my offices, in respect of the various and many offices I administer in Your Grace's service, all of which are costly to operate and which could demand much greater payment were they in the hands of others than myself. Even that of the Abthania, which requires the administration of wide lands of the old Church. I would remind all present that as well as Governor I fulfil the duties of High Chamberlain, Captain General of the forces of the Crown, Keeper of the Great Seal, Keeper of Stirling Castle, Custodian of the Royal Mint, Justiciar of Fife and Strathearn and Chief Warden of the Marches. Others likewise. All these demand much expenditure of moneys. Mind it."

"Dear God, Sire — I had no notion that your noble brother and my good uncle was so imposed upon, so overburdened by the duties of your government!" David cried, as though astonished. "All this, on the shoulders of one ageing man! Small wonder if that government has broken down. Surely Your Grace and this parliament must needs relieve the excellent Duke of much of this crushing weight of responsibility! Lest he collapse entirely beneath the load!"

"Your Grace's government has *not* broken down, Sire. And I require none of this young man's false sympathies!" Albany snapped.

"My lord Duke is too conscientious," his nephew insisted, kindly. "Nobly prepared to bear more than his share, not only in matters fiscal. In the still more vital affairs of the realm's security from assault and invasion he is sorely overwhelmed. He has just reminded us that he is Chief Warden of the Marches and commander of Your Grace's forces. Yet, less than a year past, he did naught to counter the threatened invasion of the English under the Duke of Lancaster and Sir Harry Percy — if he knew aught of it — and the matter had to be dealt with by, h'm, other hands. At considerable cost and danger to certain of your lords. Moreover the Governor, all unwittingly I make no doubt, had renewed the truce between the two realms, in a fashion most disadvantageous to Scotland, maintaining the *status quo* whereby the castles of Berwick and Roxburgh remained in English hands, thus permitting Englishmen to ride abroad on Scottish soil and even to demand compensation for damage done by Scots hands to Scots works, to wit the bridge of Roxburgh, from Scots subjects. In especial, to the Earl of Douglas his cost. Is that not so, my lord Earl?"

The sudden indrawings of breath from all around indicated that the moment of truth had come, at last. All eyes turned on

137

Archie the Grim's long crouching figure. So much depended on which way the great house of Douglas jumped now. Albany's old friend, almost his only true friend in the years past, could muster or sway up to a score of votes in that parliament.

"Aye," the Earl grunted, grinning, without rising from his seat.

Men waited, and then gazed at each other as they realised that that was all that the Earl of Douglas seemed to be going to say. Stir, disquiet, question surged over the assembly.

Even David Stewart looked less assured than he had been — although his uncle Albany was frowning uncertainly also.

Jamie Douglas cursed his chief below his breath. The old man had always been an awkward character, unpredictable save in that he could be relied upon to be difficult. But with so much at stake for all, this was too much.

The prince recovered himself. "My good-father-to-be agrees," he observed, and mustered a laugh. "As Warden of the West March, who should himself have been Chief Warden — he could hardly do otherwise. And with a claim for £2,000 sterling against him by the Percy! Moreover, when the realm is in danger from over the Border, Douglas does not shrink his duty."

"The realm was in no danger of invasion," the Governor intervened shortly. "John of Gaunt was concerned and mustering troops because my nephew's late friend, Dunbar, was landing large numbers of men on his Isle of Man, opposite Lancaster. And the Percy is ever raiding across the March, no more than a brigand. As for the truce, I could not alter the *status quo* without mounting an armed expedition against Roxburgh and Berwick — war, in fact. I either signed, or provoked a new war. Which would Your Grace have preferred?"

As the monarch, thus shrewdly appealed to, shook his head and tugged at his grey beard, a clatter from the ladies' enclosure distracted attention momentarily. Looking thereto, Jamie saw that it was the Countess of Mar who had dropped her crucifix and chain. He was surprised to perceive also that, stooping to pick it up, her glance was directly aimed at himself, and the slight jerk of her head was as unmistakable a beckon as it was imperative.

The prince smoothly used the slight interruption to make up for his father's lack of answer by declaring that the invasion had been planned by the English *before* Dunbar's force moved to Man, to coincide with a descent on the Douglas province of

Galloway by Donald of the Isles and his barbarous hordes.

Jamie slipped round behind the benches to the ladies' seats, where he managed to insinuate himself to the Countess's side. He had not seen her since that day at Kildrummy in October.

"See you," she said to him quietly but urgently, "*I* cannot speak in this man's assembly. But I have something that could be said. Against Robert Stewart. Tell Alex Stewart to come to me, quickly. He can speak to it. Then tell your prince to call him."

"Your husband, Sir Malcolm . . . ?"

"He hates Douglas — and this could benefit Douglas. Get Alex — he has his back to me, here, or I could sign to him."

Jamie moved down and whispered to Alexander, sitting amongst the lords as Lord of Badenoch. He recognised that he must be very conspicuous doing so; but David was still speaking and he was known as the prince's man. Moreover, he was by no means the only messenger who had moved between principals during that session.

David finished speaking about Donald of the Isles, and the further invasion of Lochaber and the North-West by his brother Alastair Carrach, which the Governor had done nothing to halt. Donald himself was not present, although entitled to be. Nobody took up his cause, and Albany declared that if the King's government involved itself in Highland feuding it would have time and strength for little else. Jamie moved close to the prince.

"My lord," he murmured, "the Countess of Mar says to tell you to call on Alex Stewart to speak."

"She does? Why?"

"For your benefit, she says."

"Why should she be concerned? It could be a trap. She may be my mother's brother's wife — but I do not know that she loves me."

"I think she would not trap Alex, my lord."

"Ha — you say so? Is it so? Very well . . ."

The Governor was ever brief, and Bishop Trail, the Primate, had risen to speak, pointing out that Alastair's incursion was no mere clan feuding but a major assault on part of the kingdom, in which an establishment of Holy Church, the Valiscaulian Priory of Ardchattan, was assailed, to its loss and great

139

injury. If Holy Church could not rely upon the King's government to give it protection, then it must reconsider its attitudes and support.

Although many of the assembled company appeared less than concerned with the Church's problems, David rose to declare his sympathy, and pointed out that the Islesmen's threat had been lifted thanks to the valiant efforts of Sir Alexander Stewart of Badenoch, ably assisted by Sir James Douglas of Aberdour, whose efforts on behalf of the realm, including the relief of the royal castle of Urquhart, deserved the thanks of all present. To scattered acclaim, he suggested to the Chancellor that Sir Alexander should speak.

Alex had just got back to his seat. Men considered his slenderly graceful person keenly. The fame and dread of the Wolf of Badenoch was still sufficiently fresh in all minds to endow his son with more than usual interest, and his delicate good looks were the more intriguing.

"Your Grace and my lords," he said, with his soft Highland intonations, "I fear that the defeat of Alastair Carrach was a very minor matter — save in the splendid charge of Sir James Douglas with a troop of the royal guard and some Lochaber clansmen, which saved the day. Scant credit accrues to myself." He paused. "But with Your Grace's permission, instead of dwelling on this, I would now ask a question of whosoever is best informed to answer it — a question I believe relevant to this discussion on government. I would ask whether or no, after the death of the late second Earl of Douglas at Otterburn, the Countess of Mar, that Earl's sister, was offered a large part of the Douglas lands, including the Forests of Ettrick and Jedburgh, by the then Earl Robert of Fife and Menteith, in return for her acquiescence in the said Earl Robert's taking to himself of the castle of Tantallon and the Chief Wardenship of the Marches, with their revenues — both hitherto included within the earldom of Douglas? Which great lands were assumed by the Countess — but later taken from her, the said Earl Robert and the Crown assenting. I ask if this is the fact, since it bears heavily on the administration of justice and officers of government in this realm?"

The choking cry from Archibald, Earl of Douglas, all but drowned the last of that lilting query.

"I do not believe it!" he bellowed, rising to his feet. "This, this young whelp of an excommunicate freebooting father —

how dares he! None would so use *me*, Douglas!" But it was at his old friend the Governor that he glared.

"My lord Chancellor — I suggest that the Earl of Douglas directs his spleen elsewhere than at my humble self," Alex said. "The Countess of Mar is here present. Although she may not intervene in this parliament's debate, at least, with His Grace's permission, she can answer or no what I have said is true?"

"Well, woman — is it true?" Archie thundered, not waiting for any royal permission.

"It is true." Isobel of Mar's voice might be husky but her words were clear enough. "Robert Stewart offered me such compact. And then broke it when it suited him. Can he deny it?"

"I confirm or deny nothing," Albany said levelly. "Earl James of Douglas died ten years ago. Before I was Governor. In the previous reign. What arrangements may have been made in the matter of his estates and offices are long done with and no concern of this parliament."

"They concern *me*!" Douglas grated. "Have I nursed a viper to my bosom all these years? Why have I never heard tell of this?"

"Because it did not concern you," Albany said. "You were not Earl of Douglas then, I'd remind you. Likewise I'd remind you *how* you became Earl of Douglas!"

"Christ God . . .!"

"Your Grace, Your Grace," David intervened, loudly for him, and necessarily. "I agree with my lord Duke of Albany. This matter, although interesting no doubt, is of no immediate concern to our discussion. I suggest indeed that we have discussed sufficiently. If you, my lord Chancellor, and all present, are satisfied that there has been enough evidence of the King's government's mismanagement — as I am satisfied — then let it be put to the vote of parliament without further debate. I am sure that the Governor would not delay further."

There was a long moment of silence, with the Earl Archibald still on his feet, scowling blackly, and Albany pointedly looking elsewhere. The latter shrugged.

"Then I call upon the Earl of Crawford, if still so minded, to put his motion," the Chancellor said, though doubtfully.

"Gladly," Lindsay exclaimed. "There has been overmuch of talk, I say. I move, as before, that this parliament declares that there has been grievous misrule, and hereby makes due censure

141

on the King's Grace and his government as responsible."

"And which seconder?"

Before Sir Malcolm Drummond of Montgomerie could rise, Archie the Grim, already on his feet, spoke. "I second that, by the Mass! Aye — Douglas seconds!" That was almost a shout.

The entire assembly seethed. The Governor had lost Douglas. For a full minute there was pandemonium in that refectory.

At last the Chancellor, banging with his gavel, made himself heard. "Quiet! Quiet, I say, my lords — in the King's royal presence! Is there any contrary motion?"

"Aye! Aye!" came from various parts of the chamber.

"My lord Earl of Ross. Your motion?"

"The direct negative, sir," Albany's son-in-law declared, in duty-bound. "That this parliament has fullest confidence in the King's Grace and his government, in especial in the Governor, the Duke of Albany."

"I second," Sir William Lindsay of Rossie cried — and none failed to note that here was a house divided also, with Crawford's brother voting against his motion. That was the price paid for Eupham Lindsay, no doubt.

"And I," the Bishop of Moray added, with a quick glance at the Primate. "Holy Church must ever support the King's Grace."

When the uproar died down, the Chancellor said that he would take the vote on the negative first. All who supported the Earl of Ross's motion to show hands.

Decision at last. It is safe to say that, as well as the Chancellor's tellers, practically everyone in that apartment was counting hands — and turning to scan their neighbours keenly, speculatively. Indeed not all hands went up at once; clearly what others did was important to many. When not only the Earl of Douglas but also the Lord of Dalkeith, kept their hands by their sides — the Earl of Angus and the Douglasses of Drumlanrig and Cavers were, of course, sure for the prince — not a single Douglas vote could be counted for the negative, something none would have prophesied only a short time before. On the other hand, despite the new earldom conferred on their chief, fully one-third of the Lindsays raised their hands. The Stewarts themselves were divided right down the centre, and it would be hard to compute which side had the advantage. The churchmen's vote, so important, looked to Jamie to be on the whole favourable, with well under half of the bishops and mitred abbots raising beringed hands. Of the few royal burghs repre-sented, only those in Fife, Menteith and Strathearn showed for the negative. Nevertheless, there was a solid mass of Central Scotland lords and knights-of-the-shire, many in receipt of the Governor's pensions, or vassals of the earldoms of Fife, Menteith, Strathearn, Lennox, Atholl and Ross, about whose allegiance there was no doubt.

"I make it thirty-five — no, thirty-six — against us!" Jamie exclaimed excitedly, at the prince's back. "Dear God — it is enough, is it not? There are more than eighty present . . ."

"Wait you," David said steadily. "Some cautious folk may abstain. Seek safety in that."

"Your Grace, my tellers count thirty-six votes for the direct negative of my lord of Crawford's motion," the Chancellor announced. "I now call upon all in favour of the said motion to show."

Again not all who had not yet voted put up their hands, at first. Led by the Earl Archie, Douglas did, a fine phalanx that swelled Jamie's heart. Five Mar vassals likewise. The Primate and fully half the churchmen. All the remaining burghs — for the prince was popular with the people and the Governor was anything but. The South-West was fairly solidly in favour. But it was soon apparent that there were indeed to be abstentions. No fewer than six Lothian and Merse representatives sat still heads down — these were the Earl of Dunbar and March's vassals. Some few churchmen did likewise. Surprisingly, the Lord of Calder, new husband of the King's sister Jean, had not voted although his sympathies had been taken for granted. Similarly Thomas Earl of Moray and Sir Patrick Gray.

Jamie all but shook his fist at these last, as he counted. "Thirty-four, thirty-five, thirty-six, thirty-seven, thirty-eight. God is good — thirty-eight, my lord! You have won! A curse on those faint-hearts — but you have won!"

"A-a-aye!" David let out a long sigh. "Won — but only just. By only two votes — and thanks to Isobel of Mar! One vote, truly, for the Chancellor himself has not voted, and he is for my uncle. Or *was*! One vote — by what a margin to rule a realm!"

"My lord King," the Chancellor reported, "my tellers agree on thirty-eight votes in favour of my lord of Crawford's motion, as against thirty-six negative. I do therefore declare the motion to be carried. That this parliament declares misrule and misgovernment, and censures Your Grace and your government."

Amidst the mixture of cheers and cries of anger and dissent, a new voice, clear and strong pierced the din. "My lord Chancellor — since the difference is so small, I take leave to challenge the vote of one man — Sir Alexander Stewart, who has voted for the motion." Sir John de Ramorgnie, the expert on laws, from Fife, sitting near Albany and one of his vassals, spoke authoritatively. "Sir Alexander is not entitled to vote. He only *claims* to be Lord of Badenoch. He is illegitimate. His father was Earl of Buchan and Lord of Badenoch; but being base-born he succeeds in law to neither the one nor the other. None accept him as Earl of Buchan. Why should we do so as Lord of Badenoch?"

"A plague!" Jamie muttered. "Mary said that Ramorgnie was not to be trusted."

David answered the protester, almost conversationally. "Sir John — I think you err in this. Sir Alexander was born out of wedlock, yes. But so were many here. Some even claim that my royal sire, and the Duke of Albany were so born!" He smiled. "Sir Alexander voted as representing the great lordship of Badenoch, one of the largest in the realm. None other seeks, or dares to seek, to represent that ancient lordship. Is it to be for-ever without suffrage? My uncle, the Earl of Buchan, left no legitimate issue, and Sir Alexander is his eldest son. Moreover he has but recently served the realm well indeed, against the Islesmen. Without the help of any from Fife! I say that he has the right to vote."

"Nevertheless, my lord Duke, he is not *de jure* Lord Badenoch."

"Then His Grace the King, sirrah, can make him so by a lift of the royal hand! He is his nephew, after all." David looked at his father.

The monarch raised his head, sighed, and waved a vague hand.

"You are answered, sir. Sir Alexander of Badenoch's vote stands."

There was another intervention. Sir James Sandilands, Lord of Calder, rose. "My lord Chancellor," he called, "I wish your clerk of parliament to note in his writings that I, for one, abstained from voting. Not because I was not in favour of the motion in general, but in that it included in its wording a censure of the King's Grace, in person. This I can by no means counte-nance. I will never have it said that Calder made public censure of his liege lord!"

144

Others of the abstainers hastened to add their voices to that.

The King raised his hand again, but only continued banging of the Chancellor's gavel gained him silence. "Nevertheless, my lord of Calder, and all my good lords and subjects," the monarch said in a strained and unsteady voice, "I accept that censure as just. Upon myself, as having failed to ensure good government. And on those who have governed in my name. The will of parliament has been expressed. It now behoves me to offer new arrangements of government for parliament's approval." He looked about him distinctly nervously. "It is my wish that the office of Governor of the realm be abolished — in that there can indeed be only one governor, he who wears the Crown. This office has proved to be an unfair burden on my good brother, who has borne it these many years. In its place, since I myself am, by God's will, infirm and of poor health, there will be a Lieutenant of the Crown, who shall rule in my name but subject to my authority at all times. To this high and onerous position I appoint — if I have the approval of parliament — my well-beloved elder son David, Duke of Rothesay, heir to my throne and High Steward of Scotland. I am confident that . . ." '

Despite the impropriety of interrupting the King's speech, a tumultuous cheering drowned the royal words, and continued. Robert Stewart sat still, utterly expressionless throughout, as he had done indeed throughout the voting also.

When quiet was restored, the King went on. "I am confident in my son's ability, goodwill and love of justice. But because, as my lord of Albany has said, he is inexperienced in the art of government, I would appoint a special council of his own, a Council of the Lieutenancy, to aid and advise him. On which council, distinct from my own Privy Council, I would wish to see his uncle the Duke prominent. Also my lord of Crawford, High Justiciar; my lord Bishop of St. Andrews, Primate; my lord of Douglas, Chief Warden of my Marches; and others, experienced in administering the realm's affairs. All for the better rule of my kingdom." The monarch sat back, as though exhausted. "Is this, then, approved by this parliament?"

There was a muttering and nodding of approximate agreement. But the Chancellor, wishing to see things done in order, was declaring that a motion should be moved and passed, when he was interrupted by the thin, severe voice of Robert of Albany.

"I so approve," he jerked. "I wish my nephew well. And now,

if Your Grace will permit, I shall retire. There has been a sufficiency of talk." And with a brief bow to the throne he turned and walked with stiff dignity to the dais-door, and out.

In the commotion, with several of his closer supporters apparently desirous of following him, David Stewart took charge.

"Sire," he said, "my lord Duke is right. It is sufficient for this day, is it not? Your Grace is wearied, I can see. This session has been adequately decisive. We assemble again tomorrow. I propose that Your Grace adjourns the sitting until then."

Thankfully his father nodded, and heaved himself out of his throne. Hurriedly Lyon came forward, and the trumpeters reached for their instruments. All rose.

As the fanfare blared out, men bowed and women curtsied, it was not so much on the limping monarch that eyes were turned but on the new ruler of Scotland. Very much aware of it, David Stewart smiled brilliantly and waved a genial hand. But Jamie Douglas, standing behind, noted that the other hand was clenched tight behind his back, knuckles showing white.

VII

IR JAMES DOUGLAS rode fast across the fair land of East
Lothian, between Lammermuir and the sea. He was in a
hurry, and yet loth to arrive at his destination. The wide,
undulating landscape of the coastal plain had never looked
finer, with the corn turning to gold on all the rigs in the mellow
August sunlight, the cattle sleek in the vales of Peffer and Tyne,
and the lambs on the green foothills strong and well-grown. It
was country to be savoured and enjoyed, not pounded through
with drumming hooves; the most rich and fertile in the land — a
land which had had four months of fair and reasonably honest
government, four months of the longed-for relief from oppression and lawlessness, at least in theory. Yet Jamie rode as
urgently as he had ever ridden during the long, unhappy regime
of the Lieutenant's uncle.

It was late in the warm afternoon, and he had been in the
saddle for thirty-five miles, from Linlithgow, where the Duke
of Rothesay was presently amusing himself with the Lady
Matilda Douglas — not the Lady *Mary* Douglas, the Earl
Archie's daughter, whom he had married at Bothwell Castle in
May, but the younger and more ardent wife of Sir James
Douglas of Strabrock, keeper of the royal palace of Linlithgow,
the Lady Mary being bestowed well out of the way at Turnberry
in Ayrshire. That Jamie was on the way to remonstrate with the
neglected bride's father was purely coincidental, and no more
satisfactory in that young man's estimation.

The traveller, with his two troopers of the royal guard, had
no time to call in at his own little castle of Stoneypath Tower,
tucked within a Lammermuir glen; nor yet at the mighty castle
of Tantallon on the sea cliffs, now safely back in Douglas hands,

having been taken from Albany and restored to the Earl of Angus and his mother. He drove on, east by south, along the south shore of the wide sandy estuary of Tyne, by the fishers' boat-strand of Belhaven, until the red-stone towers and battlements of the strange sea-girt fortress of Dunbar rose ahead of him. It was over two years since he had acted messenger here before.

The situation could hardly have been more different from that stormy March day when he had found George of Dunbar and March roosting almost alone in his draughty, wave-splashed hold. Now, in the genial evening sun and dark-blue calm of the whispering sea, the place was transformed. And not only thus, but in that it was seething with men, an armed camp in fact. Far too many men were there to be able to get into the castle itself, and the little town and all the slopes around were full of Douglas men-at-arms and mosstroopers. Jamie had come fearing to find the place under attack.

Asking for the Earl of Douglas, he was directed to the castle itself — and his heart sank. Clattering across the lowered drawbridge above the tide, it fell still further as he perceived signs of warfare, splintering, broken arrow-shafts, the blackening, fly-buzzing stains of spilled blood. Frowning, he rode in under the gatehouse arch, his dark features sufficiently Douglas-like to demand no challenge, whatever his escort's royal liveries might do.

But when, dismounted, he requested to be taken to the Earl Archibald, he was eyed strangely and told that he should see the Master. He was taken along the same vaulted corridors to the very room where previously he had been interviewed by the Earl George, to find it full of booted and spurred Douglas lairds sitting at meat, with the Master and his fat brother Sir James the Gross, at the head of the table, and no sign of their father.

Jamie and the Master were scarcely friendly; indeed it might have been difficult to find anyone who claimed real friendship with Archibald, Master of Douglas and Galloway, a self-contained, silent, brooding young man of now twenty-seven years, bullet-headed, heavy-featured, unsmiling. But they got on well enough, indeed had some dark Douglas affinity. James the Gross, however, he cordially disliked.

"What brings Davie Stewart's errand-runner here?" the latter exclaimed, in his squeaky, curiously high-pitched voice.

"No good, I swear! You'll find no loose women for him here, if that's your mission!" And he chuckled an unpleasant laugh.

"Quiet!" his brother commanded. "So, Jamie — welcome to Dunbar. Too late for the tulzie, I fear. How may I serve you?"

"It was your father I came seeking. My sorrow that it is too late. Is he not here?"

"He is above. Taken to bed. Sick."

"Sakes — the Earl Archie sick? Who would have thought that! I am sorry . . ."

"He is an old man — seventy-four years now. This ploy has been overmuch for him. At the height of the storming, himself in the van, he took a seizure, fell choking. We got a monk of the Red Friars here to bleed him. Yesterday. Maitland, George Dunbar's nephew, surrendered the place this morning."

"And is he . . . recovering?"

"We do not know. He has his wits again, in some measure — but does not speak. The monk says that he must not be moved or troubled."

"An ill chance. So hale and stout a man."

"What was your business with him?" the younger son demanded.

Jamie hesitated, then shrugged. "I was sent to tell him not to assault this castle. Not to do damage to any of the Earl of Dunbar and March's properties. At the Duke's . . . request."

James the Gross hooted.

His brother toyed with his meat. "Do you think that he would have heeded you?"

"I believe he would. Since it is the Lieutenant of the Crown's wish. And for good reason."

"We had good reasons for coming here. The best."

"Perhaps. But the situation has changed . . ."

"Dunbar is still turned traitor. Gone to England. Is working with Hotspur Percy, to raise a force to come back and spread devastation. Against his own countrymen. Why should David Stewart seek to protect him? From Douglas? He threw Dunbar over and chose Douglas, but a few months ago."

"It is scarce that. But he, the Duke, has now the safety of the kingdom to consider. And there is grave danger. King Richard of England is deposed, some say dead. The Duke has just had word that Bolingbroke, John of Gaunt's son, has now had himself proclaimed King, as Henry the Fourth . . ."

"Richard? The Plantagenet dead? Is he not in Ireland?"

149

"He was. When John of Gaunt, Duke of Lancaster, died, Richard confiscated his estates and declared his son, Henry Bolingbroke, forfeit and outlaw. His own cousin. Henry was in France. He came home, and set up the banner of revolt. Richard had gone to Ireland, yes, to put down some rising there. He returned — and Bolingbroke was waiting for him. Defeated him at Flint, and took him captive. Now he is deposed, or abdicate, or may be dead. And his Lancastrian cousin is king."

"Stirring tidings," James the Gross commented. "But what is it to do with us? Or Dunbar?"

"Bolingbroke — or Henry — is a very different man from Richard. He is strong where Richard was weak. A fighter not a talker. And popular with the people where Richard was not. He represents real danger to Scotland. One of his first pronouncements as king was to declare himself Lord Paramount of Scotland!"

"That old insolence and folly of Edward Longshanks!" the Master said.

"Folly and insolence, yes. But threat also. Why should he make that old claim about paramountcy now? So soon? The Duke believes that he contemplates an invasion of Scotland. What better way for a warrior-king to commence his doubtfully-lawful reign than by a military campaign? To win his people's support and rally his nobles behind him."

"If that is so, then the sooner he perceives that the Scots are warned, ready, and indeed striking first, the better." The Master said that flatly but heavily. "Teach him to think again. As we are teaching Dunbar that treason is costly!"

"The prince thinks otherwise. He was much concerned when he heard that Douglas was moving to assail Dunbar Castle. He sent me at once, when he was told. We did not believe that you could have gained entry thus soon — so strong a place."

"The hold strong, yes — but not the man who held it. Sir Robert Maitland. Dunbar left it in his keeping, his nephew, and took the rest of his family with him into England. Maitland is a weakling. And his manors in Lauderdale and Lothian are surrounded by Douglas lands. So he yielded — for a consideration! After but one sally."

"But — what authority did you have to attack Dunbar Castle? What business of Douglas?"

"You, a Douglas, ask that?" the fat young man demanded. "Dunbar is a forsworn traitor, a friend of the Percy. Controlling all the Merse and much of Lothian, from here. A menace to the realm — but to Douglas first."

"You did not seek the Lieutenant of the realm's consent before you attacked."

"Seek Davie Stewart's consent! In the Borders! Have you lost your wits, man?"

His brother intervened. "Have done, James. You ask our authority? Have you forgot that Dunbar is Warden of the East March? Gone over to the English. And as Chief Warden, is it not Douglas's duty to ensure that his desertion is made good, and punished? You — nor even my peculiar good-brother — will not deny that?"

Jamie shook his head. He, and no doubt the prince also, had overlooked the fact that, since the parliament at Perth, the Chief Wardenship had reverted to the Earl Archie, and that therefore he was supreme authority on the Border — under the Crown.

"The Crown conceives that the situation requires more delicate handling than this," he said carefully.

"Are *you* the voice of the Crown now — to Douglas? I shall require more than Jamie of Aberdour's words to convince me of that!"

Jamie was in a difficult position and knew it. This stolid young man did not get on well with his ebullient brother-in-law — brother-in-law twice over, since he was married to David's sister, as well as David being now wed to his. And with the old man ill, he now wielded the full power of Douglas, a difficult, moody, serious-minded but obstinate individual — and Jamie's own acting chief.

"I but bring you the prince's message," he said. He had been going to say command, but thought better of it. "He wished you to leave Dunbar Castle alone, and allow *him* to deal with the Earl of Dunbar's treachery."

"Then he is too late. And he should have come himself, if he seeks to over-rule Douglas and the Chief Warden, not sent you. But no doubt he is too busy with his pleasures and his whores, shaming my sister within months of her wedding." He paused, glowering. "But sit down, man. Eat. You may bring unwelcome tidings but you are still a Douglas . . ."

Jamie was indeed hungry and weary, after nearly forty-five miles of hard riding. He sat and ate gladly enough. He could not really dislike Archibald Douglas as he did his brother.

151

"How does the Earl do?" he asked, as he ate. "You say he does not speak. How long . . .?"

"Who knows at his years? I have never known him sick before. He ever laughed at sickness. Always the man of iron!" If there was a hint of bitterness there, it was scarcely to be wondered at, in a young man who had himself suffered much sickness. The Master had had a hard time with his fierce father who, besides being scarcely an affectionate parent, had never made any secret of the fact that his favourite was his first-born but illegitimate son, the late and famous Sir Will of Nithsdale.

"May I speak with him? Give him the Duke's message?"

"No. He is not to be troubled with affairs, with anything. And if he could understand you, he could not answer you. You must needs deal with *me*, Jamie, now. As must your Duke."

"M'mm. What then shall I tell him? The Duke?"

"Tell him what you will — since it is too late to alter anything. But . . . aye, tell him that I am leaving Dunbar Castle, as he requests! To go about my further business as Chief Warden of the Marches. Tell him that."

"Your father's business, surely?" Jamie amended. "Since he is the Warden . . ."

"Not so. *My* business. I am the Warden. He passed it on to me. I have been Chief Warden for two months."

"You . . .?"

"Why not? I had been Deputy Warden of the West March for three years. And this is no task for an old man."

"But . . . he did not inform the prince?"

"I do not know. Why should he? It is a Douglas matter. David Stewart could do nothing about it, even if he cared."

As Jamie digested that, it occurred to him that the other had put some significance into his phrase earlier as to going about his further business as Chief Warden. "And this further business you speak of? Can you tell me that?"

"Why not? It is but further to my duty here. We cross the Border. The morn's morn."

"You what? Cross the Border! You mean, in strength? Invade England!"

"Invade is a large word. But in some strength, yes. Make a demonstration of strength, indeed. It was needed before — and from what you tell us about the new king, it is now needed even more."

152

"But . . . man, this is crazy-mad! For Douglas, the Chief Warden! A reiving, a cattle-raid, is one thing. But this — this would be an act of war! But without the Crown's authority. Against the Crown's wishes, most certainly."

"And is Dunbar not engaged in an act of war? He and Percy are mustering men to invade *Scotland*. This we know for sure. In the vales of Aln and Till and Breamish and Coquet. And now you say that this new King Henry is calling himself Lord Paramount of Scotland and may lead an invasion likewise, to rally his people. Is not this the time to show these folk that the Scots are not waiting tamely to be trampled on? Make them think anew?"

"Arouse them to greater fury, you mean — Henry, at least. What more likely to fix him in his determination, to play into his very hands? Do this, and he has the most excellent excuse for retaliation. In greatest strength. It is folly, I say."

"I say otherwise. And, to be sure, it is what *I* say that signifies!"

"You cannot do it. Not now. Not when the Duke has but newly replaced his uncle. Before he has had time to set the realm to rights. When nothing is ready for war . . ."

"Now, indeed. Now is the time. Can you not see? The truce has just expired. The new English king cannot be ready either. Moreover, there is plague in England, bad plague. It has spread into the North, to the Yorkshire dales and Durham and Northumberland. They, the English, are in much fear of it. They will never look for a raid, in such case."

Jamie stared at the other, helpless.

"Go tell Davie Stewart that," James the Gross advised. "Aye, tell him to join us. A change of sport from wantoning and drinking!"

"Better — come with us," his brother amended. "We ride in the morning. So stout a fighter as Sir Jamie Douglas would be better employed than riding messenger."

"Ride where?"

"Across Lammermuir and the Merse, to Birgham on Tweed. There, tomorrow night, I meet with Will of Drumlanrig and Archie of Cavers, Rutherford of that Ilk, and others likewise. To double my strength."

"And then?"

"Cross Tweed and go seek out George Dunbar."

"Your father — had he intended this?"

153

"To be sure. It is at his summons that the others come to Birgham, not mine."

Jamie pondered. Will and Archie Douglas were his good friends, knighted with him at Otterburn, Will Warden of the Middle March and Archie Sheriff of Teviotdale. They were men he could talk to, important in their own right. They might heed him. Aid him to dissuade the Master from this folly. It was worth the attempt.

"I will ride with you as far as Birgham," he agreed.

* * *

On the morrow, leaving a small party in charge at Dunbar and another to convey the stricken Earl back to Threave in Galloway when he was fit to travel, they set out southwards, about five hundred strong, all mounted, a tough and fast-moving column of Border mosstroopers. Through the quiet Lammermuir hills they rode, to the headwaters of the Whitadder, to follow that lively river down to the low ground at Preston, and then to strike directly across the green and rich Merse, by Duns and Leitholm and Eccles, to the wide Tweed valley, and so to the riverside township of Birgham.

When Jamie saw the series of encampments, their banners, the long lines of tethered horses and the camp-fires, his spirits sank despite the spirited scene. He did not fail to recognise that the chances of success for his self-appointed task were small. Here was a much larger force than he had looked for, all set for war — and composed of warlike Borderers whose whole background and tradition was embued with raiding and reiving across the March; and who, moreover, had been held in, to some degree, for years by the series of official truces. To hope to turn back this exultant martial array by sweet reason and pleas, without a blow struck, seemed suddenly improbable to say the least.

And so it proved. His friends of Drumlanrig and Cavers were glad to see him, assuming at once that he was taking part in the adventure and hailing his adherence as like old times. When he disillusioned them, and endeavoured to convince them that this was an ill-considered and highly dangerous project, they were astonished and clearly considered that his judgement was at fault. It was not merely that Douglas had ordered it, they asserted; but this move of Dunbar and Percy had to be countered, before it got out of hand and set the entire Borderland on fire. There was no question but that the English were mustering. If the Mersemen refused to resist them, as was possible with their own Earl and Warden leading the invasion, then the rest of the Scots Borders would be in the gravest danger, their flank turned, their ancient enemies pouring in on them from behind. They it was who would have to bear the brunt of the bloodshed, pillage and rapine, not the Lieutenant of the Crown and the rest in faraway Linlithgow, Stirling or Perth. It was David Stewart's fault that it was happening, in the first place, by his having offended Dunbar and retained the dowry-moneys for his daughter. He could scarcely object to the Borderers defending themselves. This threat had to be halted before it properly began.

Jamie, of course, could not altogether refute their arguments, for there was much truth in what they said. And to assert that, for the greater good of the kingdom, the longer view should be taken, was neither popular nor entirely convincing. Moreover his position was complicated by the fact that he was only *assuming* that the prince would be opposed to this cross-Border raid; for of course nothing had been known of the project when he left Linlithgow. His own remit had been to dissuade the Earl of Douglas from attacking Dunbar Castle. He presumed that the same reasoning would be against this unofficial invasion — but he had no specific instructions to that effect.

When it was obvious that nothing he could say was going to alter the situation, Jamie came to a decision. He could conceivably do more good by staying with the raiders, seeking to influence them against possible follies and excesses, than by hurrying back northwards to Linlithgow — where David would be in no position to do anything swiftly effective anyway. He sent back his two royal-guard escorts with a message to the prince, and signified to the Douglas leadership that he would remain with them, although critical of their course.

The Master eyed him, at that, with a hint of grim humour — almost the first resemblance to his father that Jamie had seen in the man — but shrugged acquiescence. His Teviotdale friends clapped him on the back.

The waiting Teviotdale and Jedburgh party — which included Sir William Stewart of Jedworth, the Laird of Rutherford, Turnbull of Bedrule and a famous freebooter known as Out-with-the-Sword Turnbull — had had the good sense not to camp at the riverside and so be visible from across Tweed, but inland

155

a short distance where they were screened by woodland. In typical Border fashion, a wait was made until the small hours of the next morning when, with a pale waning half-moon adding its wan light to a not very dark night, a flying column was sent quietly across the ford of Tweed nearby, to surround and isolate the village of Carham on the far side, to ensure that no alarm emanated from there. Then the main force, some 1,300 strong, splashed across the shallows into England.

Their first concern had to be the Castle of Wark some two miles further downstream, a powerful hold belonging to the English Crown, which dominated this stretch of the river in general and in particular served for the exaction of tolls for the fords and ferry between there and Coldstream, a source of much revenue, though little more popular with the local English than with the Scots. It was not a fortress of the calibre of Berwick or Roxburgh, but it was a strong place with a sizeable garrison under a renowned and veteran keeper, Sir Thomas Grey. It was not a comfortable place to leave free to menace their rear and possibly to interfere with their use of the forts on return. The present hope was to surprise it at what was ever the most vulnerable hour for any fortified strength, when the new day began, with its cattle being driven out from their night's security in the outer bailey, night-soil being ejected and forage and fuel being brought in from outside — moreover with the night watch weary and off their guard, duty over, and the day staff still sleepy-eyed and less than alert. Many a stronghold had been surprised and cheaply won in these circumstances.

In the event, the surprise was otherwise. The Scots, halting to wait for sun-up in nearby woodland, did observe the drawbridge lowered and a quite numerous herd of cattle being driven out to pasture. A swift-moving troop under the Master himself galloped forward to capture the bridge before it could be raised again and the portcullis lowered against them. This they achieved — but the surprise was to find that there was little or no subsequent resistance. It transpired, in fact, that the castle was practically empty of its garrison, Grey and most of his men having been summoned to a great muster-at-arms being organised by Sir Ralph Percy, brother of Hotspur, at Wooler, the chief town of Glendale, where the Glen joined the Till, about a dozen miles to the south-east, leaving only a few men at Wark. These put up only the merest token fight.

The Douglases, naturally, were much heartened by this speedy and painless success, an excellent omen and proof, the Master claimed, that their raid was timely and necessary. They would now drive on for Wooler and break up Percy's muster before it could become a menace.

But before they rose, it appeared there was a task to be performed here. Wark, ever something of a threat to the Scots, must be burned, razed to the ground. It was too good an opportunity to miss, and worth spending a little time on. Moreover, it would serve as an excellent warning to Percy and Dunbar.

Jamie protested strongly. To destroy the castle would serve the Scots cause nothing. But it must seriously anger the English, the new King especially — for it was a royal castle. A raid was one thing; but deliberately to raze a major stronghold which had yielded without bloodshed was altogether another. Henry Plantagenet could not fail to seek to avenge that — his credit quite forfeited otherwise.

These contentions were rejected. The forenoon was devoted to the methodical and thorough demolition and burning of Wark, its castle and supporting castleton, of manor-place, cothouses and mill. A small detachment was despatched back over Tweed with the cattle, ever dear to Border hearts. At noon the advance was continued, due southwards over Wark Common, for the Bowmont Water, leaving a great column of black smoke soaring into the August sky.

That ominous beacon had its effect. All the way down the twisting valley of the Bowmont Water and through the wide vale of Till and beyond, the Scots found the folk fled before them, cottages, farmsteads, whole villages and manors hastily abandoned — and the Master of Douglas found it difficult indeed to control his mosstroopers and prevent them from indiscriminate pillage and helping themselves — after all, that was what Border raiding was all about, on whatever the scale. And he was not the old Earl, lacking his authority. The pace of the advance slackened inevitably.

At least they took suitable military precautions, riding in four distinct groups, with constant liaison — an advance-guard under the redoubtable Out-with-the-Sword Turnbull, old in experience of such reiving and knowing this territory like the palm of his hand; a strong flanking force to east and west on the heights above the vale; and the main body in the centre, following the rivers, where lay the villages and townships —

157

although sending back many a little party with cattle, horses and plunder.

Long before the dozen or so miles to Wooler was accomplished, it became obvious to Jamie — and to others likewise no doubt — that they were going to be in no position to fight any major action, with numbers being steadily depleted and with the minds of most preoccupied with plunder rather than battle. Fortunately for them, it appeared that Sir Ralph Percy did not realise this, or else was very doubtful about his musterers' ability to put up any sort of effective opposition, for Turnbull's scouts presently sent back information that the quite large numbers of men assembled on the Glendale flats were in fact streaming away southwards towards Alnwick. When, in the late evening, the Scots eventually arrived at Wooler, it was to find not only the encampment but most of the little town deserted.

Douglas took over the abandoned camp, and his men made merry in the town and surroundings.

The Glendale area, with Doddington, Chatton and Chillingham, was richer than the land they had traversed hitherto, and as good as a magnet for the mosstroopers. Sleep, save for the hopelessly drunken, was scarcely considered that night, with such plentiful pickings to be had for the minimum of effort. Women too were soon discovered. The Master and his colleagues did not appear to be greatly concerned, their attitude being that since this raid was in the nature of a demonstration of strength and readiness, it did not matter if there was little or no real fighting, so long as the English in general were suitably intimidated and alarmed. Their cause could be as well served by pillage and destruction as by actual bloodshed and battle. Jamie, with no hankering after either, nevertheless felt, and said, that this was mistaken policy. But then, the entire expedition was a mistake, in his opinion.

In the morning the leaders of the Scots force had the greatest difficulty in rounding up their followers into any coherent array. Pillage and rapine are highly infectious states of mind, and men with almost unlimited booty available were naturally intent on getting it safely back home. Since none were actually paid to be there, giving only armed service to their lords and lairds, they tended to see their duties in a different light from hired or professional soldiers; also Borderers were renownedly of a fiercely independent mind. Moreover, many of their lairds were similarly inclined. Had there been any sign of serious opposition, any hostile threat evident, it would have been different. Not many more than half of the original numbers were accounted for by mid-forenoon. When Out-with-the-Sword Turnbull himself sent word back that his advance-party was so sorely depleted as to be unable properly to carry out its scouting and protective functions, the Master bowed to the inevitable. He ordered a retiral to the Tweed.

If the outwards journey had been a slow progress for an armed advance, the return was more so, with vast numbers of cattle to be herded along — and more being added all the time, for it would have been a poor Borderer who would see any available left behind. It took them all day indeed to reach Tweed, at less than two miles in the hour, spread wide over the country-side, no longer any sort of coherent force but an agglomeration of drovers. Such farms and homesteads and hamlets as had escaped in the advance now went up in flames. A whole land blazed and smoked behind them.

More than once Jamie Douglas almost left the others in disgust and frustration, to ride northwards on his own, back to Linlithgow. But he told himself that he would see them safely out of England, at least. He had good friends here, and he *was* a Douglas.

The business of getting the herds across the fords of Tweed was a seemingly endless nightmare, and took most of the night in fact. There were thousands of reluctant and weary beasts to force and steer and harry over, with many breaking back in mid-stream in bellowing panic. Fortunately the water was low, so that a number of fords could be used, some not normally available, between Wark and Birgham.

On Scottish soil thereafter they rested until well into the following forenoon, all along the riverside — for such huge numbers of cattle took up a great deal of space. They had left a rearguard behind them, of course, as necessary precaution.

When eventually they moved off again, westwards now, it had to be by innumerable stages along the Tweedside drove-road, for they could not trample widespread and roughshod across the land here as they had done in the Auld Enemy's territory. Jamie thankfully decided that his presence was no longer required, in any way, and took his leave.

"Go back to your prince, Jamie," the Master said, in farewell, "and tell him that Douglas has taught both traitors and proclaimed Lords Paramount a lesson! At no cost to his realm. Tell him that the English have been given warning that the Scots are ready and in good fettle. Aye — and tell him to appoint a new Warden of the East Màrch forthwith — and that a Douglas one would be advisable! Say that I suggest your Uncle Will of Mordington."

"All that I shall tell him," the other agreed. "But I do not promise that my news will rejoice him!"

"Then he knows not when he is fortunate. We do his work for him, while he whores and idles. Tell him so."

Jamie rode with his Teviotdale friends of Drumlanrig and Cavers as far as Edenmouth, and there left them to follow up the Eden Water while they continued up Tweed. He was making for Ednam, a barony belonging to the Lady Isabel Stewart, former Countess of Douglas, gifted to her by her father at her wedding and one of her main sources of revenue. He was still her knight and kept an eye on her affairs, for he admired her greatly and owed her much — and her present husband, Edmonstone, although amiable was elderly, drunken and lazy. He would take the opportunity to look in on Ednam on his way home, since it was near at hand.

In the event, he found quite a lot demanding attention there, with the old steward dead and the new one less effective as yet; and he delayed overnight and most of next day, for it was an extensive property with much requiring decision. He had just finished, and left for the north, when, a mile or two on his way, the new steward came pounding after him at the gallop. He had just had word, the man gasped, that a large English force had crossed Tweed and was hot on the heels of the Master of Douglas, pausing for nothing.

Jamie cursed. He had feared something of the sort, and Archie Douglas's over-confidence. They would be in no state to fight effectively now, their force disintegrating and dispersed. The Teviotdale contingent would have left Tweedside to follow up their own river, at Kelso — for Jamie knew that the Master intended to head westwards for Douglasdale in Lanark's Upper Ward by following Tweed right up almost to its source and then crossing over the watershed to Clydesdale.

What to do? He could not just ride off homewards and leave his friends and fellow-clansmen to their fate. On the other hand, one extra sword would be of scant benefit. One thing he might try — he could hurry after the Teviotdale party, warn them, and possibly bring them to the aid of the Master. The probability was, if the English followed the others up Tweed, those in the long side vale of Teviot would know nothing about it — not for some time, at any rate.

Decision made, Jamie turned back for Ednam, hurriedly rounded up a dozen sturdy Mersemen there, and with these set off at top speed south-westwards for the Teviot.

On the outskirts of Kelso, with the sun setting before them, they halted discreetly when they could see from the higher ground that the town seethed. Enquiries from cottagers elicited the information that the English were in fact in the town, at the junction of Tweed and Teviot, and appeared to be going to spend the night there whilst their leaders went on to consult with their countrymen garrisoning Roxburgh Castle. A kind of hell was loose in Kelso, according to their informants, with folk fleeing; but so far the town had not been set afire. Possibly the invaders were reserving that for their return journey. The English force was said to be under the joint command of Sir Robert de Umfraville, Deputy Warden of the English East March and Sir Thomas Grey, Keeper of Wark.

At least this pause ought to give the Master of Douglas a breathing-space, a little more time to organise some defensive action. But it by no means lessened the need for swift reinforcement. Jamie turned his horses' heads westwards again, to keep well to the north of Kelso. Roxburgh Castle, sitting at the joining of the waters, had to be avoided also. In the shadow of the August dusk they rode on, round the great crescent-shaped haugh of Floors and so back to Tweed about three miles above Kelso, where they crossed the ford at Trows and so reached Roxburgh Moor well west of the fortress. In a couple more miles they came to Rutherford, and here Jamie roused up Sir Robert of that Ilk and his five sons whom he had parted from the previous noonday, quite unaware of the English presence so near. The old man, although preparing for bed, promptly sent his sons out to reassemble his men. They would ride as soon as they might, up Tweed after the Master.

Jamie hurried on southwards now through the night, to ford Teviot at Nisbetmill and so to ride up Jed to Jedburgh. Here they had some difficulty with the town-watch before they could get at Sir William Stewart in his house in the centre of the burgh. But when reached, he agreed immediately to muster as many citizens as he could mount, and to ride north likewise. Over the Dunion Hill by a drove-road to Bedrule in Rulewater they proceeded, after midnight now, there to rouse the Turnbull laird and have him summon the many other Turnbull lairdlings of that remote valley. Then on, up Teviot again, to Denholm-on-the-Green and Cavers. Despite the small hours of the morning, Jamie's friend Sir Archibald, illegitimate younger son of the late James, Earl of Douglas, left his new wife's bed to take over the task of warning the rest of the Teviotdale Douglasses, including his brother Drumlanrig at Hawick, whilst the weary group from Ednam rested.

By sun-up four hundred men were assembled in Hawick's Sandbed, most of them the same who had just returned from the raid into England. Jamie gladly resigned the initiative to his friends. The brothers decided that, in the circumstances, the Master, once warned, would almost certainly try to keep ahead of the pursuit until he could win into the wilds of Ettrick Forest proper, where he might make the land fight for him in some measure — with six hundred or so against 2,000 he would need to do so. Presumably, to free his hands and gain speed, he would send off the great cattle droves into side-valleys and hidden hollows all the way up Tweed — although this must further deplete his numbers. If this estimate was correct, he would leave Tweed where the Ettrick Water joined it, near Selkirk, and follow up the lesser river to its confluence with Yarrow — for Yarrow provided an alternative route over the empty hills to the west and eventually Douglasdale — with the forest thickening and the hills heightening and steepening. If he could get that far. There, if he chose his ground well, he might make a successful stand; there was nowhere similarly suitable before that. The Rutherfords, Jedburgh men and Turnbulls should have been able to join him before that. So much depended on how long the English might linger at Kelso and Roxburgh — although they must be equally well aware of the need for haste.

So the Teviotdale force rode for Ettrick by the most direct route, up over the rough hills by Stirches to Ale Water at Ashkirk, and again climbing, by the Haremoss heights and Hartwood to Selkirk Common. It was a dozen hard miles before the wooded vale of Ettrick opened before them, with, deep below, the little town of Selkirk nestling snugly in its enclave of the great forest. By then it was nearly noon.

This was Pringle country, vassals of Douglas, and at the Haining of Selkirk the aged Pringle laird gave them urgent tidings. The Master of Douglas was at Foulhopehaugh, at bay, with an English force caught up with him. He, Pringle, had already sent his sons, with as many Selkirk men as could be raised at short notice, to his Earl's son's aid. But by all accounts they were vastly outnumbered.

Foulhopehaugh was some two miles to the south-west, where Yarrow joined Ettrick, but on the other side of both rivers. Because of the woodlands, it was not visible from Selkirk. Thitherwards the Teviot force rode at speed.

Will and Archie Douglas said that the Master, when he could flee no further, would have taken up a defensive position where the Foulhope Burn came down to the haugh just below the junction with Yarrow, to use the burn and the damp and soft ground of the haugh as protection. Unfortunately it had been a dry season and the flats would be less soft than usual. They splashed across the Town Ford and swung left-handed along the farther bank.

They heard the noise of battle some way off — so, at least, the Master was not yet defeated. His friends would have ridden hot-foot straight on, to assail the English rear — for here they must be behind them; but as ever, Jamie urged caution, consideration. They might achieve more by less headlong measures. His reputation from Lochaber, however unwarranted, gained him their heed.

The entire terrain, save for the level haugh itself, was densely wooded with tangled scrub and old pines, poor ground for gaining any prospect. But there was a knoll to the west, a low outlier of Harehead Hill, which would overlook the haugh near the rivers-meeting. It was tree-clad also, to the summit, but it should provide some sort of viewpoint. A little reluctantly the others agreed to rein right-handed to make for this.

The trees on the knoll at least gave them some cover from view, likewise. Leaving their men at the east side of it, the leaders rode up to the crest.

The scene that met their gaze, in the early afternoon sunshine, was not at first glance that of a normal battle between two sides. It was, in fact, a furious and widespread confusion down there on the river's flood-plain. There was no line, no front, no recognisable sides as such, merely a vast number of isolated tussles, individual fights often between quite small groups, covering much of the south end of the haugh. Which was friend and which foe it was almost impossible to say, from any

163

distance, with the innumerable struggling clusters and knots surging this way and that and facing in all directions. Banners and pennons seemed to have been discarded. Bodies lay or crawled everywhere. The battle was being fought on foot, even by the leaders — which presumably meant that, dry season or not, the haugh must be too soft still for cavalry tactics. Certainly it could be seen that the levels were split and scored by many ditches and water-channels. The Ettrick, coming down from the high hills so close at hand, was very liable to spates.

One thing was clear about that fight however. The struggle was taking place on both sides of the Foulhope Burn — which must mean that the burn had in fact failed as a defensive line and therefore that the Scots were in general, losing ground, getting the worst of it. Clearly there was no time to be lost.

"Down at them!" Will Douglas exclaimed. "No more delay, in God's name!"

"Aye — they're in sore trouble," his brother agreed. "Come — quickly!"

"Wait," Jamie advised again. "For just a little." He pointed. "See — their horses. Left yonder, to the north, 2,000 of them! And under scant guard. There's our opportunity!"

"Eh? You mean . . .?"

"Send down some of our people, horsed, first. While the rest wait here, hidden. Say a hundred — we can spare that. To gallop down, shouting, to a little way north of the horse-lines. Then, at the foot, swing southwards, right-handed. Drive directly on to the pack of their beasts. Panic them. Send them bolting down on the battle, 2,000 galloping horses! Break up the fighting."

"Lord . . .!"

"Then charge down our people from here. On foot, shouting, into the midst of it. No battle left, after that, perhaps!"

"Save us, Jamie — what a ploy! But . . .?" Sir Will looked doubtful. "What if they do not bolt? The horses? Or bolt in the wrong direction?"

"They will bolt. I'll lead. If we keep well to the north, at first, then turn on them. They will not stand. They will shy, turn tail, flee. Bolt southwards. They will not plunge into the river. Nor be apt to climb this hill. They will take the open haugh."

"Yes, yes," Cavers cried, "come, then . . ."

The three young knights ran back to their men. Will shouted for roughly five score to follow Sir James of Aberdour, the rest to dismount and come with him up to the crest again.

164

"Do not charge too soon, or you might turn the horses back on us," Jamie panted, as he vaulted into his saddle.

He led his party to thread the trees northwards till they came to the tail of the little ridge. Drawing rein for a moment there, where they could see the low ground clearly, he jerked his instructions. Then, drawing his sword, he raised it high and dug in his spurs. It crossed his mind that he was becoming expert at leading false charges.

Downhill, in a fairly compact mass, they thundered, yelling A Douglas! A Douglas!, not directly towards the long lines of the English horses but angling north-eastwards. So far as Jamie could see, no more than a score or so of men had been left in charge of the animals. These began to scurry about, in agitation, at the sight of them coming. He had no time to observe whether their eruption on the scene had had any effect on the battlers to the south.

Reaching the levels, he sought to wheel his party round into a sort of sickle-shaped front, facing south, with the higher, westernmost end furthest forward, to counter any possible tendency of the English horses to bolt that way, uphill — all this without pausing. His men were not trained cavalrymen, but being mosstroopers all they were born horsemen, and quickly perceived what was required. Still shouting, and waving their swords, hooves drumming on the softish ground, they swept down on the great mass of riderless mounts.

There was no question as to the panic — and panic is just as infectious amongst horses as amongst men. The few guards left with them had no hope of exerting any sort of influence, much less control. Well before the Douglases were upon them, the first ranks of the horses were turning and rearing, whinnying and lashing out in terror at their fellows blocking their escape from the pounding, yelling, steel-waving menace. In only moments all was indescribable chaos, with animals kicking, screaming, falling. Jamie was suddenly afraid that he and his men were in fact going to crash into a solid if heaving wall of struggling horseflesh. He began to pull in on his reins in incipient panic of his own.

But, just in time, the danger eased as the alarm spread to the farther side of the pack, and the beasts there, with nothing in front to stop them, swung away and went plunging off southwards, reins trailing, stirrups and saddle-cloths flapping. The jam of unhappy creatures thereby easing, slackening in that

165

direction, every tossing head turned that way. In mere seconds that inchoate lashing mass evolved into a coherent movement, a flood that streamed away southwards shaking the entire haugh with the beat of 8,000 hooves. What happened to the guards in it all was not to be known.

Thankful that there had been no dire pile-up, Jamie and his men cantered on behind the stampede, throats hoarse with shouting, flats of swords beating at the rumps of any laggards — not that there were many of these. It was far from smooth going, of course. The ground was soft and pitted and scored by ditches and dried-up runnels. Some of the English beasts had fallen or been trampled down. There were isolated thorn-trees, and driftwood from spates, to be negotiated. It was a hectic, crazy, headlong scramble.

The first realisation for Jamie that they had reached the battlefield itself was when he began to see blood and men's bodies and weapons beneath his own mount's hooves. He risked a glance upwards, westwards. A horde of yelling Douglases were already plunging downhill, on foot, over quite a wide front. It would be only a matter of moments until the impact. He had neither time nor opportunity for further attention.

If the battle had seemed unclear, confused, before, now it ceased altogether to be a battle. No fighting could continue under the headlong onslaught of 2,000 maddened horses. Men on both sides were indiscriminately swept away, knocked over, trampled on and dispersed, under the flailing hooves. Those who had time to flee before the clash did so, desperately, uphill into the trees or actually into the river — these latter in the majority. The Ettrick was not very deep here, save in patches, and probably few drowned. Most splashed or swam to the far side, tending to lose swords and battleaxes in the process. Others clung under the near bank or stood about in the shallows, at a loss — this applying to the Scots and English alike, leader and led, for the moment at one in seeking escape from the terror. By the time that the seething flood of horseflesh had swept over the battleground and onwards unflagging, there was no semblance of a fight remaining — nor any real probability of it being reconstituted and resumed in the immediate future, whoever had been winning; especially as now the Teviotdale hundreds descended on the littered field in a fairly coherent and solid force, to find themselves in complete mastery of the situation without a blow struck. As surprised as anyone by the

166

abruptly total cessation of hostilities, they halted, to stand about in a kind of stupor. It was a little while before men went to peer at, aid and attend to the trampled wounded — all the wounded, since it was almost impossible to distinguish friend from foe still.

Jamie was able to disentangle himself and his followers, and pull up, after another couple of hundred yards, to turn and trot back, himself not a little appalled by the results of his action.

Drumlanrig and Cavers and the other Douglas newcomers, however, although slightly dazed by it all, were far from appalled. They came running to hail him, shouting their praise and plaudits. But sitting his panting, trembling mount, he shook his head.

"It . . . it is shameful! Terrible! No victory this. I . . . I have ridden down friend and foe alike!"

"You stopped the battle, man. Left us holders of the field. Saved the day . . ."

"Ignobly. Where are our friends? Where is the Master? Have I trampled him to death, with the others?"

None could answer that — though more and more of the Teviotdale men were examining the fallen.

Those who had fled successfully into the river and woodland began to reappear, clambering out of the water and emerging from the trees — or some of them, for these were nearly all Scots, the English naturally not anxious to place themselves in enemy custody. It fairly quickly became evident that larger numbers on both sides had managed to win clear than at first might have been thought. Hundreds of very wet Englishmen were now streaming away southwards on the other side of the river, and no doubt many more were doing the same through the forest glades.

Amongst those struggling out of the Ettrick, on this bank, were some whose fine half-armour or gleaming shirts of mail revealed them to be leaders or of knightly rank. One stocky figure, black hair plastered over his features, became recognisable as the Master of Douglas and Galloway. Thankfully Jamie flung himself down from his saddle and went hurrying to meet him.

"God's eyes!" the normally stolid heir to Douglas declared, gasping, and dripping water. "What a — a broil! Saints a mercy — it's a miracle!"

167

"You are unhurt? And your brother? God be praised! I feared, I feared that . . ."

"*You* feared, man? What think you *I* feared! Seeing that crazed host of horses bearing down on us. I near . . . shamed myself! I vow it! How did you contrive it? Was it of a purpose . . . ?"

"It was all Jamie's doing, Archie," Sir Will exclaimed. "He devised it. Led it. We saw you were much outnumbered, losing ground. He rode down hill, with five score men, and herded their horse-lines down upon you. To end the battle."

"Lord save us — here's a ploy! Jamie Douglas! But . . . how came you here, man? You left us at Birgham . . . ?"

"I heard, at Ednam, that you were being pursued by Umfraville and 2,000 horsed English. So I came after."

"He came after *us*, Archie. Roused all Teviotdale, to come to your aid," Sir Archibald of Cavers amplified. "You have him, and him alone, to thank for your deliverance."

"Not so," Jamie contested. "I merely brought the news. And this, this of the bolting horses, I perhaps misjudged. I insufficiently considered. How I put at risk my own friends equally with the enemy. And even these English deserved better than to be beaten down by brute beasts . . . !"

"Nonsense, Jamie. This is war, not a tourney," the Master averred. "We were all but lost, could not have withstood for much longer. You saved Douglas this day, my friend."

"Aye, he did. He did."

Embarrassed, Jamie shook his head. "This is folly! Besides waste of time. We should be ensuring that the English do not rally again — not talking here. All could yet be lost. They will still outnumber us."

"They will not rally now, I think," the Master said. "Not sufficiently to challenge us. They are dispersed, wide-scattered. And if I know them, they will before all seek to recover their horses — and that will take much time. They are Borderers too, and lost without their mounts. Besides, they will need them to get back to their own country. I do not see another attack on us. For all that, we must *see* that they do not. Will — your men are fresh. Divide them into two companies, to keep the English running, on both sides of the river. Keep them from joining up, for as long as you can. I will gather my people together again. See to the wounded and prisoners. There is much to be done, yes . . ."

168

It was only later that Jamie discovered that the victory — if so it could be termed — was far from one-sided. Indeed, on balance, it might be more truly said that the advantage was with the English. Their casualties were undoubtedly lighter. And it seemed that, before ever the Teviotdale contingent had reached the scene, the Scots had suffered a severe reverse. The earlier reinforcements from lower Teviot, those Jamie had warned first, under Rutherford, Turnbull and Stewart of Jedburgh, had coalesced into a single force of about two hundred and fifty, and following directly on the Master's route, had fallen into an English trap. Umfraville, a veteran campaigner, had ambushed them at Faldonside, where wooded hills came down close to Tweed between the confluences of Gala and Ettrick Waters, and, hopelessly outnumbered, they had been overwhelmed, only a few escaping to bring the news to the Master. Old Rutherford and all five of his sons had been captured. Likewise Out-with-the-Sword John Turnbull and other Turnbull lairds. Sir William Stewart also. Where they were now was not known — presumably held somewhere in the rear, or already sent back under guard to England. The Master would send out scouting parties to try to find them, or recover them — but feared for the result.

The toll of those fallen in the battle was grievous; but Jamie, perhaps foolishly, was relieved to discover that most, on the Scots side at any rate, had already fallen before ever the horses made their impact. The fate of the already-wounded, under those stampeding hooves, did not bear thinking of, however.

It was a distinctly grim-featured young man who eventually took his leave of his Earl's son and other friends, laudatory as were their farewells, sent off his Mersemen home to Ednam, and rode alone northwards, by Tweed and Gala Water, for Lothian and Linlithgow.

VIII

"**A**YE, JAMIE — a bad business," Rothesay nodded. "Foolishness, I agree. A beating of the air. My good-brother Archie lacks his father's wits and his strength, no doubt. But — look not so glum, man! There is no great harm done." David Stewart certainly did not look nor sound glum — but then he seldom did. He appeared to have listened to Jamie's tale of the abortive Border raid and its consequences with only a part of his attention.

"Might it not do *much* harm, my lord?" Jamie insisted. "The harrying in England. The destruction of Wark. With this new King Henry already threatening us. This cannot but grievously offend him. Give him excuse, if he needs it, for retaliation. Invasion . . ."

"It will not help, to be sure. But Henry Plantagenet may have more to think about than Douglas raiding or Dunbar's treason, as it transpires. But, come, down here. Leonora is installed in the tower there meantime. Until we contrive more suitable accommodation."

They were walking down from the upper or palace courtyard of Stirling Castle, on its lofty rock, to one of the lower groups of buildings — for the rock-summit's uneven surface meant that the fortress was built on various levels. Jamie had arrived at Linlithgow the previous evening, to discover that the Duke had moved unexpectedly to Stirling, where his father had come evidently from Turnberry. He had come on, and the prince had welcomed him gladly enough, in good spirits, but seeming to be only marginally interested in what he had to report on the Dunbar and Border incidents. He was clearly much more eager to show him his latest divert, as he described her.

Jamie, still in his travelling clothes, dust and all, tried again.

"Perhaps, my lord Duke. But, although the Master of Douglas is my own kin, and I like him well enough, there is danger surely in letting him have his head thus. He is claiming to be Chief Warden of the Marches now, in his father's room; and as such could rule all the Borderland, where *your* father's realm joins England. A most delicate province. With a spirited English king, that could spell trouble indeed. For although he does not look it, nor sound it, he is rash, headstrong . . ."

"Young Archie rash? That dull fellow! He is as rash as you are, Jamie Douglas!"

"It was a rash act, was it not, to storm Dunbar Castle? Rasher to invade England without warrant. There was no need to burn down Wark Castle, the King of England's own property. And then to allow his men to stray far and wide, stealing cattle and pillaging, in enemy country when the English were already mustering . . ."

"Aye, indiscreet, no doubt. But he lacks experience. He will learn. I will have a word with his father."

"How is the Earl Archie?"

"Recovering, I am told. He is at his house of Threave, in Galloway. But see now — here is my Leonora's lodging."

The prince produced a key, and opened the heavy door of a flanking-tower of the most northerly range of buildings, perched on the very edge of the precipice above the flood-plain of Forth. Immediately a puff of hot air came out, with a thick, throat-catching smell, strange, feral. Jamie, like all others, was used to strong smells, mankind being prone to emit them in fair variety; but this was different.

"Is she not handsome?" David demanded, gesturing.

The vaulted basement of the tower was lit only by two arrow-slit windows narrow and unglazed; but though dark, there was no difficulty in seeing the great tawny shape crouching on the straw-covered stone floor behind the interlaced iron grating, any more than in hearing the deep-throated snarling growl. Involuntarily Jamie started back before the glare of yellow, unblinking eyes and the savage grin of white teeth, of a full-grown lioness in tail-lashing menace.

"Fear not!" the prince said. "She will not eat you — not yet! Eh, my beauty?" And he held his hand out to the brute, through the bars.

The lioness did not move. But the rumbling growl lessened nothing.

171

"Do not do that!" Jamie exclaimed, pulling at the Duke's arm. "She could have your hand off in a single bite! For God's sake . . . !"

"Not so. I feed her. She learns to know me. I should have brought some meat." But he withdrew his hand. "I sent to Barbary for her. Some time ago. She reached Dumbarton the day after you left."

"But . . . but why? What want you with this creature?"

"*You* would scarce understand that, my sober Jamie! I shall be the Lion of Scotland, one day. Fit that I should have my lioness! Besides, I like taming wild females — and I find most of our Scots ones over-eager to please! Leonora will teach me much of use, I feel sure."

Jamie shook his head, wordless.

"I shall build her a travelling cage. On wheels. So that she may go where I go. Perhaps even a litter-cage, to be carried between horses so that she may travel the faster — if I can train horses to accept her. We shall have some amusement with this lady from Barbary, Jamie, I swear! How think you my Uncle Robert will enjoy Leonora's company? He was never one for females, to be sure — save as conveyors of lands and earldoms! I shall watch his sour face, with interest! Tomorrow. I have had shackles made for her, for all four paws, so that she cannot leap. A collar and chain likewise. That she may walk abroad with me. Until I have tamed her. We shall try them out, tonight."

"But — how will you put the shackles on? How?"

"The way the Moors do in Barbary. And as they did in Rome, lang syne. A great net is thrown over the creature. It struggles — and the more it does so the more entangled it becomes. Until it is wholly bound. Then the shackles are put on the net and cut away. Wasteful in nets — but they are only rope and easily remade."

"Lord! All this for what, my lord?"

"For my pleasure and satisfaction, man. There is more in life than stern duty and endeavour, than statecraft and power over men, than pious devotion or even the gaining of riches. Does your Mary, my aunt, never tell you so? I vow *she* is well aware of it! Although her brother Robert has never discovered it. Nor yet my unhappy sire. My Uncle Alex, now — he was different."

"Aye, the Wolf would have approved of your lioness!"

172

"No doubt. But Leonora may have her uses also. We shall see." David paused. "You are not overtired, Jamie?"

"Tired? No. Why?"

"How far to Aberdour? Twenty-five miles? Thirty? With a fresh horse you could be there before sundown. Easily. And back here, with your Mary, soon after tomorrow's noon. No?"

"Mary? Why Mary, my lord?"

"Because I have a task for my favourite aunt. See you, to my sorrow my mother is fallen sick. Has not been able to accompany my father from Turnberry. Nothing grievous, so far as I can learn. My royal sire is sore lost, here, without her. He requires a woman's sustaining hand ever at his elbow, I fear. Especially for such occasions as this. He is in a sorry state, to tell truth. I had the devil's own task to get him here, at all. *I* cannot seem to act nurse to him, before all, to keep him right in tomorrow's ceremonial. Moreover, a hostess is required. My own wife would not serve for this. She scarce knows my father, nor he her. Besides, she something lacks the, the graces, that one! She is going to demand a deal of training to make a queen, one day! To act suitably at the King's side, it must be a princess. So I have sent for my Aunt Isabel, from Edmonstone. My father approves of her, better than his other sisters. But she must have a lady-in-waiting. Not only for the appearance of it, but to pass on *my* instructions anent my father. Someone with quick wits, and no shrinking flower! For this is going to require careful handling. Mary has acted lady-in-waiting in the past. And her wits are quick enough for any, I swear!"

"But — why? What is this great occasion?"

The Duke shut and locked the lioness's door. "It is a strange business, Jamie — but one which I cannot afford to neglect. We are to have a visitor to my father's Court. No less than King Richard the Second of England, indeed!"

"King Richard! But . . . but is he not dead? I thought that he was slain. At Pontefract."

"So it was given out. So indeed it may be. But now there is another story. True or false remains to be seen. It was your friend Alex Stewart of Badenoch who sent me word. He had heard the tale that the deposed but rightful King of England had arrived, of all places, on the isle of Islay, at Donald of the Isles' castle of Finlaggan. It seems that he said that he had effected his escape from Pontefract where Bolingbroke held him, crossed England to the west coast, and there took ship for

173

the Hebrides. He and my cousin Donald, to be sure, had long been in league, traitorously so — Donald made treaties with Richard like an independent monarch. So he fled to him, as secure haven."

"Is there any truth in this? Surely word would have leaked out of England if Richard had still lived, had escaped? It may be but an impostor . . ."

"This I must seek to find out. If I can. But meantime, my hand is forced. For I have since learned that my Uncle Robert has also heard the story — sooner than I did, it seems. And acted upon it, swiftly. Presumably for reasons good for himself. He invited this alleged Richard Plantagenet to his own castle of Doune, in Menteith. And the man has come there. He arrived five days past, Donald with him. Now, why has Robert done this? And why has Donald agreed? My uncle never acts without sufficient reason. Nor, indeed, my Cousin Donald. They make an unlikely pair, in collusion. Hitherto they have been at each others' throats! Now Donald is in Menteith, with this mammet calling himself King Richard. As Lieutenant of the realm I had to act. I do not trust either of them so far as I can spit!"

"You fear some plot?"

"I most certainly do. Robert has not forgiven me, nor my father, you may be sure. And Donald was humiliated over the affair at Haddonstank, having to call off his invasion of Galloway, and then his brother's defeat at Arkaig. They would both unseat me if they could. Anything that brings those two together is dangerous."

"I see that, yes."

"So I am taking a risk. In my father's name I have commanded the man to be brought here. To be presented to the King of Scots as King of England. He will be received and treated as King. And once here, he will bide here! I shall see to that. He will not be allowed to become any sort of puppet in Robert's hands, nor in Donald's either. Robert cannot refuse this command. If he is indeed King Richard, then he cannot sojourn in Scotland without the King of Scots express permission. So tomorrow my father receives him, in state, as rightful King of England."

Jamie shook his dark head helplessly. "But is that not direly dangerous, my lord? Risking the repute of the Scots Crown? If he is proved an impostor, then how foolish you will seem. And your royal father."

174

"That is a hazard, yes. But none so grievous. And there are advantages, other than taking the initiative from Uncle Robert. See you, so long as Richard, the lawful monarch of England, is held to be alive, and *recognised* as such by his fellow-monarch of Scotland, then Henry of Bolingbroke remains a usurper. And this is to Scotland's much benefit. It must lessen Henry's authority with his nobility and people, tend to divide the English, offer a rallying point for Henry's enemies. Also possibly prevent Papal recognition — for Richard was the Lord's Anointed. If Henry indeed plans to invade Scotland, then this may give him pause."

"Ye-e-es." Jamie emitted breath in a long sigh. "But might it not have the opposite result? Might he, Henry, not invade Scotland just to show what he thought of this claim? Even to demand that the other be handed over? As price of his withdrawal from our land. Henry, from all accounts, is not the man to lie down under threats."

"If his nobles remain doubtful of his Crown's legality he would scarcely dare, I think. Leaving such unrest behind him. The house of Lancaster has no especial right to the throne. Richard had other uncles than John of Gaunt. No — with Richard still alive, Henry is in a difficult position. And we shall *keep* him alive! Meantime, at any rate. It should prove an interesting situation."

As they climbed back to the palace-yard, Jamie Douglas remained sceptical. Doubts, of course, were his weakness.

* * *

The Great Hall of Stirling Castle was loud with talk, rumours, surmise, as the high-born throng stirred and eddied. Jamie moved amongst them, listening, though not too obviously. Snatches of conversation and argument he overheard indicated that confusion was general, clear-cut opinion all but non-existent. Most seemed to assume that the Mammet, as he was already being called, was an impostor, and the reasons for him being received otherwise a mystery. But whether it was in Albany's interests, in Rothesay's, or in Donald MacDonald's for that matter, was roundly debated. That there was a deep plot of some sort was apparently accepted. Some complained even at being thus summoned to attend on such an evident sham.

The royal trumpeters were filing in at the back of the dais, with a gorgeously-clad pursuivant in brilliant blazonry, the recently appointed Rothesay Herald, Ninian Stewart of Kildonan. These blew a fanfare, and the herald in ringing tones announced the entry of the high and mighty Lord David, Duke of Rothesay, High Steward, Prince of Scotland and Lieutenant of the Crown.

There was a little delay and then a curious scuffling and clanking sound. In at the dais doorway backed two distinctly alarmed-looking servitors in the royal livery, pulling on chains. Suddenly one stumbled forward and all but fell as the chains went slack, whilst his colleague leapt as though bitten. Into the Hall after them, at a hampered, crouching, belly-down rush came the lioness, shackles dragging on the stone floor, tufted tail whipping from side to side, fangs bared, rumbling deeply in its throat. Behind, holding a gold-tasselled lead attached to the animal's jewel-studded collar, strolled David Stewart, magnificent in cloth-of-gold and scarlet, smiling genially.

Men gasped and exclaimed, some women screamed. The stumbling servant only just managed to get out of the creature's path in time. The strange group came forward to mid-dais, as the herald and trumpeters drew hastily aside. Then, at a flick of the prince's free hand, the attendants circled back, with their leashes taut, to pull strongly to halt the brute's onward movement. Still smiling, the Duke stooped to pat the slow-swinging, ears-flattened yellow head — while everywhere breaths were held. The lioness showed more of her great white teeth in a lip-curling snarl, but the man did not cease to stroke, and the snarl sank to a low muttering sound. Straightening up, David turned to take a raw leg of mutton from a third servitor at his back, and stooping again, held it out to the beast. At first it turned its fierce head away, and the rumbling deepened in its chest. Then abruptly it flashed back and snapped the offering from the prince's hand. Head hanging low, it sought to move off sidelong, with the meat, towards a corner. Restrained by the leashes and shackles, it sank down to the floor, mutton between its mighty forepaws, and started to tear at the red flesh. Instead of the growl, a throaty purring sounded.

David Stewart stood up, and waved casually towards the trumpeters.

A spontaneous if ragged cheer rose from the watching company — from the men, at any rate.

The trumpeters produced another fanfare — but loud and

strident as it was it by no means could drown the hoarse coughing roar as the lioness started up again, angered, meat dropped, yellow eyes gleaming. The Duke stooped, to speak soothingly. The trumpeting died away but the building-shaking roars continued for a little, accompanied by the prince's silvery laughter. Lyon King of Arms, who had come in behind during the fanfare, perforce waited until the alarming challenge at length faded, before he announced, in noticeably less ringing fashion than was his usual, the arrival of the puissant and right royal prince, Robert, *Ard Righ*, by God's grace High King of Scots.

Again there was delay. But at length the monarch came limping in, on the arm of his sister Isabel, former Countess of Douglas. He wore, although untidily, a splendid purple cloak embroidered with gold and trimmed with fur, and on his brow the royal golden circlet as crown. He peered short-sightedly at the waiting company, looked askance at the lioness, and veering well away from the brute's vicinity, made for one of the two chairs-of-state set in mid-dais, bowed sadly to the perfunctory cheers, and sat down. The Lady Isabel seated herself on a stool at his elbow, and her illegitimate half-sister Mary came and stood behind.

Jamie made his unobtrusive way to the rear of the dais.

Lyon stepped forward, made obeisance to the monarch, and turned, hand on high.

"I am commanded by the King's Highness that His Grace is now pleased to receive the august person of the high and mighty prince Richard, by God's grace King of England," he cried.

Into the stir the trumpets blared out again — and once more the roar shook the hammer-beam timbers of the roof. Clearly Leonora did not like trumpets. Fortunately this was a fairly brief fanfare. King Robert half-rose in agitation, with Isabel and Mary Stewart seeking to calm him. David stood, at ease, waving the gold-tasselled leash gently to and fro.

At the far foot of the Hall the main door was thrown open and another herald strode in, equally imposingly garbed and likewise supported by trumpeters — Sir John Stewart of Ardgowan, newly-created Albany Herald. This time, the instrumentalists' flourish being so much further away, only produced a tail-swinging snort. The newcomer announced the most noble and excellent Lord Robert, Duke of Albany, Earl of Fife and Menteith, Justiciar of Fife, Menteith and Strathearn and High

Chamberlain of Scotland, escorting his guest Richard, by the Grace of God, King of England.

Three men entered, two and one. Albany was in his usual dignified and sober black-and-silver, stiffly upright. At his side walked a heavier though slightly stooping figure, with notably pale features, peculiar heavy-lidded eyes, long fair hair to his shoulders, a down-turning moustache and a small pointed beard. His dress was nondescript and far from kingly, but he too wore a simple gold circlet round his brows. Behind, considerably more eye-catching than either, came Donald, Lord of the Isles, in the full panoply of Highland dress, vivid tartans and flashing jewellery.

All eyes were on the stranger nevertheless. Most there were undoubtedly surprised to see so comparatively young a man; for though Richard Plantagenet had been on the throne for twenty-two years, he was now but thirty-three. This man, although he held himself with a careful dignity, had little aspect of a king — but then, neither had their own monarch. All searched his features for an answer to the question, true or false? He had a pursed-up, slightly petulant mouth and a nervous frown. The trouble was that none there had ever seen King Richard. He had only once crossed into Scotland, and that was in 1385 when he had come with fire and sword, burning Melrose, Dryburgh and Newbattle Abbeys and many towns— for which invasion Otterburn had been delayed retaliation. He could only have been nineteen then. Anyway none of the few who might have seen him were here present.

People drew aside to allow the trio clear passage up the Hall; but the stir and eager whispering was very evident. Attention was concentrated on them and their progress, until a sudden, angry snoring snarl jerked every glance elsewhere. The clank of iron shackles, and the scuffle and thud as one of the Duke of Rothesay's servitors was pulled off his feet, ensured a change in concern. The rumbling growl continued.

Jamie Douglas, standing behind, was one of the very few who could have observed David Stewart's quick foot movement. He had shrewdly kicked the partially devoured leg of mutton from between his lioness's paws at a moment when the brute had her head raised, and thereby successfully resumed possession of the centre of the stage, as it were. Leonora was up on her feet again, tail lashing, meat back between her jaws.

The three newcomers had faltered in their dignified pacing,

178

staring, obviously only just become aware of the great animal's presence. As the menacing noise continued they came to a halt, astonished.

The prince waved an encouraging hand, smiling. "Come, Uncle," he called. "Fear nothing. You and your guests are entirely safe, I do assure you!"

It was cunningly, wickedly done — and the narrowing of Albany's eyes and tightening of his mouth revealed his full recognition of the fact. He grasped his companion's elbow and all but propelled him onwards to the dais at an increased pace.

Jamie exchanged glances with his wife behind the throne. The lioness sank down, to resume her interrupted meal. The King emitted something like a groan.

It was noticeable how well to the far side from the prince the new arrivals made their ascent to the dais. Distinctly to the King's left front, they stood, and bowed — if Albany's could be called a bow — and so waited.

King Robert cleared his throat and hoisted himself unsteadily to his feet. "Brother — I thank you," he said thickly. "Cousin Richard — I greet you well. Welcome you warmly to my Court. I, I rejoice that Your Grace has survived the assaults of evil men — aye, evil men. And found secure refuge in this my realm."

The other bowed again. "I thank Your Grace, from my heart," he said, in a very slightly lisping voice. "I throw myself upon your royal compassion and mercy. Until such time as I shall win back my rightful throne." That came out in something of a rush, as well it might.

There was a silence as all considered the implications of that last sentence made thus so soon.

"Oh, aye." King Robert looked about him doubtfully.

Albany spoke. "Sire — it has been my pleasure and privilege to succour and aid King Richard, and to bring him into your royal presence. With the help of our nephew Donald, here, Lord of the Isles."

"I saw Donald," the monarch said. Although the Islesman was not actually an outlaw at present, he was not far off it, and dubiously welcome at Court.

There was another pause. Oddly enough, the Duke of Rothesay had now turned partly away from the central group, and was stooping, to murmur at his lioness. He was clearly not enthusing over the new arrivals.

The Lady Isabel, who had risen with her brother, now touched his arm and glanced towards the second chair-of-state.

The King nodded. "Cousin Richard," he said, "here is my sister Isa, umquhile Countess of Douglas. Woe is me, my lady-wife is sick. See you — sit here, by my side."

Bowing to the princess, the visitor seated himself on the second chair without a word. Albany moved over to stand at his side. The King glanced over towards his son, got no response there, and sighing, resumed his seat.

The silence returned, save for the crunching of a sheep's leg-bone. Men fidgeted.

Donald of the Isles spoke up. "Uncle — I hope that I see you well? And grieve to hear of my royal aunt's sickness." His gentle Highland voice belied his reputation. "It is long since we forgathered. I welcome this opportunity to visit your Court from my island territories." It was the civil speech of a fellow-ruler rather than any subject.

The King pulled at an already slack lower lip. "To be sure," he muttered. "But your brother — yon Alastair. He did much mischief. He took possession of our castle of Urquhart. To our displeasure."

"Alastair is young, sire. Headstrong. I have him confined on Islay . . ."

David Stewart snapped his fingers, ostensibly at the lioness but looked quickly towards Jamie, and jerked his head barely perceptibly. That man moved the two or three steps over to his wife's side, and whispered briefly. As he stepped back, Mary spoke quietly to her half-sister. Isabel murmured in the King's ear.

"Aye, then," the monarch said, when Donald had finished. "That is as may be." He turned. "Now, Richard — I'd have you to meet my son and heir, David, Duke of Rothesay and Lieutenant of my realm."

The prince strolled forward and bowed elaborately. But it was to his father that he looked. "Your Grace." Then he turned his head slightly — but sufficiently to make the distinction clear. "My lord Richard — here is a notable occasion. So miraculous an escape from peril. So unexpected a sanctuary for you to seek, in our dangerous northern kingdom! We are honoured indeed!"

"I thank you, my lord David. I rejoice to see you. I have heard much of you."

"Little to my good, I fear!" He raised an eyebrow towards his

Uncle Robert, and grinned. "But perhaps it was from *your* uncle that you heard it?"

The other hesitated for just a moment. "I, I hear it on all hands," he said. "Your lordship's fame is widespread."

"You are too kind, sir. It was your Uncle Edmund I meant, of course. Edmund, Duke of York."

"Indeed, my lord? I did not know that you were acquainted with York. I assumed that you meant John of Lancaster."

"Ah, yes — John of Gaunt, God rest his soul. We met, to be sure. But I should think that it was my Uncle Albany here who made the greater impression on *him*! They found much to . . . debate. As no doubt Duke John reported to you?"

The other moistened his lips. "The Duke of Lancaster reported nothing to me, my lord."

"Ah . . ."

Albany intervened. "Sire, our nephew Donald was most fortunate in having on his island a lady who had met King Richard when in Ireland recently. Before he returned to deal with his cousin Henry Bolingbroke's shameful treason. This woman, Irish, wife to one of the MacDonald chieftains, rejoiced to see His Grace of England again, and to discuss with him the situation prevailing in Ireland. A happy chance."

"Indeed, yes," Donald agreed. "Sadly as the King's position had changed in the few months, whatever."

"Most . . . fortuitous," David commented. "It interests me greatly to learn why our distinguished guest chose to come to Scotland, a realm which he has called barbarous and with which he has been at war? Rather than to France, shall we say, where his good-brother is King?" Richard had married fairly recently, as his second wife, the child-sister of the mad King Charles the Sixth. "Or to Ireland, from which he had just returned, and where he had an army."

King Robert looked unhappy at this only slightly veiled public testing of the visitor. "Cousin Richard will tell us all these matters anon, Davie," he said. It was not often that he thus asserted himself. "We mustna weary him, new-come."

"I came here, sire, because I had little choice," the other said, carefully. "I escaped from Pontefract Castle and fled, with the help of two loyal servants, to the west. Across the moors and fells to Furness in Lancaster, in secret. At Cartmel, the good Brothers found for me a small craft sailing for Man. I dared not go to a larger haven, where I might be sought for. At Man was

181

a MacDonald galley sailing back to the Sudreys — to Islay, my lord Donald's isle. None to France or Ireland. My lord and I had had dealings. I journeyed there, and he entreated me kindly."

"A notable progress, sir," David conceded. "We all congratulate you, I am sure." He glanced at Mary Stewart, one eyebrow raised.

She spoke quietly to her half-sister, and Isabel spoke to the King.

"Aye — that is so," the monarch nodded. "Before we retire to eat, Cousin, I'd have you to meet certain of my great lords and kin, here present. My good-brother the Earl of Crawford. My nephew the Earl of Moray. My brother's good-son the Earl of Ross. My lord Bishop of St. Andrews. Aye, and others . . ."

The coming to the dais of these notables set the lioness off on a further angry growling — to considerable alarm. But since it was clearly the High Steward's and Lieutenant's animal, none might protest — save one, Robert Stewart.

"Sire," Albany declared. "This ill-disposed and ill-trained brute-beast, seemingly my nephew's, may be well enough at a fair or in a bear-pit — but is insufferable and unsuitable at your royal audience. It stinks! I pray you, have it removed."

The King looked almost relieved. "Aye, Davie — it's an unco' fierce creature that. I'd liefer it was . . . elsewhere, lad."

"Why, surely, Sire — if that is your wish. But my uncle need not be so fearful. And as for being unsuitable, what could be more suitable at a royal audience than a lion, the proud symbol of your Crown and of the royal house of this realm? It could even be more rampant! Perhaps we could find a leopard for your Plantagenet guest? And it might be, some less forthright animal for the Duke of Albany. A jackal, perhaps . . .?" And with a happy laugh, the prince bowed and sauntered back, to superintend the far from straightforward exit of Leonora.

During the upheaval and subsequent presentation of notables, Jamie moved close to his wife again, behind the thrones.

"I do not understand what David is at," he muttered. "Is he drunk, think you?"

"He is always drunk — and never drunk!" Mary said. "You know that. He is using the lioness to distract attention from the Mammet and his uncle, to upset them — for his own purposes . . ."

"I know that, yes. It is not the lion I mean. It is this of the

Englishman, king or none. David told me that he was to be accepted as Richard Plantagenet — a matter of policy, he said. Against Henry. Now he seems to be throwing doubt on him before all. Seeking to catch him out. Spoiling his own policy . . ."

"If I know Davie, it is all planned. I think he covers himself, in case the Mammet *is* proved an impostor. The King to accept him, yes — but if aught goes wrong, as well it may, David Stewart knew better! And all here to witness. And to make Robert look a fool . . ."

"His father likewise."

"I fear most consider the King a fool already. Though he is scarce that . . ."

The repast that followed, held in an ante-room, was not a banquet but a more modest and intimate meal for only about a dozen or so of the royal family and guests. The Lady Isabel, deputising for the Queen, and Mary seated on her left, were the only women present. The alleged Richard Plantagenet sat between Isabel and the King, with Albany at his brother's other side. David sat across the table, flanked by Donald of the Isles and Crawford. Jamie Douglas did not sit at all, standing throughout behind the prince as acting cupbearer — just as Sir Andrew Moray of Pettie, the hereditary cupbearer, did behind the King.

It was not a riotously successful meal. Indeed, had not David kept things going with wit, sallies and toasts, all barbed but genially so, it would have proceeded largely in silence. Donald was a good talker, and intelligent, and did his best; but he was largely shunned by all save the prince, looked on askance. Isabel also, with her instructions from her nephew, sought to engage the Mammet in conversation to discover what she could as to his *bona fides* — with scant success. Civil enough, he was not forthcoming. Throughout, primed by Mary with points relayed by Jamie from the prince, she asked leading questions in as innocent a way as she could, questions which one who was not King Richard could have difficulty in answering. At the end she was little the wiser, the guest parrying not so much skilfully as blankly — although on occasion he did vouchsafe a reply which sounded genuine, and indicated intimate knowledge of Richard. The trouble was that none might cross-question, or persist in probing in converse with a monarch, even a displaced one. If he was genuine, he was one of the Lord's Anointed. So long as he claimed to be so and they were not in a position to prove otherwise, the position remained in a kind of deadlock.

Oddly enough, he who perhaps ought to have been in the best position to judge, the other and true Lord's Anointed, seemed to be well enough content and well-disposed towards the newcomer. It might be that his own personal inadequacies and sense of being found wanting made him sympathetic towards the other, in fellow-feeling for a man overtaken by events too large for him. Whatever the cause, he appeared to get on well with his guest, and in fact throughout treated him as a fellow-monarch — which made it all the more difficult for others to do less.

None, however, felt like prolonging the meal unduly. Albany was the first to show evident signs that enough was enough — but even he, with two monarchs present, could not rise from the table until they did. He did work on his brother, nevertheless, declaring sufficiently loudly for the visitor to hear, that if they were to get back to Doune Castle before dark it was full time to be on their way.

The King was nodding acceptance when his son across the table cleared his throat.

"We must not detain Uncle Robert nor yet Cousin Donald, Sire," he said. "Perhaps they will wish to see the Lord Richard to his quarters in the North Tower before they take leave of him? It will be my pleasure to conduct them thither."

His father looked nervous. "Oh, aye," he said.

Albany sat up straight. "What mean you by that?" he demanded. "His Grace of England returns with me to Castle Doune."

"Ah, but no, Uncle. All is prepared for him, here at Stirling. As is suitable."

"He is my guest . . ."

"He is His *Grace's* guest, surely. Whilst sojourning in His Grace's realm. Would you have Richard of Bordeaux in any lesser place than the King's house, now he is in the King's care? We shall care for him very well, I assure you."

Albany rose to his feet and turned to his brother. "Sire — this is *not* suitable! King Richard is well settled in my house. He must remain with me."

The King looked unhappily between brother and son. In head-shaking disquiet he turned to the man at his other side. "Cousin Richard — how say you? Will you bide with me? Or with my brother?"

The other swallowed and looked no more happy than the questioner. "I . . . I am in Your Grace's hands," he said. "I am much honoured by Your Grace's goodwill and hospitality. I . . ."

"Good," David declared. "Well said, sir. All then, is settled. If His Grace permits, we shall proceed then to the North Tower and the Lord Richard's privy comfort. And no longer delay my lords of Albany and the Isles!"

As King Robert rose to his feet, he turned to his brother. "Davie is the Lieutenant now, mind . . ." he said, wearily.

The North Tower was that in the basement of which the lioness was immured.

IX

D AVID STEWART NOW *wanted* it to snow. At least it was not
raining. It was cold enough for snow, but there had been
frost again that morning, as for the last few days. Jamie
Douglas argued that white frost would be better than snow,
anyway.

Apart from the weather, all appeared to be as it should be,
everything practically in readiness; the vast canopy as secure
as it could be; the fires laid and the charcoal-braziers set up,
with ample fuel stacked; the long lantern-lines hung from post to
post and torch-poles planted; the evergreen shrubs and little
fir-trees set out in their tubs in clumps and groves and mazes,
with love-seats in the midst; the statuary disposed judiciously;
the many trestles placed ready to be laden. Men worked busily
everywhere, carrying, hammering, strengthening, their breath
steaming in the slightly misty air, as the prince and Douglas,
Pate Boyd at their heels, strolled around inspecting.

It was an hour past noontide, on Hogmanay, 1399.

"I would not concern myself too greatly over snow, my lord,"
Jamie said. "It will do very well lacking that, I think. It is wind
that I fear. We should be praying all the saints that the wind
does not rise! To blow all this into the Forth!"

"You are a Job's comforter, on my soul!" the prince declared.
"Why should a wind arise? Today! We have had scarce a
bellyful all winter. Besides, the tentage is strong enough,
stronger than it may look. I have had them roping and staying
it all week. It will withstand a fair blow."

"An ordinary blow, perhaps. But if a north-west wind off
yon Hielant hills sweeps down over the Flanders Moss and hits
this castle-rock, there could be down-draughts that could
flatten this frail canopy, see you. Worse, if a side-blow, *round* the

rock, came underneath, it could lift all up and over the castle itself, your ropes and all!"

"God's wounds, man — have done! You grow worse, I swear!" The Duke turned. "Is not Sir James the most devilish gloomy woemaster in all Scotland, Pate?"

His henchman grinned, and wisely held his peace.

They were standing on the greensward directly below Stirling Castle rock on the south-west side, beside the curious geometrically-stepped King's Knot, centre of the King's Garden. It was a large parterre, over four hundred feet square, raised above the level of the rest in extraordinary fashion, octagons within squares of turf rising to a sort of central plateau, round which the rose-gardens were laid out. It was of ancient, some said prehistoric, origin, sometimes called the Round Table from its alleged connection with King Arthur, its summit often used for declamations, play-actings and the like. All around it, for the past week, workmen had been busy transforming this park and garden. Tentage and the tough canvas and sail-cloth used for pavilions had been erected on poles to cover a large area with a multi-coloured canopy — although not entirely covered, for there were gaps and strips left open to the air so that smoke might escape. A long covered-way of more sail-cloth led zig-zagging down from the castle; and another such corridor from the main area went northwards, around the rock-base, for a couple of hundred yards, to a shallow hollow, always water-filled in winter. Towards this the trio walked.

The hollow had been artificially enlarged, as far as its rocky surroundings permitted, and posts bearing pitch-pine torches placed all round it, whilst in the centre a model of a Highland gallery or birlinn had been set up on the ice, almost full-size and looking very fine. But it was the ice itself that held David Stewart's attention.

"See — it is melting. A curse on it — water on top!"

"It usually does, at noontide. It will freeze up again at nightfall — unless the weather changes. Better without your snow, my lord, I say."

"Snow would make it look finer."

"Melting snow on yonder canopies, dripping down, would please none . . ."

Out of character, David was fretful, unrealistic, like a spoiled child, angry that he could not control the weather as he did so much else. He turned, to hurry back and on up to the castle again, his two companions exchanging glances. Money had been outpoured like water for this occasion. None could remember having heard of such lavish spending. The prince was determined to celebrate the start of the new fifteenth century in spectacular fashion, to emphasise the new era represented by his assumption of power, and to show Christendom, England in especial, that Scotland was no impoverished, backward kingdom which Henry Plantagenet or others might assail with impunity. Nowhere else would the year of our Lord, 1400, with all its hopes and possibilities, be welcomed in such style.

The entire town of Stirling was packed with people, to say nothing of the castle and the nearby Abbey of Cambuskenneth and sundry monasteries. Everyone who counted for anything in Scotland had been invited to attend; and since the invitations were in the joint names of the King and his Lieutenant, few had seen fit to refuse, however inconvenient and difficult might be much of the journeying at this season of the year.

Many of the principal guests, of course, had been at Court over the entire Yuletide season, and a lively, not to say hectic interlude it had been, with nothing stinted in victuals, entertainment or display. Indeed not a few declared that this Hogmanay cantrip could scarcely be other than an anti-climax in the circumstances, with little left to contrive. And where all the siller was coming from, nobody knew — for the Treasury had been empty when David had inherited it, and he had scarcely stopped spending since.

It was this aspect of the situation which intrigued Sir Alexander Stewart of Badenoch, newly arrived from the North with a group of Highland chieftains, whom David, for some reason, had been urgent that he should bring. He had not taken long to forgather with Jamie and Mary in the prince's own tower's topmost storey.

"I do not know," Jamie admitted. "About moneys he reveals little, although in most matters he is frank enough. Certainly he is constraining the customs-farmers hard. For years many have been filching moneys right and left, imposing heavier dues than they should and handing on less to the Treasury than was due. The merchants and guilds of the burghs have long complained, but the Governor, Albany, did nothing. He was too deeply in the like business himself. Now David is making the collectors squeal. But I cannot think that all his money can come from them."

"There is a tale that the Church is aiding him," Mary put in. "Bishop Trail is his friend and may help."

"Holy Church give him moneys for spending so?" Alex wondered. "I think he must have others to turn to."

"Not his father, at the least," Mary said. "The King is ever short of siller. The Stewarts never had much of their own, and needs must marry it! As did I! And *your* father, Alex. But not John. Annabella Drummond brought him little."

"David wed a Douglas," her nephew-of-a-sort pointed out. "Can it be her money he spends so lavishly?"

"I think not," Jamie said. "The Earl Archie was too canny to let his new good-son get his hands on more than the dowry-money. He is not pleased with the way his daughter is being treated, I think."

"How is the old man? I heard that he was sorely sick."

"Better. He is here. But not the man he was. I fear it may not be long before we have a new Earl of Douglas."

"David kept the money he got as dowry for his proposed wedding to the Earl of Dunbar's daughter," Mary added. "How much, I never heard tell. But they say it was a deal. And now that Dunbar has fled to England, and breathing threats, he can be called a traitor — and no moneys need be paid back to traitors! I do not think that Davie has much to learn from Robert!"

"That was ill done . . ." Jamie agreed heavily.

The timing of the evening's festivities presented something of a problem. It was dark soon after four in the afternoon, and the programme could begin any time thereafter. But the New Year did not come in until eight hours later. Since quite an ambitious procedure was planned, it was important that at least a major proportion of the company should still be sober enough to appreciate and take part. Which meant no early start. On the other hand, if justice was to be done to the refreshments provided, as well as the laws of hospitality not outraged, feeding could not be delayed until late at night; yet to provide an extra banquet in the castle, before moving down to the King's Knot garden, would spoil the effect for later. No large proportion of those attending could be provided for in the castle anyway, numbers being what they were, and the majority therefore had to make their own arrangements in the town. So only a modest meal was set before the principal guests in the late afternoon, with the liquor supply strictly limited — to considerable complaint — and all were instructed to assemble in the great hall at ten o'clock.

It was still not snowing at that hour — but neither was there wind nor rain, and the frost was beginning to sparkle in a rising half-moon. Folk had come variously garbed, some as for winter outdoor activities, others in Court or evening dress — although few of these had omitted to come provided with warm cloaks. Despite all precautions, some were already noticeably drink-taken, if not drunk. Jamie Douglas and his wife were, as usual as it were on duty, he to act general factotum to the prince, she to attend on no fewer than three of her half-sister princesses, present without husbands. But meantime their services were not required, and they waited, along with Alex Stewart and the generality of the palace guests, in the smoky but warm great hall. The less privileged perforce had to wait outside on the level tourney-ground fronting the castle gatehouse — although here large bonfires had been lit to give at least the illusion of warmth.

Promptly, as ten struck on the town bells below, a resplendent figure appeared from the dais doorway, clad in the gorgeous tabard of Lyon King of Arms, but below it baggy striped pantaloons, on his head a fool's cap-of-bells and in his hand instead of Lyon's baton a notably large and springy bull's tool with which he made great play. In ringing if falsetto tones he commanded,

"Silence, lords and gentles — silence, obeisance and humble duty for their sublime Majesties the King and Queen!" Thereafter he belched loudly and cut a caper.

The somewhat doubtful laughter, and remarks on the phrasing of "Majesty" instead of the accustomed "Grace", a Continental style, was lost in music, not the usual brassy fanfare of trumpets but the cheerful cascading melody of violins playing the lightsome measure of a favourite jig. In came a company of a dozen fiddlers dressed in the copes and chaubles of high clerics, with mitres on their heads somewhat askew, and dancing as they played. And after a suitable gap, the royal couple appeared, wearing gleaming crowns and the magnificent purple and furred robes of monarchy, the King's beard long, brushed and snowy, the Queen's hair glittering with jewels and piled high up through her crown. They also came skipping and swaying to the music, though in a more stately fashion, skilfully adjusting to only every second beat of the rhythm. But stately movements or none, the motion inevitably swung open the splendid cloaks of both quite frequently — to reveal that the King possessed a woman's shapely bare legs beneath and a definitely black triangle at the groin despite the white beard, while the Queen boasted particularly sinewy and hairy legs and well-developed masculinity above. The faces of both were not exactly masked, but coated with a sort of paste, ruddy for the monarch and white for his consort, very effective.

"I see that we are to have a lively evening!" Mary commented, into the cheering and laughter. "If this is paid for by Holy Church, then I fear that stream is like to dry up!"

"Cousin David has a nice wit," Alex observed. "I daresay his father will forbear comment. But what of his mother? She is here?"

"Yes — although less than well. She will chide him, but gently. Jamie — do not look so shocked! It is but Up Halie Day and Twelfth Night guizardry a night or two early! The Lord of Misrule . . ."

"It is unseemly. An ill mockery of the Crown, when the Crown needs propping up and supporting, not pulling down. Yon is young Michael Stewart, son to your own half-brother, Sir John of Bute, the Sheriff. Who ought to know better."

"Is he so? From what is to be seen, I would not have known! But no doubt you have the better of me, there. Are you equally knowledgeable as to the lady, Jamie?"

"Not so. But she could do with a skelping, I say."

"And I say, not from you, my dear!"

Out after the pseudo-regal pair came a column of gaily-clad revellers, led by the Duke and Duchess of Rothesay. David was resplendent, dressed all in white satin, seeded with Tay pearls and gold — which might on some have looked effeminate but on David Stewart certainly did not. He appeared to have made no provision for cold or inclement weather. At his side, the Lady Mary Douglas, looking positively dowdy by comparison, her sallow features good enough but heavy, unsmiling, her clothing rich but worn without grace. Behind came the dark-eyed, good-looking young Prince James, now aged six, walking alone, with a sort of wary excitement, followed by his three sisters and their Douglas husbands, the Earl of Angus, the Master of Douglas and Sir James, Younger of Dalkeith, Jamie's legitimate half-brother. Then the three princesses of the previous generation, the Ladies Isabel, Marjorie, Dowager of

Moray, and Gelis, widow of Sir Will Douglas of Nithsdale. The last seldom indeed attended Court, having become something of a recluse although she was the youngest and most beautiful of the King's sisters. Behind trooped the other important house-guests. Not all smiled so happily as did Scotland's High Steward.

The capering master-of-ceremonies turned, and raised his peculiar baton to quieten the fiddlers. David bowed low in an elaborate genuflection towards the mock King and Queen.

"May it please Your Serene Majesties," he said. "We shall all follow you down to the Round Table of your renowned ancestor King Arthur, where due entertainment and refreshment will be provided. My royal sire and mother will come to pay their respects later. Proceed, Highnesses."

The music struck up again, and preceded by the Lyon-fool, they all streamed out into the chill night air, to pass down through the upper and lower courtyards, the inner, counter and outer guards and through the gatehouse arch to cross the drawbridge to the forecourt tourney-ground, where the great throng waited by the light of bonfires, the steam of their breath rising into the air like a cloud. Much cheering greeted their arrival, but the light was insufficient to reveal much of the style and costume of the leaders. No pause was made here, and the tabarded guide swung away right-handed with his busy skipping musicians, towards the edge of the dark void which was the southern rim of the castle-rock. Reaching this lip, he paused for a few moments as a shadowy figure materialised out of the gloom, uncovered a hidden charcoal brazier, lit a pitch-pine torch therefrom and tossed it high into the air, blazing.

As folk exclaimed and the fiddlers jigged, there was an astonishing reaction to that signal. All down the steep path that zigzagged back and forth across the rocky face of the hill, torches flared up in the darkness, hundreds of them on their poles — which implied hundreds of men waiting there to light them from little hooded braziers. Admittedly they did not all burst into flame at the identical moment; but the pitch-impregnated turpentine-pine bunches of slivers took fire in almost every case immediately, and the effect was extraordinary. The town did not extend round to this side of the rock, only the royal park, so that all had been a pit of gloom, with the half-moon to the east. Now this brilliant alleyway of light led down into the gulf, beckoning, conjuring a myriad coruscations from the hoar-frost — yet making the surrounding night seem but the blacker.

Loud acclaim greeted this transformation, and the descent commenced, between the twisting and turning double line of torches. Mary had gone to join the princesses, but their nephew seemed to have no need for Jamie's services meantime, and he remained with Alex Stewart, now joined by his Highland chieftains, all in manifest wonder and delight at what they saw.

The progress down the cliff was a lengthy process for so large a company, for the path was inevitably narrow and a little slippery, with innumerable sharp dog's-leg bends, and fairly steep even so. Fortunately there were guard-rails at the danger-points. There was fully 350 feet of descent, practically sheer, and the track had to pick its route this way and that, sometimes making quite lengthy traverses along shelves and ledges to find a passage. Some few of the guests had come this way, of course, on previous occasions, to the King's Knot gardens; but it is safe to say none had done so of a winter's night.

When the front of the long, chattering procession was two-thirds of the way down, and the path slanting ever more towards the west now, a shout went up ahead. There was a great pressing forward and questioning, to learn what this heralded — clearly those in front could see round the contours of the great rock something as yet invisible to the majority. But that there was a widespread glow of light, and growing brighter, was evident.

When Jamie and Alex rounded the bend in the cliff, with less than another hundred feet to descend, even the former was surprised by the effect, although he had helped in its contrivance. The little plain below and in front, really a wide terrace of the castle-hill before the undulating grasslands of the New Park and the Raploch Moss, looked tonight like a veritable fairyland, the province of the little folk, brownies, trolls and the like of which the minstrels were so fond of singing. This was caused by the light of many hundreds more torches shining and filtering through the great acreage of tenting and coloured awnings, diffusing, blending, irradiating. Even the smoke — for pitch-pine torches are by no means smokeless — seemed to be disciplined by the gaps and lanes in the covering, and thereafter, shot through with reflected tints and rosy hues, coiled and eddied upwards in unnatural or supernatural fashion into the frosty air as though with its own curious and infernal life. Bonfires by the score were beginning to blaze all around the perimeter, their leaping flames contrasting with the mellower glow from under the canopy. The glitter of the frost added the final touch of unreality to a scene such as never before had been beheld.

The entry to the covered area itself, thereafter, was productive of even louder cries and gasps. For here, suddenly, they were in another land, a land of light and warmth and growing things, of plants and shrubs, bushes and trees, gleaming statuary, sparkling fountains and grassy paths, all beneath a multi-hued heaven on which painted gods and goddesses disported themselves with marked abandon and from which tinsel stars and planets dangled and spun in the heat eddies. The warmth came from the many glowing charcoal braziers, almost smokeless, and although smoke did come from the torches, the draught system coped remarkably well. The curious physical feature of the raised turf platform, the King's Knot itself, or part of it, was hidden by screens.

The weary fiddlers were now superseded by the music of hidden instrumentalists in the groves and shrubberies, playing gentler, softer music. It did not take long for many of the guests, after the initial impact, to discover the presence of numerous tables, amongst the tubs and bushes, laden with food and drink in great variety and lavish quantities, and to descend on these in force. Although not a few were distracted by the large central fountain spouting red-coloured jets and sprays, which proved to be wine.

The master-of-ceremonies, after allowing a little time for these delights to be perceived and sampled, leapt up on to the edge of the oddly-shaped grassy mound, its geometrical intricacies not so obvious from here as from high above, and there performed a few cart-wheels and similar gyrations to attract attention, singularly ridiculous-seeming in his dignified herald's tabard which tended of course to fall over his head and envelop him. Then, having gained the notice and heed of at least a fair proportion of the company, he beckoned the mock King and Queen up, with much bowing and scraping, on to the Knot, where he led them to twin thrones at one side, where he prayed them to be seated. As they sat down, the rear legs collapsed under both chairs and the pair toppled over backwards with a spectacular waving of their own white legs in the air, to the edification of the beholders. It took an unconscionable time to right them, during which it was amply proved, to the satisfaction of even the most distant or short-sighted, that not only the lower quarters of the couple were bare. Considerable fuss was made too about fixing the legs back on the chairs so that the royal pair might gingerly reseat themselves, their herald reassuringly patting them the while and carefully arranging the purple robes so that they remained parted from the waist downwards. Then, clapping his hands, he gestured towards the screened half of the mound.

The curtaining was thereafter drawn aside by invisible hands, and there, lit by more torches on particularly high poles, was a scene which immediately held every eye and had the effect of stilling all the chatter and laughter remarkably. A great circle of standing-stones was set on the inner and higher tier of the Knot, which was some 200 feet square, tall, stark, timeless, fifteen of them, with two lofty portal-stones or pointers facing east, and near these a large horizontal recumbent, flat like table or altar. Stern, immutable, the monoliths stood, as though they had been there for generations untold — although in fact they had been brought from far and near and erected there, with infinite labour, only two days before — and some aura of awe and power and even menace about them, speaking to the race-memory in them all, kept the gathering silent.

The hush was broken, for the music had died away, by the sound of a strange chanting which rose and fell, singing sweet yet somehow relentless, quietly emphatic. From beyond the Knot, from a thicket of bushes contrived there, emerged a slow-moving shadowy procession; first white-robed figures with mistletoe wreaths around their white headcloths and snakeskin girdles; then the chanting choir, men and boys clad in the skins of wolf and deer; then four young men wearing only loincloths, their glistening bodies painted with broad vertical stripes of black and white, pacing spaced out to form a square and each holding the realistically-devised head of a snake. Each snake was stretched out so far, until its tail was clamped in the mouth of a second serpent, the young men rippling their serpentine chains in lifelike fashion as they walked. The second four snakes' tails joined at a single central girdle composed of more of the coiled reptiles, and this around the white waist of a fair and completely naked young woman of most lovely form and carriage, walking in mid-square and sobbing as she walked. Behind came more choristers and two further white-garbed Druid priests carrying long and curling bulls' horns.

The procession moved deliberately on round the perimeter of

195

the stone-circle, to halt outside the tall portal-stones, the chanting continuing. Its members, and the company, waited tensely, the girl's sobs punctuating the singing. Then, infinitely slowly a great shining disc began to appear beyond the circle, at the far side of the Knot. Of beaten metal, painted red, unseen torches before and behind made it seem to glow. Actually this rising sun had to be to the west of the circle, since all the crowd was gathered to the east; but this detail in no way detracted from the illusion. As gradually the disc rose, so rose the volume and tempo of the chanting.

When at last all the round sun was visible, seeming to hang between the twin horns of the portal-stones, the now fierce chanting was cut off abruptly and into the quivering silence which succeeded sounded the hollow booming ululations of the bulls' horns, an unchancy, sepulchral resonance. The chief of the Druids paced slowly forward through the portals to the recumbent table-stone and there turned to face the company. He raised his left hand high.

While the horns continued to wail and moan, the four young men drew the weeping girl out after the priest, into the circle. With stylised motions they took her in hand, lifted her between them and laid her, writhing, on the altar, where each held her flat by wrist or ankle.

The Druid raised his right hand, and in it was seen to gleam the blade of a long knife. When it was at the full height of his arms, and now gripped by both hands, he paused. The horns ceased to sound.

The choristers burst out into a single brief yelping shout, and down flashed the knife. There was a high thin scream. Then the silence returned.

Blood, red and wet-looking, had somehow appeared on the gleaming white breasts. Leaning forward the priest dabbled a hand in it, and turned to sprinkle each of the young men at the far side of the altar in turn. Then, moving round, his back to them and the altar and sacrifice, he held both reddened hands up and out towards the sun, and so remained.

A triumphant savage hymn rose now from the choristers, who also paced on into the circle. Unseen hands closed the curtain-screen once again.

Men and women turned to eye each other strangely, as a vast corporate sigh rose on the night air. There was none of the normal applause or clamour.

"That was . . . telling," Alex Stewart said, a little thickly. "Oddly conceived. Forgive one reared in the ignorant and barbaric Highlands — but what did it signify?"

Jamie moistened his lips. "There is an ancient tale that this Stirling was once an important centre of Druidic sun-worship, under the name of Mons Dolorum, the Mound of Pain, later Snawdoun. This mound, now the King's Knot, was the sacrificial shrine. David but puts the clock back some score of centuries."

"He himself devised this?"

"To be sure. Prompted by the man who has become his dark shadow."

"Ramorgnie, you mean?"

"Aye, Sir John de Ramorgnie, the Prolocutor-General. That man is evil. But clever — too clever. And bold. Ambitious. He has come to be ever in the prince's company of late, pandering, urging, whispering. Yet he was and is Albany's vassal, from the Howe of Fife. I believe that he is still Albany's man."

They looked to where Rothesay stood, amidst a high-born throng, his wife no longer with him, replaced by a bevy of more demonstrative and alluring ladies, at his elbow a darkly handsome man of early middle years, slender, elegant in crimson and silver that contrasted with the fair prince's white satin.

"You credit Ramorgnie with a hand in this?"

"Oh, yes. He is a great scholar and student of history and legend — the darker the better. I say that it was a bad day when he was put on the prince's Council, as its secretary — at Albany's instigation I have no doubt."

Jamie would hardly have admitted it, of course, but part of his dislike of the lawyer and Prolocutor might well have stemmed from the fact that in some degree he had begun to supersede the Douglas in David Stewart's close service. As tonight.

Alex shrugged. "Ramorgnie would need a long spoon to outsup Cousin Davie," he said. "Albany himself is not here tonight?"

"No. Invited, with all others, of course. But he keeps his distance from Court now — save at Council meetings. Although he has no lack of spies and informants, I swear!"

A wheepling on a flute drew all eyes to the agile master-of-ceremonies, who waved and announced that their sublime and serene Majesties were pleased to welcome to their Hogmanay Court and presence two more terrestrial sovereigns, the earth-bound King and Queen of Scots and King Richard of England, whom all the powers of the upper and nether world preserve and protect.

All turned, to see King Robert and his wife, with the Mammet, come limping down, with a group of attendants — and now it was not the King who leant on Annabella's arm, but the reverse. The Queen was indeed grievously changed, and though she still held herself with calm dignity, her pale frailty was evident. And emphasising this sad physical deterioration, as the newcomers emerged into the brighter illumination, it could be seen that immediately behind the royal couple, with the alleged Richard Plantagenet, came hirpling the Earl of Douglas, walking with the aid of a stick. He had always had a stooping, almost crouching stance, a stooping eagle had been one punning description; now he was merely a bent old man, thin, his great shoulders shrunk. Archie the Grim was grim no longer. His Duchess-daughter now was with him, holding his arm. In that group the Mammet looked almost robust, if depressed somewhat.

The King's party mounted the Knot, to group themselves around the three chairs placed opposite those of the mock-royalties. Somebody fetched a stool for the old Earl.

Jamie heard his companion draw a quick breath, as a variation in the light-and-shadow revealed that one of the ladies behind Annabella was Isobel, Countess of Mar. He glanced at his friend.

"Her ladyship has her husband with her, this time," he observed. "That is Sir Malcolm Drummond at Crawford's side."

"Indeed," Alex said evenly. "I have yet to meet Sir Malcolm. The Queen looks ill. I am sorry, for she is much needed. By both husband and son, I think." He paused. "And that, then, is your Mammet? I do not see him very well, from here — but he looks younger than I had thought."

"Richard would be but thirty-three years."

"Would be? You still believe this to be an impostor?"

"Who knows? Say that I cannot quite believe him to be the King. Nor does the prince. But his father does, I think, and accepts him as something of a friend."

"The King is scarcely a fool, however weakly he acts. He must have his reasons."

"Fellow-feeling, perhaps, for another man in distress."

"But surely he would have discovered the man's falsity by now, if he sees so much of him? It must be evident whether or no he *knows* the close things of Richard's life?"

"He does know much. See you, the prince, to try to discover the truth, has had his spies and informants in England to make enquiry — especially when he heard that King Henry himself seems to be in some doubt on the matter. And the spies have uncovered a strange story. It seems that Richard of Bordeaux had a favourite chaplain, of whom he was very fond. Called Master Richard Maudlyn, or Richard the Magdalene. He was notably like the King in looks, almost a double. Indeed they were whispered to be half-brothers, both sons of the Black Prince, this Maudlyn illegitimate. It seems that on occasion they would exchange clothing, and this Maudlyn play the monarch and the King the priest — a useful means of discovering much of interest for a ruler. So, it seems, none can be fully certain which it was that was slain at Pontefract, Richard or this chaplain. Or whether the Mammet here is indeed king or priest."

"Save us — what a coil!"

"The prince considers the Mammet to be Maudlyn, not King Richard. He never calls him Sire or Grace, but only the Lord Richard, whatever others do. Yet it serves his purposes to hold him here, little better than a hostage or prisoner, as possible threat against Henry. For there is a party unfavourable to Henry in England, who are prepared to support the notion that this *is* Richard for their own ends. And this could help keep Henry Plantagenet from Scotland's throat."

"I suppose that there is nothing so strange in all this. *We* are both bastards . . ."

A blowing of horns halted their talk, and drew all eyes to the King's Knot again. The curtains were drawn aside. The stone-circle was still there — since its great monoliths could by no means be moved without enormous labour — but within it a very different scene was portrayed. A throne was set up in the midst, with a noble-looking man sitting, having shoulder-length hair and a small square beard, wearing a curious long coat, girdled with a gold belt and ornamented with intricate Celtic patterning, on the breast a most peculiar beast embroidered, never known to man, having a long snout, curled feet and tail and a lappet on the crown of the head. Around the throne were grouped many men, all clad in these long coats almost to the ankles, some being warriors bearing swords and spears, with small square shields, others holding aloft banners and poles topped with curious devices, the mysterious Pictish symbols of double-disc and Z-rod, crescent and V-rod, serpent and Z-rod, mirror and comb, tongs and the like. These designs, which everyone knew from the many symbol-stones scattered about the land but none could interpret, established the group as their ancestors the Picts, presumably with one of their kings. The men spoke by turn, and the king answered — but in a language none there could understand, even the Gaelic-speakers. In the background harps thrummed softly, vibrant. Then the sound of chanting voices began to filter through and supersede both talk and harping. This chanting was very different from that of the previous interlude, sweet, harmonious but assured as it was dignified. Once again light grew in the west; but not a sunrise this time, merely increasing illumination, widespread, refulgent. And to be discerned outlined against it a cross, black against the light, held high. This cross grew in size and clarity, and up on to the Knot from the far side came more pacing figures. First a youth, holding aloft this tall cross; then a man dressed in a simple white girdled robe, tonsured at the front of the head in the fashion of the Irish Celtic Church, and bearing a crozier; then four choristers wearing swords and bearing torches.

This party paced steadily towards the throne, and before it all the Pictish warriors drew their swords, lowered their spears and waved their strange symbols. But the cross-bearing singers neither paused nor wavered. Before the King of the Picts himself a threatening frieze of pointing spears barred the way, and the walkers perforce halted. But the white-robed cleric took the tall cross from the acolyte and gave him his crozier, and holding the crucifix directly before him strode on into the spear-points. One by one these wilted and sank as the cross turned them aside, and its bearer came right up to the throne, there to hold his cross right over the head of the sitting man.

"Hail, O King Brude, son of Mailcon, in the name of the One, the True and Almighty God and of His son Jesus Christ!" he cried, in a strong, clear voice. "I am Challum, son of Felim, son of Fergus the King, son of Connail King of Tirconnail, son of Niall of the Nine Hostages, High King of Ireland. Sometimes called Columb, the Dove. I bring you and yours light, O King, light in your darkness, peace in your war, love in your land, joy in your hearts and life everlasting. I have come from across the Western Sea to bring you this mighty gift — the Cross of Christ."

The seated man leaned forward to stare at the newcomer, pulling at his square beard. But the bearers of the strange symbols set up an angry shout of protest, and bore down on this Challum the Dove, or Columba, using their poles like lances. To each in turn the cross was presented, and one after another the double-disc and Z-rod, the crescent and V-rod, the serpent and Z-rod, the mirror and comb and the rest, fell back and down, and their priestly bearers shrank away abashed.

King Brude of the Northern Picts rose from his seat, held a hand up for silence, and then sank on his knees before Columba and the cross. The missionary-saint laid his hand on the other's brow, making the sign of the cross, and the *Te Deum* rose in triumph from the acolyte and torch-bearers.

The curtains were drawn once more.

"That, now, I can conceive of Holy Church paying for, and gladly!" Alex commented.

"It was well done," Jamie admitted. "But . . . look at His Grace."

King Robert was sitting forward in his chair, enthralled, tears streaming from his eyes. He turned to his wife, hands extended. Jamie had never seen the monarch so moved.

"David has pleased his father in this, at least," Alexander nodded. "How much does the King approve of his son's activities, now he is Lieutenant?"

"Little, I think. But, through the Queen and Bishop Trail, he can moderate David at times, as he never could his brother Albany. So there is that improvement."

"You do not sound so enamoured of your prince as once you were, Jamie. You are disappointed?"

"Aye, I am disappointed. It is not what I had hoped for. David is better than his uncle — but with all his gifts it should be more than that. He has it in him to rule well — but scarce takes the trouble to do so. He is too greatly taken up with his own pleasures and devices, his women in especial, ever the women! Clever as he is, he is young, to be sure — perhaps too young to be wielding the supreme power in the realm. When he is older, belike, he will make a good king. God willing . . ."

An angry coughing roaring heralded the arrival of the lioness. It had been deemed unwise to attempt to bring her on foot down the narrow winding cliff-path, where she could so easily have jettisoned her keepers. So she came in the wheeled iron cage David had had constructed for her — and which she did not like, and demonstrated the fact loudly. The cage had to be drawn by men, since they could get neither horses nor oxen to abide in the creature's near vicinity. This carriage likewise could not be brought down the steep path, so it had to make the long round-about journey down through the town and then back round the base of the castle-rock, Leonora the while making entirely clear her disapproval of all. She particularly did not like flaring torches.

The animal's arrival in the midst of the throng created the usual stir and more, her roaring, loud, fierce and continuing. Efforts to quieten her were quite ineffectual; indeed they made her worse. The prince himself could probably have soothed her — for there was an extraordinary empathy between the young man and the beast, probably because he was the only one who showed no fear of her; but he had disappeared from the scene meantime. Raw meat had been brought for the creature, but she would have none of it. Jamie tried to calm the brute, since she knew him better than most, but without success. The King was making distressed gestures, the inspiring effect of the St. Columba episode being negated by this roaring din. In the absence of better remedy, Jamie ordered the keepers to drag the cage and its occupant to some distance off north-westwards, round the rock, at least out of the crowded area and the torches' glare — where, however, although muted, the noise continued.

When he got back to his former stance, Jamie found Sir Alexander Stewart gone although his Highland chieftains were still there. Then he perceived him up on the Knot, moving quietly in behind the royal party. Mary was up there, with her princesses. But it was not to Mary's side that Alex found his way but to that of the Lady Isobel of Mar. So that pot still simmered.

The master of ceremonies captured attention in his own capering fashion and the curtains were pulled aside again — after a much briefer interval this time. Jamie had been wondering about the timing, for it could not be far off midnight by now, the vital hour.

On this occasion the scene was much more brightly lit, and more formal. In the centre of the stone-circle was set a notably large circular table, garlanded, with lesser tables grouped around. Behind it were erected twelve poles topped by banners, and

202

beneath each hung a full shining suit-of-armour, of plate and chain mail, with plumed helmets and shields painted with colourful heraldic devices. The tables were set with flagons, chalices and beakers.

Trumpets sounded, the first heard that night, and up on to the Knot filed eleven finely-dressed men, each supported by a small page carrying his knight's sword. All were clad identically in cloth-of-gold tunics, long parti-coloured hose, with curling-toed slippers, and wore gold chains round their necks with crucifixes. These took their seats on either side of a central chair at the round table, their pages standing behind.

Another fanfare announced the arrival of a file of eleven good-looking young women, dressed all in white, red rosettes in their hair. Laughing and calling to each other musically, these went to sit at the side tables.

A longer, louder flourish of trumpets heralded a splendid figure, alone save for two pages behind, in complete shirt of chain-mail painted glistening gold, a red rampant lion stitched on the breast and a gold circlet around the fair brows. He had a cloth-of-gold cloak slung behind. It was David Stewart, looking every inch a king. As the knights and ladies stood, he waved to them left and right, and with dignity took the central chair.

There was only the briefest pause, and David raised his hand. There followed the clash of cymbals and discordant shouting, and from the side came a new procession. First there were warriors with spears and drawn swords, armoured. Then a statuesque woman of magnificent build which even the shapeless brown sackcloth in which she was garbed could not hide, long dark hair unbound, who walked head down and hands clasped low before her — but held in those hands nevertheless a rope which led back to a tethered man who stumbled along behind, with two soldiers cracking whips over his bent head. He was in one of the long coats of the Picts, and on his breast was painted a great bull, head down to charge, flanked by the crescent and V-rod devices.

This curious group moved on up to the round table, where the seated twelve watched, silent. There the guards fell back, and the woman turning, jerked the rope and gestured fiercely at the captive, pointing to the ground. The man wailed, and cast himself down, prone, clenched hands out in supplication. The woman moved, to place a foot on his neck, and thus faced the table again.

"My mighty lord Arthur," she called, in ringing tones, "I, Vanora, your unworthy wife, greet, acclaim and worship you. I have sinned against you, and against my marriage vows, and am no more worthy to be your queen. I deserve death and shall embrace it. But I have brought you, on my way to the grave, Unuist, High King of the Cruithne, or Picts, with whom I betrayed you. Into your hands I deliver him. And his people. To do with as you will. And not only him, but these also." She swung about, and pointed to where two more long-coated men had materialised, not bound these but standing free. "Nechtan the Second, King of the Northern Picts; and Loth, King of the Southern Picts. These come of their own free will, to yield themselves to you, Arthur, that you may rule over a united land, of Alba, Strathclyde, Lothian as well as Dalriada — the kingdom of the Scots. This, my dying gift, in restitution for a great sin. Now, my lord King, I present myself for your stern justice. I crave but one boon, husband — that you and you only strike the just blow with your own blade. Here!" And dramatically the woman wrenched open the sackcloth gown to bare her fine bosom.

David rose — and all others with him. He paced slowly round the table to his erring queen's side. Standing before her, he looked at her unspeaking. Then, leaning forward, he reached out to take the drawn-aside gown in both hands and jerked it apart and down, so that the stuff dropped to her feet, leaving her there completely naked, but upstanding, proud. And after another brief pause, he twitched off the cloth-of-gold cloak from his own shoulders and with a flourish draped it round her ample gleaming form.

As cheers arose from his knights and cries from the young women, with applause from the audience, he placed an arm around Vanora's or Guinevere's shoulders. Then he turned to the prostrate Pict. Stooping, he raised him to his feet, and spoke.

"Unuist, High King of Pictland, I greet you in peace," he cried — and had to raise his voice considerably, for, whether by coincidence or because she recognised his tones from afar, the lioness roared the louder. "I, Arthur Pendrachan, accept your homage and forgive you your sin, as I have forgiven the sin of this woman, my wife. I hereby take you into my peace." He turned. "And you also, Nechtan and Loth — your submission and fealty I accept, your love I seek. Your lives I return to you, all three. You shall remain kings, lesser kings, or great earls;

and with my Kings of Strathclyde, the Nordreys, the Sudreys and the Cattenes, shall rule this united realm of the Scots under me, as the Council of the Seven Kings or Earls. For all time. This I declare in love and peace."

The woman and the three Pictish monarchs all sank to their knees before him, and stirring music struck up from all around, ragged at first but soon harmonising. Raising the kneelers one by one, but without delay, David, arm-in-arm with Vanora, led them to the round table — rather more quickly than he had moved heretofore. He picked up chalices and handed them to the four — and was only just in time to grasp his own. A bell began to toll solemnly up on the castle, the music died away, and percolating through the lioness's grumbling growls sounded the pealing of all Stirling-town's church and monastery bells.

When the castle bell finished its twelve strokes — although the other pealing, like the roaring, continued — David Stewart raised his voice and cup again.

"My friends all," he cried, "great and small, rich and poor. It is the Year of Our Lord Fourteen Hundred! I give you all a good and better New Year, a good and better century, and a good and better Scotland, God willing!"

To deafening cheers that toast was drunk, by all who could find the wherewithal, and acclaimed by the rest.

Jamie Douglas thereafter pushed his way through the noisy throng and up on to the King's Knot, to reach and embrace his wife, amongst all the rest of the embracing, exclamation and cheer.

David came over from the stone-circle to embrace his father, kiss his mother, less warmly his wife, and then any and every woman available. Congratulations were showered upon him, the old Earl Archie croaking that he had just managed it in time, nevertheless.

The King rose, raised up the Queen, and bowed left and right. Then, at the prince's signal, a corps of torch-bearers and musicians hurried forward to form up and conduct the monarch and his party, with all such as preferred to accompany them, back up to the castle. They moved off slowly, at the King's limping pace.

This royal departure was the signal for the entire character and tone of the proceedings to change completely, from order to disorder, from a disciplined programme to licensed chaos, from normal behaviour to general abandon. As though to set the ball rolling, the tabarded master-of-ceremonies ran over to the pseudo royal couple and began tearing off the King's beard, crown and wig, and then the purple robe, to reveal a strapping wench all white beneath — who promptly raced off, squealing, pursued by a shouting throng of men. Others dealt similarly with the queen, who, naked, revealed much muscular and masculine endowment, and bounded off before a mainly female pack led by some of the erstwhile damsels of Arthur's Court. Soon caught, this young man, fortunate or otherwise, was dragged off and held under the wine-fountain — which had been turned off during the tableaux but now was spouting redly again. Some of the ladies fell in with him, shrieking laughter. His former female partner and following disappeared into the bushes and did not reappear.

Jamie was watching this changed scene with mixed feelings when a panting at his elbow revealed a distinctly breathless Mary.

"Save us!" he exclaimed. "You back? I saw you go off with the princesses. Here is no place for you, lass."

"They did not need me any more. And I was not going to miss the rest of it," she declared. "I noticed that *you* did not follow the King and Queen!"

"My place is with the prince — or so I thought!" he told her, but a little doubtfully.

"And I say mine is with my husband on a night like this, no?"

"Then keep close, girl — or you may get more than you look for!"

"That I shall, never fear. Already, coming back to you, I have had hands grabbing at me. Torchmen, servitors, even."

"Aye. This Hour of Misrule decent wives and mothers should be safely in their own houses."

"But not their lords and masters?" She looked around on the wild and colourful scene. "Where is Alex?"

"I do not know. I have not seen him since the King Arthur affair."

"M'mm. I noticed that one of the royal party did not go back with the King and Queen — the Countess of Mar! Although her husband accompanied his sister Annabella."

"Aye, well. Alex will gang his ain gait. As will his Cousin David."

They looked towards where the prince was eating and drinking, at one of the many tables, with a noisy party, and paying

206

marked attention to one especially, the former Vanora or Guinevere — who appeared not to have found opportunity to add to her clothing in the interim.

"Who is the woman?" Jamie wondered. "She has a strange voice."

"She has more than that! But, did you not know? That is the wife of the new English envoy. I fear that her spouse may be less than enchanted."

"Aye — that could be unwise . . ."

Some dancing followed, led by the prince and his lady-for-the-night. Most who could joined in with enthusiasm, Mary and Jamie glad to take part. But before long it became too rowdy for any comfort, with too much drink taken amongst the dancers, and the licence for disorder and misrule adopted too literally. David himself withdrew, although without any evident displeasure, and his party with him. Calling out, he announced that those who still had control of their feet would now go skating — if they could find their way.

And so a laughing throng headed north-westwards into the bushes — and in almost less time than it takes to tell, were lost and dispersed. That maze had been cunningly devised, most of its grassy paths, amongst the tubbed shrubs and evergreens and fir-trees, false leads, circuits and blind alleys, the widest leading nowhere, the true tracks narrow and well disguised. Also there were distractions, hidden musicians, arbours, grottoes, sequestered seats, groups of statuary, some well lit with lanterns, some deep in shadow. Even Jamie, who had been at the making of it, could not recollect his way around in lamplight and gloom.

With a spirited and mainly youthful company of both sexes, less than fully sober and in a state of arousal and excitement, that maze accounted for many casualties — as it was intended to do. Couples, and trios for that matter, went exploring and did not return, protesting ladies went skirling off down dark lanes and their cries soon were heard no more, grinning men coaxed and beckoned from corners and entries.

The lioness's roars at least had some virtue here, since they helped to establish general direction. By their aid, a proportion of the prince's party managed to win through, in laughing pairs and groups. Many were the strange and stirring sights stumbled upon in the process — including a brief vision of Alex Stewart grappling with active white limbs which Mary at least had no doubts in identifying as those of Isobel of Mar.

The survivors now issued out from the great canopied area. The difference in temperature was dramatic, the effect of the wide spread of awnings and tentage, with the braziers and fires, quite extraordinary — although some draughts had been inevitable. Most there had tended to forget that they were outdoors on a cold winter's night. Now the tingling frosty air struck them like a blow, and the hoar decked all nearly as white as the snow David had foolishly hoped for.

There was no difficulty in finding the way now, for an avenue of lanterns led the couple of hundred yards further to the pond. But David, when he had assembled a number from the maze, insisted on first going to collect the still grumbling Leonora, over at the shadowy base of the rock.

This took time; no dealings with that animal could be rushed. With David present the creature stopped its growling, and even purred tentatively for a little. But it was suspicious of most of the company — a mutual sentiment — and at first would not come out of its cage. The rapport between prince and lioness had now advanced to the stage whereby he — but he alone — could lead it about on a leash, in suitable conditions with folk keeping their distance. She still had to wear shackles, to be sure, but David had had a lighter set made, less clankingly irritating to the brute.

At length the progress to the pond was resumed, with the Duke of Rothesay and his charge given a wide berth in the lead by the rest. Jamie ventured much nearer than the others when the prince signed to him — and noted with some satisfaction that Sir John de Ramorgnie kept well away.

"Back to the Knot, Jamie," David said. "There are not nearly sufficient folk here for this of the galley. Bring along all you can — not through the maze, but round above. It has been too successful, I fear! Bring all sober enough to come."

Simple instructions as these were, Jamie found it no easy task to carry out. There were still many revellers back in the centre of the canopied area, but these tended to be intent on their own chosen entertainment, or else too drunk to heed. Coupling, dancing, fighting, eating and drinking, even sleeping, Hogmanay merrymakers were not all inclined to abandon it at short notice, even on the Lieutenant of the Crown's relayed command. However in time he did manage to gather together a somewhat unruly company which he led round-about back to the pond.

When they arrived it was to find skating in full swing, to the music of instrumentalists hidden in the galley in the middle. A large number of wooden skates had been provided, and though not all were expert, or even in a state to perform adequately, at least this left more room for those who could. David was doing a sort of graceful *pas de deux* with Mary — his voluptuous Vanora apparently being no skater, and now evidently feeling the cold not a little, as well she might with only a cloth-of-gold cloak to protect her. The Prolocutor-General was however doing his best to keep her warm meantime. The lioness was out on the ice also, tethered to the galley and seeming at something of a loss.

With the arrival of the newcomers the fun developed fast and noisy. More refreshments were produced from the ship, and the wine flowed. Bonfires blazed all around, and wild dances about them became the order of the night for non-skaters.

Jamie really began to enjoy himself, for he and Mary were excellent on skates. Especially when Alex Stewart and the Countess of Mar joined them, anything but shamefaced, and they made a quartet for figure-skating and races and dancing. The prince favoured them with his company off and on — but he had other things on his mind, and disappeared now and again into outer darkness.

Wines and spirits however, although an undoubted aid to gaiety, in time become the enemies of skating, and even dancing. As more and more of the company began to have difficulty in keeping upright, David, drunk himself of course but as usual revealing little of it, decided that if climax was not to become anti-climax, it was probably time to come to a conclusion. He clambered up on to the prow of the galley and shouted for quiet.

"My friends," he called, "we have an ancient custom in this land, handed down to us by our distant ancestors, lost in time, known as Up Halie Days, or the end of the holy days marking the Twelfth Night of Yuletide. This is a time of girth, or sanctuary, wherein none may be apprehended or punished for breaking the law. I have given command, with the King's agreement, on this especial Yuletide, not only that none should be taken into custody, but that all in custody already should be released. This in all jurisdictions in the land, justiciars', sheriffs' and barons'. An amnesty, token of our new age and rule in Scotland."

There was a dutiful rather than an enthusiastic cheer, plus some muttered comments.

"In the past, as sign and promise that the new start was made and the old done with, it was the custom to burn a longship or galley, with all that spoke of strife, hatred and ill, in it — as is still done in some parts, they say, in the Orcades and elsewhere. We shall do so here. Follow me to the fires, for torches, my friends. It is not yet the true Up Halie Day — but we can celebrate it in advance!"

Now there was real cheering, as everyone thronged to the bonfires. Climbing down from the ship, David released the lioness tied there, and led her a discreet distance away, to secure her to a tree. Then he went to the nearest fire, to pick up and light one of the many torches lying ready. The musicians had emerged from the galley, and with these to play them on in a stirring, dancing tune, the prince raised his flaming brand high and led the torchlight procession back round the pond to the eastern side and then down on to the ice towards the vessel.

Now could be seen a new feature. Up on the high curving forepeak of the ship where David had recently stood, two figures had replaced him. Seen clearly in the light of the now innumerable torches, these drew all eyes, opened all eyes wider. Both were notably clad, one slender in black-and-silver, the other large, almost burly, in full Highland panoply. As the procession drew close the identity of these was evident to all. Dummies they might be, but they had been most skilfully made — Robert, Duke of Albany and Donald, Lord of the Isles, uncannily lifelike, unmistakable.

Something of a hush fell on the laughing, singing, skipping throng, although the music continued. The prince smiled benignly.

"Diu you know of this?" Mary demanded of her husband. "It is dangerous."

"I knew of Donald. The galley is meant to be his. The device of the Isles on the sail. And he as good as an outlaw. But not this of the Duke Robert. That is bad, too much. A great folly. It is bound to come to the Duke's ears . . ."

"Come, Jamie. We must speak to him. Get him to remove Robert's effigy, at least . . ."

They were not alone in their concern. Sir John de Ramorgnie was already at the prince's side, hand on his sleeve, making urgent representations. It was not often that Jamie Douglas joined forces with Ramorgnie, but he and Mary did so now. But to no effect. Laughing, David waved them away.

Reaching the galley, the prince turned. "So let us end the

troubles of this kingdom!" he cried, and hurled his torch. It rose in a flaming arc, showering sparks, to fall within the galley's hull. After it sailed a few others — but not all.

David looked round, narrow-eyed, most pointedly at those who still held torches in their hands. He did not speak, but his glance was eloquent.

With a sudden whoosh the combustibles in the open vessel caught fire, and roaring flames leapt up. In moments the galley was an inferno from end to end.

Shrugging, Jamie tossed his torch in with the rest, Mary and the others following suit. All drew back, for the heat was intense.

The prospect of the burning vessel there on the ice was impressive, exciting, somehow basically frightening. The great square sail caught alight quickly, and the dread device of the black Galley of the Isles painted thereon was consumed in a broad sheet of flame, the single mast and rigging taking longer to go. Almost the last to be enveloped was the lofty prow with the two so real-seeming figures standing there. For a little they seemed as though imperishable; then abruptly they were alight together, their turpentine-soaked clothing erupting. A long sigh arose from the watchers, but no words. The musicians had stopped their playing. Even the prince was silent. Only the lioness growled her anger and fear at the blaze.

David was the first to recover himself. He laughed loudly, just a little forcedly for him. "Thus ends misrule!" he cried. "Let each and all witness! Now — back to the Knot. The night is young yet. This year of Fourteen Hundred must be well launched. Jamie — take Leonora back to her cage. You she will not eat — I think! Come, all."

"I think that I have had sufficient," Mary said, when the others were moving off. "Our own bed calls, husband!"

"Aye. Enough is enough — and more! I must get the lion first. But — keep your distance from the brute, lass."

"You are sure you are safe with it, Jamie? I would leave the creature where it is, tethered."

"No, no. It knows me, knows that I am not afraid of it. Besides, it is shackled. And it is not far to the cage. Where is Alex?"

"Alex is gone again. And the Countess with him. He is a Stewart, after all! As am I, Jamie Douglas! Haste you with that roaring creature — but have a care. I wish it did not make such ill noise . . ."

211

X

THE TWO BROTHERS, both Sir James Douglas, rode hard through the Lothian countryside in the early darkening of the February afternoon, Candlemas 1400, behind them a hastily-gathered force of some two hundred Dalkeith men-at-arms and retainers. It was by pure chance that Jamie was with his legitimate brother. He had been summoned to Dalkeith from Aberdour, their father being seriously ill again, and declaring death imminent. And then had come the urgent message from Archibald, Master of Douglas, from Edinburgh Castle where the Lieutenant of the Crown had recently appointed him Keeper. The English were invading Scotland, under Hotspur, the traitor Dunbar with them. Not in major force yet, so far as was known, and not King Henry. Reported numbers varied, but about 10,000 seemed to be the figure. They were already through Dunbar's Merse and into Lothian, nearing Haddington indeed. It might well be but the spearhead of a larger invasion under the King. He, the Master, was hastening to meet them, with all the force he could muster at short notice. He called on all possible support, to join him at Haddington, the East Lothian county town, at the earliest moment. The old Lord of Dalkeith had recovered his spirits wonderfully at these reviving tidings, and insisted that his sons should leave his bed-side forthwith, gather as many of his adherents as they could, and be off, while his younger son, Will, mustered more from further afield, to follow on later.

Sir James, Younger of Dalkeith, although nominally in command, deferred to his elder bastard brother in most things. Jamie's experience in matters military especially, was much the greater; and his reputation as some sort of hero, however

212

unwarranted, was a major factor with men to lead. They rode side-by-side, therefore, but Jamie would take the decisions.

They came to Haddington, over the bleak wastes of the Gled's Muir, with the dusk, to find the town gates shut and the burghers putting the place into a hasty state of siege-defence. The Master of Douglas had moved on, watchers shouted to them, on to Traprain. The English were assailing Hailes Castle of the Hepburns and had burned Spott and Stenton and the Lammermuir townships. It could be Haddington next, unless Douglas stopped them.

In the gathering gloom the Dalkeith contingent pounded on eastwards, the abrupt bulk of Traprain Law, old Pictish King Loth's one-time hill-top capital, looming vaguely ahead four miles, its lofty flat summit outlined against a flickering ruddy glow which could only be the burning Lammermuir villages. At the sight, men's hands tended to loosen swords in sheaths.

Halfway to the hill, they swung leftwards down to cross the Tyne by the Bere Ford. The Haddington folk had said that the Master of Douglas would do this likewise, to approach Hailes, not by the normal road but by the higher ground of Pencraik Hill on the north side of the river, as precaution in case of English scouts and patrols. Jamie commended this caution in his less-than-cautious young chief.

Hailes Castle was in a curious situation for a quite major stronghold, set deep in a narrow valley below the north face of Traprain Law, on the south steep bank of the Lothian Tyne, which here ran through what was almost a gorge. The road threaded this ravine, and the castle was therefore in a position to close that road at will, one of the main highways from Dunbar, Berwick and the Border to Haddington and Edinburgh — and likewise to levy toll on travellers, cattle-droves and the like. It had its own strength, despite being thus overlooked by high ground, for owing to the constricted nature of the gorge and valley no enemy force could deploy effectively around its rock above the river. Evidently the English had discovered this.

The Dalkeith party came up with the larger force on a wooded spur of Pencraik Hill, a lesser height directly opposite Traprain, from which they could look down on the castle in the valley some two hundred feet below. The Master welcomed them with relief, even though he was frankly disappointed in their numbers; but Jamie's unexpected presence partly made up for this, for he had not forgotten his rescue at Foulhope haugh in Ettrick and

213

had acquired a high opinion of Jamie's abilities in the field. He made no pretence of treating the other Sir James as commander, although the pair of them were the two senior representatives of the house of Douglas in the younger generation, and were moreover linked by marriage, both to daughters of the King. The Master had some 1,200 men on Pencraik Hill, so, welcome as was a reinforcement of two hundred, it was not much with which to tackle 10,000.

Nevertheless, Archibald was sufficiently aggressively-minded, as befitted a Douglas leader. "At least you have come at the right time," he told them. "Fortunately, the enemy is divided, for the night, and show no signs of knowing that we are here. I chose to come by this Pencraik, to keep our presence secret — even though it is on the wrong side of the river. Fighting in the dark will be difficult, but it may yield us some advantage — which we shall need, by God!"

"To be sure," Jamie agreed. "What do you purpose? It will not be so dark, besides, with those fires."

The Master pointed directly downhill first, to where the castleton of Hailes, the cabins and cot-houses of the Hepburn retainers, had been set alight and blazed redly.

"Part of their force is there, sitting round the castle. They have made three attempts against it already, a shepherd here tells me, but without success. I think that they will try again, under cover of darkness, when archers cannot repel them." He raised his head and hand to look and point eastwards by north. "Yonder is the town of Preston, and the mill-town of Linton. The English main body is camped there — you can see their fires. There is no room for them all in this narrow valley. They are over a mile away. We could move down quietly, and attack these around the castle — Hepburn perhaps sallying out to aid us. And, pray God, surprise and defeat them before help could arrive for them from the town. How say you?"

"A bold and notable tactic, Archie," young Dalkeith declared enthusiastically. "The fires will show them up, but not our approach. Dismounted, and quiet, we should win close before ever they learn of our presence. Eh, Jamie?"

His brother fingered his long chin. "It might avail, yes. But . . . see you, why not rather assail the main body in their open camp, rather than this tight detachment in the difficult valley?"

"Eh? But, man," the Master protested, "there are thousands

214

there! My scouts say so. Three or four times as many as here around the castle. Why pit our smaller strength against the greater?"

"Sufficient reasons, I think. These are men encamped for the night, no longer girt and standing to arms. Moreover, encamped at a town, they will be dispersed for a surety, scattered, seeking drink and women, pillaging probably. Whereas those below are tightly grouped and still in fighting trim. Also, you must cross the river to get at them — and you will not do that, with many hundreds, in the darkness, silently or easily. Again, surprise and break up the main body, and this detachment will be loth to continue the invasion alone; but defeat it only, and the main body is still there, still many times your number, and alerted against you."

"Aye, you are right. That makes good sense. How then may this best be attempted?"

"I know this country. I have lands nearby, at Stoneypath, in Lammermuir. The river leaves this valley a mile on, and curves round to the north before turning east again for the sea. In that curve, this side of it, lies the mill-town of Linton, then the kirk-town of Preston. We cannot attack from the east therefore, the Tyne barring the way. Nor down this valley itself, in case there is coming and going between the camps. But if we go north-about from here, on this high ground, by Markle, then divide into two and come down upon both ends of the mill-town and the kirk-town from the Markle slopes, we should do best. It is the town's pasture there, open grass slopes, so that we can make a mounted assault, at least to start with. Always best against a dispersed and surprised enemy."

"Very well. I do not know how this land lies. But — let us pray that Hailes Castle does not fall, meantime."

"That is a hazard we must risk. But this business may not take so very long, see you. Given luck . . ."

The order was passed through the quiet waiting ranks to mount and move. It was quite dark now, but the various glows in the sky, from the distant foothills villages, from the burning castleton and the many camp-fires at the mill-town and kirk-town of Preston, provided some illumination in an arc to east and south. With its fluctuating and modest help the long column of 1,400 horsemen picked their way slowly north by east over the rounded summit of Pencraik Hill, on tussocky grassland with cattle and sheep continually moving off in alarm before

215

them. They contoured round a north-going spur of the hillside beyond, and then were faced with a complication. In the wide further valley was the small monastery of Markle, and a community clustered around it, below quite a steep escarpment. This now proved to be on fire likewise, the flames dying down to a red glow. Presumably therefore the English were there also. It meant that they must veer off eastwards, or risk giving the alarm, even a clash. There was the advantage, however, that it indicated that the enemy were more split up than ever.

Eastwards, they could not go much further before the slope dropped away, before them and the camp-fires gleamed around the south end of the double township, known as Linton, where there was a group of mills along the waterside, with an inn and the mill-hands' cot-houses. The larger part of the place, where was the parish church, another mill and more houses, was half-a-mile to the north, and not quite so easy to ride down upon, because the river began to curve away again and an incoming shallow valley from the Markle direction intervened. There appeared to be as many camp-fires in this more distant Preston vicinity. It takes a lot of riverbank ground to camp 7,000 or 8,000 men.

"What now?" the Master demanded. "We cannot reach Preston without crossing that valley. There are three fires in it. If that means English troops there also, the alarm will be given and surprise lost."

"Yes. Who would have thought that they would have been so spread out?"

"Let us just descend on this camp below us, at Linton," Jamie's brother said. "Overwhelm it, and then sweep along the riverside road to Preston. What is wrong with that?"

"This — that the leaders may not be here. Hotspur and Dunbar. We do not want to give them time and opportunity to rally their men. Always seek to destroy the leadership, I say. They *may* be back at Hailes — but I think not. That is not work for the proud Percy, of a night. After failing at the first assault, he would leave it to some captain and this detachment, and seek comfortable quarters for the night for himself and Dunbar. Where, think you? Not in some broken-down inn or miller's cot-house, when there is the Rectory of St. Baldred's Kirk of Linton nearby. Either that, or the monastery of Markle — but that is aflame. Hotspur and Dunbar will be at Preston Rectory, and we dare not leave them there unmolested to rally their

216

people, warned by our attack on Linton. Which they are bound to hear."

"Damnation, then — what to do?" the Master cried. "We could stand here and talk it to and fro all night!"

"Better talk now, and take a right course, than regrets after! But here's what I suggest. I will take our Dalkeith men, two hundred — it is enough — and ride quietly down and across this accursed side-valley, seeking to avoid the camp-fires and giving alarm. With all their own troops hereabouts, they might not think of us as Scots, in the darkness. Then, if we pass them, make on over the lesser slope beyond to the back of Preston's houses. Above the Rectory. When in position, I give you a signal — a blast on a horn. Then we both charge down, at the same time."

"Aye — but if you do *not* get across this valley unseen and unchallenged, what then?"

"Then you will hear it, and make your own charge, at once. Down there upon the camp at Linton. And when you can spare it, send a company along the riverside, to aid me at Preston."

The Master nodded. "So be it. The best we can do. You go now? Then, St. Bridgit go with you."

"And with you. Do you come with me, James?"

The brothers detached their people without difficulty and moved off at a walk, north-eastwards, down the gradual slope of the side-valley. There were three fires down in the floor of it, strung out, and they made heedfully for the larger gap between them. None spoke, but two hundred men cannot ride, however slowly, without some noise — the plod of hooves, the creak of saddlery, the clink of bits and bridles and men's armour, the snort of nostrils. There were more cattle on this slope, and these made more disturbances than the horsemen, lumbering off into the gloom in clumsy fright.

The more level ground at the foot was ridged with the strips of the township's runrig cultivation, with early ploughing already started. This was unsuitable ground for camping on — but whinnying from not far off revealed that there were horse-lines nearby on the left. Two of their own beasts acknowledged the greeting, amidst muttered anathemas from their riders.

They had to cross a burn, but it was small and caused no trouble. The track up the valley to Markle ran on the other side, and over this they moved, still at only a walk, glancing right and left warily. Jamie reined up to wait — since even two hundred

217

horses, three or four abreast, take some time to pass a given point. He was just about to ride forwards again, with the last files coming up, when they heard singing from quite close at hand, to the right, townwards. The men hearing it almost automatically began to kick their beasts into faster movement, with consequent jostling and more noise.

The singing stopped short. Jamie cursed — but took a swift decision. He raised his voice.

"Slow, there!" he called, quite loudly. "I hear voices." He turned in his saddle, towards where the singing had come from, down the track. "Hey, there!" he shouted. "A plague on it — you, there! Here, to me. Where are you?" He sought to give his voice not only authority but the typical Northumbrian burr — with what success he knew not.

There was some indistinct speaking, and then three men materialised out of the gloom, walking less than steadily. They appeared to be carrying heavy bundles, loot no doubt.

"You," Jamie exclaimed. "Where are we in this accursed place? Who are you? Where from?"

"We are Sir William Heron's men, sir," one answered, hiccuping. "What's to do?"

"Heron? Where is the Percy? The Lord Harry Percy? I have word for him. We were sent this way by some fool. Where is Hotspur, a God's name?"

"He is yonder, sir." The spokesman pointed northwards. "In the village, some place. Some house yonder."

Jamie grunted. "This night is as black as Satan's belly!" he grumbled. And without a word of thanks moved on after his disappearing last files.

No alarm broke out behind.

He was trotting up, to get to the head of his now quite extended column again, when noise did break out, ahead. There were cries, shouts and then the clash of steel. Uproar developed — including the skirls of women.

Spurring hard now, Jamie pounded over grassland, not cultivated rigs, gently rising. He found his brother and the first horsemen milling around quite a large crowd of men and some females, presumably coming back from Preston to their Markle camp, with captives. Markle being a monastery, would be short on women. Swords were drawn and there was much indiscriminate fury and noise.

All virtue in silence gone, Jamie found and raised his horn, and blew a single high blast — for the Master's sake, but it also had the advantage of drawing his own men's attention to his commands amidst all the other shouting.

"Come!" he yelled, drawing sword. "Leave here. Follow me. James — all speed!"

A gallop might have been disastrous in that lack of light, and even the canter at which Jamie led was dangerous. But then the entire situation was fraught with dangers. On he drove, directly for the rear of Preston township now, with a bare quarter mile to go.

They met no more straggling English. More camp-fires appeared before them presently, having been somewhat hidden behind a fold of the pastureland. The thunder of their hooves, as well as the shouting and clash must have given some warning to the men there, but no coherent defence met them — not unnaturally, for it was only evening and many of the men would be roaming the town in search of amusement, and not a few undoubtedly drunk, the time for posting of sentries and night patrols not yet come.

Slowly, only sufficiently for him to wave and order his horsemen into a wide front instead of a column, he swept them on through the camp area, swords slashing, the dread Douglas slogan shouted, riding men down, trampling the recumbent, overturning stacked lances and pennons, scattering fires, stampeding horses. Actual fighting there was none. In only moments this camp at least was a shambles, men fleeing in all directions, opposition none.

Jamie perceived a small knoll ahead half-right, with a towered building dark on top — the church. He did not know just where the Rectory was, but it would not be far from the church, for certain. He plunged on without reducing speed.

There was the usual walled graveyard round the church, reaching down the sides of the knoll. Cottages began where the kirkyard ended. There were men moving about here, in the shadows, some mounting horses in haste. Jamie swore. He was too late. The leadership was warned, alert.

He noticed a larger building downhill to the left. Against the glow of the riverside fires of the main camp he could see that it had a less bulky roof-line than the cottages — slate not thatch. The Rectory, for sure. Spurring towards it, he saw that it had a range of subsidiary buildings, thatched, and a yard, a farmery. There were more horsemen here.

Reining his mount up to block the entrance to this yard, he shouted for the first files of men behind to join him. With a score or so of them jostling and rearing around, he urged his brother onwards, with the rest of the two hundred.

"Down into the riverside haughs!" he shouted. "Break up the camps. Ride down all you can. Cause confusion, panic. Back and forward."

Then into the Rectory yard he drove his own mount, sword pointing, his twenty piling in behind. There were half-a-dozen men there, mounted or mounting. Some stood their ground, others leapt down and bolted into the houses at sight of the superior numbers. Advancing horsemen always have the advantage over the stationary, and Jamie had no difficulty in unseating the first man he came to. The others were overwhelmed in the rush of Scots.

Jumping down, he yelled for his men to follow him in at the open door, prepared for tough fighting in the easily-held narrow lobbies within. But no-one was there to oppose him. Stumbling through, in his heavy riding-boots, he peered into this room and that. The first two were empty, although candles and lanterns lit them. In the third, a kitchen, two women and an old man huddled in alarm, servants obviously. Beyond, and up the twisting turnpike stairs, more empty rooms, more candles and fires.

Fighting his way back through the press of his own men, Jamie made for the servants in the kitchen again.

"They've gone? Bolted?" he cried. "Where?"

Wordless the old man pointed a trembling hand, in the other direction from which they had entered. Presumably they had come in at the back door and their quarry had bolted through the front.

"Who were they? Hotspur? Dunbar?"

"Lords, sir. Proud lords," the ancient quavered. "English knights . . ."

Snorting, Jamie flung out of the kitchen, along the lobby and out at another open door. Just too late. If he had been only moments earlier. It was damnable! But at least they would be on foot. The horses would be at the back, not this front door. Though they would soon find themselves new mounts.

Waving his people back through the house to their own horses, he wasted no time. Hurling themselves into the saddles, they rode on down towards the river.

Jamie had told his brother to spread confusion and alarm. It might not be all Sir James's doing, but that was certainly the situation along the west bank of Tyne that evening. Everywhere men rode, ran or scurried in every direction, amidst shouts and wails and conflicting commands. Cries of "A Douglas! A Douglas!" resounded — and Jamie's party added their breathless quota. Most of the camp-fires had been scattered, and there was little light. Heaps of booty, piled saddlery and arms, and runaway horses trailing their tether-ropes added to the chaos. It was no sort of battle, only sheer and multiple pandemonium.

Jamie was concerned to keep his own score of men together, for in such conditions a tight, disciplined group of even so few can wield an influence out of all proportion to their numbers. To and fro over the narrow half-mile of haugh they cantered, therefore, with considerable shouting but precious little actual bloodshed, content to have men flee before their solid certainty rather than do battle. And most men there did, a great many having been fleeing before ever they arrived on the scene. The majority of these undoubtedly poured along the haughland southwards, towards the Linton camp area, but fugitives hurried wherever they could, and not a few plunged into the river itself, running high as it was after the winter rains.

They kept collecting groups and individuals of Sir James's company who had become detached. Obviously it had been much more difficult to keep one hundred and eighty together as a unified force, in such circumstances, than a mere twenty. Although, when they found Sir James himself, presently, at the far northern extremity of the township, in a state of high excitement, he did not appear to be greatly concerned that only about seventy of his one hundred and eighty remained with him now. The others were about somewhere, he declared cheerfully. Why worry? It was victory, all the way!

James was less delighted, inevitably. The enemy still outnumbered them many times, and their leaders were still at large. There could be a rally at any time. They must drive back up the haugh, collecting their people as they went, and seek to join forces with the Master again.

He blew his horn, to bring in stragglers, and formed up into line abreast, but four or five deep, and set off at a disciplined trot southwards.

All the way they were herding fugitives and runaway horses before them, flushing out skulkers, passing hiders. None stood to fight. There was a bare half-mile between the two sections of the township, a narrow strip along the riverside, with encampments all the way. All were already deserted. Almost from the first they could hear the clash and shouting from the struggle ahead, where the Master was savaging the Linton area. Nearing this, they began to meet men fleeing their way, both mounted and afoot, although mainly the latter. At Jamie's command they recommenced their "A Douglas! A Douglas!" slogan, in a regular, deep-throated rhythmic chant as they rode. Few English waited for closer inspection.

They achieved no real fighting. If there had been any spontaneous resistance to the Master's sudden attack, it had disintegrated before they arrived. All was a noisy horror of dead and wounded men, screaming horses, uncontrolled fires and the debris of war rather than of battle.

They rejoined the Master of Douglas at the wooden Linton bridge over the Tyne, near the south end, where he was endeavouring to collect and reform some major portion of his force — and finding it a difficult task. Once men become dispersed, attackers equally with defenders, in a town especially and in darkness, reassembly is no simple matter, however many horns may blow. He hailed the Dalkeith company thankfully, the more so when he heard that the Preston end of the encampments was over-run and cleared.

"But we failed to get Hotspur and the leaders," Jamie panted. "Which was my main aim. We were too late."

"Never heed, man. We have them beat. That is what matters. It is victory . . ."

"It is *not* victory! It could still be total failure, defeat. We have taken them by surprise — that is all. We have scattered them meantime, yes — but we have killed few. They are still many times our numbers — and now *we* are scattered likewise! Their leaders are still free, and will recover from their surprise — experienced fighters. Hotspur is no fool. He could regain all."

"Jamie was ever a prophet of woe!" his brother assured, laughing. "We could scarce have done better than we have done, I say."

"I am trying to gather my people again," the Master said. "What more can we do? Who knows where Hotspur and Dunbar may be?"

"We must try to find them. And forthwith. Not give them

222

time to rally any large numbers. Keep pressing them — not standing here waiting."

"But . . . how? In this darkness. Where do we seek them, man?"

"What would *you* do if you were Hotspur, in this pass? He does not know how many may have attacked him — but will think more than we are. He finds his Preston camp over-run. Then his Linton camp. What then? He still has a fighting-force up at Hailes Castle, facing an enemy, not camped and standing down. There is a camp at Markle too, but that is different, resting and smaller probably. If I was the Percy, I would have no doubts. I certainly would not just flee. I would leave someone to seek rally the folk scattered hereabouts, and send someone to bring down the Markle folk. Myself, I would ride with all speed to Hailes, to put myself at the head of a force still in order and in arms. Then bring it back here, to do battle when *we* think we have won and are off guard, scattered."

The others stared at him, in the flickering fires' light, silenced.

"You said that you reckoned perhaps only a quarter of the English force was left at Hailes?" Jamie went on. "But that could be over 2,000. And how many are we here, gathered here — four hundred, five hundred? We cannot face an attack from Hailes, here, with these numbers."

"No. But it would take Hotspur time to mount such an attack."

"Aye — and that is our chance. We must grasp it, and at once. The Hailes valley is very narrow, little more than a ravine. We must ride for it, get up into it, block it. Then their larger numbers will serve them nothing. They will not be able to learn *our* numbers. They will only be able to engage our front, and with their own front, equally small. To get out of the valley they will either have to flee south-westwards, up-river, or clamber up the steep sides, leaving their horses — which they will be loth to do, far from home, in enemy territory. And the river in its gorge to cross, at one side."

"God save us, Jamie — you keep a cool head, I declare!" the Master cried. "You are right — on my soul, you are right! We shall leave James here, and Kilspindie, to rally our own folk and keep the English from rallying. To deal with the Markle camp, likewise. The rest of us make for the valley to Hailes."

They did not count their men, but the Master probably had about four hundred mustered at the bridge, and with the

Dalkeith contingent this made a reasonable force to tackle the valley. They crossed the bridge and spurred south-westwards along the south bank of Tyne, soon leaving the houses behind. It quickly became very dark, as the light from the fires behind faded and they could not ride so fast as they would have liked; but at least there was a road to follow, the main Haddington road indeed.

After half-a-mile they could sense the jaws of the deep narrow valley drawing in on them, thankful that they had reached thus far without any sign of the enemy. Whatever else, they had now closed the gap, blocked the passage and isolated the Hailes group from the rest.

Although the road itself continued, it narrowed and its verges all but disappeared, with the rushing river in its steep rocky bed on the right and the whin-dotted hillside rising abruptly on the left. The column inevitably lengthened noticeably, jostling men unable to ride more than three abreast. In the circumstances, any fighting would have to be done by the leading files.

The valley, and therefore the road, twisted continually, and the leaders were ready for trouble around each corner. It was just under two miles from the Linton bridge to the castle, and about halfway they began to see a glow ahead from the campfires around Hailes. Gradually this provided some light of a sort, to aid them. It would also make them more evident to others, admittedly, but on balance was probably in their favour since they would still have the dark background.

It indeed proved so a minute or two later, when suddenly round a bend a fast-riding party was silhouetted approaching. In the moments before they themselves were perceived, Jamie and the Master had opportunity to shout their orders and be ready for the clash.

There was no clash, however, for there was sufficient reflection on their armour and drawn swords to give the newcomers warning whilst about two hundred yards still separated them. There followed a great rearing and wheeling of horses. The party proved to be no large one, and clearly recognised that the people in front were unlikely to be fellow-countrymen, and in numbers exceeding their own. Before ever the Scots could come up with them, they were turned around and heading back fast whence they had come.

The Master was beginning to shout for pursuit at all speed,

to prevent these being able to warn the rest at Hailes, when Jamie grabbed his arm.

"No — let them warn them," he jerked. "Better so. They will say a large force is coming up this valley. There will be panic, at first. Ride slowly. Calling our slogan. Sound full confident. In the dark, in this close gullet, with their other camps already overwhelmed, that will add to their fears. God willing, they'll bolt!"

The other was doubtful. "It could give them time to form up against us."

"We will not give them *that* long. They will hear our Douglas slogan. They are deep in enemy country, the smell of defeat already in the air. I say they will flee, not knowing that they still outnumber us. And if they do not, we are little the worse."

"Play-acting!" James the Gross, the Master's brother snorted. "We came to fight, not to play guizards! This is worthy of Davie Stewart!"

"*You* may have come to fight 10,000 with 1,400!" Jamie retorted. "*I* did not. I came to help rid our land of these Englishmen as a fighting force. Are we not doing so?"

"Jamie's right," the Master said. "We may have to fight — but try this!"

So they slowed to a steady trot and started up the rhythmic chanting of "A Douglas! A Douglas!", that dread cry which had been striking terror into Northern English hearts for the century since the Good Sir James had commenced his campaign of cross-Border raids in the cause of his friend the Bruce. And from some five hundred throats, in the narrow confines of the valley, it made a grim and menacing sound indeed. It had its own effect, moreover, on the chanters themselves, making their deliberate advance seem inexorable, undefeatable, each man half as puissant again. It might be guizardry and play-acting, but it was excellent for morale.

They had only another half-mile to go, so that even at a slower pace there was only two or three minutes in it. With the firelight increasing before them, and prepared for immediate action, they rounded the final bend of the road before Hailes Castle.

A notably strong and effective site had been chosen for the Hepburn stronghold. A small stream in a shallow, tree-lined ravine came down steeply to join the Tyne in its gorge here; and perched on the tip of the rock above the junction, the castle walls rose — so that it was protected on three sides. The fourth side was defended by a deep artificial dry ditch, spanned by a drawbridge, presently raised. Without ballista and heavy siege machinery, it was most evidently a hard nut to crack; at the same time completely dominating the road and wooden bridge which here crossed the lesser stream. Because of this side ravine, the main valley was a little wider here, which had given the English invaders room to concentrate and camp.

As this scene opened before the chanting Scots there was however no sign of concentration. Indeed there was little sign of the English invaders at all. The fires still blazed, arms, gear and booty littered the open area flanking the road, and some shadowy figures could be seen scurrying away up the wooded ravine on the south. Otherwise the castle-hollow seemed to be deserted.

"Praise be — they've bolted, as you said!" the Master cried, panting from his chanting. "Some up yonder gully . . ."

"Not many there. They could not take horses up there. And this is a horsed force. They will have fled up the road, for Traprain."

Cheering and shouting from the castle itself interrupted him, and men waving torches appeared on the parapet-walks and tower battlements. The clanking sound of the drawbridge chains being lowered had the Master spurring forward to greet Sir Patrick Hepburn, when Jamie again intervened.

"Now that they are fleeing we must keep them so," he urged. "Keep them running. Give them no time to recover. Nor to try to rejoin the others at Markle or round the town. A bare mile on, this valley opens and levels off. We must prevent them from rallying there. This south side opens to gentle slopes. They can ride out, and up round the skirts of Traprain Law, and so make for Lammermuir."

"They will never rally now, man."

"For a wager, Hotspur and their leaders are still there in front of us. With 2,000 men, scattered and in flight, but capable of turning the day against us. We cannot risk it."

"Oh, very well. James," the Master turned to his stout brother. "Go you speak with Hepburn. Then come on after us — bringing some of his men if you can."

They rode on, into deeper darkness now, with the fires left behind. They did not attempt to flush out fugitives on foot up the ravine; there would be comparatively few and they constituted no danger. They could not ride fast in the gloom, but they quickened their pace somewhat and resumed their chanting, however unevenly and breathlessly. Despite this so evident challenge, however, they were very much on the look-out for any attempt at ambush, this valley being apt therefor.

Nothing of the sort developed. They emerged into the more open country presently, to discover no stand being made there either. There were now three possibilities. The English flight could have gone straight on, or else turned left or right. Straight on up the Tyne would bring them past the Bere Ford and Stevenston to Haddington's walled town, in three miles, clearly an unlikely course. Right, northwards, meant crossing the river, still running through a difficult rocky bed, and then climbing back up the quite major ascent of Pencraik Hill, whence they could reach Markle and the Preston area again. Would they hazard that, when the way lay open on the left, southwards, to escape to safety in the hills or the Berwickshire Merse, the Borderline only some thirty miles away? From their performance hitherto this night, the chances were that they would seek to cut their losses and continue with their flight whilst they had opportunity. Generalship throughout had been poor; it was unlikely suddenly to become boldly vigorous at this stage.

So the Scots turned southwards, leaving the road, to climb the open grassy and whin-dotted slopes which lifted towards the thrusting hump-backed hill of Traprain Law. It was a dark night, without moon or stars, and with even the glow of distant fires now all but died away it was too dark to discern hoof-marks, horse-droppings or other signs of the enemy passage. They could only hope that they had calculated aright.

But up at the top, under the very crags of the Law, the hamlet of Cairndinnis lay. It appeared to be deserted, but when they shouted their Douglas identity, folk crept out from hiding, thankfully, to declare that an English patrol had savaged them earlier in the evening, whilst a much larger company, riding fast, had driven past only a short time before — without halting, God be thanked! Yes, they were riding southwards, as though making for Whittinghame and Lammermuir.

"Dunbar will be with them, and knows this country like his own hand — since his own it is!" Jamie exclaimed. "They are not stopping. In full flight still."

"Then we must keep them so doing," the Master agreed. "Show Hotspur Percy can spur as hotly backwards as forward!"

227

They sent back word to the various groups behind, and hurried on.

All that weary night they followed the fleeing English through the Lammermuir foothills and beyond, flagging as to speed inevitably — but then so must be the enemy. They got near enough their quarry to ensure that they did not lose them in the darkness and broken country — and to ensure that the fleeing men were well aware that they were on their heels. But anxious as they were to catch up — the Master now especially eager to add a feather to his bonnet by capturing the celebrated Hotspur and the traitor Dunbar — they never quite managed it. Dunbar would know the country even better than did Jamie Douglas; and frequently the pursuers had to waste time by casting about to pick up the trail. The enemy in fact did not push directly on into the empty Lammermuir Hills, but swung away south-eastwards round their flanks, parallel with the coast but a few miles inland, by Stenton and Spott, behind Dunbar itself, and the hillfoot villages of Innerwick and Dunglass.

At Colbrandspath, where there was a steep and deep ravine and rushing river to be crossed, they had their first real fighting of the night. The English had left a party behind here, to destroy the wooden bridge by fire and demolition. These had not had time to achieve their objective when the Scots arrived — had they been able to do so, it would greatly have aided them, for the gulf below was almost sheer and quite impassable for horses, entailing a lengthy detour. But the Percy had left a group of mounted archers with the demolition party, and though these could not see to aim their shafts at individual targets, by pouring arrows at random over at the northern bridgehead area, they could and did greatly hold up and harass the Scots. Indeed, had the main English force stood their ground on the far side, they could have halted the pursuit indefinitely. As it was, the Master had to send parties of men on foot left and right, clambering precariously down the steep and difficult banks amongst the clinging rowans and birches, to struggle across the fast but not deep stream and up the equally steep opposite side, eventually to outflank the bowmen and bridge-wreckers. After a sharp tussle, they managed to drive them off.

The substantial bridge was only partly damaged and quite passable. The main Douglas force crossed over, and set off again without delay but left behind over a score of casualties, the first of the night.

After that it was just hard slogging over the dreary high wastes of Coldinghame Moor, to the River Eye crossing at Ayton Castle — which was not held against them. Then on along the high cliff-top road by Lamberton Moor, the Borderline drawing ever closer. This was the main north–south road now, and the going consequently much easier. But men and horses were tired indeed and the pace eased and dwindled. They had come about twenty-nine miles from Hailes, and Berwick town lay only some three miles ahead. It was almost a relief to recognise that they could go little further.

One last flurry there was, almost within sight of the very gates of the fortress-town, with the grey dawn beginning to lighten the leaden plain of the sea to their left. It takes time to arouse the guards of a walled city to open the gates at night and to admit 2,000 horsemen through a narrow access-tunnel. To allow for this process, a rearguard had been left at a marshy stretch of the Borough Meadows, common pasture where the road crossed the wet ground by what was almost a causeway, a well-known defensive position for those concerned with the security of Berwick. Here, once again, the Scots could have been held up long enough for reinforcements to come out from the fortress garrison — and indeed, there was little point in them pressing the issue, since they must needs turn back anyway in a mile or so. But the very proximity of the walled city and its security was a heavy temptation for the rearguard manpower, sapping its resolution and fighting-spirit — for why should they now throw away their lives, at this late stage, in order to allow the rest of their companions to have comfortable access to safety? Accordingly, the defence at the causeway was a mere token one, a gesture, which was hardly made before the weary troopers were streaming off along the road the remaining mile to the Scots Gate of the town. The Douglases gave chase in only similar fashion, sufficient to capture the red-and-gold banner of the rearguard's leader — which proved to be that of Sir Thomas Talbot, brother of the Lord Talbot.

It made a notable trophy for the Master to take home — for Talbot was one of the premier barons of England — even though its owner himself escaped. There was no point in going further — indeed real danger, for Hotspur was still Warden of the English East March and therefore Governor of Berwick, and could order out the permanent garrison against them, fresh men and numerous, for a strong force was always maintained in this captured Scots city. They turned back, therefore, tired, stiff but satisfied. And just to demonstrate the realities of the situation to all concerned, they started up their hoarse chanting of the Douglas slogan once more. For two or three minutes they bellowed it out, towards the awakening town, before reining round and trotting off northwards on the long road home.

XI

JAMIE DOUGLAS WAS aiding his wife to tidy up the walled-garden at their small castle of Aberdour in Fife, scything the weeds which were already growing high beneath the gnarled old apple-trees, while she raked up the scythings into heaps — which the children almost as consistently scattered in their joyful fighting. Jamie was a less than enthusiastic gardener, and scything was sore on the back; he would much have preferred to leave it to Tom Durie, the steward's son, whose job it was, and gone fishing this sunny June day. But Mary enjoyed the garden and its tasks, and complained that he seldom was available to help her there, and when he was, usually found excuse to do something else. So this fine forenoon he had succumbed — on condition that she came out in the boat with him in the afternoon, to fish for flounders in the bay between Aberdour and St. Colm's Inch. They would land the bairns on the island with their nurse Janet Durie, beforehand, and win some peace from the clamour of small tongues on the sparkling waters of the firth. Then they would return to the island to cook the hoped-for flukies on stones heated on a fire amongst the rocks, to the delectation of all. This programme, skilfully angled to coax Mary Stewart who had an especial interest in Inchcolm, had been accepted. But meantime there was the back-breaking business of wielding a scythe, an instrument designed by fiends, with all the wrong dimensions, shapes and angles to ensure maximum distress to the wielder, not to mention risk to life and limb.

Much straightening of back, groaning and mopping of brow — for it was sheltered in the walled-garden and the June sun was hot — was the order of the day, then, with curses at hidden stones amongst the weeds, apple-tree trunks, ill-behaved brats and pestiferous flies, when the noise of clattering hooves, jingling accoutrements and halloes came from the direction of the courtyard at the other side of the castle.

"Ha!" said Sir James Douglas.

His wife frowned accusingly. "Ha, indeed! What now? Who comes noisily to our door at this hour, spoiling our day? Is this some ill ploy of yours . . . ?"

"Not so," he asserted. "I have no notion who it is. Interrupting the good work. Perhaps I will be able to send them about their business in no time, at all." But he was discarding his scythe and rolling down his shirt-sleeves efficiently as he spoke.

"No need to be in such haste then, my goodness!" she protested — but he was already striding off for the garden-gate.

Round at the front of his stocky, square stone keep, he found a whole troop of horsemen in the colours of the royal guard. Even so, he was unprepared for the Lieutenant of the Kingdom himself to be sitting his stallion there within the cobbled court-yard, with the handsome Sir John de Ramorgnie on one side and the Archdeacon Thomas Stewart of St. Andrews on the other. It was the Duke David's first visit to Aberdour Castle. Normally he summoned people to his presence, not called on them in person.

"Jamie Douglas!" the prince cried, "A picture of rude health, and sweating like a hog! So this is your roost by the silver sands. Hay-making — or love-making?"

"Being a better husband than some, my lord Duke!" the other gave back. "But — welcome to my house." Jamie nodded distantly towards Ramorgnie but more warmly to the Arch-deacon, whom he liked and who was indeed his own brother-in-law, having the same father and mother as Mary, which father was the late King. He looked very undiaconal in scarlet velvet.

"We are on our way to St. Andrews," David said. "Bishop Trail is sick. I needs must have speech with him. But meantime, I have an errand for you, Jamie."

"I feared as much!" Mary's voice spoke from behind.

"Ah, my comely aunt!" the Duke exclaimed. "On my soul, you look almost as warm as your spouse — and none the less fetching for that! I vow we have caught you at a hot work, the pair of you! Haymaking . . . or other!"

232

"Scythe and rake work, Nephew. More honest than some! Greetings, Tom. You keep unlikely company! A good day, Sir John."

"You spoke of an errand, my lord," Jamie said. "I am sorry to hear that the good Bishop is ill. We could do with more of his like in Scotland."

"To be sure. But the errand does not concern Trail. It is more important than that, than any one man."

"You had better come within, Davie," Mary said. "A beaker of wine and a bannock whilst you wean my husband away from his honest duties! Durie will serve your men ale . . ."

Dismounting, the leading visitors were conducted upstairs to the first-floor Hall, bright in the forenoon sun with the glittering sea acting mirror.

"You are on the road early," Jamie observed, "to have won here at this hour." The Duke of Rothesay was not noted for his early rising.

"Aye — we were at Dunfermline. Yesterday, I had a letter which made it more than ever urgent that I see Trail — which I was for doing anyway. Money, Jamie — siller. We are going to require a deal of siller. And Trail, as Primate, has the key to Holy Church's coffers in his episcopal hand. The realm's coffers being, as usual, empty!"

"I know that he has been aiding you, yes, this year and more past. You need more?"

"Much more, I fear. I am going to have to muster the realm in arms."

"Dear God! The English again?"

"Aye, the English again. But not just Hotspur and his friend Dunbar, this time. King Henry, with his whole might."

"War? Full armed invasion?"

"No less. Clearly Henry has decided on it. Mainly as a means of drawing attention away from his own troubles with his nobles, I think — but none the better for us, in that! Ever since yon affair with Hotspur in Lothian, that you were at, we have been getting word that Henry was assembling men at York. I hoped that it might be to deal with his own dissident barons, who still name him usurper. But now he has moved his army to Newcastle. And yesterday, from there, he sent my father a letter — as good as a declaration of war."

"Is it not another trick? A feint? With so much unrest in his own realm? They say that even the Marcher earls are making common cause with the Welsh against him — and when that happens, anything could happen in England."

"Maybe so. Henry Bolingbroke may be a trickster, yes. But he is also a gambler. And this time I believe he intends to risk much, possibly all, on a toss. This is no mere feint. He could lead his armies away south again, to be sure, at little cost. But not ships. My information is that he is assembling shipping from all the east side of England, at Newcastle, and loading them with arms, supplies, forage and siege-engines. That is too costly a ploy for any trick."

Jamie was silent.

"His letter does not sound like play-acting, either," Ramorgnie put in.

"Aye — the letter is a deliberate provocation. Designed to cover his invasion with some cloak of legality. He writes to my father in seemingly friendly terms, but styles him his vassal. He declares that since the days of someone he names as Locrinus son of Brutus the Kings of England have been Lords Superior of Scotland — God knows who these were! And declares that he will come to Edinburgh before the 23rd day of August, the Eve of St. Bartholomew, to receive my father's homage and fealty."

"But . . . this is sheerest folly!" Jamie exclaimed. "All must know it — the English no less than others. There is no thread of truth in any of it. How can this serve him?"

"Use your wits, man," Ramorgnie said. "Edward the First started this ancient canard — or revived it. And got the English parliament to accept and confirm his claims. As did his son Edward the Second and his grandson Edward the Third. Richard likewise. All obtained their parliaments' agreement and authority. This Henry merely follows precedent — and thereby establishes himself in the good Plantagenet tradition. A worthy successor of these more lawful monarchs. But, more important than that — he needs parliament's backing in money to pay for his armies and ships, for he has little of his own. He would not have got the moneys for putting down his own rebellious lords. So he takes the Scots for his whipping-post. That letter was written for the English parliament rather than for the Duke's royal father."

"It is no mere flourish of the pen, nevertheless," David added. "He is giving us warning not to oppose him. A swift triumph in Scotland would suit him very well. As victor he would then seem to unite the English, and turn and deal with his factious lords and the Welsh. But his victory would have to be swift, for a prolonged and costly campaign in Scotland would *harm* his cause as grievously. We must see that it is so. But for that I need a deal of siller!"

"You need more than siller, my lord!"

"To be sure. But the money will help, if our full muster is to be achieved. Most of our good Scots lords will require priming with siller to produce their greatest numbers of men. The burghs likewise. But Holy Church will help in the matter, I am assured — with my beloved Uncle Tom's good offices! God knows whether Trail's present malady will aid or hinder in the matter!"

"Bishop Trail has ever been a leal friend to your father and mother," the Archdeacon Thomas said. "And to the realm. He will not fail you now, I think."

"And his see the most wealthy in that realm!" Ramorgnie pointed out, smiling thinly.

"And *my* errand?" Jamie put in.

"I wonder that you need ask! The Douglas power in men is the greatest in the land. *And* readiest to take the field! I want you to go in haste to Threave, in Galloway, and get the Earl Archie, my good-father, to call out the whole of Douglas. The old devil is bed-ridden, they say, but he keeps the power in his own hands. The Master will lead, of course, but his father's authority is required to muster Douglas, as you well know."

"Yes. Where is the Master?"

"In the Borders, somewhere. Find him, and send him to me, Jamie. I shall be at Edinburgh Castle. And Jamie — call on your own father in the bygoing, and see what Dalkeith can raise. In men . . . and siller too."

"How long, think you, have we to muster our force?"

"Who knows? Henry says he will be in Edinburgh by St. Bartholomew's Eve. But he could invade much earlier. However, an English parliament is called, at York, for next month, July. The Feast of St. James. If we judge aright, Henry will wait until after that. It will be a packed parliament and will get him what he wants. He will prefer to wait for it, I think. So we have a month, perhaps. Even six weeks. But no time to waste."

"We cannot prevent it? This invasion? By guile, as you did yon time at Haddonstank. Or by striking first?"

"Not if Henry is determined — as I conceive him to be, this time. And to strike first, in sufficient strength — at Carlisle or

the Middle March say — requires that we be *mustered* first.
Which is scarce likely. And we have not got the Isle of Man to
use as threat this time, with Dunbar on the wrong side. We have
to watch Donald of the Isles, too. This might seem to him his
opportunity. No — I fear on this occasion we must stand and
fight, Jamie."

"Sir James is the warrior-hero!" Ramorgnie said. "He will
relish that."

"While Sir John will no doubt write us a prolocution!" Mary
added tartly.

* * *

In the event, they were granted nearer eight weeks than six —
and required it all. What delayed Henry Plantagenet was not
clear, from Edinburgh — if indeed he ever did intend to start
before mid-August. But it was then that he gave command for
his great army to march and his fleet to prepare for sea. Not that
the Scots could point any fingers of scorn over delays in mustering and preparation, their own performance being little more
expeditious. It was hay-harvest time, to be sure, at first, and the
lords and lairds, as well as vassals and farmers, claimed it vital
to get the hay-crop in, to provide the necessary forage for the
horses and cattle on which all depended. The same would apply
to the English, of course. Then the corn-harvest began to loom
ahead. The Douglases assembled fairly swiftly, although not
quite in their fullest strength even yet. But others were more
dilatory. They greatly missed the fine Mersemen's contingent
which the Earl of Dunbar could have fielded, and which would
not rise in any numbers for anybody else. Arousing full
mobilisation of the North-East was always a problem when the
danger was in the South, from over the Border — to the
Ogilvys, Keiths, Gordons, Hays, Cummings and the like it was
all too far away to constitute an evident threat, with internecine
clan warfare much more pressing. And much of the South-West
particularly was inhibited from major participation for fear of
what the Lord of the Isles might do to their unprotected lands
whilst they were away fighting the English. The word from the
Hebrides, indeed, was that Donald was assembling his war
galleys at Islay by the hundred — and that made almost as
ominous a sound in Lowland ears as did the slogan "A Douglas!"
in Northumbrian.

In the great fortress of Edinburgh Castle on its lofty rock

236

above the crouching grey city, so like Stirling, the groups of men around the Duke of Rothesay gazed north-eastwards from the battlements in some doubt and dismay. For long they had been watching and counting and wondering. Out there on the wide firth they could see at least thirty-two large vessels, their sails white against the blue water, a vast fleet. They had been beating up the Forth estuary against a light south-westerly breeze for hours, and now the foremost ships were almost opposite the harbour of Leith, Edinburgh's port, less than three miles away. This huge flotilla represented menace, however fair a sight to the uncommitted observer. But more than just menace, it represented a grievous problem, a possible upsetting of the Scots defensive plans. The latest reports from the Master of Douglas put King Henry and his army of allegedly 60,000 no further north than Lauder. The English had chosen to invade, not up the east coast from Berwick but by the Tweed fords of Coldstream and Carham and thereafter through the Middle March, by Kelso and Dryburgh, Melrose and Ercildoune, and so up Lauderdale. They appeared to be in no great hurry, proceeding at the deliberate pace of the large numbers of foot and the clumsy destriers of the heavy chivalry, the Douglases skirmishing warily before them, not risking any set engagement but nibbling, harassing and seeking to delay. The Master advised that at this rate they would not be in Edinburgh before the following evening. Yet here was this fleet already off Leith.

Alex Stewart, who had brought six hundred Badenoch and Clan Chattan clansmen to the muster, with more to follow, shook his fair head. "I do not see why you are so concerned," he said. "Shipping cannot be timed, like marching men, whatever. Contrary winds, flat calms, can greatly delay a fleet. Therefore they must allow ample time. They have arrived first — and so will wait for their King."

"If we could be sure of that we would not be concerned, man!" David snapped, impatiently. "The question is — what is aboard those ships? Supplies — or men? Troops. If troops, then all could be changed. They could be landing in large numbers any time now. Long before Henry and his array arrives. Worse, long before *our* main strength arrives."

"We can oppose their landing," Jamie said. "Landing men from large ships at a port is slow work, and difficult. Against opposition, more so. We could prevent those ships from tying

237

up at the quays. Only a few could do so at a time, forby — that haven is not sufficiently large to take many. Not like Berwick or Dumbarton. This will force them to use small boats — to our advantage. We could greatly delay a landing."

"Perhaps . . ."

"That means dispersing more of our own men," Ramorgnie put in. "And we have few enough with us here, as it is."

That was true, at least. The main Scottish defensive forces had been assembled at Stirling and Lanark, and were not expected to reach Edinburgh before that evening at the soonest. The Master of Douglas had his force detached in the Borders, though now falling back on Edinburgh. And of the 2,000 or so meantime in Rothesay's immediate command, quite a large proportion were engaged in the town, superintending the reluctant evacuation of the citizens. This had been an unhappy decision David Stewart had had to take; for though Edinburgh was a walled town, it was not nearly strong enough to resist the assault of a major army; and Henry had said that he was coming there. The great castle on its rock was indeed defensible, the more so once the additional pits and barricades hurriedly being contrived were completed. It would be folly, with their present numbers, to attempt to defend the city itself. So an exodus had been ordered for the folk, with their most precious belongings, and this being unpopular with many, troops had to be used to enforce it.

"A few hundred could much hold up a landing at Leith," Jamie contended. "Better than standing here idle."

"Very well. Take a horsed force down to the port," the prince said. "Do what you can. But be ready to return here at any moment. You can see this castle and rock from Leith. A column of smoke by day, or a fire by night — two fires, say — to bring you back. You have it?"

So Jamie and Alex took some four hundred men, mainly Dalkeith horsemen and Highlanders from Badenoch, and hurried down the three miles to Leith haven, where the Water of Leith entered the firth, directly across the eight-miles-wide estuary from his own house of Aberdour. By the time that they got there, the leading ships of the enemy fleet were standing off only half-a-mile out, and a daunting sight they made. Even as they watched, small boats were being lowered from one or two, no doubt to come and inspect at closer quarters the landing facilities and state of defence. To discourage all such, Jamie had bonfires heaped up and lit all along the waterfront, to at least warn of a hot reception.

The haven of Leith lined both sides of the river-mouth with quays and jetties; but these were mainly for small craft and fishing-boats and no more than half-a-dozen of the large English ships would be able to tie up at one time. There were a number of fishing craft and coastal vessels already in the harbour and these Jamie ordered to be moved so that a tight wedge of the former blocked the harbour mouth, and the latter were disposed to occupy the deeper berths which the large enemy ships would require.

This activity would be fairly obvious from the sea, and the English rowing-boats did not approach too closely. Alex had a few archers with him — the Highlanders were more proficient with bows than were the Lowlanders, since they used them for stalking deer. These he caused to wing a few arrows with blazing tow out towards the boats — which, although they fell hopelessly short, served to show that any landing would be opposed by bowmen.

The small boats duly kept their distance.

All the rest of the day Jamie's force, reinforced by such of Leith's manpower as had not moved out, showed themselves determinedly riding or marching to and fro with great activity, not only at the port itself but along the shoreside links east and west, lighting more fires, even digging trenches in the sand and erecting sham barriers on the dunes, to look like counter-archery defences. The entire English fleet, now thirty-four vessels, came to cluster at anchor in the roads; but though there was much passage of small rowing-boats between them, no move was made at a landing meantime.

No summons showed from Edinburgh Castle commanding a return.

As the late-summer dusk settled on land and sea, there was no respite for the busy defenders. The English might well attempt their landing under cover of night, either in force on the harbour or, more likely, dispersed along the coast. On the other hand, as Alex pointed out, they might not, considering a descent in the dark upon an unknown, warned and defended shore more hazardous even than by day. Jamie took no chances. Continually replenished fires seemed to be the best indication that the defence was alert and eager, and these were increased in numbers all along the shoreline for at least a couple of miles.

Fuel was becoming a major problem, and everything which would burn was pressed into service — drift-wood, old boat-timbers, tree-branches, straw, whin-bushes, even house furnishings, unpopular as was their requisition. The Gaelic-speaking Highlanders were good at this — and impervious to the complaints and threats of the outraged citizenry.

No attack came, but Jamie would permit no relaxation. The enemy might well be waiting for the dawn, when the defenders could be expected to be weary and at their least acute. Weary they were. When no early morning developments took place, Jamie did allow some standing down and sleep. They would now have sufficient warning of any attempt. It looked as though the foe were, in fact, prepared to wait until their land host arrived — in which case the probability was that the fleet did indeed bring only supplies, not troops, and all their own defensive façade was unnecessary.

It was in mid-afternoon that a tall smoke-column could be seen rising above Edinburgh Castle rock on the southern horizon, summoning the defensive force to return — to the alarm of the remaining Leithers. Jamie was sorry, but had no option. He made a final replenishment of the fires, advised the townsfolk to move out, but unobtrusively, and then withdrew his own people as secretly as possible so that their going should not be obvious to the ships.

They arrived back at the fortress to find all in a state of excitement. The castle was now packed with men and horses, the Master of Douglas and his force having arrived, with the word that King Henry's forward troops were only a few miles off. Jamie's half-brothers were with the Master; and his father, frail now but on his feet again, had come also, with his wife and womenfolk, since Dalkeith was directly in the path of the advancing army, which had streamed over the west Lammermuir pass of Soutra from upper Lauderdale. The Lady Isabel Stewart and her husband from Edmonstone had also been brought, for security.

David Stewart was in a quandary. There were no tidings of the main Scots muster from Stirling and Lanark, although he had sent urgent messengers to make contact. He had not intended the Douglas force all to crowd into the castle precincts like this, in especial their horses; for though the fortress covered a large area of the rock-summit, there was no room, nor forage, for hundreds upon hundreds of horses. The Douglases had been intended to join the main army, coming from the west, under Lindsay, Earl of Crawford, and so to constitute a major threat to the English flank. But they had been harassing the enemy advance day and night for three days, and were exhausted. They must be given time to rest. In the end, it was decided to send away the horses, under a small guard, to a safe distance westwards. Whether the riders joined them there later would depend on circumstances.

David's designed strategy was to get the English army cooped up in Edinburgh town — which was now almost wholly empty of its townsfolk — immobilise it as far as was possible in siege warfare, and then have it attacked by night by the main Scottish forces, on at least two flanks, whereupon the castle defenders would sally out and hope to complete a rout. Whether or not this was feasible depended on a number of factors; but nothing could be attempted until the reinforcements did arrive somewhere nearby — hence the prince's agitation. Lindsay was a veteran soldier and should be well aware of the situation.

Meantime, however, to delay matters, he resorted to a device. Under his personal banner and his own Rothesay Herald, he sent a challenge to King Henry, whom his scouts sent news had in fact halted at Dalkeith for the night, some seven miles to the south. In true if somewhat outmoded chivalric fashion, he sent his cartel and requested a face-to-face duel between himself and Henry, to settle their differences, carefully referring to the Plantagenet, not as King but as his 'adversary of England'. And if this was unacceptable, he suggested a knightly fight between selected noble contestants of 100, 200 or 300 a side. It was not expected that Henry would agree to this — few of his family had been noted for their chivalric qualities — but it might serve to delay, by producing an exchange of notes and so give time for Crawford to arrive.

It was dark before the herald got back from Dalkeith. He brought a letter from Henry thanking the Duke of Rothesay for his message but pointing out that he could not, as monarch and Lord Paramount, accept challenges from his own vassals however high-born. As for knightly combat, he was here to receive due submissions of fealty not to engage in tourneys and the like. He would present himself before Edinburgh Castle next forenoon, and expect to receive all necessary tokens of leal duty. He remained his esteemed cousin David's loving friend, protector and liege lord, Henry R.

Next morning they watched the endless columns of the English might stream down over the low escarpments of Edmonstone, Gilmerton and Liberton towards Edinburgh's Burgh Muir. Then one of David's own messengers arrived hot-foot from the west, to announce that the Scottish main army was at last approaching into Lothian. When he had left, it was nearing the Calder area some fifteen miles to the west, but in no great haste. He had urged all speed, but the Duke of Albany had refused to be hurried.

"Albany!" the prince exclaimed. "He is there? What in God's name has he to do with it?"

"He is in command, my lord Duke. He has superseded the Earl of Crawford and the Earl of Moray in the command."

"But — fiend seize him, *I* appointed Lindsay to command! My Uncle Robert has no authority to do anything of the sort. He is no soldier. Lindsay still must command — and you will go back and tell him so!"

"My lord," the messenger quavered, "how can I do that? The Duke Robert will not heed me. He is a proud man and more like to slay me!"

"I shall give you a writing. I am Lieutenant of this realm, and will not have my orders set aside by any soever. Lindsay must resume command and carry out the plan I told him of. I will not have my uncle interfering."

The prince ordered Ramorgnie to write a mandate for him to sign. The Douglases, with Alex Stewart, drew aside, long-faced.

"This is damnable!" the Master declared. "What is the meaning of it? Albany is not a fighting-man, no commander. Why do this?"

"It may be that he wishes to make a gesture to the nation," Alex suggested. "Smarting at having been put down as Governor, in favour of David, he would show that he is still a force to be reckoned with. Come hastening to aid the realm in this pass. He may only *seem* to take command, in name — since he could scarcely serve under Crawford. But leave the true direction of the army to Crawford and Moray."

"I think not," Jamie said. "Albany never acts without careful thought. He does not make gestures. He hates his nephew and will pull him down if he can. I fear that he will seek to use this trouble to do so. He will ignore David's written orders, I swear."

242

"You mean, not carry out David's plan against the English? You would not make him turn traitor?"

"Not traitor, no — for he hates the English also. But not use the army as David wishes. Something has brought him out from Doune Castle at this time, to take a hand. I cannot think that it bodes well for us of David's company."

That foreboding was reinforced a short time afterwards when, soon after the messenger had departed once more for the Calder area, a new arrival reached Edinburgh Castle — none other than David Lindsay, Earl of Crawford himself. Never a patient or gentle man, he came in a towering rage, announcing that he had never been so insulted and abused in his life, that he would not stay another hour in Robert Stewart's company, that the man was impossible, arrogant, presumptuous. He had taken over command of the entire Scots force as of right, and had even appointed his own oafish offspring Murdoch Stewart as second-in-command. That weakly puppy Moray had elected to stay on under this precious pair. But he, the Lindsay, was damned if he would!

The prince tried hard to make the irate Crawford go back and resume his command, with his own express authority, but to no avail. He was then considering going himself — although he felt that his place was here, to confront Henry in person — when the matter was settled for them. The English advance cavalry arrived in force in front of the castle, the last Scots troops in the city scurrying into safety before them, and all entry to or exit from the fortress was barred. For better or for worse, the situation was crystallised.

Crawford could tell them little of Albany's intentions. He had come to them not at Stirling but at Linlithgow, on their way here, and had insisted on all marching southwards to join the Lanark muster instead of coming on direct to Edinburgh, thus causing much delay. Montgomerie of Eaglesham was commanding the Lanark and South-West contingent, a good man who would do his best; but what could he achieve against Albany's steely will? The total muster of the combined force was about 20,000. It was Crawford's belief that Albany had little intention of fighting, but rather of seeking to use the Scots army as a bargaining piece.

"Bargaining?" David exclaimed. "What has *he* to bargain with?"

Crawford shrugged. "I cannot see into Robert Stewart's dark

mind. But this I do know — that he believes that Henry has come now principally to lay hands on the Mammet."

"The Mammet! God's eyes — that mountebank! Mount his great invasion for that?"

"Your royal father does not call him a mountebank. And even if Henry does, he could wish to remove him, as a figure-head for his dissident lords to rally round, a threat against his throne. So Albany believes. He said as much. *I* believe he would use the Mammet to bargain with."

"But — he it was who cherished the man! Entertained him in his house. Brought him to my father. To hand him over now to Henry would mean his execution — nothing surer."

"Think you that would trouble your uncle? It was not for love that he cherished him, I vow! I wondered why, at the time. This may be the answer."

"The man is with my father at Turnberry."

"Perhaps that was why Albany delayed the army? To give him time to send to Ayrshire and take this Richard out of the King's keeping? He could do it, could he not?"

"Yes — oh, yes. My father keeps but a small guard."

"Then that may be Robert's strategy. That *he* may seem to deliver the realm, not you. And without bloodshed it may be, offering the Mammet and a clear return to the Border, and holding our army as threat . . ."

Discussion was halted by the personal arrival of Henry Bolingbroke. He came in style up to the castle forecourt in a colourful company, mounted on magnificent destriers, all gleaming armour, tossing plumes, heraldic surcoats and banners, with mounted musicians playing a stirring march and a forest of slender lances at his back. Just outwith bow-shot of the drawbridge and gatehouse, this splendid cavalcade halted, and trumpeters blew a prolonged fanfare, whilst the bareheaded, fair-haired, gilten-armoured figure sat his white charger beneath the fluttering Leopard standard of Plantagenet England.

A tabarded herald, with two pursuivants, rode a little further forward, and when the trumpets fell silent, raised his voice.

"In the name of the high and mighty Prince Henry, by the grace of God King of England, France, and Ireland, Prince of Wales, Duke of Normandy and Aquitaine, Lord Paramount of Scotland — greetings! The Lord Henry, fourth of his name, requires whosoever represents his vassal, Robert, King of Scots, in this hold, to come speak with him, in peace and duty."

244

David Stewart and his party had moved down to the gate-house-tower, but now, on its parapet-walk, deliberately turned his back on the visitors, and laughed aloud. No other response was made to the high-sounding summons.

After an uncertain pause, the herald tried again, repeating the same wording, save that he changed requires into commands, and added the phrase, ". . . under penalty of His Grace Henry's severest displeasure."

David had had a brief word with his cousin Alex, and now two of his Clan Chattan pipers started to blow on their instruments, and out of the preliminary wails and groans developed a lively skittish jig tune, tripping, skirling, toe-tapping, which rose and continued as the musicians strutted, all but skipped, to and fro along the parapet-walk.

After a little of it, the herald turned and moved back to his master.

Still the pipers blew and jigged — and perforce the King of England must stand and wait, or else leave the scene, since by no means could voices carry above the disrespectfully cheerful ranting. Trumpets might possibly have out-blasted the pipes, but assuredly, requiring so much more puff, they could not have continued for so long, and would have had to yield ingloriously eventually. It was a difficult situation for Henry, but after his first black frowning he made the best of it, turning in his saddle and chatting smilingly to some of his near company.

At length David signed for the pipers to stop, and assumed the initiative.

"Henry, Duke of Lancaster and Earl of Hereford, usurper to the English throne," he called clearly, "I, David, Prince and Lieutenant of Scotland and Duke of Rothesay, declare that you have grievously injured and insulted my father's ancient realm of Scotland by entering it uninvited and by armed invasion, contrary to all treaties and compacts. Indeed contrary to all honest behaviour between neighbouring states in Christendom. You have refused to meet me, or mine, in knightly encounter or combat, and so further besmirched your own escutcheon. In the name of the King of Scots, I command that you leave this city and realm forthwith and retire across your own borders. Whereafter, if you have any due cause or reason for debate, we may discuss it at some chosen point, as honest men should. Or take the consequences."

245

"What consequences, sirrah?" That brief question brought a shout of laughter from the English ranks.

"Threefold consequences, my lord Duke. First, lest the main forces of my father the King, presently assembling to the west, fall upon you in great numbers. Second, lest I send signal to our strength waiting in Galloway, to descend upon and sack your towns of Carlisle, Lancaster, Newcastle and Durham. And third, lest we raise the standard of your rightful liege lord, King Richard of England, presently in our care, and march south in full might, summoning all leal Englishmen, lords and commons, to his support. The Welsh likewise."

"Hollow threats!" Henry called back. "None of which you can achieve. Besides, I have not come in war. Had I done so, you would have discovered it ere this, I promise you! I have come to receive the fealties due to me as Lord Paramount, as is my undoubted right. Make such due fealty — I shall accept yours, in your father's name, since I understand him to be a sick man — and I shall return to England, in amity and goodwill."

"Amity and goodwill!" David cried. "Do you require 60,000 men to show your amity? You do not know what the words mean . . ."

"You think not? Why then have I come all this way, sparing your people? There has been no burning, no sacking, no ravishing. I have used all in my path kindly. As the Abbots of Kelso, Dryburgh and Melrose. I have no wish to fight the Scots. I have the greatest regard for your lady-mother the Queen Annabella, of whom all speak well. I have Scots blood in my own veins, Comyn blood. I come to offer my hand in friendship."

"In friendship we might accept your hand. But none, in this independent realm, will kiss it. Or hold it in fealty."

"We shall see. It was not you that I came to speak with. But a certain magnate of your land, anxious to give him opportunity of establishing his innocence or proving my guilt. For he has grievously libelled me to the so-called King of France. But he has not dared to answer me, or face me . . ."

"If you refer to my uncle Albany, my lord Duke, you must seek him elsewhere. *I* now rule this realm, in my father's name, and by due nomination of parliament."

"And little the better for the realm, I swear!" Abruptly Henry Plantagenet had had enough. He turned to his herald, with an impatient gesture of his hand, and wheeled his destrier around.

The trumpets blared out their high flourish before those deplorable bagpipes could start up again, and the English ranks parted left and right to allow their King to ride off.

Prolonged cheering arose from all Edinburgh Castle's battlements and towers.

"So much for talk," Jamie observed, to Alex. "Now we shall see what deeds may achieve."

"I have never been concerned in a siege," the other said.

"I have — but never as a defender."

"This hold would look to me impregnable?"

"To direct assault, perhaps. But prolonged siege is another matter. We have much too many men cooped up here to feed. Of water there is plenty, for excellent wells pierce the rock. But food and forage . . ."

"How long do you give us?"

"God knows. It scarcely rests with us, now. So much depends on what Albany does. And in how much haste is Henry Plantagenet."

*   *   *

Albany, in the event, did nothing — or if he did anything, no hint of it became evident to the besieged in Edinburgh Castle; nor, it appeared, to the besiegers either, for no sign of alarm or concern was to be seen amongst them. The deeds which were to succeed Henry's words were also slow in developing. All next day the English were occupied in bringing up the heavy and cumbersome siege-machinery from the ships at Leith — mangonels, ballistae, sows, rams, scaling-towers and the like, massive equipment shipped in pieces which had to be drawn up from the port by great teams of oxen at a snail's pace, and then assembled. All was entirely evident to the watchers up on the castle-rock, spread below them as on a map. No assault was mounted that day, and all night the besieged could hear the hammering of carpenters and smiths as they put together the engines by the light of torches and bonfires.

Even so it was mid-day before the first of the vast lumbering devices was moved up into position on the forecourt which spread like a fairly narrow apron before the gatehouse-towers. The huge rock was precipitous on all sides save a segment to due east, where a sort of ramp slanted down, the commencement of the long spine of ridge on which the city was built and which sloped for almost a mile down to the Abbey of the Holy

247

Rood at the foot of the crags of Arthur's Seat. Only on this ramp-like terrace, levelled to form the forecourt, could anyone approach the fortress; and here the engines were brought. The first two were mangonels, great slings for the throwing of heavy stones to batter the defensive masonry and towers, mounted on massive wooden scaffolding. The English pushed and manoeuvred these unwieldy monsters up to just outwith bow-shot, and began trundling up their supplies of stones and small boulders. These averaged about twice the size of a man's head.

The besieged were not entirely defenceless against these. The castle had four lesser mangonels and some ballistae of its own, though these had not the range or power of the enemy's. The Master of Douglas — who, as keeper of the castle was responsible — waited for the English to fire their first ranging shots — which went wide and did no damage. Then he loosed off all four of his own engines, hidden hitherto behind flags and banners. Two missiles fell short, one overshot, but the fourth smashed into the base of one of the enemy mangonels, scattering the men grouped there — to loud cheers from the castle.

In the circumstances, the lighter Scots weapons were more quickly reloaded and adjusted as to aim, and another salvo was hurled at the enemy. Two of these shots missed altogether, but the other two both hit the same target, putting it at least temporarily out of action. It was good shooting — but then the defenders had had ample time to practise and range their machines.

There followed hasty English efforts to withdraw their difficult contrivances out of range of the Scots, and more damage was sustained during the slow process, and casualties caused, before the things were dragged backwards sufficiently far.

A good start had been made, and first blood to the defenders. But none allowed it to go to their heads. The larger enemy mangonels could still operate from further off; and the element of surprise was now lost.

It was some time before the first English shot came from the new position, about one hundred and fifty yards back and at the very edge of the forecourt area. This missile fell considerably short, but the impact and the hole it made in the cobblestones of the approach to the drawbridge, showed that its force was far from spent. That lesson was reinforced with the next shot, which crashed into the walling north of the gatehouse, doing no

248

real damage but proving that they were certainly not out of range.

After that the defenders just had to stand and take the bombardment. Fortunately for them only the one enemy engine was now in working order, and ballistae were of no avail at this range. Moreover the mangonel, operating from fairly near extreme range, had less force in its impact than might have been the case. But even so, considerable damage was done to the gatehouse-towers and parapets and the contiguous walling; and some men were hit, mainly by flying chips and splinters from their own masonry. The raised drawbridge itself was protected by the iron grating of the portcullis, fortunately. But by evening, the outer east frontage of the fortress was beginning to have a distinctly battered appearance.

No sign nor signal came from the Duke of Albany on Calder Moor.

The Scots feared an assault under cover of darkness, when the battering-rams and sows and scaling-towers might be brought up into position fairly secure from the attentions of defensive bowmen and ballistae. To seek to counter this, bonfires were lit and kept blazing all along the battlements. But this meant that the target area was well illuminated for the English mangonel, and the bombardment continued. Their own engines kept up flinging in the intermittent shot, to discourage closer approach.

They could hear the clanking, creaking and thudding of heavy equipment being moved up, and sensed the continual stir just beyond vision.

It was Alex Stewart who, just after midnight, suggested the idea of a sally, put to Jamie. After discussing its feasibility, they went together to the prince.

"We have the men," Alex declared. "The English will scarcely expect it. A swift stroke out, and then back. Put their preparations in disarray. It could be good for our people's spirit. Better than inactivity."

"It could be costly in men's lives."

"I think not. There, where they are working and assembling, is narrow. Where the town street joins the forecourt. They will be much congested, unable to bring up large numbers. If we give them little warning, we might overwhelm those there, do much damage before they could recover, and then retire."

"Damage? To the engines, you mean?"

"Fire," Jamie put in. "Take many torches, kindling, pitch.

249

Make fires under the legs of yonder mangonel. Others, too. Hold the English back until they are well alight, if we can."

"By the mass — a ploy! How many do you need?"

"Not many, too many would be but a hindrance. Say two hundred. Highlandmen and Douglases."

"As I see it, the danger is here," Alex said. "The noise made by the portcullis and drawbridge chains, giving the English warning."

"We could make other loud noise. To drown it."

"That likewise could warn that there was something to do . . ."

"Grease," Jamie said. "Melted fat. Poured on the chains and hinges."

"That should help, yes. You will lead the venture, Jamie?"

"Both of us," Alex declared. "One to see to the burning, one to command the guard. Let us be doing, I say . . ."

It did not take long to prepare the sally, and there was no lack of volunteers. The greasing of the drawbridge and port-cullis machinery took longer, the chain-drums being in an awkward position. The fighting-men fretted lest the enemy should make their move first.

At length all was ready, with two hundred men, armed with swords and axes and some lances, and carrying torches, turpentine-pinewood and pitch-soaked rags, massed at the gate-house pend. The signal was given for the raising of the portcullis and the lowering of the bridge. The former creaked and scraped metallically as it came up, and the latter clanked and rumbled as it came down, its chains far from soundless. Nevertheless, the noise was a lot less than normal, and probably would not be noticeable at any distance, especially if the enemy were busily engaged on their own noise-making activities. The Scots prayed so, at any rate.

Even before the bridge was fully lowered, Jamie and Alex were out on its timbers, men thronging close at their backs. In chain-mail armour and laden as they were, they could not actually run; but at almost a trot the close-packed force hurried out onto the forecourt cobbles.

They had almost two hundred and fifty yards to cover. Every yard of the way they could go undetected, the better their chances. All but holding his breath, Jamie cursed every scrape of boot on cobblestone, every clink of steel, even the puffings and pantings of their followers.

Half-way, and no sign of alarm ahead. Dark figures could now be distinguished moving around the tall silhouettes of the siege-engines, outlined against the glow of the fires. Hammering and sawing resounded. But no shouts.

"*Dia* — we will do it!" Alex jerked. "We have them, whatever!" He was right. The two hundred were within a score of yards or so of the working men before they were noticed. Astonished Englishmen dropped tools, ropes-and-pulleys, baulks of timber. Clearly they were repairing the damaged mangonel. Some rushed to snatch up weapons. But it was too late for any immediate defence. Most of the men around the great engines realised it and fled.

"All drop torches and wood!" Jamie shouted, need for silence over. "Alex — on with you! My fifty — here. Flint and tinder. Stack the wood. Quickly!"

Stewart and the majority of the force pressed on, as arranged. Beyond the forecourt entrance, the Castlegait narrowed between tall buildings, then opened out to the wider space of the Lawnmarket. That would be where the forward English troops would be assembled, waiting, where they would not hinder the work on the engines. Pursuing the fleeing men down the narrow hundred yards or so of the Castlegait, Alex halted his people within the far mouth of it, stoppering it like the neck of a bottle, one hundred and fifty men packed tightly, ten deep, lances like a jagged frieze before the front ranks.

Beyond, all was now noise and confusion, as the carpenters, wrights and smiths burst in on the long ranks of resting soldiery, in panic, shouting that the Scots were upon them. The files of armed men stretched far down the Lawnmarket and into the High Street beyond, past the great High Church of St. Giles, thousands of waiting men, ready to advance, but meantime relaxed, idling, many asleep on the causeway. They were scarcely to be blamed if their reaction was slow and unco-ordinated. The Lawnmarket and High Street were considerably wider than the Castlegait, but were only city streets for all that, and a city on a spine of ridge — not the best marshalling-place for troops. Moreover it was dark, and the leaders were not meantime spaced out amongst their commands but assembled, actually in St. Giles Church, for final orders, and awaiting word that the repairs to the siege-engines were completed. No swift counter-attack on the Castlegait party developed.

Meanwhile, Jamie and his people were busy. It did not take

251

long to light the torches and use them as the nuclei of bonfires which they heaped around the massive timbers of the mangonels, ballistae and scaling-towers. But it seemed to take an unconscionable time for the heavy structures really to catch alight. There were more items to damage than they had realised, assembled there, and their fuel supply had to be rationed out. All the time, Jamie was expecting Alex and his men to come streaming back, urging hasty retiral, before the fires could get a grip.

In the event, there was ample time. Indeed, presently Jamie sent men down the Castlegait to discover what had happened to their friends, with the word that the fires were now burning fiercely and the engines' supporting frames, smeared with pitch and wrapped around with the rags, were themselves blazing strongly.

Alex was glad enough to retire, for though no full-scale assault on his position had transpired, English bowmen had been summoned to harass his blocking party. It was dark, and the archery was more or less blind, indiscriminate; but even so it was unpleasant and, despite the steel plate armour and chainmail, they were suffering casualties. So a staged withdrawal was ordered.

They reached the fires area to find all blazing merrily, flames leaping high around each of the siege-engines, their timbers adding satisfactorily to the conflagration. How soon there would be the inevitable counter-attack they could not tell; but whenever the enemy came, it would be too late now to save their equipment. Well content, Jamie commanded a return to the castle.

They had to carry back half-a-dozen wounded men from the archery, fortunately none fatal. For all that, their going was very different from their coming, open, cheerful, unhurried, with even reassuring shouts to the waiting men on the battlements. They were welcomed back like conquering paladins.

It took the enemy some time to quench those pitch-induced fires. No other and more aggressive activity developed that night.

Nor indeed next day. Daylight showed that the damaged engines had been dragged away, no doubt for more basic repair in some less exposed spot. No assault by armed men with scaling-ladders would have been practical, without enormous losses; and Henry was obviously no hot-head. It was to be assumed that, at least until he could remake his siege-machinery,

252

it would be a case of simple investment, containment, in the interests of starving out the defence.

Surprisingly, this proved to be a wrong assessment of the situation — and to be demonstrated in most unexpected fashion. In mid-afternoon, the watchers on the castle's topmost towers, their eyes tending to be turned westwards, looking for the hoped-for appearance of the Scots main army, were diverted in their attention to another direction altogether, the south-east. There, long and substantial columns of men were beginning to appear beyond the city walls, marching *southwards*. At first it was assumed that this was some sizeable force being sent out possibly to try and outflank Albany's host, although moving in an odd direction to do so. But as time went on and the column grew longer and denser and showed no signs of stopping, it became evident that some sort of major withdrawal was in progress.

The Scots leaders could see it all now from the ordinary battlements, and great was the wonder, discussion and speculation. None ventured to suggest that the English were actually leaving; but that they were reducing their numbers in Edinburgh very substantially was not to be questioned. When, in late afternoon, however, the standards and banners of a large leadership company could be made out, in horsed array, climbing the long slow hill beyond Liberton, there could be no other interpretation. Henry Plantagenet was moving out.

There was wild elation in the Scots camp — but still more mystification than delight. The most general estimation was that Albany was at last moving, and into some strategic position to the south-west, which the English felt to be a threat to them and which they preferred not to face cooped up in city streets. Jamie Douglas, for one, did not hold this view, declaring that a long open withdrawal like this, in column of route, would not be the way any experienced commander would react. He would send out scouting parties, then swift flanking forces of light cavalry, left and right, before setting his main infantry columns amove, and certainly not marshal all his leadership in one bannered throng. This was a line-of-march movement—whether withdrawal or not he would not hazard a guess.

Then, further surprise, a group of ordinary citizens were seen to be hurrying up the forecourt from the Castlegait. They began to shout long before they reached the gatehouse. The English were gone, all gone, they yelled. They had pulled out, for good.

253

Marching for the Border, at speed. The King and all his people. Edinburgh was saved. They had not waited even to sack and burn it before leaving. It was God's great deliverance . . .

Whether it was that or not, it was one of God's servants, the Abbot of Holy Rood no less, who presently brought them the explanation, trotting up in person on his white palfrey. Henry and his chief lieutenants had, of course, been lodging in the comfort of the Abbey beneath Arthur's Seat, and their reluctant host had not failed to learn the news which had set the English by the ears. That afternoon an exhausted courier had arrived from the South with the tidings that Owen Glendower, the true Prince of Wales, had crossed into England with a large army, taking advantage of the King's embroilment in Scotland; and instead of opposing the Welshmen as was their duty, the English Marcher earls had joined forces with them, declaring Henry usurper. All England was in a turmoil. Henry had no option but to head for home at his fastest, with all his strength.

The rejoicings in Edinburgh Castle and town that night were wild and prolonged. But David Stewart was not the only one to have bouts of thought which seemed less than joyful. Robert of Albany remained, even if Henry Plantagenet did not. He had been prepared to take over Scotland's army, contrary to the Lieutenant of the Realm's orders, and had held it idle, inactive, when it was gravely needed. There was still no sign nor word from him. What was his intention now? Was there to be outright war between the King's son and the King's brother? Civil war, in Scotland as well as in England?

For responsible men, that 26th of August 1400 was scarcely the time for carefree revelry.

XII

REVELRY, CAREFREE OR otherwise, was, however, the order of the day, or twelve days, four months later, at Stirling — on the Duke of Rothesay's express orders. There was no attempt, this year, to repeat or rival the ambitious and elaborate festivities of the previous Yuletide, when the century turned; but the prince required that gaiety, feasting, mirth and celebration should be unconfined, amongst high and low. David Stewart of course approved of revelry by nature, a born reveller. But on this occasion it was to be more than natural ebullience. He, and others, were in fact much concerned for that intangible but supremely important matter, the spirit and morale of the Scottish people.

It had been a difficult and depressing back-end of the year that had started so auspiciously, despite the all but miraculous delivery from the invading English in August. The enmity between the Dukes of Rothesay and Albany had become a thing palpable and dire to all men, bearing within it the ominous seeds of widespread conflict, possible war. There was no question as to which was the more popular. The people preferred the young and dashing prince to his stiff and sour uncle. But amongst their masters, the nobility and ruling class, there was a fairly strong conviction that *Robert* Stewart was the man wise men should support. This was not concerned with popularity or even equity, but with sheer expediency, advantage, practical politics. Robert was strong, utterly determined, experienced, ruthless. David was brilliant, yes — but the Scots had always been chary of brilliance. Moreover habit, custom, had something to do with it. Robert had been the true ruler of the land for long years, and though they had scarcely been years of happy rule, the lordly and lairdly caste had on the whole been well looked after — or allowed a free hand to look after themselves, which was almost better. Not so with David, who had awkward ideas about the alleged rights of burghs and traders and craftsmen and the like. He could be ruthless too, of course, and was notably good at hanging malefactors, irrespective of their breeding; but he seemed to fail to recognise where ruthlessness was best applied, and tended to alienate the powerful.

So the nation was divided. The siege of Edinburgh Castle in August had made that crystal clear to all. That Albany should have been able to assume control of Scotland's assembled army and prevent it from going to the aid of the beleaguered prince and Lieutenant was eloquent sign as to where the true power lay when it came to the test.

And further to all that, the situation was by no means happy as regards the English. Henry had retired — but he had not been beaten, by either the Scots or the Welsh; only humiliated and angered. He had indeed managed to put down the Welsh and Marcher earls' eruption meantime, and Owen Glendower and his people had been pushed back into Wales. At the end of November, Henry had called for a six-weeks truce — in order to treat, he said. That this was an ominous request, none could deny. Truces hitherto had been for a period of years, when negotiated at royal level. So short a period as six weeks could only mean that Henry required a mere breathing space. And when envoys of the two nations duly met thereafter on the Border, it was made clear from the start that the Plantagenet had forgone not one whit of his demands. The kernel of all his proposals was that Scotland should and must accept him as Lord Paramount and pay him due fealty. This done, all would be well, and the Scots would find him a generous and forgiving liege-lord. The Bishop of Glasgow, whom David had reluctantly sent to represent him, declared that there was nothing to treat about, in that case, and marched off. But the shadow remained. Henry was resolute, implacable, and would undoubtedly be back — and Scotland had already revealed its inability to present a united front. The six-weeks truce was nearly over.

There were other, less political, causes of anxiety. Queen Annabella, beloved by all, was now seriously ill and thought unlikely to recover. None could fail to recognise that the effect of her death on her unhappy husband would be drastic indeed, to the realm's further hurt. Also she had had some restraining effect on her son's extravagances, and that withdrawn would be no light matter. Almost as serious was the growing weakness, amounting almost to senility, of the Primate, Walter Trail, Bishop of St. Andrews, whose firm and moderate hand had guided the Church for so long and aided and supported the Crown — and there was no obvious and sound successor, although many contenders. Finally, the old Earl of Douglas had died on Christmas Eve. Archie the Grim had hardly been beloved; but he was strong, reliable, shrewd and of course immensely powerful. The Master, now 4th Earl, was not of the same calibre, possibly a better man morally than his father, but moody, lacking the confidence in himself which being head of the house of Douglas demanded. These three indeed, Queen, Primate and Earl, had been David Stewart's great support, stay and moderating influence in his Lieutenantship. Who was adequately to take their place?

To add to this catalogue of woe, there was the pestilence. Plague had been raging in England for many months now, although it died down somewhat in winter. Presumably some of the English soldiers had brought the infection to Scotland. It was not a serious outbreak as yet, confined mainly to Edinburgh, Leith and Lothian. Nevertheless, it cast its own menacing shadow on a land unused to such visitations.

So David decreed Yuletide jollity, good cheer and festivities, not only for the Court but for all the land — and said that he would pay for it, if out of an all but empty Treasury. It may not have been the surest, soundest way to meet the nation's difficulties, but it was typically David Stewart's.

Jamie Douglas had been summoned to Stirling Castle, along with the rest, although he would much have preferred to celebrate Yule quietly at his own home at Aberdour. At least he was able to bring Mary with him. There were two notable absentees from the assembled company — the new Earl of Douglas and Sir John de Ramorgnie. The former, to be sure, could claim to be in mourning — although he had never got on well with his irascible father. Naturally, the Duke of Albany was not present either.

There was no snow, but the weather was on the whole wet, cold and miserable, restricting the outdoor activities David planned — hunting, hawking, skating, curling, hurly-hacket and the like. Those interested did get some wildfowling, with hawks, on the vast marshes of the Flanders Moss, but it was a chilly and puddling business and the hawks had the best of it. It was on their early return from one of these damp expeditions, and before the feast and entertainment scheduled for every evening, that Jamie sought out the prince in his private quarters — having ascertained that he was not in fact at present engaged with one or other of the ladies currently interesting him. The Duchess of Rothesay was, as frequently the case, elsewhere.

He found David, his wet clothing off, stretched before a roaring fire, in a furred bed-robe, wine-beaker in hand and in less than his usual spirits. Indeed, despite all the arranged merry-making, the Duke had been subject to quite frequent bouts of preoccupation, if scarcely depression, for some time. He looked up at his visitor narrow-eyed and scarcely welcoming.

"Jamie Douglas — I have seldom known you as harbinger of good tidings," he jerked, "when you seek me out thus. I can do without your forebodings, if that is what you are at. I have sufficient of my own!"

"No doubt, my lord. Yet the word I bring could be important to you, and to this realm."

"I feared as much!" The other sighed. "It concerns my accursed uncle, I'll be bound?"

"Yes. At the hawking, I was riding with a Graham, young Patrick Graham of Kilmadock, in Menteith. His house is near to Doune Castle. He told me that the Duke, your uncle, has his own visitors this Yuletide."

"Aye, no doubt. And he told you that Archibald Douglas, my good-brother and your new chief, was one of them?"

"You knew, then?"

"Oh, I am none so ill-informed, Jamie — even on what goes on at Castle Doune. I know that the Douglas arrived there three days ago — after excusing himself from coming here on account of his father's death. Scarcely brotherly, would you say? What is he at?"

"As to that, I know not. He mislikes your handling of his sister, my lord . . ."

"His sister is a sour and unfriendly bitch!" the prince said briefly.

"M'mm. That may be so. But as she *is* sister to Douglas, if naught else, she might be better cherished . . ."

"Jamie — when I require your sage counsel on how I should deal with my wife, I shall ask for it. Have you anything more valuable to tell me?"

"Aye — but you may be aware of it, since you knew of the other. Sir John de Ramorgnie is also at Doune."

"Ramorgnie!" This time David Stewart sat up. "You say so? Are you sure, man?"

"Graham appeared sure enough. When I questioned him, he said that he assumed that he was there as courier from yourself. I doubted that."

"And you were right, by God!" The prince opened his mouth to speak further, and then thought better of it.

Jamie eyed him keenly. "I thought it strange that he should be there, rather than here. He has been . . . very close to you."

"And you do not like him — and trouble not to hide the fact!"

"I do not trust him — have never trusted him. And grieved that you seemed to do so, my lord. He is a clever man — but dangerous. And he used to be close to my lord of Albany. What is he doing at Doune?"

"Why ask me, man? He may visit my uncle, if he so desires."

"Or your uncle desires! He could have been your uncle's man, all the time he was with you."

The other drummed silent fingers on his settle. "Scarcely that, I think. Or he proposed to show his devotion in a strange way!" He paused. "After the business at Edinburgh, Jamie, when Robert held back my army from coming to our aid, John de Ramorgnie came to me with a plan. A proposition. He said that my uncle had surely acted traitor, and should be tried for it. But since it would be difficult to arraign and convict him before a parliament, he suggested that he should be disposed of, quietly! He, Ramorgnie, said that he would seek to do it for me!"

"Dear God — assassination?"

"He did not call it that. He is a lawyer, to be sure! He said that it would be a judicial act, only done discreetly. And he offered to do it for me."

Jamie stared. "You mean . . . ?"

"No, I do not! That is not what he is at Doune for. Christ's Blood — what do you take me for? I told him that I would have none of it. That although I much misliked my uncle, I would not have murder done, or anything such. I forbade him to consider anything of the sort."

"And now he is at Doune, in your uncle's house. Do you think that he intends to disobey your command?"

"I wonder? That perhaps. Or even . . . ?"

"Worse? What could be worse, of a mercy?"

"Much, perhaps. For me! It occurs to me that that offer of his, to slay my uncle, is fell dangerous knowledge. Dangerous for Ramorgnie — and therefore for me. If it came to my uncle's ears, Ramorgnie would not long continue to draw breath! Robert is none so nice in these matters, I think. It was secretly said, to be sure. And I have told no-one but now you. But if Ramorgnie feared that, having refused his offer, I might one day tell my uncle of it, his life would be worth but little. So, it could be that he has gone to Doune on his own behalf — perhaps to save his skin at the expense of mine!"

"You mean betray you, somehow? Explain it away in lies . . . ?"

"I mean that a man who could offer to slay one royal duke might conceivably offer to slay another! Suppose, Jamie, that Ramorgnie went to Robert and told him that *I* had proposed that he should assassinate him for me? And *he* had refused. It strikes me that if he then offered Robert to get rid of me, for him, my loving uncle might possibly consider the matter!"

Jamie gazed at him, speechless.

The prince shrugged. "It may not be so, to be sure. I may be doing Ramorgnie injustice. But this going to Doune instead of coming here for Yule, requires a deal of explaining. I believed him in the North, at Kildrummy, with Isobel of Mar."

"The Countess? Alex Stewart's friend?"

"Alex is not unique in his appreciation of the lady's charms, Jamie — mature as they are! John de Ramorgnie finds her to his taste — and she does not noticeably rebuff him. She is more of his own age, after all, than Alex Stewart's."

"Alex is deeply engaged with her, nevertheless, I think. This of Ramorgnie would hurt him."

"Ramorgnie — and others, man! Isobel Mar is a lusty woman. And Malcolm Drummond her husband little satisfies her. Cousin Alex will have to accept that, like other folk. But — that is another matter. It is not Ramorgnie's bedfellow I am concerned with, but with whom he is closeted now!"

"At least you will be on the watch for him. How can we find out if what you fear is truth?"

"Lord knows! Robert can keep things mighty close. But I shall seek to discover it, never fear. And shall keep a sharp eye on Sir John. As do you, Jamie, if you can. Tell no-one else of this — not even my good aunt, your Mary. Now — off with you. Send in my man. I must dress for this night's delights . . . !"

At the banquet-table that evening, Jamie sat preoccupied beside his wife and her brother the Archdeacon, paying but little attention either to the viands or the entertainment — or even to his companions, if truth be told. Mary taxed him with it, at length.

"I have had enough of this false gaiety," he told her. "It sticks in my throat. The realm is in danger, dire danger, and all we do is feast and gape at spectacles. The Roman Nero did as much!"

"What would you have?" Mary asked. "I would rather be at home with the bairns, yes. But David has sense in this, too. It would serve us nothing to sit wringing our hands in woe! Better to seek keep the people's spirits up this dark winter, is it not?"

"All this must be paid for. And David is going to require every siller piece he can lay hands on, presently. The English are going to be back, sooner or later. Henry will not accept that reverse. We cannot look for another convenient Welsh rising. The realm should be looking to its arms, girding itself, not feasting and play-acting."

"We can scarce be standing to arms in mid-winter, Jamie," the Archdeacon pointed out. "The lords must be kept content, if David is to gain what he wants from this parliament he has called for February. The burghs likewise. This Yuletide money is well enough spent, I'd say."

"And since it is *your* money, I suspect — or at least Holy Church's — who are we to say otherwise?" his sister remarked. "Jamie is ever gloomy until it is time for action — and then he becomes a very paladin! Unlike most, who are quite the other way."

"What you mean is that I look more than one step ahead of my nose!" her husband asserted. "If this indeed is at the Church's cost, then the money would be better spent paying for the troops and arms we are going to need."

"That is debateable," Thomas Stewart said. "Spent now, thus, it may aid David's cause, keep the lords happy, maintain the people's spirit as Mary says, their confidence in their ruler. Later, when the time comes for paying troops, or paying the lords to lend their men-at-arms, it may not be available. Or not from the present source."

"So you say spend now, in case it is not there to spend later? If that is your advice, David is the man to approve it!"

"Something of the sort. See you, my master, Walter Trail,

cannot last much longer. Even now he is scarce in his right mind most of the time. As Archdeacon, I hold the purse-strings, under him, of the richest see in Scotland. And so, with his favour, may aid David today. But tomorrow, who knows? A new bishop could appoint a new archdeacon, favour a new policy. And all know that Robert is determined to have his own man into St. Andrews — that creature, Dennistoun."

"Surely the appointment is the King's?" Mary said. "With the acceptance of the Holy See?"

"No. The appointment is with the Dean and Chapter of the diocese. Admittedly they usually accede to the royal nomination — but need not. And this will be a very special occasion, with Robert striving his utmost. For there is no clear successor. Moreover, since the primacy by custom goes with the appointment, the College of Bishops is concerned. There will be much competition, much making of compacts. The Earl of Douglas, or the King himself, is succeeded by his eldest son, if he has one; the Bishop of St. Andrews is otherwise."

"Could *you* not be bishop, Tom?" Mary asked. "You have all in your hands. The Chapter knows and likes you well. You are the King's brother, though illegitimate — Robert's likewise. He might be hindered from working against you. The King would nominate you gladly, I swear — and David rejoice."

"No, lass — no. I have said it before. I am not of the stuff of bishops, primates. Indeed I am no churchman, in truth. I was put into this position by our father, not by any choice of mine. I do well enough on diaconal duties, look after the Church revenues, lands, buildings and the like — and need not be too careful for my sanctity! But I am no pastor, no shepherd of souls. And I have just sufficient conscience to keep it so. I cannot accept nomination, and have told David so."

"Thomas is right," Jamie said. "Would that the Church had more like him, honest men!"

"That is just it!" Mary exclaimed. "He would make a better bishop than most who will be put forward, as well as saving the realm a deal of trouble. But, no — there has to be some quibble about conscience! I know what it is, Tom — it is those women that you keep at St. Andrews! Or at your manse at Boarhills. Are they so important to you? And do not other bishops have their women? I could name a few!"

"No doubt, Mary. But I am not the man to be Primate and Bishop of St. Andrews — and that is the end of it. If I may stay on there as Archdeacon, with the new man, I shall. And aid David all I can. But that is all. I have myself to live with, see you." He smiled to her. "Now, of a mercy, let us enjoy these dancers I have paid for there, expensive as they are despite the little clothing the females appear to be able to afford! I like yon plump one — eh, Jamie? An archdiaconal choice, if scarcely a bishop's . . .!"

XIII

PERHAPS DAVID STEWART'S policy of bread and circuses was
more effective than Jamie Douglas expected; for the
February parliament at Scone was a major success for the
prince, with a clear majority of those attending voting for most
of his measures and supporting his designs. If this, by the same
token, might have been seen as a set-back for the Duke of
Albany's cause, that astute individual was far too wily an
operator to let it appear so save to the deeper thinkers. He
attended the sessions off and on, manipulated where he could
behind the scenes, but, with an uncanny ability to test the way
opinion was forming, never allowed himself to appear openly
on the losing side in any cause. That he was much displeased
and frustrated could not be doubted; but he preserved his chill
imperturbability, and indeed himself frequently voted, in the
end, for measures which it was suspected he had previously
done his best to wreck. Ramorgnie also played a careful part,
seeking to be helpful in the correct framing and legal wording
of the new statutes, not allowing himself to be seen much in
Albany's company, and accepting the prince's new coldness
towards him with urbane lack of offence. Nevertheless, David,
who was having him watched closely, knew that he frequently
visited Albany's quarters secretly at night. Moreover, the new
Earl of Douglas was much in the former Governor's company
— which especially worried Jamie.

The parliament however achieved great things — at least on
paper — and should have done much to enhance the Duke of
Rothesays's reputation with the ordinary people, for he was
quite clearly personally responsible for many overdue reforms
in government and the administration of justice. Jamie, and

Alex Stewart likewise, who was attending as *de facto* Lord of Badenoch, expressed considerable surprise at the depth and range of the pleasure-loving prince's concern for and interest in the plight of the common folk, the trade and well-being of the towns and burghs, and the humdrum but essential general administration of the realm's affairs. This was the sort of thing normally left to underlings — and therefore apt to be neglected, mismanaged and a prey to corruption. Admittedly, David did not actually involve himself in the practical working out of these matters; but he was *concerned* in a way which few others of his kind had been, and he encouraged others to be more deeply engaged. This was exemplified in the measures passed, pushed, through this February parliament, often against the inertia if not opposition of the powerful landed interests. Despite all his whoring, drinking and personal extravagance, David Stewart was more of a reformer than any of his forebears since the Bruce himself. He had the backing of the Church, of course, which counted for much; and the lower ranks of the lairdly class, as well as the burghs' representatives. But he was making many enemies amongst the nobility.

Like other reformers however, the prince was not immune to the great brake and handicap on all improvement — lack of money. The existing system, however corrupt and inefficient, was entrenched, its ramifications widespread, much more easily legislated against than altered and amended. Reform of the sheriffdoms, the game laws, illegal seizures for debt, freedom on bail for lofty persons, the correcting of false weights and measures, the standardisation of the currency, the doing away with private tolls on roads, bridges and fords, repairs to harbours and works, the removal of unlawful charges at markets and the like, all demanded revenues to establish. The collection of such revenues, customs duties, cess, export dues and other taxes had long been farmed out to a vast army of individuals from whom no-one expected to produce more than a small percentage for the Treasury, the rest going into their own and their lordly patrons' pockets. No-one, that is, until the Duke of Rothesay. With his reforms to pay for, and an army to collect, train and equip, in the face of English threats, he demanded a true accounting — and did not get it. So after the parliament was over, he began a personal campaign against the customs-farmers.

Jamie was much involved in this, heading a flying column

which roamed the country inspecting, enquiring, threatening, demanding payments, taking them where necessary and possible. It was unpleasant work, uncovering much wickedness, greed and vice, and inevitably bringing down upon himself resentment, hatred and accusations of fraud and corruption on his own part. But he collected a lot of money for the prince's cause, and felt that what he was doing was worthwhile. It was unusual to find even one-half of the customs dues extracted from the payers being forwarded to the Treasury. And in cases innumerable the full dues themselves had been partly remitted to the payers in return for various privileges and favours. Illegal and exorbitant extortions, too, were commonplace; and threats and intimidations, all in the King's name, the quite normal corollary. Jamie, not of course the only one employed on this task, learned much that he had not hitherto realised as to human cupidity, deceit and man's inhumanity to man. Indeed, although it may have been only his suspicious nature, he came to wonder whether even all his fellow-inspectors were as honest and incorruptible as he was himself. When he discovered that not a few of the prince's friends, relatives and supporters in high places were to some extent involved in the system, his disillusionment could go little further. The fact that some churchmen, as quite frequently the only persons who could read and write in their districts, acted as customers and were not always faultless in the matter, not only upset Jamie but caused some rift in David's relationship with their superiors.

At least the plague seemed to be on the wane.

So the spring of 1401 passed. The word from England was of constant preparation for war. The Welsh were still seething, and a proportion of the English baronage was by no means reconciled to Henry. But he appeared to have the situation fairly well in hand and be acting with discretion, forcing nothing. This situation David judged as ominous for Scotland.

Then the prince gained secret information from London that Sir Adam de Forrester of Corstorphine, a Lothian magnate, was concerned in some strange activity. He had sought, and obtained, permission to leave the country on a visit to kinsfolk in England, and received a safe-conduct from King Henry. But according to David's informant he had been visiting Henry himself and seeking to negotiate, on behalf of the Duke of Albany, the exchange of the Mammet Richard for certain unspecified advantages. He was still in England.

This news much disturbed the prince. It showed that his uncle was actively plotting against him, and prepared to deal with Henry behind his back. What bargain he sought was not declared; but it could be assumed to be something substantial, Robert Stewart being who he was, and Henry Plantagenet's desire to put down the possible rallying-figure of his dissident lords well-known. David suspected that it would be some English agreement to support Albany in ousting himself from the rule in Scotland, possibly by armed force, more probably by more devious means. It was not something with which he could challenge Albany openly; that inscrutable individual would merely deny all coldly, and proof would be impossible.

David was therefore very much on his guard — or as far as that was possible for a man of his outgoing and carefree nature. He was concerned to keep the Mammet under closer watch and guard, likewise. But this was difficult, for the King was now much attached to his alleged fellow-monarch and unfortunate, and kept him by his side, most of the time at Turnberry in Ayrshire. David would have tried to persuade or manoeuvre his father into bringing the man to Stirling, the most secure castle in the kingdom, but Queen Annabella was too ill to move from Turnberry and the King would by no means leave her. The prince sent an added guard, and warned his father — but John Stewart was so other-worldly and feckless, so trusting, refusing to believe sufficiently ill of Albany or anyone else, that such precautions might be of little avail.

An uneasy summer settled on Scotland.

Then Annabella died, the realm grieved, and the unhappy monarch became quite inconsolable, almost unhinged. As well as his wife and only true friend, she had been his prop and stay and adviser. Without her he was not only heart-broken, desolate, but lost, out of his mind. He shut himself up at Turnberry and would see no-one save the Mammet and his younger son James, now aged seven, apparently harbouring a grudge against David — which was not like him. He blamed his elder son for heedlessness in not having done more for his mother, and in not even reaching her death-bed in time.

David himself took the Queen's death, not unexpected as it was, harder than might have been anticipated. She had been, probably, the greatest influence in his life, and even though the results perhaps were not superficially very apparent, her place was unfillable. Unfortunately for himself, and a great many

267

others in the circumstances, his reaction was to drown his sorrow in wine. He had always been a heavy drinker, even as a youth, but until now few had ever seen him actually drunk. That autumn he drank in such excess as to be drunk much of the time, his notorious riotous living the worse. No doubt it was not only his mother's death that was responsible, or even the estrangement with his father, but the long period of strain, the chill hatred of his uncle, the ever-present threat of assassination and the lonely burden of rule. His women perhaps helped him; clearly his wife did not.

Then, only a month after the Queen, her friend and confessor, Walter Trail died also — so that three of David's principal supporters had gone within a few months, with the old Earl of Douglas. Immediately the manoeuvring started, or came out into the open, to replace him as Bishop of St. Andrews and Primate of Holy Church in Scotland — with David in no fit state to use his wits to best effect in the matter. Albany came out strongly and at once with his nominee, Walter de Dennistoun, Parson of Kincardine O'Neil, an unscrupulous time-server wholly unfitted for the position, but shrewd in his own way, cunning, who could be relied upon to manipulate the vast revenues of the see for Albany's benefit. The College of Bishops put forward Gilbert de Greenlaw, Bishop of Aberdeen, who was already Chancellor, an able churchman if on the worldly side. But he had been appointed both Bishop and Chancellor when Albany was Governor, and so owed his rise to that man. David had no particular friends amongst the clergy, and in his preoccupied state could think of nothing better than to insist on the Archdeacon Thomas, his uncle, being nominated. Thomas Stewart declined, but David imperiously commanding it, the Chapter of St. Andrews Cathedral duly elected him to the see. Then a hitherto unsuspected obstinate streak was evidenced in the King's illegitimate brother. He flatly refused to take up the appointment, and be consecrated. David, furious, would not budge — and in the subsequent confusion and mismanagement, Albany got Greenlaw to withdraw and Dennistoun became Bishop almost by default. It was a sorry business, of credit to none.

The price fell to be paid for that folly.

The King was back in his royal castle of Stirling — but it was not his son and heir who had persuaded him to return there, but his brother Albany. The Duke Robert, acutely, had recognised that the written word, carefully chosen, might have more effect upon his scholarly brother than any personal approach, and had sent a succession of letters to Turnberry, their gist the mismanagement of the realm, the shameful behaviour of the prince, the disarray of Holy Church, the dangers of war posed by the rejection of the hand of friendship held out by Henry of England, a hand still extended, and the monarch's ultimate responsibility in all these matters. So the King had reluctantly allowed himself to be coaxed back to Stirling in the interests of his people, bringing the Mammet and young James with him. David, bemused, was on the look-out for attempts on the person of the Mammet; he was quite unprepared for what did in fact transpire.

He had arrived back from a November day's hunting, and a buxom lady was aiding him, in his private quarters, to recover from the exertions of the chase, when Jamie Douglas put in one of his inconvenient appearances.

"My lord Duke," he said, briefly, bluntly, ignoring the lady, "your pardon, but I bring a summons for you to attend upon your royal father in the Great Hall. Forthwith."

"Damn you for a pest!" the other got out thickly, over a plump white female shoulder. "Summons! Forthwith! That is not how anyone may speak to David Stewart!"

"Nevertheless, my lord, that is the message I was given."

"By whom, man?"

"By your brother, the Lord James, Earl of Carrick. Sent from your father."

"M'mm. Tell him I shall come so soon as I may." He found a hand free to gesture the messenger away.

"My lord — there is this you should know. In the Hall are come many of your unfriends, with the Duke of Albany. Also his brother, the Lord Walter of Brechin, whom we seldom see. Likewise the Earl of Douglas. And Ramorgnie. And the new Bishop of St. Andrews."

"Ha — the buzzards gather!" The prince sat up, interest engaged. "Off, Jeannie — off! Here is something I must see, to be sure. God knows, I prefer my unfriends where I *can* see them, before my eyes rather than behind my back!"

"I would walk warily, nevertheless," Jamie warned. "The Duke Robert it was who brought your father here. Not to your advantage, I think. If he has brought these others today, also, he will have his reasons."

"Stop preaching, Jamie, of a mercy! You should have been a priest, on my soul! I'd have made *you* Bishop of St. Andrews! Think you that you are the only one who can see an inch before his nose?"

Bowing, the Douglas withdrew.

Even so it was some time before David Stewart put in an appearance in the Great Hall — which was notably full of folk, lords and lairds, clerics and courtiers and pages, many of them but infrequently seen at the prince's Court. Albany and his brother Walter sat at the dais-table, the latter already drunk — but then he was usually drunk and incapably so, the youngest and only other surviving legitimate brother of the monarch, a poor character and unpleasant. The boy-prince James, dark-eyed, sensitive-featured, wary, lurked near the dais-door, on watch for his brother. He slipped away when he observed his entry, presumably to inform their father. Archibald, Earl of Douglas, stood by, frowning.

David's entry on the scene was carefully calculated to offend his elder uncle, at least. He came strolling in, only partially dressed, his rich clothing thrown on anyhow, one arm around the shoulders of the plump and now blushing lady, hand actually inside her notably low and loose-necked bodice. He was laughing and jollying her, and though he nodded genially here and there, he paid no attention to the illustrious company up on the dais. He paused to chat to various of his friends, still leaning on the lady — who was in fact one of the very few women present, and uneasily aware of it.

Jamie, from a corner, watched doubtfully.

Slowly, casually, David made his way through the throng to the dais, his gait just a little unsteady, using his companion as support. They mounted the platform with some small difficulty, and moved over to the well-doing fire of birch-logs — for the dais area had its own fireplace — the prince only glancing at the table-sitters in passing.

"My good uncles," he observed, easily, "or, leastways, uncles, good bad or indifferent! A notable sight! Make your bow, lass."

The confused girl bobbed towards the older men nervously — and in so doing all but upset the prince's unsteady stance.

"Stand still, m'dear. A pox on it — stand still, woman, I say!" David requested, but affably enough. "Would you have me on my back, *here*? Again! Before all!"

"Where we'd see the best o' you, by the Mass!" the sprawling

270

Lord Walter of Brechin hiccuped. To add, "My lord Governor. Or Lieutenant, or whatever you call yourself — God save us!" He had some difficulty in enunciating all that.

"There speaks jealousy, Uncle! *You* are past it, man, I swear! Too fat. Is he not, Jeannie? Even you'd make naught of old Uncle Wattie, hot as you are . . ."

"Peace!" the cold voice of the Duke of Albany cut in, like a whiplash. "Peace, I say. Young man — your father." The Duke rose, all sitters rose — save Walter Stewart, who could not.

David turned to look behind him, as a temporary silence fell on the crowded chamber. The King, stooping wearily, features ravaged, thinner than ever, had aged grievously. Limping, he was led in by his younger son — who looked hurriedly, anxiously at his older brother. David bowed to his father, and nodded to the boy, still managing to keep his hand deep within the bulging bosom. But it was to Albany that he turned and spoke, with a mocking smile.

"Ah, yes, my lord Duke — peace!" he said. "Who indeed more apt to cry peace than my Uncle Robert — who has not the meaning of the word in him, on my soul! And would have this bedevilled realm of Scotland not to know it, either! God save us — peace from *you*, man!" It was a sign of the prince's state of inebriation that he allowed himself thus to react unwontedly.

"Silence! You'll speak me respectfully, sir. Or suffer for it."

"Ha — respect! For you? This is rich, i' faith! And you would threaten, my lord! Me? Rothesay? Beware how you do that, by Christ's Rood! Have you forgot, Uncle? You are no longer Governor, no longer master of this realm. *I* bear the rule now. Heed it, I say."

"Master, you say? I think not. Have *you* forgot His Grace the King?"

David's laughter rose almost to a hoot. "God's eyes — this from you, Uncle! Spare us, for very shame. I swear it was largely to spare my royal sire from your slights and afflictions that I assumed the governorship. Is that not so, my lord King and noble progenitor?" He gestured an unsteady flourish towards his father.

"Aye, Davie," the King said, low-voiced, troubled. But he looked at his brother rather than at his son.

Quiet had fallen on the Hall during this exchange. The clash between the royal dukes had of course been known to all

Scotland for years. It looked as though, now, it might be coming to its inevitable head.

Albany spoke, sternly but levelly, no hint of emotion in his rasping voice. "I will pay no heed to your foolish words, sir. But since you have come here on matters concerning the well-being of this realm, I suggest that you put that young woman from you and behave more as befits your place and station."

"I am here, Uncle, because as Lieutenant of the Realm I choose to come. For no other reason. I came at my father's request, but of my own decision. And as for this lady, she is at least honest in her behaviour and function — which is more than can be said for all this company! I brought her — and she stays."

"You'd have done better to have brought your wife, Davie," the King said mildly but vexedly. "Aye, you would."

"My wife is . . . otherwise, Sire." David withdrew his hand, however, from its warm resting-place, the young woman sniggered and would have edged away, but he held her by the arm firmly, even yet.

Albany pointed an accusing hand. "Your father has summoned you here, Nephew — and for sufficient reason. Overdue, I say. You stand accused, with much to answer for. I would advise you to comport yourself accordingly."

"Accused? Me? Here? Who dares?"

"I do. And many another. You are charged with the shameful misgovernance of this realm, Nephew. With wastage of the kingdom's substance. With the alienation of Crown lands and revenues. With subversion of justice . . ."

"Charged, is it!" the younger man interrupted. "How charged, sirrah? I was appointed Lieutenant by the King in Council, confirmed by parliament. If I, the Lieutenant, am to be charged, it can only be by the said King in Council. Is this the Privy Council of Scotland?" He gestured around. He appeared to have sobered quickly.

"A warning, Davie," his father mumbled unhappily. "A warning just. No more, lad."

"You would prefer to answer these charges, in detail, before the assembled Council, Nephew?" Albany asked thinly.

The prince frowned. "These are no charges. They are but vague accusations, unfounded. Representing but the spleen of an old man, jealous! One who indeed knows what misgovernance, subversion and the rest mean!"

272

"You would have chapter and verse for them, then? Such can be produced readily enough . . ."

"You lie, as ever! These are but wild denunciations. Stone-throwing. I cast them back in your teeth! You, who trampled on the country for ten sore years. You would never dare face me before Council and parliament — you who have too few friends in either. You know full well that the folk of Scotland much prefer me to yourself."

Jamie winced in his corner. This was not the David Stewart he knew and relied upon.

The older man was not to be deflected for a moment from his purpose. "You are summoned here, Nephew, in order that the King's will and decision be made known to you . . ."

"Before all these? Can my father not express his will and wishes to me save by *your* lips? And in his own chamber? Not before a gawping crowd." David swung on the King, who gnawed his lip and shook his head, but said nothing.

"It is the King's royal will and decision," Albany went on, as though there had been no interruption, "that you should be warned and restrained, given due notice to amend your ways. The governorship is not taken from you — but you are to be restrained in certain respects. You will accept the guidance, in pursuance of your duties, of myself, and the lords of Brechin, Douglas, Moray, Crawford, St. Andrews and Aberdeen, as you should have done all along. These acting in the King's express name. You will order your daily life decently and discreetly. Should you fail to do so, and not mend your way, I shall, with His Grace's and the Council's authority, resume the governorship. You understand?"

"My . . . God!" David whispered, into the hush which now gripped the great room, staring. "This is beyond all belief! And all bearing!" He looked at his father. "You, Sire — you heard? Spoken in your royal presence! To your son, to the heir to your throne. You heard?"

Swallowing painfully, audibly, the monarch shook his white head. "Aye, Davie, I heard," he got out slowly, sighing. "It must be. You have brought it on yourself, I fear — the sorrow of it. See you, the rule of this realm is not a game to be played, a sport for braw laddies. God forgive me, who say it — for my failure is greater than yours, lad. Aye, the greater. The fault is largely mine, I do confess before all. But . . . God's will be done."

"*God's* will!" his son burst out. "Is that what your brother's intrigues and schemings are named, now? The Devil's will, rather! But . . . I'll not have it. There are more wills than Albany's in this realm — even if *you* have none! Aye, and more than words to count. There are such things as swords in Scotland, I say!"

In the complete silence which followed that statement, the prince's glance left his agitated father's face, to slowly circle that vast chamber. Few men there, of any note, met his searching gaze.

"My lord of Crawford," he said, at length, to his Aunt Jean's husband, "how see you this matter?"

"But dimly, and with little pleasure," that gruff individual replied. "But I prefer *your* kind of misgovernance to the sort that went before!" Crawford did not greatly love David, but he hated Albany.

"Aye. And you, Cousin Thomas?"

Thomas, Earl of Moray, was the son of David's Aunt Marjory, and no very stalwart character. He coughed, looked down, and mumbled. "Some improvement there must be, David."

"Indeed!" The prince's scornful glance passed over Lord Murdoch Stewart, now calling himself Earl of Fife; also Albany's son-in-law the Earl of Ross. Likewise the new Bishop of St. Andrews and the Chancellor, Bishop Greenlaw of Aberdeen. It came to rest on Archibald, lately Master now Earl of Douglas.

"And you?" he enquired. "My lord and good-brother. How says Douglas?"

That stolid and moody young man did not move a muscle. Not so much as an eyelid flickered. Silent, impassive, he stood, whilst everywhere in the hall breaths were held and men awaited decision, the fall of the scales. For the Douglas, though not the man his father had been, was still the most powerful and influential individual in the kingdom, head of the most puissant and warlike family in Scotland, which differed from the Stewarts in being united. By position and the vast manpower he could wield, he was the realm's war-leader, however lacking in expertise. As all knew, he was angry with David over the way that he had treated his wife, Douglas's sister; but he was known not to love Albany either, although recently he had been seen much in his company. Whose side he took in this present power-struggle could all but decide the issue, for many would follow his lead.

As the tense moments passed, it dawned upon all, not least David Stewart, that his brother-in-law was not merely being more than usually slow of speech. He was not going to answer at all. Straight ahead of him he gazed now, wordless.

A long sigh escaped from the assembled company. Walter of Brechin barked an abrupt laugh. Albany changed neither stance nor expression.

The prince drew himself up, head high. He did not trouble to look at the lesser men present. Their support or otherwise would not decide the day. Drawing a long quivering breath, he swung back to face his accuser, and took a couple of steps up to the table. Without taking his eyes from Albany's aquiline features, he groped until his hand contacted a goblet half-filled with wine, set down by someone. Raising this to his lips, he gulped down the contents in a single draught, before them all. Then, holding it there, he spoke.

"My father's words I have heard," he declared, strongly now. "He says that the rule of this realm is no game. That I accept. As its Lieutenant I shall see that none play it — I promise you all! Warning has been given — and taken. I add mine. Let none seek to govern save the Governor! When King, Council and the Estates of Parliament, duly assembled, command me to lay down that office, then I shall do so. Not before. His Grace says 'God's will be done!' To that I say Amen — but let us not confuse Almighty God with my Uncle Albany! I charge you all to say, rather — God save the King! And, by the Holy Rood — to remember who will be King hereafter!"

With a sudden explosion of force, violent as it was unexpected, he hurled the heavy silver goblet, empty, down the littered length of the dais-table. Scattering and upsetting viands, flagons and the like in its course, it crashed to the floor beside the Duke of Albany.

In the resounding clatter, David, Prince of Scotland, flung around, and jumping from the dais went striding down the Hall without a backward glance, making for the outer door to the main courtyard. Right and left men parted to give him room. After a little hesitation, the unfortunate young woman went hurrying after him, biting her lip.

In the uproar that succeeded, King Robert, empty open hand raised tremblingly after his elder son, dropped it, moaning in-

275

coherent words. He took an uncertain step forward, to pluck at Albany's velvet sleeve — and was ignored. The boy James, features working, took his father's arm again, and gesturing towards the dais-door, led him away.

Jamie Douglas felt moved to hasten after the prince, but restrained himself. David would not want his sermonising company just now. It was a bad business — a notable exit, but a deal more than that was required to right this grievous situation. In the end, David's power emanated from the King — and the King had evidently withdrawn his favour, however sorrowfully. Just why, at this stage, was not clear. It could scarcely be all on account of Annabella — although the loss of the Queen's advice and strength was undoubtedly important. And Albany had clearly been able to get at his brother and in some measure fill the gap. Jamie found himself almost hating his new chief, Archibald Douglas. Who would have thought that, in the end, he would have thrown in his lot with Albany? For, even if he had not actually done so, his denial of the Douglas support to David came to the same thing. That David had treated his sister shamefully was true; but it was surely no sufficient reason to risk overturning the government of the realm.

Until the end, the prince had not behaved well or adequately, seeming almost to have lost his grip. Drink had been responsible, no doubt — but drink had never previously affected his capabilities. More than that was wrong.

Whatever happened now, David's position was gravely weakened. Albany now was obviously working, and openly, to bring him down and supersede him; and if Albany seemed to have the support of the monarch, then many would see the end as inevitable, and act accordingly. If one of them had had to die, why could it not have been their feckless, spineless weathercock of a monarch instead of his noble and reliable wife? John Stewart himself undoubtedly would have preferred it that way — had declared as much. And David, mounting the throne, would have been unassailable, supreme, with all the authority he required, able to deal with Albany once and for all. If, if . . .!

Desiring speech with none save his Mary, Jamie slipped away from the Hall. It was Aberdour for him.

XIV

IT WAS AT Aberdour Castle, on a forenoon of early spring, that David Stewart came, from Linlithgow, to pick up Jamie, after crossing Forth by Queen Margaret's Ferry.

"I am bound for St. Andrews," he announced. "In God's good mercy the man Dennistoun has died, before he had time to replace my Uncle Thomas as Archdeacon — a great comfort! I intend to collect what treasure I can from the see's deep coffers, before my other uncle gets his hands on it. Also to try to ensure that the Canons and Chapter will not accept another of Robert's minions. Come with me, Jamie. Mary too, if she will, to see her brother."

"Dennistoun dead? Already?"

"Fear you not — I had nothing to do with it! A higher power, shall we say? He ate too much, I swear!"

Mary had ploys of her own in hand, and excused herself.

Jamie was concerned that the prince had come so little escorted, with a mere half-dozen of the guard at his heels; and he provided another four of his own men to accompany them. David declared that he did not want to draw attention to himself or his errand, on this occasion, and had slipped out of Linlithgow at first light discreetly. The smaller the party the less notice would be taken of it — and in Fife it might be wise to go unobtrusively. If Dennistoun's people got word that the Lieutenant was on his way, they might well take steps to hide away what he sought.

So they rode north-eastwards, by unfrequented ways, by Balmule and Kinglassie and the eastern flanks of the Lomonds, carefully avoiding the Fife seat of Falkland Castle, and so into the long Eden valley which led through the centre of Fife to St. Andrews, a journey totalling about twenty-eight miles.

As they went, David held forth on the new situation which arose from the death of Dennistoun. Another Bishop would have to be appointed, and to avoid all the previous trouble he was purposing to nominate Henry Wardlaw, Precentor of Glasgow Cathedral, nephew of the late Cardinal Wardlaw, a sound man who had shown no interest in the appointment hitherto. He was well liked by the senior clergy, and the College of Bishops would almost certainly support him as Primate. A secondary reason for this St. Andrews visit was to convince the Prior, Canons and Chapter to elect him, and quickly. Otherwise Albany would be fielding a new candidate, probably Greenlaw again.

To Jamie's query as to whether Henry Wardlaw would accept, the prince made his customary gesture of dismissal.

In the late afternoon, with the sinking sun at their backs and the towers and spires of the ecclesiastical metropolis already in sight before them against the blue plain of the sea, they were riding through woodland in the Strathtyrum area when, rounding a bend in the road, they suddenly were confronted by a large body of mounted men barring the way.

Jamie's hand dropped to his sword-hilt in immediate reaction, as they reined up, but Sir John de Ramorgnie came forward, doffing his bonnet and waving.

"That viper!" the Douglas jerked. "I do not like this. What is he doing here?"

"He lives somewhere hereabouts, I think? His barony of Ramorgnie is in the Howe of Fife, is it not?"

"A dozen miles and more to the west. But . . . see you who is with him. Lindsay of Rossie — another of your unfriends! And why all these men? This smells ill to me . . ."

"Perhaps so — but put back your sword, nevertheless, man. There are over a hundred of them, I'd say. Too many even for you, Jamie! We shall see what they want . . ."

Ignoring that, Jamie wheeled his horse around, and spurred back whence they had come. Round the bend he found more horsemen streaming out from the woodland to bar their retreat in that direction.

Without pause, turning again, he dashed back. "Into the trees!" he yelled. "Quickly. Through the wood. They are behind us, as well."

But it was too late. David was already riding forward to meet Ramorgnie and Lindsay — the same cousin of Crawford's whose sister the prince had played with and declined to marry years before.

"Well met, my lord Duke!" Ramorgnie called. "We greet you. We shall escort you into St. Andrews. Well met, I say."

"Met, certainly, John — whether well or not! Why are you here? And how did you know that I came to St. Andrews?"

"A traveller journeying to Falkland mentioned that your lordship had left Linlithgow for St. Andrews," the other returned easily. "And what more natural, with Dennistoun dead and the succession to consider anew?"

"Your traveller must have foundered his horse to get to Falkland in time with this important news!" the prince observed. "And you, Sir William — you are a long way from Rossie. Or Doune Castle, where you are apt to be!"

"I was at Falkland," that man said briefly, with no attempt at the civilities.

"Ah, then I take it that my good Uncle Albany is likewise there? And that this kind reception is of his making?"

Ramorgnie shrugged. "It is our pleasure to act escort, my lord Duke."

"Here is no escort but an armed ambush!" Jamie said bluntly, at David's back. "There are as many men blocking the road behind us as in front."

"Then let us on to St. Andrews with our escort," David said. "And discuss these matters of bishops and ambushes over a flagon of wine at a priestly board — for I am hungry."

"With pleasure," Ramorgnie said. "It is not far . . ."

It was only a couple of miles in fact, and the prince's party rode there tightly surrounded by their guard, David and Ramorgnie chatting with every appearance of ease, Jamie and Lindsay riding side by side with nothing to say to each other and plenty of mutual scowling. Through the streets of the city they clattered, so much broader and better paved, the houses finer, than those of Stirling or Edinburgh or Dundee, to the great episcopal castle on its coastal promontory.

Dismounting in the courtyard, David was ushered quite ceremoniously into the Sea Tower, the Bishop's private quarters. But once he was inside, there was nothing ceremonious about Jamie's treatment. He was grabbed by Lindsay's men, disarmed, and hustled urgently to one of the lesser lean-to buildings of the courtyard, protesting but unheeded. There he was pushed along a passage and thrust into a vaulted cell or storeroom, lit only by a narrow slit-window, the heavy door slammed on him, and the key turned.

Alone, with miscellaneous lumber, he was left to cogitate, to the sound of the waves breaking below his window.

* * *

He had plenty of time for gloomy rumination, for there were no developments, no-one came near him, neither food nor drink were brought. What was happening to David he could only guess at; but since these people treated himself in this un-knightly fashion, a recognised adherent if not friend of the prince's, it looked ominous. They would never have dared this unless they had Albany's fullest backing. It looked, therefore, as though that man had decided on an all-out trial of strength — in which case he must be very sure of the outcome, for Robert Stewart was no rash adventurer. Which was not an encouraging thought.

Darkness came early to that ill-lit cell — although not before Jamie had satisfied himself that there was no possible exit save by the securely locked and solid door. Thereafter, as philo-sophically as he might, he lay down on the stone-flagged floor in a corner, and sought the release of sleep, at least.

He was awakened some unspecified time later by the door being unlocked and a shadowy figure with a lantern entering, and closing the door quietly behind him. Prepared immediately to leap on the newcomer, the prisoner was restrained by the stealthy manner of his visitor, which surely did not indicate a normal gaoler.

"Jamie?" the caller whispered, holding the lantern high. "Are you awake?"

"Thomas? I am here, yes." It was the voice of his brother-in-law, the Archdeacon. "Here's a bad business."

"Aye. Keep your voice down. The porter's lodge is just across the courtyard and they have a guard set." Stewart moved over to the slit-window, and stuffed into its narrow, draughty aper-ture a cloak he was carrying. "That is better — and the light will not shine out. I was at my manse at Boarhills, when a servant brought me word of this. I fear we are going to have great trouble."

"No doubt. Your brother, Duke Albany, making sure that St. Andrews and its treasure remains in *his* grip?"

"That, yes. But much more, I think. These minions of his

280

would not have dared lay hands on David if there was not much more to it. They must be sure that he, the Lieutenant and Governor — for he is still that — will not be in a position to repay them for it hereafter. Which means that *Robert* is sure. How, and why, I know not."

"David is held prisoner? Held, as I am?"

"Yes. Locked up under close guard. I could not get to him, as I have done to you. Lindsay and that Ramorgnie are very sure of themselves — insolent. They have taken over this castle. They say I shall not be Archdeacon much longer. They are holding David until my brother comes, tomorrow."

"And then?"

"God knows. But I have no doubt Robert has prepared this well. He does not act on impulse."

They were silent for a little.

"What can we do?" Jamie asked.

"I do not know. I came to you, to ask that. *You* are the man of action, Jamie — not I."

"There is no hope of rescuing David?"

"Not from here. I tell you, he is guarded close."

"*I* must get out of here, then. Raise the country to his aid."

"It will not be easy. Robert is greatly feared."

"The King, your brother? Weak as he is, this cannot be to his liking."

"I do not know. But I greatly fear that Robert would not be daring this if he had not got some assurance from John, some agreement. John is lost without Annabella, a poor thing, clay in Robert's clever hands. Put no reliance on him, Jamie."

"He would not abandon his own firstborn? To this, this monster!"

"He will not see him as a monster, man. Only as the sure strong hand he relied upon for years. Robert was ever the strongest of our family."

"Then I will go to Douglas. Archibald does not love David, but he would never agree to this laying hands on him, the Lieutenant and heir to the throne. The Douglas power is greater than anything that Albany can wield. I will go to my father, and the Earl of Douglas. And Crawford, Angus and the rest."

The other looked doubtful. "If David had not offended Dunbar, and Moray . . ."

"Can you get me out of here, Thomas?"

"From this cell, perhaps, yes. From the castle itself, less easy. It is after midnight, and I will not be expected to leave again this night. The gatehouse is manned, the bridge up . . ."

"Is there no postern?"

"This is an episcopal palace, Jamie, not a baron's hold. But . . . there is the Sea-gate. It is used only by the servitors, for cleaning the privies and the like. Taking the night soil out, to throw in the sea. It is below the Sea Tower."

"That will content me well enough. I shall act the servitor, gladly. It will not be watched, likely? Can you get me there, unseen?"

"At this hour, I would say so. Through the basement vaults . . ."

"Good. Let us be gone, then. And can you win me some food? I have eaten nothing since I left Aberdour before noon. Aye, and a sword and dirk, if you can. They took mine."

So the Archdeacon opened the cell-door as quietly as he could, peered out, with his lantern, along the vaulted corridor, found no-one there, and led Jamie forth, locking the door again behind them. He took him by sundry dark passages with doors off, where no doubt much of Holy Church's wealth was stored, up and down winding turnpike stairs and through damp cellars. Presently through narrow slit-windows they could hear the sigh of the waves again.

Thomas Stewart came to a door with an iron yett as outer gate, a key in its lock and a strong draw-bar securing it. That all was in constant use, however, was clear, all greased. The yett opened with only a small creak, the draw-bar slid smoothly into its deep slot in the masonry, and the lock clicked only quietly. Opening the door, the cold sea air blew in their faces. Closing it again, the Archdeacon said,

"Wait here until I see what I can find for you. If another comes, do not wait. Out with you. If I do not come back within a short time, the same. I could be stopped. It is but the rocks of the beach outside — but watch where you tread!"

"If you have to choose between a sword and victuals, Thomas — take the sword!" Jamie told him.

His brother-in-law was back sooner than might have been anticipated, for it seemed that the Bishop's kitchens were quite close. He brought an old sword, clumsy but effective enough, a dirk and a satchel with bannock and a flagon of ale.

"What will you do, Jamie?" he asked.

"Go hide somewhere in the town until the gates open at sun-up. Then slip out and wait outside, for Albany's coming. They may search the town for me. Wait until I can learn what Albany does with David. I can do little until I know. I will come into the town again, later, to learn the gossip . . ."

"*I* might be able to tell you, better than tavern gossip. If I am allowed my freedom."

"Aye. Think you that you will suffer for releasing me thus, Thomas?"

"They will not love me for it! But I *am* the King's brother — or, more important perhaps, Albany's! Also, lacking a bishop, this is in some measure *my* house. And you are my good-brother. They will not wish to offend Holy Church more than they must. I do not think that they will lay violent hands on me."

"No. My sorrow to have brought this upon you."

"I brought it upon myself. And David is my nephew, mind. Let *one* of his uncles be as loyal as yourself!"

"To be sure. Shall I look for you, then, tomorrow? In the town?"

"Come to the Cathedral, before Vespers. None will look for you there. The Lepers' Chapel — St. Lazarus. Folk avoid it. If I do not come, then you will know that I am held. You must make your own way, then." He shrugged. "I am no true churchman — but God go with you, with us both, Jamie."

"Yes. I thank you. And if you see David, tell him that I will seek to raise Douglas to his aid."

Jamie opened the door and slipped out into the chill night air and on to the slippery rocks of the beach.

It was much too late to expect any house or tavern to open its doors for him. So, when making his way with difficulty, in the dark, over the ribs and reefs of the shore, he came to the harbour, it occurred to him that one of the vessels there might offer him as good shelter as any, and be unlikely to be searched as might the churches, should his escape be discovered before morning. There were many craft tied up at the quays, for the Church did much foreign trade, especially in the wools and hides from her innumerable farms and granges. Fishing-boats, not being decked-in, provided little cover or shelter; but the second of the larger vessels he tiptoed aboard was a wool-ship, part-loaded, and he was able to bed down, under the poop, among oily-smelling fleeces, with a fair degree of comfort. Rats hopped and squeaked all about him, their eyes gleaming red, but did him no harm. He ate his viands, leaving none for the rats, and resumed his night's slumber, having done much worse in many a campaign.

Up with the dawn, still no sign of life about the harbour area, he found the Harbour Port to the town still shut, barring access. Deciding that, in the circumstances, he could probably work his way round the walls without having to enter the town at all, he set off on a south-about course, so as not to pass the castle again. It was awkward going, and smelly — for it was clear that however fine a place St. Andrews was, its folk found that the easiest way to get rid of garbage and refuse was to hurl it over the town-walls, and not only where the tide might eventually clear it away. It was a long time since the city had had to use its walls for more military purposes.

Jamie had worked his way almost round to the South Port when the bells began to chime. He heard the first with some alarm, fearing that it might have something to do with himself, a warning that a fugitive was at large. But when innumerable others joined in, presently all dominated by the great booming of the Cathedral carillon, he recognised that it was just St. Andrews' way of greeting each new day. It was a dull grey morning, with no sign of sunrise, but presumably that was the hour. He hurried to get past the South Port before the gates opened, for no-one waited there yet to gain entry and the last thing he wanted was to make himself conspicuous.

. Away from the coast now, he kept further back from the walls. The West Port was the main entrance to the city, the way Albany would almost certainly come. His plan was to hide up somewhere on the western approaches, to watch for his arrival. He might learn *something*. He would have liked to slip into the town first, to purchase food and drink for the day, but reluctantly decided against, as not worth the risk. It occurred to him that probably the best place for him to go was the selfsame spot in the woodlands of Strathtyrum where Ramorgnie had ambushed them the day before, no doubt chosen with care. Thither he made his way, as the country folk began to move in towards the town for the day's market. He drew some odd glances, for although he always dressed modestly, there was no hiding the fact that he was of the gentry, unhorsed yet wearing thigh-length riding-boots of fine doeskin, however unshaven and unwashed. But his dark Douglas glower, or perhaps his prominent sword, discouraged enquiries or spoken remarks.

In under two miles he found the place he was looking for, the tight bend in the Cupar road in the Strathtyrum woodland. Here he constructed himself a hide amongst the dead bracken and scrub birch, and settled himself to wait.

Soon he slept.

The first time he was awakened, it was by a monkish party passing, on palfreys, their leader a heavy and rubicund churchman carried in a fine horse-litter, four singing-boys chanting before him to lighten the journey's tedium. This was about an hour before noon. The second time, it was a much larger and faster-moving company, all jingling harness and clanking armour, led behind two streaming banners. The first was not unexpected, the yellow-blue-white of Stewart of Albany. It was the other, hidden at first behind, which shook Jamie — the red crowned heart under the blue chief of Douglas, undifferenced. Behind these, riding beside the Duke Robert and in front of a large group of gallants and at least one hundred men-at-arms, was Archibald, Earl of Douglas.

Angry and depressed, Jamie watched this authoritative column disappear down the road to St. Andrews. The presence of Douglas there meant that he must drastically change his outlook, abandon many of his hopes for the situation. The new Earl would not be riding with Albany to St. Andrews unless he was in the plot, agreeing to David's apprehension. So nothing was to be hoped for from Douglas arms — at least, the main Douglas arms. There were others, of course — his own father and brothers, the Earl of Angus, the Lairds of Drumlanrig and Cavers and so on. But how far would these be prepared to act against their chief? The position was suddenly very much darker.

There was nothing more to wait for now, and after a while he started to walk back to the town, hunger hastening his steps. The West Port was wide open, and unwatched. He had no difficulty in entering. The streets were full, for a market, and he mingled with the crowds unhindered. At an alehouse he re-provisioned his satchel, and then made his way to the Cathedral.

That great fane, the finest in Scotland since Elgin had been burned by Alex's father, the Wolf of Badenoch, was by no means empty, with merchants haggling in the main nave, chanting going on in one of the side-chapels, fish being sold in the south porch, this being Lent, market-women resting, with their bundles and gear, before starting for home, candle-hawkers crying their wares. One or two people were even praying. But there was nobody in the small lepers' chapel dedicated to St. Lazarus, with its squint-window giving narrow view of the main high altar, as far as these accursed of God were permitted to approach. Here Jamie settled himself, after having explored all possible exits.

He flogged his mind as to how he might affect the situation in David's interests. The fact that Albany had dared this against the kingdom's lawful ruler must mean either that the King had given consent again, or could safely be ignored. In which case there seemed little point in seeking *his* intervention. With no Primate, and the Chancellor in Albany's pocket, plus Douglas aiding, there was really no-one with sufficient authority to counter Robert Stewart. In some kingdoms, in England indeed, someone would see to it that the feckless monarch was put away, or quietly assassinated — whereupon the prince would automatically become King David the Third, with all authority vested in his person. But this was not a thing to be contemplated in Scotland, where the monarchy, although less powerful and autocratic than in England and elsewhere, was more sacrosanct, more honoured of the people, *Ard Righ*, High King of Scots, not King of Scotland, a major difference, a more patriarchal figure. What source of aid was left, then? The fact that Sir William Lindsay was involved, the Earl of Crawford's illegitimate brother, did not augur well in that direction. Moray was a broken reed. No doubt some of the lesser lords and many of the bishops would be sympathetic; but would they, *could* they, provide sufficient pressure on Albany, or armed men, to counter the combined strength of Douglas and Stewart? He knew the answer to that without asking. Just as he knew that few would commit their men or their powers into the hands of a small knight such as himself, however well disposed towards the prince. He saw no way out of the predicament.

He was little further forward, therefore, when the Archdeacon Thomas arrived at the chapel, in mid-afternoon, earlier than he had said.

"They have gone," he announced. "Robert stayed only long enough to eat and bate his horses. He has taken David back to Falkland, a close prisoner."

"The Lieutenant. With what authority, other than some hundreds of armed men!"

"The King's authority, he says."

"But . . . what has changed since November, at Stirling Castle? David has been more careful since then. Done nothing amiss. The King has had no reason to allow Albany to go further than he did then."

"There was the matter of Sir John Wemyss."

"Wemyss imprisoned Walter Lindsay in his castle of Reres, unlawfully. It was the Lieutenant's *duty* to free him and to punish Wemyss. If the King's Lieutenant cannot do such a duty without incurring the King's censure, what rule is there in Scotland?"

"Wemyss is neighbour to Ramorgnie, in Fife. No doubt a supporter of Robert's. This has but been used as an excuse. There may be other such excuses — but that was the only one that I heard mentioned. But what matters it? The facts are there. Robert has taken David into custody, allegedly with the royal authority. No doubt he has been waiting to do so for long, waiting for opportunity. David was foolish to come to St. Andrews so ill-escorted. He should never have travelled abroad without a strong force at his back. That, or else himself taken the very steps Robert has done — taken Robert himself into custody. That would have been the wiser course."

"Aye — even Ramorgnie suggested that. And worse! David had sufficient excuse: Albany's failure to come to his aid at Edinburgh, and word that he was in negotiation with King Henry, secretly, with Forrester of Corstorphine — sufficient to hold Albany on a charge of treason. But he would not. He said that it would provoke war, civil war, and give Henry the opportunity he wanted. David has had to rule from a position of great weakness. With his father so feeble, useless . . ."

"Aye. My royal brother may be saintly disposed — but saints can on occasion do more mischief than other men!"

"What to do now, then?"

"The good God knows! Did you see who was with Robert? Douglas! If he has decided to support Robert in this, I cannot see that there is much than any can do."

Jamie nodded unhappily. "That is the crowning blow!" He jerked a mirthless laugh. "Crowning, indeed! If only . . . if only . . ."

"You mean, if only the King would die? Yes, we can all think of that. But — he is the Lord's Anointed. And though frail, in fair enough health, I think. And but sixty-five. David could wait for many years yet, for the throne!"

287

"Is Albany assuming the rule? The governorship? As he said. He cannot do that lawfully without the authority of parliament, where David's cause will be upheld . . ."

"In law, no. But in fact, he can rule now. And so order matters that a parliament is delayed until he is so entrenched that he will be harder to dislodge than last time. Robert is no fool. We must face the fact."

"How did he treat David, today? He is never anything but harsh and cold. But . . ."

"I do not know. I was not allowed to see David again. I had a word or two with Robert, but to little purpose. Our brotherly ties are of the weakest. He has little love for me — indeed, I doubt if he has love for any. A strange, sour, friendless man — but able, determined."

"And without scruple. David, in his power, may fare but uncomfortably. He has taken him to Falkland, you say? For what purpose?"

"I know not. They have all gone. They gave him a ragged cloak and mounted him on the sorriest nag in the stables. To make for Falkland."

"Aye. Then I had better follow, learn what I can. I shall need a horse. What has happened to my men?"

"They are all at the castle still, David's likewise. Your horses also. Robert took only David. The castle is mine again. So, come you . . ."

Back at the castle — and strange to be able to walk therein openly again — it was decided that there was no point in riding to Falkland that night. They could not get there before dark, and there would be little to learn, so soon, anyway. Better to wait, eat well, have a good night's rest, and ride in the morning.

Despite impatience, that was Jamie's programme.

* * *

Falkland, the main seat of the earldom of Fife, lay some twenty miles west of St. Andrews, a little grey town clustering round the large castle, lying in the shadow of the East Lomond Hill. It was not the sort of place that a party of mounted men could ride into without attracting a deal of attention, and all being seen from the castle. So, next day, about noon, nearing its vicinity, Jamie sent his own men and the half-dozen of the royal guard, back to Aberdour, another fifteen miles, retaining only the one groom to guard their two horses, in a wood half-a-mile from the town. Then he went forward alone to investigate.

There was no fair going on here unfortunately, and Jamie went very warily. But he perceived that no banner was flown from the castle keep, as might have been expected, with its master in residence. And when he asked some of the townsfolk whether Albany was there, he was told that the Duke had left that morning, where none knew, but it was presumed back to his main seat of Doune in Menteith. Carefully seeking to discover who had gone with the Duke, without seeming to press too keenly, he gathered that the Earl of Douglas and Sir John de Ramorgnie had accompanied him, and seemingly his entire entourage; but there was no mention of the Duke of Rothesay. None volunteered the name, and Jamie refrained from bringing it up. He did ask who remained in charge at the castle, however, and was told the constable, John Wright, and the steward, John Selkirk.

Jamie had heard of the man Wright, a harsh and boorish character, highly unpopular in Fife, known for his heavy hand and brutality in his master's service.

At an alehouse opposite the castle gatehouse, he made more discreet enquiry. Men-at-arms from the castle used this place, and he was able to learn that a captive, identity unknown but a young man, had been brought in with the Duke's party the previous afternoon, riding a baggage-horse and covered in a rough russet cloak. He had not gone with the Duke and the rest this morning, so was still a prisoner in the castle. Despite his humdrum appearance he must be somebody of importance for the Duke to have gone to St. Andrews in person to fetch him. Albany, it seemed, had now gone only to Culross, in Fothrif, where some sort of meeting of great ones was summoned.

Very thoughtful indeed, Jamie made his way back to his horse and groom.

Later, at his own fireside at Aberdour, he recounted all to Mary, who listened grave-faced.

"Robert must be very sure of himself to do this," she said eventually. "It is not really like him, to act so directly, so openly. He prefers intrigue, using others. This is more like my late half-brother Alec! What is to be done, Jamie?"

"I have racked my wits to think of something," he told her. "You think the King will know of this imprisonment? By agreeing to it?"

"I fear that he must. Robert would never dare to lay rough

289

hands on the heir to the throne, and hold him captive, and in his own castle, otherwise. He will have played on John, told him lies and half-truths. Saying that it is for David's own good . . ."

"If we went and saw the King? You, and possibly Thomas and myself. Told him the truth?"

"I doubt if it would serve much purpose. Having gone so far, Robert will not be likely to draw back now, save on the strongest of royal commands. Which are not likely to be forthcoming, from John. Especially if he can sway this Council at Culross to support him — Robert, I mean."

"The devil of it, that Douglas should be on his side! This is the final blow. I can still go to my father, and Angus, with Cavers and Drumlanrig and the others. But, against their chief, I would not wager that they would do much."

"Would David Lindsay help — Crawford?"

"Help, perhaps — but no more than that. He will not take any lead, I think. With his half-brother in Albany's pocket and the Lindsays disgruntled over the Lady Euphemia business."

"And the Church is leaderless and divided. Oh, that Annabella and the good Bishop Trail were still alive! Even Archie the Grim. That they should all have died at the one time! It is as though God's hand is against David."

They sat staring into the fire for a while, unhappily. Then Jamie shrugged. "Tomorrow, at least, I shall go see my father. He has a wise head — although too cautious now, with age. He is still a member of the Council, although he but seldom attends. He does not like Albany. Perhaps he will think of something that we can do. Then I will try Angus, at Tantallon."

She looked up. "Jamie — has it not occurred to you that *you* are now in danger? All know how close you are to David. All know that you are a man of action. Robert has always disliked you — as you him. Ramorgnie likewise. You have escaped from them once. They will take you again, if they can. And perhaps treat you less gently."

"They may try. But I am warned now, at least. They will not take me so easily again. What would you have me do? Sit still, here? Attempt nothing for David? Flee somewhere safer . . .?"

"Just be careful, lad," she said. "Just ever be taking care . . .!"

XV

IN HIS FATHER's overheated chamber at Dalkeith, Jamie wagged his head in exasperation. The Lord of Dalkeith was old now, admittedly — in his seventieth year. But he still had sound wits, and was moreover still a powerful figure in the realm, probably its richest noble, experienced in government.

"You cannot just sit there and say God's will be done!" his illegitimate but favourite son protested. "If you make Albany's will God's will, then you make the good God a murderer! For nothing is surer than that Albany committed murder."

"Hush, lad. That is no way to talk. I do not say that Albany's will is God's — but only that God may even use such as Albany to work *His* will. David needs a lesson, it may be. He has been foolish, headstrong. A term in captivity may do him no harm, bring him to a better appreciation of his duties, so that when he is King, he may rule the more wisely. All his days he has had his own wilful way."

"So you would do nothing? Accept any wickedness on Albany's part, however unlawful, as possibly serving God's purpose? Is this how you, a Privy Councillor, are prepared to rule the realm?"

"Not so. But in ruling a realm, as in all else, what cannot be mended is best accepted, Jamie. And betterment worked for, thereafter."

"I prefer to work for the betterment first!"

"Tell me how, lad? As I see it, there is only one key which will unlock David's prison-door, and that is the King's. For no-one else will Albany yield — if even then. And Falkland is a strong castle and will be well guarded, you may be sure. You will not bring David out of there, even with a host at your back."

"Then we must go to the King."

"And what will you say to him? How persuade him? How prevail against Albany's stronger will? Think you he would heed *you*, Jamie. Or even see you?"

"He might see his own brother and sister — Mary and the Archdeacon Thomas."

"See, perhaps. But *heed*? Use your wits, lad. If the King has so turned against his own son that he allows his brother to lock him up in a castle, will he be likely to heed lesser men's pleadings?"

"If we could show him that Albany was a monster, an evil man seeking only power for himself . . ."

"He would take a deal of convincing of that, at this stage. But . . ."

"If we told him that he, Albany, wanted to hand over the Mammet to Henry? In return for aid against David. Would that not sway the King?"

"If he believed it! But see you, Jamie — there is one matter which might sway our weak and foolish monarch against his brother. And that is fear. Fear not for himself — for I believe that he might well wish to die — but for his little son. Young James is now John Stewart's all, the apple of his eye. His link with his dead queen. Was he to see a threat to James in this, all might yet be changed."

"And could there be?"

"It could be represented so. And with some justice perhaps. If David were to die, there is only young James between Albany and the throne, when the King goes."

"Aye. And you think . . .?"

"I say only could be. But Albany is perhaps ambitious for more than just power. He had the power before. He has always resented John's primogeniture, when *he* would have made the strong and able king. John must know this very well. Here is the only chance I see . . ."

"Aye, it could be. It could very well be so. You think the King would rise to that lure?"

"If it was skilfully presented to him, he might."

"You will come? And so present it? The King is at Turnberry again. With young James and the Mammet . . ."

"No, no. Not me, lad. I am past traipsing the country — an auld done man. You must make do your own self. With your wife and her brother Thomas. I will send your brother James with you to represent me, if you wish. He is not so bright as

292

you are, but he is a good lad. And he can take a troop of Douglas horse — for I jalouse that there's some who might seek to interfere with you, Jamie. You'll have to watch out for yourself, lad, in this business."

"Mary said as much." Jamie was fond enough of his half-brother, his father's heir, but had no particular desire for his company on a difficult ploy like this. But the hundred men-at-arms was a welcome suggestion and James would captain them suitably.

He was impatient, of course, to be off to Ayrshire to put the matter to the test, but had to restrain himself. Apart from the assembling of the men-at-arms, it was important that he gain the support of such magnates as he could. A day or two would make little difference, he told himself.

Next day, then, he rode to Tantallon, in East Lothian. He found the young Earl of Angus most evidently happy in his marriage, and well content with life, immersed in the management of his lands and people — and in consequence not disposed for adventures. He was concerned to hear Jamie's tidings, outraged at Albany's behaviour and anxious for the future of Scotland implicit in all this; but saw no personal involvement, nothing that he might usefully do. He offered the use of some fifty of his men — that was as far as he would go. Jamie accepted these with what grace he could, and moved on.

There was nothing more to be done in Lothian, since Douglas and Dunbar divided all between them, all lesser lairds being in vassalage to one or the other, or at least indisposed to take a contrary line. Crawford, it seemed, was at his Angus castle of Edzell, which was a long way to go. But, after Douglas, he was the next most important noble in the land, as well as being David's uncle by marriage. Jamie would go there, via Aberdour and St. Andrews, and arrange for Mary and Thomas to accompany him to Turnberry. At least he could ride secure with a bodyguard of a hundred and fifty men.

The Lindsay chief was of more practical help than was Angus; but even he lacked real enthusiasm. It was Albany's reputation for caution, strangely enough, that was the main handicap. In view of this, the fact that he now dared to act so drastically, convinced Crawford, like others, that he was entirely confident, assured of success, unbeatable — which inhibited opposition. Crawford saw nothing to be gained by approaching the King — who must have given his consent. He said, however, that he would demand a meeting of the Privy Council, and do what he

293

could to ensure that that body took strong steps to have David released, and insist upon the calling of a parliament. A parliament would be David's best hope, undoubtedly. On Jamie's expressed determination to see the monarch, he shrugged. He could not stop him — but it was a waste of time; and he, Crawford, would by no means accompany him.

So it was a small party of four, three of them bastards, who eventually set off westwards for Ayrshire, however strongly escorted. They suffered no interference *en route*.

*   *   *

They had some difficulty in gaining entry to Turnberry Castle, for although the King personally was much more accessible than many of his nobles, those concerned with his government were ever on watch for attempts to kidnap him and use him as hostage for their own ends. The present royal guard, needless to say, was of Albany's appointment; but even they could not permanently deny the monarch's half-brother and half-sister audience.

Eventually they won their way into a private apartment, where young James, Earl of Carrick, received them. He was a serious, dark-eyed, watchful child, old for his years, with good and regular features and a surprisingly direct gaze, however modest in manner — so notably different from his brother David at a similar age. He bowed gravely.

"Aunt Mary. Uncle Thomas. Sir James. I greet you." He looked at Young Dalkeith. "You, sir — I regret that I do not know your name?"

Jamie introduced his half-brother. Mary went to kiss her nephew.

"Have you travelled far?" the boy enquired politely. "You will require refreshment."

"Thank you. Your father, the King — he is well?" Thomas asked. "We have come far to speak with him."

"I shall tell him. But . . . His Grace is much troubled. Scarce himself. It is . . . it is about Davie?" The grave young voice trembled a little.

"Yes, James — it is about Davie," Mary said, as gently as she might. "Things go very ill with Davie. Does your father know it all? Is he fully aware of what is done?"

"He knows that my brother has been taken into custody. It does not please him, but he believes it necessary."

294

"Does he understand how close is the custody? How rigorous and harsh for the heir to the throne, the realm's Lieutenant?"

"He knows him to be in Uncle Robert's keeping at Falkland."

"He agreed to that?"

"Yes. Uncle Robert said that it was necessary. For Davie's own good . . ." That was tremulous again. James was known to all but hero-worship his brilliant elder brother.

"And the King accepts Robert's word as against his own son, my lord?" That was Jamie Douglas.

The boy bit his lip. "I, I fear so," he whispered. He turned away. "Come — to the Lesser Hall, for your refreshment. And I will go tell His Grace."

It was some considerable time, and the visitors were finishing a meal of cold meats and wine in the Lesser Hall, before the King came to them, leaning on the Mammet on one side, his other hand held by the boy-prince. He looked the utter wreck of a man, bent, drawn, his lower lip trembling all the while, his great eyes rheumy. As the callers rose and bowed, he shook his white head.

"If you have come about Davie, Tom — aye, and you Mary — I canna do aught," he said. "He'll have to bide at Falkland meantime. He's a good lad, but foolish, headstrong. He'll need to learn his lesson before he can rule this realm again. There's no two ways to that."

Mary it was who spoke. "Perhaps, Sire. But — greetings! We offer our leal duty, and wish you well."

The others mumbled agreement.

The King shook his head, then seemed to recollect the Mammet Richard. "His Grace of England," he said.

They all bowed again.

"Thomas — if you have come about St. Andrews, we could still have you Bishop, I'd say. Robert wouldna stand in your way, I think."

"I have no wish to be Bishop of St. Andrews, Sire. I am not of the stuff of primates! We are here on a much graver matter — the life of the Prince and High Steward of Scotland. Whom you have allowed to be shut in a prison cell."

"I told you — he'll have to bide there awhile, Thomas. Until he's learned his lesson. He's been fell foolish."

"What has he done since yon day at Stirling when you warned him? What especial folly to deserve this? He has been careful, discreet . . ."

"No, no. Robert knows better than fhat. He has had him watched, see you. He has but been hiding his follies. Robbing the Customs, mishandling those who will not give him the moneys he wants, whoring and drinking. I canna have my Lieutenant and heir. so behaving. When, when he's like to be more than heir soon enough!"

"Sire — I swear that you have been misinformed," Jamie exclaimed. "I am the Duke David's man — Douglas of Aberdour. I have aided him in his campaign against the wicked misappropriation of customs dues. There has been shameful thievery for years — but not by him. The Duke has been most honest in this, I promise Your Grace. He has been stamping down a notorious evil which, which . . ." He swallowed. "The Duke of Albany's information on this is not correct. I have been concerned in it, and know."

"Shall I prefer *your* opinion on this, sir, to that of my own brother?"

"Sire, I also am your brother, if on the wrong side of the blanket!" Thomas said. "And I would remind you that Robert hates David, resents his position and covets his power. Robert is without scruple and does not hesitate to lie to gain his ends. And worse. You prefer to trust him, rather than your own son?"

John Stewart gnawed his lip. "Who *can* I believe?" he quavered. "Not Davie, who has deceived me times without number. I can trust none, I tell you — none! Save James, here. Aye, and King Richard."

"Sire, you can trust me, your half-sister," Mary said strongly. "I have never lied to you. Nor ever would. I tell you that Robert is concerned only to bring David down. He cannot do that without your aid. He appears, by his lies and plotting, to have gained that aid. David is no saint — but he is a deal better man than Robert."

"David is weak, Robert is strong, lass. And the realm, any realm, requires a strong hand to rule it. I, God pity me, who have *no* strength, know that! I have tried, the saints know how I have tried, to teach Davie how to rule — I, who myself can by no means rule. But he has never heeded me. It is not only Robert, Mary. It is for Davie's own good. For the time grows short. I shall not live much longer — Heaven be praised! And when I am gone, Davie will be King — and none then will be able to control him. Somehow he must learn his lesson before then. This way, I pray, he may at last learn, and quickly."

"Learn to be a king — from a prison cell?"

"Aye, lacking better. A monk's cell would have been more seemly — but he would never have agreed to it. He had to be removed from temptation, away from all women and wine, communing only with himself and God — vigil, fasting, repentance, learning to know himself. I pray that he comes out of that cell in Falkland a man fitter to be King of Scots. For he has wits, courage, ability, lacking only responsibility. He may be learning it now, at last." That was a long speech for John Stewart, and he was panting at the end of it.

His visitors stared at him and at each other, speechless, scarcely able to believe their ears. That the King was in earnest was not to be doubted. Yet it was all but incredible that he should believe this, out-of-touch with the world and sheltered from reality as he was.

Thomas found words at last. "Is this . . . Robert's ploy?" he asked thickly. "Did he put it thus to you?"

"Not so," the King said wearily. "Robert was concerned only with restraining Davie from more folly. It was I myself, after much prayer, who saw how much good might come out of seeming harshness."

Jamie muttered under his breath, and his brother nudged his arm, brows raised.

Mary spoke. "Sire, the harshness you speak of could be more grievous than you think."

"Why say you so, Mary?"

She glanced at her husband.

Jamie cleared his throat. "Your Grace, I bring a message from my father. Which my brother here will substantiate. You may think more highly of the advice of my lord of Dalkeith, long a member of your Privy Council, than of my own. He asks, in all duty, whether you have considered that your sons, *both* of your sons, could be in danger? Great danger. Even of their lives?"

The monarch peered short-sightedly. "Are you out of your mind, sir? And the Lord of Dalkeith likewise?"

"My father, at least, Sire, is a notably level-headed man. Your Grace has known him long. He asks — have you considered that there are but two steps between the Duke of Albany and your throne, when you, h'm, vacate it — the Princes David and James, your sons. And the Duke of Albany is a man who seeks power above all things."

297

The King held out a hand that trembled violently. "No!" he exclaimed. "No! How dare you, sir! You, such as *you*, accuse my brother! To me — the King!"

"With respect, Sire — not me. It is my *father's* message," Jamie insisted, woodenly. "Although I agree with it. The Duke Robert already has the Duke David in his power. One step all but taken. It would be less difficult to take the Earl of Carrick, here, a mere child. Then, Sire, if aught should occur to *your* injury, your brother is in a position to reach for the throne himself. None to gainsay him."

"This is beyond belief! I *will* not listen to you, sir. Or your father." The King was clutching his young son closer to him, however. He turned to the Mammet. "Richard — have you ever heard such, such wicked imputation?"

That strange man spoke low-voiced. "I would remind you, my friend, that my throne was wrested from me. And by a kinsman!"

Unhappily the older man eyed him. "Dear God Almighty!" he said.

"Sire," Thomas put in, anxious to exploit even this opening. "It is a real danger. You must see it. But even if Robert has no such intention, it is surely most damaging to David's reputation and authority to be shut up in a cell in Robert's castle? He is the *Lieutenant*! It cannot but injure his name as ruler. Even here in your house, it would be less hurtful. But in Robert's own hold — the man who would supplant him as Governor, if naught else . . ."

"It must be where Davie could not suborn the guards, or he would be out. And I do not see any guards but Robert's proof against him!"

"*Must* he be locked in a cell?" Mary asked. "Tom is right. Apart from the danger, it cannot but harm his authority afterwards — for him to have been imprisoned while he was still Governor. Who will respect his powers after that? Unless, of course, you do not intend that he has any? That you are removing him from the governorship entirely?"

"No, not that. Robert will act Governor again meantime. But thereafter in due course, Davie will rule again."

"If he survives!" Jamie murmured.

Mary laid her hand on his arm. "How long do you intend that he be confined, Sire?" she asked.

The King gestured vaguely. "Who knows? Not for long. A month. Two months. Until he has learned his lesson."

298

"And you will not heed us, Sire?" Thomas demanded. "Pay no heed to all we have said? Ignore the danger . . . ?"

"I will consider it. Aye, I will take thought. And pray. Pray to God to guide an erring servant."

"But . . . before too long? David meantime *may* be in danger."

"Do not harass me, Thomas. I will not be harassed! I have said that I will consider the matter. God knows, I have sufficient on my mind." The monarch began to turn away.

Greatly daring, Jamie spoke again. "Your Grace, I hesitate to cast more upon your royal mind. But before he was arrested by Sir John de Ramorgnie, the Duke of Rothesay told me that he had sure information that the Duke of Albany was negotiating with King Henry of England, for the return to him of, of King Richard, here, Sir Adam de Forrester of Corstorphine acting as messenger. To exchange King Richard for certain advantages. I conceive it my duty to tell you."

The Mammet had drawn a quick and audible breath, and grasped the King's arm.

"Merciful Lord Christ!" John Stewart gasped. "No — it cannot be! I do not believe it. Robert would not do such an evil thing."

"The prince had it on most reliable information from London, Sire. Forrester gained safe-conducts to visit kinsmen elsewhere in England. But he made his way to Henry's Court. The word there is that he came to offer the return of King Richard."

"That I will *not* permit!" the monarch cried, with a deal more decision than he had shown in regard to his son. "Never fear, Richard, my friend. I will not have it."

Thomas Stewart drove the point home. "Nor would David, Your Grace. But Robert, our *strong* brother, will do anything he thinks to his own advantage — if he has the power."

John Stewart muttered something unintelligible, and turning, hurried from the hall, his attendants following.

The visitors waited for three days at Turnberry, hoping for definite word from the King that he would command the release of David. All that they gained eventually was that he would write to Robert, urging that his elder son be transferred to Stirling Castle. He would also declare that under no circumstances was King Richard to be the subject of negotiations, and would remain in his own royal care and keeping.

With this they had to be content, as they turned their horses' heads eastwards again.

XVI

I T WAS TOM DURIE, the steward's son at Aberdour, who brought the first word of the appalling news. He had been attending a cattle-fair at Freuchie, near Falkland, and he said that the whisper there was that the Duke of Rothesay was dead. Dead in Falkland Castle.

Neither Jamie nor Mary believed it, of course. It was assuredly the foolish gossip of ignorant folk. But Durie declared that some of the men of Falkland that he had spoken with at Freuchie were of the better sort, responsible. They even gave the cause of death — starvation.

Nothing would do but that Jamie must go and try to find out the facts despite Mary's warnings of danger. It might be that the prince was only ill, and the tale had been exaggerated. But even so, they must find out, and seek to aid him. So, dressed in his oldest clothes and riding his poorest nag, Jamie set out for Falkland.

At the little grey town under the hill, he scarcely required to make secret or even discreet enquiries, for the whole place buzzed with the stories. There were various versions, but all agreed that the prince had been given no food of any kind by his gaolers since coming to Falkland eighteen days before. Some had it that he had been consistently maltreated by John Selkirk and John Wright, Albany's minions, from the start, as well as starved. Others declared that he had been given nothing to drink either, and had run mad. Others explained that he had managed to survive thus long because his cell had been beneath the castle granary, and grains of corn trickling down between the floorboards had fallen to him. There was even a story that one of the women in the castle, a nursing mother, had been so distressed by the prisoner's state that she went to his aid by squeezing milk from her breast, by means of a straw poked through a crack in the masonry from the next cellar, for the prince to suck — although this sounded more ingenious than practical to Jamie Douglas. But all agreed that David Stewart was dead — and had in fact been taken to Lindores Abbey that very morning for burial. And it seemed to be substantiated sufficiently that a corpse of some sort *had* been removed from the castle during the forenoon, in a horse-litter.

Jamie grimly decided to go on to Lindores, only seven miles to the north, and the Fife family burial-place. If the corpse had indeed been taken there, it was significant —for of course ordinary folk who died at Falkland would be buried in the local kirkyard.

In a sort of numb horror of fear, Jamie rode over the hill, past Rossie, Sir William Lindsay's barony, the little town of Auchtermuchty, and Pitcairlie. But he was not so numb as to fail to take avoiding action when, still a couple of miles from the Abbey, he perceived a fast-riding company coming towards him from that direction, on the road for Cupar, the sheriff's town. He drew off the track into whin and scrub, and dismounted.

The horsemen, about a dozen strong, drummed past him at speed — but not so fast that he could not identify the man at the head, Sir John de Ramorgnie.

He rode on more desolate than ever.

The Abbey of Lindores was a handsome and extensive Benedictine establishment, founded by David the First, but largely maintained by successive Earls of Fife. In due gratitude, the Abbots maintained in their turn the highly practical and useful sanctuary arrangement, known as the Law of Clan MacDuff, whereby felons within the ninth degree of kin to the Earls of Fife, man-slayers included, could claim sanctuary at the MacDuff Cross nearby, and secure all remission by payment of a fixed and modest compensation to the victim's heirs. Many had found this convenient provision to their advantage.

Jamie was in some doubts as to whether to discard his disguise and go openly to the Abbot, as Sir James Douglas of Aberdour, requesting information; or to retain it, and seek some humbler informant. He decided on the latter course, arguing that the Abbot, whom he knew only by repute, was bound to be more or less in the pocket of Albany, as Earl of Fife, and might well have been warned against enquirers. In the circumstances it seemed wiser to try more subtle methods.

Lindores, down on the Tayside plain, had the usual hospice for travellers, and here Jamie presented himself, seeking the plain but substantial fare offered by Holy Church to all comers. From the black-robed serving-brother there he gleaned little, save that there had indeed been a funeral of a sort that day, although the body was not yet actually buried but lying coffined in the Abbey chapter-house — presumably some great one, for there was a guard of armed men. But later, out in the orchard, he discovered a more talkative monk, digging beneath the trees, who, when Jamie jocularly asked if he was excavating a grave for the newly-arrived corpse, looked disapproving, almost shocked.

"Not so," he said severely. "That's a fool question, man. This isna hallowed ground. Yon puir soul deserves better than a bit leek-patch to lie in!"

"I but jested, friend."

"You shouldna jest about suchlike matters." The other had a broad Fife accent. "Yon one had had ill and unChristian handling, to bring him here. At least we'll gie him good Christian burial."

"M'mm. You mean that the body had been mishandled on its way here? I heard that it had come from Falkland or Freuchie or some such place?"

"Na, na. The mishandling was afore that. Whilst the puir mannie was alive." The monk lowered his voice. "Man, I helped lift him frae the litter he came in, and put him in the bit kist he's in now. And the shroud he was happit in came unwound someways, and an arm pokit out — an unchancy thing! And every finger was gnawed down to the white bone, see you — gnawed clean awa'! Now — what for would a man do the likes o' that, tell me?"

Jamie drew a long quivering breath. "God knows!" he got out. "Unless he was starving. Desperate for food. And drink. Mad with hunger and thirst."

"Aye, mebbeso. Mishandled, I said, did I no'? UnChristian, whoever did it. God will judge them, aye."

"Do you know whose this is? The body?"

"Nane hae said the name. And the body and face has aye been covered. But . . . it's no' some common loon. Else why set a guard on the chapter-house door, with nane to enter?"

"Who set the guard?"

"Him they ca' the Proculator, or suchlike name. One o' the King's officers."

"The Prolocutor-General is Sir John de Ramorgnie. One of Albany's men, rather than the King's."

"Aye, mebbeso. But what's the differ? It's a high matter, but an ill one. No' for such as oursel's to speir into. But God's judgement will fa' on whoever did this thing, high or no' — mark my words. *Dominus regnavit!*"

"I hope that you are right, friend," Jamie said heavily, and turned away.

He left Lindores sick at heart, to ride southwards for Aberdour.

* * *

"Jamie, Jamie!" Mary cried urgently. "Listen to me. You now are in direst danger. We all are. If they can slay horribly the heir to the throne, think you that they will hesitate to slay you, his friend and servant? You have escaped from their clutches once. Robert knows well that you are his enemy. Ramorgnie hates you — has never hidden the fact. You know too much for your own good. You cannot stay here. We must get away."

"Where, lass — where?"

"I do not know. But away from here. Away from Fife. Away from wherever Robert's men may lay hands on you."

"That, I fear, is anywhere south of the Highland Line, my dear."

"Then let us go north. Go to Alex Stewart in Badenoch. We could be safe with him. Anywhere, so long as Robert cannot reach us."

"But . . . I cannot just turn myself into a hunted fugitive, Mary," he protested.

"Better that than a corpse, like David! You must see it, Jamie. Robert will stop at nothing, now. He will learn that you have been to see the King. Knowing what you do, he will esteem you a danger. A man who can starve to death his own nephew, will kill such as you as he would a fly! And you have no powerful protector, now, in the Earl of Douglas. He is on Robert's side."

"We could go to Dalkeith, I suppose — my father's house."

"And have to go guarded by many men every time you

303

ventured out? It would be only a matter of time until they got you."

"If we knew what were Albany's plans, now? Whether he but aims to have the rule? Or the throne itself?"

"The rule first, then the crown, I'd say. I would not give much for young James's life, poor laddie! Nor his father's — although John would give up the ghost gladly enough."

"He will not act precipitately — Albany. He never does. Always hides behind others. He will find some excuse for this terrible deed, claim that he knew nothing of it. Condole with the King, lull his suspicions. And then, in due course, strike again."

"Perhaps. But I do not see how *you* are served . . . ?"

"If that is how it goes, he may not wish more trouble meantime. If I also was to be slain, now, David's known friend and servant, then it would look very black. He might not wish that. He might well leave me alone, meantime."

"Do not cozen yourself, Jamie. Robert has gone too far now for half-measures and caution. Poor David was the turning-point. He need not fear the King, and James is only a child. Whom needs he go warily for, now, with Douglas supporting him? I say his days of caution and the hidden hand are over."

"David should be avenged," he said.

Exasperatedly she shook her head. "Not by you, Jamie Douglas! Will you never learn? You sought for years to avenge the Earl James Douglas, against Robert. To what end? He is far too strong, too secure, for such as you to reach. If David could not master him, how could you do so? Forget vengeance, Jamie — or leave it to God. David's end is terrible, beyond all contemplation. And I was fond of him. But you cannot bring him back, and you cannot reach Robert, now less than ever. You must consider yourself. And me. The children. We must not stay here where Robert can reach *us*."

"Archie Douglas, the Earl, does not hate *me*. However much he misliked David. Indeed, I believe he thinks well of me. If I put myself under Earl Archie's protection . . . ?"

"Do not believe it. Archie Douglas is not like his father, Archie the Grim. He is not much better than a weakling, I think. As clay in Robert's hands. If Robert wanted you, Douglas would not save you — that I swear. No — the only man who can protect us now is Alex Stewart, a hundred and more miles behind the Highland Line. We must go there,

Jamie, and quickly, before it is too late. Leave our home, meantime. Change our life. There is nothing else for it."

Unhappily they eyed each other.

He sighed. "It may be that you are right . . ."

*   *   *

Two evenings later, the 1st of April, they slipped out of Aberdour Castle with the dusk, leaving old Durie the steward in charge, Jamie and Mary, the two children, now eleven and nine years old, their former nurse Janet Durie and her brother Tom, and six of the barony's men as escort, to ride eastwards. The youngsters were greatly excited by this night-time journey, but none of the others found it to their taste. The county of Fife was too full of potential enemies to risk travel by day.

All night they rode, by infrequent ways, due eastwards towards the East Neuk of Fife, avoiding the coastal towns and fishing-havens, the children asleep most of the time in front of their parents. Fortunately the weather was dry, although there was a chill easterly wind, and conditions might have been a deal worse. They suffered no interference, saw few signs of life, were barked at by sundry wakeful dogs, that was all.

They came to the village of Boarhills, not far inland from Fife Ness, soon after dawn — it seemed to be Jamie's fate to lurk secretly about this coast at daybreak. Here was Thomas Stewart's archdiaconal manse. Roused, he was astonished to see them, but agreed strongly that their flight was necessary and wise. He was as shocked as they were over David's death, although he had heard no details. The rumour had indeed reached St. Andrews that the prince had been starved to death; and whilst that might be inaccurate, he acceded that death was unlikely to have been from sudden illness or by accident, in the circumstances. Jamie's account of what he had learned at Lindores appalled him.

In practical matters Mary's brother was a great help — seeming not in the least embarrassed by the presence of the lady who was currently sharing his bed with him. Jamie had not forgotten the ship in which he had taken refuge at St. Andrews harbour, and reckoning that sea transport was the safest method of eluding Albany's possible clutches, wondered if Holy Church could help. Thomas said to leave it to him. One way or another the Church controlled much of what went on at St. Andrews haven, and it would be a strange thing if he

305

could not find a skipper to sail at short notice and put them ashore somewhere on the Angus or Aberdeenshire coast, from which it would be comparatively simple to reach Badenoch. Jamie suggested the North Angus port of Montrose, not very far from Edzell, where the Earl of Crawford was apt to have his domicile. He would aid them on their way.

So Thomas left them, presently, to go to St. Andrews, four miles distant, while the fugitives rested. He was back in mid-afternoon, with all in train. A coasting vessel going to Aberdeen would take them, with the next morning's tide. They would not even have to risk going to St. Andrews; the *Good Cheer* would come to the nearby harbour of Crail for them, this evening. They could go aboard after dark, and sail with the early tide. If this south-easterly breeze held they could be at Montrose, only thirty-five sea miles to the north, by the following evening.

None found fault with that programme.

That night they said goodbye to Thomas Stewart at the fishing haven of Crail, round the other side of thrusting Fife Ness. The *Good Cheer* was already tied up at the quayside, a medium-sized, sturdy-looking craft, unlovely and smelling of hides but adequate for their purpose. They bade farewell to their escort, too, save for Tom Durie who would go with them to act general aide and factotum — for there was no accommodation for horses on the ship, and it was hoped that, anyway, a mounted escort would not be necessary where they were going. The children were happier than ever, secretly boarding a ship by night. Their elders were less appreciative of smelly and cramped quarters, but grateful enough nevertheless.

They sailed at first light, beating precisely up the glittering path of the rising sun.

It was only a fair day's sail, across the Tay estuary and up the Angus coast, to Montrose, although it would have been a ride of more than a hundred miles by land; and with a south-easterly breeze backing south, they made it in excellent time, although latterly the sea became distinctly jabbly, with a strengthening wind crossing a long ocean swell. Fortunately, living at Aberdour, they were all used to boats and sailing, and the motion upset none of them. With the Highland mountains, still snow-streaked, beckoning them on, they put into the large harbour at the mouth of the great and almost landlocked Montrose basin where the South Esk reached the sea, in late afternoon.

This was Lindsay country, and when Jamie announced that he was making for the Earl of Crawford's castle of Edzell, in the Mounth foothills, he met with no difficulties from the burghers of Montrose. Hiring a guide and horses, they set out within an hour or so, westwards up the Esk valley. There was no need for secrecy here.

It was some sixteen miles to Edzell, and they put up for the night at the inn at Dun, five miles on their way, well satisfied with progress.

They came to Edzell next midday, in the mouth of Glen Esk, with the great Highland hills drawing close now, a lovely country of woodlands and green braes under the white-patched brown giants of the heather mountains. They were fairly sure of their reception here, for not only did the Earl David approve of Jamie, in his gruff way, as a fellow-warrior, but he was wed to the Lady Katherine Stewart, another of Robert the Second's daughters, and therefore half-sister to Mary. As sisters they had never been close, for Katherine was considerably older; but the fact that she, like her husband, heartily disliked her brother Albany, helped.

They were indeed kindly received, and when the circumstances were explained, pressed to stay indefinitely. Their host and hostess had not heard of David's death, and were much startled and distressed, the Earl vowing that Robert Stewart would pay dearly for such a deed. It was tempting to stay there at Edzell; but Jamie recognised that he would not feel really safe before he had put a broad barrier of the Highland mountains between them and the Albany-dominated Lowlands. They agreed to stay for a day or two however, before commencing the long journey across the uplands to Badenoch, another hundred difficult miles at least. Meanwhile the Earl would send messengers ahead to Sir Alexander Stewart at Lochindorb, to acquaint him of their coming; and when they went, they would go with a good Lindsay escort through that wild land. With this they were well enough content.

Edzell Castle was a pleasant place to linger, within its green enclave, its attendant township nearby. It was by no means the Earl's major seat; but he had been Lindsay of Glenesk before he succeeded to the chiefship of his line, and this had always been his home. He found it preferable to his many and larger houses in the south, particularly as he found little to tempt him towards Court attendance these days. The travellers, feeling distinctly less like fugitives now, indeed remained there longer than they had intended, whilst Jamie discussed endlessly with the Earl methods by which Albany might be made to pay for his crimes. It was decided that, in the first instance, Crawford should combine with the Lord of Dalkeith in demanding either a parliamentary or Privy Council investigation of the prince's death, with a view to arraigning Albany and his henchmen on a trial for murder and high treason, this to be set in motion forthwith. If that failed to produce adequate results, a meeting of the Estates of Parliament should be called for — which would be necessary anyway for the appointment of a new Lieutenant or Governor. Moreover, the King should be urged vigorously to place the young James, now heir to the throne and Prince of Scotland, in some sure place of safety, if necessary overseas, perhaps even in France.

It was on the fifth day of their stay at Edzell, with an escort assembled and plans made to start off the following morning, that the Earl's messengers returned from the North — and Alex Stewart himself with them. He greeted the travellers with warm sympathy and affection. When he had heard of their present predicament, he had dropped all and come hot-foot. He mourned his Cousin David, damned his Uncle Albany, feared for Scotland, and welcomed his friends to the Highlands. They might be driven from their own home, but they would find another meantime at Lochindorb, where they should stay for as long as they cared — the longer the better. His mother sent warmest greetings, and was preparing the North-West Tower for them. Badenoch was theirs, and nothing that anyone south of the Highland Line could do or say need concern them. There *he* ruled, and no writ ran contrary to his own.

With that welcome and assurance next morning they made their farewells at Edzell, and turned their backs on even the sight of Lowland Scotland — for how long they could not tell.

XVII

JAMIE DOUGLAS COULD scarcely credit it, but the next few months of 1402 were amongst the happiest of all his life. He felt somehow that it should not be so, exiled from his home, his prince and friend unavenged, all he had worked for in the melting-pot and the realm abused, under threat of invasion and in a state of chaos. Moreover, it seemed the more improbable circumstance that he should feel so well content, so much one of the family almost, in this castle of Lochindorb amongst the heather moors of Braemoray, where once he had been a prisoner and indeed feared for his very life. But this was the situation, with not only himself thoroughly and comfortably settled, but his wife and children also, all enjoying a Highland summer on the roof of Scotland in excellent and friendly company — and seeing a deal more of their husband and father than was their wont at Aberdour. Mariota de Athyn, Alex's mother, was kindness itself, a magnificent woman still, only in her early fifties, who frankly informed Mary that it was as well that she was there, or she herself might be inclined to lose her silly old head over dark Jamie Douglas — but who nevertheless quickly became Mary's bosom companion. Alex was his unfailing, friendly, courteous self. And Sir James, his youngest brother, had developed into quite a personable young man — whilst the other three tough and somewhat oafish sons of the Wolf were little in evidence at Lochindorb, all having fled the osprey's nest and now roosting in other Badenoch castles. The only daughter of the unofficial union had now also gone, married to the youthful Earl of Sutherland. Mariota, like her eldest son, was clearly delighted at the influx of young folk into the loch-girt stronghold.

With hunting, hawking, fishing, visiting clan chiefs and accompanying Alex on his judicial duties — for he was still acting Deputy Justiciar of the North, none other having come north to supersede him — the time went in pleasantly. Alex was clearly both respected and popular — as indeed had been his father, the Wolf, up here, despite their astonishingly differing characters. In the South he might be only the bastard son of the late and unlamented Earl of Buchan, not even lawful Lord of Badenoch and Lochaber; but in the North he was accepted as a power in the land, the figure around which the otherwise feuding clans would rally, with his own proud patronymic of *Mac Alastair Mhic an Righ*, Son of Alexander, son of the King. He spoke Gaelic like a native — as indeed he was — and dressed normally in tartans. But he could play the King's grandson when so he wished, with marvellous authority and dignity, much more so than any of his innumerable cousins, save for the late David himself. Somewhere there was a hint of steel behind the gently assured and thoughtful manner. Jamie rejoiced to have him as friend — but would not have liked to have him as enemy.

Despite their distance and comparative detachment from southern affairs, the visitors were surprised to find how well-informed they were at Lochindorb. Holy Church was largely responsible for this, for, unlike his father, Alex made a point of keeping on good terms with the churchmen, and there was a constant coming and going between North and South of monkish couriers, wandering friars and diocesan officials, the clerics recognising no division in the realm as did secular folk. Alex had an understanding that, in return for his concern and protection as Justiciar, the Church kept him up-to-date with news. He also had his own sources of information in the Moray sea ports, where news from Aberdeen was quickly relayed.

By these means they learned that the death of his son, although it had undoubtedly further shattered the composure of the unhappy monarch, at least seemed to have aroused in him a spark of spirit. He was said to be refusing Albany audience, and had put Turnberry Castle almost into a state of siege. He had given authority for the Privy Council to command a judicial enquiry into David's fate, and this was to be held at Holy Rood Abbey on the 16th of May, Albany, Douglas, Ramorgnie and Lindsay all cited to compear. He had, totally unexpectedly, taken the matter of the bishopric of St. Andrews into his own hands, had turned down Albany's candidate, Bishop Greenlaw of Aberdeen, the Chancellor, and appointed Henry Wardlaw, his former chaplain, Precentor of Glasgow and nephew of the late Cardinal-Bishop of Glasgow, to the see — to the delight of most churchmen, who did not want Greenlaw, already powerful enough, to have authority over them as Primate. Wardlaw was a quiet studious man, no ambitious cleric, and undoubtedly the College of Bishops would happily appoint him Primate in due course. A further item of interest was that Douglas seemed to have taken over the matter of the defence of the realm, Albany being no soldier. He was instigating a series of raids over the Border, with the object of keeping the Northern English ill-at-ease and unprepared to leave their home areas to join King Henry's muster, in case of attack. The first of these raids had already taken place, under Sir John Haliburton of Dirleton, penetration having been made as far south as Bamburgh, much devastation done and considerable booty taken, with some prisoners captured for ransom. There was no lack of volunteers for further such adventures.

"You wish that you were there, Jamie?" Alex asked. "You are good at that, are you not?"

He shook his head. "Raiding, reiving, I have never loved. To sally against an armed enemy, yes, pitting wits against his, defeating him if may be. But descending upon an undefended countryside and laying all waste, burning and harrying — that is not to my taste."

"Yet it is an established Border custom, is it not? At which the Douglases have ever been foremost?"

"Perhaps. But that commends it nothing to me. Any more than your Highland clan feuding appeals to you."

"If the clans did not feud, I fear that they might turn their steel on other targets less able to defend themselves! This is something I aimed to speak to you about, Jamie. For most of the year the Highlander has insufficient to do. The pastoral life scarcely demands enough of a man. Tending flocks and herds on the high pastures is boys' work, not men's. There is little tilling of the soil, as in the Lowlands. Most work is done by the women. Men cannot be hunting and fishing all the time. Once the peats are dug, the wood cut, the sheep clipped and the hides tanned, the women can do the rest. Save perhaps distil the spirits! Which leaves much time for other activities!"

Alex shook his head. "It is my fear that some day someone will learn how to unite the clans, halt the feuding, and turn them against the South. That would be an ill day for Scotland."

"You surprise me," Jamie said. "I believed that you misliked the South and loved your Highlandmen?"

"To some extent that is true. I mislike the arrogant Southron belief that all north of the Highland Line are barbarians, savages. There is a deal that we could teach the South, yes. I resent the notion that we are scarcely part of the realm of Scotland because we speak a different language. It is the *ancient* language of Scotland. We are the true Scots, having the pure blood, not mixed with Saxon or Norman. I mean, my mother's people. She was a Mackay. My father, being a Stewart, was as Norman as the rest!"

"The Douglases are a true Celtic race," Jamie asserted. "Lords of Douglasdale when the Stewarts were still French land-stewards."

"Yes. But do most Douglases love their Highland cousins? Or despise them? That is the test."

The other was silent.

"I say that there is but one realm of Scotland, Highland and Lowland, under the one High King of Scots — who draws his title and line from the Highlands, mark you. *Ard Righ*. The division, the gulf between us, is bad. And dangerous. If the Highlanders, aroused by resentment, united to attack the South, it could be a disaster. For the Highlanders would win, in the first instance. They are the fiercest fighters, by far."

"And you fear this, Alex?"

"I do. Have done, ever since my brothers made their great raid on the South after the burning of Elgin. Partly to gain *my* release from my Uncle Robert's castle, the same in which David died. That showed me what might be, Jamie. They carried all before them, defeated the best the South could throw against them. You know that."

"But is there the least fear of it, today?"

"There could be. Donald. Donald of the Isles could do it — and might. He is no fool. He can see the possibilities, the threat. He is the descendant and representative of the ancient Celtic and Norse Kings of the Isles, who once governed much of the Highlands. He is also lawful grandson of Robert the Second, great-great-grandson of the Bruce. As indeed am I — but he is legitimate. He greatly resents Robert Stewart, who has stolen his Ross earldom from him. He *could* send out the fiery cross, to unite the clans and march against the South."

The other stared. "But . . . *would* he? Might he?"

"There are rumours that he considers the matter. With David dead, he sees Albany as undisputed master of Scotland — and does not like the sight!"

"Nor do others. I had no notion that you feared this, Alex."

"I have done, for long. I spoke of it to David. But David's death makes it all a deal more urgent. More likely."

"A stroke against Albany I would not greatly grieve over. But a Highland attack on the South, civil war — that is different."

"Yes. Robert would be the last one to suffer, if I know my uncle! The clans could never be controlled, once they were victorious, south of the Line. It would be massacre. Your Border raiding would pale before it. Centuries of debts to pay off. The land would be submerged in blood. I know my people. And whatever the final result, the cause of the unity of the realm would be set back for generations."

"This, this is something quite new to me. I swear none in the South think aught of it, perceive any threat. Is there anything that can be done?"

"I do not know. It is one reason why I welcomed you the more, Jamie — I admit it. You are a fighter, and with sound wits. I value your advice and aid, as well as your company!"

"Then you think this is urgent? For now, not for some future time?"

"It could be any time. Donald keeps calling councils of his Islesmen, at Islay. And consulting the mainland chiefs — especially those in what he still considers to be his earldom of Ross. Albany's goodson, the so-called Earl of Ross, is never there to check them, a Lowlander and a weakling. And Donald keeps sending messengers to Drummond, at Kildrummy. What for, I do not know. But . . ."

"Drummond? Sir Malcolm, of Cargil and Stobhall? The late Queen's brother? The Countess of Mar's husband?"

"The same. She is my friend. That is how I know of this. It troubles me, as it does her. If Drummond was to unite with Donald in this matter, it could be direly dangerous. Drummond has great power in the South-East Highlands — his own large clan of Drummond, and some sway over the great Mar earldom.

He is linked in kinship to half of Atholl and Breadalbane. With Donald in the west and Drummond in the east, all the Highlands could be taken in . . ."

"But why, Alex? Why should Drummond make common cause with the Islesman?"

"For the same reason as might you! Fear, and hatred, of Albany. You are not the only one to be concerned over David's death, Jamie, to see the writing on the wall. Albany will have this kingdom, if he can; has gone a far way to getting it. He must be stopped, if possible. Many will see that. But — it must not be at the cost of savage war between Highlands and Lowlands, I say. Not delivery at Donald's hands."

"I see that, yes. But this of Drummond. I cannot see him in Donald's camp. He is no longer young, a man who takes little part in affairs of the realm now, however powerful. A strange man, yes — but scarcely one to resort to arms. What has he in common with the Lord of the Isles — save this hatred of Albany?"

"They are kin. Drummond's aunt was Queen to David the Second, his sister Queen to King Robert. Donald is linked to both. And each man has a grudge, through their wives. Donald's wife is daughter of the last Earl of Ross, and is deprived of her inheritance by Albany's machinations. Drummond is deprived of the unentailed lands of Douglas, which *his* wife, your Earl James's sister, should have heired. They *may* not be in alliance — but it is very possible. If I knew what these messengers were about. Donald's messengers are apt to mean trouble. He is certainly planning some adventure in force — all reports say that. I believe he may strike when the South is engaged with the English. That has always been the Islesmen's strategy. That is why I do not like these sallies of Douglas over the Border. They are bound to provoke retaliation from Henry. If we have full war with England — then, I say, look out for Donald! And possibly Drummond. And who knows what others . . ."

Uneasily they left it at that.

* * *

It was three weeks later, and well into the second half of May, with no significant news reaching them meantime, that another visitor arrived at Lochindorb — Thomas Stewart. He came, not as any sort of fugitive or refugee, but to see how his sister fared, breaking his journey to the Chanonry of Ross in the Black Isle,

314

on an errand for the new Primate-elect to the Bishop of Ross. He had come by sea to the port of Findhorn on the Moray coast, and from there had found his way up the river of that name, and the Dorback Burn, with a friar as guide provided by the Abbot of Kinloss.

The Douglases rejoiced to see him, the Lady Mariota to welcome what she might almost look upon as a hitherto unknown brother-in-law, and Alex as an uncle.

At the dais-table in the hall that night, after the meal and with the lesser folk withdrawn, all sought the Archdeacon's news, which so far he had only hinted at. Although the visitors were happy enough with their present life in the North, their desire and need for news of the South was not to be denied.

"What of the trial, Thomas?" Jamie demanded. "The judicial enquiry of the Privy Council, or whatever it was to be called? Was it over when you left?"

"It was over before it started!" his brother-in-law declared. "What else did you expect? It was never other than a mummery — Robert saw to that."

"But . . . were they not questioned? Something of the truth brought out?"

"The truth? What is the truth, Jamie? The truth, the realm is assured, is now ascertained, made clear to all and for all time. David, Prince of Scotland, by God's will, died of a sickness, a flux of the bowels, no doubt due to his wayward living. Although well looked after at his uncle's castle of Falkland by kindly servitors, he sickened, waned and died — an act of God, for which none were to be blamed. The Duke of Rothesay departed this life by Divine Providence, and nothing else. All witnesses called testified to it."

"But . . . but . . . this is crazy-mad! Of course Albany and Ramorgnie would so claim. But what of the rest of the Privy Council? What of Crawford? My father? They would not accept such shameful travesty?"

"They had little choice. The Council could not all sit in judgement. So they appointed a panel. And no doubt Robert knew how to get at the panel. The witnesses were carefully chosen . . ."

"What of David's fingers? Gnawed at. How did they explain that?"

"They did not require to. It was not mentioned."

"Witnesses at Lindores Abbey could have testified to it."

315

"No witnesses from Lindores were called, David being dead two days before his body was brought there."

"Dear God — I should have stayed. *I* would have testified to another tune. I should never have fled here . . ."

"Your testimony would have been only hearsay, inadmissible. But think you that you would ever have been allowed to testify, man? You would have been disposed of, long before that. Robert, whatever else, knows what he is at."

"I thank God that we did flee," Mary said. "Otherwise I would have been a widow by now, I swear!"

"And the rest of the Council did nothing?"

"What could they do? They had appointed a panel, and the panel found thus. They could disagree, privily, at the next Council-meeting. But one or two individuals could not disown the lawfully appointed panel and its findings, however much they might dissent."

"I never expected otherwise," Mary said. "It is not by such methods that Robert will be brought to book — if ever he is."

Her brother nodded. "It was a shrewd move to have the Earl of Douglas arraigned with Robert and the others — shrewd on Robert's part. Few would wish to challenge both Stewart *and* Douglas power. Your chief, I have no doubt, had nothing to do with David being starved to death — and so he helped to exonerate the others."

"So nothing is to be done? David's murder goes unpunished? The King and the realm accept this play-acting as truth, and none suffer for vilely slaying the heir to the throne?"

None answered those rhetorical questions. But Thomas Stewart dryly made the position crystal-clear. "The Council finished not only by declaring all innocent, but by announcing that all subjects of the King without exception were forbidden to detract, by word or deed, from the fair fame of the Duke of Albany and the Earl of Douglas. God Save the King!"

Out of the grim silence that greeted that, the Archdeacon went on. "But at least the King is warned. I have word from the new Bishop Wardlaw that John intends to place his new heir, James, in *his* care and keeping, at St. Andrews Castle, where I also can help keep watch over him. That far he has seen the light."

"And will young James be safe at St. Andrews?" Mary asked.

"Safer than anywhere else, I would think. Robert will not

wish too greatly to antagonise Holy Church, at this stage. Particularly while this trouble with England simmers."

"Yes," Alex put in. "This of England? What is the latest, there? We heard of Haliburton's raid — naught since."

"It is a great folly. Douglas is determined to keep on with these raids, possibly lead one himself. He says, to prevent Henry from invading Scotland. But it seems to me more like to *provoke* the Plantagenet into so doing. They say that Robert himself is in doubt about it. But he needs Douglas and so will not restrain him, even if he could, for Douglas is Chief Warden of the Marches."

"It is folly, yes," Alex agreed. "Is this Douglas a fool?"

"I think he feels that it is expected of him — as Douglas. A reputation to keep up. Always they have been great warriors. The first Earl led many raids. Earl James won Otterburn. Archie the Grim likewise. The present Earl's illegitimate brother, Will of Nithsdale, a notable hero. Even Jamie here, something of another. This Earl is not of the same quality, but would have men believe that he is. And he has his family feud with the Percy. And now also with Dunbar, who is aiding Hotspur."

"His feuds could cost Scotland dear! Dearer than he knows."

"There is word that Henry has sent instructions to his March Wardens and sheriffs, and all Border lords, to muster their fullest strength. And keep their men in armed readiness. He is dealing with Owen Glendower again, meantime. But after that . . ."

"Glendower?" Jamie asked. "Have the Welsh risen again?"

"Yes. Had you not heard? All the Welsh Marches are aflame once more, seeking to throw off the English yoke. Owen claims that he alone is Prince of Wales."

"Thank God for Owen Glendower!" Alex said. "If Donald knows of this — and I shall make sure that he does — then it may delay him. He will wish to move south at the same time as Henry moves north, for greatest effect. This may give us time . . ."

"Donald? You mean the Islesman?" Thomas asked. "What is this . . .?"

His nephew explained his fears.

Thomas stayed a few days with them at Lochindorb, apparently in little hurry to move on to the Black Isle. When he did decide to go, Alex said that he would escort him down into the Laigh of Moray, and then turn south and visit Kildrummy

317

Castle in Mar. He wished to discover, if he could, just what Sir Malcolm Drummond was up to. He suggested that Jamie should accompany them.

The night before they left, Mariota de Athyn came to the North Tower, where the Douglases were ensconced, to speak with Jamie. Recognising that privacy was desired, Mary excused herself and went to the children.

The woman who had been the Wolf of Badenoch's mistress and best influence, came straight to the point, being of a direct nature.

"I am concerned about Alex and the Countess of Mar," she said. "You know of the association, Jamie?"

"Yes," he said, warily.

"I am in no state of grace to offer blame," she sighed. "But Alex is the best of my clutch, a son to be proud of — and with large responsibilities. I can see this entanglement harming him. Isobel Douglas is much older than is he, and married to a powerful man. She is a lusty and indiscreet woman. So am I, no doubt! But I do not control a great earldom, and am not wed to the King's good-brother."

"No."

"I have reason to be anxious, Jamie. This woman has her claws in Alex. It is not some passing fancy — it has been going on now for three years."

"You are sure that the claws are not Alex's? He is no child, no youngling, to lead by the nose. A man of much strength . . ."

"All that, yes. But still, in some ways, innocent. Unversed in the ways of the world, and of women. Reared here amongst the mountains. No courtier. Perhaps I am in some measure to blame. But he is no match for Isobel of Mar."

"You may be right. But . . . he will do what he wants to do."

"You have much influence with him, Jamie. He admires you greatly. If you would watch him, seek to guide him . . .?"

"In such matters one man cannot guide another. You should know that. I would, belike, do more harm than good were I to interfere."

"Not interfere, Jamie, just watch. A word here and there, discreetly. That is all I am asking, as a friend."

"If I see opportunity," he said, doubtfully. "I do not like this of the Countess, myself. I have naught against her, my former master's sister. But she is scarcely right for Alex."

"No. And the business with Malcolm Drummond is dangerous. He is a strange man. Alex conceives him to be a poor husband to Isobel Douglas, declares her a deprived and wronged woman. I say that one can look after herself! But I think that she uses that to hold Alex."

"Drummond could be all that . . ."

"Yes. But they have been married for long, twenty years. Late to be rescuing her! And this of Donald of the Isles. She uses that also, if you ask me. An excuse for messages, letters. He too, perhaps . . ."

"I'd swear that Alex is honestly concerned. Over the possibility of the Drummond and Donald planning an uprising."

"Yes. But he is well aware that it offers him opportunity also. As now. It troubles me. Alex may run into serious danger, interfering with Drummond. He is too powerful to antagonise so."

"But if the realm is endangered?"

"The realm has managed well enough without Alex Stewart hitherto!"

"A Highland invasion of the South would have to be stopped, if possible."

"No doubt. But not necessarily by Alex. Nor by Jamie Douglas, for that matter! Let Robert of Albany see to his own defences."

"Neither of us would lift a hand to save Albany. It is the bloodshed, rapine and pains of civil war which we would wish to save, the clans unleashed on an undefended land."

"A land that never fails to slight us. Despises the clans and calls us savages?"

"Even so . . ."

"I know. Forgive me, Jamie. But you will try to guide Alex? In the matter of this woman? Do what you can?"

"I will try, yes . . ."

*   *   *

They came to Kildrummy in the Garioch of Mar four evenings later, to a casually warm welcome from the Countess Isobel, her husband again not at home — and Jamie with a shrewd notion that his friend knew that he would not be. *An Drumanach Mor* had his great estates in Perthshire to manage, of course, not to mention the Countess's southern lands. Jamie also had the impression, perhaps inevitably, that though Isobel Douglas greeted himself civilly enough, she would have preferred his absence. That Alex had asked him to come, in the circumstances, might have held some significance.

Kildrummy was a large fortress of a place on the Upper Don, and Jamie had long thought it strange that so lively and strong-minded a woman as the Countess should coop herself up in this remote upland valley when she, as well as her husband, had so many south-country properties. But here, of course, she was undisputed queen, and over a vast territory.

In the silver-gilt evening of early June, they sat on the parapet-walk of the castle's Snow Tower, and gazed out over the fair and farflung countryside, so green, so different from the true Highlands to north and west, despite the range upon range of blue Aberdeenshire hills which rimmed the horizon, it seemed, to infinity. As far as they could see, it was all Mar — and a deal further still.

"A noble heritage," Alex said. "The realm's most ancient earldom, a lordship lost in time, before even earls and mormaors were."

"To be sure. But a *lordship*, not a ladyship!" the Countess answered. "It requires a man's hand, a man's strong hand."

Surprised, they looked at her.

"You have a husband," Alex said, almost roughly for him.

"Malcolm Drummond and I were wed almost as children," she replied. "He is not the man I would have chosen for husband. Nor the man to manage my earldom. I have never made him Earl of Mar, in my right, as I could have done. Some say should. He is not of the quality for that."

Jamie coughed, embarrassed. "Sir Malcolm is namely as a proud lord. Has fought boldly. I have never heard his qualities questioned."

"Ah, but then you are not a woman, Sir James!" That was tart.

"But he has *some* say in the earldom, has he not, Isobel?" Alex demanded. "He has raised men from it, ere this?"

"To be sure. He looks after my rents. He is good at that! Some of my vassals look to him, rather than to me."

"If he sought to raise men from the earldom, today — how many would follow him?"

"If I said yes, four thousand."

"And if *not*?"

"One thousand, perhaps, Or less."

"M'mmm. Even a thousand, horsed men of Mar, could

320

greatly aid a Highland invasion of the South. In especial, with another thousand *Drummond* horsed men-at-arms. Cavalry Donald lacks."

"But . . . have you reason to believe that Sir Malcolm will join the Lord of the Isles?" Jamie looked at the Countess rather than at his friend. "Has this fear aught to support it? Other than, than . . ."

"Other than a woman's malice towards a failed husband?" she finished for him. "I believe so, Sir James. Constant messengers arrive from the Isles. He has never had such exchange before, with Donald. And he is concerned with matters of arms and men, as I have not known him before. He does not confide in me, in this. He is unusually secretive."

"It could mean much, or little," Jamie insisted. "He does not love the Duke of Albany. He may therefore be looking but to his own defences — as many another must be doing in Scotland today."

"And this of Donald? What of the Islesman?"

"They are kin, after a fashion."

"Have been all these years. And never required such coming and going. And this secrecy. We have gone our own ways, for long. But do not seek to hide too much from each other." There was a certain significance in the look she gave Alex as she said that.

He coughed, "If we could lay hands on one of these messengers," he said, "or get one of your vassals whom Sir Malcolm is close to. Get them to talk . . ."

"Less than easy, I should think. But try, by all means. You act Lieutenant and Justiciar of the North — perhaps you have methods to make folk speak?" She paused. "How long will Robert Stewart leave you in that position, Alex?"

He shrugged. "He tried to unseat my father in that, and could not. I think he will be no more successful with me. No doubt he has already appointed some other. His son Murdoch again, perhaps? But that is little to the point, north of the Highland Line. The danger to my position, I'd say, does not come from Albany but from Donald of the Isles. He could overturn all."

They sat until the last light faded from the sky to the northwest, and a coolness stirred them. Isobel Douglas rose.

"I shall retire to my virtuous couch, my friends," she said. "I may even sleep — who knows? Your chambers await you.

Inform me if I may do aught further for your comfort. My room is in this tower."

They bowed, wordless.

There was a long silence after she left them.

"You are very quiet, Jamie," Alex said, at length. "You do not greatly approve of our hostess, I think?"

"Not so. I find her a fine woman — fair, strong, able. Aye, that and more."

"But . . . ?"

"It is you that I am concerned for, Alex — not her. You are . . . fond of her?"

"Yes."

"You know best. But . . . is it wise?"

"Wise? Is it wisdom you seek, in a woman?"

"No. But unwisdom can always be dangerous. The price to pay for it."

"You mean that she is forty-two years old — fifteen more than am I? And wed to *An Drumanach Mor*, chief of his name and a powerful lord. A countess in her own right — too high for the Wolf of Badenoch's bastard? All this I know, Jamie. But I am fond of her, nevertheless."

"Aye, no doubt. But where will that bring you? Save into disrepute and possible danger. If you tamper with his wife, Drummond is not going to like it — even though he does neglect her. And if you further interfere with his plans, it could cost you dear. The dearer."

"Are you concerned for my soul? Or my safety? Or this realm of ours?"

The other was silent.

"I am sorry, Jamie. We will not come to blows over this. Your concern for me I cherish. But in this matter I must follow my own path."

"Yes. As you will." He touched the other's shoulder. "I am for my bed."

"Good night, then, Jamie. Tomorrow we shall go see some of the Drummond's friends. Discover what we may."

Although Jamie lay awake in his room for long that night, he did not hear Alex Stewart come into the next chamber.

* * *

In the next few days they called upon three or four fairly prominent vassals of Mar, indicated to them by the Countess as being supporters of her husband, beginning with Forbes of Glencuie, known as Chamberlain of Mar, who acted steward to the earldom. They did not visit only these, of course, which might have been too obvious; so they had to make many calls, combining it all with hawking and hunting and the like. They learned comparatively little, save that something was definitely afoot, concerned with the mustering, arming and training of men, the reasons therefor always given as merely the uncertainties and dangers of the times consequent upon the death of the Duke of Rothesay, anarchy in the realm and the English threat. Few of those interviewed were actually subtle or devious characters, and the enquirers came to the conclusion that, in the main, they were not being deliberately misled. The Chamberlain was rather different, admittedly, a wary man, obsequious as far as his mistress was concerned, but less than open towards her guests, and clearly knowing more than he admitted. But at no time did they get the least hint of a link with Donald of the Isles; and without making their suspicions altogether too plain, they dared not themselves introduce the name of that faraway western potentate.

On the sixth day of their stay, they returned from a boar-hunt in the Ladder Hills to discover Sir Malcolm himself back at Kildrummy. He was a rather fine-looking man, now in his middle sixties, stockily built, with a leonine head of greying hair and the curious habit of looking slightly over the heads of those he spoke to. He greeted Alex Stewart only coolly civil, but was quite affable towards Jamie, whom he had known slightly since the latter's boyhood when he was the Earl of Douglas's page and esquire, and of whose activities he seemed generally to approve. But the arrival of *An Drumanach Mor* nevertheless put something of a damper on the visit.

They saw little of him that first evening, for after the meal he disappeared. That night was the first in which, so far as he could judge, Jamie's companion spent all the time in his own bedchamber.

Next morning, Sir Malcolm appeared to be in good fettle and declared that he was going to visit his new castle of Kindrochit, in Brae Mar, some twenty-three miles to the south, and suggested that the visitors might like to accompany him. They could scarcely refuse, even had they wished to — although the Countess Isobel rather pointedly announced that she would stay at home.

As they rode into the forenoon sun, through the green rolling hills of Cromar, it was noticeable that it was Drummond who was now the questioner. In a conversational but quietly persistent way, he wanted to know what they were seeking in Mar; how they saw the situation consequent upon David Stewart's death; what they thought of the Duke of Albany; whether the realm would accept the verdict of the parliamentary enquiry; whether they believed English invasion to be imminent or merely a useful threat; whether Alex was likely to remain Justiciar. And so on.

They answered him with some degree of caution — although he asked nothing which was an actual embarrassment. Until he said,

"And what part do you see our Highlands as playing on this changing scene, Stewart? Great or small? None of our concern? Or much our concern?"

"Much," Alex answered, after a moment, briefly.

"So say I," the other nodded. "For too long the North has turned its back on the South, and the South scorned the North. We can do better than that."

"To be sure. But . . . it depends what you mean by betterment? Better for whom?"

"Better for the Highlands. Better for our people. It is time."

"Perhaps. But not at the rest of the realm's cost."

"That need not be."

"My lord, you have had long experience of fighting and war, I know. But it has not been Highland war, I think? You have fought in England and on the Border. Have you ever seen how the clans fight? Not just feud, but war. In a defenceless land. I have. The Islesmen, now? Have you seen what they can do to a country? My Lochaber, see you. Slaughter of women and children, fire, rapine, destruction, death to everything that lives, man and beast. I have seen this time and again. Would you see it unleashed upon the South, where there are the many more people?"

Drummond frowned. "No. But that could not happen. Under good and sufficient leadership."

"What would you name good and sufficient leadership? The Lord of the Isles himself? Clanranald? Maclean of Duart? I have seen Alastair Carrach, Donald's own brother, leading just such warfare. Maclean likewise."

The other snorted. "Your father, Sir Alexander, would have seen little so wrong with that, I warrant!"

Alex drew himself up in his saddle. "I am not my father, sir," he said stiffly. "Nor was he so ill a man as some would make out." And he reined back a little from Drummond's side — Jamie of course doing the same.

They rode on, after that, for some considerable distance, unspeaking.

They came to Kindrochit, in the upper valley of the great Dee, where the Clunie Water dropped to the river, where there was a ferry. Here a fine new castle was arising on the massive foundations of an earlier stronghold of Malcolm Canmore's, the tall outer curtain-walls already completed. Drummond explained that it was necessary to control the caterans who were forever raiding down from the mountains, here where two great droving routes across the Mounth met, down Glen Clunie and Glen Shee to Atholl and over the Fir Mounth to the Cairn o' Mount passes to Angus. He did not actually state that the caterans involved were apt to be those of Badenoch, and quite frequently led by one or other of Alex's deplorable brothers, but that was clearly implied, and no doubt the reason for this excursion. That the Justiciar should keep his own kin in order, as well as others, was the lesson to be inferred — and then law-abiding men would not have to build expensive castles in out-of-the-way places to maintain the King's peace.

Alex swallowed all this with admirable self-control and seeming imperturbability — although Jamie knew that he seethed beneath the calm surface.

An Drumanach Mor was clearly no turner of the other cheek.

The long ride back to Kildrummy was more notable for its silences than for pleasant converse.

That night, Alex Stewart announced to his hostess that they would have to be on their way back to Braemoray next morning. Being a realist, the Countess did not urge them to stay. Jamie at least was well content.

They arrived back at Lochindorb to find two items of news awaiting them. One was from one of Alex's regular sources of information in the South, to say that there had been a disastrous Scots raid over the Border, led by young Sir Patrick Hepburn of Hailes, which had not only been driven back with heavy casualties from Northumberland but had been followed up by a large English force under Hotspur Percy and Dunbar and utterly decimated at Nisbet Moor in the West Merse. Many prominent Scots knights had been slain and many more captured.

The second item was a letter for Jamie from the Earl of Douglas no less, sent by a special messenger who was waiting to take back an answer. In it, after the usual honorifics and preamble, he wrote, in the same stilted and awkward manner in which he spoke:

. . . They tell me that you blame me in some measure for David Stewart's death. I had no hand in that, I promise you. I but believed him to be held at Falkland for a time. If there was ill done, it was not with my knowledge. I do not deceive you. They say also that you have gone to Badenoch in fear for your life. You need have no fear. You are ever my good friend. The Douglas power will protect you against any soever. This on my honour. I wish that you come back. I need you. As does the realm. It is to be war with England. Not raiding but full war. We have suffered a grievous defeat under Hepburn. Now George Dunbar and the Percy lay waste the East and Middle Marches. Henry Paget musters his fullest forces at York, to invade our land. It is necessary to strike first. Before he returns from the Welsh Marches to lead it. I am assembling a great host. We muster at Dunbar. All Douglas to be there. Moray, Graham, Haliburton, Maxwell, Gordon, Montgomerie, Swinton. Even Murdoch Stewart of Fife. But I lack experienced leaders in war. Few have fought in true warfare as have you. I need your present aid. Your brothers come. Come you, Jamie.

I remain your friend,

DOUGLAS

Signed and sealed at Dunbar on Saint Swithin's Eve.

Long Jamie considered that letter and its implications before he showed it to Mary and then to Alex.

"I must go," he told them. "I cannot hold back. It may be foolish, but I am a Douglas, and this is my duty."

"This Earl may be your chief, and declares himself your friend," Mary said. "But what has he ever done for you? Would he have saved you from Robert?"

"He might. I did not give him opportunity. We do not know . . ."

"*Could* he save you from Robert, even now? How do you know that this is not a trap?"

"I think not. He stakes his honour on my protection. In writing. And it is not only Douglas. The realm needs me. We invade England in force. My brothers to be there. Would you have me to hold back when all others go?"

She shook her head at that, helplessly.

"My friend," Alex intervened. "It may be that you could serve the realm better here. In the North. This venture may well be what Donald has waited for. All the main forces of the South engaged over the Border. If he was to strike then, he would be all but unopposed. Save by me!"

Jamie frowned. "I see that, yes. But . . . it may not be. *You* fear it, but there is no certainty that the Islesmen will come. Or Drummond aid them. I cannot wait here, kicking my heels, when naught may happen. Besides, yours is a Highland matter. *I* am no leader of Highlanders. The clans have their own leaders."

"As you will," Alex said. "But I would have been glad of your support. When will you go?"

"So soon as I may. It is a long journey."

"We shall surely find a ship for you. From one of the Moray ports. That will land you in Lothian. Leith or even Dunbar itself. Save you much trouble and the dangers of crossing Uncle Robert's territories. Even with your Earl's messenger as escort!"

"Yes. I am sorry, Alex. It is something that I must do. You understand?"

XVIII

JAMIE LANDED AT Leith, not Dunbar, some ten days later, and hired a horse to take him the nine miles to Dalkeith. There his father rejoiced to see him, claiming that he had missed him sorely, and was glad to equip him with the armour, horses, body-servants and all that he required for a campaign. His two legitimate half-brothers, Sir James and Sir William, and his younger full brother Johnnie, had already gone to Dunbar, leading the Dalkeith contingent of some four hundred horsed men-at-arms for the national army.

The old lord was, however, considerably depressed about the state of Scotland, talking gloomily about wishing that he was well away and in his grave, with no desire to see what he feared was coming upon the kingdom. Jamie, who was fairly full of foreboding himself, found himself reassuring his sire that things were not so bad, that they would warstle through, that Albany would over-reach himself and meet his due deserts one day — and so on.

Old Sir James was much concerned about the safety of young James Stewart. He was now, at last, in the care of the new Primate, at St. Andrews Castle, ostensibly being tutored, the King having been sorely loth to be parted from the boy. But, though Bishop Wardlaw was a good man and reliable, if Albany was determined to take the child, the episcopal castle was insufficiently strong to withstand him, any more than the anathemas of Holy Church. Robert Stewart would pay as much attention to these as his brother Alec the Wolf had done. The child should be got out of the country, to safety — to France possibly, with the Pope, or the Low Countries. Otherwise, sooner or later, Albany was going to be king. And when that happened, all honest men beware! He, Dalkeith, had written to King Robert, but had received no reply.

Jamie admitted that, in this, his father's fears were no doubt justified — but did not see what was to be done about it.

Next day he rode the score of miles to Dunbar.

Despite himself and his forebodings, he could not quell a lift of the heart when he trotted down on to the coastal plain from the Lammermuir foothills. He had not seen such a colourful and spirited martial assembly in the fourteen years since 1388 and the great adventure which had ended in Otterburn, the murder of the Earl James Douglas and his own knighting. The entire plain around the little red town and its harbour and castle, outlined against the blue sea, was alive with men. In great ranks and squares and formations the tents and pavilions were pitched, each of the last in the colours of its lord, baron or knight, with his banner fluttering above. The horse-lines appeared to stretch for miles, the stands of arms were like a forest, the smoke of cooking-fires rose blue over all, and everywhere steel glinted in the sun. Men by their thousands were marshalled there, the might of a realm in arms. Whatever the cause, it was a stirring sight.

Picking out the various blazons as he approached, Jamie distinguished Seton, Haliburton, Sinclair, Montgomerie, Swinton, Scott, Leslie, Erskine, Graham and others that he did not recognise — as well as Stewart and Douglas, Moray and Lindsay. The Earl of Douglas had managed to assemble a notable and representative host, then — an excellent augury. Scotland was not done yet.

The Douglas banners were the most easily discerned, for there were many more of them than any others. They seemed to have almost a tented city to themselves, and Jamie made therefor.

Almost the first persons he saw, to recognise, were his two friends Will of Drumlanrig and Archibald of Cavers, who had been knighted with him after Otterburn. They were as joyous to see him as they were surprised, and soon had the entire Douglas camp in an uproar of welcome. Jamie was astonished to discover that, instead of being all but forgotten and possibly criticised for bolting off to the Highlands, his good name and fame were enhanced. He was the man who had given up all for the dead prince, the man who had escaped from St. Andrews Castle, the individual who defied the Governor, the hero of

Foulhope Haugh, Arkaig and Prestonkirk. Even his brothers added to this paean of praise — which was certainly not their custom. Quite overwhelmed by it all, Jamie had to recognise that it meant something when even the Earl Archibald came hot-foot, summoned from elsewhere, and greeted him almost effusively for that moody man.

"So you came, Jamie — you came!" he cried. "Good! Good! I rejoice to see you."

"I came because you besought me, my lord. And in the realm's need. Although I cannot see my service as so important . . ."

"But yes, my friend. We need you. We are scarce rich in seasoned fighters. We have many stout lords and knights, excellent in any tulzie, notable raiders, well versed in arms; but experienced in war — that is different. You have proved yourself on many fields. We could not spare you, hiding way in those ungodly Hielands, with the kingdom in danger, Jamie."

"I hid in the Highlands for my *life*'s sake, I'd mind you! Not from choice. Your friends, the Duke of Albany, Ramorgnie and Lindsay of Rossie had me imprisoned in St. Andrews Castle, with the Duke David. Had I not won out, as *he* did not, would I have been alive to come to you today?"

"M'mm. That was an ill business. Mismanaged. Naught to do with me, man . . ."

"I saw you ride into St. Andrews with the Duke of Albany, my lord. You rode out again, with those others, taking the Duke David to Falkland. Had I not escaped during the night, would I not also have been taken captive to Falkland? And fared any better than my master?"

There was a stirring amongst the assembled Douglases.

The Earl looked, and sounded, uncomfortable. "Not so, Jamie. I would have looked to your safety. But you had gone, none knew where. I could not help you when none could tell me where you might be. David was but to be warded, for his own good. *You* were in no danger, I swear."

"David was warded to his grave! You will forgive me, my lord, if I doubt your friends' goodwill and honest purpose."

"Damnation, man — these are not my friends!" the other cried. "You will find none of them here, in my host. Ramorgnie and Lindsay are ill limmers, Fifers with naught to do with me. Albany, acting Governor, called on me to aid him carry out the King's command. What happened after was none of my doing, or with my knowledge. You have my word for that. You are secure with me, Jamie, I promise you."

"Very well, my lord — I accept that. I would not have come else." Jamie glanced round the circle of faces, however, to ensure that there were sufficient witnesses. "Enough of that. Now I am here, what would you have of me?"

"Aye. In this venture I would have you ever close — to advise me, as you have done well, ere this. I do not give you a command — there are plenty for that. What I need is your wits and counsel."

"I cannot refuse you that — such as they are. But — what is intended? This venture? Just what do you attempt?"

"We wait a few more days, for more men, for further arms and supplies, above all, for more horses. I am having great numbers to come from Galloway. Then we march."

"Aye, but march where?"

"Into England — where else? Through Northumberland, to Newcastle, perhaps to Durham. English Henry is mustering all the North to arms. At present he himself is engaged in bringing Owen Glendower and the Welsh to heel. Then he will turn on Scotland — he has promised it. We must strike first. Ensure that the Northumbrians and Percy, with the traitor George Dunbar, will be so concerned for their own lands and homes that they will not rally to Henry, forestall invasion of our realm. We have been raiding, to this end. But that was not enough. This great host will do it in proper fashion. We will make Henry think again!"

"And what says the Duke of Albany to this? He does not ride with you, I think? He, who exchanges letters with Henry Plantagenet secretly!"

"He is getting old. But he has sent his son, Murdoch of Fife. He approves never fear. But . . . why look so doubtful, man?"

"Because I fear that this could turn into but one more Border raid, larger, deeper, but otherwise the same — more cattle gathered, more villages sacked, more homes burned, more corn trampled, more women raped. Of such I have had my fill."

"Not so. That is not how it is to be. This is invasion. Our counter-invasion. Is that the word? In the name of the King of Scots. Led by four earls — Angus, Moray and Fife, as well as myself. And the lords of Maxwell, Seton, Eaglesham, Dundaff, Buccleuch, Swinton and many more. With the whole house of Douglas. Here is no raid, Jamie, but a great host on the march."

He nodded, but less than fully convinced.

"Come, then — wine, refreshment. You will eat in my own tent, tonight . . ."

*   *   *

They were five more days at Dunbar before a move was made, waiting for a large contingent of Gallovideans under Fergus MacDowell, with a huge herd of Galloway ponies, sturdy, broad-hooved garrons — the Earl Douglas being also Lord of Galloway. With this addition they made a host of just over 11,000 — and what was vitally important for this sort of campaign, all horsed.

Before they set off, news reached the camp — which not all found so significant as Jamie Douglas. Alexander Leslie, Earl of Ross had died, although still a young man, leaving only a little girl as heiress, by Albany's daughter. His father-in-law had acted promptly, declaring the child, Euphemia, Countess of Ross, and taking her into his wardship. This meant, of course, that the Governor would now personally control and administer that great northern earldom, to add to the others of Fife, Menteith and Strathearn — which could not but further infuriate Donald of the Isles, who claimed part of it in his own right, part in his wife's. Alex Stewart would be the more anxious. Uneasily, Jamie put the matter to the back of his mind. There was nothing that he could do about it.

The great array rode off next morning in fine style, under a waving forest of banners, company by company, extending mile upon mile along the road southwards, the baggage-trains and spare horses increasing the column to almost five miles. Although in theory Jamie's position was at Douglas's side, he did not in fact ride with the earls and lords up at the front, but with his brothers at the head of the Dalkeith contingent — fairly near the front of the column as that was, the Douglases of course coming first. An advance-guard scouted ahead.

They followed the coast, by Skateraw and Thornton, negotiating the deep ravines of Bilsdean and Pease Dean, scenes of many a fight and ambush, the major strategic hurdles between Berwick and Edinburgh. Thereafter, at Colbrandspath, they climbed high on to Coldingham Moor. Throughout it all, Dunbar's and his vassals' country, the folk eyed them sullenly; for *their* lord was on the other side, in England, and Douglas usurping his lands.

332

Evening found them a few miles north of Berwick, and they turned inland, by Mordington, on the eastern edge of the Merse, where the Lord of Dalkeith's younger brother, Sir William, was master, and there camped for the night, being made much of by that cheerful character. Berwick, although an important Scots seaport, was still in English hands — had been for many years — and, one of the most strongly-fortified towns in two kingdoms, was best left alone on this occasion, since none wished to start this gallant expedition with a prolonged siege. Hotspur Percy, as East March Warden, was also Governor of Berwick, but tended to appoint deputies, the present incumbent being none other than George, Master of Dunbar, cousin both to the Earl of Moray and the Lord Seton, here present. It was all rather embarrassing. Master George would be well aware of their approach, and had no doubt sent urgent messages south to his father and Percy. But he would not be in any position to challenge their passage. So he could be left quietly in Berwick.

They crossed Tweed next day at the fords near Fishwick, taking four hours to get all over. Now they were in England, and subtly all men's attitude and behaviour changed quite distinctly. They were in the land of the Auld Enemy. Everyone here was a potential foe. More specifically, all was fair game for the strong — and *they* were the strong today — cattle, horses, property, valuables, women. All had been warned that this was no pillaging raid; but with a column miles long, there could be little surveillance of the majority.

They went by Shoreswood and Duddo to the fertile valley of the Till; and it was the sight of tall smoke-clouds behind them in the Crookham area, in mid-afternoon, that sent Jamie spurring up to the Earl of Douglas at the head of the array.

"My lord," he exclaimed, interrupting Angus and Moray, "look yonder!" And he pointed rearward.

"Ha — smokes!" the other observed. "We have a fire or two. Our own folk no doubt. I suppose it was to be expected. A pity — but no matter. Our presence must be known to Percy, so the smoke will only warn the country-folk — no bad thing."

"I am not concerned with whom it warns — save yourself, my lord! Those fires, so soon, are a sorry augury. They mean that your command is insufficiently firm. You are being disobeyed already. Those who lit those fires, against orders, will do more than that."

The Earl frowned. "Jamie, you make too much of it, The men

333

are high-spirited. We must let them have their heads a little. The English burn, slay and harry whenever they cross the Border — always have done. This first day we must not be too strict. There are generations of debts to pay off."

Jamie could frown as blackly as his chief. "Not today!" he jerked. "We are not here for debt-paying. We are here to counter invasion. Think you those who have set those houses, farms, villages, afire will have done *only* that? They will have entered those houses first, taken all that they wanted, of goods, cattle, women. Will they leave these lying, for others to take? I say that even now many may be riding back over Tweed with their booty. And others seeing it, will do likewise."

"They would not dare . . .!"

"You think not? I have seen it time and again. You must stop this, or you will see your army melt away before your eyes."

"How can I stop it, man? We are stretched for miles . . ."

"Stop it as the Earl James did. Tell all that you will hang any guilty of looting or burning. And do so. You will not require to do it twice! That, and do not all your lords ride ever together here at the front of your host. They would be of better service spread throughout."

"Sirrah — you are insolent!" Moray barked.

"Aye, Jamie — I sought your presence with us because I valued your counsel in battle. Not to order our line of march!"

"Very well, my lord. Have I your permission to retire to the tail of your army, less illustrious than its head, and seek to ensure that it follows your noble lead?"

"Sir James — I'll thank you to watch your words! But, yes — do that. Take what men you need, and stop any looting and burning. If you can!"

So Jamie went back, gathered two of his brothers and half of the Dalkeith men-at-arms, and rode to the rear of the column.

There it was as he had feared. No sort of order was being maintained. Men were scattered over a wide area, in bands, doing what they would, often their own lairds abetting. Many were already streaming back northwards, with laden pack-horses, stolen or even commandeered from the army's horse-lines. How many had already departed, none could tell — although any halted assured that they would come back, once their booty was safely deposited across Tweed. Fires were to be seen on all hands, thatched roofs, farmsteads, haystacks; cattle

334

were being rounded up, beasts that were not worth taking or able for the journey, hamstrung, left lying. Human bodies lay here and there, likewise — although clearly most of the local people had fled — and not all of them men who had put up a struggle to save their homes and property.

Jamie and his men, under a Douglas banner, drew their swords and went into harsh and vigorous action, laying about them, shouting, commanding not arguing, beating down protests. They moved to and fro, backwards and forwards across that fair vale, herding the marauders back to the line of march and onwards, leaving bewildered cattle and abandoned goods and valuables everywhere around. Jamie was determined, thorough, remorseless, shouting the authority of the Earl of Douglas until he was hoarse, caring not on whose toes he trampled. And presently they turned the tide of anarchy, loot and lust, and stopped the rot.

For the rest of the afternoon and early evening, the Douglases policed the miles of the column, and found that it was not only at the extreme rear that men were turning aside. At last, weary and angry, they came up with the great camping area near Milfield.

Jamie did not go near his Earl's tent that night, to report, but stayed amongst his own kin, in no very congenial frame of mind. It was there that the Earl Archibald had to come seeking him, in time.

"So there you are, my friend," he said, awkwardly. "How did you fare? With the looters and burners?"

"We stopped them looting and burning, my lord," he was answered stiffly.

"Yes. To be sure. Jamie — I regret that I had to speak to you as I did. But . . . you are cursedly outspoken, man! Before these proud lords. They are not bairns, to be told their duty by, by . . ."

"By bastard lairdlings? But nor are they fighting-men, my lord — and this is fighting-men's work. This is no tourney or lordly parade, but war. I had not thought that, in war, I must needs measure my words to match court manners!"

"No. But there is discretion, Jamie. I could not have one of my Douglas lairds seem lacking in due restraint and respect, in my very presence."

"I did not know that it was discretion, restraint and respect that you required of me, my lord, when you besought me to

335

come south. Nor was it any of these that we required this afternoon, towards the rear of your army!"

The Earl cleared his throat. "No doubt. But . . . you halted the trouble?"

"For this day, yes. But how many men and horses you had lost before we stopped it, who knows?"

"Some had gone?"

"We saw not a few disappearing. This will have to be stopped, or you might as well turn for home, now!"

"I shall speak to all leaders and under-officers."

"Speaking will not serve. Announce that you will hang the first men seen looting and burning, tomorrow. Only so will you stop the rot."

"I cannot hang our own folk, Jamie. Besides, their own lairds would never permit it."

"Then command that their lairds do the hanging."

Douglas shook his head. "That is not the way. I shall not command my host through fear of hanging."

"Your father would not have been so nice, my lord."

"Perhaps not. But I seldom agreed with my father. See you, this I will do. I shall tell the lords to ride not with me but all down the column. Have them to ensure obedience. Myself ride up and down, on occasion. That should serve."

"It should *help*," he said. And then, "Your permission to ride in the rear again?"

"If you will. Take your whole Dalkeith company, if so you wish." He glanced around him. "Or, h'm, your brother's. There will be no need for hangings, I swear. Besides, soon now we shall be into the Percy's home country. Hotspur is bound to oppose us. We shall have fighting, or at least skirmishing. Men will be too busy for looting."

"Perhaps . . ."

The next day was better, undoubtedly; but still there were breaches of discipline, individual sorties, burnings and decampings for home with booty. With an unpaid army consisting of hundreds of independent units with little sense of cohesion, and a tradition for Border reiving, it was inevitable. And when the host was strung out over many miles, with inexperienced and carelessly over-confident leaders in the main, passing through rich territories, nothing short of the most drastic measures could be effective. Jamie Douglas and the Dalkeith contingent became the most unpopular part of the army.

No sign of real opposition developed. Small parties of unknown horsemen were frequently glimpsed on skylines well out on the flanks, sometimes even far to the rear, and the advance-guard reported minor skirmishing companies falling back steadily before them but never waiting to give battle. The countryside was warned and most of the villages and manors they passed had been deserted — which provided added temptation for looters. But of the Percy and Dunbar there was no sign. Rumour had it that they were at Newcastle assembling their forces — or Henry's forces. Newcastle, therefore, was the Scots' objective. It seemed improbable, however, that the English would sit tamely in that walled city, waiting to be besieged.

Moving a force of 10,000 men, even a horsed force, presents many problems in logistics, sheer numbers complicating and delaying every move. In consequence they made much less mileage per day than a smaller force might have done, averaging no more than twenty miles. Which again left too much time and opportunity for rapine and indiscipline.

Jamie grew the more concerned. Somehow he felt more responsible for this expedition than any other he had been on. Which was foolish, just because the Earl had sought his aid as some sort of adviser. Especially after he was proving by no means eager to take that advice.

The day following, when they reached Morpeth in the Wansbeck valley, they were only fifteen miles from Newcastle. But Jamie reckoned that they must have lost 1,000 men — and without a blow struck, or at least, exchanged.

That night the Earl of Douglas held a council-of-war in his pavilion, going so far as to seat Jamie at his right shoulder. All the lords, lairds and leaders were there, with the tent-sides open so that all might take part. He told them that on the morrow they might well come face to face with Hotspur — which was after all what they had come to do. They would give of their best, naturally, and the day would be theirs. But there might be some hard fighting, for the Percy was no sluggard. They would meet him in fair fight, and show the Northumbrians what it meant to threaten the Scots. If he came out of Newcastle to meet them, well and good. If not, they must needs go in and pick him out. Either way they would ensure that the English North would be in no condition thereafter to aid King Henry in his invasion plans.

337

Considerable cheers greeted this spirited statement — in which Jamie Douglas forbore to join.

The Earl went on to say that Angus would command the right wing, Moray the left, he himself leading the centre, thereafter allocating to the lesser lords and knights their places in one or other grouping, and indicating sundry supporting duties. He intimated that should he by any chance fall, the Earl of Angus would take over command. He insisted that the Earl of Dunbar was to be captured alive, if at all possible, and brought to him personally, for execution as a traitor. And so on. He asked if all was clear.

There were sundry questions, as to procedure, precedence, positions of honour, numbers of men commanded, and the like; but no lack of enthusiasm.

Jamie listened, scarcely believing what he heard. Time and again he almost intervened, but restrained himself, telling himself that his duty was to advise his chief personally, and certainly not to show him up before all the others. But it was hard to keep silence when folly was being cheerfully expounded all around.

At length, however, Douglas actually turned to him. "Sir James," he said, "you are much experienced in warfare. Have you any matter to add, which has not been touched upon?"

He swallowed. "My lord," he jerked, "my lords all, I . . . I am concerned for certain matters, yes. Matters which seem somewhat to have escaped your notice. This is war, not chivalric tourney. Hotspur is no fool. You do not know that he *is* in Newcastle town. But if he is, think you that he will sally out to meet you, at your challenge? And throw away the strength of one of the strongest walled cities in England?"

"I said, Jamie, that if he does not, we must go in and pick him out. It will take longer . . ."

"My lord — have you ever besieged a strong fortress like Newcastle? I have. Newcastle itself, and Percy inside. If they are prepared for us, and the gates shut — as they will be, for our presence here must be well known — there is no way of gaining entry, save by using heavy siege-machinery, rams, sows, trebuchets, mangonels — of which we have none. And even so, a long and bloody business. If Hotspur Percy chooses to shut his gates in our faces, there is nothing that we can do — save shout at him, and come away."

There was a long moment's silence, then murmurs, less than accepting and friendly.

338

"Hotspur is a noted warrior," Douglas said. "Why should he behave so?"

"Why not? I would, in his place. If he does bide in Newcastle. You have entered and harried his lands. Why come out and fight you on *your* terms? Better stay there, secure, until he can attack you on *his* terms. Or wait, as is more likely, until he is reinforced from Henry's army on the Welsh Marches. Messengers are probably summoning such now."

"What would you have us do, then, man?"

"Forget Newcastle. Swing westwards up the Tyne valley. Ride to and fro all over Northumberland, over into Cumberland even, on the widest front. Show that the land is at our mercy. Not pillaging or looting but leaving all afraid for their homes. Is that not what you came to do? Not to assail fortress-cities. Moreover, that way you may coax Hotspur out of Newcastle. If he is indeed therein — which I doubt."

There was a spate of talk and discussion.

"To turn away from Newcastle now would seem as though we were afraid," Moray called.

"Then send a small party to sit before it. Make a demonstration. Help coax them out. The rest up Tyne . . ."

"We have come to fight, not traipse the country like packmen," the Lord Maxwell declared.

"Aye! Aye!"

"I believed that we came to counter the wills of the North Country English to invade Scotland, my lord."

"We shall not do that other than by fighting, I swear!"

"Nor will you do it sitting around Newcastle, waiting."

More controversy.

To halt it, Douglas went on, "And if Hotspur and Dunbar are not in Newcastle, Sir James?"

"Then we must find them, and quickly. Send out many swift scouting parties, whilst we range Northumberland, else we may be caught unawares. If they have a large force assembled, they will not be hard to find."

"Very well. We shall see what the morrow brings forth." The Earl rose. "To your tents then, my lords. We ride at sun-up . . ."

On the heights of the Town Moor above Newcastle to the north, the Scots army was halted, gazing down to the walled city in the valley of the broad and silvery Tyne. Even from here they could see that the gates were shut — at least the New Gate and the West Gate, those within sight. No doubt thousands of eyes were watching them from the walls and towers and close-packed houses. No Percy banner flew from the topmost turret of the tall-castle near the New Gate, which gave the town its name — but that was not to say that Hotspur was not present. It might merely mean that he did not wish it to be known.

It had been obvious to Jamie from the beginning that his advice was not going to be taken. The entire force had come on to Newcastle, and there was no move to turn away westwards. Now, all the talk amongst the leaders was of which gate they should assail, whether a summons to surrender was necessary, or a challenge to single combat likely to be accepted. When the Earl of Douglas himself declared that if there was to be single combat with Hotspur, then *he* had an unassailable right in the matter, because of the ancient Douglas–Percy feud, Jamie recognised that the case was hopeless.

"You are going to assault the city, my lord?" he asked then, levelly.

"Aye, Jamie — we cannot turn away now. Our people would not have it."

"And if Percy is not there?"

"We shall see."

"At least, send out patrols far and wide. To find him. Otherwise we could be trapped here."

"This great host would take a deal of trapping, I think. But, see here — since you are so anxious, take *you* a swift company and go find Hotspur for us. If you can. Take so many as you wish, your own Dalkeith people."

Jamie knew that it was just to be rid of him and his objections. But he accepted the suggestion nevertheless, glad to get away from a venture in which he had lost all faith.

"To be sure," he said. "I do not need four hundred. Half that would be sufficient, and two hundred fewer will make little difference to your force here. Elsewhere they might serve you notably well."

"Where will you go?"

"Up Tynedale to Hexhamshire first. If they are not there, then south to the valley of the Derwent. If Percy has a large force to muster and forage, he will need space and much fodder to do it in. He will be in one or other of these great vales, I think."

The Earl frowned, tapping his saddle-bow. "If he is in Tynedale, with a large force? Not far away . . . ?"

340

"I shall endeavour to send you warning, my lord. Although I would prefer that you came yourself, and wasted no time on this walled town."

"Newcastle is the greatest city of the North, Jamie. Next to York, the greatest north of Trent. If it falls to the Scots, it will do more to damage English spirit than much riding to and fro in Northumberland."

On that note they parted.

XIX

JAMIE AND HIS hard-riding two hundred Douglases, a tough, self-contained and fast-moving company just the right size for the task, too strong to assail save with a much larger force but not so big as to be unwieldy or unable to live off the land without time-wasting foraging, found no trace of any large muster of men in Tynedale, although they rode its length, well up into the hills beyond Hexham. Small groups of English horsemen they did see, but these kept their wary distance. In the main this fertile land appeared to be almost cleared of its menfolk and horsemen — no doubt gone to join their lord elsewhere. Or, rather, their lord's son and heir, for the old Earl of Northumberland was still alive, although little seen. Jamie sent a courier to his own Earl, informing him.

So they turned southwards, as he had said, by Allendale and the high commons of the Pennine foothills, threading upland valleys, seeking to reach the roughly parallel vale of the Derwent unheralded. It made for slower going, against the grain of the land; but it had the advantage of them making the many river-crossings where they were young and shallow, rather than by the major fords further down which might well be guarded. The second night after leaving Newcastle, they were at Sinderhope, after covering some fifty miles.

Next morning, coming down into the Derwent valley, they began to find, not assembled men but the traces of them. At first, however unmistakable, they were modest in scope — trampled grass, horse-droppings, the black circles of recent camp-fires, gathered firewood left unburned, dotted here and there. But as they progressed down the widening valley, these signs grew and multiplied on every hand, until they came to what had been a very large encampment in the broad meadows below Blanchland — had been, for it was now deserted quite. But the trail of a great host led onwards, eastwards, down the vale towards Durham. It was impossible to say how many its numbers, even as to thousands; but the indications were that here was an army at least as large as that of the Scots.

This naturally gave Jamie and his brothers furiously to think. There could be little doubt that this was Hotspur's array. None other was likely to be mustered north of York. But why had he chosen to muster here, so far to west and south? There was no need for such secrecy; the Percy and his ally the Prince-Bishop of Durham, were supreme lords of all hereabouts, and could assemble where they would. And up in these high valleys could be convenient for few indeed. Why, then? One answer could be that this was in fact a rendezvous, that here the Northumbrian and Durham muster had waited for others, coming from the west and south-west, across the Pennines — for instance, across England from the Welsh Marches. Reinforcements from Henry, indeed. It could well be. And in that case, the reinforcements had now arrived, since the host had moved on. And what would Henry send from afar, at short notice? Not slow-moving infantry, which might take many days to the journey — but fast light cavalry, possibly mounted archers, the troops they had most to fear.

Although they had found what they came for, anything but relievedly they rode on in the wake of the English force, slowly.

By mid-afternoon Jamie had the first vital information he required. The host in front had left the eastwards-going vale and struck north-eastwards through the rolling Durham moors, by Ebchester and Chopwell, a line which would bring it to Newcastle. He immediately sent off two sets of urgent messengers, by different routes, who, riding fast, would get well ahead of the English and warn Earl Douglas. He reckoned that, here, they were some twenty-one miles from Newcastle, so that there should be time. He and his party continued to dog the enemy force. By the state of the horse-droppings they calculated that they were now only about three hours behind it.

With nightfall they pressed on at a better pace, assured that they were unlikely to stumble upon a great camp unawares; and any small outpost or patrol they could deal with. Actually they soon saw the glow of innumerable camp-fires ahead of them, somewhere in the High Spen area, and they were able to move forward until they could take up a good position in woodland above a great hollow, site of the encampment, where they could see without being seen. Here they settled to rest, taking it in turn to watch and patrol.

In the morning, they watched the all-too-familiar routine of a large army waking, eating and breaking camp — and noted that it took the English just as long as it did the Scots. But they noted much more — number, armament, colours, banners. They reckoned that there were fully 14,000 men involved, all horsed, with many knights and much half-armour, most men equipped with lance and sword, axe or mace, but an ominously large number with bows, mounted archers. Troop by troop, company after company, they watched them mount and ride off northwards.

"They make a goodly show, Jamie," his brother Will declared. "But no better than our own host. Nor so greatly more in numbers."

"Perhaps. But they can draw added numbers from the land, as we cannot, since it is their land. A fine force like this will attract many. Nor will they be hampered with booty. And they are strong in archers. Of which we have none."

"You are ever gloomy, Jamie — a prophet of woe."

"No. I do not prophesy woe. I only say that if we do not underestimate our enemy, we are the more likely to beat him."

Now their task was simple and straightforward — to ride round the slower-moving English force and get to Newcastle with all speed, to rejoin Douglas with their fullest information. They had only some fifteen miles to do it in. Percy could easily cover that in one day, even with all his host — but was unlikely to do so. He would go warily, as he neared his enemy. And would not wish to reach the possible battle area with his men weary, towards evening. So he would camp short of Newcastle, south of Tyne, to make his dispositions. They had time, then.

Without any hold-up or trouble, however tired their horses, going west-abouts and fording Tyne at Horsley Wood, without further sight of the foe, they came to Newcastle in the late afternoon. And there found only their own messengers sent from the Derwent valley awaiting them. The Scots army had left for home that morning.

Jamie heard this news with mixed feelings. He was surprised, but relieved also — since he was anything but confident that the Scots were in any state to meet the English in pitched battle.

This now looked less probable. On the other hand, it all seemed a notably feeble and abortive end to their great expedition, with little attained. It might still be possible, of course, to achieve some worthwhile result. His messengers told him that they had arrived here the previous evening, to find the Scots already packing up, to go. They had, it seemed, tired of sitting round Newcastle's walls, unable to make any impression on the city, hooted at by the defenders and shot at by bowmen if they ventured too close. The massive gates remained shut, and there was no other entrance, without heavy siege-engines to batter holes in the walling. Two days of this had been enough. Now they were withdrawing slowly northwards. The news that Percy had been located and was on his way had been received with acclaim, but had not altered the programme. They would continue to move north and draw the English after them, until some suitable position was reached where they would turn and fight, with their backs to Scotland.

Jamie had to admit that this might be the best course.

Horses and men desperately weary, they rested that night amongst the debris of the great camp on Newcastle's Town Moor.

An early start revealed no signs of the advancing English before they set off. But they had not gone ten miles on their way northwards before it was not the English behind but the Scots in front who were worrying Jamie Douglas. For, away ahead, columns and palls of dark smoke were once again rising to stain the forenoon sky, many smokes and covering a wide area of the front. The situation was self-evident. The Scots army was not going home empty-handed.

"Fools!" Jamie burst out. "Purblind, headstrong fools!" And he dug in his spurs angrily.

It was beyond Morpeth that they began to see the traces, on the ground as distinct from in the sky — burned farms, granges, villages, manors, mills, smouldering heaps of grain and hay, trampled corn, littered furnishings, dead bodies. And everywhere tracks of cattle on the move. This was clearly the work of the night before.

Hurrying on, they came up eventually with the main Scots force about seven miles north of Morpeth in the Longhorsley area — and before reaching it they had to work their way through enormous herds of cattle, thousands strong, driven by cheerful and drink-taken men-at-arms. It was, however, a grievously reduced main force, not much more than half the

345

total strength and even this slow-moving indeed, weighed down with plunder.

Earl Douglas, although he greeted Jamie and the others warmly enough, was slightly on the defensive. "So, my friends, you have accomplished your task, and done it well," he commended. "We are all grateful, I swear. And, as you see, we have followed your advice and wasted little time on Newcastle. Now we retire by slow stages towards the Border, seeking the best place to turn and face Hotspur."

Jamie had for some time been schooling himself to ensure that his too-frank tongue was properly under control. "Yes, my lord," he said.

The other shot a quick glance at him. "You do not again disapprove?" he jerked.

"Not with your policy, my lord — no."

"What, then?"

"It is the policy you are permitting others to pursue. Half your host is off raiding, looting, pillaging. It is now less an army than a horde of caterans and reivers!"

"We cannot hold them in all the time, man. Now we are facing for home, we must give them their heads a little."

"And when the Percy catches up?"

"We shall call them in again, never fear. And they fight the better for having gear at stake, perhaps."

"Or prefer to ensure their gear, and not fight at all!"

"Never that. You miscall our people, I say."

"My lord, a party with a sizeable herd, nearing the Border, will think twice of turning back to fight before it has bestowed its beasts in some safe beef-tub. And few men fight their best weighed down with plunder. Moreover, once a force has got out-of-hand it is ever the less reliable."

"God, Jamie — you are a sour, thrawn devil!" the Earl cried. "Enough of this. We have had peace from gloom and blame while you were away. It has not taken you long to be back at it! I will speak with you again when you are in better temper!" And he rode off.

Jamie's brothers grinned at him. "You never yield, do you?" Johnnie said.

"Not while there is still a chance to halt sheer folly. Folly that could cost us all dear. Lord save the army of an incompetent commander!"

The Scots host was now reduced to moving at the pace of a

cattle-drove, which in turn allowed ever more time for acquisitive-minded groups and companies to hive off and see what they could appropriate and damage. They would certainly allow the English to catch up with them long before they reached the Border, if that was Hotspur's intention.

That night they camped on the flanks of Shirlaw Pike, only some fifteen miles north of Morpeth, deafened by the bellowing of hungry and alarmed cattle, the night lit above them by the glow of fires innumerable. The Earl of Douglas did not come near the Dalkeith company.

They made no better progress next day, with the host now spread over a front almost as wide as it was long — and as such practically uncontrollable. No word from the rearguard, however, intimated the close approach of the enemy, although Jamie, for one, kept riding back to check. The Percy seemed to be in little greater hurry to come to grips as they were. Jamie feared that he was delaying for still further reinforcements. Nightfall found them still a few miles south of Wooler.

The Earl still did not come to Jamie, and Jamie was too proud to approach the other — especially as Murdoch Stewart, Earl of Fife, who never ceased to display his illwill and contempt for Jamie, was now ever closest to the Douglas's side.

It was near the following midday that an urgent rider came at a canter down the long straggling line-of-march. "Enemy in front!" he yelled, as he rode. "Enemy in front! Close up. Douglas says, close up." That was all his message as he drummed past.

Cursing, Jamie forgot his pride, and with his brothers spurred forward, like many another.

They found the head of the column — although it was no longer a column — halted in some agitation on the moorland heights west of Wooler. This time there was no cold shoulder from the Earl Archibald as they rode up.

"Jamie," he cried. "Here's strange tidings. They tell me that the English are in force ahead, in great force. Filling the entire wide vale of Till, from Doddington across to Milfield. The way we came. God knows how they got there . . .!"

"Hotspur? Is it he?"

"They say his banner flies, yes. And many another."

"Then it seems, my lord, that he has been less dilatory than have we. Worked his way round our flank whilst we herded cattle, and so won in front of us."

"Yes, yes — we can all guess that! He seeks to halt us. We will give him battle, gladly. It is what I intended. But scarcely that he should be in *front* of us."

"In front or behind matters little, my lord. So long as *we* choose the battleground, not he."

"Aye. To be sure. I had hoped to prospect a place, once we heard that he was near. But now . . .? Who knows this country well?"

A few Border voices were raised.

"Where is our best place to go? Where should we make our stand? Where Percy has not the Till and Glen rivers to aid him."

Various suggestions were made, some good enough, others less so, some quite impracticable.

The Earl looked directly at Jamie, although he did not say anything.

"My lord," that man said levelly. "Your host is direly scattered. It must have time to be brought back and reassembled. Time. That limits your choice. Hotspur will know that we are here, you may be sure. And he is stronger in numbers. He will wait for you to ride down into his trap."

"Well, man — well?"

"Bear with me. A little time spent now could be a deal more valuable than much time later. We must move from here. This open moor is no place to face the Percy. Forward we cannot go, down into the Vale of Till, into the re-entrant of those rivers — a trap if ever there was one, why Hotspur has turned there. Backwards we may not go either, without trampling through our own rear and all the cattle-herds. Besides, it is moorland for miles. The Percy knows his country, knows what he is at. Therefore, we must move left or right. Right, we have to cross Till, left to cross Glen. We shall not cross Till easily. Therefore it must be the smaller river. We must turn left, into the hills."

"And then? Can we stand there? In the hills?"

"If we choose our hills well. It will mean that Hotspur will have to leave his positions on the rivers and follow us. To *his* disadvantage."

"Yes. Well, then. But we will have to cross the Glen River. If he was to catch us at that, we would be lost."

"There are fords at Coupland and Canno and Kilham. Others too, maybe, but these I know. Kilham furthest west. And before that, the Glen winds through a narrow ravine — from which it

348

gets its name, for it is the Bowmont Water before that. A small company could hold that ravine, while the others cross higher. Then, at least, we have nothing to fear from the rivers."

"I know the place," Scott of Buccleuch called. "Between Canno Mill and Reedsford. It is called Canno Glen."

"Very well. And once we are across. Is there a place to hold and fight, beyond it?"

"Aye," said Jamie. There are two hills there, nearby — I misremember the names. You can see them, from here. Beyond them, and this side of yonder green scarp, Flodden Edge, is a high but open valley. In it is Howtel Peel. Whoever built it chose well. It is a place to withstand an assault, protected by marshes."

"Housedon Hill and Homildon Hill," Scott amplified, obviously an expert reiver. "The Howtel valley between them and West Flodden."

"We are not interested in withstanding assaults, man," the Earl of Fife growled. "Our task is to bring Percy low, not to withstand him."

"The Howtel valley will serve for that also, my lord," answered Jamie, "if you are still of that mind after withstanding his assault!"

"So be it," Douglas cried. "We move westwards. All to your places, my lords. Enough of talk. Let us be doing."

*   *   *

It was, to be sure, natural, perhaps inevitable, that Jamie and the Dalkeith contingent should be ordered to hold the Canno Glen position while the great strung-out host crossed the fords further up. He had recommended its defensive advantages, and the four hundred or so of his company was just about the right number to entrust with the task.

They hurried ahead, skirting the village of Kirknewton, reaching the Glen River beyond, and proceeding upstream. In a mile they were opposite Canno Mill and into the jaws of the defile between Kilham Hill and Housedon Hill, a deep, twisting, wooded pass enclosing the rushing river, here almost a torrent, with a track on both sides. It was ideal for their purpose, but they were on the wrong side. The English, if they came, would be on the north. So they had to go on until they emerged from the ravine, and at the wide, shallow reach beyond, were able to splash across at the farmery and mill of Reedsford. Leaving a couple of men here to guide the main body, and sending a small party further up to take and hold the major ford at Kilham, they turned back into Canno Glen.

It was, indeed, as good as made for an ambush, with no length of view anywhere, steep rocky slopes and a sheer drop to the foaming river. But it was not really an ambush that they were here for, only to ensure that no English won through this gap to disturb the Scots army at the delicate business of fording the river. Fighting was not the object. Leaving the horses hidden at the west end, Jamie placed his men to best advantage above the narrow track, where they could gather and eventually roll down rocks upon the enemy. Through the trees they could occasionally glimpse their own folk winding round the base of Kilham Hill in a seemingly unending stream.

They had to wait for some considerable time, and were beginning to wonder whether their vigil was in fact necessary, before they heard the deep drumming of hooves which bespoke many horses hard ridden. The Dalkeith Douglases, their rocks and boulders already loosened, tensed, ready.

Normally in this sort of warfare, they would have allowed some files of the horsemen to pass before hurling their stones, to obtain maximum effect, break the enemy column in two and so destroy command. But on this occasion that was not what was wanted. Jamie himself was at the extreme west end of the line, so that, by the time that the first of the English riders, steel-capped and jacked, led by two knights in half-armour, came into his vision, the rest of his people had been restraining themselves for agonising moments — for 400 men can stretch for a considerable distance along a hillside. No actual signal was required. When, with the leading English directly below them, Jamie and his immediate neighbours pushed their boulders into hurtling motion, in only moments the entire ravine resounded to yells and screams and crashes. All along the line the rain of rocks commenced.

It was, of course, utter disaster for those below, There was no means by which they could avoid the bombardment, or attempt to hit back, nor yet turn back on the narrow choked roadway. On their left the ground dropped sheer into the torrent. Most were swept over the edge into this in the first volleys, not all by the stones themselves but by their own colleagues desperately seeking to take avoiding action, or by terrified horses out of control. Succeeding rocks found fewer targets merely because the gaps in the column were suddenly so wide. But even the survivors were in a hopeless situation. Some turned back, and found the track completely blocked by their own struggling and fallen folk and animals. Some spurred furiously forward — and there could be left for others to deal with, and could do little harm. Many leapt down from their now completely useless mounts — and found themselves little better off.

It was a complete and bloody shambles, savage, inglorious for all, but highly effective. Jamie had been ready to order a general descent, with sword and dirk, upon the survivors, after the third volley of rocks. But this he saw to be unnecessary, and despatched only a few men to deal with the scurrying unfortunates, instead sending along the line the command to collect more stones, boulders and logs. Then he himself went at the run eastwards, making for the far end of his line.

His brother Johnnie was in charge there. Gleefully he announced complete triumph. How long the enemy column had been they could not tell, for there was no distant vision in this close country; but all behind the stone fusillade had turned and fled, in direst confusion.

"They will be back," Jamie assured. "Probing. I shall stay here meantime. I left James in charge at the other end, Will in the centre. These English will go back and report. When they come again, it will be warily."

He made arrangements for this east end of the line to be prepared to swing round at right angles, up and down the hill, at short notice. The next enemy move might well be on foot and in depth.

Actually they again had to wait quite some time for developments — which made it look as though the main English command was still some considerable way off. Jamie was not really familiar with the area, but he remembered enough to be fairly sure that to move westwards out of the Vale of Till hereabouts it would be necessary to climb out either by this pass or by a wider and shallower depression to the north, between the village of Milfield and the escarpment of Flodden Edge. From Milfield to Howtel Peel that way must be at least four miles. If Hotspur was actually doing that — and this prolonged interval might imply it — then he could conceivably reach the Howtel valley before the main mass of the Scots did. Jamie sent a messenger off hot-foot to warn Earl Douglas of the possibility.

When the enemy did reappear, however, it was horsemen cautiously feeling their way along the road again, eyeing each yard and bush and shadow, moving at a walking-pace — obviously scouts for a larger party. Jamie signed to his people to keep down, to let them pass. Where the debris of the earlier slaughter began, they went more warily still, staring uphill, ready for immediate flight. Unfortunately, at this stage somebody further along the Scots line skirled a laugh — and that was enough. The riders wheeled their mounts around and spurred off at speed.

Jamie cursed. Not only was that the end of all hope of a second surprise attack, but it meant that they must change their position and tactics. Those scouts would go back to their leaders and report that the road was still held. And the leaders would then order either a general retiral to the main body, or an attempt to outflank the force in the ravine. This, on the hillside terrain here could only be done on foot by infiltrating men through the steep woodland and undergrowth above; which meant that he must swing his line right round to face a new and inclined front.

This took some time to achieve, resulting at length in an L-shaped front being established, two hundred men still lining the ravine track and another two hundred strung out up the hill amongst the trees at the east end. They were barely in position before the first tentative probings began, figures flitting from tree-trunk to bush to hollow, darting, creeping, at various points of the steep braeside. The Scots made little attempt to hide their presence, only their numbers — for Jamie did not really seek battle, merely to deny this pass to the foe and so protect the fording-places for the Scots army. There were one or two minor hand-to-hand skirmishes, but no major fighting. Presently, after an interval, it became clear that these scouts also had withdrawn, no doubt to report once more. It was to be hoped that the enemy verdict would be that the woodland was strongly held and no passage practicable, above or below.

Be that as it may, no attack in force developed along either front.

After something over an hour's waiting, Jamie decided that it was long enough. Surely the Scots must be well across the fords by this time. All the cattle might not be — but he was not greatly concerned with them and their herders. He sent out orders to move back westwards to the horses.

They did find cattle-droves still crossing at Reedsford Mill, but the drovers assured them that all except stragglers of the main force had been across for some time, on their way to this Howtel.

So they turned north again. But it was quickly clear that it was not the Howtel valley that was their army's immediate destination, but the hill above it to the east — Homildon Hill, according to one of Jamie's party. Up there, on the quite steep upper slopes of the hill, the Scots force was building up, rank upon rank, an extraordinary sight, thousands of men and horses darkening the green braes.

Jamie stared. "Dear God!" he exclaimed. "Look there! What does it mean? What do they up there?"

"They are assembling there. Halted," his brother James said. "But why?"

"A good viewpoint?"

"*All* need not climb to see the view!"

"A strong defensive position . . .?"

But Jamie was already reining round, to face the hill. "Wait here," he shouted. "There is already a sufficiency up yonder."

Spurring up and up through the press of men and beasts, he came at length to the lofty ridge some hundreds of feet higher, where there were the green embankments of a one-time British camp. It was beyond this, a little way down the farther side, that the banners of the lords were clustered. To them he pushed his way, warning himself to watch his tongue.

The Earl Douglas saw him coming, and raised a hand. "Jamie," he called, in seemingly good spirits. "I hear that you held your pass to good effect. First blood in this tourney!"

"No tourney, my lord. But — we held the pass. I looked for you at Howtel." And he pointed downhill, northwards.

"Aye. But your messenger said that Hotspur might reach there before us. Besides, this is a better defensive position, by far."

"I beg leave to differ, my lord. And my message was only warning that the English might move that way, and to be ready." He gestured downwards. "The Howtel position is still un-occupied, as all can see."

"We are better here," Murdoch of Fife rapped. "Hotspur will assail us here to his sore hurt."

"And when he is sufficiently discouraged and weary, we shall sweep down and defeat him utterly," Douglas added. "Even you, Jamie, must approve such strategy."

"Possibly — were it not for *that*!" Jamie swung half-right in his saddle and jabbed a pointing finger upwards.

Immediately to the west of this Homildon rose the higher summit and ridge of Housedon Hill. Indeed, the one was but a spur of the other. There was a steep dip between Homildon's crest and the grassy side of the other, a shallow col.

"Would you have us up there, then? Better than here?"

"I would have you down there, around Howtel Peel. As we said. It is still clear. See you, my lords — whoever built that tower knew what he was at. It stands on firm ground, with ample space — yet is protected to north and south by wide marsh, waters drained off these hills. There is a mound to the west, to offer flanking support. Any cavalry attack must come by quite narrow causeways, entrants, easy to hold."

"And how should *we* attack, from there?" Moray demanded. "Since we are here to fight, not to hide in bogs!"

"Let the Percy expend his strength — as you say to do up here. Then sally out from the Peel area, and the mound, both. On foot over the marsh, cavalry by the causeways. Sufficient fighting then, my lord."

"What advantage have we down there that we do not have up here? We have height. A charge downhill, to sweep them away."

Again Jamie turned, to point upwards. "That hill . . ." he began — but was interrupted by shouts all around, as other hands pointed.

Round a low ridge to the north, two miles or more away, this side of the scarp of Flodden Edge, steel gleamed in the afternoon sunshine, much steel. More and more glittered and flashed even as they watched.

"Too late," the Lord Maxwell exclaimed. "I would think to agree with Sir James — but now it is too late."

"Not so," Jamie cried. "You could still be at Howtel before them. Let us go down."

"No!" Earl Douglas decided. "We are very well here. It would be folly to change now, in disorder. Here we have all under our eyes . . ."

"Except the far side of that Housedon Hill, man! They could come up there, hidden. And be *above* us!"

"What of it? There is this gap between. They cannot reach us without climbing this steep."

"Not with swords and lances. But what of arrows?"

"Eh . . . ?"

"I told you, my lord. The Percy is aided by a host of mounted archers. From the West. If he places them on that hill . . ."

"It is too far. Out of range."

"On the ridge, yes. But if he sent them part-way down that slope. How far then, say you?"

"Four hundred yards? More?"

"Less. And English yew long-bows will drive a shaft five hundred yards and more, with a falling shot." He paused. "So, I say, let us down to Howtel while there is time."

"If . . . if . . . if!" Murdoch Stewart jerked. "*If* Percy comes up behind the hill. *If* he sends archers there. *If* he places them half-way down the hill. *If* we stand and let them shoot at us! I say this doomster would have us fleeing from shadows, by God!"

"I say Jamie is right," the Earl of Angus said. "The English could fill the valley below us. Then we are trapped up here."

"It is too late to move now, George," Douglas declared. "The host is drawn up here in good order. To change now would mean confusion. Jamie is too fearful. We shall stand our ground."

"Then let me climb that hill with my Dalkeith people. And seek to hold it," Jamie requested.

"Very well. No harm in that . . ."

So he rode back down the south side of Homildon, through the crowded ranks again, to his own folk. Quickly he told his brothers of the situation, and they wasted no time in starting up that long climb of the higher hill. It was fairly steep from this side, and they had to set the horses zigzagging up, slithering and sliding. A burn-channel now aided, now hindered them. The summit ridge ran north and south for almost a quarter-of-a-mile. At length they reached it.

At the very crest Jamie, in front, reined back violently. Not five hundred yards away down the far and gentler slope, the first of a great host was climbing.

Urgently he waved back his company, and reined round his own beast.

He was almost bound to have been seen — which might delay the enemy a little perhaps, make them more wary. Time for themselves to get away — for there was nothing that they could do about this except flee. There were thousands mounting the hill, and no delaying tactics by his four hundred would avail anything.

So back downhill they went, as fast as they dared on the steep terrain, not directly down the face as they had come but to the col between the two hills. As he went Jamie could not but note how vulnerable the Scots position was, across the gap, to long-range archery.

On their own hill again, his company could by no means push their way through the crowded ranks already drawn up there, so Jamie had to leave them, to force his own way upwards. By the time he could reach the leadership group, his information was out-of-date, for the first ranks of the English were now plain for all to see on the ridge of Housedon Hill.

"My lords," he shouted, as he came near. "We must get off this hill. Without delay. There are thousands coming up — and Hotspur would be the veriest fool not to send his archers. We have little time left. Down with us!"

"Look there, man!" Douglas said, briefly.

There was a much lower spur of hill immediately to the north-east, Kype Hill, jutting into the Howtel valley; and over the green swell of this a mass of enemy horse was now swarming. Before the Scots could possibly reach the valley floor they would be outflanked by these.

Jamie swore. "Nothing for it but to turn back, then. Down the south side, whence we came. Back across the Glen Water. Hold the river line. This hill could be a death-trap."

"I will not turn back," Douglas declared. "Flee in the face of the Percy. And from a strong position. Besides, there is the cattle. Thousands of beasts between us and the river. We would have to push our full array right through them."

"Better that than be trapped here."

"No. Here we stand. Forget your fears, man!"

Groaning, Jamie turned away. He could say and do no more. Not for these, anyway. He would go back to his own people from Dalkeith. His duty now was to them, surely. Not that there was much that he could do for them, or for any, since he could by no means desert the army now.

As he pushed his way down the south side of Homildon once more, none had any eyes for him. All were gazing up at the ridge of Housedon, black now with massed men and horses. Even as they looked the horses were being led away, down the far east side, to make room for more men on the summit. Clearly no foolish attempt was going to be made to assault the lower hill with cavalry. It was indeed to be the archers, then.

Reaching his brothers, he barked out his grim tidings.

"What now, then?" Johnnie demanded. "Do we just die where we stand?"

"Not if I may help it. We are in one of the worst positions, here. At least let us move round this accursed hill, if we can. To the west side. It will be surrounded. But there the bowmen up yonder will not reach us. We may be attacked from below, but that is better than being shot from above."

"We cannot just go hide there, Jamie!" Will protested.

"Hide? What do you propose that we do anywhere else?"

"Are we not going to make sallies, at least?"

"Against massed archers? That is worthy of the Earl Archibald! Let the English make the sallies, meantime. Come — get our own folk round to the west."

By going slightly downhill again, and round, they were able to move their compact squadron reasonably quickly. Others, of course, saw and sought to do likewise. But long before the bulk of those seeking to do so could move away, the arrows from the summit of Housedon began to fall amongst them. These were only sighting shots, of course, fired high to curve over and down, testing the range. They did not do much damage, even though they could hardly fail to find a mark, so tightly was the hill packed with men and horses; for they were not only losing their impetus but, being dropped shots, tended to fall on the heads and shoulders of the Scots, which were in the main protected by steel morions and jacks. It was principally the unprotected horses which suffered. Nevertheless there was much shouting, jeering and even screaming, to indicate that hostilities had at last commenced.

The Dalkeith contingent found that the English cavalry had now practically encircled Homilcon Hill to the west. But they were not attempting to come up the slope as yet, the nearest some six hundred yards below.

"They but contain us," Jamie said. "Few bowmen down there, I jalouse. Percy will have sent all his archers up the hill — as I would have done. A plague on it — we could still break out of this col, if we had the will!"

"Ourselves, mean you — or all the host?" James asked.

"The host. *We* could do likewise, I believe, in wedge formation. Down the steep and through them. Nothing would stop us. And out to the west, the Cheviot foothills. Reassemble there. But the Earl will not."

"Perhaps, when he has had enough of arrows . . .!"

Johnnie was right, of course. Jamie, no more than his brothers, could bear to sit his horse idly there in comparative safety whilst the bulk of the army was facing the major threat. Admittedly more and more men were pressing round to this side of the hill; but even so, sheer numbers meant that the greater part must inevitably face the menace of Housedon Hill. So, leaving one of the Dalkeith under-stewards, Mattie Douglas, in charge meantime, the four brothers set off uphill again.

They found conditions direly changed. The enemy had moved the first companies of bowmen almost half-way down the west face of Housedon, safe in the knowledge that the Scots would have no archers of their own, as Jamie had said they would, and were in process of moving most of the rest. Already the difference in range and angle was grimly evident. Casualties were mounting steadily. It was not only the harder hitting-power of the shafts but the fact that they now could be aimed directly, so that instead of dropping on helmets and breast-plates they could come straight at the unprotected parts. And it was impossible to miss, man or beast. The men-at-arms, of course, suffered the most, being less well-protected by steel; but even the lords and knights were not in full armour — since it was impossible to ride far and fast so garbed. As the newcomers rode up men were dying under the lethal, swishing hail with yells and moans, horses falling in lashing, screaming agony, the press of men and beasts surging this way and that, pushing, trampling, stumbling. And none could hit back.

Hotspur's tactics were entirely clear now. He had the invaders where he wanted them. His main force surrounded the hill-foot area in a belt of steel, waiting, whilst the archers pinned them down. There was nothing particularly brilliant about it; indeed it was the obvious thing to do, given the folly of the Scots for ever putting themselves in such a position.

Jamie and his brothers had swift intimation of the desperation of the situation, had they required it. For, riding through the tight press towards the Earl of Douglas's stance under the massed banners, Johnnie was hit by an arrow. It struck his cuirass, was deflected by the steel, and drove in slanting upwards at the joint with the gorget, piercing the leather beneath and into the shoulder. He toppled from the saddle of his rearing, frightened mount.

Most men were dismounted now, as making less prominent marks, and hurriedly the Douglas brothers did likewise.

Assuring himself that Johnnie was not dangerously injured, Jamie left the others to deal with him, and pushed on through the angry seething crowd. He found a heated argument going on beneath the banners, all the leaders seeming to be shouting at once.

It appeared that Sir John Swinton of that Ilk, in the Merse, kin to Douglas, was advocating action, declaring that he for one was no longer prepared to stand there and be shot down as target-practice for English bowmen. They must mount a charge, he said, down this east face of the hill and up the slope of Housedon, and sweep away those accursed archers. It would be costly, he agreed — but the only way they could be saved from outright disaster. Although most of the others were disagreeing, some were supporting him vehemently, notably and strangely one, Adam, Lord of Gordon and Strathbogie. The Swinton and Gordon lands adjoined in the Merse, indeed the two families were of the same root, but they had been at feud for generations. Yet Gordon was now vociferously agreeing with his enemy that this desperate assault was necessary. And not only that, but that he was prepared to lead it. All this under the tide of arrows.

Jamie's arrival at least provided a distraction.

"Ha — Jamie!" the Earl Douglas cried. "We suffer much loss. Do you hear what is proposed? My lords of Swinton and Gordon are for a direct assault on those archers. I say that they would lose half their men. How say you?"

"Better than losing the same men standing here idle!" Swinton barked.

"It would be useless," Jamie said. "You would never reach the archers."

"Some would," Gordon asserted. "They would never bring us all down. And once amongst them we would scatter them like chaff. Bowmen are useless at close quarters fighting. They will never stand for steel."

There was more vigorous debate, as men died around them. With their long shields and better armour, of course, the lordly ones were much the less vulnerable.

Jamie gained approximate quiet by banging his dirk-hilt on his own shield, slung from his shoulder, with its colourful heraldic device for identity.

"I tell you, none would get to the archers," he insisted. "This hillside is steep and whin-grown. You could not ride down it, horsed, at speed. Every bowman would be aiming at you. And not only these, part-way down, but those above also. Climbing *their* hill beyond, you could not rush them either. The ground is bad for horses. At such short range it would be massacre."

"But, by God and His saints, we cannot just stand here, waiting to be shot down!" Swinton exclaimed.

"No, I agree. We should move, yes. But down this other side of the hill. North by west, in a series of wedge-formations. It is less steep. The English main host is there, yes — but it is spread round the entire base of the hill, none so thick at any point. At speed, in tight formation, we could charge right through. Then on, beyond, into the Cheviot foothills. There to reform."

"It is too late for that," Earl Douglas declared.

"No. They think they have us trapped up here. If we did it swiftly, we could surprise them, and through."

"And if we did *not* win through, we are lost, finished. No — that is not the way. We would risk total defeat."

"And this way . . . ?"

"I say we can clear away those archers," Swinton interrupted. "And then we are secure, up here. I will do it, with my own Mersemen."

"I said *I* would lead!" Gordon shouted.

"We cannot both lead — and I am senior. The older. And knight."

"God's sake — *older!* Will someone here knight *me*, then? So that I may show this aged Swinton how to fight?" the Gordon cried.

There was a great shouting, even some laughter, despite the occasion. But Swinton's voice rose above all.

"A pest — but I will knight you myself!" he declared. "So that you may at least die a knight, Gordon!" He drew his sword. "Kneel, you!"

The Gordon hesitated. Then, throwing back his head, he laughed deep-throated. Both men looked at the Earl of Douglas.

It was a curious tense situation in more ways than the obvious. In the field, it was the accepted custom for any knightings to be bestowed by the commander in person. Douglas had made no such gestures. Swinton's tossed out suggestion was in fact something of a challenge to Douglas almost as much as to Gordon. Implied was that the commander was not the man to bestow the honour — for proud men were very concerned as to the calibre of those who gave them the accolade.

Implicit further was that he was but a poor general to have got them into this fix.

Archibald Douglas must have been aware of at least some of this. But he gave no sign save a frown — and he was apt to wear a moody frown anyway. It was within Swinton's right, of course, looked at from another viewpoint. Any knight can in theory create another knight — and only a knight can do so.

"Very well!" There amongst the hissing arrows and cries and shouting, with a flourish Adam Gordon whipped off his plumed helmet and sank on one knee. "On this field, beggars may not be choosers! But — haste you, Swinton, or I shall be skewered as well as dubbed!"

The other slapped down the sword on the steel-clad shoulder with a clang. "By this token I dub thee knight!" he rapped out. "Arise, Sir Adam! Be thou good and true knight until thy life's end. Which 'fore God, is like to be but shortly!"

Laughing, the other rose. "Come, then — let Gordon and Swinton deal with these insolent bowmen. And I swear that I reach them first!" He held out his hand.

Snorting, the older man took it. "Better than waiting here to be slain like deer!" he said. And together they turned to push their way through the crush, calling for their horses.

"This is madness!" Jamie declared. "You should stop it, my lord."

Douglas shook his head, tight-lipped. Swinton had married the first Earl of Douglas's young widow, and retained with her certain lands which succeeding Douglases coveted.

There was now a surge of the Scots leaders south-eastwards, the better to view this attempt — which meant, to be sure, that they were forfeiting something of their beneficial position on the hill, at the receipt of directly-aimed arrows instead of merely dropping fire. However, their shields and superior armour would still aid them. And there was no backwardness among the rank-and-file in giving place and occupying their former stance.

Actually, of course, once the Swinton–Gordon company of under two hundred was mounted and marshalled, the rest of the Scots array could forget about arrows for the time being — or at least their own vulnerability to them; for, from that moment all the archery was concentrated upon the mounted squadron. Even before Gordon's horn-blast sounded the advance, half-a-dozen men and horses had fallen. Men not involved advisedly drew back to give them ample space, as well as clearing a passage for them.

They went at a heartening trot at first, and in good formation, Swinton and Gordon banners streaming side-by-side at the head. But this could not be kept up as the hillside steepened and the whin-bushes and fallen boulders proliferated. All the time, the concentrated rain of arrows poured upon them, the range ever shortening. Saddles were being emptied continuously, amidst yells and screams — although more were emptied by the mounts' collapse than by the riders', for, whether it was policy or merely that the horses provided the larger and less protected targets, these suffered much the greater number of hits. Furiously yelling their slogans, the leaders sought to urge all to greater speed, despite the terrain, and it became hard to tell whether crashing horses and pitching riders were casualties of the bowmen or the hillside.

It is safe to say that not one-half of the Mersemen reached the col between the hills.

All the time reinforcements of archers had been running down from their ridge to join their fellows, bringing fresh supplies of arrows — for they were expending vast quantities of the shafts. These additions produced an intensified and accelerated rate of fire, and it was a positive storm of bolts which swept the horsemen, their ranks now scattered and terribly gapped, as they began to breast the opposite braeside, and now at only some two hundred and fifty yards range.

It was quite hopeless, of course. Nothing could withstand that vicious hail. By the time Sir John Swinton fell, not seventy of the two hundred remained. By half-way up the slope, when Gordon's horse was shot under him, not forty survived. Waving his sword and roaring defiance the new knight lurched on on foot. When, eventually, he crashed to the ground, a bare hundred yards from the first bowmen, three arrows projecting from his person, only a dozen men straggled behind him, none now mounted. None turned to flee. All fell in a swathe, as from a single lash, facing the enemy.

A great corporate groan rose from the watching Scots — to be drowned in yells of triumph and derision from the English.

The archers lifted their aim once more, to the major target.

That gallant débâcle had a profound effect on the Scots — much more than the numbers involved might seem to warrant. Men saw it as underlining the hopelessness of their position.

Flight began to be considered. Scowls were directed towards the leadership. Men commenced to push and struggle away from those south and east flanks of Homildon Hill, further from the bowmen, caring little for orders.

More significant still, perhaps, was the effect on the Earl of Douglas himself — or it may have been as it were, the effect of the effect. After such long uncertainty and temporising, he seemed to come to a conclusion. He turned suddenly to his trumpeter and ordered a summoning blast.

"To me! To me!" he shouted, thereafter. "All leaders to me." They had lowered the banners now, as too obviously pinpointing targets.

When most of his lords and knights had gathered round, he spoke.

"We cannot wait longer here," he declared. "Swinton and Gordon have died bravely. But they have shown us the way. We shall not waste their sacrifice. There were too few of them. And mounted was not best. But their notion was right. We shall all go. Afoot. Down and across that col, and up at the archers. Some will die, undoubtedly. But some are dying now. There are many of us. We shall up and overwhelm them. And when we have taken that higher hill from them, and are no longer overlooked thus, we can bring our horses over. Enough of standing waiting."

There was a ragged cheer, the reaction of frustrated, impatient men, desperate for action.

Jamie did not cheer. "My lord," he began, "if it was folly for Swinton and Gordon, it is more so for you! I say that . . ."

"Sir James," the Earl interrupted, strongly now, "enough! The decision is mine. If you do not like it, bide you here and guard the horses."

There was a grim laugh at that.

Jamie's face set. "Is that your command, my lord?"

"Yes. To be sure. Someone must do so, lest Percy's cavalry come up this hill while we are at it." Douglas turned away. "Come then, my friends — let us all deal with these accursed bowmen . . ."

Hot anger in the head but leaden cold at heart, Jamie watched and listened as the Scots nobles and gentry made their hurried dispositions. After the long inaction and abdication of leadership, they were anxious to prove their courage, prowess and determination. They themselves would form the forefront of

363

the assault — with their finer armour and shields they were the better equipped for it, anyway. Behind them the serried ranks of the men would march, in their thousands. They would march indeed, not race nor run nor scurry, until they were within a hundred yards or so of the enemy; then they would charge, and drive those archers before them like chaff. With their numbers, they could not fail.

With an added pang, Jamie found that his brothers James and Will had brought him the wounded Johnnie, to leave in his care; they themselves were hurrying off to join the other lairds.

"Come back, you fools!" he shouted after them. "You are going to your deaths! To no purpose."

But they did not so much as glance behind them.

"Are they all crazy-mad?" he demanded of Johnnie. "God pity us all — this day Scotland goes down in senseless ruin! And the Douglas leads the way!"

Johnnie muttered something incoherent.

Recollecting, Jamie turned. "Your wound? How grievous? Is it sore pain?"

His brother was very white, reeling on his feet. "Shoulder," he got out, from tight lips. "I am . . . well enough."

"They got the arrow out? Broke it off?"

"Yes."

"See you — sit, Johnnie . . ."

A trumpet-blast heralded the Scots advance. Banners raised again, and beginning to chant their various slogans, the marshalled lines moved downhill, pacing deliberately behind the illustrious front rank — although to be sure men were falling before they even began. Helplessly Jamie watched, praying that somehow he should be wrong in his judgement and prophesy.

He was not. What he was watching was steady, unremitting bloody slaughter, on a vast scale. How many archers were now facing them they did not know, but it obviously ran into thousands. Aiming and shooting with swift competence and monotonous regularity, each sent a succession of deadly shafts into the advancing mass. They could not miss with a single shot — the target was solid.

The nobles and knights fared only a little better than the men-at-arms and mosstroopers. Their half-armour did not cover their lower quarters, and arrows were able to pierce joints and openings in helmets and cuirasses. So they were falling long before they reached the floor of the col, and the banner-bearers with them. Jamie saw Livingstone of Callander drop and Ramsay of Dalhousie, while still on their own hill-side; and others whom he could not recognise at the distance. He saw Douglas himself go down, with an arrow projecting from his gorget, and then rise again and stagger on. Behind men were pitching and crashing all the time, the slogans and yells now tending to be lost in a horrible cacophony of screams and groans.

Jamie's own groan rose to join the others as he saw his brother Will lurch, reel and drop on all fours, to be lost under the advance of the others. Crossing the col with half the knightly forefront gone now, the Earl of Douglas again dropped — and again he struggled to his feet, limping now as well as staggering. His standard-bearer had been replaced three times already.

The Earl of Angus fell as they began to breast the opposite rise. Maxwell followed him in no more than a couple of paces. Then Sinclair. Everywhere the ground was littered with the Scots dead and dying.

Gulping down his emotion, Jamie dragged his gaze away from the shambles to look back and down. The host of English cavalry below still awaited developments. From down there, of course, they would not be able to see what went on up between the hills — and since sizeable numbers of the Scots rank-and-file, including the Dalkeith contingent, had elected not to join the suicidal assault, it might not seem from below as though the situation had much changed. At any rate, no advance was attempted up the hill meantime — although it was only a question of time before word must reach Hotspur, or whoever was in command down there, of the Scots move, and vigorous reaction would follow.

When the unhappy watcher faced front again, loathing himself for his own safety and entire lack of activity in face of all this horror and desperation, he was just in time to see the Earl Archibald reeling backwards into the arms of those immediately behind, a shaft actually protruding from under the upraised visor of his Douglas-plumed helmet. That must be the end of him, surely. But no — part lurching forward on his own, part propelled and supported from behind, he struggled on, the arrow, half-broken off but still obtruding from his helmet like some additional crest. Clearly the archers were making an especial target of him. There was nothing wrong with Archibald Douglas's personal courage, only with his wits and generalship.

Jamie beat his fist on his breastplate in an access of fury, bafflement and helplessness. The urge to do the obvious was now all but overwhelming — to gather together as many as he might of the Scots left on the hilltop, with his Dalkeith men, mount, and hurl themselves down to the rescue of the hard-pressed ranks below. So simple an action — if men would follow him. But useless, he knew — quite useless. It would merely mean many more dead, to salve his conscience. Half the archers would but transfer their aim to his company for a little. The Swinton disaster had demonstrated the hopelessness of anything such. His own witless folly would not help any.

Even as he stared, biting his lip, he saw the reeling Douglas go down once more — and this time he did not arise. Earl Murdoch of Fife, Albany's son, appeared to be the only noble-man left on his feet, and even he was hirpling on, using his sword as a crutch. Only two or three knights remained, including the Douglas brothers of Drumlanrig and Cavers. There was now no sign of Jamie's own brother James.

Still there were perhaps three hundred uphill yards to go before the first of the massed bowmen.

It seemed to dawn upon the thinned ranks of the survivors, then, that they could by no means make it. Further struggle was quite pointless. The recognition appeared to sweep across the ragged front as though by some signal. In only moments the forward momentum, sorely flagging as it was by now, came not so much to a halt as changed into dispersal. Without pause men turned left or right or round about. Suddenly what was left of the assault was a flight, a rout. What remained of the leadership stumbled on until it fell.

Jamie Douglas's agonised watching and waiting was at an end. He knew what he had to do now — action at least and at long last. Raising Johnnie up, he shouted,

"To me! To me, Douglas! To horse! To horse!"

The men left above on the hilltop were, of course, desperately awaiting a lead. Swiftly the word spread, and there was a rush to do his bidding. Jamie grabbed a spare horse — and there were literally thousands of these — and somehow hoisted and heaved his wounded brother up into the saddle.

"Can you hold on?" he gasped, and at Johnnie's nod, found a mount for himself. To the men now surging all around them,

366

he pointed downhill, westwards, towards where he had left the Dalkeith company.

He was spurring to ride thither himself, leading Johnnie's horse, when he perceived many men hoisting wounded on to their horses, to carry before them at their saddle-bows. Frowning, he hesitated, then shouted.

"No! Leave them. Leave them, I say. Only wounded who can ride. It is hard. But what we do, we cannot do burdened by wounded. Only those who can ride, I say. Bring spare horses, rather . . ."

If men cursed him, then, he had to accept it as part of *his* burden.

As he rode down to his Dalkeith people, he saw that there was now movement in the mass of the English cavalry below the hill. They were beginning to stream south by west — or some considerable proportion of them. That meant, he feared, that they had been informed of the débâcle up on the higher ground, and were moving round to cut off the escape of survivors and stragglers. Which but made his task all the more urgent, although not necessarily more difficult.

Swiftly he calculated that there might be five hundred men behind him. That, with his Dalkeith contingent, would give him almost 1,000. Fewer would have been more easy to handle. But no point in splitting up meantime.

Placing himself at the head of the Dalkeith men — whose thankfulness to see him was evident — he yelled his instructions.

"Follow me. Round the hill. Save what we can of the others. Battle lost. Then, down and through. In wedges. Come!"

Whether these orders reached far back amongst the nine hundred or so was doubtful; but the following on, meantime, was obvious. They set off fast round the swell of the hill, at about the six hundred-feet contour.

It was not long before they were into the first of the fleeing survivors from the disaster, none mounted of course. The spare horses were grabbed gratefully.

On they swept, round to the south end of the col, or just below it. As Jamie had calculated, the bowmen had dispensed with their archery at last, broken their serried ranks and had in the main descended upon the killing-ground, swords in hand, to capture lords and knights for ransom, hunt down stragglers, kill off wounded, and collect their spent arrows — of which they must now be in very short supply. They were accordingly in

367

poor state to cope with the unexpected Scots mounted force.

Chaos ensued — at least, chaos on the part of the English. For the archers left behind higher on Housedon Hill could not now shoot down into the mêlée without risk of skewering their own colleagues. Jamie did not have as firm control over his miscellaneous crew as he would have liked, but sufficient to retain the initiative meantime.

They could have saved a great many men undoubtedly — had they had time. And they did save more than they had horses for, and had to send others running up Homildon again to collect beasts still roaming riderless up there. But Jamie was oppressed by the thought of the English cavalry host streaming below, making for this re-entrant and less steep approach. They would be here in a matter of only brief minutes. And then all would be lost. He had no doubts as to his task, duty and priorities.

There was no time for search or quartering the field, no time for seeking out and rescuing highly-placed wounded, no time for any consistent slaughter of the enemy archers, however tempting the opportunity. Jamie wanted desperately to look for his brothers, but could not do that either. He would have extricated the bodies of the Earl Douglas and other lords if he would — not for their own sakes so much as for the fact that a defeat was considered to be less damaging if most of the leadership escaped. But amongst the thousands of slain and wounded, he discerned only the Lord Sinclair of Roslin and Ramsay of Dalhousie, and both were dead. They did collect Will of Drumlanrig, dazed but only slightly wounded supporting his brother of Cavers, more so; but there was no time for more. Hating himself, yet resolute, Jamie blew his horn, to break off the engagement.

"To me!" he cried. "To me! Muster!" He pointed southwards, whence they had come. "Leave all. Come!"

There were murmurs, even amongst those close to him, at that harsh command. But he was insistent.

Already their time was short. There were fewer murmurs when they faced south behind the lip of the col. There, coming up the hill to them, in the groove of the re-entrant, was the broad front of the English cavalry, banners at the head, and not four hundred yards away.

Shaken, men stared.

Jamie wasted no more precious moments. "Back to our former position!" he shouted, pointing westwards once more, and led his enlarged and distinctly unwieldy company round the contour of the hill again, at right-angles away from the enemy advance.

Part of the English array broke off to swing and follow them.

At approximately the position where the Dalkeith men had waited formerly, he drew up. At the foot of the hill below them the English main body was still streaming southwards, before turning up the re-entrant, squadron upon squadron. If there had been little time before, there was less now that they were being pursued.

"Wedges," he ordered. "Form wedges. Three of them. Quickly. Will — take one. About four hundred men. Wattie — you too. Hurry! We go down in three wedges. Together. God willing, right through! Halt for nothing."

It had to be a very rough-and-ready business, only really a gesture at arrowhead-formation. It was to be hoped that they could improve on it as they went down. Into three approximate triangles they split up, uneven in numbers as in shape, wounded in the centre, leaders at the apex, under-officers at the rear flanks. Jamie, with his Dalkeith people, had that furthest to the north. He waited as long as he dared — which was only for a few moments — before raising horn to lips again. Then, with barely one hundred and fifty yards between their last wedge and the oncoming English from the battle approach area, he slashed his sword forward and down, and drove his horse onwards. In some sort of fashion, in an attempt at unison, the other two formations did the same.

Riding knee-to-knee, save for the lone individual at the tip of each apex, as close and tight-packed as horses at speed over uneven ground could move, they thundered directly downhill, three phalanxes in line abreast, yelling — and since all three were led by Douglases, it was "A Douglas! A Douglas!" that they shouted, a chant which until this day had brought fear and quaking to every North of England heart.

Below, the English reaction was, not unnaturally, confused. None of their senior leadership was present — for this, after all, was fully half-way down their lengthy column. They were meantime in line-of-march, not in the right formation to withstand such an attack in flank. And they would have been congratulating themselves that victory was already theirs. All of which would help the Scots. Only, there were many more of

369

them than in the wedges. And they were not burdened by wounded.

With less than six hundred yards to cover, at a scrambling canter, there was only about one minute between start and impact — which gave little opportunity either for the enemy to change front and regroup, or for the Scots to improve their formation. So that the crash, when it came, was less than a copybook example of arrowhead-charge and defence. Nor was the attack completely synchronised. Inevitably, Jamie's wedge, first off the mark and best led, hit the English line ahead of the others. This was no serious matter in the circumstances, but it did have the effect of buckling the enemy front somewhat and so lessening the impact of the others.

Impact, impetus, was the essence of this tactic, rather than fighting or swordery. Indeed it might be argued that weapons were all but immaterial — or at least that, in theory, it could still be effective with all the attackers unarmed. Jamie, in the lead, went in swinging his sword in a figure-of-eight pattern, left and right; but whether it made contact with any of the foe was not important. What was vital was that the encounter should be violent, the momentum overwhelming and, above all, continuing. To lose impetus would be fatal. In this, the steep hill down was much in the Scots' favour. Also the fact that men, stationary or nearly so, are almost bound to flinch before the final impact of a head-long charge — and if, by superhuman willpower they do not, their horses can be guaranteed to do so.

All depended upon these two factors, therefore — willpower and horses — on both sides, but with the balance strongly in favour of the attackers.

Jamie was aware of wild-eyed animals rearing and swerving and backing before him as he smashed in, sword swinging, breathlessly gasping his own surname. The lances which could have skewered them wavered, veered or were tossed aside. One snapped off short against his shield, all but unseating him with the jolt. Recovering himself partly by major effort and partly by the enormous pressure behind, he was almost immediately into further trouble as his mount pecked and stumbled over an English horse fallen directly in its path. Flung over its arching neck, he clung on desperately, somehow managing to retain his sword. If his beast had gone down, nothing could have saved him from being trampled by his own followers. But the animal recovered itself, and a strong arm at his side, or a little behind, helped him to regain his saddle once more. He plunged on.

Even had he sought to reduce speed he could not have done so, with such weight of driving, snorting horseflesh behind him. The enemy was not now in any recognisable ranks, and he had little idea as to what width was the barrier of men he had to plough through. But since they had been in column-of-march and not forming a front, it could not be so very wide.

Borne on, he found that the further back the English the less inclined they were to stand and face it out — a very natural reaction, no doubt. If he had achieved little with his sword hitherto, he was offered no targets sufficiently near now. A swift glance behind, however, showed that the riders at the flanks of his V were able to do better, were more in actual contact with the enemy, slashing and thrusting continuously.

The vast majority of the Scots, including the wounded, in the tight-packed centre, scarcely saw their foes.

Suddenly Jamie was through, with only scurrying fugitives before him — and was scarcely able to believe it. Behind him his wedge emerged all but intact, their few casualties almost wholly caused by horses stumbling and falling over obstacles.

Pounding on without pause, he gazed to the left. There, so far, was only a confused mass of milling men and beasts, with the other two wedges not to be distinguished as such. His impulse was to swing round to their aid — but he stifled it. That was not the priority, and could be dangerous. The enemy who had been pursuing them round the hill were now in turn streaming down. They could rally their colleagues down here. To maintain velocity and the initiative was still his objective — and this could still be lost.

So they thundered on westwards towards the welter of foot-hills which rose to the Cheviots, the first barely half-a-mile away. But every few moments Jamie was glancing over his left shoulder. Thankfully he saw the wedge next to his own, Will of Drumlanrig's, emerge from the mêlée, still in some sort of order. The third was not yet extricated.

The urge to turn back, to go to the help of the group under Wattie Douglas, the largest but almost certainly the least effective of the formations, was stronger than ever. But it would be folly — and Jamie reminded himself that there had been more than enough folly for one day. He pressed on.

Shouts caused him to turn his head again. All along the rear of the confused and gapped English line riders were emerging,

371

breaking through in ones and twos and groups. The third wedge had broken up, then, but some of its people were winning out.

Presently they could see many men streaming after them across the Howtel valley-floor, just south of the marshland. Undoubtedly these were their own folk, not English in pursuit. Not yet.

On the skirts of the first of the foothills, Jamie breathlessly blew his horn, and signed all to draw rein. Everywhere men thankfully pulled up. The second wedge came pounding up. Jamie at last could look to his brother. Johnnie was slumped in his saddle, held upright by the muscular arm of one of the Dalkeith men. Many another was in like case, including Archie of Cavers. Men of the third formation were now coming up, many of them also wounded. They made a grim company of perhaps eight hundred, survivors of eight thousand and more. Wattie Douglas was one of the last to join them, helmetless and bleeding.

Jamie raised a hoarse voice. "My friends," he called, "you did that passing well. I say you did that well. *We* live to fight again! This has been a sorry day. But . . . let us thank God for what we can."

There was a murmur through the ranks — although somewhere a man was gabbling hysterically, no doubt part-concussed.

"We are not out of trouble yet," he went on. "We are a long way from home, and many of us are hurt. The English, once they have recovered from their surprise, will be after us. We are in no state to do battle. Therefore, it seems, we must continue to ride — however sore a trial."

None commented.

"*My* sorest trial was, and is, leaving behind our wounded on yonder hill," he jerked stiffly, harshly. "I left two brothers there. But . . . we could do no other. We could by no means have won through that line burdened by grievously wounded men. We all know it. If anything was to be saved, it had to be this way."

Again the silence of unwilling assent.

"By the same token, we cannot go back there. Naught that we can do. They are more than ten times our number. It . . . it is a most grievous matter. To ride off, for home, and leave our friends in this fell place, hurt, dead or prisoner. But this is war. Many will escape the field, no doubt. Is there any here who can tell me any other course?"

No voice was raised, save that of Will Douglas of Drumlanrig. "Jamie — they are massing now. In the centre. I think they are coming after us."

"Aye. So be it. Time we were amove. We shall head north by west. Branxton lies west of Flodden Edge, I know, and Cornhill beyond Branxton. Tweed cannot be more than six miles. God with us, we can ford it at Wark or Coldstream. These English will not follow us beyond, I think — not this day . . ."

So they rode away from the Vale of Till and the sorriest defeat Scottish arms had suffered in over a century. They were followed, but warily, and by a company apparently not seeking to bring them to battle again, only to see them off English soil. In less than an hour, broad Tweed was gleaming before them, at Learmouth. Avoiding Cornhill village, they forded the river at Wark, their numbers sufficient to prevent any attack from the castle garrison there, their pursuers remaining almost a mile behind.

On Scots soil at last, Jamie turned and looked back. "We may go more gently now, Johnnie," he said. "And soon you may rest. Six more miles to Swinton. Is it bad?"

"Not so bad that I cannot make Swinton. Bearing but ill tidings."

"Ill, yes." He bit his lip. "Johnnie — did I do rightly, back there? Did I make the right choice, at Homildon?"

"Any right done this day, *you* did!" his brother said thickly. "James and Will would say the same. Now — let us on, for God's good sake!"

XX

IT WAS SOME days before Jamie stood before his father in the castle of Dalkeith, for he had had much to see to. He had waited on in the Merse, between Swinton and the Border, in case the English did decide to make a retaliatory raid, and to collect stragglers. He had bestowed the wounded in the nearby Abbeys of Kelso, Dryburgh and Melrose, where the monks were skilled in the healing arts. And, on his slow way northwards thereafter — for his brother Johnnie was in no state for riding fast or far — he had gone to inform Margaret, Countess of Douglas, the King's eldest daughter, at Dunbar Castle, of her husband's fate, but had found the princess gone elsewhere, with the news already preceding him. And so he had brought his brother home to Dalkeith at length, and now stood in the lord thereof's book-lined study, aware, as he had never been before, of being less than welcome there.

For the ill news had preceded him here also, and the old lord's fine features were cold, cold.

"So you have come!" he said stiffly, tightly, although there was just a hint of a quaver behind the strained voice. "I doubted whether you would dare. Aye, I doubted it."

"Why should I not, Father? To tell you of all, ill as it is? And to bring Johnnie home."

"Aye — to bring *Johnnie* home!" the other exclaimed. "Johnnie — your bastard brother! Him you saved. But what of James, my heir? And Will? My lawful sons! What of them? They were your brothers, too, were they not?"

"Yes. Yes, to be sure. But they . . . they went their own way. Johnnie was wounded . . ."

"They were wounded also, were they not? You left them there, on the field. Fallen. And you fled. Bringing back with you only the other bastard like yourself! And now come to tell me of the deed!"

Jamie drew a deep breath. "My lord — I believed that you would wish to hear how your sons fell. Bravely, if foolishly. But then, all was folly, at Homildon . . ."

"But *you* were wise — and turned tail!"

The young man opened his mouth, and shut it again, almost with a click. He turned, and strode to the window, to stare out, not trusting himself to speak.

"Tell me then, boy," the old man cried hoarsely. "Tell me what you have come to tell. Since you deemed it worth the coming."

Jamie turned back. "My lord — you are sore at heart, at your loss. But so am I, at mine. For I love my brothers. As I love you." That took some getting out, for this was not a man who talked of love and affection easily. "You have always shown love to *me*. Do not hurt yourself, and me, the more, by deeming me false. That I was not, I promise you. I may have made a mistake, many mistakes. But I was not false, nor craven. You know me, surely? I did not flee. I cut my way out. And saved near nine hundred. I did not *flee* from Homildon."

"Yet you came home safe. And left your brothers on the field. You, the most experienced, the warrior. And left your chief, the Earl of your name. You are not denying that?"

"Deny, no. The chief of our name is a fool. He mismanaged all, from the start. I was there to counsel him — he had sent for me, for that. Yet he would heed me nothing . . ."

"And because he was a fool and would not heed you, you deserted him? And your brothers?"

"No! How can I make you understand? The Earl's last command to me was to bide there on the hill-top. To see to the horses, left behind, and the residue of the force. That was folly, likewise — but it *was* his command. Not that I would not have disobeyed it, had there been cause. But he was leading the rest to disaster. Hopeless, inevitable disaster. Charging massed archers, with a valley between and a higher hill beyond. The veriest child should have known the outcome. I told him, but he would nowise heed. I sought to keep James and Will from following him — but they did not so much as answer me. The Earl ordered me to bide where I was, to see to the rearward and

375

the residue. Then dismounted, marched down with his main array, to fall under the arrows of thousands of bowmen. Should I, then, have followed on, to fall likewise, with the residue? None could ever have reached those archers on the hill."

"God knows, boy! But, as I heard it, you did go down. Later. When it was too late. Saved Drumlanrig and Cavers. But fled when the cavalry came up?"

"There is some truth in that, yes. I did not ride down, into the arrows, but round the hill. To come in from the far side. To seek save what I might. The bowmen had stopped shooting, were slaying and plundering. But the English cavalry were on their way up — we had seen them coming. We had only a little time. I had but some six hundred men then — against thousands. Many wounded — Johnnie amongst them. If we were to cut our way out, at all, it had to be done in good order, in tight wedges. We dared not be caught, scattered, beforehand. So that we did — and must needs leave the rest. Did I mistake?"

"You could have saved your brothers. And the Earl."

"I did not see where they lay. There were *thousands* dead and dying in that col! In the moments we had, would you have had me seek and search only for them? Leaving all others? Would my name have smelled the sweeter, then?"

His father ran a hand through his scanty hair. "I do not know. But this I do know — your name now stinks in the noses of honest men. And others! Notably the Governor's. For as well as your brothers, and Douglas, you left behind his precious son Murdoch Stewart, his heir. You returned, but Murdoch of Fife did not. For that he will not forgive you — and he mislikes you sufficiently already."

"I would have saved the Earl of Fife if I had seen him there before us. As any other. Would you have had me seek him out specially?"

"Not me, lad. But *Albany* would. And Albany rules this land, and with a heavy hand. I am told that decree is out for your arrest already, as craven and traitor! A son of mine . . .!"

"Dear God — traitor! Me, traitor? Any English slain at Homildon, *I* slew! Craven, because I cut my way through the enemy cavalry instead of falling helpless under their arrows without striking back? Is that Albany's judgement?"

"You left his son on the field. As you left your chief. There is no getting past that, boy. What think you the whole house of Douglas will call you now?"

376

"Surely not . . . ? Not Douglas! I saved many Douglases . . ."

"Not the right ones, it may be!"

"I will go tell them. Go round Douglas. Tell the truth . . ."

"That you will not, Jamie. Do you not understand? You are an outlaw. Decree out for your apprehension. By the Governor's personal warrant. Every man's hand is by law turned against you. None may aid you, an outlaw, under penalty of that same law. Douglas *might* have risked supporting you against Albany — but will not now. Albany has wanted you brought down, for long. Now he has you. You cannot bide here. Anyone sheltering an outlaw acts against the realm. Treason. And you have no Duke David to protect you now."

Shaken, Jamie stared at his father. "He can do that? On no more than ignorant hearsay?"

"To be sure he can. And will. You will have to go back whence you came — and swiftly. Back to the Hielands. Hide yourself with your friend Alexander Stewart. As before . . ."

"I would go there, anyway. Mary is there, and the children."

"Aye. But this time, not to come back! Not until your outlawry is lifted. Which could be years. Do you understand? Albany does not forgive."

They looked at each other in silence.

"James and Will?" Jamie said, at length. "Have you heard anything of them? Any sure tidings?"

"Yes. They are prisoners at Alnwick Castle. Both wounded but not grievously, thank God. Hotspur sent word. They are his prisoners. For ransom. As also is the Earl Archibald. He has lost an eye, and is otherwise wounded, but will live. The Percy demands large ransom. I have to collect it. He prices Douglas high!"

"The siller, gear, is the least of it."

"True. But it has its importance. We cannot overlook it, boy. As you have ever been apt to do. Lacking it, we should be a deal lesser men than we are! Mind it. And, Jamie — while we are on this of gear and property, I require something of you. I am sorry, lad — but it has to be. And you have brought it on yourself. I have a paper here for you to sign."

"A paper? Are you charging my brothers' ransom to *me*, because I did not bring them home?"

"Not that, no. I shall pay their ransom. This is otherwise." He rose stiffly, and went to a table, where he sought and found a paper. "This is a letter. From you, Jamie. Resigning to your

377

brother Johnnie all your lands, properties and titles whatsoever In the baronies of Aberdour, Stoneypath and Baldwinsgill. Given to you by myself at sundry times."

"What? *Resign?*" the younger man gasped. "Aberdour? My home! You cannot mean this . . . ?"

"That I do, lad. It is necessary, see you. There is no other way."

"This . . . this I did not think of you, my lord!"

"Fool, boy — do you not see? An outlaw's whole property is forfeit. To the Crown. Albany will have it, nothing surer. This way, it will be in Johnnie's name, not yours. Safe. Who knows, one day you may get it back. But meantime, Albany will not get his hands on it."

"And Mary and our bairns are homeless! Penniless . . . !"

"You are that, anyway, so long as you are outlaw. Use your wits, Jamie. It is for the best."

Biting his lip, son stared at father. "I pay a price for coming south to give the Earl of Douglas counsel!" he said.

"The price is rather for your headstrong fight against the Duke of Albany, I think."

"A man you yourself despise and hate!"

"But have the wits not to cross unnecessarily! He is too strong for you, Jamie — too strong for me also. It is a wise man who knows his own strength and weakness. Now — sign you this . . ."

Heavy-hearted and heavy-handed, Jamie Douglas signed away his home, lairdships and status. Though they could not take away from him his knighthood, at least . . .

* * *

Jamie had proved, before this, that it was impossible to approach Lochindorb Castle in its Braemoray hills unannounced, with news relayed thither, from far and near, by means undisclosed but little short of wonderful to southern minds. On this occasion, now fully a month after Homildon, weary and dejected, with only a single groom as companion, he topped the long ridge of Creag an Righ to see the silvery gleam of the loch ahead, it was to see also three horsed figures riding up through the heather towards him, and all beginning to wave at sight of him. His heart warmed as it had not done for many a day, as he spurred to meet them.

They met in a welter of incoherences, throwing themselves from their mounts to embrace and exclaim, to laugh and hug

378

and cling, Mary and their two children and the travel-stained fugitive reunited at last. The groom discreetly held back and looked away.

It was some time before any sense was spoken — although Mary had the name of being an eminently sensible young woman. But eventually the emotional tide ebbed a little, and they could look at each other in more rational fashion.

"You are thin, Jamie," she charged. "My dear, my dear, you look but poorly."

"And you, my love, look more beautiful than ever, I swear! And these two, grown, on my soul! Larger, taller. Or do my eyes deceive me?"

"It must be your eyes, I think," the practical David said. "For we cannot have grown much in but three months, see you."

"Three months? Only that since I left? Save us — it seems a lifetime!"

"Has it been so bad, Jamie?" Mary asked, holding him to her. "Was it all a great evil? I am so thankful to know you safe and see you back to us, that I can think of little else."

"It was bad. All of it, from start to finish. How much have you heard?"

"But little. Only that there was a great defeat. In England. That the Douglas fell, and Angus with him. Indeed the flower of Scotland lost . . ."

"But that *I* came out with a whole skin! Left the field, and home in safety! All Scotland rings with that word, today!"

Troubled, she looked at him searchingly. "We heard only that you had escaped — thank God! Amongst the few. No more."

"Albany would be sore disappointed! He expects better than that from his whisperers, I warrant!"

"What do you mean, Jamie?"

"I mean, my dear, that the land is loud with your husband's infamy and treachery! Or the Lowlands are — where Albany's word reaches. I am the man who deserted the others, ran off the stricken field, leaving better men to their fate. Rode for home in haste, leaving his chief, even his own brothers, to the English spleen."

"None who know you would believe a word of that!"

"No? Then many know me less well than I had thought. My own father, it seems. *He* blames me. For bringing home only another bastard and leaving his heir, and Will, on Homildon Hill."

At the bitterness in his voice Mary drew a deep breath and glanced at the children. Noting her look, he changed his tone, nodding.

"To be sure. I am tired, hungry. They say that an empty belly gives but a poor report. Let us down to that kindly Stewart table, then."

As they remounted and set off, he asked, "Alex and his mother — how are they?"

"Sir Alex has been fighting the Islesmen," the boy informed. "There have been battles and burnings. But he won. You would have been better here."

"So-o-o! Donald did strike, then?"

"Yes," Mary confirmed. "Not himself. He sent Alastair Carrach again."

"And Drummond? Did Drummond join him? What of Drummond?"

Mary hesitated. "I shall tell you later. It is a long story."

At her tone, he glanced at her quickly. Again her eyes went to the children.

"Aye," he said. "Time enough for that. What is important is that all is well with you here?"

"Yes. All is well, now that you are back. It has been an anxious time. Still may be. But — so long as you are here, the rest we can thole. Alex is still chasing Islesmen back to their Isles. Mariota will welcome you . . ."

They came to the shore of Lochindorb and were ferried over to the castle-island. It seemed a secure haven indeed to the man who had travelled furtively two hundred miles to reach it.

Later, with the children safely out of hearing, they sat in Mariota's own chamber before an aromatic birch-log fire, at ease in body at least.

"This of the Islesmen?" he enquired. "It was all as Alex feared?"

"Yes. The death of the Earl of Ross, and Albany's assumption of the heiress's wardship ensured it," Mariota said. "A great fleet of galleys landed in Moidart, where MacDonald is kin to Clanranald. They crossed the land swiftly. Inverness they burned. They turned south for Forres and Elgin, harrying, slaying. There Alex caught up with them, with a Highland host, in the main Clan Chattan, and defeated them — but not before

Alastair had burned much of Elgin and the canons' houses. He chases them still."

"Aye. That is Alex! And Drummond? Did Drummond not rise, after all?"

There was a pause. "Drummond could not rise. Because Drummond was dead!"

"Dead!" He stared. "What is this?"

"Drummond was slain. And I fear that Alex will get the blame for it."

"Save us — not that! That is not Alex's style."

"No. But still he is like to be blamed. We do not know all of it. Or much. Alex has not been back here since it happened. When he heard of Alastair Carrach's landing, he sent a small force under three of his brothers to watch Drummond, whilst he gathered the main force to halt the Islesmen. Drummond was taken, in some fashion, whilst riding in Brae-Mar. Captured and held in some lonely house in the mountains. And there given neither food nor drink. He died . . . of starvation!"

"Merciful God! Starvation — Drummond! The same death as David!"

"The same death as David," the woman repeated, level-voiced. "And not by chance, I fear. You will see, therefore, why Alex may well be blamed."

"But . . . but . . . who did it?"

The mother of five sons shook her handsome head. "We do not know. None have been back to Lochindorb since. We cannot tell who, or why. Save that it was not Alex's work. That I know well."

Jamie looked from Mariota to Mary and back. "This is beyond all! I can well see what his enemies will make of it. And the Countess . . . ?"

"We have no word of that accursed woman! Who knows what her part will be? Or was?"

That was not like Mariota de Athyn, a generous and friendly soul. Her hearers could understand, however. For even though it was not Alex, it looked as though one or other of her sons had done this terrible deed. And she had always hated Alex's entanglement with Isobel of Mar.

"She would have no part in this, any more than Alex," Jamie asserted hurriedly. "What of Drummond's people? Have they risen? In wrath?"

"Not that we have heard."

"You would have heard if they had, I think! The Drummonds are a potent clan. Alex will have to counter this, clear his name. And he is in the West? Would that I had never left his side."

"Amen to that!" Mary said. "What went wrong, Jamie? With *your* venture?"

"All was wrong, from the start. The Earl Archibald is no commander, no soldier at all. Nor those near him. He could not, or would not, control his men. Brave enough, yes — but more than that is required of a general."

"But he knew all that, did he not? And sent for you to advise him?"

"Sent for me, yes — but did not heed me." Unhappily, Jamie went on to describe for them something of the follies of that ill-conceived campaign, and its aftermath.

"Mother of God!" Mary cried. "But at least there was no blame for you in all this?"

"But I *am* being blamed. Do you not see? I am the survivor, the one who got away. Ran away! The man of experience, who saved himself."

Unhappily she considered him. "Jamie — this is not like you. To care what others say."

"I care what my father says . . ."

"A man can only do what he deems right, at the time," Mariota declared. "What he thinks of later is nothing to the point."

"You could say that of the Earl of Douglas also! He chose the wrong course, whilst no doubt deeming it right. Perhaps *I* chose wrongly? I chose to save something, a remainder, eight hundred and seventy men. It may be that the better part would have been to go and fall with the others?"

"*I* thank the good God you so chose!" his wife said fervently. "And you are safe here, at least — where Robert's writ does not run . . ."

"God Almighty!" he burst out. "Can you not see? Even you! It is not safety I seek, but, but . . ." With a great effort he controlled himself. "I am sorry, lass. Forgive me. I am weary, scarce myself. Some sleep, and I shall be a better man. Give me a little time . . ."

"Time indeed, Jamie — all the time you need, my dear. And the love, affection, peace you need also. I think that *you* were wounded in this sorry battle, as sore as any! These you shall have, in good measure, I vow!"

"Yes — but the safety too," Mariota insisted. "You may not seek it, my friend, but you shall have it, in this house and country. That *I* vow!"

He looked from one to the other. "Forgive me," he said again. "I do not deserve it, but I see that I am rich indeed. When, in my self-pity, I esteemed myself poor, penniless, a beggar indeed . . ."

Mary laughed, if with a catch in it. "Scarcely a beggar, Jamie? Sir James Douglas of Aberdour, Stoneypath and Baldwinsgill!"

"No longer of Aberdour, Stoneypath and Baldwinsgill, lass. My father prevailed on me to sign all these away. To Johnnie. *He* is laird of all, now. Lest Albany take them, as the property of an outlaw — as my father says he most certainly would. Albany now rules all unchallenged, with not even the power of Douglas to restrain him. The rewards of unwearied evil-doing! My noble sire has a great respect for property, and would not see it forfeited for my . . . failures. So all is now Johnnie's."

"Aberdour? Our home . . .!"

"Our home, lass, I fear is now wherever your outlawed husband can find shelter for his wife and bairns! I have, all along supported the wrong — or leastways, the *losing* side — in this your royal brother's Scotland. And now you and our children must pay the penalty. The truer riches you provide for me are to my much advantage. But, for yourself, I fear they offer but doubtful exchange for a roof, bed and victual! You wed the wrong man, my dear."

"I think otherwise. Besides, your father will give you back your lands when all this trouble is past, will he not?"

"There is no certainty of that. And he is old, and may not live so long. His heir, once ransomed, may feel less than grateful to his bastard brother who left him lying on Homildon Hill."

"I care not. We shall do very well, I swear. Turn Hieland, and make a new life for ourselves . . ."

"Yes, start anew," Mariota agreed strongly. "Put the past behind you. As, I fear, Alex will have to do also. He will not be able to remain acting Justiciar, I think. That was possible so long as the Highland chiefs supported him. But now, with *An Drumanach Mor*'s death hanging over him, the Clan Donald his enemies, and Albany controlling the earldom of Ross, it would be difficult indeed. Besides, knowing Alex, he will wish to have no part in it until his name is cleared. So . . . you both must make a fresh start. And if you do it together, hold to each other, I have no doubts for either. You will make a pair hard to beat

383

Jamie — Douglas and Stewart. With, between you, what is best in both. I am no spaewife, but I foresee great things for you if you hold together. Fear you nothing and none, lad, Albany, Donald or other. You have all that is required to beat them." She rose, and came to kiss him frankly on the lips. "Now — to your bed. And tomorrow start afresh, Sir James and Lady Douglas!"

The Captive Crown

PRINCIPAL CHARACTERS

In Order of Appearance

SIR JAMES DOUGLAS OF ABERDOUR (JAMIE): Illegitimate eldest son of the Lord of Dalkeith.

SIR ALEXANDER STEWART OF BADENOCH: Eldest and illegitimate son of the late and notorious Earl of Buchan, Wolf of Badenoch.

ALASTAIR CARRACH MACDONALD OF ISLAY: Brother of Donald, Lord of the Isles.

WILLIAM DE SPYNIE, BISHOP OF MORAY.

LADY ISOBEL DOUGLAS, COUNTESS OF MAR: Countess in her own right. Sister of late 2nd Earl of Douglas.

MARY STEWART, LADY DOUGLAS OF ABERDOUR: One of Robert II's illegitimate daughters. Married to Jamie.

MARIOTA DE ATHYN (or MACKAY): Mother of Sir Alexander Stewart of Badenoch. Late mistress of the Earl of Buchan.

LORD JOHN STEWART OF COULL AND ONELE: Second son of the Duke of Albany.

LADY ISABEL STEWART: Sister of the King. Former Countess of Douglas, now married to Edmonstone of that Ilk.

JAMES DOUGLAS, LORD OF DALKEITH: Former statesman and wealthy noble. Father of Jamie.

SIR JAMES DOUGLAS, YOUNGER OF DALKEITH: Half-brother of Jamie. Husband of the Princess Elizabeth.

SIR ARCHIBALD DOUGLAS OF CAVERS: Illegitimate son of 2nd Earl of Douglas.

ROBERT III, KING OF SCOTS: Great-grandson of the Bruce.

RICHARD II OF ENGLAND: Deposed by Henry IV. Called The Mammet, in Scotland. Possibly impostor.

ARCHIBALD, 4TH EARL OF DOUGLAS: Son and heir of late Archie the Grim.

SIR JAMES (the Gross) DOUGLAS OF ABERCORN: Brother of above.

HENRY WARDLAW, BISHOP OF ST ANDREWS: Primate.

SIR JAMES SCRYMGEOUR: Hereditary Standard-Bearer, and Constable of Dundee.

ROBERT STEWART, DUKE OF ALBANY: Next brother to the King. Governor.

GILBERT GREENLAW, BISHOP OF ABERDEEN: Chancellor.

DAVID, EARL OF CRAWFORD: Lord High Admiral, and chief of the Lindsays. Brother-in-law of the King.

SIR ANDREW LESLIE OF BALQUHAIN: Powerful Mar laird.

SIR ALEXANDER FORBES OF THAT ILK: Powerful Mar laird.

JAMES I, KING OF SCOTS: Surviving son of Robert III.

HENRY IV, KING OF ENGLAND: Usurper.

MURDOCH STEWART, EARL OF FIFE: Eldest son and heir of Duke of Albany.

EDMUND HOLLAND, EARL OF KENT: Great English noble.

ROBERT DAVIDSON, PROVOST OF ABERDEEN: Merchant and shipmaster.

IAN BORB MACLEOD, YOUNGER OF DUNVEGAN: Heir to chief of Siol Tormod.

ANTON DE VALOIS OF BRABANT: Brother of the Duke of Burgundy.

JOHN DE VALOIS, DUKE OF BURGUNDY: French prince, and Count of Flanders.

ISABELLA OF BAVARIA, QUEEN OF FRANCE: Wife of King Charles VI.

CHARLES VI, KING OF FRANCE: Insane.

BERNARD, COUNT D'ARMAGNAC: Powerful French noble. Father-in-law of young Duke of Orleans.

HENRY BEAUCHAMP, EARL OF WARWICK: Great English noble. Envoy to France.

HECTOR MACLEAN OF DUART: Great Highland chief; son-in-law of Donald of the Isles.

SIR ALEXANDER IRVINE OF DRUM: Grandson of Bruce's Armour-Bearer.

SIR ALEXANDER KEITH OF GRANDHOLM: Heir to the Knight Marischal.

PART ONE

I

SIR JAMES DOUGLAS, lately of Aberdour, Stoneypath and Baldwinsgill, and now a landless fugitive, reined in his sturdy, broad-hooved Highland garron on the heather ridge and, shielding his eyes against the mellow October sunlight, gazed southwards over the wide and fair vale of mid-Strathspey, golden, scarlet and olive-green amongst the blue mountains. In a land of colour, with the heather fading from purple to brown, October was the most vivid of all months, the chromatic range and vehemence of the turning leaves almost unbelievable to Lowland eyes.

The Douglas was not on this occasion thinking about all that far-flung brilliance — or at least not Nature's overwhelming contribution. It was man-made colour that he looked for, and had no difficulty in finding. For a couple of miles at least beside the wide, silver river, moving colour rippled and surged and gleamed, a great host — and by the flicker of sunlight on steel, an armed host, thousands strong, only a small proportion of it mounted. Yet it was moving fast, eastwards, down-river, and with a decided air of purpose about it all. It was further on by some miles than the man had looked for it. Nodding to his two companions, running gillies in ragged tartans, he kicked the barrel-like flanks of his shaggy mount, and set off at a trot, slantwise downhill, his gillies loping long-strided, tireless, at his sides. Parallel with the falling Tulchan Burn, they dropped from the wide heather wilderness of Dava Moor.

It took him some time to reach the head of that long column, passing company after company of kilted clansmen, Mackintoshes, Macphersons, MacGillivrays, Shaws, Cattanachs, MacQueens, MacBains and the like, armed with broadsword, dirk and Lochaber axe, most naked to the waist, leather targes slung

9

over lean, sweating shoulders, the fastest-moving infantry in Christendom, going at the slow-trot which ate up the miles. They were almost opposite Ballindalloch, on the other side of Spey, before he saw the leadership.

Under a single great banner in front, the Stewart fess-chequey impaling the green-and-red of Badenoch, a group of chiefs rode, proud of bearing, eagles' feathers in their bonnets. Amongst them, more modestly garbed than most, was Sir Alexander Stewart of Badenoch, acting Justiciar of the North, and nephew, although illegitimate, of the King of Scots, Robert the Third.

At sight of the newcomer, this young man pulled up sharply. "Jamie! Jamie Douglas!" he cried. "God be praised — yourself, by all that is blessed!" He reined his horse over, alongside to Douglas's, and embraced his friend, from the saddle, there before them all. "Back from the dead — or nearly! Jamie — we feared for you."

The other grinned, embarrassed, his dark and rather sombre good looks lightening up. His was a less forthcoming nature than that of the sunny Stewart's, but he was no less pleased at the reunion.

"Alex!" he said. "It is good."

They were so very different, these two, in more than their greetings. Both now in their early thirties, where Jamie Douglas was swarthy, stocky, strong-featured, of medium height, Alex Stewart was fair, slender, tall and of a fineness of feature which was almost beauty, but redeemed from any hint of weakness by the firm line of mouth and jaw. He did not look as though he was the eldest son of the late and notorious Wolf of Badenoch; but then Alexander, Earl of Buchan, himself had *looked* good, too — the Stewarts having a tendency that way.

"You have come from Lochindorb? How long? How long have you been there, Jamie?"

"Almost two weeks. I near came west, seeking you — but reckoned that Mary and the bairns were entitled to their husband and father for a space. And you with your battles won."

"To be sure." The other turned. "You will know most of these my friends — the Mackintosh, Cluny Macpherson, Shaw of Rothiemurchus, MacGillivray Mor, MacBain of Kinchyle, the Cattanach?"

One by one the chiefs bowed from their saddles, or inclined stiff heads towards the Lowlander, and he nodded back. Mac-Gillivray, at whose side he had fought at Glen Arkaig, reached

10

out to grip his hand, and murmured greetings in the Gaelic.

Then Stewart swung on another smaller group, distinguishable from the rest only in that they looked fiercer somehow, and wore winged helmets of an antique aspect.

"And here you see others of whom you have heard and even drawn sword against, but have not met, I think — Alastair Carrach MacDonald of Islay and Lochaber, brother to Donald of the Isles. And sundry of his captains."

Jamie stared. "Alastair Carrach himself? Here? Your prisoner?"

"Say that I have persuaded him to return with me to the scene of his indiscretions, to the city of Elgin. To express suitable regrets to the representatives of Holy Church there, for having caused fire at the canons' manses, and other parts of the town — as befits a Highland gentleman! Even from the Isles!"

The Islemen gazed back at the newcomer expressionless, from almost uniformly pale blue eyes, the Scandinavian Viking admixture in their Celtic blood very evident, not so much as a nod amongst them. Yet this Alastair, and of course his brother the Lord of the Isles, were likewise grandsons of the late Robert the Second, their mother the Princess Margaret who had married John of the Isles. The present monarch, Robert the Third, had some strange kinsmen.

"Guidsakes!" Jamie muttered, striving to repress a grin at the audacity and wry humour of this son of a father who had himself burned the same Elgin and its great cathedral almost to the ground, in malice, now imposing penance for a lesser deed on the Lord of the Isles' brother. "*You* well won your campaign, then, Alex!"

"Say that we brought matters to a decent conclusion. You, unhappily, were less fortunate I gather, Jamie?"

"I served a fool as commander," the other said briefly.

"Yes. Archibald Douglas something lacks the style of his proud line. But — tell me as we ride on, Jamie. I am eager to hear what went wrong with the English invasion. You will come with us to Elgin?"

As they resumed the march eastwards, Jamie gave his friend a typically cryptic account of the late abortive Scots campaign in Northumberland ending in the disaster of Homildon Hill five weeks before, under his chief, Archibald, 4th Earl of Douglas.

"Mismanaged from the start," he said. "Ten thousand men wasted. No discipline. Angus, Moray, Murdoch of Fife, with no

11

experience of war amongst them. They conceived it something between a tourney and a Border cattle-raid, where it was meant to be a vital counter-invasion stroke. Within hours of crossing Tweed, hundreds, possibly thousands, dispersed, looting, driving home beasts. I advised a hanging or two, but the Earl Archie would not. Folly all the way to Newcastle. Besieged that town, hoping Hotspur was inside — as only a fool would have been. I went seeking him. Found him at the head of Derwent, far to the west. Meeting a large force of mounted archers from King Henry's army on the Welsh March."

"Ha — archers! And you had none?"

"Aye. I took the word back to Douglas, at speed. He had wearied of sitting round Newcastle, without siege machinery, and was retiring north. Still burning, looting, burdened with cattle — untold thousands."

"I can guess what happened, friend."

"Wait you. The Percy got in front of us, in the Vale of Till. Barred the way. A great force. To win round, westwards, we had to ford the Glen Water. I took my father's Dalkeith men, four hundred, and held the approaches to the fords. When I regained the host it was not where we had arranged, but crowded up on top of a hill. Homildon Hill."

"Go on, man."

"Safe from Hotspur's cavalry, up there, yes. But a higher hill rose just to the east — Housedon Hill. A deal higher. And within arrow-shot."

"God's mercy — a death-trap!"

"That is what it was, yes — and thousands died, to prove it. Nor could strike a blow in return. I pleaded for a break-out. Down, in wedge-formation, through the encircling cavalry. Douglas refused. And he fell, at last, leading a foot-attack on the *bowmen*! The blind folly of it! After that, I led what I could off the field — nine hundred or so. Downhill, in wedges, through the cavalry. To escape. Leaving the rest — Douglas and the others. Two brothers of my own. That was Homildon Hill."

Stewart considered him. "Folly, yes. We heard that it was a great defeat. But not all this of folly and weakness. Douglas did not die?"

"None of the earls died. Nor my brothers. But all were wounded, and captured. Many brave men did die. Whereas I — I escaped with a whole skin! And pay the price now."

"You mean . . . ? You are blamed? For surviving?"

12

"Blamed, yes. Damned as a craven and a traitor! The man who fled the field, leaving all to their fate. His chief, even his own kin. Worst of all, leaving Albany's son and heir, the Earl Murdoch of Fife! I am a hooting and a hissing, in the South. Albany has seen to that. Even my own father miscalls me, for failing to bring home my brothers."

"But this is crazy! You, of all men!"

Jamie shrugged. "Crazy or no, I am now a landless hunted man. Outlawed. My wife and bairns dependent on others for their bread."

"Then your misfortune is my *good* fortune, man! For I need you here in Badenoch, as never before."

"You mean, because of Drummond's death?"

"Wha-a-at! Drummond — dead? Sir Malcolm?"

"Save us — did you not know? Have not heard? I would have thought that you must have heard of it. Been sent word . . . ?"

"No. When? When was this? When did he die? How?"

The other cleared his throat. "See you, Alex — this is a bad business. I had not thought to be the bearer of such ill tidings . . ."

"Scarce so ill as that, Jamie! Sir Malcolm is, was, no friend of mine, as you know. His death will make for . . . changes. But . . ."

"Changes, yes. For you, I fear, Alex." His friend's discomfort was not to be hidden. "You see, *you* are getting the blame for it."

"Damnation — me? How could that be? I knew naught of it. He was slain, then?"

"Slain, yes — after a fashion. Your lady-mother says that you sent a small force, under your brothers, to keep watch on Drummond when Donald of the Isles struck, and you yourself marched to deal with the Islesmen."

"Yes. You mean . . . that it was my brothers who slew Sir Malcolm?"

"Who knows? But somebody did. The word is that he was taken unawares, as he rode between Kildrummy and Kindrochit, in Mar, by a band of caterans. Carried to some remote hold in those mountains. And, and there fed neither food nor drink. Until he starved to death."

"Christ God!" Shocked, appalled, Stewart involuntarily drew rein, to state. "Starved . . . ?"

"So it is said. Like the Duke David, your cousin. And you are being blamed. Can you wonder? If your brothers did it — and

13

you sent them. Your fondness for the Countess, his wife, is well known."

"But, but . . ." He paused, as the implications of it all began to dawn on him. "Saints of mercy — so evil a thing!"

"Evil, yes. I grieve to bring you such tidings. Your brothers have told you nothing of it?"

"I have not seen them since I left Lochindorb with my main force. They do not much find it necessary to inform me of their doings! But if they have done this thing, I, I . . ." He swallowed. "God pity us all, they shall suffer for it! It would be Duncan, of course. Andrew and Walter are hard — but would not do that. And James, new wedded, is still at Garth, in Atholl, not concerned in this fighting. It would be Duncan, if any. He has a devil in him. Like, like . . ." He did not complete that, but Jamie knew that he was thinking of his father, the Wolf.

"See you, Alex — perhaps your brother thought to do you a service?"

"A service! This will damage me as nothing else could. All the Southern Highlands, Atholl, Breadalbane, Angus, Gowrie, as well as Mar itself, will turn against me. Malcolm Drummond, *An Drumanach Mor*, was a great chief, head of a large clan, connected to other chiefs by marriage and kin. The King's goodbrother. To starve him to death will never be forgiven. Every chief will look askance at me — even those who follow us now. I can no longer remain the King's Justiciar of the North. A service, you say!"

"Yet he may have considered it so, in ignorance — your brother. To have Drummond dead, for you — caring not how, freeing the Countess of Mar from her loveless marriage. For you . . ."

"Fiend seize you, man — how can you say such a thing! This is beyond all — to murder the husband in order to gain the wife!"

"Others will say it, Alex — nothing more sure. Mar is a great earldom. For you to gain some control of it, your brother may have seen it as worth a murder! When he could name it an act of war, the realm threatened by Donald's Islesmen, and Drummond in secret league with them."

"And what, think you, will Isobel say?"

The other did not risk an answer to that, and they rode on together, silent.

When at length Sir Alexander spoke again, he said, "Say

14

naught of this, Jamie, meantime — until I know my own mind in the matter." He smiled a little, ruefully. "When I said that I needed you as never before, I scarce knew how much it was to be! If you will hold to me, still?"

"Think you I would not? Forby, *my* need is as great as yours. We are both in trouble. And more like to win out of it better together than apart!"

"So say I, friend . . ."

*   *   *

Branching off the great Spey valley at Rothes, to head due northwards, they camped for the night in the mouth of Rothes Glen. The Douglas, who did not speak the Gaelic, could not have much converse with the assembled chiefs, but heard from Alex Stewart that evening, by the camp-fire, an account of his campaign against the Islesmen's invasion — how he had caught up with them at Elgin, defeated them whilst they were in disarray at the sacking of the city, chased them right across the Highlands to Moidart, where they had left their galleys, and defeated them again as they were hastily embarking, capturing most of the leadership. Unlike his father, Alex made a point of maintaining excellent relations with the Church authorities, and he was taking Alastair Carrach back to Elgin to make some sort of reparation.

With their accustomed speed, astonishing for an infantry host, they covered the ten miles between Rothes and Elgin, in the fair Moray plain, in just three hours — having sent faster messengers ahead to warn the Church and burgh authorities. The city, The Lantern of the North, awaited them with evident suspicion and alarm, behind closed gates, Highland armies of any sort being held in grave doubts by the plainsmen, and justifiably. Their cathedral, after all, the finest in the land, was still being rebuilt after the Wolf of Badenoch's burning of 1390, a dozen years before. But the Church dignitaries, led by the Bishop of Moray himself, William de Spynie, were moderately forthcoming, having had many dealings with Alex Stewart, who had done his best to redeem his father's offences. They were waiting to greet the Highlanders at the Panns Port, the same southern gateway at which, as the Wolf's prisoner, Jamie Douglas had waited that day, twelve years before, for sunrise to herald the attack on the city.

"Ha, my lord Bishop," the Stewart called, dismounting. "A

15

good day to you and your people. The better for being the Eve of the Blessed Saint Kenneth. I have brought you for your forgiveness and absolution, I hope, a sincere penitent, one Alastair Carrach MacDonald of Islay and Lochaber, who, having offended against Holy Church, is now concerned to redeem that offence in due and suitable fashion. With some of his brother's island chieftains."

"Indeed! You say so? Then you rejoice us, Sir Alexander," the Bishop replied, carefully. "We always welcome the penitent — provided he is truly so. And, h'm, prepared to make required and adequate restitution." The prelate, a heavily-built, square-jowled, florid man, inclining to fat but with eyes shrewd enough for a horse-dealer, sketched the sign of the cross vaguely over all.

"Ah, yes — that is important, my lord. I think our friend Alastair here, will prove sufficiently repentant. And . . . open-handed! You agree, Alastair?"

The Islesman stared blankly, expressionlessly. He had the thin down-turning moustache and tiny beard, which, with the pale glitter of his eyes, effected a sort of smouldering savagery which might send shivers down the impressionable spine. He did not speak.

"I hope that you may be right," the Bishop replied, a little doubtfully. "You do not intend to bring all these men into the city?"

"No. They will wait out here. A few of my colleagues only. The Mackintosh, Cluny Macpherson, MacGillivray Mor, Shaw of Rothiemurchus . . ." He named the chiefs of the Clan Chattan federation, who offered little more acknowledgement than had the Islesman — and whom the clerics eyed with equal wariness. "And here is my friend Sir James Douglas of Aberdour, of whose fame you will undoubtedly have heard."

"Ah, to be sure — we have heard of Sir James. And but recently! You have come north quickly, sir. The last we heard of you was in . . . Northumberland!"

"Then I hope that you are *well* informed, my lord," Jamie said briefly.

"Holy Church is always that," Alex observed. "Where, my lord Bishop, do you wish this little, er, celebratory office to take place?"

"Why, in the cathedral, Sir Alexander — where else? Thanks to your generosity, and that of others, it now has a roof again. The Lady Chapel is all but complete. We shall go there."

Leaving most of the force outside the town-walls, the leaders and prisoners rode inside, with the clerical party, a mob of citizens following on, some jeering once it became known that their oppressor, MacDonald, was present. The Bishop glanced back at Alastair Carrach, and spoke, rich voice carefully lowered.

"Sir Alexander — what do you propose? The word you sent was that you held this MacDonald, had brought him to repentance and would fetch him here to make restitution. What would you have me do?"

"Why, do what the Church does with penitents of substantial offence, my lord. No doubt you will have seen fit to pronounce some suitable anathemas upon him? You will have some form of ceremony for lifting it? I seem to recollect my esteemed father taking part in some such exercise at Perth, once!"

"H'mm." The Bishop looked away. "Perhaps. And reparation? Restitution?"

"*I* shall vouch for that. We captured much booty with the Islesmen."

"Ah. Some may well have been stolen from Holy Church."

"Then it shall be restored. With a sufficiency of further compensation."

"Very good. Suitable, commendable, my son." The other glanced sidelong at Alex. "And, ah, timely. Aye, timely, I think."

"Why that?"

The prelate cleared his throat. "Later might have been . . . different. Difficult."

"I do not understand you, my lord. Later?"

"In the matter of the unhappy death of Sir Malcolm Drummond. So very unfortunate. No sure word has reached us yet. But, when it does, Holy Church may be placed in a position of some awkwardness, Sir Alexander."

"You mean, as regards myself?"

"I fear so, yes."

The Stewart drew a deep breath. "I had nothing to do with the death of Drummond, my lord Bishop," he said flatly.

"Ah, to be sure. Excellent. I would not have expected it of you. Indeed, no. But . . . until that is established, before all men, you will understand, Holy Church cannot be seen to accept gifts and service from one whom men may think of as a murderer. And whom she might be called upon to, h'm, excommunicate! You will perceive our difficulty, my friend?"

17

"I perceive that you have been listening to idle tales, my lord Bishop. I was in the west, dealing with your unfriends here, in Moidart, when Sir Malcolm Drummond died."

"How fortunate. But the caterans who took him were your men, were they not? Led by your own brothers? And so, it might be deemed, under your command?"

Tight-lipped, Alex reined up at the great west portal of the cathedral, still smoke-blackened. "I do not myself know what took place," he said. "I have not seen my brothers. But . . . you said, my lord, that my coming here today was timely? In these circumstances, why?"

"Do you not see, my friend? Because thus far it is only hearsay. Mere reports — which Holy Church need not heed. Meantime we may accept your good offices, this excellent restitution, still deeming all to be well. Later it could be *too* late."

"Ah, yes. I see it. I see that the Church is glad to receive what I have to give — so long as it is sufficient — whether I am a murderer or not. So long as she may. *Before* she excommunicates me! Timely, indeed!"

"That is less than just, sir. The Church must not countenance sin. But she can and should exercise charity towards the alleged sinner, until the sin is proven. Just as she will exercise clemency towards this MacDonald repentant who has so shamefully used her."

The Stewart, dismounting from his garron, did not have to answer that.

Jamie Douglas had listened to all this with grim interest, a little distracted by the emotions aroused by this his return to Elgin Cathedral, after twelve years. When last he had been here, this great and noble fane was spouting smoke and flame, its stained-glass windows exploding, coughing, choking Highland-men staggering out clutching its treasures, not to save but to steal. Alex Stewart had been there then, too, at his side, as guard, deploring his father's savage fury but unable to halt it, almost as much a prisoner as he was himself. Now they were here in almost opposite roles; they were the captors, not the prisoners.

Ordering their captives to dismount, they followed Bishop Spynie within. Scaffolding and workmen's gear festooned the vast building outside and in; but one of the side-chapels was almost wholly rebuilt, and here they were led.

18

The clerics disappeared into a vestry, and Alex arranged his party to face the candle-lit altar. The Islesmen were not bound but kept hemmed in by a sufficiency of guards to ensure their security. They remained strangely impassive, almost as though they were the merest onlookers at the proceedings.

The Bishop and his assistants emerged, resplendent in full canonicals, in glittering and jewelled magnificence. For the first time the MacDonalds' eyes betrayed interest, calculating the worth of all that finery. The prelate took up his position at the altar, and turned to them.

"In the name of Almighty God, the Father, the Son and the Holy Spirit," he intoned impressively, "we are here to receive back into the outspread arms of Mother Church a repentant sinner such as is beloved of our Lord Christ. Although his sins be as scarlet they shall be whiter than snow." He paused. "Sir Alexander Stewart of Badenoch — you have one such great and penitent sinner here present?"

"I have."

"Name him."

"Alexander MacDonald of Islay and Lochaber, known as Alastair Carrach, brother-german to Donald, Lord of the Isles and son of the late John, Lord of the Isles and the Princess Margaret, eldest sister of our Lord King."

"This is he who entered this city by force with an armed host, slew many, burned many houses including the property of Holy Church, the manses of the canons of this cathedral, and so didst grievously sin against the Holy Ghost?"

"The same."

"And he does now heartily and sincerely repent him of the said great sins, confesses his grievous fault before Almighty God and all present, and is prepared to make due, ample and fullest recompence and restitution, here before God's holy altar and in the sight of all men?"

"He is."

"Bring the said Alexander MacDonald forward."

Alex, his hand on the Isleman's shoulder, climbed the three steps nearer to the altar, the other allowing himself to be pushed forward, grinning now.

Noting that grin, the Bishop frowned. "Alastair of Islay and Lochaber," he said sternly, "do you understand? Do you fully and truly repent you?"

"*He* says that I do, whatever. And Stewart is an honourable

19

man, is he not? So it must be true!" Alastair Carrach had a most gentle, lilting, West Highland voice, in notable contrast with his reputation and appearance.

The prelate looked uneasily from one to the other, and cleared his throat. "You must say it yourself, man. Another's word is not sufficient — even Sir Alexander's."

"I will be saying whatever he wishes, Clerk. Words cost a deal less than the ransom I am paying."

"Ransom . . . ?"

"He means reparation and sacrifice, my lord," Alex said evenly. "In good measure."

"Ah. Yes. Yes, indeed. That is important, to be sure. Deeds rather than words. Yet words are necessary also. Repeat after me these words. 'I do confess before Almighty God and these present . . .' "

"I do confess before Almighty God and these present . . ."

" 'That I have sinned . . .' "

"That I have sinned — as who has not?"

"Repeat *my* words only, my son."

"So long as they are *your* words, whatever!" That was cheerfully said.

"Be silent, sir!"

"Very well. I am silent."

"Repeat, 'I have grievously offended against the laws of God and man.' "

Silence.

"I say, 'I have grievously offended against the laws of God and man.' "

"No doubt, Clerk."

Alex Stewart coughed. "My lord — he has come here, and confessed that he has sinned, before God and all present. Moreover he has agreed to make fullest restitution and reparation. I respectfully suggest that this is the heart of the matter, and that the rest is less vital. Would not absolution now serve the case sufficiently — and save us all further delay?"

"H'mm." The Bishop frowned again, eyed the Isleman's arrogant amusement, and sighed. "Very well. It may be that you are right." He raised his beringed hand high. "In the name of God the Father, God the Son and God the Holy Ghost, I absolve you, Alexander, of your grievous sin. And, and . . ." by way of postscript he added, ". . . and may God have mercy on your soul! Amen!" And turning, with the briefest of nods to the altar, he stalked off to the vestry-door, and through. Hurriedly, in some confusion, his subordinates followed him.

Alastair Carrach barked a single hooting laugh, and then relapsed into his accustomed uninterested silence.

A move was made, out into the open air, relief showing on not a few faces.

Before the west portal was now drawn up a train of laden pack-horses. Stewart gestured towards it.

"Alastair Carrach's booty — or most of it," he murmured to Jamie. "An offering for the Bishop. He will be round to inspect it in but moments, I swear!"

"Why?" the other demanded, low-voiced. "Why this . . . play-acting? So, so like your own father's folly at Perth?"

"Good reasons, friend. It is the best way to deal with Alastair. In a day or two it will be all over the Highlands that he has come and made humble abasement before Holy Church at Elgin, and yielded up his booty — a deal more hurt to his name and reputation than sustaining a couple of small defeats. It is sheerest mummery, to be sure — but no matter. *I* learned that after my father's case. His repentance was the greatest mockery — yet the word was accepted far and near that he had humbly atoned. Nothing so infuriated him, that I can recollect. Keeping Alastair a prisoner will not serve my cause. I do not need ransom moneys. Better that I should send him back to his brother, unwanted, with this tale of atonement and grovelling, however untrue. And I make the Church my still better friend. I think that I am going to need the Church's friendship, Jamie!"

Bishop Spynie did indeed put in a prompt appearance at the west front of his cathedral, to set about examining the baggage-train with an expert eye and considerable diligence — an eye that lightened and brightened as he peered and poked into each pannier, package and bundle. There was the spoil of a score of churches, villages, townships and communities there, some undoubtedly from Elgin but most from otherwhere. Holy Church, however, was clearly glad to accept all, with no awkward questions about former ownership.

"Very good, very good!" The prelate beamed on all. "This is most . . . suitable. A worthy atonement. Most commendable. It will be cherished, I assure you — much cherished. And *your* faithful love of Mother Church not forgotten, Sir Alexander."

"Then, I pray, remember it, when you hear further slanderous reports about me, my lord Bishop. Which my unfriends will put

21

about, I have little doubt. Now — if you will tell me where you wish this treasure bestowed, we shall take it there and then be on our various ways. My people have marched far and fast to deliver it here, from Moidart. They would return now to their glens . . ."

So, presently, the Highland host turned southwards again from the Panns Port of Elgin, and soon began to break up and disperse, each contingent hiving off to take the shortest route back to its own clan territory amongst the great mountains of the Monadh Ruadh, the Monadh Liath or Braemoray.

Riding by Dunkinty, the now quietly thoughtful commander of it all turned to Jamie Douglas. "My friend," he said, "I think, before I return to Lochindorb, that I should pay a privy call at Kildrummy in Mar. There is much that I would learn there, if possible. If you can bear to be parted from your Mary a day or two more, I should be glad of your company. How say you?"

"You want me? *There*, Alex?"

"Yes. Two heads could be better than one. And yours could be cooler than mine, in this."

"Very well . . ."

Presently Stewart halted the rump of his force. He spoke, in the Gaelic.

"Alastair Carrach — here I leave you. From henceforth, you and your friends are free men. The Mackintosh will provide you with an escort to Moidart. Go you back to your Isles, and tell your brother not to trouble us again."

The Islesman eyed him searchingly. "This is no trick, Stewart? No ransom? No further conditions?"

"None. Save that you and yours spare us your attentions in future. And tell Donald the same."

"You are a strange man, Cousin. I cannot think that you are a fool. Yet . . ."

"Think me fool if you wish. But for the rest, recollect how many times this fool has fought you, and won! Now — go in peace."

The other's strange eyes glittered as he turned away.

II

WITH A TINY escort of only half-a-dozen gillies, all mounted now, the two friends made their unobtrusive way through the empty hills dominated by pointed Ben Rinnes, across Glen Fiddich and over the high desolation of the Cabrach, and so by the Mounth of Clova into the great province of Mar. On the second day they rode down to the upper Don at Lulach's Stone, and up a side-valley to the ancient earldom's principal fortalice of Kildrummy.

The castle was set on a neck of high ground between ravines, overlooking a wide prospect of the fair vale of Don, a commanding and splendid site. They were not permitted to approach it unobserved and unchallenged. But the guards knew Sir Alexander well, and sent back word — so that the newly-widowed Countess of Mar herself was waiting for them at the drawbridge end as they rode up.

Alex threw himself from the saddle and all but ran towards her. Then he seemed to recollect himself, and slowed, to halt and bow.

"Isobel!" he said, eyes searching her face.

She nodded, wordless, the faintest smile on her reddened lips.

It was not often that Alex Stewart showed uncertainty. He bit his lip. "I . . . I am sorry, Isobel," he said. "An evil thing. I grieve for you."

"Need you?" she asked. "Since I do not grieve for myself!"

Isobel Douglas, Countess of Mar in her own right, was a handsome and splendidly built woman, now in her early forties, her powerful femininity nothing diminished by maturity. She certainly gave no indication of distressed widowhood; but then, she and her husband, the Drummond chief, had gone their separate ways for long.

Alex, who had been in love with her for years, although

23

fifteen years her junior, all but bounded forward again, to take her substantial form in his arms. "My dear!" he cried.

She returned his embraces and kisses heartily, careless of the watchers, although with just a hint of mockery perhaps, mockery of herself as well as of the man. Then over his shoulder her eyes caught Jamie's, and, fine brows raised, she pushed the other away firmly.

"I see that you have brought my heroic fellow-Douglas with you again, Alex — his heroism now, sadly, a little tarnished, we hear! I am ever a mite wary when you bring him here — for I judge it to mean that you need his help against me!"

"No, no — not so, Isobel! You, you much mistake. Jamie is your good friend, no less than mine, I swear . . ."

"Liar!" she said, but not harshly. She had a deep, husky voice which had its own unsettling effect on susceptible men.

"If I am not welcome, my lady, I shall remove myself," Jamie said stiffly.

"Tush, man — be not so thin-skinned! We are both Douglases, are we not? And can speak plain. I do not believe the tales of you, running from this battle. You will tell me the truth of it. Come you . . ."

Kildrummy Castle was a mighty and extensive fortress, larger even than Alex's Lochindorb, perhaps the greatest in all the North-East, the key to the most important of the Mounth passes between the Aberdeen, Mearns and Angus plain, and Moray, the Spey, Findhorn and Ness valleys. It was a strange place for a woman to control, even such a woman as Isobel of Mar. And she did control it and its vast dependencies, and had done all along, never having elevated Sir Malcolm Drummond as Earl of Mar in her right, as she could have done. Very much the Countess, she made a better lord for Mar than it had had for generations.

Alex made one or two attempts to introduce the subject of Sir Malcolm's death, before the Lady Isobel took it up, as they ate.

"My husband was a strange man, and not one *I* would ever have chosen to wed," she observed. "And I cannot in honesty claim that I mourn him greatly. But his was an ill death to die. He deserved better than that."

"It was devilish!" Stewart agreed. "If it was as Jamie tells me. Locked in a cell, without food or drink, until he died. Is that true?"

"Sufficiently. He starved, that is certain. Locked in the small, remote hold of Badenyon, in the mountains."

"And . . . who did it?"

"The question comes strangely from you, my dear, does it not? It was a band of your caterans who took him, when he was riding back to Kildrummy from his new-building castle of Kindrochit in Brae-Mar, conveyed him to Badenyon, and held him there."

"Isobel — I knew nothing of it. Nothing. I tell you! You cannot believe, you cannot think . . . ?"

"No, I cannot, Alex. Do not distress yourself. I know well that it was none of your doing. You have your faults, my dear, but you are not a cold-blooded killer! Nevertheless, your brothers led the party, all aver, in your name. There is no question of that, is there?"

"I sent a company under my brothers, yes — to watch your husband, in case he joined forces with Alastair Carrach in Donald's invasion — as we feared. But this . . . !"

"Why should they do it? Thus? To slay him, I could understand — if they deemed him enemy. But starvation . . . ?"

"God alone knows. But if it *was* my brothers, it would be Duncan. He has a devil in him. He hates, as none of the rest of us can."

"What reason had he to hate Malcolm?"

"I do not know. None, that I can think on."

"Could it be that he somehow blamed Sir Malcolm for Prince David's death?" Jamie put in. "Revenge. It was the same death. Could there be any link? Even in mistake?"

"David was my husband's nephew, his sister's son. Why should he wish him dead?"

"Who can tell? But . . . Duncan Stewart must have had some reason for this shameful deed. Does nothing at all come to mind, Alex?"

"I have racked my wits. The only link between them, that I know of, was when Duncan led that great raid into Angus and Gowrie after our father's excommunication, when he won the victory at Glasclune. Sir Malcolm Drummond was prominent in gathering and leading the host which assembled against my brothers then — his Drummond country, to be sure, was overrun. I was in Uncle Robert's prison at Falkland at the time, so know not all that happened. But there may have been some incident. And Duncan never forgives. And so took this opportunity for revenge."

"It scarce sounds sufficient . . ."

The Countess shrugged. "I cannot think that it had aught to do with David Stewart's starving, at least. There is no least connection. Nor even with Malcolm's other nephew, the young James . . ."

"James? The new heir to the throne? What of him, Isobel?"

"Only that there was some talk of the King sending him up here to Kildrummy, for safety. From his Uncle Robert of Albany. He is at present in the care of the Bishop of St Andrews — but it seems the King still fears for him, and would find more secure lodging, out of Albany's reach. No doubt he fears a second death in the family — and then Albany himself is next heir. So there was talk of sending him up here, to bide with his uncle. But . . . I do not see why this should cause your brother anger?"

"No. No — there is nothing there to concern Duncan. Or any of us."

"Well — it is done now, and cannot be undone," the woman said. "In time you will learn, no doubt — and take what steps are necessary. But that is not important, meantime. What *is* important is that we should seek to counter the ill effects. For they will be grievously ill, Alex — as, I vow, you well understand."

"Yes. It can make shipwreck of my whole state and position. I can no longer remain Justiciar. It gives my Uncle Robert of Albany what he needs against me. I could well be outlawed. Sir Malcolm, being the Queen's brother, uncle to the heir to the throne, will enable Albany, as Governor, to accuse me almost of treason! And being chief of Clan Drummond, I will have all the Atholl, Gowrie and Stormonth clans against me. Chiefs everywhere outraged. Not to speak of this great earldom of Mar!"

"Leave Mar to me. Malcolm never had much say or sway over my people. What concerns me most are the accursed churchmen. Excommunication. If they excommunicate you, Alex, it could cost us all dear."

"I think, I *hope*, that I have the Church my friend. Unlike my father! We have just come from my Diocesan, the Bishop of Moray. Any excommunication would have to be imposed by him. I would say that he is sufficiently . . . sweetened."

"Good. Then they cannot prevent us marrying, my dear," she commented, matter-of-factly.

His indrawn breath was audible. Although Jamie Douglas barely heard it, for his own.

"Lord, Isobel — we, we cannot think of that! Not now!"

26

"Why not? There is now no . . . impediment."

"But — save us, do you not see? It is impossible. This was one of the first evils of it all that came to me. So long as men blame me for your husband's death, I cannot wed his widow. It would be said . . ."

"Said that you had had him slain, to wed me? Perhaps. Some might say that is the height of love, indeed! There will be talk, to be sure. But talk there would be, anyway — how Sir Alex Stewart had wed a woman almost · old enough to be his mother . . .!"

"Isobel! You are but a dozen years older."

"Fourteen, my heart. Important years. And I might have had a child at thirteen — I was sufficiently keen! So, talk there will be. What signifies a little more talk?"

"No. But this is different. It cannot be, my dear. Not until my name is cleared. Our good repute would be gone — both. You must see it. I will not be named as the man who murdered to gain a bride! We could have no true marriage that way."

"For how long must I wait, then? *My* time is shorter than yours! I cannot delay for years, whilst you establish your innocence to your fullest satisfaction."

Jamie Douglas coughed. "It may be that I should leave you . . .?" he suggested.

"Do not be a fool, man!" the Countess jerked.

"No, Jamie — do not go," Alex urged. "We need cool wits to try unravel this tangle. You can see the problems. Can you aid us towards an answer?"

"Me? No." He did not know whether this of marriage was his friend's wish, or only the Countess's. Alex had never mentioned the word marriage to him. He was careful. "Save to agree that it would be folly to wed, in such case. Even those who accept you as innocent would doubt it then."

"I would not have guessed that Sir James Douglas would have been so concerned for what folk thought!" the lady said.

"Since what folk may think determines how they may act and speak, it could be important, lady. *I* know that, to my cost! And Alex's position is delicate."

"Why so delicate?"

That man had difficulty, with the features he had, in ever looking really apologetic; but he did glance at his friend uneasily. "He is less than securely based, Countess. Albany, the Governor, hates him. He was his uncle's prisoner once, who was forced to

27

free him, against his will. The Duke never forgives nor forgets. This matter will be a joy to him — if he ever wins joy from anything! Then, his son Murdoch, Earl of Fife, now prisoner in England, has long been Justiciar and Lieutenant of the North — in name. He dared not come north to take up his appointment — nor greatly wanted to. So Alex has been *acting* Justiciar since his father died, for both the Prince David of Rothesay and this Murdoch. But only acting. Now, with Murdoch Stewart captive, Albany is bound to appoint someone else — and it will be someone more strong, you may be sure." That was a long statement for Jamie Douglas.

"That matters not, Jamie," Alex put in. "Since I shall resign the office anyway."

"No doubt. But have you considered what a *strong* man, sent up here as Lieutenant and Justiciar, could do? To *you*! If you have lost the support of the clans through this slaying of Sir Malcolm?"

"M'mm. You think that I could be endangered? My own self?"

"It is the first thing that your successor would attempt, I'd say. Seek to be rid of you. And you are not strong in manpower, Alex. So long as you had the clans behind you, you were strong. But you have few men of your own. This is not Stewart country. Up here you are incomers. Lochindorb is a strong castle — but it can raise no large forces. You are Lord of Badenoch, yes — but only *de facto*, not *de jure*. For, like me, you are a bastard. The Crown has never confirmed you in your lordship. You have never been summoned to parliament as Lord of Badenoch. Which means, I fear, that Badenoch will remain yours only for so long as you are strong enough to hold it!"

There was silence at the table for a few moments.

"You are a damnably gloomy counsellor, Sir James!" Isobel of Mar exclaimed.

"No — let him continue," Alex said. "He has the sort of sober head we much require. And he is right in what he says. It is all true. Go on, my friend."

"As I see it, until you clear your name of this murder, with fullest certainty, you are in dire danger. Not yet, perhaps, but in a short while. Even though not excommunicated, you will be outlawed — as I am. Albany will see to it. That means any man may attack you, with impunity. And be rewarded for doing so. My father made it mightily clear to me, I assure you. So, either

28

you clear your name swiftly, gain strong forces to your side, in some fashion — or go into hiding. That, or leave this your country meantime."

"You make matters accursedly stark, Jamie!" the other commented grimly. "What, then, is your advice?"

"Clear your name. And quickly."

"But how, man — how?"

"How much do you love your brother, Alex?"

"Eh? You mean . . . ?"

"I mean, find him. Hold an open trial. Whilst you are still Justiciar. As is your duty, indeed. And hang him, if proven guilty."

"Lord God!" Stewart breathed.

"There speaks Douglas!" the Countess nodded. "And I am a Douglas, too! This time, I agree with him."

"No," Alex got out. "Not that. Not hang."

"Yet, as Justiciar, you have had to hang many, have you not? And if he was other than your brother you would hang him?"

"I cannot, I *will* not, hang my own brother." That was flat, final.

"I feared as much. Then the choice must be other. Which?"

"I do not know. What can I say? Where can I gain forces to my support, whilst this hangs over me?"

"That, at least, is easy of answer," Isobel of Mar said. "Marry me, and I will make you Earl of Mar, in my right. None can gainsay my right to do so. Then you will have all Mar at your back. And little lack men to your support."

Both men looked at her, and then at each other. Alex swallowed.

"You would do that for me, Isobel? After . . . this? What you would never do for Sir Malcolm?"

"I never loved Malcolm Drummond," she said simply. "My father chose my husband, not I."

"But . . . but . . . I thank you, my dear, with all my heart. But I could not do it — accept the earldom. The thing is not possible."

"Tell me why not?"

"Isobel — the same objection as to our early marriage. Men would accept it as all but proof of guilt. It would be believed that you yourself were party to it — to Malcolm's death. That must not be — such calumny."

"If I am prepared to risk such calumny, why should you balk

29

at it? Were you Earl of Mar you might snap your fingers at Albany, Alex."

"I fear it is less simple than that," Jamie put in, "so long as Albany controls parliament. Earldoms require to be confirmed by the King in parliament. King Robert is but a cypher. A saint perhaps, but weak, a recluse, leaving all to his brother Albany. To think that he is the great-grandson of the Bruce! Albany, the Governor, is strong, ruthless, cunning. I know, who have been fighting against him, suffering his ill-will, for years, ever since he had the Earl James Douglas, my master, murdered at the Battle of Otterburn. I vowed . . ." Jamie Douglas cut himself short. On the subject of Robert Stewart, Duke of Albany and Earl of Fife and Menteith, he was perhaps, preoccupied, prejudiced — and knew it. "I say Albany would counter Alex's confirmation in the earldom," he ended.

"I fear that is true, my dear . . ."

"That would only affect your right to vote in parliament, sit on the Privy Council and the like. In the North you would still be Earl of Mar, in all that matters."

"No, Isobel — my thanks, but no. We must work this thing out otherwise. Somehow. Perhaps another time we shall see more clearly. When we are less weary and our wits are sharper . . ."

They left it there.

Later, Jamie discreetly declared himself ready for his couch and retired sufficiently early to leave the other two to each other's company.

*   *   *

Although the Countess Isobel tried very hard to make them stay longer, Alex Stewart pointed out that matters for his urgent attention were piling up, and after their second night at Kildrummy insisted that they must be gone. He wanted to interview his brother Duncan before either of them was very much older, for one thing. The lady accompanied them for some way on their journey westwards.

Some sixteen miles on their way, at the summit of the Glenfenzie pass over the Gairn Mounth, she drew rein, on the watershed between Don and Dee.

"Far enough, Alex," she said. "I think that you are being foolish. But men are often that, to be sure. You will come back to me, I prophesy, before long — no longer so proud as to

30

refuse what only I can give you. Until then, God go with you."

"It is not pride, Isobel — or not merely so. Our reputations are at stake in this — both of them. And your good name, as well as mine, is important to me. But . . . I thank you, my dear."

"Thanks I do not ask for. But — remember that I am forty-two years of age. I see time something differently from you. You can be Earl of Mar whenever you wish. But . . . you could leave it too late! And there will be others on that hunt, I think!"

He frowned at that, despite himself.

"I expect to hear from Robert of Albany, any day!" she went on. "He can scarce marry me himself — although I suppose he could dispose of that poor creature of a wife, as he has disposed of others! But he has another son — other than Murdoch, prisoner in England — unmarried. Or other nominees for my earldom — that you may be sure. Do not give him too long."

As she turned back, they rode on very thoughtfully.

"I had not thought of that," Jamie admitted. "Of Albany."

His friend did not reply.

Long and hard riding brought them to the upper Dee, and into the mighty mountains of the Monadh Ruadh, where that great river rose. Beyond Linn o'Dee they left the river, to follow up a lesser stream, the Geldie, south of the main massif of the mountains. By its birchwood side they camped, and next morning rode up, westwards now, to the bare moorland and peat-hags of its watershed, and so down the infant Feshie beyond, with all the spread and colour of upper Strathspey opening before them, back into Badenoch again.

The Feshie's lovely dozen-mile valley brought them at last to the pine forests of Rothiemurchus and the tree-girt Loch-an-Eilean with its island-castle. With Ruthven, at Kingussie, Castle Roy in Strathnethy, Drumin in Strathavon, and others, it was one of a series of strategically placed strongholds set up by the late Wolf to control the huge province of Badenoch, each under the captaincy of one of his bastard sons. Jamie had been brought here twelve years before, as captive, when its captain had been Rob Stewart, a half-brother of Sir Alexander's. Now, apparently, it was the seat of Sir Duncan.

Nevertheless, it was Rob Stewart himself who rowed over for them, when they shouted across the still waters for attention, the echo resounding from the close-thronging hillsides. The

31

Earl of Buchan had knighted only his five sons by Mariota de Athyn, to constitute the ruling family of Badenoch, illegitimate as they all were.

"Duncan is not here," Rob Stewart informed. "Has not been, for long."

"No? Where is he then, Rob?"

"I do not know. Somewhere in the South." This was a stolid and somewhat surly individual, no typical Stewart.

"The *South*! Duncan? Surely not?"

The other shrugged. "That is where I was told he had gone."

"But . . . why? Where? Duncan hates the South, the Lowlands. He has no friends there. This is crazy! When did you last see him?"

"Three weeks past. More. After, after . . ."

"After the Drummond business? You were there?"

"I had naught to do with it, Alex. It was none of my doing."

"Perhaps not. But it was *somebody's* doing. And you did not stop it."

"No. See you, Alex — I was at the *capture* of Drummond, yes. We all were, Duncan, Andrew, Walter, Tom. Duncan was the leader — he always is. We took Drummond to a small tower called Badenyon in Brae-Mar. But we left him captive, under guard. We went eastwards then, deeper into Mar, to Kildrummy country. Then south towards Atholl, looking for any muster of fighting men, as you had ordered . . ."

"And Duncan with you?"

"He came with us at first. Then he left us, saying that he had other business."

"But, if he was in command . . .?"

"He handed over to Andrew. Saying that he had private business. And went back."

"Back? You mean . . .? What business?"

"He did not say. You know Duncan. He keeps all close, gives little away. I have not seen him since that day."

"You believe that he it was who killed Drummond? Or ordered him to be starved to death?"

His brother looked distinctly alarmed, glancing at Douglas. "I did not say that, Alex. I know no more than I have told you. When we left Drummond, locked in that hold, he was well enough. An old man getting, mind . . ."

"And being fed?"

"I know not. I tell you, I had naught to do with him."

"And you think that Duncan went south, afterwards? When Drummond was dead?"

"Yes."

"Who told you?"

"Gillies here said it, Seumas and Colin."

"Alone?"

"He took two gillies only."

"Then he was going secretly. Why? Why kill Drummond? And why go to the South? Duncan, of all men?"

"The one because of the other, belike?" Jamie suggested. "Flight. He fled from *your* wrath."

"But . . . that would mean . . .? No — Duncan has no friends in the South. He has never crossed the Highland Line — save with a drawn sword. He knows none . . ."

"You are wrong, Alex. Duncan does know someone," his brother said. "A man was here, some months back, two months, more. Here at Loch-an-Eilean. A Lowlander. He stayed for three days. Lindsay by name."

"Lindsay? You mean, from Glen Esk, in Angus?"

"No. Not that airt. I thought at first that he came from the North, some place — for his style was Lindsay of Ross. But no, it was from the South . . ."

"Ross — not *Rossie*?" That was Jamie, almost with a bark. "Lindsay of Rossie? Sir William?"

"He was a knight, yes. William Lindsay . . ."

"Dear God!" the Douglas exclaimed. "Lindsay of Rossie is one of Albany's jackals! He and Sir John de Ramorgnie were mainly responsible for Prince David's death at Falkland. By starvation!"

His friend stared at him. "Albany!" he whispered. "Mary-Mother — not that! Not my uncle Robert!"

"If Lindsay was here? What brought him all this way? A Fife laird."

"What was he doing here, Rob?" Alex demanded.

"I do not know. He was here when I came, one day. Duncan told me nothing. Said that he was a friend, that is all."

"Why have I not heard of this Lowland visitor?"

"Duncan said . . . better not say anything."

"A plague on you, Rob! *I* am Lord of Badenoch, not Duncan! You know that I require to be told of every stranger who crosses into my territories. Saints give me patience! A

Lowland knight, a creature of the Governor's — and I knew naught of it!"

His half-brother scowled. "Duncan is a hard man to counter."

"And so am I, by God! As you, and others, will learn!" With an obvious effort Alex controlled himself. "Forgive me, Jamie. I am sorry." He turned back to his brother. "Duncan captained this castle. For *me*. Yet he has left it, without my authority. And put you in command? Of this, at least, I ought to have been informed."

"You were in the West," Rob said heavily. "Busy."

"You could have sent a messenger."

Silence.

"I see that I shall have to put my own house in order!" Alex said grimly. "You will hear more of this, Rob. Is Andrew at Ruthven? And Walter?"

"They are both at Drumin, with Tom. Or were."

"Indeed. What do they there?"

"I know not."

"No? Then, if you have nothing else to tell me, we shall leave you, meantime. I shall send for you to come to Lochindorb, in due course."

As they rode on, northwards now through the great forest, minds busy, Alex said, "I shall have to take my brothers in hand, it is clear. If I may no longer control the North, as Justiciar, I can at least control my own family. We are going to require a united house, I think!"

"*Can* you?" Jamie asked bluntly. "As I remember them, they are all hard, strong men."

"Ha, my friend — but perhaps you have not seen *me* at my hardest and strongest! Moreover, I have a hold over all of them. Our father, in his wisdom, left all the lordship to me, its castles, lands and privileges — did not break it up. He knew them, you see!"

"And knew you! But, Alex — this of Albany? How think you? Could he have had anything to do with Drummond's death?"

"The good God knows! The thought had not so much as come into my mind, before this. Why should he?"

"Why should any? Save *you*! But — they were unfriends. Drummond had a grudge against Albany, over the unentailed lands of Douglas, which were prevented from coming to his wife. And this is the same death which he caused his other

34

unfriend to die! And you also are an unfriend — and this strikes at you! This link with Lindsay of Rossie must mean something. Why should one of Albany's men come all this way into the Highlands to see your brother?"

The other shook his head.

"I wonder . . . ? You remember what the Countess Isobel said? About the King considering to send the young Prince James into his uncle's care at Kildrummy, for safety? Safety from Albany, to be sure, who slew his brother. Could that have to do with it?"

"You mean . . . ?"

"I mean that only young James now stands between Albany and the throne, should the King die. And he is a sick man. The King greatly fears for the boy's safety, that is evident — and has him put in the care of Bishop Wardlaw at St. Andrews. He appears to feel that insufficiently secure, if he thought to send him north. Albany could be proving that his arm can stretch as far as that! To teach others not to interfere, to offer sanctuary to the prince. And to dispose of Drummond, the King's last remaining close friend. And embroil *you* whom he hates and fears."

"Save us — you would make Robert Stewart the Fiend Incarnate, Jamie! Even he could scarce be so devilishly clever as that."

"Why not? Think how he had the Earl James Douglas slain — and the slayer's mouth closed. And the mouth-closer slain likewise! All by others' hands. Your Aunt Gelis at least, believed that he had her husband, Will Douglas of Nithsdale, assassinated equally cunningly, in Danzig. He had his nephew David starved to death at Falkland — and parliament to absolve him afterwards. Think you this would be too much for him?"

"I do not know. If Albany is in this, then all is changed, and we require to look a deal more closely at many things."

"Yes. It may not be so. But, I say, we would be fools to overlook that it is possible . . ."

III

LOCHINDORB WAS AN extraordinary place by any standards. Deep, remote within the high heather and rounded hills of Braemoray, almost ten miles from any real village or community, a wide green amphitheatre opened in the prevailing brownness. In the floor of this lay a loch two miles long by half-a-mile wide, with only a scattering of trees around; and towards its centre a single island. Following the irregular contours of this, the walls of a major castle arose in stark masonry, the massive and lofty curtains enclosing a sizeable area, with heavy squat drum-towers at the angles and what amounted to a township of subsidiary buildings within — greater and lesser halls, dormitories, kitchens, armouries, barracks, stables, store-rooms and a chapel. There was even a garden, ladies' pleasance and orchard within the perimeter walling, little to be looked for in this wilderness. A cluster of thatch-roofed cot-houses, cabins, byres and the like formed a castleton on the east shore opposite the island, where there was a stone jetty — with the ferry-scow always berthed at the castle side. Cattle grazed the enclosing braesides up to the heather-line.

To the uninformed it might seem a strange, indeed a pointless place to site a powerful castle. But, in fact, it was a highly strategic situation, in a position to command almost every important route from the fertile and populous Laigh of Moray to upper Strathspey, Moy, Strathdearn, Strathnairn, the Great Glen and the Highland West. Edward the First of England had recognised this, during the Wars of Independence, and here, in then Comyn territory, had built up a small clan-chief's fortalice into this great stronghold. And Alexander Stewart, Earl of Buchan, had perceived its potentialities and made it his head-quarters for the domination and control of the North-East, transferring here from Ruthven or upper Speyside the principal seat of his vast Lordship of Badenoch. Here he had installed Mariota de Athyn, his famous concubine and chief mistress, daughter of the chiefly house of Mackay of Strathnaver; and here were reared their five sons and one daughter. At Lochindorb Alex Stewart now reigned in his stead, the Wolf eight years dead. Illegitimate, he could not inherit the earldom of Buchan, or even be *de jure* Lord of Badenoch; but *de facto*, he ruled a huge territory as lord, and governed all the North-East as acting Justiciar and Lieutenant for the late heir to the throne, David, Duke of Rothesay, so far not effectively replaced save by the absentee Murdoch of Fife.

That castle could never be approached unwarned, and well before they reached the landing-stage, a boat had put out to come for the travellers. In it, with the rowers, was a young woman and her children, a boy and girl, aged eleven and nine. Their shouted welcome echoed from all the enclosing hillsides.

It was Alex who called back, waving his bonnet, laughing, Jamie Douglas not at his best in scenes and occasions — unless drastic action was called for. He grinned affectionately at his wife and youngsters, however, and at his friend's demonstrative greetings.

"Mary!" the other cried. "Had I wife as comely and excellent as you, I swear that I would never leave home! As for these two, Lochindorb would be a poor place without them."

"Let us hope that you continue to think so, Alex," Mary returned. "For it seems that you are burdened with us for no little time yet."

"Would that my other burdens were of such sort! That, at least, is good news. We will make Highlanders of you all, to be sure, in time!"

"You are kind . . ."

Jamie, although less forthcoming verbally, was nowise backward in embracing his wife appreciatively. And she was of the sort a man much appreciates within his arms, warm, eager, shapely, big-breasted and all woman. The Stewarts had a tendency towards beauty of feature and person, and this illegitimate daughter of the late King, sister of the present monarch, and aunt, after a fashion, of Sir Alexander himself, had the family excellences in full measure, without some of the more notable failings. Less actually beautiful than one or two of the princesses, her half-sisters, she had a lively attractiveness none of them

37

could rival. Her children had to tug and squeeze their father with some vigour to gain their due share of attention.

The Lady Mariota welcomed them at the castle landing-stage, another attractive woman although now in her fifties, handsome, large, forthright, of a natural and far from unpleasing lustiness of character and bearing, which reminded Jamie at least of the Countess of Mar, in some measure. Indeed, it might well be that something of this was in part responsible for Alex's preoccupation with so much older a woman — for he greatly admired his mother. Not that there was anything the least motherly about Isobel of Mar.

Although Mariota de Athyn, or Mackay, was known throughout the kingdom as a notorious courtesan, and concubine of one of the most spectacularly wicked men that even Scotland had ever produced, king's son though he was, she gave little impression of that role; but rather of an assured and effective chatelaine, respectable as any in the land. She had, indeed, been as good as wife — and a good wife — to the Wolf, who had never lived with his wedded spouse, the Countess of Buchan and Ross in her own right. Undoubtedly Mariota had been the best influence in that wild man's life, had given him a fair home amongst his innumerable dens, and brought up their family in as normal, domestic and stable a fashion as had been possible in the extraordinary and testing circumstances. If some of her sons behaved like their father on occasion, that was not altogether her fault.

She was demonstrably happy to see her favourite son safely back from the wars, whilst greeting Jamie with almost equal affection, and an added womanly appreciation wasted on a son. The two young men might have their problems, but they had priceless assets in their womenfolk.

That evening, round the fire in Mariota's own private chamber, the real heart of that great fortalice, what amounted to a council-of-war developed. Alex told them what he had learned at Kildrummy and Loch-an-Eilean, and explained Jamie's theory of Governor Albany's possible involvement. The women expressed their inevitable doubts, if not actual disbelief, and even when these were in some part countered, remained by no means convinced.

"Jamie is prepared to believe anything of Robert," Mary Stewart declared. "He will attribute every evil to him. He is a hard and twisted man, and has done much ill in his day, but I

38

cannot conceive him as black as Jamie thinks, nor possessed of so long an arm."

"Myself, I cannot see that Drummond's death and Alex's downfall could be so important for him. To go to these lengths," Mariota said. "It all would have taken a great deal of planning and working out, beforehand."

"As did the murder of Earl Douglas. As did your . . . as did my lord Earl of Buchan's excommunication plot. That is the kind of mind Albany has," Jamie asserted. "How he works. You cannot deny it, Mary."

"No. Not his devious, malicious mind. It is his purpose and need, in this, that I doubt."

"Let us leave the matter open, then," Alex put in. "Accept only that Robert Stewart *may* be concerned. But if he is, then we must tread a deal more warily. Possibly be prepared for further blows."

"No doubt," his mother said. "But — first things first. What is most important, Alex, is to establish your innocence in the eyes of men."

"Agreed, yes. But none so easy, is it? With Duncan gone, who is going to believe my denials?"

"You cannot perhaps *prove* who did it, in law. But you can perhaps make it clear that *you* did not. Knew naught of it. You are still Justiciar. Before you think of standing down, Alex, hold a trial. Before a great company . . ."

"I agree," Jamie said. "I have said as much."

"How can I, when there is none to stand accused?"

"You have other brothers, besides Duncan, my dear, who also led that company. My own sons, yes, but they have served you ill, done nothing to aid you in this. You must use them to clear your name."

"You mean . . . ?"

"I mean take Andrew and Walter into custody. As Justiciar. Charge them with the murder of Drummond. In your Court. They will, pray God, be shown to be innocent. But they must be made also to establish *your* innocence, before all. Then they can be set free. Mary and I have talked much of this. We believe this is what is required."

Alex frowned. "A sore, hard business that. To arraign my own brothers. They will not love me for it!"

"They will understand," Mary said. "Besides, they *owe* you this, at least. You must do it, Alex — for their sakes, as well as

39

your own. If you go down, to be a mere outlaw and Highland freebooter, *their* state and security is also endangered. All our safety."

"But . . . who will take heed of the findings of such Court? In my own Court, absolving myself and my brothers! All will scorn it, as a merest device."

"No," Jamie intervened. "There is much point to this, I think. It *has* to be your Court, as Justiciar. The highest Court in the North, dispensing the King's justice. No other would serve — the sheriff's or other. The King's good-brother has been slain. It is the King's Justiciar's duty to seek out and try the guilty — none other's. So you must remain Justiciar until then, at least. Although some may scoff, none can controvert such trial. *You* will not seem to be on trial, moreover . . ."

"It will be assumed to be but covering my own fault, nevertheless. As Robert Stewart did after David's murder, at the Holyrood trial."

"Then sit with others in judgement. Say, two others. A triumvirate. Men of repute. Your Bishop? He would serve in this. And would show that you had the power of the Church behind you — a considerable matter. And some other. It would be a duly lawful trial. And whatever Albany might say, or do, its decision could not be questioned in *law*. Any more than his could, at Holyrood. So he could not use parliament against you, at least. That would prevent outlawry, meantime. A sound move, Alex."

The other nodded. "Perhaps you are right. Who could I ask to sit with me? The Mackintosh? Chief of Clan Chattan . . . ?"

"A pity that Thomas, Earl of Moray is prisoner in England," Mary said. "Another nephew of the King, he would be of the right stature."

"I can think of what would carry more weight still," Jamie said. "A representative from Mar! The Countess Isobel could find you one, I swear. That would look notably well."

At this mention of the Countess, Mariota stiffened. Her son went on hurriedly.

"I will think on that. But — after? What then? We find Andrew and Walter not guilty. And myself, by implication, more so. If we have established Duncan's probable guilt — what to do? He has disappeared."

"You will have to order his apprehension and arrest, in the King's name," his mother declared steadily. "You can do no less, as Justiciar. Since, it seems, he has left your jurisdiction for the South, you will not be able to enforce it. He will stay away. But, better that than hanging, God knows!"

"And Robert of Albany? What will he do?"

"Who knows? But you will be on the watch for him."

"Albany will surprise, nothing is more sure," Jamie asserted. "But . . . I fear for your Duncan. If he deserves it! When Albany has finished with one of his tools, he does not usually live to tell who paid him!"

"We do not *know* that Robert paid him, Jamie," his wife pointed out. "We do not even know that Duncan did this thing."

The men had to admit that this was so, and that they had only suppositions to work on.

They could plan no further meantime.

*   *   *

It was nearly two weeks later, of a fine autumn early afternoon, that Jamie Douglas fished assiduously for salmon in the swift run of amber water where the quite major Dorback Burn issued from the foot of Lochindorb. He had been at it for almost three hours, without so much as a nibble, and had been telling himself and all the watching hills that it was a hopeless waste of time, that it was too bright a day, that the water was too clear, that it was the wrong hour, that his lures were quite useless, and that he should give it all up and row back to the castle while still he retained his sanity — this for over an hour, when his young son David came paddling across the loch in a basket-and-hide coracle, to announce breathlessly that his father was required forthwith, that there were visitors arrived and he must come.

Jamie produced the required grumbles about being disturbed at his well-earned recreation, but packed up his willow-wand and line the while, ignoring his son's interested queries as to how many fish he had caught, and gingerly embarking in his own frail craft for the paddle back to the island. Alex Stewart was away at Elgin, making arrangements for the great trial to be held there. Jamie's son, splashing alongside, insisted that his father was to go to the castle, not to the landing-stage on the shore opposite, where a fair-sized company could be seen to be waiting.

Mariota and Mary met him just within the castle gateway, out of sight of the waiting visitors, and for once the former displayed unwonted agitation.

41

"Jamie," she said, "you must deal with this, whatever. I will not have that woman in my house! She ought not to have come here. Send her away, Jamie. She is not to come here."

Bewildered, he looked from one woman to the other.

"It is the Countess of Mar," Mary said. "No doubt to see Alex. She will have to be told . . . not to come out here. And you know her, Jamie."

Her husband moistened his lips. "You say I have to turn her away? From this door? Having come all this way from Kildrummy? A great lady, like Isobel of Mar. Alex will not like this, I think!"

"Alex is not here. And I would not have her in my house if he *was* here. You may tell her so!" the normally generous and imperturbable Mariota de Athyn said.

"But . . . but this is going to be most difficult, trying," the man protested. "I have partaken of her hospitality, more than once. As has Alex."

"*I* have not! And would not! Send her away." And their hostess turned and swept off, back across the courtyard.

The man stared at his wife.

"I am sorry, Jamie — but I can prevail nothing with her," Mary told him. "I have tried. She hates the Countess, and her influence on Alex."

"No doubt. But to turn her away from the door! One of the greatest in the land. And new widowed . . ."

"What has either to do with it?"

"Sakes — if you do not see it!" He shook his head. "Women!" he exclaimed. "This countess could throw the whole of Mar behind Alex. One of the most powerful earldoms in the realm. Or . . ."

"By the sound of her she will do that anyway! She has her claws in Alex, for her own designs. Now — go across, Jamie, and tell her that the Lady Mariota is indisposed and unable to see her. But that Alex is at Elgin, and if she goes there she will see him. She will understand very well."

"That she will! Alex *loves* this woman, Mary. Has done for long."

"Then he will see her the sooner — at Elgin! Go you, Jamie."

"If I go, you come with me."

"That is foolish. I can do nothing . . ."

"You can do as much as I can. You can speak to her as a woman. And this is woman's work! Come."

So they both were rowed across the four hundred yards of water to the main landing-stage.

The sizeable party, perhaps fifty strong, was dismounted and waiting there. The Countess was easily distinguished, the only woman present, seated on a log with every appearance of patience for so proud and forthright a character. She was dressed in a travelling cloak and man-style tartan trews, cut on the cross to cling to a substantial but shapely leg, and wore a feathered bonnet with an air. Standing beside her was a young gallant, also with an air to him, features vaguely familiar.

"Who is that? A Stewart, I swear!" Mary Stewart said.

"I do not know him. Yet I should know that face, I think."

As they landed, the Countess exclaimed, "On my soul — I wondered whether all had died a death in yonder hold! And now it is Jamie Douglas and Mary Stewart! Has Alex taken to his bed, or what?"

"I am sorry, my lady, that you have been kept waiting," Jamie said, bowing stiffly. "Sir Alexander is not here. He is presently at Elgin."

"Elgin? A plague on it!"

"He has been gone two days. And we do not expect him back before two more."

"Ah. Unfortunate."

"Yes. The Lady Mariota, I fear, is indisposed and cannot receive you at the castle."

"Indeed? You mean . . . ?"

"It is a pity that you have been thus delayed, Countess — when you could have been on your road to Elgin," Mary put in.

"Still a long road, I fear."

"Ah. I see. Yes, I see." Isobel of Mar smiled. "That makes the position entirely clear! Alex should have been more . . . explicit, in his letter."

"Letter . . . ?"

"Why, yes. Alex sent a messenger, with a letter, asking me to find someone, some representative of the earldom of Mar, to sit with him as judge, in the trial anent my husband's death. I have bettered his suggestion — eh, John?" And she turned to her lounging companion.

"As to that, who knows?" he said. He was a tall, well-built and good-looking young man in his early twenties, with fair hair, long features and fine eyes. He laughed — and clearly he laughed easily. "Sir Alexander may find me young, for justiciaring."

43

"Alex is none so old himself, boy," she said. "Unlike my aged self!"

"You have the secret of endless youth and delight, Isobel," he said — and this time he did not smile, strangely enough. Indeed his fine eyes smouldered.

"Flatterer!" she returned. "And you so young. Who taught you, I wonder? Not your father. Nor yet your brother Murdoch, I vow!" She looked at the others. "Perhaps you do not know each other? Although you, Mary Stewart, should know, one would think. This is the Lord John Stewart of Coull and Onele, in Cro-Mar. Known in Mar as Brave John o' Coull. And whether he is notably brave or not, he is sufficiently bold — that I can vouch for! Second son to the Governor of us all, the Duke of Albany!"

To say that Jamie and Mary caught their breaths would be an understatement. Utterly taken aback, they stared, at a loss for words.

The young man bowed elaborately, smiling again — but at Mary rather than at the Douglas. "I believe that I may be privileged to name you Aunt!" he said. "Like all too many another, I fear!"

"Johnnie Stewart!" she gasped. "Can it be true? I have not seen you since you were a child-in-arms."

"No. I was reared far from Court. My mother, daughter to the Marischal, enjoys the barony of Coull and Onele, in the valley of Dee, in Cro-Mar. It has become my home and inheritance. My mother was never greatly enamoured of Court life, and retired there."

"So that is where your mother took . . . refuge!"

"Exactly, Aunt!"

The Countess Isobel laughed. "The Stewart family never ceases to surprise! Sir Jamie — does it not surprise you? But . . . how think you this one will serve the Justiciar as second judge?"

That man took moments to answer. To have Albany's own son as co-judge in this case was so improbable-seeming as to be almost inconceivable. If he could be relied upon to co-operate and assist in the project of establishing Alex's innocence, his adherence would be invaluable — for Albany's hands would thereby be much tied, since he was hardly likely to denigrate the judicial findings of his own son, or not publicly. It would give vastly greater validity to the entire exercise. On the other hand, he would be in a position to wreck all, should he so elect, if he sought to play his father's game. He would well recognise this — for he looked to be no fool. Yet the Countess Isobel was no fool either, and she had chosen him. So she must believe that he would be good for Alex's cause, rather than Albany's. He, it seemed, had been reared much apart from his father — indeed, Jamie had scarcely ever heard him referred to, or indeed the Lady Muriella Keith's other, younger children; only Murdoch, the son by the Governor's first wife, the Countess of Menteith in her own right, was seen much about the father. Albany was neither a man with much use for women, save for what they could bring him, nor yet for family life. So the Duchess Muriella had to make her own life. And this John of Coull might possibly make a useful ally.

As all this flashed through Jamie's mind, he nodded. "I think notably well," he said. "Provided that his intentions are . . . kindly disposed."

"I think that my lord's intentions are kindly — towards myself, at any rate!" The Countess's tone and glance were significant, archly so.

"H'r'mm. Yes. To be sure," Jamie muttered. If Alex ever eventually married this one, he was not likely to lack problems.

The younger man grinned cheerfully.

Mary spoke. "Nephew John, how think you your father will see this?"

"He can scarce object to me assisting the King's Justiciar, Aunt."

"You think not? Acting Justiciar, only!" Mary amended.

"To be sure. But then, if my brother Murdoch is in truth Justiciar — as I believe he was appointed? — then, since Murdoch is a captive in England, is it not the more my duty to assist his . . . deputy?"

"Your father may see it otherwise, perhaps."

"Then my father will have to communicate his pleasure, or displeasure, to me — which he does but seldom, God be thanked!"

Mary's faint smile at that held a hint of admiration; and Jamie decided that this Stewart was certainly no fool or simple innocent — which made him consider the Countess the more thoughtfully.

"So now you would have us ride to Elgin? Without further . . . delay?" the lady asked.

Jamie coughed. "Yes. That is best. Alex should hear of this at the earliest. I will ride some way with you. Put you on the best road. By Glen Erney, Dallas and the Lossie, to Kellas and Pittendreich. It is near thirty miles. But there is the Valliscaulian Hospice of St. Michael at Dallas, where you could pass the night."

"You are thoughtful, my friend!" She turned to Mary. "You will convey to the Lady Mariota my concern for her health? Should we inform Alex to return with all haste to his mother's side?"

"That will not be necessary, I think."

"Ah — I am relieved to hear it! Tell her to take good care of herself. We older women must not over-tax ourselves!" And the Countess snapped imperious fingers for her groom to bring forward her horse.

Jamie exchanged glances with his wife, and hastened to collect a mount for himself from the castleton stables.

* * *

Elgin, as well as being the chief town of Moray and the diocesan centre, was also in theory the official seat of government for all the North-East and site of the principal royal castle. So, for maximum effect, Sir Alexander Stewart chose to stage his great trial there, on a day of early November, in the said royal castle, on the modest height of the Lady Hill towards the west end of the town, a place he seldom used, like his father before him. It was, in fact, no impressive stronghold, old and in disrepair; but it had a large old-fashioned hall and an indefinable air of authority about it.

From an early hour, whenever the town's gates were opened for the day, folk had been flocking into Elgin — for Alex had sought to publish the word of it far and wide. The townsfolk were out in force also. Only a limited number could gain admittance to the hall, of course, and these mainly burgh, chiefly and lairdly representatives and churchmen; but the crowds could wait outside, see the principals arrive, and hear what was relayed to them from within.

Jamie, Mary and the Lady Mariota were installed at the side of the dais-platform, where they could see all, yet remain hidden from most of the hall by the serving screens. Unfortunately they were not hidden from the Countess of Mar, who sat by herself directly opposite at the other side of the dais — to the marked embarrassment of Jamie at least. *She* did not seem concerned at her isolation, any more than did Mariota or Mary, women being a law unto themselves in such matters, but rather mildly interested and amused by all that went on, the jostling for position in the body of the hall, the bickering, greeting and general stir.

It was all well managed. A trumpeter blew a flourish, and a herald — really more of a Highland sennachie than a Lowland pursuivant — strode in and announced in ringing tones but a musical Highland voice that all should be upstanding for the entry of His Grace the King's Lord Justiciar of the North, the excellent and right puissant Sir Alexander Stewart of Badenoch, Braemoray and Kinneddar, supported by the Lord Bishop of Moray, Master William de Spynie, and the Lord John Stewart, of Coull and Onele, sworn Justiciars Extraordinary. God Save the King's Grace!

He was a little early, but no matter — the stir at the naming of the third judge was sufficient to keep tongues wagging until Alex paced in, with the other two behind.

Alex, who usually dressed in Highland fashion, was today clad in his finest — actually old court clothing of his father's, crimson velvet, silver filigree and cloth-of-gold, slightly tarnished but not too obviously so. The Bishop was magnificent in his most gorgeous cope, stole and mitre, aglitter with jewels; John Stewart, much more modestly garbed, carrying himself with confidence enough for any. Seen together there was a distinct family resemblance between the Stewart cousins.

Three throne-like chairs from the cathedral were placed in the centre of the dais. The triumvirate sat. After a few moments pause, Alex lifted his hand, and the trumpeter blew a single blast for silence.

"My lords spiritual and temporal, chiefs, barons, tacksmen, freeholders, burghers of this city, and people here assembled, leal subjects of the King's Grace — hail!" the Justiciar called, clearly, still sitting. "I, Alexander Stewart, *Alastair mac Alastair Mor mac an Righ*, acting His Grace's Justiciar, do hereby declare that His Grace's lawful and superior Court of Justice in this northern part of his kingdom, is now duly in session. Let any who may question that authority stand forth."

Silence.

"So be it. I do declare that I, and my colleagues here before you, the Lord Bishop William and the Lord John of Coull and Onele, will hear, question, consider and make and pronounce

47

judgement, with open minds, firm purpose and honest hearts, on the evidence to be put before us, as we value our immortal souls — so help us God!"

"Amen!" intoned the Bishop.

"I agree," said Brave John of Coull.

"That ensured, I now declare to all that in order that the King's justice be done, it is necessary that we herewith consider and enquire into the recent and horrible murder of Sir Malcolm Drummond, Knight, Lord of Cargill and Stobhall, *An Drumanach Mor*, Chief of Clan Drummond of Strathearn and Gowrie, husband of the most noble Countess of Mar and the Garioch, and good-brother of the King's Grace. Which horrible and shameful murder, said to be by starvation, took place within our jurisdiction, to wit, within the hold of Badenyon in Brae-Mar, on a date unspecified between the Feast of St. Barnabas the Apostle and that of St. Palladius, Bishop and Confessor, in this year of Our Lord, fourteen-hundred-and-two. To which end we now make due inquisition."

He paused and turned to the herald, a brother of the Mackintosh, now to double as prosecutor.

"You, sir, have in custody two suspects whom it is conjectured may have committed this grievous murder and offence?"

"Yes, my lord. Two. Sir Andrew Stewart of Ruthven and Sir Walter Stewart of Glenavon. A third, Sir Duncan Stewart of Loch-an-Eilean, is not to be found, and believed to have left the territory under the jurisdiction of this Court."

"Yes. We note the third name. I hereby now state and affirm that these accused, the said Andrew, Walter and Duncan Stewart, are brothers-german to my own self. But that it is my simple and undoubted duty to put them on trial for this shameful offence against the King's peace and his lieges. But in case any should question my honest purpose and impartial judgement in this matter, I have empanelled two further honourable and unprejudiced judges, who have no least connection with the accused, to ensure a right verdict. Should there be disagreement amongst the judges, the vote of any two shall prevail. Is all understood? Then — bring in the accused."

The buzz of exclamation, comment and speculation was loud in the hall.

Mackintosh went out, and returned with the two young men. They stalked in stiffly, proudly, heads high, with nothing of guilt, fear or uncertainty about them. A couple of years between them, they were very much alike, although one had reddish hair, the other golden-fair. Although both bore an evident family resemblance to Alex, it would be wrong to say that either was *like* him, in the way that they were like each other, likeness, implying similarity of appearance or impact, being quite absent. They were stockier, rougher, less fine-honed versions of a superficially similar model, that is all, features good and regular but somehow blurred in comparison, expressions entirely different, with a distinct air of intolerance and arrogance. These, one could well believe, were truly sons of the Wolf of Badenoch. Jamie Douglas, seeing them anew after a long interval, perceived them as somehow liker to Alastair Carrach MacDonald than to their eldest brother. All were grandsons of King Robert the Second, of course — as was John of Coull.

The pair strode rather than were led, to the side of the dais, where they inclined brief nods towards their brother — none could say that they bowed — and so stood. They did not so much as glance at the crowd.

Mackintosh, at a nod from Alex, spoke. "Andrew Stewart, Knight, and Walter Stewart, Knight — you are hereby charged that on a day between the Feast of St. Barnabas the Apostle and that of the Blessed St. Palladius, you both and in concert, with your brother Duncan Stewart, Knight, did lay violent hands on Sir Malcolm Drummond of Cargill and Stobhall, the King's good-brother, whilst on his lawful occasions, did convey him to the lonely hold of Badenyon in Brae-Mar, and there did ill-use him so grievously that he died, and so did murder him. What say you to this fell charge?"

"No," Andrew, the elder, answered briefly.

"You deny guilt? Both?"

"Yes."

"Do you deny taking Sir Malcolm, when about his lawful affairs, and conveying him to this Badenyon?"

"No."

"Why did you so do?"

"We did so on the King's business."

"The *King's* . . .?"

"Yes."

"Explain yourself, sir. How the King's business?"

Andrew had clearly taken upon himself to act spokesman, with whatever brevity. "Donald of the Isles had invaded this country. Alastair Carrach was sacking and slaying, had sacked this city. Drummond was known to be dealing with Donald. It was feared that he would rise, to aid Alastair. We were sent to see that he did not."

"Who sent you?"

"I did," Alex intervened. "As King's Justiciar and Lieutenant it was my duty to seek preserve the King's peace. I had reason to believe that Sir Malcolm Drummond might support the Lord of the Isles in his revolt. I sent a strong company, under my brothers, to keep watch on Sir Malcolm, and myself came to the relief of Elgin and the countering of Alastair."

"The accused then, my lord, were sent to *watch* Sir Malcolm Drummond — not to slay him?"

"That is so."

Mackintosh turned back to Andrew Stewart. "Do you agree? That your orders were to watch Drummond? Not to slay him?"

"Yes."

"Then why did you slay him?"

"We did not."

"You do not deny that he was slain? In that remote hold in Brae-Mar. Locked therein, given neither food nor drink, and starved to death?"

"It may be so. But it was not our doing."

"Whose, then?"

Neither of the accused spoke.

"You must answer my question, whatever. If you did not slay Drummond, who did?"

"We do not know."

Mackintosh glanced at the judges.

Bishop Spynie spoke. "Is it your plea that you knew of the slaying but were not party to it?"

"No. We knew naught of it."

"But you were at the taking of Sir Malcolm and the immuring of him in this hold?"

"Yes."

"How then can you claim innocence for his death?"

"We knew naught of it. We left him there, well enough."

"Ah. So someone else was responsible for this starving? After you left. When you were not there?"

"Yes."

"Who?"

Silence.

John of Coull spoke. "Who commanded your company, Sir Andrew?"

For the first time the other looked uncertain. "There, there was no true commander," he said.

"No commander? Of an armed force? How many men?"

"Three hundred perhaps."

"Someone must have been in command."

"We were all brothers. In command."

"Who, then, was the eldest?"

"I was," Andrew admitted. "But . . ."

"But you were not in command?"

The other prisoner, Sir Walter, raised his voice at last. "Our brother Duncan is . . . forceful," he said.

"Ah. So, in effect, Sir Duncan it was who commanded? In fact if not in name? Sir Duncan, who is now missing."

"I can confirm, my lords, that Duncan is the most vehement and headstrong of our family," Alex put in. "Therefore I seldom give him overall command."

"But was it not he, my lord, who led the great raid on Angus and Gowrie some eight years back?" the Bishop asked. "And won the Battle of Glasclune and other fights?"

"Yes. He is an able fighter, strategist — and bold. But . . . headstrong."

"Did Sir Duncan, then, order the apprehension and immuring of Sir Malcolm Drummond?"

Walter nodded.

"And you left him at this place, in your brother Duncan's care?"

"No. We all left, Duncan with us." That was Andrew again. "We rode for the Kildrummy country. To discover whether forces were massing there, to the aid of Alastair."

"Leaving Drummond in this hold — the name of which I misremember? Alone, without food or drink? You left him to die?"

"No. We left him under a small guard. With ample victual."

"So — you are saying that it was these men of your guard who abandoned Sir Malcolm and left him to die?" The Bishop now considered himself as chief inquisitor.

Silence.

"Answer, sirrah!"

It was Alex who eventually spoke, and there can have been few who did not sense the reluctance with which he did so.

51

"I heard tell that Duncan left you, however, the next day. Turned back. Is that so?"

"Ye-e-es."

"Back to Badenyon?"

"I do not know."

"But you *understood* that is where he was bound?"

No reply.

"Later, the guard you had left returned to you?"

"Yes."

"And what did they say?"

"I do not exchange idle gossip with gillies!"

"A plague on it, man . . .!" Alex stopped himself. "Your pardon, my lords. I forget myself. Andrew Stewart — I charge you to answer my question. Do you not see? If you seek further to shield Duncan your brother, *our* brother, you condemn these your gillies. Without cause, it may be. Innocent men. For either he, or they, would seem to have starved Drummond to death. Answer me on two points. How long until the guard returned to you, in the Kildrummy area? And what did they tell you when they came?"

When Andrew continued to scowl obstinately, Walter spoke. "I will tell you — and thereafter *yours* is the responsibility, Alex, not ours! Mind it! They came in five days after we left them. And said that Duncan had sent them back to us."

Something like a sigh rose from the packed hall.

"So now we have it," the Bishop said. "Sir Duncan sent them back. So he went there, after he left you. And was still there when these left. No man will starve to death within five days. And Sir Duncan was left alone with the prisoner, the man he had insisted on taking and imprisoning. *Was* he alone?"

"He had his own two running gillies only," Walter said.

"And these are now where?"

"Neither he, nor they, have been seen since."

"I agree that no man is like to die after only five days without food. Or even water," John Stewart of Coull said. "So it seems that Sir Malcolm Drummond was caused to starve to death thereafter — by Sir Duncan Stewart. But why? What was his reason for this barbarous act?"

When none answered that, the young man went on, "He must have had cause for so ill a deed. Some hatred, or some score to pay. Such a thing is not done for simple enmity or malice."

52

When still he obtained no response from any, he turned to Alex. "My lord — have *you* any notion as to why?"

Thus directly challenged, that man spoke carefully. "I do not know. So far as I am aware, he never met Sir Malcolm before. He fought against him at Glasclune — but so he did against many another. If indeed he is guilty, he must have had a reason unknown to me. Unless . . . he was put up to it by another."

"Who would so do?"

"Your notion is as good as mine, my lord. But it would require to be someone who hated Drummond and would benefit by his death. And possibly who would wish to injure *myself*, by seeking to implicate me in this evil thing."

There was a stir at that.

"And have you no notion at all, my lord, as to whom that might be?"

"I shall make it my business to find out!" Alex said grimly.

"It may be that the accused could tell us?" the Bishop said. "Do either of you know? Or have any notion?"

Both stared at him, wordless.

"You must answer," Mackintosh told them.

"No," Andrew said.

"No," Walter said.

The prelate frowned and puffed. "Insolent! This is an outrage!"

Alex intervened. "My lord Bishop — I think that they probably speak but the truth. If *I* do not have such information, it is unlikely that they will have it. Duncan keeps his own counsel. If it is some secret matter, an intrigue, they will know no more than I do. Moreover, I think, interesting as this knowledge would be, it is scarce our present duty to discover. We are here, are we not, to seek find out *who* murdered Sir Malcolm — not why he did so? That would be valuable to discover, and I shall endeavour it. But meantime we have a decision to come to. Do we require further questioning of these accused?"

The Bishop puffed.

"Are there further witnesses?" John Stewart asked.

"Not that I know aught of. Or can conceive of. Perhaps the accused can tell us that — if there are others who might inform us in the matter, to their advantage? Andrew? Walter?"

The brothers both shook their heads.

"The only other witnesses who could take us any further, it seems to me, are the two gillies Duncan Stewart took with him

53

back to Badenyon," Alex went on. "And these, it appears he has likewise taken with him to the South. No others could speak to the actual death of Sir Malcolm."

"I agree," John of Coull nodded. "Which makes our decision here simple, does it not? We cannot declare finally who murdered Drummond — but must say that it would appear to be Sir Duncan Stewart of Loch-an-Eilean. We *can* say that it was not the doing of the two accused here before us, however. Nor does any responsibility rest with the higher command of the Justiciar's forces."

"I thank you, my lord. A clear exposition of the situation. And you, my lord Bishop?"

"The same. Save that I would have it recorded that we here recognise that the reason *why* this shameful murder was committed should be discovered, as of vital importance, in order that we may learn who, if any, was behind Sir Duncan Stewart in the commission of this crime."

"Agreed. The clerks will record that — although I fear that it may be difficult to ascertain. There is one further matter which I would wish to have established before all, before we dismiss the accused — and which they can tell us. This involves myself, in person. I would have it established what were my orders to this company I sent to Mar — since it bears on the matter. All three brothers I summoned together at Lochindorb before sending them off. Do you agree with that?"

The pair nodded.

"Do you also agree that you were ordered to *watch* Sir Malcolm? And if he had a fighting force raised to aid Alastair Carrach in his invasion, you were to seek prevent such force from joining up with Alastair? Only that. No word of arresting Drummond."

Again the nods.

"I would have you confirm that, in speech. Before all. For it is important. Did I give any order for the arrest and imprisonment of Sir Malcolm Drummond? Or that could be held to mean that? Andrew?"

"No."

"No," Walter declared.

"Very well. I declare now, in the name of the King's justice, that Sir Andrew Stewart and Sir Walter Stewart are hereby found to be not guilty of the murder of Sir Malcolm Drummond, and are free to leave this Court. And further declare that we find that the murder would appear to have been committed by Sir Duncan Stewart of Loch-an-Eilean, now fled furth of this jurisdiction. The reason for the crime being presently unknown, and to be fully enquired into, in the furtherance of justice — by order of this Court. Also that the said Duncan Stewart be found and apprehended, by all means possible. In the name of the King's Grace." He paused, and stood, waving to his companions to remain seated. "That concludes the business of this Court. There is, however, another matter of His Grace's business and concern which it is my duty to declare. In the present circumstances, with my own family and name involved in a grave matter contrary to the King's peace, I deem it right and proper that I should no longer continue in the office of Justiciar and Lieutenant of the North. Accordingly, I herewith declare that I demit and vacate that office of the Crown, so that another may be appointed thereto. This decision I shall communicate to the King's Grace, at the earliest."

There was a considerable stir and clamour in the hall, in which even the two co-judges took part. Clearly this renunciation was not popular.

Alex held up his hand for quiet. "On this I must insist," he said strongly. "The King's justice must be accepted and maintained as fair, honest and unprejudiced — this is above all important. My present state could cause some to doubt that. Therefore I must stand down. But I shall continue to see that the duties are carried out until His Grace's royal will in the matter is known and implemented. This is my decision. God save the King's Grace!" He turned. "My lords . . . ?"

The herald, accepting his cue, signed to the trumpeter, who blew strongly. The justiciars strode off. After a moment or two the prisoners, finding nobody any longer interested in them, strolled away likewise, slightly bemused but keeping up a proud front.

It was some time before Jamie Douglas could see Alex Stewart alone. "You took a step wrong there," he asserted. "Unnecessary, I say. You should not have stood down."

"I had to, Jamie. For my good name's sake, this was something I had to do."

"You are too nice in your judgement, man. As all present would tell you."

"All present, perhaps. But it is not on account of these that I am standing down. It is on account of many folk much further away. For my name's sake in the South, before the Council and parliament. You must see it?"

"I see that the North will suffer grievous loss. And to whose advantage? But . . . you have done it, now. Although I do not see any replacement for you arriving for sufficiently long, or being acceptable to the folk here. We shall see." He shrugged. "For the rest, it was well done. Skilful. Albany's son was a great help."

"Yes. A useful young man. But worth watching, I think, nevertheless."

"Perhaps. But today, excellent. The trial went very well."

"You believe so? To me, it seemed that there were many holes left to be stopped."

"Some, perhaps. But small holes only. Not sufficient to sink your boat. Save, it may be, for one. The matter of who might be behind Duncan."

"Yes. That I perceived. It was . . . difficult."

"You leave it open, to be discovered. So that it could be Albany, yes. But, equally, it could be *yourself*! And more believedly, for many. There was nothing established, back yonder, which proved that you did not give Duncan *secret* orders to slay Drummond. You could have done, more readily than could Albany, or other. And you had a motive, all will recognise, in seeking to gain the Countess. Albany will not fail to perceive it — and exploit it, I fear."

"I know it well. But what else could I have done? Stating so before all would not have aided me — but only brought it to people's minds. Other than by standing down, I can see no way to show my honesty. Can you?"

"No. None. But it is a grave weakness."

"One we must needs accept. Now, Jamie — will you escort my mother to the Bishop's town-house? And Mary, of course. I must see Isobel alone, for a little. If I can get John of Coull prised loose from her!"

"The price to be paid! He is much taken with her?"

"As to that I care not. Many men are. But she — she now appears somewhat taken with *him*! Little more than a stripling! It is . . . unsuitable."

"She but uses him, I think, into provoking you, Alex — into marriage. She will use any weapon to her hand, that one! And she has not a few!"

Alex Stewart frowned at him, unseeing, for a long moment, before stalking off.

IV

JAMIE DOUGLAS GAZED southwards to the Lothian coast with mixed feelings. He had not thought to see that coast again for long — nor was certain that he wanted to, in the circumstances. But it was good to see his home country again, after ten months of the Highlands, especially in early July when Lothian looked so very fair. And, of course, the object of his hazardous journey was in itself unhappy — to attend at his father's death-bed. He had, to be sure, done this twice before, in the last eight years — as Mary had not failed to point out; but from his brother's letter and urging, this time it was really serious. And he was fond of his father who, considering the fact that he was only a bastard, had always treated him exceedingly well — until that last meeting. It would be a shame and a sorrow to part on the poor terms of that day ten months ago.

The skipper of his ship, the *Fair Maid*, of Dysart, carrying hides, tallow and wool from Invererne, the produce of the Priory of Pluscarden, to the metropolitan warehouses of St. Andrews, had agreed to carry his passenger the extra distance as a favour to his ecclesiastical charterers, and to set him down at the little haven of Aberlady, the port of Haddington. Here, in the cowled black robe of a Benedictine friar, if questioned he would be on his way to the Priory of Luffness nearby, where he had reason to believe the Lindsay prior would aid him. It was a dangerous procedure, of course, for an outlawed man; but the country between Aberlady and Dalkeith was largely Douglas-owned. Even so, he might not have risked it — or, more accurately, Mary would have forbidden his coming — had the Church authorities in the North not told Alex Stewart that it would probably be comparatively safe. Always amazingly well-informed as to what went on all over the kingdom, they announced that another major invasion of England was being arranged, astonishingly enough, allegedly to avenge Homildon Hill, and that Albany himself was leading it. This had seemed scarcely believable to Jamie, but the churchmen insisted that reports described musters in progress all over the Lowlands, and the Governor making sundry but definite statements of intent. The Earl of Douglas was said somehow to be involved — although how this could be, when he was still a prisoner in England, was not explained. At any rate, the indications were that it would be as good a time as any for a fugitive to risk a visit to the South, with all in authority otherwise preoccupied. Holy Church was seldom wrong in such matters, and Jamie had decided to take the chance, arguing that he owed it to his father. His wife was less sure, but had reluctantly acceded.

He was duly landed at the jetty at the western mouth of the great Aberlady Bay, friar's robe carefully donned and cowl up. To seek to hire or borrow a horse would be but to draw attention to himself; wandering friars seldom went other than on foot. Not being challenged in any way, on disembarking, he had no need to make for Luffness Priory. He calculated that it was about a dozen miles to Dalkeith — but that would not kill him. In the Highlands he had got into the habit of large walking. Admittedly there was a Douglas property at Kilspindie, close to Aberlady, and he might have got a horse there; but he decided that it was not worth the risk of identifying himself.

By Longniddry and Seton and Tavernent he went, then, glad enough to stretch his legs after the constrictions of his four days in the vessel, through the July afternoon, admiring with new-seeing eyes the full stackyards, golden-turning rigs and sleek cattle, as compared with the thin and scanty crops and lean beasts of the Highlands. Folk working in the fields, rigs and orchards, pigs rooting in the woodlands, poultry everywhere, mills clacking, salt-pans steaming, coal-sleds being dragged — these were sights little seen in the North, and reminded the traveller more keenly than anything yet had done that he was indeed an outlaw and fugitive, that such scenes, formerly part and parcel of his life, were now to be noted and remarked upon.

Along the long and quite lofty ridge of Elphinstone and Fawside, wearying a little now but with the wide valley of the Esk opening before him whilst still the Forth estuary gleamed and glittered on his right, he trudged. Dalkeith lay in the

Esk valley four miles up from its confluence with the firth at Musselburgh.

He came to his old home with the sinking sun, a great sprawling palace this, compared with Lochindorb, Loch-an-Eilean or even Kildrummy, scarcely a fortress at all, although it had grown out of one, in green parklands where the North and South Esk rivers joined. But there was still a gatehouse and drawbridge — although Jamie could scarcely remember the latter ever being fully raised. Not until he felt its timbers sound hollow beneath his feet did he remove the cloying monkish robe.

He was well received, at least. The great house seemed to be full of relatives, kinsfolk and friends, drawn to the old lord's bedside. The first he saw was his one-time master's widow, the Lady Isabel Stewart, sister of the King and former Countess of Douglas, now nearing fifty but still a beautiful woman.

"Jamie!" she cried, and ran to him, arms outstretched. "How good to see you! Good, yes. It has been so long." She embraced him and kissed him eagerly, almost hungrily. "My dear! So you came? From those barbarous Highlands!"

Embarrassed, he shook his head. "Scarce barbarous, Isabel. I, I have received much kindness there. You are well? You look well. But . . . my father? How is he?"

"Better, Jamie. A deal better, I am glad to say. More himself. He supped a bowl of soup this morning. All of it . . ."

"Better! Himself — and supping soup!" the traveller exclaimed. "And I, I have put my head into a noose to come all this way . . .!"

"No, no, Jamie — you will be well enough. We shall look after you, my dear. Robert is not here. He has gone to the Border, with a great host. A strange business, that is not like Robert. But let us thank God that he is gone . . ."

"Jamie! A God's good name — Jamie himself!" That was his brother Will, last seen falling under the hail of arrows on Homildon Hill. "The saints be praised! Give me your hand, man — if the Lady Isabel will release you for a moment!"

Jamie actually flushed. "The Lady Isabel is my good-sister, Will," he asserted. "I . . . ah . . . it is well to see you on your feet, looking little the worse. You are well again? Whole from your wound? And back from captivity."

"We have been back a month and more. Paid for in good siller! Lord — I had not known that I was worth so much money! That Hotspur drives a hard bargain. The wound healed

59

well — quicker than James's. An arrow through the shoulder, passing neatly between lungs and gullet. We Douglases take a deal of killing!"

The James whom Will referred to was his elder brother, legitimate heir of the house. Jamie, older than both, but illegitimate, had been brought up at Dalkeith with the others, the old lord making little distinction between his offspring, lawful or otherwise. But, of course, when it came to inheritance and title, the lawful James must prevail.

Will at least seemed to bear no ill-will for being left by his half-brother on the stricken field of battle.

"And James? I received his letter, to bring me here. But he said naught of his own health . . ."

"He had two wounds. One in the neck which is not yet fully healed. And one in the thigh. But he is well enough. Come, we will find him . . ."

"I had better see my father first. Having come all this way . . ."

"Oh, the old one is well enough, likewise. He will not die this time! We thought that he would, mind you — it was near enough."

Between his brother and the Lady Isabel he was escorted to his father's chamber.

Father and son were almost equally reserved at their greeting. The last time they had been together it had been a difficult interview, with the old man blaming Jamie for having deserted his half-brothers on the battlefield, and forcing him to resign his baronies of Aberdour, Stoneypath and Baldwinsgill to his full brother Johnnie to save them from being forfeited on account of his outlawry — making in fact a pauper of him. Now they eyed each other warily in that over-heated bedroom.

"So, I am not dead yet, you see!" the Lord of Dalkeith croaked, almost defiantly. "Your journey wasted!"

"I rejoice to see you so much the better than I had feared, my lord."

"Aye, perhaps. But James should not have sent for you. Even if, if . . ."

"To be sure he should. It was right and proper."

"You come at the risk of your neck, boy."

"I have risked my neck many a time for less good cause, sir. How do you feel? In pain?"

"Not now. Two days back I took a turn for the better, God

60

be praised." He made a to-do of coughing, all but dislodging his nightcap. "Son — do you not bear me a grudge?"

"No, my lord — no grudges."

"Can we not be done with this my lording? See you, boy — I perhaps spoke you more sorely than I should have done, that day. I, h'mm, I regret it. I have thought much on it these weeks, lying on this bed. And I believe that I may have been over-hard on you."

"It is forgotten."

"Not by me, lad — and not, I think, by you either! It is not the matter of resigning your lands to Johnnie. That had to be. Only so could they be saved from forfeiture. It is the blame I laid on you for leaving your brothers on yon field. Now that they are ransomed and returned to me, I can see it differently. They have told me how it was . . ."

"As did I, if I remember rightly!"

"Yes, yes. But they confirmed your tale of the Earl Archibald's folly — more than confirmed it. Folly indeed. And they tell me more. Of what you did before — the ambush in the valley, the scouting deep into Durham, the warnings. The seeking to halt the reivings and break-up of the army. *You* told me none of this."

"I scarce had opportunity, I think, or desire to."

"No. Perhaps not. I was . . . less than kind. But, we will say no more of it. You won your way here without trouble? None sought to take you?"

"I came by sea, from Invererne to Aberlady, then walked, in a friar's robe. How much danger am I in, think you?"

"Who knows? You are still outlawed. I have tried to have it lifted, but without success. If Earl Archibald had been ransomed, *he* might have prevailed on Robert Stewart — since he ever needs Douglas aid. But *I* can not."

"The Earl — why is he not ransomed, then? You were gathering the money?"

"You have not heard, in your Hielands? A strange business. I . . . I . . ." The old man was getting distinctly breathless. "James . . . will tell you, lad. I . . . I canna speak for over-long. A strange business — but ask James. He has more wits . . . than has Will. Come again . . ."

Jamie's priority, however, was to the kitchen, for food and drink, not having eaten adequately for a considerable time.

It was there, at the long table, that his limping brother James

61

found him presently, with their uncle Sir Will Douglas of Mordington.

"Jamie, boy — for an outlaw and next to being a damned Hielantman you look surpassing well!" the older man cried. "You look like a gipsy — but then, you never did know how to wear clothes!"

"And you, Uncle, grow fat!" he was told succinctly.

"Jamie — I fear I have brought you a long way, and at some hazard, for little purpose," the heir of Dalkeith greeted. "Our father has made one of his recoveries! Which, of course, is excellent," he hastened to add. "But we much feared for his life."

"You did what was right. Although Mary was not for allowing me to come!"

"Aye, women ever fear the worst. But — I am sorry, Jamie, about all this. The outlawry. The miscalling. The ill repute. You have received much ill-usage. Even from our father, he tells us. It was shameful. You, of all men!"

"Quite right," Sir Will agreed. "I did not believe a word of it."

"Many did, and still do. Albany would find it all a useful stick to beat me with."

"Aye. He did not take long in proclaiming you outlaw." Sir James shook his head. "God, Jamie — I wish that we had heeded you, that day on Homildon Hill, Will and I. Had not followed the Earl Archibald down the steep, like, like . . . what were they? Pigs, of some sort . . .?"

"Gadarene swine, you mean?"

"Aye — the Gadarene swine. It was just as stupid — and hopeless. And if we had stayed back with you and Johnnie, much of all this might never have happened. You might never have been outlawed, and our father saved a deal of siller!"

"I still might — since the Earl Murdoch of Fife, Albany's son, would still have fallen and been captured. And it was *that* his father could not stomach — not that I left the Earl Douglas and yourselves on the field." He shrugged. "What happened to Murdoch Stewart?"

"He was wounded, and captured too, with Angus and Moray and the rest. Angus the most sore wounded . . ."

"Was he, Fife, with you at Hotspur's Alnwick Castle?"

"No. The traitor, my uncle Dunbar, got his hands on these others. Moray of course was his own brother's son. Where they are now, God knows."

62

"These are not ransomed yet, then? Any more than Douglas himself? Yet our father collected the siller. What went wrong? He said to ask you."

"It is a strange business. And has had stranger results."

"By the powers, it has!" their Uncle Will agreed. "There is something fell odd going on."

"Over the ransom moneys?"

"Not that," James Douglas said. "Or not that I have heard. There are two parts in this, Jamie. The first we knew of, before ever we were released from Alnwick. Henry, the English king, sent word to Hotspur — and no doubt to Dunbar and the others too — that all important captives from Homildon were to be treated as the Crown's prisoners-of-war and not ransomed. Hotspur was fell angry. He does not love Henry Plantagenet anyway, and this he took as a great insult. Henry said to send all important prisoners to him. Hotspur refused to do this. Us he let go — having our ransom. But he did hold up the Earl Archibald's release. I take it he did not consider us important!"

"Yet your wife is the King's daughter."

"He knows how little important is the King in Scotland, today!"

"What is Henry's purpose in this?"

"Lord knows! Always it has been the captor's right to ransom prisoners, the victorious commander to have his choice."

"But that is not the best of it, man," Sir Will interrupted. "Tell Jamie about this of Albany — and Cocklaws."

"Aye. Hotspur, see you, is up to some strange ploy, with Albany. He has invaded the Middle March, with a large force, and sat down around the Tower of Cocklaws — and taken the Earl of Douglas with him . . ."

"Cocklaws? Should I know Cocklaws?"

"Well may you ask! It is nothing but a small Border peel-tower, near your friend Archie of Cavers' house, held by Sir James Gledstanes of that Ilk, vassal to Cavers. In a strong position on a ridge in Teviotdale, yes — but no great fort or stronghold. But there they are . . ."

"You are saying that Hotspur, with Douglas, and a great force, are besieging this little Teviotdale tower? Only that? Why, of a mercy?"

"Answer that, boy, and you are more clever than we are!" his uncle said. "But there is more than that. Albany has assembled a great army, and gone to relieve this rickle o' stanes!"

Jamie stared.

"He has fifty thousand men and more," his brother went on, "said to be going to invade England. In answer to Homildon. And to force the release of his son Murdoch, whom Henry is holding fast. But first, to save Cocklaws! Have you ever heard the like?"

"No. It sounds to me nonsense. Albany does not embark on adventures like this. He does not lead armies — not alone. Who has he got with him?"

"None of any note. The Marischal, his good-brother, Sandi-lands, Ramorgnie. No true soldiers."

"There is more to this than meets the eye, then. There always is, with Albany. But — Hotspur? This, of Cocklaws, is as unlike him as the other is of Albany. And you say the Percy has our own Earl with him?"

"Yes. That is the word. God knows why!"

"Could it be something to do with the ransom? Hotspur seeking to get past his King's command? There will be much siller involved, for the Earl of Douglas. And the Percy with his own ransom money to make up, when he was prisoner here after Otterburn."

"Who knows? Father has collected near on twenty thousand gold nobles. He thinks that Hotspur and Albany are in league, some way, in this."

"But against whom? It could be Henry. I can conceive that Hotspur might engage to hand over the Earl Douglas to Albany, at this place, Cocklaws, at a play-acting engagement, in which Douglas seemed to be recaptured — so long as he got the moneys. Twenty thousand gold nobles is a vast sum. But you say, do you not, that the money is still here? Albany has not got it?"

"No. Father still holds it. And has had no further word."

"Strange indeed. Unlike both Albany and Hotspur. But . . . there must be an answer. Suppose, suppose Albany was doing this on his own behalf? Making his own bargain with the Percy. Using his own money — or the realm's — to buy our Earl's release? What better way to bind Douglas to him? He much needs the power of Douglas. Might he not think to buy it, thus?"

"It could be, yes. But . . ."

"Would he need fifty thousand men for that?"

"No-o-o. That is true. Much more than is needed for such

64

demonstration. But it could be that — and something else as well. This of invading England? That sounds but little likely. You have no further word on that?"

"Only that it is supposedly in return for Homildon."

"Not Albany's way. And what happens now? What is Albany at, at this moment?"

"We have heard nothing for three days. There are but few Douglases with his array. The last we heard was that his force was in Tweeddale, near Melrose. Making but slowly south for Cocklaws."

"I cannot believe in this. There is something false, somewhere . . ."

The lady of that great house put in an appearance. Jamie's relationship with the Lady Egidia Stewart had always been a little uncertain, in name as in nature. His father's second wife, and he but a bastard, she was scarcely his stepmother, any more than her predecessor had been. She was Mary's aunt, after a fashion, a sister of the late monarch, Robert the Second; but this did little to regularise their mutual positions. She *was* stepmother to his half-brothers, and great-aunt to James's wife; and with children and grandchildren by her two previous marriages, was at the centre of a tangle of relationships indeed.

"So — the wanderer returns!" she greeted him crisply. "And looking none so ill, considering the company he keeps, and a diet of oatcakes and braxy sheep — or so they tell me! Thank God I have never had occasion to set foot in those ungodly Hielands! It is good to see you, boy." That last was high praise from Lady Egidia.

"I find the Highlands a deal kinder than the Lowlands, my lady," he told her. "And the King's governance better carried out than here!"

"Ah. By which you mean that outlawry is not enforced there — since all are more or less outwith the law, anyway?"

"If by the law you mean the Duke of Albany's decrees and wishes, then perhaps you are right!"

"Aye — you still harp on that string, boy! I would have thought that you might have learned more wisdom, by now."

"By wisdom, do you mean that I should agree with evil when it seems to be winning?"

"The same obstinate, self-righteous Jamie Douglas, I see! Your father has been much concerned for you."

"When last I saw him he was more concerned for . . . others!"

"Perhaps. He has had time to reconsider, however, and to decide that you were not wholly at fault."

"But I am still a landless outlaw."

"And must continue to be so, until the sentence is withdrawn. Which means, until you make your peace with my nephew Robert of Albany."

"That I will never do."

"Then you must accustom yourself to being landless and an outlaw, Jamie. For *you* will never beat Robert. And he will never relent."

"The King could remove the outlawry, for all is done in his name. There *is* still a king in this realm!"

"*Could*, but will not. John was always timorous, and afraid of Robert. Now he quakes at mention of his brother's name. Not for himself, for he wishes that he was dead. But he still has one son, you see — the child James. So long as James is there, his father will do as Robert says."

"But — this is monstrous!"

"No doubt. But it is reality, boy — Scotland, in this year of our Lord! There is none to challenge Robert now."

There was silence in the great vaulted kitchen for a little.

Jamie changed the subject. "Johnnie — he is not here? How is he?" he asked his brother.

"He has all but recovered from his wound, likewise. He was here until two days back. Then he returned to Aberdour."

"Aberdour . . . !"

James coughed. "Yes. He has been dwelling there, in your absence. Our father thought it best. In Fife, in Albany's territory, with so many of his people nearby — Lindsay, Ramorgnie and such. Safer to have the new laird there in possession . . ." His voice tailed away.

"I see." A pause. "At least I am glad that he is recovered."

"Yes. He is . . . much grateful to you."

The Lady Egidia smiled.

*　　*　　*

Jamie stayed at Dalkeith for a few days, in case his father had a relapse, never venturing beyond the immediate vicinity of the castle. But, not a particularly patient man ever, he quickly wearied of inactivity and being cooped up. There was still no reliable news from Teviotdale and the Border as to Albany's army, though there were rumours innumerable. The Lady Isabel

66

Stewart wanted him to accompany her on a round of her properties, as he had done in the past, in the interests of better management and vassalage, her present husband being slothful; but the others all agreed that this would be unwise, hazardous, since most of the former Countess of Douglas's lands and jointure properties were in the Borders, and that was the last place for Jamie to venture to in present conditions — though Isabel asserted that he would be entirely safe with her, the King's sister. In this instance, the outlaw was well enough content to accept the advice of the more cautious — since he had tentative plans of his own, and in quite another direction. He would not stay immured in his father's house like some captive, but would make a discreet and modest journey northwards rather than southwards, and in only his own company, dressed in his friar's robe again. He would go to Aberdour.

There was considerable attempted dissuasion for this course, too. But he was determined. He would return to Dalkeith before he went back to Badenoch. But meantime he had affairs to see to.

So, through the good offices of the Sub-Prior of Newbattle Abbey, illegitimate kin of his father — the abbey was only a mile or so away, and largely indebted to the Dalkeith Douglases for support — one fine July morning, dressed in the Benedictine habit, Jamie joined a monkish party *en route* for the ecclesiastical metropolis of St. Andrews in Fife. There was a constant coming and going between the abbeys and religious houses and the metropolitan see, on account of the vast trading operations of Holy Church, for which St. Andrews was the clearing-house. Newbattle specialised in two very valuable products, coal and salt. Fortunately it was a vessel loaded with sacks and baskets of the latter commodity which carried the travellers across the Forth, from the monks' saltpans at Salt Preston, eight miles up the estuary from Aberlady; the coal-boats made for less pleasing travel. The salt was destined for the burgh of Dysart, almost directly opposite across a dozen miles of the firth, where there was a major industry, again largely Church-run, of salting and casking herring supplied by the many little Fife fishing harbours, for export to the Low Countries and France, one of the country's most important trading assets.

The clerical voyagers were set down at Dysart then, after a breezy passage, where jennets were supplied by the Benedictine Priory of St. Dennis for their onwards journey to St. Andrews. Jamie, refusing the offer of a mount as tending to be conspicuous, resumed his role of wandering friar and set off on foot westwards the ten miles to Aberdour, by Kirkcaldy and Kinghorn.

It made a strange home-coming, that late afternoon — for this little castle above the silver sands of Aberdour Bay *was* his home, in a way none other could ever be, where he had brought his bride thirteen years before to set up house, where their children had been born and reared, where the happiest years of his life had been spent, where they had planted and improved, fashioned and built, farmed and husbanded. And now, abruptly, it was his brother's house, and he came to it in stealth.

Aberdour Castle was a typical oblong stone keep, massive and thick-walled, of four storeys and a garret, with parapet-walk and cap-house, set within a small curtain-walled courtyard containing lean-to outbuildings, with a chapel nearby older than the castle, the whole surrounded by gardens, orchard, farmery and fields, a quite ancient barony which had belonged to the Anglo-Norman families of Vipont and Mortimer before the Douglases acquired it fifty years earlier. It was a fortified house rather than any major stronghold, standing upon a defensive site above the ravine of the Dour Burn, back from the shore. There was no moat and drawbridge, although a tiny gatehouse did guard the arched entry to the courtyard. The massive gates were shut and barred at night, but seldom were even guarded by day. Jamie walked in unchallenged, save by a barking deerhound which he did not recognise. He rasped the tirling-pin on the open keep door. He was surprised that it was a fresh-faced young woman who came in answer, she, like the dog, unknown to him.

"Yes, father — and how may I serve you?" she asked, pleasantly enough.

Jamie had forgotten his monkish habit, rather. "Ah . . . yes . . . I seek John Douglas," he said. "Is he here?"

"To be sure. He is down at the bee-skeps, seeing to the clover-honey. We must see to such things whilst the good weather lasts, father. But — come you in, and I will send for Johnnie."

"My thanks — but I will go see him, myself."

"But . . . you do not know where to go?"

"Yes. I, I have been here before." He realised that she was looking at him curiously. Perhaps he did not sound very like a cleric. It came to him also that she had called his brother Johnnie, not the master or the laird; and had said that she would send for him, not go for him.

In a corner of the old orchard, behind the chapel, he found Johnnie and two other men at the sticky business of extracting the clover combs from the skeps and spinning them in drums to run the honey out. He had thrown back his cowl now, so that his brother recognised him at once — the two helpers likewise, men of his own.

"Jamie!" Johnnie cried. "God be good — it is yourself! Here's a wonder. How good!" He came to embrace him, sticky hands and all.

John Douglas was his full brother. They were sons of a Dalkeith steward's daughter whom their father had fallen in love with in his youth, but whom the heir to such wealth and power could by no means wed — especially as he had been betrothed from an early age to the daughter of the then Earl of Dunbar and March. The young woman had died after the difficult birth of Johnnie, and the bereaved father had insisted on rearing the boys in his own house, making little difference between them and his later and legitimate offspring by the Lady Agnes of Dunbar. So Jamie was the old lord's first-born and indeed, until recently, favourite child, however unlawfully begotten — although he could never be heir. Johnnie, however, was very different in appearance, as in nature, a tall, sandy-haired happy-go-lucky extrovert, more like his half-brother Will, lacking any great depth of character but excellent company. It was now ten months since Jamie had brought him back, wounded, from the fatal field of Homildon.

"You are well? Fully recovered?" Jamie asked, always stiffer than he intended to be on these occasions. He also sought to make recognitions towards the two other men.

"Yes, yes. Arrow-wounds heal quickly — if they do not kill you! And you, Jamie? How do you manage? In those Hielands, in mist and snow and floods, among Erse-speaking savages? We often speak of you. Feel for you."

"I am much beholden!" his brother jerked, more stiffly than ever. "But — it is not like that. The country nor the people."

"How does Mary abide it?"

"She abides it very well. Alex Stewart is a kind host and good companion. We live passing well."

"So long as he is your *friend*! Can you trust him? After what he did to Drummond."

"So you have swallowed that tale also! It is false. Put about by Albany — if indeed the killing itself was not Albany's planning."

69

"Oh, come you, Jamie — you were ever crazed about the Governor! He is a hard man — but scarce so ill as you would have him."

"It is good to have your word for that!" the other snapped.

"M'mm. I, I can but judge by what I know, not what I, or you, may fear, man. He has never done me any hurt."

"No. Indeed, he has served you passing well! You would not be sitting here, so snugly, in Aberdour, were it not for Robert Stewart and his sentence of outlawry upon me!"

Johnnie shot a sidelong glance at him. "No. But . . . that is . . ." His voice tailed away.

His brother drew a deep breath. "I ask your pardon," he got out. "That was ill said."

"It is all yours still, you know, Jamie," Johnnie said uncomfortably. "I but hold it for you."

"Not so. In law the barony, all three baronies, are yours. I signed all my rights away. Our father said it was the only way. And better to you than to James or Will, who have plenty."

"Even so, when you are free of the outlawry, you can claim it all back." Thankfully he changed the subject. "Tell me, Jamie — how got you here? How did you win through? I never thought to see you. Did none seek to hold you?"

"I came by ship . . ."

As they walked back to the castle, Jamie paused. "Johnnie — that young woman who answered the door when I chapped — who is she?"

The other shrugged, a shade uneasily. "Ah, that was Jeannie. Jeannie Boswell, of Balmuto."

"So?"

"She . . . ah . . . we, we like each other well. Balmuto is a barony, some few miles inland. As you will know."

"I know Balmuto, yes. And the Boswells thereof. But Jeannie I know not."

"She is the youngest daughter. Old Boswell died. His son's wife now rules at Balmuto. She and Jeannie do not agree. A hard, managing woman."

"So Jeannie has come to live with you?"

"Yes. I needed a woman about the house . . ."

"But you are not wed?"

"No. I . . . ah . . . no. I fear that our father would not approve. He desires me to marry some heiress, with lands and siller. You know how he is about such things. Jeannie has nothing."

70

"So you live with her but do not wed her."

His brother frowned. "See you, Jamie — it is plaguily difficult. I have just had all this property put in my name. I do not wish to offend my father. He is old, and like to die, soon. No time to wed against his wishes . . ."

"Lest he disinherits you? Overlooks you in his will?"

"There is that, yes. But it would be an ill time to hurt the old man."

"Oh, yes. And Mistress Jeannie? Is she not . . . concerned?"

"She is prepared to wait, until, until . . ."

"Until my lord dies! She is very understanding, compliant!"

"We understand each other. Sufficiently to wait."

"Ah, yes. But I vow that you have not waited for everything!"

The other grinned. "You know how we are made!" he said.

Jean Boswell was somewhat abashed when she learned of the visitor's true identity, not unnaturally, and Johnnie became almost boisterous in seeking to put her at ease. Jamie, for his part, knew a certain sympathy with her, despite the pangs it gave him to see her acting mistress of his Mary's house and home — which she did seemingly with fair competence. Presently he found that he was liking the girl. She was bonny, straightforward, and clearly doted on Johnnie. He reckoned that his brother could have done a lot worse for himself, whatever might be their father's verdict.

He explained that he had come to Aberdour mainly to recover certain personal belongings, especially of Mary's, which they had left behind them in their hurried departure, certain clothing, some jewellery and one or two items of furniture, household goods to which she was particularly attached. Also some treasures of the children. The small items he could take with him, when he went; but the heavier things would have to be packed for despatch by ship from Dysart to the Moray coast.

Johnnie and Jeannie declared themselves only too glad to see to this, if he picked the items out for them.

He had to admit then that this was not the only reason for his quite risky visit. The fact was that he had certain enquiries to make, in Fife. Sir William Lindsay of Rossie's house was situated not very far away, in the Eden valley near Auchtermuchty; and while Lindsay himself would probably be away with this odd expedition of the Governor's, being a creature of Albany's, there might well be information to be gleaned at Rossie anent a possible Highland visitor to that establishment.

Jamie explained briefly about Sir Duncan Stewart of Loch-an-Eilean.

The couple heard him out, intrigued and excited, Johnnie declaring that he would be happy to go and make discreet enquiries for him. But Jamie asserted that this was something that he must do for himself. Only he knew the right questions to ask, and what to look for. Besides, there were dangers in this, and he was not going to have them involved. He was quite definite about that. But Johnnie could assist, in a minor way.

So next morning, in the guise of a groom, he rode behind his brother northwards across Fife, against the grain of the land, climbing gently, past the barony of Balmuto, Jeannie's home, through the Carden Forest, to cross the River Ore at Cluny and on to Leslie, mounting towards the spine of the great peninsula. Dipping down beyond into the broad vale of the Eden, at Dunshalt, some score of miles from Aberdour, he dismounted, leaving his brother to turn back the four miles to Falkland, where was Albany's main Fife seat, there to ask only certain carefully rehearsed and discreet questions; whilst he himself donned his friar's robe and cowl and started his walk towards the estate and small castle of Rossie some two miles to the north-east, on the edge of its wide and shallow loch, which he had to circle.

There was no village of the name, but a millton and small castleton, half-a-mile apart. At the first, where a stream entered the loch, Jamie ascertained from the miller that the laird indeed was from home, gone south with the Governor; but that his lady was there. He explained that it was not Sir William Lindsay himself that he sought, but for a friend who he believed might be in Sir William's company. Had the laird taken a party with him on this Border expedition?

He had indeed, the miller said — had not their own son gone, and a score of others. But his reverence's friend would be of the gentry, no doubt? In which case he could not help him, knowing nothing of what went on at that level. He should go speak with Sir William's steward.

Carefully avoiding the said steward, Jamie made for the castleton cot-houses, where he changed his tune somewhat, adopting a travesty of a sing-song Highland lilt, and declared that he was seeking a kinsman who had, he thought, come here some two months before, from the Highlands. Had anyone seen a Highlandman, a gentleman mind, visiting Rossie?

The place had the usual low-browed alehouse, and the slut who ran it hooted at this quest for a Hielant gentleman. There was no such thing, she asserted loudly, and the reverend father-in-God ought to ken it. The only Hielantmen who had crossed her door these many months were two black-avised, half-naked caterans with not a word of Christian speech between them, drunken hairy rascals that she had put to sleep in her henhouse.

Jamie sadly averred that these could be no kin of his, to be sure. He was after looking for a tall, fair-haired, fine-looking figure of a young man, who could speak with as good a Scots tongue as himself. He was turning away, at the woman's skirled laughter, when a thought occurred to him.

"What were they doing at Rossie, these two *borachs*?" he asked, mildly.

"Och, waiting just," he was told. "Idle. Naething to do but idle themsel's. And get between a decent woman's feet."

"To be sure. But why, here?"

"Waiting for their maister, what else? Up at the castle. Some freend o' the laird's, who had to be taken to Falkland to see the Duke."

"Ah. And this master? Was *he* tall and fair?"

"Och, I but saw him once — a guid-way off. Yon kind dinna frequent *my* hoose, reverence. A right tall swack lad, he lookit. But nae Hielandman, mind. Na, na — nae bare-shankit heathen yon, but a decent Christian gentleman by the looks o' him."

"You did not hear the name of this Christian gentleman with the Highland servants?"

"Fegs, no — the laird took him to Falkland, that's a' I ken."

"And after? Did he come back from Falkland? And then go south with Sir William, in the Duke's array?"

"As to that, I dinna ken. But he and his billies went when the laird did — Goad be thankit! I canna tell your reverence mair."

Thereafter Jamie risked a brief call at the kitchen premises of Rossie Castle itself, enquiring for a mythical visitor named MacAlastair, of some weeks back. And when knowledge of such was denied by the domestics, went on to ask if any Highlander had been there recently, whatever the name — again to draw a blank. It seemed that these good folk classed all Highlanders as bare-kneed wearers of tartan who spoke only a barbarous tongue and were definitely non-gentle. Mention of the tall swack gentleman that the laird had taken to Falkland produced no name; evidently Lindsay had not named him to any — perhaps in itself significant? The only point gained from his somewhat dangerous interrogation was that the gentleman had had a strangely soft sort of voice. Further Jamie dared not go. To ask to see Lady Lindsay would have been too hazardous. Apart from the fact that she might possibly have recognised him, from some Court appearance, he would have to uncowl his head before her and reveal that he had no tonsure.

He had to be content, then, with what he had learned — or, not learned but garnered and deduced. The probability was that it *was* Sir Duncan Stewart who had come to Rossie with his two gillies, had been taken for interview with the Duke of Albany, and thereafter had gone with Lindsay and the rest on this peculiar Border expedition, presumably more or less anonymously. There was no proof, but it all made sense and had a likelihood about it.

Reasonably satisfied, he retraced his steps to Dunshalt, where he found Johnnie waiting. As he had feared, his brother had failed to glean anything of value at Falkland. The place was too large, with far too much coming and going at the ducal castle for any but the most kenspeckle callers to be noted by the citizenry — and clearly Duncan Stewart would avoid being that.

They turned homewards, and rode as far as the burgh of Leslie before night overtook them, where they put up in an inconspicuous change-house, Jamie very much the groom again.

Two days thereafter, he set off on his return to Dalkeith, promising to say nothing to his father or brothers about Jeannie Boswell of Balmuto.

* * *

The journey back was less expeditious than had been the outwards one. First he was delayed at Dysart, waiting for a suitable vessel. And when eventually he found a skipper who would take him across Forth, they were held up grievously by contrary winds, reaching almost gale force, causing the craft twice to put back to harbour. It was all highly annoying when, between the driving rain-squalls, he could actually *see* the Fawside and Edmonstone ridges cradling Dalkeith, from Dysart.

When at last he reached his father's house, it was to find all in a state of some excitement. There was news from the Border, and from further afield still — astonishing news. Hotspur Percy was dead. And the Earl of Douglas was wounded once again, and more prisoner than ever — Henry Plantagenet's prisoner this time.

In the old lord's bedchamber Sir Archibald Douglas of Cavers, who had brought the news, Sir Will of Mordington, and the brothers James and Will, were in voluble discussion when Jamie was ushered in. All talking at once, it was some time before he gained any fuller information than these salient points.

"By the Mass — quiet, will you!" he burst out, at length, scarcely respectfully. "You, Archie — since you seem to be the fount of this — you tell it, of a mercy!" Bastard though he might be, not to mention landless outlaw, the others involuntarily acknowledged him to be the strongest man there by doing as he said.

"It was a ploy, Jamie — a trick. The whole Cocklaws business," Sir Archibald of Cavers, illegitimate son of the murdered hero, Earl James of Douglas, declared. Three years younger than Jamie, he had been knighted at the same time, after the fateful field of Otterburn. "When Albany arrived at Cocklaws — and he had taken his time, by God — it was to find Hotspur and the Earl Archie gone. Gone by many days . . ."

"Gone, where?"

"Gone back to England. And not just to Northumberland, but south, far south. To Shrewsbury, no less."

"Shrewsbury? But, that is on the Welsh Marches!"

"Aye, so I am told. So Albany and his fifty thousand sat down around Cocklaws — a small Border peel-tower! The most crazy-mad thing any Scots army has ever done, I swear! It is only a mile or two from Cavers, mark you. And there they waited, idle. Idle save for stealing my cattle, for their pots! When I went to see what was to do, there was some fool story that Hotspur had made a knightly compact with Albany that if he had not come to claim it again by the first day of August, Cocklaws would revert to the Scots. And with it his claim to the whole earldom of Douglas! He was claiming, mind, that King Henry had given him the earldom, as reward for winning Homildon — an English king gifting the Douglas earldom! The bairns-play insolence of it!"

"Scarce bairns-play. That was Henry's way of mocking the Percy, whom he hates — and deriding Scotland. That is *all* he gave Hotspur for the victory — the earldom of Douglas, if he could take it! To support this English claim that their kings are Lords Paramount of Scotland. The old story. But — why Cocklaws? A small place, of no importance, not even one of the Earl Archibald's own houses. Gledstanes thereof is a vassal of *yours*, is he not? Even if he had assailed your Cavers, there would be more point to it . . ."

"That is just it! He, Percy, did not *want* a fight. As he would have got at Cavers, foul fall him! It was just a ploy, a play-acting, an excuse."

"To what end, man?"

"All was but excuse to assemble an army. And to have Albany assemble one also. Against *Henry*."

"Guidsakes!"

"Hotspur had turned rebel! He is kin to Roger Mortimer, who has better right to the throne than Henry the usurper. He and the Percy have ever been unfriends."

"But would Albany play this game? Aid Percy's revolt? He was to invade England — behind Hotspur, from Cocklaws?"

"That is what is claimed. The reason for the entire strange business. Cocklaws was but an excuse for both sides to muster large armies without causing Henry to take fright."

"I see, yes — I see. Yes — and I vow that there is more of Albany's twisted mind behind this than the Percy's! Only — Albany would stand to gain the more, that is equally certain! What — beyond a share in the possible defeat of Henry? And gaining his son back, and the Earl Douglas? There will be more than that?"

"Who knows? To show him as a successful commander, perhaps? And he could do with that, by God! But, if so, it was not to be."

"You mean, this of Hotspur's death? What went wrong?"

"There was a great battle at this Shrewsbury, they say. Hotspur was slain. Our Earl fought gallantly, leaving Hotspur's van. Indeed he all but captured Henry, but fell, wounded once more. His usual luck! Dunbar fought on the King's side. But Henry won. The Earl is *his* prisoner now, and the revolt over."

"And Albany?"

"Cannily, Albany had not moved from Cocklaws. Possibly he never intended to. When this word reached him he sent a small force to make a demonstration over the Border, whilst he packed up his pavilions. He is now on his way home, with his fifty thousand — having cleansed Scotland of the English! And not a drop of blood shed!"

"Aye — that sounds like Robert Stewart!"

"And by the same token, Jamie, it means that *you* were better on your way!" his father intervened, fairly strongly for a man who had been at death's door so recently. "Once Robert is back in these parts, it will not take him long to learn that you are in the Lowlands. For he has spies everywhere — even in Dalkeith, I have no doubt. It is an ill matter to send you from my house again — but it is for your own good."

Jamie nodded grimly. "And . . . sundry others! But, yes — I will go. Forthwith. Besides, since you look like to live a while yet, there is naught to hold me."

"Yes. God willing. You saw Johnnie?"

"To be sure. All is well with Johnnie — passing well. Quite the laird!"

"Good. I have had the Sub-Prior over, from Newbattle. He is seeing to ship-passage for you to St. Andrews, then on northwards. He will see to all."

"You waste no time, my lord!"

"It is for the best, boy. Robert Stewart must not get his hands on you. It will not take him long to reach Lothian. Is there aught that you require? Gear? Siller? James will see to it . . ."

Jamie nodded.

V

JAMIE DOUGLAS HAD become very much a travelling man — as of course befitted a landless adventurer. Hardly had he won back to Lochindorb, via the port of Nairn, in mid-August, than he was off again, south by east, for Kildrummy, in haste. The Lady Mariota had a touching faith in his ability to influence Alex Stewart for good, wisdom, moderation — something he found hard to understand. And on this occasion, Mary abetted her, despite her husband's late absence in the South. And those two women represented a daunting coalition.

It seemed that some ten days before, a messenger had arrived from the Countess of Mar, with a letter — a letter which, whatever else, had the effect of setting Alex by the ears. He had not divulged its contents to them, but had hastily summoned together some two hundred armed men and marched off with them, without delay, in the direction of Mar, merely saying that he had urgent business to attend to. Mariota, of course, was convinced that it was some new deep and nefarious plot of the Countess Isobel's, to the detriment of her son's repute and well-being. He was a fool about this woman, if in little else. That she was bad for him, the veriest child could see. Mary evidently agreed with this last, at least. Jamie was considered to have more weight with Alex than had anyone else. He must go after him, therefore, to Kildrummy or wherever he had gone, to seek dissuade him from major follies. Let him remind the former Justiciar that, since he had obstinately insisted on resigning that office, he no longer had the right to range the country with large bodies of armed men. It was a blatant breaking of the King's peace, and could give the Governor just the excuse he required to declare Alex forfeit and outlaw.

So here he was riding the now quite familiar route, by mid-

Strathspey, Glen Livet and the Mounth passes, with Tom Durie, the Aberdour steward's son, and two running gillies as escort, a man on an urgent errand to do he knew not what.

He had no certainty even that it was Kildrummy that Alex had made for; but it seemed sensible to call there in the first instance. On the second day of his journey, therefore, after passing the night at Invernahaven in the Braes of Glen Livet, he crossed the watershed of the Ladder Hills and slanted down Glen Buchat to the wide valley of the middle Don. And even from a distance, it was fairly evident that he did not require to go further than Kildrummy. For, camped around the castle on its mound was a sizeable force, the blue smokes of its cooking-fires ascending on the golden evening air. The music of bagpipes, thin and high, made it clear that it was a Highland host, too.

In the castle itself he found himself welcomed with a heart-warming enthusiasm by Alex, if with less obvious delight by the Countess, as he joined them at their meal at the dais-table in the great hall. Alex seemed to look on his arrival as perfectly normal and to be expected, and was anxious to hear all his news from the South. It took some considerable time and conversational tacking before Jamie could work round to the reason for Alex's presence, with an armed force, at Kildrummy.

"Sir Jamie is agog, Alex," the Countess said, at length. "He has been sent here by your mother expressly to save you from my clutches — if he can! He is at a loss to know what he is at or where to begin! Have pity on him, and tell him what's to do."

"Is that true, Jamie?" the other asked, shaking his fair head. "Did my mother send you?"

Jamie Douglas was no expert prevaricator. "She would have me to come, yes. But myself I wanted to see you, Alex, at the earliest. I have much to tell you, concerning Albany . . ."

"We can tell you something about Albany, our own selves!" the other interjected. "For that is why I am here."

"You say so? Is his arm stretching up here, then, from the Borders?"

"He has a long arm, yes — if a crooked one!" His friend toyed with his goblet. "He uses men, and women, like inanimate things, tools, weapons, dirks — aye, dirks!"

"Go on, my love. To the point," the lady urged. "Or must I?"

"Aye. You will recollect our, our indebtedness to John Stewart of Coull, Jamie — or mine, at least — at the trial? And you may possibly know that he greatly favours the Lady Isobel here?

Well, my uncle Albany is damnably well-informed, it seems — even when on his expeditions. Learning of this, he has sought to turn all to his own advantage. He has sent the Countess word, as Governor of the realm that, in the realm's interests, powerful earldoms cannot be allowed to languish in weak women's hands! As bound to be coveted and fought over by the unscrupulous and power-seekers. He therefore sends his regrets at her husband's unhappy death, and proposes, for the Countess's comfort and protection, no less than the realm's weal, that she should be wed forthwith to a suitable and reliable candidate — to wit, his own son John Stewart of Coull! Who would thereupon become Earl of Mar, and ensure the Countess's safety from adventurers, the well-being of the earldom and the best advantage of the kingdom. The said John would also be appointed Justiciar of the North."

"So-o-o! That sounds like Albany, yes. Clever, I swear — yes, clever! John Stewart, I take it, will be far from loth!"

"To be sure," the Countess agreed, smiling. "Even at my age!"

"That is the devil of it!" Alex said. "John does not greatly love his father, and might well disobey him on occasion. But not in this instance! He had already proposed marriage to Isobel."

"A pleasant youth, my dear."

"Aged twenty-two years. Half your age!"

"But offering marriage — where you do not, my so-elderly Alex!"

"Isobel — be serious, of a mercy!"

"I am, my love — since it is *my* life that is being disposed of, is it not? It seems that married again I must be. The Governor insists!"

"He has no power to force you, has he?" Jamie asked.

"Not directly, no. But indirectly he can do much to . . . persuade! He could have the Privy Council declare the earldom of Mar to be improperly managed, and a danger to the realm. Because the earls of Scotland are, in a sense, lesser kings, as regards the *Ard Righ*, the High King, the Crown has certain concern in their disposal . . ."

"He would do that if *I* was to wed you, and become Earl of Mar!" Alex interposed.

"Perhaps. But then, you could muster my forces, and your own, and oppose any interference from the Council or the Crown, which a mere woman can scarcely do. Also, using the King's powers, he could take away sundry of my lands and revenues. He might even take me into custody—he has done stranger things than that! It might be less trouble to marry his son!"

Jamie looked from one to the other, Alex visibly upset and concerned, the Countess almost seeming to enjoy herself, playing her double game blatantly.

"What is the reason for the armed force you brought with you, Alex?" he asked.

"That is to show Albany that two can play his game. That we know what he is at. I am showing him that he is too late. That I am taking over this castle and earldom."

"You mean . . . ?"

"He means, Sir James, that he prefers to do this, to seem to take by force what he could gain in free gift! A strange man, is he not? Was ever a woman thirled to so unnatural a lover! He must rape and ravage where he might sweetly enjoy!"

"Isobel! A God's name — how can you speak so!"

"I speak in figure, of course! Sir James will understand? Alex is prepared to come and take over my house and heritage by force, rather than to marry me and gain it lawfully. Can you understand *that*? He scarce flatters a woman, does he?"

"That is not the way of it at all, Jamie! I will rejoice if I may wed Isobel — one day. But not within but a few months of the murder of her husband, whom my unfriends declare that I starved to death. Surely that is not difficult to understand? My name and fame and honour demand it . . ."

"Name, fame and honour — how very much a *man's* notion of marriage!" the woman mocked. "And not every man! *I* see our union otherwise. Concerned with warmer, tender things."

Jamie cleared his throat. "I still do not understand this of your force outside, Alex. What are they here for?"

"They are here to seem to take over this castle by armed strength, man. Is that not clear enough? To serve warning to Albany, John of Coull and any other, that *I* am in possession. That I, by *force majeure*, have prevailed upon the Countess of Mar to make over to me, by charter hereafter, her castle, property and earldom, in default of her own issue. I would have believed that sufficiently plain." That was said in a forced voice and manner so unlike Alex's normal as to cause Jamie to blink. He looked at the Countess, who smiled.

"The lady agrees . . . to this?" he got out.

"It was the lady's suggestion."

"Only as but a poor second choice, my dear. If you had agreed to marriage, right away, none of it would have been necessary. But, since you are so concerned with your honour, I proposed this alternative. Although I cannot see how honour is enhanced . . ."

"It is *your* honour that gains by it, woman!" That was almost exasperatedly said. "Do you not see? *Will* you not see? Yours. To be sure, you see — or you would not have suggested it! This way your name is preserved. You have been forced. But it will give John Stewart and his father pause. And any others with designs on you. They will recognise that they will have to come in force, be prepared to fight, to gain you and your earldom now. After, in due course, if you still will have me, we can wed."

"In due course! How long is this sorry woman to wait upon your honour?"

"Give me a year, Isobel. Twelve months. Then the thing can be done with some decency."

"Your description of our nuptials, Alex, might not content *every* woman! When Brave John would wed me tomorrow! But . . . if you insist . . ."

Jamie stared from one to the other. "Dear . . . God!" he said. And, after a pause. "You understand what this will mean? You fully realise, Alex, that it will give Albany most ample opportunity and cause to outlaw you? If he so desires. You will be declared cateran and brigand."

"By some, no doubt — but they would say that anyway. Others will see it differently. As I shall inform the Privy Council. I, as recent Justiciar, see it as necessary to preserve the King's peace, here in the North. I have had word of attempts to be made on the earldom, to coerce the Countess. I need not mention John of Coull. But it is necessary to protect the Countess. The earldom of Mar, in wrong hands, could be a grievous danger. It can raise many thousands of men. *I* have had no word from the Governor. Until I am replaced as Justiciar, it is my duty to safeguard and ensure the King's peace — thus."

"M'mm. I fear not a few will see it much otherwise, Alex!"

"That is how *I* see it — which is what signifies, at this present!"

"I cannot think it wise . . ."

"Then what do you propose instead? Out with it, Jamie."

Helplessly that man shook his head. "Since it cannot be lawful, how can you claim it your duty as former Justiciar?"

"Ah, but it is lawful, Sir James," the Countess said. "If *I* agree to it. The earldom is *mine*, and all within it. If I give Alex a charter of it all, duly signed and sealed, the thing is lawful —

for all is within my gift, meantime. Although it grieves me to say it, marriage is not *necessary*. A countess in her own right — or indeed an earl — can bestow the earldom on whom she, or he, may designate, resigning it into other hands. The King must confirm, yes. But for the King *not* to confirm would require an especial hearing before parliament. Albany himself would be the last to contest the legality of this, for *he* gained the earldom of Fife thus, not marrying the Countess thereof, who was his brother's widow. Robert Stewart was already married to the Countess of Menteith — gaining *that* earldom from her; but he prevailed upon the unhappy Countess of Fife, by what means has never been made clear, to make over Fife to him. She was known greatly to dislike him. That, indeed, is what gave me the notion for this."

"It was *your* notion, then?"

"To be sure. Think you I would allow this to be imposed on me?"

Jamie shrugged. "You both know more of it all than do I — the legality. But I do not like it."

"You mean, the Lady Mariota de Athyn will not like it, Sir James? And you to fail her in your mission!"

"No. That is as may be. It is myself who sees it all as dangerous. For Alex. Even if not unlawful. It will take him long to live this down — if ever he does."

"What is the alternative then, Jamie?" his friend insisted. "If I do not this, and do not marry Isobel forthwith, Albany will make all endeavour to have his son wed her. With all the resources of the kingdom behind him."

Jamie could not say that this might be no such bad outcome, that the Countess was not the wife for Alex, that John of Coull might indeed make none so ill an Earl of Mar. His friend loved and wanted this woman. And needed, or conceived himself to need, the manpower and resources of her earldom to retain his position and safety in the North. He spread his hands eloquently.

"This charter — is it to be something of a deed of gift? A marriage contract for the future? Will it specify marriage hereafter?"

"It does not. It is already drawn up and ready. We have considered it well. It is no marriage contract, nor betrothal document. Isobel honours me by resigning all her properties and powers into my hands, without stated condition. It will seem as

83

though I had forced it upon her, by main strength and armed might. But I would liefer have that than be named as the man who had foully slain her husband in order to marry her. I cannot make it more clear."

"You make it entirely clear, my love!" the lady said, grimacing.

Jamie held his peace.

"Now — what have *you* to tell us about Albany's doings in the South? And your own position now?" Alex demanded, as though thankful to change the subject.

"My own position is that I am still outlaw, and my brother sits snug in Aberdour Castle! But says he will give it back when I am a free man again — if ever. As to Albany, I tell you sufficient to show that the man is cleverer even than *I* had thought! He used Hotspur Percy as excuse to raise a large army — which he had little intention of using. He seemed to avenge Homildon, by driving the English from Scots soil — without a sword drawn or a drop of blood shed! He put himself in a position to gain greatly had Hotspur triumphed in his rebellion against King Henry, mustering to possibly aid the revolt. But when the Percy was slain and the revolt failed, he was able to return quietly home with his army, never having so much as set foot on English soil. Whatever Henry may suspect, he has no case against Albany. He comes back, position at home strengthened — and at no cost."

"On my soul, perhaps I should indeed embrace the man as a good-sire, so clever is he!" the Countess exclaimed. "You sound almost sorry that there was no bloodshed, Sir James?"

"No. Only that he can fool the realm so cheaply."

"Is that not part of the art of kingship? For Albany is king in all that matters. I think that he might have made a fair enough king — better than his brother or father, at least. For if he had done all this, as king, you would have been the first to praise him, I swear!"

"No," Jamie denied. "Not so. It would still have been chicanery, deceit. My father also says that he might have made a good king. But I say that is wrong. A deceiver, a man dishonest, without scruple, can never well rule a kingdom."

"There I differ with you. Kings must often be all these — since state craft itself is partly thus. We cannot judge rulers as we do other men."

"Whether we can or no," Alex intervened, "at least we are further warned how cunning is the man we are seeking to counter. To be better on our guard. Did you learn anything, Jamie, of our especial business? Or *mine*, of Duncan?"

"I cannot prove it, but I believe that he went south with the Governor, in Lindsay's train. I am fairly well persuaded that he went from here to Rossie, in Fife, as we thought that he might, to render his report on Sir Malcolm Drummond's death, was taken to Falkland to see Albany. And later went with Lindsay and his men in the Border adventure."

"And then . . .?"

"I heard nothing more. I did not linger to await the Governor's return!"

"To be sure. So Duncan is now of my, and his, uncle Albany's party! And a further danger to us all."

"And to himself, I think. Albany's tools are apt to have short lives!"

*   *   *

Next day Jamie was shown the charter which the couple had drawn up, and the two copies which the castle chaplain was making of it. In effect, it delivered the earldom — although not the title and powers of Earl of Mar — into Alex's hands, to manage as he saw fit, and to retain for so long as it was not required of him by any heirs of the Countess's body. Since, at forty-four, she had had no offspring, despite indubitably a considerable variety of bedding, the probability was that this clause would remain inoperative. But it gave the impression that the heritage of future generations of the ancient line was being considered. The original paper, duly witnessed, was to be retained by Alex, whilst one copy was for the King's consideration and the other for Albany. The timing and method of delivery of these two documents to their appropriate destinations was the subject of considerable debate.

The hope was that the monarch, feeble as he was, might be given his in secret and prevailed upon to endorse it before ever Albany saw his own copy or heard what was to do. Obviously this would not be easy to achieve. To get the paper down to Turnberry Castle in Ayrshire, the recluse King's retreat, unsuspected, would be a problem in itself; whilst to have it smuggled into the sovereign's presence, behind Albany's myriad spies and minions, and get it out again, endorsed, would be no mean feat. But that was what was required if the project was to have fullest effect.

Out beyond the lowered drawbridge-head, looking over the

stirring scene of the Highlanders' camp there, in the mellow autumn forenoon sunshine, watching the Braemoray and Badenoch clansmen at their strenuous amusements, tossing cabers, putting heavy stones, wrestling and the like, Jamie Douglas made up his mind, although reluctantly.

"It will have to be myself," he declared. "I do not see how any other could achieve it. Only through one of the princesses can the King be reached. The Lady Isabel best. She hates her brother Albany sufficiently. On none of the others could I prevail, I think."

Alex looked at him. "I am not sufficiently hypocrite, Jamie, to pretend that I had not thought the same, myself. It is a scurvy fortune that it should have to be *you* who should make this hazardous venture, you not myself. But I have no especial links with the princesses, nor with the King either — although he is my uncle. I scarce know him, or them. Nor do I know the Lowlands as do you. Neither am I a Douglas, with a Lowland voice. I will come with you, but it is you, I fear, who must achieve the business."

"Yes . . ."

"That would be folly, Alex," the Countess said. "For you to go, also. Dangerous and needless. Besides, your place is here. This mission might take a considerable time, and who knows what could happen here in the North the while? Do you not agree, Sir James?"

He nodded. "I do. It would achieve nothing — but good company for myself."

"Two heads can improve on one, on occasion."

"Perhaps. But I have learned that a single wandering friar can go far, unchallenged. But two such are seldom seen together. That would attract notice. No, I am better alone, Alex. You must see it?"

"Your Mary will not like this."

"Mary will understand very well. She is as concerned for your cause as I am. We are your guests, after all."

"I had not thought to have you pay for your lodging thus, man!"

"No. But it is something only I can do. Or attempt — since I may not be successful. God knows. Give me a few days at Lochindorb with Mary and the bairns, and I am your man."

"I mislike it," the other said. "But I see no other way, with the smell of success to it . . ."

VI

TEN DAYS LATER, therefore, the travelling man was on his way again. This time, out of much thought, he was following a different route, despite the fact that he now had the east coast sea route all but perfected, for secret travel. He reckoned that the major danger-point of his venture might well be in getting away from the royal castle of Turnberry after his mission was completed — should he ever get that far. He might have to leave in haste. In which case experience of unobtrusive flight by the *west* coast could be valuable.

So, instead of journeying eastwards to find a ship at one of the Moray ports, he headed south-westwards by upper Strathspey and down the great rift of the Laggan valley, across the watershed of Scotland, making for Lochaber in the first instance, and then further south to Appin. Alex insisted on accompanying him on this early stage of his journey, with a score of gillies — for Lochaber was ever a dangerous place for raids by the Islesmen, not major invasions like Alastair Carrach's but constant petty incursions by individual bands who looked on this area as their legitimate prey, much as the Borderers did the English Marches. He would take him to the Priory of Ardchattan, in the Benderloch district of South Appin, whence it was hoped that onward transport would be available.

It was early November but still colourful autumn in the warm Highland West, with the weather open and the rivers not yet running full to make travel difficult. Nothing of course enabled them to avoid the constant great detours made necessary by the long sea-lochs which constituted the principal obstacle to travel in this land; but Alex knew the terrain well — since in theory he might lay claim to be Lord of Lochaber, this having been one of his father the Wolf's many titles — and he was able to take many short-cuts by little-used passes and drove-roads, by causeways through peat-bogs and by ferry-scows. The latter were usually run by churchmen, with adjacent hospices of a sort for travellers, even in this wild country, and Alex's policy of keeping on good terms with the Church was again proved wise. They were not attacked by any, Islesmen or others.

They turned due southwards in the Braes of Lochaber country, crossed Spean, and took a lonely climbing drove-route through the empty mountains by the Lairig Liacach and Mamore to Loch Leven. Avoiding the terrible wastes of the Moor of Rannoch they went west through Duror of Appin, made the circuit of Loch Creran and came at last through Benderloch to great Loch Etive and the Firth of Lorn.

Ardchattan was one of only three Valliscaulian monasteries in Scotland. But since the largest was at Pluscarden, near Elgin, and Alex had taken the precaution of obtaining a letter of introduction from the Prior there, of old acquaintance, they were well received. The Priory was situated on the northern shore of Etive, not far from the great castle of Dunstaffnage, the keepers of which, since the Bruce's time, were Campbells. Alex was uncertain as to this potentate's allegiances, and was not disposed to linger long in the vicinity. He handed over Jamie to the Prior, stayed but the one night, and departed early the next morning after an affectionate and rather anxious farewell.

The Valliscaulians were great tillers of the soil, stock-breeders and wool-growers, and much of the produce of their, and their tenants' farms granges, tanneries and mills had to be sent to the South to obtain the revenues desired by Holy Church. As a consequence there were frequent shipments sent from the lochside pier, especially in the autumn when the various harvests were over and before the winter storms closed a dangerous seaboard to prudent mariners. This was Jamie's objective in coming here.

A vessel had sailed, unfortunately, not long before their arrival, and he had to wait for five days for another to come in and be loaded. But the brothers, despite their notably rigorous discipline — much more so than other Orders — were not too demanding as to his falling in with their regime, as for instance in eschewing meat and rising an hour before dawn. They were not permitted to venture beyond the monastery precincts, and this applied to Jamie also — but this aided the secrecy of his presence. For an impatient man the time passed but slowly, and the visitor was left in no doubts that he was not cut out for a monastic life. But the brothers, a score of them, were friendly, and he was not ungrateful.

Eventually, covered again in his black Benedictine robe and cowl — the Valliscaulians wore white — he took leave of his hosts and boarded the *Brigid of Lennox*, of Dumbarton, with a great train of pack-horses unloading wool-sacks, bales of hides, and skins of cured leather. The vessel flew two large banners of a white Paschal Lamb on blue, the flag of the priory — which, he was assured, would alone save it from the attentions of the Lord of the Isles' galleys and the independent pirates who infested the narrow Hebridean seas. The Church's judicious admixture of tribute and anathema appeared to be effective insurance. Jamie found that a fellow-passenger had been rowed across the loch from the south shore, a Campbell merchant on his way to Glasgow; but this proved to be an uncommunicative individual prepared to keep his own company — which suited Jamie.

They had to judge their sailing time exactly, for the narrow mouth of long Loch Etive was guarded by an extraordinary submarine waterfall, which at certain stages of the tide made the passage quite unusable. Even when the timing was right, the negotiating of the Falls of Lora was quite a navigational hazard in a large vessel, and the sense of plunging downhill was alarming to the novice.

Jamie had never sailed the Sea of the Hebrides before, and he found it all a notable and even exhilarating experience and quite the most colourful journey he had ever undertaken. Had the weather been otherwise, of course, all would have been very different, he recognised. But in slight north-easterly airs and mainly clear pale-blue skies, they tacked and twisted in sparkling waters over a long, lazy swell, round islands innumerable, great and small, where seals basked and seabirds circled, past foaming skerries and towering stacks, through narrow sounds between steep mountainsides, below mighty cliffs, skirting gleaming white-sand beaches decked with multi-hued seaweeds and shallows showing every shade of blue, purple, amethyst and green. They were never far from land, had to make wide circuits and detours to avoid tidal overfalls, races and even whirlpools, and were subjected to sudden and disconcerting down-draughts from flanking hillsides and hidden valleys. More than once they sighted lurking galleys, long, lean, evil-looking craft, low-set but with soaring prows and sterns, under a single great square sail and with serried ranks of oars. But though some pulled near, possibly to check on their flag, none molested them.

The third day out they rounded the dreaded Mull of Kintyre, graveyard of shipping, on a shining sea as innocent as a baby's smile, and sailed up into the sheltered waters of the Clyde estuary between the Isle of Arran and the Ayrshire coast, Jamie actually able to see the King's castle of Turnberry, his ultimate destination, in the passing, with mixed feelings.

Beating north-eastwards now, directly into the breeze, it took them a full day and a half to reach Dumbarton. Jamie had scarcely seen the Campbell merchant throughout, for he had remained seasick in his berth most of the time — possibly the reason for his unforthcoming attitude. At the busy Clyde port they disembarked, and the cargo was unloaded for transhipment to smaller craft for the pull up-river to Glasgow and the Bishop's warehouses. Jamie made discreet enquiries at the port as to shipping likely to be sailing northwards again in a week or two, and was concerned to learn that the traffic was practically over for the season, few shipmasters being willing to risk a voyage round the Mull of Kintyre after mid-November. The cargoes and few passengers for Hebridean waters during the winter months must go by the sheltered route through the Kyles of Bute and up long Loch Fyne to Tarbert, there to land, cross the isthmus, and await another craft to carry them onwards into the Western Sea — or else travel on by land. This was normal practice — and clearly a wandering friar was expected to know it.

Jamie took passage on one of the many small craft plying the Clyde between Dumbarton and Glasgow, some fifteen miles.

He had never had occasion to visit Glasgow, and found it a small place of crowded narrow streets and twisting wynds, yet set amongst the gardens and orchards of the rich senior clergy. It was much smaller than Dumbarton, clustering round the great cathedral, with its soaring wooden spire, which tended to dwarf all else. Clearly all here was the Bishop's — at present one Matthew Glendinning, uncle to Jamie's colleague at Otterburn, Sir Simon Glendinning (but better avoided, nevertheless) — from the eight-arch stone bridge, to cross which all had to pay toll, to the strong castle or palace near the cathedral, from the expensive pilgrim shrines to the seminaries for training priests, from the leper hospital to the great rows of warehouses and stores by the riverside. It was not so large or impressive as the ecclesiastical metropolis of St. Andrews, but it gave a greater impression of dedication, notably towards amassing wealth. It did not seem the sort of place to look for aid against the ruling power.

Jamie was tempted to turn directly southwards here, to make for Turnberry, some fifty miles away — so much less difficult and hazardous than crossing Scotland to the east coast again, first. But he recognised that this would be foolish and might well bring his whole project to naught. He even toyed with the idea of making for Nithsdale, which was not so very far southeast of Turnberry, to seek the widowed Lady Gelis Stewart there, the youngest and former favourite of the King's sisters, on whom once he himself had doted. But, although she hated Albany sufficiently, blaming him for her husband's death — though this was doubtful — she was known to have become very strange, practically a recluse, seldom leaving her house. Even though she might agree to go with Jamie to Turnberry, he felt that he could not rely on her to carry out a difficult task of persuasion. It would have to be her sister Isabel.

So the next morning he left Glasgow, for the east, with staff and satchel, great walking ahead of him, since there was no alternative, a very energetic and determined friar. Deliberately he avoided the direct routes between Glasgow and Linlithgow or Stirling, where the Governor's influence might be expected to be strong and informants numerous, keeping well to the south, following up the Clyde valley as far as Cambusnethan and then taking to the higher and little populated lands of Upper Lanarkshire, country he knew but little but judged would be of small interest to Albany. Putting up at remote inns and humble change-houses, philosophically accepting the grim conditions as no worse than many he had encountered on sundry campaigns, and now carefully eschewing religious establishments or hospices where his sham status and lack of tonsure would be obvious, he pushed steadily eastwards in poor weather now, mainly in a thin cold drizzle, averaging around twenty miles each day. He spoke to few and met with no sort of challenge save the physical. Three days after leaving Glasgow he was well into Lothian — but upland Lothian. He crossed the Pentland Hills by the high pass of the Cauldstane Slap, and came down into the valley of the North Esk.

Now he had to traverse populous country, where he was

91

known. On the other hand, he knew every inch of it, where to go and what to avoid. Carefully he kept away from Dalkeith, and by roundabout ways presently arrived at the servants' door of the House of Edmonstone on its long ridge two miles to the north-east. Here he could throw back his cowl at last, for all knew him well. Asking for the Lady Isabel, he was thankful to learn that she was at home — which was by no means always the case.

His princess sister-in-law received him joyfully — as he had had little doubt that she would, for she had been almost too fond of him for many a year. He liked her too, but found her no rival to his Mary, and was a little embarrassed by her frank displays of affection. She was some fourteen years older than he was, but that was not the sort of thing to worry any of the Stewart women. Her present husband, Sir John Edmonstone of that Ilk, was no inhibiting factor, for he was elderly, lazy and seldom sober, though amiable enough. It had been only a marriage of convenience.

"Jamie! Jamie!" she cried, flinging her arms around him. "I was desolate, thinking not to see you again for an eternity! And now here you are back to me so soon. I can scarce believe it. Did you not return to your Hielands?"

"I have been and come again," he assured, stirring somewhat in her embrace.

"For an outlaw, my dear, you come and go in remarkable fashion!"

"I choose my paths carefully. Your husband, is he well?"

"He is, I believe, as he prefers to be — unconscious! Have you come from Dalkeith?"

"No. I came straight here. From the West — from Glasgow, which I reached by ship."

"Ah! Then I cannot suppose that it is any poor attractions of mine that have drawn you here across wide Scotland, Jamie?"

"I ... ah ... no. Leastways, not only that, Isabel. I need your help."

"Yes. You are ever honest, if naught else! I conjectured that was it. But ... what can I, a weak woman, do to aid so determined an outlaw?"

"You can help in a further countering of your brother, the Duke Robert Stewart."

"Ha — you say so? For that I am seldom loth! Come to my room, Jamie, and tell me whilst you refresh yourself."

92

He explained Albany's plan to marry his younger son to the Countess of Mar, and Alex Stewart's plan to stop it. The Countess was Isabel's sister-in-law, also, the late Earl James of Douglas's sister.

"So-o-o! Isobel Douglas would have your friend and my nephew, Alex, Earl of Mar?"

"Yes. *She* would have him that now, wed him out-of-hand. But he will not. Declares it too soon after her husband's death. So they have conceived this plan — to forestall Albany. The Countess has made over the lands and powers of her earldom to him, in advance of marriage, in trust, by charter. And he brought a force of his Highlanders to sit around Kildrummy, to seem to invest it, to seem to force her in the matter. To aid her good name . . ."

His companion emitted what, in anyone less lofty and attractive, could have been called a hoot. "Anyone who knows Isobel of Mar would conceive it a deal too late for that!" she declared. "Alex need not be so nice!"

"So *she* says, also! But he is determined — and I well understand his mind. He is a man ever seeking to make up for the ill fame of his father."

"No doubt. But this arrangement will but injure his repute without aiding hers."

"So I told him, but he would not heed me. Forby, it is done now. The misfortune of it is, being an earldom, any such charter needs the King's assent. I have two copies of it here in my satchel. Somehow to gain the royal signature before Albany can stop it."

"And I am to persuade him?"

"I can think of none other who could."

"I do not know that I may be able, Jamie. John is a man lost, now. Drawn in on himself. Caring nothing for what goes on outside the walls of Turnberry Castle — unless it affects his son James. Now that the boy is at St. Andrews Castle in Bishop Wardlaw's care, his father appears to have nothing to live for. David's murder struck him hard, on top of Annabella's death. Now he leaves all to Robert. And prays, always prays!"

"How in God's good name does he match that with his coronation oath? To love and cherish, to rule and govern his people justly and well?"

"Do not ask me, Jamie, for I do not understand him. He never wanted to be King. He is a poor creature, weaker even than was his father. A saint without a saint's strength!"

"But . . . you will come? And try?"

"For you I will, Jamie. Not for Alex's sake — who seems to be a fool! And certainly not for Isobel Douglas's! But for you — and to spoil Robert's plans, I am willing to attempt it."

"I thank you. Alex has shown me, and Mary, great kindness. And he is no fool, I assure you. Of all the Stewarts he has the most good in him, I think. The most able and honest . . ."

"He need not be a paragon to be that!" she said. "But . . . perhaps you are right. When must we go?"

"Soon, Isabel — the sooner the better. We must act before Albany can."

"Act! You make it sound as though all we need do is go to Turnberry! How am I to persuade my brother to sign this paper? It is no clearly just cause. Indeed, it smells but ill, does it not? He will say that it is an unholy alliance, belike. Scarce made in heaven . . .!"

"Say that the other would be worse. Albany's son, John of Coull, is but twenty-two years. Only half the Countess's age. And he is to make him Lieutenant of the North and Justiciar, if he becomes Earl of Mar. Little more than a boy." Jamie paused, uncomfortably, his inconvenient and essential honesty not to be submerged thus. "Although I liked him well enough, and believe him able," he ended, lamely.

"The King will say that is naught to do with him, the Governor's business."

"We believe Albany was responsible for Sir Malcolm Drummond's murder. Like others. It would be an evil thing for his son to wed the widow."

"You think that . . .? Another murder?"

"It looks that way. We cannot prove it, once more. Albany covers his tracks well. But . . ."

"Then *I* cannot prove it to my brother, either. He will but wring his hands and hope it otherwise!"

Jamie frowned. "There is one thing that we might try," he said slowly. "Something that Alex suggested. I do not greatly like it. But it might serve. Playing on the King's weakness — to get behind his guard. You spoke of this about the Prince James. Alex, like many another, believes the boy to be in great danger — from Albany. The only life between him and the throne, now. St. Andrews Castle and the good Bishop are not strong enough to protect him, if Albany decides to remove the lad. Alex suggested that he might offer to have the prince up in Badenoch, at Lochindorb. He would be safe there, beyond the Highland Line. If the King is anxious for his remaining son, he might be thankful to have it so. Alex is his nephew too, after all."

"You mean, offer this to my brother in exchange for his signature?"

"Scarce so crudely as that! But . . . if Alex was Earl of Mar, and with the power of the earldom added to his own Lordship of Badenoch, he could offer a more notable and safer refuge for the heir to the throne than any bishop's palace. None would take the boy out of Lochindorb Castle unbidden, that I swear!"

"So might my brother fear! Delivering his darling, and all the power that would give, into the hands of the Wolf of Badenoch's son! Myself, I would hesitate!"

"Would you leave your son at St. Andrews Castle? With Albany as threat?"

"No-o-o. Oh, I do not know, Jamie. Perhaps we might try it. If all else fails." She shook her fair head. "We go quickly, then? Forthwith?"

"Aye. And secretly."

"How secretly?"

"Albany must learn, or suspect, nothing. And he has people everywhere. My father says even in Dalkeith, watching *him*. He, Albany, knows you hate him. So no doubt you are watched also. Why I came to you secretly. So you must not seem to be going to Turnberry. Some otherwhere. Do you ever visit your sister, the Lady Gelis?"

"I have not seen her this year past. She is . . . difficult. Her mind a little turned, I fear."

"Yes. But it would serve as pretext. You travel to Nithsdale. I, in your company, as your domestic chaplain. None will seek stop the King's sisters from visiting each other. Make for Nithsdale, and at Sanquhar or Durrisdeer turn west for Turnberry."

"It might serve, yes . . ."

The Lady Isabel was very much her own mistress at Edmonstone, and two mornings later they were on their way. Jamie had thought of borrowing a company of Douglas men-at-arms from Dalkeith, as escort — but decided against it as only liable to draw attention to them. The smaller the party the better, consistent with the princess's position. So, with only four of Edmonstone's men, they rode off south-westwards.

Isabel was a good horsewoman and fit enough for long days in the saddle — which was as well, for putting up overnight was bound to be a major problem, and therefore the largest daily mileage possible called for. Such as she could not sleep at lowly inns and wayside change-houses; and suitable lairdly houses or religious establishments and hospices, where they could rest secure from too much enquiry and subsequent report to the Governor's minions, were not of frequent occurrence. Fortunately most of the land to be covered was Douglas country, or that of their vassals, where Albany's influence would not be strong. Jamie had put much thought into this, reckoning the entire journey to be about one hundred miles. At this time of year it would be impracticable and unfair to seek to cover more than forty to fifty miles a day, even if Isabel was able for more — and without changing horses. Which meant two overnight halts at, say, forty and eighty mile stages. The first stage would bring them, by Kirkurd and Biggar, to the upper Clyde valley, in the Symington-Abington area. This was Lindsay of Crawford territory; and since the Earl of Crawford's wife was Isabel's sister Katherine, that should be a help. Not that the Crawfords themselves would be thereabouts — they lived mostly at their favourite castle of Edzell in Angus; but their vassals and servants would not be apt to fail or betray their master's sister-in-law. Also, Crawford was no friend of Albany's. Tower Lindsay, one of their original strongholds, was near the little burgh of Crawford itself, three miles beyond Abington. They would make that their first night's objective.

In the event, they could have gone further, for the weather improved, the land had dried considerably in a fresh breeze, the rivers were not running so high as to be difficult, and the horses were still fresh. After an early start they reached Crawford with still a couple of hours till sunset. But after this Clyde valley, their journey lay through the high and lonely Lowther Hills, and there would be little shelter for many a mile. They made for Tower Lindsay therefore, which guarded a ford of Clyde.

It could not be claimed that they did very well there. The place was little more than a stark, draughty and gloomy shell, in the keeping of a rough and oafish steward. They were received willingly enough, and the keeper probably did his best at short notice for their comfort, impressed by having a princess as guest; but clearly nobody of any quality or even modest refinement had occupied the hold for long, and its furnishings, like its provender, were of the plainest and most elementary. Fires were lit for them in chilly dank rooms which had not seen the like for years — and the resultant clouds of smoke indicated that jackdaws had taken over the chimneys. Isabel showed her spirit by making the best of it and even affecting a gay and holiday attitude. But running eyes from the wood-smoke, swirling draughts, pervading damp so that everything near the fires actually steamed, and only narrow wooden benches to sit upon, had their cumulative effect, and prevailed on her to retire early to an equally smoke-filled bedchamber where she announced that she would wrap herself in her travelling-cloak and horse-blanket rather than risk the mildewed sheepskins and soggy bed-coverings. She clung to Jamie tightly for a little at the door, and he kissed her hair before gently pushing her within.

At least they were secure from any hostile attentions.

A far from restful night saw them up with the dawn, anxious only to be on the move again. Isabel demanded to know just how far was the shortest route to Turnberry now, and when told over fifty miles, and hilly miles at that, declared that she would ride that distance and more, until she fell out of her saddle, rather than pass another night like that. Although sympathetic, Jamie was doubtful, but agreed that they should press ahead now by the most direct route and at best speed. He had intended that they took the Mennock Pass road through the Lowther Hills, as giving the impression that they were heading for Nithsdale and Dumfriess-shire, not Ayrshire and Carrick. But from discreet enquiries, and the conclusion that the Governor's grip was singularly loose in these upper Clydesdale hills, he felt that they could risk a direct westerly journey without much fear of alerting their enemies. Down-river some way there was a drove-road for the upland cattle to be taken across the Lowthers to the Cumnock fairs, partly on the line of an old Roman road. This should shorten their journey considerably.

It was a dull day with a cold wind, the clouds low on the hills; but it was dry and they made good time. Once they left the actual valley of the Clyde they saw no-one but the occasional shepherd or hillman. Hardy cattle grazed the hill-slopes, but apart from the infrequent herd's shack, there were no houses, much less communities. For some of the time they rodé in the chill skirts of the clouds, which slowed them somewhat. But by soon after noon they were out of the major hills and following the Guelt Water down toward the foothill town of Cumnock, which they

97

made shift to pass well to the south, and so down into the Ayrshire plain and populous lands again.

This was the danger area, the royal earldom of Carrick, and they certainly did not linger, chewing cold ribs of beef as they rode. They both knew the district well now, for Isabel had been reared partly at Turnberry and Dundonald, her father's favourite houses; and Jamie had quartered the vicinity in the late Prince David's spirited company years before. So they were able to avoid towns and villages as far as possible, and the houses of those who might be suspicious or inimical.

In the late afternoon, however, and only some few miles from Turnberry, their precautions proved to be inadequate. They were circling Crossraguel Abbey, wondering whether to risk a call there — for it was one of the King's favourite haunts — having already given Maybole town, the capital of Carrick, a wide berth, when one of their men announced that they were being followed. Looking round, they saw a mounted party of about a score, riding up at speed.

Jamie snorted. "We have been here before, I think!" he observed grimly. Years before, in the old King's reign, he had been escorting Isabel to visit her brother at Turnberry when they had been rudely intercepted and assailed by a party under her nephew, the Lord David Stewart — the start indeed of Jamie's love-hate relationship with that spirited and now dead prince. The memory of their alarming experience on that occasion made them draw up now in tight protective formation around the princess, swords loosened in sheaths, even the friar's.

The newcomers rode pounding up, to encircle them, amidst shouts and clanking steel. Their leader, a swarthy youngish man, handsomely dressed, spoke shortly.

"Where go you? And on what business?"

"To Turnberry. And on the *King's* business," Jamie returned, no less sharply. "Who are you to ask it?"

"Watch your tongue, sir priest! I represent the Governor of the realm."

"Then you do so but ill. Like any churl! Uncover your head, man — in the presence of the King's own sister, the Princess Isabel."

The other blinked, opened his mouth, and then shut it again. But doubtfully he removed his bonnet. "My lady," he jerked, then, "I . . . ah . . . greet you. I did not know." He turned back

98

to Jamie. "Have you the Governor's authority to visit His Grace?" he demanded.

"I do not need my brother's authority to visit my brother, sir." Isabel schooled her voice haughtily.

The other coughed. "Your pardon, Princess, but my lord Duke's orders are definite. None may visit the King save by his written and signed permission."

"Fool! Insolent!" That woman could play the princess adequately, when necessary. "I could have you horsewhipped for this! Think you such instructions apply to His Grace's own family?"

At her demeanour the man looked both uncertain and unhappy. "My orders," he said. "His Grace is sick. I, I . . ."

"A plague on your orders, man! I shall speak with my brother anent this scurvy order, and *your* behaviour. Both my brothers. To be sure His Grace is sick — hence my visit. But he is still King of Scots, and can suitably punish any who insult his royal dignity. Mind it, sir! Who are you, who makes so bold as to insult the King's sister?"

"Kennedy of Ballure, Lady. The steward of Maybole . . ."

"Then, if you wish to retain your stewardship, Kennedy, escort us to Turnberry Castle, forthwith," Isabel commanded, and reined round her horse to kick it into a trot, Jamie and their four men only a little less prompt.

Their interceptor bit his lip, hesitating, and then scowling, waved his party on after them.

So they rode the four miles to the great sprawling castle on the low cliff-edge, which looked out across the Firth of Clyde to Arran, scarcely a word exchanged between any of the principals the while. As they neared the gatehouse, from the tower of which the royal Lion Rampant banner of Scotland streamed in the breeze, the drawbridge lowered, the man Kennedy spurred up.

"I will ride forward, Princess, to ensure your suitable reception," he said.

"You will not. I require no introduction to my brother's house, sir. Keep back where you belong."

Without pause she led the way, thudding over the drawbridge. Men-at-arms poured out of the guard-room and porter's lodge to bar their way; but the seeming confidence of the lady, aided no doubt by the presence of the Maybole steward at her back, gave them pause. She waved them aside imperiously and clattered through the gatehouse-pend into the great open court-

99

yard beyond, to rein up. Then she beckoned to one of the soldiers.

"The captain of the guard, fellow," she commanded.

"Aye, Lady — oh, aye. But he's no' here the noo," the man said.

"Then he ought to be! See you, then — have the King's Grace informed that his sister, the Lady Isabel, Countess of Douglas, is here. Off with you. And you, man — do not stand gawping there! Aid me down from this horse."

In such fashion they arrived at Turnberry.

With their escort dismounting behind them, and the man Kennedy looking awkward, Jamie came close to Isabel.

"You do this passing well," he murmured. "But now for the test. They will watch the King closely, you may be sure."

"Yes. But . . . we must not stand here, as though humbly seeking admittance." And she set off across the cobbled yard, not for the main keep doorway but for that of the long low hall-house, within the perimeter walling, which had always contained her brother John's personal apartments, with its chapel, library, minstrels' room and bedchambers, befitting a man who had never been any sort of warrior.

There was a guard with a halberd at the door, but he was one of the old members of the castle staff, knew the princess and hastened to let her pass, jerking a bow. But he looked strangely at Jamie, whom he knew also. Jamie gestured to their four men to wait outside.

They were making for an inner door when hurried footsteps behind them turned them. A big and burly red-faced and red-bearded man came, puffing somewhat. At sight of him, Jamie drew a quick breath.

"Ah, Isabel — God, here's a surprise!" this character gasped. "They've just told me. What do you here . . . ?"

"What think you, John — but to see my brother? My *lawful* brother John! I did not know that I was to see my unlawful one also!"

The big man coughed, but managed to grin at the same time, for he was a cheerful customer, if unpredictable. "I take it in turn with John of Bute and John of Cardney to . . . to see to our brother, lass. His Grace prefers his own kin."

"You mean that *Robert* prefers it — for no doubt sufficient reasons! For why he has made you, I hear, Clerk of the Audit and Lord of Burleigh!"

"No harm in that is there, Isabel woman?" the other protested. "A king's bastards can have their uses. Like a lord's — eh, Sir Jamie Douglas? And I, at least, am not one of the King's outlaws, however unlawfully begotten!" He hooted loud laughter.

Jamie threw back his cowl at last. This was Red John Stewart, Captain of Dundonald Castle, often called the Red Captain, one of the late monarch's many bastard sons — just as Mary was one of his many bastard daughters — and therefore one more of Jamie's brothers-in-law. He was a notable if wild and boisterous individual, and hitherto Jamie had got on well enough with him, although they had never been close. But now, if Albany had appointed him as one of those to guard the King, and from what Isabel had said, got him made Lord of Burleigh, and one of the officers of the Crown, it might mean a very different relationship.

"I gather that I have to congratulate your lordship?" he said carefully.

"Na, na, Jamie — no need. Any more than I have need to congratulate *you*, by all I'm told! Nor yet you, Isabel, by the Mass — for consorting with one prescribed and forfeit by law!"

"Sir James is outlawed solely by Robert's ill-will — as you well know," his half-sister said. "Partly, that is what we have to see the King about."

"Indeed. Ah . . . h'm. See you, Isabel — it is less easy than that. My instructions . . ."

"John Stewart — do not you *dare* to start quoting Robert's wicked and unnatural orders to me!" he was interrupted. "I will not have it — from you or from anyone else. I will speak with my brother the King if I so desire, in this house that was once my home, or otherwhere. I am a Princess of Scotland, and do not forget it, bastard half-brother! Now — take us to His Grace."

The other grinned uncomfortably. "Och, Isabel — the Governor is the Governor, mind. The King has resigned his powers of rule to Robert. It isna just a matter of ill-will and a high hand. Robert's word is the law."

"But not over the King! John is still the crowned and anointed King of Scots, and Robert is his subject. Nothing can alter that. John is absolute ruler, the Lord's Anointed, even if he chooses seldom to exercise that rule. He can countermand anything that Robert says or does. He can dismiss Robert from the governorship this very day! Do not doubt it. He can likewise forfeit your lordship of Burleigh and dismiss you from your precious clerk-ship of Audit, if so he wills! Now — where is he? In his library?"

John Stewart shrugged wide shoulders. "You have become a right fierce dame, Isabel! Aye, he is in the library, at his poems and parchments. He does little else. But, see you — I canna permit Sir Jamie Douglas into his presence. No outlaw can ever have audience of the King. It isna possible."

"Sir James comes with me, in *my* company. He has word for the King's private ear. Come far to deliver it. He has long been my own knight and adviser. If you seek to stop him, I will have the King send you back to Dundonald and revoke your offices! He will heed me, I think. For John owes me much."

Doubtfully the Red Captain eyed her, tugging at his fiery beard. She did not wait further, but turned and marched to an inner door, Jamie close at her heels. Her half-brother followed on, protesting, but mutedly for so noisy a man.

The door led into the castle chapel, where candles glowed softly before a richly-hung altar and the scent of incense was strong. After an initial brief curtsy, Isabel strode to another door at the far side. This opened on to a corridor, at the far end of which was a fine large room where a great fire of logs burned on a hooded hearth, the walls lined with books, parchment rolls, missives, and where no fewer than five tables were littered with papers, charters, seals, ink-horns and quills. Over one such a man crouched short-sightedly, pen scratching. In a chair by the fire another and somewhat younger man, slept, mouth open.

They were in the presence of monarchy.

John Stewart, by the Grace of God Robert the Third, High King of Scots, *Ard Righ* and great-grandson of the hero Bruce, looked up, peering uncertainly, prepared to be alarmed. Un-kempt in careless clothing, white-bearded, sunken-eyed, frail, he was sixty-six but looked ten years more — indeed Jamie was shocked to see the change in him. He had a noble brow and good features, like most of the Stewarts, but there was a slackness about the mouth and chin. He raised his pen now, to point it waveringly.

"Isa!" he exclaimed, with something like a groan behind it. "It's Isa."

She curtsied again, and behind her Jamie bowed low.

"Your Grace," Isabel said. "I hope that I see you well, brother? Or . . . none so ill." She moved forward, to bend and kiss his drawn cheek. "It is long since I have seen you, John."

102

He eyed her less than welcomingly. "Aye, I am abroad but little, Isa. I am but poorly. Yet God keeps me in this vile body, when I'd fain have my sorry soul elsewhere, lass. Why, Isa — why?"

"No doubt because He has work for you to do yet awhile, John — as His anointed King of this realm," she suggested briskly. "You are not finished your work yet, brother, I think."

"No, no — that is done with. I am no monarch any more. Just an old done man, left with his sorrows. I'd be gone, Isa — gone. And the only epitaph I'd have you put above me is — Here lies the worst of kings and the saddest of men!"

"Tush, John — what way is that to talk? You *are* still the monarch. Nothing can alter that . . ."

But he was looking past her, eyes widening with their ready fears. "Who . . . who is this I see? This man, Isa . . . ?"

"It is Sir James Douglas of Aberdour, Sire. You will remember Jamie Douglas, Mary's husband, your good and leal servant, who has ever served you well, and David likewise."

"Puir Davie . . . !" That was quavered.

Jamie sank on one knee and reached out to take the trembling, veined hand and raise it to his lips.

Behind them Red John spoke. "I regret, Sire, that this man has pushed past me into your royal presence — an outlaw. I told him that he must not appear before you. I shall send him away . . ."

"That you shall not!" Isabel said.

"What, what is this? Outlaw . . . ?" the King faltered.

"Sir James was declared outlaw by Robert, in his spleen. Because of his support of your son David. And because he could not rescue Robert's oafish son Murdoch from Homildon field," his sister said strongly. "Did you not know?"

"No. I know naught of this. But, but . . . I do not meddle in Robert's affairs, mind, Isa."

"This is not Robert's affair but *yours*, John. The justice of your realm. And Sir Jamie has come a long way to speak with you, on an important matter. Important to *you*. Concerning your young son James."

"Eh? *James?*" As she had anticipated, that penetrated the armour of his fear and alarm. "What of James, the laddie? He's not sick? There is naught wrong with James, Isa? He's at St. Andrews, with good Bishop Wardlaw . . ." The young Prince James was the unhappy monarch's almost only link with responsibility and affection, for although he had three married daughters, all wed to Douglases, with none of them was he close, as with this belated second son.

"No doubt, Sire. It is not his present health we are concerned with. But . . ." She turned. "What Sir Jamie has to say is for your royal ear alone. Have Johnnie leave us, if you please."

"Aye, Johnnie. Do as Isa says."

"Sire — I cannot leave you in an outlaw's company! The Duke Robert would be most wrath! I will take him . . ."

"Sirrah — be off!" his half-sister exclaimed. "Do you dare to dispute the King's royal command? Who is master — Robert, or the King's Grace?"

"Aye, go, man," the monarch almost pleaded. "I mislike any dispute, see you. Best away, Johnnie — for a space."

The Captain grimaced, shrugged, and with the briefest bow, retired.

The sleeper in the chair had now awakened, and rose to his feet. Isabel bobbed one more curtsy, but a slight one, and Jamie made obeisance of a sort likewise.

"Shall I leave you also, Sire?" this younger man said heavily.

"No, no — bide you. His Grace of England can hear anything that I am to hear, Isa." Fairly clearly the King did not want to be left entirely alone with his sister and Jamie.

"Very well." The other sat down again. This was the man known in Scotland as the Mammet, allegedly King Richard the Second of England, deposed by the usurper Henry the Fourth and supposedly foully murdered at Pontefract four years before. Whether he was an imposter or not none knew for sure — although most suspected it. But King Robert accepted the strange and silent man as genuine, treated him as fellow-monarch and even made a friend of him. Indeed this strange pair were each the other's *only* friend. Albany did not object, seeing the Mammet as a possibly useful card to play against Henry in the unending tug-of-war between the two kingdoms. At least the man seemed to be harmless, and content to live thus in quiet retirement, putting on no airs.

Isabel nodded. "It is all a family matter," she said. "If His Grace of England will bear with us . . .?"

"What of James?" the King said, almost urgently for him.

It had been intended that the subject of the young prince's safety should only be brought up later, if necessary, very secondary to the Mar earldom question; but perhaps it could be handled at the same time. When Isabel glanced at Jamie, he inclined his head.

"Yes, Sire," he said. "I speak not for myself but on behalf of your nephew, Sir Alexander Stewart of Badenoch. The eldest son of your royal brother the late Earl of Buchan, until recently acting Justiciar of the North."

The monarch looked more wary than ever. "Alex," he muttered. "Alex's boy. Alex was aye difficult. Headstrong. A trouble-maker . . ."

"Yes, Sire. But his son, *this* son, is very different. A man of great worth, noble, responsible . . ."

"Yes, yes, no doubt. But this of my laddie James? What of that, man?"

Jamie recognised that this matter would have to come first. But he was relieved also that the King had not immediately denounced Alex for the murder of his beloved Queen Annabella's brother Drummond of Mar. Could it be possible that he had not heard of this either, any more than of his own outlawry? He appeared to live in a small, restricted world of his own, here at Turnberry, and would be apt to hear only what Albany and his guards wanted him to hear. Their policy might well be to keep him ignorant of much that went on, to minimise possible interference in the Governor's rule.

"Sire," Jamie said, "Sir Alexander is much concerned for the safety of the Prince James. You have sent him to the Bishop's care at St. Andrews, so it is clear that Your Grace is also concerned. But if he is so endangered, St. Andrews may be insufficiently secure a refuge. The Duke David, his brother, did not find it so!"

At mention of his elder son, the monarch's lips trembled, and his tired eyes filled with tears. He shook his head unspeaking.

Isabel added her voice. "All who wish the realm well, John, are anxious for young James. Robert was behind David's shameful death. Now only James stands between him and your throne. A bishop's palace is scarce the surest refuge. If Robert so desired, he could pluck the boy out of there with little trouble."

The King tugged at his beard. "Robert is none so ill, Isa. He is hard, strong — as I am not. But . . . none so ill." That was beseeching rather than convincing.

"Yet you sent James away from you, Sire. To St. Andrews!"

The unhappy man looked down at his twisting hands.

"Aye. After Davie, I . . . See you, James is all I have, Isa."

"Precisely, John. Therefore, heed you what Sir Jamie Douglas has to say, I'd counsel you."

"Your Grace — Sir Alexander Stewart suggests that there is only one place in this kingdom where the prince could be entirely safe — and that is north of the Highland Line. The Duke of Albany, or others in the South, have no hold there. The Governor's rule does not run north of Atholl. Nor is likely to do, unless . . ." He paused. "Unless the new Justiciar of his appointment is accepted, by the clans, the Highlanders. Sir Alex suggests that Your Grace should send the prince into *his* keeping. He will be safe at Lochindorb."

The monarch stared, slack jaw dropping. "Lochindorb? Alex's ill hold? Yon wolf's den! In the Hielands? My James, in the barbarous Hielands, man?"

"They are not so barbarous, Sire. I have lived there these many months. I have received nothing but kindness. In the Wolf's — in the Earl of Buchan's time, it was . . . different. Your nephew Sir Alex is a true man, and Lochindorb a fine house for a lad. My own son and daughter like it well. All that a boy could wish for. Better for a lad than any bishop's house. And secure, Sire — secure."

"But, but . . . the *Hielands*!"

"Part of Your Grace's realm, peopled by your subjects. Lealer subjects than many nearer here."

"I'd never see James again! If, if they took him away to the Hielands."

"Do you see him *now*, John?" Isabel demanded. "At St. Andrews? When last did you see him there?"

Her brother shook his head, wordless.

"They are not so far, these Hielands, Sire," Jamie said. "I come and go from them without overmuch trouble. Your Grace could visit the prince, if so you desired."

"No, no. Traipse the Hielands? I couldna do that, man. I am a sick man. Done. My days for traipsing the land are long by with . . ."

"And you would condemn James to remain in danger because you would not visit him, John?" the woman charged.

"No. But . . . he's maybe in no danger at all, the lad."

"Then why did you send him away?"

The King drew a deep breath. "I will think on it," he said. "Aye, I will think on it, Isa."

106

She glanced at Jamie. "More than thinking is required, Sire. And time may be short. Tell him, Jamie."

"I said, Your Grace, that the Highlands would be less secure a haven if the Governor appoints a new Justiciar, replacing Sir Alex, whom the Highlanders can accept. As they did not accept the Lord Murdoch. Then the Duke's rule might begin to run in the North, and Lochindorb be no longer so sure a refuge."

"Well, man — well?"

"Sir Alex has resigned the Justiciarship. Because of Sir Malcolm Drummond's death. The Governor proposes . . ."

"Death? Callum Drummond dead?" The King actually gripped Jamie's arm. "What is this . . .?"

"You did not know, Sire? None told you? Sir Malcolm was slain, in May month, shamefully. A bad business."

"He, he was my good-brother — my Anna's brother!"

"Yes, Sire. It was ill done. And some would seek to blame Sir Alex — although he had naught to do with it. Indeed was saving your realm from invasion by the Lord of the Isles at the time, in the West. While most of us were at Homildon . . ."

"You say so? Yon Donald is another trouble-maker. God save us — when will my troubles cease?"

The visitors exchanged glances.

"So Sir Alex resigned the Justiciarship, Sire, feeling that Your Grace's justice should be administered by other than he until this calumny was cleared — for he is a man of much resolve."

"No doubt. But that is no concern of mine, man. Appointments are Robert's business now — the Governor's, no' mine."

"Your pardon, Sire — but earldoms are the King's business, and only the King's."

"Earldoms . . .?"

"Yes, Your Grace. The Countess of Mar has granted to Sir Alexander, by her signed charter, control of the castles, properties and privileges of her earldom, With a view to future marriage. To wed at some decent interval after her late husband's death."

"Isobel Douglas! That woman! She would do that, at her age? She must be a deal older than he, is she not?"

"Thirteen or fourteen years, I think, Sire. But they are fond. She desires him to be her protector, meantime, and her husband later. And he is well agreed." Jamie reached into his robe and brought out the papers. "Here are the charter and a copy, Sire, duly signed and sealed. But because an earldom is concerned,

Your Grace's assent is required. Your royal counter-signature."

"She would make this young man earl? Earl of Mar? As she never would Callum Drummond?"

"Yes, Sire. That is her wish."

"And what does Robert say, my brother, the Governor?"

Jamie drew a breath. "It is no concern of the Governor's, Sire. The earls of Scotland are the *righ*, in the Erse tongue, the lesser kings. Only the *Ard Righ*, the High King, can say them nay. The Countess of Mar has every right to do this, without reference to the Governor of the realm. But to be complete in law the *Ard Righ's* concurrence is necessary. His only. Your Grace's signature."

"I . . . I'll have to think on this, Sir James."

A quick exchange of glances.

"John — need you debate it?" Isabel asked. "There is no reason to say the Countess nay."

"What is the haste, Isa?"

She bit her lip, so Jamie answered for her.

"The haste, Sire, is this. Many men will seek to wed the Countess, to gain the power of her earldom — that is certain. Adventurers. Already there have been approaches, suggestions. The Countess fears for her safety even. She could be in danger of being forced. That is why she has moved thus, well before marriage. To halt all such attempts on her."

"And this Alex hasna forced her? As his father would have done, I swear!"

"No, Sire. He is her choice. Here is her own signature and seal, to prove it, myself and other as witness."

The King shook his head. "I mislike this," he muttered. "Robert would name it meddling . . ."

His sister's gasp was explosive. "John — were *you* crowned and anointed at Scone, or was Robert? Who took those vows before God, to judge and uphold your people? You, or Robert? What has Scotland got for a king? A man — or a frightened bairn!"

He recoiled physically before her outburst and scorn, and went limping about the room, with his damaged knee, kicked by a Douglas horse so many years before, which had turned this man into a cripple when Scotland needed a warrior to lead her.

"You do not understand, Isa," he said brokenly. "I am sick, weary. The rule is beyond me, has aye been beyond me. I have handed over the rule to Robert. He acts the king, now . . ."

108

"No, John — no! He acts the *Governor*. Only you can act King, the Lord's Anointed, whilst the breath of life is in you. Only you are the King of Scots. You cannot hide behind Robert in that."

Jamie, fearing a complete breakdown, greatly daring sought to intervene. "Sire — the Prince James is to be considered, in this. If Sir Alexander is Earl of Mar, he is in greatly better position to protect the prince — should Your Grace send him north. An earl of Scotland, controlling Mar and Garioch as well as Badenoch and Braemoray, he would be well placed to offer your son the security he requires. Also to help keep the King's peace in the North, Your Grace might well be very glad of his aid." That was as near to *lèse majesté* as that man was ever likely to get.

Strangely enough, the monarch did not seem to recognise it as such; or if he did, he was suddenly prepared to accept it as valid, the balance no longer to be contested. Or it may have been merely that his weariness took over. At any rate, abruptly the struggle was over. The King limped back to his table and took up his quill. Hastily Jamie spread the papers open while Isabel held out an ink-horn. Where the younger man's finger pointed, the older signed ROBERT R, in a shaking hand, without even glancing at the charter's wording.

"And here, Sire. This is a copy. For the Governor," Jamie added.

So the thing was done. Isabel took the pen, to witness the royal signature, and then bore the papers over to the Mammet, who made no bones about adding RICHARD R as witness below her own name. Alex could hardly have looked for two kings and a princess to underwrite his unconventional charter.

Jamie's impulse now was to get away without delay; but he recognised that this would scarcely do. Isabel went on to make polite converse, but obtained little encouragement from her brother. An uncomfortable pause followed, until the princess could decently request the royal permission to withdraw. It was granted almost eagerly. Her brother's eyes already were reverting longingly to his own interrupted writings. The visitors bowed themselves out.

Beyond the door, Isabel grasped her companion's arm. "Jamie, Jamie — that was a sore business!" she exclaimed emotionally. "I feared that we were never going to convince him. Poor John — he is a sorry creature! To harry him so was,

was unsisterly. And for folk I care naught for. Only for you . . . !"

"Yes. And I am grateful, my dear. You did nobly. None other could have achieved it. Alex has reason to bless you. But now, we must move fast."

"Move? How mean you? We have gained what you required. What now?"

"See you — John of Dundonald and the man Kennedy will have put their heads together. They will not like this, and will fear Albany's wrath. They will seek to undo what has been done, if they can, for sure."

"How can they? They cannot take back the King's signature. Nor interfere with the King's sister in the King's house — or elsewhere."

"Not *you*, no. But I am another matter. They will pull me down if they can. I am only safe so long as I am with you. And yet, I must leave, and quickly."

"Why that? So long as I am here?"

"They will assuredly have sent word of this to others. Albany himself is like to be too far away, at Doune or Falkland, to be reached quickly. But he will have important men nearer — the Sheriff of Ayr, your other half-brother of Bute, Sir James Sandilands of Calder. Red John will seek such aid and authority. My arrest will be ordered, as outlaw — nothing surer. So I must be gone, with this charter, before they can gain such authority. Meantime, they will probably seek to hold me here."

"Jamie — what can we do, then?"

"Get out of this castle. Somewhere. Say that you must see the Abbot of Crossraguel, on the King's business."

"Now? But it will soon be dark."

"That matters not. Say that you will be back. It is only three or four miles. I do not see how they may stop you. I go with you — but I do not come back with you. Abbot Mark is a friend of the King. He will help."

"And you? Where will you go, Jamie?"

"Never fear. I will make my own way. I got here, from the Highlands, secretly. I will get back. I have siller — and much may be done with siller!"

She was very doubtful, and clearly unhappy at the thought of losing his company so soon. But she could think of no better plan. They moved on.

Red John and Kennedy were waiting in the chapel, and eyed them warily.

"John," Isabel said, at once. "You have been unhelpful. You had best improve upon it! Have suitable repast prepared for us. And bed-chambers readied. But first, a guide to take us to Crossraguel. I have to see the Lord Abbot, on the King's business at once."

"*Now*, Isabel? At this hour?"

"Now, yes, before they close the Abbey up for the night. This cannot wait."

"But . . ."

"No buts, sirrah! Or must we find our own way, in the dusk, man?"

She swept on towards the outer door and the courtyard, where their four-man escort waited.

"Horses!" she called.

With ill grace John Stewart told off one of the Maybole men to accompany them as guide, and watched them mount. Jamie half-expected any moment to be summoned to remain. But Isabel's imperious-seeming confidence won the day. They trotted out over the drawbridge, followed only by hostile stares.

Crossraguel Abbey was a medium-sized monastery of the Cluniac Order, very different in character from the last abbey Jamie had visited, at Ardchattan. It was indeed more like a fortified strength, with gatehouse, curtain-walling and towers — as was perhaps necessary amongst the quarrelsome Kennedys. The mitred Abbot Mark was himself a Kennedy, but owed much to the King, who was apt to use this Abbey almost as a personal sanctuary. An elderly man, he had known Isabel almost from childhood — knew Jamie also, from his stays at Turnberry in the past. Secure in the King's favour, and in Holy Church's own strength, he was prepared to be helpful.

Presently, then, Jamie was saying his farewells and thanks to the princess, in an emotional scene, promising that he would be careful, that he would make every endeavour to return to see her again before too long, and assuring her of his faithful regard and undying gratitude. He was indeed very fond of her, and greatly admired the part she had played in this project. He left the copy of the Mar charter with her, to hand over to Red John when she left Turnberry, for onward transmission to Albany; and with a lay brother of the monastery as guide, slipped out of a postern gate in the rear curtain-wall, into the November late gloaming, a travelling friar once more.

His companion led him seawards again, north by west, over

an hour's walking by round-about ways, to the bay of Culzean, well north of the Turnberry area. Here, between the two Kennedy castles of Culzean and Dunure there was a little haven, where he was quietly installed in a barn and warehouse belonging to the Abbey. Groping about in the dark he made himself as comfortable as he could for the night, chewing at a cold leg of mutton and seeking to accustom his nostrils to the warring smells of oily wool bales, the tang of tanned hides and the sweet scent of innumerable barrels of cider apples, all awaiting shipment. His guide went to arrange with one of the boatmen who worked for the monastery for the fugitive to sail with him at first light up the Firth of Clyde to the island of Cumbrae, a score of miles. From there he ought to find no difficulty in taking further passage to Dumbarton.

So, in a few hours, clutching his robe around him against the chill of a grey November dawn, Jamie Douglas put to sea next morning in a heavy, slow, but seaworthy craft under a single great square sail and four long sweeps, on his way to what he was beginning to think of as home. It would be a long, weary and uncomfortable road, but with luck its dangers ought to be no more than those usually faced by any law-abiding traveller in winter. Without being in any way smug, he was satisfied. He had in his satchel what could give his friend what he wanted and at the same time outwit the Duke of Albany. He asked for no better than that — meantime.

VII

THE GREAT DAY was no more than a month later — for others besides Isobel of Mar had united to convince Alex Stewart that time was of the essence now and any further delay for the sake of appearances sheerest folly. Appearances were still important, admittedly, but delay formed no part in it all.

Considering that it was only two weeks since Jamie had arrived back in Badenoch, indeed, appearances were remarkably effective — especially as there had been problems. Bishop William of Moray had, most inconveniently, fallen ill; and since Alex felt that in the circumstances a bishop's attendance was imperative, he had had to go in person all the way to the Black Isle to convince Alexander of Ross to put in an appearance. Then Mariota de Athyn had been anything but helpful, and this had had an inhibiting effect on Mary — which in turn had unsettled Jamie. Mary was with him now, but it had all been rather difficult. Mariota, needless to say, was *not* present. Then the weather might well have been unkind. After all, December was scarcely the month for travel and outdoor festivity in the North; but in fact conditions remained dry, crisply cold and almost windless, with frosty nights.

Alex's party, large and colourful, the churchmen, Highland chiefs and Badenoch vassals at their picturesque finest, came to Kildrummy from the north-east, by Strathbogie and Rhynie, not risking the direct route through the Mounth passes and the Ladder Hills in mid-winter. Long before they reached the castle the crowds were to be seen, hundreds upon hundreds converging on the scene from all quarters. Outside the fortress great numbers were already assembled. Clearly the Countess Isobel had well carried out her share of the arrangements.

113

"There is to be no lack of witnesses, at least!" Mary observed. "A bishop, a choir, music, feasting also, no doubt. All it lacks is . . . decency!"

"You women are hard on each other," her husband said.

"Alex should know better, too. But men have little sense of fitness."

"It may be that our fitnesses differ, my dear."

Kildrummy Castle's grey walls were aglow with flags and banners, flapping from every tower and bastion. The blue and gold crosslets of Mar dominated, but the fess chequey on yellow of Stewart and the red heart of Douglas were well represented. The chapel bell was ringing out strongly. Heaps of wood and brush were piled up at intervals along the battlements, to be lit as beacons and bonfires. If one thing was evident, it was that there was no lack of enthusiasm for this day at the Mar end.

As the Stewart party drew near, Alex signed to his two trumpeters to sound. They blew a resounding fanfare — which they had been rehearsing for days, to Lochindorb's considerable affliction — and this echoed and re-echoed from the surrounding braesides. Cheering arose from the throng outside the castle, and continued as the newcomers rode up.

It was to be seen, now, that the castle drawbridge was up and the portcullis lowered, shutting off all entry.

They sat their horses amongst the crowd, waiting. Alex ordered the pipers with them to play, and these dismounted, to strut up and down before them, puffing lustily.

Then a clanking sounded from the castle gatehouse, and slowly the heavy iron grating of the portcullis was raised. When it was fully up, a different groaning and creaking succeeded, which was the drawbridge being lowered. Cheers rose from all around. Signing to the pipers to discontinue, Alex dismounted — followed by the Bishop of Ross, the Prior of Pluscarden, the chiefs of Mackintosh, Macpherson, MacGillivray and many another, including Jamie and Mary Douglas. The great banner of Badenoch was brought to flap above its lord.

When the drawbridge finally settled into its place with a thud, the great castle doors within the gatehouse pend were thrown open, and out paced a choir of singing boys chanting sweet music, high and clear. These divided to line both sides of the bridge, facing inwards. Then a single figure strode forth, the portly Chamberlain of Mar, holding his staff of office. This he raised high, and the singing stopped. There was silence save for the champing of horses' bits and the calling of curlews from the hillsides.

"My lords, chiefs, knights, gentles and all true men," the Chamberlain called. "Your duty and respect for the most noble and puissant Lady Isobel, Countess of Mar and of the Garioch, Lady of Mid-Mar, Cro-Mar, Brae-Mar, and March-Mar, Baroness of Strathdon, Strathdee, Strathhelvich and Crimond, whom God empower and support."

Alex, bonnet off, led the cheering.

As a single bugle-note shrilled, Isobel Douglas came walking slowly through the pend between the drum-towers, backed by a dense pack of Mar vassals. She was superbly gowned in black and silver, which well suited her mane of tawny hair, a-glitter with jewellery, her magnificent bosom notably bare for exposure to the December air. She had never looked more handsome, more vivid, or more sure of herself. Even Mary perforce admired. But she qualified her admiration.

"Does Alex know what he does, I wonder?" she murmured.

The Countess stepped out on to the drawbridge timbers, and there halted. Unspeaking, she held out her hand, open, towards the waiting throng.

Alex Stewart strode forward then, on to the bridge, seeming almost to have to restrain himself from running, flinging aside his tartan plaid. He was seen to be dressed in Lowland garb, at his finest, in velvet and cloth-of-gold. He carried in his hand a small velvet satchel.

Everywhere people watched in silence. Both supporting parties moved slowly up behind the principals, but not so close as to block the view for others.

Alex came up to the Countess, and bowed low. She inclined her head.

He cleared his throat. "Isobel, Countess of Mar," he said loudly, "I hereby hand back into your own keeping the keys of this your castle of Kildrummy." He withdrew the great iron keys from his satchel, and held them out. "I do so before all, of my free will and in good heart, for you to dispose of as you will. This in restitution for my taking them, and it, for what seemed to me good reason, and in token of full submission and goodwill."

Reaching out she took the keys from him. "I accept these keys and your goodwill, my lord of Badenoch," she said slowly, clearly. "I hold them again, as wholly mine, in token. And . . .

115

I hereby hand them back into your hand, also in token. That I hereby choose and select you, Alexander Stewart, to be my lord and wedded husband from this day forth, keeper of my body as of my castles and lands. In token also that when presently God has joined us together in holy wedlock, I freely and heartily bestow upon you, Alexander Stewart, the styles, title and dignity of Earl of Mar and the Garioch, as is my undoubted right."

Taking the keys again, he retained her hand and raised it to his lips.

It was the signal. Loud and long the cheers rang out — and if some of the Mar vassals ranked behind the Countess seemed slightly less enthusiastic than the crowd outside and the party which had come from Badenoch, it was barely enough to be noticeable. Alex moved to her side, and together they faced the company smiling and bowing, before turning and doing the same towards those behind.

"It was decently done, at least," Jamie said. "You will not deny that?"

"Those Mar-men are less impressed than you, I think!" his wife commented. "Alex may have his hands full — with them, *as* with her!"

"If he can master her, she will master *them*, I wager!"

The choristers had, at a sign from Isobel of Mar, struck up their chanting once more, and turning, began to pace back whence they had come, the crowd behind the Countess squeezing back on either side to allow them passage through the pend again. After them the two principals walked slowly, arm-in-arm, acknowledging the salutations of those they passed, whilst the Bishop of Ross led forward after them the company assembled outside. There was some jostling for position with the Mar people as they streamed into the courtyard.

The singers progressed across the wide cobbled triangular area, making for the chapel on the east side, next to the great circular Warden's Tower. At the narrow chapel doorway there was some hold-up, but eventually most of the company managed to get inside. Here, after more jockeying for precedence, the clerics pushed forward to the vestry, the principal guests and witnesses struggled and elbowed their way to the front, near to the chancel steps, where the Countess and Alex stood waiting, facing the altar, and the choir, at each side, continued to chant a little breathlessly.

116

Isobel of Mar looked around her in a sort of sardonic amusement, Alex appearing strained.

The Bishop of Ross, gorgeous robes over his travelling clothes, supported by the Abbot of Monymusk, a Mar foundation, and the Prior of Pluscarden, the castle chaplain and other clergy behind, came out, to process up to the altar. The stir and chatter died away, as did the singing.

There followed quite the briefest and simplest marriage ceremony Jamie for one had ever attended, despite its notable significance and the lofty rank of the participants. The Bishop gave the impression of scarcely approving of the entire proceedings, and being anxious to get his part over as quickly as possible. Undoubtedly Alex had had to bring strong pressure to bear to obtain his presence at all. There were no attendants on bride or groom, nothing other than the bare essentials of the exhortation, the vows, the ring, the pronunciation of man and wife and the benediction. Indeed, it seemed as though the main import of the proceedings was what happened after, when the woman turned away, stepped over to a bench, and picked up from it in both hands what was obviously a very heavy object. This, gleaming subduedly in the dim religious light from the candles and the three narrow lancet windows, proved to be a sword-belt of solid gold links, enhanced with coloured enamel heraldic medallions of Mar and its constituent lordships and baronies. This earl's belt she brought to raise, with some little effort, and placed over Alex's head and one shoulder.

"My lord Earl of Mar!" she announced firm-voiced.

At the stir, with this the signal, Jamie Douglas stepped forward to mount the chancel-steps, drawing from his doublet the folded paper which he had carried across half Scotland. With a bow he handed it to the Countess.

"This charter," she called, opening it up, "embodies the bestowal of my earldom on this my lawful wedded husband, to descend in due course to whatever child may be begotten between his body and mine. It is countersigned by His Grace, Robert, King of Scots, as required by the law of this realm, and duly witnessed. Let none seek to dispute it." She handed this to Alex also.

Folk could scarcely cheer before a bishop in church, but there was a continuing murmur. Jamie took the Countess's fingers to raise to his lips, then stepped over to shake Alex's hand.

"My lord Earl!" he said.

117

His friend threw an arm round his shoulder, wordless but eloquent.

At their backs the Bishop cleared his throat loudly, and the trio moved aside to allow the tall, stern-faced prelate to lead the clergy back to the vestry.

The congregation threw off its reserve and surged forward.

Later, in the great hall, after the feasting but before the entertainment began and whilst most of the guests were sufficiently sober to understand him, Alex made his speech.

"My lords, ladies and friends all — hear me for a little," he said. "As you know, there has not been an Earl of Mar for over twenty-five years, to the realm's loss. It is my wife's desire, as it is my own, to have her ancient heritage, the premier earldom of this kingdom, play once again its due and proper part in the affairs of Scotland, here in the North in especial. For too long there has been a lack of due authority here — save of course in matters spiritual. There is at present no Justiciar and Lieutenant. The reason for my own resignation is known to all, and I still believe it to have been the correct course. Who the Governor may appoint we know not — nor whether he will be accepted here, as others have not. John Dunbar, Earl of Moray, seldom shows his face north of the Highland Line. The Earl of Ross is dead, leaving only a child countess of whom the Governor has the wardship. The earldom of Buchan, since my father's death, is vacant and vested in the Crown. The earldom of Angus is in Lowland hands, and its lord a captive in England, as is Moray. There are Earls of Sutherland and Caithness. But Caithness is a Norseman, looking to that king as his liege; and Sutherland, although married to my own sister, never looks south of the Great Glen. The Lord of the Isles is a high-born brigand who raids and robs our land. There is none, then, not one, to bear the King's rule and governance in this great part of the realm, twice as large as all the Lowlands put together. Can any say otherwise?"

None spoke.

"As a consequence," he went on, "there is lawlessness, feuding, rapine, murder. It is widespread. Even amongst my own family, as you know, to my sorrow. This must not be allowed to continue. I speak now to tell you all, that this my wife's creation of myself as Earl of Mar, although an honour, is not only that. An earl of Scotland has many powers that other lords have not, and that a countess, although they belong to her position,

118

cannot wield. Those of Mar will now be wielded, to her satisfaction and mine, to the best of my ability. In the interests of order, justice and the weal of this land. This I swear to you all. Not all will trust me so far, but it is my aim to make them do so before I am finished. This I would have you to know."

He paused and looked round them all. It was serious talking for a wedding-feast speech. None of the guests commented; but neither was there any of the raillery common on such occasions. The Countess toyed with the silver loving-cup which she was sharing with him.

"If you will bear with me, in all this there is one duty which I wish to declare before I sit down," he went on. "It is to acknowledge the debt my wife and I owe to our good and valued friend Sir James Douglas of Aberdour, here present, most unjustly outlawed by the present Governor, but not with the knowledge of the King's Grace. Without Sir James's notable aid, the risks he has taken and his great trouble, this bestowal of the earldom could not have been ratified and so made fully lawful. He it was who went to the King, supposedly outlaw as he is, explained all to His Grace, and with the help of the Princess Isabel, former Countess of Douglas, my good lady's brother's widow, gained the royal endorsement and signature. For this great service it is my hope that one day not only myself but all Scotland will recognise its debt. To spare Sir James further embarrassment — for he is a most modest man — I will say no more. I thank you all for hearing me, for honouring our marriage with your presence, and for the good wishes all have showered upon us."

He sat down, to relieved applause.

"Isobel Douglas did not like that last," Mary murmured to her husband. "I was watching her. I swear that she did not know that he would say it. I am beginning to have hopes for Alex Stewart, after all!"

Jamie was scowling. "He should *not* have said it."

"He should indeed! He could do no less. But *she* does not think so. She does not love you, Jamie, I vow!"

"As to that, I care not. He it is I care about, not her."

"But you will have to care about her, my dear, if you are going to continue close to Alex now. Since God and this bishop have joined them as one! For she is a clever and determined woman — and I swear that her ambitions for the earldom of Mar are other than his. She seeks to use him for her purposes — and he

119

seeks to use her earldom. It will be interesting to see who wins."

"He much loves her, see you — and she him, surely. It need not work out so ill."

"You are a bairn yet, Jamie! As is Alex. What know you of strong and scheming women?"

"Plenty!" he declared, with apparent heartfelt conviction. "And learning more every day that I am married to one Mary Stewart!"

"Then I will have to take your education further in hand, husband! For Scotland's sake, if we are to believe Alexander, Earl of Mar!"

PART TWO

VIII

FOR THE REMAINDER of the winter Jamie Douglas led a quiet, peaceful and relatively normal life — and was glad indeed to do so. He was far from idle, by any means, for with Alex now most of the time at Kildrummy and elsewhere in Mar, he was acting almost as his deputy at Lochindorb — the other sons of the house being conspicuous by their absence. The Lady Mariota seemed well enough content with this arrangement. When Alex made visits to his home, she received him warmly, but never referred to his marriage, his wife or his new status, nor asked about his doings at Kildrummy. Mary was delighted to have Jamie living a normal husbandly life with her and the children, and prayed that it might long continue — without a great deal of conviction nevertheless. The man himself might not have gone quite so far as that.

Once or twice he went to Kildrummy himself; but in winter with the high passes and bridgeless rivers to cross, it was a three-day journey, detouring by the coastal plain. He never found himself really welcomed by the Countess, however happy Alex was to see him. Nevertheless, he could not honestly claim to sense anything wrong or strained in the atmosphere there, with Alex active in the role he had set himself, the Countess reasonably amenable in all matters, and no visible signs of Mary's feared clash of interests. The new Earl was in process of getting on good terms with the Mar vassals, seeking to dissolve any suspicions they might have of him as a mere adventurer — for although they now owed him full feudal duty, their goodwill and positive support could make all the difference to his proposed programme. And it was a vast undertaking, for the Mar territories and sphere of influence covered something not far short of sixteen hundred square miles, only half of that Highland country.

123

That programme became real and significant, for Jamie at least, in early April, with spring at last beginning to loosen winter's grip on the Highlands. On a day of sunshine and showers, with the snows left only on the mountain-tops and gleaming ice-cornices left as rims to every corrie, Alex arrived at Lochindorb, this time with a fine company of Mar lairds, suitable for an earl's 'tail'. He had news, relayed to him by his ever-well-informed churchmen friends.

"There is to be a Council called for the Feast of St. Mark, at Linlithgow," he announced, "not a Privy Council but a *General* Council. Not a parliament. Why my Uncle Robert has called such is not clear but he has. I have not been summoned, I need not say — but as Earl I am entitled to attend. I *shall* attend — and I want you to come with me."

"Me? Put my head into that noose, Alex? Have you mislaid your lordly wits?"

"Not so. For one of the matters I wish to raise at that Council is to have your outlawry lifted."

"But . . . what hope is there of that? The Council, whatever sort, will be packed with Albany's men, you may be sure. You will achieve nothing, but much endanger yourself. Albany could not conceive of anything better, I swear!"

"Be not so sure, man. You do not know, but there is more news. Your chief, the Earl of Douglas, is released and will be there, for sure. King Henry has allowed him to return to Scotland temporarily, in exchange for three other Douglases, whom he will hold hostage until the Earl returns — one, your friend Sir William of Drumlanrig. The Earl will speak for you."

"Why should he? I left him on Homildon Hill likewise, you will recollect!"

"He will know well enough whose fault was all that sorry business. And that you, in fact, came out of it with credit, Jamie — you alone. He is a strange, moody man, but honest, I think. He will bear you no grudge, I wager. And if he attends this Council, other Douglases will do so, you may be sure. Your father — have you heard how is his health?"

"Not for long. But his days for attending Council meetings are past, I fear!"

"Dalkeith must be represented on the Council, surely? The second house of the Douglas clan."

"My half-brother James is now on the Privy Council, I am told."

"Better still. He will speak for you. Other Douglases will be entitled to be there. Angus is still prisoner in England — sick, they say. But there are many others . . ."

"Not sufficient to out-vote the Governor's men."

"Not out-vote, perhaps. But sufficient to make my Uncle Robert change his mind, it may be. See you, I have thought well on this, Jamie. Apart from the Governor's minions, there are some entitled to sit on the Privy Council by right — earls, certain lords and officers of state, and, of course, the churchmen. This is not a Privy but a General Council, so it applies even more to that. Many have ceased to attend, out of disgust with Albany — David Lindsay, Earl of Crawford; Sir Thomas Hay, the Constable; the Lord Maxwell; Scrymgeour the Standard-Bearer; Montgomerie, Lord of Eaglesham, your old associate; Ramsay of Bamff — and others. Wardlaw, the Primate, in particular. I shall write to certain of these. Send secret and fast messengers. Urge their attendance, even though like myself, not summoned. Declaring the opportunity to strike a blow for the good of the realm. Prove to Robert Stewart that he has not yet *all* in his pocket! We might get your outlawry lifted, amongst other matters. Do you not see it?"

"I see that you might well achieve something, yes, Alex. I see that much might be possible. But . . . *I* need not be there, for that."

"I would wish you to be there, Jamie. To guide and advise me. You know these Lowland lords a deal better than do I. Moreover, the Douglases might well make a better showing with you present than with you absent. You must be there to refute any charges against you. I cannot swear that you will be safe from Albany's spleen, any more than I will be myself. But if *I* am safe — and I intend to safeguard myself — then you will be. That I *can* promise you. Will you come with me, Jamie?"

The other spread his hands. "I do not see how I can refuse," he said.

*   *   *

So, ten days later a gallant and sizeable party of about a hundred and fifty rode jingling southwards down through Atholl, a notably Lowland-seeming company for those surroundings, for Alex was concerned that no prejudice should attach to his entourage in the South on the grounds that they were nothing more than a set of wild Hielandmen, always a hazard. So no

125

clan chiefs were included, vassals of the low country of Mar, Badenoch and Braemoray were there in strength, and the armed escort likewise was drawn from such territories. Not a yard of tartan was to be seen in the entire contingent.

That is, until at Dunkeld in South Atholl they found another party awaiting them. And of these some did wear the tartan. Jamie was much surprised to discover the leader of this group to be none other than John Stewart, Lord of Coull and Onele — whom he had never thought would fit into Alex's plans, nor would wish to do so. But he was, of course, an important vassal of Mar, and entitled to be included in any of the earldom's corporate activities, as also to attend the General Council. Indeed it transpired that he had been *invited* to attend — which was more than his new Earl could say. He appeared to bear no least grudge over being outmanoeuvred concerning Isobel of Mar, and greeted Alex, and Jamie likewise, with cheerful good-will. It was difficult to remain suspicious of so amiable and friendly a character, although they could not but recognise that he was no fool — and that he was Albany's son, even though reputedly not on the best of terms with his father. Jamie, by nature more suspiciously-minded than his friend, determined to keep an eye on him. Jamie himself had been a little doubtful about appearing openly, in the South, with this fine company, foregoing the secrecy of his recent travels. But Alex convinced him that he was safe, meantime, from Albany's attentions, with the Douglases in a strong position and the Earl Archibald able to declare the truth about Homildon, moreover with Alex's own and Brave John's influence in his favour.

Brave John of Coull seemed in excellent spirits altogether, addressing Alex as 'my lord Earl' with no evident edge or tartness to his voice, as they trotted on their way. There was a distinct family likeness between these two, brothers' sons as they were, and both frequently reminding Jamie at least, in feature and gesture, of the son of still another brother, the murdered Prince David. The Stewarts were, in so many ways, an extraordinary family.

John was, in fact, able to tell them much more about this Convention or General Council of his father's than Alex had learned from the churchmen. Its primary object was to renew the Governor's mandate for another period, the present three-year term of office expiring within months. This should really have been done by a parliament, but that would entail the King's calling and presence, and Albany much preferred to have an assembly of his own calling, the King's alleged agreement having been obtained beforehand. In announcing this, John Stewart did not attempt to make it sound like anything other than a mere device of his father's. There was other business to conduct, especially relations with England — where there appeared to be interesting developments; matters of taxation and finance, with the Treasury empty; and sundry new appointments to be made, notably that of Justiciar and Lieutenant of the North.

"Do you yourself expect to be so appointed, Cousin?" Alex asked calmly.

"I have no wish to be so, my lord. I would prefer to go soldiering."

"Soldiering . . . ? Where, man?"

"There is talk that there will be work for sharp swords in England, before long. I would find that more to my taste than holding courts of law! So, if you seek reappointment to the position, Cousin, I will not oppose you. Indeed, I will support you."

Alex eyed him thoughtfully. "I have no such intention," he said. "But . . . I thank you."

At Perth they put up at the same Blackfriars monastery where eight years before Alex had come with the Clan Chattan contingent for the great contest on the North Inch. He had been afraid of apprehension then, by the Governor, and here he was now, an earl of Scotland, still on the alert for the same interference. They had no reason to believe that Albany would have learned of their coming, for though well served by spies, the Highland North was largely outwith his sphere of influence. But learn he must, sooner or later, and it behoved the Mar party to go warily.

Alex was in something of a quandary, however. They had made rather better time so far than he had allowed for, with the weather kind, and there were still two days to pass before the Council — and they could reach Linlithgow from Perth in one day's fairly hard riding. They could dawdle, of course — but the longer they took on the road, the more likely Albany was to hear of their coming, and possibly to make his own arrangements to counter any impact they might effect. The same applied to waiting for a day at Perth. Jamie made a suggestion. The keeper of the royal castle of Linlithgow was James Douglas of Strabrock, a distant kinsman of his father's. Strabrock lay in the Almond valley of West Lothian only some six miles from Linlithgow, but with a ridge of the low Riccarton Hills between, and little coming and going from one vale to the other. They might rest hidden and secure at Strabrock for two nights at least, for it was on no major route to Linlithgow; and from there descend upon the Council unannounced. This seemed good to all — although glances were turned in the direction of Brave John. That young man declared, however, that this programme would suit him very well, for he had no desire to meet his father before the public sessions in case he sought to persuade him to certain courses he had no liking for — in especial to agree to go to England as a hostage for the temporary return of his half-brother, Murdoch, Earl of Fife, as was being suggested. If the Earl of Douglas had been allowed to come home under these exchange conditions, Albany wanted his heir back also. And he, John, had no wish to act surety for a half-brother whom he cordially disliked.

So, next day, they rode on southwards, by Forteviot and the skirts of the Ochils and Sheriffmuir, to cross the Forth at Stirling. They began to see other groups and parties riding in the same direction now, but carefully kept to themselves, prudently eschewing all banners and displays of identity and heraldry, unrecognised they hoped. In late afternoon they emerged from the constrictions of the vast forested areas of the Tor Wood into the Falkirk brae country where the great Wallace had been defeated, with the low green hills of West Lothian ahead of them. Keeping well to the south of the direct route to Linlithgow, by the Roman Wall and the Avon valley, they crossed the skirts of the Slamannan moors and turned eastwards through quiet cattle-pastured hills, avoiding the Hospitallers' Preceptory of Torphichen heedfully, and the sleepy village of Ecclesmachan, to come down into the valley of the Brocks' Burn, tributary of Almond, with the sinking sun at their backs.

Strabrock Castle crowned a knoll in the midst of this quiet vale, no very large establishment to receive some two hundred men. The laird thereof was not at home, having gone to Linlithgow to prepare all for the great gathering; but the visitors were well received by his lady, who was another Douglas, from Long-niddry in East Lothian, and who had once been a maid-in-waiting to the Lady Isabel when she was Countess of Douglas, and in consequence was an old colleague of Jamie's. A comely, uncomplicated creature now inclining to stoutness, she was probably more pleased to see them than her husband would have been, and did not appear to find the unannounced entertainment of some two hundred men for a couple of nights any trial, especially when two of them were as personable and good-looking as the Earl of Mar and the Lord of Coull and Onele. The visitors were concerned to pay their way, of course, forage for hundreds of horses alone amounting to a major item.

The lady of Strabrock was able to give them quite a lot of useful information — in especial the news that the King himself was to attend this Council; indeed he was already present at Linlithgow Castle. This had been a wholly unexpected development, certainly not suggested by the Governor. The monarch had arrived unheralded two days before, from Turnberry, and her husband had had to hurry off to receive him. It was thought that he had been prevailed upon to do this by Bishop Wardlaw, the Primate, who was now with him, for purposes as yet not clear — but presumably not in the Governor's favour. Since almost the only thing which was known to stir the sovereign these days was the welfare of his son James, who was in the Bishop's care, it might be assumed that something concerning the prince was involved. Also there were rumours that the Mammet's future was to be under discussion, and the King was known to have an interest there also.

All this much intrigued the visitors, naturally, Jamie especially. He wondered whether his secret journey to Turnberry had had anything to do with it. The King's presence at the Council would undoubtedly make a major difference, whatever the reasons. It looked as though Alex was not the only one seeking to counter the Duke of Albany — which was hopeful.

The lady's further tidings revealed that the Earl of Douglas was already in the vicinity, with a large train, lodging at his house of Abercorn, east of Linlithgow a few miles, on the firth coast.

The following evening, wrapped in their cloaks, Alex and Jamie rode alone over the shadowy braes the four miles northwards by Niddry and Duntarvie to the wooded shore at Abercorn. Here was quite a large castle, beside an ancient monastery, actually the seat of Douglas's oafish brother, Sir James the Gross. The place, castle and friary, was astir with Douglas men-at-arms, encamped around; but Jamie was well known to many of these, and they had no difficulty in obtaining access to the castle itself — from which the sound of hearty, bellowed singing emanated.

129

Disclaiming the need for any escort or introduction, Jamie led Alex up the turnpike stair to the great hall on the first floor, whence came the noise. Squeezing through the pack of servitors watching at the doorway screens, the first person he saw was his own brother Sir James, pewter tankard in hand, standing on top of the dais-table, bawling out an explicit if anatomically unlikely version of a rousing drinking-song, beating time with the slopping tankard and with his other arm around a half-naked serving-wench giggling beside him, while the company roared encouragement and chorus. James had always fancied himself as a vocalist. The next Jamie perceived was his other legitimate half-brother, Will, supporting or being supported by Sir Archie Douglas of Cavers, making for this same doorway, no doubt intent on the relief of overtaxed bladders, but singing as they lurched.

"Think you we will appear spectres at the feast?" Alex murmured. "Your Douglases would seem to be warding off despondency!"

"Drowning the memory of Homildon, perhaps . . .!"

Will recognised Jamie, raised a pointing if unsteady hand, and then emitted a high-pitched yell and came plunging forward to throw his arms round and embrace his brother, all but upending Sir Archie in the process. Words were unhearable but not really necessary.

Archie of Cavers thought otherwise. He turned to shout at the carolling Sir James — who continued to bellow lustily. Further cries proving equally unavailing, he gained his ends by the simple expedient of grabbing a beaker of ale from the nearest drinker and, stepping across, tossed the contents over singer and lady both. Douglas Younger of Dalkeith spluttered to an abrupt close, his partner screamed, and quiet of a sort was achieved.

"Look who is here!" Cavers cried into the momentary lull. "Jamie! Jamie of Aberdour! Outlaw Jamie!"

The roar from the company at that shook the building, frightening had it not been for the grinning expressions of what was presumably goodwill and welcome on all faces. Jamie had been more than a little doubtful as to what the majority of the Douglases thought of him, after Homildon; but as the noise and acclaim went on and on, and men surged forward to thump his back and shoulders, to pat and paw him, there could be no further question. He was no pariah amongst his own clan. Alex Stewart, Earl of Mar, held back, scarcely noticed.

130

At length, as the racket continued, Jamie himself made a move. Taking Alex's arm, he pushed bodily forward through the pressing throng, to the dais-table, where his brother James, dripping ale, jumped down to enfold him with a wet hug, leaving the forlorn female neglected on the table-top to gather her clothing around her and clamber down as best she could, forgotten by all. But Jamie, grinning at his brother, pushed him aside and struggled on, to the front of the table, still drawing his friend after him. There, in the centre, was the Earl of Douglas and Lord of Galloway, on his feet now, with his brother James the Gross and sundry other Douglas lords. Both Jamie and the Earl held up their hands for quiet, and so stood, looking at each other, while slowly the shouting died away.

It was a dramatic moment. Last time these two had seen each other it had been on a blood-soaked Northumbrian hillside, with dead and dying all around, and the Earl ordering Jamie scornfully to remain behind and look after the horses and baggage since he disapproved so strongly of the attack to be made against the massed English archers, when the flower of Scotland had gone down in useless bloody ruin and complete disaster, never winning near enough to the enemy for a blow to be struck. The fact that the Earl had been wrong and Jamie right, and that since then his chief had gathered the soubriquet of The Tyneman, the Loser, was by no means calculated to ensure harmonious relations now, especially as the Earl was a notably moody and awkward man at the best of times.

As he looked, Jamie was shocked at the change in the appearance of his chief. He had fallen with five English arrows projecting from his person at Homildon, one from his left eye-socket; and then had been wounded again at the Battle of Shrewsbury ten months later. Not only did he now lack an eye, but his face was twisted to that side, his right shoulder drooped and he held himself with a curious stiff forward stance. Never a good-looking man, stocky and somewhat hulking, now he was unprepossessing indeed, almost deformed.

He leaned across the littered table at length, however, as the noise died away, and held out his hand.

"Jamie!" he said — the one word, but sufficient.

With a gulp of relief and emotion, the other gripped that hand strongly. "My lord," he said thickly. "This is . . . good."

"Yes. It has been long. A bad business."

"Bad, yes." Neither of them effusive men, they nodded at each

131

other. Then Jamie recollected his duty. "Here, my lord — here is my lord Earl of Mar and the Garioch, whom it is my honour to present to you." He turned. "My lord — the Earl of Douglas and Lord of Galloway."

The two earls eyed each other, the one so darkly ugly, the other so fairly handsome.

"Alex Stewart!" the Douglas said. "I have heard tell of you."

"No doubt, my lord. But it may not all have been true!" That was said with a smile which only the sternest could have resisted.

The other said nothing, however.

"My lord of Mar is my very good friend," Jamie observed, significantly.

"Ah. Then he must be my friend also."

Alex bowed.

There was a pause as all men watched and listened — a pause on which so much depended. Then Douglas lifted one shoulder in an awkward movement, and gestured with his hand.

"Come you round here, my lord. And you, Jamie. Sit one on either side of me, and let us have your crack. We have much to hear, and tell, I wager. Come, you."

The crowded hall breathed freely again, and men went back to their seats.

There was an uneasy pause at the dais-table — at least between the Earl of Douglas and James the Gross and the new arrivals, although James and Will Douglas of Dalkeith kept up a cheerful chatter. At length Jamie himself said what had to be said.

"My lord — we disagreed when last we were together. I am sorry for that. It was a bad business, in every way. Unhappy."

"The unhappier for my folly," the other jerked. "Many good men died for it, many suffered."

Jamie said nothing — for it was no less than the truth.

"I have had much opportunity to regret my folly," the Earl went on, heavily. "Had I heeded you, Jamie, all might have been otherwise. I listened to other men, who lacked your wits and experience. And all paid the price. You also, it seems."

"The price I paid, am still paying, was scarce your fault, my lord. It was spleen, engendered long before. Homildon but provided the opportunity to display it. The Earl Murdoch was a prisoner and *I* was not! I bolted, where he fell fighting. As simple as that. So I am outlaw, a traitor . . ."

132

"Worse folly than even my own, by God!"

"Not folly, my lord — but worse, yes," Alex interposed, quietly. "Malice, hatred, and ill governance. Which is in part why I am here."

Warily the Douglas turned to look at him.

"At tomorrow's Council, I shall seek to have this shameful outlawry lifted. Can I rely on your lordship's support?"

The other stared ahead of him for a long moment. "Yes," he said, at last.

Jamie cleared his throat. "I thank you, my lord."

"Do not thank me. I could scarce do other. But ... there is little hope, I think, that we shall prevail. Robert Stewart is too strong."

"Less strong than he seems," Alex contended. "Like lesser men, he has to pay for his misdeeds, in unpopularity. Few men love the Governor. Many *fear* him, yes. You call him strong. But is he so? Determined, yes. Cunning, yes. Without scruple, yes. But strength, now, is something different."

"Strength in a ruler, sir, depends on how many swords and lances he can deploy. And on how many votes he can command in council and parliament."

"Agreed. But by those very tokens my Uncle Robert lacks strength, in fact. He relies for both on the goodwill or fear of others. That goodwill he lacks. The fear depends on his ability to wield armed strength. Armed strength of his own he lacks. He needs others' strength. Notably that of the house of Douglas!"

There was no visible reaction to that. Jamie shifted on his seat uneasily. Along the dais-table men listened, all ears.

"The Douglas power Albany requires," Alex went on, almost conversationally. "Lacking it, he is hamstrung in much that he would do — for it is the greatest power in this realm. With it *against* him, he is finished."

Douglas drew a deep breath. "Are you, sir, suggesting that I throw the power of my house against the realm's lawful Governor?"

"I am suggesting, my lord, that you consider well where that Governor is leading the realm, and use your power to control and better it — as is surely the simple duty of any leal subject of the King, with any power. Especially the earls of Scotland. That is the other reason why I am here tonight. Being bastard, I could not inherit my father's earldom of Buchan. It is now in Albany's hands. As are the earldoms of Menteith, Fife, Carrick,

Strathearn and Ross. Moray is a prisoner in England. Angus also."

"Angus is dead," Douglas said. "He died of the plague, a captive, some six weeks past."

"Dear God! George Douglas dead!"

"Aye — more of the price of my folly. And leaving only an infant son, a bairn of four."

"Worse and worse, then. For, I swear, Albany will not be long in seeking the wardship of that bairn also — and so controlling yet another of the earldoms. After all, Angus's countess is the King's daughter, as is yours, Albany's niece. You are still prisoner on parole — to return to England in due course, I understand? He will claim wardship for the Crown — which means himself."

"M'mm."

"Which leaves how many independent earldoms? Lennox's daughter is married to the Earl Murdoch, and he will do what Albany says. Dunbar and March are gone over to the English. Sutherland and Caithness do not count, as Norsemen. What are we left with? Crawford, the new earldom — Albany's goodbrother. And Mar and Douglas! That is all. You will perceive, then, why I have made it my business to become Earl of Mar — with my lady's kind goodwill? For Mar was intended for John Stewart of Coull, Albany's other son."

"Lord — young John? He is scarce of age . . . ?"

"He reached majority less than a year past. Which makes the death, then, of Malcolm Drummond . . . interesting!"

"By the Powers!" Douglas turned to stare at the other with his one eye. "You are saying . . . ?"

"I am saying that *I* had naught to do with Drummond's death. And that the Governor is in process of gathering all the realm's earldoms into his own grasp and control. So that, in turn, he can control the Privy Council, by the earls' votes, and parliament or convention by the earls' vassals' votes. Do you not see it? The strategy? And see where stands Douglas!"

There was a long pause.

Jamie took a hand. "My lord — after the Cocklaws ploy, you and Hotspur Percy expected Albany to join you against Henry, did you not? Before Shrewsbury?"

"Aye. But he was delayed. Hotspur could not wait longer. I sought to hold him back awhile, to wait longer. But Henry struck . . ."

"Albany was not delayed — or not save by his own will. He took three weeks to march the fifty miles to Cocklaws! Roundabout. And on the way — if you could call it on the way — he sat down and besieged Innerwick Castle, near to Dunbar. *Your* Dunbar — since you were controlling that earldom. Your Innerwick. Why, I have not discovered. But be sure that there was gain for Albany in it. But not for you. Or Hotspur! Can you still trust and support the Governor, my lord?"

The Earl of Douglas's fists were clenched, knuckles white.

"I am assured that my Uncle Robert has been seeking to move heaven and hell both to gain his son Murdoch's release from England," Alex mentioned. "I have not heard of any such move on your behalf, my lord — although you are Chief Warden of the Marches, commander of the realm's forces and greatest noble of the kingdom. This parole and exchange of hostages was not his doing, I think?"

"No." Abruptly, Douglas thrust back his chair and rose, a little unsteadily, a hand up to his brow. "Enough!" he jerked. "I must think. I, I seek your pardon. I fear I have drunk overmuch wine. I am not . . . the man I was. I need to think on these matters, when my head is clearer. Before tomorrow's Council. That arrow in my head . . . I, I bid you a good night my lords . . ."

In some discomfort the company watched him leave the hall.

"You think that we went too hard at it?" Alex murmured to his friend. "Overplayed our hand?"

Jamie shrugged. "Who knows? He was ever a strange man . . ."

They left soon afterwards, despite Jamie's brothers' pleas to stay, and picked their way back through the April gloaming to Strabrock.

IX

THE GREAT CHURCH of St. Michaels, Linlithgow, which shared the hillock above the loch with the royal castle, was full to overflowing, at least, as it were, at its perimeters, although the central parts were less so, and the chancel all but empty. The nave was reserved for the commissioners, that is those attending the Council with right to vote, and there was a decent sufficiency of space for these. But the transepts and side-chapels, the aisles, the embrasures of the tall windows and the clerestory galleries were packed with onlookers, churchmen, townsfolk of the royal burgh, representatives of other burghs and communities, knights, officers and lairds not entitled to be commissioners, sons, kinsmen and senior supporters of the lords and magnates present. Jamie Douglas was skied up in the last clerestory window-embrasure on the south side before the crossing, which afforded him an excellent view of the proceedings, but, with his back to the noonday light, did not make his identity too obvious. His brother Will was at his side, James being down amongst the lords.

All now awaited the arrival of the principals, amidst much noise and stir, with the clergy in St. Katherine's Chapel, the south transept, frowning disapproval. Already in the choir were the bishops, five of them, on one side, and the earls on the other, only three with Lennox sick — Douglas, Crawford and Mar. Behind the bishops were eight mitred abbots, entitled to vote in parliament, and behind the earls sundry officers of state. Below the chancel steps forms had been brought to seat the lords, at the front, twenty-one of them, of whom no fewer than seven were Douglases. The rest of the commissioners could stand behind, numbering perhaps fifty. Men-at-arms of the royal guard stood likewise, in strength.

136

As they waited, Jamie weighed up chances and probabilities. Without being actually optimistic — something he tried always to suppress — they were better considerably than he had feared when he left Badenoch. As it transpired, Albany almost certainly would be handicapped by the King's presence, whatever the reasons for his coming. He would be *there*, representing higher authority than the Governor's. It might as well have been a proper parliament, after all — although that would have entailed a larger attendance, all who had the right to attend being sent summonses and given the stipulated forty days notice. As it was, unsummoned folk were here, including Alex and his Mar vassals; but the Governor would be in a quandary regarding challenging every voter, when such could claim that they *should* have been summoned, by right, and had been deliberately excluded. Permitting an audience of non-voters could also be deleterious to the Governor's interests; yet the public were entitled to watch at a parliament, and presumably at a Council General — although not at a Privy Council, of course. Albany must have considered this, to be sure. He could have tried to squeeze all the commissioners into the great hall of the royal castle, and so left no room for onlookers, but it would have been a tight fit. It was all very much in the balance — which at least was an advance on what had seemed probable. So much might depend on the attitude of the Earl of Douglas. So many would take a lead from him . . .

His assessings were interrupted by a herald of the Lyon Court coming out, with two royal trumpeters, who sounded a short fanfare. Two splendidly robed prelates paced in from the vestry, Bishop Wardlaw of St. Andrews, the Primate, a stocky, grey-haired, quietly authoritative man, nephew of the late Cardinal; and Gilbert Greenlaw, Bishop of Aberdeen, the Chancellor, tall, pale, brisk and competent, but coldly so, a creature of Albany's. He went to his place at the end of the table placed between the high altar and the choir-steps, already spread with papers. Wardlaw moved over to a stall set in front of the row of bishops.

There was another and longer fanfare, which set the hammer-beam roof quivering, and all who sat rose to their feet. The Lyon King of Arms and the Albany Herald strode in. Then Sir James Scrymgeour, the Standard-Bearer, now bearing the Mace, which he laid on the table. Then there was something of a wait, before two very much less resplendent figures emerged from the vestry,

137

the hobbling, limping, stooping monarch leaning on the stiff arm of his brother the Governor.

"God save the King!" Lyon declared loudly. "God save the King's Grace!"

The cry was taken up with vigour throughout the church.

The monarch never dressed regally, and looked today like a distinctly seedy brother of a mendicant order. Albany, only a year younger but looking more so by a dozen years, did not go in for sartorial display either; but he was richly clad in black velvet with white lace, a spare, lean, upright man of a rigid dignity, good-looking in a tight-lipped way unusual amongst the Stewarts, with a self-contained, ageless quality to him, that belied his sixty-six years. He kept his head high, where the King's was sunk, and stalked just sufficiently far away from his brother to indicate how distasteful he found such contact with debility and weakness. Neither acknowledged the dutiful acclaim of the assembled company.

Leading the monarch to his throne-like seat in front of the earls, the Duke of Albany inclined his head briefly, stared blankly from almost colourless eyes at Alex Stewart behind the King, moved over to his own chair behind the central table, and sat down. Without pause, or even looking at the Chancellor, he raised a hand and flicked a finger. He was a man to waste neither time nor words.

As Bishop Greenlaw bowed, all others who had seats sat down.

"Your Grace," he intoned, towards the King, "my lord Governor," he bowed again, "my lords spiritual and temporal, and all fellow-subjects of his royal Grace, as Chancellor of this realm I declare that this Council General of the Estates of Parliament is now in due and proper session. My lord Bishop of St. Andrews will now pray for God's good guidance and blessing on our deliberations." His tones were a nice admixture of the authoritative, the respectful and the businesslike.

The Primate offered up a short and simple prayer in a much plainer voice.

The Chancellor remained standing. "Your Grace, my lord Governor and my lords — to proceed, I . . ." He paused at another flick of Albany's hand.

"Have you ascertained well, my lord Chancellor, that all who are here are entitled to be here?" That was thinly said, as the speaker looked directly at Alex Stewart.

138

The Bishop coughed. "Such is my belief, my lord Governor. The Lord Lyon King of Arms has checked all credentials, I am assured."

"Then proceed."

It was a warning, that was all. Albany would have received his copy of the Mar charter and would know well that Alex's assumption of the earldom had the King's confirmation. He was but indicating displeasure, and demonstrating who controlled this assembly.

"Yes, my lord. The first business is the appointment of Lord High Admiral of this kingdom, for some time vacant. My lord Governor, with His Grace's agreement, recommends that the office and all dues, privileges and emoluments pertaining thereto should be held by the King's good-brother, and his own, the Lord David, Earl of Crawford. It is not within the power of this Council to withhold agreement, but objections may be heard."

There were, of course, no objections raised. David Lindsay of Crawford, although now elderly, was popular enough, and reliable. Jamie looked at Will.

"Clever," he murmured. "The said emoluments include customs dues at every port of the kingdom. So Albany seeks to stop Crawford's mouth, and to buy his vote, before ever a start is made — and none can say him nay."

The Lindsay stood, bowed, and sat down again.

"The next business concerns the King's peace. And relations with the realm of England," the Chancellor went on. "And in such case it would be meet, and His Grace's wish, that we should express here the pleasure and satisfaction of all at the presence with us of my lord Earl of Douglas, who has led valiantly in the defence of the realm. He is here but on parole and must return to captivity. But we salute him."

Men could cheer that, at least — although Douglas himself looked grim.

"As is well known, the Earls of Fife and Moray are still prisoners in England, with many lords and knights, captured at Homildon," Greenlaw went on. "And the Earl of Angus has died a prisoner, to our sorrow. The Governor has been seeking the release of these, but without success. It may now be revealed that there was an attempt made against the usurper Henry of Bolingbroke some months past, after Shrewsbury fight, a compact between the Earl of Northumberland, the late Lord Henry

139

Percy's father, Scrope, Archbishop of York, and sundry North of England lords, to go to the aid of the Welsh under Glendower, the King of France to send an expedition likewise. My lord Governor was privy to this endeavour, and sent envoys to York to assist. By misfortune, this good attempt was betrayed to Henry by Neville, Earl of Westmoreland. The Archbishop and the Lord Mowbray were beheaded, and the other leaders now fugitive. Some escaped to France, but others, including the Earl of Northumberland, the Lord Bardolph and the Bishops of St. Asaph and Bangor, are believed to be making their way to Scotland and His Grace's protection, to join His Grace King Richard, already here."

There was a murmur at this depressing catalogue — and some wondered why it was being announced. Crawford spoke.

"My lord Chancellor — Henry may be usurper, but he is now firmly on the throne of England. He may well construe protection given by the Scots Crown to his rebels as an act of war. Are His Grace and the Governor prepared for the possible consequences?"

Greenlaw glanced at Albany, who remained silent, expressionless.

"It is believed that Henry will not take action on such account, with insurrection at home and the Welsh still undefeated, my lord. He has not done so against King Richard's presence here, to be sure. Whereas the holding of the Earl of Northumberland, Lord Bardolph and others in Scotland would be a distinct advantage in any bargaining with Henry, would it not?"

"Holding? Advantage? Bargaining?" That was the Primate, Wardlaw, in his quiet but firm voice. "My lord Chancellor — do we take it that these Englishmen are to find refuge here? Or to be held and used as pawns in a game of statecraft? I cannot think that His Grace's honour would be enhanced, if this is so."

Bishop Greenlaw looked again at the Governor. He was in a difficult position in any debate with his own Primate and superior.

With obvious displeasure Albany spoke. "His Grace's honour is at no risk," he said. He had the slightest hesitation in his speech, and always spoke slowly, deliberately, coldly. "I mislike the term pawns. Offering shelter to Northumberland and others is no less than a duty, since they are allies against the common enemy. But none will deny the advantage of having the chief nobleman of Northern England in our midst. Will *you*, my lord of Douglas, Chief Warden of the Marches?" That was quite a speech for Robert Stewart, who preferred others to do the talking, whilst he manipulated.

The Douglas frowned his twisted brows. He could by no means controvert that, whether he would or not. Douglas lands lined the Border, east, mid and west, that Border kept in a state of perpetual turmoil and trouble largely the age-old feud between the Douglas and Percy families, excuse for any barbarity on either side. With Douglas himself a captive and unable to lead in the protection of his lands, nothing could be more suitable than for the Percy earl to be in Scots hands.

"Damn him — he knows what he is at, that one!" Jamie whispered. "He has our earl gripped tight! And . . . he has not said so, but by naming Douglas like that, he as good as hints that an exchange might well be suggested."

"Why not?" Will demanded — to his half-brother's look of pitying scorn.

"Because, if there is any such exchange, dolt, it is his *son*, the Earl Murdoch, who will benefit, not Earl Archie. Of that you may be sure."

The Earl of Douglas, who was no fool, whatever else, contented himself with a shake of the head.

Albany waved his hand to the Chancellor.

"Is it agreed then, my lords, that this matter is best left in the Governor's capable hands?" Greenlaw asked. "Since no other is in a position to effect the issue." He turned. "With, of course, my lord of St. Andrews, fullest concern for the King's honour, as always."

"Aye — but why raise it in the first place?" Jamie muttered. "I say it was only done to show the Earl Archie where his advantage lay. Albany controls all, like any puppet-master. There is none here clever enough to upset him."

"Not your friend the new Mar, I warrant!" Will said.

"Further to this of England," the Chancellor resumed, confidently now, "His Grace is concerned for the welfare, good guidance and upbringing of his grandson, the new Earl of Angus, in consequence of the sad death of his father, captive. His Grace deems it proper that the child, of but four years, should be taken into the care and wardship of the Crown, his widowed mother being the King's daughter."

Alex Stewart looked at the Earl of Douglas beside him — who sat still. Just as the Bishop began to speak again, he himself rose.

141

"My lord Chancellor," he said in his clear and musical Highland voice, softly sibilant but carrying, "guide the Council, if you will. Does the care and wardship of the Crown refer to His Grace the King's own keeping? Or that of my lord Governor? Or of another? For instance, the Bishop of St. Andrews — who indeed presently has the care and keeping of His Grace's own surviving son, the Prince James, Earl of Carrick?"

That mildy-spoken enquiry might have been the harshest of challenges by its impact upon the crowded church. Men stared at the speaker, the Governor, the King and each other. Here was a bold man, with a vengeance! Seeming to question even the royal prerogative, and in the King's own presence — although none could fail to grasp the significance of the point implied, that if the monarch could not ensure the keeping of his own son and heir, he was unlikely to do better for his four-year-old grandson.

"My lord, I . . ." the Chancellor began, when he was halted by a peremptory snap of the fingers from the Governor.

"Who speaks?" that man said.

Greenlaw looked uncomfortable. "The Lord Alexander, Earl of Mar, formerly Lord of Badenoch and acting Justiciar of the North, my lord Duke," he replied, in almost a gabble. "Earl by charter of the Countess Isobel of Mar, confirmed by the King's Grace." The Bishop's diocese of Aberdeen was near enough to Mar, and with rich endowments therefrom, to ensure that he wished for no trouble in that direction.

"Vacated the Justiciarship on possible implication in the vile murder of Sir Malcolm Drummond, the lady's husband and good-brother of His Grace," Albany said tonelessly. "Then married the widow."

"Precisely, my lord Duke," Alex agreed genially. "If . . . abbreviated."

"Found to be innocent of any such implication by the highest Court in the North, on which sat the Bishop of Moray and the Lord John Stewart of Coull, both here present. Which Court also learned that the said vile murder had been carefully arranged from south of the Highland Line!"

Moments passed in tense silence, before the Governor inclined his head.

"Proceed," he said.

It had been an exchange of warnings.

A sigh of relief escaped from many, not least from the

142

Chancellor. But he still had a difficult question to handle, since Alex remained on his feet.

"Royal wardship, my lord, means that the minor is placed within the protection of the Crown. In whose care the child resides is not the vital matter, and is at the Crown's best judgement."

"Ah. I thank you. Then, my lord, I suggest that this Council advises the Crown to place the child George Douglas in the care and wardship of his own chief and uncle, the Earl of Douglas, whose wife is sister to the Countess of Angus, and likewise the King's daughter. Thus putting no unnecessary further burden on the already much burdened shoulders of His Grace and the Governor." He sat down.

"If that is a motion for decision, I second it," the Bishop of St. Andrews said.

It was hard for Jamie, who could not hide a foolish grin, to decide who was most put out, the Governor, the Chancellor, or the Earl of Douglas — although undoubtedly Albany hid it best. All were placed in an obvious quandary. Albany needed Douglas's aid and power, therefore would be loth to offend him; the Chancellor did not know how he should proceed; and Douglas was having his hand forced cleverly — for he could scarcely refuse wardship of the third most important Douglas before all his own lords and vassals without jettisoning respect.

Slowly that twisted man got to his feet. "I will accept the wardship, if Your Grace permits," he said thickly, looking at the King.

Almost imperceptibly the monarch nodded, biting his lip.

Greenlaw looked at the Governor anxiously. "Is the motion contested? Or any other motion?"

Albany eyed his finger-nails, and said nothing.

"Then, then with His Grace's approval, I declare the matter settled. The young Earl of Angus, his earldom and lands, are placed in the care of the Earl of Douglas until such time as the Crown declares him fit and of age to manage all for himself. With, to be sure, good and proper provision made for his lady mother, the Countess Mary. Is it agreed?"

Jamie was not the only one who could scarce forbear to cheer. The Duke of Albany had suffered his first open defeat in years. It was no large matter; but the significance was there — not least in that the gently-spoken stranger had contrived it, and in his support by the primate.

The Chancellor was rather evidently hurrying on to the next business when he was interrupted by the said Primate.

"Your forbearance, my lord," Wardlaw said, standing. "But on the matter of wardship and the safety of minors, there is more to debate. I have the honour to speak for the King's Grace in this. As all know, owing to ill health and infirmity, His Grace has been pleased to place his heir, the Prince James, Earl of Carrick and High Steward of Scotland in my care and keeping, at St. Andrews Castle — to my great satisfaction. It has come to the ears of His Grace and myself, however, that possible attempts might be made upon the prince's safety by ill-designing persons. My bishop's palace, and resources in armed men, could well be inadequate in such evil attempt, we fear. Other houses likewise. Therefore it is His Grace's design that the prince be sent into the care either of His Holiness the Pope, or of His Most Christian Majesty, the King of France, for true security. This is His Grace's considered desire, and my own advice. But before sending the heir to his throne outwith the realm's borders, he would seek the agreement and understanding of this parliament or council."

As though thunder-struck, the great company sought to gather its wits. This was why the King had come here in person, obviously. Whatever else was behind it, none could fail to see it as the direst commentary on the state of the realm, when its monarch felt his own son would be safer elsewhere. Therefore, at the very least, it was an open indictment of the Governor's rule and inability to protect his nephew — although few there of any knowledge of affairs doubted that it was the Governor himself who was believed to pose the threat. Nothing could more strongly underline the gap and enmity between the royal brothers, he who reigned and he who ruled. Men would be forced to take sides — loyalty to the weak King, or adherence to where the power lay.

The quivering hush was broken by Albany's dull, factual voice.

"Who, my lord Bishop, are the ill-designing persons whose evil intents have come to your clerkly ears, and His Grace's? Sharper ears than mine and the realm's government, it seems!"

"My lord Duke, you would not have me to name names, I think, here in open assembly, for a crime not yet committed?" the Primate answered. "But that must not prevent us taking due precautions. I may say, however, that one who might consider laying violent hands on the prince, not necessarily the most

144

dangerous, is your own nephew the Lord of the Isles, who has already made attempted invasion, twice, and failed, thanks only to the strong and bold efforts of my lord Earl of Mar."

A buzz of comment and approval swept the church. It was a shrewd tactic. Donald of the Isles was an ominous figure in Lowland Scotland, something of a bogeyman. Albany could not pooh-pooh the constant threat he posed, nor publically dismiss Alex's service in thwarting him. Whether or not Donald had ever had any intention of abducting the prince his cousin, none could doubt that such an attempt would be in character.

"The Islesman is a long way off," the Duke observed. "If ever he made any such attempt, there would be ample time to move my nephew to a more secure hold than St. Andrews — Stirling Castle, or Edinburgh. Would any claim that the boy could be lifted out of these? Why send him to France?"

Wardlaw hesitated, but only for a moment. He could not say baldly that Albany himself was the danger, and could lift the prince out of Stirling or Edinburgh even more easily than out of St. Andrews Castle.

"His Grace considered that," the Primate said slowly. "But these are fortresses, military strengths. He could have sent the prince there in the first place. But great fortresses are no places to confine a growing lad. He would become all but a prisoner. The prince needs space, freedom, the company and influence of cultured minds, my lord. The Papal or French Courts would be excellently to the advantage of our future King. This is His Grace's decision." He emphasised that last word slightly.

Albany was a determined man, but not obstinate. He knew well when to abandon an untenable position. He shrugged. "His Grace's wish, of course, is our command. Proceed, Chancellor."

The Bishop of Aberdeen swallowed. Evidently there was not to be any further discussion on the subject by the company.

"Yes, my lord. The next business concerns the good governance of the realm. My lord Duke's term of office as Governor expires within a month or so. It was for three years. It is necessary that further arrangements be made. I have a letter here from my lord Earl of Lennox, absent through sickness, thanking my lord Governor for his valuable and unremitting services in the past, and praying that he favours the realm by accepting office for a further term of three years. He authorises Sir Malcolm Fleming, Lord of Cumbernauld, to so move, in his name."

"I so do," Fleming declared briefly.

"And I make it my privilege to second," the Bishop of Dunblane added. Doune Castle, Albany's favourite seat, in Menteith, was near Dunblane.

"I thank you, my lords. Is there any contrary motion?" Greenlaw actually smiled as he said that.

There was silence. It would have been a rash man indeed who would have proposed any other name — and a rasher who would have accepted nomination. In fact, there was nobody else of sufficient seniority and experience for the role, unless perhaps the Earl of Crawford, who almost certainly would refuse, and was indeed older than the Duke, and with no fondness for the business of statecraft. The only other brother of the King was Walter, Lord of Brechin, not present, never present, a drunken irresponsible who could not manage himself much less a kingdom. Douglas conceivably could have been appointed — but he had to return to his captivity in England. It was all part of Scotland's tragedy.

"Very well . . ." the Chancellor was saying when Alex Stewart rose to his feet.

"My lord — one moment," he said pleasantly. "We are all very much aware of the Duke of Albany's prolonged activities in the realm's name. But too much can be laid on one man's shoulders, however willingly he bears the burden. I cannot, for the life of me, think of any name adequate or fit to take his place — as yet. But, in view of his advanced years — sixty-six, if I mistake not, my lord Duke? In view of this, I propose that his appointment be renewed for only *two* years, not three. Perhaps the Earl of Douglas, or other, will be available to take on the task by then." Smilingly bowing to the Governor, he sat.

Albany had half-risen from his chair. Sternly impassive of appearance always, he could not wholly control his features now, his cold fury the more frightening for being under such evident restraint. He raised a trembling finger, to point.

Before he could speak, another bold voice broke the tense silence, from the lord's seats at the front of the nave this time.

"It is my filial duty, and my pleasure, to second such motion," John Stewart of Coull declared.

As men caught their breaths, Robert Stewart sank back in his chair, his eyes closed.

In agitation the Chancellor looked at him, as men stirred and whispered. "This is . . . this is . . ." He bit his lip. "I, I have no

146

option, my lord Duke, and Your Grace. I have two motions before the Council. Both duly seconded. Is it your wish that I proceed to the vote, my lord?"

Clear, precise, definite, so much in contrast with Greenlaw's, the words came from behind the table. "No vote. I accept the two years' term. Proceed, man." Those colourless eyes remained closed.

The Chancellor looked unhappy and relieved at the same time, shuffled his papers as though in doubt as to what to do next in an assembly all too evidently not going as planned. "Er . . . there is the matter of moneys," he said, almost tentatively. "Moneys for the costs of government. Further moneys to reimburse my lord Duke for much expense. He is sorely at loss."

"Provision was made for this," Crawford said shortly.

"It has proved . . . inadequate, my lord."

"It is unsuitable that the Governor should be put to expense as well as trouble in the realm's service," the Bishop of Dunblane said. "My lord of St. Andrews — cannot Holy Church help in this matter?"

"The Church is already helping, my friend. More than is her due, I may say," the Primate observed. "Save, perhaps, for the See of Aberdeen, where I am informed, dues and contributions, not only to the Exchequer but to Holy Church's own Treasury, are unaccountably held up."

Mirth, for the first time that day, broke through, especially amongst the laity.

"Not so!" Greenlaw expostulated, flushing. "My diocese is most concerned to make full and generous contribution. But it must be understood that much of the see's revenues come through the port and haven of Aberdeen and its merchants and shipmen, its fishers also. For lack of a Lord Admiral of the realm, these past years, such duties and customs have not been properly farmed, and we, the Church, have suffered grave loss..."

"My lord of Crawford will attend to it," Albany intervened levelly, his eyes open again. "Observing therein the requirements of the Exchequer and of the Church, both. My lord Chancellor — the matter of Atholl."

Some grins were turned in the direction of Crawford, but that was the end of the mirth. Such seldom survived long in the Governor's presence.

"Ah, yes — Atholl. Further to this of moneys, my lords — and Your Grace — it is considered that the revenues of the earldom of Atholl could well be used for the realm's weal. As all know, the earldom of Atholl has been merged in the Crown for many years — since 1342 indeed. It seems now good and proper that its revenues should be made available to the Governor for defraying the costs of government with His Grace's agreement."

"My lord — is that a statement or a question?" That was Wardlaw the Primate.

"Is what . . . ?"

"Is His Grace's agreement obtained, or to *be* obtained?"

Greenlaw looked, as always, at the Governor — who looked at his brother. The King's head sank lower, but shook. Whether it was a shake or a wag, in denial, helplessness or agitation, was for individual assessment.

Wardlaw chose to interpret it as a denial. "I would point out, my lord Chancellor, a slight error in your pronouncement," he went on. "You say that the earldom of Atholl has been merged in the Crown since 1342. But this is not so. In 1342 King David Bruce was on the throne. This earldom was conveyed to Robert, the High Steward — who did not become King, as Robert the Second, until 1370. The earldom, then, is merged in the Steward-ship, not the Crown. I feel it to be my simple duty, in whose care the present High Steward has been placed, the Prince James, to here assert his undoubted claim and title to this earldom and its revenues."

Once again there was all but consternation.

"A minor," Albany said briefly, apparently to no-one in particular.

"Yes. To be sure. My lord Bishop — the High Steward being a minor, and so unable to manage the affairs and revenues of an earldom, they therefore must be in the hands of his guardians and elders," Greenlaw said.

"In this case, the King's Grace, the minor's father — not the Governor, his uncle. May I ask how the Atholl revenues have been disposed, hitherto?"

"M'mm. Into His Grace's privy purse, I believe."

"For the benefit of the prince. Then, I say, that they must remain so. That when the High Steward comes of due age to require and use such moneys, they are awaiting him — not drained off otherwise. If it pleases the King's Grace?"

The monarch raised his head, moistening slack lips. "It does," he said — although only those nearby could hear him.

"Albany's fourth defeat!" Jamie declared elatedly, to his

brother. "And in none of them did he dare put it to the vote. Alex and the Bishop Wardlaw between them have him hobbled!"

"Here, perhaps, Jamie. But, wait you! Wait until we are all gone home, and the Duke is ruling the land again. Then see who wins!"

Grimly, unwillingly, the other nodded.

"Next business," the Governer said, apparently unmoved.

The next business was controversial also — but one in which at least Alex's hands were tied. It was the appointment of an acting Justiciar of the North. The Chancellor explained that the new Earl of Mar had resigned the office for good and sufficient reasons, and must be replaced. The office was only an acting one, because of course the true Justiciar was the Lord Murdoch, Earl of Fife, presently unfortunately captive in England. In the circumstances, and since it was advisable that the Justiciar should be a man known and accepted by the people of those parts and acquaint with their curious language, it was appropriate that the brother of the said Earl of Fife, the Lord John Stewart of Coull, Onele and Oboyne, who was now of age to play his due part in the governance of the realm, should be appointed . . .

"No!" the Governor rapped. "I have decided otherwise."

Greenlaw, put out of his stride again, spread plump hands, looked pained, but said nothing.

Albany allowed moments to pass before again raising that strange voice. "On due thought, it may be that my son John is still young enough to lack mature judgement for such office — where judgement is important. I shall retain the Justiciarship in my own hands meantime. Appoint deputies when and as required. It may be, test the Lord John as to improved judgement in due course. You may proceed, Chancellor."

John Stewart rose, and bowed, half-smiling, to his father, and sat again, whilst the hum of talk and comment arose.

Greenlaw had to beat the table for quiet. "Your attention, my lords. There is the matter of the fortress and castle of Roxburgh. The people and vassals of Teviotdale, through the Sheriff thereof, Sir Archibald Douglas of Cavers, have petitioned the Governor to assail and eject the English garrison therefrom, long established. My lord Duke declares this to be the business of the Wardens of the Marches, in especial the Chief Warden, the Earl of Douglas. Do you wish to speak further on this, my lord of Cavers?"

149

"I do," Sir Archie said vigorously. "The English have shamefully held this Scots castle for sixty years, despite all truces and treaties. They frequently raid out from it, to assail and ravish in Teviotdale and the Merse, in especial my town of Jedburgh. It is a very strong hold, and cannot be taken but my major assault and siege, with engines. My lord Earl of Douglas, being captive on parole, may not lead any such warlike attempt against his captors. His brother, Sir James Douglas of Abercorn, who acts deputy Chief Warden, is in no position to mount any such major siege. We say that this is a matter for the Crown."

"If the Earl of Douglas, or his deputies in the house of Douglas, are unable to control the Marches of the Borders, then his right course is to resign the Wardenship to others who can," the Governor said, almost primly. "Do you so, my lord of Douglas?"

"No," that uncommunicative man said shortly.

"Then I suggest, Sir Archibald, that you confer with your own lord on this matter, instead of taking up the time of this Council."

"But — surely it is the realm's business? A great castle within the Scots Border, held by an enemy garrison. *You*, my lord Duke, led a large army of fifty thousand not so long since, to relieve the small tower of Cocklaws, in my lordship and sheriffdom. It was a strange business — but no doubt you had your reasons! Why cannot you do the same for Roxburgh?"

"I went to Cocklaws, young man, on the invitation and with the agreement of the Earl of Douglas, then in the care of the Lord Henry Percy. This of Roxburgh is quite otherwise."

"Then I urge the Earl of Douglas again to seek your aid, my lord Duke!"

"That he cannot do, while on parole. It would be construed an act of war. We are at truce with England. The Crown will not break that truce until it is fully prepared to do so. You may sit down, Sir Archibald. The matter is not for discussion here. Chancellor — is there aught else?"

"Other than confirming in office sundry sheriffs and officers appointed since the last parliament, I think not, my lord Duke . . ."

"I have a matter to raise," Alex announced, rising. "It concerns the outlawry wrongfully pronounced upon Sir James Douglas of Aberdour — pronounced in the King's name but without the royal knowledge. I move now that this be revoked, as mistaken and unsuitable."

"This surely is a matter entirely within the prerogative of the Governor," Greenlaw said, looking grieved.

"As I understand it, nothing that the Governor, or any other subject of the King may do, cannot be overturned by the King in parliament. Am I misinformed, my lord?"

"I . . . ah . . . mmm."

"This man is a trouble-maker," Albany observed.

"I presume that my lord Duke refers, not to myself, but to Sir James Douglas?" Alex said, genially. "In which case, I would agree — but point out that the trouble he makes is invariably for the King's and the realm's enemies, the English, the Islesmen and others nearer home who endanger the peace and well-being of the kingdom. His valour on the fields of Otterburn, Glenarkaig in Lochaber, and Preston in Lothian, as elsewhere, is well known. His sound judgement — which my lord Duke recognises as so important — both in the field and in council, is known by many here, in especial by such as are soldiers themselves. His services to the King and to the *late* Governor, the Duke of Rothesay, are without question. I ask, as I think is my right, for the reasons for his outlawry to be stated."

There was actually a sort of cheer at that.

"I am not obliged, sir, to give account to you, or any other, for the actions I require to take in the day-to-day rule of this realm," the Governor said.

"Not even to the King in parliament? This may not be a true parliament, but it is a convention of parliament. And the decisions already taken here have the force of a parliament, do they not? Else the King, you my lord Duke, and all others, but waste their time. I appeal to His Grace for a ruling, as one of the earls of his realm."

The King of Scots wrung his hands, but nodded. "Yes," he said.

His brother shrugged. "As His Grace wishes. Douglas, formerly of Aberdour, now forfeit, fled from the affray at Homildon Hill, with a thousand men, without a blow struck. Leaving his commanders, like all his comrades, on the field, their rear and flanks open to attack. So I am informed."

Various cries of denial rose from Douglases throughout the church. But these stilled as, at last, the Earl of Douglas rose to his feet.

"You have been misinformed," he said, heavily. "I commanded there. I ordered Sir James Douglas to remain behind after rejecting his advice earlier. When all was lost, by the failure

151

of his commanders, he contrived to save what he could of the Scots force. I say that his conduct on that field was more to be admired than that of any other present. I second my lord of Mar's motion that his outlawry be revoked herewith."

Now there were cheers indeed, every Douglas, and many another, rising in acclaim.

Albany pointed at the Chancellor. "My lord — have this unseemly uproar stopped! Forthwith. This is a Council General, not a bear-baiting!" And as the noise died away before his cold but frightening anger, he added, "Since it is the wish of my lord of Douglas, the outlawry is withdrawn. Chancellor — this of the confirmation of sheriffs' and officers' appointments. And let us have done!"

Although the dull task of listing and agreeing, or otherwise, many minor appointments took some time thereafter, the Linlithgow Council General was in fact over with that last statement by the Governor — for he did not again open his thin lips. Many of the onlookers undoubtedly would have streamed out had not the monarch's presence forbidden it. But at last it was done, the Chancellor thanked the Commissioners for attending, hurriedly, the trumpeters sounded, and the King, Governor and principals filed out.

Outside the church, Jamie was surrounded by a back-slapping, vociferous and congratulatory crowd, to his embarrassment. But when, presently, he was joined by Alex Stewart, and it was his turn to congratulate and thank, he found his friend not embarrassed but preoccupied.

"See you, Jamie," Alex said, when they could be private, "we gained what we wanted there, and more than we could have hoped for. Thanks to Wardlaw, and, of course, your Earl. Aye, and the King himself. But let us not lose our heads, in one fashion or another! My Uncle Robert is still Governor — and will love us even less than heretofore. He never forgets nor forgives, as you well know. If he cannot win one way, he will, I fear, try to gain his ends in another — less openly."

"You mean, my safety is still at risk, you think?"

"Yes. My own too, perhaps. After all, he murdered his other nephew, David, who challenged him! But you are in more immediate danger, I would judge. Your outlawry may be over — but you are still a stone for stumbling in his path. I say, the sooner we are back over the Highland Line the better, my friend. Before there is any possible . . . mischance!"

"Is all that we have achieved today of little value, then?"

"Far from it. That was just the beginning, I hope. But we can continue to assail our foe from *our* hold, not from inside his! Do you not agree?"

"Aye, you are right. Back to Strabrock, then. And ride north tomorrow? Banquet tonight or none."

"I saw my uncle in close converse with Lindsay of Rossie, before I came out to you. I think that we might with profit ride *tonight*, Jamie . . ."

X

STRANGELY ENOUGH, THE first overt move by Albany *vis-à-vis* the new Earl of Mar and his ex-outlaw friend was not made until well into the following summer; and when it was, it seemed to negate their apprehensions. It came in the form of an olive-branch, indeed, unexpected as this was.

Jamie was comfortably settled and well enough content, acting more or less as steward for Alex at Lochindorb. Albany might not take active steps against him; but he was far from assured that he and his family would remain secure and unmolested if he returned to live in the South. Besides, he had come much to enjoy the Highland way of life, the folk and the country. Alex strongly urged him to remain. The fact was, he trusted Jamie to look to his interests there adequately, where he did not similarly trust his brothers. Where Duncan might be, none knew; but he might possibly seek to bring some dangerous pressure on Andrew and Walter Stewart. James, the youngest of the family, had married and gone to manage a detached portion of their father's lands, at Garth in Atholl. Andrew now managed the Strathaven and Lower Spey lands to the east, and Walter those of Upper Donside; but for the central Badenoch and Strathspey territories, his main inheritance, Alex was happier with Jamie as his representative.

One day, early in July, Jamie was interrupted, at the business of building a new timber jetty to serve the castle-island, by the arrival of Alex from Kildrummy, in company with John Stewart of Coull — the first they had seen of that young man since Linlithgow. The cousins seemed to be on excellent terms.

As they were rowed over to the castle, Alex explained. "Cousin John brings interesting tidings, Jamie. He is but recently from the South. He tells of some change of attitude by the Governor. Or so it would seem."

The Douglas eyed the other without comment but in entire disbelief.

"My esteemed sire has qualities which even you must grant him, Sir James," John Stewart said, smiling. "He has a notably clear and discerning eye, however chilly! He sees things as they are and wastes no time and concern in wishing them otherwise. He may be devious, but none is more practical than my lord Duke. What he cannot beat down or bring low by guile he will work with — and seek to use to his own ends. If one path is blocked he will take another, and care naught for what men say. He is a proud man — but does not allow pride to injure ultimate advantage."

"So?"

"Jamie, I think, is almost as practical a man as your father, Cousin! He will be hard to convince that the Governor loves us."

"That he does not. But he has decided that you can be of use. And are better working if not for him, at least not against him. He was quick to learn the lesson of Linlithgow. You, and perhaps myself, offer a threat to his rule. He does not like that. He cannot remove you, here behind the Highland Line, and so takes other steps. To use you and me."

"We should rejoice at that?" Jamie asked bluntly.

"Why not? If you can use it to your advantage. Learn from him." They had reached the castle landing-stage, but John of Coull sat still, intent on what he had to say. "He sent for me, from Coull — for, like you, I did not linger after the Council General. He is never affable, even with his own family, and he did not fall on my neck! But nor did he assail me for countering him that day as he might have done. He has never concerned himself with me hitherto, as a father might, and I have kept out of his way. Now, it seems he would have me for him, not against him."

"I can understand that," Alex said. "I would wish the same."

"Thank you! So I am sent up to Elgin and Inverness, to take the justiciary courts, after all. To try me out, he says. I am not Acting Justiciar yet. He keeps that for himself — and all the revenues pertaining. He has a great stomach for siller, has the Duke! I am but to be his deputy, this time. And if I do well, or at least please him, he will consider giving me the acting office. Also the earldom of Buchan — which my lord of Mar's father held and is now reverted to the Crown. Moreover, he threatens to find me a suitable heiress to wed!"

"Another one!" Jamie said, unkindly.

"Ah, the first was *my* choice. My father only thought to make use of it. Woe is me, I lost to a better man!"

Neither of his hearers commented on that. But Jamie went on, "Where do we come into this? Or, leastways, the Earl of Mar?"

"My father, if you will believe it, advised me to seek my lord's advice and help, saying that his aid and guidance would not be forgotten. Also that all question as to the death of Sir Malcolm Drummond was now closed."

"Which might have its own convenience for himself!"

"There is something for you also, Jamie."

"Yes. He says that forfeiture on properties, consequent upon your outlawry, is now revoked, that you may come and go freely, within the realm."

"Was that not understood when the outlawry itself was lifted?"

"A mere understanding and the Governor's stated assurance are different!"

"The Governor's stated assurance could mean anything or nothing." That was flat. "His words and deeds are apt to differ! With all respect, I have had to deal with him longer than you, my lord. I think I will continue to bide in the North yet awhile."

"Good — in that at least I rejoice," Alex said. "Since Cousin John brought these tidings, I have been concerned that I might lose you. And I need you here. But . . . it will be to your much advantage, Jamie, to have your property restored, and to move freely in the South, without fear of apprehension."

"I shall go warily, nevertheless . . . !"

At this stage Mary arrived at the landing-jetty to greet them, wondering why they sat there in the boat. She welcomed the new arrivals warmly, both her nephews, declaring that she liked personable young men so long as they had not come to take away her husband from her, as seemed to be their custom — and his delight. Alex reassured her. There was no suggestion of taking Jamie away — although if he would come with them to Elgin next day, it might be advantageous and pleasant. She could come herself, if she cared. It seemed that John of Coull intended to adopt the widest interpretation of his father's suggestion, and would have Alex actually to sit with him on the judicial bench at this assize, possibly with some churchman or other of his choice — Bishop Spynie of Moray being a dying man. This procedure, of course, would fairly well ensure his own acceptance as Justiciar; but it would also be of advantage to the new Earl of Mar, in building up his image as a power in the North irrespective of authority in the South. There might well come a time when these two Stewarts' interests would clash, and then sparks would fly indeed; but meantime their mutual co-operation could achieve much.

John Stewart told them, that night, much more of events in the South than had emerged in the boat. He informed them that the Earl of Douglas had returned to captivity in England, and the first three hostages were on their way home, with another three to be ready to stand in for him next year — these to include Jamie's brother James of Dalkeith, the Earl's own son the young Master of Douglas, and Sir Simon Glendinning, Jamie's old colleague at Otterburn. Just why King Henry was allowing this especial privilege to the Douglas, while still refusing to ransom him outright, was not clear; possibly he believed that the power of Douglas, much the greatest in Scotland, could thus be kept restrained. But it much offended the Governor, for whose son Murdoch of Fife no similar concessions were being offered, despite many pleas and letters.

The old Earl of Northumberland, with his grandson young Harry Percy, son of the late Hotspur, the Lord Bardolph and the Bishops of Bangor and St. Asaph, had duly arrived in Scotland; the boy was now sent to study with Prince James at St. Andrews, while his grandfather and the others were domiciled at the Blackfriars in Perth, ostensibly guests of the Governor but in fact little better than hostages. The King had sent an envoy to King Charles of France asking him if he would accept the prince at his Court for a few years, in theory to learn chivalry and kingcraft, such as he could not learn from Bishop Wardlaw — renewed squabbling between the rival Popes at Avignon and Genoa had ruled out a papal destination for the boy.

John Stewart was very good company, and Alex and he made a notable pair, amusing, quick-silver, tossing the ball of repartee, allusion and challenge between them in lively fashion, with Mary joining in not infrequently, another Stewart with her own shrewd contributions to make. Jamie, on the other hand, was content to listen and watch. Not for him this conversational sparring and gymnastics. He could appreciate and admire but not take part. Also he had a fairly pronounced critical faculty, and he was by no means certain that he was as happy with John of Coull as was Alex most obviously. Perhaps it was merely that this was Albany's son, and he could not forget it. There might even have been a kind of jealousy. Jamie Douglas did not make friends easily, and Alex he had grown to be very fond of, without putting it into so many words. This comparative newcomer, although a kinsman to be sure, seemed to have jumped into an association and understanding with his cousin almost overnight. Moreover, clearly one day he would be an earl likewise, a major figure in the land, on an equal footing with Alex — which the Douglas could never be. So he reserved his acceptance somewhat, like his judgement — in which he was abetted by Mariota de Athyn, who remained cool towards the visitor.

The Countess Isobel was not once mentioned throughout the evening, but her shadow was very much present.

*   *   *

As they rode to Elgin the next day, Mary gladly accepting the invitation to accompany them, it became clear that John Stewart's desire to have Alex sit in judgement with him was not entirely disinterested and out of friendly good-fellowship. It transpired in fact that, in addition to the many straightforward and lesser cases and disputes remitted to the Justiciar's assize from barony and sheriffs' courts, there was a major dispute to be pronounced upon concerning two of the principal vassals of the earldom of Mar, Sir Andrew Leslie of Balquhain and Sir Alexander Forbes of that Ilk. Alex, Hereditary Sheriff of Aberdeen as well as Earl of Mar, could have sat in judgement on these two himself; but had avoided doing so for fear of alienating the support of one or the other, which in his present stage of building up goodwill and a solid base in his new feudal situation, he could not afford — for these were both very powerful men, heads of their respective houses. So, since the dispute concerned alleged murder and mayhem, as well as other mutual irritations — the two houses had been at feud for generations — the thing was referred to the Justiciar for decision, the hearing to be held at Elgin rather than at Aberdeen, where rival influences might well be brought to bear. John of Coull, himself a Mar vassal, and much younger and junior save in royal descent to either of the litigants, had not failed to recognise that he was going to require support and guidance in this matter, and the Earl of Mar was the obvious choice. Alex saw it as a means of influencing the decision without having to accept the responsibility of judging against one or the other, which must remain the Justiciar's duty. They decided to ask the Prior of Pluscarden as third and independent member, he having no links with Mar, and Pluscarden being on their way to Elgin.

So once again Jamie and Mary sat in the great hall of the royal castle of Elgin, next morning, as the Justiciar and his two co-adjutors were ceremoniously ushered in to take their seats on the dais, with due pomp and dignity. John Stewart played his part well, easy, confident but not arrogant, and deferring pleasantly to his colleagues. When truly Highland questions arose, he put them all in the first instance to Alex, whose knowledge of clan justice, traditions and attitudes he could not hope to rival — thereby gaining a vital acceptance which could so easily have been withheld, a problem which was always inherent in the Crown-appointed Justiciar of the North's office. The dichotomy between the true Highlanders and the clans and communities east of the various Mounths, in Angus, the Mearns, Aberdeen-shire and the Moray plain, although nothing like so sharp as between Highland and Lowland, North and South, was very much a reality. Alex's strength of position was that he had been brought up as a true Highlander, with a Mackay Highland mother, and yet was of Lowland and royal descent — illegitim-acy meaning nothing here. Now that he was also Earl of Mar, he was enabled to straddle the divide the more effectively. Undoubtedly Albany had not failed to recognise this unpalatable fact in his instructions to his son.

There was a succession of cases remitted by sheriffs, barony courts and clan chiefs, which for one reason or another required the Justiciar's decision — not because these authorities lacked judicial powers, for every baron had the ultimate sanction of pit and gallows — but for reasons as to side-effects, conflicting interests of the involved authorities themselves, prestige and seniority; and where the Crown's own interests were concerned, as in unlawful customs dues collection, offences on royal lands and forests and complaints against Crown officers. Claims against raiding Islesmen and other mainland MacDonalds and clans allied to the Lord of the Isles, constituted the most trouble-some sector of the day's proceedings, since there was really little that could be done about these, short of major armed inter-vention which the Governor certainly was not prepared to con-sider. In all this, decisions were in the main expeditiously reached, crisp, clear and generally acceptable, whilst in line with realities. John Stewart proved an apt pupil, and the Prior Moray of Pluscarden a wise and succinct diviner of the truth and heart of the matter.

It was, consequently, late in the day before the testing issue of the two Mar vassals came before the Justiciar — deliberately withheld until now so that the doughty protagonists might have ample time to partake of their earl's hospitality in food and especially wine — kept well apart, of course — and so, hopefully, be in a state of mind not to insist too much on finicky details and hierarchal precedences and the like. Their dispute, although somewhat ridiculous, was important for the peace of a large area, for the well-being of the earldom and to some extent that of the entire North-East. All recognised that this was likely to be an exercise not so much in justice as in tact and ingenuity.

On Alex's advice the thing was suitably stage-managed. A single trumpet-blast introduced a pursuivant, who announced in ringing tones that the King's Justiciar, aided by the most noble Earl of Mar and the Garioch, and an illustrous representative of Holy Church, would now hear and consider the notable cause and arbitrament between the puissant and high-born lords, Sir Andrew Leslie of Balquhain, Lord of Urie, Conglas and Harlaw, on the one part and Sir Alexander Forbes of that Ilk, Lord of Forbes, Putachie and Kinnernie; in which the said Sir Andrew made accusation against the said Sir Alexander of injury and offence; and the said Sir Alexander counter-charged the said Sir Andrew with grave intrusions against his rights and privileges, to his hurt and undoubted loss. There had been some doubt, even at this stage, as to which name should be enunciated first; but Leslie was the original complainer and considerably the elder. So a risk was taken.

"Sir Andrew and Sir Alexander!" the Mackintosh pursuivant concluded, loudly, as though at a tournament.

Out from the opposite corner-doors of the dais-area, precisely at the same moment, strode the distinguished litigants, heads high. Their progress towards the front of the table was a little less exact, for Leslie was undoubtedly a little drunk and lurched rather, and Forbes was slightly lame in one leg. They did not so much as glance at each other, nor yet at the company, but somehow managed to reach their indicated places before the table, well apart but simultaneously, bowed stiffly to the judges and so stood, glaring.

Leslie, known as Red Andrish, was a man in his mid-fifties, bulky, florid, hot-eyed, with a shock of wiry red hair so far not in the least diluted with grey, bull-like of shoulder, carelessly clad. Forbes was a dozen years younger, tall, good-looking in a hatchet-faced way, dark-eyed, beak-nosed and notably well dressed. He was a Crowner or Coroner of Aberdeenshire, chief of his name. Unfortunately, although their principal seats of Balquhain and Forbes Castles were over a dozen miles apart, in mid Strathdon, downstream of Kildrummy, their baronies touched at various points, with evident friction.

John Stewart, wisely, was notably careful about how he handled these two, from the start. "A good day to you, my lords," he said. "I greet you well, in the name of the King's Grace, and regret if you have been kept waiting. I am informed that you have certain matters between you on which you desire the ruling of this court of High Justiciary, and I am happy to oblige you by all means within my power. But before doing so, I must remind you, and all others, that we have here present the person of your feudal superior, the most noble Earl of Mar, whose undoubted privilege it is to hear and pronounce upon all such controversies within his earldom, if so he chooses, by the powers vested in him as one of the great earls of Scotland."

"I do not so choose," Alex said easily. "Both these lords are my very good friends, and long-time supporters of my lady-wife. I have eaten the salt of both. I therefore find myself in no position to pass judgement on one cause or the other. But, if I may, I will assist you, my lord Justiciar, in the honest assessment of each or either."

"Very well. Do your lordships wish to speak to your own causes, or be represented by others?"

"Only Forbes speaks for Forbes!" the dark man barked, deep-voiced.

"None other would!" Leslie declared.

"H'mm. Then, my lords, may we proceed with the hearing? In all order and due respect for this High Court of the King's Grace. Sir Andrew, as the elder and with whom complaint to this Court originated, will you commence? Sir Alexander agreeing?"

"By God, I will!" Red Andrish cried. "I demand justice on this, this upjumped cattle-thief and all his misbegotten tribe! He insults me. *Me*, Leslie! He injures . . ."

"I say that it is impossible to insult a Leslie!" Forbes interjected. "All men know that."

"Fiend seize you — Leslies were noble before ever your fore-bear issued from the arse of the bear or the pig or whatever brute you claim to descend from, Forbes!"

"Noble? Leslie! You come of a line of Low Country huck-sters, Hungarians or Flemings, or such, Bartolph by name . . ."

"My lords!" Brave John interrupted strongly. "These may be matters of opinion, sincerely held. But this Court is only con-cerned to hear *facts*. I ask you to confine yourselves to such. Sir Andrew — what are the facts you wish to bring before us?"

Leslie swallowed audibly, almost as though in reluctant alter-native to spitting. "This man's bastard brother, Out-with-the-Sword John Forbes of Callievar, has stolen the bell I gave to God and the church of Forbes in blessed memory of my mother, from that parish. He has removed it and taken it up the Hill of Callievar above the said church, and hung it from a tree. The godless ruffian rings it there. To the hurt and distress of the lieges. *My* bell!"

"How can it be your bell, Red Andrish?" Forbes demanded. "Given to my church of Forbes years back. What we do with our bell is no concern of yours."

John Stewart drew a hand across his mouth. "My lords, bear with me. But I scarce perceive, as yet, what the present location of the church-bell of Forbes parish has to do with the King's Justiciar? Nor how His Grace's lieges are so grievously hurt?"

"Hear this, then," Leslie cried. "This man's ill brother mis-rings it. He jangles and clangles it. At the wrong times, whatever. Turning decent folk out to the kirk when there's naught to go for, when no priest is present. Whanging it during sermons so none can hear . . ."

"When were *you* at sermon in the kirk o' Forbes, man Leslie?" the other demanded. "If you ever attend the kirk at all, which I misdoubt, it is not *my* kirk . . ."

"I am a god-fearing Christian, Sandy Forbes — not a heathen barbarian worshipping idols like your own self, fiend seize you!"

"That's a lie, by the Mass! I am as good a Christian as any man in Mar — and a deal better than you, you adulterous old goat! We all ken fine what you do of a Lord's Day — aye, and every other day, and night too!"

"I say you are an idolator. An open worshipper of false gods, Forbes! You'll no' deny that you keep yon shameful and heathenish image in your own hall. And bow down before it

162

when you eat. The stinking, shrunken head of a bear — forby it looks more like a pig, to me! The bear out of whose filthy arse you and your line issued . . .!"

"Fool! That is the mighty bear my great ancestor Ochonachar slew, in the days of the Cruithnie. And was given the lands of Forbes in consequence, and the name *Fear-boisceal*, Brave Warrior, by the Cruithnie king. In the days when you Fleming Leslies were still painted Goths scratching for acorns!"

"Liar again! *Boisceal* means savage, unlettered savage, not warrior. All know that . . ."

The Justiciar banged on the table, to make himself heard. "My lords — I must rule that all this controversy is out of my jurisdiction. Church-bells, interrupting sermons, worshipping bears — these are not matters for this Court. If aught, they appear to be subjects for Holy Church's consideration. But . . . not here! Unless, to be sure, my Lord Prior wishes to make observation?"

The Valliscaulian, a stern-faced, muscular prelate, shook his fair but tonsured head. "I recommend remitment to the Diocesan, my lord Bishop of Aberdeen," he said, in pained fashion.

"Now you see why Alex did not want these two beauties before his earldom court!" Jamie said to his wife — who for some time had been sitting with one hand pressed tightly over her mouth and the other held against her stomach, in an effort to contain her emotions.

"Yes. Excellent," John Stewart was acceding. "The Bishop of Aberdeen it must be. You agree, my lord of Mar?"

"Not so!" Leslie objected. "I demand my rights. From the King's Justiciar, not any snivelling churchman! This man Forbes is Crowner of Aberdeen, a bishop's man. Think you I will win my rights from Greenlaw?"

"H'mm. My lord of Mar?"

"I would agree, my lord Justiciar, that these matters complained of are not such as we can pronounce upon here. Reference to an ecclesiastical court would appear to be proper. If not the complainant's own Diocesan, then to another. The Bishop of Ross, perhaps? Since I cannot see the Justiciar's jurisdiction extending to church matters. Unless, to be sure, there is further complaint of a more secular nature?"

"There is indeed!" Forbes put in. "I demand to be protected from the calumnies and assaults of this madman. And that the

King's Grace punishes him suitably. He is naught but a thorn in the flesh to all decent men — and women. Forby, it is not so much a thorn as a *rod* in the flesh he is to them!"

"*You* say it? Whose whorings are known from Dee to the Spey!"

"*I* cannot claim seventy bastard sons — to say nothing of the queans! He cannot deny that, my lords, I warrant!"

For the first time Leslie had no ready answer. It might be that he could not indeed deny the charge; more probably that he did not wish to do so, as a man of some spirit.

"I have heard no complaints!" he said, shortly.

"No — not from your wife, by the Mass!" the other charged. "Who is rejoiced to have you out of her bed, I am assured, whosoever else's you are in!"

"Do not soil my wife's fair name with your foul lips, bear-worshipper! I have been a good husband to her — which is more than you have been to yours. I have given her seven good sons and seven daughters living. *She* has no cause to complain!"

"My lords . . ." Brave John attempted, but hardly hopefully. He was, of course, overborne. "Deny that your wife, Isabella Mortimer, so rejoiced to be quit of you, even for one night, that she sent seven of your doxies a thank-offering of meal and meat!" Forbes exclaimed.

"You do not have even that right, man. It was an especial occasion, my lords. Those seven women I bairned all in the same night and in four parishes. By God's mercy they were all brought to bed the same day, and delivered with fine sons. My lady was pleased to send each a half-boll of meal, a half-boll of malt, a wedder-lamb and five shillings siller. I say that shows a good and satisfied wife."

Mary Stewart emitted an unusually inelegant squeak and squawk from behind her hand. "Sakes, Jamie!" she gasped. "Is he not a joy? Seven! *You* could not rise to that, I swear! Lord — my belly aches!"

"So it should — and more than your belly, woman!" he asserted severely. "For so great a Christian, this Leslie sounds to be a menace to all decent husbands — and wives abetting him, to their shame. The man's no more than a stallion! I would find for Forbes, whatever, bear or not, if I was John Stewart."

"For why? What is the charge? We have not heard it yet. Or have I missed it?"

164

Clearly something of the same sort was preoccupying the judges, who were conferring together, whilst Sir Alexander proclaimed his disgust.

John of Coull waved a hand. "No doubt these, h'm, informations are interesting and instructive, my lords," he said, "but still they do not concern this Court. We are not here to try matters of adultery or illegitimacy, any more than offences against the Church. Either we hear of injury to the King's peace and lieges, or we must refer all to an ecclesiastical court." He pointed at Leslie. "*Have* you a personal injury to complain of, Sir Andrew? Other than to your name and pride? Which are not our present concern."

"I have, Christ God! I was assailed by this man's bastard brother, John Out-with-the-Sword, of Callievar, at the funeral of a kinswoman of my own, at the kirk of Forbes on the feast of the Assumption of the Blessed Virgin, I tell you."

"Assailed? How assailed, my lord?"

"He lies," Forbes observed, but almost dutifully, wearily, now.

"By that damnable bell! He rang it at me, shouted. Mocked the dead, and me, from his hill — all through the interment."

"Unseemly, yes," the Justiciar sympathised. "Lacking due respect. But . . . a matter for private adjustment, surely? For you and your seven good sons?"

"When I sought to do the same, and sent my son Davie and my servants up the hill at him, this damnable John assailed them, first with arrows then with the sword. He struck Davie to the effusion of blood."

"Ah. So there *was* an attack upon the person? Of your son."

"In self-defence," Sir Alexander pointed out.

"The creature assailed us."

"In self-defence. You sent your people up at him, from the kirk. If your miserable son Davie sustained some small hurt, he had but himself to blame. Or you, for sending so poor a sworder against Johnnie!"

"He shot arrows whilst yet distant. Was that self-defence?"

"Was your son injured by an arrow?"

"No, by the sword. But three of my servants were slain by the arrows on the way up, I'd mind you, Forbes."

"Johnnie is a fair archer, yes. Good with the axe and quarterstaff, likewise. Though best of all with the sword . . ."

"Wait you — wait!" John Stewart exclaimed. "Sir Andrew —

165

you say *slain*? Three servants killed? By this John Forbes?"

"Aye, as they climbed the hill."

"But . . . this is altogether different! Why did you not say so, long since? Here was slaughter, of the King's lieges. Why all this talk of bells and idolatry and the like, when you had this slaying?"

"They were but servants," Leslie pointed out.

"Servants," Forbes agreed — the first agreement between them that day.

The judges exchanged glances.

"Nevertheless, subjects of the King's Grace and entitled to the King's protection," Alex said, sternly for him. "Why were we not told?"

Silence — this too for the first time.

"Do I take it, Sir Andrew, that you in fact are not petitioning about these deaths, but only of the injury to your son? And the offence to yourself?" John of Coull enquired slowly.

"That is so."

"And you, Sir Alexander, are not concerned with the fact that your brother slew these men?"

"It was unfortunate. But the responsibility was Leslie's. They were armed. He should not have sent them up the hill to attack Johnnie. He shot no arrows until they climbed the hill."

"Then, my lords, since you both hold barons' courts, with power of pit and gallows, you could have settled this between you. Or you could have appealed to the Sheriff of Aberdeen. I am at a loss to know on what this Court is expected to adjudicate."

"The Sheriff of Aberdeen is Forbes's good-brother," Leslie reminded.

"I understood it was my lord Earl of Mar, himself."

"Now. Not then."

"When, then, did this offence take place? The Feast of the Assumption did you not say?"

"Aye. But two years back."

"Two years? Why, then, wait until now, to bring it before this Justiciary?"

"Because . . . I wasna like to win justice before."

"I do not understand you, my lord. If your barony courts were of no avail, and you could not rely on the Sheriff, there was still the Mar earldom court, and finally this royal court of appeal. Why wait two years?"

166

Red Andrish looked almost uncomfortable — as, oddly enough, did Forbes. "It was difficult, see you," he said.

"I do *not* see it, I fear."

The litigants actually exchanged glances.

"Come, my lord — answer me."

"There was no earl, mind. And, and my lord of Badenoch was Justiciar."

"So?"

"Sir Malcolm Drummond was no superior of mine."

"Nor mine," added Forbes.

"But the Countess was, and is. And she controlled her own earldom."

"She did, aye."

"And you did not appeal to her, to Lady Isobel?"

"No."

"Why?"

Leslie's florid features were purple now. After a pause, he burst out. "Because this Forbes knew her bed ower well, that's why!" He glanced at Alex, half-apologetically, and then away again.

There was a profound hush in Elgin Castle's hall.

John Stewart was at a loss as to what to say. He did not look at his fellow-judges, but considered his finger-nails and cleared his throat.

It was Alex Stewart who spoke, eventually. "We need not here consider such hearsay," he said evenly. "It is not evidence. By the nature of matters Sir Andrew Leslie can have no proofs to support his unfortunate statement. I request that it be removed from any record of these proceedings."

"Most certainly, my lord Earl," Brave John acceded, almost eagerly. "This Court regrets that it was said, Sir Andrew. We can consider only testimony which can be substantiated."

"I . . . ah . . . mmm." Red Andrish said.

"I, my lords, wish to repudiate what this man has said," Forbes declared strongly. "It is a calumny on our feudal lady. And false, like all else he has said this day. All lies."

"Damn you, Forbes — it is no lie, as well you know!" his enemy cried. "As I could prove, if I wished."

"How prove? You but disclaim our lady's honour."

"It is not *her* honour I disclaim but yours, man! You made but a poor showing in her bed, compared with my own self. She told me so, herself!"

There was uproar in court.

167

It took some time to achieve silence, even the Justiciar seeming to be in no great hurry to make himself heard. Mary, gleaming-eyed, shook her husband's arm.

"Now you see what your Alex has taken on," she said. "I told you he would not have his troubles to seek, with that one."

Jamie shook his head unhappily. "Damn the man!" he muttered. "This is beyond all."

John Stewart had found his voice. "Sir Andrew — I forbid any further such ill-considered and unmannerly statements in this Court. Your spleen has deprived you of your wits, it is clear. You will no more traduce the fair name of this great lady, or any other. Mind it." He turned to his colleague, doubtfully. "My lord of Mar — do you wish to make any comment?"

Alex drew a deep breath. "Little," he said. "Save to assert my lady's good name and honour before all, and to declare its safety from the slanders of so great and self-confessed a lecher and defiler of women. All that has been spoken of took place before my marriage to the Countess, but I personally vouch for their untruth." He paused. "And now, my lord Justiciar, I suggest that overmuch time has been taken up by this unsuitable and unnecessary cause. I say that we should come to swift decision and have done."

"So say I, my lord, and most heartily." Brave John frowned. "Only . . . I confess to being uncertain as to what it is we are to decide upon. We have heard so much that is irrelevant to this Court — and what *is* relevant, the slaying of these three servants of Sir Andrew's, does not appear to be before us. I fail to see what pronouncement we can make."

"I, likewise," Prior Moray said. "May we not dismiss the entire matter as irrelevant and beyond the jurisdiction of this Court? Or remit it to a court of Holy Church?"

"Perhaps. As former Justiciar, my lord of Mar, how would you have dealt with this?"

Thus appealed to, Alex spoke carefully. "I would say that, despite Sir Andrew's intemperate and ill-judged statements, he has shown himself to have suffered wrong, which we cannot dismiss. On the other hand, nothing has been proved against Sir Alexander's good repute. We are not concerned with matters under the jurisdiction of the Church. But we are concerned with the keeping of the King's peace. And it has been established, I think, that this John Forbes of Callievar has indeed offended against and broken that peace, to the distress of the lieges and

168

the effusion of blood. We can, and I believe we should, therefore, require Sir Alexander Forbes, in whose baronial jurisdiction his half-brother undoubtedly is, to take full and due steps to remedy this situation, and to ensure that the said John Forbes no longer breaks the King's peace. Less than this we cannot do. More is not within our competence."

"Exactly. Excellently said," his cousin agreed thankfully. "You accept, my lord Prior? Very well. I so pronounce, in the name of the King's Grace. You, Sir Andrew, accept this judgement?" That was not so much a question as a challenge.

Leslie pursed thick lips, frowned, and then shrugged. "I do."

"And you, Sir Alexander — you will take due action to control and punish John Forbes of Callievar?"

"I will."

"So be it. This cause is closed. As, also, is this present assize of Moray." Relievedly, John Stewart rose to his feet — as must all others. "God save the King's Grace!"

The trumpets blared.

"What are you going to say to Alex now?" Mary asked, as they filed out after the judges.

"I do not know. That was an ill mouthful for any man to stomach," Jamie said, "regarding his wife. But . . . if any man can face it with dignity, he can."

"Yes. But it is the effect on *other* men, and on his control of her earldom, that is important."

"I think that will be none so great. Isobel of Mar's reputation has been well known for many a year. In her own Mar in especial, no doubt. I mind Duke David told me of it, long ago. But she was strong enough, as woman as well as countess, to carry it off. This, today, must have been a sore offence for Alex — but I do not think that it will injure him."

"Perhaps. So long as she does not continue on her course, now she is wed to him!"

"I think not. She is older now. And she loves him — that I swear. She says openly that she has never loved another. She will wish to hold Alex now — a younger man. And that would not be the way to do it. No — Alex knew her reputation when he wed her. Part of the price he had to pay."

"For . . . what?"

"For power, no less. Power for good, yes. But power, nevertheless. Alex is as much a Stewart as the rest of you! Though better than most . . ."

169

XI

JAMIE DOUGLAS'S PROGNOSTICATION was proved fairly accurate. Alex Stewart went quietly ahead with the consolidation of his hold over the earldom of Mar in the months that followed, apparently unaffected by the unfortunate revelations of Sir Andrew Leslie. Whatever he may have felt personally in the matter, he revealed no sign of it. As for the Countess Isobel, she only laughed when she heard of the allegations, called Red Andrish an old goat and Sandy Forbes too touchy by half — a verdict which was reinforced when it was learned that Forbes had gone home to Strathdon from Elgin, straightway summoned John Out-with-the-Sword into his presence, and without further ado took the said sword and struck off his half-brother's head with a single stroke, by way of interpretation of the Justiciar's order to remedy the situation. Thereafter he had had the body buried without ceremony at the back of the kirkyard — which was considered by most of Mar to be almost a more drastic punishment than the beheading itself, for only the least respected outcasts and the nameless were interred in such a position — indication, it was realised, of the Laird of Forbes's resentment at being caused inconvenience and public affront by any, kin or otherwise, rather than any kind of acknowledgement of injury done to the Laird of Balquhain. Alex, after a due interval, made a point of calling upon each protagonist, avoiding all reference to the dispute, and being well received by both. Which was the most satisfactory outcome, in the circumstances — for between them these two could field five hundred armed men at least, more at a pinch. The feudal system was much concerned with realities.

Jamie Douglas did not venture south during the months that followed, despite his officially-proclaimed immunity from arrest, being, as has been indicated, of a somewhat suspicious nature. He did send letters, however, mainly by travelling churchmen, to his father and brothers, requesting the payment to himself of the dues and rents from his restored estates of Stoneypath and Baldwinsgill. But, after due consideration, and discussion with Mary, he did not ask that his brother Johnnie vacate Aberdour Castle. For two reasons; one that it was set in Albany's county and earldom of Fife, and was just too close to Falkland and Rossie and other seats of his enemies for comfortable living; the other that he had a fondness for Johnnie and did not want to deprive him of his new style and status — or of his young woman there, Jeannie Boswell, which might well have resulted from any dispossession and return to Dalkeith. Unexpectedly this gesture produced an appreciative reaction from their father — who appeared once again to have regained a new lease on life — in the announcement that he was settling the barony and lands of Roberton, in Borthwick Water at the head of Teviotdale, on Jamie in compensation, a more valuable and extensive property than Aberdour. Mary, when she had heard of Jean Boswell's occupancy of her former house and home, had announced, in possibly typical feminine fashion, that she wanted nothing more to do with it, and was quite content to remain living at Lochindorb, where she and the young people were now firmly installed and beloved of Mariota de Athyn. She did not trust her half-brother Robert any more than did her husband. So, with Alex in Mar much of the time and Jamie a useful steward of his interests in Braemoray, enabling him to avoid having one of other of his awkward brothers in control at Lochindorb, the new Earl was well pleased to leave the situation as it was. The fact that the Douglases no longer felt themselves to be paupers, and dependent on Alex's charity, helped. Jamie, in fact, led a more normal, congenial and satisfying life than he had ever done.

But in the Scotland of this new fifteenth century, normality, congenial living and peace were conditions which not many were permitted to enjoy for long. That winter was punctuated by reports coming north that the Duke of Albany, far from taking his defeats at Linlithgow to heart, or at least amending his gubernatorial ways thereafter, was wielding an increasingly heavy hand. He was not a tyrant in any sense of oppressing the ordinary people; but no more did he seek to protect them from the ravages and savageries of others — especially some of his own minions. It seemed that he could not have been less interested in the state of the common folk, whom he was so determined to rule. He made a great proclamation of his resolve not to impose general taxation on the realm — which, of course, applied only to the land-owning interests and nobles, the burghs and the larger merchants and guilds, for the commonality had no wherewithal to pay tax anyway. Yet he increased customs dues, both greater and lesser, import licences, immunities and fines; but instead of applying the increased revenues towards the necessary maintenance of public works, roads, bridges, city walls, ports and harbours and so on, and the building up of a nucleus of a standing army which could bind together and service the feudal levies of the lords — as various parliaments and councils had decreed — he farmed out the customs collection lavishly to new men of his own raising, many of whom were blatant and harsh extortioners avid to grow rich quickly. Clearly the Governor was buying support in a big way. But support for what? He was already, and had long been, the power behind the throne. The King was unlikely to live long, and the new monarch would be only a boy, whom Albany could dominate as he did the father. Why then this suddenly much increased purchase of supporters, not only with Treasury and Exchequer revenues but with those of the earldoms and lordships Albany controlled personally? He himself was a man of fairly frugal tastes and habit — unusual in a Stewart. Another ominous theme was his new wooing of Holy Church, something he had little troubled with hitherto, never previously attempting to hide his contempt for upjumped prelates, clerics and clerks. Jamie wondered if he, the Governor, feared a link-up between the North, as represented by Alex, and the Church as represented by Bishop Wardlaw, with the young prince as pawn, and was taking countermeasures? Suspicious as ever, the Douglas considered that in such circumstances a very watchful eye should be kept on John of Coull, excellent company as he might be. Nothing altered the fact that he was Albany's son, legitimate and therefore in line, at two removes, for the throne.

Alex did not commit himself to more than general comment.

Then, with the winter well advanced, in late February they learned that young James, Earl of Carrick — he had not been advanced to his late brother's dukedom of Rothesay although some called him that — had started on his journey to France. The French King had sent the necessary invitation to his Court, and was indeed despatching a special ship to collect the boy. Until the vessel arrived James had been moved secretly from St. Andrews and in the care of the Earl of Orkney to — of all places — the Bass Rock, the towering isolated stack in the mouth of the Firth of Forth, with its small fortalice perched high thereon. Nothing could illustrate more significantly the fears felt by the King and Bishop Wardlaw for the safety of the prince. The Bass Rock was an utterly impregnable if extremely uncomfortable roosting-place, from which none could snatch him; the Earl of Orkney, Henry St. Clair, although a Scot was a subject of the King of Norway for his earldom, and so could not be attacked in any way without international complications; and the same applied, of course, to the ship being sent by the King of France, to interfere with which would breach the cornerstone of Scots foreign policy, the Auld Alliance. No chances were being taken.

This news was welcomed with great relief by Alex and Jamie, as by innumerable other loyal lieges of the Crown. The prince seemingly now was safe, the succession assured. Whatever else, Albany could not now gain the throne for himself, or at least not by any obvious means.

However, the tidings which reached Lochindorb, via the Church, a few days later, perturbed Jamie. Sir David Fleming of Cumbernauld, a friend of the King, who had been responsible for conveying the young prince to the Bass Rock, by sea, had been set upon and foully slain on his way home, at Herdmanston in East Lothian, not much more than a dozen miles from the Bass. And his slayer had been Sir James the Gross, next brother to the Earl of Douglas, who was making no secret of the fact, indeed boasting of the deed, clearly in no danger of retribution from the Governor. Which implied Albany's anger at the prince's escape, and at the same time, unhappily, the house of Douglas's involvement on the Governor's side, at least under its present direction. Jamie decided that he had been wise to remain in the North.

It was almost a month after this last news reached Braemoray, and the first promises of spring were beginning to stir in that world of the mountains and glens, when, on a windy fresh day of late March, Alex Stewart came in haste to his former home, and was rowed out over the slap-slapping wavelets of the loch, with a dark young man at his side, a stranger to Jamie. Alex was in Highland garb — he had been away in upper Strathspey in his capacity as Lord of Badenoch, seeking to settle a dispute between the Cattanachs and the Macphersons which his brother Sir Andrew had signally failed to do. The stranger wore Lowland dress.

"Jamie — this is Patrick Leslie, Younger of Balquhain. He came seeking me, with tidings. Sir James Douglas, my good friend." Alex looked preoccupied, less at ease than his usual.

"I had not thought to see you so soon. When you left here three days back, you thought to be away as much as two weeks," Jamie commented, nodding to young Leslie.

"Yes. I have had to make change of plan." He frowned. "I will tell you presently. Come, Patrick man — you will be hungry. I know that I am . . ."

When Alex decently could, he got Jamie alone.

"I am in a sorry pickle," he declared. "I am at a loss just what to do. I would value your good counsel, Jamie — as often ere this. It is about Isobel, my wife."

"Ah! I'd be something loth to advise between man and wife, Alex."

"No doubt. But I know no other I can turn to. And I need to talk this out with someone. You have a notably level head."

"Where women are concerned, Mary says that I am but a bairn!"

"They say that of us all. Perhaps it is true. But — bairn or not, I need guidance. Red Andrish Leslie sent his son seeking me, followed me to Ruthven — to tell me that Isobel, after I left Kildrummy five days back, went secretly to the old castle of Piell, in Kennethmont, to meet Sir Alexander Forbes. It is a remote hold in the northern tip of the Lordship of the Garioch, bordering on Strathbogie, a hunting-house. She said nothing of this to me. And it is scarce the time of year for hunting!"

Jamie made no comment.

"See you — I do not wish to play the jealous husband, spying on my wife. If I am insufficient for her needs, I must bear it with such patience as I may, Jamie, I recognise. At least, before others. She is a, a lusty woman. No doubt but you are aware of that. And I have been leaving her much alone these months, as I sought to bring her earldom into shape. But . . . that is what divides my mind — the earldom. Red Andrish, you see, is concerned with more than proving to me that he was telling the truth that day at Elgin. He claims that Forbes has been boasting that he has my Countess in his breeches pocket, or thereby!

174

That he is going to get her to transfer the keepership of the Forest of Kennethmont to himself, from Leslie. And this Piell Castle is the main house for that Forest."

"Is this so great a matter?"

"It is, yes. Not the keepership itself, perhaps, but this of transfer. Whether it is true, or not, I do not know. But it could do the earldom the greatest hurt. Do you not see? Here I am trying to hammer this Mar into a strong and united whole, a force to wield in the North, a rallying point for other forces, a link between the Highland clans and the low-country lairds. And here are two of the most powerful vassals of the earldom like to be thrown at each other's throats. They have always been at feud, yes — but this is different. This transfer of the keepership could be like throwing a meaty bone between two savage hounds. They have been content to growl at each other for long; this could set them tearing and rending. And with it, my earldom."

"Scarce so bad as that, Alex?"

"I say that it could be. Kennethmont abuts the Leslie lands — and it is far from the Forbes properties. Moreover, it lies next to the great Gordon lordship of Strathbogie — delicate folk to handle. There is an heiress at Strathbogie now, as you know, since her father Sir Adam Gordon was slain at Homildon. Leslie hints that Forbes would like her for one of his sons! I have been trying to bring the Gordons into my fold. This is no time to play such games. Do you realise how many Leslie lairdships there are in Mar? Red Andrish is not the head of the family; but any such open affront to him would bring in the rest. Forbes is less strong — but he is linked in marriage with other great houses of power. So, indeed, is Leslie. I would not have Mar divided into warring halves, and all my labours spoiled."

"The Lady Isobel must herself know this."

"No doubt she does — since she has managed Mar herself for long. But it is folly, nevertheless. Perhaps she recognises the danger, perhaps not. Perhaps she cares not? That is why I am at a loss. She does not see my use of the earldom with quite the same eye as I do! She is not greatly concerned with uniting the North against my uncle Albany. She may even be seeking, in her own way, to halt me somewhat. You see my difficulty?"

"To be sure. But it may not be so ill as you fear. This Leslie may be making overmuch of it, for his own purposes. He is a wild man . . ."

175

"There you have it. He *is* a wild man, and would not hesitate to sound to arms from what his son tells me. Much of any earl's, or other great lord's, time and effort is taken up with keeping his vassals from quarrelling and so weakening his power. That is what I have been doing at Ruthven, between the Macphersons and Cattanachs, for my lordship of Badenoch. Leslie asks me to intervene now, in Mar — and uses this of my wife's dalliance with Forbes to force my hand. I do not wish to seem to go rushing after my wife like any jealous husband. You know how she would deal with that! Yet I must do something."

"To me, it seems that you have to choose, Alex. Which means most to you? Your wife or your earldom?"

"I am fond of her, Jamie. We match each other well, for the most part. But . . ."

"Aye — *but*, my friend?"

"You must know how much the power of Mar means to me, man. For what I can do with it. Have already begun to do. With it I can build up the North into a force to halt Albany. Young James Stewart may well need that force, one day. The realm will need it, I say. Only I can provide it, I think."

"You have sufficiently answered my question, my lord of Mar! You go to this Kennethmont."

The other stared at him, nibbling his lip.

"You will require some excuse, to be sure. Could you not say that the Ruthven business was settled speedily, and coming back, you were given word that she, the Lady Isobel, was at Kennethmont? You could say that coming by Lochindorb, the place, this Piell Castle, was on your way home to Kildrummy, could you not? So, like any loving husband, you thought to join her."

"It might serve, yes. But . . . it is damnable to be thus held. To have to choose . . ."

"You chose before ever you came here, Alex, I think. When you cut short your time at Ruthven and rode here in haste, you had already chosen. Else why come?"

"On my soul, you are devilish blunt, stark, Jamie Douglas!"

"What would you prefer that I told you, then . . .?"

*   *   *

Nothing would do but that Jamie must accompany the Earl on his uncomfortable errand. It seemed that the latter still found him an aid and comfort in certain dealings with his wife — little as that man relished the role. The high passes were still blocked with the winter snows, and many rivers running too high to ford, so that a roundabout route had to be followed — and one which would make a passing near to the Forest of Kennethmont seem realistic. This involved going down Spey to Craigellachie, and up Glen Fiddich to Auchindoun, and then crossing the low pass of Glass to the Raws of Strathbogie and up that Gordon valley by the narrows of Gartly and Noth, a journey of nearly sixty rough miles. In the present state of the terrain and the hours of daylight, they would take two days to do it, halting for the night at the castle of Bucharin near Craigellachie.

They sent off Patrick Leslie homewards on his own, advisedly. Two days later, then, after paying due respects to sundry Gordon lairds — that proud clan, half-Highland, half-Lowland, being in a touchy state following the death of their chief at Homildon, with only a child heiress and two powerful and assertive but illegitimate uncles, to steer it meantime — they rode up the Water of Bogie, the sun already dipping behind the steep ramparts of the Tap o' Noth rearing on their right, notable country for ambushes, as well the Gordons appreciated.

The Forest of Kennethmont lay just outwith mid-Strathbogie to the east, covering a vast area of the low Foudland Hills around the vale of the Shevock Water. It was a forest in the hunting sense, by no means all woodland, with braes and valleys, moorland plateau, peat-bog and empty wilderness, dotted with Caledonian pines, oak and ash and endless silvery scrub birch, a place alive with deer and boar, wildcat and foxes, a great haunt of wildfowl. Wolves too, infested its fastnesses — and one of the principal tasks of the keepership was to keep these down, or at least to prevent too many complaints from neighbouring landholders as to depredations amongst their flocks and herds. The Gordons, of course, poached the forest shamelessly, always with the excuse that they were really only putting down the wolves for their own protection. Nothing could be done about this; but Sir Andrew Leslie, as Keeper, had a working agreement with them whereby they were reasonably discreet in their activities and helpful in keeping lesser offenders away. Matters such as these were of quite major importance in the smooth running of a widespread lordship in the North.

Piell was a commodious but fairly elementary establishment, a hall-house capable of a moderate defence rather than any fortified strength. It lay in a hollow re-entrant of the wooded hills on the north side of the main valley, under Knockandy Hill, a pleasant place surrounded by the cabins of the foresters, its kennels and stabling. Almost the first person the newcomers saw about the place, other than the servitors and woodmen, was the Lord John Stewart of Coull, handing his horse over to a groom.

It would be hard to declare who was most surprised by this cousinly encounter. Being the men they were, both Stewarts recovered quickly, and greeted each other with some appearance of pleasure and normalcy. But there was no doubt that each was concerned at the possible implications of the other's presence. Jamie made little attempt at a like cordiality.

In the hall, cheerful with chatter and clatter and the roaring of two great log fires, they found quite a sizeable company about to sit down to a meal, servitors bustling. Gradually, however, a profound hush developed as the newcomers' appearance and identity was perceived.

Isobel of Mar's ringing laughter ended that silence. "Alex!" she cried, rising. "My devoted lord and master!" And she moved from her place at the centre of the dais-table to come round to meet and greet him, neither hurrying nor with any evident hesitation. They embraced with every sign of affection.

John of Coull watched them, and smiled with what need not necessarily have been relief. Jamie Douglas watched them, and John Stewart, and did not smile.

"How great and unlooked for a pleasure, Alex," his wife declared, standing back a little. "I thought you deep amongst your wild Highlandmen in Badenoch."

"No doubt you did," he agreed. "But I finished there more speedily than I had thought to. And coming home by Lochindorb, by chance learned that you, my dear, were here at Kennethmont, for some reason. And so came by Strathbogie, as none so far out of my road to Kildrummy. For the pleasure of seeing you the sooner!"

"How considerate of you, my love! And how . . . well-informed!"

"Aye. News travels apace in my Highlands. Is it not fortunate?" He turned. "Cousin John, too — you seem to have been equally fortunate! Or were you at Kennethmont purely by chance? It seems a long way from Coull."

"John came, quite in haste, at my request," the Countess said easily. "He is, as ever, kind."

178

"Ah, yes. And what for was the haste? Which brought you all here?"

"Sufficient — as you shall hear. But come, sit you. And you, Sir James. When *you* appear, with Alex, I am apt to fear the worst! Were you also on your way to Kildrummy?"

"I am, as ever, at my lord's command, Countess," Jamie said briefly.

"I see. One day, you and I must come to some conclusion, Sir James! Alex — here is Sir Alexander Forbes, and his sons."

"So I see. Greetings, Sir Alexander. How fortunate that you too found yourself at Kennethmont!"

"Sir Alexander it was who brought us here, Alex. To our much advantage." Isobel of Mar was very much in command of herself and of the situation. "Sit by me here, husband. John, you at my other side. Sir James — find yourself a place. How far have you ridden today, Alex . . .?"

Determined small talk was maintained whilst the meal was being served, Alex clearly awkwardly placed to force the pace, or to seem to cross-question his wife in front of others. Jamie, between two of the Forbes sons, ate stolidly.

It was the Countess herself who presently returned to the subject of their presence there. "We owe a debt to Sir Alexander," she announced, pushing back her platter. "He sent me timely word, suggesting that I should come here to Kennethmont, secretly. Or *we* should come — but you were already gone to Badenoch. Come, for the well-being of the earldom. Yourself absent, I came at once."

"It must have been a grave matter?" Alex said carefully.

"Yes. He believed so. As do I. Sir Alexander has discovered that Sir Andrew Leslie desires to gain control of the great lordship of Strathbogie, by seeking to wed his second son, Norman, to the heiress, Elizabeth Gordon. He has made offer of this Forest of Kennethmont to the Gordons as inducement to the match. It is not his, to be sure, but mine. Or ours. But his family have been the keepers of it for so long that he appears to deem it his own, in fact if not name. And the Gordons have long wanted it, reaching into their own lands as it does."

Forbes nodded strongly. "That is so, my lord."

Alex caught Jamie's eye, down the table, and then went back to considering his rib of beef. "I do not see Sir Andrew Leslie here, to answer such charge," he said, slowly.

"He would but deny it," Forbes declared.

179

"Perhaps. But he might possibly have a different tale to tell, some other side to the story."

"What do you mean?" the Countess asked sharply.

"I but mean that before we make any judgement on this, we should at least hear the other side. As we did at, h'm, Elgin! Moreover, there may well be others than Leslie wishful to marry this heiress of Gordon. And bidding other offers for the privilege."

"What has that to do with it?"

"I but wondered, my love. Wondered why Sir Andrew was not here. Indeed why any of us are here. Sir Alexander lives but six miles away from Kildrummy, at Forbes. Why come sixteen, to Kennethmont, to discuss this? Why indeed *you* required to come here at all, my dear? As Countess, should not Sir Alexander have come to you, at Kildrummy? By the same token, much as I rejoice to see him, how comes my good Cousin John here, likewise? From Coull — all of forty miles, I'd say."

Isobel of Mar was tapping finger-nails on the table. "As to the last, I *sent* to ask John to come — to aid me with advice. *You* were far away, and like to be gone many days. John acts Justiciar, does he not? And ought to be able to give a mere woman good counsel. I did not summon Sir Alexander to Kildrummy, but came here, because he besought me to. *He* was here, and this is where any decision should be made. It was expedient that I, as Countess of Mar, should be known to be here, by the Gordons. That they should recognise that Kennethmont is *mine*, not Leslie's. Perhaps they, like Red Andrish, have forgotten it! I have not summoned Leslie yet, until I learned fully on the matter. An' it please your lordship!" That last was less than sweetly added.

"I see," Alex said. "And what have you decided? Or been advised?"

"That it may be necessary to have a new Keeper of Kennethmont Forest."

"Not, by chance, Sir Alexander Forbes?"

"That is possible. Have you better counsel?" That last word was stressed.

Her husband drew a long breath. "I have not yet had opportunity fully to consider the matter. Any decision demands considerable thought, you will admit? For its divisive effect on the earldom, if for naught else. Have you considered what the Leslies, the whole house of Leslie, would have to say to any such transfer of the keepership? A dozen lairdships, at least."

"I do not require to be advised as to the number of my vassals! Sir Andrew might be otherwise . . . compensated."

"It would have to be large compensation, to appease that one's pride."

"I am not greatly concerned for Red Andrish's pride."

"But I *am*, my dear. Or, more truly, the pride of the house of Leslie. As Earl of Mar, I will not see the earldom divided, if I can help it."

"Earl of Mar by *my* gift!"

"To be sure, Isobel. But Earl of Mar, nevertheless — by the King's edict and confirmation."

She started to speak, and then restrained herself.

It was John Stewart who spoke, conversationally. "The Gordons are uppity — whoever weds their heiress. Jock of Scurdargue and Tam of Ruthven make a rough pair of uncles. They will require watching, I think. The presence of the Countess here today, and of your lordship, may serve to make them more careful."

"I am glad that you, Cousin, and all others, recognise that they are dangerous," Alex acknowledged steadily. "I have done so, for long. They have represented one of my principal problems in this earldom. They are not of it, yet they much affect it, encircling it to the north, and, moreover, coming between it and my lordship of Badenoch. They can muster two thousand men. And these two half-brothers of the late Sir Adam are strong and violent men. Let none here think to handle them lightly — or you may bite off more than you can chew!" It was not often that Alex Stewart sounded almost grim.

"Exactly my own estimate, Cousin. Else I might have thought to marry this Elizabeth Gordon my own self!" John of Coull exclaimed, laughing. "After all, she is also my cousin. Her mother, Sir Adam's wife, was sister to *my* mother, both daughters of the late Keith, the Marischal. But . . . I would wed none with two uncles such as those!"

This jocular note served to release the tension in the hall. Both the Earl and Countess of Mar accepted the relief.

"Traitor, Johnnie!" Isobel said.

"A Justiciar's judgement, indeed!" Alex commended.

The talk at the dais-table became general and at least superficially easy.

It was some time thereafter before Alex could have a word

with Jamie Douglas apart. On the excuse of having to see to their men's comfort and lodging in the overcrowded purlieus of Piell, they later strolled to and fro in the courtyard, in the April dusk.

"What think you of it all, Jamie?" his friend asked. "This tangled web?"

"I think that you were wise to come."

"Aye. That at least is sure. But the rest? How think you? What is Isobel at? Did she come here in lust, in concern for the earldom, or to counter *my* efforts?"

"Who am I to tell you that, Alex? It could be any — or all!"

The other pursed his lips. "Perhaps. That is the curse of it. I still do not see why she had to come here, to Kennethmont, at all. This declared warning-off of Gordon, or indeed of Leslie, could have been done equally well by letter."

"But that would not have allowed her the company of Alexander Forbes."

"If she wanted that, why send for John of Coull?"

"He did not arrive until a deal later. She has been here for four days, it seems. The Lord John came only yesterday."

"So?"

"Perhaps your lady planned it that way? Reckoned that she would have had enough of Forbes by then. And would be glad of alternative company!"

"God's Eyes, man — you are suggesting that my wife is so hot for other men than her own husband that she planned this meeting, in a remote house, when I was gone for sufficient time — and arranged to have not one but two paramours, in succession?"

"I suggest nothing that you have not considered yourself, Alex, when you asked your question. But — it may be that we greatly wrong her, in this. It could be that Forbes indeed planned it, and that the Countess came, judging it necessary for the earldom's sake. But sent for the Lord John to join them, to safeguard her name and repute. As well as to advise."

"You think that is the likelier explanation?"

"No," the other answered simply.

"Damnation — you are as bad as my mother! You have never liked Isobel."

"I admire much in the Countess." That was stiff. "But I see her as other than most men's wives — of an independent mind and lusty body. She has been as a queen up here in Mar, for

182

long. Her former husband did not interfere, it seems. If you do not like that, you should perhaps have heeded your lady-mother — who has known the Countess Isobel much longer than have you!"

Angrily the other increased his pace, and Jamie dropped heedfully behind. But presently Alex paused for his friend to catch up again.

"You are right, to be sure," he said, shaking his head. "I knew Isobel's repute before I married her. Foolishly, I believed that I could change her. And, and . . ."

"And you wanted her earldom."

"I did, yes. It was the answer to so much. But . . . I am fond of her, Jamie. Still. That is the devil of it . . ."

He was interrupted by the clatter of hooves, as three horsemen came riding into the courtyard on steaming, mud-spattered beasts. Drawing up, one, travel-stained and weary-seeming in his saddle, pointed at the two strollers.

"You, there. I seek the Lord John Stewart of Coull. Is he here?"

Alex was not the man to stand on his dignity. "Yes. He is within," he called back.

The trio dismounted stiffly, and the man who had spoken tossed his reins to one of his escort and stamped heavily in at the hall-house doorway.

"You saw?" Alex asked quietly.

"Aye." It was not so dark that Jamie had failed to distinguish the royal livery. "From his father. Ridden far and fast. No doubt from Coull."

"It could be Justiciary business . . ."

When, presently, they went inside again, one of the Forbes sons came to Alex.

"My lord Earl — the Lord John Stewart asks that you will be pleased to go to him — in yonder small chamber, with the Countess and my father."

Alex nodded. "Come, Jamie."

In a withdrawing-room off the hall the three men rose as the newcomers entered. The Countess herself was placing food and drink before the latest visitors, no servants being present. The indications of fatigue in face and posture were most evident in the candlelight.

"My lord Earl of Mar — a courier from the Governor," John Stewart said.

"I regret, my lord, any offence given," the man said, words slurred somewhat, "I did not know your lordship."

"No offence taken, sir. Sit you to your refreshment. You look tired."

"A bearer of ill tidings, Cousin," John said. "My father sends word that the Prince James's ship, sent by the French king, and sailing from the Forth, has been attacked and captured by English pirates off Flamborough Head. James is now a prisoner of King Henry, at London."

Appalled, the others stared at him.

"The boy is unharmed, but a captive. The Earl of Orkney with him. They are held in the royal palace at Westminster."

"But, but . . . the realm is at truce with England!" Alex exclaimed. "Henry has no right to hold our prince."

"Does Henry Bolingbroke require a *right* for what he does?"

"Fall foul of him — this is as good as a declaration of war! The heir to the throne, aye, and a ship chartered by King Charles of France. So he challenges France also. As well as the King of Norway, whose subject Orkney is. Has this king lost his wits?"

"I know not. But it seems that *our* King has! On being given the tidings of his son's capture, old King Robert, our uncle, fell under a stroke. Now he lies between life and death."

"Dear God!"

There was silence in that room for long moments, as all that was implied sank in.

It was Jamie who spoke. "His Grace will die," he said, flatly. "He has wanted death, for long. This will end all for him. So now the Governor will both rule and reign in this realm."

None challenged that realistic summary.

"My father has called a parliament, in the King's name, at Perth. For Saint Columba's Day, at the beginning of June."

"Is Henry saying that he will continue to hold the prince?" Alex demanded of the courier.

"We do not know, my lord. The Governor has had only the bare word, a short letter, from King Henry. Saying that the Earl of Carrick is safely in his custody, after his adventure with the pirates. Saying indeed that he is in safer hands than those of the French! Saying also that he will take it upon himself to instruct the prince in manners and chivalry, better than would any Frenchmen!"

"The insolence of him! That means, then, that he does intend to hold him as hostage, for long. This is intolerable!"

"Intolerable or not, my dear, we must need accept it, tolerate it — since we can do no other," the practical Countess said. "Or would you suggest outright war? Thousands to die? And Donald of the Isles awaiting his chance!"

They eyed each other.

"We shall see," Alex said heavily. "This parliament will decide. But . . . till June is a damnable time to wait."

"A true parliament requires forty days of notice to be lawful," John of Coull reminded. "And nothing less than a full parliament will be required in this pass. No mere council will suffice."

"A Privy Council should be held at once, at least . . ."

By unspoken consent their immediate controversies and the reasons for them all being at Kennethmont were, if not dismissed or forgotten, at least laid aside meantime in the face of this national crisis. John Stewart had been summoned south forthwith by his father; and Alex wanted to get back to Kildrummy without delay. The Countess recognised that changed circumstances made the Forbes-Leslie-Gordon controversy presently untimely and, possibly, romantic adventures scarcely convenient. She agreed to a return to Kildrummy.

Jamie went back alone to Lochindorb, with Alex's instructions to warn the Badenoch clans into readiness for possibly swift mobilisation.

Confrontations fell to be postponed, in public at least.

XII

THE SCOTS PARLIAMENT of 1406, held in the Blackfriars monastery, Perth, was a very different affair from the Council General at Linlithgow of the year before. This time the Duke of Albany was in undisputed control — for King Robert the Third had died some weeks before, and his brother had immediately proclaimed himself Regent as well as Governor, as indeed was his almost incontestable right and duty. Now he was both actually and lawfully supreme in Scotland — or would be, once parliament had confirmed his regency — wielding more power than anyone had done since Robert the Bruce. The King's authority could no longer be used against him, either as rallying-cry or modifying influence. None were left in any doubt of the fact.

It was a much larger assembly than that at Linlithgow for, in the national emergency, all who had the right to be present had flocked to Perth — earls, officers of state, lords of parliament, representatives of the sheriffdoms, shires and burghs, and, of course, the churchmen. The Highlands were, however, as usual, grievously under-represented, and Donald of the Isles a notable absentee. Oddly enough Jamie Douglas, who had again gone south in Alex's train, found on arrival at Perth that he was now entitled to attend as a commissioner, no longer a mere spectator, on account of his new barony of Roberton, gifted by his father to replace Aberdour. It was a freeholding, held direct of the Crown, and as such carried this privilege — like many another, not always utilised. So now he sat amongst the barons and freeholders.

Albany made it clear from the start that all was changed. For one thing, the Chancellor referred to him as Your Grace, and was not corrected. Instead of his accustomed chair behind the

186

central table, the Duke now sat on a splendid throne, brought from Scone, well apart, flanked by two magnificently tabarded heralds who bore above him between their staffs the Lion Rampant banner of Scotland. The Lord Lyon King of Arms stood directly behind.

After Bishop Greenlaw had said a brief prayer and declared that this duly called and lawful parliament of the Three Estates of Scotland was now in session, he announced that His Grace the Prince-Duke of Albany, Regent and Governor, would address the commissioners.

At least Robert Stewart's flat, factual voice, with its strange slight hesitation of speech, had not altered; nor his preference for brevity.

"My lords," he said, "owing to the capture of my nephew James, Earl of Carrick, by English pirates, and his subsequent holding by Henry Bolingbroke, calling himself King of England, and the consequent death of my brother, the King's Grace, it became my duty, both as heir presumptive to the throne and Governor of the realm, to assume forthwith the position, style, title and authority of Regent of the Kingdom of Scotland. Which appointment it is the first business of this parliament to confirm. My lord Earl of Crawford will now so move."

As Crawford began to rise, another voice intervened. "One moment, my lord Earl." It was Henry Wardlaw, the Primate. "Is this indeed the first business of this parliament, my lord Chancellor? Is it not our first and most important duty to proclaim and declare the accession to the throne, consequent on the sad death of our late monarch, of his only remaining son and undoubted heir, captive though he may be — James, by the Grace of God, King of Scots?"

A muted cheer rose from the body of the refectory.

The Chancellor looked at Albany.

"The Bishop of St. Andrews is mistaken," that man said coldly. "Until my position of Regent is confirmed, this parliament lacks its full authority, and is merely another Council General, unable to proclaim the succession. Only by the Crown's express pronouncement does it become a parliament. Proceed, my lord of Crawford."

"I so move," the Lindsay said, with notable lack of apparent enthusiasm, "that this Council declares Robert Stewart, Duke of Albany, to be Regent, with all the powers of the Crown — until such time as our lawful monarch returns to his realm.

187

There is no other who may so act. He is the heir presumptive."

"I second," the Bishop of Dunblane added. "Any other nomination is inconceivable."

There was silence in the great chamber.

"Very well," Albany said, at length. "I, the Crown, declare this a parliament of the Three Estates. The Chancellor will further pronounce."

"Yes, Your Grace." Chancellor Greenlaw nodded eagerly. "I hereby declare that this parliament assembled duly confirms the appointment of His Grace the Duke of Albany as Regent as well as Governor of the realm, with all the powers of the Crown duly vested in his person. God save His Grace!"

Men looked at each other doubtfully. Some rose to their feet with alacrity, others did not. By no means all there — including of course the Earl of Mar and Sir James Douglas of Roberton — were prepared to stand and urge the Creator to look upon and save Robert Stewart as His Grace, whatever his new powers. On the other hand, it was just possible that the Chancellor's last four words referred to young James in London. Some were prepared to rise, on that assumption.

Bishop Wardlaw called out, "God save the *King's* Grace!" and so stood, putting the matter to rights.

All now rose, save Albany himself.

There was a pause, as men muttered to each other. Some sat, some remained on their feet.

The Duke pointed a finger at Greenlaw, who banged on the table with his gavel and motioned all to sit.

"His Grace will speak," he announced.

Albany waited impassively for silence. "It is my duty now to proclaim that, the throne being left vacant by the decease of my royal brother, my nephew James, Earl of Carrick and High Steward of Scotland, although a captive in England, succeeds to the style and title of nominal King of Scots. Being a minor as well as a captive and outwith the realm, no powers as King may be exercised by him, but fall to be exercised by myself as Regent. This for the well-being and good governance of the realm." As an afterthought, he added levelly, "God save the King."

Seldom can a new monarch have been less heartily proclaimed.

Those who did not mind risking the Regent's displeasure did their best, led by the Primate and the Earl of Mar, getting once again to their feet, chanting 'God save the King' again and again, and cheering. But it was only a moderately successful demonstration, realities being altogether too evident. Gradually quiet was restored.

"To business," the Chancellor said. "On His Grace's instruction, a new Great Seal of the realm has been cast, to establish the new rule and reign, and the former Great Seal duly broken. From now onwards this Seal's impression will represent the Crown's authority . . ."

"May we see this new Seal, my lord Chancellor?" the Primate requested. "I have heard tell that it is . . . unusual, in wording and design."

Greenlaw looked at the Regent, who nodded. He leant over to open the handsome silver casket on the table, and took out the large and heavy disc of shining bronze. He carried it across to his senior bishop, lips compressed.

Wardlaw took the thing, turning it up this way and that to gain the best light from the not over-generous windows. "This shows a man sitting on a throne, flanked by the arms of Albany and the kingdom," he reported, for all to hear. "The man bears in his right hand the Sword of State. And around are the words SIGILLUM ROBERTI DEI GRACIA INTERREX SCOTTORUM. That is the Seal of Robert, by the Grace of God . . . !" He paused. "My lord Chancellor, is this not the seal of a monarch, rather than a regent? Robert, by the Grace of God!"

There was a hush. No word came from Chancellor or Duke.

"My lords," the Primate went on, "this seal appears to me to be neither one thing nor another. The Great Seal of the realm should surely bear the monarch's image and superscription — James, by the Grace of God. If this is but the *Regent's* seal, as the name Robert implies, then surely he should not be sitting on the throne, nor should he be described 'by the Grace of God'. It appears to me that a mistake has been made."

Albany spoke, without turning his head to glance at the Bishop. "No mistake, Sir Clerk. That is the Great Seal of this realm. Until James my nephew has received his coronation, he is but presumptive and postulate monarch, not true King. In present circumstances it may be long before such coronation. And since he is a child and his authority vested in myself, it is proper that meantime my name appears on the Great Seal."

There were murmurs from various parts of the chamber.

"I would wish to enquire further into this, my lord Duke,"

189

Wardlaw said, "into the correctness of it. Proper you may consider it. But is it lawful?"

"Enquire then, sirrah. But — have you, and others, considered who now *makes* the laws of this realm?" That question was none the less ominous for being tonelessly said.

"The Crown in *parliament* makes the laws. Only so, my lord."

"As it will do. Proceed, my lord Chancellor." The flick of Albany's hand indicated that the subject was closed.

Greenlaw retrieved the seal and put it back into its casket, making something of a ploy of it. Then he banged with his gavel to gain quiet.

"There is the matter of the succession," he announced, consulting his papers. "With the King in enemy hands, and a child, unwed, this becomes of vital import. His Grace the Regent is, to be sure, the heir presumptive and in the event of the demise of the Crown would forthwith become King in name as well as in fact. But since His Grace is in his sixty-eighth year, and although we pray God that he may be preserved to reign over us for many more years, yet he esteems it right that parliament should recognise and confirm the further succession. His Grace's eldest son, of course, Murdoch, Earl of Fife, is next in succession. But he is prisoner likewise. He has infant sons who would be in line for the succession. But . . ."

"My lord Chancellor — I do protest!" That was Alex Stewart, on his feet. "I say that this of the possible succession, in the Duke of Albany's family, may be important, in some measure. But it is scarcely so vital as the recovery and saving of our young sovereign lord James from enemy hands! Surely the first and foremost matter this parliament should be discussing is what steps are to be taken to show our anger at the outrage done to our prince, in time of truce; and how best we can ensure his speedy return to his realm and throne . . ."

Shouts of approval from all over the refectory drowned his voice. There was no question but that he had the vast majority with him in his protest.

"Yes, yes," the Chancellor began, when he could make himself heard. "All in due course . . ."

He was interrupted by Albany. "My lord of Mar is impatient. A youthful failing, which may perhaps be forgiven, but unsuitable in those who seek to bear rule and governance. All is to be done in proper order. Measures will be taken regarding my nephew's unfortunate position. But before we consider what we may do to that end, we must set our house in order, here at home. The change in rule, kingship and authority here must be firmly established, consequent upon the King's death and his son's capture, that duly authorised steps may be taken in our relations with England. And that includes the due succession. Proceed, my lord Chancellor."

Alex frowned, but resumed his seat.

"To resume," Greenlaw said, looking about him warily. "Since His Grace's eldest son, the Earl Murdoch, is also in enemy hands, and his children as yet but bairns, the Regent, aware of the transience of this life and man's impermanence, sees himself as in duty bound to make due provision for the carrying on of the regency and governance should he himself — which God forbid — suffer removal from our midst. He therefore would make provision for his second son, the Lord John of Coull and Onele, next in succession to the throne, to be able to step into the regency, with the consent of parliament, in the event of his own demise. The Lord John is now a man of full age and ability, and an increasing experience in affairs of state. In pursuance of this aim, His Grace has decided now to advance the said John Stewart of Coull and Onele to the position, style and dignity of Earl of Buchan. Which earldom, since the death of His Grace's brother, the late Lord Alexander of Badenoch, has been vested in the Crown. Moreover, since it is no longer suitable that the Regent should fill the office of Great Chamberlain — which His Grace has supported for many years — with the agreement of this parliament he now confers it upon the said Lord John."

The stir in the chamber was pronounced, but not in the main hostile, for the personable John Stewart was gaining in popularity and much to be preferred to his arrogant, yet moody half-brother Murdoch. None failed to perceive, of course, the principal implications of this promotion; for so long as his brother remained a prisoner in the South, it made Brave John of Coull second most important man in the kingdom — an extraordinary advancement for one who had been almost unknown a year or two before.

Jamie Douglas looked from John to Alex Stewart, anxiously, his mind busy. This move, shrewd in more ways than one, he well perceived would reverse their respective positions in the North. No longer would the new Earl of Mar be the most important figure above the Highland Line; the new Earl of Buchan, Great Chamberlain and in line for the throne, would outrank him. The fact that the earldom of Buchan would have been Alex's own had he been legitimate, must be the more galling. Had Brave John known of all this when he came south? The new appointment would not do away with Alex's great influence with the Highland clans, of course, which his cousin did not possess. But it must have a major effect on the former's plans, and tend to set these two on a collision course — which no doubt was partly the objective.

Almost as though he himself had been following Jamie's line of thought, Albany intervened.

"The earldom of Buchan marches with the earldom of Ross, to north and west, formerly held by my daughter's husband, the late Alexander Leslie, and now in the name of their only child, my grand-daughter and ward, the Lady Euphemia. The said Lady Euphemia has declared her desire to wed only Holy Church and to retire to the life of sanctity in a nunnery, to her exceeding renown. Therefore the earldom of Ross also falls to the Crown. It is suitable that, situate so importantly for the Highland polity, it should be held in strong and capable hands. I therefore place the earldom of Ross also in the hands of my son John, for the North's security. It will also aid him in his position as Justiciar of the North, the revenues thereof to help in defraying the costs of the chamberlainship. The Lord John now to step forward."

As everywhere men craned their necks to see this newly exalted star in the Scots firmament, Will Douglas spoke in Jamie's ear.

"There is no doubt as to who is to be King of the North! Your friend Mar's days are numbered, I think!" Will was sitting beside his half-brother once more, now also a baron commissioner; their uncle, Sir Will of Mordington, had died suddenly, leaving no heir, and their father had conferred his Merse barony on his second legitimate son.

"Alex will not be so easily brought down," Jamie was saying, but through tight lips, when there was a dramatic development. Brave John was on his way from the barons' benches to the dais, when Alex stood up again amongst the tiny group of earls.

"My lord Chancellor," he called strongly, "may I be the first to congratulate my cousin and friend the Lord of Coull on his advancement to the earldom of Buchan — particularly as it was long held by my own father and I was, as it were, partly suckled on its revenues! The Great Chamberlain's office, also, I am sure that he will adorn. But this last of the earldom of Ross is a very different matter. I say that we must consider well before handing over Ross to any soever — unless we are prepared for major warfare."

John Stewart had halted, looking from Alex to his father doubtfully.

"The Earl of Mar is over-fearful," Albany said.

"I think not, my lord Duke. I have three times had to fight the Lord of the Isles or his brother. I have no wish to have to do so again. Especially if Donald has a fair cause. I would remind this parliament that the late Earl of Ross, Alexander Leslie, left a child heiress, yes, the Countess Euphemia — who would appear, at ten years, to have chosen a life of religion at a notably early age! But he also left a sister, the Lady Margaret, who is wed to the Lord of the Isles. Therefore, if the Lady Euphemia indeed resigns the earldom, her aunt, the Lady Margaret, is surely entitled to claim it as heir of entail. And nothing is more certain, I do swear, than that Donald of the Isles will ensure that she does!"

"The Earl of Mar, I think, forgets," the Regent commented, apparently unmoved. "He ought not to do so, since he was at some pains to ensure the matter for himself, not so long ago! The disposition of earldoms is subject to the Crown's agreement. The natural heirs are always given first consideration. But the safety and well-being of the realm is the Crown's prime concern. Donald of the Isles is a man guilty of ravagement and rapine, but also of armed invasion and insurrection — treason. The earldom of Ross is so placed that, if he had his hands on it, in the right of his wife, he could do enormous hurt to the North, to the entire kingdom. He would be no longer confined to his heathenish Hebrides, but would have a base reaching across the breadth of Scotland. It must not be. The earldom must be in sound and strong hands. Therefore I have so ordained."

"Your ordaining, my lord Duke, will, I fear, not prevent the Lord of the Isles seeking to take what he believes should be his by right. Safer to leave the earldom vacant meantime. Better still, that the child Countess should be, h'm, dissuaded from her sudden and youthful desire to embrace Holy Church! Then no new destination need be made."

"I support the Earl of Mar in this," the Earl of Crawford said, at Alex's side. "We have trouble with England before us. We want no trouble with the Islesmen, meantime."

"I agree, my lord Chancellor," the Primate added. "This child's vocation will be the more acceptable to Holy Church at a more mature age!"

"May I speak, my lord Chancellor?" John of Coull requested, from his midway stance. "It seems to me that there need be no dispute. The earldom of Buchan marches with that of Ross for long distances. As Earl of Buchan and acting Justiciar of the North, I should, with the Earl of Mar's aid, be able to maintain good and sufficient watch over it, and ensure its peace and the security of the realm, without myself being appointed Earl of Ross at this time."

There was a pause. Then his father nodded briefly.

"Step forward," he commanded. Undoubtedly one of Robert Stewart's greatest strengths lay in his ability to judge shrewdly when to change his stance in any controversy, and to do so swiftly and without evident animus, whatever his private feelings; not, of course, allowing such minor deflections to alter his major intentions.

None making further objection, John Stewart paced up to the dais. With the minimum of ceremony Albany rose, moved over to the Chancellor's table, picked up a golden earl's belt where it had lain hidden amongst the papers, and placed it over his son's head and one shoulder.

"Earl of Buchan," he said.

John bowed, kissed his father's hand, bowed again, and walked over to the earls' seats.

A somewhat ragged cheer arose.

"Proceed, my lord Chancellor," the Regent ordered.

Some shuffling of papers followed. "The matter of steps to be taken regarding the unhappy situation of our young liege lord, the King," Greenlaw intoned. "Protest has been made to the so-called King Henry, but this has been spurned. His Grace the Regent therefore purposes that a strong and important embassage should be sent forthwith to the English Court, under safe conduct, in terms of the signed truce still pertaining, to make representations, to ascertain Henry of Bolingbroke's intentions and to seek negotiate the King's release . . ."

Strong applause resounded from all quarters.

"His Grace declares that this embassage must be of the most illustrious, that due weight may be accorded to it. He proposes that it should be led by the Earl of Crawford, Lord High Admiral; the Earl of Buchan, Great Chamberlain; and the Earl of Mar; also, of the Lords Spiritual, the Bishop of Dunblane and my humble self, duly supported by a knightly company . . ."

"How may we be sure, my lord, that such embassage would be safe from molestation?" the Bishop of Dunblane interrupted. "If the English are prepared to waylay and capture Scotland's heir to the throne and now monarch, will they be more gentle with this company, however illustrious?"

Greenlaw looked at the Duke.

"Ambassadors, even in time of war, are protected in all Christian nations," Albany said. "But we shall seek a safe-conduct. If he grants it, even Henry could scarce dare to break it." He paused. "I should not be sending my second son into his hands, who already holds my first, were I not assured on this."

That seemed convincing, and the thing was accepted, Jamie for one recognising that the inclusion of Alex in the embassage was a clever move and could well be viewed with suspicion. It might to some extent close his lips, yet he would be established as less important than the new Earl of Buchan, the Great Chamberlain. It would embroil him in Southern affairs, which might lessen his influence in the North.

The Chancellor went on to ask parliament to renew the mutual-aid treaty with France, due to expire shortly; and this, which had become almost the corner-stone of Scots foreign policy, was passed without dissent. There followed three or four routine matters concerning trade, customs dues and claims for royal burgh status, which were unproductive of dispute. Then, with Greenlaw gathering his papers together and Albany clearly preparing to announce adjournment, Alex rose to his feet again.

"I have a matter with which I believe, this parliament should be concerned," he said. "I am surprised that it has not already been raised or remarked upon, since it concerns persons here present and one who should have been. I refer to the slaying of Sir David Fleming of Biggar and Cumbernauld, at Lang Herd-manston in Lothian, who had escorted the Earl of Carrick, now King James, to the Bass Rock, and was thereafter waylaid and murdered. I say that parliament should receive details of this outrage and learn what steps have been taken to bring the offenders to punishment."

If hitherto the assembly had had its moments of drama and tension, these were as nothing to the effect of this bombshell.

Few there did not know that this killing had been perpetrated by Sir James Douglas of Abercorn, nicknamed the Gross, next brother to the captive Earl of Douglas himself, and therefore acting head of that so potent house. Moreover it was accepted that it had been done at Albany's instigation, as indication of the Governor's disapproval of the secret move of the young prince from St. Andrews. So that, in publicly raising this issue, the Earl of Mar was in effect challenging both the Regent and the house of Douglas, the two greatest powers in the land.

"Your man is no faint-heart, I will say that for him!" Will Douglas murmured to his half-brother.

"I am glad that my lord of Mar has raised this matter," Bishop Wardlaw supported, rising. "I should have done so, myself. Sir David Fleming was my good friend. More important, he was a leal and true friend of our late King, of our present King, and of his brother the late Duke of Rothesay. His murder was a most grievous crime against the King's peace and the King's interests — which I call upon the King's Regent and government to punish."

In the hush that followed, the Chancellor spread his hands, eloquent of non-involvement and disassociation.

Albany took his time about speaking, as the silence became almost a living thing. "I know of no such murder or crime," he said evenly. "The Earl of Carrick, my nephew, had been removed from his place of safe-keeping at St. Andrews secretly, by stealth, without my authority or knowledge, and conveyed to this barren rock of the Bass, and there held — by this Fleming of Cumbernauld. I would have failed in my plainest duty, as Governor, had I not made due enquiry. I requested Sir James Douglas of Abercorn to find Fleming and bring him to me, for question. Sir James did find him, riding from the Lothian coast to Biggar, but he refused to accompany the Douglas. Indeed he drew a sword, and in the resultant mêlée was unfortunately fatally wounded — a mishap wholly of his own making. No blame attaches to Sir James Douglas." Almost as though exhausted by this, for him, lengthy disquisition, the Regent sat back in his throne, eyes closed, the matter finished with.

Alex and the Primate eyed each other, waiting one for the other.

"My lord Duke," Wardlaw said, after a moment, "with respect, there are one or two relevant points which require to be stated, on Sir David Fleming's behalf, since he cannot make them himself. You say that the prince was removed from my castle of St. Andrews without your knowledge and authority, by Sir David. I would point out, however, that it was done on the authority, indeed at the direct command, of the King's Grace, father of the prince. Secretly, yes, for the best of reasons. Sir David, therefore, was carrying out his liege lord's orders — as was I in permitting the prince's removal. No blame can attach to him."

"Then, sir, he should have yielded peaceably to Sir James Douglas's request, and come to explain the matter to myself."

"Perhaps he had no opportunity to do so, my lord Duke."

"Explain yourself, sir."

"He may have been . . . silenced!"

"May have been . . .! Perhaps . . .! This is a parliament, sir, not a churchmen's chapter! We are here concerned with facts, not suppositions. You will not impute motives to others which cannot be substantiated."

"My lord Chancellor," Alex intervened, comparatively mildly. "Sir James Douglas of Abercorn is here present. Let him speak, and tell us the circumstances in which Sir David died."

"No! Douglas will *not* speak," Albany rapped out. "He was obeying my orders, as Governor, to bring Fleming to me. I will not have this parliament's time wasted with base calumnies and aspersions."

"Nevertheless, my lord Duke," Crawford put in heavily, "the allegation has been made publicly that Sir David Fleming — who was *my* friend also — may have been silenced. Surely it is this parliament's concern to learn what caused the Primate-Bishop to make such allegation?"

"My lords," Henry Wardlaw declared, giving no time for any ban to be pronounced, "Sir David spoke to me before he left my castle, with the prince. He told me that I would be wise to send the young Henry Percy, Hotspur's son, and heir to Northumberland, off to France with the prince. He said that there was a plan to deliver up the boy — who was also in my care — along with his grandfather, the Earl of Northumberland, the Lord Bardolph and the Bishop of St. Asaph, who took refuge in our realm from King Henry's spleen, to the English — in exchange for the Lord Murdoch, Earl of Fife. I said that I could not do this without higher authority. But I did send here to Perth, to warn the Earl of Northumberland and the others, here resident. I understand that they have . . . departed."

Another prolonged silence.

"If the Bishop of St. Andrews is finished with his hearsays, prittle-prattle and clerks' clishmaclavers, I shall now rule that this parliament be spared further waste of time," Albany said sternly. "If, on the other hand, he has any true *evidence* to support his extraordinary allegations, if he will submit it to me in due course, I shall see that it is laid before the Privy Council or other suitable court of law. I should but add that had these addle-pated plans for the removal of my nephew not been put into practice, the prince would still be safe within my lord's palace of St. Andrews, and my brother the late King no doubt still on his throne. I leave you all to consider that well. My lord Chancellor — adjourn the session."

Without waiting for the further formalities, Robert Stewart rose from his throne and stalked from the chamber, banner-bearers hurrying behind.

The parliament of 1406 was at an end — which meant that talking had had its day and the rule of law began, the Regent's law.

XIII

IT WAS DIFFICULT to maintain any suitably sober and dignified air for the Scots embassage, however illustrious, as the brilliant company trotted down through the fair English countryside at its summer finest. They were on a grimly serious mission in a traditionally hostile land, and they represented an angry nation. Yet they were in the main young men, clad in their colourful best, presently released from their normal day-to-day duties and responsibilities, on a prolonged flag-waving expedition in a strange country. It would have been unnatural had a holiday spirit not prevailed. Even if some of them did not rely too entirely on King Henry's safe-conduct, with their escort of seventy they were secure enough from anything but major assault. They did not dawdle but nor did they indulge in any unseemly rush; a steady forty miles a day was the target — something of a daunder for some there, though sufficient for the two bishops no doubt. This permitted ample time for sight-seeing, wine and women sampling and appreciation of the good life generally.

The two young Stewart earls very much set the tone and tempo of the venture, for though David Lindsay, Earl of Crawford and Lord High Admiral, was nominally the senior member of the delegation, he was now an elderly man and had become somewhat quiet, almost morose, with the years; and Bishop Greenlaw, the Chancellor, although an able administrator, was no leader and somewhat out of his depth with lively young men — while the other Bishop, Finlay Dermoch of Dunblane, likewise a creature of Albany's, was so much in awe of the company he now kept as to be an embarrassment. For the rest, both John and Alex Stewart had vied with each other in bringing along a cheerful crew of youthful gallants, in the interests of prestige — although Jamie Douglas would certainly have excepted himself from such description, and Sir Alexander Forbes of that Ilk, in his early forties, scarcely qualified either. The former had been included simply because Alex desired his company and support, the latter, ostensibly as one of the senior vassals of Mar but in fact so that his master might have an easier mind as to the activities of the Countess Isobel in the interim. Whatever feelings of rivalry existed inevitably between the Stewart cousins, no sign of it was revealed; they made a gay, handsome and attractive pair, and the embassage very much took its character from them.

They went by Berwick-on-Tweed, coastal Northumberland and Newcastle — and for Jamie at least it was an odd experience to be riding peacably through territory over which he had campaigned, sword in hand, so frequently. By Durham and Cleveland and York they rode, and so down into the English Midlands, new country for all save Crawford, putting up at abbeys, priories and monkish hospices, where the bishops' presence assured them, if not welcome at least sustenance and shelter — the English lords and landed gentry eyeing them very much askance. Ten days of this and, beyond the endless level lands flanking the Fen country, they came by Peterborough and the one-time Scots-held earldom of Huntingdon and St. Neots, to the broad vale of the Thames — although it was unlike any vale, dale or strath they knew in Scotland — and approached their goal.

London appalled, affronted and yet exhilarated them. Indeed they could scarcely take it in, so overpowering was the impact, in size, noise, smells — above all, smells. Extremes were the rule here, extremes in numbers, in quality of building, with magnificence and tumbledown hovels side by side, in riches and poverty, in splendour and filth, in music and laughter, screams and groans, in the variety at least of the stenches. The Scots were used to towns and burghs, to crowded narrow streets and tall tenement lands and burrowing closes and wynds; but even in the greatest cities like Perth, Dundee and Aberdeen, there was nothing to compare with this teeming, throbbing, deafening, stinking ant-hill of humanity. Although ant-hill was quite wrong — that was part of the trouble. There was no least hill of any sort worth calling even a brae, to relieve the endless sprawl, the ranked and serried clutter of streets and lanes and alleys, of dark arched vaults and tunnels and vennels. Scots towns were usually built around a fortress or castle, which almost always perched proudly on top of a hill or rock, with the streets climbing towards it or clustered under its walls. Here, although the dread of the famous Tower of London was known to all, it presumably did not sit on any upstanding rock — at least it could not be seen to do so from the stifling huddle of the causeways. The buildings were no taller than those at home — less so, often, indeed — but they tended to extend outwards over the streets, one storey projecting above and beyond the next in extraordinary fashion, so that with the roadways narrow enough in the first place, the two sides often nearly met at the top, leaving the merest strip of sky to be seen, and daylight at street-level only a pale memory. Down there the causeways were all but choked with the refuse thrown from windows or pushed out from the doorways and closes, or else deposited by the poultry and even pigs which roamed and proliferated everywhere. The flatness, lack of hills and vistas, and tight huddle of buildings, all kept out the air and sea-breezes which made the Scots burghs tolerable. In the height of summer, the resultant odours hit the newcomers like a blow, a continuing hail of blows. They rode on in a sort of stupor of noise, of fetor, of claustrophobia. Yet the sense of vigorous, teeming, pulsating life was such as they had never before experienced.

In less time than it takes to tell they were quite lost in that chaotic labyrinth, at a loss which street to take, which way to turn. There was no lack of people to direct them, but their requests were singularly unproductive of result, their Scots voices being as little understood apparently as were the Londoners' answers — although they had made themselves understood well enough all the way down through England. But here not only their accents but their very appearance, it seemed, was a source of wonder, indeed of general hilarity. Laughter, jeers, even occasional hurled refuse, tended to greet their enquiries — though most of the reaction was not probably intentionally ill-natured, however disrespectful. Young lairds, unused to such behaviour, were inclined to drop hands to sword-hilts, but their leaders sternly commanded restraint. Their mission must not be started on the wrong foot.

Eventually, after much time-wasting and casting around, they reached the riverside and a sudden widening of vistas. They could at last see a considerable distance up and down stream. Ahead of them, still a distance off but now eye-catching, beyond a bend of the river, rose the massive white walls of a huge, slab-sided square keep, with four angle-towers topped by onion-like domes, and surrounded by high curtain-walls, set apparently at the edge of Thames. Amongst all the welter of buildings, of gables and turrets, spires and steeples and roofing, this could only be the redoubtable Tower of London itself. Crawford said that the monarch no longer dwelt there but in the palace of Westminster, attached to the abbey. Amidst the innumerable churches visible from here, the tall triple towers of one larger than all the others stood out plainly, not far from where they had emerged, again near the river, almost certainly the Minster. It was sixteen years since Crawford had been here, and he had forgotten how he had reached the palace, it having been a private visit. But, evidently, by keeping to the waterside, they could make directly for it.

When the visitors reached the great cathedral-like church, it was to discern little sign of any palace, only the lengthy ranges of the abbey's monastic buildings, purlieus and cloisters linked to a great hall of ecclesiastical aspect. Yet Crawford declared that this was indeed the place — and certainly there was much coming and going around its environs, with none wearing monkish habits and some indeed clad in fine scarlet-and-gold livery. On Jamie's asking one of these if this was indeed King Henry's palace of Westminster, the fellow looked him up and down, pointed within the courtyard arch with a pitying gesture, and hurried off. It seemed that this was journey's end.

Dismounting in a wide courtyard, watched by a multiplicity of guards but no guides nor welcomers, the Scots leadership decided to make for the largest doorway. Here, halted by the crossed halberds of the guard, Crawford announced that they were the Scots embassage come to treat with the King of England, and seeking His Grace's hospitality. From the many interested onlookers an officer came forward, the statement was repeated, and this man, shaking his head doubtfully, turned and made his way within, leaving the visitors standing on the doorstep, still facing the crossed halberds.

They had to wait some considerable time there, with proud Scots tempers rising. At length the officer returned, told Crawford to follow him and waved back the others. As curtly, the remaining Scots leaders informed him that they were not going to be left waiting like beggars at the door, and marched in behind the Lindsay.

Conducted by this disappointing guide through long corridors and across inner courts, they gained little better impression of this as a palace than they had done of London as a whole, considering it but a poor sprawling place compared with the towering royal strongholds of their own land. Admittedly those parts which were furnished seemed to be richly plenished, with a great deal more of hangings, tapestries, floor-coverings and the like than they were used to, but the effect was still of a converted and overcrowded monastery.

They were brought eventually to a lobby in no very splendid portion of the rambling establishment, where an overdressed individual of middle years awaited them. To him Crawford repeated, rather stiffly his statement of identity and purpose.

"Were you looked for, sirs?" this gentleman asked.

"*Looked* for?" the Earl barked. "We have come here from the Regent of Scotland, under your King's safe-conduct and invitation. I should say that we are looked for!"

"Perhaps. But did any here know of your coming?"

"God's sake, man — why ask *us* that? King Henry well knows of our coming. What arrangements he has made is his business, not ours."

"The King's Grace is not here at this present, sir. He is hawking on the marshes of Erith."

"Then find someone who knows the King's business, sirrah. Who are you?"

"I am Sir Everard Bacon. Deputy Master of the King's Wardrobe."

"Saints a' mercy — a wardrobe master!" Crawford exploded.

John Stewart intervened. "Sir Everard, I am Buchan, Great Chamberlain of Scotland. The Earl of Crawford is Lord High Admiral. This is the Earl of Mar and Lord of Garioch. This is Bishop of Dunblane. And this the Bishop of Aberdeen, Chancellor of Scotland. Since your King is absent, our accommodation would seem to be a matter for his Chamberlain. Kindly inform him of our presence."

"The Lord Chamberlain, the Earl of Kent, is not here, sir, er, my lord. He is with the King's Grace."

"Then go find somebody who is here, Wardrober, of some rank and position," Crawford exclaimed.

"*I* am in charge of the palace meantime, sir," the other said shortly.

"God's eyes — is this how Henry of Lancaster manages his

household! Be off, fellow, and find someone who may decently receive us, and suitably bestow us. Or I swear your King will be needing a new deputy papingoe!"

Flushing hotly, the other turned and stalked off.

Seething, the older Scots huffed and puffed, although Alex and John Stewart counselled patience. It was all no doubt a mistake, some foolish misunderstanding.

"Do you mean to tell me that Henry Bolingbroke is so ill-served with spies and informants, to say nothing of his flunkeys here, that he knows nothing of our progress down through his realm, these ten days?" Bishop Greenlaw cried. "It is a calculated insult!"

"Scarcely that," Alex demurred. "More probably mere mis-management and poor manners."

"They are barbarians . . .!"

Again they were kept waiting, this time for even longer than before. At last the same Sir Everard Bacon reappeared, now supported by quite a phalanx of liveried guards with halberds, all looking aggressive.

"I have been able to have word with the Lord Chancellor himself, sirs . . . my lords," he declared, almost grandly. "The Lord Henry, Bishop of Winchester. He says that you are to be bestowed in the Tower, meantime. I will send a guide to conduct you there, to the Governor."

"The Tower? You mean — the Tower of London?" Crawford got out, all but choking.

"Yes."

"By the Rood — this is too much! It is a prison!"

"Not so. Or not only so, sir. It is a house of His Grace. Much used. Besides, I would have thought that you would wish to bide there — since the youth, your so-called King, is lodged there! Sergeant, convey these Scots lords to the Tower. Present them to Sir Thomas Rempton."

"The King . . .? James? In the Tower . . .?"

But the Deputy Master of the Wardrobe had turned and hurried off. The visitors were left with the glowering guards, the sergeant of whom was gesturing for them to follow him.

Angrily the assemblage stamped out.

* * *

Within the gloomy portals of the Tower of London there were further delays. It proved to be a vast citadel, almost a city in itself, the tall foursquare central keep, visible from afar, only the grim heart of it, with its inner and outer moats, its tiered curtain-walls, its baileys and wards, its proliferating lesser towers and gatehouses, its barracks and armouries, stables and yards. The Scots' escort of seventy men-at-arms would have made a major mouthful for most establishments to swallow; but here they were absorbed without difficulty, even if equally without cordiality. It took a considerable time for the sergeant to find the Governor, however, so that the men-at-arms' betters had to kick their heels, in mounting ire and frustration, in an inner courtyard.

There, after a while, a curious coughing, grunting sound, allied to a new smell, animal, throat-catching, attracted their speculative attention, and eventually their physical presence, towards an archway and vaulted passage opening from a corner of the yard. Pushing along this stone-flagged way, they came to a great open well of a place below the main White Tower walling, sunk below general ground level — but not below the underground dungeons obviously beneath their feet, over the gratings for which they trod in that passage, and from which unpleasant sounds and more smells arose at them. But it was not this which drew them. The large sunken central pit was subdivided by heavy iron bars and partitions into sundry cages of varying sizes; and in these up to a score of lions and leopards paced and wheeled and padded, snarling, in a sort of terrible, ritualised, contained and hopeless rage. A keeper with a great steel trident over his shoulder, paraded his own monotonous circuit of the pit's terraced perimeter gallery, whilst two boys, at the far side, sought unsuccessfully to interest a huge, dark-maned lion in a piece of red meat dangling on a line.

It was Jamie Douglas who recognised one of the lads as their new monarch. Oddly enough, despite the fact that the two Stewart earls were his first cousins and Crawford his uncle by marriage, few there really knew James Stewart, who had been brought up very much away from Court, almost as much a recluse as had been his father. Jamie, however, through his service and friendship with the late David, Duke of Rothesay, the boy's elder brother, had known him quite well.

"That is the prince," he called. "James — the King. With the thin-faced wiry boy."

The party of nearly a dozen went hurrying round the rim of the pit.

The lads, looking up, watched their approach with interest. The younger was an attractive, sturdy boy, not tall but well-made, with good regular features, dark-eyed and dark-haired, but with a wary, self-contained expression, twelve years now though looking older. The other, a year or so his senior, was bony and gangling of build, dark also but intense. Neither was dressed with any distinction.

As the visitors approached, James's eyes widened and lightened. "Jamie!" he cried. "It is Sir Jamie Douglas!" And thrusting the meat on its string at his companion, he darted forward, hands out.

Jamie, glancing at his betters, went to drop on one knee before the boy, and taking one of those slender hands between his own two, in the gesture of fealty, kissed it. "Sire," he said, "Your Grace's leal and humble servant."

· "It is good to see you, so good!" James exclaimed, eagerly. "Have you come to take me home?"

The Douglas swallowed. "I . . . ah . . . not yet, Sire, I fear," he said unhappily, rising. "But soon, no doubt. I . . . we rejoice to see you also. Here is Your Highness's uncle, my lord of Crawford. And my lords of Mar and Buchan, your cousins . . ."

The kneeling and hand-kissing proceeded, as each of the visitors, in order of precedence, murmured allegiance, the boy seriously and with unassumed dignity, acknowledging each token. When it was finished, he turned to the older lad.

"This is Griffith Glendowèr, my lords, son to the Lord Owen Glendower, the true Prince of Wales. He is also held hostage here. He is my friend."

They all bowed to the Welsh boy, who smiled brilliantly.

It was to Jamie that the boy-King turned. "My father is dead," he said, biting his lip. "But the Bishop? The good Bishop Henry. All is well with him, at St. Andrews?"

"Yes, Sire. He is greatly concerned for your welfare . . ."

"As is the Regent, your royal uncle," Greenlaw put in. "He sends greeting, Sire."

The boy eyed the Chancellor levelly for a moment, and then turned back to Jamie. "You have come all the way from Scotland? To see me?"

"Yes, Your Grace. Bringing the love of all your people. We have come also — or these great lords have — to seek negotiate your release."

"I do not think that King Henry will let me go," James said flatly. "Do you, Griff?"

"No," his friend agreed.

The visitors exchanged glances.

Alex cleared his throat. "Do they treat you well, Sire, in this fell Tower?"

"Oh, yes. We have sufficient to eat. I have a dog the Governor gave me. And there are these lions, and leopards. There are bears too, in another part. They had a bull-baiting in the tilt-yard a few days ago . . ."

A cough, other than that of the brutes below, turned all heads — although perhaps it should not have done when their monarch was speaking. A tall, handsome, soldierly-looking man stood behind them, with the sergeant.

"A good day to you," the newcomer said, from thin lips, with the briefest of bows. "I am Rempton, Governor here. You will be the deputation from Scotland. I would prefer it if you do not have speech with this boy save with my express permission."

"You do, damn you!" Crawford gave back. "I'd have you to know, sirrah, that this boy, as you call him, is our liege and sovereign lord, James, King of Scots, and we shall not seek any permission save *his* before we speak with him. In our presence, at least, you will refer to him as His Grace."

"Indeed I shall do no such thing. My lord King and only Grace, as yours, is the Lord Henry of England and France, who is also Lord Paramount of Scotland. I take instructions only from him. As, if you are wise, will you. Boy — be off. And Glendower with you."

"Your Grace — be pleased to stay with us a little longer," Alex said, mildly enough. "We have come a long way to see you."

"Aye, Sire — if you will," John of Buchan added. "You, sir — leave us. We shall send for you when we are ready."

"That you will not! I have my orders and I shall obey them. James Stewart, go to your chamber. Or shall I send for the guard?"

"Sir Thomas," the boy said, his voice quivering just a little. "These are great lords in my country — my cousins, and uncle, and the Chancellor of the realm. Pray speak them more . . . heedfully. My lords — I will leave you now. We shall speak again. There is much that I would have you to tell me. Come, Griff."

The Scots bowed low as the boys hurried off, the Governor and the sergeant not at all.

"You, sirrah, may bear the knightly style, but you are as ill-reared and upjumped a lout as that papingoe Bacon we saw at Westminster! Has your prince never taught you how to behave? Or does himself not know? I am Crawford, Earl and Lord High Admiral of Scotland. These lords similar. See that you do not forget it. Now — convey us to our quarters."

Rempton began to reply, but thought better of it. He turned to the sergeant. "Fetch the Captain of the Guard to take these Scots lords to Byward Tower, where their chambers are prepared for them." He stalked off without another word.

"So we were expected here, at least!" Jamie observed.

* * *

The Scots found that they had a single flanking-tower of the Byward allotted to themselves, with a basement dining-vault, damp and chill, where food was brought to them from some central kitchen, and four upper chambers for sleeping — which meant that none might have a room to themselves, even the bishops — who protested strongly. It was scarcely the accommodation for high-born ambassadors; but, as Alex pointed out philosophically, it was good by campaigning standards. The food provided proved to be adequate, plain but plentiful enough, presumably the same as that supplied to the garrison, possibly even to the state prisoners. There was ale, but no wine.

Whilst they were eating, and discussing their reception, a stranger arrived, a fine-drawn elegant man of early middle years, pale, with a thin dark moustache and only the hint of a beard, almost Spanish-looking but announcing himself to be Henry St. Clair, Earl of Orkney. Crawford had once met him, although none of the others knew him — but then he was scarcely to be considered as a Scot, seldom appearing at Court and looking across the sea to the King of Norway, of whom he held his island earldom, as liege lord — which was why he had been chosen to escort the prince to France, as diplomatically safe — an evident misjudgement where Henry of Lancaster was concerned.

After greetings, he told them that he feared that they had come on a fools' errand.

"Henry will never let our young King go, now he has him," he asserted. "He went to sufficient trouble to get him."

208

"You mean . . ." Alex said, "you mean that this capture of James, at sea, was more than just chance piracy?"

"To be sure. It was no chance. This shipmaster, Hugh-atte-Fen, is no common pirate. He is a large merchant venturer, out of Great Yarmouth, Norfolk, with two other ships besides the *Kingfisher* which captured us. They were waiting for us, off the Yorkshire coast, knew who we were when they boarded us. And sailed straight for the Thames with us, captive, to bring us to King Henry. He knew just what he was at."

"You are saying that Henry planned it all?" Buchan demanded.

"Yes. No common shipmaster or merchant, much less a pirate, would have acted so, brought us straight to this Tower, not even returning to his own haven first. I tell you he was waiting for us. He said that he had been looking to welcome us for days. And he called the prince by name. Think you that Henry, having gone so far, will let James go again?"

As they digested that, Crawford spoke. "What does he want, then? Some great ransom?"

"I think not. He is sufficiently rich without your Scots siller. Besides, like all the Plantagenets, he is a man concerned with power rather than riches. He has refused to ransom Douglas, the most powerful lord in your kingdom. Also Murdoch of Fife. Others likewise. Now he has better even than he planned — since he could not know that this would kill King Robert. Now he holds the monarch, the most valuable of all."

"To what purpose, man? If it is not to ransom them?"

"He calls himself Lord Paramount of Scotland. As did Edward First and Second. I believe that he intends to be so, in fact, not just in name. And these are steps on that road."

"My God — then he will have to be taught differently!" Crawford cried. "Will these English never learn?"

All down the table these sentiments were echoed with angry vigour.

"Do not underestimate the man," Orkney warned. "This Henry may be a usurper, but he is clever. He is not of the stature of Edward Longshanks, but he is shrewder, cunning. He uses his head, rather than just his fist — and might gain more in Scotland with the one than the other."

"What then do you suggest?" Alex asked.

"I do not suggest anything, my friend. I but warn you."

"May I ask my lord of Orkney how does he think King Henry

knew of our prince's being on that ship?" Jamie Douglas said.

"I know not. I have thought long on this. We were a month roosting on the Craig of Bass, awaiting this *Maryenknyght*. I can only suppose that word of us being there got out. The Bass is but two score miles from the Border."

"But to know the right ship to assail?"

"I cannot tell you, sir. I have seen Henry but the once, and he was scarcely forthcoming! He made it seem that it was but a chance encounter, mocking us."

Grimly the leaders of the Scots embassage regarded each other.

No word came to them that evening, from Westminster.

All next day they waited for a summons to the royal presence. By early evening, with none forthcoming, they hotly demanded an interview with the Tower's Constable. Even that was difficult to attain. When at last they saw Rempton, it was to be informed coldly that they must wait their turn, that the King's Grace had much to attend to, that he was aware of their presence here and would no doubt summon them when he was ready and pleased so to do. And not before. Meantime, they had sufficient victual and comfort, did they not?

The day following was equally unprofitable and frustrating. As the time passed they decided that they must assert themselves somehow, and should find their own way back to Westminster, there to make their presence felt. But they discovered that they were not permitted even to leave the Tower, every gate held against them. Their vehement protests met with the reply that this was for their own good. His Grace could not ensure their safety from the populace if they wandered the streets, Scots being less than popular. It was unsuitable that their armed escort should parade London's streets. They would, in due course, approach England's sovereign lord under *English* escort. They must learn a modicum of patience. Had they any cause for complaint? The open spaces of the Tower Hill and garden was available to them for exercise if such they required, the tilt-yard and bear-garden likewise, a dozen acres no less, within the walls. No, it would not be possible for them to speak again with the boy James Stewart, without the King's express permission.

Feeling extraordinarily helpless for men accustomed to wielding authority, the ambassadors fretted and fumed.

Most of yet another day passed before the Deputy Constable, one Davies, came to inform them that they were to repair at once to Westminster. The King would see them. There was, however, no reason for a dozen of them to go; half that would be more than sufficient. When Crawford once again burst out with indignation, Alex Stewart explained patiently that the embassage, in the Scots fashion, was carefully composed, of great officers of state, lords spiritual and temporal, and knight nominees, as representing the realm and parliament of Scotland; all should take part. Davies declared that the King of England did not grant audiences to regiments. But, with tempers rising again, he conceded that they might all go, at least as far as Westminster. Who actually entered the royal presence would be a matter for the proper authorities there. This was no time for debate. They must move at once. His Grace must not be kept waiting.

Arriving at the outer bailey, however, the Scots leaders discovered that, despite all this sudden haste, no horses were forthcoming. They were expected to walk to Westminster. Hot protests had no effect. They either walked or did not go at all. Horsed foreigners were not to be considered in the narrow streets, would be much resented. Besides, they would be quicker walking, in the congestion. Crawford all but refused to go, under these conditions, but the others persuaded him, for the sake of their young monarch.

So, in most ill humour, the illustrious envoys set out, tightly hemmed in by a strong guard of liveried spearmen and halberdiers under a peremptory captain, more like a troop of prisoners than the representatives of a sovereign power, marching at a pace unusual for bishops and for an elderly earl. Admittedly their guards were very effective at clearing a way for them through the crowds, pushing the populace aside ungently with the butts of their spears from the crowns of the causeways; but nothing prevented the filth and ordure of the kennels and cobbles from soiling and splashing the marchers feet and legs, much to their offence.

It was a full two miles from the Tower to the palace, by Eastcheap, St. Paul's Church, Blackfriars and the riverside, and though the younger members of the party were glad enough to stretch their legs after three days of cramped confinement, their elders were not appreciative. They went, barked at by dogs and shouted and jeered at by the citizenry — who no doubt took them for captives on their way to a well-earned hanging.

At Westminster they were handed over to the palace guards

— who betrayed no increase of interest or favour, but who at least made no attempt to divide up the party. A functionary was found at length to take charge of them, wielding a wand of office, who conducted them through a different selection of passages and corridors than heretofore, these becoming ever fuller of folk as they progressed. A series of ante-chambers and assembly-rooms followed, before they came eventually to a stone-arched lobby from which opened a vast hall, larger than any of the other former monastic apartments, through the open doors of which they could see it full of people, diners sitting at long tables waited on by hurrying servitors, with much noise of music, talk and laughter coming out in gusts. The hall was certainly one of the finest any of the visitors had ever seen, stone walls hung with arras and tapestries, a magnificent hammer-beam roof, dark with smoke, minstrel-galleries high on both sides. The tables were arranged lengthwise just out from the walls, with the usual dais-table crosswise on a raised platform at the other end of the chamber, leaving the central rush-strewn area free. Here an entertainment of leaping, vaulting tumblers was in progress, to music from the galleries, Eastern-seeming men, stripped to the waist, their brown bodies gleaming with sweat.

The usher told them to wait, and stepped within, bowing low, to move off round the walling. The Scots sought to wipe their feet and legs with the floor-rushes, with appropriate comments.

"It seems that we are to be dined, tonight, rather than listened to," Alex said. "Or first, leastways."

Their man with the stick came back, and signed for them to follow him again.

Once more, within the doorway, he bowed, lower than ever. Up at the centre of the dais-table what was presumably the King of England was paying no least attention, nor were those flanking him. The visitors were more moderate in their genuflection.

The entertainment still proceeding, the Scots were led not directly forward up the centre of the hall but round the right side behind the tables there. Few accorded them more than a glance. As they neared the far end, they could see that the central figure lounging at the dais-table did wear a slender gold band round his brows and the shock of straw-coloured hair. He was a heavily-built, red-faced man of about forty, in aspect more like a yeoman-farmer than any monarch, hulking of shoulder, broad of feature, with a square thrusting jaw. He appeared to have finished eating, platters pushed away from him, and was toying with a wine-cup, listening casually to a smooth-faced, richly-clad prelate who sat on his left. Between them a great deer-hound, larger than usual, sat with its shaggy head resting on the table.

It occurred to Jamie Douglas that the Stewarts, whatever their faults, at least looked royal. This Henry Plantagenet, although he was grandson of both Edward the Third and Henry, Duke of Lancaster, gave no such impression.

About a dozen others, all men, sat at the King's table, at one side only, and facing down the hall. But there were two other and smaller tables on the dais, at right-angles to the main one. That at this side was empty; at the other half-a-dozen men sat, one of whom Jamie was quick to recognise as his own chief, Archibald, Earl of Douglas. Beside him were Thomas, Earl of Moray, Murdoch, Earl of Fife, and other major captives of Homildon Hill battle four years before. These at least were watching the new arrivals.

It became evident that the visitors were being conducted to the empty table facing these last, to the left of the main one. As they mounted the dais steps their guide sank on one knee once more, signing to his charges to do likewise. They contended themselves, however, with fairly businesslike bows. This time the King did glance briefly in their direction, but without change of expression, and continued to talk with the cleric.

It made a distinctly tight fit for the Scots to seat themselves at their table, which was clearly not intended for a dozen; but they crowded around it, since it seemed that no other was provided. It meant that the lesser men, Jamie included, had to sit with their backs to the King — which might be considered unsuitable but which could scarcely be helped. Jamie sat opposite Alex and John Stewart.

"Think you this King Henry is but a boor?" Buchan wondered. "Perhaps always acts thus? Or does he behave so to humble us?"

"They say that he is a clever enough man. No boor, I think," Alex answered. "So I fear that he does all this of set purpose. Our friends over there would be able to tell us, no doubt — Douglas, and your brother . . ."

"My *half*-brother," Buchan corrected. It was no family secret that John had little love for Murdoch of Fife.

"The fact that they are here at all may mean something,"

213

Jamie suggested. "I would not think that this King has his captives to dine with him."

"You think that they are here further to humble us? Or themselves be humbled?"

"Both, belike."

Servitors brought them food and drink, and the entertainment proceeded, with dancing bears, jugglers and a choir of singing boys. King Henry seemed as little interested in these as with the Scots envoys.

At length the monarch abruptly pushed back his chair and rose. The singing died away, and everywhere the diners got to their feet. Without sign of acknowledgement Henry Plantagenet turned away and stalked to the guarded dais-door, and out. The cleric and some of the others from his table followed him, one of whom Jamie recognised as George, Earl of Dunbar and March, the renegade.

Men resumed their seats and the singing continued.

"The manners of a hog!" Crawford growled, sufficiently loud for all around to hear. "Why were we brought here?"

He got no answer to that.

Presently Murdoch Stewart rose and came strolling across the dais to their table. He was dressed, or over-dressed, in the dandified height of English fashion, in parti-coloured clothes, his hose green and red, such as he never would have worn in Scotland. Even his carriage seemed to have changed, so that he all but minced.

"Ha, Johnnie," he said. "On my soul, 'tis good to see you! Grown into a man, after all!" The voice was an unsuccessful attempt at the higher-pitched but languid English overlaying the broader Lowland Scots.

"Would that I could say the same for you!" his brother gave back, not rising. "For all that you seem to thrive on captivity."

"Captivity?" Murdoch repeated. "Scarce that. Henry treats me as cousin and guest."

"Better than he treats your liege lord, then!"

The other raised his eyebrows, and shrugged. He turned to nod to Crawford. "My lord." He gestured airily with a hand at the two bishops, gazed blankly at his cousin Alex — whom he had never met, but as to whose identity he had undoubtedly been informed — and moved on to look down at Jamie. "Ah — Sir James Douglas! Last seen departing from Homildon's field with much celerity!" which was at least more than he would

214

have been able to get his tongue round in the days before his sojourn in England.

Jamie inclined his head but did not attempt an answer. Rising, he looked at his own earls. "With your lordships' permission, I shall go pay my respects to my lord of Douglas," he said.

He crossed the dais and bowed to his chief, then to Moray and the rest.

"So, Jamie — we meet once more in less than happy case," Douglas said. "I had not expected to see you here. You were better hiding in your Hielands, man."

"It would seem so, my lord. But some effort had to be made, on King James's behalf."

"No doubt. But why you? I fear that you will gain little for your pains. Henry is a strange man. Devious."

"More devious than the Duke of Albany?"

"Ah, now there I am sweert to judge! They make a pair, I think. I see that you have his other son, there, John Stewart."

"Now Earl of Buchan — and a man to be reckoned with."

"So? I scarce know him. His father ever kept him at arm's length."

"No longer. Not since my lord of Fife was captured. He has brought him on notably. He is now Great Chamberlain and Lieutenant of the North, as well as Earl. But he is able, and well disposed. Though not one to cross, either."

"Chamberlain . . . ? That Albany kept ever to himself. The office carries considerable revenues, does it not?"

"No doubt. But I understand that my lord Duke keeps these to himself. As yet."

"That sounds like Robert, yes."

"My lord," Jamie said. "How are you treated, here, by these English?"

"None so ill so as we do as we are told! We are never allowed to forget that we are captives, to be sure. Henry blows hot and cold. And the others follow his lead. We have all had to give our word, of course, not to attempt escape. Some it irks more than others!" He looked, with his one eye, across the dais, to the colourful figure of Murdoch of Fife.

Jamie nodded. "Do you know, can you tell us, anything of King Henry's intention towards *us*? The embassage has been mocked and made light of ever since we reached this London. We are in the Tower, as good as prisoners. It can scarcely be without the King's knowledge. What does he intend for us? He acceded to our coming. Granted us safe-conduct. And now, this. After much waiting, he summons us to this hall — and then ignores us."

"Do not ask me, Jamie, what Henry Plantagenet is at! He never ceases to surprise me. But . . . he will rule Scotland one day, if he can. That is certain. All is to that end . . ."

One of the English lords who had left with the King emerged from the dais doorway and came to the embassage table, a tall, handsome man with a noble brow and less noble mouth, prominent pale eyes seemingly set in an unblinking stare, implicit with arrogance.

"That is Edmund Holland, Earl of Kent," Douglas said, "the King's cousin. He is Lord Chamberlain here. You had better go. Beware Kent, I advise you."

The newcomer all but overlooked the Scots in that he appeared to stare just above their heads, and with every aspect of distaste, the Earl of Fife discreetly sidling away.

"His Grace commands your presence," he jerked, briefly.

They eyed each other doubtfully. But clearly they could not refuse even this peremptory summons into the presence they had come four hundred miles to gain. Led by Crawford, they followed Kent to the door, Jamie tacking himself on at the rear.

In the ante-room Henry stood fondling his deer-hound, backed by his lords all laughing at apparently some royal witticism. The Scots perforce bowed again, however stiffly.

"Ha — Lindsay, is it not?" the King said genially, but as though he had only just recognised Crawford. "Sir David Lindsay! Whom we have had the pleasure of seeing in London once before. Long since, I think?"

"Yes, Sire. In 1390, it would be. Although now I am usually called Crawford! We respectfully salute Your Grace. Here are my lords the Earl of Buchan, Great Chamberlain; the Earl of Mar; the Bishop of Aberdeen, Chancellor; the Bishop of Dunblane; and representatives of the Scottish realm and parliament."

"Almost the *entire* Scottish realm and parliament, no?" Henry observed, to loud laughter from his companions.

The emissaries stood silent.

"Shall I eject the, the surplus, Sire?" Kent asked. "Although, dammit, I scarce know where to begin!"

"No, no, Edmund — let them be, now they are here. So be it they do not all wish to speak!"

216

Crawford opened his mouth, and then shut it again, as though he did not trust himself with words. Alex Stewart spoke instead, pleasantly enough.

"Your Grace, it is the Scots custom to mark the importance of such a mission by the number as well as the quality and representative position of those forming it. Here in England you may do otherwise. The Earl of Crawford, as well as being uncle to our King, is Lord High Admiral of Scotland — since matters on which we seek to treat include piracy on the high seas. The Chancellor is chief minister of the kingdom. The remainder of us represent the lords spiritual and temporal and the baronage and parliament of our liege lord's realm."

"Indeed. Then I perceive that I must consider myself flattered that so large and distinguished an array has descended upon my poor Court, sir. But, correct me if I mistake — as I am sure that you will do, being Scots! — but it seemed to me in your so helpful explanation, that you used certain words in error. Words which cannot apply here, such as treat and piracy. Or did I mishear?"

"I used those words, yes, Your Grace."

"Then it is your turn to be instructed, friend. I do not treat with any save equals, certainly not with such as owe me allegiance. And no question of piracy arises."

There was a moment or two of silence.

"How would Your Grace describe the waylaying and attack at sea of a peaceful trading vessel by another, but armed, trader, not a King's ship? And the forcible removal of passengers?" Crawford growled.

"That might conceivably be piracy, sir — but it does not describe the circumstances. Hugh-atte-Fen, of Norwich, the shipmaster, bore letters of mark and reprisal from me, as privateer. He was entitled to act as a King's ship. Vessels from the Low Countries and France have been preying on our English shipping. His duty was to intercept and investigate any such in our waters. This *Maryenknyght* was a Danziger. The passengers he found aboard were such as owed allegiance to me, as Lord Paramount of Scotland, who were travelling forth of my realms without my permission or safe-conduct. Rightly the shipmaster brought them to me."

Another silence.

"Lord Paramount of Scotland is not a phrase which we in Scotland recognise or accept," Crawford said heavily, "save

217

insofar as it may apply to our own liege lord, King James."

"Then you are ignorant, if not contumacious, sir. If not worse, indeed. Since it has been a style, designation and lawful status of the Kings of England for over a century, adopted and established by my great-great-grandsire, Edward the First, of blessed memory. And held by his successors in inalienable right, and to be so held for all time coming, God willing."

Helplessly the Scots eyed each other.

"Self-assumed and self-styled, Your Grace," John of Buchan said, quietly but firmly.

"Acknowledged, admitted and confirmed by charter. By John Baliol, sub-King of Scots, and sworn to in allegiance by all the whole nobility and community of that realm, sir. As by John's son, Edward Baliol, sub-King."

"John Baliol was a puppet, Your Grace, nothing more. His son a usurper," John returned, strongly. "The good King Robert the Bruce, *my* great-great grandsire, made that truth amply known to England, as to Scotland. Would Your Grace name *him* sub-King?"

"Young man, I would advise you to watch your tongue!" Henry said, almost gently. "My friends," he turned to his lords, "what shall I do with a guest at my table so ill-disposed as to declare the King of England liar to his face? And to seek deny him one of his rightful styles and positions bestowed on him at his coronation?" That was mock-sorrowful.

There was a chorus of wrathful advice. "Back to the Tower with them! Hold them in chains! It is treason! Bring them to trial . . .!"

"No, no, my lords — let us be merciful. Our guest is young. As is this other who spoke — I misremember the name. Although Sir David Lindsay and these bishops ought to know better! We shall bear with them, this once. So be it there is no more such unseemly contradiction of my words. I would advise, Sir David, that you or your Chancellor be spokesmen. With, I hope, the wisdom of years. Proceed."

When Crawford stood silent, but breathing deeply, lips tight and brows black, Bishop Greenlaw cleared his throat.

"My lord King," he said, picking his words, "we come from the Duke of Albany, Regent for young King James and Governor of the realm of Scotland, to seek renew the truce between the two realms, due to expire in four months time. And to ascertain Your Grace's terms for the release of our liege

218

lord James. Also, if it please you, the release of the Earls of Fife, Douglas and Moray, as of other captives held by Your Grace."

"*Release*, Sir Bishop? Do I hear aright? Release does not come into it. The Earls of Fife, Douglas and Moray are prisoners-of-war, yes, on parole. And I shall decide, in due course, their destination. But the boy James Stewart, Earl of Carrick, is in totally different case. He is not a prisoner. He is my guest, dwelling in a house of mine at my expenses. Cared for by my servants. How can you speak of release for such as he?"

Greenlaw swallowed, audibly. "You, Your Grace will allow him to leave?"

"To be sure. In due course. When it seems good and proper — for him."

"To return to Scotland?"

"As to that, I shall have to consider well. For the boy's weal. He is, to be sure, sub-King to myself, as Lord Paramount. And he was fleeing from Scotland, secretly, was he not? With reason, it is to be presumed. He believed himself to be in danger of his life, I have learned. As did his father, whom God rest. Would not I be most unkind, harsh, cruel, to force him to return to this dangerous realm of Scotland? The more so with his father no longer there to protect him?"

"But . . . but he is now King, Sire. All is changed. Not that he was ever in danger . . ."

"The Earl of Orkney, who accompanied his flight, believed him to be so, sir. As did others. Some of whom died thereafter, I heard! Who, then, am I to believe? You, Sir David? Do you say the boy was in no danger?"

Crawford glanced at his colleagues doubtfully. "I know not," he said. "He may have been — then. I am not fully apprised of the matter, at that time. I was in Angus. But now, certainly, he is in no danger in Scotland. He is the monarch."

"I rejoice to hear it, friend. But even monarchs may be in danger, amongst their own folk, I have heard!" It was Henry's turn to glance at his companions, who duly indicated their appreciation of this remark from the man who had toppled and allegedly slain King Richard. "You will understand, however, that I shall have to ascertain, to my fullest satisfaction, the assured safety of this my young vassal prince, before I could advise him to leave the security of this my own Court and realm."

219

As neither Crawford nor Greenlaw appeared to know what to say to that, Alex elected to raise his voice again.

"I may be young, Your Grace, but I am a fully accredited member of this mission of a sovereign nation, and accordingly entitled to speak to its purpose. I would point out that the said mission is here for the very purpose of satisfying you on the desire of that Scots nation to have its King back amongst his people. As is proper. That is why we are so large and representative an embassage, of all manner of opinion in Scotland. Your Grace cannot have greater assurance of King James's safety than is given by the present company."

"Indeed? Yet all here were in Scotland when the lad *was* in dire danger, were you not? I fear that I shall require greater assurance than this, my friends."

"Then — who is able to give you that assurance?"

"That I will have to consider. The Duke of Albany, perhaps? Fortunately I have the pleasure of his heir's company here! It may be that this will facilitate such assurances — who knows? But, see you — until I am so assured, I shall advise James Stewart to remain here where he is safe and well cared for. He was being exiled to France, was he not? For his further education, he tells me. I vow that I am competent to educate the lad as well as any Frenchman!" He nodded at them, with a half-smile. "I think that is all, my Scots friends."

The visitors looked from one to the other. Was this, then, the end of their audience? Was this what they had come all the long road to achieve? Precisely nothing.

Alex spoke up once more. "My lord King — are you sending us away thus, with no more than this considered? Nothing gained — on either side. We were sent to treat in the matter. You say that you will not treat with Scots. Yet treat you have done, each time the present truce has been negotiated and renewed."

"That is not treating, sir. That is conceding — no more." Henry was frowning now, the superficial bonhomie gone.

Alex inclined his head, non-committal. "May we discuss these other matters, Your Grace?"

"No, you may not. There is naught to discuss. The release of the prisoners-of-war is no matter for discussion, but my own decision only. When I deem the time ripe, I shall consider it. As to this truce, I continue it for the space of one year from this day. You may so inform your Duke of Albany. Now — you have my permission to retire."

"But . . . but . . ."

"Young man," the smooth-faced prelate said, cold-voiced, "whatever you do in Scotland, no man gainsays the King of England. Hold your peace, sirrah! My lord of Crawford — retire, with your company, from His Grace's presence."

"We had, indeed have, certain proposals to put to His Grace . . ." Crawford began, when his words were overborne.

"Precious soul of God!" the Earl of Kent cried hotly. "Do these cattle not understand plain speech? Out, Scots — out!" He strode forward, hand pointing from them to the door. Behind him some of the other English lords moved forward threateningly also.

Henry watched, with a half-smile.

Crawford glanced at his colleagues, and shrugged. He bowed to the King, and the others followed suit, features strained, lips tight. But as Alex Stewart straightened up, the Earl of Kent, scarcely by accident, in his hectoring advance, cannoned into him, all but knocking him over.

Hotly Alex turned on him, hand beginning to rise automatically. He restrained himself from striking the other only by an effort.

Kent made no such effort. He reached forward and grabbed the still slightly raised arm, and jerked its owner round. "Out, oaf!" he exclaimed. "All of you — be off!"

White-faced, Alex wrenched his arm free, and with a strangely deliberate action, slapped the Englishman across the face, left cheek and right.

The two slaps, small sounds as they were in all the stir, might have been the loudest of explosions, in their effect upon the company. Immediately all was still, silent.

"Christ God!" Kent got out, at length, hand up to his face. "Struck! You . . . you shall die for that!" he whispered.

"My lords . . .!" the Bishop of Winchester said.

"You may attempt my death, by all means, sir," Alex returned, tensely. "I presume you are knight? Can offer knightly satisfaction?"

"You will receive my cartel forthwith, lout! And pay for your base effrontery in full."

"It shall be my pleasure to teach you otherwise."

A snort from behind them halted this exchange, as King Henry decided to assert himself. "Fiend seize me — as well that I did not perceive this scuffle!" he cried. "Brawling in the royal

221

presence! Edmund — you may leave us. And you, Scots — begone! While still I retain my patience."

The embassage backed out, without another word.

On the main hall dais, they paused, to eye each other, wordless still. Then, without waiting for escort, Crawford led the way down and through the still crowded and noisy apartment, whence they had come.

EDMUND HOLLAND WAS as good as his word. His cartel and formal challenge was delivered to the Scots' quarters in the Tower, by an esquire, that very evening. It consisted of a demand, in high-flown terms, for Alexander, styling himself Earl of Mar, to meet him, Edmund, Earl of Kent, two days hence, the Feast of St. John the Baptist, at noonday at London Bridge, in knightly and mortal combat, mounted, armed *cap-à-pie* in due armour, with lance, sword and dirk, the joust to be *à l'outrance*, that is, to the death. Since the said Alexander Stewart would presumably not have come equipped for such contest, the Constable of the Tower would offer the resources of the Armoury there, the best in all England, whilst he himself, Edmund of Kent, would provide a destrier or war-____ fully trained and armoured, exact match of his own.

Alex expressed his thanks to the esquire, agr____ meeting, the venue and the conditions, declaring ____ look forward to the occasion.

The Scots reacted to the affair with very ____ *À l'outrance* was the grimmest of contests, wit____ tenders not to be content with unhorsing or ____ fighting on until one or other expired. The fac____ chosen to go to such drastic lengths indicated, ____ he was an expert jouster and supremely co____ Whereas none there knew anything of Alex S____ this respect — but they feared the worst. Th____ been reared in the Highlands where chivalri____ unknown, was unhopeful. Heavy full armo____ to him, and a trial, seldom indeed worn ____ however good the horse provided, it woul____ his touch, and so be less swift to react — ____ ne

223

fatal difference. As well as these personal forebodings, there was the general annoyance that they had to wait another day and more as part-prisoners in this Tower. Their mission totally unsuccessful, their pride affronted, their tempers on edge, all were anxious to get away from London and home to Scotland just as quickly as possible. None wanted any further contact with the English Court, indeed Londoners in general. They none of them blamed Alex Stewart for what he had done; but they all could have wished it undone.

That night, in the cell-like chamber he shared with Alex, Jamie voiced his more particular doubts and fears to his friend.

"Pride, Alex, honour and the like, are all very laudable and to be expected from such as yourself. But we can pay too high a price for it. This folly could well result in your death. Indeed, it would seem almost likely, dear God! That Kent is a hard man, and not like to have challenged you thus unless he was very sure of himself. The Earl Douglas warned me to beware of him."

"He is perhaps *over*-sure of himself," Alex observed easily. "So he seemed to me. A bullyrook and braggart."

"Perhaps. But fighting on his own ground, at his own trade, on his own horse with his own weapons. You could have objected, not have accepted all so readily."

"For why, Jamie? I am not afraid to meet him on these terms. I am younger than he is. And have less belly — which means a better wind. Important in such a ploy. And I am not just a babe at this business. I know how to joust with lance and sword."

"Fighting the Earl of Kent will require more than but knowing how, man!"

"True. But perhaps you have forgotten, Jamie, whose son I am? The Wolf of Badenoch, see you, was renowned for more than his misdeeds. He was also Earl of Buchan, one of the finest jousters in Scotland. He won tourneys innumerable, in his day. Think you that he did not seek to pass on something of his skills to his sons? Even in the barbarous Highlands! We used to tilt together on a terrace of Aitnoch Hill, above Lochindorb. We were never as good as he was, but we learned the way of it. We did not use heavy destriers, to be sure — I doubt if there is one above the Highland Line. But we rode the heaviest garrons we could find. Just as, in this contest, I do not intend to use Kent's chosen destrier."

"What, then?"

"Why, my own grey stallion, on which I rode south. It is a

good beast, strong, well-winded. It is not trained for the tilt-yard. But it will be a deal lighter on its feet, faster, more swiftly turned, than any clumsy war-horse. Kent can scarce object, since he has had the choosing of all else."

Jamie remained doubtful, but his friend settled to sleep apparently with a quiet mind.

The day following was a trial for them all, long hours of a summer's day to be got through in restricted quarters, with the feeling on all that they should be somehow preparing themselves for the morrow, doing something at least to make ready, to seek to even the scales somehow. But there was nothing that they could do — save for Alex himself who spent some time in the Tower Armoury, extensive indeed, selecting and trying on plate-armour, shirts-of-mail and helmets, and trying out swords and lances for weight and balance.

Next morning they were hustled off much too early — on the principle, presumably, that they must not keep Kent, the King's cousin, waiting. Once again they were not permitted to ride through the streets, nor use their own Scots escort. Alex was allowed to lead his grey horse, with another led beast behind burdened with his armour and equipment.

This time they found crowds flocking in the same direction as themselves and in holiday mood, and realised that they, in fact, were today cast in the roles of entertainers, providers of spectacle and amusement. At least there was a less hostile atmosphere. And the journey was less long, London Bridge lying no great distance west of the Tower.

When they reached the place, through the dense network of crowded narrow streets and lanes of the waterside, the smells atrocious this warm morning, it seemed a more extraordinary venue for any sort of passage of arms than even they had anticipated. It was indeed quite the most strange bridge that any of them had seen, more like a village spanning the broad river, the bridge itself, raised on nearly a score of piers, lined on both sides by tall tenements of housing, projecting outwards as they rose. It was, in fact, merely another long and narrow street stretching across the Thames, little different from all the others. It was already packed with people, who crowded the causeway, filled the booths on either side and all but spilled out from the windows and balconies at various levels above — and this apparently all the way along the bridge, which seemed to imply that the contest was to be staged, not at some open space at a bridge-end, as the Scots had assumed but on the cobblestones of the crossing itself. These certainly had been covered with some inches of new-looking sand for a considerable length.

The Tower party was, of course, much too early. They had to wait, near the north bridge-end gatehouse, within their circle of guards. All of London appeared to be converging on its curious bridge that forenoon — this proving to be one of the city's many holidays, John the Baptist's Day, and possibly had been chosen by Lord Kent for that very reason. Alex remained calm if a little withdrawn, although his stallion was restive with the noise and crowds.

At length the gentry and nobility began to arrive, in colourful, laughing droves, the women dressed as though for some festive occasion. Though they eyed the Scots curiously, these offered no greetings. Eventually, half-an-hour before noon, Edmund Holland himself appeared, at the head of a glittering company, mounted, with horsed musicians playing a stirring air on flutes, horns and drums as they came, to the cheers of the populace. Behind, grooms led two massive war-horses, like great carthorses indeed, thickset, ponderous, splendidly turned out as though for a show, even their mighty shaggy-topped hooves painted with the blue and white colours of the house of Holland. They were followed by a heavy, lumbering cart, bearing armour, weapons, mantling in vivid hues, and heraldic shields.

Kent did not so much as glance at his opponent as he passed. But one of the grooms with the destriers peeled off with his charge and led it towards the Scots. The cart stopped.

"For the Earl of Mar," the man said briefly.

"I thank you," Alex called. "But I prefer to ride my own beast. Less handsome, no doubt, but . . . more fitting."

The groom blinked. "That . . . ?" he said, pointing at the riding-horse.

"That, my friend."

"But — that will not carry this 'ere h'armour, m'lud. Too big for it, too 'eavy."

"I am aware of that, and shall make do without. My thanks to your lord. But I require nothing of his."

Staring, the man bobbed his head and went off with the destrier, after his betters, signing to the carter to follow. A buzz of talk rose from the watchers.

"I hope that you are wise," Jamie said flatly, at Alex's side.

He was to act esquire and aide to his friend. "I cannot think so."

"You were ever a prophet of woe — before the event, Jamie. Perhaps the bridge will collapse under the weight of yonder pounding destrier, and my challenger go right through and drown! Look on the bright side, man!"

"I am looking! As did Kent — and as must you! Presently. Southwards, into the sun! You will perceive that the Englishman has passed on — a plague on him! Leaving you at *this* end. So that you will face south, the sun in your eyes. That is the chivalry of him!"

"I noticed, yes. Let us hope that he requires that advantage."

There seemed to be no provision made for a viewing-place for the Scots party, and all reasonable stances had been fully occupied before ever they arrived. They huddled where they could — and were left in no doubt when they might be obscuring the prospect of those already in the booths lining the bridge. No sort of pavilion was provided, either, for Alex to don his armour, as was usual at a tourney; it was certainly the oddest venue for such a contest. Jamie was for forcibly ejecting some of the on-lookers from one of the booths, and using it as both dressing-tent and viewing-stand; but Alex said just to wait until they were told what to do. If the proceedings were held up thereby, that would be no fault of theirs.

Information eventually arrived in the person of a gorgeously-garbed herald, who announced that he came from the Earl Marshal of England himself, and sought Sir Alexander Stewart styling himself Earl of Mar.

"I am Alexander Stewart," Alex conceded. "But why do you say 'styling himself'? I *am* the Earl of Mar. Does Edmund Holland likewise only style himself Earl of Kent?"

"No, sir. My lord of Kent is belted earl. You, it is understood, only assume the style in the right of your wife."

"Ah, is that it? So you know more about us than you pretend! I was not aware that our Scots custom was so different from yours, in this. Was not the King's father only Duke of Lancaster in courtesy of his wife? However, my earldom was confirmed and ratified by the King of Scots and his parliament. Is that not sufficient for you, Englishman?"

"I but bear the Earl Marshal's instructions, Sir Alexander."

"Then I could send you back to your Earl Marshal to have his instructions amended, sirrah, before we proceed further. Since in an affair of honour identity is important, is it not? But I

227

suppose that I should be thankful that my knighthood at least is acknowledged!"

"Were you not accepted as knight, sir, my lord Earl could nowise cross swords with you," the herald pronounced stiffly. "May I proceed?"

"You make yourself, and your masters, sufficiently clear, Sir Herald. But continue, yes."

"The Earl Marshal informs you, and all others, that by the command of the King's Grace, the proposed joust *à l'outrance* is forbidden. His Grace will not have the death of an envoy on English soil. The jousting therefore will be as in any tourney, with blunted lances and swords. Dirks will not be used. Is it understood?"

If Alex was distinctly relieved, as was Jamie Douglas, and others there also, he gave no sign of it.

"This is disappointing, sir," he said conversationally. "I had intended to relieve this realm of England of one of its more unpleasing encumbrances. Many, I am sure, would have thanked me. But I can understand your King Henry's concern for his cousin — for, I think, it is that rather than any fear for foreign envoys, which accounts for this. But I shall abide by his royal wishes, to be sure — and seek only to teach my lord of Kent a lesson, and better manners."

The herald seemed to be having difficulty with his breathing. "You will abide by the terms of the contest, sir, as laid down by the Earl Marshal, sole authority for such in this kingdom. In the event of a broken lance, that contender may elect to fight on with the sword. But no requirement lies on his opponent thereupon to abandon *his* lance. In the event of an unhorsing, the unhorsed may yield him, or may choose to fight on afoot. But no requirement rests on the other to dismount. Disarming of both lance and sword constitutes defeat. If a contender falls and remains fallen for sufficient time for the other to place his foot on his neck, that is defeat. Is all understood?"

"It is. But how shall I do? I have here only a sharp sword and a pointed lance."

"My lord of Kent has spare weapons. I shall have lance and sword sent down. Thereafter, at sound of trumpet, you will ride forward over this bridge, to a bar, where you will salute the Earl Marshal and the Earl of Kent, and at my signal will return to your starting-point two hundred paces back, there to await a further trumpet, which will commence the joust."

228

"Understood."

Nodding abruptly, the herald stalked back whence he had come.

"Thank God that King Henry at least showed sense," Jamie said, as he began the elaborate process of aiding his friend into his armour, piece by piece.

"You are less than flattering," Alex protested. "As well that I am armoured in faith, even better than in this steel! But I have this to thank God and King Henry for, at least — that I need not now wear the chain-mail under the plate, and shall be a deal more comfortable. And possibly agile."

"I would watch that Kent, nevertheless," his ever-suspicious friend advised. "Blunted weapons or none, he will seek to injure you if he can, that one. There has many a man died in a jousting that was not à l'outrance."

"I am warned," the other nodded. "Tighten that greaves-strap, will you?"

Presently the herald returned with a man bearing a nine-foot-long wooden lance, and a two-handed sword, cutting edges blunted.

"The Earl Marshal is displeased that you have refused the destrier," he announced.

"I grieve for the Earl Marshal," Alex returned. "But prefer my own horse."

"You understand, sir, that it is to your own disadvantage? This beast will tire quickly, under the weight of the armour."

"That I realise. I must see to it that the joust is not unduly prolonged."

"It makes the contest less . . . even."

"My lord of Kent does not conceive it to be even in any degree, does he? Or your Earl Marshal? Or indeed your King? In their eyes, I am beaten before I commence, am I not?"

The other did not attempt an answer to that, but strode off.

Alex, fully accoutred save for the helmet, was standing by his stallion when the trumpet blew for the first time. Jamie held out a hand to grip the steel gauntlet, wordless now, while the other Scots called their good wishes — and spectators offered light-hearted advice, largely to the effect that the Scotchman would be well advised to turn in the other direction entirely and not stop his nag until he got back to Scotland and safety. Lance high, Alex, helmet within his shield-arm, waved to all and sundry, and rode his horse off over the bridge at a trot, Jamie and Sir

Alexander Forbes, acting as esquires, coming along behind, on foot.

London Bridge was built in three sections, with a drawbridge-like raising portion two-thirds of the way across on the south side, coinciding with the deepest part of the river's channel, so that shipping could pass upstream. The chains for this lifting section were housed in slender towers on either side — and there were, of course, no houses here. The centre of the longer main stretch for this contest was railed off today with hurdles for most of its length, covering about three hundred and fifty yards or four hundred paces. This length, two hundred paces on either side, was important, being estimated to be just sufficient for a heavy war-horse to attain major if not maximum speed — not a gallop, which it would never reach under any circumstances, but a lumbering canter — impetus being a vital factor naturally, although not necessarily the most vital. Midway in this four hundred paces a cord in the Kent colours was stretched across the sanded causeway. Here stood the herald, a trumpeter, two mounted marshals in half-armour, and a resplendent gentleman in Court clothing whom Alex recognised from two nights before at the King's table, presumably the Earl Marshal himself.

Cheers from all around heralded the arrival of Edmund of Kent as he rode up from the south side, at the head of a large and laughing group of sauntering knights and esquires. At least as far as tournaments were concerned, he appeared to be a popular figure. Certainly he looked the part. Indeed, the contrast between the two protagonists was very marked, almost laughable. Kent was clad in the most magnificent armour, gleaming with black lacquer, gold inlaid, bearing in the crook of his arm a great helm of similar design, crowned with the crest of a silver demi-lion guardant arising from a flourish of tall ostrich-feathers, blue-and-white for Holland. His shield was vivid with the quartered device of his house and earldom, in contrasting colours. A silken scarf around his neck presumably represented the favours of some lady other than his wife, being different from his own in hue. His charger was as splendid. Pure white but clad in matching black armour on head and body, over this it bore heraldically painted linen mantling, very colourful, whilst from between its steel-guarded ears sprouted more ostrich-feathers. The harness and trappings were of rich maroon leather studded with precious stones. The total effect was overwhelming, perhaps just a little overdone.

Alex Stewart, on the other hand, inevitably was without any such display. His armour, chosen from the Armoury for effectiveness and as much suppleness as was possible in such commodity, was entirely plain and unpolished, not exactly rusty but dull and dented as was the long shield and uncrested helmet. His mount, looking positively fragile beside the massive, thick-legged destrier, carried no plate armour at all and certainly no plumes. The only gesture Alex had made was to drape the blue-white-and-gold fesse-chequey banner of Stewart, with its bend sinister, brought south only for identification purposes, round his stallion's chest and withers.

At the rope barrier both contestants reined up, facing each other, their horses' noses almost touching. They inclined heads stiffly, and then each turned in the saddle and raised his lance in salute towards the Earl Marshal. Nothing was said. That magnate bowed in return, and waved a hand.

Kent, as challenger, leaned forward and extended the butt of his upright lance to tap Alex's shield, twice; and as he sat back, Alex made the same gesture.

A chorus of groans and shouts arose from the spectators near enough to observe these moves. It was the indication that the joust was not to be to the death, as had been said, and great was the disappointment. The populace felt itself to be cheated, having come to see blood shed.

At a nod from the herald, the contestants reined round and with their supporters headed back to their starting-places, accompanied — at least as far as the Scots were concerned — by catcalls and insulting comments from the crowd. A mounted marshal followed each.

Two hundred paces back, at another marked spot, Alex turned, and put on his helmet, visor still up, clamping it secure. Jamie and Forbes made a final check of all accoutrements and fastenings, and signed their satisfaction to their principal.

It was as Jamie was moving back to his own new stance at the side of the starting-line that, his glance lifting, he saw amongst the many other faces watching them from the booth behind one which riveted his attention. It was an extraordinary sensation — for it might almost have been a trick of his vision, some sideslip of timing. The features could have been those of Alex Stewart, save for some slight blurring of outline and a difference of expression. For a moment Jamie floundered, mentally. Then he realised that he was looking at a face he knew. He had not seen

Sir Duncan Stewart of Loch-an-Eilean for many a year, but he had no doubt as to his identity now. Alex's brother was here in London, and had come to see the fight.

As recognition came to the Douglas, the other's glance locked with his own, and for a long moment they stared at each other, the fair man and the dark. Then quickly, almost furtively, the former ducked away behind the spectators next to him, and was gone.

Jamie's first impulse was to push his way into the booth, through the press, to grab and hold Stewart. But the briefest thought told him that this would be foolish, even if practicable. It could only distract and upset Alex at a time when he required all his concentration. Duncan Stewart would not submit tamely, that was certain, so there would be trouble, disturbance — and the crowd was scarcely friendly anyway. He turned away, doing nothing. He did not even make a sign to his friend.

A trumpet-blast sounded from mid-bridge, and the mounted marshal beckoned.

Alex Stewart snapped down his helmet's visor, lowered his lance to the level, and leaning forward, kicked with his heels his beast's flanks.

Two hundred paces, on a horse, is no great distance, especially on a spirited riding-horse. But it was quite sufficient to get the grey up through trot and canter to a gallop. On the other hand, although the distance did mean more to the slower, heavier destrier, it still did not allow it to attain quite its fullest impetus. As a consequence, Alex reached the central barrier considerably before Kent did. But the rope was withdrawn now, and there was nothing in the rules to say that the contestants must remain on their own sides of the division. He pounded on over the sanded cobbles. The sun in his face, striking through the slits of his visor, was a major handicap, barring his vision in confusing dazzle and shadow.

His opponent was thundering towards him on the most determined of collision courses, carrying more than twice his weight and strength. Orthodox jousting tactics were for the two to meet head-on, lance-tips aimed at wherever each deemed to be the most vulnerable spot, with the object of smashing the opposite number right out of his saddle and to the ground, if possible — where he might well be stunned by the impact or by the battering effect of his own plate armour. It was not a delicate or precise operation, the precision lying in the handling of the horses, the timing of the strike, the aim, and of course the ability to withstand the shock and keep in the saddle.

Since any such headlong collision would almost certainly result in Alex's overthrow, his methods had to be less than orthodox. Yet no mere dodging, by-passing and, as it were, skirmishing, would serve or be acceptable, as against all the laws of chivalry. His opportunity to manoeuvre was strictly limited.

He continued, then, on his head-on course, the yells of the crowd loud and echoing within his helmet. A corner of his mind noted that Kent had transferred the silken scarf from his neck to his lance-head, where it streamed in confusing fashion — an allowable device but one which could mask, even for a moment, the all-important point of aim.

With less than a dozen yards to go, their squared-off lance-tips only about seven yards apart, Alex acted. Fiercely he dug in his spurs, at the same time jerking up his beast's head. The stallion responded nobly, leaping forward and upward with an abrupt access of speed and change of level. The scarf-tied lance-head wavered in instinctive reaction. Even as the grey's forefeet touched down again, Alex pulled to the left. Only a trained, agile and light-footed horse could have conformed sufficiently swiftly. The beast swung off to the side before Kent's lance could adjust, and the scarfed tip missed by inches. Alex, on the other hand, who had so planned it, was able to bring his own lance to bear. Because of the angle, and turning away, it could not be the sort of major thrust which might have unseated his opponent; but he managed to strike a glancing blow. Kent was able to deflect it on his shield, and scarcely even rocked in his saddle. Nevertheless, it was a hit, the first point to the Scot.

They hurtled past each other, to the yells of the onlookers.

Alex did not even draw breath before flinging himself and his mount into the next move. Urgently he reined back and back, and snorting violently the grey reared high on its hind legs, staggering forward on two feet for half-a-dozen paces, its forelegs pawing the air even as its upper half turned in response to the furious tugging to the right. By the time its forefeet touched sand again, it was half-way round, and in an involved but remarkably well-adjusted side-stepping dance of the hindquarters completed the turn. Seldom if ever could the spectators have witnessed so rapid and complete a reversal of course, at speed. Spurring hard again, the Scot went pounding after the destrier a mere dozen yards behind.

Kent was not seeking to rein up or round. His obvious course now was to get well to the other, northern end of the lists before swinging round in a wide arc, both so as to maintain the fullest possible impetus on his war-horse and to avoid putting himself directly into the sun's dazzle. Unfortunately for him, he did not know that his antagonist was on his heels — his helmet prevented any part-backward view and the thunder of his own charger's hooves allied to the deadening effect of his armour, drowned the sound of the chase.

The grey stallion was infinitely faster, and swiftly overtook the destrier. Alex could not, of course, attack the other from the rear. So just as Kent began his swing round to the right, the other pulled off in the same direction. The Englishman must have been astounded suddenly to discover his enemy rearing to another pawing turn directly in front of him. And surprise would not stop at that. For the Scot had in fact tossed away his lance, and drawn sword instead. That Kent was unready for instant action went without saying. His lance was half-raised. If he could have brought its nine-foot length down to bear in time, with the necessary velocity, he would have had the other at his mercy and hopelessly out-ranged. But those instants he was not given. Alex plunged at him, sword high, and as the lance came down to the couched position, but before it could be aimed, drove down his steel upon it with maximum force. Edge blunted or none, the weight of the massive blade snapped the wooden shaft of the lance clean through. Kent was left with only the stump.

Raising his sword high again, in mocking salute, the Scot reined round and trotted off towards the south end of the lists.

The howls of the crowd were angry now. However unusual, there was nothing improper in what Alex had done. Nothing in the rules insisted that the lance must be used in preference to the sword. It normally was, of course, because of its greatly longer reach. But that was little to the crowd's taste; undoubtedly the inevitable wagering was heavily on the Earl of Kent.

The situation was now much transformed, and in Alex's favour. Kent it was who now faced the wrong way, into the sun. And the heavy destrier held no advantage for swordery.

By mutual consent the contestants waited a little, giving their mounts rather than themselves some small breathing-space. But no lengthy pause was permitted, and soon the trumpet blared again. Both plunged forward.

This time Alex did not urge his grey to a gallop, or even a

canter. He trotted out in no hurry at all. Kent, however, drove his animal at the same earth-shaking charge, sword outstretched before him as like a lance as possible.

Alex was well aware where both danger and opportunity lay. Sword-fighting was close work, inevitably; and at close quarters the great destrier could be lethal, its weight and strength overwhelming. Struck by it, cannoned into, the grey could be easily knocked over and trampled. However close the fight, therefore, the horses must not touch. On the other hand, manoeuvre, speed, agility, were far more important with the sword than with the lance. Although, of course, clad in armour as they both were, delicate and intricate swordsmanship was neither possible nor productive, the use of the weapon limited.

Now, by deliberately going slowly and holding back, Alex allowed the other to gain almost maximum speed and momentum, so that to suddenly change the course or deflect the hurtling monster would be all but impossible. He had to hold his stallion hard in and on its straight course, for the beast was all too well aware of the menace beating down upon it. Then, as Kent almost crashed upon them, the Scot jerked and kneed his grey to the left and, thankfully and just in time, the creature almost leapt sidelong out of the way. It meant, to be sure, that Alex could not use his sword. But, as he plunged past, the Englishman lashed out in a furious back-handed swipe. It missed the man by inches, but the tail-end of it struck the grey's croup near the tail, causing the brute to rear and whinny with pain and fright. The lack of horse-armour was being paid for.

Then they were past. To Kent's slight advantage — but only apparently.

Alex was reining round immediately. But now he had a hurt and alarmed mount to cope with — and quickly knew the difference. The stallion, agitated, responded much less swiftly and effectively, side-stepping, dancing, head-tossing. Nevertheless its rider enforced his mastery, seeking to reassure by word and hand — although a steel gauntlet is scarcely made for gentling — but at the same time forcing the beast round with rein and knee and spurring it on. Training, familiarity and reliance told. They plunged on after the destrier.

Now Alex's problem was two-fold. He wanted to retain the advantage of the sun, and at the same time close with his opponent at a moment of the destrier's minimum impetus. He pulled over to the right therefore, to the west, as widely as he might, so as to circle round to actually confront the other. Kent was seeking to rein-in his charger for the turn.

Alex was scattering the spectators lining the western side of the bridge, for there was precious little space for his manoeuvre in this the most constricted lists he had ever known. His aim was to get as far to the south as he might, and for the other to see him doing so, despite his helmet-restricted view, and to turn in that direction to meet him.

Alex ran out of space, of course, at the end of the marked-off area. He had to pull south-eastwards, cursing the narrowness of the bridge — even though, as bridges went, it was broad. Fortunately Kent, of intent or otherwise, had drawn over to the other, east side, and was now turning, speed reduced to a ponderous trot. Alex spurred in at him, yelling "A Stewart! A Stewart!" little like him as this was.

There were only a few yards available, little time to muster significant speed; but the situation was a deal better for the Scot than for his enemy. Kent was almost stationary, in a corner, and facing south-westwards, so that the sun slanted in through his left-hand visor-slits.

Deliberately forcing his grey to rear and plunge and sidle right in front of the other, Alex leaned forward in his saddle, blade as nearly flickering as was possible with a heavy two-handed sword. All but dancing his beast there, he sought to feint, confuse, aid the sun's dazzle. Kent, restrained from making any mighty lunge by the need to parry, his mount at a standstill now, had been forced to a defensive posture.

This play could not be kept up for any time, the weight of those great swords, meant for double-handed work, being too sore on the wrist. Because of their shields, neither could use the left hand to aid the right. But Alex was the younger man, and, not being a courtier, almost certainly the fitter. He cherished his advantages, kept his horse sidling and his blade weaving.

When he recognised that his own wrist would stand little more of it, he chose his moment to make a direct lunge for the throat when the other's sword was flagging after a mid-body parry. The only way Kent could cope with this was by an instant reversal, a directly upward stroke. This only by a great effort. It was achieved, at a price. Alex, expecting it, swung his blade away to the right, as though to smash down instead on the other's left shoulder, above the shield, pausing fully extended thus for an instant. He was entirely vulnerable at that moment,

236

had his opponent been in a position to take advantage of it. But Kent's awkward upward sweep could nowise be altered to any sort of forward thrust. It had to reach its full height and then come down through sheer weight and muscle failure. The man chose to bring it down in an attempt to parry the wavering point threatening his shoulder. Which was what Alex had manoeuvred for.

Jerking back in his saddle at last, the Scot drew back his weapon just in time to avoid that slashing downward cut — which nothing could bring up again quickly. Then, kicking his beast nearer, with all his strength remaining he lunged forward his blade in a fierce but controlled thrust to the throat again. Or just a little lower, directly at the base of the gorget, where the helmet joined the body-armour. With all his concentration he guided the blunt, flattened-off sword-tip right in under the flange of the helmet, slightly upturned to reach in. And then, with a final explosion of that weary wrist, he jerked the whole weapon up, from the hilt. With a snap the leather strap securing the helmet to the rest burst at Kent's right side, and over the helmet itself toppled, to hang, still held by the strapping on the other side, over its owner's left shoulder, resting on the shield-top, and leaving the man bareheaded, blinking open-mouthed and gasping, sweat running down into screwed-up eyes.

For a long moment Alex held the sword poised above his opponent's unprotected head; then, as the other's blade came up automatically, he slashed down on it, driving it aside. Pulling back, he flung his own weapon down on the sand in front of his defeated foe — for to be unhelmeted was as final a verdict as any — and raising gauntlet in salute, reined round and went trotting back over the bridge, whilst the populace and spectators groaned, shook their fists and roared their disappointment. He paused to bow briefly to the Earl Marshal and herald, in passing, but received the merest nod of acknowledgement.

Jamie and Forbes ran out to greet the victor, shouting their congratulations and admiration, scarcely able to express their delight and relief. Alex took off his helmet and gave it to Forbes, smiling, and shaking a shower of sweat-drops from brow and plastered fair hair, generated by the heat inside that steel box.

"I would not have believed that you had it in you!" Jamie, tactless as ever, cried, leading the grey back towards the other waiting Scots. "You are a notable jouster, man. That was a joy! You had him all ways."

"I but recollected what my great ancestor, Robert Bruce, did at Bannockburn, at the first onset," the other replied, still panting a little. "You'll mind, he was caught on but a palfrey against de Bohun's charger — yet won the day. His tactics I used. He was my great-great-grandfather, after all."

The reception by the Scots party of their champion was in marked contrast to that of the crowd round about them. Since, apart from the sword Alex had brought with him originally, they were none of them armed save with dirks, the two bishops were not alone in urging that the sooner they removed themselves from the vicinity the better. Their escort, provided by the Constable of the Tower, looked as though it might be less than enthusiastic in their defence from a mob's anger. Jamie and Forbes, therefore, with all speed aided Alex in divesting himself of the armour, the officer of their guard looking apprehensive.

It made a distinctly hurried and undignified departure from the scene of triumph — but already some missiles and filth had been thrown at them, and fists and sticks shaken. Whether the Earl Marshal would feel any responsibility to protect them the visitors were not prepared to wait to discover.

It was as they were moving off from the bridge-end, Alex leading his stallion and in his own clothing again, that Jamie felt a tug at his elbow. He was prepared to turn and defend himself against attack, hand on dirk, but discovered there only a middle-aged individual, grizzled and tough-looking, in the garb of a man-at-arms. Although he had a hand on a short cavalry sword, he was nodding his head in greeting.

"Sir James? Sir James Douglas, is it no'?" this new arrival said, in a strong Lowland Scots voice. "I jalouse you'll maybe could do wi' a bit mair steel handy, in this pass? I'll bide wi' you, a whilie."

"Why, thanks, friend. You could be right. This crowd looks ugly. You know me, then?"

"Aye, I do. I'm Rab Douglas, frae Peebles. I was wi' you at yon stramash at Preston, against Hotspur Percy. Aye, and I was at Otterburn, forby. I was wounded at Homildon, and taken prisoner wi' the Earl. He should ha' done as you said, man. I've been wi' the Earl these four years. But, och I'm wearying for hame, mind."

"That I can believe. Is the Earl here today, then?"

"No' him. Forby, he'll wish he had been, when he hears. He said he didna want to see decent Scots gien mair ill usage and

238

mockery. Little did he ken! Sakes, Sir James — your man fair skelpit yon baistard Kent!"

"Aye, it was a bonny fight. The Earl of Mar is no bairn at the jousting."

"He was the Earl o' Buchan's son, was he no'? I've seen his faither at the same ploy, one time — at a tourney at Stirling. He was an awfu' man that — but a right stark fighter!"

They dodged, as a handful of dirt was thrown at them. Cursing, the new arrival whipped out his sword and flourished it threateningly.

"Dirty low swine!" he snarled. "Have you no' a guard? Decent Scots, no' this Englishry?"

"They are still at the Tower. We were not permitted to bring them. The English have sought to humble us, ever since we came."

"Och, you should never have come, at all. Anyone could ha' tell't you that."

"We had to come. To seek the young King's release. Scotland could not just leave her liege lord a prisoner. Not that we have achieved anything."

"Nor would you. Anyone here could have tell't you that same, too. The laddie will never be loosed. When they went to siclike pains to get him."

"How mean you — pains?"

"Trouble, man. Siller. Plotting."

"How that? James was captured at sea, on his way to France. A mischance . . ."

"Nae mischance! They kenn't he was in that ship, and lay wait for it. We a' kenn't, here aboot the Court, what was to do."

"What mean you? How could you know? James was a month on the Craig o' Bass, waiting for that ship."

"Aye, we kenn't that, forby. A messenger came to this King Henry, frae Scotland, wi' the word o' it. Killing beasts to get here in haste, they said."

"A messenger? From whom, man?"

"Whae'd tell the likes o' me that? But I've heard it said it was one o' the Governor's men."

"Lord — Albany!"

"Aye, that's the whisper amongst the English lords' servants. That the Governor sold the laddie to Henry. The price I dinna ken. But he's no' like to hand him back, I'm thinking."

Appalled, Jamie did not speak for a little. It was scarcely

believable. And yet, and yet . . . Was it not logical enough? If Albany had murdered Prince David, and threatened young James's life sufficiently for his father to send him to France, would he boggle at betraying him to the English? Was it worse than starving to death, poison, or the knife? And if it was true, what likelihood was there of James Stewart ever coming back to Albany's Scotland? Instead of astonishment should he, James Douglas, not be blaming himself for having failed to think of it?

"Did you ever see this messenger of Albany's?" he asked presently, heavily. Before his mind's eye there had arisen the features, so like Alex's, of Duncan Stewart hiding amongst the throng in that saddler's booth, to watch his brother.

"No."

"Does the Earl of Douglas know of this?"

"It would be unco strange if he didna, Sir James."

Thereafter, wending their way through the narrow streets, Jamie was notably silent, considering it all and wondering how and when to tell Alex Stewart. Not in front of the others, certainly. Presently, with the Tower in sight and the disappointed tourney crowds far behind, the Douglas man-at-arms left them, with good wishes and handshakes. Jamie gave him no message for his master.

When the Tower gates clanged shut on them, Crawford and Buchan went to inform the Constable that they would be leaving for Scotland at sunrise next morning.

* * *

Although they were prepared for delaying tactics and general obstruction from the Tower authorities, in this matter as in all others, the reverse in fact applied, and speeding the parting guests was the theme. Indeed, the Scots were requested to leave, not at sunrise but an hour before it — this again to ensure that mounted and armed foreigners did not make unsuitable appearance in London's streets. They were nothing loth to comply. Apparently King Henry and higher authority had no further interest in their presence.

So they made a very early start, their Scots men-at-arms even more thankful than the leadership to be on their way — for, of course, their seventy-strong escort had been cooped up in cramped quarters ever since arrival, to their great resentment. It was on the whole, therefore, a cheerful company which,

240

despite the hour, shook the dust of London from their feet and headed northwards for home.

The Earl of Mar was the exception. Since Jamie's revelations of the evening before he had been in an unusual withdrawn mood of abstraction and reserve; if not depressed, certainly distressed, grieved, angered. Clearly the thought of treachery such as was indicated towards their young prince shook him to the roots of his being, both from the dynastic and the family standpoint; and that his own brother was probably the means by which that treachery was effected hurt most of all. As well as this, a sensitive and friendly man, he had been much galled throughout by the deliberate discourtesy shown to them all by Henry and his Court, and especially by the unchivalric behaviour at the tourney the day before and the utter ignoring of them after the victory. Respecting his friend's state of mind, Jamie maintained a fair degree of silence himself, something he had an aptitude for.

They were over a dozen miles on their way, crossing the rolling hunting country of Enfield Chase when there was an unexpected interlude. Shouts from their rearward turned all heads. Behind them a hard-riding company of perhaps a score pounded after, two large banners at the head. It did not greatly tax the Scots' English heraldic knowledge to recognise the colours of the earldom of Kent and the house of Holland.

"How think you? A recall by Henry?" Buchan wondered.

"He would have sent more than this," Crawford said. "He knows our numbers."

"He would require to send an army to turn us back now!" Forbes declared. "We have had sufficient of English hospitality!"

So said they all as they trotted on.

As the newcomers caught up, Kent himself was seen to be leading them. He actually smiled, something they had not seen before, as he flourished a feathered and bejewelled velvet bonnet at them.

"Greetings, my lords," he cried. "Whither away this fine morning, so early? Do not say that you are on the road to Scotland, so soon? Without the courtesy of a farewell?"

His hearers' gasps were audible, none finding words easily to match such effrontery.

"We heard but an hour or so back that you were gone," the other went on. "I rose with all haste."

"Why, sir?" That was Alex Stewart, baldly for him.

"For sufficient reason, surely, my lord? To pay my respects and to wish you God-speed, if naught else."

"The first belated, the second unexpected!" Alex jerked.

"Come, come, my lord of Mar!" Kent reproved, reining nearer. "You did not wait to allow me to congratulate you on your, your prowess yesterday."

"I gained no notion that such would be forthcoming, sir. And the crowds scarcely encouraged delay."

"Pooh — wagering losses, nothing more. They showed me little love, either. But you should pay no heed to such cattle. What made you think, sir, that I would not acknowledge your superior . . . cunning?"

"Cunning?"

"To be sure. Cunning, wits, artifice, wile, sleight of hand. Which gained you the victory."

"You are suggesting, my lord of Kent, that it was by cunning contrivance that I gained the advantage yesterday? Rather than by knightly skill and honest fight?"

"Did you not make that sufficiently evident to all, man? You rejected fair matching, refusing equal horses. You mocked the accepted terms of fight, playing at horsemanship instead of jousting. You discarded the lance without informing me, the true tourney weapon, and deliberately broke mine. And then you used the sword merely to unhelmet me and gain a cheap end to it all. Had I known that we were to engage in jugglery and hall-floor entertainment, I would have come prepared, sir."

Alex drew a deep breath. "*I* came prepared to fight to the death, my lord — as you had challenged. *You* chose the terms, the weapons, the place, the time, the sun even. Henry of Lancaster forbade *à l'outrance*, not I. If I used my head to redress the balance, you have no call to complain, I say. I broke no rules. I fought fair."

"You fought like a jester, a mountebank, sir — scarcely a knight. But if you will agree to meet me again in honest jousting, anywhere, equally mounted, equally armed and armoured, to abide by knightly custom, I shall rejoice. And perhaps show a different result."

"I see no virtue in anything of the sort," Alex returned. "I never desired such contest in the first place. Let it be, my lord."

"So — you choose not to meet me in fair fight?"

"I would choose not to meet you again in any circumstances,

242

sir! Fair or otherwise. I have seen enough of you." Alex's voice quivered a little. Despite his generally equable and courteous disposition, he did not lack the spirited Stewart temper. "But if ever we do encounter each other, it will be my earnest endeavour to do more than unhelmet you!"

"I see, then, why you are in such haste for Scotland! You will be secure there from test, to be sure. Unless my Cousin Henry decides to show his barbarous northern realm the weight of his hand. In which case it will be my pleasure to seek you out."

"We shall await your coming, sir. And thereafter continue your education in jugglery and hall-floor entertainment! Your Cousin Henry's, likewise. Tell him so, if you please. Tell him also that the price for pirating and holding captive our young King may prove more expensive than he bargained for with his friend north of the Border! Tell him, likewise, that more than usurping a throne is required to make a true king. A good day to you, sir."

Alex reined round and rode off, followed gladly enough by the other Scots.

The Earl of Mar returned to Scotland a different man from he who had left it.

XV

THE HIGHLAND HARVEST over that autumn, Jamie Douglas was summoned to a meeting at Aberdeen. He had stayed on at Lochindorb, where he was useful, kept pleasantly busy, and where Mary and the children were happy. Reported conditions in the South, under the Regent's complete sway now, were not such as to entice him to leave Badenoch. His brothers were looking after his lands of Roberton, Stoneypath and Baldwinsgill for him, and he was well enough content superficially, however much he seethed in his inmost heart over the state of Scotland, its mismanagement and what he considered to be the triumph of wickedness and bad faith. He got on well with the Highlanders, was learning the Gaelic, and was gradually becoming something of a minor power in his own right in Braemoray and Badenoch. He saw Alex at intervals and continued to enjoy their association but recognised that his friend had become a preoccupied man, in some measure at war with himself, and not as prepared to be forthcoming about it as was usual. Also that he was still not altogether happy about his wife and her activities.

The Aberdeen summons, in early October, was to meet at the provost of the burgh's change-house in the Shiprow; which struck Jamie as a strange rendezvous for the Earl of Mar. He was surprised at the composition of the party assembled, likewise. Apart from Sir Alexander Forbes of that Ilk the others were merchants, burgesses and shipmasters. Their host, Provost Robert Davidson, was a big powerful man of about forty, with a ruddy, weatherbeaten face unlooked-for in a townsman; he had been a shipmaster himself until a few years before, when he had inherited his father's merchanting business and quayside inn, and thereafter by his drive and energy had quickly made

244

himself a powerful figure in Aberdeen, now being its chief magistrate and spokesman of the merchants' guilds.

With beakers and flagons of excellent wine before them the company of about a dozen sat around a long table in a handsome panelled upstairs room, richly if soberly furnished, which would have bettered many a lord's hall, overlooking the busy fish-market and quays of the port. Alex sat at one end and his host at the other. Jamie was intrigued by the composition of the party, never having had occasion to sit down with a roomful of burgesses before. They seemed substantial, shrewd men, in their own way formidable, and clearly somewhat suspicious of such as himself. For his part, he had no least notion as to the reason for this assembly.

Robert Davidson, deep-voiced, almost grim, opened the proceedings. "My lord Earl of Mar has a matter of much import to put before us," he said, in a strong and unmistakable Aberdeen accent which gave no hint of his Highland antecedents — the Davidsons were, of course, a branch of the great Clan Chattan of Badenoch. "It could concern us all. My lord — we are listening."

"Mr. Provost and my friends," Alex said pleasantly. "What I have to say may not be approved by you all. Or indeed, by any. In which case you will tell me. But I have come to you because I believe that if you *do* approve, together we can strike a blow for our realm and our young King. And also for your own interests. You are all merchants, shippers, traders with foreign lands, France, the Low Countries, the Baltics and the like. And you all have been suffering grievous losses in your shipping at the hands of English pirates, losses for which you can obtain no redress."

Throaty growls of agreement for this, at least.

"As no doubt you are aware, I have recently returned, with Sir Alexander Forbes and Sir James Douglas and others, from an embassage to England, to London, to the Court of the usurping King Henry, to seek negotiate the release, by ransom if need be, of our rightful King James, shamefully taken by English pirates from the Danzig ship *Maryenknyght* chartered by the King of France, in which our liege lord was on his lawful way to France. We were most rudely used by King Henry and his servants, who refused to consider the release of our sovereign and who said openly to us that the ship which took our prince was no pirate but a privateer under letters of mark and reprisal

245

from himself, the King. And this in time of signed truce between the realms. That ship, the *Kingfisher*, of Great Yarmouth, under Hugh-atte-Fen, is a notorious pirate, as you all know too well."

As his hearers scowled and muttered, Alex leaned forward over the table.

"You perceive what this means? It means that King Henry is himself involved in piracy. He encourages these English ship-masters to attack and rob on the high seas, and divides the spoil with them. This is why you have had no redress, no response to your complaints. The King of England is chief pirate!"

General exclamation broke out round the table. Alex gave it its head.

Presently he went on. "You are angered, as was I. But . . . Henry Plantagenet, by that admission, gave us the means to strike back. If he can employ privateers, so can we! He can have no lawful complaint if we trade with him in his own coin. And that, my friends, is what I propose to do. With your help."

There was no doubt now about the company's rapt attention. However doubtful most of them looked, they all sat forward eagerly.

"Henry mocked and ignored our embassage. He is a man who heeds only deeds, not speeches. So we will give him deeds. And seek to regain our young King's liberty by means he cannot fail to understand. I intend to charter and fit out a stout ship, here in Aberdeen, and sail her against English shipping, under letters of mark."

Alexander Forbes slapped the table delightedly and roared his approval. Davidson was stroking his chin thoughtfully. Jamie Douglas, however, when he could make himself heard, un-doubtedly spoke for more than just himself.

"Where, my lord, would you get the said letters of mark? Not from the Regent Albany, I think!"

"Not from Albany, no. But from his son."

"What! But . . .?"

"Jamie — hear me. This is more than a device. These letters of mark and reprisal are issued by the government of a realm in the name of the King. Who governs this northern portion of King James's realm? Not the Duke of Albany, but John, Earl of Buchan, Lieutenant and Justiciar of the North. I have spoken with him. He is ready to give me such a letter. He misliked our reception, and Henry's manners, as much as I did. Wait, man!

I know that such a letter would be unlikely to stand good in an English court of law. But — would any? Henry in his arrogance claims that he is Lord Paramount of Scotland. Would he accept any letter of mark from whomsoever in Scotland? Albany's or other? I say he would hang us as pirates, out-of-hand — if he caught us. So we must not be caught. But the letter will serve well enough for anything less than Henry's warships. And it is not his warships that we go to assail, but his traders — as he does with us. Aye, and his privateers."

Noisy debate arose around that table. It was clear that it was not the ethics of what was proposed which was preoccupying the company, but the likelihood of being captured by the English king's ships. At least none doubted Alex's verdict that any captured sailors would hang.

"My lord of Mar," the Provost said presently, "none of us will question the worth of this ploy, if it is possible. Nor the need for some stroke against these pirates. Nor, indeed, your lordship's good heart in proposing this. But to have any success, we would have to be able to out-sail not only the English privateers but their king's ships, forby. And I know of no vessel like to do that, in Aberdeen or elsewhere."

There were murmurs of agreement.

"Surely we do not wholly lack for fast ships in Scotland?"

"Sufficiently fast for this — yes, my lord. Craft that could out-sail ships of war have to be built to do so. Our ships are for trading, carrying goods, cargo. They have to be right stoutly built to withstand stormy seas, and of bulk to carry sufficient cargoes over long voyages. Heavy vessels."

"Are the English privateers not the same?"

"Not so. They use lighter, narrower craft, not made for long voyaging. These dart out from their ports of Kingston, Yarmouth, Harwich and the like, to prey on vessels using the seas off their coasts on their way to France and the Low Countries. They do not have to make long voyages, and can choose their weather. So they can be fast and light — aye, and sleep in their own beds of a night! We build no such craft."

"But we *could*, could we not? Build a vessel to outmatch these pirates. For that purpose?"

The merchants eyed each other.

"How long would you be prepared to wait, my lord. One year? Two?"

"So long . . . ?"

"Does Scotland hae nae ships o' war o' her ain?" one of the others demanded.

"Few, if any, I fear, sir," Alex said. "And if such there are, they would be under the control of the Duke of Albany, who would not allow that they be used against Henry, I wager!"

There was silence for a little.

It was Jamie who broke it. "I am not assured that this project is altogether sound," he averred, frowning. "Although I am as strongly in favour of teaching the English a lesson as any here. But . . . in this matter of fast ships, it seems to me that we need not look further than the galleys and birlinns of the Islesmen."

"Galleys, 'fore God!"

"Yes. They are the fastest craft that sail, I was assured by shipmen in the West. Long and lean as wolfhounds, driven by thirty-six long oars, two men to an oar, besides their square sails, they can outpace and overreach anything that floats. When I journeyed, yon time, from Ardchatten Priory to Dumbarton, to see King Robert, my ship was challenged more than once by the robber galleys of the Islesmen. The Priory's flag saved us. But I saw the speed and power of these ill craft."

"A notion, Jamie, bless you . . .!"

"That was in the sheltered Hebridean seas, Sir James," Davidson objected. "Galleys would not serve in our stormy main."

"They get swifter storms and steeper seas there, shipmen told me, than anywhere. Because of mountain winds and the fierce currents . . ."

"Nevertheless, sir, their galleys are not the craft for our great main seas. They are open vessels, men exposed. There is little decked-in cover, cabins or holds. They could not make long voyages, as would be required. Fast they may be, but they are cockle-shells compared with our sea-going carracks and the like."

"Yet, it was in vessels like galleys that the Norsemen crossed your same main, Provost, to raid our land long ago," Alex pointed out. "I understand that the Islesmen's galleys are but improved Viking longships."

Davidson shrugged, obviously unconvinced.

Another shipmaster spoke. "Thae light galleys couldna hold the cargoes they might pirate frae the English ships," he pointed out. "Sae where'd be the guid o' that?"

Jamie intervened again. "Why not use *both* kind of ships,

then? In partnership. Your heavy but slow trading-vessels to act as base, a floating haven, well out to sea, and the galley to make the attacks. Like cavalry and foot, in a host. Might it not serve?"

They all considered that for a few moments. Alex was smiling beatifically. Gradually the others nodded, scratched heads, or grinned.

"It is just possible, sir," the Provost admitted. "Forby, the ship, the proper ship, would be at risk all the time — from king's ships, whilst it lay off."

"Possible, man — it is more than possible," Alex cried. "It is the answer. Trust Sir Jamie! Cavalry and foot — to be sure!"

"It is only a notion," Jamie pointed out, embarrassed a little. "As to this of the large ship being at risk as it lay off, it could do with a light cavalry screen, like any infantry host. Another galley, always with it, for protection. If we could find one galley, we could find two."

"Excellent!"

"You would require crews," Forbes said, "for the galleys, trained oarsmen. Aye, and men used to fighting from such devilish craft. You would need Islesmen, many Islesmen. And the Islesmen scarce love you, my lord! Or any here."

"Not only Islesmen have galleys," Alex contended. "Every Highland chief in the West has his birlinns, which are but smaller galleys."

"It is not the Islesmen who are our enemies, my lord, but their chief, Donald of the Isles, and his brother Alastair Carrach. And not all Islemen owe Donald MacDonald allegiance," Jamie pointed out. "Some hate and resist him, I have heard, notably the MacLeods. The Campbells also, to be sure — although they could be kittle cattle to herd with! Others. The Mackenzies are ever at war with the MacDonalds. And all their palms itch for good siller."

"Sir James is right," Alex exclaimed. "We will get our galleys, I swear, since I think that I may find a little siller — and the men to sail and fight in them."

"My lord, the English king's ships — aye, and some of their privateers forby — carry these new bombards, cannon, using gunpowder. They can throw a great ball or bolt far. Much further than any siege ballista or catapult. To smash a vessel's timbers, and men," Davidson reminded. "I have seen it. To such, a galley would be no more than an egg-shell."

"But a lively egg, friend! An egg that would not stand still to

249

be smashed! I have heard that these cannon are ill things to serve and aim, even on land. On a tossing ship, to hit a speeding galley might tax such not a little. Nevertheless, we must seek to gain a cannon or two for ourselves — although it may not be easy. Perchance two can play at that game."

"It will all take time, my lord. When do we start?" Forbes asked.

"We start our preparations forthwith. We cannot sail, with hope of success, until the winter's storms are over. So we have until the spring. But much work to be done before then, in finding, equipping and victualling the vessels, mustering and training the crews, planning our warfare!" Alex raised his wine goblet. "Here's to the spring of Our Lord's year fourteen hundred and seven, my friends! Are we all agreed?"

However doubtful some of those present, none failed to drink to that. It was not every day that an earl of Scotland offered Aberdeen burgesses such a toast.

Outside, on their way to the stables behind the inn, Alex threw an arm around his friend's shoulders.

"What a man you are, Jamie Douglas!" he said, shaking his fair head. "You are a black-frowning, thrawn, suspicious devil! Yet you have the wits of us all, and the keen and far-seeing eye. You are a joy to me, lad — and the finest friend a man ever had!"

The other scowled. "For an earl, and a Stewart one forby, you talk great havers!" he accused.

"Perhaps. But you, now, for so chary an adventurer, talk all others into that adventure! By the sheer worth of your proposals."

"I but spoke of simple facts."

"Quite. Facts, however which others had not thought of. But now we must turn your simple facts into a plan of action, Jamie. I shall come back to Lochindorb with you, for we have much to discuss and settle. Before we head for the West and your MacLeods."

"We . . . ?"

"To be sure. You do not think that you are not in this matter up to the hilt, my Douglas friend? If you did not want to go travelling again, you should have held your tongue between your teeth back there! Dunvegan, is it not, in the Isle of Skye, where MacLeod roosts . . . ?"

XVI

THE GREAT VENTURE was set to commence on St. Serf's Day, 20th April, Serf or Servanus being a notable Celtic saint much experienced in voyaging, and his day an auspicious one for sea-going. Despite sundry inevitable hitches and delays, all was ready, or as ready as it would ever be, a couple of days before, and Aberdeen in no small excitement. Some seventy of its seafaring men were involved, to crew the substantial carrack *Greysteel*, of three hundred and eighty tons, captained by Provost Davidson himself, who had agreed to relinquish both his burghal and inn-keeping duties for a while, having debts to pay in southern seas. His prominent adherence had been of the greatest value to the entire enterprise, of course, much facilitating the support of others, the enlistment of a first-rate and experienced crew and the provision of the best equipment. Other shipmen and merchants had rallied round, and the result was this fine sea-going vessel, Aberdeen-built and formerly chartered by the Abbey of Deer for trading with the Baltic ports and Muscovy. The MacLeod galleys had been obtained also, without too much difficulty but at great cost, with the necessary large complement of rowers and fighting men to the number of over three hundred, no less; but it was considered inadvisable to let loose this host of wild Gaelic-speaking warriors on the decent burgh of Aberdeen, in the interests of continuing goodwill, so that the galleys — which, being shallow-draught vessels, did not require deep-water quays and anchorages — were meantime waiting in the shelter of Nigg Bay, a mile or two to the south, having arrived from the West nearly a week early, to the embarrassment of all.

Alex had held a farewell banquet the night before, in the Town House, graced by his Countess, at which were present most of

251

the city's notables as well as officers of the *Greysteel* and the various higher-born adventurers whom Alex had persuaded to take part. It had been a noisy affair, and Jamie Douglas's head still ached. Now, at last, they had reached the final leave-taking, the Dean of Aberdeen and the Abbot of Deer had ceremonially bestowed their blessing upon ship and company, and all was ready for casting off.

Mary Stewart was clutching her husband's hand tightly. "Do not think that *I* am calling down blessings on this stupid venture!" she told him — as though it was news. "I have let you go on all too many ploys, without protest. But this is nonsense, quite unnecessary, the pair of you behaving like bairns. I mislike the sea, have never trusted it. You are knights and lairds — not pirates. You will either hang or be drowned, and I shall never see you again!"

"Yes, my dear."

"You will take great care, Jamie? Remember that you are not on a horse, this time. Do not go jumping from one boat to another. You all but fell in, at the quayside here — so what you will do on the sea I do not know."

"Yes, my dear."

"Do not stand there saying 'yes, my dear'!"

"No, my dear."

"You should never have allowed yourself to be talked into this. You said yourself that you doubted the wisdom of it. Because Alex is eager to get away from his wife, that is no reason for you to do so!"

"Hush, lass . . ."

"Why should I hush? Is anybody else hushing? I am fond of Alex. But he is being foolish. He should never have married that woman. But if he must put distance between him and Isobel of Mar, there is no need to go to sea to do it, or to go pirating against the English. Are his Highlands not sufficiently wide for him? *She* would not chase after him, I warrant!" And Mary nodded her comely head towards the Countess.

That woman stood laughing in the midst of the group of young lairds enlisted for the venture, in mid-deck — John Menzies of Pitfodels, Alexander Irvine of Drum, Alexander Keith of Grandholme, Alexander Straiton of Lauriston and Patrick Leslie Younger of Balquhain, all Mar vassals. She certainly did not look upset at the imminent departure of her lord. Alex himself, with the younger Forbes of that Ilk, was

252

busying himself with superintending the charging of the two small cannon which he had managed to hire at great expense, and which were presently to fire a blank-shot parting salute.

"Like a bairn with his toys!" Mary insisted.

"Let him be," Jamie said. "He has worked long and hard on this project. It means much to him. And he is our good friend."

She was silent.

Isobel Douglas's throaty but uninhibited laughter prevailed.

At last the cannoneers declared themselves satisfied, and Alex called out that all was ready, and that those who lingered longer must needs sail with them. From the poop Robert Davidson shouted for warps to be readied for casting off.

Mary flung herself into her husband's arms. "Oh, Jamie! Jamie!" she cried.

"Hout, lass — this is not like you," he said, stroking her hair. "What ails you?"

"It is the sea. You have never gone sea-fighting before. I hate and fear the sea."

"You did not hate or fear it one time, at Aberdour, I mind!"

"That was different, different altogether. Promise me that you will take heed for yourself, the greatest heed . . ."

"I will, yes — for I am a careful man. Anyone will tell you so."

She shook him in exasperation, but allowed herself to be led to the gangway and quayside.

There Alex was ushering his Countess ashore likewise, assisted by her bevy of admirers. Their embrace was fairly brief, formal.

"I require a shipload of the best that England can provide," Isobel proclaimed, to all and sundry. "Do not come back until you have it, I charge you!"

Mary muttered uncharitable comments towards her sister-in-neglect, kissed Jamie hurriedly, and broke away.

Alex sensibly cut things short, by waving to his trumpeter to sound. Amidst cheers the great banner of Mar was run up to the mainmast-head, that of Stewart to the mizzen, and the saltire flag of Scotland to the foremast, whilst, at Davidson's commands sails were unfurled and ropes cast off.

With the stern warps still holding and the *Greysteel*'s high bows gradually beginning to swing out from the quay, Alex signed to the cannoneers up on the forecastle. These had their fuses ready and smouldering. Blowing them lustily into a red glow, the chief man on each piece applied his to the touch-hole at the base of the wide-mouthed, short-barrelled clumsy horn-like device made of wrought-iron bars bound together by steel hoops. The port-side piece flashed immediately and mightily, a vivid red flare singeing the cannoneer's beard and hair and sending him and his assistants staggering back — but unfortunately making no desired report. Its partner did, a moment or two later, bang loudly however, setting all the gulls screaming and sending a peculiar ball of smoke rolling out over the harbour waters, to the mixed admiration and alarm of the onlookers. The plan had been to have a small succession of salvoes; but, concerned for the state of the crew of the first gun, Alex signed for no more, and hurried forward to look to and condole with his humiliated artillerymen. Most there shook their heads over this new-fangled invention, which clearly never could be relied upon, as the carrack's stern warps were cast, her sails began to fill and she moved out into the brief estuary of the Dee. Gradually the cheers from the shore died away.

Alex Stewart's private war had started.

Rounding Girdle Ness beyond the estuary, they came to Nigg Bay. Warned by the cannon-shot, their two galleys had hoisted sail and were driving out to meet the carrack. They were extraordinarily different-looking craft from *Greysteel*, long, slender, graceful in a menacing fashion, low in the water, each with a single great square sail painted with the black bull's head crest of the Siol Tormod, the senior line of the Clan MacLeod. They were not of equal size, one a hundred and sixty feet long, with thirty-six great oars in two banks, the other a hundred and twenty feet, with twenty-four oars, but both no more than twenty feet wide. Each had a fierce, upthrusting, high prow, to finish in an outstretched eagle's head, this sharp prow sheathed in steel to form a savage cutting-edged ram. In the stern was a raised platform, on which stood the commander, pilot, helmsman, boatswain and other leaders, and beneath which were scanty sleeping quarters. The bows also had a smaller platform, with a little storage accommodation below. The oarsmen, two to each sweep, sat their thwarts open to the sky, with a gangway down the centre of the craft between the seventy-two or forty-eight men. Beneath them the vessels were decked-in to provide a very shallow hold. Because the oar-teams were duplicated for continuous rowing, where necessary, a lot of men had to stand

and sit around in notably restricted space. Davidson's comments about galleys being unsuitable for long-range voyaging could be seen to be valid.

The two strange craft came out of the bay at a speed which had to be seen to be believed by more conventional sea-goers, amidst a cloud of spray from the flashing oars, which drove in long, rhythmic strokes in time to a curious chanting, throaty, angry-sounding, unending, which rose and fell, every other beat punctuated by something between a gasp and a growl, as the rowers expelled breath and took the strain, with on the poops, oarmasters or boatswains beating the time. Out they swept, to drive fore and aft round the carrack — and nothing could more plainly demonstrate that they moved at more than twice the speed of the bigger ship. Out to sea they sped, presently to curve back, leaving long white washes, to take up position astern of *Greysteel*. Now they rested most of their oars. Clearly they were going to find keeping that position as tedious as it was difficult.

"Wolfhounds you named them, that time, Jamie," Alex commented. "Myself, I would say wolves, and be done with it! How think you we shall manage these expensive allies we have acquired?"

"I would not think that we *could* manage them, at all. Work with them we must, and may learn much, gain much."

"I would not like to be in one of those in a storm," Davidson said.

"Yet storms are frequent in their own Hebridean seas," Alex answered. "They must be seaworthy. I think that we should pay our Islesmen friends a visit. It would be civil. How do we go about it?"

"I can heave to and lower a wherry, my lord . . ."

"Why trouble?" Jamie asked. "These galleys can do all that your wherries can do. Hail them alongside. That is their custom, is it not, when they board vessels?"

Waving and shouting brought the galleys up without any difficulty, one on either side of the carrack — and without the latter even having to shorten sail — the nearside oarsmen raising their long sweeps vertical, the offside ones sculling expertly to hold their craft in position, upper bank working against lower. Grinning half-naked Islesmen were about to toss up grappling-hooks on chains, but Davidson stopped them with oaths, concerned for his decking, and ordinary ropes were thrown down to them instead, then rope-ladders. The smell of sweating men came up on each side, chokingly.

Alex told Sir Alexander Forbes, who was a Gaelic-speaker, with one or two others to go down into the smaller galley, whilst he and Jamie climbed carefully down the swaying ladder to the larger. Both then cast off from the carrack.

On the galley's crowded tiller-platform they were greeted by a cheerful red-headed young man in faded tartans and long piebald ponyskin sleeveless waistcoat, with sword-belt — as indeed were most of those present, save the actual rowers, who were stripped to the waist above short kilts. Only the fact that the sword-belt was jewel-studded distinguished this individual from the others. He was John MacLeod Younger of Dunvegan, known as Ian Borb, elder son of the fifth chief of the name, William Achlerich. *Borb* meant fierce or furious, and *Achlerich* meant the cleric; but this young man gave no special impression of ferocity, and his father, whom Alex and Jamie had negotiated with the previous November, had looked anything but clerical.

"Greetings, sir," Alex said heartily. "Sir James Douglas you know? We rejoice to have you join our venture. And we much admire your two fine craft, and how well you handle them. An excellent augury. The speed at which you came out to join us impressed us all."

"Speed is it, whatever? That was no speed, friend." There was never any my-lording amongst the Islesmen, who accorded no-one that title save — and the MacLeods only grudgingly — the Lord of the Isles himself. "We shall show you speed, if you would see it." Without waiting for agreement he slapped Alex on the back, and turned to the oarmaster, who as well as beating time and leading the chanting, carried a bull's horn slung at his side. A wailing blast on this drew the attention of the other galley — which seemingly was called the *Clavan* or Hawk (this one being the *Iolair* or Eagle), and was commanded by a natural brother, one Ruari Ban, or the Fair. Ian Borb made some energetic signals with a clenched fist, which seemed to be understood, for they were answered by a great shout from the *Clavan*, and a distinctly derisive horn ululation, clearly a challenge.

There followed a pause, as flagons of whisky were passed from rower to rower, men spat on their hands, and Ian Borb, the pilot and the boatswain held a brief conference. In these galleys the overall commander was not the shipmaster, or pilot, but the leader of the fighting men, usually of chieftainly status. Then the horn was blown again, loud and long, to be answered from across the waves, and what evidently was to be a race was on.

The oarmaster, a brawny, almost bald-headed character of middle age, with a great paunch but no hint of flabbiness, raised his mighty voice to a bellow, at the same time lifting a short broadsword high above his head. Every rower's eye on him, tensed, ready, his shout maintained. Then abruptly ending his cry on a single explosive word, he brought down the sword on to a large bronze gong-like object, set on legs like a table and barbarically carved. The booming clangour coincided with the deep first powerful thrust of every oar, and all on board, from commander downwards, took up the outlandish but exciting, pulsing chant. At each stroke the sword clanged down, and gradually the intervals between lessened and lessened, the rowers soon dispensing with their contribution to the singing, save for the regular punctuation of coughing grunt which was synchronised breath and effort. The sweeps creaked in their sockets, the blades splashed and feathered in unison, the bow-waves creamed back hissing, and the wind whistled in the rigging.

Jamie Douglas, sober man, had seldom experienced such sudden exhilaration. The sense of power, united effort and determination, of tension, the clanging of the gong, the vehement singing and ever-increasing speed, was heady in the extreme. Even the almost overpowering smell of sweating humanity wafted back on their own wind added its own measure to the excitement.

The oar-strokes had gradually changed character, the blades dipping less deeply and at a different angle, with much shorter pulls in the water, to enable them to quicken tempo dramatically, seeming almost to skim the waves. So dense was the curtain of spray around them now that they could only intermittently see the other galley a quarter-mile to starboard. The visitors had neither of them realised that man could move so fast save on horseback.

Ian Borb, yelling encouragement, kept gazing to the right and frequently shaking a fist towards his half-brother's vessel. They seemed to his passengers to be running neck-and-neck.

"How can they keep up with us?" Alex shouted. "They have fewer oars, and men."

"Och, in a light sea . . . such as this . . . *Clavan* has some advantage," the other panted. "Less weight. Sits higher in the water. Shorter oars . . . ten strokes to our eight. Heavy weather, *Iolair* gains. But . . . we will beat them, by God!"

It seemed impossible that the rowers could maintain their herculean efforts, purple in the face, arm-muscles bulging, sweat streaming, mouths wide. Yet that slamming sword and the relentless chant went on and on, so that it became, for the visitors at least, almost a physical pain to watch, their own tensed muscles aching in sympathy.

"This . . . this is faster than a horse could gallop!" Alex exclaimed. "They will burst their hearts!"

Jamie nodded, but pointed over to the right. "We are drawing ahead, I think."

"Praise God!" He peered through the spray. "Yes, we are." Turning, he grasped Ian Borb's shoulder. "We are winning, man. It is enough. Call a halt, of a mercy! They will kill themselves!"

The other laughed, shaking his red head, and shouted mixed abuse and encouragement to his men the louder.

At last, when it was amply clear to all that the *Clavan* was indeed being left behind, Ian Borb threw up his hand, and signed to the boatswain who, reluctantly it seemed, blew on his horn a prolonged blast. As though it had slain them all, the rowers collapsed forward over their oars in heaps, the singers changed to cheering — such as could summon the breath — and the poop party beat each other about the back and beamed on their guests with simple joy. An answering horn-call from across the water signified acceptance of victory and defeat.

In the sudden relaxation and comparative quiet, Alex actually mopped his brow, although he had done nothing more exhausting than hold his breath.

"I would not have believed it," he said. "It is beyond all. Such speed. Every man, on both ships, shall be rewarded, I promise. If they live! Jamie — this, in a sea-fight, could give us untold advantage."

"Aye — if these craft can twist and turn at a like pace."

"Can you, man — twist and turn?" That to Ian Borb.

The other shrugged, and jerked a word or two to the bald boatswain. That man bellowed for a change of oar-crews. Now all the singers began discarding shirts, jerkins and plaids, and went to replace the panting heroes on the thwarts, the whisky flagons going round once more.

While this was going on, Jamie pointed away astern, where *Greysteel*'s sails were just to be seen.

"We came further than I had known, as well as faster. How many miles have we outdistanced our ship?"

"Lord knows! Jamie — we shall have to consider all this with much care. In planning our warfare and sallies. To use it all to greatest advantage . . ."

The new rowers in place and anxious to show their prowess, *Iolair* swung hard round, to make for *Clavan*. Nearing her, Ian Borb hailed his half-brother, in mocking condolence over the evident age and decrepitude of his crew and his misfortune to command such a lumbering wash-tub, before declaring that they were now going to show these Lowland Sassenachs a few tricks, chasing their own tails and the like.

Thereafter, the great sails run down, followed a highly alarming interlude, as breathtaking as the other had been breathless, with the two galleys weaving and circling, describing figures-of-eight, turning at speed, reversing stern-first, cavorting on the waves like frisky colts, even going through the motions of ramming each other with those cruel steel-shod prows, and only pulling aside at the very last moment, with oars swiftly raised high and dripping, to avoid a splintering crash. Time and again it seemed that nothing could save them from disaster, but always most skilful steering and oarsmanship prevailed. Time and again, likewise, Alex cried out that it was enough, that he was more than satisfied; but there was no stopping their gleeful allies. One bank of oars countering another, starboard oars countering port, helm aiding, tempering or reversing, the dangerous, crazy sport continued. To his employer's protests, Ian Borb declared that this was nothing compared with dodging strewn reefs and skerries of the West in a Hebridean storm. From ever having to experience such, then, his passengers prayed that they might be delivered.

At length, with *Greysteel* drawing near, the demonstration was called off. But before returning the visitors to their own ship, Ian Borb had one more piece of galley-craft to display. The spare crew was set to unlashing and raising tall poles which lay along the low bulwarks, and which proved to be spare light masts, to be set into sockets in the stern and fore platforms. Extra small square sails were then hoisted, along with the main-sail, to give additional power when there was a suitable follow-ing wind. It was explained that this was only really useful in

259

special conditions, since it tended to alter the trim and steerage of the craft and could confuse the rowers.

Alex invited Ian Borb and Ruari Ban aboard the carrack for a meal, loud in his praise. But as they surmounted the rope-ladder, he murmured to Jamie.

"We are going to have problems with these people, I fear. Do you see them obeying my commands?"

His friend shrugged. "Possibly not. Unless you can make them love you. But — you are good at that, Alex. Otherwise, we could be out-pirated, I think!"

"My own thought, whatever. We shall have to consider this, too. But, by the Mass, they are bonny seamen!"

"Yes. When we start fighting, I would wish to be in that galley."

"Aye, man — so would I . . ."

*   *   *

Greysteel led a course almost due south-east. They wanted to get, and remain, well out of sight of land. Also Alex did not wish to become involved with North of England shipping; his quarrel was specifically with King Henry, the Earl of Kent and the East Anglian privateers. So it was the open sea for them meantime. But leading the way did not necessarily mean that the carrack was followed as though by obedient dogs at heel. The galleys sometimes were there, one or both, sometimes were not, ranging about near and far, frequently not even in sight. Clearly it was difficult for them to adjust their speed to the slower vessel; but more vitally it was a matter of the mind — these Islesmen not being of the sort patiently to follow anyone, independent to a degree.

The second day out, the weather broke, with rain squalls, gusting winds and angry seas. Conditions in the galleys must have been highly unpleasant, and it was the turn of the Aberdeen crewmen in *Greysteel* to laugh and look superior. But despite their slender, rakish appearance, the smaller craft proved themselves to be surprisingly good sea-boats, however exposed their companies to the elements, riding the seas like ducks rather than ploughing through them as did the carrack. Low-set as they were, frequently they were out of sight in the wave-troughs, to reappear at odd and even alarming angles. Most of the oars were shipped in these conditions, and the remainder used more for steerage and balance than for propulsion. In consequence, the Islesmen tended to fall far behind now, or else swing off on different courses altogether in their running battle with the seas. There was the minimum of contact with *Greysteel*.

For two days and nights the half-gale continued, from the south-west, the carrack stolidly beating its way south-eastwards through the cross-seas. Inevitably they were blown quite a lot further east than intended, when at length wind and seas moderated and fair visibility returned. Robert Davidson reckoned that they might be as much as one hundred miles off the North Yorkshire coast. Many of his passengers were, however, too seasick to care greatly.

Neither Jamie nor Alex were troubled that way, thankfully, and their concern was for the galleys, nowhere to be seen on the empty, tossing horizon. Some distinctly anxious hours passed, with Alex suggesting that they should put about and go back to look for their missing associates, and Davidson declaring that this would be a pointless exercise, with no least indication as to where to search in hundreds of square miles. However, just before midday the fourth day out, a look-out on *Greysteel* reported the galleys fine to starboard, due westwards perhaps eight miles off and coming up fast. It was not long before this was evident to all; and soon the Islesmen were milling around the carrack in fine style, evidently not only none the worse for their battering but in lively, indeed challenging mood, shouting across to the effect that did the Sassenachs know not that they were nowhere near where they ought to be, leagues out of their course? They had been hunting the seas for them.

Davidson's comments were unrepeatable; but Alex was much relieved.

This content did not last long, nevertheless — a bare couple of hours, in fact. Then, soon after the Aberdeen look-out spotted a single sail hull-down far to the north-west, suddenly, without permission or warning, their MacLeod friends swung around both galleys and went streaking off in that direction, oars flashing. No amount of shouting or signalling from *Greysteel* had the least effect on them, and after a while both they and the hull-down ship disappeared over the horizon.

Again there was debate as to whether to turn and go after them; and again Davidson pointed out that it would be useless, since they could nowise catch up. Alex's concern that North of England vessels should not be interfered with made him angry.

"They are like ill-trained hounds!" he declared. "Chasing any game that moves."

"Wolves, you decided, not hounds," Jamie reminded. "And wolves hunt at will, not at command."

Davidson muttered darkly.

It was early evening before the truants returned. They came in high spirits, obviously, dashing up with horns trumpeting and much waving. Alex beckoned for *Iolair* to come close alongside.

"MacLeod!" he shouted down. "That was . . . unfortunate. A mistake. A mistake, I say . . ."

"No mistake, friend. And excellently fortunate!" Ian Borb waved towards a stack of casks and barrels on his poop. "Have you a taste for French wines? Brandies? Lower a net and you shall have your share. And, look you — catch this! A gift, just." And he tossed up a handsome silver goblet which Jamie managed to grasp. "Would you wish for a jewelled sword? A toy, but pretty . . ."

"I thank you. But . . . it is not a matter of booty, man. I told you, my quarrel is with the English king and the Southerners. Not these of the North. And if we rouse the North against us, behind us, it could be the worse for us later."

"I do not hear you, friend."

Alex sighed, and raised his voice to a shout. "Do not attack in these northern waters. Do not attack, I say. Save on my orders."

The MacLeod did not comment on that, other than by a wave of his hand and a wide grin.

"You will never hold these devils!" Sir Alexander Forbes said. "They are but sea caterans."

"Perhaps. But we may be glad of them, nevertheless, before we are done."

The Earl's orders were not put to the test thereafter, for they sighted no more sails that day or the next. They were, of course, deliberately keeping well away from land, and most shipping tended to keep within sight of the coastline. They had reached a point which Davidson reckoned to be about seventy miles east of the Thames estuary by the following evening. At last they were ready for action.

At first light, next morning, after cruising quietly westwards all night, Alex and his lairds transferred themselves to the two galleys. Land was still not in sight, but the low-lying shores of Essex and Kent could not be more than twenty-five miles off.

Greysteel was to beat up and down at this range, waiting, whilst the galleys went in search of prey.

Jamie found a holiday atmosphere prevailing on *Iolair*, the whisky flagons already circulating. He judged that most of the scanty storage space beneath the rowers' deck must be loaded with barrels of the fiery spirit. Ian Borb welcomed Alex and himself like old friends unseen for long, and they set off westwards without delay.

They spied their first sail in only a short time; but the general opinion was that it was only a small, low-set Netherlands smack, little more than a heavy sailing-barge, of the sort used for carrying hides, grain and suchlike bulky cargo across the narrow seas, not worth attacking. Then, with land beginning to show as a dark line ahead, they saw, somewhat to the north, a group of half-a-dozen dark sails, fairly close together. These also were small, however, and almost certainly a fishing-fleet from one of the outer Thames havens. The galleys swung away south-westwards.

It was mid-forenoon, and men becoming restive, before they saw their first tall ship, heading north-by-west as though for the Thames. Even if Alex had decided not to intercept, it is doubtful if he could have restrained the Islesmen. As though slipped from the leash, the galleys darted forward on a converging course. Each lowered its sail, now, for better manoeuvrability.

The vessel proved to be a large three-masted bark, flying the red cross on white of England. The galleys made a wide circuit of it at speed, and the *Iolair* drew in close, the *Clavan* lying off at the far side.

"What ship is that?" Alex cried. The bark's rail, high above, was lined with suspicious faces.

"I am the *Clara*, of London. Master, Peter Holden. But — what is that to you?" a hoarse voice answered.

"Sufficient. I am the Earl of Mar, out of Scotland. On my King's business. Heave-to — I am coming aboard."

"That you are not! I heave-to only at King Henry's orders. Be off, Scotchman, or it will be the worse for you."

"Indeed, sir? How could that be?"

"I will sink your oar-boat, sirrah — earl or no earl! I have cannon aboard."

"Unfriendly, Master Holden. Prepare to be boarded."

"Two cannon," Jamie reported. "Not large. One on the poop, the other at the bows."

"Easy, just," Ian Borb commented. "We go in and keep below them." He raised his voice, to bark orders at his crew.

Thereafter everything happened at great speed. Oars shipped on the near side, *Iolair* was swung in directly under the bark's port side amidships, timbers actually bumping. There she was quite safe from the cannon at least, which could by no means be depressed sufficiently to shoot down at them. Men, stripped to the waist, were already climbing up the rigging of the galley's central mast, to loosen booms which swung down and outwards, over the *Clara*'s deck. The booms were suspended from a circular platform, something between a fighting-top and a crow's-nest, two-thirds of the way up the mast. On to this spearmen clambered, to hurl down javelins upon the Englishmen, to provide cover whilst their colleagues swarmed out along the booms, to drop on to the bark. At the same time grappling-irons on chains were being flung up, to hook on to the other's deck, binding the ships together. Before these could be detached and tossed down again, more men were streaming up the chains, scaling the bark's side like monkeys, swords being thrown up for them. In almost less time than it takes to tell, a score and more of the Islesmen were aboard, steel in hand.

Trained fighting-crews on king's ships might have managed a more effective defence and created casualties amongst the boarders; but these were ordinary merchant seamen, and such tactics quite beyond their experience. Ian Borb himself was one of the first up the chains and, sword in hand, took vigorous charge. The English shipmaster and his mates did their best, but were wholly outclassed by their experienced attackers, and very quickly isolated on the high aftercastle, without having been able to strike a blow.

It was at this stage that wild shouts and the sound of bagpipes from the other, starboard side of the *Clara*, heralded the arrival of the *Clavan*'s contingent of boarders. Ruari Ban appearing up on the aftercastle itself. That was more than sufficient for the skipper. Throwing down his sword, which he had held in less than accustomed fashion, he folded his arms and so stood, waiting and chewing his lip. His people were thankful to follow his lead. By the time that Alex and Jamie had clambered up on to the deck of the bark, all was over, in only a few hectic minutes.

"Skilful work, MacLeod," Alex commended. "I think that you are scarcely new to this practice! I would not like to sail your Western Sea lacking your safe-conduct!"

"Yours for the asking, friend. Any time, whatever. What shall we do with these?" Ian Borb gestured around. "Cut their throats?"

"Not so. They have yielded decently. Our quarrel is with their masters. They have two wherries, I see. Lower them, and they can row to land. It is within sight. Master Holden — my sympathies. But your king should not have pirated mine, and held him prisoner. If you have opportunity, tell him so. Tell your betters that they will continue to lose ships until they release King James. You have it?"

Wordless, the unfortunate shipmaster nodded.

"Very well. Get your men into the wherries and be off. You should make land in but a few hours. You will take nothing with you but your lives."

As the Englishmen hastily lowered their boats, the Islesmen were already scouring the ship for what they could find. The cargo proved to consist of woven cloth and linens, bale upon bale; also carved ironwork, clearly for church furniture, glassware packed in straw, great cheeses and innumerable bundles of furs. The MacLeods found this exceedingly disappointing, although the cheese they appeared to appreciate and the furs they were prepared to appropriate. The master's and crew's belongings did not add up to much, either — so that, to the Islesmen at least the *Clara* was poor reward for their expertise.

"Sink her, whatever," Ruari Ban recommended.

"No, burn her," his half-brother said. "Near land, as here, a burning ship will bring others to investigate. Smoke will be seen far off. Further pickings, see you. It seldom fails, I tell you."

"Perhaps not," Alex objected. "But this is a fine ship, in excellent order. Our Aberdeen friends have lost many such to English pirates and privateers. It would be folly and a wicked waste to destroy her. We shall send her back to join *Greysteel*. These two more cannon I covet."

There was some demur, but at this juncture shouting from above sent the two young MacLeod chieftains hurrying up to the deck.

"This cargo could sell for much in Aberdeen," Alex said. "And Holy Church would be glad of much of these plenishings. I have found it ever advisable to keep the churchmen my friends!"

Jamie nodded. "These Islesmen have different values. Let them have the furs and cheese, and what else they want, if they

265

will sail us back to *Greysteel*. And praise them, Alex — much praise. They like it. They are like bairns . . ."

When they returned to the deck, it was to find the situation changed. Another sail had hove in sight to the west, and Ruari Ban MacLeod, envious of his brother's success, had hurried back to his *Clavan* and gone off alone to intercept. He was already a mile away.

In the circumstances Ian Borb accepted that it would be unwise to set the *Clara* alight meantime. He agreed to provide a small crew, under his navigator, to sail her back to *Greysteel*. As he conceded this, his eyes were on his brother's receding galley. Clearly he was anxious to be after him.

Hastily, then, a dozen men under the *Iolair*'s pilot were detached to man the captured bark as best they could; and MacLeod and the rest swarmed down to their galley and cast off, Alex and Jamie, with the other lairds, electing to stay on *Clara* meantime.

The prize-crew were not used to handling full-rigged ships, of course; but they were good seamen, and the moderate breeze and sea enabled them to control the vessel sufficiently to steer a fair course, if slowly. Indeed, after the galleys' speed, it seemed painfully slow.

So the lairdly party had opportunity to watch what was happening to the west. Far beyond the two small wherries, now looking as tiny as water-beetles as they pulled clumsily for the land, both galleys had come up with what seemed from this distance to be much like a lighter version of *Clara*. They were too far off to see details, but all three vessels were massed as one, and if not halted were moving very slowly. The reports of two cannon-shots came booming across the water, but no effects therefrom were evident. Presently, however, with the scene of action almost hull-down, a dark cloud of smoke began to mount above the ships. The Islesmen, it seemed, were trying out their burning-decoy theory.

"It seems to me that there is little need for us in this venture!" Jamie observed, grimly. "We could sail back to Aberdeen and leave all to the MacLeods!"

"Somehow we must bring them under control," Alex agreed. "But how? Though, see you, they are serving our cause excellently well. So long as they do not make our name infamous, by savagery."

"Are there degrees of piracy, my lord?" Forbes asked.

"We are privateering, not pirating. Under letters of mark. There should be a difference."

"Convincing the MacLeods of that will be difficult, I think."

It took them some time to find *Greysteel*. Davidson and the other Aberdonians were delighted with the *Clara* and her cargo, however bored with beating up and down the empty seas in idle waiting. They felt even more useless than did the lairds.

They waited, that evening, for the Islesmen to turn up, lookouts high on the masts of both ships. But when darkness fell there was still no sign of the galleys.

That night Alex held a council, in the low-ceilinged main cabin of *Greysteel*, aware that morale demanded it, allowing all, leading shipmen and gentry, to say their say. Jamie felt distinctly guilty. It had been at his suggestion that the galleys had been hired, and although their effectiveness had been amply proven, it was as evident that mixing Islesmen in an East Country expedition was of doubtful wisdom. The men's respective attitudes and characters were incompatible, their outlook and code quite different. But such recognition was late in the day. They were here now and must make the best of it — although there was one train of opinion to the effect that they would not see the galleys again anyway, and could forget the problem; the MacLeods, having flexed their muscles and been brought to the hunting-grounds, would now go their own way. Both Jamie and Alex contested this view, claiming that the Islesmen had their own loyalty and would respect the bargain made with their chief back in Skye.

Meantime an effective strategy had to be worked out, if they were not going to become mere onlookers at their impulsive allies' activities. It was decided that *Greysteel* should provide a prize crew for *Clara*, not just to sail her but to fight her, cannoneers on both ships and Sir Alexander Forbes in command. They would go hunting as a pair, irrespective of what the galleys might do.

Next morning there was still no sign of the Islesmen, although they gave them some hours of daylight to find this waiting area. At length, disappointed, Alex gave the order to abandon their beating-up-and-down stance. *Greysteel* leading, they headed off under full-sail south-westwards.

Towards midday they spotted two sails at once, although on different sectors of the horizon — for now, of course, they were coming into the main trade routes between the Low Country and French ports on the one hand and London and the English east coast havens on the other. Deciding to intercept the nearer and larger of these vessels, they altered course, preparing for action, cannon charged, fuses burning, boarders ready.

As they drew near, however, they perceived that the ship, a fine carrack somewhat larger than *Greysteel*, was flying a banner bearing the Lilies of France. At first, balked, Alex was for making a polite signal and then veering off to look for something they could legitimately attack. Then he changed his mind and asked Davidson to move in close, *Clara* to stand off.

Greysteel stood about, to gain a parallel course with the Frenchman on her windward side, and then drew in to within hailing distance — her people staring into the open mouths of French cannon at the ready. Alex, on the aftercastle, took off his velvet bonnet and waved it.

"A good day to you, messieurs!" he called, in fair French. "I am the Count of Mar, in Scotland. Greetings from one ally to another. May I ask whither you are bound?"

"Your reasons for asking, monsieur? And your right?" came back thinly.

"On the King of Scots' business, friend. I hold letters of mark against English shipping. You understand? Letters of mark?"

"Privateer? You are privateer, Monsieur le Comte?"

"Yes. But only against the English, who have captured our King James, on his way to your country, on *your* King's invitation. You are bound for an English port?"

"For London, yes. On our lawful business. *St. Barthemely* of Etaples. What do you wish of us? You have no right to trouble us ..."

"No, monsieur. I desire only the courtesy of your assistance, as ally of Scotland. When you reach London, will you be so good as to inform the English officers that the Earl of Mar is happy to permit *your* passage, with his compliments. But English shipping will continue to be assailed until such time as King James is released. To tell their King. You understand, monsieur?"

"Yes. If it is your wish, I shall tell them. Is that all?"

"Why, yes. I am indebted to you. We wish you well. Pray, proceed." Alex flourished his bonnet again, and turned to wave Davidson on.

"What will that serve, my lord?" young Irvine of Drum wondered.

"It will reach King Henry's ears the more surely, and swiftly. And foreign shippers' likewise. The English will mislike this, on their very doorstep, almost more, I think, than losing a ship or two."

The second sail which they had spotted earlier was now too far off to be worth following up, so they continued on their prowling progress in a south-westerly direction. They saw no more shipping for a considerable time, to the frustration of all. When a sail at length did appear, it proved to be only a small coasting lugger scarcely worth the chasing. Nevertheless, with his colleagues eager for some action, however modest, Alex acceded.

They had no difficulty in running the craft down, which, when challenged by two larger vessels, promptly and discreetly hove-to, with the minimum of fuss, and did not obstruct a boarding party. She proved to be the *Gillyflower*, of Deal, in Kent, with a smelly cargo of untanned hides. Despite the disgust of the Aberdonians, Alex was interested in this, questioning the unhappy master closely. Had he any dealings with Edmund, Earl of Kent? Was Deal connected with the Earl's domains? Had he any hand or interest in Kent trade? The shipman said that he had never seen the Earl, but that he was of course overlord of all the region, as was his father before him, every village, farm and field owning him as superior. Where had these hides in the cargo come from then, he was asked? From Kent's farms and fields? The other agreed that this would be so, although they were really the Earl's *vassals'* property. They were being sent to Rye for tanning. Satisfied, Alex ordered the lugger's crew into their small boat, to row for the shore, there to send word to the Earl of Kent that his vassals' hides were at the bottom of the sea. Then he allowed the *Clara*'s cannoneers to try out their armament by sinking the lugger. This was achieved after much misfire, noise, smoke and waste of powder and shot — but providing much-needed practice. It all did not represent much of an achievement and no glory, but might have its own repercussions.

It was decided that they were getting too far to the west, into the mouth of La Manche, the Channel, and they turned on a reverse course, on the look-out for their galleys. They were fortunate, just before darkness came down, to come up with a large and heavy vessel, from Greenwich bound for Danzig which, being slow and lumbering, made little attempt at flight, and hove-to obediently whilst the letters-of-mark announcement was made — but had the spirit to put up something of a fight on being boarded, which enabled the Aberdonains to regain their self-esteem somewhat and get rid of mounting frustration. The prize, the *Maid Mary*, had no cannon and was not really a very adequate adversary. But it had a rich cargo of salt, always valuable, especially in Aberdeen where fish-curing was important; casked ale, always welcome; ironware pots and cauldrons; and handsome horse-harness and saddlery. Transferring all this to *Greysteel* and *Clara* would be a lengthy process and must await daylight. The English crew were battened down below, therefore, and the three vessels lay-to for the night. They were approximately twenty miles off the North Foreland, Davidson said, although the south-westerly breeze and the current would inevitably drift them a considerable distance northwards.

Daylight revealed no sign of either land nor sail. The work of transferring the cargo went on apace, the Englishmen being forced to labour, however unwillingly. It took a long time, even so, in open sea conditions.

Sail was sighted just before midday, with the task nearly finished. Two full-rigged ships were reported by the look-outs, close together to the north-west; and presently a third, somewhat smaller but in the same vicinity. Davidson did not like the look of this, and said so. Trading vessels did not usually sail in convoy, and two of these were large ships. If they were king's ships or privateers it could be serious. There had been ample time for word of their activities to reach London.

Alex did not dispute it, and gave orders to abandon the work on *Maid Mary*, its crew to take to the boats forthwith, and gunpowder to be used to set the vessel on fire quickly. This might possibly distract the attention of the newcomers.

This could not be done in a few minutes, and before the Scots ships were able to draw away, leaving the other blazing at various points and sending a black column of smoke into the air, the three strange sail had halved their distance. It seemed clear that they were making directly for them, too.

"I fear they *are* king's ships," Davidson said. "Do we run or fight, my lord?"

"Run if we can, fight if we must!" Alex answered.

Greysteel and *Clara* headed due eastwards now, to gain sea-room — and fairly quickly the approaching vessels reacted. The two larger, both bigger ships than *Greysteel*, swung on an intercepting course, whilst the third and smaller, a galiot by the look of it, proceeded on towards the burning *Maid Mary*.

"No question but they are king's ships," the Provost decided grimly. "They have come looking for us. This will be less easy than picking off unarmed traders. Eagles, not barn-door fowl!"

"To be sure. But perhaps more satisfying!" Alex rejoined cheerfully. "Can you out-sail them? Or must we come to grips?"

"We can try. But I am no' happy about yon *Clara*. Manned by a crew no' used to her."

"We cannot abandon her. And have no time to transfer her people to this ship."

Davidson shrugged, and ordered an alteration in course southwards.

So commenced a curious chase, anything but straightforward, with continual tacking, gybing, twisting and veering away, *Greysteel* making the running, concerned to keep distance between herself and the Englishmen but at the same time not to outsail *Clara*. It became evident, fairly quickly, that although the newcomers were probably able to sail faster than *Greysteel* they were less manoeuvrable and unable to lie so close to the wind; but that they outdid *Clara* on both counts. The Englishmen were frequently near enough, despite all the dodging, for their great banners of the Leopards of Plantagenet and the St. George's Cross of England, to be distinguished. Also, unfortunately, that each had at least a dozen cannon. Keeping out of range of these would have to be a major preoccupation for the Scots.

Clara, of course, was given the first taste of the medicine, one of the enemy opening up with her four port-side armament in a notably ragged salvo. Cannon were a comparatively new development in warfare at sea, their effectiveness as yet far from perfected, their standard of handling seldom high. Indeed their usefulness was probably very largely in the sphere of morale, their noise, flame and smoke being apt to have more impact than their shot — save in siege warfare and battering at castle walls. Flash-backs and misfires were frequent, and could be very dangerous for the cannoheers.

In this case one of the weapons misfired, one ball plunged into the sea only a few yards away, one went wide astern and only one fell close to the target. This amidst impressive expolsions and vast smoke. *Clara* fired back with one cannon —

presumably the other misfired — and was no more successful in scoring a hit.

"I say that we should forget these toys!" Jamie snorted. "They are for scaring bairns, just."

"Not forget," Alex returned. "When they do hit they can do much hurt. But we should not let them frighten us, I agree, cause us to feel inferior, or to change our tactics."

"What *are* our tactics, my lord? Other than seeking to keep our distance?" Davidson demanded. They were standing in a group on the poop, beside the *Greysteel*'s helmsman.

"We are hampered by *Clara*," Alex said. "But . . . we must fight, eventually. Look for our best opportunity."

"Board them, you mean?"

"What else . . . ?"

He was interrupted by a banging of cannon-fire from the Englishman nearest to themselves. Five booms there were, in an uneven succession — but well before the last Davidson had his helm hard over and they were bearing away to starboard putting them stern-on to the enemy, to minimise the target. One ball made a neat hole in one of their sails, another a mighty splash to port, as total result.

Alex shouted to the stern cannoneer to open fire. But he had had his weapon facing the enemy over the port rail, and his men had to man-handle the heavy, clumsy contraption round at right-angles. By the time he was ready to apply his glowing fuse, the ships had drawn considerably further apart and the shot fell hopelessly short.

"At least it will show that we can hit back," Alex muttered.

Jamie was watching the gunners at the reloading process, thoughtfully. It took a considerable time. The touch-hole and breach had to be cleared out with cloths, a fresh charge of powder carefully ladled in per measure, and tamped cautiously down, then a wad of tinder packed in on top, to channel the explosion and prevent a flash-back. At the same time a stone ball had to be selected, pushed down the gaping muzzle and rammed firmly home with a ramrod. It could not be done hastily, even when the cannon were cold. They got scorchingly hot after two or three shots, and then handling became slower still — and with the added danger of premature explosion.

As *Greysteel* swung again on to a different tack, and her cannon had to be moved once more to face the enemy, Jamie was calculating.

272

"Timing," he said to Alex. "Timing is the heart of the matter, if the English are no quicker than these. They have their cannon at the sides, port and starboard. Where we, with only two, have them fore and aft. So they must turn their ship around, after each volley, to use the other side while the first reloads. Whilst they are turning they cannot fire. Nor can they fire the same cannon without this delay."

"Yes. You mean . . .?"

"I mean that here is the measure of their weakness. If we can keep them having to turn, firing at an awkward line or angle, and getting their cannon over-hot. Keep ourselves as much as possible bows-on or stern-on. Close in. Close range does not matter, if they cannot bring their bombards to bear. Then, whilst they are reloading, directly after a salvo, move in, fast, to board . . ."

"Aye — something of this was coming to me, also. You hear, Davidson man?"

"Boarding?" the other said, at his Aberdonian dourest. "These are king's ships. Bigger than this. More men than have we. Men-at-arms . . ." He broke off to shout a change of helm.

"The more their surprise," Jamie contended. "They will scarce expect to be boarded. And they may not be such bonny fighters, depending on all those cannon. How often will they have had to fight off boarders, think you? I tell you . . ."

His voice was drowned in more gunfire as the second English ship made another attack on *Clara*. They were the best part of a mile away now, and details were difficult to see, but it looked as though at least one hit had been made. Then their own adversary opened fire with his starboard armament on themselves, *Greysteel* swinging violently away — but not before a ball smashed into them amidships with a splintering crash of timbering, seemingly between rail and waterline. Their stern cannon fired in return, but again the shot fell well short.

"Out-ranged!" Alex exclaimed. "They have bigger pieces. Davidson — we have no choice. We must go in, as Jamie says. Can you steer for the Englishman? As near bows-on as you may? But not midships. So that he must shoot at a slant. You understand? He will be coming about, now. Jamie — prepare the boarders . . ."

So instead of circling and twisting, *Greysteel* turned directly in for the enemy. Directly only in the broad sense, however, for Davidson was concerned both to present as narrow a target as he might and to present that target at as acute an angle to the other's broadside as he could. Only an expert master and an experienced crew, in a sufficiently swift-helmed vessel, could have attempted it. Fortunately the wind was consistent, fresh without being strong, reducing the complications.

The Englishman was neither laggard nor fool, and after some initial and understandable — but very valuable — hesitation, did all that he could to counter the tactics of the suicidally-inclined Scot. But it took him almost half as long again to effect any sharp change of course, and he was always just sufficiently behind to leave the advancing *Greysteel* with the initiative and a fairly consistently favourable angle of approach. He did manage to fire off both port and starboard armament once, but because of the slantwise aim involved, this was ineffective. On the other hand, *Greysteel*'s own forward cannon was able to fire almost directly ahead, at ever-shortening range, and scored two hits despite two misfires. The stern weapon could not be brought to bear.

The final stage of the approach had to be timed to a nicety. It was essential that they should run alongside the enemy on the flank from which a salvo had just been fired — which meant that they would be at very close range when it *was* fired, the most dangerous stage of the tactic. Fortunately for them, this seemed to coincide with the realisation by the Englishmen that there was actually an intent to board them — with disconcerting effect. Cannoneers were particularly helpless and vulnerable against a boarding foray, not concerned with hand-to-hand fighting. At any rate the shooting, which could have been the most telling of the battle, was the feeblest and most erratic yet, resulting in only one spar and minor sail being brought down.

Robert Davidson's handling of his ship thereafter was beyond praise. It is no easy matter to lay two sailing ships alongside smoothly at sea, even when both so desire it. When one is seeking to turn away, so as to bring its alternative armament to bear, a very high standard of seamanship is called for. But the thing was achieved, at the second try, scarcely smoothly but fairly speedily. Timbers grinding and creaking, the vessels came together, amidst wild shouting and cheering.

The strategy for such an engagement had been planned and gone over, on *Greysteel*, times without number, and every man knew his part. First into action were men who had climbed the rigging and mast-stays with blazing torches and pitch-soaked tow tied to javelins, to cast down, lit, on to the Englishman's deck. This was more to cause confusion and alarm than anything else, smoke as important as flame — although with tubs of gunpowder beside every cannon, there were fair chances of an explosion. Needless to say it was at these that the aimers directed their blazing brands. None actually ignited a barrel, but some fell very close. This again had the effect of upsetting many of the enemy crewmen who, well aware of the danger, pushed away from the vicinity urgently. At the same time, grapnels, hooks, ropes and scaling-nets were being tossed up on to the taller ship. Or, more accurately, the heavy nets were cast *down* from *Greysteel*'s fore and aftercastles into the other's well-deck amidsmips, whilst archers and spear-throwers endeavoured to keep the English from casting these off again. The two Scots cannon were set to firing as regularly as they might at point-blank range directly into the enemy's hull, this being possible on account of the bigger ship's decking being some eight feet higher than their own. The cannons' wide mouths were capable of little elevation and no depression, so they could fire only straight ahead; but the Scots could pump balls into their opponent's timbering, which could not be reciprocated. It might not do much real damage at that level, but the effect on morale could be considerable.

The boarding-party, of course, was the principal assault, but this had to wait until the ropes, nets and ladders were in position. Then, led by Alex and Jamie and the other lairds, they swarmed up.

The English, needless to say, were not inactive meantime. But their defence, at this stage, was less coherent, co-ordinated, than it might have been. Undoubtedly they had never anticipated being boarded, and had not made adequate plans to deal with it. Bugles blew, commands resounded, but confusion raged. A group of archers on the high aftercastle were fairly effective, causing a number of Scots casualties; but at that short range they were within throwing distance of javelin-men on *Greysteel*'s poop, their position very exposed.

Once aboard, Alex's policy was to try to put out of action the enemy leadership, which also was mainly concentrated on the poop or aftercastle. In the swirling smoke-clouds, swords slashing, they hacked and thrust and parried their way aft, at last engaged in the task they had come to perform. They had the distinct advantage in that these young lairds were all trained swordsmen, experts, and fighting ordinary men-at-arms and sailors; and the fact that they were few in numbers was of little account on the narrow crowded deck where only a small proportion of the defenders could actually engage them at any moment. Jamie, shouting "A Douglas! A Douglas!" drove steadily onwards, unquestionably the most veteran fighter present.

A sudden violent explosion, much greater than the intermittent banging of the *Greysteel*'s cannon, swept the deck with its blast and forced a temporary pause in the swordery as men were knocked over, shaken and distracted, One of the powder-barrels had blown up, turning a small fire quickly into a large one.

The effect was immediate and obvious — and a deal more noticeable on the defenders than on the attackers. Nobody likes being on a burning ship; but it is much worse when it is one's own ship and the enemy has a means of escape — and when there are other barrels of gunpowder all too close at hand. It would be too much to say that demoralisation set in, but undoubtedly the English rank-and-file now had only part of their minds on the fighting.

To the Scots, on the other hand, the effect was to some extent the reverse. It made them anxious to finish off the engagement before worse might befall and the entire ship become an inferno. With redoubled fury they renewed the attack.

Alex and Jamie had fought their way to the foot of the poop-stairway, and were faced with the difficult task of mounting this against opposition, when there was a new development, another convulsion. Not an explosion this time, but a concussion. The entire ship jarred and shook, knocking many off their feet. At the same time, there was much shouting from the direction of *Greysteel*. In the subsequent second pause, the Scots had opportunity to glance over their shoulders — and were dismayed at what they saw through the drifting smoke.

The second English warship had abandoned its assault on *Clara* and come to the aid of its partner. The bump had been this vessel laying itself alongside *Greysteel*, at the other side, the impact transmitted through the Scots ship now sandwiched between the two. Englishmen were already beginning to pour across the intervening deck to assist their fellows.

Now, of course, the situation was transformed, with the Scots facing attack from the rear and their original opponents gaining new heart — even though the fire tended to preoccupy all. Jamie shouted to form a schiltrom, a sort of back-to-back hedgehog, an admittedly defensive device. There was little alternative meantime.

There followed a period of major confusion, with the main Scots boarding-party as it were under siege but two smaller detached groups seeking to aid them, and Davidson and such of his crew as remained in *Greysteel* fighting their own battle. The English on the aftercastle were now exploiting their lofty position, and the lairdly group seeking to edge away forward from under it. The smoke and crackle of flames made an ominous and distracting background. The Scots cannon had ceased firing.

There was no question but that the Scots position was now serious. They were greatly outnumbered, their ship wedged between the others and the enemy's nerve recovered, even though the fire's progress was in all minds. Help from the *Clara* scarcely could be looked for — where she was or what her state was not evident. Jamie almost wished for another and larger explosion, which might injure the enemy more than themselves. Or the fire to cause an abandonment of the fighting. They were suffering mainly from the javelin-throwing now. Most of the boarders wore half-armour, the lairds having shirts-of-mail also. But javelins cast down on them from the aftercastle could find chinks and joints in the steel-plating, and injure below, even if they did not actually penetrate, the chain-mail.

Desperate situations may demand desperate remedies, and Jamie was beginning to consider the possibilities of seeking to cut their way back, in a fighting-wedge, first into the sandwiched *Greysteel* and then over on to the second English ship, in an attempt to take it over, only part-manned as it would now be, and to sail clear — this, when, in all the noise, clash and shouting, his ears heard a new sound. It took moments, in his preoccupied state, for the significance to sink in. Then his heart lifted in a great bound. It was the skirl of bagpipes on the wind. Panting, he raised his voice.

"The Islesmen! They come! Listen — pipes!" he shouted. "The MacLeods! The MacLeods!"

From scores of dry and weary Scots throats strangled, gulping cheers arose and new strength surged into flagging arms. The Englishmen were less affected — as yet.

The sworders were far too busy to see their allies arrival, but they certainly heard them come in no uncertain fashion, pipes shrilling, horns ululating, men yelling. Like one of their own Highland rivers in spate the half-naked MacLeods came pouring over the various decks, irresistible, terrifying.

The English, appalled and clearly out of their depth in face of this savage horde, fought on bravely enough, but with defeat implicit almost from the start. It was all too much. Fairly quickly the boarders from the second warship came to the conclusion that they would be better back on their own vessel, and began to disengage as best they could and straggle off. Another explosion expedited matters, and gave even the Islesmen pause for a little. The shipmaster of the enemy vessel took the opportunity to cast off in haste, and stood away in no hesitant style, however many of his men were left behind. Seeing this, the commander of the burning ship wisely decided that he had had enough. He shouted that he surrendered, ordering all his people to lay down their arms, and sending men to strike their flag.

Only the Islesmen seemed disappointed that the battle was thus suddenly over.

The *Greysteel* party had suffered heavy casualties, nine dead and almost all wounded in some degree, a number seriously. Both Alex and Jamie were slightly hurt, the former with a flesh-wound in the thigh, the latter with a grazed and bleeding brow where his helmet had been knocked off.

Three distinct movements commenced, each little concerned with the other. The *Greysteel* people sought to get themselves, their dead and severely wounded, back to their own vessel and such attention as was available. The Islesmen, who had never had so large and impressive a ship to loot, even if part aflame, set about despoiling it with a will, before it was too late. And the English crew, finding nobody now very interested in them, and recognising also that time was probably short, began to lower their small boats at the poop, to pile in, taking their own wounded with them.

The fire was growing apace, even though the MacLeods had tossed overboard the remaining powder-barrels on deck.

At length even the acquisitive MacLeods decided that it was better to be content with what they had than to die getting more and, heavily laden, retired to their own galleys. Ian Borb and his brother came aboard *Greysteel*.

"I do not know whether to fall on your necks, thanking you for coming to our aid, MacLeod," Alex said, having his leg dressed and bound, "or to curse you for deserting us, in the first place! Where a God's name have you been, man?"

"Och, we have been doing well. Very well, friend," the other assured cheerfully. "Taking many ships for you. No trouble, at all. But, you — you left your place, whatever! We have been searching for you, for long. Had it not been for the smoke of that ship you fired yonder, we might not have found you in time. Foolish, just."

Alex's gasp was the only rejoinder he allowed himself.

Jamie did his best for his friend. "My lord of Mar was scarcely required to lie idle, awaiting *your* pleasure, sir! He commands this expedition, does he not? We waited a night and a day for you to return to his authority. If all had ended in disaster, the fault would have been yours."

The Islesman seemed amused rather than contrite. "Disaster? You were near to disaster? Without us? As well we saw the smoke, then. You have a sore head, friend?"

Helplessly they gave it up.

The situation at large seemed now to have resolved itself. The second English king's ship was off at best speed west-by-north, clearly making for the mouth of the Thames estuary; and her smaller colleague, which had never joined in their fight but had apparently taken over the assault on *Clara*, was now in full sail after her. *Clara* herself was in a poor state, one of her masts down and listing somewhat to port. The Greenwich *Maid Mary* was now but a smoking hulk on the horizon.

Decision fell to be made, and swiftly. Once those fleeing warships reached the Thames, there could be little doubt but that a major hunt would be mounted for the raiders. King Henry would have many such ships and privateers at his disposal, and it would probably be a fleet which would come seeking them. Such they were in no state to face, whatever the MacLeods' reaction. A move should be made at once, north-by-east, homewards. The question was what to do about *Clara*? The Islesmen were for abandoning her, as only a handicap, and Alex tended to agree. But the Aberdonians were concerned to hold on to her, both as a useful prize and on account of the rich accumulation of booty with which her holds were now stuffed. And since it was the Aberdeen contingent which had had the greatest casualties and the least joy out of the whole expedition, he felt bound to humour them. They might *have* to abandon *Clara*, but meantime they would make her as seaworthy as possible and head eastwards, in convoy, for the open sea. With the night before them, and no chase likely for a full day, at least, they ought to be able to lose themselves in the wide ocean.

While this decision was being taken, a series of internal

explosions rent their late foe, toppling her masts and leaving her a sorry sight. With mixed feelings, the Scots limped from the scene.

* * *

It took them almost two weeks to win home to Aberdeen — long before which they had lost the galleys, the MacLeods going off on their own one evening and just not returning. No doubt they considered their duties to be over, and sped back to Skye, laden with loot.

Fortunately, *Greysteel* did not sight a single ship-of-war or privateer throughout, and the weather being fairly kind, *Clara*'s jury-mast and patched-up state were not severely tested. Wounds, in healthy young bodies, healed up quickly, in the main. In a general way the expedition was voted a success. Certainly they had done more damage to English shipping than could have been anticipated. The effect on Henry remained to be seen.

Aberdeen greeted them warmly, as returning heroes. Bishop Greenlaw himself, the Chancellor, came down from his palace, a notable sign of favour. But, after a word or two, he drew Alex aside, and changed tone.

"My lord," he said, lowering his voice, "I have ill-tidings for you. A grievous matter. Your lady-wife, the Countess . . ."

Alex schooled his features. "She is a, a woman of spirit," he said.

"She was," the Bishop agreed. "She has gone to other . . . activities, in the providence of Almighty God. I grieve for you, my son."

"Gone . . . ?"

"Gone, yes. She died, two weeks past. Fell from her horse, whilst hunting, at Balquhain Castle. Broke her neck. Death would be painless . . ."

"Good God! Isobel . . . !"

"God is good, yes. And this is the will of God, my friend. Accept it."

Alex was much distressed. Although whether he was actually heart-broken Jamie Douglas was uncertain. He remained very silent on the matter.

The company broke up, and these two friends parted, for Kildrummy and Lochindorb respectively, Jamie at least a richer man than when he had set out. He was longing to see Mary and the children again.

PART THREE

XVII

ALEX STEWART AND Jamie Douglas could hardly have
anticipated being anxious to see their MacLeod friends
quite so soon as the following mid-November of 1407,
sufficiently to be travelling in person across the width of
Highland Scotland for the purpose. But since their return from
their privateering venture, events — or better, the shadow of
coming events — had so loomed and developed in Albany's
Scotland that clarification and some planning ahead had
become vital if so much that these two stood for was not to be
overwhelmed. And since the most immediate threat appeared
to be from Donald of the Isles, some illumination on the
Hebridean scene was necessary, and scarcely to be obtained
without personal contact. Hence this secret journey to see
William Achlerich MacLeod of Dunvegan, in Skye.

It was, of course, hardly the best time of year to be making
such an expedition. But they had little choice in the matter; any
offputting now would delay them until mid-March at the
earliest. The weather, if not good, was at least not impossible,
windy and cold but with little rain, or worse snow, to make
the rivers, bogs and passes impassable — the major hazard in
Highland travel. Even crossing the high watershed of Scotland,
the Great Glen and Glens Moriston, Cluanie and Shiel, they
had seen no snow — although the savage mountain-tops were
consistently veiled in low cloud and might be white-tipped.
Now, down the shores of the long, linked sea-lochs of Duich
and Alsh, weed-hung and rocky, they had come to the narrows
of the Kyle of Lochalsh, with the Isle of Skye looming mightily
only half-a-mile away across the slate-grey, white-capped waters.

They sat their garrons considering the situation in the fading
light of a dull afternoon, their two gillies behind. They were

inconspicuously dressed and with only this pair as escort, for the last thing they desired was to draw attention to themselves, here in the Highland West where Donald MacDonald was the major power. The small castle of Dunakin soared on a fang of rock at the other side of the narrows, dominating the passage. There were other crossings than this to Skye, for it was a very large island; but those further south led into the MacDonald territory of Sleat, and last time they had come to see MacLeod, to arrange the hire of his galleys, they had crossed there, from Glenelg to Kylerhea, and been all too much involved with MacDonalds. Further north the crossings were much longer. That castle opposite, Dunakin, belonged to MacKinnon, not a MacDonald nor yet a MacLeod — but the lands west of his were MacLeod's. They had heard that MacKinnon was at odds with Donald of the Isles.

Before them was a jetty but no ferry-boat. Beside the jetty was a low-browed thatched cottage, little more than a turf-hut, heather-roofed, from the black doorway of which a plaid-wrapped man was watching them heedfully. As they reined closer, this man spoke in the soft lisping Gaelic.

"It is none so poor a day, friends, and not that cold, at all," he declared conversationally. "Good enough for travelling. Och, yes."

"As you say. We would cross over to Skye. Are you the ferry-man?"

"Sometimes just, sometimes. Och, yes. For the time of the year I have seen it worse, mind."

"No doubt. And we are thankful for it. But — the ferry?"

"There is many a time when it is not possible to cross the water at all, no. Wild it can be, just wild."

"I am sure of it. But — not today. How *do* we cross, friend? Where is the boat?"

"Och, the boat, yes. MacKinnon has the boat. Your name now, will be . . . ?"

"My name is MacAlastair," Alex said, with exemplary patience. "How do we get MacKinnon's boat?"

"MacAlastair is it? Och, yes — MacAlastair. Which Mac-Alastair would that be?"

"*My* MacAlastair! Now — do we cross this ferry, with your aid? Or with the aid of some other?"

"None cross to Skye save at MacKinnon's pleasure, what-ever."

"Not even MacLeod? MacLeod of Dunvegan."

"MacLeod . . .?" The man's voice and attitude changed noticeably. "Och well, MacLeod . . ."

"Yes. We travel to see MacLeod, at Dunvegan."

"Yes, yes, MacAlastair. MacLeod it is. William Achlerich of Dunvegan."

"And Ian Borb and Ruari Ban likewise."

"Surely, surely. MacKinnon will be glad, just, to put you over on your way to MacLeod, MacAlastair." The man ducked back within his low-doored hovel.

"A mighty to-do to cross a ferry!" Jamie commented. "You might think this carle a chief at his castle gate!"

"In the Islesmen's West we must do as they do. The stresses and strains here, between MacDonalds and MacLeods, Mac-Kinnons and MacKenzies, perforce make us to walk warily. But it seems that MacKinnon supports MacLeod."

The man emerged with a blazing torch, with which he set alight a bundle of pitch-soaked rags hanging in a chain from a sort of gibbet. It was not long before an answering flare showed as a red gleam from the castle across the dark water. They were informed that it would be no time at all before they were on their way to MacLeod.

As they waited the man enthused carefully on the power, puissance and potency of William Achlerich MacLeod of Dunvegan, fifth chief of the Siol Tormod — at the same time trying hard to discover the identity of MacAlastair. The MacLeod, he declared, was a mighty man of valour who had slain his hundreds, despite his name — Achlerich meaning the cleric, he having been intended for the Church but, God be praised, had been spared from that fate by the death of an elder brother. The travellers knew all this well enough, but preferred to encourage their informant to talk rather than continue his devious but probing questions. At length a large flat-bottomed scow, propelled by four oarsmen, arrived at the jetty, and the young man in charge — who proved to be a son of MacKinnon of Dunakin — after a muttered conversation with the beacon-lighter, announced himself as agreeable to carry them across the kyle — at a price. Embarked, he too began, almost at once, to seek to establish just who they were and whence they had come.

As they were pulled slantwise across the choppy narrows in the fading light, horses standing uneasy in the heaving boat,

Alex was glad to divert the conversation by pointing to a massive seaweed-hung chain which, anchored to a great cairn of stones on this east side, sank away gradually out of sight into the water.

The young man laughed. "That is MacKinnon's Sword-Belt," he explained. "No ship passes through these narrows without paying tribute to MacKinnon. The chain lies just beneath the water, and can be raised or lowered from the castle. None may pass Dunakin."

"Save, I think, MacLeod? Or should it be Donald of the Isles?"

The other looked at him sharply, and then shrugged. "Only these, yes."

"MacKinnon must do well, then — if he demands as much tribute from shipping as he does for his ferry! But perhaps shipmasters avoid your Sound of Sleat, in consequence?"

Young MacKinnon laughed again. "They dare not. They must sail round this side of Skye, or the other. This side they pay only *our* tribute. The other side, Donald takes them — and demands more than tribute!"

"I see. Who would be a shipmaster in the Isles?"

Lachlan MacKinnon of Dunakin, chief of the name, a tall old hawk of a man, greeted them with a sort of wary arrogance until he ascertained that they were bound for Dunvegan. Then he was all hospitality, although his small, rude castle's facilities were of the most primitive, it being merely a stark square tower of three storeys and an attic, one chamber to each floor, with nine-foot walls. He pointed out that Dunvegan was two days journey to the north-west, fifty miles, at the other side and other end of the island, and darkness was falling. They must be his guests for the night — his house was theirs. But although Alex still did not wish to divulge his identity, not being sure of MacKinnon's allegiances however much he might approve of MacLeod, he found it impossible to put him off with the pseudonym of MacAlastair against no devious probings but a direct demand.

"I am loth to give you my name, MacKinnon — for fear that it could be to your hurt to know it, and you befriending us," he said carefully. He took a chance. "I am friend to MacLeod, you see — but scarcely so to Donald of the Isles."

"Donald is it? Devil burn his bones!" MacKinnon cried. "I am your better friend if you are Donald's foe. He executed my own father — or had Maclean of Duart do it for him — and then stole our lands in Mull, wide lands. Yet MacKinnon had always supported his line."

"Ah. Then I understand your feelings for him, sir. And I accept that my name is safe with you. I am indeed MacAlastair — *Alastair MacAlastair Mor-mhic-an-Righ*, Earl of Mar and Lord of Badenoch. And this is Sir James Douglas, son to the Lord of Dalkeith."

"God in his heaven — Mar! Who was Justiciar? Buchan's son — the Wolf?"

"The same." Alex found himself actually embraced.

"Your father — I knew him. A man after my own heart, whatever!"

"M'mm. Not all would say that, I fear, MacKinnon! I thank you."

"Now I know why you are seeking MacLeod. His son, Ian Borb, did great things with you against the wretched English, we heard. You want more of him? My own sons would be happy to have a hand in that noble work."

"I thank you again. But it is scarce that. I am here to seek to watch and contain Donald. The English yes — but they can wait. Donald first, whom we have found out is in league with them. And intends invasion."

"Ha! Then you will be for Ireland?"

"Ireland . . . ?"

"Ireland, yes. Have you not heard? Donald is gathering a great host to go to Ireland, to Ulster. To aid the English king in his trouble there, who is faced by an alliance of the Irish princes. These have recovered most of Ulster and much else. They boast that they will throw the English into the sea. Donald is to go to the help of the English."

His visitors exchanged glances. "So-o-o! We heard nothing of this. What we heard was . . . otherwise." Alex explained the situation more fully to Jamie, whose Gaelic was not yet sufficient to cope with these details.

"If true, this could change much. Explain much. But it could be no more than a feint, a bluff to put us off our guard." Jamie was ever cautious. "Ask him when? When is this Irish expedition to be?"

MacKinnon did not know that, but assumed that it would be in the forthcoming campaigning season, from April onwards. Indeed he could give them little further information. It was all

287

only hearsay. But he could confirm that there was much activity, much coming and going of island chiefs at Finlaggan Castle on Islay, Donald's main seat, and a great repairing, refurbishing and preparation of galleys and birlinns up and down the entire seaboard. All of which left the main question as to destination open.

They retired that night to couches of heaped deerskins and plaids in the draughty attic of the tower — having gratefully declined the offer of suitable female bed-warmers of unspecified identity — wondering whether in fact their journey had been necessary.

They were awakened in the morning by the strains of Mac-Kinnon's piper parading around the small castle's constricted parapet-walk in a smirr of rain. After a breakfast ambitious enough to last them all day, not to mention whisky offered by the flagon, their host would not hear of them setting off forthwith on their journey to Dunvegan. He wished them to meet sundry of his MacKinnon notables, would have them go hunting stags in Strathsuardal, even to demonstrate the sport of salmon-spearing in the Anavaig River, seemingly an Isles specialty. When Alex regretfully declined, pointing out that they still had a long ride ahead of them and time unfortunately precious, the other had to reveal that they would not in fact be riding at all — which was no way for gentlemen to travel in the Isles; they would go by water, infinitely more swiftly. When his guests eyed the chief's birlinn, lying at anchor in the lee of the castle-rock, with no sign of crew or activity about it, MacKinnon was forced to admit that it would be a MacLeod boat which was coming for them, that he had indeed sent one of his many sons hot-foot through the night for Dunvegan with the word. Why this, instead of despatching them onward in his own vessel Alex was too polite to ask. Probably the MacKinnon had sent his messenger before learning of his guests' true identity, and was merely passing the responsibility to MacLeod.

So they went salmon-hunting in a rushing crystal-clear river under the shadow of thrusting Beinn na Cailleach, and saw young MacKinnon transfix two fine fish, although they themselves failed miserably to overcome the refraction of the water combined with the darting speed of the quarry, try as they would — this from a series of tiny jetties built at an angle to the current beneath various runs and rapids. Both keen fishermen, they were much put out at being found so ineffective at the business, but decided to practice it in their own more peat-stained waters in due course.

When, at dusk, a smallish sixteen-oared birlinn arrived at Dunakin from the north, it proved to be under the command of Ian Borb himself, who greeted the visitors with every appearance of simple pleasure, clearly anticipating a new pirating expedition for MacLeod co-operation. However, he swallowed his disappointment, expressed himself delighted to see his former co-heroes, and, in an evening's great drinking and talking, entertained the company to a highly-coloured account of their exploits in English waters in which the visitors scarcely recognised their own parts. Here obviously was a saga in the making. It was no occasion for questioning as to the state of affairs in the Isles. The hospitality, liquid in especial, was such that coherent thought, much less meaningful converse, was all but impossible, to say nothing of the fiddling, piping, singing, dancing, story-telling and the like. Eventual bed, even with sore heads, was something of a relief.

But on the morrow, on their spirited way up the widening Inner Sound of Skye, with the lesser islands of Scalpay and Raasay on the one hand and the mainland mountains of Apple-cross on the other, now glistening and gleaming in watery sun-shine, now hidden in driving rain-storms, they had ample time to learn something of what they required to know, from Ian Borb, as his oarsmen thrashed their way north-about round Skye's long and spectacular east coast in fiercely proprietorial style. They learned that Donald MacDonald was undoubtedly preparing to mount a major expedition to Ireland where, as well as aiding the English, it seemed that he had his own feud with certain Ulster princelings. He was actually seeking to hire galleys and men for this from chiefs who were not normally his supporters — presumably with English gold since he was not believed to have overmuch of that commodity of his own. When Alex wondered whether this could be a ruse, a blind to disguise the mustering when in fact his host was destined for an invasion of mainland Scotland, MacLeod was sure that it was not so. For there was considerable coming and going with Ireland, allies being sought in Ulster. His own father had been approached to co-operate, through third parties, with rich pickings promised, although normally Donald's foe. There seemed no doubt that Ulster was the destination and early summer the planned time.

They learned also why MacKinnon had not sent the visitors

to Dunvegan in his own birlinn. Donald, it appeared, resented the lesser chief's enterprise, not so much in putting his chain across the Kyle narrows as in charging a lower scale of tolls for shipping to pass it, and so undercutting his own barriers and toll-gatherers and causing much trade to use the inner channel past Skye. He threatened, in consequence, to sink any vessel of MacKinnon's found in the outer seas. MacLeod, scorning such pedestrian methods of producing an income, did not compete in the matter — and anyway was strong enough for Donald not to challenge without major cause.

Ian Borb's craft always seemed to move at top speed. The birlinn was scarcely so fast as a full-sized galley, but its sail and sixteen oars drove it along in stirring fashion, to the usual chanting and sword-clanging; and in just over three hours they were passing the dramatic heights of the Quirang and rounding the cliffs of Rudha Hunish at the northern tip of the Trotternish peninsula and moving into the very different conditions of the open Sea of the Hebrides, to head south-westwards now into the long Atlantic swell, the disadvantages of winter-time voyaging becoming quickly more evident to the travellers. What had been merely a keen, chill breeze developed into a fierce, piercing half-gale, steep short seas overlying the swell and the birlinn pitching and rolling in the cross-seas in highly uncomfortable fashion, flying spray soaking all continuously. However, the oarsmen appeared to be in no way distressed, skilfully adjusting their strokes and rhythm to suit the troughs and summits of the waves. Ian Borb remained his usual cheerful self, the whisky flagons going the rounds.

Twice they saw other craft, the second time two larger galleys together, their sails painted with the black lymphad of the Isles; but when these drew near enough to discern the black bull's head of MacLeod on the birlinn's sail, they veered off discreetly. It was clearly a matter of dog not eating dog.

Passing presently another great headland at the tip of the Waternish peninsula, they turned in at the mouth of six-miles-long Loch Dunvegan, a fairly narrow fiord but island-dotted, at the head of which reared the MacLeod castle, crowning the usual rocky bluff, an oblong keep larger than most in these parts, with irregular flanking curtain-walls outlining the rock's summit, and a beetling sea-gate entrance. A fair-sized township clustered around the skirts of the rock and a dozen galleys rode at anchor in the basin of the loch, *Iolair* and *Clavan* amongst them.

The visitors discovered themselves to be highly popular at Dunvegan, the booty brought back by the temporary privateers not forgotten and the prowess attributed to the entire Mar expedition by no means fading with time and repeated telling. William Achlerich treated them distinctly differently from on their previous visit, more like dear kin long lost. He was a plump, rubicund, smiling little man, smooth of feature, all bows and gestures, unlikely-seeming sire for his clutch of stalwart sons, yet with a martial reputation of his own to outdo any of them. He too was disappointed that they had not come to hire more galleys and fighting men for further adventures; but rejoiced to find them inimical to and suspicious of *Mac Dhomhuill*, as he called Donald of the Isles. Anything that they could contrive against that man and his whole house would have his whole-hearted co-operation.

Mightily fed, warm and relaxed around the long table in Dunvegan's blue peat-smoke-filled hall, antique but capacious drinking-horns to hand, the visitors found that they were expected to give as much information as they got — with William Achlerich both more interested and knowledgeable about mainland affairs than they had assumed. Why were they so expectant of an Isles invasion of Scotland, he wanted to know. It must exercise them greatly to have brought the great Earl of Mar himself all this road to Skye?

"We have had sure word from London, from King Henry's own Court," Alex told him. "A letter to myself from the captive Earl of Douglas. It reached me some three weeks back. The Earl, Sir James's chief, is an anxious man, and with reason. He fears for the whole future of his great house. But he fears for Scotland too. Fears so much that he is prepared to take most drastic steps. Captive as he is, he has agreed to swear to be Henry's man, to support him and his sons against all, save only the King of Scots himself!"

"God Almighty — then the man is a traitor, whatever!" MacLeod exclaimed.

"Scarcely that, I think — although it is an ill choice. But it was the only way he could gain temporary release. To come home to Scotland for a time. To see to Douglas affairs and to try to counter the Duke of Albany's moves. Albany is playing a strange double game. With Henry . . ."

"But Douglas was Albany's man, was he not?"

"Not truly. He has supported Albany when he thought it best.

Against Prince David, who insulted his sister. Against others."
That was Jamie speaking. "I do not say that he is always wise
or far-sighted. But I do not believe that he is Albany's man.
Indeed I think that he much dislikes him. And he is no traitor —
that I swear. But Albany has allowed Henry to send back the
Earl of Dunbar, who *is* a traitor, to Scotland. Douglas's enemy.
Dunbar acting as go-between for Henry and Albany can only
mean trouble for Douglas — and Scotland. I say that this swearing to be Henry's man, ill as it is, may be something of a warning
to Albany, something of a declaration of war!"

"All because of this of Dunbar?"

"More than that," Alex said. "Albany has gone much further
towards the English. He has offered his daughter to marry
Henry's son, the Prince John. And, in order to get his captive
son Murdoch of Fife released, he has offered to send up his
second son, John, Earl of Buchan as hostage instead — without
Buchan's knowledge or agreement. For Buchan is critical of his
father. *I* let my cousin know of this — and he will not go, if he
can help it. But it means that Albany is playing a deep game —
and Henry perhaps deeper."

"For why?" MacLeod demanded. "What does he seek, your
Albany?"

"I think to ensure that young King James is not allowed to
come home. Either that he should be kept captive in England
indefinitely, or else disposed of otherwise, so that Albany can
perhaps assume the throne himself. So Douglas thinks. There is
more to it — but that is the heart of the matter."

There was silence round the table for a little.

"What has this to be doing with Donald, then?" their host asked.

"Albany is not the only one who sees opportunity in the boy-
king's plight. Donald, remember, is the King's cousin, his
mother a sister of Albany — as of my father's. He could see
himself on the throne."

"Donald — King!" MacLeod hooted at the notion.

"It is not so far from possible," Alex pointed out. "A successful invasion, and Albany and his sons disposed of — and who
else is there? The Lord Walter of Brechin, whom Albany has
now made Earl of Atholl, is a drunken sot, whom none would
support. And all the rest of the royal women are wed to
Douglases. Anyway, Donald also has been dealing with Henry
Plantagenet. Did you know that his nephew, Hector Maclean of
Duart, has been to London?"

"God in heaven — Maclean! Red Hector! That, that . . .!"

"Yes. He has been negotiating with Henry, Douglas writes. He believes that a full alliance is planned. He says that Henry will have Scotland one way or the other. While seeming to work with Albany, he plans for Donald to raise most of the Highlands and the Isles against Lowland Scotland, while Henry himself prepares to attack from England. Dunbar's return to Scotland is to work so that there will be a large and strong party in the Lowlands to support such double attack. Now do you see why the Douglas was prepared to pay so high a price to return home?"

William Achlerich shook his round head. "This is beyond all!" he said. "Treachery on every hand."

"When a crown and a kingdom are at stake treachery is seldom absent. Henry knows that, if any does. Consider how he usurped Richard's throne. Nobody can teach Henry Bolingbroke about guile and plotting and double dealing — even Albany. Myself, I think that Donald is the innocent, in this. Ambitious, yes — but not a match for these other two. But dangerous, in that he can field thousands of men and hundreds of ships. Henry will use him, and discard him. Henry will win, whoever loses. If we, the rest of Scotland allow it. Henry has sent envoys to France, to offer a new peace treaty. On condition that the old alliance with Scotland is broken. So Douglas comes home — paying the price. He believes that *I* can rally the North against Donald, and only I. It may be true. I must try, at the least. So I must know what Donald plans — and when."

There was another long pause as they eyed each other. "This of Ireland?" MacLeod wondered, at last. "I swear that Donald aims at Ireland, not Scotland. All the signs are there. It is no cheat, no stratagem, to be sure. Ireland will be invaded — that I am sure, whatever."

"I rejoice if it is so. For it will give us time — time we need greatly. It could be that this is part of the bargain with Henry. Ireland first." Alex frowned. "Henry is known to be in trouble in the Irish North, many of his garrisons wiped out, occupied towns in revolt. It could be. So that Henry could withdraw many of his troops to England — for his attack on Scotland later. Yes, it could be."

"Would Donald be prepared to play that game?" Jamie demanded. "To fight two wars, not one? On Henry's behalf?"

"On his own, Jamie, it could be . . ."

"Och, Donald is much concerned in Ulster, mind," MacLeod pointed out. "He has had two of his younger brothers to wed heiresses there, moved them across the Irish Sea. Ian Mor the Tanist is wed to the only child of Bisset of the Glens of Antrim. Marcus MacDonald wed to much of Tyrone. See you, if he could land and take Tyrconnel, with these other two he could have most of the North in his hands. Use this to extend his sway over O'Neill and the other Irish princelings — with the help of the English, from the south. He would be overlord of Ulster. God — he has been after dabbling in that water for years, the man! Could he be . . . ? Could he be . . . ?"

"Aye!" Alex breathed out. "It could be, indeed! High King of Ireland! As well as King of Scots! Donald, King of the Celts, one day! Dear God — it is possible! That could be where he lifts his eyes."

"Save us — that, that turkeycock!" Jamie exclaimed. "That island bog-trotter!" Recollecting the company he kept, the Douglas swallowed.

"He is no bog-trotter, man," Alex reminded. "He is a deal more learned than any of us. He studied at the University of Cambridge. He speaks many languages. History he dotes on, they say. The history of the Celtic peoples, in especial. Aye, it could be. And, as well as being grandson of Robert the Second, he comes of the ancient line of the Kings of the Isles and of Man. Do not underestimate Donald in this. Seeing the disunity and treachery in all the lands concerned, he may see his opportunity."

MacLeod had become very thoughtful. Clearly this new conception shook him — as it would shake all the Celtic polity. His own house had supported the Isles lordship loyally enough. It was Donald's claim to the earldom of Ross and overlordship of Skye which had aroused his fears and enmity, since these implied vassal status for himself. When Donald, or at least Alastair Carrach his brother, had heavy-handedly emphasised the claim a few years before by descending upon Skye with a sizeable force, burning, sacking and rounding up cattle, as some sort of tribute-taking, William Achlerich had risen in wrath, assailed the invaders near Loch Sligachan and roundly defeated them. Since then the feud had intensified. Oddly enough, however, Ian Borb and his brothers were less concerned; indeed they, whilst declaring no love for Donald, had in fact been toying with the notion of taking part in the Irish expedition, in which the pickings were almost certain to be substantial.

There was another aspect of the situation on which Alex desired elucidation — the attitude of the other mainland seaboard clans towards an invasion by Donald. After all most of the West Highlands, right down to the Clyde estuary, had once been part of the ancient Kingdom of the Isles. On how much support, or otherwise, could Donald rely, not against Ireland but against Scotland?

William Achlerich was reluctant to commit himself on that. He pointed out that Donald was not popular, and his brother who had been doing most of his fighting for him, was less so. But on the other hand, if there was a triumph in Ireland, and a vision of renewed greatness for the Celtic peoples generally, with English assistance assured, anything might happen. The situation was intricate, he reminded — reminded at length, proceeding to give as example the position of Clanranald, the great house of Garmoran, mainland neighbours of MacLeod — whose attitude must necessarily affect his own, if it came to hostilities. Their chief, the late Ranald, had in fact been Donald's elder brother. Their father, John, Lord of the Isles, had led a fairly united principality and married Amy MacRuarie, heiress of Garmoran — the vast province which included mainland Moidart, Knoydart and Morar, as well as the island Uists and Barra — herself the descendant, like John, of the great Somerled, King of the Isles. Then, in a fatal political move, John had divorced Amy and married the Princess Margaret, eldest daughter of Robert the Second of Scotland, and raised a new family of whom Donald was the eldest — although he had three sons already by Amy. He had thereafter declared the second family to be senior to the first, a folly for which all the realm was to pay. Donald was made heir to the lordship of the Isles, while his elder-born Ranald was made to sign a deed of resignation and given instead his mother's lands of Garmoran — or some of them. Godfrey, the eldest of all, was driven out because he refused to sign, made landless. Ranald himself, however resentful, had never rebelled against father or step-brother, being content to found his own lesser branch of the house, known as Clanranald. But he had died a few years before this, and his sons Alan and Donald were otherwise minded and positively hostile to Donald senior. So the Lord of the Isles by no means led a united patrimony.

The visitors had to take what comfort they could from that.

MacLeod would not forecast reactions. They went to their couches thoughtful indeed.

After three days at Dunvegan they took their leave of William Achlerich who promised to keep them informed of any significant developments, and were rowed back to Dunakin in Ian Borb's birlinn, to pick up their horses for the long ride home to Badenoch. The cold rain and blustering winds emphasised that the sooner they were safely back across the high spine of the mountains, the better — for the tops, when they could be seen, were already gleaming white.

"How say you?" Alex demanded, when at length they rode away eastwards from the grey waters of the Kyle of Lochalsh. "We came a long way — for what? Much trouble, for what achieved? Was our journey worth the making, Jamie?"

"I say it was," the other answered. "We have learned much of value, I think, which we needed to know — and which we would not have learned otherwise. We have learned that Earl Douglas was wrong — that this alliance between Henry of England and Donald is not against Scotland but Ireland — at least in the first instance. Later, who knows? So we have time. We have learned something of Donald's weaknesses. Strengths, too. But the weaknesses we can seek to exploit. We have learned that he may have much greater ambitions than we thought. That he may be looking a deal further ahead. But, again, that gives us time. I say that it was worth coming."

"Agreed. Donald is still a threat, yes. Perhaps a greater one. But not immediately so. The immediate and principal threat remains as it was — my uncle Albany. Who, the saints be praised, is Donald's enemy also! The house of Stewart, my friend, may almost be left to defeat itself!"

"I wonder . . . ?" Jamie said. "Robert Stewart of Albany will survive, I swear, whether Donald does or no. Leave *him* out, at your peril!"

Alex Stewart nodded as they rode on.

XVIII

GAZING WESTWARDS FROM *Greysteel*'s forecastle rail towards the hazy line that was the last of the Scottish coast, off Angus, it seemed scarcely credible to Jamie Douglas that he should be so doing, within six months of their Hebridean journey — more especially with his arm around the shoulders of his wife Mary Stewart. Nothing could have seemed less likely even that Yuletide. Yet now, in early May of 1408, here they were, heading south-eastwards once more, and in fine style — although this time with no accompanying galleys. The fine style included ladies advisedly, for on this occasion they were on no privateering expedition — even if *Greysteel* was again well equipped to deal with any attackers they might encounter. They were bound for France.

Alex came strolling forward to them. "Mary, my dear Aunt," he said, "does it stoun your heart to see your native land fading from your sight? You have never left Scotland before, I think?"

"Not so," she replied cheerfully. "So long as I come back before too long. I am rejoicing in this, Alex — to feel as free as my dear husband, for once! To come and go. The going is no hurt, believe me, provided I come again — for I have left two bairns hostage back yonder at Lochindorb."

"We shall return, never fear. I am no more for exile than are you. Or Jamie here. This is but a flourish, a demonstration."

"As well an absenting," Jamie added dryly.

"That too, yes."

They were both right, although the absenting had taken precedence over the demonstration originally. The fact was that John of Buchan had come to see Alex, just after Yule, and strongly advised him to leave Scotland for a while, in his own

297

interests. He had it on good authority that a trap was being set for him, all in due process of law. Albany, as Regent representing the Crown, was commanding a Privy Council enquiry into the proper destination of the earldom of Mar — which would be rigged against Alex, of course — legal niceties were being concocted and marshalled and a major sitting of the Council was scheduled for June, before which Alex would be ordered to appear, to state his case. This he could scarcely refuse to do, without hopelessly prejudicing his position by defying the Crown in Council — as distinct from Albany himself — and making an official outlaw of himself. In which case, naturally, the earldom would be found to be rightfully destined for Sir Robert Erskine, the claimant. On the other hand, if Alex did appear, he would be admitting the competence of the hearing to rule against him, would find the majority of the Council already decided for Erskine and might well be arrested thereafter on the old charge of murdering Sir Malcolm Drummond and forcing the Countess. If, however, he should be out of the country at the time, the hearing could scarcely be held, or if it was, its findings could be contested as improper and not binding. All would fall to be delayed — and in the present turbulent conditions, delay might well mean never. It was the Earl of Douglas, back on the Privy Council, who had conveyed this advice to Buchan for onward transmission, and suggested France as an excellent objective for the traveller.

Alex's first reaction had been outright rejection. He would not run away, to France or anywhere else. He would remain in possession in Mar, and challenge Albany and the Council to come and eject him. But it was pointed out that, though he might be successful in this, it was again to put him outside the law. The case would be adjudged against him as having refused to contest Erskine's claims; and for so long as he could remain holding Mar it would be as an embattled outlaw. Much better to be outwith the realm, prepared to come back at short notice if indeed an attack on Mar in force was made — which seemed unlikely. Moreover, France would give him an excellent and legitimate excuse for travel — on young King James's behalf. He had been prominent in the official embassage to Henry on this subject — to say nothing of the privateering enterprise. What more natural than that, as the King's cousin, he should go seek the King of France's aid in obtaining James's release? To urge the French not to renew the truce with Henry unless James

VISITORS TO NORFOLK LAVENDER

Yearly we welcome thousands of visitors to
Caley Mill. They come from all over the world
to enjoy the tours, the gardens, the shops and
the cream teas. Our visitor leaflet has full details.

OUR LAVENDER PLANTS

From the National Collection of Lavenders
(Norfolk) we have selected lavender plants to
suit all size of garden. The colours vary from
white through to very deep purple. The plants
are available to visitors to Norfolk Lavender and
by post throughout the UK.

HOW TO OBTAIN OUR PRODUCTS

If you do not have a local retailer and would
like our full colour mail order brochure,
please complete the form below and send it
with two 1st class stamps/$2 (check or M.O.)
to the appropriate address.

**If you live in the U.K. or any other country except
USA and Canada, please return this form to:**

Norfolk Lavender Ltd.
FREEPOST 196, Heacham, Norfolk PE31 1BR
Tel: 01485 572383   Fax: 01485 571176

**If you live in USA or Canada, please return this
form to:**

Norfolk Lavender Ltd.
"Pickering & Simmons LLC"
2031 Route 130, Suite D, Monmouth Junction,
NJ 08852. Tel: (1) 732 422 0824 Fax: (1) 732 422 2290

Our products are also available in many other countries.
Please ask for the name of your local distributor.

- ✂ -

☐ For full colour product brochure enclose
   2 x 1st class stamps/$2 (check or M.O.).

Please also send details of:

☐ Visitor and tour information.

☐ Plants (U.K. only - not available in USA)

NAME:
Mr/Mrs/Ms _____

ADDRESS: _____

_____

County/State _____

Post Code/Zip _____

Welcome to our collection of fine English fragrances.

FOR LADIES
English Lavender
Rose
Night Scented Jasmine
Lily of the Valley

FOR GENTLEMEN
Men of England
Lavender for Men

CLASSICALLY ESSENTIAL
Essential oils and blends (Aromatherapy products)

These fragrances come to you from Norfolk Lavender, England's Lavender Farm. For more than 60 years, our family business has accumulated a unique breadth of experience in growing and harvesting essential oils, the most important natural ingredient of fragrant soaps, colognes, talcs, lotions and other gifts. We have taken this experience and used it in the making of these products, thus enhancing the great tradition of English floral perfumery.

OUR ENVIRONMENTAL STATEMENT

❖ All toiletries can be safely used by vegetarians and vegans

❖ The soap is vegetable based

❖ We do not test our products or ingredients on animals

BY APPOINTMENT TO
H.R.H. THE PRINCE OF WALES
GROWERS & DISTILLERS OF
ENGLISH ESSENTIAL OILS
NORFOLK LAVENDER LTD.
NORFOLK

was freed — who had been on his way to France. Albany could scarcely declare publicly hostility to this mission, however unofficial he named it; and the Council would at least have to acknowledge it as a noble gesture, and so be disinclined to take active proceedings against him in the interim. Who could tell, he might succeed with King Charles?

So Alex had been persuaded. But he would make it all a flourish, a demonstration, as much to Scotland as to France. He would not go like any fugitive or minor applicant for help. He would go as a prince, the King of Scots's cousin indeed, a great earl of Scotland, would spend his all on it if need be. It would be an embassage worthy of Scotland, even if unofficial. Fortunately he was given time, for he was not to be sent a summons to appear before the Council until close to the due date, so that he should have no time for preparation. There had been opportunity to charter *Greysteel* once more, and to fit her out in much finer style, as regards accommodation, than on the privateering trip, and to assemble quite a glittering company to sail in her. No fewer than eighty knights, lairds or sons of lairds were included, and three other ladies besides Mary Stewart — Lady Margaret Forbes, mother of Sir Alexander; the Lady Straiton of Lauriston; and Lady Melville of Glenbervie. There were two chaplains; also a full company of musicians and singers. Even Sir Andrew Stewart, the eldest of Alex's awkward brothers, had been persuaded to come along — more to ensure that he did not get into mischief in the interim than anything else. Mariota de Athyn had declined to take part, saying that she was too old for such cantrips and would stay at home and look after the young Douglases. John of Buchan himself would have liked to have joined the company, but as Lieutenant and Justiciar felt that he could hardly leave the North for so long. No summons by the Council had arrived at Kildrummy before Alex left. Also well before they started he had heard that Donald of the Isles had indeed sailed for Ulster with a large galley fleet, so clearly there was no threat to Scotland meantime.

Although *Greysteel* was well armed with cannon and had a sufficiency of fighting men aboard, they sought no engagements with the English on this journey and were to follow a dog's-leg course which would take them south-eastwards at first, well clear of the English waters before turning south-westwards for Sluys, the port for Bruges. Robert Davidson was acting shipmaster again. He was combining the role with that of merchant,

299

in a joint trading venture with Alex which, it was hoped, would help to defray some of the costs of this ambitious project.

Fortunately their voyage proved uneventful and reasonably speedy, with a fair breeze maintaining and no challenges from English shipping. They saw sundry sails, at a distance, but only single ships and none greatly larger than themselves. And the seas were never rough enough to upset the travellers to any degree. Six days after leaving Aberdeen they beat into the West Scheldt estuary, at the head of an inlet of which Sluys lay, on the level Flanders coast, so different from the last upheaved land they had seen. Now, in the estuary there was shipping in plenty, for this was a busy waterway and haven indeed, the port for perhaps the greatest trading centre in Christendom. The low flatness of the land struck them all, with the buildings, churches, houses, windmills, seeming to tower everywhere, the only objects to dominate that strange featureless and all but treeless landscape.

They met with no difficulties in docking and disembarkation, for the Flemings' entire economy was geared to international trade, and foreigners were as common in the streets, wharves and lanes of Sluys as were natives. They continued to use the ship as sleeping quarters whilst arrangements were made for their onward journeying. Horses were hired — over one hundred of them, no less, for riding and pack animals — guide-interpreters engaged, messengers sent ahead to smooth the way and announce the coming of the illustrious Earl of Mar, and so on. Sluys was linked to Bruges by canal, but *Greysteel* was rather too large to use this.

Two days later they moved on to Bruges, the Flemish capital, about ten miles inland, in a quite impressive procession, all in their finest clothing under an array of heraldic banners, Mar, Badenoch, Garioch, Stewart, Forbes, even Douglas, and with their mounted instrumentalists playing stirring music in the rear, the two priests in full canonicals. This was all an exercise in public relations to try to ensure the right reception in Paris eventually.

They did not have to complain about Bruges's reception, at any rate. The Flemings had strong links with Scotland, with many trading colonies settled therein. They were not a warlike people, although sturdy in defence of their own interests, and scarcely looked upon the Scots as allies, as the French did — more as business partners, which perhaps was a sounder and more enduring relationship. They traded with England also, of course — but relations were less happy with that dominant nation which was ever concerned with overlordship, military threats, special terms and the like, and whose privateers took indiscriminate toll of all shipping. It turned out that the Earl of Mar's own naval exploits against *English* shipping the year before had made a great and exaggerated impact upon the Flemings. Bruges now hailed him as hero, sea-warrior and benefactor. The Burgomaster, masters of the merchant guilds, and magistrates came to meet them outside the principal of the seven gates of the city, to make speeches of welcome and to conduct them to the governor's palace — on the way to which the Archbishop of Bruges waited for them oütside his great cathedral of St. Sauveur, to give them his blessing and an episcopal stirrup-cup. The visitors were pleasantly surprised.

They were surprised at more than this welcome. Save for Robert Davidson who knew it of old, they had had little idea as to the size, wealth and importance of this Flemish metropolis and centre of the Hanseatic League. It was, they were informed, at this time the largest city in all Christendom, outdoing Paris, London, Rome, Lubeck, Genoa and Venice, and certainly the greatest merchanting centre. There were said to be over two hundred thousand inhabitants, almost one-third of the population of all Scotland. Although the prevailing flatness spoiled it somewhat for the Scots, they could not fail to be impressed by its extent, the richness and variety of its buildings, churches, monasteries, hospices, palaces, towering tenements, cloth-halls, warehouses, market-places and the rest. They were amazed at its network of canals with their innumerable fine bridges — that is what the name Bruges meant — the public statues, the soberly rich dress of much of its population, the notable lack of beggars and all the other signs of long-continued prosperity. It all made Aberdeen, Dundee, Perth, Stirling, Edinburgh seem poor places — save for the scenic qualities of the Scots hills and castle-crowned rocks, their trees and orchards. Although they reckoned that St. Andrews, the Scottish metropolitan see, could probably rival it in the magnificence and number of its ecclesiastical buildings, if not in size.

Outside the huge and ornate cathedral, as Alex bowed his fair head for the Archbishop's benediction, Jamie could not help conjuring up before his mind's eye the scene before that other splendid cathedral at Elgin, Scotland's pride, eighteen years before, in blazing ruin, sacked and set alight by this man's father, a younger Alex torn by dire distress. Like many another, Jamie was apt to forget, in the assured and courteous leader he had become, whence Alex Stewart had sprung and the dramatic background to his upbringing.

In procession they moved on over the bridges to the governor's palace. The government of Flanders, part of the Empire, was in a curious state, for the Count of Flanders, under the Emperor, had died, and his daughter's husband was the French royal prince, Philip de Valois, Duke of Burgundy. He had acted heir to his father-in-law; and dying, his son John the Fearless, Duke of Burgundy, became ruler, although an uncle of the French king, so frequently at war with the Empire. The Duke at present was, it seemed, absent in Paris — indeed he usually was — and his brother, the Lord Anton of Brabant, was deputising for him. He it was who greeted the Scots with a strange mixture of haughtiness and flattery, a curious, pale slight man in his late thirties, overdressed and very slightly deformed, with burning eyes and features which gave the impression that he was racked with pain. However, he handed over a wing of the vast rambling palace, which itself bridged two canals, to the visitors, regretting that he could not entertain them, at such short notice, in the manner to which they were no doubt accustomed; but the Burgomaster and guild leaders would do the honours in the Hotel de Ville, and the next day it would be his pleasure and privilege to offer the hospitality to such close relatives of the King of Scots.

So in due course they all moved across to the Town Hall. But before doing so, Alex came to Mary Stewart and Jamie in their palatial if distinctly gloomy chamber.

"My dear," he said, "tonight I would wish you to act the princess. This Anton of Brabant is clearly a man much concerned with rank and standing. His brother, the Duke, is one of the two most important men in France, highly influential at the French Court — where he is at present. It will be to our advantage to make much of our royal blood, however illegitimate, I think. *I* shall be very much the King's cousin — and you must likewise act the King's aunt — which you are. On what side of the blanket you were conceived is little to the point, in this issue. But it would be best for you to *be* the Princess Mary Stewart. You understand?"

"But I am *not* a princess, Alex!" she protested. "I am Robert the Second's natural daughter, yes — like many another! But I have never looked on myself, or called myself, a princess. The nearest I have come to that was to be maid-of-honour to my sisters Gelis and Isabel — and I am able to be that no longer, being wed to this, this Douglas bastard and outcast here!"

"Nevertheless, Aunt, you will much oblige me by allowing yourself to be treated as your father's daughter whilst on this ploy. A princess of Scotland will, I swear, serve our cause a deal better than just Jamie Douglas's goodwife, however comely!"

"You have depths of deceit in you hitherto unsuspected, Nephew!" she accused. "But — do not overdo it."

In the event they were entertained not in the Hotel de Ville but in an extraordinary composite building nearby called Les Halles — this because there appeared to be no apartment in the former sufficiently large to accommodate all who were to attend the banquet, other than the great council-chamber itself which for some reason could not be got ready in time. Les Halles was a vast square range of building on an island-site, incorporating an enclosed market surrounded by the guild halls which the name implied, some of these of great size. Out of this far-flung extravaganza in stone, of arches, buttresses, crenellations and pinnacles, soared a mighty clock-tower and belfry in three tiers like some enormous wedding-cake, overdecorated and overwhelming, rising to no less than three hundred and fifty-three feet, they were assured, and apparently the pride of Bruges. From it bells jangled in a deafening cacophony to welcome the distinguished guests.

Installed in one of the largest of the halls, that of the Lacemakers' Guild, some four hundred sat down to a feast. It said much for the power, wealth and organising ability of the Bruges burghers that they could, at one day's notice, produce and mount such a repast, lacking nothing in quantity, quality or variety, even if something heavy for a warm evening of May. Mary, addressed by all as Princess, found herself seated at the centre of the topmost table between the Lord Anton of Brabant and the Burgomaster, with Alex at the latter's other side and Jamie well down the board. As the interminable meal progressed, she began to wish that she was safely at her husband's lowly side, for the Lord Anton had a roving hand as well as a burning eye, and she had frequently to discourage its exploratory ventures whilst maintaining a polite conversation on the iniquities of successive Kings of England and the rebellious nature of the lower classes — in which she rather gathered Anton of Brabant included their hosts for the evening.

Unlike Scots banquets, great eating was very much the prime preoccupation here, with drinking — at least at this stage — very secondary, and no distracting entertainment the while. Never had most of the Scots seen such eating, such determined demolition of endless provender, or heard so much slurping, munching, champing and belching.

It was a relief, especially to Mary Stewart, when at length the succession of viands began to tail off and musicians made their appearance, with the advent of serious drinking. Unfortunately the music and the wine had a rousing effect on the Lord Anton, who had been inclining towards the soporific; and presently, in desperation, speaking across the nodding Burgomaster, Mary was urgent in suggesting to Alex that they should volunteer a demonstration of Scots music and dancing, in which they all might take part — in especial herself. Alex was glad to agree, and in the announcements and arrangements, the temporary princess was thankful to escape.

The Scots dancing went down very well, with members of the resident Scots colony in Bruges taking part, inspiring some attempts at emulation — although by no means all the company were in a condition to react positively. Fortunately, the Lord Anton did not feel called upon to take part; fairly clearly he thought it was no way for people of birth and breeding to behave.

When they were finished, Mary would not hear of returning to her place at the table and the further gallantries of the Governor's brother. She insisted on being taken back to their lodging in the palace, in sufficiently royal fashion, and the other Scots ladies were well content to accompany her. She also declared that if Anton of Brabant was himself to give them a banquet the next day, she for one would be indisposed. If this was the price for being a princess, the sooner she reverted to a humbler status the better. Jamie escorted them back to their quarters gladly enough, emphasising to her the pleasures of freedom and foreign travel.

Next forenoon Alex informed the Lord Anton that, grateful as they were for his proposed hospitality, time pressed and it would be advisable for them to be on their way to Paris, still some two hundred miles off. Their host, who appeared to combine an appreciation of economy with that of feminity, made no real protest. The good burghers of Bruges were very much more loth to see the Scots go. Robert Davidson remained behind. He was to negotiate a cargo of Flemish goods and ship it back to Scotland, returning to pick the others up again in ten or twelve weeks' time.

The cavalcade rode southwards over the level lands of Flanders, where every community stood out from the flats abruptly, as though only recently dropped there ready-built — although many of the villages and towns seemed ancient enough at closer inspection. At every sizeable place they passed their musicians played and Alex acted the gracious prince, even bestowing largesse and paying bountifully for their entertainment. Despite what he had said about time pressing to the Lord Anton, they did not hasten — deliberately — for Alex wanted word of their style and repute to reach Paris before them.

Crossing an unending pattern of canals, ditches and meres, by innumerable bridges and causeways, gradually, imperceptibly, the ground rose and dried out beneath them, until eventually they rode on land of sufficient altitude to reveal an actual valley ahead, however shallow and wide, down which a sluggish river coiled and twisted — the Lys, a principal tributary of the Scheldt. This they crossed, and presently came to the upper Scheldt itself, up which they turned, westwards, by Roubaix, Valenciennes and St. Quentin. They put up at abbeys and monasteries each night, being consistently well received. There were great numbers of such religious institutions, which had clearly gathered much of the wealth of the countryside into their hands, many of them having cloth, lace and tapestry weaving manufactories attached.

When they crossed into France from Flanders, at Cambrai, it was remarkable how quickly the entire face and character of land and people changed. Instead of husbandry, manufacture, prosperous towns, field cultivation and drainage, was neglect of land, forest and scrub, swamp, bad roads and everywhere the signs of local warfare. The villages and towns were poor huddles of houses, in the main — but many were the proud castles, châteaux and mansions of counts and barons, something but little seen in the Flemish plains. The abbeys and religious houses were less frequent, but still larger and more splendid. But elsewhere were all the signs of poverty and oppression, beggars abounding, gallows with their rotting fruit at every cross-roads and market-place — in monastery yards likewise. It was much

305

more picturesque country, with much woodland and some un-dulation to the landscape; but there was a fear and sadness about it not seen hitherto. The peasants scurried into hiding at sight of the cavalcade, instead of thronging and waving; agri-culture was wretched and hunting appeared to be the preoccupa-tion of those with leisure.

The Scots began to wonder whether their ancient allies of France were all that they had believed them to be.

Across the Picardy plain they followed the River Ouse to its junction with Seine, still resting at religious houses but on the whole with less satisfaction and at greater expense. The evi-dences of the internecine warfare which was splitting France, the indiscipline of the nobles and the sheer anarchy which prevailed, began seriously to worry the travellers, not for their own safety — for they made a sufficiently strong company — but for the value of their mission. They had known that King Charles the Sixth was lacking something in his wits and strength — but they had not realised that he was now quite mad, and that the factions of his two cousins, the Dukes of Burgundy and Orleans, with that of the Archbishop of Paris, were at each other's throats and tugging the monarch — or, more important, the Queen — this way and that. They had as guide and interpreter one John Duncan, a member of the quite large Scots trading colony in Bruges, who told them hair-raising stories about French affairs. It became fairly clear why France had proved something of a broken reed as an ally against the English.

They came to the Seine at St. Germain, with only thirteen more miles to Paris. They were still travelling deliberately slowly.

If Alex had expected a similar reception at the French capital to that at Bruges, he was disappointed. He had sent messages ahead, of course; but there was little sign of them having had any effect. No deputation awaited them at the city gates, from Court or municipality, no crowds lined the streets, and even though their musicians played their best, they aroused little more than a passing interest from the citizens — who no doubt were entirely used to nobles' cavalcades parading the town. They gathered a vociferous tail of urchins, and that was about all.

Even apart from the lack of reception, Paris did not impress them, certainly not as Bruges had done. It was, as a whole, dirty, smelly and airless, more like London. There were fine buildings, especially palaces, but many of these were shut up and with an appearance of neglect — and the squalor of the town came right to their doors. There were many great and fine churches and religious houses, the Sainte Chapelle quite lovely, shrine for Christ's alleged Crown of Thorns; but these tended to give the impression that they were scarcely part of the community, turning their backs on the streets, as it were gathering their skirts from contact, the monasteries behind high walls and barred gates like lesser fortresses. There was no lack of inns, hostelries and wine-shops however, in the narrow alleys and lanes, seemingly largely patronised by innumerable bands and groups of men-at-arms in a great variety of lords' colours, many of these drunken and noisy. Beggars, the maimed, loose women — who made their profession notably plain — and yapping dogs abounded.

The Scots' hearts sank. They had come a long way for this.

Since no offer of quarters seemed to be forthcoming from the authorities, Alex was certainly not going to present himself at any palace-door begging for hospitality. With a princely image to maintain, he consulted their guide, seeking some hostelry sufficiently large to accommodate the entire party, and sufficiently near the royal residence of the Louvre to be convenient. Duncan, a dealer in tapestries and wall-hangings, whom they had chosen because he made frequent business visits to Paris, after consideration suggested that they try an establishment in the Ile de la Cité rejoicing in the designation of At the Sign of the Tin Plate, almost under the walls of the cathedral of Notre Dame, which was in fact a former monkish hospice of a serving order where the poor had been given shelter and fed on tin plates. The monks had gone but the name had stuck. Now it was a very large inn, indeed a sort of caravanserai.

They made their way across bridges to this establishment therefore, to the sound of music, yelling boys and barking dogs, and found it in what was almost a town within the city, on an island site, within the precincts of the towering cathedral, in a great bend of the river. It was a sprawling place, somewhat decayed, but with ample accommodation, yards, outbuildings, stables, even an overgrown orchard. The innkeeper was quite overwhelmed by the size of the company and the work involved in catering for them — but his shrewd and businesslike wife was not long in convincing him that all could be managed — and in striking a notable bargain with the visitors. Alex, in pursuance of his chosen role as illustrious envoy, had come prepared to

307

spend money — he had, after all, married one of the richest earldoms in Scotland and had made considerable profits from the privateering expedition — and he agreed to take over the entire hostelry meantime, with suitable servants to be found, food and drink to be provided in abundance, and cost no object. He required for it considerable cleaning-up, however, without delay. A judicious disbursement of silver coinage reinforced his demands, and worked wonders.

The next step was something of a problem. Foreign envoys normally proceeded to present their credentials to the ruler of the state concerned; but they were not official ambassadors and had no letters of introduction to present. Private persons could not just thrust themselves into the presence of a monarch, even a partially mad one, requiring a royal summons — and none such seemed to be forthcoming, as yet. The innkeeper's wife informed them that King and Court were in fact presently at the royal hunting palace of St. Germain-en-Laye — which they had passed nearby — but were due to return to Paris two days hence it was said, to celebrate the Feast of Saint Boniface — Queen Isabella of Bavaria being notably pious. The King, of course, might not come, being much more interested in killing things than in worshipping; but the Queen would — and it seemed that it was the Queen who counted in France now. Or, at least, the Duke of Burgundy and the Orleans faction who sought to influence the Queen.

Alex decided to wait.

The next day the Scots spent finding their feet in Paris. They nearly all spoke French fluently — after all, it was not so long since it was an everyday language for the gentry in Scotland — and they found the common people friendly enough, much more so than in London, although in the main they seemed desperately poor and ragged, with an extraordinary proportion homeless, diseased and deformed. For the rich capital of Christendom's Most Christian King, this seemed strange; but presumably misrule and constant warfare, national and feudal, along with a sort of endemic indiscipline, were responsible. Even Albany's Scotland, by comparison, was beginning to look less shameful.

All this poverty and obvious hunger stirred Alex on to making a gesture, partly politic, partly out of a kind heart. Calling on the city's mayor, he announced that meantime at least the former hospice of the Tin Plate would revert to one of its earlier roles, with food and drink available for all comers, gratis, the poor to be provided for in the stableyard at the rear, open house for the better sort at the front, all at the Earl of Mar's expense. Jamie thought this a wild extravagance, and said so; but his wife reminded him that Alex was a Stewart, and the Stewarts were always notable for large gestures and seldom did things by halves. And it would certainly make his name and fame ring throughout Paris. So the Scots found themselves thrust into the role of caterers, suppliers and general benefactors — and were all but bowled over in the rush. It was amazing how swiftly the word swept Paris and the crowds converged, not all content peaceably to await their turn, either at the back door or the front. Dealers in meats, victuals and wines flocked in on them also. Few gestures could have been calculated so to move the city.

The day following it was confirmed that the Court was indeed returning to the Louvre Palace, and should arrive in mid-afternoon. Leaving the noisy crowds besieging the hostelry for food and drink, the Scots, arrayed at their finest, rode off northwards again.

The metropolitan seat of the French monarchy was an extraordinary establishment by any standards, almost a separate fortified town. It stood nearly a mile down-river from Notre Dame, in many-towered splendour, occupying a vast area of ground within outer and inner baileys and high curtain-walls, the entire many-acred site cut off from the city by a broad moat diverted from the Seine, with an enormous detached gatehouse range at the riverside, itself almost another palace. There were eighteen major towers around the double perimeters, and a legion of lesser ones. Enclosed in all this and flanking many courtyards, was the royal palace itself, but also other buildings by the score, lodgings, government offices, barracks, armouries and the like. Also kitchens, allegedly a round dozen, breweries, bakehouses, laundries, warehouses, blacksmith's forges, even a slaughterhouse. The stables were said to accommodate five hundred horses. So vast an establishment was quite beyond the visitors' experience — indeed it was some considerable time before they were fully aware of its dimensions and ramifications.

This first day they took up their stance on the broad riverside avenue at the north-east corner of the gatehouse range, where the main drawbridge crossed the moat near its junction with the Seine. Here, watched somewhat askance by guards at the bridge-end and tower, but not interfered with, Alex drew up his company in an orderly formation, dismounted meantime, and set the musicians to play. He sent his brother Andrew and two others to keep watch at the approaches beyond their view from the north, to give them warning of the royal arrival — in particular as to whether royalty was accompanied by its own music.

Thus they waited, whilst an admiring throng gathered.

It was some time before Sir Andrew Stewart rode back, to say that a large horsed company was not far off, apparently not accompanied by musicians. He had had to wait until they were fairly close before he could ascertain this last, so they would be in sight very soon. Alex ordered all to remount, and the instrumentalists to redouble their efforts in a rousing marching tune.

An escort of the sovereign's guard, all gleaming armour and tossing plumes, trotted into sight some three hundred yards off, and drew rein at sight of the Scots phalanx, obviously at a loss. Alex rode out a little way to meet them as two of their number came spurring forward.

"What is this?" a haughty officer demanded. "*Parbleu* — who are you to stand in the way of the King of France? His Majesty approaches." He had to shout loudly to make himself heard above the orchestration.

"I am the Earl of Mar, cousin to the King of Scots, sir. With an illustrious Scottish company, including His Grace's aunt, come to greet His Most Christian Majesty of France, our ancient ally," Alex returned.

"Scots? An embassy? But . . . but . . . ?"

"We but seek to bask in the sun of His Majesty's presence for a moment, as he passes to his house, sir. As the humblest citizen of this town may do."

"But . . . this noise, Monsieur le Comte!"

"It is our Scots custom, friend. Music for those we would honour."

The officer looked undecided, glanced back, saw the main royal cavalcade now in view and almost on top of the halted escort and, calling something to his colleague, reined round and rode back at a canter. Alex returned to his former stance at the front of his carefully marshalled company, between Mary Stewart and Lady Forbes, flanked by his brother, Jamie Douglas and Sir Alexander Forbes. The band of fiddles, lutes, flutes, trumpets and cymbals continued to play loudly.

The new arrivals came on now, almost warily for so splendid and authoritative a company. The escort, now doubled in size by bringing forward the rearguard also, rode up ahead, to take up protective positions flanking and opposite the Scots. Then the front ranks of the main procession drew level, slowing to a walk, all eyes on the strangers. Foremost were four gorgeously clad riders, three men and a woman. And just behind, in a fine two-horse litter with canopied and heraldic fittings, lounged an extraordinary trio, a middle-aged man dressed all in white, but slovenly, stained white, with sprawling at either side of him a girl and a boy, each perhaps ten years or so of age and both stark naked. Behind rode rank upon rank of men and women, the proudest and fairest in France.

Alex doffed his bonnet with a flourish, and all the Scots bowed from their saddles — and behind them the musicians reduced their notes to the merest background murmur, trumpets and cymbals silent.

"Your Majesties of France and my lord Duke and other lords — most humble and respectful greetings! We hail you in the name of James, High King of Scots. I am Alexander, Earl of Mar and the Garioch, Lord of Badenoch. And here is the Princess Mary Stewart, sister of our late liege lord Robert and aunt to King James. And others of renown from Scotland."

The reaction of the new arrivals was varied. The lady in front, a handsome woman in her late thirties, somewhat massive as to build but upright in carriage and dressed entirely as a man in hunting green, conferred with her magnificent companions. The lounging man, who was scratching in his unusually long and lanky black hair, paid no least attention, whilst the naked children sat up interestedly.

One of the men in front, a florid, well-built man of about Alex's own age, notable for his remarkably heavy eyebrows, spoke.

"Her Majesty is interested to meet the renowned Comte de Mar," he said. "She bids you welcome. Also the Princess." He bowed. "I am John of Burgundy. And this is the Archbishop of Paris and the Comte d'Armagnac." He glanced back over his broad velvet-clad shoulder. "His Most Christian Majesty. We, ah, heard that you were in France, monsieur."

"Yes. We had the honour to be entertained by your brother, the Lord Anton, at Bruges, my lord Duke." Alex bowed again towards the Queen and then the reclining King. This was rather

311

difficult. He could scarcely carry on a conversation with Burgundy in front of the monarch and his consort. "We greatly rejoice to see Your Majesties, and to convey to you the good wishes and greetings of all Scots. But . . . we most certainly would not wish to seem to delay Your Majesties thus in your progress. Only to salute you in passing. You will be wearied with your journey. Perhaps you would be sufficiently gracious as to grant us audience, in due course?"

The older of the two other men with the Queen, stocky, stern-faced, of middle years, dressed wholly in purple and white lace, frowned. "Her Majesty cannot stand thus, waiting," he said, looking sourly at Burgundy. "Madame, let us proceed."

"No haste, Archbishop," the Queen suggested. "Monsieur de Mar and his friends have had the civility to wait upon us. And to provide pleasing music for our ears. Strangers from another land — although renowned. The least we may do is to thank them. And welcome them to Paris." Isabella of Bavaria had a light, lilting and very feminine voice, like a girl's, markedly at variance with her present somewhat masculine appearance — although, the mother of five sons, she was no girl.

"Your Grace is most kind . . ." Alex began, but the third man with the Queen broke in. He was younger than the cleric but slightly older than Burgundy, and brilliantly good-looking, tall, broad-shouldered but slender, with very fair wavy hair and a flashing smile but no hint of weakness about him. He bent in the saddle, to murmur close in the Queen's ear, and then spoke more loudly.

"Her Majesty is ever kind. No doubt she will consider your request favourably, monsieur — at some more convenient occasion." He reined round his horse, as to ride on.

"Not so fast, D'Armagnac," the Duke of Burgundy said, strongly. "You are ever impatient. Her Majesty finds the music pleasing, even if you do not. Because you have no ear for music, there is no reason why we all should be deprived. Perhaps Monsieur de Mar will oblige us with a further rendering of his Scottish airs? I cannot think that Isabella is so wearied after but a mere fifteen-kilometre ride."

Brows raised, the Queen glanced from one to the other. "Peace, you two," she pleaded. "But, yes. If Monsieur le Comte will be so good. Some short piece, from Scotland."

Very much aware of this cross-play, Alex bowed, and waved to his instrumentalists. "*Hey Tuttie Taitie*," he called. This was

312

Bruce's marching-song at Bannockburn, a tune to stir even the most sluggish blood.

With an admirable minimum of delay the musicians broke into a spirited version of the traditional air. Although the Archbishop frowned and the Count d'Armagnac stared away expressionlessly, most of their hearers appeared to be appreciative. The Queen nodded her head, smiling, and the Duke John beat time vigorously. King Charles seemed to be quite unaffected, and was fondling the naked boy beside him in preoccupied fashion.

After three verses, Alex signed to his people to finish. There was considerable applause, led by Burgundy, who seemingly was requesting an encore. Alex, in some doubt, was looking at the Queen when a loud cackling laugh rang out — and all eyes abruptly switched to Charles de Valois. He had sat up in the litter in a crouching posture and was pointing a shaking finger at Mary Stewart, grinning crazily. He continued to point, gabbling incoherently through his laughter, which sank to a chuckle and then to a mere giggle, Mary seeking not to show her alarm. Then suddenly he changed expression to a fierce glare, and jerking his hand, now pointed forward with a repeated jabbing motion, eloquent enough. Immediately all his company turned to urge their horses into movement, Queen, Duke, Archbishop and Count included — for this was still the Most Christian King, supreme ruler of all France.

"We shall send for you, Monsieur de Mar," Queen Isabella called, as she rode on. And, shrugging and grimacing, John of Burgundy waved to them.

The musicians played the long royal procession past with more of *Hey Tutti Taitie* by way of encore.

As the Scots presently trotted back towards Notre Dame, Jamie asked, "That was a strange business. Are you satisfied with what you achieved? This is going to be no simple mission, I think. If we gain any good here, I shall be much surprised."

Alex shrugged. "We may do better than might appear. The Queen seems well enough disposed. We shall get our audience now. And Burgundy is clearly for us."

"And therefore the Archbishop and that d'Armagnac against us. They sharpen their dirks on each other — that I swear! And pull the Queen between them. This D'Armagnac — how has he so much influence?"

"The Counts of Armagnac have long held powerful sway in

313

Gascony. This one, Bernard, was friend to the Duke of Orleans, whom Burgundy was instrumental in having slain — slain horribly. Indeed, his daughter is wed to Orleans' son, the new Duke — both but children. It is whispered that D'Armagnac was formerly lover of the Queen — as was Orleans. For she is ... generous! The Count has allied himself with the Archbishop of Paris, who also hates Burgundy. But Burgundy, the King's first cousin, is still the strongest voice at Court, and moreover favoured by the citizens of Paris — which seems to be important. Though the other faction is said to be growing in strength. In matters of state the Queen has to heed him most. She must be much beset."

"Poor woman," Mary put in. "Consider having that king as a husband. I all but swooned with fright when he pointed at me, with his crazed laughter. I vow I shall keep out of his sight hereafter — if I can! And those poor children — the shame of it!"

"For a princess, you are too easily shocked, my dear. Remember that the Lord's Anointed are never to be judged by everyday standards!"

"Nor the Lord's Anointeds' wives, either, apparently!" Jamie added. "From what I have heard, Queen Isabella finds ample compensations for her deranged husband ... religious or otherwise!"

*   *   *

They did not have to wait long for their audience. The very next forenoon a messenger came to the Tin Plate with the Queen's command for the Comte de Mar, the Princess Mary of Scotland and a few of their company to wait upon her that evening after vespers.

When, with his four ladies and half-a-dozen of his lairds, Alex presented himself at the Louvre, it was to discover that Isabella of Bavaria had her own wing of the enormous palace, where she maintained an almost separate establishment. Conducted thither across no fewer than five courtyards, the visitors were brought to a great apartment, a salon rather than a hall since it was unlike any hall they had ever seen, vast, lofty, the walls lined with tall mirrors of polished brass and silver, as well as of glass, interspersed with magnificent tapestries and vivid mural paintings of eye-catching immodesty and religious themes mixed, all illuminated — although it was still bright daylight without — by thousands of candles in huge hanging chandeliers, their light reflected to infinity by all the mirrors. All was set for a great banquet, and many courtiers were already present, chatting, laughing, strolling on the rich Eastern carpets. These eyed the Scots with frank interest as they were led, through a further doorway into an ante-room and there left for a space.

Presently ushers came to announce Her Illustrious Majesty the Queen of France. Isabella entered with a minimum of fuss, accompanied by a splendidly dressed group, which again included the Duke of Burgundy, the Count d'Armagnac and the Archbishop. If the Queen had worn masculine clothing before, now she was sufficiently feminine with a velvet and pearl-sewn gown cut so low as barely to contain her fairly heavy bosom. She moved over to a throne-like chair, but there, instead of sitting, she paused, and seemingly on impulse came forward to the visitors and held out her hand to Alex, who dropped to one knee to kiss it. She raised him up in more than mere token fashion, her generous person very close to him. Then she turned to Mary.

"And this is the Princess? Marie, did I hear? Your cousin, monsieur?"

"My aunt, Majesty. Wife to Sir James Douglas, here."

"*Mon Dieu* — is that possible? Aunt — so young? And so charming!" Isabella leaned forward again to embrace Mary, who was all but smothered.

"Scarce that, Your Grace," she got out. "I have a son of sixteen years! And I am a princess only by courtesy — since my royal father omitted to wed my mother!"

The Queen tinkled a laugh which, like her voice, was a deal more girlish than her appearance warranted, but cheerfully un-affected. "Splendid! You and I are going to be friends, I think, Madame Marie. I like an honest woman."

Alex presented the rest of his party to the Queen, who then returned to her chair and sat, while the Duke John introduced the remainder of the royal group, including two countess ladies-in-waiting, the younger of whom, besides being strikingly beauti-ful, with odalisque eyes and raven-black hair, was additionally eye-catching through wearing a satin gown, the bodice supported at one shoulder so that the other breast hung free, aureole and nipple painted scarlet. There was no sign nor mention of the King.

"We have heard much of Scotland, our ancient friend and ally in the North, and rejoice to welcome so distinguished a company to the Court of France," Isabella went on, in more formal tones. "We trust that you will much enjoy your stay amongst us. Are you the bearers of letters which I may pass on to my royal husband, who is somewhat indisposed? Or is your visit a private one?"

Alex spread his hands in rather French fashion. "No letters of credence, Majesty. Nor yet our visit entirely private," he said carefully. "We do not come as representing my uncle, the Duke of Albany, Regent of Scotland, since he is in truce and treaty with the King of England. Whereas we are concerned — as of course is he — for the release of our young liege lord King James, shamefully taken on his way to your Majesties' Court here, and held prisoner in London. Such concern has to be expressed in private visit rather than by official embassage."

"I see — and perceive the difficulty. We are all, to be sure, distressed at the situation of King James, and at the sad death of King Robert. But, of course, we too are in truce and treaty with King Henry of England. There is a twenty-eight-year truce, of which fifteen years are still to run. And so we recognise the wisdom of the private nature of your visit."

"Your Grace is understanding . . ."

"Majesty — may I ask Monsieur le Comte a question?" the Archbishop intervened heavily. "If his visit is that of a private citizen of Scotland, should not his concern for the state of the King of Scots be equally private, and not voiced thus openly to Your Majesty? Since it affects the relations between the states of France, England and Scotland?"

"What say you to that, Monsieur de Mar?" the Queen asked.

"Forgive me if I mistake, Highness, or unknowingly trespass upon your French usage. But I would have thought that a cousin of an unlawfully imprisoned boy, monarch though he is, might legitimately, indeed suitably, express his concern in public or private — and especially before the royal lady to whose house and care he was bound when piratically captured?"

"Well said, monsieur!" Burgundy cried.

"How say you to that, my lord Archbishop?" Isabella asked mildly. "Does it not sound reasonable?"

"So long as he does not seek to embroil Your Majesty in activities to which King Henry could take exception," the prelate declared flatly.

"God's Blood! Would you have the Crown of France seeking

316

the permission of Henry Plantagenet for what it may or may not say or do?" John de Valois exclaimed.

"Not so, my lord Duke. Only to observe the proper and accepted procedures between sovereign nations. It is my simple duty to remind Her Majesty, and all others, of this."

"His Beatitude has the rights of it," Bernard D'Armagnac put in, but in a lighter tone, and with a faint smile on his handsome features. "Private views should be kept private and private visits eschew public policies. But let us not mar a pleasant occasion, with Monsieur de Mar and the Madame Marie!" And he waved a hand to emphasise his stress of the first syllable of that last name.

The loud laughter helped to dissipate the tense atmosphere which had developed. And Isabella further added to this, by saying, "You will perceive, Monsieur le Comte, how well I am advised and guided, on all hands! But enough of this, for the moment. We hope that you had an untroubled journey? Clearly you were more fortunate, on the sea, than your royal cousin James! If the good Archbishop will permit such comment."

Again the laughter.

"We came well prepared, Highness," Alex answered genially. "Having, as it were, spied out the land, or the ocean, a year previously!"

"Ah, yes. We heard of that, monsieur. A notable . . . excursion!"

"A gesture, Majesty. We made sure that no French ships suffered, nor Flemish either, my lord Duke." As Alex said it, Jamie Douglas hoped devoutly that none of the Islesmen's unspecified targets had been French or Flemish.

"Piracy at sea is no matter to laugh over, monsieur," the Archbishop observed severely.

"No, sir. I agree. But privateering is rather different, is it not? We had letters of mark, you understand? And operated only against English east coast shipping. Since it was from thence that our liege lord had been attacked. Our object to bring King Henry to release King James. Which he has not done, unfortunately."

"On a *private* visit, Monsieur Priest, should you be pronouncing upon the Scots policy of privateering?" Burgundy demanded.

There was mixed laughter and frowns at that sally.

Again D'Armagnac intervened. "Our Scots friends' progress here has aroused much admiration, we have heard. Monsieur de

Mar has been . . . open-handed. Much liberality and distribution of largesse. Even now he holds open house here in Paris, I am told. For good reason, no doubt?" Despite the smile, there was no hiding the barb in that question.

"To be sure, my lord," Alex nodded, "I took much wealth from the English ships. Not on my own behalf. To distribute some of it to your humbler compatriots, while we are pilgrims in France, seemed only suitable. Many, it seemed, could do with it! You do not object?"

A titter of amusement greeted that.

"Ah, no. No, monsieur — but so much liberality might be expected to have a purpose?"

"It has. I seek goodwill, in this fair France. Their Majesties', yours, that of all present here. A little liberality may help, with the humble. For those more illustrious, I can only proffer my unworthy self. And, to be sure, the excellencies and charms of the Princess and others of our company."

"Good! Spoken like a proper man! Bernard, you are answered." The Queen rose. "But enough of this talk. Come, Monsieur de Mar — you will escort me to the table." And she held out a quite formidable arm.

As Alex hurried forward to take that arm, the Duke of Burgundy stepped over, to bow to Mary and offer her his. Others of the royal party, male and female, selected partners — and Jamie, to his embarrassment, found the younger Countess with the exposed bosom choosing himself, presumably finding his sombre and rugged good looks to her taste. She placed herself on his right, taking his arm enthusiastically, so that when they moved off after the more illustrious pairs, the man was all too vividly aware of the warm, bare and shapely breast which brushed and quivered against his wrist in time with the lady's animated talk. She had to sustain the burden of the conversation, it is to be feared. Jamie's wife, on the other hand, further forward, was almost equally perturbed lest the Duke of Burgundy should come to display social behaviour similar to that of his brother, the Lord Anton of Brabant.

The royal column moved into the great salon amidst general bowing and curtsying, to take seats at the top table. There was no dais here, as in a castle's hall, but the Queen's table ran transversely across the apartment, at considerable length, whilst the others were placed lengthwise. Mary found herself on Isabella's left, with the Duke at her other side. This she found reassuring — for surely Burgundy would scarcely engage in any embarrassing exploration which would be obvious to the Queen. Alex was on the royal right. Jamie, considerably further down the table, for his part found some relief also, in that he perceived that the Countess Eloise was not quite so kenspeckle as he had supposed — for the company was now seen to contain quite a number of bare breasts, some indeed in pairs; and even when not actually fully displayed, most bosoms were apt to be distinctly evident, owing to the fashion of bodices being open down the front and laced up criss-cross, seldom tightly or with any infilling. He felt considerably better for this recognition, and in fact began to acknowledge a more healthy appreciation of his companion's various endowments.

The repast which followed was such as none of the Scots had ever previously experienced, in scale and magnitude, sumptuous assortment, exotic variety and ingenious presentation. Courses came and went, over a score of them, in bewildering profusion, cooked in every conceivable fashion, garnished and supported with every extravagance to titillate the palate and the eye, hot and cold, delicacies, savouries, fish and shell-fish, fowl, game, red meats, confections and dainties. There might be starvation in the wake of war in much of France, but there was no hint of it here.

The Queen appeared to have a hearty appetite, and advised Alex as to what he should try and what not, very much as a man might do. She did not neglect Mary either, and was indeed notably friendly; but she concentrated her attention upon Alex.

"What is your name, monsieur?" she asked, presently. "I cannot continue to call you that, if we are to be honoured with your presence."

"My friends call me Alex, Highness. I am Alexander Stewart, knight, at your service."

"Then Alex you shall be. You have not brought a wife with you?"

"My wife died a year past. She also was named Isobel."

"Ah. And you were desolated?"

"I was much saddened, Highness. It was through her that I gained the earldom of Mar. She was a woman of much spirit."

"I see. You did not inherit the earldom, then, from your father?"

"He was Earl of Buchan, King Robert the Second's third surviving son. He had no lawful children — and I was his eldest bastard. From him I got the lordship of Badenoch."

"So! You Stewarts are clearly a virile race, Alex! Which of

319

the ladies you have brought with you is your mistress? Not your aunt, here?"

"None of them, Majesty."

"None? And you widowered for a year? Here is a strange state of affairs. Do not tell me that you are one who prefers men to women? You, with those eyes and that way with you!"

"No, Highness. I find women very much to my taste. In especial, strong women! Rather than dainty misses and simpering girls."

"Ah!" The Queen moved distinctly closer, her ample charms prominent. "When we are speaking together thus near, Alex, call me Lady Isabella. It is less stiff, is it not? We shall have to find you a strong woman, then, shall we not? Of . . . experience!"

"I am in Your Majesty's capable hands!" he said, mildly.

Smiling, Isabella turned to speak with Mary — who was finding the Duke of Burgundy little trouble, a determined trencherman rather than an amorist evidently. Alex turned to the Count d'Armagnac, on his other side.

"You seemed concerned, my lord, that I should be offering liberality to the poor," he said. "I should be interested to hear why."

"Tell me, monsieur, why you do it — and I will tell you why I am concerned," the other answered.

"It is simple enough. I am here to seek French aid in the Scots' struggle to gain the release of our young King. But I am not here as a beggar. Scotland has much to offer France, as closer ally and also in trade. On the seas, especially. So, I demonstrate that we are no beggars. No more than that."

The Gascon looked at him keenly. "You are either very frank, monsieur — or very cunning!"

"I have no reason not to be frank. Our mission, although not official, is open for all to know. And I have no other concern or ambition here — save friendship with the French monarchy and people." Alex paused. "Now, my lord — *you* tell me why you are concerned at the alms-giving."

D'Armagnac took his time about answering. "The situation here in France is . . . delicate," he said, at length. "As you must know. The country is split in two great factions — Orleans and Burgundy. King Charles is . . . handicapped. I shall not speak at length on our differences. But they are deep, the more so since Louis of Orleans was murdered. I am of the Orleans persuasion, my daughter married to the young Duke."

320

"And this, my lord, is affected by the Scots liberality to the poor?"

"It could be, monsieur. In the north and east of France, Burgundy is most powerful; in the south and west, Orleans. In any question of power in France, Paris is ever important. Burgundy makes friends of the people here, woos them shamefully — the guilds, the merchants, the Lombards, even the Jews. And you — you come here from Flanders, Bruges, which he rules, distributing largesse to the people also."

"I see," Alex said slowly. "So you believe that I do this on the Duke's behalf? Or, at least, to gain his aid and support?"

"Why, yes. And he appears to favour you, monsieur."

"I had hoped that you *all* might favour me, favour my mission. May I assure you, my lord, that I have no least enmity against Orleans and its cause? Indeed, I do not understand your differences with Burgundy."

"I am glad to hear it, monsieur. May it continue. But . . . let me warn you against too great friendship with John of Burgundy. Me, I would prefer that one as enemy rather than friend. As he is! For he is dangerous, a man of blood. Do not trust him."

Alex toyed with his swan's leg, seethed in wine. "I have heard well of him, my lord. Is he not John the Fearless, who led a Crusade against the Infidel some years ago? A noted general."

"An incompetent general! And coward. Fearless for other men's lives! That Crusade of 1396 was a disaster. His whole army captured, almost without a blow struck. Did you know that the Sultan Bajayet had ten thousand Frenchmen and Flemings decapitated before Burgundy's eyes — ten thousand! At Nicopolis. Yet Fearless John returned to France unharmed!"

Alex swallowed — and was grateful that the Queen was once again turning to him.

"Your delightful aunt tells me that you are a musician, Monsieur Alex. A noted performer on the lute, likewise a poet. I am the more intrigued."

"My delightful aunt should hold to stricter truth, Lady Isabella! I strum a lute on occasion, yes — but feebly. As for my rhyming, it is but heavy stuff, uncouth versifying . . ."

"That I shall believe when I hear it. You shall write a song, for myself, and sing it to me, with your lute. Then we shall see who is the liar, your aunt or *you*, my friend! And that is a royal command." She lowered her voice huskily. "What has Bernard been telling you so seriously?"

"He, er, spoke of France's difficulties. Between the houses of Burgundy and Orleans. I fear that I am very ignorant."

"No doubt. And difficulties there are, the good God knows! But — do not believe all that Bernard tells you. He is a good soul. But on Burgundy he is scarcely to be trusted." She shrugged those fine white shoulders so near to his own. "For that matter, my friend, do not believe all that John of Burgundy tells you either. Of Bernard or of Orleans. If you are wise, Alex, you will heed all — but believe only *me*!"

"Ah! And wisdom, Highness, is enforced on us by Holy Writ, is it not . . . ?"

Alex was interrupted by a commotion at the far end of the salon. Men were pushing back their chairs and benches and rising to their feet, some women curtsying, everywhere people turning to look.

"So!" the Queen observed. "His Serene Majesty!" She laid a hand on Alex's arm. "No need to rise yet."

The odd figure of the Most Christian King took some time to appear from behind the standing guests, for he was making what might be termed a halting progress. Charles de Valois was quite alone, and moving along between the tables, pausing here and there to stare, to grin or frown, to stroke or fondle or slap, apparently indiscriminately, to take food from this platter or that, sometimes to sample, sometimes to throw away. After he had passed them, men and women sat down — although sometimes they had to rise again, for the monarch was just as apt to turn back as go forward. Once he grabbed somebody's goblet, drank a little, grimaced, spat out the mouthful, threw the half-empty goblet to the floor, and swinging round abruptly struck its owner across the face before lurching on.

"A pity," the Queen murmured. "Wine is good for him — it sends him to sleep! But he does not greatly like it, usually. Fear nothing, Alex — there is little real harm in him. He has returned to being a child, that is all. Although, even so, he can be acute still. Rise only if he comes near."

The Queen's 'if' rather than 'when' was revealed to be valid when presently her husband, pausing beside an overdressed gallant, suddenly pushed the young man roughly aside and sat down in his chair, turning to pull down beside him his curtsying partner. This lady was under- rather than overdressed, in the same fashion as Jamie's Countess Eloise, with particularly thrusting and pointed breasts, one of which projected proudly

322

independent, ringed in red paint. This the King began to play with enthusiastically, and quickly leaned over to wrench the bodice off the other shoulder, to reveal and compare its partner, the lady simpering but not unhelpful. Charles himself was scarcely overdressed, wearing stained white satin breeches with an old and tarnished military style long tunic, fastened askew.

"Good," Isabella commented. "He will be content for a little. If she will ply him with wine, all will be well."

The lady's escort discreetly removed himself elsewhere.

For once Alex was at a loss for suitable and courteous words. "Your Highness is . . . very understanding," was the best that he could do.

"My Highness has to be," she answered. "But we do none so ill. France has greater problems than Charles de Valois!"

The meal went on, with its interminable succession of courses, now mainly sweetmeats and most elaborate sculpted confections, the King spooning up a bowl of mixed fruits in honey in between fondling, squeezing and even sucking at his chosen partner, a sticky proceeding.

"Charles by no means always honours us," the Queen explained. "He has his own apartments and company. Peculiar company, as you may guess! He may well have left his own banquet to come here. Who knows why? And may return."

In France, evidently, as in Flanders, the entertainment took place after the repast was over, not throughout as it was apt to do in Scotland. And here it was not dancers, jugglers, fiddlers, performing bears or cavorting gipsies, but troubadours, wholly — or approximately — masculine, who sang stylised love-songs, soulful, sad or passionate, often to their own accompaniment on the lute, sometimes in close company of good-looking youths, with gestures romantic and semi-dramatic. Most of the performers were themselves courtiers, members of the dining company, not all unaffected by wine. It was a new experience for the Scots — who tended to find it slightly embarrassing and insufficiently robust.

Apparently King Charles was not a troubadour enthusiast either, for quite quickly he seemed to have had enough, and tiring of the lady's mammary delights and honeyed fruits both, got up to resume his perambulations — occasioning again considerable up-rising and sitting down. This time, after a wandering start, he came directly to the Queen's table — and all save Isabella herself rose to greet him. Charles ignored their bows and curtsies, his strange dark eyes fixed on Mary Stewart. Moving round the end of the long table, he came straight for her, with his odd stumpy walk.

Mary was no shrinking maid; but she tensed nevertheless as Majesty came up, her curtsy sketchy, her glance wary. Further down the table, Jamie Douglas had clenched his fists, his brow blacker than ever. Alex watched them all, carefully.

Charles stood beside Mary, chuckling, face close to her's. He reached out a not overclean hand — and hooted as involuntarily she started back. The hand went up to her head. She was not wearing the tall steeple-like headdress nor the lace-hung horns sported by many present, but was bareheaded save for a scatter of Tay pearls threaded on gossamer silk, as a sort of coif. The King stroked her hair, fingering the pearls.

As the hand strayed down towards the bare neck and throat, and Mary's smile grew fixed, Jamie stood back from his chair abruptly — despite the Countess Eloise's restraining hand on his arm. Up the table, Alex coughed warningly, and bowing to the still-seated Queen, moved behind her to the King's side, and Mary's.

"Sire," he said genially, "are not these pearls pleasing? Their colours? They grow only in one of our Scottish rivers. My aunt, the Princess, would perhaps present them to Your Majesty — as a token of our great esteem."

Mary's hands were up to disentangle the gossamer net of pearls from her hair before ever Alex had finished speaking, to thrust it at the monarch eagerly.

Charles took it with alacrity, holding the delicate thing up so that the pearls caught and reflected the light from the chandeliers, turning them this way and that to reveal the colours so much more pronounced than in normal pearls. He made a sort of crooning noise, his delight evident. Then he tried to put the net over his own lanky hair — but of course could not see it there, and snatched it off again.

"With your permission, Sire, allow me," Alex said. And taking the coif, held it against the straggling and honey-soaked royal beard, with most of the network hanging down the front of the stained tunic.

This seemed to please; but unfortunately there was no obvious way of keeping the thing in position. Mary solved the problem by reaching up again and extracting two slender bone pins, stained so as to be all but invisible in her own hair, used for

324

keeping the coif in place. She handed them to Alex. Showing them to the King, deftly he affixed the net to the beard, smoothing the rest to hang like a cravat, so that Charles could look down and admire it. Intrigued, the Most Christian King stroked and chortled.

Greatly bold, Alex took the preoccupied monarch and manoeuvred him to his own chair beside Isabella — who aided by ecstatically admiring her husband's new acquisition. Mary forgotten, Charles sat down happily.

With all seating themselves again, Alex would have moved away to find a seat elsewhere, but the King reached out to grasp his arm, continuing to hold it. Then, with the other hand grabbing Alex's goblet from the table, he gulped a mouthful before holding it up for his benefactor to drink likewise. Still he clung to his arm.

So Alex remained standing at the royal side, drinking draught for draught, with servitors hurrying to refill the goblet. The troubadours resumed their entertainment.

Presently, as Isabella had foretold, the wine sent her royal spouse to sleep. And once asleep, it seemed, he remained asleep. At the Queen's command, he was carried off to his own quarters, snoring.

In the commotion this entailed the Scots took the opportunity to request permission to retire. This was graciously granted — save for one reservation. Isabella insisted that Alex Stewart remained behind, at her side. He would be escorted back to the Tin Plate in due course. The night apparently was yet young.

Bowing their way out, Mary murmured to her husband. "I think that Alex will require to defend *himself* against royal favours hereafter! Believe you he will be so instant on his own behalf as he was on mine?"

"Perhaps not. He admires older women, with minds of their own. But — thank God he dealt with that Charles as he did, back there! Another moment and I would have been taking a hand. And less . . . delicately! *Lèse majesté* or none."

"Yes, I feared that — what fear I had to spare! You might have been locked in some cell by now. And I also — for I could not have borne his handling."

"Aye. God — and Alex — preserve us from a mad king!"

"Amen! At least, Jamie, my curious half-brother Robert does not behave so!"

Her husband grunted.

XIX

SO STARTED A stay in Paris of almost twelve weeks. The
duration of their visit had been undetermined from the first,
dependent upon various factors. Most important of course
was the achieving of results, the object of the mission, the gaining
of aid towards the release of young King James. In the peculiar
governmental state in which they found France this was obviously not easy of attainment. Had King Charles been entirely
insane it might have been simpler, in that the rule would then
have been taken right out of his hands and exercised either by a
regent or a council of State. But though mad in some respects,
reverting to infantile and fatuous ways much of the time, he
had periods of comparative lucidity if not normality, even a kind
of cunning and shrewdness — and he had, after all, been quite
a good and able monarch prior to his mental collapse, popular
enough with his people to have gained the title of Charles the
Well Beloved. He still ruled his country after an erratic fashion,
pulled this way and that by competing interests, his wife, the
Church, and the Burgundian and Orleans factions. All these
Alex sought to influence, with varying success — although he made
little progress with the churchmen. But in the nature of things,
any real decision, or even consideration, was hard to
attain.

Another factor affecting the length of their stay was the news
from Scotland. Alex had arranged, as far as was possible, for a
relay of messages to reach him, via Aberdeen vessels trading
with the Low Countries; and fairly regular information did
arrive by this means. There was no permanent Scots ambassador
to the Court of France, meantime, the system being to send
special envoys as required; but there was considerable coming
and going of churchmen to and from Avignon — where Pope
Benedict the Thirteenth, recognised by both Scotland and

326

France, was established, in opposition to Pope Gregory the Twelfth at Rome — and these were a further source of information. From both sources they learned much of interest. First and most important, that the Privy Council had had to defer consideration and decision on the earldom of Mar, in the Earl's absence — postponed until September. That the Earl John of Buchan had become betrothed to the young Elizabeth, daughter of the Earl of Douglas — clearly a match of policy since the child was only nine years old. On the same theme, the said Earl of Douglas had finally broken his parole with King Henry, refusing to return to captivity in England, and sending instead a ransom reputed to be of fifty thousand merks, presumably the value he set upon himself — Henry's reaction not specified. Douglas had declared that he could not possibly leave Scotland whilst his old enemy and rival, the turncoat Earl of Dunbar and March, was welcomed back by the Regent. Yet the same Douglas was reported to have entered into a mutual support bond with Albany, and been given Dunbar's great lordship of Annandale in return. In the light of all this, the betrothal of his daughter to Albany's son John might have especial significance. Other news was that the Regent's nephew, Donald of the Isles, was said to be involved in heavy fighting in Ireland, with fair success but objectives unclear.

All this, although interesting, did not add up to any urgent requirement for Alex to return home; indeed, clearly any return before the autumn's meeting of the Council was inadvisable. But there was another factor to be taken into account regarding the length of their stay, and that was money. Alex did not want to draw in his horns, seem to tarnish the princely image he had been at such pains to build up, by any evident economies. But maintaining the large company and keeping up open house at the Sign of the Tin Plate, was digging deeper and deeper into even the large funds he had brought. And siller, or the lack of it, might eventually cut short their visit — however galling this might be in the midst of all the wealth and extravagance of the French Court.

Meantime, however, the situation was not without achievements and gains. Alex's success with the Queen, perhaps was not to be wondered at, good-looking, personable and attractive to women as he was. But his impact on the King was scarcely to be expected. Nevertheless, from that incident of Mary Stewart's pearled coif onwards, he became a favourite of the curious monarch, embarrassingly so. The very next day he received a command to attend on the King, and thereafter had difficulty in escaping. Charles found him understanding, patient and companionable — though courteously firm when the monarch became too indecent or outrageous, and surprisingly was then usually heeded. Isabella, indeed, rather ruefully admitted that he had a better influence on her husband than had any other at Court, herself included. And fairly clearly Charles tended to be on his best behaviour when Alex was present — which was all too often for the latter's comfort. The King had a besetting fear of being poisoned, not unnatural perhaps considering what had happened to so many of his family, which was one reason for his habit of drinking from other people's wine-cups and eating from their plates; and he appointed Alex to be an extra Cup Bearer, requiring him to stand or sit at his side at meals, when he frequently fed him tid-bits once they had been duly passed as edible by his new friend. Fortunately Charles slept a great deal, otherwise Alex's life would have been restricted to the point of desperation; his abnormality seemed to tire him excessively, and not only wine made him sleepy. Once his eyes were closed he was apt to sleep for hours, like a child, scarcely wakenable — as often as not now clutching the pearled coif.

At least, Alex felt, if he could persuade others to help with King James, King Charles would not withhold royal permission.

His endeavours to convince the real rulers of France were only partially successful. The Queen was fairly sympathetic but played him along, emphasising the divided state of the country, the inadvisability of foreign adventures at present, the dangers of English reprisals. The Duke of Burgundy was encouraging but vague, indicating general agreement but never committing himself to actual plans. Count d'Armagnac temporised and showed no enthusiasm. And the Archbishop was consistently hostile. All dreaded the English power, clearly, with Henry still claiming much of France as his own, despite the extended truce. The divided country was in no state to take on an aggressive Plantagenet.

It was during one of their many forenoon discussions of this intractable problem at the Tin Plate — Alex being apt to be elsewhere of an evening and night — that Jamie Douglas mooted a new approach.

"I was speaking with a captain of the King's Scots Archer Guard. He told me that some years ago he took part in a French expedition to aid Owen Glendower's rising against the English.

328

They landed in Wales and fought with the Welsh for two months, winning as far as Worcester. Glendower was defeated, to be sure, and the French returned home. But — it gave me a notion . . ."

"Wales? I fear that horse is dead, Jamie . . ."

"Not Wales — Ireland. See you, the French would *like* to strike against the English, for they know that Henry intends to attack France sooner of later. But they dare not mount an invasion of England. You will never get that, Alex — or even the threat of it. But Ireland, now — that might be a different story. Ireland is the weakest link in England's chain, ever in revolt, a quagmire for English blood and treasure. A French expedition to Ireland could be a grievous threat to Henry. Yet a deal less costly than any attack on England itself."

"True. True — but Henry would conceive it as such, and retaliate in the same fashion."

"I think not. For one thing, as we learned in London, the English nobles are weary of fighting in Irish bogs, where they gain nothing and lose much. But, more important, it could be made to seem no attack on the *English* themselves. But aid for the Irish against Donald of the Isles! Donald is laying waste in the North, we hear — no doubt at Henry's behest, as part of the price to gain English aid for his later attempt for the Scots throne. But meantime it is but an Islesmen's invasion of Ulster. O'Neill, or other of the Irish kinglets, could appeal to France for aid — or be said to have done so. A French force could land in the North of Ireland — and not, on the face of it, seem to be aimed at England at all. Though Henry would not fail to see the threat. But his nobles would not feel bound to act. And this would suit Scotland very well, would it not? Keeping Donald engaged in Ireland, instead of troubling us."

"Dear God, Jamie — you are right! That black head of yours is shrewdly set. This is something to work on. We might persuade the French to *this*. A limited endeavour, not costly — but a major threat to Henry nevertheless. And Donald given pause in his ambitions. Yes, I like that. If only . . . if only my siller will last out, whilst I seek persuade them! My purse is running low. These Paris burghers have vast bellies! Keeping them filled costs more than I had bargained for."

"Need you continue with this expense, man? This keeping of open house here? It has served its turn. You are close to the King — if not closer to the Queen!"

329

"No. I would not wish to stop this liberality, Jamie. It has paid us well, got us where we are, proved that we are not beggars. It has enabled me to ask aid, openly, as a prince would. Lacking any mandate from the Scots Regent and Council, I require to make such gestures. To stop them now would be unfortunate, much commented on. It might cost our cause dear."

Mary, who had been listening to all this, spoke up. "I know naught of statecraft and war, of how to persuade the French to aid you in that," she said. "But in another way, I think, they might do so. John of Burgundy tells me how besotted they all are here with tourneys and displays of knightly prowess. The other side of this languishing troubadour nonsense. The King, in especial, dotes on such contests. Burgundy says that Charles offers goblets of gold pieces to the winners of bouts, on occasion. You, Alex, are proficent at this, I believe? And have the King's ear. You can scarce ask him for money, but you might *win* it."

"Ah!" that man said thoughtfully.

"You unhorsed the English Earl of Kent, did you not? Something of a champion, was he not? Would these Frenchmen prove more difficult?"

"M'mm. I cannot seem to fight for money, Mary. I would have to have a reason for jousting. To challenge or be challenged. Dispute for a lady's favours would serve. But . . . I can scarce choose any other than the Queen, in this present pass. And I could by no means challenge any openly for *her* favours! And, too, I wish to make no enemies here, while our business is unresolved."

"A pity that Holy Church does not go in for jousting!" Jamie observed. "That Archbishop has been against us from the first. No risk of making a new enemy there. You will just have to seek opportunity to make a challenge, Alex. That D'Armagnac should not prove difficult!"

"No. I must not offend the Orleans party any more than the Burgundian. The Italians, now, are scarcely popular — over this Papal dispute. Perhaps I could find a Lombard to fight, or a Florentine. Or for that matter a Castillian. But . . . he would have to be a man of repute in arms . . ."

In fact, this aspect of the problem solved itself only two days later. The Queen announced to Alex that an envoy had arrived from England, the Earl of Warwick, on a mission concerned with Henry's claim to the revenues of the duchy of Aquitaine — an unpopular subject, naturally. He would be given an official audience the next evening. She suggested that some of the Scots might be interested to attend. The usual banquet would follow.

So Alex and some of his party joined the splendidly-dressed throng waiting in the Throne Room of the Louvre the next afternoon, to see how an *official* ambassador was received. The royal couple came in, to the usual flourish of trumpets, flanked by the Archer Guard, Charles finely clad for once but eating an apple, Isabella's arm firmly tucked through his. They seated themselves on the two thrones on the low dais — although the King almost immediately got to his feet again, to peer around him. Mary Stewart involuntarily drew in behind her husband.

Then, after a pause, another door was thrown open and a herald announced the presence of the most illustrious Monsieur Henry Beauchamp, Comte de Warwick — he pronounced it Vark — Envoy Extraordinary of the King of England, seeking audience of His Most Christian Majesty. Long live the King!

Warwick stalked into the Throne Room, escorted by two more Archers, bowed stiffly, advanced three more steps, bowed again, and advanced to near the dais. He was a heavily-made man of early middle age, clean-shaven, square-featured, indeed square-built altogether, with a stumping short-legged walk. He had a reputation as a soldier and looked the part, with a distinctly aggressive mien and determined mouth. He looked in little doubt, likewise, as to the unpopularity of his mission. Charles sat down and eyed him somewhat askance, spitting apple-skin on the floor.

From behind the thrones the Archbishop, who was acting Chancellor, spoke. "His Most Christian Majesty graciously welcomes your lordship to his Court. And would scrutinise your mandate from his royal cousin, Henry of England."

Warwick nodded, stepped closer, drawing from his doublet a heavily-sealed roll of parchment, and making a gesture of dropping on one knee, held this out to Charles.

"With this, Highness, I bring warm and cordial greetings from my lord King Henry," he jerked. He spoke clipped but clear French — for he had spent years of exile in France, with Henry, when the latter was Earl of Derby and banished from Richard the Second's England.

Charles found the great seal of interest, peering at both sides of it. But he did not unroll the parchment. Nor did he say anything.

The Archbishop came forward to take the roll. But frowning, the King clung to the seal, and at a tug the two parted company.

Coughing, the prelate drew back, and unfolding the document, commenced to read its contents aloud. It was in fair French, to the effect that Henry, by the Grace of God King of England, High King of Ireland, Prince of Wales, Lord Paramount of Scotland, Duke of Aquitaine, warmly greeted . . . and so on.

Charles quickly wearied of this, and rising to his feet the better to scan the company, soon identified Alex Stewart. Grinning happily, he stepped down from the dais, brushing past Warwick without a glance, and hurried to Alex's side, England's seal held out to show him. Isabella raised resigned shoulders, the courtiers, used to this sort of thing, merely smiled discreetly, and the Archbishop went on reading the credentials. But the Earl of Warwick frowned darkly, toe tapping on the tiled floor.

Alex made a point of examining the beeswax seal at much length, to give the prelate time to finish, Charles pointing out details. But it was a particularly long-winded document of introduction, concerned to make it entirely clear that in sending this eminent envoy to negotiate payment of his Aquitanian revenues, Henry was in no way admitting or conceding His Majesty of France's lawful superiority, rights or concern in the matter, Aquitaine being a Plantagenet fief, independent of the Crown of France.

Charles de Valois was not long in having enough of this also. Taking Alex's arm, he turned and pushed through the bowing throng, for the door. Sighing, the Queen rose, held out her arm to the affronted ambassador, and followed her lord. The Archers hurried to take up some sort of position, theirs a difficult and unpredictable task.

The King made for another huge salon, even larger than that in which the Scots' first banquet had been held, all set for the feasting, with servitors waiting. All but dragging Alex, he went directly to his place at the centre of the top table, and sitting down clapped his hands for service to commence. He pointed for Alex to take the seat at his right; but that man carefully stood back.

The Queen came up, with a glowering Warwick, and took her chair, two to the right of her husband, and indicated for the Englishman to take the seat between — the same to which Charles had gestured Alex.

Warwick sat down and Alex remained behind the King's chair.

Charles looked up at his friend, and then glared at the envoy. Leaning over, he pushed at Warwick, telling him to be gone in no uncertain terms.

Urgently the Queen spoke. "Charles — this is where King Henry's representative *should* sit, at this audience banquet. Alex may sit at your other side. Or here, next me."

The King scowled.

Alex bent to his ear. "Sire — I would prefer to stand here. At your back. To serve you the better. I can see better that all is well."

Charles stared from him to Warwick, made a face at the latter, and then pulled the Scot forward so as to place him, standing, between the two chairs. Thus he hid the Englishman — to whom he had clearly taken a powerful dislike — from his sight.

So the repast proceeded, Alex plying Charles with food and drink, eating and drinking little himself, ignored by Warwick, frequently smiled at by Isabella.

In due course the King fell asleep and was carried off, as usual. Alex was able to sit down in the vacated chair, Warwick pointedly turning a square shoulder towards him.

Presently, with the time for the entertainment arrived, at the Queen's command, Alex led off by rendering, troubadour fashion, the song he had composed about Isabella:

> One thousand three hundred and four-score year
> > After the birth of our Lord dear,
> > The dark Ysabel of Danubius' banks
> > Was matched to the heir of all the Franks;
> A child of wit and elegance,
> > At the age of twelve she came to France;
> Like an alpine rose of high Bavaire
> > She bloomed anew in a lowland fair;
> Changing Danubius' banks for Seine,
> > To live and love and charm and reign . . .

And so on, pedestrian stuff enough but redeemed by flashes of humour, drollery and eloquent expression, the man accompanying himself on the lute. He had a fine tenor voice, and if he sang with less than the usual languishing sentimentality, he made up for it by his allusions, extravagances and near-comic postures, whilst always skilfully remaining the Queen's worshipful gallant. He soon had his hearers laughing delightedly, Isabella most of all. He was rewarded with much applause, a warm royal embrace and powerful kiss, on his return to his place.

The plaudits were not joined in by Henry Beauchamp, however. Continuing to ignore his neighbour until a break in the

333

proceedings, preparatory to a change over to dancing, allowed him decently to seek and obtain the Queen's permission to retire, he turned at last to Alex.

"You, sir, are, I understand, the notorious freebooter, Earl of Mar so-called, who has been pirating our English shipping and attacking King Henry's interests?" That was bluntly said.

"Say privateering, my lord," Alex answered, as lightly as he might. "It scarcely becomes your good King Henry to complain of pirating, moreover, after his waylaying, capture and imprisonment of the King of Scots. But . . . perhaps we might discuss this elsewhere, at another time?"

"That boy, sir, is safer in the Tower, as you know well, than in his own barbarous realm. And I hope that I may be spared any further discussion with you at any other time."

"You have my sympathy, in the last. The first, however, is but your contention. I contest it, my lord. But, might I remind you that King James would have been *here*, not in Scotland, had Henry not unlawfully and in time of truce seized his ship?"

"He is very well, in all respects, where he is — pirate!"

"Ha! So you would challenge me, my lord of Warwick?"

"Not I. I challenge only my peers! I but name you what you are — a pirate, a rogue and the bastard of a rogue!"

The smack of Alex's back-handed slap across the other's square face resounded through the hushed salon.

"Then *I* challenge you, Warwick! Eat your ill-mannered words. Or support them before all, with lance and sword, so soon as you may."

"Curse you, oaf!" The older man's clenched fists and quivering voice testified to his tight-held fury. "You shall weep blood for that! Ill-begotten bastard's blood. I will teach you not to strike an earl of England!"

"I shall look forward to the lesson, sir. So soon as it can be arranged. With Their Majesties' royal permission. Meanwhile, we both should humbly seek Queen Isabella's gracious clemency for our boorishness in her presence." Alex spread his hands wide, to the Queen. Belatedly Warwick jerked a nod, and turned to stride to the door.

Isabella, frowning, looked regally displeased. But when, after a moment or two, she came closer to him she looked anxious rather. "Alex, my dear, I may perhaps forgive you the ill behaviour — since you were much provoked. But . . . was that wise? I have heard that man is a noted warrior."

334

"Ah, but you must not believe all that you hear, Highness — you told me so yourself! After all, the same has been said about myself, I am told — despite my bastard blood! And . . . once you have forgiven me for the behaviour, you will thank me for the sport to come, no?"

She did not answer, but took his arm to lead off the dancing.

*   *   *

It took almost a week to organise the joust — for, of course, the opportunity was taken to turn the occasion into a full-scale tournament with numerous lesser contests supporting the main event. It all aroused great enthusiasm and heavy wagering, King Charles in especial waxing gleeful and, in theory at least, superintending all. The lists were set up in the huge parade-ground and archery butts of the royal bodyguard, and large quantities of soil and sand brought in and strewn on the ground — peat being little known here — and pavilions, awnings and tentage erected, with floral and heraldic decorations. One side of the four-sided enclosure was reserved for the populace. Fortunately it had not been necessary tactfully to prime the King on the subject of chalices of gold pieces, he volunteering these prizes from the first, with a specially large one for his *cher ami* Alex, apparently whether he won or lost.

It was a steamy hot late-August afternoon when the trumpets sounded and the royal party arrived. To, as it were, warm up the great company, comic jousters first took the arena, to clown and caper mock battles wherein lances bent and snapped, sword-hilts parted from their blades, armour fell off to reveal stark naked heroes, and ancient bony nags competed against tiny ponies.

The spectators suitably humoured, an introductory bout was staged between two groups of sword-fighters, wholly armoured, four a side, Gascons against Normans, who were to fight it out to a finish, the side with one or more remaining on their feet at the end winning. It was, to be sure, a fairly unedifying spectacle, of slow-motion banging and clanging, with little of finesse or skill demonstrated or possible — since men totally sheathed in steel cannot wield heavy swords in any other than a ponderous and hacking fashion, the motion indeed growing slower and slower as weariness set in. Sheer percussion and shock within the armour-plating represented success since no penetration was likely and one by one the contestants dropped, stunned, or lost the use of numbed limbs, until there were only two left upright, both Gascons — who possibly were less affected by the heat than were the Northerners.

This triumphant if exhausted pair, egged on by the crowd, then turned on each other, to slog it out, until one's sword dropped from nerveless grasp and he sank down creakingly on all fours on the soil and so remained, and the victor went staggering off towards the royal box in zigzag style to receive his prize. When he removed his helm, before the excited monarch, it was to reveal, surprisingly, the bald head and sagging cheeks of a man in late middle years. The cheers were loud and long.

Then it was the turn of the principal contenders, and a change in the entire atmosphere became evident. The procedure was now formal and deliberate. Trumpets preceded a royal herald who announced in measured but ringing tones that the illustrious Henri, Comte de Warwick, of England, envoy of the King of England himself, would meet the equally illustrious Alexander, Comte de Mar, of Scotland, cousin of the King of Scots, in full battle on a field of honour, with lance and sword, the challenger being the Monsieur de Mar. Let the best knight win. Then, from opposite ends of the lists the champions rode out, fully armoured and accoutred, helmed but visors up, to meet in the centre, bow stiffly in their saddles, and turn to salute the royal pair, lances raised, before pacing slowly back to their own bases, where their respective banners hung limply over their supporters. Both were splendid in polished, gleaming steel-plating and chain-mail, borrowed necessarily, but with the breast-plates and shields painted for the occasion with the colours and emblems of their houses.

It was not Alex Stewart's fault that what followed was anti-climax, that he was prevented from demonstrating to a keyed-up and critical audience that he was his father's son in this at least and a match for any England, or France itself, could throw against him. It was not really Warwick's fault either — only unfortunate circumstance and ill luck. For, despite the fact that Alex had sent him information beforehand that he intended to use a light horse, in the Scots fashion, recognising that the other would choose what suited him best, the Englishman had elected to borrow a huge and most massive mount from the royal stables. This, covered in the conventional plate armour also, made a mighty and impressive sight, which caused Alex's ordinary riding-horse, fine Barbary stallion as it was, with only

336

linen, lion-rampant-painted trappings, to look like a whippet before a mastiff. The crowd did not fail to draw uncomplimentary comparisons.

These changed their tune however once the trumpets blew again, and at vastly differing speeds now the antagonists rode at each other, lances levelled. Alex, meeting his opponent more than two-thirds of the way to his base, proceeded to demonstrate all the advantages of pace, lightness, manoeuvrability and a familiar mount, feinting, veering, rearing away, making rings around his enemy, in a fashion which soon had the spectators laughing almost as much as at the clowns' efforts. If Warwick had been content to stand in one place, pivoting his destrier round on its rear hooves, horse and rider secure behind their armour-plating and all but unassailable, he might well have tired out his spirited attacker and remained fresh for a final powerful thrust. But instead of doing so, he lost his proud temper at this wretched display of monkey-tricks, and lashed out savagely but ineffectually time and again, forcing his ponderous steed to twistings and turnings and labourings for which it was quite unfitted. As a result, the brute not only tired first and quickly, but soon became totally unmanageable. It eventually lumbered to the side of the lists, where it stood immovable, despite all its rider's frenzied efforts. Alex ranged to and fro for a little, concerned at this ridiculous and utterly tame outcome; but as the crowd's jeers and epithets rose to a crescendo, drove in from the flank and swiftly, simply, unseated the unhappy and all but helpless Warwick, who crashed to the ground. Here, at the listside where no real fighting had been anticipated, little soil or sand had been spread. The impact was accordingly heavy. Henry Beauchamp lay still within his fine armour.

Men came running, Jamie Douglas from Alex's own support team amongst them. They loosened and removed Warwick's helmet, to reveal an unconscious man, purple of face and breathing stertorously. Raising his own visor Alex shrugged, saluted his fallen adversary, and to mixed jeers, laughter and cheers, reined round and trotted off towards the royal box.

He received a rapturous and uncritical welcome from Charles de Valois at least, and rather more than the traditional queen-of-the-tournament's salute from Isabella. Also the so-necessary chalice of gold pieces, to which was added a gold chain and jewel as keepsake from the Queen. But nothing could make it a triumph or a credit to anyone, Alex was the first to assert.

Few were the sympathetic enquiries for the Earl of Warwick, symptomatic of contemporary French hostility for England — although Alex himself made a point of ascertaining that the other was not seriously injured.

A Scots stay of a week or two longer in Paris, was paid for. But it was necessary to make such stay productive.

*　　*　　*

Try as he would, Alex's success remained only partial. Perhaps he should not have expected more, in the then state of France. He obtained agreement to the principle of an Irish expedition, limited in size but to be mounted soon, before winter set in. If it proved effective and successful, the small French expeditionary force could be reinforced in the spring, as greater pressure on Henry. The Duke of Burgundy it was who accepted responsibility for this — although he could not commit himself to personally leading the venture, since he could not afford to leave France for any length of time lest D'Armagnac and the Orleans faction took advantage. The Queen added her acceptance of this. And that seemed to be as far as they were going to get.

The Scots decided that it was time to be gone. But breaking loose was not easy, with King and Queen both urgent for them to stay — at least, for Alex to stay. Their popularity was now something of a disadvantage.

The disengaging process lasted for a full week longer than they had intended, and lack of funds was again beginning to loom large when, at length, they were able to close up their over-successful establishment at the Sign of the Tin Plate and make their farewells. Alex was able to use as excuse the information that apparently the bulk of Burgundy's proposed Irish force was to come from his province of Flanders, and the advisability therefore that he himself should go there in person to help whip up enthusiasm for the venture, time now being pressing, with September already upon them.

The farewell Louvre banquet was a notable occasion, prolonged until dawn on the day of their departure — although long before that time King Charles had been carried off, not so much asleep as unconscious, and indeed Isabella and Alex himself had been unseen for some time.

With sore heads, empty pockets but a distinct feeling of relief, then, the unofficial Scots embassage rode out of Paris north-eastwards, leaving behind multiple promises to return when possible, the Auld Alliance most certainly the firmer for their visit. Some, at least, were longing to be home in Scotland.

The journey back through Vermandois and Picardy to the Flanders plain, however, with its contrasts of war, anarchy, ruin and near-famine, renewed their doubts as to the reliability and effectiveness of a regime which could so mismanage a fair land.

At Bruges they were faced with unexpected problems. They found the great city in a stir, and far from being in a position to muster troops for any Irish adventure. It was involved, albeit unwillingly, in raising forces for a military confrontation much nearer home — something John of Burgundy had omitted to mention. It seemed that the peculiar Lord Anton of Brabant, amongst his other responsibilities, was eager to assume episcopal ones. He had indeed had himself elected Prince-Bishop of Liège — by what electorate was not entirely clear, and the fact that he was not in holy orders apparently no handicap. The bishopric, admittedly, was no ordinary one. It had enormous revenues and carried with it a princeship of the Holy Roman Empire and the title of Duke of Bouillon, also the suffraganship to the arch-bishopric of Cologne, which was one of the Electors of the Empire and probably its greatest eccleciastical power. Unfortunately for Anton, the citizens of Liège, egged on by the diocesan chapter and canons, had elected a different nominee as Bishop, in the person of one Heinrich Horn, who was daring to contest the Lord Anton's right. This might have been dealt with in suitable summary fashion, had it not been for the fact that this Horn's father was a rich and powerful lord, with his own influence and support within the Emperor's hierarchy, as well as in Holy Church: moreover the latter had obtained for him the backing of Pope Gregory the Twelfth, in Rome — whereas, of course, Anton was a supporter of and supported by Pope Benedict the Thirteenth, at Avignon. So there was nothing for it, apparently, but to settle the issue in the only really effective way, by the sword. Anton, as it happened, was not much of a soldier and though besieging Liège, was not achieving much thereby, and calling for ever more troops. In the circumstances, Bruges was not in a state to take recruiting for any Irish expedition very seriously.

As well as this, a spell of unseasonably bad weather had hit Northern Europe, and the *Greysteel*, which should have been waiting for them at Sluys, had not put in an appearance. The Bruges authorities were as hospitable as ever, but advancement of the travellers' plans was annoyingly held up. Endless eating and drinking was beginning to pall on the more frugal Scots.

They all summoned up what patience they could muster.

With still no sign of Robert Davidson in *Greysteel* a week later, they were surprised by the arrival at Bruges of the Duke of Burgundy himself, in some style. And it did not take him long to reveal the reason for his journey from Paris. It was to persuade the illustrious Earl of Mar and his renowned Scots knights to go to the aid of his brother Anton outside Liège. Their military ability and prestige was famed all over Europe, it seemed, and nothing would more quickly bring to an end this ridiculous and wicked rebellion, he contented, than their appearance in his brother's camp.

Needless to say the last thing that Alex desired was to get himself involved in a military campaign in Flanders at this stage — even though the prospect of some more spirited activity appeared to commend itself to some of his younger lieutenants, after too much courtiership, feasting and the like. He made known his reluctance very plainly, whereupon the Duke, in the friendliest possible way, pointed out that the troops with Anton represented his main available forces, and until they were free of their commitments at Liège they would not be available for adventures anywhere else.

This, naturally, greatly upset the Scots, Jamie in especial. It was sheerest blackmail, and he said so in no uncertain terms. They all resented being tricked and made use of, thus.

But Alex pointed out, in his reasonable way, that if the Irish expedition was indeed dependent upon a quick finish to this Liège controversy, and their involvement could aid in that, then it might not be too high a price to pay. It all required thought and discussion.

To assist in this process, John the Fearless brought in reinforcements in the shape, the voluptuous shape, of his sister, the Duchess of Holland, a large lady of ample proportions and major curves, supported by a bevy of beauties — whose duty clearly was to convince the Scots that it would be well worth while lingering for somewhat longer in Flanders. It seemed, indeed, that all this pulchritude was intended to accompany the warriors to Liège, warfare here evidently being conducted on a different scale and tempo from the Scottish custom — which perhaps helped to account for the Lord Anton's lack of any swift success in his endeavours.

Whilst all this was being coped with and debated, *Greysteel* arrived at Sluys, and Robert Davidson came on to Bruges, cursing the weather and declaring that he had been blown across almost to Norway. The main items of his news from Scotland were that the Privy Council had still not sat to decide on the Mar earldom case; and that Donald MacDonald was said to be back in his Isles, but he had left most of his force in Ulster under his brothers Alastair Carrach and Ian Mor, presumably to winter there — which seemed to imply that there might well be a seasonal lull in his campaign for Irish hegemony, to be resumed in the spring.

The effect of this information on Alex was somewhat to relax the pressure on him, both for any speedy return to Scotland and for the need for haste over the Irish-French project. The immediacy of requirement, for a start before the winter storms, was removed, making a larger and better-organised spring campaign more practical. He did not tell the Duke this meantime, however, since clearly he was a man who required no encouragement to put off action. In the circumstances, the Liège interlude might not be so objectionable.

Jamie Douglas was otherwise minded. They were being tricked and used, and to his more uncompromising mind, that ruled out any co-operation. Moreover, Mary wanted to get home, and so did he. *He* had a family at Lochindorb, even if Alex had not. Their womenfolk should not be dragged off on a warfare adventure, to Liège or elsewhere. Moreover, Donald of the Isles could not be assured to lie quiet until the spring.

The other accepted the force of much of this; but believed that if he could indeed put Burgundy much in his debt over Liège, one of the main objectives of their entire expedition would be brought much nearer fruition. It was not often that these two disagreed. But at length a compromise was worked out. Jamie and some few of the older Scots would return, in *Greysteel*, with the womenfolk, forthwith, to Scotland. And Alex with the others would go assist the Lord Anton to gain his bishopric — and with it apparently, the vitally important electorship of the Empire — thereafter to return home when Robert Davidson could bring his ship back for them, hopefully before Yule.

Not everybody was happy about this — especially the Scots ladies, who viewed the Duchess of Holland and her entourage with grave suspicion.

341

XX

IT WAS GOOD to be home amongst the great heather hills of Braemoray, so much more dramatic and satisfying than the level landscapes of the Low Countries and France. It was a joy, too, to be with the young people again now in lively adolescence and requiring their parents — even if they gave little impression of realising it. Mariota de Athyn rejoiced to see them, and Mary at least declared that she had had enough of foreign lands and foreign ways to last her for the rest of her days.

Jamie, however, was inconsistent, according to his wife. It did not take him long to be almost wishing that he was back with Alex and his friends in Flanders. He recognised that this was folly, that he was so much better here, that this was where he *ought* to be. But his mind constantly was drawn over the seas to what might be going on at Liège and Bruges and Sluys. Not that he lacked for work here, and useful occupation, or failed to appreciate the satisfaction of a full, ordered and family life. But . . .

He was by no means housebound at Lochindorb, either. He got in touch with Earl John of Buchan, gave him some account of their doings abroad and gained in return a summary of the present situation in Scotland. Albany his father, Buchan said, was growing ever more concerned about the activities of Donald of the Isles, which he had seemed to dismiss for so long as of little account. He was not actually seeking to interfere in the affairs of the North, but was urging on his son the need for constant vigilance and the drawing up of plans for mobilising men at short notice and in major numbers. He had little faith in the Highlanders themselves as any bulwark against attack by the Islesmen; but the low country lairds of Angus, the Mearns, Aberdeenshire, Buchan, Banff and Moray must be warned, and ordered to have their maximum forces ready. The Earl of Douglas was similarly making mustering arrangements in the Borders, to be in a position to repel any English invasion timed to coincide with Donald's. These considerations, with the financial ones attendant upon supplying and maintaining large armed forces, was tending to preoccupy the Regent's government to the exclusion of others, and there was little else of importance going on apparently. The Highlands themselves were now alive with rumours of Donald's intended descent upon them, as never before; and certainly threats were being spoken of on all hands as to what would happen to Highland chiefs who opposed, or even failed to support, the Islesmen.

John Stewart thought that it was high time that his cousin Alex came home.

Jamie, for his part, did what he could towards readying forces for mobilisation. But his influence with the Aberdeen and Moray lairds was slight, and with the Gaelic-speaking clans of the glens less so. He made some impact on various of the Clan Chattan federation chieftains such as Macpherson of Cluny, MacGillivray of Dunmaglass, Shaw of Rothiemurchus, and the Cattanach — all very much within the orbit of the lordship of Badenoch; but with the Captain of Clan Chattan, the Mackintosh himself, a kinsman of Donald's and making hostile noises, it was difficult for a lowlander to achieve much. It was even reported that their former MacLeod allies, Ian Borb and his brother, were lining up on Donald's side, despite their father's disapproval. It was that sort of situation which was developing in the North and West, houses divided against themselves; and it would be a bold stranger indeed who would seek to intervene. Actually Mariota de Athyn's influence was much more effective than Jamie's. She was a Mackay of Strathnaver, her name but an Anglo-Normanisation of Mac Aodh, the Sons of Hugh. She sent warnings and urgings to her own people in the far North, in Caithness, Sutherland and Ross, and obtained encouraging assurances.

Winter closed the passes and the seasonal sort of hibernation set in over the Highland scene, at least insofar as travel was concerned. Yuletide passed pleasantly enough, but without any sign of Alex Stewart. Robert Davidson had taken *Greysteel* to the Low Countries once again, in November, complaining about weather conditions and the hare-brained schemes of lordly ones with insufficient to do; but had not, so far, returned

343

to Aberdeen. It was, in fact, a Flemish shipmaster trading with Aberdeen who brought the letter from Alex. It was addressed from the Castle of Duffel, in Brabant.

It read:

I fear, Jamie, that it will be after Yuletide before you receive this, if receive it you ever do. I shall not be home so soon as I thought. Much has happened to delay me. For one, I am wed again. You will not approve, I swear, my sober friend. Indeed, a whisper in your ear, I am beginning to have some doubts my own self, in a small way. The lady is the Countess Marie of Duffel, and I have no complaints as to her person and attractions. The difficulty is otherwise. She is most handsome, and by no means unkind in her body. She was one of the Duchess of Holland's ladies, and indeed the greatest heiress in the dukedom. You may remember her. When at length we won for them the Liège battle — of which I shall tell you hereafter — nothing would do but that I must have this lady and her wealth in reward. It cost the Dukes nothing. All call Liège a notable victory, and Alex Stewart's fame as general resounds through the courts of Europe, I am assured. I was to be a rich man, in consequence, and Count of Duffel forby.

Alas, I am not certain whether or no I am even Count of Duffel, and as yet none the richer. For my lady, who was but recently widowed, from one Baron Thierry de Lienden now whispered to have been poisoned no less, it appears omitted before that to gain a bill of divorcement from the earlier husband, the Count of Beveland. Some confusion, with this problem of the two Popes, at Rome and Avignon, the divorcement by way of falling between them. So I can scarcely claim to be wed, after all. And the lady's family have close fists and are loth to loosen their grip on her fortune.

I can, I think, now hear Black James Douglas muttering that if he had been there none of this folly would have been allowed to happen.

There is more to it than this, I fear. The Dukes knew of it all, to be sure, and it was all but another trick, a ruse. This Count of Beveland, the true husband still as I must believe him, despite my Archbishop's wedding, is a notable scoundrel and thorn-in-the-flesh to the Dukes of Burgundy and Holland and all the Low Countries. He is indeed a pirate, preying on the great shipping of this coast. And it so happens that most of my Marie's — of his Marie's — wealth is in shipping and trade, in the Dutch fashion. And this

344

Beveland has kept his hands on it all, and uses the ships for his pirating ventures. So you will see why I had to be wed to the lady. My reputation as a pirate matches his. And, they considered, I ought to be disposed to out-pirate this wretch, slay him, recover the lady's wealth, save the coastal trade, and so cause all to rejoice.

You, my friend, may well conceive my state when I but lately made discovery of all this. I was for coming home so soon as Robert Davidson could carry me. But second thoughts have prevailed. I have decided to play these French and Netherlanders at their own game. I shall indeed go and seek pirate this pirate, and take his treasure and ships if I may. But I shall endeavour not to slay him. I shall leave him truly wed to my deceiving Countess, and sail home with such of his loot as I can stow in Greysteel. You, Jamie, will at least approve of this ploy, I think.

Liège, although called a great victory, was to my mind a sorry business, and I hope never to see such another. They say that 25,000 died, and I believe it. In these lands a general's fame is counted by the numbers slain in his battles. So I am much esteemed — for that Anton left all to me to achieve, save the slaying afterwards. In truth nearly all the dying was done after the fighting was over, when I had gained Anton and the Duke's entry to that unhappy city. Men, women and bairns, the streets running with blood, the town set afire. I was sickened. I shall tell you how we won it, when I see you. For the rest, I had rather forget it.

I hope to be back in Aberdeen, in Greysteel, in not many weeks after you read this, God willing. Also, God willing, the richer — though the poorer of a wife.

I ask that you convey my affection to my good mother and my fair aunt. To you, my sure friend, my much esteem.

                    At the Castle of Duffel, Brabant.
                         ALEXANDER STEWART

There was a sufficiency in that letter to keep Jamie Douglas thinking, and his wife commenting, for long.

Later, they heard through Buchan of the great victory of Liège, which Alex had won for Burgundy and his brother, and the Duke of Holland, who seemed also to have been involved. Albany's informants on the Continent all wrote of it. Whatever the victor's own modest assessment of the affair, his fame as a commander, rather than as just a privateer captain, seemed to be established. No word of pirating activities, however, were as yet forthcoming.

It was March before *Greysteel* arrived back to her home port, and in fine style, laden with the richest of booty, and Alex in excellent humour. It transpired that they had achieved a surprise attack on the awkward Count of Beveland, in the shallow sand-banked coasts of the eastern mouth of the Maas, more or less ambushing the Count's squadron of ships laden down with the fruits of a trading-cum-pirating expedition to the Baltic lands and Lower Muscovy — including a great hoard of gold, silver, jewellery, church ornaments, ikons, silks, rich furs, liquors and the like, not to mention chestsful of coinage of various realms and dukedoms. Never had the Scots seen such treasure. They had set the Count and his crews ashore on one of the innumerable sand-islands, to fend for themselves — so that the Countess could not claim to be truly widowed again; and they had handed over the captured ships and the bulkiest part of the treasure to the authorities at Bruges, for the Countess, the Dukes, and the Flemish and other merchants who had suffered loss for so long. Then, without waiting for embarrassing meetings or the inevitable arguments over the division of the spoils, they had slipped out of Sluys, for home. Although he did not admit as much, Alex appeared to have more or less given up hope that Burgundy would honour his commitment to send an expedition to Ireland. Although perhaps the very threat of him proposing to do so might have its effect on the well-informed Henry Plantagenet.

At any rate, Alex came home rich indeed, and so in a better position to encourage the maximum effort on the part of his northern compatriots to rise to resist Donald of the Isles, when and if the time came. Jamie was the last to contest the theory that gold and silver could be a major aid to patriotic endeavour.

It was good to have his friend home again.

PART FOUR

XXI

"MUCH AS I love my nephew Alex, I must say that I have come to dread these messengers of his, from Kildrummy," Mary Stewart declared, to her husband. "They ever presage some further headstrong venture, of much flourish but little need, which will remove my helpmeet and support, father of my bairns, far from my side. This will be just such another, I swear! If Alex would indulge in his cantrips on his own, I would have no complaint. But he seems to be unable to move more than a few steps from his new door without Jamie Douglas by his side. To *my* cost!"

"I left him in the Low Countries, to come home with you," Jamie reminded.

"Nor will you ever let me forget it! You came home because you *wanted* to."

"And Alex did very well lacking me, did he not? Moreover, some of what you name his cantrips have proved profitable, my dear — to us, as to others. Do we not all live the more comfortably therefor?"

"We could live comfortably enough without that. And better to our liking. At least, to mine. You, I do declare, enjoy these flights away from your wife and children. Leastways, you never say no to him, do you?"

"This may be nothing of that sort," he protested. "It is but a request for me to attend him at Kildrummy, for an important meeting, in which he seeks my counsel. I may be back in a night or two."

"Do not be a hypocrite, Jamie Douglas, as well as a shameful wife-deserter! You know very well what happens after Alex's important meetings. You disappear from my ken, north, south, or furth of the realm, on some ploy, usually dangerous. And I am left to weep alone."

"Weep! You? When did I last see Mary Stewart weeping?"

"You are never here to *see* me weeping, wretch . . . !"

It was June. Mary perhaps should have been grateful that she had had eight months.

Despite all this, the man rode off quite cheerfully to Donside. The first person Jamie saw at Kildrummy was Gilbert Greenlaw, Bishop of Aberdeen and Chancellor of Scotland — which seemed sufficiently significant. Then he recognised none other than Sir Robert Erskine of Balhaggarty and Conglass, the claimant of the Mar earldom, still more unexpected. When he heard that Alex was closeted with the Earl of Buchan, Justiciar, it became evident that some major development was projected. Mary's fears might even be substantiated.

Presently, alone with his friend, Alex explained. "We have become acceptable, Jamie," he announced cheerfully. "My Uncle Robert deems himself to have need of my services. So all is forgiven! For which we have to thank my Cousin Donald."

The other looked predictably suspicious, unimpressed.

"He has, apparently, been getting ever more ominous reports as to Donald's activities, intentions and ambitions, and has at last recognised the menace. He now accepts that Donald's Irish venture was merely a prelude to a major invasion of Scotland, to coincide with an English assault from the South, from Man, possibly from the Dublin Pale. It has taken him a long time to reach this conclusion. But now he is much concerned. Since Crawford's death and Douglas's failure at Homildon, he finds himself and the realm singularly lacking in soldiers — or, at least, in commanders. And he has gained the notion that I might have my uses. Especially as I have the reputation of being able to raise large numbers of Highlandmen, and ships, galleys. In token of which he sends the Chancellor, as messenger, and Sir Robert Erskine as bribe, to inform me that he will drop the Mar claim if I will agree to work with them, and I can remain earl for life. And his son John, to reassure me of his sincerity in the matter and my, h'm, safety."

"I still would not trust him," Jamie said bluntly.

"No doubt. But, since we are of a mind to stop Donald anyway, is there any reason why we should not do so aided by the Regent's authority, arms and siller?"

"The day I see that, Albany offering arms and siller — or *providing* them — I shall sing a different tune, Alex!"

"We shall see. He desires me to go south, to discuss all with him, of my goodwill. And *I* desire you to accompany me, old friend, as adviser. If you will."

"My advice you can have now. Do not go. If he needs you so badly, let him come to you."

"He is an old man getting, Jamie. This must be his seventieth year. Moreover, there are others I would wish to sound, on this. Your chief Douglas, for one. The new Crawford. And ... would you not wish to see your father again? He too is getting old."

"You are satisfied that you, we, will return safely?"

"John of Buchan pledges his word on it. I trust *him*. He has never failed me yet. He will come with us. And we can take a fair company. To show our dignity!"

"You have made up your mind?"

"Yes. I see no ill in it — and possibly much good. Authority, the Regent's authority, could serve us well, even lacking other aid. Remember our letters of mark, how valuable these can be. This is of the same sort. We can call on men to aid us, aid the realm, everywhere. Instead of merely buying them with our siller. You will come, Jamie?"

"If you are set on it. When do we go?"

"Soon. So soon as may be. They believe that there is urgency in this ..."

So Mary was right, as usual. Three days later a quite impressive cavalcade set off southwards through the Mounth passes, out of the security of the Highlands.

They did not have very far to go into the Lowlands, for Albany had come to Perth, from his castle of Doune in Menteith.

The meeting, however significant, was scarcely dramatic — Robert Stewart was never a man for drama. In the company of Buchan and the Chancellor, Alex was led to a small study in the Prior's quarters of the Blackfriar's Monastery, where the Regent sat alone at his papers, wrapped in a furred robe, spare, ascetic, the picture of a dedicated scholar rather than one of the most ruthless and unscrupulous rulers in Christendom. His cold grey eyes narrowed momentarily at sight of Jamie Douglas — but thereafter he totally ignored him. He greeted Alex with thin affability.

"Ha, Nephew — it is long since we foregathered, although I hear much of your doings, from near and far. Notably that you have been distinguishing yourself in France and the Low Countries. Cup-bearing to King Charles, instructing his Consort, teaching the Earl of Warwick how to joust and the Duke

351

of Burgundy how to treat rebels. Aye, and marrying again — after a fashion!" That was a long greeting for Albany; and Jamie, for one, marvelled at the man's information — as no doubt was the intention. He also noted how much older the Regent looked; it was years since he had seen him in the flesh, however frequently he had been in his mind's-eye. But, though more brittle-seeming, stiffer, thinner, there was no least impression of any diminution of mental powers and will.

"You are well served by informers, Uncle," Alex answered. "I am flattered that you find my poor doings of sufficient interest to warrant such attention. I hope I see you in good health?"

"Fair. Although weary with overmuch of the weight of government — requiring some younger shoulders to relieve me of some part of it." He laid down his quill. "You are namely for putting down of rebels, it seems. We have some nearer home, worthy of your attentions, I think."

"You refer to your nephew and my cousin Donald, sir?"

"I do. The Chancellor and my son have explained matters to you?"

"They tell me that you now accept what I have known for long."

"M'mm. That is as may be. Yet, if it is so — you went away to France and left this danger behind, which you knew of so fully. For others to face."

"I believed the danger to Scotland to be not yet. Ireland first. And have been proved right. Sir James Douglas and I made a journey in the Hebrides before we sailed for France, to seek learn the truth."

"To MacLeod of Dunvegan. I know of that. MacLeod told you that Donald aimed at Ireland first?"

"Not only MacLeod. That was the general belief in the Isles. For two reasons. One, to ensure that his rear was secure, when he came to invade Scotland, that there would be no attack on the Isles, from Ireland. Also, possibly, to make a claim for the eventual high kingship of Ireland, a stepping-stone in his ambitions. And two, to prove to King Henry that he was a sufficiently sound and effective ally, fit to be ruler of Scotland, under the English. Before, he had always sent Alastair Carrach to do his fighting for him. This time, he went himself."

"No doubt. Yet *you* went to France. For more than a year. In costly style."

"I went to France, sir, for good purpose. To seek French aid for the release of our liege lord James. Since *you* would do naught in the matter."

"How know you what I do or have done, young man? In this or other matters. I do not shout all from my castle parapet! Forby, you would win no aid for James from France. That I knew well."

"I gained the Duke of Burgundy's agreement to send a force to Ireland in the spring, against Donald and the English forces. He has not done so yet. But . . ."

"John of Burgundy will agree to anything — and perform nothing! You wasted your time, Alexander. We shall have to do better than that, against Donald."

"I, my lord Duke, always intended so to do. But you — what do *you* intend to do?"

"I intend to protect this realm and throne. I have two flanks to protect, possibly three. For, as well as an English attack across the Border, there may well be an assault against Galloway and Carrick from the Isle of Man and even the Irish Pale. The Earl of Douglas commands in the Borders, as is his right and duty. Montgomerie of Eaglesham will command in the West. My son John, here, is Lieutenant of the North. But he is as yet inexperienced in war. You, I would place in command there, to act with him. How say you?"

"In command? What does that mean? Save that on me would fall the task of halting Donald's main array and strength. Who would I command? What are my forces? Would my lord of Buchan be in a position to over-rule me? What moneys, arms and supplies would be at my disposal?"

"All Scotland north of Clyde and Tay would be at your disposal to levy men and moneys. My son John, as Justiciar as well as Lieutenant, would have the fullest authority to supply you, aid you. But *you* would have fullest control of the forces of the Crown in the field. And in return, Robert Erskine would waive his claim to the earldom of Mar, the lordship of Badenoch would be confirmed in your name, and all outstanding issues between yourself and the Crown remitted."

Alex was silent for a moment. "You must fear Cousin Donald greatly, I think, Uncle!" he said then.

"Fear? I fear no man, only almighty God," the other assured, with a chilly certainty which robbed the words of their pomposity. "But I perceive that my foolish sister's son may pose the greatest threat to this ancient realm of Scotland since Edward Plantagenet. He claims only that he would be Earl of Ross. But

353

it is my information that he has boasted that he will be King of Ireland and King of Scots both. And he is willing to put Scotland in thrall to England, to gain his ends. In that day, to be sure, the fool will be cut off — so!" Albany made a vicious chopping motion with the side of his hand on his table. "And Henry alone will rule all three. But meantime, Donald can raise scores of thousands of men, from his Isles, from the mainland clans, from Ulster — who knows, perhaps even from my enemies here in the Lowlands. The threat is great, and growing. I do not fear, young man — I *know*! Henry has found a monkey to pull his chestnuts out of the fire for him!"

"Henry, with whom you deal! To whose son you offered your daughter!"

"Henry, with whom I *have* to deal, fool! Can I choose who is King of England? Can I make him other than he is? You speak like a child. In statecraft a ruler faces the possible, not what he desires. Something you should have learned ere this. So — do you accept this command, or do you not?"

Alex glanced from Jamie to Buchan. "I shall have to consider it, sir, consider it well. Give me a little time."

"Do not take too long. Time may be short."

"One matter. You said that all outstanding issues between us would be remitted. I would expect this to apply also to my friends and lieutenants. Sir James Douglas, here."

His uncle picked up his quill again and inclined his grey head briefly. "Even Sir James," he said grimly.

Alex did not really require time to make up his mind, since he had more or less decided before ever he came south. But it looked better; and allowed him to take soundings, interview others and test opinion. Jamie took the opportunity to go to Dalkeith and see his father and brothers; also to Edmonstone, where he was distressed to find the Lady Isabel ill and looking almost an old woman, although she greeted him with a pathetic warmth and wept at his departure. He feared greatly that she was not long for this world. The others were eager to hear of his adventures overseas, having heard garbled and exaggerated tales. The general belief now, indeed, was that he was very rich, on the proceeds of piracy, trade and foreign adventures. He was even approached for a loan by Sir Robert Stewart of Durrisdeer, to initiate a foreign trading venture. His brother Johnnie, sadly, had died while he was away in France, and Aberdour was his own again. He did not visit his Lowland properties, however;

354

stewards were managing them satisfactorily, his father assured. One day, his son David would inherit a fine patrimony.

There seemed to be little of alarm or despondency at large over the Islesmen's threat. Donald had been a bogeyman for too long.

Alex saw the Earls of Douglas and Crawford and a few other nobles, and gained little impression that they were greatly concerned or doing anything very much about the situation meantime. As Chief Warden of the Marches, as well as the greatest landholder in the Borders, Douglas always had his ear fairly close to the ground, and had heard nothing to suggest that the English were preparing any especial activity. Since the Battle of Bramham Moor, when the Percys had finally been brought low, there had been a fair measure of peace in the North of England and little cause for armed comings and goings. Henry kept a military presence at York, but there was no indication that this was being reinforced or otherwise activated.

None of this convinced Alex that he and Albany were being unnecessarily fearful. Henry Plantagenet was a wily character and would not be apt to reveal his plans a day earlier than was necessary. Moreover, it would be entirely in keeping if he held back deliberately, allowing Donald to do all the major fighting, and only moving in over the Border when success was assured.

At any rate, nothing that they heard or saw convinced Alex and Jamie that they ought to reject the Regent's offer of co-operation. They returned to Perth, signified Alex's agreement to accept the official command of the realm's forces in the North — forces not yet in being — and received an authoritative document under the Great Seal to that effect. Albany, showing no sign of pleasure in the decision, told him that his latest reports put Donald back in Ulster, holding a great meeting with Irish kinglets and chiefs. He was still shipping troops to Ireland, however, so it looked as though there would be no Scottish invasion this year before the campaigning season ended. So they had some months, at least, to prepare. Incidentally, there was no indication of any troop movements out of France, to Ireland or anywhere else.

If, indeed, a marked inactivity seemed to characterise the entire international scene, Albany at least believed it to be only the lull before the storm. Others might scoff and shrug, but for once both Alex Stewart and Jamie Douglas agreed with him.

They headed north thereafter determined not to emulate this apparent inactivity.

XXII

ALBANY'S FORECAST THAT they would be granted a few
months' grace was fulfilled. Donald did not return from
Ireland until the late autumn, announcing to all concerned
that he had concluded a treaty with his friend the King of
England whereby each would support and protect the subjects
of the other — first step towards the independent ruler status.
He was now affecting royal style, in employing uniformed
heralds in his entourage, the Islay and Ross Heralds and the
Kintyre and Dingwall Pursuivants. All that winter and the following spring the Highlands were agog with rumours of the
mustering and massing of hosts, on Islay, Mull, Skye and the
Outer Isles, from every corner of the Hebrides and much of the
west mainland also, and later from Antrim, where Ian Mor,
Donald's brother, was being called his viceroy. Galley-fleets
were assembling, in alarming numbers. Word of fence-sitters
amongst the Highland chiefs being cajoled, pressed, threatened,
was brought to Alex almost daily — even as near home as his
own Badenoch, where the Mackintosh himself was alleged to be
under strong pressure, friendly with Alex as he was. Donald was
waving the flag of Highland dominance in Scotland, instead of
Lowland, something unknown since Malcolm Canmore's Queen
Margaret had effectively contrived the southern supremacy, a
powerful incitement for the clans. The hegemony of the Celts
was being held out as practical politics, at long last, with Ireland,
other than the English Pale, brought within the scheme of things.
With no effective King of Scots to be rebelling against, King
Henry giving his support, and Donald himself nephew of the
late King, the thing was possible as never before.

Alex, aided by John of Buchan, did all that he could to counter
this pressure. He sent his emissaries, Jamie Douglas amongst

them, all over the Highlands, warning, directing, commanding, exhorting. He sought to gain promises of contingents for his army, requiring each sheriff to raise his quota, in the name of the Crown; but quickly was made aware that it was one thing to be lent men to fight against Lowlanders, the English, or even in private feud, but altogether another when it was a matter of defeating a demonstration of Highland independence. He came to the conclusion before long, that, commander-in-chief and Lord of Badenoch or not, friendly as he was with many of the chiefs, he could only rely for his fighting-force on the eastern lowlands of his area — Mar, Angus, the Mearns, Buchan and Moray, and the cities of Aberdeen and Elgin. No help came from the South in all this, Albany having passed on the responsibility to Alex and leaving him severely alone. There was no doubt as to who would get the blame if things went wrong — though that might well be of academic interest in that event. Jamie even suggested that they would be wise to watch their rear when and if fighting began, with a stab in the back entirely possible.

The Douglas made more constructive suggestions than that, however. He urged Alex to form and train an officer-corps, based on their privateering group of lairds, which could assemble frequently and regularly, discuss strategy and tactics, plan for various eventualities, and learn to co-operate in the field, so that their force, once mustered, would be an effective fighting-machine with a highly-trained leadership, that what it might lack in numbers might be made up for in efficiency. In this the leading lights were those old foes, Sir Alexander Forbes and Sir Andrew Leslie, with their sons; Sir James Scrymgeour of Dundee, the Standard-Bearer; Sir Alexander Keith; Sir John Menzies of Pitfodels; Sir Alexander Irvine of Drum, and Provost Robert Davidson. Only one Highland chief was prepared to be included at this stage, Donald Og Macpherson of Cluny. Alex's brothers, Andrew and Walter, co-operated after their awkward fashion, and James, the youngest, promised aid from Atholl.

So the winter passed and the campaigning season of 1411 opened.

Messengers from the West were now arriving regularly at Kildrummy, many from old MacLeod in Skye, intimating great activity all over the Isles; but the major concentrations of men and shipping were at Islay, with its many harbours, where was the main seat of the Isles lordship, at Finlaggan. Decisive action must be soon now.

357

But still nothing happened — while Alex fretted. He had decided on his strategy, made his plans as far as was possible in advance, held almost daily councils with his lieutenants. Yet April passed, and May, with the passes clear, the river-levels falling and the cuckoos calling on all the glen-sides. Still Donald did not move. The tension at Kildrummy was acute.

And then Donald MacDonald managed to surprise, despite all their eager preparedness. From Islay his vast galley-fleets sailed at last — but northwards, not east nor south. All up the Western Sea reports came in of his progress, gaining strength all the way, through the northerly isles. This was totally unexpected, for any assault on the mainland must aim for the South eventua-ally, and any round-about and delayed approach would only give warning and time to the defenders. Islay was almost the most southerly of the Sudreys, the southern half of the Hebrides, and to have assembled there, and then to head north, did not seem to make sense. Alex had anticipated a landing in Lochaber or Argyll, and then a swift strike eastwards across the spine of Scotland, by Laggan or Rannoch. Yet Donald made straight for the north of Skye, and this turned, landed on mainland Ross.

It became clear that his first objective was to take the earldom of Ross — which, of course, he claimed to be his in the right of his wife, the original reason for his dispute with Albany. Possibly he intended to use it as a secure base. Certainly it would provide him with additional manpower. But the personal pride and prestige aspect of it must be very great to account for this major preliminary gesture. At least, it encouraged Alex in the belief that his adversary might be a man who might throw away military advantage for heroics and superficial lustre.

Nevertheless Alex was faced with a difficult decision. To head north towards Ross, to deal with the invaders, could be dangerous, removing him from his own base and greatly extend-ing his lines of communication. He would be fighting on Donald's chosen territory rather than his own, and his levies would be unlikely to react with enthusiasm. Moreover, he had no experience of moving, supplying and foraging large armies — nor had any of his people. On the other hand, just to wait idly whilst the other consolidated his position, and took over large tracts of the mainland, was not good either, and could be injurious to morale.

On balance, he decided to wait. At least it gave him time to gather and train more men — and now that the threat was self-evident, men were more ready to come forward.

Alex was unprepared, however, for the news that, in the midst of elaborate celebration and initiation ceremonies as Earl of Ross at Dingwall, the ancient seat of the earldom, Donald had made a sudden and vicious raid on the town of Inverness, eighteen miles to the south, sacking and burning it, with considerable slaughter. This savage move, apparently with no other purpose than to show his teeth and appease the blood-lust of his Islesmen, could not be ignored. John of Buchan, as Justiciar, declared his cousin the Lord of the Isles to be outlaw, and all aiding and supporting him equally so. The cities of Aberdeen and Elgin were proclaimed to be in a state of siege, and the magistrates thereof ordered to see that all able-bodied citizens were provided with arms, and made constant practice of their use, walls and defences to be strengthened, fire-fighting forces set up and curfews instituted. Alex moved from Kildrummy south-eastwards down the Don to Inverurie, the head burgh of the Garioch lordship, where at Thainston, the same spot in the green levels where his ancestor Robert Bruce had set up his camp before the Battle of Barra, he established the nucleus of his army. It was only a few miles from Aberdeen.

After that events moved fast. Donald set his huge force in motion — and a Highland army on the march was a terrible and fast-moving host. It was now reported to number anything between ten and twenty thousand. Word came that another force of West Highlanders under the famous Hector Maclean of the Battles, son-in-law of Donald, was marching up the Great Glen to join him. Alex assessed his own strength at less than three thousand, mainly the followings of Mar, Garioch, Angus, Mearns and Buchan lairds — plus what, at the last moment, he could persuade Aberdeen city to provide. It did not add up to encouraging odds.

Where to confront the invaders? Alex had worked out a great variety of suitable battlegrounds, with Jamie's help, where the terrain could be used materially to fight for them. With the threat coming from the north, however, the choice was much limited. And there was the question as to whether Donald intended to come seeking them out, and do battle, or only to fight if he was intercepted on his way south — which could much affect the situation. He was reported as declaring that he would burn Aberdeen more direly than he had done Inverness

359

— but this might be mere dramatics. Either way, to be sure, much wild and difficult country lay between the two forces. Jamie suggested — and it seemed good sense to his friend, although it might seem like a lack of spirit on the face of it — that if anybody had to expend major time and energy crossing that wilderness and the northern Mounth passes, it should be the enemy, leaving themselves fresh and in good order. In the circumstances, the nearer base the ultimate battle, the better for them.

South of Inverness, the Islesman's host, now joined by Hector Maclean of Duart's contingent, could move either directly onwards southwards, over the Moy and Slochd passes into Badenoch, or eastwards, by Drummossie Moor into the Laigh of Moray. If they were aiming for the conquest of the Lowlands, obviously the first would be the direct advance; but if seeking a speedy confrontation with the defending forces, the second course would be the choice. When an exhausted courier reached Alex with the information that, in fact, the invaders, moving notably fast now, were into Braemoray, last reported in the Barevan area, avoiding the Nairn plain and the Forres-Elgin lowlands, it seemed clear that they were looking for battle. There was no reason to believe that Donald would be any less well served by spies and informants than they were themselves. He would know who was waiting for him, and where. Also, no doubt, approximate numbers. There could only be a few days, now, before the clash, wherever it was going to be.

Jamie, no less than Alex, was put in a state of anxiety by the word that Donald was advancing through Braemoray — which might bring his host close to Lochindorb. It was not particularly near to this Barevan, but it was a noted place and Donald might consider it worth going out of his way to attack. The castle, on its island, was well nigh impregnable however, without cannon — which Donald was unlikely to have with him, on fast forced marches. So their womenfolk were probably in little real danger. But they might well be alarmed and frightened — especially as later word had come in that there *had* been opposition to Donald before Dingwall, and this had been led by Mariota de Athyn's two brothers, Black Angus Mackay and his brother Roderick, the one now prisoner, the other slain. Nothing could be done about this, however, by Alex.

Then they had news that the invaders had, oddly enough, turned seawards down Spey from Rothes, to the Enzie area near

Speymouth — which almost certainly meant that they would have missed the Lochindorb uplands. Enzie was a detached property of the Ross earldom, so evidently Donald was still concerned with demonstrating his rights — an interesting facet of the character of a man in process of throwing three kingdoms into turmoil. By the same token he would probably move on to Boyne, near Banff, another of the outlying Ross baronies. If this was so, then his onward approach to the Aberdeen area would almost certainly be by the Deveron valley and Strathbogie into the Garioch. This was what Alex had had to know, to crystallise his plans.

They reckoned that they had three days, no more. They could not ambush tens of thousands of men; but they might perhaps select a battleground which could serve them as well as a couple of thousand extra troops — and they were going to require every such help. There were a number of sites to be considered; but the choice was limited by the fact that the Aberdeen contingent, which might make a major difference, would not be horsed, and would therefore be slow-moving and not really of much use over long distances. So the battlefield must be near-at-hand. Alex sent word to Robert Davidson, and then, alone save for Jamie and Sir Robert Erskine, the earldom claimant — whose estates of Balhaggarty and Pittodrie were nearby and who knew all the land like the palm of his hand — set off northwards on a hurried tour.

They were looking for a position which would tend to negate the Highlanders' overwhelming superiority in numbers and at the same time enable them to gain the fullest benefit of their own strength in cavalry and armoured knights. Also to be able to use the hoped-for Aberdonians to best advantage. They could rule out any idea of surprising the enemy — thousands of men can neither be hidden nor taken by surprise. But they might *constrain* Donald.

According to Erskine, within reasonable marching distance of Inverurie there were five such sites possible; but inspection reduced these to only the two. One, at Manar, up the Don westwards about three miles, where the river made a sharp bend through steep bluffs and hanging woods. The other the long, low ridge of Harlaw, actually on the Balhaggarty property, a sort of whaleback in the valley of the Urie, the Don's major tributary coming in from the north, about a mile east of the Urie and parallel to it, lying north-west and south-east. It was scarcely a major feature, reaching no more than a hundred and fifty feet above the valley floor. But it was over a mile long and three-quarters wide, firm ground on a gentle curve, flanked on both sides by low-lying marshland. Cavalry could operate up there, and large numbers be much restricted. But it could be a death-trap if the cavalry had to flee, those surrounding marshes fatal for horses. On the one side, these were the usual river's flood-plain boglands; the other had presumably once been an earlier or subsidiary course of the Urie, now silted up.

"Which, then?" Alex asked. "Neither are all I would wish. But they are the best that we have seen. We must believe Sir Robert when he says there are none better within our distances. Manar would give us more constriction and a better route for retreat. But Harlaw has advantages, too . . ."

"I say Harlaw," Jamie answered promptly. "We are not really concerned with retreat, are we? If it comes to that, all is lost. We shall not be able to remuster and make a stand elsewhere — not one that could halt Donald. The Manar site is cluttered with trees, narrow, wooded, close, fine for small fights but poor for a great battle such as this must be. You require to *see* what is happening, the whole field. To move your forces as required. This Harlaw ridge will give you that. And Donald will never be able to mount his fullest strength against us — there is not room."

"He could get round, outflank us. Send some to take us in the rear."

"Yes. So we must have no rear! Like a besieged city. But our cavalry will be able to dominate that ridge, if properly used. The foot form schiltroms, strong-points."

"How say you, Sir Robert?"

"I agree with Sir James. Somehow we must shorten our front. Manar would, I fear, shorten it too much. No full battle could be fought there — so we should have to do it all again, elsewhere."

"Very well. Harlaw let it be. Unless we are faced with something unforeseen . . ."

They rode back to Thainston.

*   *   *

Alex sat his horse on the top of the great Bass of Inverurie, a green artificial mound, which had once been crowned by an ancient fort, flanked by the glittering array of his lieutenants

362

and principal supporters. He was looking magnificent, and deliberately so, for morale was all-important this day, St. James's Eve of July, 1411. He wore gleaming half-armour and heraldic linen surcoat below a gilded camail, or hood of chain-mail covering neck and shoulders, plumed helmet in the crook of his shield-arm, mount splendidly caparisoned in the Mar colours. Fully a score of only slightly less resplendent figures formed a row behind him, on sidling, fretting chargers, not only his own group of tried and trained colleagues, such as Forbes, Menzies, Keith, Straiton, Leslie, two of his brothers and Jamie, but notables like Sir Alexander Ogilvy, Sheriff of Angus; Sir Robert Melville of Glenbervie, Sheriff of the Mearns; Sir Thomas Moray, Sheriff thereof Sir James' Scrymgeour, Constable of Dundee and Standard-Bearer of Scotland; Sir William Abernethy of Saltoun, a nephew of Albany; Sir Gilbert de Greenlaw, styled nephew of the Chancellor-Bishop; Sir Robert Maule of Panmure and others. Below them, on the Don meadows all around the base of the Bass was drawn up their host, in troops and companies and squadrons, standing by their horses, the lairds of the North-East with their sons, men-at-arms and fighting-tails, with a sprinkling of Badenoch and Atholl Highlandmen, mainly of Clan Chattan — although their Captain, the Mackintosh himself, was reported to be marching with Donald to whom he was related. Jamie made the grand total two thousand nine hundred — which was less than grand in relation to the task ahead, however stirring a sight they made in the forenoon sunshine. There were still some to come, however — especially Robert Davidson and his Aberdeen contingent, for whom they were specifically waiting and who could be seen as a dust-cloud shot with the gleam of steel a mile or so back along the road from Kintore.

Before the marching Aberdonians could come up, a much faster although smaller body put in an appearance in dashing style, the banner at their head showing the three green holly-leaves on white of Irvine.

"I did not think that Sir Sandy would fail us — despite his wedding!" Alex asserted.

Sir Alexander Irvine of Drum, a cheerful, ruddy-featured young man, grandson of Bruce's renowned armour-bearer, leaving his eighty or so men at the bottom, rode up on to the mound, to the laughter, cheers and ruderies of the waiting lairds. Grinning, he saluted Alex and waved and gestured crudely at them all. He had been married only the day before.

"I hope that you are not so exhausted as to be unable to wield as lusty a brand this day, friend, as you did last night?" Alex enquired kindly.

"Not so," the other assured. "God's eyes — I have a bone to pick with Donald MacDonald this day! He ruined my bridal night!"

"Sakes, man — could you not raise your standard for fear of the Islesman!" his crony, young Alexander Keith, demanded.

"Think you so, oaf? There was naught amiss with the Irvine standard. It was the socket to fit it in that was at fault! Making the wedding five days early, on Donald's account, set my lady's calculations adrift. The Islesman will pay for it, I say!"

There was a howl of mirth and commiseration. "My heart bleeds with and for Lady Irvine!" Alex said. "Deprived so cruelly."

"Aye — and how will she do if you do not return from this tuilzie, Sandy?" the irrepressible Keith, heir to the Marischal, cried. "What will she use for the standard of Irvine, then?"

"I have attended to that," his friend asserted, solemnly. "I left my brother Rob behind at the Drum Stone of Skene, the last place from which we could see my castle of Drum, on the Dee, sent him back. If I do not return, Rob will change his name to Alexander, take my new wife for his own and raise up sons for Irvine." He shrugged steel-clad shoulders. "Och, he likes her fine, forby!"

The grins and chuckles faded, at that. Suddenly the reality of the situation was brought home to them all, even the least sensitive, and the high-spirited adventure before them took on a different colour.

Alex coughed. "Commendable forethought, Sandy. Your brother will have to find his own bride, I vow, nevertheless! Now — we wait for Provost Davidson and his burgesses, yonder. Others are still to come, likewise — with perhaps less excuse for tardiness than you! But we shall not wait for them all . . ."

Shouts drew the attention of the company on the Bass to still another horsed party, coming this time from behind, from the north, skirting Inverurie burgh by the riverside. It was larger, fully two hundred strong, at its head the blue banner with three golden boars' heads of Gordon. A shout went up.

364

"Thanks be for that!" Alex murmured. "Now, pray God, we will learn something."

Sir Alexander Seton put his horse to the mound, a fine figure of a man in the richest armour there, black inlaid with gold, the Lothian laird who had married, three years earlier, the heiress of Sir Adam, the Gordon chief who had fallen at Homildon. He was now Lord of Gordon in her right.

"How fares Strathbogie, my lord?" Alex asked eagerly.

"But poorly, my lord Earl," the other answered. "The Hieland savages have swept down it like a heather-fire, God damn them! Brute beasts!" The new Gordon would have to learn an amended vocabulary, for the North. "Scarce a house left unburned or a woman unraped! I would have brought you twice this number otherwise."

"It was no little matter that you came at all, man. I thank you. But . . . what of Donald, now? What news have you for us?"

"The Islesmen camped last night at the Whitehaugh of Montgarrie, after leaving Strathbogie. They are now marching by Keig and the back of Bennachie hitherwards, in their thousands . . ."

"Keig, and Bennachie? Not down the Vale of Alford? Then they are making for the Urie. Looking for us! We thought they might come by Alford, Tillyfour and Monymusk."

"No. They take the north route round Bennachie. We avoided them, by Auchleven and Oyne . . ."

"Then it is time that we were moving, not waiting here!" That was Jamie Douglas, strongly, behind. "Keig is little more than a dozen miles. Ten, no more, from Harlaw. And they march fast, as we know . . ."

"A little longer only, Jamie," Alex said. "This means that we can now recall the Forbes force waiting at the Tillyfour gap." He turned. "Forbes, my friend, will you now send for the main mass of your people to rejoin us? Quickly. And now — we must welcome the good burgesses of fair Aberdeen, as is seemly. Forby, we must not all be on top of Harlaw's hill too soon, or Donald may stay down, and avoid battle up there. We have to *coax* him up. Bisset — go you out to welcome the Aberdeen men. And bring Robert Davidson to me here. Tullidaff — some music, if you please, for the burgesses."

So, to the sound of fifes, fiddles and drums the hot and tired Aberdeen contingent straightened stooping shoulders, lifted

365

their steps higher and marched in, about four hundred strong, twenty-six burgesses of the city with their following of shop-keepers, seamen, apprentices, clerks, fishermen, a motley crew of all ages and shapes in comparison with the ranks of steel-clad knights, men-at-arms and horsemen, but well-armed and equipped. Alex led the cheering.

Walter Bisset, son of Lessendrum, Sheriff of Banff, brought Davidson, in fair armour, and his second-in-command ex-Provost Chalmers, up the hill. Alex dismounted and strode forward to greet them, hand out.

"Bless you, friends," he exclaimed. "I rejoice to have you at my side, this day. This is a sight to sing over! Who knows — I may yet put it into my halting verse! It is not every day that the Provost, magistrates and council of the city of Aberdeen march out to war!"

"There would be more, my lord, had we not had to leave the gates and walls manned, mind."

"To be sure. Master Chalmers — take the Provost's helm."

"Eh . . .?"

"His helm. Take it off, Robert. And kneel down."

"What is this, my lord . . .?"

"Do as I say. You are all soldiers now, under orders. *My* orders! Kneel, man. You are none so stiff yet, are you? I have seen you leaping about your ship's decks nimbly enough! Down with you."

As, staring, the Provost half-knelt, half-stooped, Alex drew his sword.

"As commander of this host and an earl of Scotland, as is my undoubted right, I, Alexander Stewart, knight, do now knight you, Robert Davidson, Chief Magistrate of the city and royal burgh of Aberdeen, and so honour you, your burgh and all your men." Intoning thus, Alex brought down his gleaming blade on the other's wide shoulders, one side then the other. "Thus, and thus, I hereby dub you knight, in the presence of God and this host. Arise, Sir Robert. Make your knightly vows hereafter. And remain a good and true knight until your life's end. Arise."

Surprise was so complete that it was moments before the cheers broke out. But when they did, there was no doubt as to the enthusiasm and delight, not so much on the part of the other knights and lairds, but on that of the thousands of the rank-and-file, in especial of course, of the Aberdonians. Never before had such a thing been seen. Loud and long the acclaim resounded, while Sir Robert Davidson gulped and moistened his lips and scratched his helmetless grizzled head.

Then men surged forward to shake him by the hand, and everywhere the great assembly hummed with excited comment and remark. Nothing better calculated to raise the spirit of the men could have been imagined. But Alex gave them only a few moments, then turned back to his horse, nodding to Jamie and signing to his trumpeter to sound the Advance.

Out of seeming confusion, then, the host eddied, moved and coalesced into four distinct groupings, and finally set off, to cross the Urie ford shallows east of the Bass, and then to turn northwards up the riverside, opposite the small burgh of Inverurie. Sir James Scrymgeour, Constable of Dundee and the realm's hereditary Standard-Bearer, commanded the van, with Sir Alexander Ogilvy, Sheriff of Angus, the senior sheriff. Next came the left wing, under Sir Andrew Leslie of Balquhain, styled Master of Horse to compensate for not commanding the right, which was given to his rival Forbes. Leslie's seven fine sons led his wing, with Johnston of Caskieben and Barclay of Towie Barclay. Sir Alexander Forbes, most of whose people were still at Tillyfour on the Don waiting to delay the Islesmen, should they have chosen that route, had Sir Henry Preston of Fyvie as second-in-command, his son's father-in-law, with the stern Sir Robert Melville of Glenbervie, Sheriff of the Mearns. Finally came the main body, under Alex himself, with most of his closest lieutenants around him. As Jamie had suggested, they did not use a rearguard.

They made a lengthy column, winding up the riverside meadows, however much less so than Donald's array would make. They had two miles to go to Balhaggarty, at the southern tail-end of the Harlaw ridge. There, above Erskine's small castle, whilst Scrymgeour and his van went on ahead, openly, to take up a position on the high ground, evident to all, the rest waited. His role was to be bait to draw the Islesmen up. The van would look like a comparatively small force, only a few hundreds, but larger than any patrol; therefore an outpost of the main army, holding this upland — which must therefore be important. The chances were that Donald would thereupon seek to take the position, even though he used only a small proportion of his host in the attempt. These would find a reinforced Scrymgeour difficult to dislodge, in a strong defensive site, and Donald would have to send up more Islesmen. Alex would feed up more and more of his force, until Donald must either commit his main array or give up the attempt. The Lord of the Isles' pride, however, had been sufficiently proved, and the likelihood of him withdrawing was remote. So, they hoped the battle would be fought there, on the ground of their own choosing, initiative and strategy theirs.

Alex, of course, had his scouts out, who now sent back reports as to the enemy's progress. Last word was that they were in the Logie area, a mile west of Pitcaple, which itself was a bare couple of miles west of the north end of Harlaw, all in the valley of the Urie. Donald's advance-guard must be seeing Harlaw, and Scrymgeour, now.

Hidden by the escarpment, the main eastern army waited tensely.

A messenger came from Scrymgeour to announce that a force of about a thousand Highlandmen was climbing the north slope of the escarpment towards them. They would let them get up before attacking.

Alex did not require a courier to inform him, presently, that battle was joined; they could all hear the clash and shouting, on the westerly breeze. Presently a man arrived to inform, however, that the fighting was hot and reinforcements should be sent, quickly. Sir Andrew Leslie sent up two hundred men, under one of his sons.

Donald reinforced his advance-guard. It was going according to plan.

Swiftly thereafter, Leslie and the entire left wing was despatched up the hill. That ought to bring matters to a head.

It did. In but twenty minutes after Leslie's departure, the news came that all Donald's host, thousand upon thousand, appeared to be on the move uphill along a mile-wide front.

"This, then, is the hour we have waited for, my friends," Alex cried. "All Scotland has waited for it. Today this realm's road will be decided. Pray God it is *our* road! And that we may prove worthy of the task. Come — waiting is over."

It was almost three hours past noon.

*   *   *

Up on the grassy plateau visibility was suddenly enormously extended, sight replaced imagination, reality conjecture. Far and wide the land was laid out, rising dramatically in the west to the towering conical summit of the Mither Tap of Bennachie, central

368

landmark of all Aberdeenshire, five miles away. But sight, however welcome, was in some measure disappointing for Alex. Not in the stirring quality and excitement of the scene or even the spirit of the actors, but in the relative positioning. The northern half of the whaleback was a seething mass of men and horses all colour and movement and noise; but the entire southern half was as good as empty. Which was not as planned. Scrymgeour, once he had drawn the enemy, was to have made a strategic retiral here, Leslie likewise, so that they could all then form a unified battle, not exactly a front but a coherent and manageable array. Instead of which, the Lion Rampant standard of Scotland — presumably with the Standard-Bearer beneath it — was most evidently still pressing forward into the thickest of the enemy ranks, totally surrounded now but certainly not retiring. The same could be said of Leslie's entire wing, in a quite separate battle, over towards the west side of the escarpment. Both were obviously engaged in slaughtering as many of the saffron-clad enemy as possible in the shortest-time — but neither were doing as ordered.

"Curses on them!" Alex exclaimed. "What do they think they are at? Some clan squabble!"

"There are many fewer horses than there should be. Already!" Jamie pointed out grimly.

"You are right. That means . . ." He did not finish that. "Greenlaw — go you and command Leslie to fall back. Menzies — go tell Forbes to advance with his right wing, round the *east* edge of this scarp, to draw some of the enemy away from Scrymgeour. But not too far. Tell him to keep level with Leslie — form a line. And to watch his horses — dirkmen! Sandy — take your company and Skene's in, at the centre, in behind Scrymgeour. He's surrounded. Try to free his rear, so that he can retire. But — keep line with Forbes."

"Gladly, my lord," Irvine said. "But . . . should we not *all* go? Rescue the Constable, and then throw these Islesmen down the hill. With our fullest force?"

"Fool!" That was Jamie Douglas, at his gruffest. "Have you forgot already? Not one-third of Donald's force is yet engaged, on this hill. My lord cannot engage his main strength until he has the enemy more fully committed."

"Jamie is right, Sandy. Off with you. We have to fight this cunningly, if we are to win."

"Or to survive!" the Douglas growled.

"If you need aid, I will send Gordon . . ."

Irvine and Barclay rode off.

All the time more and more of the Highlandmen were appearing over the crest of the rise all along the northern perimeter and quite far down the west flank, this last preoccupying Leslie's wing — which was much too greatly extended. Alex and his remaining lieutenants had found a slight eminence from which to survey the field — and did not like what they saw.

"Leslie will not be able to withdraw," Jamie declared. "He is losing his horses fast, hamstrung and disembowelled. You will have to send him aid — a diversion, hard-hitting, along the edge, there. But not too many, of a mercy . . .!"

"Yes. Sir Thomas Moray — take two hundred and drive between Leslie and the lip of the hill, then back. Tell Leslie he *must* retire, or they will be cut down to a man. He thinks that he is fighting his own small war, there! But — for the saints' sake, watch your horses! The Islesmen are rushing in beneath them and dirking open their bellies. And, Sir Thomas — send me back word of Donald's main force."

Jamie was glaring around him in a fever of frustration. "This is going but ill," he declared. "If they will not obey your commands, how can you order the field?"

"The weakness of such an army. Made up of proud lords and lairds, with their own men. We did seek to train them . . ."

"These around you know their duty. It is their betters . . ."

The main mass of their own manpower was formed up in four great companies covering most of the southern end of the plateau, two of cavalry, two of infantry and bowmen, these being the Aberdeen force and the mixed contingent of churchmen, the servants and tenants of the bishoprics of Brechin, Moray and Aberdeen, under Tullidaff of that Ilk. Impatient as all were to be in and striking, there was nothing that they could usefully do at this stage without endangering their whole further strategy. Men cursed and swore as they stood idle, and at a distance watched their colleagues dying. But the supreme leadership was adamant. No move to be made until ordered by the Earl of Mar.

And men *were* dying, on Harlaw's hill, terribly and in large numbers. On both sides, to be sure — and probably many more Highlanders than the steel-clad Lowlanders. But with their vast preponderance in numbers, from a military point-of-view, this was not significant. Scrymgeour's van was but a sorry residue of its original gallant strength with barely one-third of its horses still surviving. Irvine's company was hacking and slashing to try to reach the encircled men, but the Constable had pressed much too far ahead and there was still a wide belt of axe-wielding Islesmen between them and rescue. Even as they watched, the proud Lion Rampant banner went down — and was not raised again. That could only mean that Scrymgeour himself, grandson of Bruce's standard-bearer, as Irvine was of his armour-bearer, was fallen. Fighting one of Bruce's great-grandsons, whilst another stood and watched, helpless.

Forbes, with his right wing, was moving in from the east now, in good order — he was, of course, the most experienced of Alex's lieutenants. But the Islesmen's numbers were being added to all the time and it was apparent that he, any more than Irvine, would not be able to save what was left of the van.

"I shall have to withdraw Sandy," Alex said, hammering his saddle with clenched fist. "Abandon Scrymgeour. Or he too will be surrounded, and lost. Christ pity me!"

"The burden of the commander, man!" Jamie rasped. "The loneliest man God made!" But his heart grieved for his friend. "Aye, recall Irvine. And have Forbes straighten his line. You can do naught else."

Unhappily Alex gave the orders.

Having jettisoned the costly van, and done what could be done to rescue the errant left, gradually a semblance of order was restored to the defending force. Forbes joined up with the retiring Irvine, Alex moved his main strength forward, and about one-third of the left wing was extricated, to take up its proper position at the east of the front. A twice-wounded Leslie was brought, horseless and limping, to the mound.

"Are you sore hurt, Sir Andrew?" Alex asked. And then steeled himself to say, "You much exceeded your orders. Hazarded your command. That was not well done, Leslie."

The older man stared up at him, hot-eyed but silent, grimacing with pain.

"How many have you left, of your seven hundred — for Moray to command?"

"You cannot take away my command! I am not so sore stricken."

"How many, man?"

"Three hundred, a few less. Aye, and two sons left!"

371

"Two? You mean . . .?"

"Aye. Five lie dead, yonder."

Biting his lip, Alex turned away, wordless.

"I have two more here, and myself. For vengeance!"

The first stage of the battle was over, and it had been costly for Alex. But at least he had achieved his objective in getting all Donald's forces committed to the hill-top site. He reckoned that he had lost up to seven hundred men in doing it. Was that competent generalship?

There was no break, nor even a lull, of course. The enemy, having swallowed up the last of Scrymgeour's van, came surging on in a vast, yelling mass over a half-mile front, terrible to behold. Not in any wild and unco-ordinated rabble however, but in close-packed companies and regiments, thousands upon thousands. Nothing, it seemed, could resist that tide of ferocious humanity. There were almost as many banners amongst the Islesmen as on the eastern side, mostly bearing the Galley of the Isles in some form or colour. But three larger standards, spaced out, rose above the rest — the great undifferenced black galley on white, in the centre, emblem of the Lord of the Isles himself; the yellow lion and galley of MacNeil of Barra on the east; and, on the right of the line, the red rock-stack and galley of Maclean of Duart, Red Hector of the Battles.

This charge, to be sure, had been foreseen, and all plans made for countering it as far as was possible. The foot quickly turned themselves into four great circles of spearmen, schiltroms, perhaps a hundred and fifty yards apart, front rows kneeling, inner ranks standing shoulder to shoulder, facing all round, spears thrusting out like a hedgehog; with, in the centre of each, the archers, all too few of these, who meantime were busy indeed, winging shafts in furious succession at the advancing enemy. In front of these schiltroms steep arrowheads of cavalry projected, armoured knights in front, to divide and break up the charge and lessen the impact on the spearmen — leaving the necessary gaps for the bowmen to shoot through. Even so, almost half the total remaining cavalry strength was drawn up behind the schiltroms, ready to plug any gaps, exploit any opportunities — and at the same time be prepared to turn and face the other way, should Donald send any force round the hill-foot to attack their rear. Unfortunately, the arrows did less damage than hoped for. The Highlanders were all equipped with targes, round leather shields which, held up before them as they ran, formed a fairly effective barrier. Many did fall, but little difference was evident in the charge.

The impact on the Islesmen's front of their meeting with the cavalry horns was shattering, cataclysmic, a most violent disintegration, an abrupt chaos of flailing limbs, flashing steel, rearing horses and the eruption of flesh and blood — more especially blood, which spurted and splashed and sprayed everywhere. Pressed on by the weight of men behind, there was no question of the front ranks being able to halt and fight. They were flung onward like the foam of breaking rollers, dead, wounded and unhurt alike, a yelling tide being slashed at all the way by the swords and maces of the mounted men above and flanking them. On and on they were carried, to break in appalling ruin on the spear-fronted schiltroms, there to pile up in shameful masses. It was a most fearful slaughter, all along that half-mile line.

But, however shattered, the red tide was not to be reversed, the pressure behind it too heavy. On came the men of the Isles, of the mainland West, of the Antrim glens, until by sheer weight of numbers the cavalry prongs were twisted and broken up. Time and again Alex flung in aid and support, but nothing could halt the dissolution of the horsed arrowheads. The infantry schiltroms still stood firm, islands in a ghastly sea; but otherwise the battle broke up into what Alex had dreaded and sought all along to avoid, a multiplicity of separate struggles, large and small, more or less unconnected in the main — but none the less savage and bloody for that. Now he had little or no control, save perhaps over the schiltroms — but these were static anyway. Long might they remain so. For the rest, he could only try to retain a small mobile reserve and hope to use it to best effect. That, and resist the almost overwhelming urge to plunge into the mêlée, with Jamie and his close colleagues, to smite, and if need be, be smitten. It might come to that — but not yet. Admittedly Donald himself must be in almost the same position; but that was scant consolation.

He did what he could, guided by an ever-shrinking band of lieutenants, sitting their horses on the eminence, watching, assessing, sending a messenger here, a group there, a troop elsewhere. When one of the schiltroms collapsed, he was able to rally the survivors, Aberdonians all, and stiffened with some unhorsed men-at-arms, form them into another smaller hedgehog.

But this type of fighting allowed the Islesmen the fullest scope for their dire tactic of darting under the horses' bellies and slashing them open with their dirks. Once unhorsed, the armoured men were vulnerable indeed, for however protected by steel, they were slow and heavy in movement. Most of the killing was being done with dirks now, in close hand-to-hand press, with insufficient room for effective sword-wielding. And the Islesmen were better with their dirks than were the men-at-arms.

The enemy leadership strove, equally with Alex, for some control of the battle. Most effective at this was the Maclean chief on their right; and though his wing had more or less disintegrated, he had managed to gather and hold together a sizeable and coherent company, which he was using to good effect. In fact, he was fairly clearly pressing towards the eminence occupied by Alex, no doubt with the objective of destroying the eastern leadership. The menace of this became only too apparent.

"My lord," Alexander Irvine said, "we must stop Red Hector. Give me a company. I will halt him, somehow. Or we lose this position — and much else."

"He is right," Jamie agreed. "Maclean could be our ruin. On this mound he could dominate the field."

"Aye. Take half our reserves, Sandy. I cannot spare more. Lord — that will be a bare hundred! Do what you can . . ."

Irvine formed a wedge of the precious horsemen, his own banner at their head, and drove in through the struggling throng of bodies towards Maclean's colourful flag, shouting "An Irvine! An Irvine!" Quickly their momentum sank away, but still onward they pushed, swords and maces smiting to keep Islesmen from getting beneath their mounts. Dirks could not reach them effectively, up in their saddles, but the long-handled Lochaber-axes could, and not all these were parried, bringing down fully a dozen of the five score.

"What can he do?" Keith cried. "He will never reach Maclean. And if he does, he will be hopelessly outnumbered. Let me take the rest of these, to aid him."

"No. We must hold *some* reserve, however small," Alex said. "Your time will come, never fear! If a schiltrom breaks, these will be needed, man."

Irvine had got to within perhaps forty yards of Maclean, but looked unlikely to get much further, so tight was the throng. Suddenly he grabbed his own banner from its bearer, and turning it over, hurled it and its shaft, like a javelin, over the heads of the struggling men directly towards Maclean. In their astonishment, men around ceased their yelling for the moment — at least sufficiently for Irvine's great shout to be heard.

"Red Hector of the Battles!" he cried. "I am Irvine of Drum. And a better man than Maclean can boast! I have come for you. You are namely as a fighter. Will you hide there behind your gillies? Or come out and fight with me, man? I challenge you — show who fights Hector's battles for him!"

There was a roar from the Islesmen. But it died away quickly as Maclean raised his arm. He was an enormous man, red-haired, red-bearded, red-furred of chest — for he was stripped to the waist above a short saffron kilt, like most of his men, only the golden-linked belt showing his quality.

"Puppy! Infant!" he called, deep-voiced, but with the soft lilt of the Highland West. "Would you die so soon? Back to your mother, boy, before you come to hurt!"

"So you are craven, after all, you big red stirk! They told me you would not fight, save behind your savages."

"You should have better advisers, whatever! But there is still time to save your life, Irvine. Be off! I am busy."

"I came to kill you. But if words are all you can fight with . . . ?"

The big man hooted a laugh. "Words!" He tossed his long, two-handed sword into the air, twirling, and caught it again skilfully. "Take your choice of death then, Sassenach. Sword? Axe? Dirk? Or bare hands? Either or all. We shall teach you manners. And then finish this battle."

Irvine dismounted and pushed his way through the crush. Maclean was ordering a ring to be cleared.

"Save us, he is going to do it!" Keith exclaimed. "Maclean will devour him."

"He is a fair enough fighter. But Hector is a famed swordsman," Menzies said. "He cannot win this."

"He is buying us time," Alex declared sombrely. "But — what am I to do with it? At such cost!"

Scarcely credible as it was, there in the midst of the vast confused battle, this private duel took place, some small percentage of the combatants breaking off their fight to watch. Mainly these were Islesmen, admittedly. Within the circle the two champions lost to time in getting down to flailing and hacking at each other with sword and dirk. There was nothing delicate

375

or refined about this swordery. These were the heavy two-handed brands, and dirks had to be gripped between the teeth. Maclean had the height and weight and reach, but Irvine, being considerably the younger, was the more nimble, so that they were the more evenly matched. Irvine had thrown off his steel jack and tossed aside his helmet, not so much to even their state as to free his own movement. He was dancing around his opponent, thrusting and feinting, as far as such was possible with so clumsy a weapon. But that he must tire quickly was certain.

Alex and Jamie, on their eminence, could only watch this intermittently; they had all the rest of the field to consider. Another of the schiltroms was weakening, pulled sorely out-of-shape. Alex sent two-score horsemen to make a swift sally around it, to seek relieve the pressure, give them a chance to rally and re-form. But clearly they would not hold together for much longer. And the others were sadly reduced also. Time was not on *their* side, it seemed. But how to amend it? How to take advantage of what time Irvine was buying?

A messenger from Forbes came to ask for urgent aid, on the right wing. It seemed extraordinary that there was still any right wing. This was on the farthest-away part of the hill. He sent fifty men under young Menzies of Pitfodels — which left him virtually with only his personal group and those who came back from aiding the schiltrom.

Both contestants in the duel were staggering and bloody. Who had the advantage it was impossible to say; but obviously both were weary, flagging. One way or the other, it would not be long. Alex wiped away the drips from his face. He had not realised that their fine day had turned to rain.

The ailing schiltrom recovered somewhat, though lessened in size — and then its neighbour broke. This was Davidson's own. Jamie and a few other knights fought their way desperately across to the shambles of it, seeking to rally what was left, but it was hopeless. The new Sir Robert lay on a heap of dead, his head split by a Lochaber-axe. Most of the survivors appeared to be wounded. They were still fighting, resisting the tide of Highlanders, but clearly they would never reform as a unit. Jamie and his friends managed to break up the front of the attackers, for the moment. He himself got the Provost's body somehow hoisted across his saddle-bow. They escorted the sad residue of the schiltrom back to Alex on the mound.

376

That man gnawed his lip at the sight of Robert Davidson, finding no words. Then Keith grabbed his arm.

"Look! Maclean is down. But . . . oh, dear God — look at Sandy!"

Sure enough, Red Hector of the Battles had fought his last battle. He had fallen, not to rise again. Alexander Irvine was, however, in only little better case. One side of his head and face was so covered in blood as to be unrecognisable, one shoulder drooped and was clearly broken, and he was lurching round in ragged circles, a scarcely human figure. The Islesmen gazed, stunned at their leader's death. Then reeling, Irvine tripped over his fallen adversary, fell all his length, and so lay.

"Let me get to him! Let me get Sandy!" his friend Keith yelled. And without waiting for permission, spurred off. Alex nodded to the little group behind Jamie, who hurried after Keith.

Fortunately the Maclean clansmen were still in something of a state of shock, more concerned with collecting their chief's body than with fighting the newcomers, for the moment. These were able to pick up Irvine and bring him back, with the residue of his company. But it was a corpse that Keith carried to Alex, in choking distress.

"Rob Irvine has . . . gained a bride this day!" he gasped.

They laid Sandy Irvine's body beside Robert Davidson's, there on the mound. They were by no means alone.

One schiltrom was left, the churchmen, with the survivors of the others and various oddments forming something like another round the eminence. For the rest, the battle was merely far-flung confusion, scores of small struggles, men dying in fearful chaos — although it was to be hoped that the right wing away to the east retained some identity.

"Thank God for this rain!" Jamie jerked.

"Why? What service?"

"It will mean earlier dark. If we can hold out so long."

"You believe it . . . hopeless? Nothing that we can do, man?"

"We can always pray!"

They gained some small comfort, presently, with the arrival of the main Forbes manpower from Tillyfour, on the Don, under Sir Alexander's heir, some two hundred and fifty strong. These had been rather forgotten, in the stress. Although somewhat tired from their fourteen-mile hurried ride, after a sleepless night, they were fresh to the fight, indeed worried that they might have missed the best of it. The trouble was that their eagerness was to be with Sir Alexander rather than to be used merely as a strategic reserve. Indeed, young Forbes had even brought his father's best suit of mail, to hand over, for some reason left behind.

Alex compromised. Retaining about fifty of the newcomers, he sent the rest, with the angry Keith, to cut their way round, somehow, to the former right wing, there to command Sir Alexander to return, to rejoin them here. There was no longer any point in maintaining a separate identity and supposed threat the best part of a mile away, especially with the light failing.

Soon after they went, the churchmen's schiltrom broke. Alex used his reserve to rescue most of the survivors and bring them to build up the defensive ring around his mound. These brought with them, amongst other leaders, the bodies of William de Tullidaff and Sir Gilbert de Greenlaw.

One of the remaining Leslie of Balquhain sons came staggering in from elsewhere with the corpse of his last brother over his shoulder. That made six dead out of seven.

Alex was indeed praying now, for darkness if not oblivion. He had not been able to strike a single blow, personally, all that grievous day, while he sent so many of his friends to die.

Stragglers from all the battle kept finding their way back to the eminence, very largely wounded, weary, dispirited. For a July night it was almost dark, the rain not heavy but continuous.

The Forbes return was heartening — even though the one-time right wing was but a shadow of its original self. But, with its reinforcements, it gave the remnants of the main body some feeling, not of strength but of solidarity.

Since Maclean's fall, the Highland right wing had been less aggressive. It kept assailing the perimeter of Alex's central position, but without the fire of heretofore. Perhaps it was waiting for a new commander. At any rate, presently, with visibility reduced to little more than a hundred or two yards, when horns began to ululate from the north, this group took it as a directive to retire, and began quite quickly to disengage. Scarcely able to believe their eyes at the suddenness of it, Alex and his beleaguered residue perceived and wondered. Wondered more as the horn-wailing continued, and elsewhere, on the edge of vision, a movement backwards could be sensed.

"My God — they are breaking off, I do believe!" Alex cried. "The saints be praised — they are retiring!"

"Only to regroup, I swear!" Jamie said. "This rain and darkness. I hoped for this . . ."

"I *prayed* for it! To give us time, a breathing-space. And, by the Powers, we need it!"

"We cannot be sure yet . . ."

Before long it became clear to all that the battle was over for the time being. Not dramatically, not with any sort of final victory or defeat. Merely that the fighting had stopped as no longer really practicable in the circumstances of darkness and sheer weariness and human weakness.

"What now?" the Lord of Gordon, bleeding from a gashed brow, asked. "How do we retire from this hill? With all our wounded."

"We do not. We cannot," Alex answered. "Donald has the entire position surrounded. We may get a messenger or two through, that is all. To seek aid. But — from whom? I raised every man I could, before. A few more may be scraped together, here and there. But not to counter Donald's thousands."

"I could win two or three hundred more from Strathbogie, allowed a day or two."

"And I a hundred, older men, from Forbes . . ."

Not to be outdone, the wounded Leslie roused himself. "I will beat that, by God!" he growled thickly.

"Keith will find *some* more . . ."

"Aye, my friends — so be it. Brief your messengers. Brief them well. We are going to require every man and boy to-morrow, not two days hence. If we survive this night."

"And meanwhile?"

"Meanwhile we set strictest watch. We tend our wounded, count our dead. Is that not sufficient?" That was Jamie Douglas.

That was, indeed, a task more than sufficient for any man. Few indeed on that field had come out of it unscathed — but it was the legion of the seriously wounded, scattered far and wide over the plateau, that taxed the survivors. There was little that they could do for them. Even to move many was dangerous. Yet to leave them lying there was scarcely to be considered. There were equally large numbers of the Islesmen wounded amongst the fallen, of course, and often the search-parties came across groups of the enemy similarly employed; by mutual consent they ignored each other. Save once, when one of Alex's Macphersons found a son of the Mackintosh, sore hurt amongst a heap of the slain, and called to some of his own people to look to him.

379

The dead, to be sure, seemed the more numerous. Most had to be left where they lay. Burial was for the future. In few battles, surely, even in Scotland, was there so great a proportion of the leadership amongst the slain. Few castles and halls of the North-East would not be in mourning tomorrow. Two of the three sheriffs present were dead — Angus and Moray; and the Banff sheriff's son, young Bisset of Lessendrum. Sir William Abernethy, Albany's nephew, was slain, like Sir Robert Maule of Panmure, Sir Alexander Stirling, Sir James Lovel of Ballumbie, Sir Alexander Straiton of Lauriston, besides those already brought in, along with many lairds of the houses of Gordon, Forbes, Abercromby, Leith, Blackhall and Meldrum. And, of course, the six sons of Balquhain.

Alex Stewart never closed his eyes that evil, desolate, watchful night.

* * *

The rain died away in the early hours, and dawn saw a white mist over all the valleys of Urie and Don, rising high enough to thinly obscure the plateau of Harlaw. The shrunken, desperate loyalist force had been standing to arms for an hour before that — even though sentries had reported no enemy probes or approaches, other than the parties succouring the wounded. As they stood in chilled, silent ranks, watching, waiting, gradually more than daylight dawned upon them. They had the top of Harlaw's hill to themselves. Wherever Donald and his hosts were, they were no longer occupying the northern end of the plateau.

Scouts sent out quite quickly returned with the word that the enemy was not encamped down in the floor of the valley either, nor any sign of them on the moorlands to the east. Only their dead remained anywhere in sight.

At first neither Alex nor any of his people could believe it. It could only be a trap, to lure them down from this strong position. But as their scouts ranged further and further afield, it became evident that, if it was a trap, it was a very strange one, for there did not seem to be an Islesman within five miles.

When, at length, there was reliable information that the Highland host had indeed crossed the shoulder of Bennachie and was streaming back north-by-west, there could be no doubts; and the sense of relief and wonder was almost overwhelming. They, the survivors, were not going to die — for none there had expected to live through another day. Some of their wounded also would live. They could go home, to wives and parents and friends, whom they had not looked to see again. They were men redeemed, by some strange trick of fate.

It was some time before the wider aspect began to register, even with Alex. They were left in possession of the field. Despite all their losses, their failures and mistakes, they were not really defeated, after all. They could scarcely call themselves the victors, but they had turned back the menacing tide — meantime, at least. For one reason or another Donald was retiring, had lost heart. He might come again another day — but surely not soon, nor in greater strength, nor with ramifications of support. It seemed that, somehow, with God's help, they had done what they set out to do, at whatever cost.

Yet, amidst all that grim array of their dead friends and colleagues, there could be no elation, no joy. But thankfulness, yes. Perhaps that, and the relief, was enough.

There was much to do before the leaders, at any rate, might turn for home and rest. Alex, amongst so much else, Sheriff of Aberdeen, felt that he must personally convey the Provost, and its many other dead, back to the city, a dire task. Jamie, with an axe-slashed upper arm which was swelling painfully, as well as a grazed forehead, was anxious to get back to Lochindorb, to ensure that no eddy of the Isles' tide had reached that place, making or ebbing. He was going back to Badenoch with the Macpherson clansmen, and accompanied Alex's sad cavalcade only as far as the junction of Urie and Don.

"My thanks, Jamie, old friend," the other said, on parting, voice breaking just a little. "This has been a, a sore trial. A test. Out of which I feel that I have come . . . wanting. But you — you have stood firm, always sure, a rock to lean upon. Without your black Douglas strength, I doubt if I could have stood yonder all yesterday, unmoving. If I thought that I might make a general, one day, now I know differently. But you are of the stuff of generals, man. And better, of the stuff of heroes. I could not have a finer friend. Nor needed one more."

Embarrassed, Jamie looked away. "I but stood by, advised. It is easy to advise. You made the decisions. Scotland was fortunate in having Alex Stewart in command yesterday. Although whether many will thank you for it is another matter!"

"Perhaps not. But that signifies little. What does is that the Isles threat is pushed back. The Celtic dream shattered, at least for the present. And, knowing Henry Plantagenet, the English will not now invade. My Uncle Robert may not love me the more. But he must now *seem* to! And you also, Jamie. He owes too much to us to have us as foes. I think that you may walk the South again unfearing. You will never trust him, I know — nor indeed shall I. But I believe his power must wane, from now on."

"And Alex Stewart take Robert Stewart's place?"

"No. Not that. *James* Stewart, only. We must continue to work for that, Jamie, always. To bring back the King of Scots somehow. Using John Stewart, perhaps, towards that end. The house of Stewart is, God willing, due to take a turn for the better with the house of Douglas's support. Now — go back, friend, to your Mary Stewart, and to my mother, carrying my love to them. And tell them to cherish Black Sir James Douglas — for this realm needs him sorely. As do I."

They gripped hands.

HISTORICAL NOTE

THE BATTLE OF Harlaw was, of course, one of the turning-points in Scotland's story. Never again was the North and West really to threaten the South — save perhaps 335 years later, when another Stewart, Charles Edward by name, led a mainly Highland army as far as Derby, before the Stewart line went down, once and for all. Donald of the Isles did try again, the following summer; but he got no further than Argyll.

Alexander, Earl of Mar, became a major force in the land, appointed full Lieutenant and Justiciar in place of Buchan; and under his rule the North remained in fair peace and order until he died, and was buried at Inverness, twenty-four years later, where his recumbent effigy may still be discovered in an abandoned graveyard in Friar's Street — the former Blackfriars Monastery. He died much honoured, almost beloved, a strange circumstance for the son of the Wolf of Badenoch, and who had gained his earldom in such doubtful fashion. The question of his wedding to the Countess of Duffel remained unresolved, although he petitioned the Pope to have it annulled. He did not marry again. He had an illegitimate son who became Sir Thomas Stewart. His brothers set up their own branches of Highland Stewarts, Atholl and Strathdon, although Sir Duncan disappeared into the mists of history.

John, Earl of Buchan, married the daughter of the Earl of Douglas, and made a reputation for himself as a military commander, but in foreign wars. Indeed he was made Constable of France in 1421, but fell there three years later, at the great Battle of Verneuil.

Sir James Douglas of Aberdour, Roberton, etc., passes from the pages of recorded history after 1415, when he seems to have been rich enough to lend money to various people. His old father, the Lord of Dalkeith, lingered on until 1420, when he finally succumbed to the 'flu, leaving the most interesting will in Scottish records. Jamie's father left him his second-best girdle, a pair of plates and a suit of tilting armour. The legitimate line duly became Earls of Morton, and still subsists.

The Duke of Albany died, over eighty, in 1420 'of a sound mind and Christian manner', still Regent of Scotland, with King James remaining a prisoner in England until 1424, despite efforts to gain his release — not made by Albany however. When James the First did at last come home, after eighteen years imprisonment, it was to take a terrible vengeance on the Albany line. But that is another story.

There was never again any doubt as to the dynastic destiny of the house of Stewart.